Leslie Stephens

Dictionary of national biography

Leslie Stephens

Dictionary of national biography

ISBN/EAN: 9783742891877

Manufactured in Europe, USA, Canada, Australia, Japa

Cover: Foto ©Raphael Reischuk / pixelio.de

Manufactured and distributed by brebook publishing software
(www.brebook.com)

Leslie Stephens

Dictionary of national biography

DICTIONARY

OF

NATIONAL BIOGRAPHY

Kennett——Lambart

DICTIONARY

OF

NATIONAL BIOGRAPHY

EDITED BY

SIDNEY LEE

VOL. XXXI.

KENNETT——LAMBART

New York

MACMILLAN AND CO.

LONDON: SMITH, ELDER, & CO.

1892

LIST OF WRITERS

IN THE THIRTY-FIRST VOLUME.

List of Writers.

A. G. L. . . A. G. LITTLE.

H. R. L. . . THE LATE REV. H. R. LUARD, D.D.

Æ. M. . . . ÆNEAS MACKAY, LL.D.

W. D. M. . THE REV. W. D. MACKAY, B.D. F.S.A.

A. H. M. . . A. H. MILLAR.

C. M. . . . . COSMO MONKHOUSE.

N. M. . . . . NORMAN MOORE, M.D.

G. P. M-Y. . G. P. MORIARTY.

J. B. M. . . J. BASS MULLINGER.

A. N. . . . . ALBERT NICHOLSON.

P. L. N. . . P. L. NOLAN.

F. M. O'D. . F. M. O'DONOGHUE.

S. P. O. . . CAPTAIN S. PASFIELD OLIVER.

J. H. O. . . THE REV. CANON OVERTON.

H. P. . . . . HENRY PATON.

S. L.-P. . . . STANLEY LANE-POOLE.

B. P. . . . . MISS PORTER.

R. B. P. . . R. B. PROSSER.

J. M. R. . . J. M. RIGG.

L. C. S. . . LLOYD C. SANDERS.

T. B. S. . . T. BAILEY SAUNDERS.

T. S. . . . . THOMAS SECCOMBE.

R. F. S. . . R. FARQUHARSON SHARP.

W. A. S. . . W. A. SHAW.

C. F. S. . . MISS FELL SMITH.

L. T. S. . . MISS TOULMIN SMITH.

G. W. S. . . THE REV. G. W. SPROTT, D.D.

L. S. . . . . LESLIE STEPHEN.

G. S-H. . . . GEORGE STRONACH.

C. W. S. . . C. W. SUTTON.

H. R. T. . . H. R. TEDDER.

T. F. T. . . PROFESSOR T. F. TOUT.

J. S. V. . . . J. SAVILL VAIZEY.

E. V. . . . . THE REV. CANON VENABLES.

R. H. V. . . COLONEL R. H. VETCH, R.E.

A. W. W. . . A. W. WARD, Litt.D.

M. G. W. . . THE REV. M. G. WATKINS.

C. W-H. . . CHARLES WELCH, F.S.A.

W. W. . . . WARWICK WROTH, F.S.A.

DICTIONARY

OF

NATIONAL BIOGRAPHY

KENNETT, BASIL (1674–1715), miscellaneous writer, born at Postling, Kent, on 21 Oct. 1674, was younger brother of White Kennett [q. v.], bishop of Peterborough. He was educated under the care of his brother at Bicester grammar school and in the family of Sir William Glynne at Ambrosden, Oxfordshire. In 1689 he entered St. Edmund Hall, Oxford, under the tuition of his brother, who was then vice-principal. In 1690 he was elected scholar of Corpus Christi College as a native of Kent, and graduated B.A. in 1693, M.A. in 1696. In 1697 he became fellow and tutor of Corpus. His learning and amiable qualities won him the regard of all parties. In 1706 he was appointed chaplain to the British factory at Leghorn, being the first to fill that office, and received the degree of B.D. by decree of convocation. He was at first much harassed by the Inquisition, and had to seek the intervention of the English government. Ill-health, caused by the climate and his dislike of exercise, obliged him to resign, and he preached for the last time on 8 Jan. 1712–13. He returned home by way of Florence, Rome, and Naples, and through France, collecting books, sculpture, and curiosities. He resumed residence at Corpus Christi in 1714, became D.D., and during the same year was elected president of his college, although he was 'even then,' as Hearne says, 'very sickly.' He died of slow fever on 3 Jan. 1714–15 (*Hearl. MS. C.* 915), and was buried in the college chapel.

Kennett was author of: 1. 'Romæ Antiquæ Notitia, or the Antiquities of Rome. . . . To which are prefixed two Essays concerning the Roman Learning and the Roman Education,' 8vo, London, 1696. This work, which passed through many editions, is dedicated to the Duke of Gloucester. A Dutch

translation by W. Sewel appeared in pt. ii. of Seine's 'Beschryving van Oud en Niew Rome,' fol. 1704. 2. 'The Lives and Characters of the Ancient Grecian Poets,' 2 pts. 8vo, London, 1697, also dedicated to the duke. 3. 'A Brief Exposition of the Apostles' Creed, according to Bishop Pearson, in a new method,' 8vo, 1705; other editions 1721 and 1726. 4. 'An Essay towards a Paraphrase on the Psalms in Verse, with a Paraphrase on the Third Chapter of the Revelations,' 8vo, 1706. 5. 'Sermons preached . . . to a Society of British Merchants in Foreign Parts,' 8vo, London, 1715; 2nd edit., as 'Twenty Sermons,' 1727.

Among the Lansdowne MSS. are the following works by Kennett: 1. 'Poem to Queen Anne' (MS. 722, f. 1). 2. 'Collections on various subjects' (MSS. 924–34). 3. 'Oratio' (MS. 927, f. 19). 4. 'Lives of the Latin Poets' (MS. 930). 5. 'Letters to S. Blackwell' (MS. 1019). 6. 'Notes on the Church Catechism' (MS. 1043). 7. 'Notes on the New Testament' (MS. 1044).

He translated from the French: 1. Bishop Godeau's 'Pastoral Instructions for an Annual Retirement of Ten Days' [anon.], 8vo, 1703; another edition in 'A Plea for Seasons of Spiritual Retirement,' 1809. 2. Pascal's 'Thoughts upon Religion' [anon.], 8vo, 1704; other editions 1727 and 1741. 3. La Placette's 'The Christian Casuist,' 8vo, 1705. 4. 'Politics in Select Discourses of Monsieur Balzac which he called his Aristippus,' 8vo, 1709, with a preface by White Kennett. 5. 'The Whole Critical Works of Monsieur Rapin,' 8vo, 1716. He also helped to translate Puffendorf's 'Of the Law of Nature and Nations,' fol. 1710 (1729 and 1749), and translated Horace's Art of Poetry' (*Brit. Mus. MS. Addit.* 28726, f. 173). Hearne

    B

states, on the authority of James Tyrrell, that the third volume of White Kennett's 'History of England,' fol. 1706, was in reality the work of Basil Kennett.

Kennett likewise edited Bishop Vida's 'Poetica,' 8vo, 1701.

[Biographia Britannica; Lansd. MSS. 987 f. 363, 989 f. 156; Hearne's Notes and Collections (Oxf. Hist. Soc.), i. 286, 295, 311, 332, ii. 179, 234.]
G. G.

KENNETT, WHITE, D.D. (1660–1728), bishop of Peterborough, born in the parish of St. Mary, Dover, on 10 Aug. 1660, was son of Basil Kennett, M.A., rector of Dimchurch and vicar of Postling, Kent, by his wife Mary, eldest daughter of Thomas White, a wealthy magistrate and master-shipwright of Dover. After receiving a preliminary education at Elham and Wye, he was placed at Westminster 'above the curtain,' or in the upper school; but as he was suffering from small-pox at the period of the election of scholars on the foundation, his father recalled him home. After his recovery he spent a year at Beaksbourne, in the family of Mr. Tolson, whose three sons he taught 'with great content and success.' He was entered a batler or semi-commoner of St. Edmund Hall, Oxford, in June 1678, being placed under the tuition of Andrew Allam [q. v.] According to Hearne he 'sometimes waited on Dr. Wallis to church with his skarlett,' and performed other menial offices (*Remarks and Collections*, i. 311), but, on the other hand, he associated with the gentlemen-commoners. While an undergraduate he began his career as a writer by publishing anonymously, just before the assembling of parliament at Oxford on 21 March 1680–1, 'A Letter from a Student at Oxford to a Friend in the Country, concerning the approaching Parliament, in vindication of his Majesty, the Church of England, and the University.' The whig party endeavoured to discover the author, with a view to his punishment, but the sudden dissolution of the parliament put an end to the incident and occasioned the publication of Kennett's second piece, 'A Poem to Mr. E. L. on his Majesty's dissolving the late Parliament at Oxford,' 28 March 1681. About this period Kennett was introduced to Anthony à Wood, who employed him in collecting epitaphs and notices of eminent Oxford men. In his diary, 2 March 1681–2, Wood notes that he had directed five shillings to be given to Kennett 'for pains he hath taken for me in Kent.' On 2 May 1682 Kennett graduated B.A. (*Cat. of Oxford Graduates*, 1851, p. 381), and next year published a version of Erasmus's 'Moriæ En-

comium,' under the title of 'Wit against Wisdom: or a Panegyric upon Folly,' 1683, 8vo. In the following year he contributed the life of Chabrias to the edition of Cornelius Nepos, 'done into English by several hands.' He commenced M.A. on 22 Jan. 1684, and having taken holy orders he became curate and assistant to Samuel Blackwell, B.D., vicar and schoolmaster of Bicester, Oxfordshire. Sir William Glynne, bart., presented him in September 1685 to the neighbouring vicarage of Ambrosden (KENNETT, *Parochial Antiquities*, p. 676). Soon afterwards he published 'An Address of Thanks to a good Prince: presented in the Panegyric of Pliny upon Trajan, the best of Roman Emperors,' London, 1686, 8vo, with a high-flown preface expressing his loyalty to the throne (*Notes and Queries*, 2nd ser. ii. 441).

Kennett's political views were quickly modified by dislike of the ecclesiastical policy of James II. He preached a series of discourses against 'popery,' refused to read the 'Declaration for Liberty of Conscience' in 1688, and acted with the majority of the clergy in the diocese of Oxford when they rejected an address to the king recommended by Bishop Parker. Hearne relates that at the beginning of the revolution Kennett lent Dodwell a manuscript treatise, composed by himself and never printed, offering arguments for taking the oaths of allegiance and supremacy to William and Mary (*Remarks and Collections*, i. 71). Subsequently Kennett openly supported the cause of the revolution, and thereby exposed himself to much obloquy from his former friends, who called him 'Weathercock Kennett' (NICHOLS, *Lit. Anecd.* i. 393 *n.*) In January 1689, while shooting at Middleton Stoney, his gun burst and fractured his skull. The operation of trepanning was successfully performed, but he was obliged to wear a large black patch of velvet on his forehead during the remainder of his life.

After a few years' absence at Ambrosden he returned to Oxford as tutor and vice-principal of St. Edmund Hall, and in September 1691 was chosen lecturer of St. Martin's, commonly called Carfax, Oxford. He was also appointed a public lecturer in the schools, and filled the office of pro-proctor for two successive years. He proceeded B.D. on 5 May 1694 (cf. *Life of Wood*, ed. Bliss, p. cxvii). In February 1694–5 he was presented by William Cherry, esq., to the rectory of Shottesbrook, Berkshire. He was created D.D. at Oxford on 19 July 1700, and in the same year was presented to the rectory of St. Botolph, Aldgate (NEWCOURT, *Repertorium*, i. 917). He resigned the vicarage of Ambrosden, and did not obtain possession of St. Botolph's without a lawsuit. On 15 Feb. 1701 he was installed in the prebend of Combe and Harnham, in the church of Salisbury (LE NEVE, *Fasti*, ed. Hardy, ii. 665).

Kennett's historical and antiquarian researches had meanwhile procured him some reputation. From Dr. George Hickes [q. v.] (afterwards nonjuring bishop of Thetford), who lived for a time in seclusion with him at Ambrosden, he received instruction in the Anglo-Saxon and other northern tongues. For several years the two scholars were on the most friendly terms, but eventually there was an open rupture between them, owing to religious and political differences. Kennett contributed a life of William Somner to the Rev. James Brome's edition of that antiquary's 'Treatise of the Roman Ports and Forts in Kent' (1693), and the biography was enlarged and reissued in Somner's 'Treatise of Gavelkind,' 2nd edition 1726. His reputation as a topographer and philologist was enhanced by his 'Parochial Antiquities attempted in the History of Ambrosden, Burcester, and other adjacent parts in the counties of Oxford and Bucks, with a Glossary of Obsolete Terms,' Oxford, 1695, 4to, dedicated to his patron, Sir W. Glynne. A new edition, greatly enlarged from the author's manuscript notes, was issued at Oxford (2 vols. 1818, 4to) under the editorship of Bulkeley Bandinel. While engaged on this work the question of lay impropriations had come much under his notice, and he published 'for the terror of evil-doers' the 'History and Fate of Sacrilege, discovered by examples of Scripture, of Heathens, of Christians,' London, 1698, 8vo, written by Sir Henry Spelman in 1632, but omitted from the edition of that author's 'Posthumous Works.'

Kennett was now chaplain to Bishop Gardiner of Lincoln, and on 15 May 1701 became archdeacon of Huntingdon. Thereupon he entered into the famous controversy with Atterbury about the rights of convocation, and ably supported Dr. Wake and Edmund Gibson in their contention that convocation had few inherent rights of independent action. In Warburton's view, Kennett's arguments were based on precedents, while Atterbury's rested on principles. On Archbishop Tenison's recommendation he was appointed in 1701 one of the original members of the Society for Propagating the Gospel in Foreign Parts. In a sermon preached in his parish church of Aldgate on 31 Jan. 1703-4, the fast day for the martyrdom of Charles I, Kennett acknowledged that there had been some errors in his reign, owing to a 'popish' queen and a corrupt ministry, whose policy tended in

the direction of an absolute tyranny. To correct exaggerated statements made about this sermon, Kennett printed it under the title of 'A Compassionate Enquiry into the Causes of the Civil War,' London (three editions), 1704, 4to. It elicited many angry replies from his high-church opponents.

In 1704 he published 'The Case of Impropriations, and of the Augmentation of Vicarages, and other insufficient Cures, stated by History and Law, from the first Usurpations of the Popes and Monks, to her Majesty's Royal Bounty lately extended to the poorer Clergy of the Church of England.' A copy of this work, bound in two vols., with copious additions by the author, was formerly in the possession of Richard Gough, and is now in the Bodleian Library. In 1705 some booksellers undertook a collection of the best works on English history down to the reign of Charles II, and induced Kennett to write a continuation to the time of Queen Anne (*Notes and Queries*, 2nd ser. viii. 313). Although it appeared anonymously as the third volume of the 'Compleat History of England,' 1706, fol., the author's name soon became known, and he was exposed to renewed attacks from his Jacobite enemies. A new edition, with corrections, was published in 1719, but it was not until 1740 that there appeared Roger North's 'Examen, or an Inquiry into the Credit and Veracity of a pretended Complete History, viz. Dr. White Kennett's "History of England."' His popularity at court was increased by the published denunciations of his views, and he was appointed chaplain in ordinary to her majesty (cf. LUTTRELL, *Brief Relation*, vi. 207). He was installed in the deanery of Peterborough 21 Feb. 1707-8 (BIRCH, *Life of Tillotson*, ed. 1753, p. 212; LUTTRELL, vi. 223, 251). A few days previously he had been collated to the prebend of Marston St. Laurence, in the church of Lincoln.

A sermon which he preached at the funeral of the first Duke of Devonshire on 5 Sept. 1707, and which laid him open to the charge of encouraging a deathbed repentance, was published by Henry Hills, without a dedication, in 1707. To a second edition, published by John Churchill in 1708, with a dedication to William, second duke of Devonshire, was appended 'Memoirs of the Family of Cavendish,' a separate edition of which was published by Hills in the same year. A new edition of the sermon, with the author's manuscript corrections, was published by John Nichols in 1797, but very few copies were sold, and the remainder were destroyed by fire (NICHOLS, *Lit. Anecd.* i. 396 n.) The imputation against Kennett was fresh in the memory of Pope when in the 'Essay on Criticism' he wrote:

Then unbelieving priests reformed the nation,
And taught more pleasing methods of salvation

(see Jortin's note, *Pope*, ed. Elwin, ii. 68, iii. 329). Kennett's subsequent preferment was naturally connected by his enemies with the strain of adulatory reference to the second duke with which the sermon concludes.

In 1707, desiring more leisure for study, he resigned the rectory of St. Botolph, Aldgate, and obtained the less remunerative rectory of St. Mary, Aldermary, London. During this period he published numerous sermons, and his pen was actively engaged in support of his party. He zealously opposed the doctrine of the invalidity of lay baptism, and his answer to Dr. Sacheverell's sermon preached before the lord mayor on 5 Nov. 1709 raised a storm of indignation. In 1710 he was severely censured for not joining in the congratulatory address of the London clergy to the queen, which was drawn up on the accession of the tories to office after Sacheverell's trial. Kennett and others who declined to subscribe it were represented as enemies to the crown and ministry (cf. DYER, *Newsletter*, 4 Aug. 1710). Dr. Welton, rector of Whitechapel, introduced into an altar-piece in his church a portrait of Kennett to represent Judas Iscariot (*Lansdowne MS.* 702, f. 101; SHARPE, *Short Remarks*, p. 30). It was stated that the rector had caused Kennett's figure to be substituted for that of Burnet at the suggestion of the painter, who feared an action of *scandalum magnatum* if Burnet were introduced. A print of the picture in the library of the Society of Antiquaries is accompanied with these manuscript lines by Maittaire:—

To say the picture does to him belong,
Kennett does Judas and the Painter wrong.
False is the image, the resemblance faint:
Judas compared to Kennett is a Saint.

Multitudes of people visited the church daily to see the painting, but Compton, bishop of London, soon ordered its removal. For many years afterwards it is said to have ornamented the high altar at St. Albans (NICHOLS, *Lit. Anecd.* viii. 369; *Notes and Queries*, 3rd ser. iii. 409).

In order to advance the interests of the Society for the Propagation of the Gospel in Foreign Parts, Kennett made a collection of books, charts, maps, and documents, with the intention of composing a 'History of the Propagation of Christianity in the English-American Colonies,' and on the relinquishment of that project he presented his collections to the corporation, and printed a catalogue entitled 'Bibliothecæ Americanæ Primordia,' London, 1713, 4to, afterwards republished with additions by Henry Homer the elder, 1789, 4to. He also founded an antiquarian and historical library at Peterborough, and enriched the library of that church with some scarce books, including an abstract of the manuscript collections made by Dr. John Cosens, bishop of that see, and a copiously annotated copy of Gunton's 'History of Peterborough.' The collection, consisting of about fifteen hundred books and tracts, was placed in a private room at Peterborough, and a manuscript catalogue was drawn up and subscribed 'Index librorum aliquot vetustorum quos in commune bonum congessit W. K., Decan. Petriburg. MDCCXII.' (NICHOLS, *Lit. Anecd.* i. 257). This library is now arranged in the chapel over the west porch of the cathedral.

On 25 July 1713 Kennett was installed prebendary of Farrendon-cum-Balderton at Lincoln. He preached vehemently against the rebellion of 1715, and in the two following years warmly advocated the repeal of the acts against occasional conformity. In the Bangorian controversy he opposed the proceedings of convocation against Bishop Hoadly. By the influence of his friend Dr. Charles Trimnell, bishop of Norwich and afterwards of Winchester, he was appointed bishop of Peterborough; he was consecrated at Lambeth on 9 Nov. 1718, and had permission to hold the archdeaconry of Huntingdon and a prebend in Salisbury *in commendam* (STVANS, *Registrum Anglicanum*, p. 111). He died ten years later at his house in St. James's Street, Westminster, on 19 Dec. 1728. He was buried in Peterborough Cathedral, where a marble monument with a brief Latin inscription was erected to his memory (cf. NICHOLS, *Lit. Anecd.* ix. 319).

He married first, on 6 June 1693, Sarah, only daughter of Robert and Mary Carver of Bicester (she died on 2 March 1693-4, *sine prole*); secondly, on 6 June 1695, Sarah, sister of Richard Smith, M.D., of London and Aylesbury (she died in August 1702); thirdly, in 1703, Dorcas, daughter of Thomas Fuller, D.D., rector of Wellinghale, Essex, and widow of Clopton Havers, M.D. By his second wife he had issue a son, White Kennett, who became rector of Burton-le-Coggles, Lincolnshire, and prebendary of Peterborough, Lincoln, and London, and died on 6 May 1740; and a daughter Sarah, who married John Newman of Shottesbrook, Berkshire, and died on 22 Feb. 1756 (HOWARD, *Miscellanea Genealogica et Heraldica*, new ser. ii. 287). Hearne, writing on 26 April 1707, says that Kennett's 'present wife wears the breeches, as his haughty, insolent temper deserves' (*Remains and Collections*, ii. 9).

His biographer, the Rev. William Newton, admits that his zeal as a whig partisan sometimes carried him to extremes, but he was very charitable, and displayed great moderation in his relations with the dissenters. He is now remembered chiefly as a painstaking and laborious antiquary, especially in the department of ecclesiastical biography. The number of his works both in print and manuscript shows him to have been throughout his life a man of incredible diligence and application. He was always ready to communicate the results of his researches to fellow-students. Probably his best-known work, apart from his 'Compleat History' already noticed, was his 'Register and Chronicle, Ecclesiastical and Civil: containing Matters of Fact delivered in the words of the most Authentick Books, Papers, and Records; digested in exact order of time. With papers, notes, and references towards discovering and connecting the true History of England from the Restauration of King Charles II,' vol. i. (all published), London, 1728, fol. The original materials for this valuable work are preserved in the British Museum among the Lansdowne MSS. 1002-1010. The manuscript volumes bring the register to 1679. The published volume begins with the Restoration, and only comes down to December 1662.

Kennett published more than twelve separate sermons preached on public occasions between 1694 and 1728, and others in support of charity schools (cf. *The Excellent Daughter*, 1708; 11th edit. 1807) or of the Society for the Propagation of the Gospel (cf. sermon issued in 1712). His addresses to his clergy at Peterborough on his first visitation were issued in 1720. Kennett was also the author of the following, besides the works already noticed: 1. 'Remarks on the Life, Death, and Burial of Henry Cornish,' London, 1699, 4to. 2. 'Ecclesiastical Synods, and Parliamentary Convocations in the Church of England, Historically stated, and justly Vindicated from the misrepresentations of Mr. Atterbury,' pt. i. London, 1701, 8vo. 3. 'An Occasional Letter, on the subject of English Convocations,' London, 1701, 8vo. 4. 'The History of the Convocation of the Prelates and Clergy of the Province of Canterbury, summon'd to meet in the Cathedral Church of St. Paul, London, on Feb. 6, 1700. In answer to a Narrative of the Proceedings of the Lower House of Convocation,' London, 1702, 4to. 5. 'An Account of the Society for Propagating the Gospel

in Foreign Parts, establish'd by the Royal Charter of King William III,' London, 1706, 4to; translated into French by Claude Grotête de la Mothe, Rotterdam, 1708, 8vo. 6. 'The Christian Scholar, in Rules and Directions for Children & Youth sent to English Schools; more especially design'd for the poor boys taught & cloath'd by charity in the parish of St. Botolph, Aldgate,' London, 1708, 8vo; 5th edit. 1710, 8vo; 14th edit. London, 1800, 12mo; 15th edit. in 'The Christian Scholar,' vol. vi. 1807, 12mo; 20th edit. London, 1811, 12mo; new edit. London, 1836, 12mo. 7. 'A Vindication of the Church and Clergy of England from some late reproaches rudely and unjustly cast upon them,' London, 1709, 8vo. 8. 'A true Answer to Dr. Sacheverell's Sermon before the Lord Mayor, Nov. 5, 1709. In a Letter to one of the Aldermen,' London, 1709, 8vo. 9. 'A Letter to Mr. Barville upon occasion of his being reconciled to the Church of England,' printed in 'An Account of the late Conversion of Mr. John Barville, *alias* Barton,' London, 1710, 8vo. 10. 'A Letter, about a Motion in Convocation, to the Rev. Thomas Brett, LL.D.,' London, 1712. 11. 'A Memorial for Protestants on the 5th of Novemb., containing a more full discovery of some particulars relating to the happy deliverance of King James I, and the three Estates of the Realm of England from the most traiterous and bloody intended Massacre by Gunpowder, anno 1605. In a Letter to a Peer of Great-Britain,' London, 1713. 12. 'A Letter to the Lord Bishop of Carlisle, concerning one of his predecessors, Bishop Merks; on occasion of a new volume (by George Harbin) for the Pretender, intituled The Hereditary Right of the Crown of England asserted,' London, 1713, 8vo (two editions in one year); 4th edit. London, 1717, 8vo. 13. 'The Wisdom of Looking Backwards to judge the better on one side and t'other; by the Speeches, Writings, Actions, and other matters of fact on both sides for the four last years,' London, 1715, 8vo. 14. 'A Second Letter to the Lord Bishop of Carlisle, upon the subject of Bishop Merks; by occasion of seizing some Libels, particularly a Collection of Papers written by the late R. Reverend George Hickes, D.D.,' London, 1716, 8vo. 15. 'A Third Letter to the Lord Bishop of Carlisle, upon the subject of Bishop Merks; wherein the Nomination, Election, Investiture, and Deprivation of English Prelates are shew'd to have been originally constituted & govern'd by the Sovereign Power of Kings and their Parliaments ... against the Pretensions of our new Fanaticks,' London, 1717, 8vo. This and the two preceding letters to the Bishop of Carlisle, Dr. William Nicholson, gave rise to a heated controversy. 16. 'Dr. Snape instructed in some matters, especially relating to Convocations and Converts from Popery,' London, 1718, 8vo. 17. 'An Historical Account of the Discipline & Jurisdiction of the Church of England,' 2nd edit. London, 1730, 8vo.

Hearne published in his edition of Leland's 'Itinerary' (vol. vii. Pref. p. xvii) a letter from Kennett 'concerning a passage' in vol. iv. of the same work (1711). Some manuscript verses by Kennett on 'Religious and Moral Subjects, translated from some of the chief Italian Poets,' belonged to S. W. Rix in 1855, and manuscript notes by Kennett, written in a Bible, were printed in 'Notes and Queries' for 1855. Sir Walter Scott first printed, in his 'Life of Swift,' p. 157, from a manuscript in the British Museum, the well-known description by Kennett of Swift's attendance in Queen Anne's antechamber (November 1713).

Many of Kennett's manuscripts, which once formed part of the library of James West, president of the Royal Society, were purchased in 1773 by the Earl of Shelburne (afterwards Marquis of Lansdowne), with whose collection they passed, in 1807, to the British Museum. They are now numbered 1028-1041 in the Lansdowne collection. Among them are: 1. 'Diptycha Ecclesiæ Anglicanæ: sive Tabulæ Sacræ in quibus facili ordine recensentur Archiepiscopi, Episcopi, eorumque Suffraganei, Vicarii Generales, et Cancellarii, Ecclesiarum insuper Cathedralium Priores, Decani, Thesaurarii, Præcentores, Cancellarii, Archidiaconi, et mediores notæ Canonici continua serie deducti a Gulielmi I conquesta ad suscepta Gul. III tempora,' 955. 2. 'Diaries and Accounts' (chiefly commonplace books), 1826, 887. 3. 'An Alphabetical Catalogue of English Archbishops, Bishops, Deans, Archdeacons, &c., from the 12th to the 17th century,' 982. 4. 'Biographical Memoranda, many of them relating to the English Clergy from 1500 to 1717,' 978-87. 5. 'Materials for an Ecclesiastical History of England from 1500 to 1717,' 1021-4. 6. 'Collections for a History of the Diocese of Peterborough; with Particulars of all the Parishes in Northamptonshire,' 1025-9. 7. 'Notes and Memoranda of Proceedings in Parliament and Convocation,' 1037. 8. 'Collections for the Life of Dr. John Colet, Dean of St. Paul's, with a Letter of Advice and Instruction to Dr. Samuel Knight [q. v.], by whom they were Digested and Published,' 1030. 9. 'Materials relating to the History of Convocations,' 1031. 10. 'Etymological Collections

of English Words and Provincial Expressions,' 1033. 11. 'Letters to Bishop Kennett from Dorcas his wife, 1702-28,' 1015.

He also made copious annotations in an interleaved copy of the first edition of Wood's 'Athenæ Oxonienses.' This copy was purchased by Richard Gough, from the library of James West, president of the Royal Society, and it is now preserved in the Bodleian Library. Kennett's notes are incorporated by Bliss in his edition of Wood. They consist chiefly of extracts from parish registers and from other ecclesiastical documents (Wood, Athenæ Oxon. ed. Bliss, vol. i. Pref. p. 13).

His portrait was engraved in mezzotint by Faber from life in 1719, and by J. Smith. There is also a portrait, engraved by James Fittler, A.R.A., prefixed to the second edition of the 'Parochial Antiquities.'

[Life (anon.), London, 1730, 8vo, by the Rev. William Newton, vicar of Gillingham, Dorset; Short Remarks on some Passages in the Life of Dr. Kennett, by a Lover of Truth (J. Sharpe, M.A., curate of Stepney). London, 1730, 8vo; Wood's Athenæ Oxon. (Bliss), iv. 792, 1003; Burnet's Own Time, ii. 81; Gent. Mag. lxxv. 971 (and general index); Biog. Brit.; Nichols's Lit. Anecd.; Nichols's Illustr. of Lit.; Gutch's Collectanea Curiosa, ii. 403; Addit. MS. 5874, f. 49; Watt's Bibl. Brit.; Nichols's Atterbury, edit. 1789-98, i. 114, 401, ii. 145; Catalogue of MSS. in Univ. Libr. Cambridge; Hackman's Cat. of Tanner MSS. p. 988; Walker's Letters written by Eminent Persons, i. 224, ii. 62, 74, 108, 113; Lowndes's Bibl. Man. (Bohn); Notes and Queries (general indexes); Le Neve's Fasti (Hardy); Georgian Era, i. 263; Hollis's Memoirs, pp. 588, 589.] T. C.

KENNEY, ARTHUR HENRY (1776?-1855), controversialist, born in 1776 or 1777, was the youngest son of Edward Kenney, vicar-choral and prebendary of Cork, by Frances, daughter of Thomas Herbert, M.P., of Muckross, co. Kerry (Burke, Landed Gentry, 1868, p. 686; Cotton, Fasti Eccl. Hibern. i. (1847), 221, 234). In 1790 he entered the university of Dublin, was elected a foundation scholar in 1793, and graduated B.A. in 1795. In 1800 he proceeded M.A., and was elected to a junior fellowship, which he vacated in 1809 for the college living of Kilmacrenan, co. Donegal. He became B.D. in 1808, and D.D. in 1812 (Dublin Graduates, 1591-1868, p. 317). On 27 June 1812 he was instituted to the deanery of Achonry, which he resigned in May 1821 on becoming rector of St. Olave, Southwark (Cotton, iv. 105). He soon became popular among his parishioners, but his living was eventually sequestered on account of pecuniary difficulties, and he was obliged to reside abroad during the last ten years of his life. He died at Boulogne-sur-Mer on 27 Jan. 1855, aged 78. He was twice married, and had issue by both marriages. Under the initials of A. H. K., Kenney edited the fifth edition of Archbishop Magee's 'Discourses on the Scriptural Doctrines of Atonement and Sacrifice,' 3 vols. 8vo, London, 1832. He also wrote a memoir of Magee prefixed to the latter's 'Works,' 2 vols. 8vo, London, 1842.

Kenney's own writings are: 1. 'An Enquiry concerning some of the Doctrines maintained by the Church of Rome: in Answer to the Charge of Intolerance brought by Members of that Church against Members of the Church of England,' 8vo, London, 1818. 2. 'Principles and Practices of Pretended Reformers in Church and State,' 8vo, London, 1819. 3. 'Facts and Documents illustrative of the History of the Period immediately preceding the Accession of William III, . . .' 8vo, London, 1827. 4. 'The Dangerous Nature of Popish Power in these Countries, especially as illustrated from Awful Records of the Time of James the Second,' &c., 8vo, London, 1830. 5. 'A Comment, Explanatory and Practical, on the Epistles and Gospels for the Sundays of the Year, and on those for Holy Days immediately relating to Our Blessed Saviour,' 2 vols. 12mo, London, 1842.

[Gent. Mag. new ser. xliv. 544-5; Taylor's Univ. of Dublin, pp. 445, 490; Brit. Mus. Cat.]
                 G. G.

KENNEY, CHARLES LAMB (1821–1881), journalist and author, son of James Kenney [q. v.], dramatist, was born at Bellevue, near Paris, 29 April 1821, and had Charles Lamb for one of his godfathers. In July 1829 he was entered at the Merchant Taylors' School, and in 1837 became a clerk in the General Post Office. He commenced his literary career at the age of nineteen as assistant foreign editor, dramatic critic, and scientific reporter on the 'Times,' contributing at the same time to magazines and writing plays. In 1851 he aided in promoting the Great Exhibition in Hyde Park. Ill-health obliging him to give up his position on the daily press, he became secretary to Sir Joseph Paxton during his organisation of the transport service for the Crimea in 1855. On 17 Nov. 1856 he was called to the bar at the Inner Temple, and was appointed secretary to M. de Lesseps. He advocated the advantages of the Suez Canal when the enterprise was opposed by Lord Palmerston, and wrote a book on the subject entitled 'The Gates of the East' (1857). Partly owing to his exer-

tions a complete revolution was effected in public opinion, and he received from Seyd Pasha a letter of thanks accompanied by a diamond ring. A misunderstanding with De Lesseps deprived him of the secretaryship, and his connection with the Suez Canal ceased. In 1858 he joined the staff of the 'Standard.' In 1862 he was active in support of the International Exhibition at South Kensington. He belonged to a literary circle which included Thackeray and Dickens, and was noted for his impromptu and satirical skits in rhyme upon the celebrities of the day. With the exceptions of Boucicault and Vivier, he was said to be the wittiest man of his period. He had a prominent share in the introduction of modern opera-bouffe, having written the libretti of the 'Grand Duchess,' the 'Princess of Trebizonde,' and 'La Belle Hélène.' Some of his dramatic pieces were brought out in conjunction with Albert Smith, Tom Taylor, Shirley Brooks, and Dion Boucicault, but the rate of remuneration at that time did not exceed 100l. for a burlesque and 25l. for a farce. Kenney also wrote 'The Vagabond' and many other popular songs. He suffered for several years from an incurable disease, and a performance for his benefit was given at the Gaiety Theatre on 20 June 1877. He died at Eldon Road, Kensington, on 25 Aug. 1881, aged 60, and was buried in Brompton cemetery on 30 Aug. By his marriage at the English embassy, Paris, in 1859, with Miss Rosa Stewart, he left two children, Charles Horace Kenney and Rosa Kenney, who made her first appearance on the stage as Juliet at Drury Lane on 23 Jan. 1879.

Kenney was the author of: 1. 'Mr. Phelps and the Critics of his Correspondence with the Stratford Committee,' 1864. 2. 'Wanted, Husbands,' musical sketch, Drury Lane, 11 March 1867. 3. 'Valentine and Orson,' pantomime, New Holborn Theatre, 24 Dec. 1867. 4. 'Our Autumn Manœuvres,' farce, Adelphi Theatre, 21 Oct. 1871. 5. 'Memoir of M. W. Balfe,' 1875. 6. 'Maid of Honour,' comedietta, Holborn Theatre, 24 April 1876. 7. 'The Correspondence of H. de Balzac,' translated, 1878. He contributed 'Covent Garden,' pp. 28–32, to Albert Smith's 'Gavarni in London,' 1859, and translated (with others) Count Hamilton's 'Fairy Tales and Romances,' 1849, and Demidoff's 'Travels in Southern Russia,' 1853. Books of words for the following operas were furnished by Kenney: 'The Mock Doctor,' 1865; 'Fair Helen,' 1866; 'Princess of Trebizonde,' 1870; 'The Grand Duchess of Gerolstein,' 1871; 'Don Pasquale,' 1871; 'La Figlia del Reggimento,' 1871; 'Lucia di Lammermoor,' 1871; 'Le Nozze di Figaro,' 1871; 'Un Ballo in

Maschera,' 1871; 'La Muette de Portice,' 1872; 'La Favorita,' 1872; 'Semiramide,' 1872; 'Le Domino Noir,' 1872; 'Ali Baba,' 1873; 'The Wonderful Duck,' 1873; 'L'Elisir d'Amore,' 1875: and 'La Jolie Parfumeuse,' 1875. He also wrote the words to a 'Requiem' by Verdi in 1875, as well as numerous songs, the most popular of which were 'Soft and Low,' 1865; 'Ever my Queen,' 1866; 'The Vagabond,' 1871; and 'A Russet Cloak o'er Motley Gear,' 1875.

[Illustrated London News, 3 Sept. 1881, pp. 223, 242; Illustrated Sporting and Dramatic News, 3 Sept. 1881, p. 583; Era, 3 Sept. 1881, p. 6; information from Miss Rosa Kenney.]

G. C. B.

KENNEY, JAMES (1780–1849), dramatist, was born in Ireland in 1780. His father, James Kenney, was for many years manager of Boodle's Club, St. James's Street, London, of which he was also part proprietor and institutor, and was well known in the sporting world. The son when a youth was placed in the banking-house of Herries, Farquhar, & Co., and while there indulged in private theatricals. His first literary attempt was a small volume published in 1803, entitled 'Society, a Poem in two parts, with other Poems.' He next wrote a farce called 'Raising the Wind,' which in 1803 was produced at a performance of amateurs, he himself taking the part of Jeremy Diddler. The success of this farce induced him to offer it to the managers of Covent Garden, where it was produced on 5 Nov. 1803, the character of Jeremy Diddler, played by Lewis, securing an immediate popularity. It ran for thirty-eight nights, and has often been revived since. On 20 Nov. 1804 Kenney's second piece, 'Matrimony,' a petite opera taken from Marsollier's 'Adolphe et Claire,' was given at Drury Lane and repeated ten times during the season. 'False Alarms, or my Cousin,' a comic opera in three acts, with music by Braham and Matthew Peter King [q. v.], had a run of twenty-one nights at the same theatre early in 1807. In this piece Bannister had a comic song, 'Major M'Pherson,' which was long chanted in the streets, and Braham introduced for the first time his popular ballad, 'Said a Smile to a Tear.' The piece was praised by Genest, in spite of its poor underplot, and it was revived in 1810, with Foote, Russell, and Madame Vestris in the cast. 'Ellen Rosenberg,' a melodrama, first performed at Drury Lane on 19 Nov. 1807, with Elliston, Bannister, and Mrs. Siddons as Rosenberg, Storm, and Ella respectively, was also very successful (cf. *Monthly Mirror*, November 1807, pp. 351–3). Kenney's next venture, an original comedy,

'The World,' which came out at Drury Lane on 31 March 1808, had a run of twenty-three nights, and was frequently played in the following season. Lord Byron, however, speaks harshly of this piece in 'English Bards and Scotch Reviewers.' He wrote that:

Kenney's World—ah! where is Kenny's wit?—
Tires the sad gallery, lulls the listless pit.

On 7 March 1812 a musical afterpiece, 'Turn him out,' described by Genest as tolerable, was acted at the Lyceum, was repeated twenty-eight times, and still keeps the stage. Before the close of the same year another excellent farce, 'Love, Law, and Physic,' added considerably to Kenney's reputation. It ran forty-four nights, and was much indebted to the Lubin Log of Liston for its popularity. In 1815 'The Fortune of War,' a farce, was produced at Covent Garden, and in 1817, in conjunction with Howard Payne, Kenney wrote a drama called 'The Portfolio, or the Family of Anglade,' taken from the French. This was played at Covent Garden on 1 Feb., the rival house, Drury Lane, producing another version on the same night. 'Match Breaking, or the Prince's Present,' a drama in three acts, and 'John Buzzby, or a Day's Pleasure,' were attractive pieces at the Haymarket in 1821 and 1822.

In 1821 Kenney was residing at Bellevue, near Paris, and he entertained Charles Lamb and his sister at Versailles in 1822. He still continued his dramatic work, and for the Haymarket on 7 July 1823 he wrote one of the most popular dramas ever produced, 'Sweethearts and Wives,' which ran for fifty-one nights and is still a great favourite. Madame Vestris was in the cast, and Liston as Billy Lackaday was at his very best. In July 1826 his farce 'Thirteen to the Dozen' was played at the Haymarket, with Liston and John Reeve in the chief characters. One of Kenney's most fortunate pieces, 'Spring and Autumn,' came out at the Haymarket on 6 Sept. 1827, and ran with much applause during the remainder of the season. On the opening of Drury Lane in October 1827 he produced a most successful farce, 'The Illustrious Stranger, or Married and Buried,' written expressly for Liston. This piece, which probably owed some of its incidents to 'Le Naufrage,' by Lafont, printed in 1710, was received with great favour, and has continued to keep the stage. On 4 May 1829 he brought out at Drury Lane an adaptation of Auber's opera, 'La Muette de Portici,' which under the title of 'Masaniello' pleased the musical and theatrical world. For the Surrey Theatre he wrote in 1840 'The Sicilian Vespers,' a tragedy, in which Power sustained the chief character with great reputation. Kenney's last production was a serious drama entitled 'Infatuation,' a tale of the French empire, written in 1845 for Charlotte Cushman, then acting at the Princess's Theatre.

Kenney was a frequent guest at Samuel Rogers's breakfasts and dinners, and met there most of the notabilities of the day. He long suffered from a nervous affection, which gave him such an eccentric appearance that he was more than once taken for an escaped lunatic. He died of heart disease at 22 South Terrace, Alexander Square, Brompton, 25 July 1849. He had received large sums for his writings, but was not in affluent circumstances; a performance for his benefit took place at Drury Lane on the day of his death, and produced 500l. for his family. He married Louisa, daughter of Louis Sebastian Mercier, the French critic, and widow of Thomas Holcroft [q. v.] the dramatist. By her he had two sons, James and Charles Lamb Kenney [q. v.], and two daughters, Virginia and Maria. Mrs. Kenney on 13 Oct. 1849 received a civil list pension of 40l. a year, which was continued to her daughters on her death, 17 July 1853.

Besides the plays mentioned, Kenney wrote for Covent Garden, 'Too many Cooks,' a musical farce, 12 Feb. 1805; 'The Blind Boy,' a melodrama, 1 Dec. 1807; 'Debtor and Creditor,' a comedy, 20 April 1814; 'A Word for the Ladies,' 17 Dec. 1818; and 'The Green Room,' a comedy, 18 Oct. 1826. For the Lyceum he wrote, 'Oh ! this Love, or the Masqueraders,' June 1810, and 'The Magic Bell.' For Drury Lane he wrote, 'The Touchstone, or the World as it goes,' a comedy, 3 May 1817; 'A House out at Windows,' a musical farce, 10 May 1817; 'Benyowsky, or the Exile of Kamschatka,' an operatic play, 16 March 1826; 'Forget and Forgive, or a Rencontre in Paris,' 21 Nov. 1827, reproduced as 'Frolics in France' 15 March 1828; 'Peter the Great, or the Battle of Pultowa,' 21 Feb. 1829; 'Hernani, or the Pledge of Honour,' a play, 8 April 1831; 'A Good-looking Fellow,' in conjunction with A. Bunn; and 'The King's Seal,' with Mrs. Gore. For the Haymarket he wrote, 'The Alcaid, or Secrets of Office,' a comic opera, 10 Aug. 1824; 'Spring and Autumn, or Married for Money,' a comic drama, 6 Sept. 1827; and 'Love Extempore.' For Madame Vestris at the Olympic he wrote 'Fighting by Proxy,' a farce, 9 Dec. 1833, followed by 'Dancing for Life' and 'Not a Word.' Other plays were 'Dominique the Possessed;' 'False Alarms,' an opera; 'Spirit of the Bell,' a comic opera; 'Hush!' a musical drama; 'The Black Domino,' an opera; 'Barbara, Macintosh, & Co.,' a farce, written for Power; and 'The Irish Ambassador.' He also wrote 'Valdi, or the Libertine's Son,' a poem, 1820.

[Gent. Mag. January 1850, p. 99 ; You have heard of them, by Q., 1854, pp. 347-53; Genest's English Stage, vii. 613 et seq., viii. 504 et seq.; Clayden's Rogers and His Contemporaries, passim (Kenney's christian name is wrongly given as John in the index); Baker's Biog. Dram. i. 430; Pascoe's Dramatic List, 1880, p. 240; Dublin University Mag. January 1856, pp. 15-24.]   G. C. B.

KENNEY, PETER JAMES (1779-1841), Irish jesuit, was born in Dublin on 7 July 1779. While serving as an apprentice to a coachbuilder he attracted the attention of Dr. Thomas Betagh [q. v.], whose evening school he attended, and by whom he was sent to Carlow College. He afterwards went to Stonyhurst College, and entered the Society of Jesus on 20 Sept. 1804. He completed his studies with much distinction at the jesuit college in Palermo, where he was ordained priest. The English, who occupied Sicily at the time, formed a plan, which came to nothing, for liberating Pope Pius VII, then held captive by the French, and Kenney was selected to act as interpreter between the pope and his rescuers. He also ministered as catholic chaplain to the British troops in Sicily, but was ordered to discontinue his services by the governor of Malta, and the prohibition was denounced by Grattan in parliament. He returned to Ireland in 1811, and served one of the parochial chapels in Dublin, where he acquired great renown as a preacher. His friend Dr. Murray, who was then coadjutor to the Archbishop of Dublin, on becoming president of Maynooth College in 1812, nominated Kenney as vice-president, which post he held for about a year. Kenney was mainly instrumental in reviving the jesuit mission in Ireland, and was its superior for many years, becoming subsequently its vice-provincial after the Irish mission was made a vice-province of the society. In May 1814, a few months previous to the restoration of the jesuit order by papal bull, he opened Clongowes Wood College, co. Kildare, which has since been the leading catholic lay school in Ireland, and in later years he aided in the establishment of St. Stanislaus College, Tullabeg, King's County, and of the jesuit residence of St. Francis Xavier in Dublin; he was also of much assistance to Mary Aikenhead [q. v.], the foundress of the Irish sisters of charity in the institution of her religious congregation. In 1819 and in 1830 he was sent by the father-general of the order as visitor to the jesuit mission in the United

States, and in July 1833, during the period of his second visit, he published the general's decree constituting the American mission a province of the society. In Ireland he was constantly employed in conducting missions and retreats. He died in Rome on 19 Nov. 1841, and was buried in the church of the Gesù in that city.

Kenney was one of the most eminent preachers and theologians in the catholic church in Ireland in the early part of this century. His style of eloquence resembled that of O'Connell, and was, it is stated, much admired by Grattan. Manuscript copies of his 'Meditations' are preserved. He began several times a history of the jesuits in Ireland, but did not continue it. There is a portrait of him in Maynooth College.

[Hogan's Chron. Cat. of the Irish Province S. J., pp. 85–6; Foley's Records, vii. 414; Oliver's Collectanea S. J.; Battersby's Dublin Jesuits, pp. 113–16; Meagher's Life of Archbishop Murray, pp. 89–93; Life of Mary Aikenhead, by S. A., Dublin, 1879; Eighth Report of Commissioners of Irish Education Inquiry—Evidence of the Rev. Peter Kenney, London, 1827; Irish Monthly, xviii. 1, 2, 4, 5, 6, 9, 10; Irish Ecclesiastical Record, 3rd ser. xii. 794–9.]

P. L. N.

KENNICOTT, BENJAMIN (1718–1783), biblical scholar, was son of Benjamin Kennicott, barber and parish clerk of Totnes, Devonshire, buried 28 March 1770, and of his wife Elizabeth, buried 13 Jan. 1749–50, over whose remains their son in after years erected a large table-tomb in Totnes churchyard. He was born at Totnes on 4 April 1718, and spent seven years as a foundation boy at the grammar school, under the Rev. Nicholas Roe. When young he was very fond of books and of music. The regulations which he drew up for the practice of the Totnes ringers, and dated 8 Nov. 1742, are quoted in Polwhele's 'Devonshire,' i. 320, and he gave a brass eight-light candlestick for the use of the ringers in the belfry. His first appointment was that of master of the bluecoat or charity school at Totnes, where he attracted attention by some short poems, the chief of which was 'On the Recovery of the Hon. Mrs. Eliz. Courtenay from her late dangerous Illness.' This was printed in 1743 and 1747, and the manuscripts of several others are in the possession of Mr. E. Windeatt of Totnes (*Western Antiq.* iii. 249). Subscriptions were opened for his support at Oxford, and, mainly through the Courtenays, Ralph Allen, and the Rev. William Daddo, master of Blundell's school at Tiverton, he matriculated as servitor at Wadham College, Oxford, 6 March 1743–4, whence he wrote a

warm letter of thanks to Daddo on 30 March 1744 (HARDING, *Tiverton*, bk. iv. pp. 89–90; *Gent. Mag.* 1791, p. 222). He was Pigott exhibitioner 1744 and 1745, Hody (i.e. Hebrew) exhibitioner 1745–7, and bible clerk 3 May 1746. In order that he might be eligible for a fellowship at Exeter College, and as he had not resided long enough to qualify in the usual way, he was made (in accordance with the recommendation of Lord Arran, chancellor of the university) B.A. by decree and without 'examination, determination at Lent, or fees,' 20 June 1747, and was duly elected to a fellowship, which he retained until 1771. His subsequent degrees were M.A. 4 May 1750, B.D. 6 Dec. 1761, and D.D. 10 Dec. 1761, and in 1764 he was elected F.R.S. Kennicott was instructed in Hebrew by Professor Thomas Hunt (1696–1774) [q. v.], and the greater part of his life was spent in the collation of Hebrew manuscripts. His preferments were for many years inconsiderable. He was Whitehall preacher about 1753, vicar of Culham, Oxfordshire, from 21 Sept. 1753 to 1783, chaplain to the new bishop of Oxford in 1763, and Radcliffe librarian at Oxford from November 1767 to 1783. In July 1770 he was appointed to a canonry at Westminster Abbey, but soon resigned it for the fourth stall at Christ Church, Oxford (1 Nov. 1770). From 1771 to 1781 Kennicott held the vicarage of Menheniot, Cornwall, which was given to him as a fellow of Exeter College, Oxford, by the dean and chapter of Exeter, on the recommendation of his steady friend Bishop Lowth. This preferment he voluntarily resigned in 1781 in consequence of his inability to reside there. After a lingering illness Kennicott died at Oxford, 18 Aug. 1783, and was buried in Christ Church Cathedral, close to Bishop Berkeley's grave, on 21 Aug.

He married, on 3 Jan. 1771, Ann, sister of Edward Chamberlayne (afterwards secretary of the treasury). Another of Chamberlayne's sisters was wife of William Hayward Roberts [q. v.], provost of Eton. Mrs. Kennicott was very friendly with Richard Owen Cambridge, Mrs. Garrick, Hannah More, and Miss Burney, the last of whom made her acquaintance in 1786, and praised her as 'famous by having studied Hebrew after marriage in order to assist her husband in his edition of the bible; she learnt it so well as to enable herself to aid him very essentially in copying, examining, and revising' (*Diary of Madame d'Arblay*, iii. 237). Bishop Barrington left her an annuity of 100l., and from Bishop Porteus she received a legacy of 500l. 3l. per cent. stock as his 'dear and pleasant friend Mrs. Kennicott.' In memory of her husband and for the promotion of the study of Hebrew she founded two scholarships at Oxford, which took effect on her death at Windsor, 25 Feb. 1830, and her name is perpetuated in the bidding prayer among the benefactors of the university. Numerous letters to and from her are in Roberts's 'Memoirs of Hannah More.'

Kennicott's great work was his 'Vetus Testamentum Hebraicum cum Variis Lectionibus,' 1st vol. Oxford, 1776, fol. ; 2nd vol. 1780, fol. To the second volume was annexed a 'Dissertatio Generalis' on the manuscripts of the Old Testament, which was published separately at Oxford in the same year and reprinted at Brunswick in 1783 by Paul James Bruns, a native of Lübeck, who was employed by Kennicott in collating manuscripts at Rome and elsewhere. A copy of the entire work, the result of many years' assiduous labour, was presented by Kennicott in person to George III. In 1753 he issued 'The State of the printed Hebrew Text of the Old Testament considered, a Dissertation,' and in 1759 he brought out a second dissertation on the same subject. These volumes were translated into Latin by W. A. Teller, and published at Leipzig, the first in 1756, the second with additions in 1765. Bishop Lowth inspired him with a desire to test the accuracy of the Hebrew text of the Old Testament. His critical examination of the manuscripts began in 1751, and when Secker, then bishop of Oxford, urged him in March 1758 to undertake their regular collation, he yielded to the request. His labours met with much support. The subscriptions made in England for his aid amounted to 9,119l. 7s. 6d. In France the Duc de Nivernois encouraged his design, and he was permitted to examine certain manuscripts at Paris in 1767. By the king of Denmark's order the use of six very ancient manuscripts was offered, four quarto volumes of various readings were sent to him by the command of the king of Sardinia, and the stadtholder of Holland gave a yearly donation of thirty guineas. His first report 'On the Collation of the Hebrew Manuscripts of the Old Testament' was forwarded to the subscribers in December 1760, and a similar statement appeared each year until 1768. The complete series was issued in one volume at Oxford in 1770, and the reports to 1768 were translated into Latin and included in the 'Bibliotheca Hagana ... a Nicolao Barkey.' Kennicott was twice (1758 and 1769) refused permission to borrow manuscripts from the Bodleian Library, but he sent to it on 17 Dec. 1760 the manuscript collations which he had then made. The rest of his collations, with his correspondence and miscellaneous codices, were at first deposited in the Radcliffe Library, transferred to the Bodleian Library on 10 May 1872, and now rest in the new museum. Bishop Barrington gave in 1820 to the Bodleian Library a mass of Arabic tracts and papers which belonged to Kennicott.

Johnson said of these investigations that 'although the text should not be much mended thereby, yet it was no small advantage to know that we had as good a text as the most consummate industry and diligence could procure;' but they were censured by some critics for inaccuracy, and by the Hutchinsonians through the feeling that they might lead men to value the letter rather than the spirit of the bible. A volume called 'The printed Hebrew Text of the Old Testament vindicated. An Answer to Mr. Kennicott's "Dissertation,"' was written by Fowler Comings in 1753 (MRS. DELANY, Autobiography, iii. 526), and Julius Bate [q. v.] published 'The Integrity of the Hebrew Text vindicated from the Objections and Misconstructions of Mr. Kennicott,' 1754. An anonymous pamphlet, 'A Word to the Hutchinsonians, or Remarks on three Sermons lately preached before the University of Oxford,' 1756, was written by Kennicott, and George Horne [q. v.] retaliated with 'An Apology for certain Gentlemen in the University of Oxford,' 1756. Horne subsequently issued 'A View of Mr. Kennicott's Method of Correcting the Hebrew Text,' 1760; but in the end they became attached friends. Thomas Rutherforth, D.D., King's professor of divinity in Cambridge, issued in 1761 a letter to Kennicott on his 'Dissertation,' to which he at once replied, whereupon Rutherforth published a second letter, and the Rev. Richard Parry came out with 'Remarks on Dr. Kennicott's Letters,' 1763.

Kennicott met with great opposition abroad. There appeared in 1771 'Lettres de M. l'Abbé de • • • ex-professeur en Hebreu ... au St Kennicott,' purporting to be printed at Rome and sold at Paris, and an English translation was struck off in 1772. In reply to this work Kennicott at once wrote 'A Letter to a Friend occasioned by a French Pamphlet [anon.],' 1772, stating that it was the composition of six Capuchins in the convent of St. Honoré at Paris ; but it is said by Jones to have been inspired by a Jew called Dumay, who had been an assistant to Kennicott (JONES, Life of Horne, pp. x-xi, 84-109). Bruns published at Rome in 1782 a Latin version of this letter by Kennicott, and added some letters of his own. Another defence in reply to this attack was written in 1775 by the Rev. George Sheldon, vicar of Edwardston, Suffolk. In Italy there appeared a censure upon Kennicott's letters in 'Des titres primitifs de la Revelation par Gabr. Fabricy, Romæ,' 1772, 2 vols.; but his chief opponents were in Germany. O. G. Tychsen pronounced his work 'ingens, cui lumen ademptum,' and in the 'Bibliotheca Orientalis' of J. D. Michaelis, pt. xi, there appeared a severe criticism on his first volume. Kennicott then sent out a long Latin epistle to Michaelis, which was printed at Oxford in 1777, reprinted in the same year at Leipzig, and inserted in the twelfth part of the 'Bibliotheca Orientalis' with the criticisms of Michaelis. After the publication of his second volume Kennicott drew up a brief defence in Latin, 'Contra ephemeridum Goettigensium criminationes,' 1782. A full list of the pieces against Kennicott is said to have appeared in the 'Catalogue of English Divinity,' sold by the Dyers of Exeter in 1820.

The four volumes of De Rossi, published at Parma, 1784–7, with an appendix in 1798, form a supplement to the 'Collations of Kennicott.' On them are based the editions of Doederlein and Meisner (Leipzig, 1793), Jahn (Vienna, 1806), and Boothroyd (Pontefract, 1810–16). Parkhurst, in his 'Hebrew Lexicon,' made much use of Kennicott's inquiries, and J. L. Schulze translated into Latin and published at Halle in 1782 the Hebrew interpretation of the books of Daniel and Ezra, which Kennicott had first edited.

His other works were: 1. 'Poem on the Recovery of the Hon. Mrs. Elizabeth Courtenay' [anon.], Exeter, 1743; 2nd edit. Oxford, 1747. Only a few copies were printed of the first edition. The lady was the Hon. Elizabeth Montagu, who had married Kelland Courtenay of Painsford, near Totnes, and contributed to Kennicott's maintenance at Oxford. Kennicott's sister was her lady's-maid. 2. 'On the Tree of Life in Paradise: a Critical Dissertation on Genesis ii. 8–24,' 1747, 8vo. This provoked an anonymous answer called 'An Enquiry into the Meaning of that Text Genesis i. 26, with an Answer to Mr. Kennicott's Interpretation of the same,' 1748, and 'Remarks on Mr. Kennicott's Dissertation,' by Richard Gifford [q. v.], 1748. 3. 'On the Oblation of Cain and Abel,' 1747; 2nd edit. of this and preceding volume, 1747 also. 4. 'Duty of Thanksgiving for Peace,' 1749. 5. 'A Letter to Dr. King, occasion'd by his late Apology, and in particular by such parts of it as are meant to defame Mr. Kennicott,' 1755; a caustic attack. [See KING, WILLIAM, 1685–1763.] 6. 'Christian Fortitude. A Sermon preached before the University at St. Mary's, Oxford, 25 Jan. 1757.' It was much criticised, and was attacked in 'Remarks on Dr. Kennicott's Sermon,' n.d. [1757],

and in 'A Critical Dissertation on Isaiah vii. 13–16, in which the sentiments of Dr. Kennicott are cordially and impartially examined,' 1757. A second edition of the sermon, 'with a list of the falsehoods in the Remarks,' came out in 1757. 7. 'Sermon before the University of Oxford,' 1765. 8. 'Remarks on a Printed Paper entitled "A Catalogue of the Sacred Vessels restored by Cyrus,"' 1765, attributed to him by Watt. 9. 'Remarks on the 42 and 43 Psalms' [anon.], n.d. [1765]. This was soon followed by a similar treatise on Psalms 48 and 89. These, when translated into Latin with an appendix by Bruns, were published by J. C. F. Schulz at Leipzig in 1772. In 1791 the Rev. Henry Dimock published 'Notes on the Psalms,' to correct the errors of the text in grammar, from the collations by Kennicott and De Rossi. 10. 'Observations on First Book of Samuel, chap. xvi. verse 19,' 1768; translated into French. 11. 'Critica Sacra, or a Short Introduction to Hebrew Criticism' [anon.], 1774. 12. 'Observations on Several Passages in Proverbs. With two Sermons. By Thomas Hunt,' 1775; they were edited by Kennicott. 13. 'The Sabbath. A Sermon preached at Whitehall and before the University of Oxford,' 1781. 14. 'Remarks on Select Passages in the Old Testament. With Eight Sermons, by the late Benjamin Kennicott,' 1787. Published in consequence of directions in his will. Kennicott also contributed to the Oxford verses on the death of Frederick, prince of Wales. His library was sold by Tom Payne in 1784.

[Gent. Mag. 1747 pp. 471–2, 605, 1768 pp. 147–9, 203–5, 251–3, 366–8, 1771 p. 520, 1783 pt. ii. pp. 718, 744, 1789 pt. i. p. 289, 1830 pt. i. pp. 282, 374; Macray's Bodleian Library, 2nd ed. pp. 118, 260, 263, 306, 372; Nichols's Illustr. of Lit. iv. 656, v. 627; Nichols's Literary Anecdotes, passim; Boswell's Johnson, ed. G. B. Hill, ii. 128, iv. 288; Diary of Madame d'Arblay, iii. 237; Miscell. Geneal. et Herald. 2nd ser. i. 146; Trans. Devon. Assoc. 1878: information from Mr. E. Windeatt of Totnes, Mr. T. M. Davenport of Oxford, and Mr. R. B. Gardiner of St. Paul's School.] W. P. C.

KENNION, EDWARD (1744–1809), artist, was born on 15 Jan. 1743–4 in Liverpool, where his father, James Kennion, was engaged in business. His grandfather, John Kennion, was for many years minister of the (unitarian) Ancient Chapel of Toxteth Park, Liverpool, and was a man of high education. A kinsman, John Kennion, took charge of Edward's education, placing him first at John Holt's school in Liverpool, and sending him when he was fifteen to Mr. Fuller's academy in London, where he probably first learned drawing. In 1762 he sailed for Jamaica, and joined the expedition against the Havannah under Sir George Pocockc and the Earl of Albemarle, in which John Kennion was commissary. After the capture of the place he returned to England for a time, but again went out to Jamaica in 1765 to superintend John Kennion's estates, and remained there almost continuously till July 1769, when he returned to England. By a commission dated 11 April of that year he was appointed an aide-de-camp, with the rank of lieutenant-colonel, to the commander-in-chief of the island.

On settling in England he engaged in trade in London. His marriage in 1774 with Ann Bengough, a Worcester lady, brought him some property, but he continued in business till 1782, when he retired to Rydd-Green, near Malvern. About 1771 he had made the acquaintance of George Barret, R.A., and in the following years accompanied him on sketching tours. At Rydd-Green he occupied himself in making drawings for a book on landscape-painting which he had long contemplated. In 1784 appeared in 4to No. 1 of a work on remains of antiquity, which contained five perspective views of ancient castles on the Welsh border, and three ground plans engraved in line by R. Godfrey, with full descriptions by Kennion (cf. Notes and Queries, 4th ser. iii. 263). The winters of 1787 and 1788 were passed in London, where he gave drawing lessons, and in 1789 he removed thither altogether, adopting the profession of a teacher and artist. He was admitted a member of the Society of Artists, and was a constant contributor of landscapes to its exhibitions, sending in all twenty-four works. He was also a fellow of the Society of Antiquaries. He exhibited eight landscapes at the Royal Academy between 1790 and 1807. Meanwhile he continued to work at his book on landscapes during frequent visits to the neighbourhood of Liverpool and the English lakes. In 1790 he etched eight plates as examples of the oak-tree, which were published with a preface as No. 1 of 'Elements of Landscape and Picturesque Beauty,' ob. 4to. The death of an uncle, Dr. Kennion, a Liverpool physician, in 1791, increased his resources, and in 1803 he issued a full prospectus of the proposed work. His project had expanded into an exhaustive treatise on the graphic art in 4 vols. He laboured at it conscientiously, and final arrangements were made for the publication of a first volume early in 1809. But before matters went further Kennion died suddenly in London on 14 April. He left a widow and four children. Of all Kennion's collections for his large

enterprise, 'An Essay on Trees in Landscape' was alone found ready for press. This was issued in 1815, many of the plates being engraved or finished in aquatint and soft ground etching by his son Charles [see infra]. The volume, which is in folio, contains fifty etched and aquatinted plates, a preface, a biographical notice, and forty-eight pages of letterpress. With a copy in the Manchester Free Library 'four large unpublished landscapes by Kennion, and six studies of trees beautifully etched by H. W. Williams,' were bound up in 1844. The four landscapes are soft ground etchings after Kennion by Vivares, folded on guards. There seems no reason to suppose the six studies were after Kennion's drawings. A soft ground etching (in the present writer's collection), numbered plate xxi, and dated 1 Dec. 1796, was published in the volume as 'plate xx, June 27, 1814.' It is signed 'C. J. Kennion,' and is mainly by Kennion's son. A small proof soft ground etching, on which is written 'Oak at Northan, near Enfield' (also belonging to the present writer), has a figure and cattle introduced, as was usually the case in Kennion's finished drawings. Kennion seldom painted in oil, and his earlier work was usually executed in Indian ink and pencil, but he subsequently tinted his drawings, and finally, under the influence of his friend, George Barret, painted with a full strength of colour. He contended that it was possible by the touch and manner of the execution to indicate the exact foliage represented, and he practically illustrated his opinion in his drawings. He had a very thorough knowledge of the principles of art, and drew with great skill and accuracy.

CHARLES JOHN KENNION (1789-1853) painted in water-colour much in the style of his father, and his drawings are interesting and well finished. He exhibited between 1804 and 1853 twenty-six landscapes at the Royal Academy, and five at the Suffolk Street Gallery. He died in Robert Street, Regent's Park, London, on 10 Sept. 1853 (Gent. Mag. 1853, ii. 538).

[Memoir in Kennion's Essay on Trees; Davis's Toxteth Park Chapel, 1884; Graves's Dict. of Artists; private information.]   A. N.

KENNY, SAINT (d. 598?), abbot of Achadh-bo. [See CAINNECH or CANNICUS, SAINT.]

KENNY, WILLIAM STOPFORD (1788-1867), compiler of educational works, born in 1788, kept for many years a 'classical establishment' at 5 Fitzroy Street, Fitzroy Square, London. He was an accomplished chess-player. He died on 16 Nov. 1867, aged 79 (Gent. Mag. 4th ser. v. 113). His compilations include: 1. 'Practical Chess Grammar,' 4to, London, 1817; 2nd edit. same year. 2. 'Practical Chess Exercises,' 8vo, London, 1818. 3. 'Why and Because, being a collection of familiar Questions and Answers on subjects relating to Air, Water, Light, and Fire, altered from the French,' 12mo, London, 1830; 18th edit. 1854. 4. 'The Manual of Science,' 18mo, London, 1844. 5. 'One Thousand Questions, with their Solutions, on Goldsmith's Grammar of Geography,' 18mo, London, 1853. 6. 'The Grammatical Omnibus; or, a Methodical Arrangement of the Improprieties frequent in Writing and Conversation, with Corrections,' 8th edit. 8vo, London, 1853. 7. 'The Improved French Word-Book . . . revised by J. Duprat Mérigon,' 18mo, London (1854). 8. 'The Improved Italian Word-Book,' 18mo, London (1854). 9. 'The Improved Italian Phrase-Book,' 32mo, London (1854). 10. 'Improved French Phrase-Book . . . revised by J. Duprat Mérigon,' 12mo, London (1856?). 11. 'School Geography . . . with a Treatise on Astronomy,' 12mo, London, 1856. Kenny edited educational works by other writers, and translated, with notes, A. Danican Philidor's 'Analysis of the Game of Chess,' 12mo, 1819.

[Kenny's Works.] G. G.

KENRICK or **KENDRICK, DANIEL** (*fl.* 1685), physician and poet, son of Samuel Kenrick of Leigh, Gloucestershire, was born about 1652, and entered as a servitor at Christ Church, Oxford, on 31 March 1686, whence he proceeded B.A. 1689, and M.A. 1674. At the age of thirty-two, when his portrait was engraved by R. White, Kenrick was practising as a doctor at his native town of Worcester, and was much esteemed there as 'a man of wit and a jolly companion.' Several poems by 'Dr. Kenrick' appear in 'The Grove, or a Collection of Original Poems, by W. Walsh, Dr. J. Donne, Mr. Dryden, Mr. Butler, Sir John Suckling, and other eminent hands,' London, 1721. Kenrick's 'talents,' it is declared in the preface, 'seem equal to panegyrick, satire, and lyric. There is a fire and sprightliness of thinking which runs through all his copies, and to this perhaps he owed that haste in his writing which made him sometimes negligent of Harmony both in Rimes and Numbers.' We gather from the same source that Kenrick was on terms of intimacy with Mrs. Behn and Purcell the musician, and that he died before the publication of 'The Grove' in 1721. There are some verses signed by Kenrick in the fifth vol. of Dryden's 'Miscellany Poems,' entitled 'Upon a Giant Angling.' These, however, are said by Granger, 'on the

information of Dr. John Wall,' to have been freely borrowed from a work called 'The Mock Romans,' London, 1653, while in Pratt's 'Cabinet of Poetry' (1808) these same lines are assigned to Dr. William King (1663–1712) [q. v.] The preface to 'The Grove' declares that Kenrick took degrees in divinity as well as physic. He may therefore be identical with Daniel Kenrick, D.D., who preached the assize sermon at Worcester in 1688.

[Granger's Biographical Hist. iv. 326; the Dean's Entrance Book, Christ Church, Oxford; Dryden's Miscellany Poems, ed. 1727, v. 136; Brit. Mus. Cat., where, however, Kenrick is entered without christian name.] T. S.

KENRICK, JOHN (1788–1877), classical scholar and historian, was eldest son of Timothy Kenrick [q. v.], by his first wife, Mary, whose maiden name was Waymouth. He was born at Exeter on 4 Feb. 1788. In 1793, the year of his mother's death, he began his education under Charles Lloyd, LL.D. [q. v.], and made such progress that in his twelfth year he was admitted (1799) to the Exeter academy as a student for the ministry under his father and Joseph Bretland [q. v.] Thomas Foster Barham (1766–1844) [q. v.] taught him German. His first experience in teaching was as locum tenens for James Hews Bransby [q. v.] at Moreton Hampstead, Devonshire, in November 1804, when he had Sir John Bowring [q. v.] as a pupil. On the dissolution of the Exeter academy (25 March 1805) he continued his theological studies under John Kentish [q. v.], in whose house at Birmingham he was a pupil from June 1805 till 1807, when he entered at Glasgow University on an exhibition from the Dr. Daniel Williams trust. Sir Benjamin Heywood [q. v.] was his fellow-lodger during his second and third years at Glasgow. The long vacations gave him time for pedestrian tours in the western highlands. He obtained distinctions in logic, classics, and physical science, and gained the Gartmore gold medal for an essay on the English constitution during the Tudor period; he graduated M.A. on 1 May 1810.

On leaving Glasgow he accepted a tutorship in classics, history, and literature at the Manchester College, York (now Manchester New College, Oxford), under Charles Wellbeloved [q. v.]. After a summer spent in preaching in Exeter and the neighbourhood, he settled in York, and at once made his mark as a scholar and disciplinarian. The duties devolving on a resident tutor rendered his position anxious and irksome. He twice tendered his resignation (1811 and 1817), but in July 1817 he was relieved of all residential responsibility, and granted a year's absence for study in Germany. He was accompanied abroad by the theological tutor's second son, John Wellbeloved, who died at Homburg. During the winter semester he studied history at Göttingen under Heeren, attending also the lectures of Eichhorn and Blumenbach; the following summer semester he devoted to classical study at Berlin under F. A. Wolf, Boeckh, and Zumpt, and attended Schleiermacher's course of philosophy. He had valuable introductions, including one to the Duke of Cumberland, then residing at Berlin, of which, however, he was unwilling to avail himself. After a tour in southern Germany and Switzerland he returned to York in September 1820.

In 1825 Thomas Belsham [q. v.], brother of his stepmother, endeavoured to secure him as assistant at Essex Street Chapel, London; but Kenrick had now fixed himself in academic life, and though an able exponent of his own theological position, had none of the gifts of a popular preacher. He remained in office as tutor at York till 1840, his place being supplied by assistant-tutors during his absence from ill-health in the two sessions 1837-9. In 1840, when the college reverted from York to Manchester, and took the name of Manchester New College, he became professor of history, and held this chair till 1850; he continued to reside in York, going to Manchester to deliver his lectures. In 1851 he was appointed one of the visitors of the college, a post which he retained until his death.

Kenrick was, beyond question, the greatest scholar of his denomination, the equal of Eliezer Cogan [q. v.] in erudition, and his superior in culture. His philological publications belong to the period following upon his studies in Germany; his historical works to his later years of increased leisure. Dr. Martineau, who has spoken of Kenrick as 'the wisest man he ever knew,' describes his historical lectures as 'models of selection, compression, and proportion,' and regards his volume on 'Phœnicia' as his most permanent contribution to history. He was a fellow of the Society of Antiquaries, one of the founders of the Yorkshire Philosophical Society, and curator of the department of antiquities in its museum; the Cook collection in the hospitium was his gift, as also the cast of the obelisk of Nimrod in the entrance hall of the museum. His theology, while essentially that of the older unitarian school, was modified in its conservatism both by his critical judgments and by the simplicity of his religious trust. In private intercourse his courteous dignity, sparing and accurate speech, and incisive humour left a strong impression of

reserve of power and force of character. In person he was of middle height, with a light but well-knit frame, and a noble forehead.

He died at York on 7 May 1877, having preserved his faculties to the great age of eighty-nine. He was buried on 12 May in the York cemetery; his funeral sermon was preached by Charles Wicksteed. His portrait has been engraved. He married, on 13 Aug. 1821, Lætitia (d. 27 Sept. 1879, aged 84), eldest daughter of Charles Wellbeloved, his colleague, but had no issue.

He published, besides seven single sermons (1814-36), including a sermon (7 June 1827) before the British and Foreign Unitarian Association: 1. 'A Grammar of the Latin Language, by C. G. Zumpt. Translated ... with Additions,' &c., 1823, 8vo; 4th edit. 1836, 8vo. 2. 'Exercises of Latin Syntax,' &c., 3rd edit. 1835, 12mo (also 'Key' to this). 3. 'An Introduction to Greek Prose Composition,' &c., pt. i. 2nd edit. 1836, 12mo; pt. ii. 1835, 12mo (also 'Keys' to both parts). 4. 'Ἡροδότου αἱ Ἀἰγυπτιοι Λόγοι. The Egypt of Herodotus,' &c., 1841, 8vo. 5. 'An Essay on Primæval History,' &c., 1846, 12mo. 6. 'Ancient Egypt under the Pharaohs,' &c., 1850, 8vo, 2 vols. 7. 'The Value of the Holy Scriptures,' &c., 1851, 12mo. 8. 'Memoir of John Kentish,' prefixed to 'Sermons,' 1854, 12mo. 9. 'Phœnicia,' &c., 1855, 8vo. 10. 'Biographical Memoir of Charles Wellbeloved,' &c., 1860, 8vo (reprinted from the 'Christian Reformer'). 11. 'Biblical Essays,' &c., 1864, 12mo (reprinted from periodicals, the most important being 'On the Gospel of Mark,' regarded as the protevangelion). 12. 'Papers on Archæology and History,' &c., 1864, 12mo. 13. 'Memorials of the Presbyterian Chapel, St. Saviourgate, York,' &c., York, 1869, 8vo (originally contributed to the 'Unitarian Herald' in 1862). In 1832 he edited for Bishop Blomfield the fifth edition of the translation of Matthiae's 'Greek Grammar,' by Edward Valentine Blomfield [q. v.], the bishop's younger brother; and published separately (1833) an 'Index of Quotations from Greek Authors' contained in it. His inaugural lecture in the chair of history is in the 'Introductory Discourses ... in Manchester New College,' &c., 1841, 8vo. He contributed biographical and critical articles to the 'Monthly Repository,' 'Christian Reformer,' 'Prospective Review,' and other periodicals.

[Manuscript autobiography to 1810, begun 1870 and finished 14 Feb. 1872; Roll of Students, Manchester College, 1868 (with manuscript additions); Christian Life, 12 May 1877, 11 Oct. 1879; Inquirer, 19 May 1877; Martineau's In Memoriam, in Essays, Reviews, and Addresses,

1890, i. 397 sq. (reprinted from the Theological Review); Palmer's Older Nonconformity of Wrexham (1889), p. 52; unprinted letters of Belsham, Wellbeloved, and Kenrick.] A. G.

KENRICK, TIMOTHY (1759–1804), unitarian commentator, third son of John Kenrick of Wynne Hall in the parish of Ruabon, Denbighshire, by Mary, daughter of Timothy Quarrell of Llanfyllin, Montgomeryshire, was born at Wynne Hall on 26 Jan., and baptised on 6 Feb. 1759. His ancestor, Edward Kenrick, was owner of the Talbot Inn, Wrexham, in 1672. In 1774 he entered Daventry academy under Caleb Ashworth, D.D. [q. v.], succeeded in 1775 by Thomas Robins. While yet a student he was chosen assistant-tutor in classics; during one session he read lectures for Robins, who lost his voice, and on Robins's resignation (1781) he continued under Thomas Belsham [q. v.] as classical and afterwards as mathematical tutor. In January 1784 he became colleague to James Manning at George's Meeting, Exeter, and was ordained there on 26 July 1785. The two pastors worked well together, though Manning was an Arian, while Kenrick followed Belsham in theology, and drew up (1792) the preamble of the Western Unitarian Society, excluding Arians.

In 1798 he declined an invitation to the divinity chair in the Manchester Academy (now Manchester New College, Oxford). In the summer of 1799 he opened a nonconformist academy at Exeter, having Joseph Bretland [q. v.] as his coadjutor. He followed the Daventry model, and had the use of a library formed for the academy carried on (1690–1720) by Joseph Hallett (1656–1722) [q. v.], and revived (1760–71) under Samuel Merivale. In Kenrick's academy, which was finally closed on 25 March 1805, eleven students, including James Hews Bransby [q. v.], received the whole, and four others, including Kenrick's eldest son, a part of their training. Kenrick died suddenly while on a visit to Wrexham, on 22 Aug. 1804. He was buried on 26 Aug. in the dissenters' graveyard at Rhosddu, near Wrexham, where there is an inscription to his memory. He married, first, in 1786, Mary (d. 1793), daughter of John Waymouth of Exeter, who died in giving birth to her sixth child; John, the eldest son, is separately noticed. He married, secondly, in 1794, Elizabeth (d. 1819), second daughter of James Belsham, and sister of his former tutor, but had no issue by the second marriage.

He published four single sermons (1788–1795), and there appeared posthumously: 1. 'Discourses on Various Topics,' &c., 1805, 8vo, 2 vols. 2. 'An Exposition of the Historical Writings of the New Testament,' &c.,

1807, 8vo, 3 vols. (with 'Memoir' by John Kentish [q. v.], a work of great ability, which well represents the exegesis of the older unitarian school.

KENRICK, GEORGE (1792–1874), fourth son of the above, born at Exeter on 28 Oct. 1792, became a pupil of Lant Carpenter, LL.D. [q. v.], studied at Glasgow College (1808–10) and Manchester College, York (1810–13), and was unitarian minister at Chesterfield (1813–1814), Hull (1815–21), Maidstone (1822–6), Hampstead (1829–45), and Battle (1845–7). He was a trustee of Dr. Williams's foundations, 1833–60. In 1860 he retired in enfeebled health to Tunbridge Wells, where he died on 2 Dec. 1874. He married, first, in 1817, the youngest daughter of Richard Hodgson, unitarian minister at Doncaster; secondly, Lucy, sister of Sir John Bowring [q. v.]; thirdly, Sarah (d. 1888), daughter of Thomas Walters. He published sermons and contributed to the 'Monthly Repository' and other periodicals.

[Memoir prefixed to Exposition, 1807 (reprinted in Monthly Repository, 1808, pp. 87 sq.); Monthly Repository, 1818 p. 230, 1822 pp. 197, 557 sq.; March's Hist. Presb. and Gen. Bapt. Churches in West of England, 1835, pp. 406 sq., 507 sq.; Inquirer, 12 Dec. 1874; Jeremy's Presbyterian Fund, 1885, pp. 202 sq.; Palmer's Older Nonconformity of Wrexham [1889], p. 76.]

A. G.

KENRICK, WILLIAM (1725?–1779), miscellaneous writer, born about 1725, was the son of a staymaker at or near Watford, Hertfordshire. He was brought up as a scale-maker, or in some such employment, but early became a hack writer. He had a strong love of notoriety, a jealous and perverse temper, and was often drunk and violent. He became the enemy of every decent and successful person, and so notorious as a libeller that few condescended to answer him. His vanity led him to fancy himself equal to any task without serious study.

His first publication was a verse satire called 'The Town,' 4to, London, 1748. He next edited a miscellany of prose and verse, ostensibly contributed by various writers, entitled 'The Kapélion, or Poetical Ordinary: consisting of great variety of Dishes in Prose and Verse: recommended to All who have a good Taste or keen Appetite. By Archimagirus Metaphoricus,' 8vo, London. It was published in sixpenny numbers from August to December 1750. He wrote a 'Monody' on the death of Frederick, prince of Wales, London, 1751; 2nd edition, same year. Under the pseudonym 'Ontologos' he published a tract called 'The Grand Question Debated; or, an Essay to Prove that the Soul of Man is not, neither can it be, Immortal,' 8vo, Dublin, 1751 : which was followed by 'A Reply to the Grand Question Debated ; fully Proving that the Soul of Man is, and must be, Immortal,' 8vo, London, 1751, dedicated to the Archbishop of Canterbury. This was his first experiment in the plan of answering himself when no one else cared to do so (cf. his *Pasquinade*, p. 18 *n*.) In 1752 he published a burlesque called ' Fun : a Paroditragi-comical Satire,' attacking Fielding and Dr. John Hill (1716?–1775) [q. v.] An intended private performance at the Castle Tavern, Paternoster Row, on 13 Feb. 1752, was suppressed, at Fielding's desire, by a special order from the lord mayor and court of aldermen. It was anonymously printed, and copies were presented to all who had taken tickets (BAKER, *Biog. Dram.* 1812, ii. 253). Kenrick next attacked Hill (anonymously) in 'The Pasquinade. With Notes variorum. Book the First,' 4to, London, 1753. A second book, apparently never written, was to have libelled Christopher Smart, with whom he was at the time involved in controversy. According to Kenrick's account, Smart had advertised an 'Old Woman's Dunciad,' directed against Kenrick, but Kenrick had immediately published a piece under the same title, upon which Smart abandoned his design (*Pasquinade*, p. 20 *n*.) During the same year Kenrick wrote an imitation of Dodsley's ' Economy of Human Life' (which then passed for Lord Chesterfield's), called ' The Whole Duty of Woman. By a Lady. Written at the desire of a Noble Lord,' 12mo, London, 1753 ; 3rd edition the same year. In 1756 he published without his name a few copies of a philosophical poem in octosyllabics, called ' Epistles to Lorenzo,' 8vo, London, which obtained the praises of the ' Critical Review' (iii. 162–7). It was republished with alterations as ' Epistles, Philosophical and Moral,' 8vo, London, 1759 [1758] ; 4th edition, as ' Epistles to Lorenzo,' 1773. Its sceptical tone having been censured in the ' Critical Review' (vi. 439–53), Kenrick defended himself in an anonymous pamphlet called ' A Scrutiny, or the Criticks criticis'd,' &c., 8vo, London, 1759.

In January 1759 Kenrick was appointed to succeed Goldsmith as a writer in the ' Monthly Review,' and states that he contributed the review of foreign literature for vols. xxiii. to xxxiii. He also reviewed Goldsmith's ' Enquiry ' in November 1759 (xxi. 389), inserting at the request of the proprietor, Ralph Griffiths [q. v.], so vile an attack upon Goldsmith that even Griffiths was ashamed of it. Kenrick was therefore instructed to explain away his insinuations in

a favourable critique of Goldsmith's ' Citizen of the World,' which appeared in the ' Monthly Review' for June 1762 (xxvi. 477).

Kenrick (anonymously) translated Rousseau's ' Eloisa,' 4 vols. 12mo, Dublin, 1761, and ' Emilius,' 3 vols. 12mo, Edinburgh, 1763. For the ' Eloisa' he received the degree of LL.D. from the university of St. Andrews (*European Mag.* x. 20 *n*.) He also translated Rousseau's ' Miscellaneous Works,' 5 vols. 12mo, London, 1767.

Kenrick assailed Johnson's 'Shakespeare' (published October 1765), not without a certain coarse smartness, in 'A Review of Dr. Johnson's new edition of Shakespeare ; in which the Ignorance, or Inattention of that Editor is exposed, and the Poet defended from the Persecution of his Commentators,' 8vo, London, 1765 (BOSWELL, *Life of Johnson*, ed. G. B. Hill, i. 497). A threatened continuation never appeared, nor did a promised castigation of Johnson's ' Dictionary,' to be entitled ' A Ramble through the Idler's Dictionary : in which are picked up several thousand Etymological, Orthographical, and Lexicographical Blunders.' Kenrick's attention was diverted by a pamphlet written by an Oxford student named Barclay, entitled ' An Examination of Mr. Kenrick's Review ' [of Johnson's ' Shakespeare '], 1766. He retaliated with ' A Defence of Dr. Kenrick's Review. . . . By a Friend,' subscribed ' R. R.,' 8vo, London, 1766. Johnson was displeased with Barclay for doing what he disdained to do for himself (*ib.* ii. 209, v. 273). Kenrick again attacked Johnson in ' An Epistle to J. Boswell, Esq., occasioned by his having transmitted the Moral Writings of Dr. S. Johnson to Pascal Paoli : with a Post-script, containing Thoughts on Liberty ; and a Parallel after the manner of Plutarch, between the celebrated Patriot of Corte and John Wilkes, Esq., M.P. By W. K., Esq.,' 8vo, London, 1768. At Johnson's request Boswell refrained from answering that and another scurrilous libel by Kenrick, called ' A Letter to James Boswell, Esq., on the Moral System of the Idler,' 8vo.

Kenrick used to lecture at the ' Devil,' Temple Bar, and other taverns on every conceivable subject, from Shakespeare to the perpetual motion, which he thought he had discovered. Soon after his attack on Johnson he issued proposals for a new edition of ' Shakespeare,' with a commentary ' in a manner hitherto unattempted.' A few people were foolish enough to subscribe. After eight years had passed he informed them that, in consequence of George Steevens's commentary, the ' intended publication ' was for the present ' laid aside.' To console his subscribers he presented them with a meagre

c

instalment of his public lectures, called an 'Introduction to the School of Shakespeare. . . . To which is added a Retort Courteous on the Criticks,' &c., 8vo, London [1774].

Kenrick wrote for the stage, and for a time was patronised by Garrick. An abridgment of his comedy 'Falstaff's Wedding,' in continuation of Shakespeare's 'Henry IV' (published in 1760), was performed once at Drury Lane, 12 April 1766 (GENEST, v. 95). Two editions were issued in 1766; others in 1773 and 1781. Garrick's refusal to risk a further representation produced Kenrick's 'Letter to David Garrick, Esq., on the non-performance of "Falstaff's Wedding," &c.,' 4to (two editions). Another of his comedies, 'The Widow'd Wife' (printed in 1767 and 1768), was acted on 5 Dec. 1767, and reached a ninth night, though only through Garrick's judicious alterations (ib. iii. 405–7). Garrick is said to have acted ungenerously in the division of the profits (European Mag. x. 19–21), and a quarrel followed. Kenrick challenged Garrick to a duel, but had not the courage to fight (Garrick Correspondence, ii. 341). When in 1772 Isaac Bickerstaffe [q. v.] was driven from society, Kenrick grossly connected it by allusion with Garrick in a satire entitled 'Love in the Suds; a Town Eclogue. Being the Lamentation of Roscius for the Loss of his Nyky,' fol. London, 1772, ostensibly edited for an anonymous author. Prefixed is a most impudent letter to Garrick signed 'W. K.' Despite Garrick's attempts to suppress it, five editions of the libel were published during the year, each with additional papers and letters. The last edition contains 'The Poetical Altercation between Benedick and Beatrice,' extracted from the 'Morning Chronicle,' and written in defence of Garrick by Joseph Reed, the ropemaker and dramatist, though he had himself quarrelled with Garrick (LYSONS, Environs, ii. 431; NICHOLS, Lit. Anecd. ix. 118). Kenrick gave a minute account of his quarrel in 'A Letter to David Garrick, Esq.; occasioned by his having moved the Court of King's Bench against the publication of "Love in the Suds,"' &c., 4to, London, 1772. Kenrick finally inserted an abject apology in the newspapers for 26 Nov. 1772, with which Garrick professed to be satisfied (Garrick Correspondence, i. 477). Kenrick afterwards told Thomas Evans (1742–1784) [q. v.], the bookseller, that he did not believe Garrick guilty, but 'did it to plague the fellow.' Evans never spoke to him again. In 1773 Kenrick published a venomous anonymous 'Letter to D. Garrick, Esq., on his Conduct as principal Manager and Actor at Drury Lane. With a Preface and Notes by the Editor,' 4to, London [1773].

Kenrick now offered his plays to Colman at Covent Garden. He had had in 1768 a violent quarrel with Colman, who in his 'True State of the Differences, &c.,' 1768 (p. 60) had ridiculed the 'philosophical experiments' of Kenrick, and hinted that Kenrick was treacherously trying to supplant him as manager. Kenrick retorted with a verse 'Epistle to G. Colman,' 4to, London, 1768; 2nd edition same year. By March 1771 they had composed their differences (COLMAN, Posthumous Letters, 1820, pp. 158–61), and on 20 Nov. 1773 (GENEST, v. 414) Colman produced Kenrick's comedy 'The Duellist,' of which three editions were printed in the same year. The play was damned at once, on account, says Kenrick in his preface, of the resentment of the audience at Macklin's discharge. His comic opera, 'The Lady of the Manor,' with music by James Hook, altered from Charles Johnson's 'Country Lasses,' failed in 1778 (ib. vi. 80). Three editions and an altered version appeared in the same year. Another farce, called 'The Spendthrift, or a Christmas Gambol' (not printed), was acted for two nights also in 1778 according to the 'Biographia Dramatica' (iii. 295).

It was perhaps with some desire to propitiate Kenrick that Goldsmith consented in 1768 to take part in editing Griffin's 'Gentleman's Journal,' in which Kenrick was a leading writer. In 1771 Kenrick, having grossly libelled Goldsmith in the 'Morning Chronicle,' was forced by Goldsmith, upon an accidental meeting in the Chapter Coffee-house, to admit that he had lied. As soon as Goldsmith had left the room Kenrick abused him to the company, repeating various slanders. He was probably also the author of the atrocious attack upon Goldsmith and Miss Horneck, published in the 'London Packet' in 1773, for which Goldsmith thrashed the publisher, Evans [see under GOLDSMITH, OLIVER, where the date is misprinted 1771]. Kenrick is said to have been in the house at the time, and to have separated the combatants, and sent Goldsmith home in a coach (FORSTER, Life of Goldsmith, 1888, ii. 347–351).

Kenrick ceased writing for the 'Monthly Review' in 1766, when he announced in the newspapers that he was about to establish a new literary review. The first number of his 'London Review of English and Foreign Literature' did not appear until January 1775. In the editing Kenrick was latterly assisted by his son, William Shakespeare Kenrick, who carried it on after his father's death until June 1780. The review contains attacks upon members of every profession. Kenrick's 'Observations on S. Jenyns's "View of the Internal Evidences of the Christian Religion "' (vol. iii., appendix), was reissued in an enlarged form, 12mo, London, 1776.

In 1770 Kenrick published ' An Account of the famous Wheel of Hesse-Cassel, invented by Orffyreus,' 4to; and in 1771 ' Two Lectures on the Perpetual Motion, as discovered by the Author,' 4to. In 1774 he collected in part the ' Poetical Works' of Robert Lloyd in two octavo volumes, with a life of the author, remarkable for being written without dates. In 1775 he commenced a translation of Buffon's ' Natural History,' and in 1778 a translation of some of Voltaire's works. His last undertaking was an anonymous translation of Millot's ' Elements of General History,' 2 pts. 8vo, London, 1778-1779. On 19 May 1779 he petitioned the attorney-general for a patent for a mechanical principle of self-motion (*Gent. Mag.* xlix. 269). He died on 10 June 1779 (*ib.* xlix. 327), and was buried on the 13th in Chelsea Old Church (LYSONS, ii. 141). His portrait was engraved by Worlidge in 1763.

In his later years Kenrick seldom wrote without a bottle of brandy at his elbow. Though a superlative scoundrel, he was clever, and especially proud of the rapidity of his writing: even his more serious works seldom occupied him more than two days (*Pasquinade,* p. 20 n.) His other writings are: 1. ' Poems: Ludicrous, Satirical, and Moral,' 8vo, London, 1768; new edition, with additions, 1770. 2. ' A new Dictionary of the English Language. . . . To which is prefixed a Rhetorical Grammar,' 4to, London, 1773. 3. ' An Address . . . respecting an Application to Parliament for the farther Encouragement of new Discoveries and Inventions . . .,' with an appendix upon ' the late decision on literary property,' 4to, London, 1774. 4. ' Observations, Civil and Canonical, on the Marriage Contract, as entered into conformably to the Rites . . . of the Church of England,' 8vo, London, 1775. 5. ' Free Thoughts on Seduction, Adultery, and Divorce,' 8vo. 6. ' Rural Poems, translated from the German of Gesner,' 8vo.

[Prior's Life of Goldsmith, 1837, pp. 293-6; Forster's Life of Goldsmith, 1888, passim; Chalmers's Biog. Dict. xix. 323-7; Baker's Biog. Dram. 1812, i. 430-1; Faulkner's Chelsea, 1829, ii. 137; Georgian Era, iii. 546-7; Goldsmith's Miscellaneous Works, 1801, i. 103; Davies's Life of Garrick, ii. 132; Murphy's Life of Garrick, ii. 32, 33; Notes and Queries, 3rd ser. xi. 480, 4th ser. x. 9, 5th ser. iv. 209, 6th ser. viii. 267, 410; Cat. of Advocates' Library, iv. 331-2; The Recantation and Confession of Dr. Kenrick (a satirical piece), 1772; The Kenrickiad (a satire by ' Ariel '), 1772; Poetical Review . . . a Sa-

tirical Display of the literal Characters of Dr. K*nr**k (no date); Evans's Cat. of Engraved Portraits, ii. 231.]   G. G.

KENT, DUKE OF (1664?-1740). [See under GREY, HENRY, 1594-1651.]

KENT AND STRATHERN, EDWARD AUGUSTUS, DUKE OF (1767-1820), prince, fourth son of George III, by Queen Charlotte, born on 2 Nov. 1767 at Buckingham House, had his early education in England under John Fisher, successively bishop of Exeter and Salisbury [q. v.], and completed it on the continent under Baron Wangenheim, with whom he spent two years (1785-7) at Luneburg and Hanover, and two years more at Geneva. On 30 May 1786 he was gazetted brevet-colonel. Wangenheim treated him with needless rigour, allowed him only a guinea and a half a week pocket-money out of the annuity of 6,000*l.* provided for his maintenance, and intercepted his letters home. The prince accordingly borrowed largely, and the debts thus contracted were a burden to him throughout life. In June 1790 he came home from Geneva without leave. The king was much displeased, gave him peremptory orders to embark for Gibraltar, and saw him for only five minutes on the night before he sailed (1 Feb.) At Gibraltar he was put in command of the 7th regiment of foot (royal fusiliers). He at once showed himself a thorough martinet, and became so unpopular with his men that in May 1791 he was sent to Canada.

He was now in receipt of an income of 5,000*l.* a year, but out of this he had to pay the interest on his debts. In October 1793 he was advanced to the rank of major-general, and received at his own request orders to join Sir Charles (afterwards Lord) Grey's force in the West Indies. The navigation of the St. Lawrence being interrupted, he travelled by land at considerable risk from Quebec to Boston, and there took ship for Martinique, where he arrived on 4 March 1794. In command of a brigade of grenadiers he took part in the reduction of that island, and also of St. Lucia, was honourably mentioned in despatches, and received the thanks of parliament. On the close of the operations he returned to Canada, and on 16 Jan. 1796 was promoted to the rank of lieutenant-general. In October 1798 he was invalided by a fall from his horse, and returned to England.

In March 1799 parliament granted him an annual income of 12,000*l.*, and on 23 April he was raised to the peerage as Duke of Kent and Strathern and Earl of Dublin. On 10 May he was gazetted general, and on 17 May commander-in-chief of the forces in

c 2

British North America. He sailed in July, but was compelled by ill-health to return to England in the autumn of the following year. On 27 March 1802 he was appointed governor of Gibraltar, where he arrived on 10 May with express instructions from the Duke of York, then commander-in-chief, to restore the discipline of the garrison, which was seriously demoralised. He accordingly issued a general order, forbidding any but commissioned officers to enter the wine-shops, half of which—there were ninety on the Rock— he summarily closed at a personal sacrifice of 4,000*l.* a year in licensing fees. The incensed wine-sellers plied the soldiers with liquor gratis, and a mutiny, to which it was thought some of the officers were privy, broke out on Christmas eve 1802. The mutiny was promptly quelled, three of the ringleaders were shot, discipline was thoroughly restored, and in the following March the duke was recalled. On his return to England he demanded a formal investigation of his conduct, which was refused. He then asked to be permitted to return to Gibraltar; this also was refused. He still remained nominally governor, but without pay; the standing orders he had issued while in command were set aside by the lieutenant-governor, Sir Thomas Trigge, and the garrison relapsed into its former condition. On 7 Sept. 1805 the duke was gazetted field-marshal, and on 25 Nov. following keeper and paler of Hampton Court. For some years he resided at Castle Hill, near Ealing, taking little part in state affairs. He was, however, the confidant and adviser of the Prince of Wales in his matrimonial difficulties. In 1810 he opposed the Regency Bill as unconstitutional. In 1812 he spoke in favour of catholic emancipation, and became a patron of the British and Foreign School Society, the Anti-Slavery Society, the Society for Promoting Christianity among the Jews, and the Bible Society. In 1815 and 1816 he took the chair at the Literary Fund dinner. Finding his pecuniary embarrassments increase, and getting no relief from government, he made in 1815 an assignment of the bulk of his property in favour of his creditors, and retired to Brussels, where he lived in the simplest possible style. In 1818 he married, for reasons of state, Victoria Mary Louisa (see KENT, VICTORIA MARY LOUISA, DUCHESS OF), widow of Emich Charles, prince of Leiningen. The marriage was solemnised on 29 May at Coburg, and on 13 July following at Kew. Returning with his bride to the continent, he resided with her at her palace of Amorbach, Leiningen, until the spring of 1819, when he brought her to England for her confinement. After the birth of the child (now Queen Victoria) on 24 May, at Kensington Palace, he took the duchess and the princess to Sidmouth, Devonshire, and applied to parliament for authority to dispose of his establishment at Ealing by lottery, a sale being unadvisable, for the benefit of his creditors. The petition was refused, and the duke had made up his mind to return to Amorbach, when he died suddenly of inflammation of the lungs at Sidmouth on 23 Jan. 1820. During his illness he was attended with the utmost devotion by the duchess, to whom he left his entire property. He was buried in St. George's Chapel, Windsor, on 11 Feb.

As a soldier the duke never had an opportunity of gaining high distinction, and his pedantic, almost superstitious, insistence upon minutiæ of military etiquette, discipline, dress, and equipments, made him unpopular in the army. He was, however, the first to abandon flogging and to establish a regimental school. He was extremely regular in his habits, a model of punctuality and despatch in the discharge of duty, and sincerely pious. He was a knight of the orders of the Garter, Bath, and St. Patrick, and a knight grand cross of the Bath and of the order of the Guelphs. There is a portrait of the duke, together with his elder brother the Duke of Clarence (afterwards William IV), at Hampton Court Palace, dated 1779. A bronze statue by Gahagan is in Park Crescent, Portland Place.

[The principal authority is the Life by Erskine Neale, 1850. There are also obituaries in the Gent. Mag. and European Mag. for 1820. Reference may also be made to Nicolas's Hist. of British Knighthood; Smeeton's The Unique, vol. i. (with portrait); London Gazette for 1793, 1796, 1799, 1802, 1805; Annual Register, 1767 p. 170, and 1794 App. 68 et seq.; Commons' Journals, liv. 311; Gent. Mag. 1790 p. 80, 1818 pt. i. p. 562, pt. ii. p. 79, 1819 pt. i. p. 479; and the Duke of Buckingham's Memoirs of the Regency, ii. 390.]   J. M. R.

KENT, VICTORIA MARY LOUISA, DUCHESS OF (1786–1861), fourth daughter of Francis Frederic Antony, hereditary prince (afterwards duke) of Saxe-Saalfeld-Coburg, by Augusta Carolina Sophia, daughter of Henry, count Reuss-Ebersdadt, was born at Coburg on 17 Aug. 1786, and married on 21 Dec. 1803 to Emich Charles, hereditary prince, afterwards prince of Leiningen-Dachsburg-Hardenburg, a widower twenty-three years her senior. The marriage was happy, and on the death of the prince (4 July 1814) he left his widow guardian of their only son, Charles Frederick William Ernest (1804–1856), and regent of the principality. Her only other child by the prince was Anne Feodorowna Augusta Charlotte Wilhelmina (1807–1872), who resided with her mother till her marriage on 18 Feb. 1828 to Ernest Christian Charles, prince of Hohenlohe-Langenburg.

Princess Victoria Mary married in 1818 a second husband, Edward Augustus, duke of Kent [q.v.], fourth son of George III. The marriage ceremony took place at Coburg on 29 May, and was repeated at Kew on 13 July. By the Duke of Kent she had an only daughter, Alexandrina Victoria, now queen of England. On the duke's death on 23 Jan. 1820 the duchess was in straitened circumstances, having only a jointure of 6,000l. and an allowance of 3,000l. made her by her brother Leopold. In 1825, however, parliament voted her an annuity of 6,000l. towards the support and education of her daughter Victoria, and a further annuity of 10,000l. was granted her in 1831. In the previous year she had been appointed regent of the realm in the event of her daughter succeeding to the throne while yet a minor. She resided at Kensington Palace, devoting herself to the education of her daughter, and during the reign of George IV saw little society; but as the Princess Victoria grew up she took her from time to time to visit most of the places of interest in England, and gathered round her at Kensington a small highly intellectual coterie. She regretted the princess's accession to the throne in 1837 as depriving her of her one interest and occupation. Thenceforward she accompanied the court on its periodical migrations.

She died of cancer at Frogmore on 16 March 1861, and was buried in St. George's Chapel, Windsor, on 25 March, whence her remains were transferred to the royal mausoleum at Frogmore.

[Almanach de Gotha for 1790, 1805–6, 1817, 1829; Commons' Journals, lxxx. 471, lxxxvi. pt. ii. p. 727; Duke of Buckingham's Memoirs of the Courts and Cabinets of William IV and Victoria, ii. 24; Greville Memoirs, 1837–52, i. 15; Gent. Mag. 1861, pt. i. p. 456; Sir Theodore Martin's Life of the Prince Consort.] J. M. R.

KENT, EARLS OF. [See BURGH, HUBERT DE, d. 1243; EDMUND 'OF WOODSTOCK,' 1301–1329; GREY, EDMUND, first EARL (of the Grey line), 1420?–1489; GREY, GEORGE, second EARL, d. 1503 (under GREY, EDMUND, first EARL); GREY, HENRY, ninth EARL, 1594–1651; HOLLAND, EDMUND, fourth EARL (of the Holland line), d. 1408 (under HOLLAND, THOMAS, second EARL); HOLLAND, SIR THOMAS, first EARL, d. 1360; HOLLAND, THOMAS, second EARL, 1350–1397; HOLLAND, THOMAS, third EARL, and DUKE OF

SURREY, 1374–1400; NEVILLE, WILLIAM, d. 1463; ODO, d. 1097, bishop of Bayeux.]

KENT, MAID OF. [See BARTON, ELIZABETH, 1506?–1534.]

KENT, JAMES (1700–1776), organist and composer, born at Winchester on 13 March 1700, was admitted in November 1711 as chorister of Winchester Cathedral, under Vaughan Richardson. In 1714 he was sent to London, and was for four years a chorister of the Chapel Royal, under Dr. William Croft [q.v.]. In 1718, through the influence of the sub-dean (the Rev. John Dolben), he was appointed organist to the parish church of Finedon, Northamptonshire. 'An organ stool is still preserved at Finedon, on which Kent carved the initials and date, "J. K., 1717," probably a record of a visit anticipatory of his becoming organist there' (BEMROSE). In 1731 he was elected organist to Trinity College, Cambridge, and held the post till 1737, when he succeeded John Bishop [q.v.] as organist of Winchester Cathedral and College. The latter appointment he resigned in 1774 to Peter Fussell, and died in Winchester on 6 May 1776. He was married to Elizabeth, daughter of John Freeman.

In 1773 Kent published, in London, a collection of twelve anthems. He also wrote services in C and D, and assisted Dr. Boyce in the compilation of the latter's 'Cathedral Music.' His anthems were republished in London by T. Gresham in 1844. A selection of eight of them, together with Kent's two services, was edited in two volumes by Joseph Corfe.

Kent's music never rose above mediocrity, and he unscrupulously plagiarised the works of the Italian composers, especially Bassani, and also of Dr. Croft, whose style he closely followed. He took the chorus 'Thy Righteousness,' in the anthem 'Lord, what love,' from Bassani's 'Magnificat' in G minor, with very little alteration; and the 'Hallelujah' in the anthem 'Hearken unto this' is transcribed note for note from Bassani's 'Alma Mater' (GROVE).

[Grove's Dict. of Music, ii. 50, and i. 150; Bemrose's Choir Chant Book, App. p. xxii; Hogarth's Musical Hist. p. 299; Winchester Chapter Books; Kent's music in Brit. Mus.] R. F. S.

KENT, JOHN, or SION CENT (fl. 1400), also called JOHN OF KENTCHURCH, Welsh bard, is said to have been born at Cwm Tridwr in the parish of Egllwisilan, or, according to others, at Kilgerran, Pembrokeshire. He was educated by an uncle named Davydd Ddu o Lwyn Davydd Ddu, who lived at Pentyrch, and was afterwards a farm-servant near Caerphilly, but being ill-treated fled to Kentchurch, Herefordshire, and entered the service of the Scudamore family there. His patrons sent him to Oxford, and eventually he became a parish priest, first at Newcastle Emlyn, and then at Kentchurch. He is said to have lived to the age of a hundred and twenty. The popular legends make Kent a magician, and many stories of his power are still current in Monmouthshire; ' as great as the devil and John of Kent ' is a local proverb. One legend relates that he outwitted the devil by being buried half within and half without the church at Kentchurch. Another tombstone, without an inscription, is shown as Kent's at Grosmont, Monmouthshire (SYMONDS, *Diary*, p. 204, Camd. Soc.) In the possession of the Scudamore family at Kentchurch there is an ancient portrait, supposed to represent Kent; it is engraved in Coxe's ' Tour in Monmouthshire,' p. 338. The Scudamores are descended from a daughter of Owen Glendower, and hence some have conjectured that Kent was Glendower in disguise.

Kent apparently sympathised with Oldcastle, and it has been conjectured that he was the pretended chaplain John, whose services at the lollard leader's house in Kent excited the censure of Archbishop Arundel (WILKINS, *Concilia*, iii. 330-1); but for this there is no sufficient authority. Kent satirised the clergy and friars; but there seems to be no evidence for describing him as a lollard. He is one of the best of the Welsh poets, and one of the first and most successful cultivators of 'cntinued' verse. Numerous Welsh poems are extant under his name. Wilkins gives a list of forty-four pieces. Four are printed in the 'Iolo MSS.,' pp. 285, 286, 290, 304 (Welsh MSS. Soc. 1848). One of his poems is a ' Lamentation on the Condition of the Welsh under Henry IV,' and in another poem he alludes to the death of Sir John Oldcastle. Poems by Kent are to be found in Additional MS. 24980, and in the Myfyr MSS. (Add. MSS. 14932, 14965-7, 14972, 14974, 14977-9, 14984, 14988, 15001-15008, 15010, 15038) in the British Museum. Besides his poems, Kent is said to have been the author of a grammar, of ' The Apologue of Einiawn ab Gwalchmai,' ' Llyfr yr Offeren,' ' Araith y Tri Brodyr,' of a version of St. John's Gospel in Welsh, and of some fables, besides Latin theological treatises.

The suggestion that John Kent is identical with JOHN KENT or GWENT (*fl.* 1348) is impossible. The latter was a Franciscan, and doctor of theology at Oxford, where he was divinity reader for his order. He was

twentieth provincial of the Franciscans in England, is said to have worked miracles, and was the author of a commentary on the ' Sentences' of Peter Lombard. He died at Hereford, and was buried there (*Monumenta Franciscana*, i. 538, 554; LELAND, *Comment. de Scriptt.* pp. 376-7).

[Information supplied by the Rev. M. G. Watkins; Wilkins's Hist. of Literature of Wales, pp. 50-9; Iolo MSS. pp. 676-7, 682, 687; Williams's Eminent Welshmen, pp. 268-9; Coxe's Tour in Monmouthshire, pp. 336-8; Cambrian Journal, Tenby, 1859, pp. 268-75; Phillips's History of Cilgerran, p. 151; two biographical sketches in Welsh are contained in Geirlyfr Bywgraphiadol o Enwogion Cymru, pt. ii. and Geiriadur Bywgraffyddol o Enwogion Cymru.]   C. L. K.

KENT, NATHANIEL (1737-1810), land valuer and agriculturist, born in 1737, was first employed in the diplomatic service as secretary to Sir James Porter at Brussels. During his stay there he set himself to study the husbandry of the Austrian Netherlands, which was at that time held to be the best in Europe. Some of Kent's letters to Sir James Porter dated 1765 and 1766 are in Brit. Mus. MS. Egerton 2157. Returning to England in 1766, he drew up an account of Flemish husbandry at the request of Sir John Cust, speaker of the House of Commons, and was persuaded by him to quit diplomacy and devote himself to agriculture. He shortly afterwards made the valuable acquaintance of Benjamin Stillingfleet (q. v.) the naturalist. Kent published in 1775 ' Hints to Gentlemen of Landed Property,' London, 8vo (3rd edit. 1793), containing, among other valuable suggestions, some designs for labourers' cottages, which were greatly in advance of his time (DONALDSON, *Agricult. Biog.* p. 59). The book brought him employment on a large scale as an estate agent and land valuer, and he did much to improve English methods of land management (cf. *Gent. Mag.* 1811, pt. i. p. 182). His work lay chiefly in Norfolk, the farmers of which county presented him in 1808 with a silver goblet in acknowledgment of his services to agriculture, but he also suggested extensive embankments in Lincolnshire, which were successfully executed. Besides the ' Hints' he contributed ' A General View of the Agriculture of the County of Norfolk ' to the ' Survey' issued by the board of agriculture in 1794, with supplementary remarks, Norwich, 1796, and several papers to vols. iv. v. and vi. of Hunter's 'Georgical Essays,' York, 1803. Kent was for a short time bailiff of George III's farm in the Great Park at Windsor. Particulars concerning the king's farm, communicated by him to the Society of Arts in 1798, were subsequently published in pamphlet form. He died of apoplexy at Fulham, Middlesex, 10 Oct. 1810.

Another NATHANIEL KENT (*fl.* 1730), scholar, born at Weedon, Northamptonshire, was educated at Eton and King's College, Cambridge. He proceeded B.A. 1729, A.M. 1733, and became a fellow of King's College. In 1744 he was for a time deranged, but recovered, and in 1748 was head-master of Wisbech school, and afterwards curate of Kersey in Suffolk. While at Cambridge he published 'Excerpta quædam ex Luciani Samosatensis Operibus. In usum Tyronum,' Cambridge, 1730, 8vo. Latin notes and a Latin version accompany the text. The work was several times reprinted in London; the third edition 'prioribus auctior et emendatior' appeared in 1757; another ed. 1788.

[For the land valuer see Gent. Mag. 1810, pt. ii. pp. 396, 452; Kent's books in Brit. Mus. Cat.; and authorities quoted; for the scholar see Harwood's Alumni Etonenses, p. 315; Cat. of Cambridge Graduates; Cooper's Memorials of Cambridge, i. 229; Brit. Mus. Cat.]   R. B.

KENT, ODO OF (*d.* 1200), abbot of Battle. [See ODO.]

KENT, THOMAS (*d.* 1489), mathematician, was elected fellow of Merton College, Oxford, in 1480. According to Tanner and Pits, he had no small reputation as an astronomer and mathematician, and issued predictions as to the severe winter and famine of 1490. He died, however, of the plague 5 Sept. 1489, and was buried in the Merton burying-ground. He is said to have written a treatise on astronomy, but if he did so it has perished.

Another THOMAS KENT (*fl.* 1460) was clerk to the privy council. He graduated as a doctor of civil and canon law, probably at Cambridge, and was clerk to the privy council as early as 1444. His name consequently appears at the foot of many acts of the privy council (cf. NICOLAS, *Proceedings of the Privy Council*, vi. 31, 37, 38, &c.; STEVENSON, *Letters and Papers illustrative of the Wars of the English in France during the Reign of Henry VI*, i. 480, 493, &c.: for his signature see *Brit. Mus. Cotton. MS.* Galba, B. I. 151). Kent was frequently employed as an ambassador to various countries. On 4 July 1444 he was appointed, with Sir Humfrey Stafford, William Pyrton, and William Colebroke, to treat for commercial intercourse with Holland and Zealand (RYMER, *Fœdera*, xi. 67). On 20 July 1459 he was one of several commissioners, among whom was the Bishop of Durham, to treat with the king of Scotland about a truce (*ib.* xi. 424); his last embassy seems to have been entered

upon 20 Sept. 1467, when he made arrangements for the marriage of Charles the Bold with Margaret, sister of Edward IV (*ib.* p. 390). His salary when on an embassy seems to have been 20s. a day (*ib.* p. 504). Meanwhile, on 7 Jan. 1444-5, he had been appointed sub-constable of England, at a salary of one hundred marks a year from the customs of Southampton (*ib.* p. 75). A Thomas Kent, who may have been the same as the ambassador, resigned the rectory of St. Dunstan-in-the-East, London, in 1443, and was presented to the rectory of Woodford, Essex, 22 Aug. 1458.

[Tanner's Biog. Brit.; Pits, Rel. Hist. de Reb. Angl. p. 914; Wood's Hist. and Antiq. of Univ. of Oxf. ed. Gutch, App. p. 203; Brodrick's Memorials of Merton (Oxf. Hist. Soc.), pp. 37, 64, 241. For the ambassador see authorities quoted; Newcourt's Report. i. 333, ii. 662; and for his other embassies see Rymer's Fœdera, pp. 138, 186, 187, 189, 229, 233, 241, 269, 272, 274, 304, 415, 424, 504, 524, 541, 542, 563, 565, 576, 578, 590.]
W. A. J. A.

KENT, WILLIAM (1684–1748), painter, sculptor, architect, and landscape gardener, was born in the North Riding of Yorkshire in 1684, and was apprenticed to a coach-painter in his fourteenth year. Five years afterwards he left his employer without leave and came to London. There he made some attempts at portrait and historical painting, which, says Walpole, induced some 'gentlemen of his country' (county?) to send him to Rome. He went to Rome in company with John Talman [q. v.], the first director of the Society of Antiquaries, studied under the Cavalier Luti, and gained a second prize in the second class at the academy. At Rome also he met with other patrons. Sir William Wentworth allowed him 40l. a year for seven years, and in 1716 he attracted the notice of the Earl of Burlington [see BOYLE, RICHARD, third EARL OF BURLINGTON], who brought him to England with him, and gave him apartments in his town house for the remainder of his life. Through the influence of the earl he soon obtained extensive employment in portrait-painting, and covered the walls and ceilings in the houses of the aristocracy with historical and allegorical subjects. Among the works mentioned by Horace Walpole are 'full-lengths' (for the Right Hon. Henry Pelham [q. v.]) at Esher, Surrey; frescoes in the hall of Wanstead House (now destroyed), Essex; ceilings and staircases for Sir Robert Walpole at Houghton, Norfolk; and a staircase at Rainham, Norfolk, for Lord Townshend. But his talents did not lie in this direction. Hogarth's verdict, that neither England nor Italy ever produced a more contemptible dauber than Kent, has not been reversed since. William Mason, in the 'English Garden,' praises Kent's landscape gardening at the expense of his painting; and even Horace Walpole, who regarded him as a 'genius in other branches of art, tells us that Kent's portraits 'bore little resemblance to the persons who sat for them, and the colouring was worse,' and that 'in his ceilings Kent's drawing was as defective as the colouring of his portraits, and as void of every merit.' He adds that Sir Robert Walpole would not permit him to work in colours at Houghton, but restrained him to chiaroscuro. His portrait-painting was also the theme of a witty epigram by Lord Chesterfield:—

As to Apelles, Ammon's son
  Would only deign to sit;
So, to thy pencil, Kent! alone
  Will Brunswick's form submit!

Equal your envied wonders! save
  This difference we see,
One would no other painter have—
  No other would have thee.

Hogarth did not spare him or his patron. In two plates,'Masquerades and Operas, Burlington Gate' (1724), and 'The Man of Taste' (1732)—the Man of Taste was Burlington, not Kent—he introduced the statue of Kent surmounting the gate of Burlington House, and supported on a lower level by those of Raphael and Michael Angelo; and in his 'Burlesque on Kent's Altar-piece at St. Clement's' (St. Clement Danes in the Strand, 1725) he caricatured without mercy the feeble composition and bad draughtsmanship, which had already led Bishop Gibson to order its removal from the church. But Kent was able by his influence at court to retaliate upon Hogarth by preventing him from executing a portrait group of the royal family and other works (see 'Notes by George Vertue' in the Brit. Mus. Add. MS. 23076, p. 66).

Nevertheless Kent easily made his way in high society by his winning manners and the authority with which he spoke on questions of art, and he soon became the fashionable oracle in all matters of taste. His skill in design was so prized that, according to Horace Walpole, 'he was not only consulted for furniture, as frames of pictures, glasses, tables, chairs, &c., but for plate, for a barge, for a cradle. And so impetuous was fashion that two great ladies prevailed on him to make designs for their birthday gowns. The one he dressed in a petticoat decorated with columns of the five orders: the other like a bronze, in a copper-coloured satin with ornaments of gold.'

When he first seriously turned his attention to architecture is not clearly ascertained, but he probably began at an early date to assist the Earl of Burlington in his architectural designs; and in 1727, with the assistance of his lordship, he published two folio volumes of the 'Designs of Inigo Jones,' with a few by the earl and himself, and one by Palladio, the master and guide of them all. Kent's designs in this volume were mostly of chimneypieces and doors, but included one for a royal art gallery, in which panels for paintings alternated with niches for sculpture. Many of the nobility and some of the royal family were among the subscribers to this handsome work.

Kent went a second time to Rome, before 1719, and in 1730 he paid a third visit there to study architecture and buy pictures for Lord Burlington. It was perhaps on this occasion that he acquired the collection of engravings formed by his old master Luti, who had died in 1724. After his return he added largely to his reputation as an architect and a landscape gardener. He altered and decorated Kensington Palace, of which the staircase was thought by Horace Walpole to be 'the least defective work of his pencil.' He built the Horse Guards and the block of treasury buildings (the central portion of a design never fully executed) which overlook the parade at Whitehall. Devonshire House in Piccadilly, the Earl of Yarborough's in Arlington Street, and Holkham, Norfolk, the seat of the Earl of Leicester, are also examples of his skill in the Palladian style, and do more than any other of his existing works to justify the high patronage which he enjoyed.

Despite his poor ability he was selected to execute the statue of Shakespeare for Poets' Corner in Westminster Abbey, and was appointed principal painter to the crown after the death of Charles Jervas [q. v.] in 1739. Besides this office he held those of master-carpenter, architect, and keeper of the pictures, all of which, together with a pension of 100l. a year for his works at Kensington Palace, brought him an income of 600l. 'Kent's style,' says Walpole, 'predominated authoritatively during his life.' He was still engaged on his most important and favourite work (Holkham) when he died at Burlington House of an attack of inflammation in the bowels on 12 April 1748. He was buried 'in a very handsome manner' in Lord Burlington's vault at Chiswick. 'His fortune,' says Walpole, 'which with pictures and books amounted to about 10,000l., he divided between his relations and an actress, with whom he had long lived in particular friendship.'

It is only as an architect that Kent's artistic reputation now survives. If, as has been asserted, he had any hand in designing the beautiful colonnade of Burlington House (now lying neglected on the embankment at Battersea), this reputation might stand higher, but there appears to be no sufficient reason for depriving the Earl of Burlington of the full merit of this work. On the other hand, there seems to be no doubt that he was the real designer of Holkham, although the plans were published after Kent's death by his pupil and assistant, Matthew Brettingham, without any mention of Kent [see BRETTINGHAM, MATTHEW, the elder, and BRETTINGHAM, ROBERT FURZE]. He was a faithful follower of the Palladian style, the principles of which he understood, and his buildings, especially the Horse Guards, have the merit of fine proportion. As a decorator and designer of furniture he was heavy, but not without style.

Other works of Kent which are praised by Walpole are a staircase at Lady Isabella Finch's in Berkeley Square, the 'Temple of Venus' at Stowe, and the great room at the Right Hon. Henry Pelham's in Arlington Street. For this statesman he also built a Gothic house at Esher; and other works in the same style were the law courts at Westminster and a choir screen in Gloucester Cathedral; but all these have been demolished. His most important 'gardens' were those of Sir Charles Cotterel Dormer and of Carlton House, but they no longer exist. Walpole calls him the 'father of modern gardening,' 'the inventor of an art that realizes painting and improves nature. Mahomet imagined an Elysium, but Kent created many.' His claim to be the inventor of that more natural style of gardening and planting which was afterwards developed so greatly by 'Capability' Brown [see BROWN, LANCELOT] and others seems to be well founded, although Bridgman, who invented the 'haha,' was to some extent his predecessor. The principles Kent followed were those laid down by Pope in his 'Epistle to the Earl of Burlington,' and had been illustrated by Pope himself in his famous garden at Twickenham. Mason, in his 'English Garden,' speaks of Kent as Pope's 'bold associate.' In connection with John Wootton [q. v.] Kent designed some illustrations to Gay's 'Fables,' and he executed the vignettes to the large edition of Pope's 'Works,' and plates to Spenser's 'Fairy Queen,' 1751. All of these are poor, and the last are execrable.

Kent designed the decorations of the chapel-royal at the marriage in 1734 of Princess Anne and the Prince of Orange, and published an engraving of the scene. He also published a print of Wolsey's hall at Hampton Court. Two pictures by Kent are still exhibited at Hampton Court Palace, 'The Interview of Henry V and the Princess Katharine' (784), and the marriage of the same persons (788); and a model by Kent for a palace in Hyde Park is also to be seen there. A portrait of Kent by himself was lent by the Rev. W. V. Harcourt to the Loan Exhibition of Portraits at South Kensington in 1867.

[Walpole's Anecdotes of Painting; Redgrave's Dict.; Bryan's Dict. (Graves and Armstrong); Redgraves' Century of Painters; Cunningham's Lives of British Artists, 1831; The English Garden, by W. Mason, Commentary, &c., by W. Burgh, 1783; Fergusson's History of Architecture; Gwilt's Encyclopædia of Architecture; Sarsfield Taylor's Fine Arts in Great Britain and Ireland; Cat. of Loan Exhibition of Portraits at South Kensington, 1867; Biographie Universelle, article 'Luti, Benoit;' Nichols's Literary Anecdotes, v. 329, vi. 159; Chalmers's Dict.; Gould's Sketches of Artists; Pye's Patronage of British Art; Seguier's Dict.; Nagler's Künstler-Lexikon; Hist. MSS. Comm. 12th Rep. (1891), App. pt. ix. p. 191; Dobson's Hogarth (1891).]

C. M.

KENT, WILLIAM (1751–1812), captain in the navy, born in 1751, son of Henry Kent of Newcastle-on-Tyne, and of his wife Mary, sister of Vice-admiral John Hunter [q. v.], was promoted to the rank of lieutenant in 1781, and after continuous service in the Channel and North Sea was appointed in 1795 to the command of the Supply, in which, on 15 Feb., he sailed for New South Wales, in company with his uncle, Captain Hunter, in the Reliance. The ships arrived at Sydney on 7 Sept., and for the next five years Kent was employed in the service of the colony, making several voyages to Norfolk Island and the Cape of Good Hope, and surveying parts of the coast of New South Wales. In October 1800 he sailed for England in command of the Buffalo, and on his arrival was reappointed to her, June 1801, for the return voyage to Sydney, where, in October 1802, he was promoted by the governor, Captain King, to the rank of commander. In the following April he was ordered to go to Norfolk Island with stores, and thence through the islands examining their capabilities as to the supply of cattle and forage. He was afterwards to go to Calcutta and bring back as many cows as possible of the best breed. On 19 May he made the south-west coast of New Caledonia, and discovered a 'beautiful and extensive harbour,' which he named Port St. Vincent, where he remained for several weeks (KENT, Journal, quoted in 'Quarterly Review,' iii. 32). In January 1804 he was at Calcutta (Addit. MS. 13753, f. 96), and returned to Port

Jackson in June, bringing back a supply of cattle and other stores. He was afterwards moved into the Investigator, which had undergone a thorough repair [cf. FLINDERS, MATTHEW], and in 1805 was sent home with important information about the state of Peru. The Investigator was paid off at Plymouth on 22 Dec. 1805, and on 22 Jan. 1806 Kent was advanced to post rank. In November 1808 he was appointed to the Agincourt, and from her was moved to the Union of 98 guns, in command of which, off Toulon, he died 29 Aug. 1812.

In 1791 Kent married his cousin Eliza, daughter of William Kent of Newcastle-on-Tyne, and left issue one son, born at Sydney in 1799. A portrait of Kent in pastel is in the possession of his grandson Mr. Charles Kent.

[Information from Mr. Charles Kent; Gent. Mag. 1810 pt. i. p. 288, 1812 pt. ii. p. 400; O'Byrne's Naval Biog. Dict. s.n. 'Kent, William George Carlile;' Collins's Account of the English Colony in New South Wales, ii. 306; Flinders's Voyage to Terra Australis; official letters, &c.. in the Public Record Office.] J. K. L.

KENTEN (d. 685), West-Saxon King. [See CENTWINE.]

KENTIGERN or ST. MUNGO (518?-603) was the apostle of the Strathclyde Britons. There is a fragment of a life of Kentigern by an unknown author of the twelfth century, and a biography written near the close of that century by Jocelyn, a monk of Furness, who tells us that he had before him two lives of the saint, one used in the church, and another in the vernacular; that in both of these there was something contrary to sound doctrine and the catholic faith, and that his purpose was to compile a life free from these blemishes, and to 'season what had been composed in a barbarous way with Roman salt.' The main facts given by these writers of the twelfth century are regarded as historical, and are to some extent confirmed by the records of Wales, Adamnan's 'Life of St. Columba,' and the dedication of churches to St. Kentigern in the localities associated with his life.

Kentigern was born probably in 518. His mother, Thenaw, was the daughter of Loth, a British prince, after whom the Lothians are called, and whose seat was at Traprain Law, then named Dunpelder, halfway between Haddington and Dunbar. Prior to that time there had been a church at Dunpelder, and though Loth is described as a semi-pagan, his daughter was a Christian, and perhaps a nun. She was sought in marriage by Owen or Ewen, a Briton of the noblest stock, but she refused his offer, preferring a life of virginity. Her father was so indignant that he handed her over to the charge of a swineherd, who was secretly a Christian. Her suitor met her by stratagem in a wood, and having violated her she became pregnant. When her father heard of her condition, he caused her to be hurled from the top of a hill called Kepduff, but she escaped without injury. He then put her in a coracle, or boat of hides, in Aberlady Bay, and left her to the mercy of the winds and waves. The boat was first carried out beyond the Isle of May, then driven up the Frith to Culross, where she landed, and where her child, a son, was born. Mother and son were brought into the presence of a Christian pastor, an earlier St. Serf, or one to whom that name was afterwards erroneously given, who on seeing the child exclaimed in Celtic, 'Mungo,' i.e. my dear one. Mother and child were baptised by him, the latter receiving the christian name of Kentigern, or head chief, in allusion to his descent. He was trained in the monastic school at Culross kept by the saint, and became one of his chief favourites. In early manhood he left his protector to become a missionary to the people of his own race, and took up his residence at Cathures (now Glasgow), beside a cemetery and a church founded by St. Ninian (q. v.), but then in ruins. There he was chosen bishop by the king, clergy, and people who remained Christian, and was consecrated, according to Jocelyn, by a bishop summoned from Ireland for the purpose. After some years he suffered such persecution from heathens in the neighbourhood, the kindred of a King Morken, that he removed to Wales. On the way he stopped for a time in the Cumberland mountains, where he converted many to the faith, and then went to Menevia (now St. Davids). Having obtained a grant of land from the king of North Wales or the king's son, he founded the monastery of Llanelwy (afterwards St. Asaph's) in the vale of Clwyd, and gathered around him 965 monks, some of whom were employed in agriculture, others in education and the conducting of divine service, while the more experienced accompanied Kentigern on his missionary tours. The battle of Arthuret, near Carlisle, fought in 573, established the supremacy of the Christian party among the Britons of the north, and Rhedderch the Bountiful, who then became king of Strathclyde, sent messengers to recall Kentigern. The latter appointed Asaph his successor in the monastery, and returned to the north with many of his monks. Rhedderch and his people met him at Hoddam in Dumfriesshire, and welcomed him with great joy. There he fixed his see for some years, founding churches and ordaining clergy; and at this period he visited Galloway, and reclaimed its Pictish inhabitants from the idolatry and heresy into which they had fallen after the death of St. Ninian. After this Kentigern returned to Glasgow, which became henceforth the headquarters of Christianity among the Strathclyde Britons. He was the great means of planting or restoring Christianity in that large district which afterwards formed the diocese of Glasgow. He also visited Alban, i.e. Scotland north-east of the Forth, and the dedication of some churches in Aberdeenshire bears witness to his labours in that quarter. He is also said somewhat doubtfully to have sent missionaries to Orkney, Norway, and Iceland. In his later years St. Columba (of whose intercourse with King Roderech we have traces in Adamnan's 'Life') came from Iona with many followers to visit him. Kentigern went out to meet him with a large retinue, and as the two bands approached they sang alternately appropriate verses of the Psalms. The two venerable men exchanged crosiers in token of mutual affection. Kentigern died on 13 Jan. 603, and his grave is shown in the crypt of Glasgow Cathedral, named from him St. Mungo's. Jocelyn says he lived to the age of 187, but historians are agreed in striking off the century. Many miracles were in after times attributed to him; e.g. he ploughed his fields with a stag and a wolf from the forest, sowed sand and reaped wheat, caused the Clyde to overflow its banks, and to bring the barns of the king who persecuted him to his own dwelling. When some of the highland clergy who came with St. Columba stole one of his rams and cut off its head, he caused the decapitated animal to run back to the flock, and turned the head to stone in the hands of the thief. When a boy at Culross he restored to life a pet robin which his companions had torn in pieces, and kindled a fire with a frozen oak branch. King Roderech found a ring which he had given to his queen on the finger of a sleeping knight, threw it into the Clyde, and then demanded it of his spouse. In her distress she applied to the saint, and he sent a monk to the river to fish, who caught a salmon with the ring in its mouth. Hence the bird, tree, fish, and ring in the arms of Glasgow.

[Bishop Forbes's St. Kentigern in vol. v. of the Historians of Scotland; Skene's Celtic Scotland, ed. ii.; Notes and Queries, 2nd series, i. 194, ii. 13, 92; Dict. of Christian Biog.]

G. W. S.

KENTISH, **JOHN** (1768–1853), unitarian divine, only son of John Kentish (d. 1814), was born at St. Albans, Hertfordshire, on 26 June 1768. His father, at one time a draper, was the youngest son, and ultimately the heir, of Thomas Kentish, who in 1723 was high sheriff of Hertfordshire. His mother was Hannah (d. 1793), daughter and heiress of Keaser Vanderplank. After passing through the school of John Worsley at Hertford, he was entered in 1784 as a divinity student at Daventry academy, under Thomas Belsham [q. v.], William Broadbent [q. v.], and Eliezer Cogan [q. v.] In September 1788 he removed, with two fellow-students, to the new college at Hackney, in consequence of a prohibition by the Coward trustees of any use of written prayers at Daventry. In the autumn of 1790 he left Hackney to become the first minister of a newly formed unitarian congregation at Plymouth Dock (now Devonport), Devonshire. A chapel was built in George Street (opened 27 April 1791 by Theophilus Lindsey [q. v.]), and a prayer-book drawn up by Kentish and Thomas Porter of Plymouth. In 1794 he succeeded Porter as minister of the Treville Street congregation, Plymouth. In 1795 he removed to London as afternoon preacher at the Gravel Pit, Hackney, adding to this office in 1802 that of morning preacher at St. Thomas's Chapel, Southwark. On 23 Jan. 1803 he undertook the pastorate of the New Meeting, Birmingham. In 1832 he declined the emolument but retained the office of pastor, and continued to preach frequently till 1844. He retained his faculties to a great age, and died of pneumonia on Sunday, 6 March 1853, at his residence, Park Vale, Edgbaston. On 15 March he was buried in Kaye Hill cemetery, Birmingham. A mural tablet to his memory was placed in the New Meeting, removed in 1862 to the church of the Messiah, Birmingham. His portrait, painted in 1840 by Phillips, was engraved by Lupton; a full-length silhouette, executed in 1851, exhibits his short stature, portly figure, and old-fashioned costume with knee-breeches. He married, in October 1805, Mary (b. 21 March 1775, d. 9 March 1864), daughter of John Kettle of Birmingham, but had no issue.

Kentish was a man of great personal dignity, and his weight of character, extensive learning, and ample fortune munificently administered, secured for him a consideration rarely accorded to a nonconformist minister. His favourite study was biblical exegesis; he was a scholar of solid attainment, versed in oriental languages, and familiar with the labours of German critics. In politics an old whig, he was in religion a unitarian of the most conservative type, holding closely to the miraculous basis of revelation. His sermons were remarkable for beauty of style.

He published, in addition to separate sermons (1786–1844): 1. 'Letter to James White, &c., 1794, 8vo. 2. 'Reply to Fuller's Examination of the Calvinistic and Socinian

Systems,' &c., 2nd edit. 1798, 8vo. 3. 'Notes and Comments on Passages of Scripture,' &c., 1844, 8vo; 2nd edit. 1846, 8vo: 3rd edit. 1848, 8vo. 4. 'Biographical Notice of Rev. George Wiche,' &c., 1847, 8vo. 5. 'Sermons,' &c., Birmingham, 1848, 8vo; 2nd edit. with 'Memoir' by John Kenrick [q. v.], 1854, 8vo. His 'Memoir' of Timothy Kenrick [q. v.] is prefixed to the latter's 'Exposition,' 1807, 8vo, 3 vols. To the 'Monthly Repository' and 'Christian Reformer' he was a frequent contributor, usually with the signature 'N.'

[Biographical Dictionary of Living Authors, 1816, p. 187; Murch's Hist. Presb. and Gen. Bapt. Churches in the West of England, 1835, pp. 504 sq., 526 sq.; Inquirer, 19 March 1853, p. 180 (article by John Kenrick, reprinted from the Birmingham Mercury); Christian Reformer, 1853 pp. 262, 265 sq. (memoir by John Kenrick, reprinted with Sermons, 1854), 1854 p. 223; Unitarian Herald, 18 March 1864, p. 99; Addit. MS. 24870; personal recollection.]   A. G.

KENTON, BENJAMIN (1719–1800), vintner and philanthropist, was born in Fieldgate Street, Whitechapel, on 19 Nov. 1719. His mother kept a greengrocer's shop, and he was educated in the charity school of the parish. At the age of fifteen he was apprenticed to the keeper of the Angel and Crown Inn, Whitechapel, and when he had served his time became waiter and drawer at the Crown and Magpie in Aldgate. A large crown of stone surmounted by a magpie of pear-tree wood was the sign, and sea-captains were the principal customers. The owner wantonly let the Magpie decay and changed the name to the Crown. Custom fell off: he died, and the business passed into Kenton's hands. The sea-captains who had previously purchased their ale for long voyages at the tavern still bought it of Kenton, who was famous as an attentive waiter. It often excited their admiration that, when they were dining above stairs, the waiter below in the bar knew when the candles wanted snuffing, and his explanation that his knowledge was due to no extraordinary instinct, but merely to the observation of a contemporary light in the bar, does not seem to have diminished their opinion of his sagacity. He restored the sign of the magpie, and because possessed of a secret which made his fortune, that of bottling ale so that it could pass through the changes of climate on the voyage to India round the Cape, without the cork flying out of the bottle. Thomas Harley [q. v. was alderman of Portsoken, the ward in which Kenton took a house, and gave him judicious advice as to investments. He thus attained to great wealth, and on retiring from active business went to live in Gower Street, and there died 25 May 1802. He had been en-

rolled a member of the Vintners' Company 3 April 1734, and was elected master in 1776. A portrait of him in their court-room shows that he was a man of solid proportions with a slight inward squint. He was married and had one son, whom he bred a druggist, but who died young, and one daughter, who became attached to his clerk, but died before her father would allow the marriage. The clerk behaved in so honourable and considerate a manner in the difficult circumstances of the engagement that Kenton made him his chief friend, and bequeathed to him 300,000l. He was a liberal benefactor of the parish school where he was educated, of Sir John Cass's school in Portsoken, and of the Vintners' Company. He gave 5,000l. to St. Bartholomew's Hospital, of which his friend Harley was treasurer, and a surgical ward in the north wing is called after him. He was buried in Stepney Church, where he has a monument by Westmacott, and the master and court of the Vintners attend an annual sermon to commemorate his benefactions. A street near Brunswick Square, London, is named after him.

[Herbert's History of the Twelve Great Livery Companies, ii. 634, 637; Benjamin Standring's B. Kenton, a Biographical Sketch, London, 1878; Monthly Magazine, 1802; information received at Vintners' Hall.]   N. M.

KENTON, NICHOLAS (d. 1468), Carmelite, born at Kenton, near Framlingham, Suffolk, became a Carmelite at Ipswich, and studied at Cambridge. On 2 March 1419, being then resident at Whitefriars, London, he was ordained sub-deacon, and on 1 Dec. 1420 priest. In 1444 he was chosen twenty-fifth provincial of his order in England in a council held at Stamford, and retained his office twelve years. He died in London 4 Sept. 1468, and was buried at Whitefriars. Weever quotes his epitaph (Funerall Monuments, p. 438). Leland wrongly gives the date of death as 1460.

Kenton is credited with a commentary on the 'Song of Songs' and a variety of theological treatises. He is also said to have written lives of saints belonging to his order; among them was a 'Life of St. Cyril.' The Bollandists suggest that this collection of lives may possibly be identical with an anonymous collection in their possession (Acta Sanctorum, January, iii. 688). Bale specifies a number of letters of Kenton's with some exactness, and in Brit. Mus. Harleian MS. 1819, f. 196 b, gives the purport of one. Kenton is also credited with 'Carmen votorum ad dominum Albertum Carmelitam et dominum Andream episcopum' (i.e. St. Andrew of Fiesole); St. Andrew is said to have worked a miracle for Kenton's benefit (*ib.* January, iii. 687).

[Leland's Comment. de Scriptt. p. 459 ; Bale, viii. 28 ; Harleian MS. 3838, ff. 91 *a*-92 *a* (Bale's Heliades); Pits, p. 658 ; Davy's Athenæ Suffolciences in Addit. MS. 19165, ff. 75-6 ; C. de Villiers's Bibl. Carmelit. ii. 499-501.] C. L. K.

KENULF (*d.* 1006), bishop of Winchester. [See CENWULF.]

KENULF or **CYNEWULF** (*fl.* 800), Anglo-Saxon poet. [See KYNEWULF.]

KENWEALH (*d.* 672), king of the West Saxons. [See CENWALH.]

KENYON, JOHN (1784-1856), poet and philanthropist, was born in 1784 in the parish of Trelawney, Jamaica, where his father owned extensive sugar plantations. His mother was a daughter of John Simpson of Bounty Hall in the same parish, also a sugar planter. Both parents died while Kenyon was a boy at Fort Bristol School, Bristol. Thence he went for a time to the Charterhouse, and after some desultory dabbling in experimental science at Nicholson's Philosophical Institute, Soho, proceeded in 1802 to Peterhouse, Cambridge. Kenyon left Cambridge without a degree in 1808, married, and settled at Woodlands, between Alfoxden and Nether Stowey in Somerset. Here he made the acquaintance of Thomas Poole [q. v.], and through him of Coleridge, Wordsworth, Southey, Charles Lamb, and an ever-widening circle of men of letters. Rich, and without ambition, he spent his life in society, travel, dilettantism, dining, and dispensing charity. Among the first to profit by his philanthropy were Coleridge's family. In later life he distributed his alms in a systematic manner through the medium of sisters of charity, who investigated every case. At Paris in 1817 Kenyon met Ticknor, the historian of Spanish literature, who corresponded with him for years, and introduced to him many Americans, to whom his house was always open. Among these were Bayard Taylor and James T. Fields.

Other of Kenyon's friends about this period were Bryan Waller Procter (Barry Cornwall) [q. v.], Augustus William Hare [q. v.], Julius Charles Hare [q. v.], and Crabb Robinson [q. v.]. At Fiesole in 1830 he met Landor, who when in England was frequently his guest, and wrote part of 'Orestes at Delphos' under his roof. Kenyon was one of Southey's travelling companions on his French tour in 1838, and when, to procure him complete relief, they persuaded him to play, as if in jest, the part of a prince, while they divided among

themselves the offices of his suite, Kenyon selected that of master of the horse, and made all the necessary arrangements for posting. Meeting Browning at a dinner-party, he discovered in him the son of one of his schoolfellows at Fort Bristol, whom he had lost sight of. This was the beginning of a warm and close friendship broken only by death. Kenyon first introduced Browning, at the house of her parents, to Elizabeth Barrett, a distant relative and *soi-disant* cousin of Kenyon, who became Browning's wife. To Kenyon Browning dedicated his 'Dramatic Romances and Lyrics.' Failing to procure for Kenyon a copy of the picture of 'Andrea del Sarto and his wife' in the Pitti Palace, Browning wrote and sent to him from Florence the poem 'Andrea del Sarto.' When the Brownings visited England, Kenyon's house was their home, and here in 1856 Mrs. Browning finished 'Aurora Leigh,' and dedicated it to Kenyon in grateful remembrance of a friendship 'far beyond the common uses of mere relationship and sympathy of mind.'

Kenyon was early left a widower, and in 1823 married Caroline, sister of John Curteis, a wealthy bachelor, whose residence, 39 Devonshire Place, he shared when in London. He had also a villa at Torquay, and others in later life at Wimbledon (Lime Cottage) and Cowes. His second wife died on 7 Aug. 1835, and her brother on 27 April 1849, leaving Kenyon the bulk of his property, amounting to 100,000*l.*, great part of which with characteristic generosity he made over to the next-of-kin, some distant relatives of the testator.

Crabb Robinson says that Kenyon had 'the face of a Benedictine monk and the joyous talk of a good fellow;' other of his friends saw in him an idealised impersonation of the Mr. Pickwick of Seymour's plates. He was the beau ideal of a host, his exuberant geniality communicating itself as by a contagion to his guests, and bringing people of the most opposite characters into sympathetic accord. He was also, like his friend Philip Courtenay, Q.C., a thorough gastronome. On one occasion he commended to his guests' attention one of the earliest brace of canvasbacked ducks ever seen in Europe, with an exhortation 'not to talk, but to eat and think.' He died after a lingering and painful illness at Cowes on 3 Dec. 1856, and was buried in the vault belonging to his wife's family in Lewisham churchyard. By his will he divided his property between his friends and various charities, the largest legacy, 10,000*l.*, being taken by Browning. A portrait of Kenyon in oils by William Fisher, the property of Mr. George Scharf, C.B., F.S.A., is at the

National Portrait Gallery. Another, by the same artist, a companion picture to the Landor in the National Portrait Gallery, is in the possession of Mr. George Scharf, and was exhibited in the Victorian Exhibition (No.223) held in London in 1892. A marble bust of him, done at Rome in 1841 by T. Crawford, was in the possession of Browning. A lithograph of a half-length in water-colours, by Moore, was presented by him to his friends; and a fine cameo profile of him was executed by Saulini at Rome.

Kenyon published 'A Rhymed Plea for Tolerance,' London, 1833, 8vo; 'Poems, for the most part occasional,' London, 1838, 8vo; and 'A Day at Tivoli, with other Verses,' London, 1849, 8vo. These productions hardly pass muster as poetry. The 'Rhymed Plea' is a didactic dialogue in the heroic couplet on the duty of tempering religious zeal with charity. The other two volumes contain some graceful verses.

[Many interesting reminiscences and anecdotes of Kenyon are collected by Mrs. Andrew Crosse in Temple Bar, April 1890, January 1892, and references to him occur in Southey's Life, Ticknor's Life, Letters, and Journals, L'Estrange's Life of Mary Russell Mitford, Horne's Letters of Elizabeth Barrett Browning, Ingram's Life of Elizabeth Barrett Browning, Crabb Robinson's Diary, Clayden's Rogers and his Contemporaries, Macready's Reminiscences, Field's Old Acquaintance. See also Forster's Life of Landor; Sharp's Life of Robert Browning; Mrs. Sutherland Orr's Life and Letters of Robert Browning, pp. 105, 145, 154, 209; Sandford's Thomas Poole and his Friends, ii. 312; Gent. Mag. 1835 pt. ii. p. 331, 1849 pt. i. p. 664, 1857 pt. i. pp. 105, 309; Notes and Queries, 5th ser. vii. 285; Edinburgh Review, xlviii. 461 et seq.; Blackwood, xliv. 779 et seq.; North American Review, xlviii. 461 et seq. Material for the present sketch has also been furnished by Mr. George Scharf of the National Portrait Gallery.]   J. M. R.

KENYON, LLOYD, first LORD KENYON (1732–1802), master of the rolls, the second son of Lloyd Kenyon of Gredington, Flintshire, a landed proprietor and farmer of good education but limited means, by his wife Jane, eldest daughter of Robert Eddowes of Gredington and of Eagle Hall, Chester, was born at Gredington on 5 Oct. 1732. He was educated under Dr. Hughes—whom in after-life he appointed preacher at the Rolls Chapel—at first at his day-school in the neighbouring village of Hanmer, and afterwards at Ruthin grammar school, of which Hughes became head-master. He learnt a little Latin—though his bad Latin was always jeered at when he was a judge—and enough French to be subsequently improved into tolerable French scholarship, but no Greek. Being a

younger son, he was at seventeen years of age articled to a solicitor of Nantwich, Cheshire, named Tomkinson, in whose office he remained even after his elder brother had died, and he had been entered as a student of the Middle Temple on 7 Nov. 1750. His mental alertness soon showed itself, and he made great progress, so that, upon Tomkinson's refusal to take him into partnership, he left Nantwich in February 1755 a rapid and accurate conveyancer. He proceeded to London, and was called to the bar on 10 Feb. 1756. (Lord Campbell, however, rightly points out that his reports of cases begin with Easter term 1753, and thence infers, with some probability, that he must have been resident in London from that time.) For some years he had no practice. He lived on the 80l. a year furnished by his father, lodged frugally near the Temple in Bell Yard, by day took notes of Lord Mansfield's judgments (from 1753 to 1759) in the king's bench, which were published posthumously by J. W. Hanmer in 1819, and read law sedulously by night. At last he obtained a little conveyancing, and contrived to pay the expenses of going the North Wales circuit and the Stafford, Oxford, and Shrewsbury sessions by the briefs procured for him by friends. The friendship of John Dunning (afterwards Lord Ashburton), which he obtained in 1759 and kept till Dunning's death in 1782, first brought him regular employment, and while acting as Dunning's 'devil' he obtained a junior practice of his own. He was retained for the Duke of Portland in election contests in Cumberland, was introduced to Thurlow, and supplied by his industry the defects of Thurlow's indolence, and in his turn became the patron and helper of John Scott (afterwards Lord Eldon). His fee-book shows both his rise and the gains of lawyers in his day. Till 1764 he made nothing. In that year he received 80l.; in 1770 1,124l.; in 1771 2,487l.; in 1772 3,134l.; in 1775 4,225l.; in 1778 5,008l.; in 1780, the year in which he became a king's counsel, 6,359l.; in 1781 7,437l.; and in 1782, having become attorney-general, 11,038l. He made 80,000l. in sixteen years; his fees for opinions on cases alone were in 1780 2,578 guineas, in 1781 2,936 guineas, and in 1782 3,020 guineas. On the death of his father in 1775 he succeeded to the family estates at Gredington, and, marrying his cousin Mary, daughter of George Kenyon of Peel Hall, Bolton, Lancashire, went to live in Lincoln's Inn Fields. On the death of Sir R. Aston in 1778 he was sounded by Thurlow and Wedderburn about taking the vacant judgeship, but on the advice of Thurlow refused it; and he again declined a similar offer in 1780, on the death of Sir William Blackstone. He was now leader of his circuit, received a silk gown on 30 June 1780, and was the same year appointed chief justice of Chester, a post which he much coveted and prized. On the trial of Lord George Gordon (5 Feb. 1781) he was briefed with Erskine, and, though the latter had been called only two years, Kenyon yielded to him, as the first orator at the bar, the lead in the case, and supplied him with learning and experience. He opened the defence in a speech which Lord Campbell calls 'very honest but very inefficient,' and cross-examined most of the witnesses, but left to Erskine the reply (see *State Trials*, vol. xxi.) At the general election of 1780 he was returned, through Thurlow's influence, for the borough of Hindon in Wiltshire, and took his seat on 31 Oct. He acted with the opposition, but until Lord North's fall only spoke once, on a motion to expedite the hearing of an election petition. He was, in fact, a very bad speaker, thick and hurried in his utterance, awkward in delivery, obscure in expression, and irritable under opposition or interruption. With some hesitation, and acting as usual upon the advice of Dunning and Thurlow, he accepted the offer of the attorney-generalship which Lord Rockingham made him on taking office (23 April 1782). He set himself against the wish of his colleagues, to remedy the abuse which permitted the receivers of the funds in the different government offices to retain balances in their hands for long periods together without accounting for them, and proposed resolutions calling on Rigby, late paymaster-general, and Welbore Ellis, late treasurer of the navy, to file statements of the balances, said to amount to 1,100,000*l.*, which were in their hands on quitting office. His resolutions were rejected, but he pressed the matter till a subsequent ministry introduced a bill to pay exchequer auditors and tellers by salary and not by fees. When Lord Shelburne came in, Kenyon adhered to him, and, quitting office with him, resigned on 15 April 1783. He resumed it reluctantly under Pitt (26 Dec. 1783), for he disliked both the business of his office and the duties of parliament. His health was impaired, and accordingly, upon the death of Sewell, master of the rolls, shortly before parliament was dissolved, he yielded to the pressure of Pitt and Shelburne, resigned his chief-justiceship of Chester, accepted the mastership of the rolls, small as its emoluments were, was sworn in on 30 March 1784, became a member of the privy council 2 April 1784, and was knighted. As master of the rolls, and sitting often for the lord chancellor, he was one of the most expeditious judges who

ever sat in chancery, and cleared off many arrears of causes. He avoided enunciating principles, and was content to decide each case barely on its merits. Retaining his right to sit in parliament, and being returned for Tregoney in Cornwall, he was entrusted by Pitt with the task of justifying the conduct of the high bailiff in the case of the Westminster scrutiny, and in the result the previous question was carried by 233 votes to 136. During the debates upon the motion for the impeachment of Warren Hastings he was a constant speaker in his defence, and especially (May 1786) resisted the motion for production of Hastings's correspondence with Middleton, minister at Lucknow, upon the ground that in a quasi-criminal proceeding discovery of documents ought not to be ordered. His best speech was made in defence of his old friend Sir Elijah Impey [q. v.] On 28 July 1784 he was created a baronet, and was already understood to be designated as Lord Mansfield's successor; but Lord Mansfield, who wished Buller to have the chief-justiceship, clung to office until 1788, when on 9 June Kenyon was sworn in as chief justice, with the title of Baron Kenyon of Gredington, and was installed in November. The appointment was not popular. His manners were rough, blunt, and somewhat boorish. 'Little conversant with the manners of polite life,' says Wraxall (*Memoirs*, 1st ser. p. 165), 'he retained all the original coarse homeliness of his early habits. Irascible, destitute of all refinement, parsimonious even in a degree approaching to avarice,' he was the subject of innumerable jests and stories. It was said of him by Lord Ellenborough that the words on his tomb, 'mors janua vita,' were not the result of a blunder, but of an attempt at thrift by sparing the expense of a diphthong. But his life was, and had been from youth, strict and temperate, and his integrity was as undoubted as his learning, quickness, and industry were great.

He was much consulted by Pitt and Thurlow upon the regency question during the king's illness in 1788, and was even summoned to attend cabinet councils. His principal trials were Rex *v.* Stockdale (*State Trials*, xxii. 253), in which he ruled in favour of making the question of libel or no libel a question for the jury, a view which he tenaciously opposed in the subsequent debates on Fox's Libel Act in 1792; the trials of Frost and of the publishers of the 'Morning Chronicle' for seditious libels in 1794, in which he pressed somewhat hardly upon the prisoners, though in the year following he voted with Thurlow against the Treasonable Attempts and the Seditious Meetings Bills; the trial of Reeves in 1796 for libelling the constitution by describing the House of Commons as a mere adjunct of monarchy (*ib.* xxvi. 590); the trial of Thomas Williams in 1798 for publishing Paine's 'Age of Reason' (*ib.* 703); and the trial of Hadfield for attempting the life of George III. Like Mansfield, Holt, Loughborough, and Eyre, he attended the examinations before the privy council of state prisoners, whom in many instances he afterwards tried (LORD COLCHESTER, *Diary*, ii. 42). He took up the position of a judicial censor of public morals, denounced gaming, directed heavy damages in actions of *crim. con.*, and in 1800 charged grand juries, by way of remedy for the prevailing scarcity, to present indictments under the long obsolete laws against regrating and forestalling. Both as master of the rolls and as chief justice he set his face against the practice of selling offices in his gift, by which his salary, which during the fourteen years that he held the chief-justiceship averaged only 6,500*l.*, might have been much increased; and though he successfully urged Pitt to raise the salaries of puisne judges to 3,000*l.*, he refused any increase of his own, and himself brought in a bill to abolish sinecure clerkships of assize. He did, however, bestow valuable sinecures—those of custos brevium and of filazer of the king's bench—upon his two eldest sons as they attained their majority. George III honoured him with his particular friendship, constantly asked his advice, and visited him at his house at the Marshgate, Richmond Park. He was commissioned by the king to endeavour to make peace between Pitt and Thurlow on several occasions between 1789 and 1792, and was much consulted by him in 1795 on the extent to which the coronation oath would forbid the royal assent to any relaxation of the laws against Roman catholics. Attendance in the House of Lords became increasingly distasteful to him, and he almost ceased to speak in debate. In 1794 he presided in the House of Lords during Lord Loughborough's illness and at Hastings's trial, which he in vain endeavoured to shorten and bring within reasonable bounds. The death of his eldest son in 1800 so distressed him that he was all but compelled to resign the chief-justiceship. In the autumn of 1801 his health failed; he in vain tried to sit in court during Hilary term 1802, and, dying at Bath on 4 April, was buried at Hanmer Church—where there is an effigy of him by Bacon—and was succeeded in the barony by his eldest surviving son, George.

In person he was about five feet ten inches in height, spare of figure, stern in countenance, chary of speech. He was a pure lawyer,

rarely wrong, but rarely venturing on any broad exposition of the law, and always leaning to the strictness of law rather than to the flexibility of equity. No judge who presided so long in the king's bench has been as seldom overruled; yet he hardly ever consulted a book, and could dispose of a score of cases in a day. He was no statesman and disliked politics. His gains, which were large, and his savings, which were larger, he invested in land in Wales, often buying estates on indifferent titles; for, as he said, if he bought property he would find law to keep it till twenty years' occupation gave him a title better than deeds. He became lord-lieutenant of Flintshire in 1797. There are two portraits of him by Romney and one by Opie.

[The principal authority is G. T. Kenyon's Life, published 1873, which corrects the errors of Townshend's anecdotic life in the Lives of Twelve Eminent Judges, and of Lord Campbell's very hostile life in the Lives of the Chief Justices. See, too, Foss's Lives of the Judges; Espinasse's Note-book of a Retired Barrister; Twiss's Life of Lord Eldon; Campbell's Lives of the Lord Chancellors, vol. v. (Lord Thurlow's Life); Wraxall's Posthumous Memoirs; Stevens's Memoirs of Horne Tooke.] J. A. H.

KEOGH, JOHN (1650?–1725), Irish divine, born at Clooneleagh, near Limerick, about 1650, was son of Denis Keogh, of an old Irish family, which had lost its possessions in the Cromwellian wars, by his wife, the widow of a clergyman named Eyres. His mother's maiden name was Wittington. Keogh entered Trinity College, Dublin, in 1669, and proceeded M.A. in 1678. He obtained some reputation for his skill in mathematics, was appointed to a living by his kinsman, John Hudson, bishop of Elphin, and settled down to a scholar's life at Strokestown, co. Roscommon. The prebend of Termonbarry in the church of Elphin was conferred on him in February 1678, and he appears for some time to have kept a school and prepared pupils for Dublin University (*Vindication of Antiquities of Ireland*, p. 140). His favourite studies seem to have been Hebrew and the application of mathematics to the solution of mystical religious problems. Among his works was 'A Demonstration in Latin Verse of the Trinity,' which 'he was often heard to say was as plain to him as two and three make five.' Keogh's son, during a visit to London, showed this work to Sir Isaac Newton, 'who seemed to approve of it mightily well.' In his 'Scala Metaphysica' Keogh demonstrated mathematically 'what dependence the several degrees of beings have on God Almighty, from the highest angel to the lowest insect.' A large number of other 'ingenious treatises' from his hand were unfortunately destroyed by an accidental fire at his residence: but his 'Hebrew Lexicon,' a book 'De Orthographia,' Latin and Greek grammars, and an 'Analogy of the Four Gospels' still exist in manuscript in Trinity College Library. He died in 1725. Keogh married in 1679 Avis Clopton, daughter of Dr. Rous Clopton, of the old Warwickshire family. He had twenty-one children.

The second son, JOHN KEOGH, D.D.(1681?–1754), entered the church, and after acting for some time as chaplain to James King, fourth lord Kingston, obtained the living of Mitchelstown, co. Cork. He was the author of three curious works: 1. 'Botanologia Universalis Hibernica' (a list of medicinal plants growing in Ireland), Cork, 1735 (see PULTENEY, Progress of Botany, ii. 201, cf. Addit. MS. 25588). 2. 'Zoologica Medica Hibernica,' Dublin, 1739. 3. 'A Vindication of the Antiquities of Ireland,' Dublin, 1748. He married Elizabeth, daughter of Dr. Henry Jennings, a cousin of the Duchess of Marlborough, by whom he had three sons and three daughters. He died in 1754, at the age of seventy-three.

[Webb's Compendium of Irish Biog.; Walker's Hibernian Mag. 1778, p. 327; Cotton's Fasti, iv. 155; Account of the Keogh or MacEochachs family in Vindication of the Antiquities of Ireland. Appendix.]   T. S.

KEOGH, JOHN (1740–1817), Irish catholic leader, born in 1740, the son of humble parents, began life as a small tradesman in Dublin. He prospered in business, and acquired, as a zealous Roman catholic, considerable influence among his co-religionists in the Irish metropolis. In 1790 or thereabouts he was elected a member of the catholic committee, at that time under the leadership of Lord Kenmare. His efforts to promote a more active agitation on behalf of catholic emancipation were not at first successful. Early in 1791 he obtained the sanction of the committee to lay the grievances of the Irish catholics before the English ministry, and after three months' sojourn in England he returned to Ireland with a favourable answer to his petition. Meanwhile, however, 'the Kenmareites,' acting, as was supposed, under the influence of the Irish government, had resolved to refrain for the time from further petitioning, and to leave the matter in the hands of the Irish parliament. To this policy Keogh was altogether opposed, and on a vote in general committee he succeeded in carrying the majority with him. The defeat of the Kenmareites was followed by their secession, and by the reconstruction of the committee on a wider and

more popular basis. Keogh himself, by every means within his power, strove to rouse the catholics from their lethargy, and it was mainly owing to his enthusiasm that the catholic convention assembled in Dublin on 3 Dec. 1792. Acting under his advice, the convention appointed a deputation, of which Keogh was a member, to present to the king a statement of the grievances under which the catholics of Ireland laboured. The deputation was favourably received, and a direct consequence of it was the Relief Act of 1793. The measure owed much to the judicious management of Keogh while it was passing through parliament. Notwithstanding his sympathy with the objects of the United Irishmen, he steadily refused to allow the catholic claims to be compromised by any connection with them. The Relief Act was the great triumph of Keogh's life. When it had passed he felt that the convention had done its work, and forthwith prompted its dissolution.

Keogh had several ardent friends among the United Irishmen, and Wolfe Tone speaks in his letters of sympathetic meetings with Keogh at the latter's house. The Irish government had long possessed certain information that Keogh was in the habit of attending the meetings of the committee of United Irishmen, and shortly before the French expedition sailed in December 1796, he and others of the United Irishmen on whose co-operation the French had counted were placed under arrest. He was subsequently liberated, but the rebellion of 1798 greatly depressed him. Bodily infirmity also confined him to his residence at Mount Jerome, and he gradually ceased to take any active part in public affairs, though he occasionally spoke at catholic meetings. He lived to see the revival of the catholic agitation by O'Connell, but was strongly impressed with the impossibility of obtaining complete emancipation until the catholics could secure the return to parliament of one of their own body. He died on 13 Nov. 1817, and was buried in St. Kevin's churchyard, under a stone erected to his father and mother. Eight years later his wife was laid in the same spot.

Keogh was a man of rough manners, but possessed much natural ability. He was somewhat vain of his personal appearance, and his conduct on the occasion of the catholic deputation to London caused much merriment to his companions; but 'when he returned home he laid aside his court wig and his court manner, and only retained his Irish feelings.' His enemies charged him with insincerity, but the charge was unfounded. To Keogh's boast that it was he that had made men of the catholics

O'Connell replied with some truth: 'If you did, they are such men as realise Shakespeare's idea of Nature's journeymen having made them, and made them badly.' But the Relief Act of 1793 was very largely due to his generalship of the catholics at a time when they were sunk in apathy and despair.

[Webb's Compendium; Wyse's Catholic Association, i. 123, 137, 144; T. Wolfe Tone's Autobiography, i. 48; Grattan's Life, iv. 81; Mac-Nevin's Pieces of Irish History, p. 18; Fitzpatrick's Correspondence of Daniel O'Connell, i. 160, ii. 430; Lecky's England in the Eighteenth Century; Dublin Evening Post, 22 Nov. 1817.]

R. D.

KEOGH, WILLIAM NICHOLAS (1817–1878), Irish judge, belonged to a Roman catholic family formerly settled at Keoghville, co. Roscommon. He was born at Galway on 7 Dec. 1817. His father, William M. Keogh, was a solicitor, and sometime clerk of the crown for the county of Kilkenny; his mother was Mary, daughter of Mr. Austin Ffrench of Rahoon, co. Galway. He was educated at the school of the Rev. Dr. Huddard in Mountjoy Square, Dublin, then in high repute, entered Trinity College, Dublin, in 1832, and obtained honours in science in his first and second years. He left in his third year without having taken a degree. While at Trinity he was a frequent speaker in the debates of the Historical Society, and was awarded the first prize for oratory at the age of nineteen. In Michaelmas term 1835 he was admitted a student of the King's Inns, Dublin, and in Michaelmas term 1837 of Lincoln's Inn. In Hilary term 1840 he was called to the Irish bar, and joined the Connaught circuit, where his family connections lay. In the same year he published, in conjunction with Mr. M. J. Barry, 'A Treatise on the Practice of the High Court of Chancery in Ireland,' but he never obtained any considerable practice in that court. His natural gifts were those of an advocate rather than of a lawyer; a powerful voice, an impressive face, and impassioned delivery were combined with a ready flow of vigorous and ornate language.

He soon acquired a fair practice, principally on circuit, where, as a junior, he held leading briefs in the most important cases, and his powers of advocacy were counted so formidable that opposing counsel were sometimes briefed to oppose him. At the general election of 1847 he was returned for Athlone as an independent conservative, being the only Roman catholic conservative elected to that parliament. After a time he was ranked as a Peelite. In 1849 he was made a Q.C. In 1851 he took an active and prominent part in opposition to the Ecclesiastical Titles Bill passed by Lord John Russell. His action largely increased his reputation and popularity in Ireland. He was the principal speaker at a mass-meeting of Roman catholics held in Dublin in August 1851 to protest against the measure, and was one of the founders of the Catholic Defence Association established in consequence of it. He also took part in the tenant-right movement, speaking at various meetings held in support of it, and in the session of 1852 seconded in the House of Commons the Tenant Right Bill of William Sharman Crawford [q. v.] At the general election of 1852 he was again returned for Athlone. In December 1852 Keogh and the bulk of the Irish party voted in the majority which upset Lord Derby's ministry. In the new ministry of Lord Aberdeen Keogh became solicitor-general for Ireland (December 1852). His acceptance of office gave great offence to the extreme wing of the Irish party, who considered it inconsistent with the speeches which he had made in Ireland during the preceding eighteen months. He was bitterly assailed by Gavan Duffy in the 'Nation' and by Lucas in the 'Tablet,' and his re-election for Athlone was opposed. His appointment was also distasteful to the conservatives, and was attacked by Lord Westmeath in the House of Lords. At Athlone he was supported by the catholic bishop (Dr. Browne) and clergy, and was re-elected by a large majority. In January 1855 the Aberdeen ministry resigned; a new ministry was formed by Lord Palmerston. Keogh was appointed attorney-general for Ireland and was sworn of the Irish privy council. He was re-elected at Athlone without opposition. In April 1856, on the death of Mr. Justice Torrens, he was appointed a judge of the court of common pleas in Ireland. Among the remarkable cases in which he was counsel while at the bar were Birch v. Somerville (December 1851), an action by the proprietor of the 'World' newspaper against the Irish chief secretary on an alleged agreement to pay him for supporting law and order in his paper; Hancock v. Delacour, in the court of chancery (February 1855), a case of a painful nature, involving the title to a large estate in which Keogh's reply for the plaintiff was so touching and eloquent as to draw tears from the chancellor; and Reg. v. Petcherine (December 1855), the trial of a Redemptorist monk on a charge of profanely and contemptuously burning a copy of the authorised version of the Bible; Keogh conducted the prosecution as attorney-general.

On the bench he soon acquired the reputation of a judge of ability and discernment. Though not a profound lawyer, he never failed to appreciate a legal argument, and his judgments were clear and to the point. He excelled in the trial of nisi prius cases; his perception was quick, he grasped the facts of the case rapidly, and presented them to the jury with clearness and precision. In 1865 he was appointed, with Mr. Justice Fitzgerald, on the special commission for the trial of the Fenian prisoners at Dublin and Cork, and before them Luby, O'Leary, O'Donovan Rossa, and the other principal conspirators were tried. Luby, in his speech after conviction, acknowledged the fairness of Keogh's summing-up to the jury. In 1872 the celebrated Galway county election petition was tried before him. The candidates at the election were Captain J. P. Nolan (home ruler) and Captain Le Poer Trench (conservative); the former was returned by a large majority. His return was petitioned against mainly on the ground of undue influence exercised on his behalf by the Roman catholic clergy. The trial lasted from 1 April to 27 May, and resulted in Captain Nolan being unseated, and three Roman catholic bishops and thirty-one priests were reported to the house as guilty of undue influence and intimidation. That Captain Nolan was properly unseated on the evidence could hardly be contested, but the judge in the course of his judgment commented on the action of the Roman catholic bishops and priests in terms of unusual severity. His remarks were deeply resented, and aroused much popular feeling. Meetings were held at which he was denounced, he was burnt in effigy in numerous places, and the excitement became so great that special precautions had to be taken by the government for his protection. In the House of Commons Isaac Butt [q. v.], the home-rule leader, brought forward a motion impugning the conduct of the judge; it was defeated by a large majority, only twenty-three voting in its favour (9 Aug. 1872). For the remainder of his life Keogh was the subject of constant attack by the home-rule party. In 1878 his health began to fail, and he died at Bingen-on-the-Rhine on 30 Sept. of that year. During the greater part of his tenure of office he had been one of the most conspicuous figures on the Irish bench. Genial and good-natured, he was popular in private life, where his ready wit and conversational powers made him a most agreeable companion; he possessed an unusually retentive memory, and his fund of anecdote was varied and entertaining.

In 1867 the university of Dublin conferred upon him the honorary degree of LL.D. He

married, in 1841, Kate, daughter of Mr. Thomas Roney, surgeon, by whom he had a son (called to the Irish bar in 1871) and a daughter (married to the Hon. Mr. Justice Murphy). Both survived him. In addition to the 'Chancery Practice' already mentioned, he was author of two pamphlets, 'Ireland under Lord de Grey,' 1844, and 'Ireland Imperialised,' and of 'An Essay on Milton's Prose Writings,' 1863.

[Law Magazine and Review, November 1878; Ann. Reg. 1878; Times, 2 Oct. 1878; Hansard, 1848-55 and 1872; New Ireland, 1877; Life of Frederick Lucas, M.P., 1886; Galway County Election Petition Judgment, and Minutes of Evidence, Parliamentary Papers (211) of 1872, vol. xlviii.; information from family.] J. D. F.

KEON, MILES GERALD (1821-1875), novelist and colonial secretary, last male descendant of an old Irish family, the Keons of Keonbrooke, co. Leitrim, was born on 20 Feb. 1821 in the paternal castle on the banks of the Shannon, which was built entirely of white marble quarried on the estate, and still known as Keon's Folly. Miles was the only son of Myles Gerald Keon, barrister-at-law, by his second wife, Mary Jane, fifth daughter of Patrick, count Magawly, and of Jane, daughter of Christopher Fallon of Runnymede, co. Roscommon. His father having died at Keonbrooke in 1824, and his mother in 1825 at Temora, he and his younger sister, Ellen Benedicta, were left to the care of their maternal grandmother, Countess Magawly, and upon her death to the care of their uncle, Francis Philip, count Magawly, sometime prime minister of Marie Louise in the duchies of Parma, Placentia, and Guastalla. On 27 March 1832 Keon was entered as a student at the jesuit college of Stonyhurst, then under the presidency of Father Parker. He won many prizes, including one for a poem on Queen Victoria's accession, reprinted in the jubilee year, in the thirty-second number of the 'Stonyhurst Magazine.' On quitting Stonyhurst he made a pedestrian tour through France and crossed to Algeria, where he served for a short time in the French army under Bugeaud. He afterwards became a law student at Gray's Inn, but soon abandoned law for literature. In 1843 he published at Dublin an octavo pamphlet entitled (see the *Tablet*, iv. 532) 'The Irish Revolution, or What can the Repealers do?' And what shall be the New Constitution?' His earliest success as a writer was a vindication of the jesuits, published in the third number of the 'Oxford and Cambridge Review,' September 1845. Appearing in the nominal organ of both universities it provoked a smart controversy.

D 2

The author's name was revealed, and the paper itself was reissued as a separate publication. Messrs. Longman announced as in preparation a history of the jesuits by Keon, which never appeared. In September 1845 Keon began a series of contributions to Colburn's 'United Service Magazine,' pp. 59–71, entitled 'The Late Struggles of Abd-el-Kader, and the Campaign of Isly. By one who has served in the French Army.' They contain vivid sketches of Abd-el-Kader, Horace Vernet, and Lamoricière. Two other instalments appeared in the July and October numbers under the title of 'An Idler's Journey on Foot through France.' From April to November 1846 he was the editor of 'Dolman's Magazine.' In 1847 he published 'The Life of Saint Alexis, the Roman Patrician.' Shortly afterwards he secured an appointment on the staff of the 'Morning Post,' with which he was connected for twelve years. In 1850 he went as its representative to St. Petersburg, whence he wrote 'A Letter on the Greek Question.' Between 22 Feb. and 32 Aug. 1851 he contributed a series of twenty-six 'Lessons in French' to 'Cassell's Working Man's Friend,' which afterwards came into extensive use in the United States and Canada. In 1852 Keon wrote in the 'London Journal' a serial novel called 'Harding, the Money-Spinner,' which was published posthumously in 1879 in three volumes. In 1856 he was sent for the second time by the 'Morning Post' to St. Petersburg, to describe the coronation of the emperor, Alexander II. He there made the acquaintance of M. Boucher de Perthes, who, in his 'Voyage en Russie' (1859), has written pleasantly of their intercourse. In 1858, under a mistaken arrangement, Keon went out to Calcutta to edit the 'Bengal Hurkaru.' He returned in 1859, and was appointed in March the colonial secretary at Bermuda by the then secretary of state for the colonies, Sir Edward Bulwer Lytton. He held the post till his death. In 1866 he published in two volumes octavo 'Dion and the Sibyls, a Romance of the First Century.' In the winter of 1869 he obtained leave of absence, and visited Rome at the opening of the council of the Vatican. In 1867 he had delivered in the Mechanics' Hall at Hamilton a course of lectures on 'Government; its Source, its Form, and its Means.' He was invited to lecture in the United States, but declined on account of his official position. On 3 June 1875 he died at Bermuda. On 21 Nov. 1846 Keon married Anne de la Pierre, third daughter of Major Hawkes of the 21st light dragoons.

[Personal recollections of the writer; Hewitson's Stonyhurst Present and Past, 8vo, pp. 244–246; Hatt's two papers on A Colonial Secretary in the Stonyhurst Magazine for March and June 1886; Burke's Peerage, under 'Foreign Titles of Nobility,' p. 1535, ed. 1890; Boucher de Perthes' Voyage en Russie en 1856, 12mo, passim, 1859; Gillow's Bibl. Dict. vol. iv. 1891.] C. K.

KEPER, JOHN (*fl.* 1580), poet, appears to have been born at Wells, Somerset, about 1547. He entered Hart Hall, Oxford, in 1564, and graduated B.A. on 11 Feb. 1568–1569 (*Oxf. Univ. Reg.*, Oxf. Hist. Soc., i. 268). He was still in residence at college in 1572. On 8 July 1580, being then M.A. of Louvain, he petitioned to be incorporated at Oxford, but the grace was refused, as he was supposed to be a Romanist (*ib.* vol. ii. pt. i. pp. 35, 156–7, 377).

Wood, on the authority of Bishop Barlow, assigns to Keper the authorship of 'The whole Psalter, translated into English Metre' (1567?), which is known to have been written by Archbishop Matthew Parker. Keper is author of three complimentary poems, besides an address to the reader, in Thomas Howell's 'Arbor of Amitie,' 8vo, 1568. J. K. (who, as Bliss conjectures, may be John Keper) translated from the Italian of Count Annibale Romei 'The Courtiers Academie,' 4to, London, 1598.

[Wood's Athenæ Oxon. (Bliss), i. 416–18; Tanner's Bibl. Brit.-Hib. p. 454.] G. G.

KEPPEL, ARNOLD JOOST VAN, first EARL OF ALBEMARLE (1669–1718), stated to be descended from Walter van Keppel (1179–1223), lord of Keppel in the Low Countries, was born in Holland in 1669. He was son of Oswald van Keppel and his wife Anna Geertruid van Lintelo. Nothing is known of his early history (VAN DER AA, vol. x.) He came to England in 1688 with William of Orange as a page of honour, and after the accession of William and Mary was made a groom of the bedchamber and master of the robes. By letters patent of 10 Feb. 1696 he was created Baron Ashford of Ashford in the county of Kent, Viscount Bury of Bury in the county palatine of Lancaster, and Earl of Albemarle, the latter being a town and territory in the dukedom of Normandy (cf. *Notes and Queries*, 1st ser. ii. 466). He was a major-general 16 June 1697, in which year he was employed in the camp at Promelles. The year after he was made colonel of the first troop of British horse-guards, which he resigned to the Earl (Duke) of Portland 'for a valuable consideration 'in 1710. He introduced the Polish envoy to King William at Loo, which sent William afterwards presented to him. On 14 May 1700 he was made K.G. In 1701 he was appointed colonel of the first regiment of Swiss in the Dutch service, and some years later deputy-forester of Holland, colonel of the Dutch carabineers, and governor of Bois-le-Duc. He was William's constant companion, and completely engrossed the royal favour. During William's last illness Albemarle was sent to communicate his future plans to the deputy Heinsius at the Hague. On his deathbed William handed to Albemarle the keys of his cabinet and private drawers. 'You know what to do with them,' he said (MACAULAY, v. 81-3; cf. Hist. MSS. Comm. 10th Rep. v. 193). After William's death (8 March 1702) Albemarle returned to his own country, took his seat as a member of the nobility in the States-general, and was made a general of horse in the Dutch army. William bequeathed him a sum of two hundred thousand guilders and the lordship of Brevost. A Dutch manuscript in the British Museum shows that he instituted a suit against the Princess-dowager of Nassau in respect of the legacy (Egerton MS. 1708, f. 104). In 1705 he paid a visit to England, and, attending Queen Anne on a visit to Cambridge, is said to have received the honorary degree of doctor of laws. His name does not appear in 'Graduati Cantabrigienses.' Soon after his return home he left the Hague to join the army under Auverquerque. Marlborough, who appears to have been on the best terms with Albemarle, courteously expressed pleasure at his rejoining the army (Marlb. Desp. ii. 437). Albemarle was present at the forcing of the French lines at Tirlemont, at Ramillies in 1706, and at Oudenarde in 1708. During the siege of Lisle, Marlborough detached him with thirty squadrons to cover a convoy of guns and ammunition which the enemy were trying to intercept, a service he successfully accomplished. He was made governor of Tournay in 1709. He was employed at the siege of Bouchain, and commanded at the siege of Aire. In 1712 he commanded and was made prisoner at the battle of Denain, but was released, and entertained the Prince Eugène during the winter season in his house at the Hague. On the death of Queen Anne, Albemarle was sent to Hanover by the States-general to congratulate George I on his accession to the British throne, and afterwards received the new king and the Prince of Wales (George II) on the Dutch frontier. A resolution in favour of Albemarle's claim to a seat in the Dutch assembly in 1715 is in the British Museum Addit. MS. 15826, f. 242. He died 30 May 1718.

Bishop Burnet describes him as a cheerful young man, who had the art to please, but was so much taken up with his own pleasures that he could scarcely submit to the restraints of a court. He shared in all the recreations of William III, which brought him under the lash of Swift; but he was equally esteemed by Queen Anne and George I; and his handsome person and openhandedness, his obliging temper and winning manners, in marked contrast with the cold reserve of his rival Portland, rendered him a general favourite with the English people.

Albemarle married, in 1701, Geertruid Johanna Quirina van der Duyn, daughter of Adams van der Duyn, lord of St. Gravenmoer, governor of Bergen-op-Zoom, and master of the buckhounds to William III. By her he had a son, William Anne [q. v.], who succeeded to the title, and a daughter.

[Van der Aa's Biog. Wordenboek der Nederlanden, Haarlem, 1862, vol. x. and Dutch authorities there given; Foster's Peerage, under 'Albemarle;' Doyle's Official Baronage; Macaulay's Hist. of England, particularly vol. v.; Marlborough Despatches, vols. ii-v.; Georgian Era, ii. 462. Collections of Albemarle's letters, &c., are noticed in Hist. MSS. Comm. Reps. ii. 188-9, iii. 193, viii. (i. ii.) x. (v.) 193.] H. M. C.

KEPPEL, AUGUSTUS, VISCOUNT KEPPEL (1725-1786), admiral, second son of William Anne Keppel, second earl of Albemarle [q. v.], was born on 25 April 1725. After a few years at Westminster School, he entered the navy in 1735, on board the Oxford, in which he served for two years on the coast of Guinea. He was afterwards for three years in the Mediterranean, on board the Gloucester, carrying the broad pennant of Commodore Clinton. On his return to England in the summer of 1740 he was appointed to the Prince Frederick, and in September was moved to the Centurion, under the command of Commodore Anson [see ANSON, GEORGE, LORD ANSON]. In her he served during the celebrated voyage round the world, and is specially mentioned as having been landed at the sacking and burning of Payta, 13 Nov. 1741, where the peak of his cap 'was shaved off close to his temple' by a musket bullet [see BRETT, SIR PEIRCY]. In March 1742 he was promoted by the commodore to be acting lieutenant, in which rank he was confirmed on the Centurion's arrival in England and his passing his examination, on 25 July 1744. On 4 Aug. he was appointed to the Dreadnought, on 7 Nov. was promoted to be commander of the Wolf sloop, and on 11 Dec. was posted to the Greyhound frigate. In February 1744-1745 he was appointed to the Sapphire of 40 guns, in which he cruised with some success on the south coast of Ireland. In November 1745 he was moved to the Maidstone of 50 guns, and in her was again employed in continuous cruising in the Soundings and in the Bay of Biscay till, on the morning of 27 June 1747, having chased an enemy's ship in-shore off Belle Isle, he ran aground, and the Maidstone being a total wreck, Keppel and his men were made prisoners. After a few weeks he was permitted to return to England on parole, and, on being exchanged, was tried by court-martial and honourably acquitted on 31 Oct. He had already been promised the command of another ship still on the stocks, which was launched in October and christened the Anson. He was now formally appointed to her, and on 25 Nov. and following days sat as a member of the court-martial on Captain Fox of the Kent, notable as the first in which depositions taken beforehand were disallowed.

The Anson was employed in active cruising till the peace of 1748, and, being then made a guardship, Keppel with his officers was transferred to the Centurion, reduced from 60 to 50 guns, and in her was sent out as commodore to the Mediterranean, with a special mission to treat with the dey of Algiers, or, if necessary, to compel him to restrain the insolence of his cruisers. The story goes that the dey angrily expressed surprise that 'the king of Great Britain should have sent a beardless boy to treat with him;' to which Keppel replied, 'Had my master supposed that wisdom was measured by the length of the beard, he would have sent your deyship a he-goat.' Thereupon the dey threatened him with instant death, but Keppel, pointing to the squadron in the bay, said there were Englishmen enough there to make him a glorious funeral pile. The dey then consented to treat; but it was not till June 1751 that the points at issue could be arranged, and in July the Centurion returned to England and was paid off.

In the latter part of 1754 Keppel was ordered to hoist a broad pennant on board the Norwich, and to take command of the ships on the North American station. He arrived in Hampton Roads in February 1755, and during the next few months co-operated with General Braddock and the governors of the several colonies in the measures for the summer campaign. The arrival of Boscawen on the station with several senior captains necessarily superseded him, and he returned to England with the intelligence of Braddock's defeat and death. Keppel was then appointed to the Swiftsure of 70 guns, and in June 1756 was moved to the Torbay of 74, in which, in command of a small squadron, he cruised off Cape Finisterre during the autumn, returning to Spithead in December.

In January he sat as a member of the court-martial on Admiral John Byng [q. v.], and, finding that the recommendation to mercy was not likely to receive attention, he vainly exerted himself to procure the intervention of parliament. In September 1757 the Torbay was one of the fleet under Sir Edward (afterwards Lord) Hawke [q. v.] in the expedition to Basque Roads, and continued attached to the grand fleet, under Hawke and Anson, till in September 1758 Keppel was appointed to the command of a squadron of ships of war and transports sent out to reduce the French settlement of Goree. The service was effected with little loss on 29 Dec., and, having reinforced the garrison of Fort Louis on the Senegal, Keppel returned to England. During the summer and autumn of 1759 the Torbay was again attached to the grand fleet off Brest under Hawke, and on 20 Nov. was the leading ship in the battle of Quiberon Bay, and was closely engaged with the French Thésée, which ultimately sank, though whether from the effect of the Torbay's fire, or swamped through her lower deck ports, has been doubted. The Torbay herself took in a great deal of water through the lee ports, and for a short time was in danger of a similar fate.

In March 1761 Keppel was moved from the Torbay to the Valiant, and appointed to command the squadron co-operating with the troops sent to reduce Belle Isle. This squadron, supported by another off Brest under Captain Buckle, and a third under Sir Thomas Stanhope off Rochefort, completely covered the military operations, and the island surrendered in June. Keppel continued in command off Brest and Belle Isle till the following January, when a violent gale forced him to bear up for Torbay. Most of his ships were much damaged; the Valiant, in particular, was making a great deal of water, and had to go round to Portsmouth for repairs. Almost at the same time war was declared with Spain, and Keppel was appointed commodore and second in command, under Sir George Pocock [q. v.], of the expedition against Havana, his brother, George Keppel, second earl of Albemarle [q. v.], being the commander-in-chief of the land forces employed. The fleet arrived off Havana on 5 June, the landing was effected on the 7th, and after a two months' siege by sea and land, in which the climate proved the deadliest enemy, the place surrendered on 14 Aug. The prize-money was estimated at upwards of three millions sterling, of which nearly 25,000l. fell to Keppel's share. His younger brother, a general officer serving on the staff, probably received the same, while the elder brother received about five times as much. Notwithstanding the blow inflicted on the Spanish navy and on Spain, it was not unnaturally said that 'the expedition was undertaken solely to put money into the Keppels' pockets.' Immediately after the reduction of Havana Pocock returned to England, leaving the command of the remaining ships with Keppel, who on 21 Oct. 1762 was advanced to be rear-admiral of the blue, the promotion being, it is said, extended so as to include his name. At the peace Havana was restored to the Spaniards, and the troops were sent home; but Keppel retained the command at Jamaica till the beginning of 1764, when he was relieved by Sir William Burnaby. In May he sailed for England.

From July 1765 till November 1766 he was one of the lords commissioners of the admiralty, and in September 1766 hoisted his flag on board the Catherine yacht, to convey the Princess Caroline Matilda to Rotterdam, on the occasion of her unfortunate marriage to the king of Denmark. He seems, too, to have attached himself closely to the political party of the Marquis of Rockingham and the Duke of Richmond, and during the years immediately following to have identified himself with the intrigues and schemes of which they were the centre. On 24 Oct. 1770 he was promoted to the rank of vice-admiral, and was nominated for the command of the fleet fitting out against Spain; the dispute was, however, arranged, and Keppel did not hoist his flag.

During the following years, in which party animosity raged with great virulence, Keppel was closely associated with the opponents of the government, and the relations between him and the Earl of Sandwich, then first lord of the admiralty, would seem to have been the reverse of friendly. Still, his standing in the service was so high that it was impossible to pass him over, and as early as November 1776, on the probability of war with France, he was asked by the king in person to undertake the command of the Channel fleet. Keppel felt bound to accept it, but he represented to his majesty the hostility with which the ministry regarded him. He had an uneasy feeling that the offer might be a trap of his political enemy. 'If Lord Sandwich has but a bad fleet to send out,' wrote the Duke of Richmond to him, '"tis doing him no injustice to suppose he would be glad to put it under the command of a man whom he does not love, and yet whose name will justify the choice to the nation. If we meet with a misfortune, he hopes to get off. . . . If blame is to be borne he will endeavour by every art he is but too

much master of, to throw it on your shoulders.' It was, however, more than a year before Keppel was called on to serve. On 29 Jan. 1778 he was promoted to be admiral of the blue, and on 22 March received his commission as commander-in-chief of the grand fleet. At Portsmouth everything was still unprepared; and in spite of Sandwich's boast in the House of Lords, 18 Nov. 1777, that 'there were thirty-five ships of the line completely manned and fit for sea at a moment's warning,' Keppel found there were not more than six 'fit to meet a seaman's eye.' The dockyard, too, was depleted of stores, and it was only by the most unremitting exertion that by the beginning of June twenty ships could be got ready. With these he sailed from St. Helens on 13 June, with instructions to prevent the French fleet in Brest from putting to sea, or the Toulon fleet from joining it. To either of these singly he was supposed to be superior. Presently, however, on detaining the French frigates Licorne and Pallas, he obtained certain intelligence that the fleet at Brest consisted of thirty-two ships of the line ready for sea, and acting on the spirit of his instructions, he fell back to Spithead, 27 June, to wait for reinforcements. His instructions were kept strictly secret; but to naval men it was clear that, under the circumstances, no other line of conduct was open to him, and the admiralty tacitly admitted as much by continuing their efforts to strengthen the fleet. The government, however, was much enraged at the imputation which his return to Spithead cast on them, and, as the Earl of Bristol said in the House of Lords, 23 April 1779, 'Instead of applause and testimonies of approbation for his conduct, the tools and scribblers of power were employed in every quarter of the town to whisper and write away his exalted character. . . . The pensioned vehicles of infamy, detraction, and villany poured forth the dictates of their more infamous and profligate protectors and paymaster, not only by asserting that Admiral Keppel's return to port was in hopes of ruining the ministry, but also by a constant abuse on all those whose experience and whose judgment in naval matters justified the admiral's conduct.'

On 9 July Keppel again put to sea with twenty-four ships of the line, a fleet which was raised to thirty two days later. On the 8th the French fleet of thirty-two sail, under Count d'Orvilliers, had also put to sea, apparently on the report that the English fleet consisted of only twenty ships. The weather was very thick; but on the afternoon of the 23rd the fog clearing discovered the two fleets to each other, distant only some four or five miles. Both formed line of battle, and an engagement appeared imminent; but as D'Orvilliers made out the numbers of the English, he acted more cautiously, and, aided by a slight shift of wind, while Keppel was lying to for the night, succeeded in passing ahead of the English line and obtaining the weathergage, though in the manœuvre two of his ships were partially dismasted and obliged to return to Brest. At daybreak on the 24th the fleets were still in sight of each other; but Keppel being now to leeward was unable to bring on the engagement which D'Orvilliers no longer offered. And thus in foggy, squally, unsettled weather the fleets continued in presence of each other till the forenoon of the 27th, when a sudden shift of wind enabled Keppel to lie up for the French line and to engage it, as the two fleets passed each other on opposite tacks. 'Our van,' wrote Jervis, who commanded the Foudroyant, next astern of the Victory, Keppel's flagship, 'passed the French line without receiving heavy damage; but this firing brought the enemy down so much that most of their centre and rear passed the greatest part of our centre and rear within musket shot, and the wind having been quite abated by the concussion of the air, a very sharp cannonade continued on the centre till near one o'clock, and on the rear till forty minutes after one, when the firing ceased.'

As the two lines drew clear of each other D'Orvilliers made the signal to wear in succession. The signal was not obeyed, a blunder which popular report attributed to the cowardice of the Duc de Chartres, who commanded the van. On the side of the English a part of the van, under Sir Robert Harland, had tacked at once, and was standing towards the enemy; the rest of it was too much disabled, and dropped to leeward. The ships of the centre also were much disabled, those of the rear perhaps still more so; and though both Keppel in the Victory, and Sir Hugh Palliser [q. v.], who commanded the rear, in the Formidable, wore as soon as they were well clear of the enemy's line, it was at once apparent that the fleet could not be got together for an immediate renewal of the action, and they wore back again.

About three o'clock the French fleet had got round, and was standing to the south, with the apparent intention of cutting off five ships much disabled, which had fallen to leeward. Keppel, seeing the danger, hastily formed so much of his line as he could, and stood towards them, a manœuvre which was afterwards described as flying before the French. The action was not renewed, for the French bore away to leeward and formed their line, waiting for the attack which was not made. It was in vain that Keppel made the signal for the line of battle, and for ships to windward to come into the admiral's wake. Palliser did not obey. The Fox frigate was sent with a distinct message to Palliser that the admiral was only waiting for him to renew the attack, but it was not till after dark that Palliser and his division bore down. The next morning, 28 July, the fleet was in line of battle, but the French were no longer there. They could only be seen from the masthead, hull down to the eastward. It was clearly useless to follow them, for Brest was under their lee and offered them a ready shelter; while in the uncertain and squally weather it might be dangerous to take so many crippled ships near a hostile lee shore. On the 29th the French went into Brest, and Keppel, leaving a few ships to cruise for the protection of trade, drew back to Plymouth, where he anchored on the 31st.

The fleet was ordered to refit without delay. Keppel was deeply hurt by the conduct of Palliser on the 27th, but the emergency called for haste, and he conceived that to institute an inquiry or to hold a court-martial would destroy the possibility of unanimous exertion. He therefore expressed no dissatisfaction, and even wrote to the admiralty in praise of 'the spirited conduct of Vice-admiral Sir Hugh Palliser.' 'I do not conceive,' he said afterwards in his defence, 'that a commander-in-chief is bound to disclose to all Europe, in the midst of a critical service, the real state of his fleet, or his opinion of any of his officers.' There can, however, be no doubt that he ought to have referred the matter at once to the admiralty, and his failure to do so was mainly, if not entirely, due to his distrust of Lord Sandwich. But the real circumstances were known to too many to admit of any possibility of concealment. On 23 Aug. the fleet put to sea, cruised vainly off Ushant for a couple of months, and anchored at Spithead on 28 Oct., when Palliser, learning that a full statement of the case had appeared in a London paper, wrote to Keppel, 'requiring' him to contradict the 'scandalous report;' and as he received no reply he called on him to insist on his doing so. An angry quarrel was the result; other letters appeared in the papers; the subject was mentioned in the House of Commons; and Palliser applied for a court-martial on Keppel on a charge of misconduct and neglect of duty. Palliser was one of the lords of the admiralty, and his colleagues had no hesitation in complying with his request. His official letter was dated 9 Dec., and the very same day the secretary of the admiralty notified the decision of the board to Keppel. The conduct of the admiralty in thus ordering the trial of the commander-in-chief on charges exhibited by an inferior, five months after date, and under circumstances which were strongly suggestive of a personal motive, called forth an expression of surprise from Keppel, and of disapproval from the House of Commons and the country at large. A memorial to the same effect was addressed to the king by Lord Hawke and most of the senior admirals; but no notice was taken of it, and the court assembled at Portsmouth as ordered, on 7 Jan. 1779; for the first day on board the Britannia, and afterwards, through a period of five weeks, at the governor's house on shore, in consideration of Keppel's infirm health, and in accordance with a special act of parliament.

He was charged with not marshalling his fleet, going into the fight in an unofficer-like manner, scandalous haste in quitting it, running away, and not pursuing the flying enemy—each one a capital offence. Palliser in person was the prosecutor; Sir Robert Harland, Rear-admiral Campbell, most of the captains, some lieutenants, and several masters were the witnesses. Of these, whether called for the prosecution or defence, the unanimity was remarkable. With scarcely an exception they were agreed that if the admiral had waited to form his fleet in line he could not have brought the enemy to action at all; that the enemy was very far from being in a perfect line; that after passing the enemy the admiral had turned towards them as soon as he could do so without blocking the course of the ships astern; that he turned from them and hauled down the signal for battle only when it was evident that many of his ships were too shattered to renew the fight at once; that his standing towards the south was a judicious manoeuvre, and neither was, nor had the appearance of being, a flight from the enemy; and that any chase on the morning of the 28th would certainly have been unavailing, and would probably have been dangerous. And after examining and considering an enormous body of technical evidence, the court, on 11 Feb., pronounced the charge to be 'malicious and ill-founded;' that Keppel had behaved as became 'a judicious, brave, and experienced officer:' and thereupon unanimously and honourably acquitted him.

Keppel became the hero of the hour. It was honestly believed that he would have won a victory had not Palliser prevented him, and Palliser's backwardness was attributed to the malign influence of Lord Sandwich. Keppel's acquittal was thus not only a triumph of innocence over vice and fraud, it was a triumph of the popular party over the unpopular ministry. The admiralty gates were torn down; the windows of the official residences were smashed; Palliser's house in Pall Mall was gutted, and his effigy was burnt. Bonfires blazed in Keppel's honour; the rioters drank Keppel's health; and the publicans painted Keppel's head on their signs.

On the conclusion of the court-martial Keppel addressed a letter to the king personally, relating the facts of the conduct of the admiralty towards him, and imploring his majesty's permission not to go again to sea under men on whom, as he had learned by experience, he could not depend for support. 'I am ready,' he wrote, 'to quit my command to-day, or to preserve it as long as may be convenient for your majesty's arrangements and consistent with my own honour; but I trust your majesty will see my reputation cannot continue safe in hands who have already done all they could to ruin it.' The king would seem to have handed the letter over to the admiralty, who wrote on 12 March expressing their desire to know with certainty whether he intended to continue in his present command. Keppel replied that he had laid his situation and the treatment he had received before the king; and after a further exchange of acrimonious letters he was ordered, 18 March 1779, to strike his flag.

He had naturally no further service under Lord Sandwich. But he had long been a member of the House of Commons, being elected for Windsor to the parliaments of 1761, 1768, and 1774, and for Surrey to the parliament of 1780, and from his place in the house he lost no opportunity of criticising the misconduct of naval affairs. On the fall of Lord North's administration, 20 March 1782, and the formation of Rockingham's, Keppel was appointed first lord of the admiralty, and on 26 April was raised to the peerage as Viscount Keppel and Baron Elden. After the death of Rockingham Keppel was succeeded at the admiralty by Lord Howe, but resumed office on the formation of the coalition ministry. On its downfall, 30 Dec. 1783, he was again succeeded by Howe, and retired altogether from public life. His health, which had suffered severely from the climate of Havana, had never been quite re-established, and during his later years was very much broken. In the autumn of 1785 he was advised not to risk the winter in England, and went to Naples, from which he returned in the spring of 1786. The change, however, effected no lasting good, and he died a few months later, on 2 Oct. He had not married, and the title on his death became extinct.

His portrait, by Reynolds, in 1753, formerly belonging to the Earl of Albemarle, was bought by Mr. Agnew in 1888. It is engraved as the frontispiece to his 'Life.' After the court-martial Reynolds again painted his portrait five times. Three of these were presented to the lawyers who had assisted him in his defence—John Dunning (afterwards Lord Ashburton), John Lee, and Thomas (afterwards Lord) Erskine; the fourth was presented to Edmund Burke; the fifth was bought by Agnew in 1888. Dunning's copy is now in the National Portrait Gallery; Burke's is in the National Gallery: Lee's was lent to the Guelph Exhibition (1891) by the Hon. William Massey-Mainwaring.

[The Life of Keppel, by his grandnephew, the Rev. Thomas Keppel, is comprehensive, and on the whole fair, though with a natural bias; the memoirs in Charnock's Biog. Nav. v. 308, Ralfe's Nav. Biog. i. 35, and Nav. Chron. vii. 277, contain little or nothing additional; official correspondence and other documents are in the Public Record Office; the minutes of the court-martial and those of the subsequent court-martial on Palliser have both been published. The circumstances of the trial, and its baneful effects, gave rise to many pamphlets, of which the most important is Considerations on the Principles of Naval Discipline, 1781, 8vo. See also Walpole's Letters, ed. Cunningham, vii. 86 et seq.; Beatson's Nav. and Mil. Memoirs, ii. 456 et seq., iv. 411 et seq.; Chevalier's Hist. de la Marine française pendant la Guerre de l'Indépendance américaine, livre ii.] J. K. L.

KEPPEL, FREDERICK (1729–1777), bishop of Exeter, fourth son of William Anne Keppel, second earl of Albemarle [q. v.], was born on 19 Jan. 1728–9. He was admitted at Westminster School in 1743, and matriculated at Christ Church, Oxford, on 26 June 1747, graduating B.A. in 1752, M.A. in 1754, and D.D., by diploma, on 19 Oct. 1762. Having been ordained in the English church, he soon obtained ample preferment. He acted as chaplain in ordinary to George II and III, and from 19 April 1754 to 1762 enjoyed a canonry at Windsor. His father-in-law, Sir Edward Walpole, wrote to Pitt in August 1761, asking whether it was 'agreeable to him to make Mr. Keppel a bishop at this juncture,' and although this application was unsuccessful he was consecrated bishop of Exeter on 7 Nov. 1762, when it was rumoured that the preferment was bestowed upon him on account of the capture of Havana by his brother; but Horace Walpole says that the mitre was promised to him the day before the news came. With this see he held in commendam the arch-

deaconry of Exeter and a prebendal stall in that cathedral, and he also obtained the promise of translation to the more lucrative bishopric of Salisbury on the next vacancy. He refused the deanery of Exeter in 1763, but relinquished this promise of the see of Salisbury for the deanery of Windsor, which became vacant first, and to it he was appointed, with the registrarship of the order of the Garter, in 1765, the general comment being that 'all things are crowded into three or four people's pockets.' He spent large sums of money in improving the episcopal palace at Exeter and in relieving the needs of the poorer clergy in his diocese. Keppel enjoyed good living, and his portrait, a half-length, in the palace at Exeter shows him as a jovial man with homely features. Polwhele says that he conferred favours in the most handsome manner, and it is to his credit that Jonathan Toup the philologist [q. v.] was among those whom he promoted. After a long illness he died at the deanery, Windsor, on 27 Dec. 1777, and was buried in St. George's Chapel, Windsor. A post-mortem examination showed that he died from dropsy in the stomach. He married, on 13 Sept. 1758, Laura, eldest natural daughter of Sir Edward Walpole, who left her in 1784 Lacy House, Isleworth, and most of his fortune. The issue was Frederick Keppel of Lexham Hall, Norfolk, who died in 1830, and three daughters.

Keppel contributed a set of verses to his university's collection of poems on the death of the Prince of Wales in 1751, and published two sermons. He was a whig, of sufficient courage in preaching before the king in March 1776 to recommend a peace with the American colonies, and on his deathbed he 'thanked God that he had not given one vote for shedding American blood.'

[Walpole's Letters (Cunningham), iii. 155, iv. 38, 40, vii. 18, viii. 372, 450, 487; Walpole's Journal, 1771–83, ii. 27–8, 175; Chatham Corresp. ii. 134–5; Corresp. of George III and Lord North, ii. 61; Admiral Keppel's Life. i. 424, ii. 7; Grenville Papers, iii. 91; Oliver's Bishops of Exeter, pp. 163, 273; Gent. Mag. 1758 p. 452, 1778 p. 43; Trans. Devon. Assoc. xvi. 130; Polwhele's Devon, i. 314; Carthew's Launditch, pt. iii. p. 251; Aungier's Isleworth, p. 232; Welch's Alumni Westmon. ed. Phillimore, pp. 327, 340, 341; Le Neve's Fasti; Foster's Alumni Oxon.] W. P. C.

KEPPEL, GEORGE, third EARL OF ALBEMARLE (1724–1772), general, colonel 3rd dragoons (now hussars), was the eldest son of William Anne, second earl [q. v.], and his wife, the Lady Anne Lennox. He was born 8 April 1724, and on 1 Feb. 1738 was appointed ensign in the Coldstream guards. He was promoted to captain-lieutenant in the 1st royal dragoons 25 April 1741, was transferred to the Coldstream guards 14 April 1743, and became captain and lieutenant-colonel therein 27 May 1745. Albemarle, then Lord Bury, was the favourite aide-de-camp of William, duke of Cumberland, with whom he was present at Fontenoy and at Culloden. On the morning of Culloden he had a narrow escape from death at the hands of a highlander, who had found his way into the camp, and, snatching a musket from a soldier, fired at Bury point-blank, believing him from his showy dress to be the duke. Bury brought the Culloden despatches to London (by sea from Inverness), receiving from the king a gift of 1,000*l.* He was also made aide-de-camp to the king, and a lord of the bedchamber to the Duke of Cumberland. He was returned as member for Chichester, which city he represented until his removal to the upper house. On 1 Nov. 1749 he was appointed colonel of the 20th foot. Wolfe, then lieutenant-colonel of the regiment, calls him ' one of those showy men who are seen in palaces and in the courts of men. . . . He desires never to see his regiment, and wishes that no officer would ever leave it ' (WRIGHT, chap. ix.) Bury, however, afterwards joined his regiment at Inverness, and signalised himself by very high-handed dealing with the magistrates, who invited him to an entertainment on the Duke of Cumberland's birthday. He insisted, under pain of reprisals from the soldiers, that the banquet should be deferred till the anniversary of Culloden (ib.) He succeeded to the earldom on the death of his father in 1754, and the same year was transferred to the colonelcy of the 3rd dragoons. He became a major-general in 1756, and lieutenant-general in 1759, and a privy councillor and governor of Jersey in 1761. He was a member of the court-martial of Lord George Sackville (afterwards Germain) [q.v.], and was said to have shown much animus against the prisoner in the cross-examination of the witnesses. On 5 March 1762 he was sent with a force of ten thousand troops on board Admiral Pocock's fleet to attack the Havana. The conquest was achieved by the capture of Moro Castle, in the face of difficulties supposed to be insurmountable, on 30 July 1762. Albemarle's share as commander-in-chief was 122,000*l.* His conduct as a conqueror was alleged to be harsh and exacting. He banished the Bishop of Havana to Florida for appointing clergy without his approval, and he exacted contributions from the merchants which the government at home denied

his right to levy. He was consequently obliged to refund the money. He returned home in February 1763. He was made a K.B. in December 1764, and a K.G. in July 1771. In politics his views were very liberal. He distinguished himself by his opposition to the Royal Marriage Act and the rescinding of the East India dividends, and in 1770 by pledging himself, with forty-seven other peers, to oppose any future infringement of popular rights at elections.

Albemarle married, in 1771, Anne (d. 1824), daughter of Sir John Miller, bart., of Chichester, by whom he had an only son, William Charles, who succeeded him. Horace Walpole, who was Albemarle's intimate friend, speaks of his marriage as disappointing ' his brothers and my niece.' Albemarle died 13 Oct. 1772, aged 48, and was buried at Quiddenham, Norfolk. His official correspondence, 1746-1768, is in the Brit. Mus. Addit. MSS. 32708-33072.

[Collins's Peerage, 1812 ed. vol. iii.; Doyle's Official Baronage; Foster's Peerage, under ' Albemarle;' Georgian Era, ii. 72; Wright's Life of Wolfe, London, 1864, chap. ix.; Campbell-Maclachlan's Order Book of William, duke of Cumberland, London, 1875; Beatson's Naval and Military Memoirs, London, 1794, vols. ii. and iii.; George Thomas, sixth earl of Albemarle's Lord Rockingham and his Contemporaries, London, 1852, vol. i.; Horace Walpole's Letters, vols. i-vii.] H. M. C.

KEPPEL, GEORGE THOMAS, sixth EARL OF ALBEMARLE (1799-1891), second son of William Charles, fourth earl, by his first wife, the Hon. Elizabeth Southwell, daughter of Lord de Clifford, and grandson of George Keppel, third earl of Albemarle [q. v.], was born 13 June 1799. His childhood was passed with his grandmother, the Dowager Lady De Clifford, who at the time was governess to the Princess Charlotte of Wales. The princess, three years his senior, often ' tipped' him liberally. He idled at Westminster School from the age of nine until nearly sixteen. When Dr. Page, the head-master, had pronounced him unfit for any learned profession, an ensigny was obtained for him in the old third battalion of 14th foot (now West Yorkshire regiment). The battalion, consisting chiefly of raw recruits, was in Belgium, and young Keppel, whose commission was dated 4 April 1815, joined it in time to be present with it at the battle of Waterloo. Footsore and ragged, he marched with the victorious troops to Paris. He returned home with the battalion at the end of the year, and when it was disbanded served with the second battalion of the regiment in the Ionian Islands. This battalion was disbanded at Chichester in 1818, when Keppel was appointed to the 22nd (Cheshire) foot, with which he was in Mauritius and at the Cape, returning home with the regiment in 1819. For a time he was equerry to the Duke of Sussex. In 1821 he was promoted to a lieutenancy in the 24th foot, was transferred to the 20th, and ordered to India. There he served as aide-de-camp to the governor-general, the Marquis of Hastings, but upon Hastings's resignation in 1823 he obtained leave to return home overland. Relying on a scanty stock of Persian acquired during the long and weary passage out, he visited the ruins of Babylon and the court of Teheran, thence journeying to England by way of Baku, Astrakan, Moscow, and St. Petersburg, a rare feat in those days. His published narrative is an interesting volume. He next served as aide-de-camp to the Marquis Wellesley when lord-lieutenant of Ireland; obtained a company in the 62nd foot in 1825, and after studying at the senior department of the Royal Military College, Sandhurst, obtained a majority on half-pay unattached, 20 March 1827. He was not on full pay again, but he rose step by step, finally attaining the honorary rank of full general (on half-pay of his former commission), 7 Feb. 1874. In 1829 he paid a visit to the seat of war between the Russians and Turks, was with the English fleet in Turkish waters, visited Constantinople and Adrianople, and crossed the Balkans. In 1832 he was returned, in the whig interest, for East Norfolk, in the first reformed parliament, and sat until 1835. In 1846 he became one of the private secretaries to Lord John Russell, the new premier, and in 1847 was returned for Lymington, for which he sat until 1849, the year of his father's death. On the death of his brother, Augustus Frederick, the fifth earl, 15 March 1851, he succeeded to the title. He was appointed a trustee of Westminster School in 1854, in succession to the (first) Marquis of Anglesey, and was long the 'father of the trust.' Few men have been longer known or more generally popular in London society. He retained his faculties to the end of his life, during the latter part of which he held receptions on each anniversary of Waterloo, at his daughter's house in Portman Square (see *Broad Arrow*, 28 Feb. 1891, p. 278, and 13 June 1891, p. 749).

Albemarle died at his London residence in Portman Square, 21 Feb. 1891, in his ninety-second year, and was buried at Quiddenham, Norfolk. He married in 1831 Susan, third daughter of Sir Coutts Trotter, bart., and by her had a son, the present earl, best known as Viscount Bury, who in 1876 was summoned to the upper house under the family title of Lord Ashford, and four daughters, two of whom predeceased their parents. Lady Albemarle died in 1885.

Albemarle was author of: 1. 'Personal Narrative of a Journey from India to England . . .,' London, 1825, 2 vols. A third edition of this work appeared as 'Travels in Babylonia, Media, Assyria, and Scythia,' London, 1827. 2. 'Narrative of a Journey across the Balkans . . . and a Visit to . . . newly discovered Ruins in Asia Minor,' London, 1830. A volume of extracts from the narrative, with added letters, appeared in Dublin in 1831. 3. 'Memoirs of the Marquis of Rockingham and his Contemporaries,' London, 1852, 2 vols. 4. 'Fifty Years of my Life,' London, 1876. A third and revised edition appeared in London, 1877. Some of Albemarle's speeches in the House of Lords, as on the Marriage Bill in 1856 and on 'Torture in the Madras Presidency' in the same year, were printed in pamphlet form.

[Doyle's Official Baronage, vol. i.; Foster's Peerage; Albemarle's Fifty Years of my Life (rev. ed.), and other works; Parl. Debates under dates; Times, February 1891.]   H. M. C.

KEPPEL, WILLIAM ANNE, second EARL OF ALBEMARLE (1702–1754), lieutenant-general, colonel Coldstream guards, son of Arnold Joost van Keppel, first earl [q.v.], and his wife Geertruid Johanna Quirina van der Duyn, was born at Whitehall on 5 June 1702; was baptised at the Chapel Royal, Queen Anne being his godmother; was educated in Holland; and on his return to England (as Viscount Bury) was appointed, 25 Aug. 1717, captain and lieutenant-colonel of the grenadier company of the Coldstream guards. In 1718 he succeeded to his father's title and estates, and in 1722, at his family seat in Guelderland, entertained the Bishop of Münster. In 1725 he was made K.B., in 1727 aide-de-camp to the king; and on 22 Nov. 1731 was appointed to the colonelcy of the 29th foot, then at Gibraltar, which he held until 7 May 1733, when he was appointed colonel of the third troop of horse-guards. He was made governor of Virginia in 1737, a brigadier-general July 1739, major-general February 1742, and was transferred to the colonelcy of the Coldstream guards in October 1744. He went to Flanders with Lord Stair in 1742, and was a general on the staff at Dettingen, where he had a horse shot under him, and at Fontenoy, where he was wounded. He commanded the first line of Cumberland's army at Culloden, and was again on the staff in Flanders, and present at the battle of Val. At the peace of 1748 he was sent as ambassador extraordinary and minister plenipotentiary to Paris, and was appointed commander-in-chief in North Britain, and in 1749 was made K.G. The year after he was made groom of the stole and a privy councillor, and in 1752 was one of the lords justices during the king's absence in Hanover. In 1754 he was sent back to Paris to demand the liberation of some British subjects detained by the French in America, and died in Paris suddenly on 22 Dec. 1754. His remains were brought over and buried in the chapel in South Audley Street, London.

Albemarle married in 1723 Lady Anne Lennox, daughter of Charles, first duke of Richmond, and by her had eight sons and seven daughters. His sons George, the third earl, Augustus, viscount Keppel, the admiral, and Frederick, bishop of Exeter, are separately noticed.

Horace Walpole calls Albemarle 'the spendthrift earl,' and says that the British embassy in Paris was kept up for his benefit (Letters, ii. 331). Walpole adds that Albemarle had 90,000l. in the funds when he was married, and his wife brought him 25,000l. more, all of which, with the exception of about 14,000l., he squandered, without leaving a penny for his debts or for his children, legitimate and illegitimate, who were many (ib. ii. 420-1). George II conferred a pension of 1,200l. a year on his widow. His correspondence in 1732-54 is in Brit. Mus. Add. MSS. 32687-33066.

[Collins's Peerage, 1812 ed. iii. 728 et seq.; Foster's Peerage, under 'Albemarle;' Doyle's Official Baronage; Mackinnon's Origin and History of the Coldstream Guards, London, 1832, vol. ii.; Campbell-Maclachlan's Order Book of William, duke of Cumberland, London, 1875; Georgian Era, ii. 49; Horace Walpole's Letters, vols. i. and ii.] H. M. C.

KER. [See also KERR.]

KER, SIR ANDREW (d. 1526), of Cessfurd or Cessford, Scottish borderer, was the eldest son of Sir Robert Ker of Caverton, Roxburghshire, cupbearer and master of artillery to James IV, by his wife Christina, daughter of James Rutherford of Rutherford. He was served heir to his grandfather 30 Sept. 1511, being then of lawful age. Shortly afterwards, to avenge the death of his father, who some years previously had been slain by Starhed and two other Englishmen, Ker sent two of his vassals, who entered Starhed's house, ninety miles beyond the borders, killed him, and brought his head to Ker. Ker sent it to Edinburgh, where it was set up in a conspicuous position (BUCHANAN, bk. xiii. c. xxvi.) At Flodden Ker fought under Lord Home with the other 'merch-men,' who, after defeating the English vanguard, dispersed in search of pillage. He was one of those who signed the letter to the king of France, 15 May 1515, proposing that Scotland should be comprehended in the treaty with England (RYMER, Fœdera, xiii. 509). In August of the same year he was appointed warden of the middle marches (Albany to Dacre, Cal. State Papers, Hen. VIII, vol. ii. entry 795). Dacre expressed surprise at the appointment of Ker, 'a young man without wisdom and substance;' but two years afterwards confessed that he had no fault to find with him, 'but that he is some forgitfyll and rukles (ib. entry 3393). In January 1520 Ker defeated a force of four hundred Mersemen who, under Sir James Hamilton of Finnart, were hastening to support Andrew Ker [q.v.] of Fernichirst in his assumption of the power to hold courts at Jedburgh, claimed as an exclusive right by the Earl of Angus. The action of Ker was submitted to the decision of arbiters. The final decision of the arbiters, given on 24 Sept., was that Ker and his friends should for their lifetimes take the Earl of Arran's 'trew and afuld part,' and in particular should henceforth assist him against the Earl of Angus and his party (Hamilton Manuscripts, Hist. MSS. Comm. 11th Rep. App. pt. vi. pp. 32-3). On 22 Jan. 1521 Ker was appointed one of a commission for a treaty with England (Fœdera, xiii. 735), which was signed on the 30th (ib. p. 739). In September 1524 he and Scott of Buccleuch, 'on account of a variance with each other,' were called before the council and committed to prison (Cal. State Papers, Hen. VIII, iv. 651). In 1526, he with Lord Home accompanied the king to Melrose when he went to hold justice eyres in the southern shires. Shortly after taking leave they learned that Scott of Buccleuch with one thousand men was approaching to deliver the king from the power of Angus. Returning immediately, they succeeded in turning the tide of battle against Buccleuch; but Ker, while in pursuit of the foe, was slain, 23 Jan., by a spear hurled at him by one of Buccleuch's servants. By his wife Agnes, daughter of Robert, second lord Crichton of Sanquhar, he had three sons: Sir Walter [q.v.], Mark, commendator of Newbattle [see KERR, MARK], and Andrew; and two daughters: Catherine, married to Sir John Ker of Fernichirst, and Margaret, to Sir John Home of Coldingknowes.

[Histories of Buchanan and Leslie; Rymer's Fœdera; Cal. State Papers, Hen. VIII; Hist. MSS. Comm. 11th Rep. App. pt. vi.; Douglas's Scottish Peerage (Wood), ii. 446.] T. F. H.

KER, ANDREW (1471?–1545), of Fernichirst, border chieftain, was eldest son of Thomas Ker, eighth laird of Kersheugh in Teviotdale, by his wife Catharine, daughter of Sir Robert Colvill of Ochiltree. Thomas Ker built a house in the middle of the forest of Jedburgh, and gave it the name of Fernichirst, by which title this branch of the Ker family was afterwards known. Andrew was probably born about 1471, for we find him appearing as bail for men charged with border robbery in 1483, and he can hardly have done so before he was of full age (PITCAIRN, *Criminal Trials*, vol. i. pt. ii. pp. 17–18, 28). In 1489 he succeeded his father as laird of Fernichirst, and in 1511 inherited through his mother the barony of Oxenham and had confirmation of the lands of Fernichirst from his feudal superior, Archibald, earl of Angus. In 1512 he sat at Edinburgh on an assize for the trial of several borderers accused of theft (*ib.* p. 88). The disturbed state of Scotland after the defeat of Flodden Field seems to have inspired Ker with a desire to secure for himself a strong position on the Scottish border. On 9 Sept. 1513, the night after the battle, he broke into the abbey of Kelso, then held *in commendam* by Andrew Stewart, bishop of Caithness, turned the superior out of doors, and set up in his stead his brother Thomas, who seems to have maintained the position thus forcibly won, and on the death of the Bishop of Caithness in 1518 became abbot of Kelso (MORTON, *Monastic Annals of Teviotdale*, p. 964). In the struggle between Angus and Arran which arose after the marriage of Queen Margaret with Angus [see DOUGLAS, ARCHIBALD, sixth EARL OF ANGUS] Ker joined Lord Home in helping Angus, and when Margaret took refuge in England in December 1515 Ker was one of her escort (BREWER, *Calendar of State Papers*, vol. ii. No. 1350). He was arrested in Edinburgh with Home in October 1516 by the orders of the governor, the Duke of Albany. Hume was beheaded, but Ker contrived to escape (DRUMMOND, *Hist. of Scotland*, p. 168). After Margaret's quarrel with Angus the Earl of Arran was made warden of the marches, and Ker took advantage of the conflict between the two to claim for himself the bailiwick of Jedburgh forest (*ib.* p. 174). For some time he was a source of disorder on the borders, and in 1521 the English warden, Lord Dacre, joined with Andrew Ker of Cessford in complaining of his lawlessness (*Calendar*, iii. 1171). In September 1523 Lord Dacre led his forces against Fernichirst, 'the lord whereof was his mortal enemy,' and after a resolute defence captured it and made Ker prisoner (ELLIS, *Original Letters*, 1st ser. i. 216–17).

He soon escaped, and in November commanded under the Duke of Albany at the unsuccessful siege of Wark (HOLINSHED, *Scottish Chronicle*, p. 311). At the beginning of 1524 he was reckoned as one of the chief supporters of the Earl of Lennox in his attempt to govern Scotland (*Calendar*, iv. 43). But when Angus returned at the end of the year and was made warden of the east and middle marches Ker promised his allegiance (PITCAIRN, p. 127). A feud soon broke out between him and Angus, and at the beginning of 1526 he joined Arran, who was raising forces against Angus (*Calendar*, iv. 1878). He was accused of treason, but the process was abandoned. After that he made peace with Angus, and rendered him signal service in July 1526, when Scott of Buccleuch made an attempt to seize the young king, who was with Angus at Melrose. Ker and the Homes had departed, but returned in answer to a summons, fell upon the Scotts in their flank, and routed them (DRUMMOND, p. 189). The death of Andrew Ker of Cessford in this encounter was the beginning of a feud between the Kers and the Scotts which long continued, in spite of attempts at pacification, one of which was signed by Ker in 1530 (WADE, *Hist. of Melrose*, p. 63). After his agreement with Angus, Ker settled down to a more orderly life, and busied himself in restoring order, for which he was praised by the English warden in September 1527 (*Calendar*, iv. 3421). On the forfeiture of the Earl of Angus he received a grant of Fernichirst from the crown on 5 Sept. 1528. He undertook the rule of Teviotdale, and was one of three commissioners empowered to make an agreement with England, which was signed on 2 Dec. (RYMER, *Fœdera*, xiv. 276). In 1530 James V took the management of the borders into his own hands and committed Ker's eldest son, John, to prison. He was soon released, and seems to have acted for his father in military undertakings. In 1533 it was computed that the Kers, the Homes, and the Scotts could together bring into the field five thousand men. When, in 1543, war broke out between Scotland and England, Ker found it impossible to withstand the superior forces of the English. He made promises to help them, and his son John assisted them in their raids upon his neighbours (HAYNES, *Burghley Papers*, pp. 43–51). In October 1544 Ker made a covenant with Sir Ralph Eure to serve England (*State Papers of Henry VIII*, v. 398), and in November was in receipt of English pay (LODGE, *Illustrations*, i. 79). In September 1545 he pleaded his services against the threatened ravages of the Earl of Hertford and made submission to him, thereby saving his lands. He died soon afterwards.

Ker married Janet, second daughter of Sir Patrick Home of Polwarth, by whom he had three sons and two daughters. His son John succeeded him as lord of Fernichirst, and had a son Sir Thomas Ker [q. v.] His daughter Isabel married Sir Walter Ker of Cessfurd [q. v.]

[Authorities in text; Douglas's Peerage of Scotland, ed. Wood, ii. 132; Jeffrey's Hist. of Roxburghshire, i. 261–5; Armstrong's Hist. of Liddesdale, pp. 213–60; Marquis of Lothian's manuscripts at Newbattle Abbey.]   M. C.

KER, CHARLES HENRY BELLENDEN (1785?–1871), legal reformer, son of John Bellenden Ker [q. v.], was born about 1785. He was called to the bar in Lincoln's Inn in Trinity term 1814, and obtained a large practice as a conveyancer. Active in promoting parliamentary reform from 1830 to 1832, he was a member of the boundary commission (House of Commons' Papers, 1832, c. xxxv.), and contested Norwich unsuccessfully in the whig interest. He was a member of the public records commission, and in 1833 he was appointed one of the royal commissioners to report upon the expediency of digesting the criminal law and consolidating the other branches of the statute law. Various bills for the amendment of the criminal law were founded on the reports of the commission. In 1845, with Messrs. Hayes and Christie, Ker drew for Lord-chancellor Lyndhurst a short bill which, when passed into an act (8 & 9 Vict. c. 106), was a most valuable amendment of the law of real property. In 1853 Lord Cranworth appointed Ker head of a board nominated to consider the consolidation of the statute law, and when that board was replaced in 1854 by a royal commission, Ker became the chief working member (Lord Cranworth's Speeches, Ann. Reg. 1853 p. 4, 1854 p. 142; Mr. Ker's First Report, 13 Aug. 1853, App. p. 209; House of Commons' Papers, p. 438; ib. 1854, vol. xv.) The action of the board and commission led to the revised edition of the statutes, the successive Statute Law Revision Acts, the issue of the chronological tables of the statute law, and to the Criminal Law Acts of 1861. Ker also suggested and prepared the useful Leases and Sales of Settled Estates Act of 1856, and Lord Cranworth's act of 1860, which were finally superseded by the Conveyancing and Settled Land Acts, modelled to a great extent upon Ker's work. In 1852 the office of master in chancery was abolished, and that of conveyancing counsel to the court of chancery was instituted. To that post Ker was soon afterwards appointed. For some years he was recorder of Andover.

Ker was an ardent advocate of popular education, and of the diffusion of literature and art. Charles Knight, in 'Passages of a Working Life,' ii. 120, 121, says that he was 'the most fertile in projects of any member of the committee' of the Society for the Diffusion of Useful Knowledge, and suggested many publishing schemes apart from the society. Two of Eastlake's most beautiful works were painted for Ker. He was himself a contributor of woodcuts as well as lives of Wren and Michael Angelo to the 'Penny Magazine.' He was an original member of the Arundel Society, was much interested in the foundation of schools of design, and helped to promote the establishment of the Department of Science and Art. He was one of the first private growers of orchids, and he wrote a series of articles under the pseudonym 'Dodman' in the 'Gardeners' Chronicle.' He was in early life a fellow of the Royal Society, but resigned his fellowship when in 1830 the Duke of Sussex was chosen president. In 1860 he retired from practice, and lived during the rest of his life at Cannes, where he died 2 Nov. 1871. Charles Knight speaks warmly of his charm in all social relations. He married Elizabeth Anne, daughter of Edward Clarke, a solicitor, but had no issue.

[Authorities cited above; personal knowledge; information from Mr. M. I. Fortescue Brickdale.]   J. S. V.

KER, JAMES INNES, fifth DUKE OF ROXBURGH (1738–1823), born at Innes House, Elginshire, in 1738, was second son of Sir Hary Innes, fifth baronet and twenty-eighth laird of Innes, by his wife Ann, daughter of Sir James Grant of Grant, and a sister of Jean, first countess Fife. During the insurrection of 1745–6 Elginshire was held by the Jacobites, and to escape falling into their hands young Innes was sent across the Moray Firth to Dunrobin Castle. He was captain of the 88th regiment of foot in 1759, and of the 58th regiment in 1779. On the death of his father in 1762 he, as the eldest surviving son, was served heir to the baronetcy 7 Feb. 1764. His family claimed to have held Innes since 1160, and at one time possessed the whole territory between the Spey and the Lossie, besides estates in Banffshire; but for a century their fortunes had been ebbing, and in 1767 Innes was obliged to sell his ancient barony of Innes to his first cousin, the second Earl Fife. On 19 April 1769 he married his first wife, Mary, eldest daughter of Sir John Wray, bart., of Glentworth, Lincolnshire, by Frances, daughter of Fairfax Norcliffe of Langton, Yorkshire. His wife inherited the Langton estate soon afterwards, and Innes thereupon assumed by royal license the additional surname of Norcliffe; but on his wife's death without issue, on 20 July 1807, the Langton estate went to her nephew, and Innes dropped the name of Norcliffe. Eight days later he married his second wife, Harriet, daughter of Benjamin Charlewood of Windlesham, Surrey, by whom he had an only son, James Henry.

Meanwhile William Ker, fourth duke of Roxburgh, had died on 22 Oct. 1805, without surviving issue. Innes's great-grandfather, Sir James Innes, third baronet, had married in 1666 Margaret Ker, granddaughter by a second marriage of Sir Robert Ker, first earl of Roxburgh [q. v.] On the ground of this distant relationship Innes, who now called himself Innes-Ker, claimed to succeed to the dukedom and its estates. His pretensions were disputed by Lady Essex Ker, by Major-general Walter Ker of Littledean, Roxburghshire, and by John Bellenden Ker [q. v.], in whose favour the last duke had entailed the property. Lord-chancellor Eldon took three days (15, 16, and 20 June 1809) to state in the House of Lords the grounds on which he preferred Sir James Innes to the other claimants. The litigation continued till 11 May 1812, when the House of Lords finally granted the title to Innes-Ker, and in the following year the deeds by which the fourth duke had attempted to bequeath to Bellenden Ker the greater part of the property were set aside. The duke died, aged 85, at Floors, near Kelso, on 19 July 1823, and was buried in the family vault at Bowden. His widow re-married Colonel Walter Frederick O'Reilly, C.B., of the 41st regiment of foot (d. 1844), and died 19 Jan. 1855. His only son, James Henry (1816–1879), succeeded as seventh duke.

[The Familie of Innes, edited for the Spalding Club by Cosmo Innes; Douglas's Peerage; Reports of Cases decided in the House of Lords upon Appeal from Scotland, vol. v.] J. C.

KER, JOHN (1673–1726), of Kersland, Ayrshire, government spy, eldest son of Alexander Crawford of Fergushill, second son of John Crawford, seventeenth laird of Crawfurdland, by Elizabeth, daughter of John Maxwell of Southburn, was born, according to the preface to his 'Memoirs,' in the family house of Crawfurdland on 8 Aug. 1673. In 1693 he married Anna, the younger of two daughters of the deceased Robert Ker of Kersland. On the death of their only brother, Major Daniel Ker of the Cameronians, at the battle of Steinkirk in 1692, the estate had been settled on the elder sister Jean, married to Major William Borthwick of Johnstonburn, but in 1697 she sold it to her sister's husband, who thereupon assumed the title and arms of Ker of Kersland. Between 1689 and 1704 Ker became so overloaded with debts that he found it necessary to grant irredeemable feu charters to sundry mortgages to the extent of half the property. His impecuniosity was probably the cause of his shameless abuse of his position as the recognised leader of the Cameronians. The support of this sect being claimed both by the government and the Jacobites, he set his wits to discover how best he could prey upon both parties, or, failing this, which party he could prey upon to most advantage. Lockhart states that he tried to gain credit with the Jacobites by opposing the union (Papers, i. 302). Ker's version is that the Jacobites concealed their own intentions in favour of the Pretender, and tried to persuade the Cameronians to a rising against the union by arguments suited to the principles of the sect (Memoirs, 1726, pt. i. p. 28). He moreover affirms that against his own conviction he was so beguiled by 'the rhetorical' (a gloss for pecuniary) 'arguments' of the Duke of Queensberry, that he cajoled the Cameronians into peace (ib. pp. 30–4). He professes deeply to regret his action in favour of the union (ib. p. 37). At the same time he naively confesses that his main motive was an assurance of the queen's favour from the duke.

Immediately after the union he says that he was sounded by some Jacobite agents as to his 'terms.' Feigning to take the bait, he endeavoured to gain their confidence in order to betray them. That he was simply a government spy may be held as proved, if we accept as genuine the royal license of 7 July 1707 (printed as a frontispiece to his Memoirs), permitting him to associate with disaffected persons. He boasts that he had spies and agents in all parts of the country. Lockhart affirms that, as 'Ker was known to be a person highly immoral and guilty of several base actions, such as forgery and the like, no person of the least note would have the least intercourse with him' (Papers, i. 302). This is partly confirmed by the Hooke 'Correspondence,' as is also the statement that 'his chief correspondence was with the Duchess of Gordon and some catholic priests.' He figures in the 'Correspondence' under the names of Thomas Trustie, Wilks, Wicks, and the 'Cameronian mealmonger.' On 20 April 1707 Mr. Strachan, a catholic gentleman, treated with him as representing the Cameronians of five shires. Ker in their name offered thirteen thousand men for the king's service, and volunteered to go to France and remain there as a hostage for the fidelity of his party (HOOKE, p. 309). Strachan also gave

Hooke a 'memoir' from Ker on the disposition of the presbyterians (printed ib. pp. 370-371); but on 18 Nov. the Duchess of Gordon wrote that 'Mr. Wicks is turned a knave' (ib. p. 517). The probability is that before his treachery was discovered he had wormed himself into some Jacobite secrets, and there is reason to suppose that he helped to frustrate a plot to seize Edinburgh Castle in 1707. In the latter end of March 1709 he came to London, and according to his own account the lord treasurer upon his arrival paid all accounts due to himself, but would do nothing 'in the matter of the Cameronian arrears' (Memoirs, p. 65). Lockhart, however, prints a copy of a letter of Ker to the Duke of Roxburgh, dated 4 May (Papers, i. 302-6), simply asking to be repaid the expenses he had incurred in 'managing of these people.' This letter, according to Lockhart, was shown to certain Jacobites by a kept mistress of Ker's, who allowed them to make a copy. Lockhart states that Ker obtained in all from the government about 500l. or 600l., and finding that Godolphin 'would give no more,' he 'tacked about to the whigs and tories,' and, on the promise to give evidence of Godolphin's connection with the Jacobites, obtained at least two thousand guineas from the leaders of both parties unknown to one another (ib. p. 308).

In 1713 Ker was, according to his own testimony, sent on a private mission to the emperor of Austria in connection with a scheme for employing buccaneers to harass the trade of France and Spain (Memoirs, p. 75). On his arrival in Vienna in January 1713-14, he told his 'story' to Leibnitz, who privately arranged with the emperor an interview between Ker and the emperor's secretary. The enterprise being unfavourably received, Ker thereupon 'drops' it, to 'inform posterity that I employed my spare hours at Vienna in sending to the Electress Sophia all the light I got.' For the ill-success of his mission he was consoled by a present of 'the emperor's picture in gold set round with diamonds' (ib. p. 87). He arrived in Hanover in July 1714, and thus, according to his own account, was useful in securing the Hanoverian succession (ib. p. 92), besides giving good advice to the elector as to the method of ruling the English nation. He asked the government of the Bermudas as a reward, but, as he scorned to bribe officials, it was bestowed on another. He professes also to have given important information against the Jacobites in 1715, but no notice was taken of his communications. Being 'disappointed' of all his 'endeavours to prevent the rebellion,' he embarked for Holland, but returned to

London, where Leibnitz told him that his presence would be 'very necessary,' in March 1715 (ib. p. 110). His offers of service were declined, and he only received 'a hundred dollars from the king.' He now offered his services to the East India Company, to arrange matters between them and the emperor of Austria; but disappointed here also, he in 1721 directed his efforts to form a scheme and charter for erecting a new company of commerce in the Austrian Netherlands.' The affair came to nothing, and henceforth ill-luck continued to dog his footsteps till his death, which took place in the King's Bench debtors' prison on 8 July 1726. He was buried in St. George's churchyard, Southwark. On his return from abroad in 1718 he sold the estate of Fergushill to John Asgill [q. v.] and Robert Hackett for 3,800l., and in 1721 Hackett conveyed his moiety of the estate to Asgill, which moiety Asgill afterwards mortgaged to Ker for 2,600l., 'which remained at his death' (ib. pt. iii. pp. 63-4). During his absence on the continent his wife had been obliged to impropriate the plate and furniture of Kersland to three friends who undertook to support her. After Ker's death she tried to save the estate from creditors by producing a forged deed in the name of her elder sister Jean. Ultimately the property, with the superiority of the barony, was sold in 1738. Ker left three daughters: Elizabeth, married to John Campbell of Ellangieg, Argyllshire, and Anna and Jean, of whom nothing further is known.

The 'Memoirs of John Ker of Kersland, part i., published by himself, appeared in 1726, and parts ii. and iii. also in the same year. The publisher of all the three parts was Edmund Curll [q. v.] Part ii. was published by Ker's 'express direction,' and though part iii. was published posthumously, it claimed to be 'faithfully printed from the original manuscript of the said John Ker, Esq.; and other authorities serving to illustrate the said work,' and also to be 'prepared for the press under his express direction.' Part iii. contained 'Maxims of Trade,' and there was also added by Curll the indictment for publishing part i. For publishing the 'Memoirs,' which contained professed revelations reflecting on the government, and for other similar offences, Curll was fined twenty marks, and had to stand in the pillory an hour at Charing Cross (State Trials, xvii. 160; Notes and Queries, 2nd ser. iii. 143-4). A third edition of part i. appeared at London in 1727 (Catalogue of Advocates' Library, Edinburgh), and another edition of part ii. in the same year (ib.) 'Castrations of the Memoirs of John Ker of Kersland' also appeared in 1727. (There is a copy in the Grenville Library in the British Museum.) His 'Memoirs' were translated into French under the title, 'Mémoires contenant des réflexions intéressantes sur le commerce et une histoire abrégée de l'île de Majorque,' Rotterdam, 1726–8, 3 vols. Ker's portrait by Hammond is prefixed to part i. of his 'Memoirs.'

[Lockhart Papers; Ker's Memoirs, and preface to part i.; Nathaniel Hooke's Correspondence (Abbotsford Club); Political State of Great . Britain, 1826, xxxii. 97; Paterson's Hist. of the County of Ayr, i. 425–6.] T. F. H.

KER, JOHN, fifth EARL and first DUKE OF ROXBURGH (d. 1741), was brother of Robert, fourth earl, and second son of Robert, third earl, by Lady Margaret Hay, eldest daughter of John, first marquis of Tweeddale. He was, according to Patten, carefully educated by his father (History of the Rebellion), and Macky refers to him as 'a young gentleman of great learning and virtue,' who 'knows all the ancient languages thoroughly, and speaks most of the modern perfectly well' (Secret Memoirs). He also describes him as 'brown-complexioned' and 'handsome.' Lockhart calls him perhaps 'the best accomplished young man of quality in Europe' (Memoirs, p. 95). He had also great personal charm. 'By all that are so happy as to be acquainted with him,' writes Patten, 'he gains their affection and applause.' He 'had so charming a way of expressing his thoughts,' laments Lockhart, 'that he pleased even those against whom he spoke.' On 22 Oct. 1696 he was served heir male and of entail of his brother in the earldom of Roxburgh, when, according to Lockhart, 'he made his first appearance in the world to the general satisfaction of all men.' In 1704 he was appointed one of the secretaries of state for Scotland, and the same year he accompanied the Earl of Rothes and Baillie of Jerviswood as a deputation to London to protest against the payment of Scots troops from the English treasury (Marchmont Papers, iii. 264). The deputation were assured that no purpose of this kind had been contemplated. Subsequently Roxburgh joined the squadrone, and as one of its principal leaders he took a very prominent part in the debates in favour of the union and the protestant succession. On 25 April 1707 Roxburgh's great services to the government were recognised by creating him in the Scots peerage Duke of Roxburgh, Marquis of Bowmont and Cessfurd, Earl of Kelso, Viscount Broxmouth, and Lord Ker of Cessfurd and Caverton. The same year he was chosen one of the sixteen Scottish representative peers, and he was rechosen in

1708, and again in 1715 and 1722. Dissatisfied with the influence exercised by the Duke of Queensberry in the management of Scottish business, Roxburgh, after the union, again set himself with other nobles to oppose his administration and to carry the elections in Scotland against him, but with very indifferent success. Roxburgh was one of the council of regency appointed in 1714 before the arrival in England of George I, by whom he was, on 24 Sept., named keeper of the privy seal of Scotland, and also appointed lord-lieutenant of Roxburgh and Selkirk. On 14 Oct. he was sworn a privy councillor. On the outbreak of the rebellion in the following year he accompanied the Duke of Argyll to Scotland, and in a troop of horse volunteers, composed chiefly of gentlemen of position, specially distinguished himself at the battle of Sheriffmuir (PATTEN, History of the Rebellion). He was also able to raise about five hundred men in support of the Hanoverian succession. In 1716 he was reappointed one of the secretaries of state for Scotland, and during the king's absence from England in 1716, 1720, 1723, and 1725 he acted as one of the lords justices. He zealously supported Carteret and Cadogan in their opposition to Townsend and Walpole. Walpole triumphed, but for some time he was unable to obtain Roxburgh's removal. At last, however, Roxburgh was dismissed on 25 Aug. 1725, on the ground that he had used his official position to encourage the discontent in Scotland on account of the malt-tax. Roxburgh's opposition to this tax seems to have been quite sincere. His dismissal arose, in fact, partly from a constitutional difficulty—the difficulty of harmonising the discharge of the functions of the office with due subordination to the cabinet. Consequently, no one was immediately appointed to succeed him, and although subsequently the office was nominally held by Lord Selkirk and the Marquis of Tweeddale, Roxburgh was the last to exercise the full functions of the office until its revival in modern times. Roxburgh spent his subsequent years chiefly in retirement on his estates; but at the coronation of George II he officiated as deputy to the Countess of Errol, high constable of Scotland. He was a fellow of the Royal Society, and acted as a pall-bearer at the funeral of Sir Isaac Newton in Westminster Abbey on 28 March 1727. He died at Floors 24 Feb. 1741, and was buried at Bowden.

He married, on 1 Jan. 1708, Lady Mary Finch, only child of Daniel, earl of Winchelsea and Nottingham, and widow of William Savile, marquis of Halifax. She died on 19 Sept. 1718, and was buried in Westminster

Abbey, leaving one son, Robert, second duke of Roxburgh, who befriended Fielding, was father of John Ker, third duke [q. v.], and died at Bath 23 Aug. 1755.

[Patten's History of the Rebellion; Lockhart of Carnwath's Memoirs; Macky's Secret Memoirs; Marchmont Papers; Burnet's Own Time; Coxe's Life of Walpole; Douglas's Scottish Peerage (Wood), ii. 451-2.]　　　　T. F. H.

KER, JOHN, third DUKE OF ROXBURGH (1740-1804), book-collector, born in Hanover Square, London, 23 April 1740, was elder son of Robert Ker, second duke, by his wife Essex (d. 7 Dec. 1764), daughter of Sir Roger Mostyn, bart. In 1755 he succeeded his father in the dukedom, and in 1761 paid his addresses, while travelling on the continent, to Christiana Sophia Albertina, eldest daughter of the Duke of Mecklenburg-Strelitz, but the lady's younger sister, Charlotte, was affianced very soon afterwards to George III (September 1761), and it was deemed necessary, on political grounds, to break off the match between the duke and Christiana. 'Both parties,' it is said, 'evinced the strength of their attachment by devoting their after-lives to celibacy.' The disappointment induced in Roxburgh a 'reserved melancholy which prefers retirement to splendid scenes of gaiety' (SIR WALTER SCOTT). Roxburgh's sisters, Essex and Mary, both acted as bridesmaids at the king's marriage. George III showed much friendship for Roxburgh, and appointed him a lord of the bedchamber in 1767. He received the knighthood of the Thistle on 24 Nov. 1768, became groom of the stole and a privy councillor 30 Nov. 1796, and was invested on 3 June 1801 with the order of the Garter, which he held—a very rare distinction—along with that of the Thistle. He died at his house in St. James's Square on 19 March 1804, and was buried at Bowden. His British titles of Earl and Baron Ker of Wakefield became extinct at his death, but his Scottish honours devolved on a kinsman, William, seventh lord Bellenden, born about 1728, who succeeded as fourth duke, and died without surviving issue 22 Oct. 1805 [see KER, JAMES INNES-, fifth DUKE].

The third duke was a man of many accomplishments. According to Sir Walter Scott, who was well acquainted with him, his 'lofty presence and felicitous address' suggested Lord Chesterfield. When in Scotland he was an ardent sportsman, but his time in London was chiefly spent in book-collecting, and he devoted 'hours, nay, days, in collating' his rare editions. George III and he were often competitors for the purchase of the same book,

and the duke was rarely unsuccessful in such contests. He secured an unrivalled collection of books from Caxton's press. Scott describes him as 'a curious and unwearied reader of romance,' making 'many observations in writing,' including a genealogy of the Knights of the Round Table (LOCKHART, Life of Scott, 1839, iii. 35). He possessed the two rare editions, dated in 1566, of the Scottish acts of parliaments 'of the five first Jameses and Queen Mary,' and printed separately the few statutes omitted in the later impression for the use of those who only possessed that impression. His splendid library was housed in his residence in St. James's Square, London, and was dispersed by sale there during forty-five days between 18 May and 8 July 1812. The lots numbered 9,353, and though the duke is said to have only expended 5,000l. on the collection, 23,341l. was realised. Brunet asserts that the sale marked the highest point reached by 'the thermometer of bibliomania' in England. Valdarfer's edition of Boccaccio, for which the second Duke of Roxburgh had paid one hundred guineas, was sold to the Marquis of Blandford for 2,260l., after a severe competition with Lord Spencer, and Caxton's 'Recuyell of the Historye of Troye' fell to the Duke of Devonshire for 1,070l. 10s. (Gent. Mag. 1812, pt. ii. pp. 112-16). Roxburgh possessed a rare collection of broadside ballads bound in three volumes. Two of these had originally formed part of the Earl of Oxford's library, and after passing into the possession successively of James West and Major Thomas Pearson, had been bought by the duke at Pearson's sale in 1788 for 36l. 14s. 6d. Pearson had, with the help of Isaac Reed, made valuable additions to the collection, but the duke devoted himself to perfecting it, and the number of broadsides in his hands reached 1,340. They fetched 477l. 15s. at the sale in 1812, and were acquired by Benjamin Heywood Bright, after whose death in 1843 they were purchased by the British Museum in 1845. The whole collection has since been carefully edited for the Ballad Society by William Chappell and the Rev. J. W. Ebsworth.

To celebrate the sale of the Boccaccio on 24 June 1812, the chief bibliophiles of the day dined together in the evening at St. Alban's Tavern, St. Alban's Street, under the presidency of Lord Spencer, and there inaugurated the Roxburghe Club, consisting of twenty-four members (Gent. Mag. 1812, pt. ii. p. 79).

A portrait of the duke by Thomas Patch, in the manner of an Italian caricature, was presented in 1884 by Sir Richard Wallace to the National Portrait Gallery.

E 2

[Douglas's Peerage, ed. Wood; Gent. Mag. 1804, pt. i. p. 383; Sir Walter Scott in Quarterly Review, xliv. 446-7; Chambers's Eminent Scotsmen, ii. 440-1; Lockhart's Life of Scott; Edwards's Memoirs of Libraries, ii. 132; Lowndes's Bibliographer's Manual, ed. Bohn; G. and W. Nicol's Sale Catalogue of the Duke of Roxburgh's Library, 1812.]   S. L.

KER, JOHN (1819-1886), divine, was born in the farmhouse of Bield, in the parish of Tweedsmuir, Peeblesshire, on 7 April 1819. His parents moved successively to Fillyside, between Leith and Portobello, and to Abbeyhill. Ker was much impressed as a child by the preaching of John Brown (1784-1858) [q. v.] He was educated at the Edinburgh High School, and in 1835 he became a student in the university of Edinburgh. He gained the first prize in Sir William Hamilton's class, and was second in both the moral philosophy and natural philosophy classes. In 1838 he entered the divinity hall of the united secession church. During the recesses he studied the French and German languages, getting the whole German dictionary by heart. He also learnt Hebrew and Arabic. He spent six months at Halle under Tholuck, and attended Neander's lectures at Berlin. He was well read in history, and fond of Scottish songs and romances. In February 1845 he was ordained in Alnwick, Northumberland, as minister of Clayport Street Church, in connection with the associate presbytery of Edinburgh. His congregation rapidly increased, and he helped to found a ragged school, besides giving literary lectures. He was called to Barrhead in 1849, and he was inducted to East Campbell Street Church, Glasgow, on 19 March 1851. He became known as a preacher and platform orator. His large church became crowded, and the centre of many agencies. He declined a call to Bristol in 1855, and an offer of the post of the first home mission secretary made by the synod (now the United Presbyterian Synod) in 1857. On 28 Nov. 1857 his congregation removed to a new church erected in Sydney Place at a cost of over 8,000l. In May 1858 his health broke down from overwork, and he had to spend many winters abroad, not being able to resume full work till 1872. A volume of his 'Sermons' ran through thirteen editions, and is remarkable both for style and power of thought. In 1869 he received the degree of D.D. from Edinburgh University. In 1876 Ker was chosen professor of practical training in the reconstructed theological hall of his church. His weakness obliged him to limit his labours; but, in spite of much suffering, he performed his duties successfully till his death on 4 Oct.

1886. Besides the volume of sermons already mentioned Ker published various sermons and pamphlets. He contributed to the 'United Presbyterian Magazine' articles on 'Echoes of the Psalms in the Experience of Life and Death,' 1884 (afterwards published as a volume entitled 'The Psalms in History and Biography,' 1886, 8vo); and on 'The Revocation of the Edict of Nantes,' 1886, &c. There appeared posthumously 'Scottish Nationality and other Papers,' 1887; 'Lectures on the History of Preaching,' 1888; and an interesting volume of his letters in 1890.

[See Scotsman, 6 and 11 Oct. 1886; Christian Leader, 28 Oct. 1886 ('Dr. John Ker as Preacher and Professor,' by the Rev. W. Dickie, M.A., Perth), and 18 Nov. 1886 ('Dr. John Ker as a Pastor'); Biographical Sketch of the late Rev. Dr. John Ker, by the Rev. Dr. Leckie. Ibrox, Glasgow, in United Presbyterian Magazine, December 1886; and other notices and reviews.]
                                            T. B. J.

KER, JOHN BELLENDEN (1765?-1842), botanist, wit, and man of fashion, was the eldest son of John Gawler of Ramridge, near Andover, Hampshire, and of the Inner Temple (d. at Bath 24 Dec. 1803, aged 77). His mother was Caroline, eldest surviving daughter of John, third baron Bellenden (d. 1740). John Gawler (as he was at first called) obtained a commission in the second regiment of life-guards; was appointed captain 20 Jan. 1790, and was senior captain in the regiment in 1793, when he was compelled to quit the army owing to his displays of sympathy with the French revolution. On 5 Nov. 1804 George III, out of regard for Gawler's mother, and at the instance of his second cousin, William, seventh baron Bellenden and fourth duke of Roxburgh, granted him a license to take the name of Ker Bellenden in lieu of Gawler; but he was invariably known as Bellenden Ker. William, fourth duke of Roxburgh, died in 1805 without direct heir. During his lifetime he sedulously endeavoured to divert the succession in favour of Ker, and entailed his estates upon him. But both the entail and Ker's claim to the title were, after much litigation, set aside by the House of Lords in favour of James Innes-Ker, fifth duke of Roxburgh [q. v.] on 11 May 1812 (cf. 2 Dow's Reports). Ker was long known as a wit and man of fashion in London. Many stories were told of the charm of his conversation, and he was the hero of some 'affairs of gallantry.'

His attention must, however, have been early turned to botany, for in 1801 he brought out anonymously his 'Recensio Plantarum,' a review of all the plants figured up to that time in Andrews's 'Botanist's Repository.'

About the same date he began to contribute occasional descriptions of new plants to Curtis's 'Botanical Magazine,' then under the editorship of Dr. Sims, who highly commended Ker in the preface to the fifteenth volume. In 1804 he printed an important memoir on a group of plants, the Iridaceæ, in König and Sims's 'Annals of Botany.' In 1812 the 'Botanical Register' was started in opposition to the 'Botanical Magazine' [see EDWARDS, SYDENHAM TEAK], and Ker became the first editor. He held the office till about 1823, when Dr. Lindley took sole control. When freed from botanical journalism, he revised his memoir on the Iridaceæ of 1804, and brought out his 'Iridearum Genera,' Brussels, 1828, 8vo, which was his last important work on botany. An illness supervened, and on resuming work he busied himself on 'An Essay on the Archæology of Popular English Phrases and Nursery Rhymes,' Southampton, 1834, 8vo, which reached a second edition, London, 1835-7, 2 vols. 12mo. Supplemental volumes are dated 1840 and 1842. Until within twenty years before his death he wrote occasional articles in the gardening papers.

During the later period of his life Ker lived at Ramridge, where he died in June 1842. The genus *Bellendena* commemorates him. He was married. His son, Charles Henry Bellenden Ker, is separately noticed.

A painting by Sir Joshua Reynolds of Ker and his brother Henry Gawler (afterwards of Lincoln's Inn) as boys, was engraved by J. R. Smith. The picture was sold in 1887 for 2,415*l.* (*Times*, 5 May 1887).

[House of Lords, Roxburgh Succession. Ker and others appellants, &c., 1808, &c.; Douglas's Peerage of Scotland, ed. Wood, ii. 453-4; Gent. Mag. 1842, pt. ii. p. 220; information kindly supplied by Mr. M. I. Fortescue Brickdale, and Mr. J. Savill Vaizey of Lincoln's Inn.]

B. D. J.

KER, PATRICK (*fl.* 1691), poet, has been supposed, with some support from internal evidence, to have been a Scottish episcopalian who migrated to London during the reign of Charles II. 'Flosculum Poeticum. Poems divine and humane. Panegyrical, satyrical, ironical, by P. K. . . .' (London, 16[?]4, 12mo), a volume of ultra-loyalist verse, though assigned by Lowndes to P. Kirk (*Bibl. Man.* ii. 1252), may be safely attributed to him. Facing the title-page appears the triangle symbolical of the Trinity, which appears in another work, 'The Map of Mans Misery,' with the author's name, P. Ker, in full. The 'Flosculum' includes a grotesque cut of Charles II in the oak, accompanied by verses equally grotesque (p. 19), and a number of scurrilous rhymes and anagrams on Oliver Cromwell. The Luttrell Collection of Broadsides at the British Museum contains two elegies on Charles II, one dated 9 Feb. 1685, and signed P. K., the other dated 15 Feb., as well as a 'Panegyrick Poem on the Coronation of James II,' all of which are by Ker. In 1690 appeared his 'Map of Mans Misery, or the Poor Man's Pocket Book. Being a Perpetual Almanack of Spiritual Meditations, or Compleat Directory for our Endlesse Week. . . . To which is added a Poem, entituled The Glass of Vain Glory. For Jn. Lawrence at the Angel in the Poultry,' 1690, 12mo. The author's tory tendencies are here suppressed, the work being dedicated to Rachel, lady Russell, and subscribed P. Ker, 24 Jan. 1689 (O.S.) In the following year was published 'Λογομαχία, or the Conquest of Eloquence: containing two witty orations (in doggerel verse) as they may be read in Ovid's "Metamorphoses," lib. xiii. By P. K.' This is attributed in Heber's 'Catalogue' (p. 109), followed by Lowndes, to P. Kirk, but there is no apparent foundation for this theory of authorship. The last work traceable to Ker appeared in 1691. It is called 'Πολιτικὸς μέγας. The Grand Politician, or the Secret Art of State Policy discovered. Written originally in Latin by Conradus Reinking, Chancellor to his Electoral Highness the Duke of Brandenburgh, and now done into English.' The so-called translation is supplementary to Machiavelli's well-known treatise, being addressed for the most part to statesmen and instructing them 'How to Dissemble,' 'How to abrogate Privileges,' 'How to reveal a secret without giving offence to him who did inform you of it.' 'How to collect taxes without offending the subjects.' The writer dedicates his 'small treatise or wandering meteor' to the Earl of Nottingham, and subscribes himself 'Pat. Ker.' This volume was published by Thos. Howkins, the publisher of the 'Λογομαχία,' with which work it was in some cases originally bound up. There seems little reason for supposing that Patrick Ker was identical with a Rev. Dr. Kerr, an eminent schoolmaster of Highgate, who is referred to by Dunton (*Life and Errors*, passim).

[Notes and Queries, 2nd ser. i. 281, 4th ser. ii. 102; Hazlitt's Bibl. Collections, 3rd ser. p. 132; Ker's works in Brit. Mus. Library, catalogued under K., P.]

T. S.

KER, ROBERT, EARL OF SOMERSET (*d.* 1645). [See CARR.]

KER, ROBERT, first EARL OF ROXBURGH (1570?-1650), eldest son of William Ker of Cessfurd, by Janet, daughter of Sir William

Douglas of Drumlanrig, was born about 1570. His father was grandson of that Sir Andrew Ker [q. v.] of Cessford who was father of Mark Kerr [q. v.], abbot of Newbattle. He had charters of lands in the barony of Caverton on 22 March 1573 (*Reg. Mag. Sig. Scot.* 1546–80, entry 2213), and also on the same date a charter of the barony of Cessford and other lands (*ib.* 2214). It was Sir Robert Ker's father (not himself, as stated sometimes) who in 1585 assisted the banished lords in driving Arran from power, and towards the close of 1587 was, at the same time as Scott of Buccleuch, committed to ward, at the instance of Lord Hunsdon, for making excursions on the borders. In 1590 Sir Robert conspired the murder of William Ker of Ancrum, which was committed in Edinburgh 'under silence of night' (*Hist. James the Sext*, p. 245). He fled to England (*ib.*), but on 18 Nov. 1591 obtained a remission under the great seal (*Reg. Mag. Sig. Scot.* 1580–93, entry 1981). He was an adherent of the Chancellor Maitland of Thirlestane, whom in 1592 he succeeded in reconciling with the queen (SIR JAMES MELVILLE, *Memoirs*, p. 405). In October 1593 Ker, with two or three hundred horse, joined the king at Linlithgow to support him against the Bothwell party (MOYSIE, *Memoirs*, p. 105), and while returning homewards in December, accompanied by only one servant, accidentally encountered Bothwell, who also was accompanied by only one attendant. They fought on horseback two by two for several hours without decisive result, until at length both parties were so exhausted with their exertions that they separated by mutual consent (*ib.* p. 111). On 27 March 1594 Ker, as warden-depute of the middle marches, received a commission from the privy council for the pursuit of Bothwell (*Reg. P. C. Scott.* v. 137), and in August Ker of Ferniehirst and others were ordered into ward for declining to subscribe an association to assist him in the pursuit (*ib.* p. 161). On 16 Oct. following he was 'denounced a rebel' for failing to present before the council Andrew Ker of Newhall (*ib.* v. 230). On 2 Dec. the Earl of Morton complained that Sir Robert had evaded the act by formally presenting Andrew Ker before some of the council in Edinburgh (*ib.* pp. 240–1). On 5 July 1596, for neglecting to appear before the king and council to give advice regarding the means to be used for the quieting of the borders, he and others were denounced as rebels (*ib.* p. 300), but on the 24th he found caution that he would keep good rule (*ib.* p. 742). The chief reason for his non-appearance was, probably, that he was himself the prime pro-

moter of the disorders. Sir Robert Carey [q. v.], afterwards earl of Monmouth, who describes Ker as a 'brave, active young man' (*Memoirs*, ed. 1808, p. 67), gives a graphic description of his exploits, and of the manner in which he checkmated him by the capture of Geordie Bourne, one of Ker's most daring subordinates. In December 1596 a settlement of the disputes on the borders had been arranged, including an exchange of prisoners, and Ker, having failed to deliver up some English prisoners, surrendered himself in the following year to Sir Robert Carey, by whom he was courteously treated. Not long afterwards he was released, and on 24 July 1599 he was admitted a member of the privy council of Scotland (*Reg. P. C. Scott.* v. 557). In the following year he was created Lord Roxburgh. Douglas and others state that the date of creation is uncertain, all that is known being that it was previous to that of Lindores (created 31 March 1600–1), before whom his name appears in the ranking of the nobility in 1606; but, according to Sir James Balfour, the creation took place on 29 Dec. 1600 (*Annals*, i. 409). His name appears as Roxburgh in the council sederunt of 10 Feb. 1601 (*Reg. P. C. Scott.* vi. 203). On 3 Aug. 1602 a commission of wardency was appointed for the middle marches in view of Roxburgh's intention to go abroad (*ib.* p. 441). He accompanied King James in his journey to London in 1603, after his succession to the English crown, and subsequently retained a position of influence in his counsels. At the parliament held at Perth in July 1604 he was appointed a commissioner to treat with the English commissioners regarding a union with England. On 24 July 1606 he was served heir to his father, and subsequently he received a large number of charters of other lands, including (15 Aug. 1630) that of the burgh of Canongate, united into the barony of Broughton. On 24 June 1606 the council ordained that a deadly feud between him and the Kers of Ancrum on account of the slaughter of their father should be submitted to arbitration (*ib.* vii. 215), and on 20 Nov. the Kers of Ancrum, although declining to submit the feud to arbitration, agreed to be reconciled (*ib.* vii. 272).

In October 1607 Roxburgh was sent as the king's commissioner to the synod of Merse and Teviotdale, to urge its compliance with the enactment of the Linlithgow convention by admitting one of the 'constant moderators' of the presbytery to be moderator of the synod, but 'got a flat *nolumus*' (CALDERWOOD, vi. 680). He was retained a member of the privy council on its reconstruction by royal letter 20 Jan. 1610 (*Reg. P. C. Scotl.* viii. 815). On 18 Sept. 1616 he was created Earl of Roxburgh and Lord Ker of Cessfurd and Caverton. He was, however, disappointed at not obtaining the place of chamberlain to the prince, and about the same time his lady lost the favour of the queen and left the court (*Cal. State Papers,* Dom. Ser. 1611–18, p. 415). In the parliament which met at Edinburgh on 25 July 1621 he was chosen a lord of the articles, and in the same parliament he voted for the confirmation of the five articles of Perth. He was a member of the committee appointed by King James, 19 May 1623, to sit every week for the purpose of hearing grievances (CALDERWOOD, vii. 576). In 1637 he was made lord privy seal of Scotland. After the afternoon service in St. Giles's Church on 23 July of this year, which followed the disturbance caused in the forenoon by the reading of the service, Roxburgh drove the bishop to his lodgings in his carriage amidst the stone-throwing of an enraged mob (GORDON, *Scots Affairs,* i. 11; SPALDING, *Memorials,* i. 80). Subsequently he favoured a conference with the ministers in order that the matters in dispute might be arranged, although he was supposed to be a secret supporter of episcopacy. In November he was sent from London by the king with secret instructions for the council to take decisive action (king's letter in BALFOUR, *Annals,* ii. 237), the result being that all meetings held in opposition to the service-book were discharged under pain of treason (GORDON, i. 32). Roxburgh was one of those who, on 22 Sept. 1638, subscribed the king's covenant at Holyrood (*ib.* p. 108). He was one of the six assessors named by the king to sit in the general assembly held at Glasgow in November (*ib.* p. 144; SPALDING, p. 118), but not allowed by the assembly to take part in the business. On the outbreak of the civil war in 1639 he joined the king, but his son having joined the covenanters, he himself was for security committed on 15 May to the mayor's house at Newcastle (*Cal. State Papers,* Dom. Ser. 1639, p. 173). In June he, however, again kissed the king's hands (*ib.* p. 265), and a little later was received into great favour (*ib.* p. 268). After the pacification of Berwick he returned home. As he had not subscribed the covenant, he was not permitted to enter the Scottish parliament when it was opened by the king in 1641, but, along with other noblemen under similar disabilities, 'stayed in the next room' (BALFOUR, *Annals,* iii. 44). Having, however, subscribed on 18 Aug., he took his seat (*ib.* p. 45), and besides having his office of privy seal confirmed to him, served on several important committees. He also took a prominent part in most of the discussions, supporting so far as possible a policy consonant to the wishes of the king. When Charles in 1642 attempted the arrest of the five members, Roxburgh kept the door of the house open that members might see the inadvisability of resistance. In the following year he was stated to have been concerned in the writing of a letter to the queen from Derby, informing her of the intention of the Scots to take up arms. He remained, however, practically neutral until in 1648 he supported the 'engagement' for the king's rescue. For doing so he was on 13 Feb. of the following year deprived of the office of privy seal. He died 18 Jan. 1650, in his eightieth year, at his house of Floors (now known as Floors Castle), near Kelso, and was buried in Bowden Church on 20 March.

Roxburgh was thrice married. By his first wife, Margaret, only daughter of Sir William Maitland of Lethington, he had one son, William, lord Ker, who graduated at Edinburgh University 28 July 1610 and died while travelling in France in 1618; and three daughters: Jean, married 1655 to Sir William Drummond, fourth son of John, second earl of Perth; Isabel, married to James Scrimgeour, second viscount Dundee; and Mary, married first to James Halyburton of Pitcairn, and secondly to James, second earl of Southesk. By his second wife, Jean, third daughter of Patrick, third lord Drummond, he had a son, Harry, lord Ker, who died in January 1643, and whose daughter, Margaret, wife of Sir James Innes, third baronet, was ultimately great-grandmother of James Innes-Ker, fifth duke of Roxburgh [q. v.] By his third wife, Isabel Douglas, fifth daughter of William, earl of Morton, Roxburgh had no issue. Having no heirs male, the titles and estates, in accordance with a new destination obtained in 1646, renewed by charter under the great seal 31 July 1646, and executed 23 Feb. 1648, passed to Sir William Drummond, the husband of Roxburgh's eldest daughter, Jean.

[Reg. Mag. Sig. Scot. vols. ii–iii.; Reg. P. C. Scotl. vols. v–ix.; Cal. State Papers, Dom. Ser. reigns of James I and Charles I; Hist. James the Sext, Sir James Melville's Memoirs, Robert Baillie's Letters and Journals, and Moysie's Memoirs (last four Bannatyne Club); Gordon's Scots Affairs and Spalding's Memorialls of the Trubles (both Spalding Club); Sir James Balfour's Annals; Calderwood's Hist. of the Church of Scotland; Sir Robert Carey's Memoirs; Douglas's Scottish Peerage (Wood), ii. 447–8.]
T. F. H.

KER, ROBERT, first EARL OF ANCRUM (1578–1654), eldest son of William Ker of Ancrum, by Margaret, daughter of Alexander Dundas of Fingask, who afterwards became wife of Sir George Douglas of Mordington, was (see *Correspondence*, p. 379) born 9 Dec. 1578. William Ker of Ancrum was grandson of Andrew Ker of Ferniehirst [q. v.]. He succeeded to the family estates on the assassination of his father in 1590 by Sir Robert Ker of Cessfurd, afterwards first earl of Roxburgh [q. v.]. In 1603 he was appointed groom of the bedchamber in the household of Prince Henry, and shortly afterwards knighted. On 1 Oct. of the same year he signed, as provost of Jedburgh, the general bond against thieves and robbers of the borders (*Reg. P. C. Scotl.* vi. 825). On 24 June 1606 he consented to drop the feud with Roxburgh [see under KER, ROBERT, first EARL OF ROXBURGH]. He was one of the commissioners appointed in 1607 to see to the acceptance of 'constant moderators' by the presbytery (*ib.* vii. 376). After a foreign journey he was appointed one of the gentlemen-in-ordinary to Henry, prince of Wales. He was also frequently employed on special missions to Scotland. On 13 Nov. 1613 he resigned the captaincy of the guard in favour of Sir Andrew Ker of Oxenhame, in order to attend on the king's son, Charles. In the beginning of February 1620 Charles Maxwell of Terregles accused Ker of saying something about the Duke of Buckingham, which led to a duel at Newmarket. Maxwell was slain. Maxwell was clearly the offending party, and a verdict of manslaughter having been returned at the coroner's inquest, Ker, after six months' banishment, received a special pardon on 23 Oct. 1620. In 1623 Ker joined Prince Charles in Spain as gentleman of the bedchamber (*Verney Papers*, Camden Soc. 1853, p. 107). In April following a pension was bestowed on him and his wife. On the accession of Charles in 1625 he was promoted to be a lord of the bedchamber. Subsequently he was made master of the privy purse, and on the occasion of the coronation of Charles in Scotland was in 1633 created Earl of Ancrum, Lord Nisbet, Langnewton, and Dolphinton. On 7 Jan. 1634–5 he obtained a grant for seven years of the ten-shilling impost on the ton of foreign starch, and of the four-shilling impost paid by the makers of starch in the kingdom to the king, 200*l.* a year of the grant being reserved for the king (*Cal. State Papers*, Dom. Ser. 1634–5, p. 454). On 23 June 1638 he received powers for thirty-one years for the discovery of ambergris and things lost at sea (*ib.* 1638, p. 527). On 22 Aug. he was nominated a member of the commission on cottages, and also of that appointed to inquire into breaches of the law against the taking of excessive usury (*ib.* pp. 602–3). On 23 Sept. he made a complaint regarding certain grants out of his perquisites to others, explaining that his diligence in encouraging the starch trade had raised the value (*ib.* 1638–9, p. 24), and the matter was referred to the attorney-general (*ib.* 1639–40, p. 92). On 28 March of the following year a pension of 2,000*l.* per annum was assigned to him and his wife for both their lives (*ib.* 1638–9, p. 620). He seems to have retired from the office of privy purse in the end of February of this year, for in April he received a discharge for all sums received by him up to the previous March (*ib.* 1639, p. 100). In October 1640 his wife received a gift of 1,700*l.* in recognition of her services as governess to the three princesses and also to the Duke of Gloucester (*ib.* 1640–1, p. 172). Although Ancrum's son William, third earl of Lothian, joined the covenanting party, himself continued faithful to the royalist cause during the whole of the puritan conflict. He, however, remained aloof from public affairs from 1641 to 1650. On the death of Charles he retired to Amsterdam. He died there in great poverty towards the close of 1654. His dead body was arrested in May 1655 by his creditors to secure payment of his debts, but through the intermediation of Cromwell with the Dutch authorities directions were given that the funeral should not be disturbed.

Ancrum was twice married. By his first wife, Elizabeth, daughter of Sir John Murray of Blackbarony, he had one son, William Kerr [q. v.], who married Anne, countess of Lothian, and was created third earl of Lothian 31 Oct. 1631. By his second wife, Lady Anne Stanley, daughter of William, sixth earl of Derby, by Elizabeth Vere, he had one son, Charles, earl of Ancrum, and several daughters.

Ancrum was a man of cultivated tastes, and lived on terms of intimacy with some of the most famous literary men of his time, including John Donne and Drummond of Hawthornden. His 'Sonnet in Praise of a Solitary Life,' sent in 1624 to Drummond, was published in Drummond's works, and reprinted in 1875 in his own 'Correspondence.' While abroad he also wrote a metrical version of the Psalms, to fit them to tunes he had heard them sung to in the Low Countries. These have been also published in his 'Correspondence.' His portrait, by Blyenbach, is at Newbattle Abbey, and has been engraved in his 'Correspondence.' There is also an engraved portrait in Walpole's 'Royal and Noble Authors,' and in Pinkerton's 'Iconographia Scotica.'

[Reg. P. C. Scotl. vi-ix.; Cal. State Papers, Dom. Ser., reign of Charles I; Sir James Balfour's Annals of Scotland; Correspondence of Sir Robert Ker, Earl of Ancrum, and his son, William Ker, third Earl of Lothian, 1875; Walpole's Royal and Noble Authors, ed. Park; Pinkerton's Iconographia Scotica: Douglas's Scottish Peerage (Wood), ii. 136-7.]   T. F. H.

KER, SIR THOMAS (d. 1586), of Ferniehirst, eldest son of Sir John Ker of Ferniehirst, by his wife Catherine, daughter of Sir Andrew Ker of Cessfurd (q. v.), succeeded his father in July 1562. His father was second son of Andrew Ker of Ferniehirst (q. v.) Sureties were given in August of the same year for his appearance before the council in November (Reg. P. C. Scotl. i. 216), in consequence of the feud between the Kers and the Scotts of Buccleuch, but on 6 Dec. he was freed from all blame (ib. i. 227). In December 1564 he was warded in the castle of Edinburgh for the non-payment of certain teinds to the commendator of Jedburgh (ib. i. 304). He was one of the members of the privy council specially chosen in 1565 on account of the rebellion of Moray and his adherents at the time of the Darnley marriage, and in October attended the queen in the 'Roundabout Raid' to Dumfries. While in the southern districts the queen commanded him to raise the royal standard at the head of his followers, and placed herself under his immediate protection. On the escape of the queen from Lochleven in 1568 Ker joined her at Hamilton. Although he signed the bond of Teviotdale, 10 April 1569, in support of the authority of the regent on the borders (ib. i. 651), his maintenance of border thieves compelled the regent to make a special excursion into Liddesdale in the following September (CALDERWOOD, ii. 505). He made no concealment of the protection given by him to the Earl of Westmorland on his flight from England in November, and Douglas of Cavers told Sir Ralph Sadler that 'his master' [Sir Thomas Ker] 'cared not so much for the regent as the regent cared for him' (SADLER, State Papers, ii. 114). Cavers also affirmed that Ker was well able to raise three thousand men 'within his own rule.' Ker and Scott of Buccleuch were supposed to have had some knowledge of the conspiracy against the regent, and on the night of the murder made an excursion into the English borders, 'not so much for greediness of booty as to provoke the English' (CALDERWOOD, ii. 513; also HERRIES, Memoirs, p. 121). In February he met with the Hamiltons and

others at Glasgow, whence they sent a letter to Morton declaring their ignorance of the agent in the regent's murder, and professing their willingness to consult with the rest of the nobility for securing justice (CALDERWOOD, p. 520). Ker also about the same time wrote a letter to his father-in-law, Kirkcaldy of Grange, offering to quiet the borders if the queen of England 'would stay her army' (ib.) In April, Sussex and Lord Hunsdon entered Scotland, and, besides ravaging the lands of Ker, demolished his castle of Ferniehirst, which remained in ruins till 1598. In 1570 Ker conspired, along with Lord Herries and others, to surprise Edinburgh, but the project miscarried (HERRIES, Memoirs, p. 130). Subsequently he joined Kirkcaldy of Grange, in the castle of Edinburgh, with 'seventy spears or thereabout' (CALDERWOOD, iii 75). He also brought with him his charter chest, which at the surrender of the castle was destroyed by Morton. By the party of the queen Ker was chosen provost of the city of Edinburgh (HERRIES, Memoirs, p. 138). He was one of those forfeited at the parliament of the opposite party held at Stirling in August 1571 (CALDERWOOD, iii. 136). Ker took part in the raid of September, in which Lennox was slain. The borderers under him and Scott of Buccleuch began to pillage prematurely, and a sally put the raiders to flight (HERRIES, p. 148). In the following October Ker assembled a force to attack Jedburgh, and on account of complaints of the inhabitants a bond was on 12 Feb. 1571-2 subscribed for his pursuit (Reg. P. C. Scotl. ii. 117). Some time before the surrender of the castle of Edinburgh he sought refuge abroad, but through the influence of Esmé Stuart, earl of Lennox, he obtained license to return home at the close of 1579. Although believed to have been directly implicated in the murder of Darnley, Ker, at the execution of Morton on 2 June 1581 on the charge of having been 'art and part in the murder,' stood ' in a shott over against the scaffold, with his large ruffles, delighting in this spectacle' (CALDERWOOD, iii. 575). Shortly afterwards he was restored to his estates, and on 26 Nov. 1583 he received from parliament a formal and full pardon. He continued to be one of the chief supporters of Lennox, accompanying him after the Ruthven raid to Glasgow. On 30 Nov. Ker failed in an attempt to seize Edinburgh (ib. p. 691). At the general assembly of the kirk held in October of this year the session of Haddington were enjoined to call before them the Laird of Ferniehirst, his wife, and his daughter, on the charge of going to mass in France and other parts beyond sea, and also to require them to subscribe the confession of faith (*ib.* p. 682). In 1584 Ker was appointed warden of the middle marches and keeper of Liddesdale. During a meeting held by him on 27 July 1585 with Sir John Forster, the English warden, a fray arose between the Scots and English, in which Francis, lord Russell, was fatally wounded. The English suspected this to be a deliberate plot of Fernichirst, prompted by Arran, to break off the conference. The Scottish king talked for a time of sending them into England to be tried, but afterwards changed his mind. On 18 Aug. Fernichirst appeared before the council and made a declaration absolving Arran from all connection with the murder (*Reg. P. C. Scotl.* iv. 4). Shortly afterwards Ker was committed to ward in Aberdeen, where he died some time in 1586. He is described by Camden as 'a stout and able warrior, ready for any great attempt and undertaking, and of an immovable fidelity to the Queen of Scots and the king, her son; having been once or twice turned out of all his lands and fortunes, and banished the sight of his country and children, which yet he endured patiently, and, after so many crosses falling upon him together, persisted unshaken and always like himself.' He was twice married. By his first wife, Janet, daughter of Sir William Kirkaldy of Grange [q. v.], he had a son, Andrew, who succeeded him, and two daughters: Janet, married, first to Sir Patrick Hume of Polwarth, and secondly to Thomas earl of Haddington; and Margaret, married to Robert, second lord Melville of Monimail. By his second wife, Janet, sister of Sir Walter Scott of Buccleuch, he had three sons: Sir James Ker of Crailing; Thomas, who inherited from his father the lands of Oxenhame; and Robert [see CARR, ROBERT, EARL OF SOMERSET], the favourite of King James; and a daughter, Janet, married to John, lord Balgy.

[Sadler's State Papers; Reg. P. C. Scotl. vols. i.–iv.; Lord Herries's Memoirs (Bannatyne Club); Calderwood's Hist. of the Church of Scotland; Douglas's Scottish Peerage (Wood), ii. 133–4.]
T. F. H.

KER, SIR WALTER (*d.* 1584?), of Cessfurd, eldest son of Sir Andrew Ker of Cessfurd [q. v.], by his wife Agnes, daughter of Robert, second lord Crichton of Sanquhar, was served heir to his father 12 May 1528. He had charters of various lands on 23 April and 21 Sept. 1542, and in 1543 he received the lands and barony of Cessfurd, with the castle of the same and their annexes (*Reg. Mag. Sig.* 1513–46, entry 2785). In October 1552 Sir Walter Scott of Buccleuch was killed in the

High Street of Edinburgh in a nocturnal encounter with the Kers, headed by Sir Walter of Cessfurd. On 8 Dec. they petitioned the privy council regarding the 'unhappy chance,' offering to submit to anything to save their lives and heritages (*Reg. P. C. Scotl.* i. 133). It was decided that they should be banished to France, but on 16 May 1553 they received a full pardon (*ib.* p. 141). On 9 Aug. of this year Cessfurd, with John Ker of Fernichirst and Andrew Ker of Hirsell, signed a bond to be 'leill and trew men' to John Hamilton, archbishop of St. Andrews, and James, earl of Arran, &c. (Hamilton MSS., *Hist. MSS. Comm.* 11th Rep. App. pt. vi. p. 39). On 28 Aug. 1559 he was appointed one of the commissioners to treat for the ransoming of prisoners taken by the English in the late war (*Cal. State Papers*, For. Ser. 1558–9, entry 1266). Cessfurd as a catholic sympathised with the queen-regent, but in April 1560 he came with Lord Home to the camp of the lords of the congregation (*ib.* Scott. Ser. p. 140). On the return of the young Queen Mary to Scotland Cessfurd was reappointed to his old office of warden of the middle marches (*Reg. P. C. Scotl.* i. 169). When the chiefs of the border clans were ordered in 1567 to enter the castle of Edinburgh on the pretext that they might hinder the success of Bothwell's expedition into Liddesdale, Cessfurd, 'a weill-meaning man, suspecting nothing,' was the only one except Ker of Fernichirst who obeyed (CALDERWOOD, ii. 360). He was one of the chief leaders against the queen at Carberry Hill (*ib.* p. 363), and also at Langside, where he fought side by side with Lord Home (SIR JAMES MELVILLE, *Memoirs*, p. 201). On 3 April 1569 he signed the bond of Teviotdale, promising obedience to the regent (*Reg. P. C.* i. 653), and he served under Morton at the siege of Edinburgh. When Ker of Fernichirst and others of the queen's party advanced to plunder Jedburgh in 1571, the inhabitants sent to Cessfurd for assistance, and by his aid and that of Lord Ruthven they were completely routed (CALDERWOOD, iii. 155). Cessfurd was one of those who, under Atholl and Argyll, took up arms against Morton in 1578. In 1582 he signed the bond which resulted in the raid of Ruthven. He died in 1584 or 1585. By his wife Isabel, daughter of Andrew Ker of Fernichirst [q. v.], he had two sons: Andrew, who predeceased him, and William, warden of the middle marches; and two daughters: Agnes, married to John Edmonstoune of Edmonstoune, and Margaret, to Alexander, fourth earl of Home.

[Reg. Mag. Sig. Scot. vol. i.; Reg. P. C. Scotl. vols. i. and ii.; Cal. State Papers, For.

Ser., reign of Elizabeth; Calderwood's History of the Church of Scotland; MSS. of the Earl of Home (Hist. MSS. Comm. 12th Rep. App. viii.); Sir James Melville's Memoirs; Douglas's Scottish Peerage (Wood), ii. 445-6.]   T. F. H.

KERCKHOVEN, CATHERINE, LADY STANHOPE and COUNTESS OF CHESTERFIELD (d. 1667). [See KIRKHOVEN.]

KERNE, SIR EDWARD (d. 1561), diplomatist. [See CARNE.]

KEROUALLE, LOUISE RENÉE DE, DUCHESS OF PORTSMOUTH AND AUBIGNY (1649-1734), was the elder of the two daughters of Guillaume de Penancoët, sieur de Kéroualle, a Breton gentleman of very ancient lineage, whose wife was through her mother connected with the De Rieux. Evelyn, who made the acquaintance of her parents on their visit to England in 1675, gives a pleasant account of them (Diary, ii. 310). Her only brother, Sebastian, took part in the campaign in Candia under the Duke of Beaufort in 1669 (FORNERON). Before this date Louise de Kéroualle had become maid of honour to Henrietta, duchess of Orleans, the sister of Charles II. In 1670 she accompanied to England the Duchess of Orleans, who was negotiating the first treaty of Dover. There is no proof of the existence at the time of any design to establish her as the mistress of Charles II. But he was growing weary of Lady Castlemaine. The effect produced on him by his sister's attendant was at once obvious, and probably contributed to a prolongation of the negotiations. A coldness on the part of Charles towards Louis XIV resulted from the sudden death of the Duchess of Orleans after her return to France (June), and Louise de Kéroualle was thereupon sent back to England, Charles ordering a royal yacht to meet her at Calais. On arriving in London she was named maid of honour to Queen Catherine.

Mlle. de Kéroualle at first played her game so cautiously as to dispirit the French ambassador, Colbert de Croissy. In November Evelyn first saw the new 'famous beauty, but in my opinion of a childish, simple, and baby face' (Diary, ii. 253). Gradually, however, her charms and her coyness prevailed, and the ministers began to pay court to her. During a sojourn of the king at Newmarket she was, in October 1671, invited to Lady Arlington's country seat of Euston, where, with the co-operation of the French ambassador and others, she was established as mistress en titre (ib. ii. 296-297). Louis XIV sent her congratulations; and though, notwithstanding her entreaties, Charles delayed his profession of catholicism,

the declaration of war against the Dutch, in accordance with the treaty of Dover, was not long in coming (March 1672; cf. MME. DE SÉVIGNÉ, ed. Monmerqué, 1862, ii. 546).

On 29 July 1672 Louise bore the king a son, Charles Lennox, first duke of Richmond [q. v.] But for a time her position was uncertain (cf. ib. iv. 128-9). Although universally unpopular in England as a Frenchwoman and catholic, she nevertheless contrived to hold her own, and having been, at the request of Louis XIV, naturalised as an English subject, she was on 19 Aug. 1673 created Baroness Petersfield, Countess of Fareham, and Duchess of Portsmouth (DOYLE). The ducal title at first granted to her, but immediately altered, is said to have been that of Pendennis. In the same year she was sworn lady of the bedchamber to the queen (ib.)

In 1674 Charles induced Louis XIV to grant the duchess, who was obliged to seclude herself at the time, the fief of Aubigny in Berry, with remainder to such of her natural children by Charles as should be designated by him. The fief had reverted to the French crown in December 1672 by the death of Charles Stuart, duke of Richmond, on whose family it had been first bestowed by Charles VII of France in 1422 (COLLINS, i. 182; DOYLE, iii. 127; LINGARD, 6th edit. 1855, ix. 256-257). The title of Duchess of Aubigny, carrying with it the coveted right of a tabouret at the French court, was for the present withheld. The disgrace of Buckingham at the time was widely attributed to her influence (RERESBY, pp. 192-3). In December 1674 — an annuity of 10,000l. was settled upon her out of the wine licenses. In the same month the king endowed the Duchess of Portsmouth's youngest sister, Henrietta, on her marriage to Philip Herbert, seventh earl of Pembroke [see under HERBERT, PHILIP, fourth earl]. In August 1675 the duchess's son, Charles, was created Duke of Richmond.

During the administration of Danby the Duchess of Portsmouth consistently exerted herself to keep Charles in dependence on France, notwithstanding his outward pretences to the contrary; but she was anxious to keep on good terms with Danby (ib. p. 165), to whom it is said that she at one time granted a share of her favours. Her ascendency over the king, which seemed assured by the retirement from court of the Duchess of Cleveland, was imperilled by the arrival in England, about the end of 1675, of Hortensia Mancini, duchess of Mazarin. The rising influence of Monmouth was also used against her. Yet in the contest which ensued (see WALLER's poem, The Triple Combat, 1675; Rochester's Farewell, 1680), although she found little support either at court or in the public at large, the duchess was in the end altogether successful (see FORNERON, p. 143). At the close of 1677 she fell seriously ill, but maintained herself in power, with the help of Barillon, the new French ambassador.

On the outbreak of the 'Popish plot' troubles the duchess was thoroughly frightened, and inclined to fly to France. On 25 April 1679 she was reflected on by name in both houses of parliament, but no further step was taken against her (RERESBY, p. 168; cf. A. SIDNEY, *Letters to H. Saville* (1742), p. 46; but see FORNERON, p. 177 note). By way of precaution, she hereupon made advances to Shaftesbury, and sought to ingratiate herself with Monmouth, with the help of her confidential servant, the notorious Mrs. Wall (cf. H. SIDNEY, *Diary*, ii. 22, and i. 190-1, and note. FORNERON regards the supposed letters of the duchess to Monmouth in the British Museum as forgeries). At the same time she took special pains to secure the confidence and goodwill of the Prince of Orange (H. SIDNEY, *Diary*, i. 10, &c.), and contrived to remain on good terms with the Duke of York (*ib.* i. 176, 189). Although she was never more unpopular, her influence over the king remained unbroken despite his periodical infidelities. In December 1679 the removal of herself and Sunderland from court was once more demanded by parliament, and she deemed it prudent to dismiss her catholic servants (*ib.* p. 217). There seems no doubt that she was brought to favour the Exclusion Bill as unavoidable in itself and likely to advance the interest of the Duke of Richmond (BURNET, ii. 259 seqq.; cf. CLARKE, *Life of James II*, i. 645). Both she and Nell Gwyn were at Oxford during the parliament of 1681 (LUTTRELL, i. 71).

During the remainder of the reign she was not exposed to any serious rivalry (H. SIDNEY, ii. 226 seqq.) Her feeling of security is best shown by her visit to France from March to July 1682, which was at first represented by her enemies as her final withdrawal, and was attributed to the Duke of York's resentment. She had already, in November 1681, pressed for his return from Scotland, with a view to his settling on her a rent-charge of 5,000*l.* on the revenue of the post-office for fifty years, to be made up to him out of the excise, and, though the plan fell through, his recall followed (MACPHERSON, *Original Papers*, i. 129 seqq.; *Life of James II*, i. 722 seqq.) In France she not only benefited by the waters of Bourbon, where she spent part of May and June with Lady Pembroke, but also strengthened her position at Versailles. St.-Simon describes her warm reception at the French

court. She also paid a visit to her estate of Aubigny. On her return to England she found the king and the Duke of York on cordial terms, and contrived to bring about the reappointment of Sunderland as secretary of state (*ib.* i. 730). She sided with Rochester in his quarrel with Halifax (RERESBY, pp. 272, 276). Nothing could now shake her sway over the enervated king, not even his jealousy of her intrigue with Philip de Vendôme, whom Charles proved unable to drive out of the country, till Louis XIV, anxious for the maintenance of the duchess's ascendency, had brought about his return to France (FORNERON; see HANSARD, *Parliamentary Debates*, xxxiv. 627). Treated by both king and duke as a member of the royal family, she took part in negotiating the marriage of the Princess Anne with Prince George of Denmark. The erection of the estate of Aubigny into a duchy was granted her by Louis in letters patent of January 1684, and a year later the Duke of Richmond was naturalised in France, in order to be able to succeed to her estates and title there.

Her splendid apartment at the end of the gallery at Whitehall (EVELYN, ii. 314, 419-420; cf. H. SIDNEY, i. 208) was, according to Evelyn, 'twice or thrice pull'd down and rebuilt to satisfy her prodigal and expensive pleasures;' it was ultimately burnt down, with all the buildings adjoining, 9 April 1691 (EVELYN, iii. 93; cf. *Autobiography of Sir J. Bramston*, Camden Soc., 1845, p. 385). When the post-office job failed, she had been allowed 10,000*l.* a quarter out of the privy purse (MACPHERSON, *Original Papers*, i. 133); but the sums paid to her varied, and in 1681 amounted to the enormous total of 136,668*l.* None of the king's other mistresses appear to have approached her in rapacity (see J. Y. AKERMAN, *Secret Services of Charles II and James II*, 1679-88, Camden Soc., 1851, and the comments of FORNERON).

During Charles's fatal illness she was excluded from the royal chamber; but, according to Barillon (cf. C. J. Fox, *History of the Reign of James II*, edit. 1808, Appendix, p. xii), it was she who informed him of the king's membership of the church of Rome, and thus obtained for him the last consolations of his faith. She is said to have suspected James of having poisoned his brother (*ib.* p. 67 and note; cf. HALLAM, *Constitutional Hist.* 10th edit. ii. 468 note). Immediately, however, after the death of Charles II she was visited by James, and received assurances of protection from both him and Louis XIV. A sum exceeding 12,000*l.*, probably due to her on her pension, was at once paid. But, notwithstanding the courtesies of the king and the goodwill of Rochester, she grew uneasy, and was further disquieted by the dismissal of Richmond from the mastership of the horse. She desired that the pension of 3,000*l.* offered to her might be added to that of 2,000*l.* proposed for her son; but claimed in vain the fulfilment of a supposed promise by Charles II of a large Irish estate or interest. Fully aware of the general hatred against her, and apprehensive of a direct attack in parliament, she crossed to France, where she had large investments, in August 1685.

In France she met with a cold welcome. Although in a personal interview Louis XIV destroyed a formal sentence of banishment against her, she soon returned to England, and remained at Whitehall (*Ellis Correspondence*, i. 178) till the end of July 1688, when her sudden departure to France gave rise to 'great conjectures' (*ib.* ii. 78, 103). At New Year 1689 the Duke of Richmond gave explanations to Louis on behalf of himself and of his mother, who was charged with scandalous utterances about the birth of the Prince of Wales (DANGEAU, ii. 286); there had been an old grudge between her and Queen Mary of Modena. At the same time she made vain endeavours to recall to William III her former (supposed) services to his interest (cf. HENRY SIDNEY in his *Diary*, &c., ii. 307–8). Her pension was withdrawn: in April 1691 a fire consumed her apartments and the treasures accumulated in them: in the previous year her father had died, and early in 1692 Richmond left France to reconcile himself to the new *régime* in England. His allowance was generously continued to his mother by Louis XIV.

The remainder of her life, chiefly spent on her estate at Aubigny, which she managed with much care, was a struggle against pecuniary difficulties, a royal decree year after year staying execution. In 1697 she received permission from Louis to visit London, but William III forbade her landing. In 1704 the estates of Brittany reluctantly paid her a compensation for her father's manor, appropriated by the government for the harbour at Brest. Under the regency her pension was raised to twenty thousand livres, and converted into an annuity. St.-Simon in 1715 speaks of her as old, embarrassed in her affairs, and 'very converted and penitent' (*Mémoires*, edit. 1863, x. 48). In 1723 she lost her worthless son, the Duke of Richmond. She died on 14 Nov. 1734 at Paris, whither she had journeyed to consult her physicians. She was buried in the church of the Barefooted Carmelites, in the chapel belonging to the De Rieux family. Among those who saw her in her old age were Vol-

taire, who thought her still very beautiful, her great-granddaughter (the mother of Charles Fox), the first Lord Holland, and George Selwyn. The influence of the duchess was due in part to her courage, to what her biographer terms her *esprit froid*, and to her business capacity. But the chief source of her power lay of course in her personal beauty (EVELYN, *Diary*, ii. 253). In contrast to the Duchess of Cleveland, she was said at times of difficulty to rely chiefly on the influence of tears (H. SIDNEY, *Diary*, ed. Blencowe, ii. 114 *n.*) There is no reason to suppose that she had any literary tastes, though Nathaniel Lee dedicated two plays to her. Albeit recklessly extravagant, she does not appear to have carried the vice of gambling to the same extent as the Duchess of Mazarin. The people detested 'Madam Carwell,' or 'Carewell,' as she was familiarly called, more heartily than any other of the king's favourites.

The earliest portrait of the Duchess of Portsmouth is a miniature by Samuel Cooper [q. v.], who died in 1672. Other portraits of her remain by Lely, Kneller, H. Gascar, and Mignard (at the National Portrait Gallery). Engravings of her appear in several series of portraits of ladies of the court of France (FORNERON, p. 195, note, and *ib.* p. 237). Her motto, 'En la rose je fleuris,' is still borne by her descendants, the Dukes of Richmond and Gordon.

[H. Forneron's Louise de Kéroualle, Duchesse de Portsmouth (Paris, 1886), is an excellent biography, of which an English translation has been published by Mrs. Crawford (1888). Capefigue's La Duchesse de Portsmouth et la Cour Galante des Stuarts (Paris, 1861) is valueless and blundering. See also the brief accounts of Mademoiselle de Kéroualle, Duchesse de Portsmouth, et le Duc de Richemont, son fils, in Écrits Inédits de St.-Simon, ed. P. Faugère (Paris, 1880), iv. 485–7; and in Letters of William III and Louis XIV, &c., ed. P. Grimblot (1848), vol. i. App. i.; J. H. Jesse's England under the Stuarts, vol. iii.; Diary of the Times of Charles II by Henry Sidney, ed. Blencowe; Reresby's Memoirs, ed. Cartwright; Burnet's Hist. of his own Time; Lettres de Mme. de Sévigné. Of the scurrilous attacks upon the duchess in verse, specimens by Rochester and others are contained in Poems on State Affairs (1697); she was also attacked in the Essay on Satire, ascribed at the time to Dryden. Of the attacks in prose, the most notable is The Secret Hist. of the Duchess of Portsmouth, London, 1690, of which a French translation was published in the same year. It was followed by a second English edition, entitled The Life, Amours, and Secret Hist. of Francelia, D. of P—h, London, 1734, and Forneron states that a second French edition likewise appeared. It is a romance in the New Atalantis style, containing, however, more facts than fiction. All the earlier part is sheer invention; the remainder is diversified by such charges as that of complicity in the deaths of Sir Edmund Berry Godfrey and of Charles II himself. The proper names are slightly disguised. The Mémoires Secrets de la Duchesse de Portsmouth, publ. aver des Notes historiques, 2 vols., Paris, 1805, and ascribed to J. Lacombe, are a mere elaboration of the above, with a good deal of padding and some original additions (e.g. Monmouth here appears as the son of the Duchess of Portsmouth). A virulent pamphlet against her, under the title of Articles of High Treason, &c., against the Duchess of Portsmouth, is printed in Somers Tracts, viii. 137-40.]

A. W. W.

KERR or **KER, MARK** (d. 1584), abbot of Newbattle, was the second son of Sir Andrew Ker of Cessford [q. v.], by Agnes, daughter of Robert, second lord Crichton of Sanquhar. In 1546 he was promoted abbot of Newbattle, and on renouncing popery in 1560 continued to hold the benefice in commendam. He was one of those who, on 26 April of this year, signed at Edinburgh the contract to defend the 'evangell of Christ' (KNOX, ii.64). Subsequently he was presented to the vicarage of Linton, Peeblesshire, by the abbot and convent of Kelso, and his presentation was confirmed by the commissioners 4 Aug. 1567, in opposition to one made by the crown. At a parliament held at Edinburgh on 15 Dec. of this year he was appointed one of a commission to inquire into the jurisdiction that should pertain to the kirk. On 20 April 1569 he was nominated an extraordinary lord of session, and he was also chosen a member of the privy council. By one of the articles of the Pacification of Perth in February 1572-3 he was nominated one of the judges for the trial 'of all attempts committed against the abstinence be south the water of Tay' (Reg. P. C. Scotl. ii. 195). At the fall of Morton in 1578 he was one of the extraordinary council of twelve appointed to carry on the government in the king's name (MOYSIE, Memoirs, p. 6; CALDERWOOD, iii. 397). He was also one of the four delegates deputed on 28 Sept., after Morton had seized Stirling Castle, to meet Morton's delegates for the purpose of arranging the terms of a reconciliation. Receiving in 1581, after the second fall of Morton, a ratification of the commendatorship of Newbattle, he continued to be a steadfast supporter of Esmé Stuart, duke of Lennox. On 15 July 1581 he was appointed to hear and report on the case of Sir James Balfour, who was endeavouring to get reinstated in his rights of citizenship (Reg. P. C. Scotl. iii. 403). After the raid of Ruthven the commendator was, with Lord Herries, despatched by Lennox with offers of concilia-

tion to the now dominant party. The proposals were rejected. Kerr died in 1584. By his wife, Lady Helen Lesley, second daughter of George, fourth earl of Rothes, he had four sons: Mark, first earl of Lothian [q. v.]; Andrew of Fenton; George, the catholic emissary, in whose possession the 'Spanish blanks' were found, and William; and a daughter, Catherine, married to William, lord Herries. There are portraits of Kerr and his wife, ascribed to Sir Antonio More [q. v.], preserved at Newbattle.

[Histories of Knox and Calderwood; Moysie's Memoirs (Bannatyne Club); Hist. King James the Sext (Bannatyne Club); Register of the Privy Council of Scotland, vols. ii. and iii.; Douglas's Scottish Peerage (Wood), ii. 130.]

T. F. H.

KERR or **KER, MARK,** first EARL OF LOTHIAN (d. 1609), master of requests, was the eldest son of Mark Kerr, commendator of Newbattle [q. v.], by Lady Helen Lesley, second daughter of George, fourth earl of Rothes. He was appointed master of requests in 1577, and the office was confirmed to him by King James in 1581. On the death of his father the reversion of the commendatorship of Newbattle granted him by Queen Mary was ratified to him by letters under the great seal 24 Aug. 1584. He was also, on 12 Nov. of the same year, appointed to succeed his father as an extraordinary lord of session. On 28 July 1587 his lands of Newbattle were by charter erected into a barony, and on 1 Aug. of the same year he was chosen by parliament one of his majesty's 'ordiner and daylie privie council.' On 15 Oct. 1591 the baronies of Prestongrange and Newbattle being united into the lordship of Newbattle, he was created a lord of parliament. He was appointed, 4 March 1596-7, one of a commission to arrange for the issue of a new coinage (Reg. P. C. Scotl. v. 369). He was one of the commissioners for holding the parliament of 1607, and the same year was appointed collector-general of the tax of two hundred thousand merks levied in connection with certain foreign embassies (Acta Parl. Scot. iv. 142-3). A commission was appointed, 2 March 1598-9, to examine Newbattle's accounts (Reg. P. C. Scotl. v. 634), the result being entirely satisfactory.

Notwithstanding the attempt of the king to influence the court of session to an adverse decision against Robert Bruce, minister of Edinburgh, in regard to his life pension out of the rents of the abbey of Arbroath, Newbattle, with the other judges, declined to be influenced in their judgment, either by entreaties or threats. Newbattle was one of the special members of the privy council chosen on 8 Dec. 1598 to sit in the palace of Holyrood on Tuesdays and Thursdays to assist the king in the discharge of business (CALDERWOOD, v. 727). On 10 July 1600 he was appointed one of a commission to consider means for the more effectual concurrence of the lieges with the sheriffs and magistrates in the execution of their offices (*Reg. P. C. Scotl.* vi. 68), and, on 1 April of the same year, one of a commission for reporting on remedies for abuses in cloth-making (*ib.* p. 98). In order more effectually to carry out the act of 1567 for the pursuit of thieves he was, on 28 July 1600, ordered to repair to and reside within his castle of Neidpath (*ib.* p. 138). On 19 Sept. 1604 he was nominated to act as interim chancellor during the absence of the Earl of Montrose in England as a commissioner for the union (*ib.* vii. 15). He was one of the assessors chosen at Linlithgow in January 1605-6 for the trial of the ministers imprisoned in Blackness (CALDERWOOD, vi. 375). On 10 Feb. of the same year he was created Earl of Lothian by patent to him and heirs male of his body. On 11 July he resigned the office of master of requests in favour of his eldest son, Robert (*Reg. P. C. Scotl.* vii. 226). In 1608 Lothian acted as assessor to the Earl of Dunbar, the king's commissioner to the assembly of the kirk (CALDERWOOD, vi. 752). On 6 Feb. 1608-1609 he was appointed one of a commission to advise the king as to the best means of assuring the peace of the Isles and planting 'religion and civilitie therein' (*Reg. P. C. Scotl.* viii. 742).

He died on 8 April 1609. By his wife, Margaret Maxwell, daughter of John, lord Herries, he had four sons: Robert, second earl of Lothian, Sir William Ker of Blackhope, Sir Mark Ker, and Hon. Henry Ker, and seven daughters: Janet, married, first to Robert, master of Boyd, and secondly to David, tenth earl of Crawford; Janet, married to William, eighth earl of Glencairn; Margaret (founder of Lady Yester's Church, Edinburgh), married, first to James, seventh lord Yester, and secondly to Andrew, master of Jedburgh; Isabell, married to William, first earl of Queensberry; Lilias, married to John, lord Borthwick; Mary, married to Sir James Richardson of Smeaton; and Elizabeth, married to Sir Alexander Hamilton of Innerwick. Scot of Scotstarvet affirms that in all the Earl of Lothian had by his wife thirty-one children. The statement is probably, however, as baseless as is Scot's story that the countess was addicted to the black art, and that, 'being vexed with a cancer in her breast,' she was healed by 'a notable warlock,' on condition 'that the sore should fall

on them she loved best:' her husband died of a boil in his throat.

[Acta Parl. Scot. vols. iii. and iv.; Reg. P. C. Scotl. vols. iv-viii.; Calderwood's Hist. of Church of Scotland; Moysie's Memoirs (Bannatyne Club); Scot's Staggering State of Scottish Statesmen; Douglas's Scottish Peerage (Wood), ii. 130-1.]

T. F. H.

KERR, ROBERT, fourth EARL and first MARQUIS OF LOTHIAN (1636-1703), born in 1636, was the eldest son of William, third earl [q. v.], by his wife Anne, countess of Lothian in her own right. In 1673 he served as a volunteer in the Dutch war. He succeeded his father in 1675, and on 23 Oct. 1678 a patent of the earldom of Lothian was granted to him and heirs male of his body, with the original precedency. On 4 Jan. 1686 he was sworn a privy councillor (LAUDER of Fountainhall, *Hist. Notices*, p. 686), but on 14 Sept. a letter was read in the council from James II removing him and four other privy councillors (*ib.* p. 750). He was a supporter of the revolution, and on 25 June wrote to the Earl Melville suggesting 'some return suitable to the capacity I think I can best serve his majesty in' (*Leven and Melville Papers*, Bannatyne Club, p. 79). He was appointed a privy councillor to King William, and in August was also constituted justice-general. On the death of his brother Charles, second earl of Ancrum, in 1690, he united that earldom to his other titles.

In 1692 Lothian was appointed commissioner of the king to the general assembly of the kirk of Scotland. The occasion was notable, on account of the recommendation of the king that episcopal ministers who were prepared to accept the confession of faith and submit to the authority of the ecclesiastical courts should be received into the kirk. The royal recommendation was enforced by Lothian in a speech the liberality and kindliness of which tended rather to awaken than allay presbyterian prejudice. After a month spent in routine business the assembly still refrained from taking into consideration the subject pressed upon their attention, and it was dissolved by Lothian, who declined to fix any date for the next assembly. Thereupon the moderator, notwithstanding the protest of Lothian, appointed the third Wednesday of August 1693. No assembly was, however, held on that date (see narrative in BURTON's *Hist. of Scotl.* vii. 450-3, founded on the *Register of the Actings and Proceedings of the Assembly*, printed for private circulation).

Lothian was created marquis by patent on 23 June 1701. He died on 15 Feb. 1703. A portrait of him, attributed to Scougal, dated

1654, is at Newbattle. He married Lady Jean Campbell, second daughter of Archibald, marquis of Argyll. His eldest son, William, second marquis of Lothian, was a lieutenant-general in the army, was elected representative peer for Scotland in 1715, died 28 Feb. 1722, and was buried in Westminster Abbey (see MACKY, *Memoirs of Secret Services*). The first marquis had four other sons: Charles (*d.* 1735), who was made a director in chancery in 1703; John (*d.* 1728), who for some time had the command of the 31st regiment; LORD MARK KERR (*d.* 1752), who became captain in the army 8 June 1693, was wounded at Almanza on 25 April 1707, acted as brigadier-general at the capture of Vigo in 1719, was governor of Guernsey in 1740, obtained the rank of general in 1743, was made governor of Edinburgh Castle in 1745, and died in London 2 Feb. 1752; and James. Of the first marquis's five daughters, Mary married James, marquis of Douglas.

[Burton's Hist. of Scotland; Douglas's Scottish Peerage (Wood), ii. 139-40.] T. F. H.

KERR, ROBERT (1755-1813), scientific writer and translator, was born at his father's seat, Bughtridge, Roxburghshire, in 1755. His father, James Kerr, convener of the trades (1746) and M.P. for Edinburgh from 1747 to 1754, was great-grandson of Sir Thomas Ker of Redden, brother of Robert Ker, first earl of Ancrum [q. v.] His mother, Elizabeth Kerr, was grand-daughter of Robert Kerr [q. v.], first marquis of Lothian. He studied at Edinburgh High School and at the university with a view to the medical profession, and became surgeon to the Edinburgh Foundling Hospital, but relinquished a successful medical career for the management of a paper mill at Ayton, Berwickshire, which eventually proved a failure. He returned to Edinburgh about 1810, and occupied himself with historical and biographical work. His valuable translations from Lavoisier and Linnæus procured his election as fellow of the Royal Society of Edinburgh in 1805. He was also a member of the Scottish Society of Antiquaries. He died at Edinburgh 11 Oct. 1813.

The following is a list of his works: 1. 'Elements of Chemistry' (from the French of Lavoisier), Edinburgh, 1790; 2nd edit. 1793. 2. 'Essay on the New Method of Bleaching by means of Oxygenated Muriatic Acid' (from the French of Berthollet), Edinburgh, 1790. 3. 'The Animal Kingdom, or Zoological System of Linnæus.' A translation of part i. of the 'Systema Naturæ,' with additions, Edinburgh, 1792, 4to. 4. 'The Natural History of Oviparous Quadrupeds and Serpents' (from the French of Lacepède), London, 1802. 5. 'Statistical, Agricultural, and Political Survey of Berwickshire,' 1809, 8vo. 6. 'Memoirs of the Life, Writings, and Correspondence of the late Mr. William Smellie,' Edinburgh, 1811. 7. 'The History of Scotland during the reign of Robert I, surnamed the Bruce,' Edinburgh, 1811, 8vo. 8. 'Essay on the Theory of the Earth' (from the French of Cuvier), 1813, 8vo. Ker compiled vols. i-x. of 'A General History and Collection of Voyages and Travels,' London, 1811-24, 18 vols.

[Scots Mag. 1813, p. 880; Irving's Eminent Scotsmen, p. 254; Timperley's Anecdotes, pp. 788, 935; Donaldson's Agricultural Biography; Foster's Members of Parlt. Scotland; Watt's Bibl. Brit.; Brit. Mus. Cat.; Gent. Mag. May 1814 (pt. i. p. 524), where the date of death is wrong. T. S.

KERR or **KER**, WILLIAM, third EARL OF LOTHIAN (1605?-1675), eldest son of Robert, first earl of Ancrum [q. v.], by Elizabeth, daughter of Sir John Murray of Blackbarony, was born about 1605. He was at the university of Cambridge in 1621, but he did not graduate, and probably completed his education in Paris. On 6 Nov. 1626 he set out from Paris on a tour through France, Italy, and Switzerland. A journal of the tour is preserved at Newbattle Abbey. In 1627 he accompanied George, duke of Buckingham, in his expedition to the Isle of Rhé, and he witnessed next year the duke's murder by Felton. He also joined the expedition in aid of the States-general against the Spanish forces in 1629, and was present at the capitulation of Bois-le-Duc to the Prince of Orange on 14 Sept. He returned to Scotland in 1630, and about January 1631 married Anne, daughter of Robert, second earl of Lothian, and countess of Lothian in her own right. On 31 Oct. of the same year he was created third Earl of Lothian, and the next brother of Robert, second earl of Lothian, Sir William Ker of Blackhope, on laying claim to the title as nearest heir male, was prevented by the lords of the privy council from assuming it (8 March 1632). The earl was one of the supplicants against the service-book in 1638, and on 28 Feb. signed the national covenant in Old Grey Friars Church, Edinburgh. He also, on 3 Oct., attached his signature to a complaint against the means taken to force the people to sign the king's covenant (GORDON, *Scots Affairs*, i. 122). He was a member of the assembly of the kirk which met at Glasgow in October of this year, and he supported the action there taken against the service-book. He was also one of the most prompt to lend aid to the covenanters when, in the spring of the following year, they resolved to take up arms. On 22 March—the day succeeding the seizure of Edinburgh—he and other leading covenanters marched out from the city to Dalkeith House, and compelled the lord treasurer Traquair to deliver it up (BALFOUR, *Annals*, ii. 321). With a force of fifteen hundred men he also joined the army of Leslie which advanced into England in August 1640 (*ib.* p. 383; *Cal. State Papers*, Dom. Ser. 1640, p. 447; ROBERT BAILLIE, *Letters and Journals*, i. 257). He was present at the defeat of the royalists at Newbury, and on the arrival of the Scottish army at Newcastle he was appointed governor of the town, with a garrison of two thousand (BALFOUR, *Annals*, ii. 388; *Cal. State Papers*, Dom. Ser. 1640–1641, p. 27). Lothian was the supposed author of 'A True Representation of the Proceedings of the Kingdome of Scotland since the late Pacification, by the Estates of the Kingdome, against mistakings in the late Declaration,' 1640. On 7 June 1641 he left Newcastle to attend the meeting of the parliament in Edinburgh. On 16 July he was chosen a member of the committee for the ordering of the house (BALFOUR, iii. 9), and on the 20th one of the committee of the articles (*ib.* p. 21). On the conclusion of a treaty with the English on 25 Aug. the Scottish army was disbanded, and Lothian's governorship of Newcastle came to an end. He was one of the commissioners appointed on the king 'anent the preparing of matters left by the treaty' (*ib.* p. 53), and also served on other important committees.

In 1641 Lothian was named one of the four commissioners of the treasury. In October he was appointed to the command of one of the regiments sent to Ireland, and according to his own statement was lieutenant-general of the Scots army in Ireland, but without payment (*Cal. State Papers*, Dom. Ser. 1655–6, p. 296). His regiment remained there till February 1644, but he appears himself to have been in Ireland for only a short period. In November 1641 his name was inserted by the estates in the list of the privy council in place of one of the names which they had deleted from the king's list (BALFOUR, iii. 149). On 5 March 1642 he obtained a charter of the lordship of Jedburgh, and in December of the same year he was sent by the privy council of Scotland, with the approval of Charles I, on a mission to the court of France in relation to the position of the Scots guard in France. On his return he went to the king at Oxford to give an account of his embassy, but the king would not receive him, and, on account of rumours known

afterwards to be unfounded, that he had been engaged abroad in treacherous designs, he was, after being kept for some time under restraint at Oxford, sent a prisoner to Bristol Castle. As his health, weakened by a severe attack of fever in France, suffered from close confinement to one room, the king granted him ultimately the liberty of the town (BAILLIE, *Letters and Journals*, ii. 124); but he did not receive his freedom till the following March, and then only by exchange with Sir Charles Goring. Lothian was present at the parliament which met in June 1644, and on 17 July the house approved of his conduct and voted a sum of money to defray his expenses (BALFOUR, iii. 222). In the same year he joined Argyll in command of the unsuccessful expedition against Montrose. He declined to accept the commission when thrown up by Argyll (BAILLIE, *Letters and Journals*, ii. 262). He was one of the commissioners sent to treat with the king at Newcastle in 1647, and, with James McDouall of Garthland, was specially appointed by the Scottish parliament to attend on the king on his journey to Holmby House, where they continued with him for some weeks. The parliament of 1647, in payment of his expenses in the public service, apportioned him 1,500*l.* out of the 20,000*l.* agreed to be paid to the Scots army by the parliamentarians, but according to his own statement he never received the money (*Cal. State Papers*, Dom. Ser. 1655–6, p. 26). He protested against the 'engagement' of 1648, and after it had been condemned by parliament was appointed to the office of secretary of state, in succession to the Earl of Lanerick, who was deprived by the Act of Classes. He was one of the commissioners sent by the parliament of Scotland in 1649 to protest against proceeding to extremities against the king. According to Clarendon there was a secret understanding between Lothian and Argyll (*Hist. of Rebellion*, Oxford ed. iii. 384–5), but there is no tangible proof of any such understanding. The commissioners were, according to their orders, proceeding to Holland to communicate with Charles II, when they were arrested at Gravesend by a troop of Cromwell's horse (BALFOUR, iii. 388). They were treated with courtesy, and sent under a strong escort to Berwick, there to be detained until the estates of Scotland should own their action. This being done, they were permitted to proceed to Edinburgh. Lothian was a member of the second commission appointed by the estates to proceed on 9 March 1650 to treat with the king at Breda. On the arrival of Charles in Scotland in 1650 the kirk desired that Lothian (who apparently declined) should be made general of the Scottish

F

forces (WHITELOCKE, *Memorials*). On 9 Aug. he was sent by the committee of the army to the king at Dunfermline to induce him to sign a declaration in favour of the covenanters (BALFOUR, iv. 77). When, on 4 Oct. following, the king escaped from the thraldom of the covenanters at Perth and joined the northern loyalists, Lothian was appointed one of a commission to induce him to return (*ib.* p. 115). They succeeded, but had to make terms with the strictly loyalist party and pass an act of indemnity for them on 12 Oct. This procedure was severely blamed by the synod of Perth (*ib.* p. 119). Along with Argyll, Lothian took an active but unsuccessful part in inducing the extreme covenanters of the west of Scotland to come to terms with the northern loyalists. Subsequently he acted generally in concert with Argyll. On 14 Oct. he was appointed one of a committee to arrange for the king's coronation at Scone (*ib.* p. 123). According to his own account, he intended to have joined the Duke of Hamilton in his expedition into England in the following year, but could not get ready in time. He was about to sail to join the king when he heard of the battle at Worcester. He also states that when he ceased to be secretary on the triumph of Cromwell, he retired to his own house at Newbattle, and never passed any writs under the great seal, which he preserved until able to offer his services to the king (*Correspondence*, p. 434). The Laird of Brodie, however, relates that Argyll told him that Lothian had been tampering with the Protector (*Diary of the Laird of Brodie*, Spalding Club, p. 153). In any case, he endeavoured in 1655 to obtain not merely payment for his expenses in the cause of the covenant, but also compensation for having been deprived of the office of secretary of state in 1652 (*Cal. State Papers*, Dom. Ser. 1655-6, p. 20). At the Restoration he went to London and presented a vindication of his conduct in the past (*Correspondence*, pp. 431-8). The king promised him some reward, and according to Sir George Mackenzie he received a grant of 1,000*l.*; but he himself affirmed that he received more promises than revenue. Having refused in 1662 to take the abjuration oath, he was fined 6,000*l.* Scots, and his finances having been previously in a crippled condition he found it necessary to part with his paternal estate of Ancrum. He died at Newbattle in October 1675.

By his wife he had five sons: Robert, fourth earl of Lothian [q. v.], Sir William Ker, Charles, Harry, and John; and nine daughters: Anne, married to Alexander, master of Salton; Elizabeth, to John, lord Borthwick;

Jean, died young; Margaret, died young; Mary, married to James Brodie of Brodie; Margaret, to James Richardson of Smeaton; Vere, to Lord Neill Campbell of Ardmaddie; Henrietta, to Sir Francis Scott of Thirlestane; and Lilias, died unmarried. A portrait of the Earl of Lothian by Jamiesone is at Newbattle Abbey.

[Sir James Balfour's Annals of Scotland; Robert Baillie's Letters and Journals (Bannatyne Club); Gordon's Scots Affairs (Spalding Club); Clarendon's History of the Rebellion; Diary of the Lairds of Brodie (Spalding Club); Correspondence of Sir Robert Ker, earl of Ancrum, by his son William, third earl of Lothian, 1875; Douglas's Peerage (Wood), ii. 137-8.] T. F. H.

KERR, WILLIAM, second MARQUIS OF LOTHIAN (1662?–1722), eldest son of Robert, first marquis [q. v.], and grandson of William Kerr, third earl of Lothian [q. v.], was born about 1662. On the death of his kinsman Robert Kerr, third Lord Jedburgh, in 1692, he succeeded to that title, and sat in parliament as Lord Jedburgh. He was colonel of the 7th regiment of dragoons, 1 Oct. 1696, and a stout adherent of the revolution. On his father's death, 15 Feb. 1703, he became Marquis of Lothian, was created a knight of the Thistle in 1705, cordially supported the union, and was chosen a representative peer of Scotland in 1708. On account, however, of some informalities this election was cancelled, but he was re-elected in 1715. He obtained the command of the 3rd foot-guards, 25 April 1707, with the rank of lieutenant-general, 1708, and was deprived of his regiment on a change of administration in 1713, but afterwards became major-general on the North British staff. Macky, the court spy in the time of Queen Anne, describes him about the date of his succession to the marquisate in the following terms: 'He hath abundance of fire, and may prove himself a man of business when he applies himself that way; laughs at all revealed religion, yet sets up for a pillar of presbytery, and proves the surest card in their pack, being very zealous though not devout; he is brave in his person, loves his country and his bottle, a thorough libertine, very handsome, black, with a fine eye, forty-five years old' (*Memoirs*, pp. 197, 198). This character is generally borne out by references to him in letters of the period. He married his first cousin, Lady Jean Campbell, daughter of Archibald, ninth earl of Argyll, who was beheaded in 1685, and he did so purely from a chivalrous desire to befriend those whom he believed were suffering wrongfully (*ib.*). The marquis died at London on 28 Feb. 1722, aged 60, and was interred in King Henry VII's Chapel in Westminster Abbey. A full-length portrait of Lothian, attributed to Seougal, is at Newbattle. He was succeeded by his son William, and left four daughters: Anne, married to Alexander, seventh earl of Home; Jean, married to William, fifth lord Cranston; Elizabeth, married to George, twelfth lord Ross; and Mary, married to Alexander Hamilton of Ballincrief.

[Douglas's Peerage of Scotland (Wood), ii. 140.]   H. P.

KERR, WILLIAM HENRY, fourth MARQUIS OF LOTHIAN (d. 1775), the elder son of William, third marquis, and Margaret Nicholson of Kempney, was a captain in the first regiment of foot-guards in 1741. He acted as aide-de-camp to the Duke of Cumberland at Fontenoy, 30 April 1745, when he was severely wounded by a shot in the head. He also attended the duke at Culloden, having command there of the cavalry on the extreme left wing of the royal army, after which he was placed for a short time in charge of all the forces on the east of Scotland. In December 1746 he again accompanied the duke to the continent. On the death of his granduncle, Lord Mark Kerr, he was promoted to be colonel of his regiment, the 11th dragoons, and was, as lieutenant-general, with the duke in his expedition to the east coast of France in 1758. He was styled Lord Jedburgh until his marriage in 1735, when he assumed the title of Earl of Ancrum. He represented Richmond in parliament in 1747, and was re-elected by the same constituency in 1754 and 1761, but resigned in 1763. He succeeded as fourth Marquis of Lothian on his father's death on 28 July 1767. In 1768 he was chosen one of the sixteen representative peers of Scotland, and on the same day, 26 Oct., was invested as a knight of the Thistle at St. James's Palace. He was promoted to the rank of general in the army in 1770, and died at Bath on 12 April 1775. He married in 1735 Caroline d'Arcy, only daughter of Robert, third earl of Holderness. The marchioness died in October 1778. By her Lothian left a son and successor, William John, fifth marquis, and two daughters, Louisa, married to Lord George Henry Lennox, and Willielmina Emilia, married to John Macleod, colonel R.A.

[Douglas's Peerage of Scotland (Wood), ii. 141.]   H. P.

KERRICH, THOMAS (1748–1828), librarian of the university of Cambridge, born 4 Feb. 1748, was son of Samuel Kerrich, D.D., vicar of Dersingham and rector of Wolferton and West Newton, Norfolk, by his second wife, Barbara, elder daughter of Matthew Postlethwayt, archdeacon of Norwich. He was educated at Magdalene College, Cambridge, graduated B.A. in 1771 as second senior optime, and was elected one of Worts's travelling bachelors. Kerrich was accompanied in his travels by a pupil, John Pettiward, fellow-commoner of Trinity, and journeyed through France, the Low Countries, and Italy, residing at Paris for six months and at Rome for two years. At Antwerp the Academy of Painting awarded to him a silver medal for the best drawing. During his tenure of the travelling fellowship he devoted most of his time to artistic pursuits and antiquarian research, and made a fine collection of drawings from old monuments.

Returning to Cambridge he proceeded M.A. in 1775, and about the same time was elected a fellow of his college. In 1784 he was presented to the vicarage of Dersingham, which had previously been held by his father; and to the vicarage of Hemisby, Norfolk, in 1786. In 1793 he served the university office of taxor. On 21 Sept. 1797 he was elected principal librarian of the university on the death of Dr. Richard Farmer [q. v.] (COOPER, Annals of Cambridge, iv. 460). In the same year he was elected a fellow of the Society of Antiquaries of London. He was collated to a prebend in the church of Lincoln in 1798, and to one in the church of Wells in 1812 (LE NEVE, Fasti, ed. Hardy, i. 197, 200, ii. 215). He died at his residence in Free School Lane, Cambridge, on 10 May 1828.

He married Sophia, fourth daughter of Richard Hayles, M.D., of Cambridge. By that lady, who died on 23 July 1835, he had one son and two daughters, one of whom, Frances Margaretta, became the wife of the Rev. Charles Henry Hartshorne [q. v.], and died 3 Jan. 1892. The son, Richard Edward Kerrich, M.A., of Christ's College, Cambridge, died in 1872.

To great antiquarian and architectural knowledge Kerrich united the most accurate skill as a painter and a draughtsman. He was also a miniature-painter and a practised etcher, contributing some highly finished drawings to Gough's 'Sepulchral Monuments.' He was one of the earliest lithographers, and executed the portraits of Henry VI and Richard III for Fenn's 'Paston Letters.' His very curious collection of early royal portraits he bequeathed to the Society of Antiquaries. A list of them is printed in Nichols's 'Illustrations of Literature,' vi. 818, and a catalogue raisonné by Mr. G. Scharf in the 'Fine Arts Quarterly Review' for 1865. To the British Museum he bequeathed his extensive manuscript collections and sketches in illustration of ancient costumes, consisting chiefly of drawings from monuments, sepulchral brasses, stained windows, seals, and armour. These are contained in forty-eight volumes of various sizes, Addit. MSS. 6728-73. The volumes 6760-73, which form part of the legacy, contain the collections of James Essex [q. v.], architect, of Cambridge. The vol. 6735 contains drawings and plans by Kerrich of various ecclesiastical buildings, and of English castles and camps illustrative of military architecture. Kerrich's son presented his father's large collection of coins to the Society of Antiquaries, and bequeathed to the Fitzwilliam Museum at Cambridge seven pictures, two hundred volumes of books, and many valuable portfolios of early prints.

To the 'Archæologia' Kerrich contributed: 1. 'Some Observations on the Gothic Buildings abroad, particularly those in Italy, and on Gothic Architecture in General,' 1809, xvi. 292-325, illustrated by eighteen plates of sketches and sections of cathedrals. 2. 'Account of some Lids of Stone Coffins discovered in Cambridge Castle in 1810,' with two plates, 1813, xvii. 228. 3. 'Observations upon some Sepulchral Monuments in Italy and France,' 1814, xviii. 186-96, accompanied by eight plates either etched by Kerrich or copied from his etchings. 4. 'Observations on the use of the mysterious figure called Vesica Piscis in the Architecture of the Middle Ages, and in Gothic Architecture,' 1820, xix. 353-368, accompanied by fifteen plates containing no fewer than sixty-five drafts of the ground plans and arches of ancient ecclesiastical edifices, both abroad and at home.

A posthumous work of his is entitled 'A Catalogue of the Prints which have been engraved after Martin Heemskerck; or rather, an Essay towards such a Catalogue,' Cambridge, 1829, 8vo.

The portraits of Robert Glynn (afterwards Clobery), M.D. [q. v.], Thomas Wale of Shelford, Dr. Waring, Joseph Browne [q. v.], Isaac Milner [q. v.], William Pearce [q. v.], James Bentham, Robert Masters, Dr. Hill, and William Cole [q. v.] were engraved by the brothers Facius, from drawings by Kerrich. A portrait of Kerrich, painted by H. P. Briggs, R.A. [q. v.], and formerly in the possession of Mrs. F. M. Hartshorne, was engraved by Facius in folio, and is copied in Nichols's 'Literary Illustrations.' There is a replica of Briggs's portrait in Magdalene College, Cambridge.

[Private information; Addit. MSS. 5824 f. 128 b, 5835 pp. 108, 109, 5874 f. 69 b; Cooper's Annals of Cambridge, iv. 557; Gent. Mag. xcviii. pt. ii. p. 185, new series, iv. 332; Graduati Cantabr.; Gunning's Reminiscences, ii. 76-8;

Nichols's Lit. Illustr.; Nichols's Lit. Anecd.; Wilson's Miscellanies (Raines), p. 161.] T. C.

KERRISON, Sir EDWARD (1774-1853), general, only son of Matthias Kerrison, by Mary, daughter of Edward Barnes of Barnham, Suffolk, was born at his father's seat, Hoxne Hall, near Bungay, in 1774. He entered the army as cornet in the 6th dragoons on 23 June 1796. He attained the rank of captain in October 1798, and was transferred to the 7th hussars in the same year. With the last-mentioned regiment he served in the Helder expedition of 1799, taking part in the actions of 19 Sept. and 2 and 6 Oct. In October 1808, being then lieutenant-colonel, he embarked with his regiment for Spain, and in the following December was severely wounded on the plains of Leon. He commanded his regiment at the passage of the Oleron, in the action of Sauveterne, and at the battles of Orthes and Toulouse. At the battle of Orthes the charge headed by Lord Edward Somerset, in which Kerrison with the 7th hussars took the chief part, was highly commended by the Duke of Wellington (Despatches, vii. 440).

Kerrison next served in the campaign of 1815, and was slightly wounded at Waterloo, where his horse was shot under him; but he continued with his regiment, and took part in the occupation of Paris. On his return to England he was nominated a commander of the Bath, and knighted 5 Jan. 1816. He was subsequently created a baronet by patent dated 27 July 1821. He represented the borough of Shaftesbury from 1812 to 1818, that of Northampton from 1818 to 1824, and Eye from 1824 to 1852, in the conservative interest. Promoted to the rank of lieutenant-general in 1837, he became general in 1851, and died at his house in Great Stanhope Street, London, on 9 March 1853.

Kerrison married, on 20 Oct. 1813, Mary Martha, daughter of Alexander Ellice of Pittencrieff, Fifeshire. By her he had issue one son, Edward Clarence Kerrison (b. 1821), present baronet, and three daughters, the second of whom, Emily Harriet (d. 1873), married in 1831 Philip Henry, viscount Mahon, the historian, afterwards fifth earl Stanhope [q. v.]

[Ann. Reg. 1853, p. 219; Gent. Mag. 1853, i. 542; United Service Gaz. 1853; Foster's Peerage and Baronetage; Cannon's Hist. Records of British Army (7th Hussars), pp. 75, 78.] T. S.

KERRY, Knights of. [See Fitzgerald, Maurice, 1774-1849; Fitzgerald, Sir Peter George, 1808-1880.]

KERRY, Lords. [See Fitzmaurice, Thomas, 1502-1590, sixteenth Lord; Fitz-

MAURICE, PATRICK, 1551?–1600, seventeenth LORD; FITZMAURICE, THOMAS, 1574–1630, eighteenth LORD.]

KERSEBOOM, FREDERICK (1632–1680), painter, born in 1632 at Solingen in Germany, studied painting in Amsterdam, and in 1650 settled in Paris, where he worked under Charles Le Brun. He subsequently went to Rome, and remained there for fourteen years, two of which he spent under Nicolas Poussin, apparently engaged in landscape-painting. On leaving Rome he came to England, where he devoted himself to portrait-painting. His best-known portrait is that of Robert Boyle [q. v.], of which there are versions at the National Portrait Gallery, the Royal Society, and Hampton Court; it was painted in 1689. Pepys, in a letter to John Evelyn, dated 30 Aug. 1689, writes that Boyle had ' newly beene prevayled with by Dr. King to have his head taken by one of much lesse name than Kneller & a strang', one Causabon.' It is this letter perhaps that has led to the notion that Kerseboom was related to the great scholar, Casaubon. He painted a portrait of Sophia Dorothea, wife of George I, from which there is a scarce mezzotint engraving by William Faithorne, jun. A few other portraits by Kerseboom were engraved. Kerseboom died in London in 1690, and was buried in St. Andrew's Church, Holborn.

[Walpole's Anecdotes of Painting, ed. Wornum; Redgrave's Dict. of Artists; Abecedario de P. J. Mariette; Chaloner Smith's British Mezzotinto Portraits; Pepys's Diary and Correspondence.]
L. C.

KERSEY, JOHN, the elder (1616–1690?), mathematician, son of Anthony Carsaye or Kersey and Alice Fenimore, was baptised at Bodicote, near Banbury, Oxfordshire, on 23 Nov. 1616 (cf. HEARNE, Coll., ed. Doble, Oxf. Hist. Soc., ii. 11). Kersey early came to London, where he seems to have had relatives (cf. ROBINSON, Reg. Merchant Taylors' School, i. 104; CHESTER, London Marriage Licenses, p. 790), and gained a livelihood as a teacher. At first (1650) he lived at the corner house (opposite to the White Lion) in Charles Street, near the piazza in Covent Garden, but afterwards moved to Chandos Street, St. Martin's Lane. He was acquainted with John Collins [q. v., the 'attorney-general for the mathematics,' who persuaded him to write his work on algebra. He was a friend of Edmund Wingate 'q. v., and edited the second edition of his ' Arithmetic' in 1650, and subsequent issues till 1683. Kersey obtained a wide reputation as a teacher of mathematics. At one time he was tutor to the sons of

Sir Alexander Denton of Hillesden House, Buckinghamshire, 'whose family,' he writes, 'gave both birth and nourishment to his mathematical studies' (Elements, Ded.; cf. HEARNE, Coll. ii. 11). To his pupils Alexander and Edmund Denton he dedicated his first and principal original work, 'The Elements of Mathematical Art, commonly called Algebra,' in two folio volumes, dated respectively 1673 and 1674. A portrait of the author, by Faithorne, was prefixed to the first volume. Both Wallis and Collins wrote in 1672 in the highest terms of their anticipations of this work (cf. Corresp. of Scientific Men, ii. 554; and NICHOLS, Lit. Illustrations, iv. 46), and on its publication it became a standard authority. It was honourably mentioned in the 'Philosophical Transactions' (viii. 6073–4), and was commended by Hutton. Kersey's method of algebra was employed in Cocker's 'Arithmetic' of 1703. Kersey is said (BEESLEY, Hist. of Banbury, p. 485) to have died about 1677, but the date must be later, as the eighth edition of Wingate was edited by him in 1683. In the tenth, published in 1699, he is spoken of as 'late teacher of the Mathematicks.'

JOHN KERSEY the younger (fl. 1720), lexicographer, son of John Kersey the elder, with whom he has been much confused, revised the work of his father in the fourteenth edition of Wingate (1720), and he, more probably than his father, contributed the 'Discourse to an unlearned Prince' to the 'Translation of Plutarch's Morals,' which appeared 1684–5 (republished 1870). He was mainly occupied with lexicography. The sixth edition of Phillips's 'New World of Words,' which was published in 1706, was edited by him (Pref. to Dict. Anglo-Britannicum, 1708). He greatly added to the number of words (cf. H. B. WHEATLEY, 'Chronological Notice of the Dictionaries of the English Language,' in Proc. Phil. Soc. 1865), and published a seventh edition in 1720. Another dictionary, the 'New English Dictionary,' of which the first edition is said to have appeared in 1702 (2nd 1713, 3rd 1731, &c.), was also assigned on the title-page to J. K., but Kersey's responsibility for the work has been questioned. In 1708 was printed his 'Dictionarium Anglo-Britannicum, comprehending a brief explication of all sorts of difficult words;' a new edition in 1715 contained ' words and phrases made use of in our ancient statutes, old records, charters;' the third edition appeared in 1721. The date of his death is uncertain. From Kersey's 'Dictionarium' Chatterton borrowed part of his archaic vocabulary (cf. PROFESSOR SKEAT's essay in Chatterton's Poems, Aldine ed., ii. xxx sq.)

[Granger's Biog. History, iv. 81; information kindly supplied by the Rev. A. Short; authorities quoted; De Morgan's Arithmetical Books, pp. 48, 58, 73; Biog. Brit. (Suppl.), p. 33; Notes and Queries, 4th ser. vii. 323.]

KERSHAW, JAMES (1730?–1797), methodist preacher, a native of Halifax, was born about 1730. He joined a Socinian club in Halifax, whose members deputed him and another, in 1761, to attend a sermon to be delivered by Henry Venn (q. v.) at Huddersfield, in order 'to furnish matter of merriment for the next meeting.' But Kershaw left the church after the sermon exclaiming, 'Surely God is in this place: there is no matter for laughter here.' He subsequently called on the preacher, was converted, and became one of Venn's constant correspondents (*Life and Letters of Henry Venn*, 1836, passim).

Kershaw soon afterwards became known as an itinerant methodist preacher, and accompanied John Wesley on more than one occasion in his rapid journeys about the north of England. He settled down at Gainsborough about 1770, and was famous in the neighbourhood for his quack medicines. He still continued to preach, but only at irregular intervals, and occupied his leisure in writing. He died at Ashby-de-la-Zouch in 1797.

Besides some tracts Kershaw wrote: 1. 'An Essay on the Principal Parts of the Book of the Revelations, in a series of Dialogues between Didaskalos and Phylotheos,' Stockton, 1780, 2 vols. 12mo. 2. 'The Methodist attempted in Plain Metre,' a sort of Wesleyan epic, published at Nottingham in 1780, but not approved by Wesley, who feared it might deter the elect from perusing more edifying works, and determined henceforth to exercise a censorship over methodist publications. 3. 'The Grand and Extensive Plan of Human Redemption, from the Ruins of the Fall . . . in twelve familiar Dialogues,' Louth, 1797. A note appended to this volume states that Kershaw died 'shortly after this work was put to press.'

ARTHUR KERSHAW (*fl.* 1800), apparently James Kershaw's son, was educated at Wesley's school near Kingswood. He contributed to the 'Monthly Magazine,' and was employed by London booksellers in the enlargement of Walker's 'Gazetteer' and similar work at the beginning of the present century.

[Atmore's Methodist Memorial, p. 128; Tyerman's Wesley, ii. 531, iii. 362; Creswell's Hist. of Printing in Nottingham, p. 37; Biog. Dict. of Living Authors, p. 188; Kershaw's works in Brit. Mus. Library.]
T. S.

KERSLAKE, THOMAS (1812–1891), bookseller, born in Exeter in July 1812, proceeded in 1828 to Bristol, and soon afterwards commenced business as a second-hand bookseller in Barton Alley, together with his brother-in-law, Samuel Cornish. In 1839 the partnership was dissolved, and Kerslake removed to a shop at the bottom of Park Street. A disastrous fire occurred here in 1860. Kerslake continued on the same site, however, until 1870, when he removed to Queen's Road, and shortly afterwards retired. For over twenty years after his retirement he devoted himself to antiquarian controversy. Kerslake died at his private residence, Wynfred, Clevedon, on 5 Jan. 1891. His wife, Catherine Morgan, a native of Bath, predeceased him in 1887. He had no issue.

Previous to the fire, in which many works of great value and scarcity were destroyed, Kerslake had amassed a collection especially valuable in its antiquarian and archæological departments. He was also distinguished as an antiquary. Though self-taught, he had a good command of Latin and of modern languages, and his series of articles and pamphlets on antiquarian subjects is remarkable alike for shrewdness and originality. Kerslake's individuality is well exemplified in his sturdy defence of the historic phrase 'Anglo-Saxon' (see infra). 'His pamphlets were usually published at his own expense' (cf. *Proc. Somerset Archæolog. Assoc.* 1892).

The following are Kerslake's chief works: 1. 'A Vindication of the Autographs of Sir Roger de Coverley's "Perverse Widow" and her "Malicious Confident" from a disparaging statement thrown out in the "Athenæum,"' Bristol [1855], 8vo. 2. 'Saint Ewen, Bristol, and the Welsh Border, circiter A.D. 577–926,' Bristol, 1875, 8vo. 3. 'A Primeval British Metropolis, with some Notes on the Ancient Topography of the South-Western Peninsula of Britain,' Bristol, 1877, 8vo. Revised and re-edited, with additions, under the title of 'Caer Pensauelcoit, a long-lost Unromanized British Metropolis,' London, 1882, 8vo. 4. 'Traces of the Ancient Kingdom of Damnonia, outside Cornwall, in remains of Celtic Hagiology,' London, 1878, 8vo. 5. 'Vestiges of the Supremacy of Mercia in the South of England during the Eighth Century,' Bristol, 1879, 8vo. 6. 'The Word "Metropolis."' 'The Ancient Word "Anglo-Saxon."' 'Anglo-Saxon Bristol and Fossil Taunton.' Three essays, Bristol, 1880, 8vo. 7. 'The Celtic Substratum of England,' London, 1883, 8vo. 8. 'The Liberty of Independent Historical Research,' London, 1885, 8vo. This is a somewhat caustic attack upon the office of her majesty's inspector of ancient monuments, and on a preliminary report entitled 'Excavations in the Pen Pits, Penselwood, Somerset,' issued by the first holder of the office,

General A. Pitts-Rivers. 9. 'Gyfla, the Scir or Pagus of the Ivel Valley,' Somerset, 1887, 8vo. 10. 'Saint Richard the king of Englishmen and his territory, A.D. 700-720' (privately printed), 1890.

[Information kindly supplied by Mr. William George. Bristol; Athenæum, 10 Jan. 1891; Kerslake's Works (for a full list of which see Index Catalogue of the Somerset Archæological Society Library, Taunton, 1889, p. 99).] T. S.

KETCH, JOHN, commonly known as 'JACK KETCH' (d. 1686), executioner, is supposed to have been the immediate successor in the office of hangman to Edward Dun, who had in his turn succeeded Richard Brandon [q. v.], the executioner of Charles I. The last known reference to 'Squire Dun's' official activity is in a curious pamphlet dated 1663, and entitled 'Qui chetat chetabitur, or Tyburn cheated.' It is believed that Ketch took office in the following year, but no printed notice of the new hangman occurs until 2 Dec. 1678, when a broadside appeared called 'The Plotters Ballad, being Jack Ketch's incomparable Receipt for the Cure of Traytorous Recusants, or Wholesome Physick for a Popish Contagion.' On the top of the sheet is a woodcut, in which is represented Edward Coleman [q. v.] drawn in a sledge to the place of execution, exclaiming, 'I am sick of a traytorous disease,' while Jack Ketch, with a hatchet in one hand and a rope in the other, is saying, 'Here's your cure, sir.' In 1679 it appears from another pamphlet purporting to be written by Ketch himself, and entitled 'The Man of Destiny's Hard Fortune,' that the hangman was confined for a time in the Marshalsea prison, 'whereby his hopeful harvest was like to have been blasted.' A short entry in the autobiography of Anthony à Wood for 31 Aug. 1681 states how Stephen College was hung in the Castle Yard, Oxford, and 'when he had hanged about half an hour, was cut down by Catch or Ketch, and quartered under the gallows' (cf. Hist. MSS. Comm. 12th Rep. App. vii. 183). In a pamphlet probably written by Ketch himself, and entitled 'The Apologie of John Ketch, Esquire' (the title of 'esquire' being still claimed by the hangmen in confirmation of the arms granted to Richard Brandon), in 'vindication of himself as to the execution of the late Lord Russell, 21 July 1683,' Ketch repudiated the charge that he had been given 'twenty guennies the night before that after the first blow my lord should say, "You dog, did I give you ten guennies to use me so inhumanly?"' He attributed the bungling of the execution (described by Evelyn as done in a 'butcherly fashion') to the fact that Lord Russell 'did not dispose himself for receiving the fatal stroke in such a position as was most suitable,' and that he moved his body, while he himself 'receav'd some interruption just as he was taking Aim.' Ketch successfully struck for higher wages in 1682—action to which allusion is made in D'Urfey's popular 'Butler's Ghost' (1682). In the 'Supplement to the last Will and Testament of Anthony, Earl of Shaftesbury' (1683, fol. p. 3), Ketch is referred to under the name of Catch as a person of established reputation, and in the epilogue to Dryden's 'Duke of Guise' he is termed an 'excellent physician.' From the fact that the manor of Tyburn, 'where felons are now and for time out of mind have been executed,' was leased for a considerable time during the seventeenth century to the family of Jacquet, Arthur Collins, in his 'Memorials of the Sidneys,' assumes that the 'name of the executioner has corruptly been called Jack Ketch.' But this, which was written in 1746, can hardly be regarded as more than an ingenious theory (COLLINS, i. 85).

At Monmouth's execution, 15 July 1685, Ketch played a prominent part. Monmouth, in his address to him on the scaffold, alluded to his treatment of Russell, and this appears to have totally unnerved him. After three ineffectual blows he threw down the axe with the words, 'I can't do it,' and was only induced to complete his task by the threats of the sheriffs. Sir John Bramston (Autobiog. p. 192) and others confirm the fact that Ketch dealt at least five strokes, and even then, according to Macaulay, he had recourse to a knife to completely sever the head from the trunk (MACAULAY, Hist.; Somers Tracts, x. 264-5). In January 1686 Ketch, for affronting the sheriff, was turned out of his place and committed to Bridewell, one Pascha Rose, a butcher, taking his place. But on 28 May following Rose himself was hanged at Tyburn and Ketch was reinstated.

His behaviour at the executions of Russell and Monmouth, combined with the prominent position he occupied in carrying out the barbarous sentences passed on Titus Oates and his fellows (cf. THOMSON, Loyal Poems, 1685, p. 291), greatly increased Ketch's notoriety. This was perpetuated by the natural application of his name to the executioner, who regularly figured in the puppet-show drama of 'Punchinello,' introduced into England just about this time from Italy, and popularised by Robert Powell [q. v.] and others during the reign of Anne. A letter 'From Charon to the Most Illustrious and High Born Jack Ketch, Esqre.,' in Tom Brown's 'Letters from the Dead to the Living' (1702,

p. 48), shows that the office of executioner was very soon specially identified with his name. That Ketch deserved his reputation for excessive and inhuman barbarity is rendered very probable by a letter from Dr. Hutton to Thomas Comber, D.D. [q. v.], dean of Durham, dated 4 Dec. 1686, in which it is said 'Mr. [Samuel] Johnson [1649-1703, q. v.] was whipped on Wednesday, but civilly used by the new hangman, Jack Ketch being buried two days before.' It appears, therefore, that Ketch died towards the close of November 1686.

A fictitious 'Autobiography' of Ketch, with illustrations from designs by Meadows, was published in 1836, and a 'Life of Jack Ketch with Cuts of his own Execution' was among the humorous titles furnished by Tom Hood for the Duke of Devonshire's library at Chatsworth.

[Luttrell's Diary, i. 271, 353; Notes and Queries, 1st ser. xii. 293, 2nd ser. xi. 151, 256, 314, 447, 5th ser. xi. 349, 510; Butler's Hudibras, ed. Zach. Grey, ii. 341; Evelyn's Diary, ii. 182; Burnet's Own Time, i. 646; Macaulay's History, chap. v. p. 306 (popular ed.); Wheatley and Cunningham's London, iii. 418; Hone's Table Book, p. 695; Brit. Mus. Cat.; authorities quoted in text. Pegge, in Curialia Miscellanea, argues that Ketch's real name was Catch; and Gent in his Canting Dict. calls him Kitch.]

T. S.

KETEL, CORNELIS (1548-1616), portrait-painter, born at Gouda in Holland on 1st March 1548, was the illegitimate son of Govert Jansz van Proyen, and of Elizabeth, daughter of Jacob Ketel. His father's daughter was married to Wouter Pietersz Crabeth, the famous glass-painter at Gouda. Ketel showed an early aptitude for painting, and was instructed in the art, especially in glass-painting, by his uncle, Cornelis Jacobsz Ketel, at Gouda. There his work attracted the notice of the glass-painter Dirk Crabeth, brother of Wouter Pietersz Crabeth. In 1565 Ketel went to Delft to study under Anthonie Blocklandt, and thence in 1566 to France, where he was associated with other young artists from the Netherlands on work at Fontainebleau. He resided for some time at Paris with the court glass-painter, Jean de la Hamée. In 1568 he returned to Gouda, to avoid the religious wars in France, and practised there for six years. In 1573 he came to England, and worked in London for eight years. He lodged with a statuary, who was a friend of his uncle, and received commissions from the Hanse merchants at the Steelyard. It is stated that a merchant friend presented to Sir Christopher Hatton [q. v.] an allegorical painting by him of 'Force Van-

quished by Wisdom,' and that he thus obtained an introduction to court circles. He undoubtedly soon obtained a high reputation among the English nobility as a portrait-painter. He painted Hatton at full length more than once; examples of the portrait are in the collections both of the Earl of Winchilsea (Tudor Exhibition, 1890, No. 345) and of Viscount Dillon at Ditchley Park, Oxfordshire. He also painted, among others, Henry Fitzalan, earl of Arundel (one is in the collection of the Duke of Norfolk at Arundel Castle (Tudor Exhibition, 1890, No. 211), and another in that of the Marquis of Bath at Longleat, Wiltshire); Edward Clinton, first earl of Lincoln (in the collection of the Duke of Bedford at Woburn Abbey); James Hamilton, second earl of Arran (in the collection of the Duke of Hamilton at Hamilton Palace); Edward Vere, earl of Oxford; Sir James Gresham (1579) (in the collection of G. W. Leveson-Gower at Titsey); and Sir George Penruddocke (Tudor Exhibition, 1890, No. 222). In 1577 Ketel was employed to paint for Queen Elizabeth and the Cathay Company portraits of Sir Martin Frobisher [q. v.] and the Esquimaux brought back by him to England from Greenland; as well as of Frobisher's ship, the Gabriel. The portrait of Frobisher is now in the Bodleian Library at Oxford (Tudor Exhibition, 1890, No. 327). In 1578 the Duchess of Somerset received Elizabeth in state at Hanworth, Middlesex, and her son, the Earl of Hertford, employed Ketel to paint a portrait of the queen to celebrate the occasion. Ketel returned to Holland in 1581, having married in England Aeltgen (Adelaide) Gerrits, by whom he had a son, Raphael, baptised at Amsterdam on 16 Nov. 1581.

Ketel now settled at Amsterdam, where he quickly became the leading portrait-painter. He was especially patronised by the guilds of marksmen, for whom he painted some large groups of portraits, and was the forerunner in this line of Frans Hals and Van der Helst. Two of these portrait-groups are now in the Ryksmuseum at Amsterdam, one, painted in 1588, showing a group under the corporalship of Dirk Rosencrans; the other was painted in 1596. Four similar pictures in the same museum are attributed to Ketel, and portraits of Jacob Bas, burgomaster of Amsterdam, in 1581, and of Grietje Codde, his wife, painted in 1586, are in the same collection. Four portraits by Ketel are in the collection of Mr. Hugo Gevers at the Hague. Carel van Mander, the intimate friend and biographer of Ketel, who wrote while Ketel was still living, gives a list of the principal works executed by Ketel in Amsterdam, including his allegorical and poetical productions. From him we learn that Ketel in his later years took to modelling in wax, painting entirely with his fingers instead of brushes, and finally in 1600 painting with his feet alone. Ketel died at Amsterdam in 1616, and was buried on 8 Aug. in the old church there. In a will dated 16 March 1610, to which he added numerous codicils, he mentions his wife, Aeltgen Jans, apparently his second wife, and a son Andries, who died young.

Ketel frequently painted his own portrait: one, at Hampton Court, was engraved by H. Bary. Two allegorical pictures by him, 'The Triumph of Virtue' and 'The Triumph of Vice,' painted for an Amsterdam merchant, were subsequently in the collection of the Duke of Buckingham. Ketel was one of the most remarkable portrait-painters of his time, and such works of his as have survived are of the highest interest. Pieter Isaacsz, the famous painter in Denmark, was his pupil.

[Carel van Mander's Livre des Peintres, ed. Hymans, 1885; Bredius's Meisterwerke des Ryksmuseums zu Amsterdam; Bredius's Catalogue of the Ryksmuseum; Taurel's L'Art Chrétien en Hollande, ii. 176; Oud Holland, iii. 74; Obreen's Archief voor Nederlandsche Kunstgeschiedenis, iii. 62, &c.; Vertue's MSS. (Brit. Mus. Add. MS. 23068); Scharf's Catalogue of Pictures at Woburn Abbey; Law's Catalogue of the Pictures at Hampton Court; Tudor Exhibition Catalogue.] L. C.

KETEL or CHETTLE, WILLIAM (fl. 1150), hagiographer, was a canon of Beverley. He wrote a narrative 'De Miraculis Sancti Joannis Beverlacensis,' wherein he says that he had only entered things of which he had personal knowledge or which he had learnt from others worthy of credit. Almost all that he relates took place during the reign of William I (1066–87). Ketel dedicated his work, according to the version in the 'Acta Sanctorum,' to Thurstin, prior of Beverley in 1101, or, according to Leland, to Thomas, prior of Beverley. One Thomas was prior in 1092 and another in 1108. But Mr. Raine points out that the treatise contains quotations from Aelred of Beverley, whose chronicle was written about 1150, and that there was a prior Thurstin who died in 1153 or 1154. Tanner is clearly mistaken in giving Ketel the date 1320. The editors of the 'Histoire Littéraire' consider that Ketel (or Kecel as they spell it) was a Norman or French name; Leland suggests that it is a corruption of Aschetel.

The 'De Miraculis' is given in the 'Acta Sanctorum,' 7 May, 172–9, 3rd edit.; in the original edition it was printed from a transcript supplied by Leander Pritchard; in the last edition this version is collated with a copy in Cotton. MS. Faustina B. iv. ff. 164 b–178 a. It is also printed by Mr. Raine in 'Historians of the Church of York and its Archbishops,' i. 261–91 (Rolls Ser.) Ketel's style is pious and diffuse, and his work is of little interest; he is named as the author by a continuator of slightly later date. Bale ascribes to him two other treatises, 'De Rebus Beverlacensis Ecclesiæ' and 'Vita S. Joannis Beverlacensis;' but his statement is not substantiated.

[Leland's Comment. de Scriptt. p. 175; Bale, v. 5; Pits, p. 411; Tanner's Bibl. Brit.-Hib. p. 176; Hist. Litt. de la France, viii. 317–18; Hardy's Descript. Cat. Brit. Hist. iii. 369; Bollandists' Acta Sanct. 7 May, 172–9, and App.; Raine's Historians of the Church of York and its Archbishops, i. p. liv.] C. L. K.

KETHE, WILLIAM (d. 1608?), protestant divine, is generally believed to have been a native of Scotland. He was one of the congregation of protestant exiles at Frankfort during the Marian persecution in December 1554 (Brieff Discours, p. 26). During the ritualistic controversies among the exiles in November 1556, Kethe, with William Whittingham [q. v.] and others, removed to Geneva (ib.) Here he was frequently employed by the English congregation as a delegate to the exiles in other parts of the country, and when Mary died (1558) was sent to visit and confer with various bodies of refugees, for the purpose of bringing about reconciliation and unity of action. He seems to have remained at Geneva till 1561 (cf. ib. p. 187; LIVINGSTON, p. 66). He returned to England in that year, and was at once instituted to the rectory of Okeford Superior, in the parish of Child Okeford, Dorset. He accompanied Ambrose Dudley, earl of Warwick [q. v.], on the expedition to Havre in 1563, as 'minister and preacher' of the English army, and in 1569 went to the 'north partes' as one of the preachers to the troops which were engaged in subduing the popish rebels. His sermon (on John xv. 22) 'made at Blandford Forum ... at the session holden there ... 1571,' was published by John Daye in 1572 (8vo), with a dedication to the Earl of Warwick. A successor was appointed at Okeford Superior in 1608, which may be assumed to be the date of Kethe's death.

Kethe is now remembered chiefly for his metrical psalms, especially for his version of the 100th psalm, 'All people that on earth do dwell.' The latter was in some carelessly revised early psalters ascribed to Hopkins (Warton attributes it to Whittingham), but the earliest published versions are signed with Kethe's initials, and all the later and best authorities agree in assigning it to him. Kethe wrote in all twenty-five metrical psalms; these were first printed in the English Psalter issued at Geneva in 1561, and were subsequently transferred to the complete Scottish Psalter (1564), ten only being adopted in the English Psalter (1562). A rendering by Kethe of the 94th psalm was published in 1558, attached to a tract called 'The Appellation of John Knox.' Kethe's 100th psalm appeared in the appendix of the first complete English metrical Psalter (1562), but was admitted into the text of the edition of 1565. Warton describes Kethe as 'no unready rhymer;' and if regard be had to the different elements of variety, fidelity, energy, and elegance, he is entitled to a high place among the psalter versifiers. His 'long' and 'peculiar' metres are superior to most of his day.

Besides his psalms he wrote some popular religious ballads; the most noted was 'A Ballet, declaringe the fal of the Whore of Babylone, intytuled Tye thy Mare, Tom-boye, with other; and therunto annexid a Prologue to the Reders.' A copy of this very rare tract, consisting of sixteen leaves in black letter, belonged to Heber. The 'Ballet' ends 'Finis, quod William Kythe,' and a concluding 'exhortation to the papists,' 'Finis, quod Wyllyam Kith.' Another of Kethe's broadside poems bore the title 'Of Misrules contending with Gods Worde by name. . . . Quod Wyllym Kethe' (London, by Hugh Singleton, n.d.), twenty-two four-line stanzas. While with the exiles he served as one of the translators of the Geneva Bible. He also produced 'William Kethe, his seeing Glasse, sent to the nobles and gentlemen of England, whereunto is added the Praier of Daniel in meeter' (MAUNSELL'S Cat.); and contributed an English poem to Christopher Goodman's 'How Superior Powers oght to be obeyed of their Subjects' (Geneva, 1558).

[Brieff Discours of the Troubles begoune at Franckford, &c., 1575; Notes and Queries, 4th ser. ix. 59, 170; Warton's Hist. of English Poetry; Heber's Cat. ed. Collier; Hutchins's Dorset, iv. 84; Strype's Annals; Holland's Psalmists of Great Britain, 1843; Notices regarding the Metrical Versions of the Psalms in Baillie's Letters and Journals, edited by Laing, iii. 527 (Banuatyne Club), 1841–2; Dissertation prefixed to Livingstone's reprint of 1635 Scottish Psalter (Glasgow, 1854); Julian's Dict. of Hymnology; Ames's Typogr. Antiq. ed. Herbert.] J. C. H.

KETT or KET, FRANCIS (d. 1589), clergyman, executed for heresy, son of William Kett, and grandson of Robert Kett

[q. v.], was probably born at Wymondham, Norfolk. He was admitted of Corpus Christi College, Cambridge, proceeded B.A. 1569, and M.A. 1573; and was elected fellow in the same year. On 27 Dec. 1575 he joined in a letter of thanks to Burghley, as chancellor, for a settlement of college disputes. In 1580 he resigned his fellowship and left the university, probably for some preferment. Though described as of Wymondham, he does not appear to have been vicar of that parish. He has been identified with the 'Francis Kett, doctor of phisick,' who published 'The Glorious and Beautiful Garland of Man's Glorification' (prose) in 1585, with a dedication to Queen Elizabeth. In 1588 Edmund Scambler, bishop of Norwich, summoned him to his court, and condemned him on charges of heresy. Scambler in a letter (7 Oct. 1588) to Burghley, as lord high treasurer, urged his 'speedy execution,' as a 'dangerous' person, of 'blasphemous opinions.' The 'Articles of Heretical Pravity objected by' Scambler against Kett (in Lansd. MS. 982, f. 162), and the 'Blasphemous Heresyes of one Kett' (Record Office, ccxvii. f. 11), are both printed in Storojenko's 'Life of Greene,' and adequately dispose of the allegation, sometimes brought against Kett, that he indoctrinated Greene and Marlowe in atheism. William Burton (d. 1616) [q. v.], who classes him with Arians, correctly describes him as a sort of millenarian, holding that 'Christ wyth his Apostles are nowe personally in Iudea gathering of his church, and that the faithful must 'goe to Ierusalem,' there to be 'fed with Angelles foode.' Underlying this theory was a view of Christ as 'not God, but a good man,' who 'suffered once for his owne sinnes' and is to 'suffer againe for the sinnes of the world,' and 'he made God after his second resurrectió.' It seems probable that Kett was a mystic of the type of Johann Scheffler (1624–1677). Strype thinks he may have belonged to the 'family of love.' Burton notes 'how holy he would seeme to bee . . . the sacred Bible almost neuer out of his haudes, himselfe alwayes in prayer.' He was burned alive in the castle ditch at Norwich on 14 Jan. 1589. Burton, who witnessed the execution, and deemed Kett 'a deuill incarnate,' says that 'when he went to the fire he was clothed in sackcloth, he went leaping and dauncing: being in the fire, aboue twenty times together, clapping his hands, he cried nothing but blessed bee God . . . and so continued vntill the fire had consumed all his neather partes, and vntill he was stifled with the smoke.' The presentation of his surname as 'Knight' arises from a mere blunder, Ket having been read Kt.

[Burton's Dauid's Euidence, 1596, pp. 124 sq.; Blomefield's Norfolk, 1805 ii. 508, 1806 iii. 293 sq.; Strype's Annals, 1824, vol. iii. pt. ii. p. 73; Wallace's Antitrinitarian Biog. 1850, i. 38 sq.; Heywood and Wright's Cambridge University Transactions, 1854, i. 190 sq.; Gabriel Harvey's Works, ed. Grosart; Cooper's Athenæ Cantabr. 1861, ii. 38, 543; Storojenko's Life of Greene, in Greene's Works, ed. Grosart, i. 42–5, and App. pp. 259–61.]
A. G.

KETT, HENRY (1761–1825), miscellaneous writer, son of Benjamin and Mary Kett, was born in the parish of St. Peter's Mancroft, Norwich, 12 Feb. 1761. His father was a cordwainer and freeman of Norwich, and he himself was admitted to the freedom of the city on 28 Aug. 1784. He was educated at Norwich grammar school by the Rev. William Lemon, and matriculated as commoner inf. ord. of Trinity College, Oxford, on 18 March 1777, graduating B.A. 1780, M.A. 1783, B.D. 1793. He was elected Blount exhibitioner 26 May 1777, scholar 15 June 1778, and fellow 5 June 1784, retaining his fellowship until 1824. His name occurs as the tutor of various undergraduates from 1784 to 1808, but the period during which he acted as college tutor probably ranged from 1799 to 1808. In 1789 Kett, who was fond of travel, visited France, to observe the first ferment of the revolution. He was Bampton lecturer in 1790, and in the same year was chiefly instrumental in raising a subscription for the venerable scholar, Dr. John Uri (q. v.), when the latter was discharged by the delegates of the Clarendon Press from his position as cataloguer of the Oriental MSS. in the Bodleian. He was select preacher 1801–2, and classical examiner during 1803–4. On 31 Oct. 1793 he unsuccessfully contested the professorship of poetry at Oxford against James Hurdis [q. v.] In 1802 he canvassed again for the same post, but refrained from going to the poll. On the first occasion he published, as his credentials for the professorship, a volume of 'Juvenile Poems,' most of which had appeared in the 'Gentleman's Magazine,' but he afterwards endeavoured to suppress it as beneath the proper dignity of poetry. On these productions Tom Warton composed the epigram in allusion to their author's large nose:—

> Our Kett not a poet,
> Why how can you say so?
> For if he's no Ovid,
> I'm sure he's a Naso.

The length of Kett's face also led the wits to nickname him 'Horse' Kett, and Copleston incurred much censure by reprinting, on the title-page of his pamphlet against him, the lines of Virgil ending with 'equo ne credite Teucri.' His person lent itself to caricature, and in June 1807 he was depicted by Dighton in 'A View from Trinity' as a tall man, with his hands behind his back. In his younger days Kett was conspicuous for gravity, but he afterwards became a beau, learnt dancing, and sought a reputation for gallantry. He rejected many college livings, and twice missed the college headship. Through the kindness of Dr. Chapman, the president of his college, he held the incumbency of Elsfield, near Oxford, from 22 May 1785 to 28 June 1804; from July 1812 to 1820 he was vicar of Sutton Benger, Wiltshire, and in 1814 he was nominated by Bishop Tomline as perpetual curate of Hykeham in Lincolnshire. He was also king's preacher at Whitehall; but these appointments did not compel him to leave Oxford, and he resided in college until his marriage at Charlton Kings, Gloucestershire, in December 1823, to Miss White. Kett was independent in principle, but of extreme vanity, and subject to fits of depression. His mind became unhinged, and he was found drowned at Stanwell, Middlesex, on 30 June 1825. His widow married at St. James's, Piccadilly, on 28 Nov. 1828, the Rev. Thomas Nicholl. Kett gave to his college, in addition to large subscriptions to various buildings and some plate, portraits of William Pope, earl of Downe, and the first earl of Chatham. The bulk of his fortune, about 25,000l., was left after his widow's death to three public charities, one being the Radcliffe Infirmary at Oxford.

Kett was the author of: 1. 'Bampton Sermons,' 1791, consisting of 'A Representation of the Conduct and Opinions of the Primitive Christians, with Remarks on Gibbon and Priestley;' 2nd edit., with corrections and additions, 1792. It has been suggested that Parr assisted him in this work. 2. 'Juvenile Poems,' 1793. 3. 'History the Interpreter of Prophecy,' 1799, 3 vols.; and numerous editions in later years. It was dedicated to Bishop Pretyman, afterwards known as Tomline, to whom Kett on his death left the copyright. 4. 'Elements of General Knowledge,' 1802, 2 vols., forming the substance of a course of lectures which he had read to his pupils during the previous twelve years. The appendix of fifty-two pages contained a list of books, in the classical part of which Porson was consulted. There were numerous editions of this work, the eighth appearing in 1815. Some of its blunders were pointed out by John Davison [q. v.] in 'A Short Account of certain Notable Discoveries contained in a Recent Work,' pt. i. 1803 [by Phileleutheros

Orielensis], pt. ii. 1804. It was defended, probably by Kett himself in the disguise of 'S. Nobody, of King's College, Oxford,' in 'The Biter Bit, or Discoveries Discovered in a Pamphlet of certain Notable Discoveries,' 1804; and by Frederick Nolan of Exeter College, in 'A Letter to Phileleuthercs Orielensis,' 1804, upholding the view that Kett's errors were due to carelessness rather than ignorance, and had been unduly magnified (see *Gent. Mag.* 1805, pp. 41–5). 5. 'Emily, a moral Tale,' 2nd edit. 1809. 6. 'A Tour to the Lakes of Cumberland and Westmoreland in August 1798.' This was published in Mavor's 'British Tourists' Companion,' v. 117–57. 7. 'Logic made Easy, or a short View of the Aristotelic System of Reasoning,' 1809. A very severe attack on it was made in 'The Examiner Examined, or Logic Vindicated. By a Graduate' [i.e. Bishop Copleston], 1809, and it was afterwards rigidly suppressed by Kett. 8. 'The Flowers of Wit, or a Choice Collection of Bon Mots,' 1814, 2 vols.

Kett contributed five papers (4, 22, 27, 39, and 42, all signed 'Q.') to the 'Olla Podrida' of Thomas Monro. His life of William Benwell [q. v.] was appended to a volume of 'Poems, Odes, Prologues, and Epilogues spoken at Reading School,' 1804, pp. 205–23; and his memoir of Henry Headley [q. v.], with some verses on Headley's death, was inserted in the 'Select Beauties of Ancient English' Poetry' (1810 edit., pp. xx–ii). To Shoberl's translation of Chateaubriand's 'Beauties of Christianity' he supplied a preface and notes. His translations of Jortin's poems were reprinted in Jortin's miscellaneous works; numerous pieces by him appeared in the 'Gentleman's Magazine,' and several letters to and from him are in Johnstone's 'Parr,' i. 328–31, vii. 577–83, viii. 212–15; and in T. F. Dibdin's 'Reminiscences,' ii. 791–2. He left many manuscripts, including an edition of Greek proverbs by Lubinus, with English translation and notes, on which he was long engaged.

[Gent. Mag. 1812 pt. ii. p. 81, 1825 pt. ii. pp. 184–5, 1828 pt. ii. p. 558; Notes and Queries, 4th ser. ix. 380, 448, 517 (1872); Annual Biog. 1826, pp. 15–25; Johnstone's Parr, i. 282, vii. 653; G. V. Cox's Recollections of Oxford, p. 16; information from the Rev. William Hudson of Norwich, and from Trinity College, per the Rev. H. E. D. Blakiston.]   W. P. C.

KETT, ROBERT (d. 1549), rebel, was a member of an old Norman family, whose name passed through the forms of Le Chat, Cat, Kett, Ket, and Knight. A branch of this family settled at Wymondham, Norfolk, and held lands there in 1483. In 1549 Robert Kett is called a tanner, and his brother William a butcher or mercer; but both were landowners and men of some position in the neighbourhood. Robert held the manor of Wymondham from John Dudley, earl of Warwick, and other lands as well. He belonged to the class of landlords, and only through accident took the side of the people. This accident arose from a local quarrel. The parish church of Wymondham was joined to the priory church, and after the dissolution of the monasteries the men of Wymondham in 1539 bought from the crown the choir of the priory church and other parts of the monastic buildings. In spite of this the tenant of the royal grantee, Serjeant Flowerden, who lived at Hathersett in the neighbourhood, stripped the lead from the roofs and carried away the bells (BLOMEFIELD, *Hist. of Norfolk*, i. 733–734). The Ketts, as the chief people in the town, resented this, and a feud grew up in consequence. There were many hardships arising from the harsh conduct of the new landlords, especially in the enclosure of common lands; and on 20 June 1549 there was a riot at Attleborough, and fences were torn down. On 7 July an annual festival, with a play in honour of St. Thomas of Canterbury, was held at Wymondham. The gathering of excited rustics ended in the destruction of more fences, among them some erected by Flowerden at Hathersett. Flowerden gave the rioters money to pull down Kett's fences as well; and Kett, in his anger at this treatment, helped them to level his own fences, and then led them back to make a clean sweep of Flowerden's. In this Kett was helped by his brother William, and the riot became important when it was headed by two men of position. The excitement of leadership awakened in Kett's mind a sympathy with popular aims. He led the rioters to Cringleford, and thence to Bowthorpe, where the sheriff, Sir Edmund Windham, boldly ordered them to disperse. He was assailed, and fled to Norwich, where the rioters followed and pulled down the fences of the Town Close. The mayor of Norwich sent off a messenger to London, and tried meanwhile to save the city. Kett occupied Mousehold Heath as a camp, and his followers soon reached the number of sixteen thousand men, who scoured the country for provisions and blockaded the city. Yet Kett maintained order. He established law courts, which sat under an oak-tree; there were chaplains, who said daily prayers and preached to the people; among others Matthew Parker, afterwards archbishop of Canterbury, ventured into the camp and addressed the rioters. A petition of grievances was drawn up and signed by twenty-two delegates of the hundreds of Norfolk and one of Suffolk. The demands were singularly moderate, and aimed at redressing the hardships of the feudal system by diminishing the power of lords of manors as regards enclosures, outgoings which were unjustly thrown upon tenants, restrictions of rights of fishing, keeping of dovecots, and such like. The only general principle laid down is, 'We pray that all bondmen may be made free; for God made all free with his precious bloodshedding.' There is no ground for finding in this rising any sympathy with the old form of the church; clerical residence and diligence in teaching are the only demands of a religious nature. On 21 July came a royal herald, offering pardon, whom Kett answered, 'Kings were wont to pardon wicked persons, not innocent and just men.' After being thus treated as a rebel, Kett began the siege of Norwich, and William Parr, marquis of Northampton, was sent with 2,500 men to its succour. Among his troops were some Italian mercenaries, who were worsted in a skirmish, and on 1 Aug. Kett attacked Norwich, slew Lord Sheffield, and drove the royal troops out of the city. The privy council was in great anxiety, and not till 16 Aug. was John Dudley, earl of Warwick, named commander against the rebels. On 23 Aug. he reached Norwich, and sent a herald offering pardon to all except Kett. While the herald was delivering his message one of his escort shot a boy who affronted him, and the herald was almost torn to pieces. Kett interposed to save him, and for a moment hesitated whether or no he should accompany him to Warwick. But his followers seized his bridle, and the chances of peace were at an end. Warwick forced his way into one end of Norwich while the rebels held the other, and there was confused fighting in the streets till, on 26 Aug., Warwick was reinforced by eleven hundred lanzknechts, and was strong enough to meditate an attack on the camp at Mousehold. Moved by a local prophecy, which foretold that 'the country gnuffes should fill up Dussindale with blood,' Kett moved from Mousehold to Dussindale below, and there awaited Warwick's onslaught. In the open field trained soldiers easily prevailed; the lanzknechts fired a volley, and charged the centre of the rebels, who gave way, and their forces were thus cut into, and fled on different sides. At least 3,500 men were slain on the field, and so fulfilled the prophecy. Kett rode away to Swannington; but his horse was weary and he could go no further. He was taken and brought back to Norwich, whence he was sent with three brothers to London.

Only he and William were brought to trial; they pleaded guilty, and were condemned to death as traitors. On 29 Nov. they were handed over to the sheriff, and were taken back to Norwich, where Robert was executed on 7 Dec. 1549, and his body was hanged in chains from the top of the castle. William was sent to Wymondham, and was similarly hanged from the church tower.

[Russell, Kett's Rebellion in Norfolk, has collected most of the documents relating to the rising. There are two contemporary accounts, Neville's De Furoribus Norfolcensium, first published 1575, and Southerton's The Commoyson in Norfolk (Harl. MSS.), 1576. Besides these: Hayward's Reign of Edward VI; Holinshed's Chronicle; Strype's Ecclesiastical Memorials and Life of Parker; Blomefield's Hist. of Norfolk, ii. 160, &c. Of modern writers: Froude's Hist. of England; Dixon's Hist. of the Church of England; Rye's Popular Hist. of Norfolk.]

M. C.

KETTELL, RALPH (1563–1643), third president of Trinity College, Oxford, born in 1563, was the third son of John Kettell, gentleman, of King's Langley, Hertfordshire. He was nominated to a scholarship at Trinity College, Oxford, in 1579 by Lady Elizabeth Paulet of Tittenhanger, the widow of Sir Thomas Pope, knt., founder of the college; and was elected fellow in 1583. One of his contemporaries and friends was Sir Edward Hoby [q. v.] The Christopher Kettell who became a commoner of the college in 1583, and the George Kettell who became a commoner in 1588, were Ralph's younger brothers, and John Kettell of King's Langley, whose family bible is in the college library, was his elder brother (King's Langley reg.) Ralph Kettell graduated B.A. 1582, M.A. 1586, B.D. 1594, and D.D. 1597, and, after filling various college offices, was elected president in 1598-9, on the death of Dr. Yeldard. Among those who as young men were under his care while he was either tutor or president were Archbishop Sheldon, Bishops Glemham, Lucy, Ironside, and Skinner, Sir John Denham, James Harrington, Ludlow, Ireton, George and Cecil Calvert, Lord Baltimore, William, earl of Craven, and Sir Henry Blount. Many documents drawn up in his very curious and marked handwriting remain in the college archives. He exercised great vigilance in dealing with the college estates and college discipline, rebuilt the college hall, and added attics or 'cocklofts' to the old Durham College quadrangle, of which the east side still remains. About 1620 he built for the use of commoners, on the site of 'Perilous Hall,' the fine stone house in Broad Street which is still known as Kettell Hall.

Kettell was one of the older heads of houses who, without being inclined to the 'factious in religion,' disliked Laud's highhanded reforms. He was a 'right church of England man;' saved the old paintings in the college chapel from the puritan commissioner, Lord Say and Sele; lectured on the Thirty-nine Articles, and talked of roodlofts, wafers, and the old rites which he could just remember. Outside Oxford Kettell held the rectory of Garsington, which was attached to his office of president, and was private chaplain to Sir Francis Walsingham's widow and to Bishop Bilson of Winchester. Aubrey, who was admitted a commoner of Trinity in 1642, and knew Kettell in his old age, narrates many anecdotes of his eccentricities, and quotes specimens of his quaint remarks. Aubrey also mentions his secret charity to poor scholars, and his contemptuous treatment of the strange visitors whom the civil wars brought to the university. His death, in Aubrey's opinion, was hastened by 'the dissoluteness of the time.' He died about 17 July 1643, and was buried at Garsington on 5 Aug.

Kettell's portrait, preserved at Trinity, is a mere daub, but agrees fairly with Aubrey's description of him as 'a very tall well-grown man, with a fresh ruddy complexion; he was soon white; his gowne, and surplice, and hood being on, he had a terrible gigantique aspect, with his sharp gray eies. The ordinary gowne he wore was a russet cloath.'

He does not seem to have published anything. A large book of manuscript pieces in his handwriting, given by President Bathurst to Wood (now Bodleian Library MSS. Wood, f. 21), probably contains nothing original.

Aubrey states that 'he had two wives, if not three, but no child,' and that his second wife was the widow of Edward Villiers of Hothorpe, Northamptonshire, whose daughter Elizabeth married George Bathurst, and was the mother of Ralph Bathurst [q. v.], president of Trinity College, Oxford; but there are probably some inaccuracies here. His wife was buried at Garsington in 1623–4, and an infant daughter in 1606; one, 'Mrs. Barbara Villiers, widow,' was the wife of his brother John Kettell.

[Registers and other documents in the archives of Trinity College, Oxford; notes in Warton's Lives of Pope and Bathurst; Life by John Aubrey, printed in Bodleian Letters, ii. 417; Pope's Life of Seth Ward; information from King's Langley and Garsington parish registers, kindly communicated by the Rev. A. B. Strettell, vicar, and the Rev. David Thomas, rector; Clark's University Register, vol. ii. pts. ii. and iii.]   H. E. D. B.

KETTERICH or **CATRIK**, **JOHN** (d. 1419), successively bishop of St. Davids, Lichfield and Coventry, and Exeter, was probably educated at one of the universities, since he is described as LL.B., and as a licentiate in decretals (NICOLAS, Proc. Privy Council, iii. 5, 20). From his later career it may be conjectured that he became a clerk in the royal service, but the first mention of him is on 1 Jan. 1402, when he obtained the prebend of Brampton at Lincoln. He subsequently received a variety of preferments: the prebends of Cropredy, Lincoln, on 14 July 1402, of Stow Longa, Lincoln, 3 April 1406, and of Osbaldwick, York, 20 Jan. 1407. On 25 March 1408 he was made treasurer of Lincoln, but exchanged this post for the mastership of St. Mary Magdalen's Hospital, Sandown, Surrey, on 14 Nov. following. From 1410 to 1414 he was archdeacon of Surrey. Between 1408 and 1411 he was frequently employed on embassies to the French king and the Duke of Burgundy (Fœdera, viii. 432, 504, 546, 571, 585–6, 599, 636–7, 677, 694). On 22 May 1413 he was appointed king's proctor at the papal court (ib. ix. 12). On 27 April 1414 he was papally provided to the see of St. Davids, was consecrated by John XXIII at Bologna on 29 April, and received possession of the temporalities on 2 June. But on 13 Oct. he received custody of the temporalities of Lichfield and Coventry during a vacancy, and on 1 Feb. 1415 was translated to that see, the spiritualities being restored on 21 June.

Meanwhile, on 20 Oct. 1414, Ketterich was appointed one of the English representatives at the council of Constance, and was apparently present throughout its sittings. He took part in the proceedings which attended the deposition of John XXIII, being one of the commissaries for receiving evidence against that pontiff. He was also one of those appointed to elect the new pope, Martin V, 11 Nov. 1417 (H. VON DER HARDT, iv. 171, 182, v. 16; WALSINGHAM, Hist. Angl. ii. 318). In 1416 Ketterich was concerned in a variety of negotiations with the Duke of Burgundy, with Alfonso of Arragon, the princes of Germany, the Hanse, and Genoa (Fœdera, ix. 374, 410–15). After the death of Robert Hallam [q. v.] in September 1417, the Cardinal des Ursins wrote to Henry V recommending Ketterich as his successor at Salisbury on account of the judgment and learning he had shown during the council (ib. ix. 489). On the conclusion of the council he accompanied Martin V into Italy at the beginning of 1418, and apparently resumed his old position at the papal court. In April 1419 he had authority to take all Normans at the court of Rome into the king's favour (*ib.* ix. 730). On 20 Nov. of that year he was postulated to the see of Exeter. But before the translation could be completed he died, on 28 Dec. 1419, at Florence, where the papal court had been since the previous February. In accordance with his will he was buried in the church of Santa Croce, where a marble slab still marks his tomb in the centre of the nave near the choir. His name is variously spelt Catrik, Catryk, Catterich, or Ketterich; the first is the form that appears on his tomb, and is probably the best.

[Le Neve's Fasti Eccl. Angl. i. 296, 373. 552, ii. 89. 117, 140, 214, iii. 29, 207, ed. Hardy; Rymer's Fœdera, orig. edit.; Wharton's Anglia Sacra, i. 452; Godwin, De Præsulibus. pp. 321, 412, 582, ed. Richardson; H. von der Hardt's Concilium Constantiense; Labbé's Concilia, vol. xxvii.] C. L. K.

KETTLE or **KYTELER, DAME ALICE** (*fl.* 1324), reputed witch, lived in Kilkenny in the fourteenth century. Her relatives were wealthy. Robert le Kyteler was a trader with Flanders towards the close of the thirteenth century. She is frequently referred to in the history of the English Pale. According to Holinshed she was accused in 1324, by Richard de Lederede, bishop of Ossory, with two accomplices, Petronilla of Meath and Bassilla her daughter, of holding 'nightlie conference with a spirit called Robert Artis-son, to whome she sacrificed in the high waie nine red cocks and nine peacocks' eies.' The accused persons abjured and did penance, but were afterwards found to have relapsed. One of the accomplices was burnt at Kilkenny, and at her death declared that Lady Kettle's son was an accomplice. He was imprisoned by the bishop for nine weeks, but delivered by Arnold le Powre, seneschal of Kilkenny (a relative of Lady Kettle's fourth husband). Lady Kettle's son then bribed le Powre to imprison the bishop. Lady Kettle was again cited to appear at Dublin before the Dean of St. Patrick's, but some of the nobility supported her, and got her over to England, where no more was heard of her. In her closet was found a sacra-mental wafer, with a print of the devil, and some ointment which converted a staff into a practicable steed. Wright gives Lady Kettle four husbands: 1. William Outlaw of Kilkenny, 'banker.' 2. Adam le Blound of Callan, whom she married about 1302. 3. Richard de Valle, whom she married about 1311; and 4. John le Poer or Powre, to whom she was married in 1324. She bore a son to William Outlaw, also called William. A 'Narrative of the Proceedings against Dame Alice Kyteler, prosecuted for sorcery

in 1324 by Richard de Lederede, bishop of Ossory,' in Latin, was edited by Thomas Wright for the Camden Society in 1843, from Harl. MS. 641, f. 187; a transcript is in Sloane MS. 4800.

[Wright's edit. of the Proceedings; Cal. of Carew MSS., Book of Howth (Rolls Ser.), pp. 147–148; Chartularies of St. Mary's Abbey, Dublin (Rolls Ser.), ii. cxxxiii–v, 362–4; Holinshed's Chron. of Ireland, p. 69; Irish Eccles. Journ. (October 1843), ii. 261, where is another letter by James Heathorn Todd, D.D.] B. H. B.

KETTLE, TILLY (1740?–1786), por-trait-painter, born in London about 1740, was the son of a house-painter, apparently Henry Kettle, sen., who in 1774 was re-siding in Silver Street, Wood Street, and exhibited at the Society of Arts a cylindrical painting. Kettle learnt first from his father, then studied in the Duke of Richmond's gallery of casts, and later at the academy in St. Martin's Lane. He practised as a por-trait-painter, and in 1761 exhibited a portrait at the Free Society of Artists. In 1762 he was employed to repair Streater's painting on the ceiling of the theatre at Oxford. In 1765 he exhibited at the Society of Artists, of which he afterwards became a fellow, a full-length portrait of Mrs. Yates as 'Man-dane,' and a kit-cat portrait of Mrs. Powell, wife of the actor, in Turkish dress. In 1767 he exhibited a portrait of Miss Eliot as 'Juno,' and in 1768 'Dead Game.' He continued to exhibit portraits and conversation-pieces until 1770, when he went to India. He re-mained there seven years, and acquired a considerable fortune. He sent home many pictures for exhibition. One contained full-length portraits of Mahomed Ali Caun, nabob of Arcot, and his five sons in 1771; another in 1772 depicted native dancing girls. In 1775 he exhibited a painting representing Sujah Dowlah, vizier of the Mogul Empire, and his four sons meeting Sir Robert Barker, his two aides-de-camp and interpreter at Fyzabad, in order to conclude a treaty with the East India Company in 1772. This group, painted for Sir Robert Barker [q. v.], was afterwards placed at Bushbridge Park, near Godalming, Surrey. In 1776 Kettle forwarded to the Academy 'The Ceremony of a Gentoo woman taking leave of her re-lations, and distributing her jewels prior to ascending the funeral pile of her deceased husband.' Kettle returned to England about 1777, settled in London, and married the younger daughter of James Paine, senior [q. v.], the architect. In 1779 he exhibited a portrait at the Royal Academy, and in 1781, with other portraits, 'The Great Mogul, Shah Allum, reviewing the third Brigade of the

East India Company's Troops at Allahabad' (now at Bushbridge Park). In 1782, the last year but one that he exhibited, he sent a full-length portrait of Admiral Kempenfeldt (now at Greenwich Hospital, engraved by J. H. Robinson as three-quarters for Locker's 'British Admirals'). Kettle built a house for himself in Old Bond Street, opposite Burlington Gardens, but fell into financial difficulties, became bankrupt, and retired to Dublin. In 1786 he started on a second visit to India, which he determined to reach overland. He was taken ill near Aleppo and died there. He left a widow and two children.

Kettle's portraits show great merit in colour and drawing, and have been mistaken for the work of Sir Joshua Reynolds. He often apparently placed his sitter with the light on a level with the face. In the National Portrait Gallery there is a portrait of Warren Hastings by him, and in the Bodleian Library one of Sir William Blackstone. He also painted for Sir Robert Barker of Bushbridge a large picture of 'The Mother and her seven Sons martyred by Antiochus,' 1 Maccabees chap. vii. Many of his portraits were engraved.

[Edwards's Anecd. of Painters; Redgrave's Dict. of Artists; Gent. Mag. 1786, pt. ii. 1091, 1145; Graves's Dict. of Artists, 1760–1880; Catalogues of the Royal Academy, &c.; information from George Scharf, esq., C.B.]   L. C.

KETTLEWELL, JOHN (1653–1695), nonjuror and devotional writer, second son of John Kettlewell, a merchant at North Allerton, Yorkshire, by his wife, Elizabeth Ogle, was born 10 March 1652–3, and was educated at North Allerton school under Thomas Smelt, a zealous royalist. Among other pupils who attained distinction were Dean Hickes, William Palliser, archbishop of Cashel, Dr. Thomas Burnet of the Charterhouse, Thomas Rymer, editor of the 'Fœdera,' and Dr. Radcliffe. Kettlewell matriculated at St. Edmund Hall, Oxford, 11 Nov. 1670, and graduated B.A. 20 June 1674. On Radcliffe's resignation of a fellowship at Lincoln College, Kettlewell was elected in his place in July 1675, largely through the influence of Dr. George Hickes [q. v.], then himself a fellow. For about five years he acted as tutor in college, and proceeded M.A. 3 May 1677, by which time he had, we are told, in preparation for his ordination, 'laid up a large fund, near one hundred, of sermons' of his own composition (*Life*). He was ordained deacon by the Bishop of Oxford in Christ Church Cathedral 10 June 1677, and priest 24 Feb. following (*Rawlinson MS. J. 63*, Bodl. Libr.) His first book, 'The

Measures of Christian Obedience,' a summary of Christian morals as involved in obedience to the laws of the Gospel, was written between Christmas 1077 and Easter 1678, but was not published until 1681, when, at Hickes's suggestion, Kettlewell dedicated it to Compton, bishop of London, but this dedication he suppressed after Compton had appeared in military array on behalf of the Prince of Orange at the revolution. The reputation which the book secured for him led to his appointment as chaplain to the Countess of Bedford, and to his presentation by Simon, lord Digby, to the vicarage of Coleshill, Warwickshire (December 1682). Through the countess he became known to Lord William Russell, who, despite political differences, esteemed him so highly that he sent him a message of remembrance from the scaffold. At Coleshill Kettlewell was exemplary in attention to his pastoral duties, and supplied all the poor families with copies of the Bible and the 'Whole Duty of Man.' By his influence with the patron he procured the restoration to the living of great tithes to the value of 100l. His second publication resulted from his parochial work; he was in the habit of preaching preparation-sermons before administering the holy communion (which he did eight or nine times in the year), and of these he printed a summary in 1683 under the title of 'An Help and Exhortation to Worthy Communicating,' dedicating the book to Lord Digby. He resigned his fellowship at Lincoln College on 22 Nov. 1683, and thenceforward devoted himself entirely to his parish. Here, in prospect of the disturbed times which shortly followed, he frequently inculcated passive obedience, and shortly after the suppression of Monmouth's rebellion preached a sermon *ad clerum*, which was printed after his death in his collected works with the title of 'Measures of Christian Subjection.' On the death of George Downing, archdeacon of Coventry, in 1684, Kettlewell made unsuccessful application to Archbishop Sancroft for that post and for the prebend of Alrewas, which Downing held as chancellor of Lichfield; a copy by Bishop Thomas Tanner of his letter, dated 15 Nov. 1684, is in 'Rawlinson MS. Letters,' xxx. 27, in the Bodleian Library.

In 1685 Kettlewell married, and gave to Coleshill Church a service of communion plate, which was solemnly consecrated by Archbishop Sancroft; a formal record of the act, drawn up at the time, was printed in 1703 (with the omission of names and date), together with the form of service used. As a supplement to his first book, that on 'Christian Obedience,' he published in February 1687-8 his 'Practical Believer,' treating of doctrines. This book became very popular, and passed through many editions. During the confusions of the revolution year he preached strongly against rebellion upon any pretence. He adhered consistently to this principle, and was deprived of his vicarage in 1690. No notice of his deprivation is found in the parish books. He then removed to London, where, or in the neighbourhood (for a letter of his of 26 May 1694 is dated from Bagshot Park, *Rawlinson MS. D.* 373, f. 100, Bodl.), he quietly spent the short remainder of his life, occupied in the composition of devotional books and of a few controversial tracts. He wrote from London, on 4 Dec. 1694, a letter to Sir William Boothby, on behalf of Dr. William Sheridan, the deprived bishop of Kilmore (a copy exists in Bodleian MS. 'English Hist.' d. f. 137). Shortly before his death he proposed to Bishop Ken the establishment of a fund for the relief of the suffering deprived clergy. The proposal was adopted, and circulars asking for subscriptions were issued. But the charitable scheme was regarded by the government as a seditious usurpation of authority, and prosecutions were instituted. Kettlewell died at his house in Gray's Inn Lane on 12 April 1695, at the age of forty-two, and was thus exempted from prosecution. His warm friend, Robert Nelson [q. v.], has given an account of his last days, which was sent to Hickes. He was buried on 15 April in the church of All Hallows Barking, in the same grave in which Laud had been interred, and is commemorated in a Latin inscription on a marble tablet erected by his widow at the east end of the church. Hearne, in a pencil-written memorandum preserved in a Bodleian MS. (*Rawl.* D. 800, 144,) gives an account of Kettlewell's funeral. Ken, who officiated for the only time in public after his deprivation (cf. *Rawlinson MS. Letters*, Bodl. xvii. 35), 'performed the office in his lawn sleeves,' and ' prayed for the king—and the queens' (*sic*), &c. 'There were besides Mr. Gascarth, the minister, between thirty and forty clergy and as many of the laity, some of them of good quality.'

Kettlewell had married at Whitchurch, near Reading, on 4 Oct. 1685, Jane, daughter of Anthony Lybb of Hardwick House in the parish of Whitchurch. His married life was one of great happiness; his wife, by whom he had no children, survived him, but the date of her death has not been found; it seems, however, to have occurred about or before 1719 (*Notes and Queries*, 3rd ser. i. 91). His papers were entrusted by his widow to Robert Nelson, who published

some of them. Several charities were established by his means at Coleshill, through gifts from Simon, lord Digby, Mrs. Rawlins, and himself. He exhibited in his character a perfect pattern of quiet Christian devotion and unfailing charity in the midst of heated controversies. Ken said, in a letter to Nelson, ' He was certainly as saint-like a man as ever I knew.' In Hearne's pencil note quoted above, Bishop Henry Gandy (from whom the note seems to be derived) appears to be quoted as saying: ' His books show him to be a very pious as well as learned person, and will outlast any monument his friends can bestow upon him. He was, as far as ever I could perceive, of a sweet and courteous disposition and very communicative.' His chief recreation lay in music; he was skilled in the theory, and performed on the violoncello, base-viol, and violin. His portrait was painted by Henry Tilson, and engravings by Vandergucht, Vertue, and J. Smith are found prefixed to some of his books.

Kettlewell's works are: 1. 'Measures of Christian Obedience,' 1681; 2nd edit. 1683-1684, 3rd 1696, 4th 1700, 5th 1709 (with portrait), 6th 1714. 2. 'Help and Exhortation to Worthy Communicating,' 1683; eight editions up to 1717, the fourth printed at Cambridge in 1701. 3. 'A Discourse explaining the Nature of Edification,' in a visitation sermon at Coventry, 1684. 4. 'A Funeral Sermon for the Lady Frances Digby,' 1684. 5. 'The Religious Loyalist ;' a visitation sermon at Coleshill, 1686. 6. 'Sermon on Occasion of the Death of Simon, Lord Digby,' 1686. 7. 'The Practical Believer; or the Articles of the Apostles' Creed drawn out to form a true Christian's Heart and Practice,' two parts [anon., with initials J. K.], 1688; published by William Allen, D.D., fol. 1703; 3rd edit., with a preface by Robert Nelson, and additions, 1712-13; translated into Welsh by Richard ap Robert, 1768. 8. 'Of Christian Prudence, or Religious Wisdom, not degenerating into Irreligious Craftiness in Trying Times' [anon., with initials J. K.], 1691. 9. 'Christianity, a Doctrine of the Cross; or Passive Obedience under any pretended Invasion of Legal Rights and Liberties' [anon.], 1691 ; 1695, with the author's name. 10. 'The Duty of Allegiance settled upon its True Grounds . . . in Answer to a late Book of Dr. Will. Sherlock, entituled The Case of the Allegiance due to Sovereign Powers' [anon.], 1691. 11. 'Of Christian Communion, to be kept on in the Unity of Christ's Church . . . and of the Obligations both of faithful Pastors to administer Orthodox and Holy Offices, and of faithful People to Communicate in the same,' three parts [anon.], 1693; reissued in 1695 with a general title of 'Four several Tracts of the Rev. John Kettlewell,' without specification of any others. 12. 'A Companion for the Persecuted; or an Office for those who Suffer for Righteousness,' 1694. 13. 'A Companion for the Penitent and for Persons troubled in Mind,' 1694; of this Kettlewell sent down copies to Coleshill, to the people of which parish it was addressed, for distribution; it was reissued in 1696, together with the 'Companion for the Persecuted' dated 1693. 14. 'Death made Comfortable, or the Way to Die well,' 1695; with an office for the sick 1702, and 2nd edit. 1722. 15. 'Declaration and Profession made by [him] at the receiving of the Holy Sacrament of the Lord's Supper, 23 March 1694,' printed, Wood says, in a half-sheet in 1695; reprinted in his 'Life.' 16. 'Five Discourses on so many important Points of Practical Religion,' with a preface giving some account of his life (by Robert Nelson), 1696; 2nd edit., with four sermons, two parts, 1708. 17. 'An Office for Prisoners for Crimes, together with another for Prisoners for Debt' (with a preface by Robert Nelson), 1697. 18. 'The Great Evil and Danger of Profuseness and Prodigality' (published by Nelson), 1705. 19. 'Works,' 2 vols. fol. 1719, with 'Life' prefixed; the several tracts have title-pages dated 1718. 20. 'The True Church of England Man's Companion' (a manual of devotion compiled from his works), 1749. 21. A treatise 'of the new oaths' was left by him in manuscript, but never printed.

[Memoirs of (Kettlewell's) Life . . . compiled from the collections of Dr. George Hickes and Robert Nelson, and edited anonymously by Francis Lee of St. John's College, Oxford, and M.D. of the university of Padua, 8vo, London, 1718; Wood's Athenæ Oxon.; Secretan's Life of Nelson, 1860, pp. 50–62; private information from the vicar of Coleshill and rector of Whitchurch. A letter from Kettlewell to Bishop W. Lloyd, the deprived bishop of Norwich, dated 20 Dec. 1694, upon sending Lloyd a copy of his Companion for the Penitent. and describing his scheme for charitable relief, is printed from the original in the possession of the late Dr. D. Williams, warden of New College, Oxford. in J. L. Anderdon's Life of Ken, 1854, 2nd edit. pt. ii. p. 666. Some letters to Colonel James Graham (brother of Lord Preston) are among the manuscripts of Captain Bagot at Levens Hall, Westmoreland, and a letter to Sancroft, dated 15 Oct. 1684, among the manuscripts at Stonyhurst College (Hist. MSS. Comm. 10th Rep. pt. iv. p. 327. 3rd Rep. p. 340).] W. D. M.

KEUGH, MATTHEW (1744?–1798), governor of Wexford, born of a protestant family in Ireland about 1744, rose by his ability during the American war from the position of private to that of ensign, being gazetted in the 60th or royal American regiment of foot on 31 Oct. 1763. On 14 July 1769 he was appointed lieutenant in the 45th regiment of foot (Ireland), from which he was transferred on 14 March 1772 to the 27th or Inniskilling regiment of foot (Ireland). On retiring from the army in 1774 (*Army Lists*) he went to live upon his property in the town of Wexford. He became a J.P., but was deprived of his commission in 1796 for his revolutionary sympathies. Upon the occupation of Wexford by the insurgents on 30 May 1798, Keugh was chosen by them military governor of the town. Though he endeavoured to protect such of the royalists as remained, he was powerless to prevent the piking on the bridge on 20 June of 97 out of the 200 prisoners who were charged with having wronged the peasantry. When the capture of Wexford by the military was inevitable, Keugh formally placed the government in the hands of the loyalist Lord Kingsborough, hoping thereby to save the town from massacre and plunder. He was ultimately brought to a drumhead trial. Lord Kingsborough, Colonel Le Hunte, and other witnesses of good social standing stated that Keugh had acted on all occasions with singular humanity, and had tried to prevent effusion of blood, and that they owed their lives to his personal interference. He was nevertheless executed on the bridge on 25 June 1798; his body was thrown into the river, and his head placed on the courthouse. In private life Keugh was esteemed for his many amiable qualities and accomplishments. He married an aunt of the wife of Sir Jonah Barrington.

[Webb's Compendium of Irish Biography; Musgrave's Hist. of the Irish Rebellions; Madden's United Irishmen; Lecky's England in the Eighteenth Century, vol. viii.; Barrington's Personal Sketches.] G. G.

KEVIN, Saint (498–618). [See Coemgen.]

KEY. [See also Caius.]

KEY, Sir ASTLEY COOPER (1821–1888), admiral, son of Charles Aston Key [q. v.], entered the navy in 1833, passed his examination in 1840, and on 22 Dec. 1842 was awarded the lieutenant's commission, at that time competed for in a special course of study, on board the Excellent gunnery-ship and at the Royal Naval College at Portsmouth. In February 1843 he joined the Curaçoa going out to the east coast of South America, where, in February 1844, he was transferred to the Gorgon, with Captain

Charles Hotham [q. v.] On 10 May the Gorgon, then at anchor off Monte Video, parted her cables in a violent gale, and was driven on shore, far above high-water mark. When the sea returned to its usual level, the ship was dry to within a few feet of her stern-post, and imbedded in the sand to a depth of thirteen feet. Key was only the junior lieutenant, but his scientific training enabled him to take a prominent share in the work of getting her afloat, and at once marked him as a rising man. He was appointed to command the Fanny tender, and after the action at Obligado (20 Nov. 1845), in which he was slightly wounded, he was promoted to the rank of commander, his commission being antedated to 18 Nov. From 1847 to 1850 he commanded the Bulldog steamer in the Mediterranean, and on 11 Oct. 1850 was advanced to post-rank. During the Russian war of 1854-5 he commanded the Amphion frigate in the Baltic, took part in the reduction of Bomarsund and in the bombardment of Sveaborg, and was repeatedly engaged with the enemy's batteries, especially in the gulf of Viborg. On 5 July 1855 he was nominated a C.B. In 1857 he went out to China in command of the screw line-of-battle ship Sanspareil, in which he was at once sent with a detachment of marines to Calcutta; and, bringing them back when the urgent need had passed, he commanded a battalion of the naval brigade at the capture of Canton (28-9 Dec. 1857), and a few days later with his own hands seized Yeh, the Chinese governor, as he was seeking to escape in the disguise of a coolie (OLIPHANT, Narrative of the Earl of Elgin's Mission to China, i. 141) [see SEYMOUR, SIR MICHAEL, 1802-1887].

From 1858 to 1860 Key was a member of the royal commission on national defence; in 1860 he was appointed captain of the steam reserve at Devonport, and in 1863 captain of the Excellent and superintendent of the Royal Naval College. On 20 Nov. 1866 he was promoted to be rear-admiral; he had already been consulted by the admiralty about the organisation of the new department of naval ordnance, and was now appointed to the office of director, which he held till the summer of 1869, when he accepted the post of superintendent of Portsmouth dockyard, from which he was shortly afterwards moved to Malta, at once as superintendent of the dockyard and second in command in the Mediterranean. In 1872, when it was determined to establish the Royal Naval College at Greenwich on a much enlarged plan, Key was called home for the purpose of organising it. The whole scheme was drawn out by him, and the college, with

Key as president, was opened in February 1873. On 30 April 1873 he was advanced to be vice-admiral, and on 24 May was nominated a K.C.B. He continued at Greenwich till the beginning of 1876, when he was appointed commander-in-chief on the North American and West Indian station. On attaining the rank of admiral, 21 March 1878, he returned to England, and for a couple of months in the summer had command of an evolutionary squadron in the Channel. In June 1879 he was appointed principal naval aide-de-camp to the queen, and in August first naval lord of the admiralty, in which post he remained till the change of ministry in the summer of 1885, when he was granted a special pension of 500l. a year, in addition to his half-pay. The G.C.B. was conferred on him on 24 Nov. 1882, and on 11 Aug. 1884 he was appointed a member of the privy council. He was also F.R.S., F.R.G.S., and D.C.L.; and was author of 'A Narrative of the Recovery of H.M.S. Gorgon, stranded in the Bay of Monte Video, 10 May 1844,' 8vo, 1847. After his retirement he resided at Maidenhead, and there he died on 3 March 1888. He was twice married, and left issue. A portrait, presented by the subscribers in 1876, is in the library of the Royal Naval College.

[O'Byrne's Naval Biog. Dict.; obituary notices in Times, 5, 7, and 8 March, and Morning Post, 5 March 1888; information from the family; personal knowledge. The official correspondence in July 1885 relating to the special pension was published as a parliamentary paper.] J. K. L.

KEY, CHARLES ASTON (1793-1849), surgeon, born in Southwark on 6 Oct. 1793, was eldest son of Thomas Key, medical practitioner, and Margaret Barry. Thomas Hewitt Key [q. v.] was a half-brother by a second marriage. Aston Key was educated at Buntingford grammar school, Hertfordshire, and was apprenticed to his father in 1810. He attended the lectures at the United Borough Hospitals in 1812, and became a pupil at Guy's in 1814. In 1815 his apprenticeship to his father was cancelled, and he became pupil of Astley Cooper at a large premium. In 1817-18 he lived with Cooper, and in 1818 married Cooper's niece, Anne Cooper. Key became demonstrator of anatomy at St. Thomas's Hospital, but resigned the post in February 1823, though he gave some of Sir Astley Cooper's surgical lectures for two sessions afterwards. Key had qualified at the Royal College of Surgeons in 1821, and in the autumn of the same year was appointed the first assistant surgeon to Guy's, succeeding to a full surgeoncy in January 1824. In this year he introduced the operation for litho-

o 2

tomy with the straight staff, using only a single knife all through; the success of his operations established his reputation as a surgeon. He gained a large practice, and was elected a fellow of the Royal Society. In 1825, on the separation of Guy's from St. Thomas's medical schools [see COOPER, SIR ASTLEY PASTON], Key was appointed lecturer on surgery at Guy's, and his classes were for many years very popular. He resigned the lectureship in 1844. In 1845 he was one of the first elected fellows of the Royal College of Surgeons, and in the same year became a member of its council. In 1847 he was appointed surgeon to Prince Albert. He died of cholera on 23 Aug. 1849, leaving nine children. His son Sir Astley Cooper Key is separately noticed.

Key was a great surgical operator and lecturer, his lectures being largely the results of his own experience. He was not a well-read man nor a scientific pathologist. He was one of the first surgeons in London to use ether as an anæsthetic. His dexterity with the knife was remarkable; he was never known to make a mistake through inattention to details. In person he was of commanding presence, thin, and rather tall, with a slightly aquiline nose.

Key contributed to the 'Guy's Hospital Reports' some valuable papers on hernia, lithotomy, and other subjects. He also wrote: 1. 'A Short Treatise on the Section of the Prostate Gland in Lithotomy,' 4to, 4 plates, London, 1824. 2. 'A Memoir on the Advantages and Practicability of Dividing the Stricture in Strangulated Hernia on the outside of the Sac,' 8vo, London, 1833; and he edited the second edition of Sir Astley Cooper's work on hernia, 1827.

[Brit. and For. Med.-Chir. Review, iv. 572-7; Lancet, 1849, ii. 300, 411; Wilks and Bettany's Biog. Hist. of Guy's Hospital.]   G. T. B.

KEY, SIR JOHN (1794–1858), lord mayor of London, eldest son of John Key of Denmark Hill, Surrey, was born on 16 Aug. 1794. He entered his father's business, that of a wholesale stationer, about 1818. The firm had been established in the last century, and then traded as Key Brothers & Son, at 30 Abchurch Lane. After several changes of abode the business was finally removed to 97 and 103 Newgate Street. Key was elected alderman for the ward of Langbourn on 8 April 1823, and served the office of sheriff of London and Middlesex in the ensuing year. He served the office of master of the Stationers' Company in 1830, and in the same year was elected lord mayor. He was one of the leading supporters of the Reform Bill in the city, and received the unusual honour of re-election to the mayoralty in the following year. During his second mayoralty, when William IV and Queen Adelaide had arranged to visit the city in order to open new London Bridge, Key suffered some loss of popularity by advising the king and his ministers not to come to the city on account of the supposed unpopularity of the Duke of Wellington. The visit passed off satisfactorily, and Key was created a baronet by William IV on 17 Aug. 1831. He was elected member of parliament for the city in 1833. He removed in 1851 from Langbourn to the ward of Bridge Without, which he represented until 1853. In that year he was elected chamberlain of London after a poll, his opponent being Benjamin Scott (q. v.), who afterwards succeeded him in that office.

Key died on 15 July 1858, leaving by his wife Charlotte, youngest daughter of Francis Green, esq., of Dorking, Surrey, a son, Sir Kingsmill Key, who succeeded him in the baronetcy, and three daughters.

[Records of the Corporation of London; City Press, 1858; Orridge's Citizens of London and their Rulers; Foster's Peerage and Baronetage; Kent's and Post Office London Directories.]   C. W-n.

KEY, THOMAS HEWITT (1799–1875), Latin scholar, born in Southwark, London, on 20 March 1799, was the youngest son of Thomas Key, M.D., a London physician, by his second wife, Mary Lux Barry. Charles Aston Key (q. v.), the surgeon, was his half-brother. The family of Key was an old one, settled for six hundred years at Standon in Staffordshire, and for about two hundred of them at Weston Hall. Thomas was educated for nearly ten years at Buntingford grammar school, Hertfordshire, where, under the Rev. Samuel Dewe, Latin, French, and mathematics were especially well taught. In October 1817 he entered St. John's College, Cambridge, and was elected a scholar, but in the spring of 1819 migrated to Trinity College, where he also obtained a scholarship. He graduated B.A. in 1821 (as nineteenth wrangler), M.A. 1824. At his father's desire Key studied medicine (1821–4) at Cambridge and at Guy's Hospital, London. In July 1824 he met in Praed's rooms at Cambridge an accomplished American, Francis W. Gilmer, who had been deputed to select professors for the newly founded university of Virginia at Charlottesville, U.S.A. Key was induced to accept the professorship of pure mathematics, and entered on his duties 1 April 1825. He taught successfully till the autumn of 1827, when he resigned on account of the unsuitability of the climate, and returned to England. In America Key had devoted part of his leisure to the etymological study of Latin (Trent, 'English Culture in Virginia,' in *John Hopkins Univ. Studies*, 7th ser. vols. v–vi., 1889; H. B. Adams, 'T. Jefferson and the Univ. of Virginia,' in No. 2 of *U.S. Bureau of Education Circular of Information*, Washington, 1888). In the autumn of 1828 Key was appointed professor of Latin at the newly founded London University in Gower Street (now University College). In 1842 he resigned this professorship for that of comparative grammar, discharging the duties of the latter chair without salary until his death. In 1833 he had been appointed, jointly with Professor Henry Malden (his contemporary at St. John's College), head-master of the new school attached to University College. From 1842 till his death Key was sole head-master. Between 1868 and 1875 the numbers of the school rose from about four hundred to over six hundred. As a schoolmaster Key was a man of ideas. He introduced the crude-form system of teaching the classical languages, and his school was one of the first in England to include natural science in the ordinary curriculum. Key maintained the discipline firmly but without severity. He died of bronchitis, after a fortnight's illness, on 29 Nov. 1875, and was buried in Highgate cemetery. He married, on 28 Sept. 1824, Sarah Troward, younger daughter of Richard Ironmonger Troward, who had been solicitor to the prosecution in the Warren Hastings trial. Key's wife and seven children survived him.

Key was an enthusiastic and widely read Latin scholar, and had especially a minute acquaintance with Plautus and Terence. His best-known work is his 'Latin Grammar' (published in 1846), a book 'recommended' (says Mr. Robinson Ellis) 'by its simplicity, the newness of its examples, and the clearness with which it presents the elementary or crude forms of Latin words apart from their inflexions.' In January 1831, in reviewing Zumpt's 'Latin Grammar' (*Quarterly Journal of Education*), Key had made the first proposal in print to apply the method of the Sanskrit grammarians to the study and teaching of Latin and Greek, but previously to 1831 the crude-form system had been expounded in his classical lectures. An account of the system is given in Appendix i. in the second and third editions of the 'Latin Grammar.' About 1846 Key had begun to prepare a Latin dictionary for schools; but he abandoned this work, and about 1856 undertook a large dictionary, the manuscript of which, left incomplete at his death, was published without additions in 1888 by the syndics of the Cambridge University Press. The letter A is tolerably complete, but only portions of the remaining letters are finished. The work displays wide reading and originality, though the etymologies have been partly superseded by later philological knowledge (see *Academy, Saturday Review*, and *Spectator*, all of 5 May 1888; *Athenæum*, 21 Sept. 1889). Key's chief works are: 1. 'The Alphabet,' &c. (partly a reprint of his articles from the 'Penny Cyclopædia,' 1833–43), London, 1844, 12mo; 2nd edition, 1849. 2. 'The Controversy about the "Varronianus"' (between Key and J. W. Donaldson, five pamphlets reprinted), London, 1845, 8vo, privately printed. 3. 'A Latin Grammar on the System of Crude Forms,' London, 1846, 12mo; 2nd edition, London, 1858, 8vo; 3rd edition, 1862, 8vo. 4. 'A Short Latin Grammar,' London, 1852, 12mo. 5. 'Philological Essays,' London, 1868, 8vo (partly incorporating papers contributed by Key to the Philological Society). 6. 'Cæsar's Helvetic War,' with translation and notes, pt. i. cc. 1–29, 1872. 7. 'Language, its Origin and Development,' London, 1874, 8vo. 8. 'A Latin-English Dictionary,' Cambridge, 1888, 4to.

Key was a fellow of the Royal Society (elected 1860), and for some years president of the Philological Society of London, to whose 'Transactions' he contributed more than sixty-three papers. He was one of the founders of the London Library, and for some years a member of the committee of the Society for the Diffusion of Useful Knowledge. For the atlas of this society he prepared the maps of 'Gallia' and 'France in Provinces,' and was a contributor to its 'Quarterly Journal of Education,' 1831–2. As a politician, Key was a zealous supporter of the Reform Bill, of the repeal of the corn laws, and of the abolition of the paper duty. He also took an active part in the movement which resulted in the formation of the volunteer force in 1859.

A marble bust of Key by T. Woolner, R.A., subscribed for by old pupils and friends as a testimonial a few months before his death, was presented to University College. Key was tall, and of striking personal appearance. Professor George Long, his contemporary at Trinity College and his intimate friend through life, speaks of him as a man of kindly temperament, unaffected and modest, though bold in his opinions, and as 'a teacher beloved by his pupils.'

[Information kindly furnished by Thomas Key, esq., son of Professor Key, and by J. Power Hicks, esq., of Lincoln College, Oxford, an old pupil and friend of Key's; obituary notice by

George Long in Proceedings of Roy. Soc. No. 169, 1876; art. 'T. H. Key' in Knight's Engl. Cyclop. Biography, 1856 (for this Key supplied information); R. Ellis in the Academy, 4 Dec. 1875, p. 576; Athenæum, 11 Dec. 1875, p. 791; Ward's Men of the Reign, 1885; Brit. Mus. Cat.]

W. W.

KEYES or **KEYS, ROGER** (*d.* 1477), architect and warden of All Souls' College, Oxford, is first mentioned in 1437, when, together with John Druell, afterwards archdeacon of Exeter, he was architect and inspector of works at the building of All Souls' College, Oxford, by Archbishop Chichele [q. v.] He was one of the original fellows of the college, and succeeded Richard Andrews as warden in 1442, holding that post for three years. In 1448 Keyes was summoned by Henry VI to act as clerk of the works for the new royal foundation of Eton College, with a salary of 50*l.* a year. For his services at Eton he and his brother, Thomas Keys, received a grant of arms and patent of nobility from the king on 19 May 1449, and he was collated to the archdeaconry of Barnstaple, 25 Jan. 1449-50. Keyes acted as precentor of Exeter Cathedral in 1467 and 1469, and apparently held the post till his death. In 1469 he made a present of books to Exeter College, Oxford. Keyes died on 11 Nov. 1477, and was buried at Exeter.

[Dict. of Architecture; Burrows's Worthies of All Souls; Bentley's Excerpta Historica; Anthony à Wood's Hist. of Oxford; Willis and Clark's Architectural Hist. of Cambridge; Le Neve's Fasti Eccl. Angl. i. 407, 411.] L. C.

KEYL, FREDERICK WILLIAM (FRIEDRICH WILHELM) (1823-1873), animal painter, born at Frankfort-on-the-Maine on 17 Sept. 1823, showed at an early age a taste for drawing animals, and became a pupil of Eugene Verboeckhoven at Brussels. In May 1845 he came to London for the purpose of studying under Sir Edwin Landseer [q. v.] Landseer received Keyl as a pupil, and became much attached to him. Through Landseer Keyl was introduced to the notice of the queen and the prince consort, and obtained many commissions from the royal family. Keyl was a frequent exhibitor at the Royal Academy and British Institution, though he was naturally averse to exhibiting his works. He died in London on 5 Dec. 1873, and was buried in Kensal Green cemetery. There are three pleasing drawings by Keyl in the print room at the British Museum.

[Redgrave's Dict. of Artists; Graves's Dict. of Artists, 1760-1880; Bryan's Dict. of Painters, ed. Graves; Men of the Reign.] L. C.

KEYMIS, LAWRENCE (*d.* 1618), naval commander. [See KEMYS.]

KEYNES, GEORGE, *alias* BRETT (1630-1659), jesuit, son of Edward Keynes of Compton Pauncefoot and his wife, Ann Brett, both of old Roman catholic families resident in Somerset, was born in 1630, and entered his novitiate as a jesuit at Rome 2 Jan. 1649. He studied at St. Omer, and, having been ordained priest, sailed for the China mission in December 1654, but died at the Philippine Islands in 1659. He published a translation of the 'Roman Martyrology,' of which a second and much enlarged edition was printed at St. Omer in 1667.

[Foley's Records. iv. and vi. 371; Oliver's Collections, p. 125; Visitation of Somerset (Harl. Soc.), vol. xi.] T. S.

KEYNES, JOHN (1625?-1697), jesuit, born at Compton Pauncefoot, Somerset, about 1625, was probably brother of George Keynes [q. v.] After studying humanities in the college of the English jesuits at St. Omer, he removed to the college of St. Alban at Valladolid, and entered the Society of Jesus on 30 July 1645. Subsequently he taught philosophy at Compostella, and theology for nine years at Valladolid, Salamanca, and Pampeluna. He was made prefect of the higher studies at Liège, and obtained permission to devote himself to the care of the English soldiers in the Low Countries while the plague was raging among them. In this service he caught the infection, and for the recovery of his health was sent to England. He was professed of the four vows on 15 Aug. 1662. At the time of the pretended popish plot he was superior of his brethren in the 'college of St. Ignatius' or London district, and although the government diligently searched for him, he succeeded in escaping to the continent in March 1678-9. His name is in the list of the intended victims of Titus Oates, who frequently mentioned Keynes. In 1680 he was appointed rector of the college at Liège, and three years later provincial of the English province, in succession to John Warner. He held the latter office for six years, being succeeded in 1689 by William Morgan. Dr. Oliver states that he governed the province 'with singular ability, prudence, and credit.' The establishment of the jesuit college at the Savoy Hospital in the Strand in 1687, and of the smaller college near the residence of the Bavarian ambassador in the city of London, was effected by Keynes, who also witnessed the destruction of the two colleges at the outbreak of the revolution in 1688. Keynes then withdrew to the continent, and died at Watten, near St. Omer, on 15 May 1697, in his seventy-third year.

He composed 'A Rational Compendious Way to Convince, without any dispute, all Persons whatever dissenting from the true Religion, by J. K.,' *sine loco*, 1674, 12mo. This work was translated into Latin by the author, Liège, 1684, and into French by Gonneau, under the title of 'La Guide des Croyans,' St. Omer, 1688, 8vo. It was answered by Dr. Gilbert Burnet, afterwards bishop of Salisbury, in 'A Rational Method for proving the Truth of the Christian Religion,' London, 1675, 8vo. Keynes was the principal author of 'Florus Anglo-Bavaricus Serenissimo Principi Maximiliano Emmanueli Duci Bavariæ, &c. et Mariæ Antoniæ Leopoldi Cæsaris filiæ, auspicato Nuptiarum faedere conjunctis inscriptus,' Liège, 1685, 4to, pp. 207. The first part of this rare work contains an account of the foundation of the English jesuit college at Liège, with a brief history of that institution, and the second part gives a curious history of Oates's plot, with biographies of the English jesuits who were alleged to be implicated in it.

Southwell erroneously attributes to Keynes the authorship of two pamphlets attacking Stillingfleet, dated 1671 and 1673 respectively. Both were by the jesuit John Warner.

[De Backer's Bibl. de la Compagnie de Jésus; Dodd's Church Hist. iii. 315; Foley's Records, v. 296, vii. 416; Oliver's Jesuit Collections, p. 126; Southwell's Bibl. Scriptorum Soc. Jesu, p. 466.]
T. C.

KEYS, LADY MARY (1540?–1578), third surviving daughter of Henry Grey, third marquis of Dorset [q. v.], by his wife Frances, daughter of Charles Brandon, duke of Suffolk, was born at Bradgate Hall, Leicestershire, probably in 1540. Her sister Lady Jane [see DUDLEY, JANE] and father were beheaded in 1554, and her mother died in November 1559. It would seem that Queen Elizabeth soon after her accession took the two remaining daughters, Mary and her elder sister, Catherine, who were the last representatives of the Brandon line of the Tudor house, as maids of honour into her court, that she might keep close watch over their matrimonial plans. Great was the dismay of all the ministers when, in August 1565, it became known that Lady Mary Grey had secretly married Thomas Keys, the queen's serjeant-porter (Letter of Cecil in WRIGHT, *Queen Elizabeth*, i. 207). The matter was ludicrous, because Mary Grey was almost a dwarf, and Keys, who had been chosen for his office for his size, was of huge proportions. Further, there was the disparity of age and station. Keys was a native of Kent, probably related to Richard Keys of Folkestone, who received from Henry VIII a grant of the monastery of St. Rhadegund in that town. He had been twenty-two years at court, and was a widower with several children. Elizabeth showed her anger by committing Keys to the Fleet, and sending Lady Mary to the care of William Hawtrey at Chequers, Buckinghamshire. In August 1567 she was transferred to the charge of the Dowager Duchess of Suffolk, and in June 1569 to Sir Thomas Gresham. Meanwhile the luckless Keys was pestered by a lawsuit which he had on hand at the time of his committal, and pleaded vainly for release. The question of the legality of the marriage was referred to Grindal, bishop of London, who reported to Cecil that it was impossible to accept a renunciation of the marriage; if its validity was questioned, he must judge according to the evidence. Elizabeth seems to have thought it best to keep the culprits in custody. Keys was liberated from prison in 1568, but was ordered to live at Lewisham; in May 1570 he was at Sandgate Castle, whence he implored Archbishop Parker to intercede on his behalf. On 8 Sept. 1571 he died, and Gresham had to write to Cecil for permission for his widow to wear mourning. She grieved over her husband's death, expressed her determination to keep and bring up his children, and from that time forward signed herself Mary Keys. As she was then harmless to the queen, she was allowed to leave Gresham's custody in 1573, and died in a little house in London on 20 April 1578. She was buried in the church of St. Botolph Without. Her will is given in Strype's 'Annals,' ii. ii. 210–11.

[Burgon's Life of Sir Thomas Gresham, ii. 386 415; Cal. of State Papers, Dom. Elizabeth.]
M. C.

KEYS, SAMUEL (1771–1850), china-painter, born in 1771, was one of the principal gilders and china-painters in the old Derby china factory under William Duesbury the elder [q. v.], to whom Keys was articled. He was an excellent workman, and much of the success of the china, especially the figures in the Dresden style, was owing to his skill in decoration. Keys quitted Derby some years before the close of the factory, and went to work under Minton at Stoke-upon-Trent. He returned later to Derby, where he died in 1850, in his eightieth year. Keys preserved his delicacy of execution to the last. He collected materials for the history of the Derby china factory, which form the foundation of subsequent accounts.

Keys left three sons, all apprenticed at the Derby factory. John Keys (1797–1825) became a skilled flower-painter in water-colour, and teacher of that art. Edward Keys left Derby, and subsequently went to work for

Messrs. Minton, Daniell, and others in the Potteries. Samuel Keys the younger excelled in modelling small figures; he left Derby in 1830, and went to the Potteries, where he carried on a small manufactory of his own, besides working for the leading manufacturers there.

[Haslem's Old Derby China Factory.] L. C.

KEYSE, THOMAS (1722–1800), still-life-painter, and proprietor of the Bermondsey Spa, born in 1722, and a self-taught artist, was a member of the Free Society of Artists, and exhibited with them from 1761 to 1764. He painted skilful imitations of still life, flowers or fruit. From 1765 to 1768 he was an occasional exhibitor at the Society of Artists, and twice sent pictures to the Royal Academy. In 1768 he obtained a premium from the Society of Arts for a new method of setting crayon drawings. About 1770 Keyse opened a tea-garden in Bermondsey, where a chalybeate spring had been found, which was known as the Bermondsey Spa. Here, among other attractions, Keyse kept a permanent exhibition of his own drawings. Obtaining a music license, he made the gardens a kind of Vauxhall, open in the evening during the summer months, and provided fireworks, including a set-piece of the siege of Gibraltar, constructed and designed by Keyse himself. Keyse died at his gardens 8 Feb. 1800, in his seventy-ninth year. The gardens remained open for about five years longer, and their memory is preserved by the Spa Road, Bermondsey. A portrait of Keyse, painted by S. Drummond, A.R.A., was engraved.

[Redgrave's Dict. of Artists; Gent. Mag. 1800, pt. i. 284; Lysons's Environs of London, i. 558; Catalogues of the Free Society of Artists, &c.; Wheatley and Cunningham's London Past and Present.] L. C.

KEYSER, WILLIAM DE (1647–1692?), painter. [See DE KEYSER.]

KEYWORTH, THOMAS (1782–1852), divine and hebraist, son of Thomas Keyworth, a bookseller, of Nottingham, was born in that town in 1782. Going to London as a young man, he was converted from unitarianism by the preaching of Dr. Draper, and entered Cheshunt College to prepare himself for the congregational ministry. Called in the first instance to Sleaford, Lincolnshire, he was afterwards minister successively at Runcorn, Wantage, Faversham, and Nottingham. He also occupied for short periods the pulpits of several London chapels. From 1842 to December 1851 he was in charge of a congregation at Aston Tirrold in Berkshire.

He retired at the close of 1851, and died at Cheltenham on 7 Nov. 1852.

Keyworth was distinguished for modesty and simplicity of character. He was an active advocate of a scheme for garden allotments to the poor, and while in London was an able promoter of missionary work. In addition to his hebraical knowledge, he was no mean scholar in general literature. His chief works are: 1. 'Principia Hebraica,' London, 1817, 8vo (written in conjunction with David Jones). 2. 'A Daily Expositor of the New Testament,' London, 1825, 8vo. 3. 'A Practical Exposition of the Revelation of St. John,' 1828, 8vo. 4. 'A Pocket Expositor of the New Testament,' 1834, 12mo; 2nd edit. 1835.

[Congregational Year-Book, 1853, p. 212; Liverpool Congregational Mag. April 1862, p. 56; Eclectic Review, November 1818; Brit. Mus. Cat.; information from the Rev. Thomas Keyworth.] T. S.

KIALLMARK or **KILMARK**, GEORGE (1781–1835), musical composer, born at King's Lynn in 1781, was the son of John Kiallmark, an officer in the Swedish navy, and of Margaret (or Marggrit, as it is written in the parish register) Meggitt, a Yorkshire heiress, who lived at Wakefield and was a descendant of Sir Joseph Banks. His parents' marriage took place in St. Nicholas's Chapel, Lynn, 4 Oct. 1775. Shortly after George's birth his father, who had run through his property, disappeared and soon died. Thereupon his widow married her butler, a man named Pottle, and George was adopted by his mother's family. He began his education under the care of a Dr. and Mrs. Gardiner (née Meggitt); but he showed at an early age a strong taste for music, and he was placed under a German professor for purposes of musical instruction from 1796 to 1798. For some time after 1798 Kiallmark maintained himself by teaching the violin and piano, and when he had accumulated sufficient funds, took further lessons from Barthelemon, Cobham, and Spagnoletti in violin-playing, and from Von Esch and (later) from Logier in composition. He held many important posts, was a member of all the principal concert and theatre orchestras, and leader of the music at Sadler's Wells. In 1803 he married Mary Carmichael, a cousin of the Countess of Rothes, and settled in Islington, London. Here he devoted himself to teaching the harp, violin, and piano, and soon acquired a large and lucrative connection. He resigned his public engagements, and devoted himself entirely to his pupils and to composition, entering into arrangements with Chappell and D'Almaine to supply them annually with a fixed number of compositions. He died in March 1835, leaving a large family.

His chief works were: 1. Introduction and variations to ' Roy's Wife.' 2. Introduction to ' Last Rose of Summer.' 3. Variations on ' Home, sweet Home.' 4. ' Les Fleurs de Printems,' in six books. Also a number of songs, of which the only one that survives is ' Maid of Athens.' Many of his compositions are still extant in manuscript.

His eldest son, GEORGE FREDERICK KIALLMARK (1804-1887), musician, born at Camden Street, Islington, 7 Nov. 1804, was educated at Margate. He began his musical career at the age of fourteen, assisting his father in the work of musical tuition; afterwards he studied under Logier and taught his system. At sixteen he went to Rouen and thence to Paris to place himself successively under Zimmermann and Kalkbrenner. Returning to England in 1825 he became intimate with Clementi, by whose advice he sought further instruction from Moscheles. In 1829 he married the eldest daughter of Dr. Bryant of the Edgware Road, and gave his first public concert at the King's Theatre in 1832.

When in Paris, Kiallmark formed a great friendship with Thalberg, upon whose method and style he moulded his own. His playing was remarkable for delicacy of touch, and he was a superb player of Chopin's works. On hearing Kiallmark play, Mendelssohn said: ' A fine sketch of what piano-playing should be, and what he will one day make it.' Niecks, in his ' Life of Chopin' (pp. 280-1), writes: ' Kiallmark is said to have had a thorough appreciation and understanding of Chopin's genius;' and he took especial delight in playing Chopin's ' Nocturnes.'

In 1842 Kiallmark opened an academy for the study of the piano at his residence, 29 Percy Street. During his long life he was associated with every great pianist from Clementi to Rubinstein, and at the age of seventy-eight he studied the sonatas of Gade and Rubinstein. At eighty he was still daily practising Clementi's ' Gradus.' He died on 13 Dec. 1887, having only a week before played a Thalberg transcription with much of his old fire and brilliancy. He was a fine extempore player, but his compositions have not survived.

Of the Kiallmarks, father and son, there exist several portraits. Of the father, one by W. Simpson, 1820, half-length, life size. Of the son: one by J. Slater, in ' Musical Keepsake,' 1834; another by H. C. Selous, 1836, three-quarter length, life size; and a third by J. P. Knight, R.A., 1845, three-quarter length, life size. There is also a bust of the younger Kiallmark by Edward H. Baily [q. v.], 1845, companion to a bust of Thalberg by the same sculptor. These are in the possession of the descendants of Kiallmark.

[Georgian Era, iv. 549; Goulding's and Chappell's Catalogues; Mus. Times, January 1888; Dram. and Mus. Rev. 17 Dec. 1842; Niecks's Chopin, 1888, pp. 280-1 notes; Mus. Keepsake, 1834; parish reg.; private sources.] R. H. L.

KIARAN, SAINT (516-549), of Clonmacnoise. [See CIARAN.]

KICKHAM, CHARLES JOSEPH (1826-1882), journalist, was born in 1826 at Mullinahone, co. Tipperary, where his father was a prosperous shopkeeper. He was intended for the medical profession, but a gunpowder accident, when he was returning from shooting, so injured his sight and hearing that this career became impossible. He took part in the ' Young Ireland movement,' and in 1848 busied himself with the preparation of pikes at Mullinahone for the use of the forces of Smith O'Brien.

He became a Fenian about 1860, and in 1865 James Stephens, the Fenian head-centre, appointed him, T. C. Luby, and John O'Leary the supreme executive of his Irish republic, and editors of the ' Irish People' newspaper. Kickham and his associates were not, however, fitted by nature for the business of revolution. Their newspaper was suppressed; the supreme executive was taken into custody, and the rising miserably failed (cf. W. O'BRIEN, *When we were Boys*). Kickham was arrested at Fairfield House, Sandymount, Dublin, on 11 Nov. 1865, was tried for treason felony, and was sentenced to fourteen years' penal servitude. His friends asserted that he was grossly maltreated in prison, and J. F. Maguire, M.P. for Cork city, called the attention of parliament to the subject in 1867 (*Times*, 8, 9, 11, and 27 May 1867). After serving four years in Woking and in Portland convict prisons, he was set at liberty. When the election of O'Donovan Rossa for co. Tipperary in 1869 was declared void, Kickham was brought forward as the nationalist candidate. He was returned, but upon a scrutiny he was defeated by Mr. Heron, Q.C., by four votes, 26 Feb. 1870. He thenceforth confined himself to literary work. About 1878 a ' Kickham Tribute ' was collected for his benefit. He died at Blackrock, near Dublin, on 21 Aug. 1882.

Kickham was the author of several poems and stories dealing with Irish subjects and scenes from a nationalist point of view. These were collected in ' Poems, Sketches, and Narratives illustrative of Irish Life,' 1870.

Sir Charles Gavan Duffy puts him 'next after Carleton, Griffin, and Banim,' and far before Lever and Lady Morgan as a painter of national manners. He also published 'Sally Cavanagh, or the Untenanted Graves,' a novel, 1869 (written in prison); 'Knockagow, or the Homes of Tipperary,' a novel, 1879; and 'For the Old Land, a Tale of Twenty Years Ago,' 1886. His portrait is prefixed to 'Sally Cavanagh.'

[Times, 24 Aug. 1882; Charles Gavan Duffy's Young Ireland; Introduction to James Duffy's edition of Knockagow, Dublin, 1879; Justin H. McCarthy's Ireland since the Union.] J. A. H.

KIDBROOKE, LORD HERVEY OF (d. 1642). [See HERVEY, WILLIAM.]

KIDD, JAMES (1761–1834), presbyterian divine, born on 6 Nov. 1761, was the youngest son of poor presbyterian parents residing near Loughbrickland, co. Down. His father dying soon after his birth, the family removed to Broughshane, co. Antrim. A friendly farmer sent him to a good classical school, and before long enabled him to open a school of his own at Elginy, a neighbouring farm-town. The school was successful, but Kidd found means to go to Belfast to study English. He next set up a school at Kildownie, twenty miles from Belfast. He stayed there about four years, and married Jane, second daughter of Robert Boyd, farmer, of Carnlea, near Ballymena. Kidd and his wife emigrated to America in April 1784; he soon joined Little, a fellow-countryman, in a school at Philadelphia, and next became usher to Pennsylvania College, where he also studied and corrected for the press. The sight of the Hebrew character set him upon learning the language; he bought a Hebrew bible, and with the help of a Portuguese Jew, and by dint of attending the Jewish synagogue in Philadelphia, acquired some fluency in the language. Oriental tongues became thenceforward his favourite study; He returned to Edinburgh, became a student at the university, read chemistry and anatomy, and joined the theological classes of the university, supporting himself by forming extra-collegiate classes in the oriental languages. In the autumn of 1793 he was appointed professor of oriental languages in Marischal College, Aberdeen. He there completed his theological courses, obtained formal license as a preacher from the presbytery of Aberdeen on 3 Feb. 1796, and was appointed evening lecturer in Trinity Chapel in the Shiprow. On 18 June 1801 he became minister of Gilcomston Chapel of Ease, in the immediate suburbs of Aberdeen, where he

preached for above a quarter of a century to one of the most numerous congregations in Scotland. His popularity as a preacher continued undiminished to the end. He was at pains to secure variety and freshness in his preaching, constantly looking out for new illustrations, and keeping up his student's habit of rising at three o'clock every morning. In October 1818 the College of New Jersey conferred on him the honorary degree of D.D. (HEW SCOTT, Fasti Eccl. Scot. vol. iii. pt. ii. pp. 489–90).

Kidd's powerful preaching and vigorous character overcame violent opposition, and ultimately gained for him an extraordinary popularity. It became an article of popular belief that no one who ever resisted 'the Doctor' had prospered. Stories of his courage, benevolence, and eccentricity are numerous. On the accession of George IV he prayed in public that he 'might be a better king than he had been a prince regent,' and when the local authorities complained, asked, 'And where's the man that can't improve?' Kidd not only lectured on vaccination from the pulpit, but employed a medical man to vaccinate his converts, and finally forced hundreds into his own house and vaccinated them himself. He is said to have given a stimulus to the study of Hebrew in the north of Scotland, but was not a very profound hebraist.

Kidd died on 24 Dec. 1834. By his wife, who died on 4 June 1829, he had two sons and three daughters. He was a strenuous supporter of the Anti-patronage Society, and eagerly advocated the popular election of ministers. He was author of: 1. 'A Course of Sermons,' 8vo, Aberdeen, 1808. 2. 'An Essay on the Doctrine of the Trinity: attempting to prove it by reason and demonstration, founded upon duration and space: and upon some of the divine perfections; some of the powers of the human soul; the language of scripture; and tradition among all nations,' 8vo, London, Aberdeen (printed), 1813. 3. 'A Short Treatise on Infant Baptism,' 8vo, Aberdeen, 1822 (also appended to Peter Edwards's 'Candid Reasons for Renouncing the Principles of Antipædobaptism,' 8vo, Aberdeen, 1830). 4. 'A Dissertation on the Eternal Sonship of Christ,' 8vo, Aberdeen, 1822 (new edition, with an introduction, biographical and theological, by R. S. Candlish, 8vo, London, Aberdeen (printed), 1872). 5. 'A Catechism for Assisting the Young preparing to Approach the Lord's Table for the first time,' 18mo, Aberdeen, 1831. 6. 'Rights and Liberties of the Church vindicated against Patronages,' 8vo, Aberdeen, 1834. 7. 'Sermons and Skeletons of Sermons,' 12mo, Aberdeen, 1835. 8. 'A Farewell Address (Recollections),' 12mo, Aberdeen, 1835. He also edited Park's 'Rights and Liberties of the Church,' 1834, and wrote the second part of the preface to 'Memoirs, Diary, and other Writings of Alexander Wood,' 12mo, Aberdeen, 1818.

[Prof. David Masson in Macmillan's Mag. ix. 143–59; Candlish's biog. introduction as above; article in Aberdeen Evening Gazette, 28 March 1892; Hew Scott's Fasti, v. 491.]   G. G.

KIDD, JOHN (1775–1851), physician, born in London 10 Sept. 1775, was son of John Kidd, captain of a merchant vessel, the Swallow, which conveyed Lord Cornwallis out to India as governor-general in 1786. His mother was the daughter of Samuel Burslem, vicar of Etwall, near Derby; she was left a widow in early life with three sons to bring up. John was first sent to the school at Bury St. Edmunds, but in 1789 obtained a king's scholarship at Westminster. There he attracted the special notice of the head-master, Dr. William Vincent [q. v.], afterwards dean of Westminster, who continued his lifelong friend. He was elected to a studentship at Christ Church, Oxford, in 1793. The exceptional ability of Kidd and the schoolfellows elected with him to scholarships at Oxford and Cambridge secured for the election the epithet of 'golden' in the annals of Westminster School (WELCH, Queen's Scholars at Westminster, p. 437). Kidd graduated B.A. in 1797, M.A. in 1800, M.B. in 1801, and M.D. in 1804. He studied at Guy's Hospital for four years, 1797 to 1801, and was for a time a pupil of Astley Paston Cooper [q. v.], with whom he continued on intimate terms for the rest of his life.

On leaving Guy's Kidd took up his residence in Oxford, where he was appointed chemical reader in 1801, and first Aldrichian professor of chemistry in 1803. He was very successful in his chemical experiments, and retained the professorship till 1822, when he resigned in favour of Dr. Charles Giles Bridle Daubeny [q. v.] He was also one of the physicians to the Radcliffe Infirmary from 1808 to 1826, and at one time had a large private practice, chiefly among members of the university. For several years before the endowment by the prince regent of the chairs of mineralogy and geology, Kidd delivered public courses of lectures on those sciences. In 1809 he published his 'Outlines of Mineralogy' (2 vols. 8vo, Oxford), which were reviewed by Dr. Thomas Thomson of Edinburgh in the 'Quarterly Review' (vol. ii.) in an article which Gifford, the editor, altered in some parts as being 'very splenetic and very severe, and much too wantonly so.' Gifford added:

'Kidd is a modest and unassuming man, and is not to be attacked with sticks and stones like a savage' (SMILES, Memoir of John Murray, i. 102). With the assistance of some of his friends he considerably increased the geological collection in the Ashmolean Museum, and also the anatomical and pathological specimens in the Christ Church Museum, when he was appointed Lee's reader in anatomy in 1816. In 1817 he was admitted a candidate of the London College of Physicians, in 1818 he was elected a fellow, and in 1836 he delivered the Harveian oration. In 1822, on the death of Sir Christopher Pegge, regius professor of physic at Oxford, Lord Liverpool, on the recommendation of Sir Astley Cooper (Life of Sir Astley Cooper, ii. 200), appointed Kidd his successor. In this office his principal service to the medical profession was the active part he took in the enactment of what was popularly called after him, 'Dr. Kidd's Examination Statute' for the degree of M.B. He did not lecture as regius professor, but continued the practice of his predecessor of giving courses of non-professional lectures on anatomy and physiology; occasionally, but not often, he procured from London a subject for dissection by the few medical students that were then at Oxford.

Kidd was a deeply religious man, and in 1824 published 'An Introductory Lecture to a Course in Comparative Anatomy, illustrative of Paley's "Natural Theology."' He undertook a similar work on a larger scale when, on the recommendation of Archbishop William Howley [q. v.], he was selected to write one of the eight 'Bridgewater Treatises' (see xvii. 155), for which he received a thousand pounds. Its title was 'On the Adaptation of External Nature to the Physical Condition of Man: principally with reference to the Supply of his Wants and the Exercise of his Intellectual Faculties.' It was published in 1833, and was one of the most popular of the series, reaching a sixth edition in 1852. It is not an original or strictly scientific treatise, as he himself admits in his preface; but the intention of the testator 'seemed to him to require a popular rather than a scientific exposition of facts.' In the appendix he gave an interesting comparison in parallel columns of some points of the zoology of Aristotle and Cuvier. In 1834 Kidd was appointed keeper of the Radcliffe Library. He superintended the compilation of a classed catalogue of the scientific part of the collection (Oxford, 8vo, 1835), and he made the library as convenient as possible to the few readers who then made use of it. This office (for which he was admirably suited, both by his learning and his exact and studious taste) he retained till his death, which took place, after a few hours' illness, on 17 Sept. 1851, at Oxford. He married Miss Savery, daughter of the chaplain of St. Thomas's Hospital, who survived him, and by her had four daughters.

Kidd was 'gifted with a real scientific insight,' and took a prominent part with W. Buckland, Philip Bury Duncan [q. v.], and Charles Giles Bridle Daubeny in the promotion of science at Oxford. His admirable behaviour during the two outbreaks of cholera in Oxford in 1830 and 1848, which is specially commemorated in the printed accounts of both those visitations, illustrates his practical benevolence. The mastership of the hospital at Ewelme, near Oxford, is annexed to the office of regius professor of medicine. The restoration of the hospital, and of such part of the parish church as belongs to it, was carried out during Kidd's mastership; and he introduced some wise regulations for the comfort and welfare of the bedesmen. He was a fellow of the Royal Society, and contributed to the 'Philosophical Transactions' (1815) an ' Essay on the Spontaneous Production of Salt-Petre;' and (1825) an elaborate paper on the '.Anatomy of the Mole-cricket.' He was eminently straightforward, somewhat hasty and hot-tempered, and averse to all show and pretence, so that he is said to have been the first physician in Oxford who laid aside the traditional wig and large-brimmed hat and gold-headed cane.

Besides the works already mentioned Kidd wrote: 1. 'A Geological Essay on the Imperfect Evidence in support of a Theory of the Earth, deducible either from its General Structure, or from the Changes produced on its Surface by the operation of existing Causes,' 8vo, Oxford, 1815. 2. 'An Answer to a Charge against the English Universities in the Supplement to the "Edinburgh Encyclopædia,"' 8vo, Oxford, 1818. 3. 'Observations on Medical Reform,' 8vo, Oxford, 1841, with 'Further Observations,' 1842.

[Picture of the Present State of the College of Physicians in London, 1817, p. 43; Munk's Coll. of Phys. iii. 178; Oxford Chronicle, 20 Sept. 1851; Lancet, 1851, ii. 286; Medical Times, 1851, iii. 315; Daubeny's Inaugural Chemical Lecture, 1823, pp. 7, 8; Acland's Oxford and Modern Medicine, 1890, pp. 12, 14, 17; G. V. Cox's Recollections of Oxford, pp. 133, 431; Pantheon of the Age, ii. 468; private information.]   W. A. G.

KIDD, JOSEPH BARTHOLOMEW (1808–1889), painter, born in 1808, perhaps at Edinburgh, was a pupil of the Rev. John Thomson [q. v.] of Duddingston. On the foundation of the Royal Scottish Academy in 1826 Kidd was elected one of the original associates, and became an academician in 1829. He practised painting at Edinburgh till about 1836, when he came to London, resigning his membership of the Royal Scottish Academy in 1838. He then settled as a teacher of drawing at Greenwich, where he resided until his death in May 1889, at the age of eighty-one. Kidd chiefly painted the scenery of his native country, and executed a few etchings of highland views. Some of his pictures were engraved. Not long before his death he painted a portrait of the queen for the Royal Hospital Schools, Greenwich.

[Redgrave's Dict. of Artists; Athenæum, 25 May 1889; Queen, 18 May 1889.]   L. C.

KIDD, SAMUEL (1804–1843), missionary at Malacca and professor of Chinese at University College, London, born 22 Nov. 1804 at Welton, near Hull, was educated at the village school of that place. In 1818 he was sent to Hull, where his thoughts were directed towards a missionary career, and in 1820 he entered the London Missionary Society's training college at Gosport. In April 1824 he married Hannah, second daughter of William Irving of Hull. At the end of the same month he sailed under the auspices of the London Missionary Society to Madras, and thence to Malacca, where he arrived in the November following. He at once began the study of the Fuhkien dialect of Chinese, and under the advice and direction of the Rev. David Collie made rapid progress. In the course of 1826 he published several small tracts in Chinese, and in the year following he was appointed professor of Chinese in the Anglo-Chinese College of Malacca. From this time he took an active part in missionary labours, preaching constantly and preparing tracts for publication. In 1829 Mrs. Kidd was obliged to return to England on account of her health, and three years later attacks of epilepsy, to which he had become subject, compelled Kidd himself to adopt the same remedy. He had fully intended to return to Malacca, but the state of his health forbade him, and in 1833 he was appointed pastor of a church at Manningtree in Essex. In 1837 he was appointed professor of Chinese at University College, London, for a term of five years. It was understood at the time of his nomination that his appointment would be renewed at the end of that term, but the condition was disregarded, and it was while the matter was in debate that he died suddenly on 12 June 1843, at his residence in Camden Town. Besides a number of small Chinese tracts, Kidd was the author of ' Critical

Notices of Dr. Robert Morrison's Literary Labours' in 'Memoir of Morrison,' 1838, ii. 1–87; an inaugural lecture at University College on the Chinese language, 1838; a catalogue of the Chinese library at the Royal Asiatic Society; and 'China, or Illustrations of the Philosophy, Government, and Literature of the Chinese,' London, 1841, 8vo.

[Evangelical Magazine, 1843, p. 585; Gent. Mag. 1843, pt. ii. p. 209; information kindly supplied by W. G. B. Page, esq., of Hull.]

R. K. D.

KIDD, THOMAS (1770–1850), Greek scholar and schoolmaster, born in 1770, was the son of Thomas Kidd of Kidd, Yorkshire. After being educated at Giggleswick school under Paley, he was entered as a sizar of Trinity College, Cambridge, on 14 Dec. 1789, where he took the degrees of A.B. (as fifth junior optime) in 1794 and A.M. in 1797. He was for some time second master of Merchant Taylors' School, and in 1818 was appointed head-master of Lynn school; he next became master of Wymondham school, and lastly of Norwich. Having taken holy orders, he was successively instituted to the rectory of St. James, Garlick Hythe, London, in 1802; to that of Croxton, Cambridgeshire, in 1813; to the vicarage of Eltisley, Cambridgeshire, in 1814; to that of Bedingham, Norfolk, in 1831; and, for a second time, to both the vicarage of Eltisley and the rectory of Croxton in 1835.

At Cambridge Kidd became acquainted with Porson, who was considerably his senior, and his affection and reverence for him influenced his whole life. Though himself a genuine Greek scholar and steeped in Greek literature, he is chiefly remembered for editing the critical works of others. Thus he edited Ruhnken's minor works, Dawes's 'Miscellanea Critica,' as well as the very valuable volume of Porson's 'Tracts and Criticisms.' He took especial interest in collecting lists of the works of several of the chief English and Dutch scholars. In his preface to 'Opuscula Ruhnkeniana' there is a complete list of Tyrwhitt's works, while his collation of Tyrwhitt's smaller pieces is in the Dyce collection at South Kensington Museum. In his review of Sluiter's 'Lectiones Andocideæ' in the 'British Critick' for October 1805 he catalogues Valckenaer's criticisms and classical editions. It was due to him that the collection of Bentley's books, which had lain neglected at Lackingtons, was in 1807 rescued and obtained for the nation (Gent. Mag. November 1807, p. 1047). At one time he contemplated an edition of Homer, and a series of very elaborate criticisms on the Grenville edition from his pen will be found in the 'Critical Review' for 1803 and 1804. He reviewed R. P. Knight's 'Analytical Essay on the Greek Alphabet' in the 'Gentleman's Magazine' for October and November 1797, and Valpy's 'Greek Grammar' in the 'British Critick' for June 1806; contributed some 'curæ novissimæ' of Bentley on Horace to the 'Museum Criticum' (i. 194), and wrote in the 'Classical Journal,' among other articles, 'On the Quantity of a final short Vowel before sc,' &c. (i. 71, 283), 'Ionic Temple in Blenheim Gardens' (ii. 521, 897), notices of Bishop Pearson's minor works in vols. vii. ix. xii. xiii. xvii., and 'Literary Coincidences' in vols. xvii. and xxxvii. His English style is sometimes confused, and always quaint. His 'imperfect outline of the Life of R. P.,' was prefixed to Porson's 'Tracts and Criticisms.' Beloe, in his 'Sexagenarian' (i. 138), in a short account full of errors, calls him 'the modern Parson Adams.' He married, in 1801, Miss Smith of Hoxton Square. In 1842 Lord Melbourne gave him a civil list pension of 100l. A strong testimonial to his merits as a Greek scholar and to his general character, from the pen of Dr. Parr, will be found in Barker's 'Parriana,' i. 372. He died 27 Aug. 1850, and is buried in Croxton churchyard.

His published works are: 1. 'Opuscula Ruhnkeniana,' London, 1807. 2. 'Tracts and Criticisms of the late R. Porson, Esq.,' London, 1815. 3. 'Horatii Opera ad exemplar recensionis Bentleianæ plerumque emendata et brevibus notis instructa,' Cambridge, 1817. 4. 'Ricardi Dawesii Miscellanea Critica,' Cambridge, 1817; 2nd edit., 1827. 5. 'A Sermon preached at the Visitation of the Archdeacon of Norwich, May 10, 1831.' Letters from him will be found in Parr's 'Correspondence' (Works, ed. Johnstone, viii. 215–19) and Porson's 'Correspondence' (Cambr. Ant. Soc.), p. 113.

[Gent. Mag. 1850, pt. ii. p. 557; Foster's Index Eccl. 1800–40, p. 104.] H. R. L.

KIDD, WILLIAM (d. 1701), pirate, is said to have been a native of Greenock, to have settled in Boston, Massachusetts, to have commanded a trading vessel in the West Indies, and to have distinguished himself in command of a privateer during William III's war with France. In 1695, when the Earl of Bellomont was appointed governor of Massachusetts Bay, with especial instructions to suppress the piracy which infested the coast, Robert Livingstone, a man of good repute in the colony, brought Kidd to the earl's notice in London as a fit man for the work [see COOTE, RICHARD, EARL OF

BELLOMONT]. Bellomont's suggestion to the admiralty that Kidd should be appointed to the command of a small ship of war was judged irregular, and it was determined to send him out in command of a privateer, with, in addition to the ordinary letter of marque, a special commission under the great seal empowering him to seize and bring in such pirates as he should meet with on the coast of America or elsewhere. Kidd and Livingstone undertook to pay one-fifth of the expenses; Bellomont paid the other four-fifths, in conjunction with Orford, then first lord of the admiralty, Somers, the lord chancellor, Romney, a secretary of state, and Shrewsbury, one of the lords justices. A vessel named the Adventure was accordingly fitted out, and sailed from Plymouth in May 1696. After visiting New York, where she raised her complement of men to 155, the Adventure proceeded to Madagascar, then known as the haunt of pirates. In the course of 1698 and the beginning of 1699 complaints reached the government that Kidd, instead of capturing or destroying the pirates and preying on the king's enemies, was himself a very active pirate, seizing and plundering native ships belonging to friendly powers. Orders were sent out to Lord Bellomont to apprehend Kidd if he should return to North America; and accordingly, when he returned to Boston in July 1699, he was thrown into gaol. He admitted that acts of piracy had been committed, but alleged that he at the time had been overpowered by a mutinous crew and imprisoned in the cabin. Others of the ships taken were sailing under French passes, and were legal prizes, but the desertion of his men, who had joined the pirates, had prevented his sending them in to be condemned. He affirmed, moreover, that the Adventure being no longer seaworthy had been destroyed, and Kidd and the few men who had remained loyal were (according to his own account) on their way home in the Quedah Merchant, a richly laden ship of some 400 tons, which had a French pass and had been captured under French colours, when, touching at the island of Hispaniola, he heard that he had been proclaimed a pirate, and that a warrant was out for his apprehension. Leaving the Quedah Merchant, he bought a small sloop, and came on to Boston to know the truth. Bellomont was anxious to learn where the Quedah Merchant had been left; her cargo, he wrote to England, was, by the best computation he could make, worth about 70,000l. Kidd, however, declined to give any information, and the ship was apparently never found. Some small part of the treasure

was seized in the sloop; a portion that he had buried in Gardiner's Island was not recovered by the government; but, like the larger amount left in the ship, it was probably at the disposal of Kidd's friends. Popular traditions which recount its burial, and the failure of attempts to recover it, enormously exaggerate its value; even of the estimated 70,000l. the greater part was in perishable bale goods. In the spring of 1700 Kidd and his companions were sent to England in the Advice frigate, and on their arrival on 8 April were taken in charge by the marshal of the admiralty, who also seized Kidd's papers (*Admiralty Minute*, 14 April 1700). The enemies of the government now charged the subscribers to the Adventure's equipment with having fitted out a notorious pirate, and attempts were especially made to implicate Somers, who had not only subscribed, but had affixed the great seal to Kidd's commission. The charge was formally preferred in the House of Commons, and was debated with all the virulence of faction, but was too evidently absurd to be affirmed by a majority. In the following May, Kidd, with several of his crew, was put on his trial at the Old Bailey. He was charged with the murder of one Moore, the gunner of the Adventure, whom he had hit violently on the head with a bucket. His defence was that Moore was mutinous and insolent, and that he had knocked him down in a fit of passion; but the judge directed the jury that it was done with malice prepense, and was therefore murder. He was further charged with piratically seizing and plundering six different ships. His defence was that the ships were sailing under French passes, and were legal prizes according to the terms of his commission. These passes, he said, he had preserved, but they had been taken from him, and Lord Bellomont and the admiralty had refused to restore them. No further inquiry was made for them by the court; he had no properly constituted legal adviser or counsel; the only witnesses against him were two of the Adventure's men, who were accepted as king's evidence. The judge summed up against him; he was found guilty of murder and piracy, was with several of his companions sentenced to death, and was duly hanged at Execution Dock on 23 May 1701. Whatever may have been Kidd's crimes, it is clear that he had not a fair trial, and was found guilty on insufficient evidence. Kidd's effects to the value of 6,472l. 1s. were forfeited to the crown, and the money was given by Queen Anne to Greenwich Hospital in 1705 (LYSONS, *Environs*, iv. 448).

[Johnson's General History of the Pirates; Macaulay's History of England (Cab. ed.), viii. 240-4. Macaulay's account is more than usually inaccurate. Kidd was brought to Lord Bellomont's notice in London, not in New York; and the whole story, as told in brilliant language with picturesque detail, is very doubtful. The contemporary pamphlets, which give the commonly accepted account. are: Articles of Agreement made this 10th day of October 1695 between the Right Honourable Richard, Earl of Bellomont, on the one part, and Robert Levingston, Esq., and Capt. William Kid of the other part (printed 1701); The Arraignment, Trial, and Condemnation of Captain William Kidd for Murder and Piracy. . . . Perused by the Judges and Council (fol. 1701); A True Account of the Behaviour, Confession, and last Dying Speeches of Captain William Kidd and the rest of the Pirates . . . (1701); A Full Account of the Proceedings in relation to Captain Kidd, in two Letters written by a Person of Quality to a kinsman of the Earl of Bellomont . . . (4to, 1701). Lord Bellomont's Official Correspondence in the Public Record Office (Colonial, Board of Trade, New England, vol. ix.) gives a full account of Kidd's arrest; one paper, 24 June 1699, is a letter from Kidd, apparently written and signed by himself. Cf. Admiralty Minutes, 8-15 April 1700. Watson's Annals of Philadelphia (ii. 212) is very inaccurate.]   J. K. L.

KIDD, WILLIAM (1790?-1863), painter, born about 1790 in Edinburgh, was first apprenticed to a house-painter, but on the completion of his term made his way to London to study painting. He was an enthusiastic admirer of the works of Alexander Carse [q. v.] and of Sir David Wilkie, and determined to paint domestic scenes from Scottish life in their manner. He first exhibited at the Royal Academy in 1817, and at the British Institution in 1818, and was from that time a frequent contributor to both exhibitions, and also to the Society of British Artists in Suffolk Street. Kidd was very successful in depicting the pathos and humour of rustic life, and his pictures have maintained their popularity. Many were engraved, such as 'The Poacher Detected,' by T. Lupton, the same picture as 'Le Braconnier Pris,' and another, 'Le Baiser Surpris,' in aquatint by P. Jazet at Paris; 'Indulging,' by J. H. Watt; 'The Poacher's Snare,' by J. Stewart, &c. In 1849 Kidd was elected an honorary member of the Royal Scottish Academy. Never able to manage his own affairs, Kidd fell at the end of his life into hopeless financial embarrassment, and was supported finally by his friends and a pension from the Royal Academy. He died in London on Christmas eve, 1863. A picture by him, 'Contemplating the Times,' was lent to the Century of British Art Exhibition at the Grosvenor Gallery in 1888-9 (No. 29).

[Redgrave's Dict. of Artists; Graves's Dict. of Artists, 1760-1880; Catalogue of Century of British Art Exhibition, Grosvenor Gallery, 1888-9.]   L. C.

KIDD, WILLIAM (1803-1867), naturalist, born in 1803, was apprenticed early in life to Baldwin, Craddock, & Joy, a firm of London booksellers. He afterwards entered business on his own account, and had shops successively in Chandos and Regent Streets. While at Chandos Street he published a 'Guide o Gravesend,' 'Popular Little Secrets,' and other short essays written by himself. Between May and October 1835 he published twenty-four numbers of a weekly 'London Journal' dealing with natural history ; from 1852 to 1854 he brought out a similar monthly periodical called 'Kidd's Own Journal,' which was subsequently reissued in five volumes, royal 8vo, and during 1863-4 he issued ten numbers of 'Essays and Sketches' on miscellaneous subjects. By that date he had sold his business, and devoted himself entirely to his favourite studies. He was always an earnest student of nature, and he possessed an astonishing gift of endearing himself to animals. In the later years of his life he resided in the New Road, Hammersmith, and set up a fine aviary, which was burnt down and never rebuilt. Kidd was an independent and eccentric thinker and talker on religious and social subjects, and delivered many lectures in various parts of the country on such subjects as 'Genial Gossip,' 'Fashion and its Victims,' 'The Value of Little Things,' and 'Happiness made comparatively easy' (*Liverpool Mercury*, 8 March 1856). He died at Hammersmith, 7 Jan. 1867. He was married and his wife survived him.

As a naturalist Kidd's chief works were: 'The Canary,' London, 1854 ; 'The Aviary and its Occupants,' two parts, 1856, and a number of small books on the goldfinch, the linnet, and other British songsters, which are still valuable. He also wrote an introduction to Westcott's 'Autobiography of a Gossamer Spider,' 1857, and, in conjunction with F. Buckland, several papers in 'Birds and Bird Life,' 1863, besides contributing papers on birds and kindred subjects to the 'Gardeners' Chronicle' and similar periodicals. A long series of tracts and essays which he published on very miscellaneous subjects are either weakly imitative of Leigh Hunt, or characterised only by ignorance and superficiality. The chief of these pamphlets are: 1. 'The Heart's Proper Element.' 2. 'The World and its Two Faces,' 1854. 3. 'Honest Thoughts for Plain and Honest People.' 4. 'The Strange Spirits of the Day, or a Rap for the Rappers.' 5. 'Friendly Appeals to the People' (only two numbers published). 6. 'Example, its Power for Good or Evil,' 1855. 7. 'The Charmed Ring.' 8. 'Man, viewed with Reference to his Words, his Deeds, and his Motives.' 9. 'Life, its Tints and its Shadows,' 1856.

[Gent. Mag. 1867. pt. i. p. 247; Athenæum, 12 Jan. 1867; Kidd's Works.]   M. G. W.

KIDDER, RICHARD (1633–1703), bishop of Bath and Wells, was born at East Grinstead in Sussex in 1633. His father belonged to the class of yeomen or lesser gentry. His mother was a woman of great piety, of puritan sympathies. He was educated at a grammar school in the neighbourhood under the mastership of a Mr. Rayner Harman, of whom he speaks in the highest terms. He was sent to an apothecary at Sevenoaks to study medicine; but his friends raised a sum of money to send him to Cambridge, and in June 1649 he was admitted as a sizar at Emmanuel College. Samuel Cradock [q. v.], then a fellow of the college, directed his studies, encouraged him in a religious life, and helped him with money. He graduated B.A. in 1652, and in 1655 was elected fellow of Emmanuel. In 1658 he was ordained deacon and priest, in one day, by Dr. Brownrigg, the deprived bishop of Exeter. The ordination took place in a private house at Bury St. Edmunds. In 1659 the vicarage of Stanground, Huntingdonshire, which was in the gift of his college, fell vacant, and Kidder was appointed to it. In 1662 he was ejected by the Bartholomew Act, because he 'did not think fit to subscribe to what he never saw,' that is, of course, the amended Book of Common Prayer. He declares that he had 'never taken the covenant or engagement, was entirely satisfied in episcopacy, and with a liturgy; had no hand in the late confusions, and was so far from it that he lamented them, and was deprived of his living only for not subscribing to a book that was not, as it ought to have been, laid before him.' For a time he took chance duty in London and the country, but in 1664, having by that time 'conformed,' he was appointed by Arthur, earl of Essex, to the rectory of Raine (now spelt Rayne), near Braintree. He found the people 'factious to the last degree,' and used to call the ten years he spent among them 'the lost part of his life.' The great plague of London in 1665 spread to Essex, and added to his troubles;

and he also lost (not through the plague) three children there. In 1674 he was offered the living of St. Helen's in London by Sancroft, then dean of St. Paul's, who had known him at Emmanuel College; but though he officiated there for a while, and was much pleased with the people, he would not be instituted on the terms of refusing the holy communion to those who would not kneel. He was appointed also in 1674 preacher at the Rolls by Sir Harbottle Grimston [q. v.], the master, and in the same year was presented by the Merchant Taylors' Company to the rectory of St. Martin Outwich, the next parish to St. Helen's. Soon afterwards he was also chosen to be a week-day lecturer at Blackfriars. In 1680 he lost three children by the small-pox. He was now a popular preacher, and was offered various preferments. In 1681 he was appointed to a prebend at Norwich by the lord chancellor, the Earl of Nottingham, and a few years later was twice chosen lecturer of Ipswich, but declined both times. In 1688 his old friend Sancroft, now archbishop of Canterbury, offered him the living of Sundridge, Kent, and he was also recommended by Robert Nelson to Tillotson, then dean of St. Paul's, for the living of Barnes, but he accepted neither preferment.

In 1689, soon after the accession of William and Mary, he was made one of the royal chaplains, without his knowledge, and was also appointed on the royal commission to consider such alterations in the liturgy, &c., as might give satisfaction to the dissenters in connection with the Comprehension Bill. He prepared a new version of the Psalms, but the commission had not time to examine it. In the same year, on the elevation of Dean Patrick to the see of Chichester, he was appointed by the crown dean of Peterborough, and finally, through the instrumentality of Tillotson, now archbishop of Canterbury, was offered the bishopric of Bath and Wells, of which Thomas Ken had been deprived. He says that he was very unwilling to accept the see, but after some days consented. He afterwards thought that he had not been wise; for 'though he could not say that he had acted against his conscience, he did not consult his ease,' and often repeated. He was consecrated at Bow Church on 30 Aug. 1691, and 'presently took up his residence at Wells.' 'I am sure,' he says, 'no man living could come into a place with a more hearty desire to do good than I did.' But his position was most unfortunate, for the whole sympathies of the diocese were probably with his deprived predecessor, Ken. Ken himself greatly disliked the appointment, and spoke of Kidder as a 'latitudinarian traditor,' a 'hireling.'

who, 'instead of keeping his flock within the fold, encouraged them to stray,' 'a stranger ravaging his flock.' Kidder seems to have been continually in trouble with the cathedral chapter; they refused to attend his ordinations, thinking that he ordained nonconformists without having properly ascertained that they had really become churchmen. The whole tone of his charges to the clergy, and also of his autobiography, shows his false position. Kidder and his wife were both killed in their bed in the palace at Wells by the falling of a stack of chimneys through the roof in the great storm of 26 Nov. 1703.

Few men were more obnoxious to high churchmen than Kidder, but it is hardly fair to charge him, as he has been charged, with being a mere time-server. He refused many offers of preferment, including at least one bishopric, that of Peterborough; and his literary work, if nothing else, certainly pointed him out for advancement. A story is told, much to his credit, that in 1696-7 it was intimated to him that he must go up to the House of Lords and vote for the attainder of Sir John Fenwick, and upon his replying that he must wait to know the merits of the case, he was asked, 'Don't you know whose bread you are eating?' To which he replied, 'I eat no man's bread but poor Dr. Ken's,' and, to show his principles, went up and voted against the bill. The story that he made the deprived bishop an allowance from the see is apocryphal.

Kidder was a most industrious and, in many respects, valuable writer. His first work of any importance was entitled 'Convium Cœleste: a Plain and Familiar Discourse concerning the Lord's Supper.' It was published in 1674, but was a reprint of what he had preached to his recalcitrant parishioners at Raine some years before. In 1684 he published the first part of his 'Demonstration of the Messias.' Other parts were published at different times, and the whole was not completed until 1700. In 1693 he was appointed Boyle lecturer, and he inserted the substance of the lectures he then delivered in the 'Demonstration.' It was intended in the first instance to promote the conversion of the Jews, and his knowledge of Hebrew and the oriental languages well qualified him for the task; but it was also directed against the arguments of the deists. In 1684 he undertook the translation of Dr. Lightfoot's works into Latin. In 1694 he published 'A Commentary on the Five Books of Moses, with a Dissertation concerning the Author of the said Books, and a general Argument to each of them,' 2 vols. This was part of a joint work which was to be executed by

London clergymen for the use of families. It was to have embraced the whole of the Old and New Testaments, but the scheme fell through because the attention of the writers was diverted to the Roman controversy. In 1692 he published 'A Charge to the Clergy of his Diocese at his Primary Visitation begun at Oxbridge June 2, 1692.' In 1698 appeared his 'Life of Anthony Horneck'[q.v.] His last work was a posthumous one, 'Critical Remarks upon some Difficult Passages of Scripture, in a Letter to Sir Peter King,' 1719 and 1725.

Kidder also published a vast number of sermons, tracts, and fugitive pieces. Of the sermons the first was entitled 'The Young Man's Duty; a Discourse showing the necessity of seeking the Lord betimes,' &c., which was published as early as 1663, and became so popular that it reached a tenth edition in 1750; 'The Christian Sufferer Supported,' 1680, a sermon preached at Guildhall Chapel on 16 July 1682; a funeral sermon on Mr. W. Allen, a London citizen who wrote in defence of the church of England, on 17 Aug. 1686; another on Thomas Pakeman in 1691; one 'On the Resurrection,' 1694; 'Twelve Sermons preached upon several occasions,' 1697; and 'A Discourse concerning Sins of Infirmity and Wilful Sins,' and another 'Of Restitution,' which were to be distributed among the poor of his diocese, and were sent to the press a very short time before his death. His 'Tracts against Popery' include 'A Second Dialogue between a new Catholic Convert and a Protestant, shewing why he cannot believe the Doctrine of Transubstantiation' (1686); 'An Examination of Bellarmine's Thirteenth Note of the Church, Of the Confession of Adversaries' (1687); 'The Judgment of Private Discretion in Matters of Religion Defended' (1687) (this was originally preached as a sermon at St. Paul's, Covent Garden, 1686); 'Texts which the Papists cite for proof of their Doctrine of the Sacrifice of the Mass examined' (1686); 'Reflections on a French Testament printed at Bordeaux in 1686; pretended to be translated out of the Latin into French by the Divines of Louvain' (1690). Among his tracts on other subjects were 'Charity Directed, or the Way to give Alms to the greatest advantage, in a Letter to a Friend' (1677); 'A Discourse of the Sacraments,' with some heads of examination and prayers (1684); 'Help for Children's understanding the Church Catechism' (undated). He also collected a number of Hebrew proverbs, which were published in an appendix to Ray's 'Collection of Proverbs.' Some Latin letters passed between him and Le Clerc on the meaning of Genesis xxxvi. 31. Both Le Clerc and Du Pin had a high opinion of Kidder's powers.

[Autobiography of Bishop Kidder, first published in Cassan's Lives of the Bishops of Bath and Wells; Dean Plumptre's and other biographies of Bishop Ken; Hunt's Religious Thought in England; Kidder's own writings.]   J. H. O.

KIDDERMINSTER, RICHARD, D.D. (d. 1531), abbot of Winchcombe. [See KEDERMYSTER.]

KIDGELL, JOHN (fl. 1766), divine, baptised on 28 April 1722 at St. Mary Woolnoth, London, was son of John Kidgell of St. Mary Woolchurch (Registers, ed. Brooke and Hallen, p. 100). He was admitted to Winchester in 1733 (KIRBY, Winchester Scholars, p. 238), matriculated at Oxford from Hertford College on 21 March 1740–1, graduated B.A. in 1744, and M.A. in 1747 (FOSTER, Alumni Oxon. 1715–1886, ii. 792), and was elected fellow. He was a man of some talent, but dissolute and dishonest. James Douglas, earl of March and Ruglen (afterwards the well-known Duke of Queensberry), appropriately appointed him his chaplain. In 1756 he was assistant-preacher to the Bishop of Bangor, in December 1758 became rector of Woolverston, Suffolk (Addit. MS. 19105, f. 250), and by 1761 was morning preacher at Berkeley Chapel, London. On 14 May 1762 he was instituted to the rectory of Godstone, Surrey (MANNING and BRAY, Surrey, ii. 337), and on 24 June following to that of Horne in the same county (ib. ii. 320–1). He habitually neglected his duty, and lived as a man about town, under the auspices of Lord March. Walpole describes him as a 'dainty, priggish parson, much in vogue among the old ladies for his gossiping and quaint sermons' (Reign of George III, i. 311). When in 1763 the government wanted a second copy of Wilkes's 'Essay on Woman,' Kidgell secured one of the proof-sheets, and by the treachery of one of Wilkes's printers succeeded by degrees in procuring the whole. This he handed to Lord March, who was in secret consultation with Lord Bute and Lord Sandwich. He then attempted to defend his conduct and replenish his purse by publishing 'A genuine and succinct Narrative of a scandalous, obscene, and exceedingly profane Libel, entitled "An Essay on Woman,"' &c., 4to, London, 1763, which completely blasted his reputation. An attempt on the part of Lord Sandwich to obtain for him the wealthy rectory of St. James, Westminster, failed (NICHOLS, Literary Anecdotes, ix. 650), and Kidgell, who was deeply in debt, had to fly the country, and is said

to have died in Flanders (BRAYLEY and BRITTON, Surrey, iv. 148). In June 1766 the churchwarden of Horne instituted proceedings against him in the court of arches for non-residence, but the cause, as being 'improperly begun,' was dismissed ' for the present' (Ann. Reg. ix. 105).

Kidgell was author of: 1. 'The Card' [anon.], 2 vols. 12mo, London, 1755, a series of tales partly in the epistolary form. 2. ' Original Fables,' in English and French, 2 vols. 12mo, London, 1763. Both were printed for private circulation only. In the ' Oxford Sausage' (ed. 1764, pp. 119–24) are some amusing lines by him, entitled ' Table Talk,' which were written in 1745.

[Kidgell's Works; pamphlets in answer to his Narrative, 1763; Forster's Charles Churchill, 1855, p. 93; Gent. Mag. 1768, p. 613.]   G. G.

KIDLEY, WILLIAM (fl. 1624), poet, was son of John Kidley of Dartmouth, Devonshire, where he was born in 1606. In matriculating at Oxford he gave his name as Kidley, alias Pointer. He entered at Exeter College on 16 July 1625, and graduated B.A. 12 Nov. 1627. He speaks, in a marginal note interpolated in the work noticed below, of returning to the college after a twelve years' absence, apparently in 1639. In 1624 he composed in his leisure ' A Poetical Relation of the Voyage of Sr Richard Hawkins [q. v.], Knight, unto Mare del Zur,' and ' History of the year 1588, wth other Historical Passages of these Tymes (during the Raigne of the B. Q. Elizabeth).' Hawkins's account of his voyage to the South Sea had been published in 1622. Kidley's poem, which is now among the manuscripts at the British Museum (Sloane Coll. 2024), and has not been printed, is entitled ' Kidley's Hawkins.' It was designed to be in eight books, but six only were completed. Kidley refers to other attempts made by him in verse, both at Oxford and at Dartmouth.

[Wood's Athenæ Oxon. ed. Bliss, ii. 367–74; Foster's Alumni Oxon. 1500–1714.]   T. B. S.

KIFFIN or **KIFFEN**, WILLIAM (1616–1701), merchant and baptist minister, was born in London early in 1616. His family appears to have been of Welsh descent. Both his parents died of the plague which broke out in June 1625. His father left property which was invested by some relatives in their business; on their failure little was saved. Kiffin was apprenticed in 1629 to John Lilburne (1618–1657) [q. v.], a brewer; he left Lilburne in 1631, and seems to have been apprenticed to a glover. In that year he attended the sermons of many puritan divines, including John Davenport

q. v.] and Lewis du Moulin [q. v.], but attached himself next year to John Goodwin [q. v.] the independent. He joined a religious society of apprentices, and became (1634) a member of the separatist congregation gathered in Southwark by Henry Jacob (1563–1624) [q. v.], and then ministered to by John Lathrop [q. v.] Kiffin preached occasionally. In 1638, during the ministry of Henry Jessey [q. v.], he and others became baptists, and seceded to the particular baptist church at Wapping, under John Spilsbury. Early in 1641 he was arrested at a Southwark conventicle and committed by Judge Mallet to the White Lion prison, bail being refused. Mallet was himself committed to the Tower in the following July, whereupon Kiffin obtained his release. On 17 Oct. 1642 he was one of four baptist disputants encountered at Southwark by Daniel Featley [q. v.]

In 1643 Kiffin began business in woollen cloth on his own account with Holland. His success was encouraging, and he rapidly became rich. In 1647 he was parliamentary assessor of taxes for Middlesex. In 1649 he made good use of the five weeks' grace before the coming into force of restrictions upon the import of foreign goods. In 1652, on the outbreak of the Dutch war, he gained money and privileges by furnishing requisites for the English fleet. Meanwhile he was pursuing his religious labours. His name heads in 1644 the signatories to a confession of faith drawn up by seven churches 'commonly (but unjustly) called anabaptists.' Joshua Ricraft, a presbyterian merchant, attacked him (1645) as 'the grand ringleader' of the baptists. Thomas Edwards (1599–1647) [q. v.] assailed him in 1646 as a 'mountebank,' and as adopting the 'atheistical' practice of unction for the recovery of the sick (Gangræna, iii. 19). Kiffin had offered in vain (15 Nov. 1644) to discuss matters publicly with Edwards in his church (St. Botolph's, Aldgate). He joined Hanserd Knollys [q. v.] in a public disputation (1646) at Trinity Church, Coventry, with John Bryan, D.D. [q. v.], and Obadiah Grew, D.D. [q. v.] In January 1649 parliament, in response to a petition from Ipswich, gave him liberty to preach in any part of Suffolk. He travelled in that county with Thomas Patience, or Patient, his assistant. He corresponded also (1653) with the baptist churches in Ireland and Wales. His settlement with the congregation, which, on 1 March 1687, opened a meeting-house in Meeting-house Yard, Devonshire Square, London, is usually dated in 1653. But as early as 1643 Kiffin and Patience ministered to this congregation, which consisted of seceders from Wapping practising close communion. On 12 July 1655

Kiffin was brought before John Dethick, the lord mayor, for preaching that infant baptism was unlawful, a heresy visited with severe penalties under the 'draconick ordinance' of 1648. The execution of the penalty seems to have been indefinitely postponed. A contemporary pamphlet ('The Spirit of Persecution again Broke Loose,' &c., 1655, 4to) contrasts this leniency to baptists with the severity used towards John Biddle [q. v.]

Between 1654 and 1659 Kiffin is spoken of as captain and lieutenant-colonel in the London militia. This may account for his arrest, and the seizure of arms at his house in Little Moorfields, shortly before the Restoration, in 1660, by order of Monck, who was quartered near him. He was released by order of the common council, and the arms were restored to him. A more serious trouble befell him later in the year. A forged letter, dated 21 Dec. 1660, and professing to come from Taunton, implicated him in an alleged plot, following the death of the Princess of Orange (24 Dec.) He was arrested on 29 Dec., and kept in the guard-house at Whitehall, but released on 31 Dec. by Sir Robert Foster [q. v.], the chief justice, the date and other circumstances proving the letter a forgery. On 7 Jan. 1661 Venner's insurrection broke out. Kiffin at once headed a 'protestation' of London baptists, but nevertheless was arrested at his meeting-house and detained in prison for four days.

About 1663 he gave evidence before a committee of the House of Commons, and before the privy council, against granting to the 'Hamburg Company' a monopoly of the woollen trade with Holland and Germany. His evidence is said to have permanently impressed Charles II in his favour, and to have gained him the goodwill of Clarendon. A year later he was arrested at the instance of George Villiers, second duke of Buckingham [q. v.], on suspicion of being concerned in an anabaptist plot against the king's life. He addressed a letter to Clarendon, and was at once released by the privy council, and though a prosecution was threatened nothing came of it. On two occasions, in 1670 and 1682, Kiffin, when prosecuted for conventicle-keeping, successfully pleaded technical flaws in the proceedings. On two other occasions (one in 1673) he obtained interviews with the king, securing the suppression of a libel against baptists, and the pardon of twelve Aylesbury baptists who had been sentenced to death under 35 Eliz. c. 1. Crosby relates that Charles wanted a loan of 40,000l. from Kiffin, who made him a present of 10,000l., and said afterwards that he had thus saved 30,000l. In 1675 he took part in a scheme for ministerial education among baptists; and in the following year went into Wiltshire, to aid in dealing with the Socinian tendencies of Thomas Collier [q. v.] In 1683 his house was searched on suspicion of his complicity with the Rye House plot; his son-in-law, Joseph Hayes, a banker, was tried for remitting money to Sir Thomas Armstrong [q. v.], and narrowly escaped with his life, 'a jury of merchants' (BURNET) refusing to convict him. Treasonable letters were forwarded to Kiffin; he at once placed them in the hands of Judge Jeffreys. Two of his grandsons, Benjamin and William Hewling, the former being just of age, were executed (Benjamin at Taunton on 30 Sept., William at Lyme Regis on 12 Sept. 1685) for having joined the Monmouth rebellion. Kiffin offered 3,000l. for their acquittal, but 'missed the right door,' not having gone to Jeffreys. The latter is said to have remarked to William Hewling: 'You have a grandfather who deserves to be hanged as richly as you' (cf. MACAULAY, cap. v. popular edit. p. 316). Though his near relatives were thus involved, Kiffin himself was neither a plotter nor, in any active sense, a politician.

On the revocation (1685) of the edict of Nantes, Kiffin maintained at his own expense an exiled Huguenot family of rank. Both on constitutional and on anti-popish grounds he refused to avail himself of James II's declaration for liberty of conscience (April 1687), and did all in his power to keep his denomination from countenancing it; not a single baptist congregation admitted the dispensing power, though prominent individual baptists did, e.g. Nehemiah Cox. In August 1687 James sent for Kiffin to court, and told him he had included his name as an alderman for the city of London in his new charter. Kiffin pleaded his age and retirement from business, and reminded the king of the death of his grandsons. 'I shall find,' said James, 'a balsam for that sore.' Kiffin was put into the commission of the peace and the lieutenancy. He delayed four months before qualifying as alderman, and did so at length (27 Oct. 1687) because there was no limit to the fine which might have been imposed on him. He gave 60l. towards the lord mayor's feast, but would not have done so had he known the papal nuncio (Cardinal Ferdinand Dada) was invited. For nearly a year he held office as alderman of Cheap ward, being succeeded on 21 Oct. 1688 by Sir Humphrey Edwin [q. v.]

After the death of Patience (1666) he was assisted in his ministry by Daniel Dyke (1617–1688) [q. v.] and Richard Adams (d. 1716). He resigned his charge in 1692. He

died on 29 Dec. 1701 in his eighty-sixth year, and was buried in Bunhill Fields; the inscription on his tomb is given in Stow's 'Survey,' ed. Strype, 1720. His portrait was in 1808 in the possession of the Rev. Richard Frost of Dunmow, Essex, a descendant; an engraving is given in Wilson, and reproduced in Orme and Ivimey. He married late in 1634; his wife, Hanna, died 6 Oct. 1682, aged 66. His eldest son William died 31 Aug. 1669, aged 20; his second son died at Venice, and was supposed to have been poisoned; Harry, another son, died on 8 Dec. 1698, aged 44. His daughter Priscilla (d. 15 March 1679) married Robert Liddel.

Kiffin published: 1. 'A Glimpse of Sion's Glory,' &c., 1641, 4to. 2. 'The Christian Man's Trial,' &c., 1641 (ANGUS). 3. 'Observations on Hosea ii. 7, 8,' &c., 1642 (ib.) 4. 'A Letter to Mr. Edwards,' &c., 1644, 12mo (dated 15 Nov.) 5. 'A Briefe Remonstrance of the . . . Grounds of . . . Anabaptists for their Separation,' &c., 1645, 4to (answered by Ricraft in 'A Looking-glass for the Anabaptists,' &c., 1645, 4to). 6. 'A Declaration concerning the Publicke Dispute,' &c., 1645, 4to (by Kiffin, Hanserd Knollys [q. v.], and Benjamin Cox [q. v.]) 7. 'Walwyn's Wiles,' &c., 1649 (ib.) 8. 'A Letter to the Lord Mayor, by Lieut.-Col. Kiffin,' &c., 1659, fol. 9. 'A Sober Discourse of Right to Church Communion,' &c., 1681, 12mo (against open communion, in reply to Bunyan). He wrote prefaces to an edition of Samuel How's 'The Sufficiency of the Spirit's Teaching,' &c., 1640, 4to, and to 'The Quakers Appeal Answered,' &c., 1674, 8vo, and edited, with a continuation, the 'Life of Hanserd Knollys,' 1692, 8vo. He spelt his name Kiffen and (later) Kiffin, which is the form given in the 1677 directory; Featley calls him Cufin.

[Kiffin wrote his autobiography to 1693; the manuscript was used by Wilson, Dissenting Churches of London, 1808, i. 400 sq., and edited by Orme as Remarkable Passages in the Life of William Kiffin, 1823; it is also incorporated in Ivimey's Life of Kiffin, 1833. See also Discourse between Captain Kiffin and Dr. Chamberlain, 1654; the Life and Approaching Death of William Kiffin, 1659 (an abusive pamphlet); Burnet's Own Time, 1724, i. 599 sq.; English Presbyterian Eloquence, 1720, p. 141; Pike's Ancient Meeting Houses, 1870, p. 689; Crosby's Hist. of English Baptists, 1738–40, i. 215 sq., ii. 180 sq., iii. 4 sq.; Tracts on Liberty of Conscience, 1846, p. 315; Records of Broadmead, Bristol, 1847, pp. xcii, 123, 149, 359; Confessions of Faith (the last three Hanserd Knollys Soc.), 1854, pp. 17, 23, 26, 310, 326; Macaulay's History; London Directory of 1677, 1878; Angus's Early Baptist Authors, 1886.]   A. G.

KILBURN, WILLIAM (1745–1818), artist and calico-printer, born in Capel Street, Dublin, in 1745, was only son of Samuel Kilburn, architect, of Dublin, and Sarah Johnston his wife. He showed an early taste for drawing, and was apprenticed to John Lisson, an English calico-printer at Leixlip, near Dublin, but devoted much of his spare time to drawing and engraving. The family was in embarrassed circumstances at the father's death, and Kilburn came to London, where he obtained a good sale for his calico designs. He also became acquainted with William Curtis [q. v.] the botanist, and executed the exquisite plates of flowers, drawn and engraved from nature, for Curtis's 'Flora Londinensis.' He was able to return to Ireland and fetch his mother and sister, settling with them in Page's Walk, Bermondsey. Soon afterwards he accepted the management of Newton's calico-printing factory at Wallington, Surrey; after seven years he purchased the business. The beauty of his designs established him as one of the most eminent calico-printers in Europe, and he acquired great wealth. He induced Edmund Burke to introduce a bill into parliament to secure to calico-printers the copyright of original designs. He died at Wallington on 23 Dec. 1818, in his seventy-third year. Kilburn married the eldest daughter of Thomas Brown, an East India director, by whom he left a large family.

[Gent. Mag. 1818, cii. 222; Webb's Compendium of Irish Biography.] L. C.

KILBURNE, RICHARD (1605–1678), Kentish topographer, born in 1605, was the fifth and youngest son of Isack Kilburne of London, by Mary, daughter of Thomas Clarke of Saffron Walden, Essex (*Visitation of London*, 1633–5, Harl. Soc. ii. 31; KILBOURNE, *Family of Kilbourn*, pedigrees facing p. 8). He was baptised, 6 Oct. 1605, at St. Mary Woolchurch Haw (*Registers*, ed. Brooke and Hallen, p. 314). He entered Staple Inn, became an eminent solicitor in chancery, and was five times principal of his inn. By 1631 he had entered into possession of Fowlers, an estate in the parish of Hawkhurst, Kent, which he greatly improved. As a J.P. for the county he was deputed for three or four years during the commonwealth to celebrate weddings at Hawkhurst without sacred rites, but married only two couples (*Archæologia Cantiana*, ix. 263). In 1650 he appears as steward of the manors of Brede and Bodiam, Sussex. In 1657 he published as an epitome of a larger work 'A Brief Survey of the County of Kent, viz. the names of the parishes in the same; in what bailiwick ...

and division ... every of the said Parishes is ...; the day on which any Market or Faire is kept therein; the ancient names of the Parish Churches, &c.' (oblong quarto); it is exceedingly rare. Two years later Kilburne issued his promised 'larger survey' entitled 'A Topographie, or Survey of the County of Kent, with ... historicall, and other matters touching the same, &c.,' 4to, London, 1659, to which his portrait by T. Cross is affixed. Although mostly a meagre gazetteer, the book contains much curious information about Kilburne's own parish of Hawkhurst (cf. *ib.* v. 59). Kilburne was also author of 'Choice Presidents upon all Acts of Parliament relating to the office and duty of a Justice of Peace ... as also a more usefull method of making up Court-Rolls than hath been hitherto known or published in print,' of which a third edition, 'very much enlarged,' was 'made publick by G. F. of Gray's Inn, Esq.,' in 1685, 12mo, London. An eighth edition appeared in 1715.

Kilburne died on 15 Nov. 1678, aged 74, and was buried in the north chancel of Hawkhurst Church, where there is a flat stone to his memory (HASTED, *Kent*, fol. ed. iii. 71). He married, first, Elizabeth, daughter of William Davy of Beckley, Sussex, by whom he had six sons and three daughters, and secondly, in 1656, Sarah, daughter of James Short, and apparently widow of one Birchett, who brought him no issue (cf. Kilburne's will registered in P. C. C. 6, King). A portrait of Kilburne was engraved by Cook (EVANS, *Cat. of Engraved Portraits*, i. 195). A few of Kilburne's letters, preserved among the Frewen MSS. at Brickwall, Northiam, Sussex, have been printed in 'Sussex Archæological Collections' (xvi. 302–4).

[J. R. Smith's Bibl. Cantiana, p. 4; Sussex Arch. Coll. ii. 167, ix. 295; Granger's Biog. Hist. of England, 2nd edit. iii. 118; Marvin's Legal Bibliography.] G. G.

KILBYE, RICHARD (1561?–1620), biblical scholar, born of humble parentage at Ratcliffe on the Wreak, Leicestershire, about 1561, matriculated at Oxford from Lincoln College on 20 Dec. 1577, and was elected fellow on 18 Jan. 1577–8 (*Oxf. Univ. Reg.*, Oxf. Hist. Soc., vol. ii. pt. ii. p. 75, pt. iii. p. 77). He was admitted B.A. on 9 Dec. 1578, M.A. in 1582, B.D. and D.D. in 1596 (*ib.* vol. ii. pt. i. pp. 139, 198, 263). On 10 Dec. 1590 he was elected rector of Lincoln College (LE NEVE, *Fasti*, ed. Hardy, iii. 557), and became prebendary of Lincoln Cathedral on 28 Sept. 1601 (*ib.* ii. 188). In 1610 he was appointed regius professor of Hebrew (*ib.* iii. 514). He died on 7 Nov. 1620, and was buried in the college chancel of All Saints' Church, Oxford. By his will he gave to the parish a double-gilt chalice and 50s. to buy a silver-gilt paten. Both utensils are still in use in the church.

Kilbye, who was an able preacher, published a funeral sermon on Thomas Holland (d. 1612) [q.v.], 4to, Oxford, 1613. He was one of the translators of the Bible appointed by James I in 1604, and took part in the version of the prophetical books. He wrote also Latin commentaries on 'Exodus,' part ii. of which came into the possession of William Gilbert, fellow of Lincoln, and prepared a continuation of John Mercer's commentary on 'Genesis' (1598), but was not allowed to print it.

[Wood's Athenæ Oxon. (Bliss), ii. 287.]

G. G.

KILDARE, EARLS OF. [See FITZTHOMAS, JOHN, d. 1316, first EARL; FITZGERALD, THOMAS, d. 1328, second EARL; FITZGERALD, MAURICE, 1318–1390, fourth EARL; FITZGERALD, THOMAS, d. 1477, seventh EARL; FITZGERALD, GERALD, d. 1513, eighth EARL; FITZGERALD, GERALD, 1487–1534, ninth EARL; FITZGERALD, THOMAS, 1513–1537, tenth EARL; FITZGERALD, GERALD, 1525–1585, eleventh EARL.]

KILDELITH, ROBERT (d. 1273), chancellor of Scotland. [See KELDELETH.]

KILHAM, ALEXANDER (1762–1798), founder of the 'methodist new connexion,' was born of methodist parents at Epworth, Lincolnshire, on 10 July 1762. As a lad of eighteen he worked at Owston Ferry, Lincolnshire. Returning to Epworth he joined the Methodist Society, during a local revival of methodism, and began to preach in his twenty-first year, his first sermon being at Luddington, Lincolnshire. In 1783 he was engaged, as travelling companion and assistant in preaching, by Robert Carr Brackenbury of Raithby Hall, Lincolnshire, a gentleman of fortune in delicate health, and one of Wesley's followers. Kilham travelled with Brackenbury in Lincolnshire, and accompanied him to Jersey, where Brackenbury conducted a mission. In June 1784 they returned to England. Brackenbury was admitted on the regular list of itinerant preachers at the conference in July. Kilham, on the advice of William Dufton, had applied (6 June 1784), and he was regularly admitted at the conference in July of the following year. He was employed in the Grimsby circuit, where he encountered opposition from his patron's brother, Edward Brackenbury, vicar of Skendleby, Lincolnshire. To secure his position he registered

himself under the Toleration Act. His appointments for the next few years were in Yorkshire.

On Wesley's death (2 March 1791) Kilham, though under thirty, at once became an energetic leader of the party opposed to the restriction, in the interests of the established church, of methodist operations. In May 1791 the Hull circular, officially issued by that circuit, advised methodists not to rank themselves as dissenters, but to meet only out of church hours, and to receive the Lord's Supper only in the parish churches. Kilham prepared a reply (anonymous), which was adopted by the Newcastle-on-Tyne circuit. He repudiated Wesley's personal dictation, on scriptural grounds, and argued that methodists were de facto dissenters, and their preachers qualified to administer all Christian ordinances. The conference at Manchester in July passed over Thomas Coke, D.C.L. [q.v.], the conservative leader, and elected as president William Thompson, a moderate man. Kilham was appointed to Newcastle-on-Tyne, where he was ordained by Joseph Cownley. The latter had been ordained by Wesley himself. The preachers in this circuit began (January 1792) to administer the Lord's Supper. An angry controversy ensued, to which Kilham contributed a printed 'Address.' He was summoned to the 1792 conference, held in London, and censured for his pamphlet by a large majority, Coke even moving his expulsion. The conference transferred him to Aberdeen, where he was stationed for three years. The conference of 1793 conceded the right of preachers to administer the Lord's Supper under certain restrictions.

In 1794 Kilham wrote, but did not publish, a pamphlet, signed 'Martin Luther,' denouncing the hierarchical scheme drawn up at a private meeting in Lichfield [see COKE, THOMAS, D.C.L.], and was especially severe on Alexander Mather, whom Wesley had ordained in 1788 as a 'superintendent.' The 1794 conference was marked by fierce debates; an address on the sacrament question presented by Kilham was ordered to be torn up by the president. The resolutions actually arrived at went too far in their concessions to suit the conservative leaders, and a stormy agitation was raised throughout the body. Kilham published a pamphlet, signed 'Aquila and Priscilla,' going over the whole ground of controversy. Shortly before the conference met in Manchester in 1795 he issued his 'Martin Luther' pamphlet. During the meeting of the conference he printed another in Manchester, signed 'Paul and Silas,' vindicating the progressive nature of Wesley's principles of organisation. The conference adopted a 'plan of pacification,' which Kilham thought had 'an appearance of duplicity.' He wished to remain in Scotland, but the conference appointed him to Alnwick, Northumberland. Here he printed a new pamphlet, 'The Progress of Liberty,' pleading for the recognition of popular rights in the organisation of methodism. For this he was arraigned before successive district meetings, but decision was referred to the conference. Kilham meanwhile issued several fresh pamphlets, including an 'Appeal' to his circuit (24 May 1796).

The conference of 1796, held in London, at once proceeded to try Kilham on charges founded on his various publications, which certainly contained an undue proportion of invective. Such expressions as 'persecuting Neros,' applied to methodist leaders, he was prepared to explain, but not to withdraw. On the other hand, his agitation was viewed, absurdly enough, as inspired by the political principles of Thomas Paine. After three days' trial he was condemned by a unanimous vote, and solemnly 'expelled from the connexion,' all the preachers (about one hundred and fifty) standing up, and each one attesting the justice of the proceeding by signing a paper which was placed on the communion-table. Efforts were made to induce Kilham to express penitence and apply for restoration. Six days after his expulsion he wrote to the president asking whether the sentence removed him from the society, and whether he could retain a place among the 'local' as distinct from the itinerant preachers. The reply was an offer to confer with him on condition that his letter might be taken as an acknowledgment of fault. He made a conciliatory response, and met a delegation from conference. Negotiation was at an end as soon as he was informed that he must bind himself by the 'plan of pacification.'

Kilham spent the next few months in visiting his sympathisers in the north of England. In October, acting on the suggestion of Moir of Aberdeen, he began a monthly magazine, 'The Methodist Monitor.' The first step towards a separation from the main body of methodism was taken at Leeds, where Ebenezer Chapel, purchased from the baptists, was opened by Kilham on 5 May 1797. In July the conference met at Leeds. Kilham had been appointed a lay delegate, but did not present himself. The conference definitely decided against the admission of lay representatives, either to its own meeting or to district meetings, or to form 'a second house of legislature.' On 9 Aug. Kilham, with three preachers who had with-

drawn from the conference, met a number of laymen in Ebenezer Chapel, and formed a 'new methodist connexion,' Kilham becoming the secretary. The total number who joined the new society was about five thousand. Kilham was now stationed at Sheffield. In January 1798 his magazine appeared as the 'Methodist New Connexion Magazine.' The organisation of the new body was completed at its conference held in Sheffield at Whitsuntide 1798, when Kilham was removed to Nottingham.

Late in 1798 he undertook a journey with a view to extending his connection in Wales. He returned to Nottingham at the end of November, completely exhausted, yet struggled on with some of his engagements. He died at Nottingham on 20 Dec. 1798, at the early age of thirty-six. He was buried in Hockley Chapel (now primitive methodist), Nottingham. A marble monument to his memory was removed (before 1838) to Parliament Street Chapel, Nottingham. His portrait, engraved by W. Collard from a likeness taken in 1797, is prefixed to his 'Life,' 1838. An earlier engraving, from a drawing taken after death, is less satisfactory. He married, first, at Easter 1788, Sarah Grey of Pickering, North Riding of Yorkshire (d. 1797), by whom he had, besides children who died in infancy, a daughter Sarah, who became Mrs. Biller; secondly, on 12 April 1798, Hannah, daughter of Peter Spurr of Sheffield, by whom he had a posthumous daughter, who died in infancy. His widow, Hannah Kilham, who became a quakeress, is separately noticed.

Kilham's publications have only a denominational interest. Had he lived it is not improbable that he might have brought his new connexion (now numbering over thirty thousand members) into reunion with the main body. The subsequent course of methodism may be taken as vindicating his cause. He injured it by an occasional virulence of aspersion that was not in harmony with his general character.

[Life of Mr. Alexander Kilham (1799), an autobiography with additions; Life, 1838, based on original materials furnished by his widow and daughter; Townsend's Alexander Kilham (1889); Myles's Chronological Hist. of Methodists (1799); Tyerman's Life and Times of John Wesley, 1871, iii. 408, 504.]   A. G.

KILHAM, MRS. HANNAH (1774–1832), missionary and student of African languages, born at Sheffield on 12 Aug. 1774, was seventh child of Peter and Hannah Spurr, respectable tradespeople of Sheffield. Although brought up as a member of the established church, she was permitted to attend Wesley's early morning services, and at the age of twenty joined the Wesleyans. Her mother's death when she was twelve (1786) placed her at the head of the household, which consisted of her father and five brothers. Two years after her father died, and she was sent to a boarding-school at Chesterfield, where she made more rapid progress than her master approved. On 12 April 1798 she became the second wife of Alexander Kilham [q. v.], founder of the 'methodist new connexion,' who died at Nottingham eight months later (20 Dec. 1798). Mrs. Kilham thereupon opened a day-school in Nottingham, spending the vacations at Epworth, her husband's early home. There she became acquainted with the quakers, and in 1802 joined their society. She returned to Sheffield, and though still teaching, busied herself in philanthropic work. She originated a Society for the Bettering of the Condition of the Poor, which proved a model for many others.

In 1817 Mrs. Kilham commenced to study the best means of reducing the unwritten languages of Africa to print, so that the natives might be instructed in Christianity, and produced an elementary grammar for the children in missionary schools at Sierra Leone. From two native African sailors who were being educated at Tottenham Mrs. Kilham acquired a good knowledge of the Jaloof and Mandingo languages, and in 1820 printed anonymously 'First Lessons in Jaloof.'

In October 1823, under the auspices of the 'Friends' committee ' for promoting African instruction,' she sailed with three of their missionaries and the two native sailors for St. Mary's, in the Gambia. Here she at once started a school, and made herself readily understood in Jaloof to the natives on the coast. She taught also at Sierra Leone, and in July 1824, after thoroughly reconnoitring the fields of labour, she returned to England to report to the committee of Friends. On her arrival she at once proceeded to Ireland, and spent several months at work under the ' British and Irish Ladies' Society ' for relief of the famine. On 11 Nov. 1827 she once more started for Sierra Leone, taking with her a number of 'African School Tracts' (London, 1827), which she had published in the interval. She visited Free Town and the villages round, and in little more than two months put into writing the numerals and leading words in twenty-five languages. The state of her health s oon compelled her to return home again, but on 17 Oct. 1830 she set out on her third and last voyage to Free Town. Having obtained permission from the governor to take

charge of all children rescued from slaveships, Mrs. Kilham, with the aid of a matron, founded a large school at Charlotte, a mountain village near Bathurst, and spent the rainy season there with her pupils. She then proceeded to Liberia (the Free State), visited the schools in Monrovia, and arranged for sending the children of the most influential natives to England to be trained. About 23 Feb. 1832 she sailed for Sierra Leone. The vessel was struck by lightning, and put back to Liberia. Mrs. Kilham never recovered from the shock, and died three days afterwards, at sea, on 31 March 1832. There is a silhouette portrait of her in the Friends' picture gallery at Devonshire House, Bishopsgate Street.

Besides the works above mentioned Mrs. Kilham was the author of several smaller educational books: 'Scripture Selections,' London, 1817; 'Lessons on Language,' 1818; 'Family Maxims,' 1818; 'First Lessons in Spelling,' 1818; 'Report on a Recent Visit to Africa,' 1827; 'The Claims of West Africa to Christian Instruction,' 1830, &c. Her step-daughter, Mrs. Sarah Biller of St. Petersburg, edited her memoirs and diaries in 1837.

[Life of Alexander Kilham, Nottingham, 1799; Memoir of Mrs. H. Kilham, by her step-daughter, S. Biller, London, 1837; a Sketch of H. Kilham by Mrs. C. L. Balfour, London, 1854; Letters of H. K., reprinted from the Friends' Magazine, London, 1831 ; Smith's Catalogue.]

C. F. S.

KILIAN, SAINT (d. 697), apostle of Franconia. [See CILIAN.]

KILKENNY, WILLIAM DE (d. 1256), bishop of Ely and keeper of the seal, was possibly a member of the Durham family of Kilkenny, but was no doubt of Irish descent (SURTEES, Hist. Durham, ii. 229 ; Hist. Dunelm. Script. Tres, pp. lxxii. lxxiv. lxxv, Surtees Soc.) He is first mentioned as one of the royal clerks in 1235, when he was sent by Henry III on a mission to the emperor Frederic (SHIRLEY, Royal and Historical Letters, i. 463, 475). Some time previously to 1248 he was made archdeacon of Coventry; he also held the prebend of Consumpta per Mare at St. Paul's, London (LE NEVE, Fasti, i. 368 ; ii. 379). In 1251 the abbey of Tewkesbury had to provide him with a benefice worth forty marks (Ann. Mon. i. 147, Rolls Ser.) Between Michaelmas 1249 and February 1252 he attests the accounts of Peter Chaceporc, one of the keepers of the wardrobe. In 1250 Kilkenny and Peter de Rivallis were temporarily entrusted with the seal (Rot. Claus. 34 Hen. III, m. 15). Shortly afterwards Kilkenny received the sole charge, according to Matthew Paris in the same year (1250) (iv. 130), but certainly before May 1253, when it was entrusted temporarily to Peter Chaceporc and John de Lexington, 'because William de Kilkenny was ill' (*Rot. Fin.* 37 Hen. III, m. 9). Kilkenny was again in sole possession in the following July (MADOX, *Exchequer*, i. 69). Matthew Paris speaks of him in 1254 as a clerk and special councillor of the king, who was then honourably discharging the duties of chancellor (v. 464). At Michaelmas of this year Kilkenny was chosen bishop of Ely, and the royal assent was given to his election on 25 Dec. He thereupon resigned the seal on 5 Jan. 1255, and on 15 Aug. was consecrated by Archbishop Boniface at Belley in Savoy; the performance of the ceremony abroad is said to have angered the bishops and the canons of Canterbury (*ib.* v. 464, 485, 508; LE NEVE, i. 329). Kilkenny made peace with the abbot of Ramsey respecting the boundaries of the abbey and the episcopal property in the fens (MATT. PARIS, v. 576), and gave the monks the churches of Melbourn and Swaffham. In June 1256 Kilkenny was appointed to go on a mission to the king of Castile, and seems to have departed next month (*Fœdera*, i. 343, Record ed.) He died at Surgho in Spain on 22 Sept., and was buried there, but his heart was brought back to be interred in his own cathedral (MATT. PARIS, v. 588). By his will Kilkenny left his church a cope, and two hundred marks for two chaplains to pray for his soul (WHARTON, *Anglia Sacra*, i. 634). He was also a benefactor of the hospital of St. John the Evangelist at Cambridge (MULLINGER, *Hist. Univ. Cambr.* p. 233).

Matthew Paris calls Kilkenny 'cancellarics,' b it Foss says that he had only found two instances in which he is called by that title, both in 37 Hen. III, 1253-4 (*Fœdera*, i. 238; *Abbrev. Placit.* p. 133); while in the quittance granted to him at the close of his service he is described as 'Custos sigilli nostri in Anglia' (MADOX, *Exchequer*, i. 71). It therefore seems probable that he was simply keeper, and not chancellor. Matthew Paris describes him as 'a truly modest, faithful, and well-read man, skilled in the canon and civil law, handsome in person, and eloquent and prudent' (v. 130, 464). It does not appear whether or no he was a relative of the lawyer, Odo de Kilkenny, who was concerned in the riot at Oxford in 1238 (*ib.* iii. 483-4).

[Matthew Paris (Rolls Ser.); Foss's Judges of England. ii. 375-7; authorities quoted.]
C. L. K.

KILKERRAN, LORD (1688-1759), Scottish judge. [See FERGUSSON, SIR JAMES.]

KILLEN, JOHN (*d.* 1803), Irish rebel, kept an eating-house at the corner of Thomas Street, Dublin. Killen was arrested for participation in Emmet's movement of 23 July 1803. His trial commenced on 7 Sept. before Mr. Baron Daly. Two informers, Michael Mahaffey and John Ryan, pedlars by trade, swore that on the night of 23 July they were met by an armed mob, of whom Killen was one, and were forced to take pikes in their hands and join the insurrection. They also testified to a definite act of cold-blooded murder committed by Killen himself. On the other side, however, numerous witnesses, among them James Crosbie, an army pensioner, swore positively that on the commencement of the outbreak, at nine o'clock in the evening of 23 July, Killen had locked his door, and had not only not gone out himself, but had tried to prevent others from doing so. He and several of the witnesses, in fact, had, it was stated, remained in the cellar at Thomas Street till the morning of 24 July. James Smith, Killen's landlord, moreover testified to his character for loyalty. The evidence in Killen's favour was ably summarised and commented on by Curran, who defended him. The judge, however, summed up against the prisoner, and the jury brought in a verdict of guilty. A careful reading of the whole case points to the conclusion that this decision was entirely unjust. Killen protested bitterly from the dock against the verdict, but no reprieve was granted. He was executed on 10 Sept. 1803.

[Hibernian Magazine for 1803: Killen's Trial, in Howell's State Trials, vol. xxviii.]
G. P. M-Y.

KILLEN, THOMAS YOUNG (1826-1886), Irish presbyterian divine, son of Edward Killen, a merchant in Ballymena, co. Antrim, was born at Ballymena on 30 Oct. 1826. His boyhood was spent at Glenwherry, to which his father removed in 1832. He was principally taught by a private tutor, and in 1842 entered the old Belfast College, where he took several prizes. At the close of his fifth session he was sent by the mission board of the general assembly as a missionary to Camlin, co. Roscommon, where he laboured for two years. On 19 May 1848 he was licensed to preach by the presbytery of Carrickfergus, and on 25 Sept. 1850 was ordained by the presbytery of Letterkenny as minister of 3rd Ramelton, co. Donegal, where his pastorate proved very successful. In 1857 he received a call from the congregation of Ballykelly, co. Londonderry, and was installed there on 31 March. He took a leading part in the Ulster revival of 1859. In 1862 he became one of the ministers of

Belfast, being installed on 26 Feb. as the first minister of the new Duncairn Church, which prospered so much under his care that it was twice enlarged. He rose to be one of the foremost ecclesiastics of the Irish general assembly, of which in 1882 he was elected moderator. In 1883 the degree of D.D. was conferred on him by the presbyterian theological faculty (Ireland). He died suddenly on 21 Oct. 1886, leaving a widow and seven children.

He was author of 'A Sacramental Catechism' (Belfast, 1874), which ran through several editions, and was republished in America. For four years he edited a monthly magazine, the 'Evangelical Witness,' and on the establishment of the 'Witness' newspaper in Belfast he wrote much in its columns. He also published several sermons and tracts.

[Personal knowledge.] T. H.

KILLIGREW, ANNE (1660–1685), poetess and painter, daughter of Dr. Henry Killigrew (q. v.), master of the Savoy, was born in 1660 in St. Martin's Lane, London, shortly before the Restoration, and was christened privately, as the offices of the common prayer were not then publicly allowed. Her father was chaplain to the Duke of York, and in due course she became maid of honour to Mary of Modena, duchess of York; but in her twenty-fifth (or twenty-sixth?) year she was attacked by small-pox, and in June 1685 she died in her father's rooms in the cloisters of Westminster Abbey. She was buried 15 June 1685 in the chancel of St. John the Baptist's Chapel in the Savoy (entry in register, communicated by the late Rev. Henry White). According to the copy of the inscription upon her monument, and given in her poems of 1686, since destroyed by fire, she died on 16 June.

In 1686 a quarto volume, 'Poems by Mrs. Anne Killigrew,' was published. To the hundred pages of verses there was prefixed a mezzotint engraving of the author by Becket, after a painting by herself, and by way of introduction there was Dryden's ode 'To the pious memory of the accomplished young lady, Mrs. Anne Killigrew, excellent in the two sister arts of Poesy and Painting.' Johnson considered this ode to be the noblest in our language—a judgment then bold and now scarcely intelligible. Her own verses are forgotten, but she seems to have been a woman of sincere piety and much charm of character. Dryden alludes to paintings of James II and his queen by Anne Killigrew, and to pictures of country scenery. Three of her paintings are mentioned in her poems, and six others were sold in her brother Ad-

miral Killigrew's collection in 1727. Besides Becket's engraving of Anne Killigrew, an engraving was made by Chambers from her own painting for Walpole's 'Anecdotes of Painting;' and there is a scarce mezzotint from the same painting by Blooteling. Lowndes mentions large-paper (folio) copies of Anne Killigrew's 'Poems,' with a portrait different from that in the ordinary copies.

[Ballard's Memoirs of Several Ladies of Great Britain, 1742, pp. 337–45; Wood's Athenæ Oxon. ed. Bliss, iv. 623; Loftie's Memorials of the Savoy, 1878, pp. 199–206; Cibber's Lives of the Poets, ii. 224–6; Granger's Biog. Hist. 1775, vol. iv. class x. p. 129; Boase and Courtney's Bibliotheca Cornubiensis, 1874, i. 286; Walpole's Anecdotes of Painting, 1849, ii. 456, 457; Miss E. C. Clayton's English Female Artists, pp. 59–70.] G. A. A.

KILLIGREW, CATHERINE or KATHERINE, LADY (1530?–1583), a learned lady, wife of Sir Henry Killigrew (q. v.), was the fourth daughter of Sir Anthony Cooke, knt. (q. v.), of Giddy Hall, Essex, by Alice, daughter of Sir William Waldegrave, knt., of Suffolk (*Visitation of Essex*, Harl. Soc. Publ., xiii. 39). Her elder sister was wife of Sir Nicholas Bacon (q. v.). She is said to have been proficient in Hebrew, Greek, and Latin. She married Sir Henry Killigrew on 4 Nov. 1565. Sir John Harington, in the notes to book xxxvii. of his translation of 'Orlando Furioso,' has preserved some Latin lines in which she asked her sister Mildred, wife of Cecil, lord Burghley, to use her influence to get her husband excused from going on an embassy to France. The verses were reprinted in Fuller's 'Worthies.' On 21 Dec. 1583 she gave birth to a still-born child, and on 27 Dec. she died. She was buried in the church of St. Thomas the Apostle, London. It was burnt down during the great fire, but Stow, in his 'Survey,' has preserved the four Latin inscriptions on her monument, including one by herself and one by Andrew Melville (1545–1622) [q. v.]

[Sir John Harington's Notes to Orlando Furioso; Fuller's Worthies; Ballard's Memoirs of Learned Ladies; Stow's London; Harl. Soc. Registers, vol. vi.; Archæolog. xviii. 100.]
T. F. H.

KILLIGREW, CHARLES (1655–1725), master of the revels, born at Maestricht on 29 Dec. 1655, was son of Thomas Killigrew the elder (q. v.), by his second wife, Charlotte, daughter of John de Hesse of Holland (Boase, *Collectanea Cornubiensia*, s. v.). He was gentleman of the privy chamber to Charles II, 1670, James II, 1685, and William and Mary, 1689, master of the revels in 1680, patentee of Drury Lane Theatre in 1682, and commissioner of prizes in 1707. He lived at Somerset House, London, and Thornham Hall, Suffolk. His varied acquirements won him the friendship of Dryden (cf. Dedication of *Juvenal*, 1693, p. xxiii), Humphrey Prideaux, and others. He was buried in the Savoy on 8 Jan. 1724-5, leaving by his wife Jemima, niece of Richard Bokenham, mercer, of London, two sons, Charles (*d.* 1756) and Guilford (will registered in P. C. C. 13, Romney). His library was sold in December following.

[Boase and Courtney's Bibl. Cornub.; Malcolm's Ancestors, pp. 427, 431; Notes and Queries, 1st ser. i. 204, 219; Gent. Mag. 1833, i. 27; Downes's Roscius Anglicanus, pp. 16, 39; Moneys for Secret Services (Camd. Soc.), p. 34; Academy, 25 April 1874, p. 458; Fitzgerald's Hist. of the Stage; Cal. State Papers, Treas. Ser.; Addit. MSS. 12201, 20726 ff. 16, 37, 28227 f. 32; Chester's London Marriage Licences (Foster), col. 792.] G. G.

KILLIGREW, SIR HENRY (*d.* 1603), diplomatist and ambassador, was the fourth son of John Killigrew of Arwenack, of an old Cornish family, by Elizabeth, second daughter of James Trewenard of Trewenard (pedigree in VIVIAN'S *Visitations of Cornwall*, p. 268). He was probably educated at Cambridge, but there is no definite information on the point. On 18 Feb. 1552-3 he was returned member of parliament for Launceston (*Members of the Parliament of England*, pt. i. p. 378). He assisted Sir Peter Carew [q. v. in escaping to the continent in January 1553-4, and during the remainder of Mary's reign appears to have been in exile. He was at Paris in July 1556, when he was described by the English authorities as a rebel (*Cal. State Papers*, For. Ser. 1553-8, p. 238). Sir James Melville states that 'Harry Killigrew, an Englis gentilman, my auld friend,' held his horse while he got his wound dressed after his escape from St. Quentin (*Memoirs*, p. 35). Killigrew was recalled to England on the accession of Elizabeth, and she employed him on various diplomatic missions, including one to Germany in connection with negotiations for a defensive league. In July 1559 he went for a short time to assist Throckmorton in France. In June 1566 he was sent on a mission from Elizabeth to the Queen of Scots, for the 'declaration of sundry things necessary to be reformed between them for the preservation of their amity' (Instructions to Henry Killigrew, *Cal. State Papers*, Scott. Ser. i. 235). He returned in the following July, and after the murder of Darnley was again sent to Scotland with a special message to the Queen of Scots, which he

delivered to her 'in a dark chamber' (*ib.* p. 243). On 20 April 1572 he was elected M.P. for Truro. In September 1572 he was again sent to Scotland, in connection with the negotiations for the surrender of the Queen of Scots to the protestant lords. They came to nothing, but Killigrew ultimately succeeded in persuading Elizabeth to send an English force to assist in the siege of the castle of Edinburgh He remained in Scotland till the castle fell, and in numerous letters to Burghley minutely described the siege, and the negotiations connected with its surrender (*ib.* Scott. Ser. and For. Ser.) Subsequently he was employed in similar diplomatic missions in Scotland, Germany, France, and the Low Countries. While in attendance on the Earl of Essex in France he was knighted on 22 Nov. 1591. He died in the spring of 1602-3, his will being proved on 16 April.

Lloyd eulogises Killigrew in his 'Worthies' for his learning and his artistic accomplishments. He states that, while a good musician, he was specially skilled as a painter, being 'a Dürer for proportion; a Goltzius for a bold touch, variety of posture, a curious and true shadow; an Angelo for his happy fancy, and an Holbein for oyl works,' but no authenticated work of his brush is known. Killigrew gave 140l. to Emmanuel College, Cambridge, for the purchase of St. Nicholas Hostel, the materials of which were applied to the construction of the lodge for Dr. Laurence Chaderton [q. v.], the first master. His London residence was in Lothbury.

On 4 Nov. 1565 Killigrew married in the church of St. Peter-le-Poor, London, Catherine, fourth daughter of Sir Anthony Cooke [see KILLIGREW, CATHERINE]. She died in 1583, and on 7 Nov. 1590 he was married in the same church to Jaël de Peigne, a Frenchwoman. She was naturalised in June 1601 (*ib.* Dom. Ser. 1601-3, p. 50), and on 19 April 1617 she married George Downham [q. v.], bishop of Derry (BOASE, *Collect. Cornubiensia*, p. 454). By his first wife Killigrew had four daughters: Anne, married first to Sir Henry Neville, and secondly to George Carleton [q. v.], bishop of Chichester; Elizabeth, married first to Sir Jonathan Trelawny, knt., secondly to Sir Thomas Reynell, knt., and thirdly to Sir Thomas Lower, knt.; Mary, to Sir Reginald Mohun; and Dorothy, to Sir Edwin Seymour. By his second wife he had a daughter, Jane, and two sons, Joseph and Henry, the former of whom, only ten years of age at his father's death, succeeded to the estates.

[A Remembrance of Henry Kylligrew's Journyes in her Majesty's service, and by commandment from Lords Treasurer, from the last years of Queene Marye, is printed in Leonard Howard's Collection of Letters, pp. 184-8, from the British Museum Lansd. MS. 106. There are numerous diplomatic letters by him in the British Museum, the Record Office, and elsewhere, the majority of which have now been calendared in the State Papers series. For the facts of his life see Vivian's Visitations of Cornwall, 1887, pp. 268-9; Boase's Bibliotheca Cornubiensis and Collectanea Cornubiensia; Parochial History of Cornwall, i. 397-400; Wootton's Baronetage; Peck's Desiderata; David Lloyd's Worthies; Sir James Melville's Memoirs; Cooper's Athenae Cantabr. ii. 345-9, 553.]

T. F. H.

KILLIGREW, HENRY, D.D. (1613-1700), divine, the fifth son of Sir Robert Killigrew [q. v.], by Mary, daughter of Sir Henry Woodhouse of Kimberley, Norfolk, was born at the manor of Hanworth, near Hampton Court, on 11 Feb. 1612-13. He was educated under Thomas Farnaby [q. v.], entered Christ Church, Oxford, as a commoner in 1628, and soon afterwards became a student. Two years later he contributed Latin verses to a volume, 'Britanniæ Natalis,' published at the university. He graduated B.A. on 5 July 1632, and became one of the quadragesimal collectors. On 4 July 1638 he was created M.A. On 13 March 1638 a play called 'The Conspiracy' was entered at Stationers' Hall (ARBER, Transcript of the Registers, iv. 385). It was surreptitiously published in quarto form from an imperfect transcript from the original copy, which, with its author, was then in Italy. It was to be performed before the king on occasion of the marriage of the eldest son of the fourth Earl Pembroke to the daughter of the first Duke of Buckingham, and it was afterwards acted at the Blackfriars Theatre. In 1653 Killigrew published a corrected version of the play, in folio, with a fresh title, 'Palluntus and Eudora.' The preface states that Ben Jonson had praised it; while, according to Langbaine, Lord Falkland defended it against some critics by saying that the author was only seventeen (really twenty-one) when he put language suited for a man of thirty into the mouth of a lad of seventeen. The play shows some skill for a youthful author. Sir Charles Sedley's 'Tyrant King of Crete' was an adaptation from Killigrew's play.

Upon the outbreak of the civil war in 1642 Killigrew became chaplain to the king's army, and in November he was created D.D. at Oxford. Immediately afterwards he was appointed chaplain to James, duke of York, and at the Restoration in 1660 was made almoner to the Duke of York, superintendent

of the affairs of his chapel, prebendary of the twelfth stall at Westminster, and rector of Wheathamsted in Hertfordshire. Killigrew resigned the rectory in 1673 in favour of Dr. John Lambe, husband of his daughter Elizabeth, who died on 28 Oct. 1701, in her fifty-first year. Killigrew had a salary of 100l. a year as chaplain and almoner to the Duke of York (Hist. MSS. Comm. 8th Rep. pt. i. p. 278), and in 1663 he was appointed master of the Savoy, in succession to Sheldon. Killigrew's sister, Lady Shannon, was one of Charles II's mistresses.

According to some writers the final ruin of the Savoy Hospital was the result of Killigrew's improvidence and greed. A bill was passed in 1697 abolishing its privileges of sanctuary. The hospital was leased out in tenements, and the master appropriated the profits: among the leases granted was one (1689) to Henry Killigrew, the patentee of Drury Lane Theatre, for his lodgings in the Savoy, at a rent of 1l. a year for forty years. Killigrew and other masters granted licenses of marriage. Each of the four chaplains had 26l. a year, and when Killigrew died all of them were holding pluralities. Among them was his son-in-law, Dr. Lambe (appointed in 1677). In 1702 the chaplains were deprived of office, and the hospital dissolved. The chaplains pointed out that about 1674 Charles II had taken for other uses parts of the hospital allotted to the master and poorer persons in the hospital. Killigrew, after vainly trying to get them back, compensated some of the sufferers by pensions and doles. He had also spent money on the chapel of the hospital and Henry VII's Chapel at Westminster. Killigrew gave 50l. towards the completion of the building of Christ Church, Oxford, finished in 1685 (WOOD, Antiquities, &c., 1786, iii. 448). He died on 14 March 1699-1700 (LUTTRELL, Brief Relation of State Affairs, 1857). Killigrew's wife, Judith, was buried at the Savoy on 2 Feb. 1682-3. His daughter Anne and sons Henry and James are noticed separately.

Killigrew published: 1. 'Sermons [22] preached ... at Whitehall ... and ... at the Chappell at St. James,' London, 1685. 2. 'Twenty-five Sermons preached before the King,' London, 1685; published by Bishop Patrick (LOWNDES, Bibl. Manual), and some separate sermons. He contributed Latin verses to the Oxford collections: 'Britanniæ Natalis,' 1630; 'Musarum Oxoniensium pro Rege suo Soteria,' 1633; 'Musarum Oxoniensium Charisteria pro Serenissima Regina Maria,' 1638; 'Προτέλεια Anglo-Batava,' 1641. A poem by Killigrew is among the

Malone MSS., Bodleian Library, No. 13, p. 71.

[Boase and Courtney's Bibliotheca Cornubiensis, 1874, i. 290-1, iii. 1256; Genest's History of the English Stage, 1832, x. 109, 150; Wood's Fasti Oxonienses, 1815, i. 465, 506; Wood's Athenæ Oxonienses, 1820, iv. 621-3; Walker's Numbers and Sufferings of the Clergy of the Church of England, 1714, pt. ii. p. 290; Malcolm's Londinium Redivivum, 1803, iii. 406, 408, 412-413, 420; Rev. W. J. Loftie's Memorials of the Savoy, 1878, pp. 152-3, 156-8, 209; Langbaine's Dramatick Poets, 1698, p. 82; Clutterbuck's Hertfordshire, 1815, i. 517-19; Pepys's Diary, 22 Nov. 1663; Le Neve's Knights, Harl. Soc. Publ. viii. 39.]   G. A. A.

KILLIGREW, HENRY (d. 1712), admiral, son of Henry Killigrew, D.D. [q. v.], and brother of James Killigrew [q. v.], was made, after some service as a volunteer, lieutenant of the Cambridge in 1666; from her he was moved to the Sapphire, and in 1668 to the Constant Warwick. In January 1672-1673 he was made captain of the Forester, from which he was moved to the Bonadventure, and afterwards to the Monck, one of the ships with Prince Rupert through the summer of 1673. After the peace he was continuously employed in the Mediterranean, on the African coast, where he successively commanded the Swan prize in 1674, the Harwich and the Henrietta in 1675, the Bristol and the Royal Oak in 1676, and the Mary in 1678-9, returning to England in her in June 1679. In 1680 he commanded the Leopard and the Foresight; in 1683-4 he was captain of the Montagu in the expedition to Tangier under Lord Dartmouth, and of the Mordaunt in 1684-5 for a voyage to the Gambia. In 1686 he went out to the Mediterranean in the Dragon as commodore of a small squadron for the suppression of piracy. A detailed account of this voyage, with a description of the several places visited, was written by G. Wood, Killigrew's clerk in the Dragon, and formerly in the Royal Oak and Mary (Addit. MS. 19306). However interesting, the commission was uneventful, with the exception of a running fight on 8 Dec. 1687 with a Sallee cruiser, which shot away the Dragon's fore and main topmasts, and thus escaped. In the course of the action Killigrew was severely wounded by the bursting of a gun. He returned to England in May 1689, was promoted to be vice-admiral of the blue, and during the summer had his flag in the Kent in the Channel. In December he was appointed commander-in-chief of a powerful squadron, which in the following March sailed for the Mediterranean to oppose the passage of the Toulon fleet to Brest. On 9 May 1690

he was refitting at Cadiz after a stormy passage, when he learned that Château-Renault was at sea, with ten ships of the line. On the 10th Killigrew, having been joined by some of his ships from Gibraltar, was able to pursue with fifteen; but they were foul, and sailed badly, and Château-Renault, having waited to ascertain their force, easily sailed away from them [cf. HERBERT, ARTHUR, EARL OF TORRINGTON]. By the next morning the French squadron was hull down from the English van, which itself was hull down from the rear; and Killigrew, judging further pursuit useless, returned to Cadiz, whence, after arranging for the several services in the Mediterranean, he sailed home. Bad weather still opposed him. He was thirty-five days on the passage to Plymouth, and when he arrived the battle of Beachy Head had been fought, and the French for the time were masters of the Channel. On the supersession of the Earl of Torrington, Killigrew, Sir Richard Haddock [q. v.], and Sir John Ashby [q. v.] were appointed joint commanders-in-chief till December, when they were superseded by Admiral Edward Russell (afterwards Earl of Orford) [q. v.], Killigrew remaining with him as admiral of the blue squadron. In 1692 he had no command, but in 1693 was again one of the joint admirals, with Sir Clowdisley Shovell [q. v.] and Sir Ralph Delavall [q. v.] On 15 April 1693 he was appointed also a lord commissioner of the admiralty. After the disaster which befell the Smyrna fleet in June 1693 [see ROOKE, SIR GEORGE], Killigrew, together with Delavall, was dismissed from the command. It was said, and by many believed, that they were both in the interest of King James, and that the loss was due to treachery on their part (BURNET, Hist. of his own Time, Oxford ed., iv. 180). It is possible that Killigrew's sympathies were, theoretically, with the banished king; but there was no reason to suspect him of giving them a practical form, and though deprived of his command, he remained at the admiralty till May 1694. In 1702 he pointed out, in a memorial to the crown, that, although discharged from the command of the fleet on 6 Nov. 1693, he had not received any pay or allowance till 1699, when he had been granted half-pay as admiral of the blue from 1 Oct. 1697. His prayer that he might be allowed full pay from 1693 to 1697, and that his present allowance might be increased to full pay as admiral of the blue, was refused, the report on the petition further stating that, as war had been again declared, he could not receive half-pay or any other allowance except by special grant from her majesty. He was accordingly given a pension of 700*l.* a year (*Home Office Records*, Admiralty, vol. xi.), rather more than half-pay. He died at his seat near St. Albans on 9 Nov. 1712.

[Charnock's Biog. Nav. i. 338; commission lists and other documents in Public Record Office; Burchett's Transactions at Sea; Lediard's Naval History; Boase and Courtney's Bibl. Cornub. i. 291, iii. 1256.] J. K. L.

KILLIGREW, JAMES (*d.* 1695), captain in the navy, son of Henry Killigrew, D.D. [q. v.], and brother of Admiral Henry Killigrew [q. v.], was appointed lieutenant of the Portsmouth on 5 Sept. 1688. On 11 April 1689 he was promoted to be captain of the Sapphire, was employed in her cruising in the Channel, and in July 1691 captured a large French privateer. In 1692 he commanded the York, in 1693 the Crown, from which he was moved into the Plymouth of 60 guns, and sent with Admiral Russell to the Mediterranean. In January 1694-5 he was cruising to the southward of Sardinia in command of a detached squadron of five ships, when, on the 18th, they sighted two French men-of-war, the Content of 60, and the Trident of 52 guns. In the chase the Plymouth, being far ahead of her consorts, closed with and engaged the enemy. She was much over-matched, and suffered severely. Killigrew and many of his men were killed. But the French ships had been delayed till the other English ships came up, and, being unable to escape, were both captured. They were taken into Messina, and were afterwards added to the English navy. The question was afterwards raised by his brother, the admiral, whether his estate was not entitled to share in the prize-money, and evidence was adduced to the effect that the two French ships were disabled and virtually beaten by the Plymouth's fire. Russell, who was commander-in-chief in the Mediterranean at the time, presided over the admiralty, and he decided that as Killigrew was killed early in the action, and the Plymouth was beaten off by the French ships, the prize-money was payable only to the captains of the Carlisle, Falmouth, and Adventure, which actually took them. Although presumably in accordance with the regulations of the day, such an award now appears unjust.

[Charnock's Biog. Nav. ii. 327; Home Office Records (Admiralty), vol. iv. 16 July, 31 Aug. 1696.] J. K. L.

KILLIGREW, SIR ROBERT (1579-1633), courtier, grandson of John Killigrew of Arwennack, Cornwall, and son of Sir William Killigrew, by Margaret, daughter of Thomas Saunders of Uxbridge, Middlesex, was born in London, probably in 1579. His father, though always in debt, kept up a large house in Lothbury, London, and held the post of groom of the privy chamber to Queen Elizabeth, by whom he was granted the right to farm the profits of the seals of the queen's bench and common pleas. This privilege was, in spite of numerous protests, confirmed to him by the queen in 1577 (see *Burghley Papers*, Lansdowne MSS. 25 and 83). In return for his perquisite Killigrew supported the court interest in parliament, where he represented Helston in 1572, Penryn in 1584, and the county of Cornwall in 1597. He was knighted by James I at Theobalds on 7 May 1603, and represented Liskeard in the parliament of 1604. Appointed chamberlain of the exchequer for 1605-6, Sir William Killigrew sat once more for Penryn in 1614, and died in Lothbury on 23 Nov. 1622 (P. C. C. Savile, p. 96).

As 'Robert Killegrew of Hampshire' he matriculated at Christ Church, Oxford, on 29 Jan. 1590-1, aged 11. In 1601 he was returned to parliament for St. Mawes, Cornwall. Knighted by James I at Hanworth on 23 July 1603, he sat for Newport in the parliament of the following year, and was sitting for Helston in May 1614, when during the debate on 'undertaking' he 'offered to pluck Sir Roger Owen off his chair,' or at any rate 'laid hands on him, used an unkind countenance to him, and sharp words.' His sequestration was demanded, but on the intercession of Sir Edward Montagu, and considering the circumstance that 'his father, brother, and uncle, all in the house do condemn the fact,' he was allowed to acknowledge his error at the bar (*Commons' Journals*, i. 483). Killigrew represented Newport again in 1621, Penryn in 1623, Cornwall in 1625, Tregony in 1626, and Bodmin in 1628. The family interest in Cornish boroughs must have been very strong, since in 1614, while his father was still alive, and other members of the family held Cornish seats, Sir Robert gave a seat at Helston to Sir James Whitelocke (*Liber Famelicus*, p. 41; cf. COURTNEY, *Parl. Representation of Cornwall*, p. 18).

In the middle of May 1613 Killigrew, who had just emerged from the Fleet prison—the cause of his confinement is unknown—paid a visit to Sir Walter Raleigh in the Tower. On leaving Raleigh he was hailed from a window by another prisoner, Sir Thomas Overbury. Killigrew had been on friendly terms with Overbury, and stood for some minutes in private conversation with him. For this offence he was on 19 May committed once more to the Fleet (WINwood, *Memorials*, iii. 455), but his detention was a short one, as on 7 July 1613 he was appointed captain or keeper of Pendennis Castle for life (*State Papers*, Dom. Ser. 1611–1613, p. 242). That he permitted Killigrew to converse with Overbury was one of the charges brought against Sir William Waad, lieutenant of the Tower, previous to his dismissal in June 1613. But Killigrew was more intimately concerned with the mystery in which Overbury's death was involved. He had obtained a great reputation among the courtiers as a concoctor of drugs and cordials, and as a man of general scientific attainments (see a letter of his to Sir Dudley Carleton on a perspective glass; *ib.* 1618–19). According to a statement made by Killigrew at the investigation regarding Overbury's last days (3 Oct. 1615) Somerset had in May 1613 sent to him on three separate occasions for one of his white powders. The first of these powders was avowedly for Overbury, and was to be forwarded, he was told, in answer to the prisoner's own request for an emetic (see GARDINER, *History*, ii. 182). Somerset alleged that it was one of Killigrew's powders that had such bad effects on Overbury on the night of 3 June 1613. But it came out in the evidence that these effects were attributable to a fourth powder, and Killigrew solemnly affirmed that Somerset had from him but three, all of which were quite harmless, and similar to those he was in the habit of dispensing (AMOS, *The Great Oyer of Poisoning*, pp. 106–7, 144). On Somerset's downfall Killigrew found a friend in Buckingham, who wrote on his behalf to Bacon in 1619 about a suit for certain concealed lands. He lost favour by a duel which he had with Captain Burton on 7 Jan. 1618, but recovered it sufficiently to be appointed prothonotary of chancery for life on 31 Oct. 1618. In 1619 he was granted some lands in Windsor Forest, and from this date until his death he accumulated small perquisites about the court. He would have obtained more both for his sons and on his own account if he had not given offence to Buckingham by his complaints against his agent, Sir James Bagge (see Killigrew's letter to Lord Conway, FORSTER, *Eliot*, ii. 67). In 1625 a grant of 550*l.* was made to him by parliament for the repair of three Cornish strongholds, the castles of St. Mawes, St. Michael's Mount, and Pendennis. In this year also, in a debate concerning the supply demanded by the new king, Killigrew moved in the interest of the court that the question should not be put, thus averting from the royal party the humiliation of open defeat (*Debates in Parliament*, 1625, Camd. Soc., p. 120). On

8 Sept. 1625 it was mentioned that he was likely to succeed Sir Dudley Carleton as resident ambassador to the States-general, and he was actually appointed on 7 Feb. following (*Cal. State Papers*, Dom. Ser. 1625–6). On 2 Jan. 1630, once more in England, he was appointed vice-chamberlain to the queen. Killigrew was an original shareholder in the New River Company, incorporated 21 June 1619, and bore a part in the draining of the Lindsey Level in 1630 (*ib.* 1629–31, p. 420). He died at his country seat, Kineton Park, Hanworth, in the spring of 1633. His will was proved 12 May 1633 (P. C. C. Russell, 49). Although he shared the fiery temper characteristic of his family, Killigrew was a man of much originality and business capacity.

He married Mary, daughter of Sir Henry Woodhouse of Kimberley, Norfolk, and niece of Sir Francis Bacon (BLOMEFIELD, *Norfolk*, ix. 353). She survived him, and remarried Sir Thomas Stafford, gentleman-usher to Queen Henrietta Maria. The Countess of Warwick remarks of her in her autobiography (Percy Soc. 1848, p. 9), 'she was a cunning old woman who had been herself too much, and was too long versed in amours.' Killigrew had five sons, including William (afterwards Sir William), Thomas the dramatist, and Henry the divine, who are separately noticed, and seven daughters, one of whom, Elizabeth, married Francis Boyle, first viscount Shannon. She had a daughter by Charles II, Charlotte Jemima Henrietta Boyle, *alias* Fitzroy (*d.* 1684), who became Countess of Yarmouth (JACOB, *English Peerage*, ii. 482; *Notes and Queries*, 4th ser. vii. 238, viii. 98).

[Boase and Courtney's Bibl. Cornub.; Archæologia. xviii. 99 (pedigree); Vivian's Visitations of Cornwall, 1887, pp. 268, 271; Miscellanea Genealog. and Herald, new ser. i. 376; Foster's Alumni Oxon. 1500–1714; Metcalfe's Knights, Append. p. 222; Spedding's Bacon, passim; Harl. MSS. 7002 and 7006; Sloane MS. 203, fol. 38; Dugdale's Hist. of Imbanking, 1772. p. 424; Nichols's Progresses of James I. ii. 641; W. P. Courtney's Parl. Representation of Cornwall, pp. 42, 169, &c.; Gardiner's History, v. 429; Returns of Members of Parl.; Notes and Queries, 4th ser. vii. 454, 550.]   T. S.

KILLIGREW, THOMAS (1612–1683), dramatist, son of Sir Robert Killigrew [q. v.], by Mary, daughter of Sir Henry Woodhouse, born in Lothbury, London, 7 Feb. 1611–12, was baptised on the 20th at St. Margaret's, Lothbury. While a child he used, according to Sir John Mennis, to go to the Red Bull, and when the manager asked for boys to personate devils, to volunteer and thus see the play for nothing. Appointed in 1633 page to Charles I, he remained constant to the fortunes of that monarch and his successor. He married, 29 June 1636, Cecilia or Cicely, daughter of Sir John Crofts of Saxham, Suffolk, by whom he had a son Henry. A dispute on jealousy between Killigrew and Miss Crofts supplied Thomas Carew [q. v.] with the subject of a duet, which, with full acknowledgment of indebtedness, is printed by Killigrew at the close of part ii. of his 'Cicilia and Clorinda,' whence it was transferred to the 1671 edition of Carew's poems. Carew also wrote a poem 'On the Muriage of T. K. and C. C. The morning stormie,' which appears in his 'Poems,' ed. 1640, and an anonymous epithalamium was among Sir Thomas Phillipps's MSS. 4001. The lady died 1 Jan. 1637-8, and in 1640 Quarles issued his 'Sighes at the contemporary deaths' of 'Mistress Cicely Killegrve' and her sister the Countess of Cleveland.

Killigrew was in France in 1635, and while there wrote a letter concerning the 'Possessing and Dispossessing of several Nuns in the Nunnery at Tours in France,' three sheets folio, dated Orleans, 7 Dec. 1635. Manuscripts of this are in the Bodleian (Ashmolean MS. 800, art. iii. ff. 21-7) and in the library of Magdalene College, Cambridge (Pepys Coll. No. 8383). It is reprinted in the 'European Magazine,' 1803, xliii. 102-106. This was followed by the 'Prisoners' and 'Claracilla,' two tragi-comedies, 12mo, 1641. In the 1664 collection of Killigrew's works the former, the scene of which is Sardinia, is dedicated to his 'Dear Niece, the Lady Crompton,' and is the only play in the collection which is said to have been written in London; the second piece, 'Claracilla,' which is dedicated to his 'Dear Sister, the Lady Shannon,' and has its scene in Sicily, was written while he was in Rome. Both were produced at the Phœnix, otherwise the Cockpit, in Drury Lane. Mr. Fleay puts the date of both performances before 1636, and dates the representation of a third play by Killigrew, the 'Parson's Wedding,' his best-known comedy, between 1637 and 1642. This piece, written at 'Basil in Switzerland,' seems to have first seen the light in the folio of 1664.

Killigrew was in London on 3 Sept. 1642, when he was committed by a warrant from the parliament to the custody of Sir John Lenthall, on a charge of taking up arms for the king. On 16 May 1643 he successfully petitioned the House of Lords from the King's Bench prison to make void all suits begun against him since he was in confinement. After his release he went to Oxford in 1644, and seems to have subsequently con-

tinued his travels; in 1647 he joined Prince Charles in his exile in Paris. A brilliant conversationist, and a man little disturbed by moral scruples, Killigrew warmly commended himself to Charles II, by whom, in spite of some remonstrances, he was appointed resident at Venice in 1651. His proceedings there, the manner in which, with royal connivance, he borrowed money for his master and for his own subsistence, and his general debauchery led in June 1652 to his compulsory withdrawal and a complaint to Charles from the Venetian ambassador in Paris. Killigrew's vindication is among the Clarendon MSS. (Cal. Clarendon Papers, ii. 143). His recall from Venice was the subject of some waggishness on the part of the English poets. Denham's lines concerning him are well known:

Our resident Tom
From Venice is come,
And has left all the statesman behind him;
Talks at the same pitch,
Is as wise, is as rich,
And just where you left him you find him.

But who says he is not
A man of much plot
May repent of his false accusation,
Having plotted and penned
Six plays to attend
The Farce of his negotiation.

His travels during this, his second continental tour, included Italy and Spain, and he spent some time in Florence, Turin, and Madrid, as well as in Paris and Venice. He occupied part of his time in writing a new series of plays. Besides his plays Killigrew brought back with him, on returning to London at the Restoration, a second wife, Charlotte, born 16 July 1629, daughter of John de Hesse, whom he married at the Hague 28 Jan. 1654-5. She was appointed keeper of the sweet coffer for the queen in May 1662, and first lady of the queen's privy chamber 4 June 1662 (Brit. Mus. Addit. MS. 20032, f. 44).

Immediately after his return home Killigrew was appointed in 1660 groom of the bedchamber to Charles II, and subsequently chamberlain to the queen. The greatest proof of royal favour consisted, however, in the grant by Charles II, in August 1660, to Killigrew and Sir William D'Avenant [q. v.] of patents to erect two new playhouses in London, Westminster, or the suburbs thereof, to raise two new companies of players, and to have the sole regulation thereof. Leave was also given to the two managers to license their own plays. This interference with the privileges of Sir Henry Herbert, the master of the revels, involved both managers in disputes and litigation with that functionary [see HERBERT, SIR HENRY.] More pliable or amenable than D'Avenant, Killigrew came to terms with his opponent, and articles of agreement between them were signed 4 June 1662, by which 'a firme amity' was concluded, and Killigrew, who is described as 'Thomas Killigrew of Covent Garden, Esq., agrees to pay before 4 Aug. next all monies due to Sir Henry Herbert from the King and Queenes company of players . . . for the new plays at forty shillings a play, and for the revived plays at twenty shillings a play.' This agreement carried costs and a solatium of 50l. to Sir Henry for the damage he had suffered. Killigrew also formally abjured D'Avenant and all his works with 'any of his pretended company of players,' or any other company of players (HALLIWELL, *Ancient Doc.*) On 15 Jan. 1662-3 a second patent was granted to Killigrew; it is identical with one given to D'Avenant at the same time (cf. COLLEY CIBBER, *Apology*, ed. Lowe, preface).

Killigrew's actors were soon officially recognised as the king's servants, but the exact date is not clear. His company seems, according to Downes, who received the information at second hand, to have first 'Acted at the "Red" Bull, and [to have] Built them a New House in *Gibbon's Tennis Court* in *Clare Market*, in which Two Places they continu'd Acting all 1660, 1661, 1662, and part of 1663.' Malone gives a list of the stock plays of the king's company at the Red Bull, twenty in all. They include Shakespeare's 'First Part of Henry IV,' 'Merry Wives,' and 'Othello,' Killigrew's 'Claracilla,' and some pieces by Beaumont and Fletcher. On 4 July 1661 Pepys saw 'Claracilla' at 'the theatre' for the first time, and on 5 Jan. 1662-3 the same play at the Cockpit done by the king's players. Killigrew's company then consisted, according to Downes, of Theophilus Bird, Hart, Mohun, Lacy, Burt, Cartwright, Clun, Baxter, Robert and William Shatterel, Duke, Hancock, Wintersel, Bateman, and Blagden; Mrs. Corey, Mrs. Ann Marshall, Mrs. Eastland, Mrs. Weaver, Mrs. Uphill, Mrs. Knep, and Mrs. Hughs, besides Kynaston, whose feminine characters did something to popularise the king's company, and at least eleven other boys.

Meanwhile, Killigrew and the principal actors of his company obtained from the Earl of Bedford a lease for forty-one years of a piece of ground lying in the parishes of St. Martin-in-the-Fields and St. Paul's, Covent Garden, known by the name of the Riding Yard, the lessees engaging to pay a ground-

rent of 50l. and to erect a theatre at an expense of 1,500l. On this site, which is now occupied by Drury Lane Theatre, Killigrew built a house 112 feet in length from east to west, and 59 feet in depth from north to south. It was known at first as the Theatre Royal, and subsequently as Drury Lane, and was opened 8 April 1663 with the 'Humourous Lieutenant' of Beaumont and Fletcher, which was acted twelve days consecutively. 'Rule a Wife and Have a Wife,' by Beaumont and Fletcher, was given during the same season, when the company was strengthened by the accession of Mrs. Boutel, Mrs. Ellen Gwin, Mrs. James, Mrs. Rebecca Marshall, Mrs. Rutter, Mrs. Verjuice, and Mrs. Knight; Hains, Griffin, Goodman, Lyddal, Charleton, Sherly, and Beeston.

Killigrew revived his 'Parson's Wedding' at the Theatre Royal or Drury Lane in October 1664, and again in 1672 or 1673 at Lincoln's Inn Fields, which was then occupied by his company. On both occasions it was acted, presumably on account of its obscenity, only by women, Mrs. Marshall at each revival speaking the prologue and epilogue (included in 'Covent Garden Drolleries') in masculine attire. On 11 Oct. 1664 Luellin remarked to Pepys: 'What an obscene loose play this "Parson's Wedding" is, that it is acted by nothing but women at the king's house !'

According to Malone, Killigrew drew from the profits of the theatre in 1666 two shares and three-quarters out of a total of twelve shares and three-quarters. Each share was supposed to produce 250l. Cibber declares that Killigrew's company was better than that of his rival D'Avenant until D'Avenant gained superior popularity by adding spectacle and music to his performances. But Killigrew also interested himself in the improvement of the scenery of the theatre, and in the introduction of good music. He told Pepys that he had been eight or ten times to Rome to hear good music (12 Feb. 1666-7), but had not been able to supply his English patrons with anything better than ballads. In August 1664 he announced his intention of building a theatre in Moorfields in order to have common plays acted. 'Four operas were to be given in the year for six weeks each, with the best scenes, music, and everything as magnificent as is in Christendom, painters and singers to be brought from Italy' (PEPYS). On 12 Feb. 1666-7 Pepys was told that Killigrew was about to produce an opera by Giovanni Battista Draghi [q. v.], but nothing further is known of the intention. In January 1672 Drury Lane Theatre was burnt down, and Killigrew's company played at Lincoln's Inn Fields till Drury Lane was rebuilt and reopened 26 March 1674 (cf. *Shakespeare Society's Papers*, iv. 147 sq.) On the death of Sir Henry Herbert in 1673, Killigrew succeeded him as master of the revels. Herbert gave to Killigrew some manuscript directions concerning the duties of the office on 29 March 1664 (see *Notes and Queries*, 1st ser. i. 279).

Oldys spoke of Killigrew as the king's jester, and Pepys was told on 13 Feb. 1667-8 that 'Tom Killigrew hath a fee out of the wardrobe for cap and bells under the title of the king's jester, and may revile or geere anybody, the greatest person without offence, by the privilege of his place.' Pepys calls him 'a merry droll, but a gentleman of great esteem with the king,' and says that he 'told us many merry stories' (24 May 1660).

Killigrew is certainly best remembered as a wit, and he appears to have treated his royal master with remarkable freedom. He told Charles on one occasion that he was going 'to hell to fetch back Oliver Cromwell, that he may take some care of the affairs of England, for his successor takes none at all.' He is said to have won a wager of 100*l.* from the Duke of Lauderdale, who was deploring Charles's continued absence from the council-table, by persuading the king to repair thither immediately. According to Pepys, when Charles spoke of the Duke of York as Tom Otter, a henpecked husband in Ben Jonson's 'Epicoene,' Killigrew remarked to him, 'Sir, pray which is the best for a man to be, a Tom Otter to his wife or to his mistress?' a reference to the king's relations with Lady Castlemaine. Nor, it is said somewhat apocryphally, did he treat Louis XIV more ceremoniously. When Louis showed him at Paris a picture of the crucifixion hanging between portraits of himself and the pope, Killigrew is alleged to have remarked: 'Though I have often heard that our Saviour was buried between two thieves, yet I never knew who they were till now' (HALS, *Parochial History of Cornwall*, under 'Falmouth'). Grammont (*Memoirs*) speaks of Killigrew as a man of honour, and tells stories concerning him that at any other period, and in most other courts, would have deprived him of all claim to the title. He mentions, however, that Killigrew, while returning from the Duke of York's, received three passes with a sword through his chair, one of which went entirely through his arm, the cause of the attack being his intemperate language. This was not the only occasion on which he had to pay for the license he allowed himself. On 16 Feb. 1668-1669, Rochester, while in the company of the king, gave Killigrew a box on the ear. Instead of resenting this violence in his presence, Charles shortly afterwards took the earl's arm, and Killigrew was forced to stomach the affront.

Killigrew survived the union of the two companies—the king's and the duke's—in 1682, though his name does not appear to the agreement for which see BETTERTON, THOMAS, and HART, CHARLES, *d.* 1683. He died at Whitehall on 19 March 1682-3, and is buried in Westminster Abbey. Fifty pounds was paid by the king towards his funeral charges (AKERMAN, *Secret Service Money of Charles II and James II*, Camd. Soc.) His wife survived him. Letters of administration were granted to her estate, 15 May 1716, when she was in her eighty-seventh year (see HOWARD, *Monthly Miscellanea*, i. 370). By her Killigrew had four sons and two daughters. She and three of her sons by Killigrew were naturalised by act of parliament, 3 June 1664 (*Lords' Journals*, xi. 420). Killigrew's eldest son Robert, brigadier-general, was killed at Almanza 14 April 1707, aged 47. His younger sons Charles and Thomas are separately noticed.

Portraits of Killigrew and Carew in the same picture are in the Vandyck Room at Windsor Castle. Faithorne has engraved many portraits. One represents Killigrew in the dress of a pilgrim, with the distich

You see my face, and if you'd know my mind,
'Tis this: I hate myself and all mankind.

His portrait, with that of Lord Coleraine, appears in an engraving known as 'The Princely Shepherds.' It is supposed to have been done for a masque. Another portrait was purchased in 1892 for the National Portrait Gallery.

In 1664 was published the folio edition of Killigrew's 'Works,' with a portrait by Faithorne of the author with a dog. It is entitled 'Comedies and Tragedies written by Thomas Killigrew, Page of Honour to King Charles the First, and Groom of the Bed Chamber to King Charles the Second,' London, by Henry Herringman. The volume contains: (1) 'The Princesse, or Love at First Sight,' a tragi-comedy; (2) 'The Parson's Wedding,' a comedy, which has been reprinted in successive editions of Dodsley's 'Old Plays;' (3) 'The Pilgrim,' a tragedy; (4) the first part of 'Cicilia and Clorinda, or Love in Arms,' a tragi-comedy; (5) the second part of the same; (6) 'Thomaso, or the Wanderer,' a comedy; (7) the second part of 'Thomaso;' (8) 'Claracilla,' a tragi-comedy; (9) 'The Prisoners,' a tragi-comedy; (10) the first part of 'Bellamira her Dream, or the Love of Shadows,' a tragi-comedy; (11) the second part of 'Bellamira.' Each of these plays, or parts of plays, has a separate title-page dated 1663 or 1664. Three of them (Nos. 1, 2, and 8) were, as has been seen, acted before the civil war, and there is no record of a performance of any of the others. Few of them, indeed, seem to have been intended for the stage, those that are in two parts consisting, as Genest observes, of plays in ten acts divided into halves, the first part bringing with it nothing in the shape of a *dénouement* of action. The 'Parson's Wedding' is outspoken enough for Wycherley, and verbose enough for the Duchess of Newcastle. It has wit of a sort, and Congreve has condescended to adopt some of its jokes. According to Langbaine, its intrigue of 'Careless and Wild circumventing the Lady Wild and Mrs. Pleasance into marriage' is an incident in several plays, as "Ram Alley," "Antiquary," &c., but in none so well managed as in this play.' Killigrew's other comic pieces are less flagrantly indecent, but also less amusing. In his serious pieces Killigrew is seen to no great advantage. Genest affirms that the 'Pilgrim' is a good tragedy, which, with judicious alterations, might have been made fit for representation. Portions of it are indeed written with some vigour, but poetry and imagination are absent, and the excisions that would fit it for performance would have to be numerous. Of the second part of 'Cicilia and Clorinda' Langbaine says that the first scene between Amadeo, Lucius, and Manlius 'seems copied from the characters of Aglatidas, Artabes, and Megabises in the "Grand Cyrus:" see "The History of Aglatidas and Amestris," pt. i. bk. iii.' In affirming that ornaments in 'Thomaso' are taken from the 'Captain' by Fletcher, and that a character and some words are copied from Jonson's 'Fox,' Langbaine acquits Killigrew of the intention to conceal his theft, and adds that 'if every poet that borrows knew as well as Mr. Killigrew how to dispose of it, 'twould certainly be very excusable.' In Moseley's edition of William Cartwright's 'Poems,' 1651, are lines of somewhat turgid praise dedicated to 'Mr. Thomas Killigrew on his two playes, the "Prisoners" and "Claracilla."' Killigrew's separate plays are dedicated mostly to ladies of rank. The opinion generally entertained of Killigrew is expressed in two lines of Denham—

Had Cowley ne'er spoke, Killigrew ne'er writ,
Combin'd in one, they'd made a matchless wit.

Manuscripts relating to Killigrew are in various collections. The most important of these, 'An Account of T. Killigrew's Residence at Venice,' with many documents in his handwriting, 1649, is in the British Museum (Add. MS. 20032). Other papers relating to his residence in Venice are among the Clarendon MSS. in the Bodleian Library. Killigrew's abstract of title to the playhouse, Drury Lane, from 14th Charles II to 1684, is in the Addit. MS. 20726, f. 1, British Museum. Suggestions for alterations in 'Julius Cæsar,' signed T. Killigrew, are in Add. MS. 22629, art. 41. Numerous indentures and agreements concerning Drury Lane Theatre also exist in manuscript, and 'Mr. Thomas Killigrew's Letters of his Travels,' in the manuscripts of Trinity College, Dublin, seem to call for publication.

[Books cited; Clarendon's Hist. of the Rebellion; Langbaine's Dramatic Poets; Genest's Account of the Stage; Malone's Suppl. to the Biographia Dramatica; Boase and Courtney's Bibliotheca Cornubiensis; Downes's Roscius Anglicanus; Wood's Athenæ Oxonienses, ed. Bliss; Halliwell's Ancient Documents concerning the Office of Master of the Revels; Lowndes's Bibl. Man.; Williams's Dramatic Censor; Notes and Queries, 1st and 3rd ser.; Cibber's Apology; Chester's Westminster Abbey Registers; information kindly supplied by C. H. Firth, esq.]
J. K.

KILLIGREW, THOMAS, the younger (1657–1719), dramatist, son of Thomas Killigrew [q. v.], by his second wife, Charlotte de Hesse, was born in February 1657 (*Miscell. Genealog. et Herald.* new ser. i. 370). He fought a duel, according to Luttrell's 'Brief Relation,' on 31 Jan. 1692, and was subsequently gentleman of the bedchamber to George II when Prince of Wales. He is the author of 'Chit Chat, a Comedy in five acts. As it is acted at the Theatre Royal, in Drury Lane, by his Majesties servants. Written by Mr. Killigrew, Lond., Printed for Bernard Lintot,' 8vo, no date (1719). It is dedicated to the Duke of Argyll, and is a pleasant, gossipping, happily named piece, with very little plot, as the author acknowledges in the prologue, but some moderately felicitous dialogue. It was played at Drury Lane 14 Feb. 1719, with Wilks, Booth, Cibber, Mrs. Thurmond, Mrs. Porter, and Mrs. Oldfield in the principal parts. Thanks to the zeal of the Duke of Argyll and other friends of the author, it kept the stage eleven nights, and brought its author no less than 1,000*l.*, which, however, he did not live to enjoy, since he died a few months afterwards, and was buried at Kensington 21 July 1719. His play went through two editions in 1719. 'Miscellanea Aurea, or the Golden Medley,' London, printed for A. Bettesworth, 1720, contains 'The Fable of Aemilius and the Statue of Venus,' which is signed T. Killi-

I 2

grew. An agreement for the sale of 'Chit Chat' to Bernard Lintot for 84*l.* was on sale by T. Thorpe in 1843. A portrait of a 'Captain' Killigrew is mentioned by Nichols (viii. 722) as in Lumley Castle. It appears to be that of another Killigrew.

[Genest's Account of the English Stage; Baker's Biographia Dramatica; Boase and Courtney's Bibliotheca Cornubiensis; Lysons's Environs of London.] J. K.

KILLIGREW, Sir WILLIAM (1606–1695), dramatist, the eldest son of Sir Robert Killigrew [q. v.], was baptised at Hanworth, Middlesex, 28 May 1606, and entered a gentleman-commoner of St. John's College, Oxford, 4 July 1623. He was knighted 12 May 1626, and made what was called the tour of Europe. He was elected by double returns member of parliament for Newport and Penryn, both in Cornwall, and sat for the latter, 1628–9; was appointed governor of Pendennis Castle and Falmouth Haven, and obtained the command of the West Cornwall militia. He succeeded to the family mansion in Lothbury, and to Kineton Park, near Hampton Court, on his father's death in 1633. He was made gentleman-usher to Charles I, and had command of one of the two troops of horse that guarded the person of the king during the civil war. While in attendance on Charles I at Oxford, he took, 1 or 2 Nov. 1642, the degree of D.C.L. After the defeat of the royal cause he compounded for his estate with the committee of sequestration. He was in much trouble with his neighbours, who resented his efforts to drain portions of the Lancashire fens for his own benefit. In the manuscripts of the House of Lords there are, among many similar papers, a petition of Henry Carr and others of Donnington, Lincolnshire, respecting their imprisonment in the Fleet for a riot in the Fens by the House of Lords at the suggestion of Sir W. Killigrew, 1641; a petition of Thomas Kirke of Burne (Bourn, Lincolnshire), respecting the impounding of his cattle and other persecutions at the hands of Sir William Killigrew, 14 Dec. 1640; petition of Sir W. Killigrew and others respecting Lindsey's Level, in Lincolnshire, 9 May 1642, with the copy of order therein; petition of Sir W. Killigrew about Thomas Kirke, the Earl of Lindsey, and the riots at Lindsey Level, 22 Feb. 1647–8, 3 Sept. 1660; and another petition against the same, in which Killigrew states that he owes 11,000*l.* Killigrew and the other drainers in Lindsey Level had lost 30,000*l.* by Kirke's conduct, and Killigrew on 22 Feb. 1647–8 'prays the house to consider the estate of himself, his wife, and family, who do beg their bread, which misery

is fallen on them through the riotous conduct of Kirke.' Killigrew was one of the first to taste of the not too lavishly accorded bounty of Charles II, who after the Restoration restored him to his former post of gentleman-usher of the privy chamber. After his marriage to Catherine of Portugal, Charles appointed him vice-chamberlain to the queen, a post he held for two-and-twenty years. On 9 April 1664 he was elected M.P. for Richmond, Yorkshire, vice Sir John Yorke, deceased, and continued to sit for the borough until 1678. After 1682 Killigrew disappeared from court. Two grants of 20*l.* were made to him by Charles II (AKERMAN, *Secret Service Money*, Camd. Soc. 1851, pp. 24, 42). He was buried in the Savoy Chapel 17 Oct. 1695. By his wife Mary, daughter of John Hill of Honilay, Warwickshire, he had three sons, Henry (*d.* 1661), William, a captain in the army, and Sir Robert. A daughter Elizabeth married Sir Francis Clinton.

In 1665 appeared, in 8vo, 'Three Playes, written by Sir William Killigrew, Vice-Chamberlain to her Majesty the Queen Consort, 1664; viz., Selindra, Pandora, Ormasdes.' These were reprinted in 8vo in 1674. Among the contributors of commendatory verses, English or Latin, are: R. Stapylton, the translator of Juvenal, whose lines are suggestively headed 'To Envy;' Edmund Waller, 'Of Pandoras not being approved upon the Stage as a Tragedy;' T. P. (? Thomas Porter); T. L., whose verses Lamb gives *in extenso* in his 'Dramatic Poets;' and Lodowick Carlisle. Of 'Pandora' as a tragedy nothing is known. It was played as a comedy at Lincoln's Inn Fields Theatre, and is for the epoch both well written and passably decent. Much of its dialogue and one or two of the female characters are vivacious. 'Selindra' and 'Ormasdes' are fairly interesting works, happy in termination, but called tragi-comedies, as some deaths by violence are introduced. 'Selindra' is mentioned by Downes as having been given at the Theatre Royal. Of the performance of 'Ormasdes' no record is extant. In 1666 was published in folio, Oxford, printed by Henry Hall, printer to the university, for Richard Davis, 'Fovr new Playes; viz., The Seege of Urbin, Selindra, Love and Friendship, Tragy-Comedies: and Pandora. A Comedy. Written by Sir William Killigrew, Vice-Chamberlaine to Her Majesty.' 'Love and Friendship' is 'Ormasdes.' The 'Siege of Urbin,' also unacted, is a capable and sympathetic play. The plays have separate title-pages, and the volume contains some further commendatory verses. In 1663 appeared 'A Proposal shewing how the Nation may be vast Gainers by all the Sums of Money given to the Crown without lessening the Prerogative . . . by W. Killigrew. To which is prefixed The late Honourable Sir James Sheenes Letter on the same Subject,' no place or date [London, 1663', 4to, 16 pp. In London, 1684, appeared 'The Artless Midnight Thoughts of a Gentleman at Court; who for many Years built on Sand, which every Blast of cross Fortune has defaced; but now he has laid new Foundations on the Rock of his Salvation, which no Storms can shake; and will last out the conflagration of the world, when time shall melt into eternity,' 8vo, 1684; 2nd edition, 12mo, 1684. The first dedication to Charles II bears no name, but the second to James II is signed W. Killigrew. Following this came 'Midnight and Daily Thoughts, in Prose and Verse, by Sir W. Killigrew,' London, 1694, 8vo (see SIR E. BRYDGES, *Restituta*, ii. 130–6). Giles Jacob (*Poetical Register*, i. 157–8), like the anonymous author of a 'Continuation of Langbaine,' p. 83, assigns to Killigrew the 'Imperial Tragedy; taken out of a later Play and very much altered by a Gentleman for his own Diversion,' &c., London, 1669, folio. It was acted at the Nursery in the Barbican. A sonnet by Killigrew is in Lawes's 'Ayres and Dialogues for one, two, and three voices,' two books, 1653–5.

In addition to these works Killigrew is responsible for the whole or portions of: 1. 'An Answer to the Objections made by some Commoners of Lincolnshire against Robert, Earl of Lincolnshire, and his Participants concerning the Drayning of those Fens which lye between Lincoln, Berne, and Boston. Set forth by Sir W. Killigrew. Printed for the Author, 1647,' 4to. 2. 'Certaine Papers concerning the Earl of Lindsey his Fennes. . . . With a Paper directed to Sir W. Killigrew, and signed William Howell. And also an Answer to that Paper by Sir W. Killigrew,' no place or date [August 1649], 4to, 8 pp. 3. 'Sir William Killigrew his Answer to the Fennemen's objections against the Earl of Lindsey his drayning in Lincolnshire. Printed at London, 1649,' 4to, single sheet and a title-page. 4. 'The Rioters in Lindsey and their Abettors,' single sheet, no place or date [1654', fol. 5. 'The late Earl of Lindsey his Title,' &c., a single sheet, n.d., signed 'Henry Heron, W. Killigrew, 1 July 1661.' Further contributions to the controversy by William Killigrew, son of Sir William, appeared in 1695 and 1705. In Heber's 'Catalogue,' pt. v., is a pamphlet privately printed for the judges, entitled 'Proofs that Jane Berkeley and Sir W. Killigrew combined to defraud Richard Lygon of an estate left him by H.

Killigrew;' 'Letters from Col. Doleman to Col. W. Killigrew' are in the 'Thurloe State Papers,' and 'Letters from Killigrew to Archbishop Sancroft and Tobias Rustat, underhousekeeper at Hampton Court, dated respectively 31 Dec. 1677 and 1682,' are among the Tanner MSS. in the Bodleian Library.

A portrait of Killigrew was in the first Exhibition of National Portraits.

[Boase and Courtney's Bibliotheca Cornubiensis is the chief source of information. Mr. Joseph Foster, editor of Alumni Oxonienses, has supplied notes of Killigrew's parliamentary career and the dates of his Oxford progress. See also Vivian's Visitation of Cornwall; Genest's Account of the English Stage, Wood's Fasti Oxonienses, the Biographia Dramatica, Watt's Bibl. Brit., and Langbaine's Dramatic Poets have been consulted.] J. K.

KILLINGWORTH, GRANTHAM (1699–1778), baptist controversialist, grandson of Thomas Grantham (1634–1692) [q. v.], was born in Norwich in 1699. He was a layman, a personal friend of William Whiston, whom he supplied with evidence of cures effected through 'prayer, fasting, and anointing with oyl' by a unitarian baptist minister, William Barron (*d.* 7 Feb. 1731, aged 51). Killingworth wrote on the perpetuity of baptism, against Thomas Emlyn [q. v.]; in favour of adult baptism, against John Taylor, D.D., and Michajah Towgood; and of close communion, against James Foster [q. v.], John Wiche, and Charles Bulkley [q. v.] He died in 1778, leaving a considerable endowment to the Priory Yard general baptist chapel, Norwich.

Among his publications are: 1. 'A Supplement to the Sermons . . . at Salters' Hall against Popery,' 1735, 8vo; 3rd ed. 1735, 8vo; 5th ed. 1738, 8vo, with appendices, including his answer to Emlyn's 'Previous Question,' 1710, 4to. 2. 'An Examination,' &c., 1741, 8vo, of Foster's 'Discourse' (1744) on 'catholic communion.' 3. 'An Answer to the Defence of Dr. Foster,' &c., 1752, 8vo (the 'Defence' was by 'Philocatholicus,' i.e. John Wiche, general baptist minister at Maidstone). 4. 'An Answer to Mr. Charles Bulkley's Pleas for Mixt Communion,' 1756, 8vo. 5. 'A Letter . . . to the late . . . Mr. Whiston,' &c., 1757, 8vo.

[Whiston's Memoirs, 1753, pp. 297, 306, 372; Bulkley's Notes on the Bible, 1802, iii. xv sq.; Toulmin's Historical View of Dissenters, 1814, p. 353; Neal's Puritans, 1822, i. xxvii; Christian Life, 12 Aug. 1876, p. 164.] A. G.

KILMAINE, CHARLES EDWARD SAUL JENNINGS (1751–1799), general in the French army, was born at Dublin 19 Oct. 1751, accompanied his father, whose surname was Jennings, at eleven years of age to France, and took the name of Kilmaine from a village in Mayo where a branch of the Jennings family had resided. He entered the army as a cavalry officer in 1774, serving in the American war of independence under Rochambeau, and in Senegal under Biron. In August 1791, as a retired captain, he took the civic oath and, being recalled to active service, became brigadier-general in March 1793 and lieutenant-general in the following May. He commanded the vanguard in the Ardennes and Flanders, distinguished himself at Jemappes, and was reported by the convention commissaries as brave, active, and dashing, though they did not think it prudent to allow an Irishman a command-in-chief. 'He is a foreigner,' they said; 'he is Irish; republicanism does not easily penetrate such skulls.' He was, however, recommended by Dubois-Dubay, though unsuccessfully, for the command in Vendée, as the only general whose ability and energy could be relied on. In August 1793 he temporarily succeeded Custine, against whom he gave evidence before the revolutionary tribunal; but being forced to retreat before the superior forces of the Duke of York, he was superseded, and was imprisoned for eighteen months. Susan Kilmaine, who was also imprisoned, was apparently his wife. In 1795 he helped to defend the convention against the Prairial insurgents. In 1796 he served in Italy under Bonaparte, and by establishing a second blockade contributed to the reduction of Mantua. Summoned to Paris to discuss a descent on Ireland, he was appointed, in the absence of Desaix, to the temporary command of the so-called army of England. On this expedition being abandoned, he had, in June 1798, the command of the territorial (inland) troops, and was for a time general-in-chief in Switzerland, but, not giving satisfaction in that capacity, was superseded by Masséna. He returned to Paris, where he died 15 Dec. 1799. His great failing was rapacity.

[Moniteur, 28 Nov. 1799; Webb's Compendium of Irish Biography; Fieffé's Hist. des Troupes Étrangères, ii. 62, Paris, 1854; Alger's Englishmen in French Revolution, pp. 152-3.]

J. G. A.

KILMARNOCK, fourth EARL OF. See BOYD, WILLIAM, 1704-1746.

KILMOREY, first EARL OF. See NEEDHAM, FRANCIS JACK, 1748-1832.

KILMOREY, fourth VISCOUNT. See NEEDHAM, CHARLES, d. 1660.

KILSYTH, first VISCOUNT. See LIVINGSTONE, JAMES, 1616-1661.

KILVERT, FRANCIS (1793-1863), antiquary, born at Westgate Street, Bath, on Good Friday 1793, was the eldest son of Francis Kilvert, coachmaker, and of Anna his wife. His uncle was Richard Kilvert, domestic chaplain to Bishop Hurd [q. v.] and rector of Hartlebury. His parents died while he was young, and, as the eldest of seven sons, he became guardian and instructor to his brothers. For a time he was educated under Dr. Michael Rowlandson at Hungerford. He afterwards proceeded to the grammar school at Bath, where he became head boy; his attainments induced the then chief master, Nathaniel Morgan, to engage him as an assistant even before he entered at Oxford. He matriculated at Worcester College, Oxford, on 6 Nov. 1811, and graduated B.A. in 1819 and M.A. in 1824. Kilvert was ordained deacon by Beadon, bishop of Bath and Wells, in 1816 and priest in 1817; his first curacy was that of Claverton, near Bath. He loved his native city; no one knew its history better, and in order to dwell there he declined the post of principal of Queen's College, Birmingham. At Bath he filled in turn several small offices, including those of minister of St. Mary Magdalen's Chapel, chaplain of the General Hospital, and evening lecturer at St. Mary's, Bathwick, but his chief source of income lay in keeping pupils. His success in that direction led him to purchase in 1837 Claverton Lodge, on the southern slope of Bathwick Hill, where he took scholars until his death. Kilvert was one of the earliest members of the Bath Literary Club, and read before its members many papers on the literary associations of the city, some of which have not been printed. He died at Claverton Lodge on 16 Sept. 1863, and was buried in Old Widcombe churchyard, near the grave of his father and two of his brothers. A brass tablet to his memory is on the walls of St. Mary, Bathwick. He married at the close of 1822 Adelaide Sophia de Chièvre, a refugee of French extraction, then living at Clapham, near London. Their issue was three daughters.

Kilvert wrote: 1. 'Sermons at Christ Church, Bath, before the National Schools,' 1827. 2. 'Sermons at St. Mary's Church, Bathwick,' 1837. 3. 'Sermon preached at Wrington,' 1840. 4. 'Selections from unpublished Papers of Bishop Warburton,' 1841; also issued in same years as vol. xiv., supplemental, of Warburton's 'Works.' 5. 'Pinacotheca Historica specimen. Auctore F.K., A.M.,' 1848; pt. ii., with name in full, 1860. A series of inscriptions on illustrious men, which have been much praised for happiness of expression and for command of the Latin language. 6. 'Ralph Allen and Prior Park,' 1857. 7. 'Richard Graves of Claverton,' 1858. 8. 'Memoirs of Life and Writings of Bishop Hurd,' 1860. After his death there was published in 1866 a volume of his 'Remains in Verse and Prose, with a brief Memoir' by the Rev. W. L. Nichols, assisted by Mr. William Long. It included a paper on Pope's connection with the West of England, and particularly with Bath; but other articles which he read to the Bath Literary Society, notably those on Philip Thicknesse and the Batheaston vase, were omitted. His last communication to the Bath Theological Book Society, lines on 'Over the Water to Warleigh,' were printed by Mr. H. D. Skrine at Bath in October 1863. He was a frequent contributor to 'Notes and Queries,' and he wrote many memoirs for the 'Bath Chronicle.'

Mrs. Kilvert published in 1841 a work on 'Home Discipline.' There was only one edition, though it was reissued with fresh title-pages in 1843 and 1847.

[Gent. Mag. 1823 p. 82, 1863 pp. 652-6; Foster's Alumni Oxon.; Peach's Bath Houses, 2nd ser. pp. 7-10; Notes and Queries, 3rd ser. xi. 188; information from Mr. R. E. Peach of Bath.]
W. P. C.

KILVERT, RICHARD (d. 1649), lawyer, rose from a subordinate position in the prerogative court at Canterbury to the office of a proctor practising there. When it was proposed to impeach Sir John Bennet [q. v.], judge of the court, in 1621 on the ground of corruption, Kilvert laid an information against Bennet before the House of Lords, and the lords at his request guaranteed him as an informer freedom from arrest (Lords' Journals, iii. 153, 185; State Papers, Dom. 1619, pp. 249, 252). Hacket states that Kilvert was subsequently branded for perjury by order of the parliament of 1621. But he probably gave evidence in the Star-chamber prosecution instigated in 1622 by the crown after that parliament was dissolved. Three years later Kilvert petitioned the privy council for power to levy Sir John Bennet's fine, some part of which was awarded apparently to him as an informer.

Kilvert was subsequently used as a tool in the proceedings in the Star-chamber against Bishop Williams on a frivolous charge of betraying secrets as a privy councillor. He raked up evidence against the moral character of Williams's principal witness, Pregion (1634), and Williams, in his endeavours to rebut it, exposed himself to a charge of subornation of perjury (see State Papers, Dom. 1634, pp. 456-99). Williams foolishly attempted to bribe Kilvert into inactivity, but Kilvert informed Secretary Windebank of the attempt. In the later trial of the bishop in 1637 in the Star-chamber for publishing an unorthodox work on 'The Holy Table,' Kilvert acted as solicitor for the prosecution, and was awarded 1,500l. out of the total fine imposed (10,000l.)

In 1637 Kilvert became concerned with Alderman Abell [q. v.] in the promotion of the wine monopoly. Since 1634 the Vintners' Company had been exposed to a Star-chamber prosecution for unauthorised dressing of meat. The crown proposed to compound the offence if the Vintners would agree to an imposition, and Kilvert was introduced to the company by Abell, in that year master, in order to coerce them by threats of prosecution. The Vintners gave way, and agreed to the imposition in return for a grant of the monopoly of wines. Kilvert was paid 1,000l. out of the purse of the Vintners' Company, although without the consent of the 'generality.' Immediately on the assembling of the Long parliament he was called into question, along with Alderman Abell, for his share in this transaction. He was arrested on 18 Nov. 1640, and only released on bail 1 Sept. 1641. In the meantime (May 1641) the commons had ordered the bill to be prepared to declare the offence of Alderman Abell and Richard Kilvert 'to the end that they may be made exemplary.' What was finally done does not appear. He was at liberty in December 1643, and in 1647 was living in apparently comfortable circumstances at his own house in St. Martin's Lane. He died there suddenly on 16 Dec. 1649. His brother Roger was a wine merchant in London, and also aided in the wine monopoly; he was released 2 May 1645 on payment of 40l.

Kilvert wrote in his own defence 'A Reply to a most untrue Relation made by certain Vintners,' 1641. He is also identified by a note in Thomasson's hand as the author of a 'Discourse concerning the interest England hath in the Siege of Graveling,' 1644. Some biographical details, together with a portrait, are contained in 'A Dialogue . . . betwixt Alderman Abel and Richard Kilvert,' 1641, and 'The Vintners' Answer to . . . Kilvert,' 1641.

[The tracts mentioned above; Commons' Journals, ii. 26-279; Lords' Journals, iii. 153, vi. 127; State Papers, Dom. 1619-41; Hist. MSS. Comm. 12th Rep. pt. i. p. 172, pt. ii. p. 163, pt. iv. p. 73, 14th Rep. p. 203, pt. vi. p. 472; Harl. MS. 1219, f. 3; State Trials; Rushworth's Collections; Smyth's Obituary (Camden Soc.); Gardiner's Hist. viii. 251, 287.]
W. A. S.

KILWARDBY, ROBERT (d. 1279), archbishop of Canterbury and cardinal-bishop of Porto, was an Englishman by birth, though nothing is known of his family and origin, except that a namesake, Robert Kilwardby, resigned in 1283 the living of All Saints, Gracechurch Street, London (PECKHAM, Register, iii. 1018, Rolls Ser.) He studied at the university of Paris, and probably also at Oxford. At Paris he taught for several years as a master of arts, and became especially distinguished as a teacher and writer on grammar and logic (TRIVET, p. 278, Engl. Hist. Soc.) It is to this portion of his life that his important grammatical and his thirty-nine philosophical treatises must be assigned. Kilwardby finally abandoned his secular career and entered the order of St. Dominic. He now devoted himself exclusively to theology, and especially to the study of the scriptures, St. Augustine, and others of the fathers. He was famous for dividing nearly all St. Augustine's works into chapters, and prefixing to each a short analysis of its contents (ib. p. 278). Among his pupils in theology was Thomas of Cantelupe [q. v.], the future bishop of Hereford (ib. p. 306).

In 1261 Kilwardby was chosen provincial prior of the Dominicans in England, and discharged the duties of that post with great success for eleven years. In 1271 he was present at the general chapter of his order at Montpellier, and was described as a 'great master of theology.' In 1272 the general chapter at Florence relieved him of his office, but in the same year the English province again appointed him prior.

The archbishopric of Canterbury had been vacant since the death of Boniface of Savoy in 1270, as the monks of Canterbury insisted on the election of their prior, Adam of Chillenden, and Edward, the king's son, was eager for the appointment of Robert Burnell [q. v.] Adam went to Rome to press his claims, but Gregory X at last persuaded him to resign them, and appointed of his own authority the provincial of the Dominicans. Kilwardby's appointment was on 11 Oct. 1272. He received the spiritualities of his see from Bishop Bronescombe of Exeter on 11 Dec., and the temporalities three days later (Winchester Annals in Annales Monastici, ii. 112–113). But he had already, on 21 Nov., joined with Gilbert of Gloucester and other magnates in recognising Edward I as king on the day after Henry III's funeral, and in appointing a regency to act until the new king's return from the East (TRIVET, p. 283). He also successfully intervened in the strife between the Bishop of Norwich and his townsmen, and procured a relaxation of the interdict pronounced against that city (COTTON, p. 150). The pope having granted Kilwardby a license to be consecrated by any catholic bishop, he chose the saintly William Button II [q. v.], bishop of Bath and Wells, to perform that office. He was consecrated on 26 Feb. 1273 at Canterbury. Besides the Bishop of Bath, twelve other suffragans of Canterbury took part in the ceremony. Yet it was not until 8 May that Kilwardby received the pallium at Teynham (Winchester Annals, ii. 115), and his enthronement only took place in September. At the pope's request he compensated Adam Chillenden for his expenses incurred in his bootless journey to Rome (Hist. MSS. Comm. 5th Rep. p. 429).

Kilwardby was the first Mendicant advanced to a great post in the English church. His interests remained exclusively theological and ecclesiastical, and he took little part in political affairs, remaining on good terms with Edward I, whom he crowned along with Queen Eleanor on 19 Aug. 1274. He joined with his suffragans in 1276 in exhorting Llewelyn of Wales to perform his feudal duties to Edward, sending his favourite clerk, William Middleton, archdeacon of Canterbury, on a special mission to the Lord of Snowdon (Fœdera, i. 536–6). On Llewelyn refusing to accept his mediation, Kilwardby excommunicated him in February 1277 (ib. i. 541).

Kilwardby devoted himself with some energy to the systematic visitation of his diocese and province. After holding a convocation in London, and making an agreement with the chapter of St. Paul's as to jurisdiction during the vacancies of the see of London (WILKINS, Concilia, ii. 26–7), he held in December 1273 a visitation at Worcester (Annals of Worcester in Ann. Mon. iv. 465). But in the summer of 1274 he attended the council of Lyons, upholding during its sessions the papal power in its strongest forms (cf. BALUZE, Histoire de la Maison d'Auvergne, ii. 113–14). Returning to England Kilwardby again busied himself with visitations. In November 1274 he visited the diocese of Winchester, being received on 26 Nov. on his arrival by the bishop, Nicholas of Ely [q. v.], and subsequently holding visitations of the neighbouring monasteries. He kept Christmas at the bishop's manor of Bitterne, near Southampton (Winchester Annals in Ann. Mon. ii. 118). In 1276 he made a prolonged visitation of the vast diocese of Lincoln. His zeal for monastic rigour was shown by his expulsion of some disorderly monks from Bardney Abbey, Lincolnshire; but the canons of Osney, whom he visited on 7 March, bitterly complained that he exacted from them procurations amounting to over twenty-four marks, while his predecessor Boniface had been contented with four marks only (*Ann. Osney* in *Ann. Mon.* iv. 270). He now visited the university of Oxford, and, with the consent of the regent and non-regent masters, solemnly condemned various erroneous opinions in grammar, logic, and natural philosophy that were then current in the university. Among the grammatical heresies was the doctrine 'quod ego currit, tu currit et curro eque sunt perfecte et congrue.' But some of the other errors were of a more serious kind. Masters found guilty of these errors were to be deprived; bachelors were to be forbidden access to the mastership and expelled the university. Similar errors were condemned a little later at Paris, and the same doctrines at Oxford were again censured in 1284 by Archbishop Peckham. The list of errors condemned by Kilwardby has been several times printed (Paris, n.d., ?1500, 4to; Basel, 1513 and 1528). Among the persons censured was one Richard Clapwell, a friar of Kilwardby's own order (*Ann. Dunst.* in *Ann. Mon.* iii. 325). In 1277 he again visited the diocese of Lincoln; and the monks of Dunstable spoke highly of his liberality and justice (*ib.* iii. 276).

On 16 June 1276 Kilwardby was present at the translation of the remains of St. Richard at Chichester (WYKES in *Ann. Mon.* iv. 268). When first provincial in England he had been one of the commission appointed to examine into Richard's claims to sanctity, and he afterwards encouraged the Dominican Ralph Bocking to write his life of the saintly bishop (*Bollandist Acta Sanctorum*, April, i. 283). He was always a good friend of his order. He bought a new and convenient site for the London house of the Dominicans near Castle Baynard, and contributed towards the building of the new church and monastery (LELAND, *Comm. de Scriptt. Brit.* p. 287). He was conspicuous for his sanctity and care for the poor. He mediated between the citizens of Canterbury in their dispute with Christ Church, when the monks refused to take any share in providing soldiers for the Welsh war. He held frequent synods, those of 1273 and 1277 marking important developments in the representation of the lower clergy, which was finally systematically organised by his successor (STUBBS, *Select Charters*, pp. 444–5; *Const. Hist.* ii. 205).

On 12 March 1278 Pope Nicholas III, a great friend of the Mendicants, nominated Kilwardby, at his first creation of cardinals, to the cardinal-bishopric of Porto and Santa Rufina —an appointment which necessitated

his resignation of the see of Canterbury and his residence at Rome. Kilwardby accepted the post, though the temporalities of the church of Porto were incomparably inferior to those of Canterbury. Some dissatisfaction with his work at Canterbury rather than a desire to do honour to Kilwardby probably inspired the pope to make the translation. As soon as the appointment was known doubts were raised as to the validity of his recent acts as archbishop (PECKHAM, *Register*, i. 48). On 25 July Kilwardby solemnly took his leave of his suffragans and departed for Italy. He sought to increase his lessened income by selling to the king the crops and rents of his estates for the year, and took away with him five thousand marks in money, precious vessels, church ornaments, and manuscripts, including a costly new bible, all of which belonged to the see (*ib.* i. 17, 277, 550). More important than all, he removed all the registers and judicial records of Canterbury. Peckham and his successor sought in vain to recover the property of their church, but never succeeded in getting any back. To this day the oldest records of Canterbury begin with Peckham's archbishopric. Yet Peckham continued to consult Kilwardby on English ecclesiastical matters, and believed that, if he had lived longer, he would have sent back the property.

Kilwardby was already an old man and in poor health. Soon after joining the papal curia at Viterbo he fell sick. He was, however, employed by the pope to write letters to the 'king of the Tartars' urging his conversion to Christianity (CIACCONIUS, *Vitæ Pontificum*, ii. 224). But he died on 11 Sept. 1279, and was buried at the Dominican convent at Viterbo. There was some suspicion of poison (COTTON, p. 371).

Kilwardby was a very voluminous writer on grammatical, philosophical, and theological subjects. Trivet (p. 278) regards his chief works to be these: 'De Tempore,' 'De Universali,' 'De Relatione,' and 'De Ortu Scientiarum,' and describes the last as 'a curious and useful book.' It may be regarded as the most important of Kilwardby's writings, and is identical with the treatise 'De Divisione Scientiarum,' which is sometimes considered as an independent work. The large number of surviving manuscripts shows that it was widely studied. Two are in the Bibliothèque Nationale at Paris, and two in the Bodleian Library. It is a commentary on Avicenna's work with the same title. M. Hauréau considers it worth printing, and speaks of its clearness and accuracy. In all thirty-nine philosophical works by Kilwardby are enumerated in Quétif and Echard's 'Scriptores

Ordinis Prodicatorum,' i. 376–80. They are mainly commentaries on Aristotle's 'Logic,' with a few treatises on Aristotle's 'Psychology,' 'Physics,' and 'Metaphysics.' His commentaries on various parts of the 'Organon' show, says Hauréau, that he was a scrupulous and minute logician, and he was one of the most important teachers of the time in developing the doctrine of the syllogism. Hauréau (ii. 2, 30–2) gives a long extract from his 'De Ortu' as a specimen of his power of abridging Aristotle clearly and faithfully. He says that he was a disciple of Thomas Aquinas, but never seems to have attempted any real investigation of his writings.

Kilwardby's treatises on grammar were frequently cited as an authority during the fourteenth century. There are manuscripts of his 'In Priscianum de Constructione Commentarius' at Merton and Corpus Christi Colleges, Oxford. Large extracts are given in Quétif and Echard (pp. 377–8) from his 'Commentary on the Sentences,' of which there is also a manuscript at Merton College. He also wrote commentaries on scripture, 'De Passione Christi' and 'De Sacramento Altaris.'

[Leland's Commentarii de Scriptoribus Britannicis, pp. 286–8; Quétif and Echard's Scriptores Ordinis Predicatorum, i. 374–80; Bale's Script. Brit. Catal. Cent. Quart. p. xlvi (Basel); Tanner's Bibl. Brit.-Hib. pp. 455–7; Hook's Lives of the Archbishops of Canterbury, iii. 304–26; Touron's Histoire des hommes illustres de l'ordre de Saint-Dominique, i. 397–404; Hauréau's Histoire de la Philosophie Scolastique, ii. ii. 28–33; Stöckl's Geschichte der Philosophie des Mittelalters, ii. 735–6; Catalogus Librorum MSS. Angliæ et Hib. (1697); Notices des Manuscrits de la Bibliothèque Nationale, xxii. ii. 39, 95, 97; Coxe's Cat. Cod. MSS. in Coll. et Aul Oxon.; Trivet, Engl. Hist. Soc.); Peckham's Register, Annales Monastici, Cotton, Chron. of Edward I and Edward II (the last four in Rolls Ser.); Rymer's Fœdera, vol. i.; Prynne's Records.]   T. F. T.

KILWARDEN, VISCOUNT. See WOLFE, ARTHUR, 1739–1803.

KIMBER, EDWARD (1719–1769), novelist and compiler, born in 1719, was son of Isaac Kimber [q. v.] He gained a scanty subsistence by compiling for booksellers, and died, worn out with such drudgery, in 1769 (R. JOHNSON, preface to WOTTON's Baronetage, 1771). His works are: 1. 'The Life and Adventures of Joe Thompson, a Narrative founded on fact, written by himself' anon., 2 vols. 12mo, London, 1750; other editions, 1751, 1775, 1783. A French translation appeared in 1762. 2. 'The Peerage of England,' 12mo, London, 1766; 2nd edit. 1769.

3. 'The Peerage of Scotland,' 8vo, London, 1767. 4. 'The Peerage of Ireland,' 8vo, London, 1768. 5. 'The Extinct Peerage of England,' 12mo, London, 1769. He also wrote memoirs of his father, together with a poem to his memory, prefixed to the latter's 'Sermons,' 1756. With Richard Johnson he edited and continued Thomas Wotton's 'Baronetage of England,' 3 vols. 8vo, London, 1771. Kimber's father, not himself, as Nichols (Lit. Anecd. v. 251) asserts, superintended a third edition of Ainsworth's 'Latin Dictionary' in 1751.

[Chalmers's Biog. Dict. xix. 349; Nichols's Lit. Anecd. iii. 441; Cat. of Advocates' Library.]   G. G.

KIMBER, ISAAC (1692–1755), general baptist minister, biographer, and journalist, was born at Wantage, Berkshire, on 1 Dec. 1692. He studied languages under John Ward, LL.D., professor of rhetoric at Gresham College, and went through a course of philosophy and divinity under John Eames [q. v.] His first settlement was early in 1722, as assistant to Joseph Burroughs [q. v.], at Paul's Alley, Barbican. He was a dull preacher, and very near-sighted, eventually losing the sight of one eye. He left Paul's Alley on 28 June 1724, and became assistant to Samuel Acton at Nantwich, Cheshire. Here he published (1727) a funeral sermon for Mrs. Milton, who is said to have been the third wife of the poet John Milton, Elizabeth, daughter of Sir Edward Minshull, who died at Nantwich March 1727. Milton's widow was certainly a member of his congregation, but her identity with the subject of the sermon has been disputed, as there were two other ladies of the same surname at Nantwich. He left Nantwich in 1727, and became assistant at the general baptist congregation in Old Artillery Lane, London, and also at a neighbouring congregation. On the amalgamation of the two places his services were dispensed with, and he left the active ministry. He started a periodical called 'The Morning Chronicle,' which lasted from January 1728 to May 1732. In 1734 Ward made over his school near Moorfields to Kimber and Edward Sandercock, but the school declined in a few years, and Kimber gave it up and took to writing for the booksellers, editing Ainsworth's 'Latin Dictionary' in 1751. He died of apoplexy early in 1755; his funeral sermon was preached at Paul's Alley by Burroughs on 9 Feb. He was unfortunate in his marriage, his wife being insane for twenty-three years. His son Edward is separately noticed.

Among his publications were: 1. 'The Life of Oliver Cromwell,' &c., 1724, 8vo (six editions); a French translation appeared in 1725. 2. 'An Abridgement of the History of England,' 1745, 8vo.

Posthumous were: 3. 'Twenty Sermons,' &c., 1756, 8vo. 4. 'Sermons,' &c., 1758, 8vo (with life). He edited the 'Works,' 1729, fol., 2 vols., of William Beveridge [q. v.], prefixing a 'Life;' and contributed the account of the reign of George II to the 1740 8vo edition of the 'Medulla Historiæ Anglicanæ' of William Howell (1638?–1683) [q. v.]

[Funeral Sermon by Burroughs, 1755; Life prefixed to Sermons, 1758; Wilson's Dissenting Churches of London, 1810 iii. 257, 1814 iv. 370; Urwick's Nonconformity in Cheshire, 1864, pp. 117, 134.]   A. G.

KINASTON. [See KYNASTON.]

KINCAID, Mrs. JEAN (1579–1600), murderess, daughter of John Livingstoun of Dunipace, was born in 1579. She married John Kincaid of Warriston, who was a man of influence in Edinburgh, being nearly connected with the ancient family of Kincaid of that ilk in Stirlingshire, and possessed of extensive estates in Midlothian and Linlithgowshire. Owing to alleged maltreatment, the young wife conceived a deadly hatred for her husband, and a nurse who lived in her house urged her to take revenge. A servant of her father, a youth named Robert Weir, was admitted by Mrs. Kincaid into her husband's chamber in his house at Warriston at an early hour on the morning of Tuesday, 1 July 1600, and he killed Kincaid with his fists. News of the murder quickly reached Edinburgh, and 'the Lady Warristoun,' 'the fause nourice,' and her two 'hyred women,' were arrested 'red-handed.' Weir escaped, refusing to allow Mrs. Kincaid to accompany him in his flight. The prisoners were immediately brought before the magistrates of Edinburgh, and sentence of death was passed upon them. No official records of the trial are extant. 'Scho was tane to the girthcrosse, upon the 5 day of July, and her heid struck fra her bodie, at the Cannagait-fit; quha deit very patiently. Her nuri-sche was brunt at the same tyme, at 4 houres in the morneing, the 5 of July' (BIRREL, Diary, p. 49). According to Calderwood, 'the nurse and ane hyred woman, her complices, were burnt in the Castell Hill of Edinburgh' (CALDERWOOD, History of the Kirk of Scotland, vi. 27). In the brief interval between the sentence and execution Mrs. Kincaid was brought, by the efforts of a clergyman, from a state of callous indifference to one of religious resignation. An authentic and interesting 'memorial' of her 'conversion,' 'with

an account of her carriage at her execution,' by an eye-witness, was privately printed at Edinburgh in 1827, from a paper preserved among Wodrow's MSS. in the Advocates' Library, by Charles Kirkpatrick Sharpe. The youth and beauty of Mrs. Kincaid were dwelt upon in numerous popular ballads, which are to be found in Jamieson's, Kinloch's, and Buchan's collections. Weir, who was arrested four years afterwards, was broken on the wheel (26 June 1604), a rare mode of execution in Scotland.

[Pitcairn's Criminal Trials, ii. 445–50; Chambers's Domestic Annals of Scotland, ii. 316–17; Memorial of the Conversion of Jean Livingston, 1827.]   G. S-H.

KINCAID, SIR JOHN (1787–1862), of the rifle brigade, second son of John Kincaid of Dalbeath, near Falkirk, and his wife, the daughter of John Gaff, was born at Dalbeath in January 1787. He was educated at Polmont school, and served for a time as lieutenant in the North York militia. On the formation of the old 3rd battalion (afterwards disbanded) of the 95th rifles, now the rifle brigade, at Hythe, Kent, in 1809, Kincaid joined with a draft of militia volunteers from the North York, and received a second lieutenancy in the 95th, with which corps he served through the Peninsular campaigns of 1811–14 and at Waterloo (medal). He led the forlorn hope at one of the assaults of Ciudad Rodrigo; was severely wounded, and had a horse shot under him as acting adjutant at Waterloo. He attained the rank of captain in the rifle brigade in 1826, and retired by sale of his commissions 21 June 1831. For his Peninsular services he afterwards received the medal with clasps for Fuentes d'Onor, Ciudad Rodrigo, Badajoz, Salamanca, Vittoria, Pyrenees, Nivelle, Nive, and Toulouse. Kincaid was appointed exon of the royal bodyguard of yeomen of the guard on 25 Oct. 1844, and, on becoming senior exon in 1852, was knighted according to custom. In 1847 he was appointed government inspector of prisons for Scotland, and in 1850 Sir George Grey [q. v.] conferred on him the appointment of inspector of factories and prisons for Scotland, which he resigned through ill-health shortly before his death. He died at Hastings, unmarried, on 22 April 1862, aged 75.

Kincaid was author of 'Adventures in the Rifle Brigade' (London, 1830; 2nd edition, London, 1838) and 'Random Shots of a Rifleman' (London, 1835). Cope, the historian of the rifle brigade, says that, although written with too much levity, they contain many facts of interest, and the dates and statements are confirmed by more formal authorities.

[Dod's Knightage, 1862; Militia and Army Lists, under dates; Cope's Hist. of the Rifle Brigade (London, 1880); Preston's Hist. of the Royal Body Guard (London, 1887); Gent. Mag. 3rd ser. xii. 658.]   H. M. C.

KINCARDINE, EARLS OF. [See BRUCE, ALEXANDER, d. 1681, second EARL; BRUCE, THOMAS, 1766-1841, eleventh EARL; BRUCE, JAMES, 1811-1863, twelfth EARL.]

KINDERSLEY, SIR RICHARD TORIN (1792-1879), vice-chancellor, eldest son of Nathaniel Edward Kindersley of Sunninghill, Berkshire, was born at Madras, where his father was in the civil service of the East India Company, on 5 Oct. 1792. He was educated first at Haileybury, with the intention of entering the Indian civil service, but subsequently he proceeded to Trinity College, Cambridge, where he was fourth wrangler, and graduated B.A. in January 1814. In October of the following year he was elected a fellow of his college, and proceeded M.A. in July 1817. He was called to the bar at Lincoln's Inn on 10 Feb. 1818, and after enjoying a considerable junior practice was appointed a king's counsel in January 1835. He took a leading position in the rolls court; in 1847 became chancellor of the county palatine of Durham, and in March 1848 a master in chancery. He was not a politician, and was recommended only by his deep learning and sound judgment. On 20 Oct. 1851 he was appointed a vice-chancellor and was knighted. His judgments are mainly reported in Drewry's 'Reports,' Drewry and Smale's 'Reports,' and the 'Law Reports,' Equity Ser. vols. i. and ii. He retired from the bench in 1866, when he was sworn of the privy council, and received a pension of 3,500l. per annum. He died at his residence, Clyffe, near Dorchester, on 22 Oct. 1879. He married in 1824 Mary Anne, only daughter of the Rev. James Leigh Bennett of Thorpe Place, Surrey, and by her had four children.

[Foss's Lives of the Judges; Times, 25 Oct. 1879; Law Times, 8 Nov. 1879; Law Journal, xiv. 657. 723; Solicitors' Journal, 1 Nov. 1879.]   J. A. H.

KINDLEMARSH. [See KINWELMERSH.]

KING, CHARLES (fl. 1721), writer on economics, a London merchant in the reign of Queen Anne, wrote several papers in the 'British Merchant,' a periodical which appeared twice a week during the summer of 1713, at the time of the proposed treaty of commerce with France. The object of the

paper was to refute the reciprocity arguments propounded by Defoe in favour of the treaty in his 'Mercator;' it was started by Henry Martin, and numbered among its contributors Joshua Gee (concerning whose influence see HUME, Philosophical Works, 1884, iii. 340), Sir Charles Cooke, Sir Theodore Janssen, Nathaniel Torriano, and other leading merchants, several of whom had a special audience in the House of Lords on the subject of the treaty (2 and 4 June 1713). Backed up by the Earl of Halifax, 'the support and very spirit of the paper' (Brit. Merch. Preface, p. xvii), Lord Stanhope, and the bulk of the commercial classes in the country, the 'British Merchant' more than neutralised the effect of Defoe's paper, and finally secured a majority of nine against the eighth and ninth articles of the treaty [see under MOORE, ARTHUR, fl. 1712]. Its object achieved, the 'British Merchant' ceased to appear, but the most important numbers were collected and edited by King in book form under the title of 'The British Merchant, or Commerce Preserved,' 3 vols. 8vo, London, 1721. King was at that time chamber-keeper to the treasury, and he dedicated the concluding volume of the work to Paul Methuen, son of the framer of the Methuen treaty, and comptroller of his majesty's household. He was allowed 395l. 16s. from the exchequer for expenses of printing, and copies were sent to 'each of the corporations of Great Britain which send members to parliament' at the cost of the treasury (Cal. Treas. Papers, 1720-8, ccxl. 32). The work may thus be supposed to represent the views of Walpole's government (though not perhaps of Walpole himself) upon economic matters. It was, however, less an exposition of theory than an appeal to contemporary common sense, and to the interests involved in the Methuen treaty of 1703 with Portugal against the supposed fallacious doctrine of reciprocity advanced by Bolingbroke, and set forth in Defoe's 'Essay on the Treaty of Commerce with France,' 1713. Such general theories as it did contain were based without alteration upon the treatise (reprinted in 1713) of Thomas Mun [q. v.], showing that the object of commercial policy was 'to encrease the exportation of our commodities and to decrease the consumption of foreign wares.' The 'British Merchant' enjoyed unique authority during the forty years following its publication, and its statistics (though by no means invariably accurate) on British commerce, the extent of markets, price of labour, and kindred subjects render it indispensable to the historian of commerce during the early Georgian era. The book was republished in 1743, but there is no evidence to show if King was living at that time, or if he was identical with the Charles King ' of Westminster Hall,' printer and publisher, who issued the 'Tracts against Popery' of Michael Geddes [q. v.] in 1715, and the 'General Treatise of Mortality' of Richard Fiddes [q. v.] in 1724.

[Information kindly supplied by W. A. S. Hewins, e-q., of Oxford; Tindal's Continuation of Rapin, vi. 83; Boyer's Quadriennium Annæ Postremum, vol. v.; W. Lee's Defoe, i. 215; Daily Courant, 3 Jan. 1734; Nichols's Lit. Anecd. viii. 298; Willis's Current Notes, 1856, p. 38; M'Culloch's Literature of Pol. Econ., and his edition of Adam Smith's Works, xxiv. n., xxxv. n.; Macpherson's Annals, iii. 30; Roscher, i. 279; Watt's Bibl. Brit.; Brit. Mus. Cat.] T. S.

KING, CHARLES (1687–1748), musical composer, the son of Charles and Mary King, was born at Bury St. Edmunds in 1687, and was baptised in St. Mary's Church in that town 5 June 1693. He became a chorister of St. Paul's Cathedral, under Dr. Blow and Jeremiah Clark, and was subsequently appointed supernumerary singer in the same choir at an annual salary of 14l. On 12 July 1707 he proceeded to the degree of Mus. Bac. at Oxford, and in the same year married Clark's sister. At Clark's death (1 Dec. 1707) King received the appointments of almoner and 'master of the children' of St. Paul's, and in 1708 was elected, in addition, to the post of organist of St. Benet Finck, Royal Exchange. In 1730 he was nominated a vicar-choral of St. Paul's, and held that office with his organistship until his death on 17 March 1748.

King composed a large number of anthems and church services—a fact which gave rise to Maurice Greene's remark that 'Mr. King was a very *serviceable* man.' The titles of his best-known works are: 1. Anthems— 'Rejoice in the Lord,' 'Hear, O Lord,' 'O pray for the peace of Jerusalem,' 'Wherewithal shall a young man.' 2. Services in F, C, B flat, and D, which are still occasionally performed. Four of his anthems are to be found in Page's 'Harmonia Sacra,' and two in Stevens's 'Sacred Music.' Other of his compositions are included in Arnold's 'Cathedral Music,' and the Tudway Collection (Harl. MSS. 7341-2). Some services and anthems by King were published separately in 1859 and 1860. Hawkins remarks that 'King's inferiority was due rather to indolence than want of ability.'

[Georgian Era, iv. 512; Dict. of Mus. 1824; Grove's Dict.; parish registers.] R. H. L.

KING, CHARLES WILLIAM (1818–1888), author of works on engraved gems, was born on 5 Sept. 1818 at Newport, Monmouthshire, where his father was engaged as a shipping agent in the iron trade. He entered Trinity College, Cambridge, as a sizar, in October 1836, and was elected scholar of his college in 1839, and fellow in 1842. He graduated in 1840 as sixth in class I. of the classical tripos. About 1842 King went to Italy, and there spent several years studying the Italian language and literature and in collecting antique gems, which he procured at moderate prices, especially in Rome and Florence. King afterwards increased his collection by many gems purchased of Eastwood, the London dealer, and acquired specimens at the sale in London of several important cabinets, such as the Mertens-Schaafhausen (Praun), the Hertz, and the Uzielli. The collection, formed between 1845 and 1877, ultimately consisted of 331 engraved stones, more than two-thirds of which were Greek and Roman, the remainder being Sassanian, Gnostic, and Oriental. About 1878, when his eyesight was seriously failing, King sold his collection, and it is now in the Metropolitan Museum of Art at New York, to which it was presented in October 1881 by Mr. John Taylor Johnston, the president of that institution. A catalogue has been printed, without change, from King's own manuscript (dated 28 Feb. 1878), with the title, 'The Johnston Collection of Engraved Gems' (*Metrop. Mus.*, New York, Handbook No. 9). Three Greek marbles which belonged to King are described by Michaelis in his 'Ancient Marbles in Great Britain,' pp. 271-2.

After King's return from Italy his life was chiefly spent at Trinity College, Cambridge. He was in holy orders, but had no cure. About 1860 he was one of her majesty's inspectors of schools (*Clergy List*, 1866). At Cambridge King passed a very retired existence, engaged in the composition of various works, but taking no part in the educational life of the place. The few friends who knew him well found him a kind-hearted man and a delightful companion, full of curious knowledge and quaint humour (ALDIS WRIGHT in *Athenæum*). He was widely read in the Greek and Roman classics, without having, however, a minute philological knowledge. He had specially studied Pausanias and Pliny's 'Historia.' His short-sightedness always rendered reading difficult for him, though he had 'a microscopic power of discernment ' for objects such as gems. His writings on ancient gems are original, and evince the experience of the practical collector. In England they have stimulated an interest in glyptography, though they are often marred by defects due to insufficient numismatic and archæological training. King died in London, after a brief illness, of a bronchial cold, on 25 March 1888. There is a portrait of him, in a travelling costume, by George Mason, one of his friends when in Rome.

King's principal publications are: 1. 'Antique Gems,' London, 1860, 8vo. 2. 'The Gnostics and their Remains,' London, 1864, 8vo; 2nd edit. London, 1887, 8vo (for a controversy as to misprints and alterations in this edition see *Athenæum*, January–June 1888, pp. 441, 468, 499, 535, 602, 606). 3. 'The Natural History . . . of Precious Stones and Gems and of the Precious Metals,' London, 1865, 8vo; also a 2nd edit. in 2 vols. published as 'The Natural History of Gems, or Decorative Stones,' Cambridge, 1867, 8vo, and 'The Natural History of Precious Stones and of the Precious Metals,' Cambridge, 1867, 8vo. 4. 'The Handbook of Engraved Gems,' London, 1866, 8vo; 2nd edit. 1885, 8vo. 5. 'Horatii Opera,' illustrated by antique gems selected by C. W. K., 1869, 8vo. 6. 'Antique Gems and Rings,' vol. i. text, vol. ii. illustrations, London, 1872, 8vo. 7. 'Early Christian Numismatic and other Antiquarian Tracts,' London, 1873, 8vo. 8. 'Plutarch's Morals,' Translated by C.W. K., 1882 (Bohn's Classical Library). 9. 'Julian the Emperor . . . Theosophical Works,' &c. Translated by C. W. K., 1888 (Bohn's Classical Library).

[W. Aldis Wright in Athenæum for 7 April 1888, p. 441; Athenæum for 31 March 1888, p. 412; Academy for 7 April 1888, p. 247; Cat. of Johnston Coll.; Brit. Mus. Cat.]   W. W.

KING, DANIEL (d. 1664?), engraver, son of William King of Chester, baker, was apprenticed on 3 Sept. 1630 as painter for ten years to Randle Holme the elder [q. v.] After carrying on business for some years at Chester, he removed to London, where in 1656 he published 'The Vale Royall of England, or the County Palatine of Chester Illustrated,' folio. This was written by William Smith, William Webb, and Samuel Lee, with an appendix on the Isle of Man by James Chaloner. The dedication alone is by King; indeed, Dugdale told Wood that he was not able to write one word of true English, being 'a most ignorant, silly fellow,' and moreover 'an arrant knave.' The engravings to the 'Vale Royall' are admirably done by King himself in the style of Hollar. The 'Vale Royall' is embodied in Ormerod's 'History of Cheshire,' 1819, and an abridgment with notes by Thomas Hughes, F.S.A., was published in 1852. King also published: 1. 'The Cathedrall and Conventuall Churches of England and Wales Orthographically Delineated,' 1656, oblong 4to, containing fifty engravings,

three or four of them by Hollar. 2. A translation of the 'Universal Way of Dyaling, by G. de Desargues,' 1659, 4to (Brit. Mus. Cat.) 3. 'An Orthographical Design of severall Viewes upon y* Road in England and Wales,' about 1660. He etched some plates for Dugdale's 'Monasticon.' On visiting Chester in 1660 he was received and entertained by the Stationers' Company of that city. Wood states that he made an unfortunate marriage, and that after his wife had robbed and left him, he died heartbroken near York House, in the Strand, about 1664.

[Wood's Athenæ Oxon. (Bliss), iii. 503; T. Hughes in Chester Archæol. Soc. Journal, ii. 25, 256; Sir W. Dugdale's Diary (Hamper), 1827, p. 108; Bryan's Dict. of Painters and Engravers (Graves), i. 732; Brit. Mus. Cat.]
    C. W. S.

KING, DAVID, LL.D. (1806–1883), Scottish divine, son of John King (1762–1827), pastor of the second united associate church in Montrose, by his wife Eliza, daughter of Mr. Young, a Montrose merchant, was born in Montrose on 20 May 1806. His ancestors had been tenants of Giffen Mill, near Beith, for several generations. King began his education in the high school of Montrose, and matriculated at Aberdeen University in 1820, but after a year was transferred by his parents to Edinburgh University. Here he became a good classical scholar and showed a taste for science. Having completed his arts course at Edinburgh, he removed to Glasgow to study theology under John Dick [q. v.] of the secession church. He was licensed as a probationer by the presbytery of Edinburgh. On 13 Jan. 1830 he became minister of the first united secession church of Dalkeith, and after the death of Dr. Dick he removed to Greyfriars secession church, Glasgow, 15 Oct. 1833. At Glasgow he displayed marked organising power and enthusiasm. He began a systematic series of missions to the poor; was the first to establish homes for poor boys there; and set up classes for the instruction of young men in both sacred and secular subjects. The first foreign mission to Trinidad connected with the secession church was originated by him, and was supported during the early years of its existence principally through his exertions. His refined and sympathetic style of preaching was especially attractive to young men, and students of all denominations attended his ministry in Greyfriars. He took a determined position in favour of the disestablishment of the church, and was associated with Lord Brougham, O'Connell, and other leaders of the time in the anti-slavery movement of 1838. The university of Glasgow conferred the degree of LL.D. upon him in 1840. He took an active part in the foundation of the Evangelical Alliance in 1845, and attended many of the annual conferences held in various parts of Europe. He helped to bring about the union of the secession and relief churches in 1847 to form the united presbyterian church. In 1848 his health gave way, and he employed his enforced leisure in visiting Jamaica and making a tour through the United States, returning to Scotland in the following year. Until 1853 he continued actively engaged in the multifarious schemes connected with his denomination. Illness compelled him to resign his position at Greyfriars Church 12 Feb. 1856. He retired to Kilcreggan in the Firth of Clyde, and in 1860 removed to London. Having settled at Bayswater, he founded a presbyterian congregation there, and laboured in this quarter, amid many discouragements, till 1869. He still preserved his connection with the united presbyterian church in Scotland, and was chosen moderator of the synod of that body in 1863, taking a prominent share in the movement (1863-73) for the union of the free church of Scotland, the reformed presbyterian church, the united presbyterian church, and the presbyterian church in England. Though this union was only partially realised, King's attitude helped to promote conciliatory feeling. In March 1869 he accepted a call to the small congregation of Morningside, near Edinburgh, but in February 1873 he was forced to resign all ministerial work. He died, after much travel in search of health, in London on 20 Dec. 1883.

King's popularity as a preacher overshadowed his reputation as a writer, though the few books which he wrote were very successful. His principal works were: 1. 'The Ruling Eldership,' 1845, which went through three editions. 2. 'The Lord's Supper,' 1846. 3. 'Geology and Religion,' 1849, an attempt at a reconciliation of the scriptural and scientific accounts of the creation, of which five editions were published. 4. 'The State and Prospects of Jamaica,' 1850. A volume of his sermons was published posthumously in 1885, with a memoir of him written by his widow, the daughter of Professor James Thomson and sister of Sir William Thomson of Glasgow University.

[Memoir as above.] A. H. M.

KING, SIR EDMUND (1629-1709), physician, born in 1629, practised, after apprenticeship, as a surgeon in London. He lived at first in Little Britain, and had a museum in his house which he took pleasure in showing to students. He used to keep dried specimens, such as the ileo-cæcal valve, pressed in a large paper book, and he dissected animals as well as the human subject (*Sloane MS.* 1900). About 1665 he took a house in Hatton Garden, and was married at St. Andrew's Church, Holborn, on 20 June 1666, to Rebecca Polsted of the adjoining parish of St. Sepulchre. In the same year he published in the 'Philosophical Transactions' a paper on the parenchymatous parts of the body, and maintained, from microscopic observation, that they contained enormous numbers of minute blood-vessels. In 1667 the 'Philosophical Transactions' contained a long account by him of the transfusion of the blood of a calf into a sheep, with a view to proving that one animal may live with the blood of another. The experiment was carefully conducted by means of an apparatus of pipes and quills. In 1669 he published further microscopic researches to show that glands consisted of tubes and vessels only. He was fond of insects, and in 1667 published a paper on ants, and in 1670 one on leaf cutter bees (both in 'Philosophical Transactions'). He had examined the eggs of ants microscopically, and studied the ways of life in ant-hills. He is probably one of the investigators described as antmen and bearmen by the Duchess of Newcastle (*Description of a New World,* 1668, p. 15). He was acquainted with Lord Arundel, Sir William Petty, Dr. Needham, and Robert Boyle, and some of his experiments were carried on at Arundel House in the Strand. Sheldon, the archbishop of Canterbury, created him M.D.; he was incorporated at Cambridge in 1671, and in 1677, on bringing a commendatory letter from the king, was admitted an honorary fellow of the College of Physicians of London. He was admitted a regular fellow 12 April 1687, being one of the nominees of James II's charter, and was thus completely converted from a surgeon into a physician. He was knighted and sworn physician to the king in 1676.

On the morning of 2 Feb. 1684-5 King was sent for by Charles II. Charles talked incoherently, but the physician did not ascertain the morbid change at work (BURNET, *History of his own Time,* edit. 1724, i. 606). By Lord Peterborough's advice he paid a second visit to the bedchamber, and at the moment that he entered Charles fell down in a fit. King bled him immediately. Charles gradually regained consciousness. The other physicians who arrived approved the bleeding, and the privy council advised that King should receive a reward of 1,000*l.*; but as that body has no command of funds, and as the subsequent fatal termination prevented any expression of royal gratitude, King never received his fee. King approved of viper powder, but liked the volatile salt better (original letter to Sir Hans Sloane). In the 'Philosophical Transactions' for 1686 he published an account of the autopsy of Mr. Robert Bacon, a demented person, who had a calcified pineal gland in his brain, renal and vesical calculi and gallstones. He mentions that he had dissected one hundred brains. In the preface to the 'Pharmaceutice Rationalis' of Dr. Thomas Willis [q. v.], who became his close friend, King's dexterous dissections are commended. His next observations (Phil. Trans.) were on animalculæ in pepper. He had looked at them 'with my best microscope,' and had noticed that when oats and some herbs were left in water, living organisms became discoverable in it. He tried the effects of sack, ink, sulphuric acid, and other fluids on these atmo-bæ. In November 1688 he published a further paper in the 'Philosophical Transactions' on the tubular structure of reproductive glands in men, guinea-pigs, and bulls. He had a considerable practice, from which he did not retire till he was seventy-two, and thenceforward he spent much time in the country. His own loss of strength compelled him in 1701 to give up attending the aged poet, Sir Charles Sedley, whose death he had foretold at his first visit, and he handed on the patient to Sir Hans Sloane (original letters in Sloane MS. 4050). He died in Hatton Garden 30 May 1709. His portrait by Lely, which he bequeathed to the College of Physicians, and which hangs in the reading-room of the college, represents him with a large aquiline nose and a dark complexion. It was engraved by Williams.

[Munk's Coll. of Phys. i. 448; Phil. Trans. of the Royal Society; Burnet's Hist. of his own Time, London, 1724; Wilkin's Sir Thomas Browne's Works, London, 1836, i. 52; Sloane MS. 1906 in British Museum; Mr. Edward Browne's Journal; Sloane MS. 4050, ff. 169, 177, 179. The last, a letter on the death of Sir Charles Sedley, is dated in error by Sir E. King himself 1601 for 1701.] S. M.

KING, EDWARD (1612–1637), friend of Milton, was younger son of Sir John King (d. 1637) [q. v.], at one time of Feathercock Hall, Northallerton, Yorkshire, but afterwards an active civil officer in Ireland. Edward King, bishop of Elphin, was his godfather, and Sir Robert King [q. v.] was his eldest brother. Edward was born in 1612, and seems to have been partly educated at the school of Thomas Farnaby [q. v.] in London (cf. Justa Edouardo King... 1638). He was admitted a pensioner of Christ's College, Cambridge, on 9 June 1626, at the same time as another brother, Roger, who was two years his senior (College Admission Book). In 1630, in compliance with a royal mandate, Edward was elected to a fellowship at Christ's. Milton, who was also two years his senior, was at that time hoping to obtain a like distinction. In the mandate, which is dated 10 June, his majesty is said to be 'well ascertained both of the present sufficiency and future hopes' of the new fellow (Baker MS. ix. 220). King, however, having been born in Ireland, his election, as the son of a Yorkshireman, gave rise to some dispute, and the questions arising out of his election were not settled until 1636 (ib. ix. 247). King did not discredit the royal recommendation. He appears to have been popular in the college, and Milton himself became warmly attached to his rival, on account both of his amiable disposition and scholarly tastes. During 1633–4 King was prælector of his college, and the admissions are in his handwriting. He was also one of the tutors, and was looking forward to the career of a parish priest. At the close of the academic year 1636–7 King set out for Ireland, on a visit to his brother Robert and two of his sisters. The vessel on which he had embarked left the estuary of the Dee, and was coasting in calm weather along the Welsh shore, when it struck on a rock and foundered. With the exception of a few who managed to get into a boat, all on board perished. King is said to have behaved with calm heroism; after a vain endeavour to prevail upon him to enter the boat he was left on board, and was last seen kneeling on deck in the act of prayer (Account prefixed to the Obsequies). His death, according to Baker, took place on 10 Aug. (4 Id. Sextilis) 1637; but his name in the audit books occurs in the list of Lady day 1638; it is also entered, but erased, in the list of midsummer 1638. His name, written by himself in a small and very beautiful hand, occurs in a college order written in an old lease book.

King's reputation for poetical ability is hardly sustained by his extant compositions, all of which were contributed to various collections of poems by Cambridge scholars. They are as follows: 1. Four metrical compositions in Latin, signed 'Ed. King, Coll. Christi Socius,' in pp. 36-9 of a volume entitled 'Genethliacum illustrissimorum principum, Caroli et Mariæ, a Musis Cantabrigiensibus celebratum,' Cambridge, 1631, on the occasion of the birth of the Princess Mary on 4 Nov. 1631. 2. Some Latin iambics on pp. 43-4 of a collection of Cambridge verses celebrating the king's recovery from the

mall-pox in the winter of 1632, and entitled 'Anthologia in Regis Exanthemata;
en gratulatio Musarum Cantab. de felicis-
ime asservata Regis Caroli valetudine,' Cam-
ridge, 1633 (reprinted in NICHOLS's *Collection of Poems*, vii. 70–85). 3. Latin iambics
n a similar collection congratulating the
ing on his safe return from Scotland in July
1633, entitled 'Rex redux, sive Musa Canta-
rigiensis, etc., de incolumitate et felici re-
itu Regis Caroli post receptam coronam
omitiaque peracta in Scotia,' Cambridge,
1633. 4. Latin iambics prefixed to 'Senile
Odium,' by Peter Hausted [q. v.], 1633.
5. Latin elegiacs in another collection on the
birth of the Duke of York on 15 Oct. 1633,
entitled 'Ducis Eboracensis Fascia a Musis
Cantabrigiensibus raptim contexta,' Cam-
ridge, 1633. 6. Latin stanzas in a like col-
ection in honour of the birth of the Princess
Elizabeth on 28 Dec. 1635, entitled 'Carmen
Natalitium ad cunas illustrissimæ principis
Elizabethæ decantatum, intra nativitatis
domini solemnia, per humiles Cantabrigiæ
musas, A.D. 1635.' 7. Iambic Latin verses
n another collection, which was entitled
Συνωδία, sive Musarum Cantabrigiensium
concentus et congratulatio ad serenissimum
Britanniarum Regem Carolum de quinta sua
subole, clarissima Principe sibi nuper felicis-
sime nata, A.D. 1637.'

On the intelligence of his death reaching
Cambridge, King's fate was commemorated
by members of the university in a series of
effusions which clearly show that he had inspired among his friends no ordinary esteem
and regard. These compositions appeared in
two parts, both printed at the university
press in 1638; the former containing twenty-
three pieces in Latin and Greek, including
one by Farnaby, was entitled 'Justa Edo-
vardo King naufrago ab amicis mœrentibus,
amoris et μνείας χάριν.' The second part
contains thirteen English poems, and is entitled 'Obsequies to the Memorie of Mr.
Edward King, Anno Dom. 1638.' Of these
Milton's 'Lycidas' is the last. Milton probably modelled his poem after an Italian
eclogue entitled 'Phyllis,' recording the fate
of another Lycidas; the author, Actius Syn-
cerus Sannazarius, was one of Milton's favourite poets of the Renaissance.

[Masson's Life of Milton, vol. i.; information
supplied from college documents by Dr. Peile,
master of Christ's College; letter by Professor
J. W. Hales in Athenæum, July 1891, pp. 159–
160.]   J. B. M.

KING, EDWARD (1735?–1807), miscellaneous writer, born about 1735, was the only
son of Edward King of Norwich. He studied

for a time at Clare Hall, Cambridge, as a
fellow-commoner. On 18 Sept. 1758 he was
admitted a member of Lincoln's Inn, and was
called to the bar in Michaelmas term 1763
(*Lincoln's Inn Register and Bar Book*). An
ample fortune bequeathed to him by his
uncle, Mr. Brown, a wholesale linendraper
of Exeter, rendered him independent of his
profession, but he regularly attended the
Norfolk circuit for some years, and was appointed recorder of King's Lynn. In his attendance on the circuit he defended a lady
from a faithless lover, and afterwards married
her. King was elected F.R.S. on 14 May
1767 (THOMSON, *Hist. of Roy. Soc.* Append.
iv. p. lii) and F.S.A. on 3 May 1770 (GOUGH,
Chronological List of Soc. Antiq. 1798, p. 23).
He contributed several papers to the 'Archæologia,' among which were 'Remarks on the
Abbey Church of Bury St. Edmunds in Suffolk' (iii. 311–14), reprinted separately in
1774, 'Observations on Antient Castles,' with
four plates (iv. 364–413), and 'A Sequel to
Observations,' with thirty-one plates (vi.
231–375), also issued separately in 1782. On
the death of Jeremiah Milles [q. v.] in February 1784, King was elected his successor
in the presidency of the Society of Antiquaries on the understanding that Lord De
Ferrars (afterwards Earl of Leicester) would
assume the office on the ensuing 23 April
(NICHOLS, *Illustr. of Lit.* vii. 461). King,
however, sought to obtain re-election, and
that by the employment of ungenerous tactics, but was defeated by an overwhelming
majority. His speech on quitting the chair
was printed, and he subsequently printed a
letter in vindication of his conduct and reflecting upon the earl, and thenceforward
ceased to make any communications to the
Society (NICHOLS, *Lit. Anecd.* viii. 57).

King's first separate work appeared in 1767
under the title of 'An Essay on the English
Constitution and Government,' 8vo. In 1780
he issued, without his name, 'Hymns to the
Supreme Being, in Imitation of the Eastern
Songs,' 8vo, of which two editions were issued
in 1795 and 1798. In 1785 he circulated, also
anonymously, 'Proposals for Establishing at
Sea a Marine School, or Seminary for Seamen,' &c., 8vo, in a letter addressed to John
Frere, vice-president of the Marine Society.
Jonas Hanway, in a report made to the society in July of that year, had proposed a
large marine school on land. King pointed
out objections to this scheme, and suggested
the fitting up a man-of-war as a marine-school
(cf. *Gent. Mag.* vol. lv. pt. ii, pp. 904–5). In
1788 he published 'Morsels of Criticism,
tending to illustrate some few passages in the
Holy Scriptures, upon philosophical principles

and an enlarged view of things,' large 4to. Among other absurdities King attempted to prove that John the Baptist was an angel from heaven, and the same who formerly appeared in the person of Elijah. The work on its first appearance was severely criticised by Richard Gough [q. v.] in the 'Gentleman's Magazine' (vol. lviii. pt. i. pp. 141–5). A notice of the book in Mathias's 'Pursuits of Literature' created some demand for it, and a second edition, to which was added a 'supplemental part designed to show, still more fully, the perfect consistency of philosophical discoveries, and of historical facts, with the revealed Will of God,' was published in 1800 (3 vols. folio), and also a second part of the quarto edition (*Literary Memoirs of Living Authors*, i. 338). In 1793 King published 'An Imitation of the Prayer of Abel,' and during the same year 'Considerations on the Utility of the National Debt: and on the Present Alarming Crisis: with a Short Plan of a Mode of Relief,' 8vo. In 1796 he wrote some whimsical 'Remarks concerning Stones said to have fallen from the clouds, both in these days and in antient times,' 8vo, occasioned by a supposed shower of stones in Tuscany on 16 June of that year. King's next treatise, called 'Vestiges of Oxford Castle; or, a small fragment of a work intended to be published speedily on the History of Ancient Castles,' &c., fol., London, 1796, was followed by his great work entitled 'Munimenta Antiqua; or, Observations on ancient Castles, including remarks on the ... progress of Architecture ... in Great Britain, and on the ... changes in ... Laws and Customs' (with Appendix), 4 vols. fol. London, 1799–1806. The book is full of foolish theories, misplaced learning, and blunders, but the importance of its plans and details, despite inaccuracies, is generally recognised by antiquaries. Louis Dutens having taken exception to King's theories on the invention of the arch in 'Recherches sur le tems le plus reculé de l'usage des voûtes chez les anciens,' 4to, 1805, King anticipated his fourth volume by publishing during the same year an 'Introduction' of twenty-one pages, in which he vigorously defended his views. Dutens continued the controversy in three more tracts, to which King replied in an 'Appendix' to 'Munimenta Antiqua' issued in 1806. In 1798 King wrote another extraordinary pamphlet called 'Remarks on the Signs of the Times,' 4to, in which he demonstrated the genuineness of the second book of Esdras. Irritated by Gough's critique on this tract in the 'Gentleman's Magazine' (vol. lxviii. pt. ii. pp. 591–3), he wrote a violent letter to the printer, John Nichols. King added a 'Supplement' to his 'Remarks' in 1799, but this was demolished by Bishop Horsley in 'Critical Disquisitions on the Eighteenth Chapter of Isaiah, in a letter to E. King,' 4to, 1799 (*Gent. Mag.* vol. lxix. pt. ii. pp. 496–503). In 1808 King published anonymously 'Honest Apprehensions; or, the unbiassed ... Confession of Faith of a plain honest Lay-man,' 8vo. It is strictly orthodox. King died on 16 April 1807, aged 72, and was buried in the churchyard at Beckenham, Kent, where was his country seat, 'The Oakery,' on Clay Hill. He had read much, was exceedingly tenacious of his opinions, and would contend with as much zeal for the genuineness of the correspondence between St. Paul and Seneca and of the apocryphal writings as for the canonical books. His collections of prints and drawings were sold by auction in 1808.

[Chalmers's Biog. Dict.]   G. G.

KING, EDWARD, VISCOUNT KINGSBOROUGH (1795–1837), born on 16 Nov. 1795, was eldest son of George, third earl of Kingston, by Lady Helena Moore, only daughter of Stephen, first earl of Mountcashell (BURKE, *Peerage*, 1891, p. 789). After his father succeeded to the earldom in 1799 he was known by the courtesy title of Viscount Kingsborough. He matriculated at Oxford from Exeter College on 25 June 1814, and in Michaelmas term 1818 gained a second class in classics, but did not graduate (FOSTER, *Alumni Oxon.* 1715–1886, ii. 794). In 1818 and again in 1820 he was elected M.P. for Cork county, but resigned his seat in 1826 in favour of his younger brother Robert (*Lists of Members of Parliament*, pt. ii.)

The sight of a Mexican manuscript in the Bodleian Library determined King to devote his life to the study of the antiquities of that country. He promoted and edited, with copious notes, a magnificent work entitled 'Antiquities of Mexico, comprising facsimiles of Ancient Mexican Paintings and Hieroglyphics preserved in ... various Libraries, together with the Monuments of New Spain, by M. Dupaix, with ... accompanying Descriptions. The whole illustrated by many valuable Manuscripts by Augustine Aglio,' 9 vols. imperial fol., London, 1830–48, including sixty pages of a projected tenth volume. Four copies were printed on vellum, with the plates coloured. It is said that the work was undertaken by the encouragement and with the advice of Sir Thomas Phillipps, in whose collection many of the manuscripts and drawings used in it were preserved (MACRAY, *Annals of the Bodleian Library*, 2nd edition, p. 322). The drift of King's speculations is to establish the colonisation of Mexico by the Israelites. The book cost King upwards of 32,000*l.* and his life. Oppressed with debt, he was arrested at the suit of a paper manufacturer, and lodged in the sheriff's prison, Dublin, where he died of typhus fever on 27 Feb. 1837, and was buried at Mitchelstown. He was unmarried.

[Gent. Mag. new ser. vii. 537–8; Ann. Reg. 1837; Webb's Compendium of Irish Biog. p. 275; Allibone's Dict.]   G. G.

KING, Mrs. FRANCES ELIZABETH (1757–1821), authoress. [See under KING, RICHARD, 1748–1810.]

KING, GREGORY (1648–1712), herald, genealogist, engraver, and statistician, born at Lichfield, Staffordshire, on 15 Dec. 1648, was eldest son of Gregory King of that city, by his first wife, Elizabeth, daughter of J. Andrews of Sandwich, Kent. His father, an accomplished mathematician, gained a livelihood by surveying land, laying out ornamental gardens, and constructing sun-dials, but his habits were irregular and his income precarious. The son was educated under Thomas Bevans, head-master of Lichfield grammar school. When he left school at the age of fourteen he knew Latin and Greek and the Hebrew grammar. In December 1662 he became clerk to Sir William Dugdale [q. v.], Norroy king of arms. Dugdale held a visitation of the whole of his province between 1662 and 1666, and in many of the northern counties his little clerk, who was very small for his age, delineated 'the prospects of towns, castles, and other remarquables,' besides emblazoning armorial bearings on vellum.

Between 1667 and 1669 King was in the service of Lord Hatton, who was forming a collection of the arms of the nobility. In 1669 he returned to Lichfield, where he supported himself by teaching writing and arithmetic, by painting hatchments, signs, and coaches, and by giving instruction in the decipherment of ancient records. He likewise transcribed the family muniments of Walter Chetwynd [q. v.] of Ingestre. At the end of 1669 he became the steward, auditor, and secretary of the Dowager Lady Gerard of Gerard's Bromley, widow of Charles, and mother of Digby, lord Gerard. He resided with the lady's father, George Digby of Sandon, Staffordshire, until August 1672, when he came back to London. On the recommendation of Hollar the engraver, John Ogilby the printer employed him to etch plates for Sir Peter Leycester's 'Historical Antiquities;' for the edition of '.Æsop's Fables' (2 vols. London, 1672–3, 8vo), the 'Description of Persia' (1673), and for a new edition of Camden's 'Britannia.' While engaged on the last work King travelled into Essex with a surveyor named Falgate, and in the winter of 1672 they constructed maps of Ipswich in Suffolk and Malden in Essex, which were afterwards 'very curiously finished.' King also assisted in drawing the map of London, subsequently engraved by Hollar, and he superintended its production. He projected and managed a lottery of books to recoup Ogilby for the expenses incurred in these undertakings, and a similar lottery which he superintended for Bristol fair proved very profitable. He next edited the 'Book of Roads,' digesting the notes and directing the engravings, three or four of which he executed with his own hand, these being his earliest experiments with the graver. He undertook on his own account the map of Westminster (1675), and with the assistance of Falgate completed it in a year. Afterwards he was employed in engraving the letter-work of maps. He continued to engrave from 1675 to 1680, and compiled a portion of Francis Sandford's 'Genealogical History of the Kings and Queens of England,' while his friend the author was prostrated by illness.

London was indebted to King for the laying out of the streets and squares in Soho Fields. Soho Square was formerly called King's Square, and Rimbault suggests that Greek Street, formerly Grig Street, was so called after King's christian name. Many of the first building articles or leases in various parts of London were drawn up by him.

At the College of Arms he formed a close friendship with Thomas Lee, Chester herald; and the Earl of Norwich, deputy earl-marshal, on Lee's recommendation, created him Rouge Dragon pursuivant on 24 June 1677 (NOBLE, College of Arms, p. 291). In Michaelmas term of that year King brought an action for libel in the court of king's bench against one who had charged him with cheating (KEBLE, Reports, ii. 265).

In 1680 he removed from his house in Covent Garden to the college. He assisted Sir Henry St. George, Norroy king of arms, in his visitations in 1681 and 1682; and in 1684 he was nominated by the Duke of Norfolk to the office of registrar of the College of Arms. He was consulted about the coronation of James II and his queen, and was the principal author of the superb volume containing descriptions and splendid engravings of that ceremony (London, 1687, fol.), though he allowed Francis Sandford to affix his name to the title-page. King contented himself with one-third of the profits, but the book

K 2

did not appear until just before the landing of the Prince of Orange, and the authors barely cleared their expenses, which amounted to nearly 600*l.* (NOBLE, pp. 323, 324).

In 1687 King assisted Sir Henry St. George in his visitation of London. After the revolution he was engaged in the ceremonial of William and Mary's coronation, and succeeded Sandford, who resigned on account of his Jacobite sympathies, in the office of Lancaster herald. He took part in the investitures with the insignia of the Garter of the elector of Brandenburg (afterwards Frederick I, king of Prussia) in 1689 and of the Duke of Zell in 1691. He was sent to Dresden on similar business in 1692, and although the elector of Saxony, who was to be invested with the insignia of the order, died before the ceremony, the achievements were hung up, and the installation took place on 5 July 1694. A quarrel with the earl-marshal respecting the arrangements at the funeral of Queen Mary led to King's dismissal from the office of registrar, and a charge brought against him by the earl of embezzling fees caused him to be temporarily suspended from service in the college. He became, however, secretary to the commissioners for taking and stating the public accounts and also secretary to the controllers of the accounts of the army. He was in 1710 a candidate for the patent of Clarencieux, and wrote a long letter to Harley stating his claims, but, as his biographer, Chalmers, puts it, the wit of his rival, Sir John Vanbrugh, 'prevailed over King's arithmetick.' He died on 29 Aug. 1712, and was buried in the chancel of the church of St. Benet, Paul's Wharf, where a handsome mural monument of stone, with an inscription in English, was erected to his memory.

He married, first, 1 July 1674, Anne, daughter of John Powel of Firley in the parish of Forthampton, Gloucestershire; secondly, in 1701, Frances Grattan, by whom he had three children, who all died in infancy.

King was a man of remarkable versatility. As a herald and genealogist he was the equal of his master, Sir William Dugdale; and as a statistician he surpassed Sir William Petty.

His chief statistical work is entitled 'Natural and Political Observations and Conclusions upon the State and Condition of England, 1696' (THORPE, *Cat. of MSS.* pt. v. for 1839, p. 62). It supplies the best account accessible of the population and wealth of England at the close of the seventeenth century. Some extracts from it were published by Charles Davenant, but the treatise itself was not published till 1801, when George Chalmers added it, with a notice of King, to his 'Estimate of the Comparative

Strength of Great Britain.' Chalmers, who drew attention to King's originality as a political arithmetician, his local knowledge, and scientific methods, appended to the 'Observations' two other tracts by King, viz. 'A Scheme of the Inhabitants of the City of Gloucester,' laid before the board of trade in 1696, and 'A Computation of the Endowed Hospitals and Almshouses in England,' presented to the same board in 1697. Another of King's statistical undertakings was 'A Scheme of the Rates and Duties granted to his Majesty upon Marriages, Births, and Burials, and upon Batchelors and Widowers, for the term of five years from May 1, 1695.' London, 1695, fol. An interesting account of the chief conclusions in King's 'very valuable estimate' is given by Mr. Lecky in his 'England in the Eighteenth Century,' i. 560-1.

King's heraldic or genealogical works are: 1. 'The Order of the Installation of Prince George of Denmark, Charles, Duke of Somerset, and George, Duke of Northumberland, at Windsor, April 8, 1684,' London, 1684, fol. 2. 'The Order of the Installation of Henry, Duke of Norfolk, Henry, Earl of Peterborough, and Laurence, Earl of Rochester, at Windsor, July 22, 1685,' London, 1685, fol. 3. 'An Account of the Ceremony of investing his Electoral Highness of Brandenburgh with the Order of the Garter,' London, 1690, 4to. 4. 'The usual Ceremony observed by the Lord High Steward and Peers of Great Britain, the officers of the Court, their assistants and attendants, on the Arraignment and Trial of some Peer or Peeress . . . for Treason or Felony,' London, 1746, fol. 5. 'The Visitation of Worcester, begun by Thomas May, Chester, and Gregory King. Rouge Dragon . . . 1682, and finished by Henry Dethick, Richmond, and the said Rouge Dragon . . . 1683. With additions by Sir Thomas Phillipps, Bart. Edited by W. C. Metcalfe,' Exeter (privately printed), 1883, 4to. 6. 'The Visitation of the County of Gloucester, begun by Thomas May, Chester, and Gregory King, Rouge Dragon . . . and finished by Henry Dethick, Richmond, and the said Rouge Dragon. With additions. Edited by T. Fitz-Roy Fenwick, and W. C. Metcalfe,' Exeter, 1884, 4to.

Some of King's collections are printed in Arthur Collins's 'Proceedings, Precedents, and Arguments in Claims and Controversies concerning Baronies by Writ and other Honours,' 1734.

An autobiography bringing King's career down to his quarrel with the earl-marshal, entitled 'Some Miscellaneous Notes of the Birth, Education, and Advancement of Gregory King,' remains in manuscript in the Rawlinson collection in the Bodleian Library. It was printed in the appendix to Dallaway's 'Inquiries into the Origin and Progress of the Science of Heraldry in England,' Gloucester, 1793, 4to, and also in the anonymous 'Heraldic Miscellanies,' London, n.d. 4to.

The following writings of King have not been printed: 1. Letter to H. St. George describing a masquerade at the Court of Dresden, 10 Feb. 1693 (Brit. Mus. Addit. MS. 6321, f. 44). 2. Ordinary of Arms (Addit. MS. 26690). 3. Transcripts of the Council Books of the reign of Edward VI (Addit. MSS. 14024-6). 4. Arms of Families of the name of Russell (Addit. MS. 26680, f. 28). 5. Heraldic Miscellanies (Harl. MSS. 6591, 6821, 6832, 6833).

King painted a pack of cards with the arms of the English nobility in imitation of 'Claud Oronce Fine Brianille.'

[King's Autobiography; Chalmers's Memoir of King; Gent. Mag. 1809, pt. i. p. 973, vol. xc. pt. i. p. 233; McCulloch's Lit. Pol. Econ. p. 210; Noble's College of Arms, pp. 294, 313, 324, 335; Nichols's Lit. Anecd. i. 98; Hamper's Life of Dugdale; Macaulay's Hist. of England, chap. iii.; Pepys's Memoirs, v. 183.] T. C.

KING, HENRY (1592-1669), bishop of Chichester, eldest son of John King [q. v.], bishop of London, by his wife, Joan Freeman, was baptised at Worminghall, Buckinghamshire, 16 Jan. 1591-2. Robert King, first bishop of Oxford [q. v.], was his great-granduncle. He was educated at Westminster, whence, in 1608, he was elected, with his brother John (see under KING, JOHN, D.D., 1559?-1621), student of Christ Church, Oxford. The brothers were matriculated 20 Jan. 1608-9, and were admitted on the same days (19 June 1611 and 7 July 1614) to the degrees of bachelor and master of arts. On 24 Jan. 1615-16 Henry was collated to the prebend of St. Pancras in the cathedral of St. Paul's, receiving at the same time the office of penitentiary or confessor in that cathedral, together with the rectory and patronage of Chigwell, Essex. He was made archdeacon of Colchester on 10 April 1617, and soon afterwards received the sinecure rectory of Fulham, in addition to being appointed one of the royal chaplains. All these various preferments he held until he was advanced to the episcopal bench. Chamberlain, in a letter to Carleton, dated 8 Nov. 1617, mentions that 'young King, the Bishop of London's eldest son,' had preached a sermon at Paul's Cross. 'It was thought,' he writes, 'a bold part of them, both that so young a man should play his first prizes in such a place and such a time, it being, as he

professed, the *primitiæ* of his vocation, and the first sermon that ever he made. He did reasonably well, but nothing extraordinary, being rather slow of utterance and *orator parum vehemens.*' About this time King married Anne, eldest daughter of Robert Berkeley, esq., and granddaughter of Sir Maurice Berkeley. There were four or five children of the marriage, but only two survived. His wife died about 1624, and was buried in St. Paul's Cathedral. From his elegy on her we learn that she had barely reached her twenty-fourth year.

After his father's death, on Good Friday 1621, and the circulation of the false rumour that he had died in communion with the church of Rome, King preached a sermon (on John xv. 20) at St. Paul's Cross, on 25 Nov. 1621, 'Upon Occasion of that false and scandalous Report touching the supposed Apostasie of . . . J. King, late Bishop of London,' 4to. He was made canon of Christ Church 3 March 1623-4, and John was made canon in the following August. On 19 May 1625 they were admitted to the degrees of B.D. and D.D. as accumulators and compounders, and on 10 July (Act Sunday) they both preached at St. Mary's, the elder in the morning and the younger in the afternoon, the two sermons being published together, with the appropriate motto, 'Behold, how good and how pleasant it is for brethren to dwell together in unitie.'

King's amiability endeared him to his friends. Among these were Ben Jonson, George Sandys, Sir Henry Blount, and James Howell. His friendship with Izaak Walton began about 1624, and continued till death. He was on terms of closest intimacy with John Donne (1573-1631) [q. v.], who appointed him one of his executors, and bequeathed to him the gold medal struck in commemoration of the synod of Dort. An elegy by King is prefixed to the 1633 edition of Donne's poems.

From time to time he published sermons. In 1626 appeared 'A Sermon of Deliverance,' 4to, preached on Easter Sunday at the Spittle by request of the lord mayor and aldermen; in 1627 'Two Sermons, preached at Whitehall in Lent, March 3. 1625, and Februarie 20. 1626,' 4to; and in 1628 'An Exposition upon the Lord's Prayer. Delivered in certaine Sermons in the Cathedrall Church of St. Pavl,' 4to; 2nd edit. 1634. On 6 Feb. 1638-1639, shortly after the death of his brother John, he was made dean of Rochester, and on 6 Feb. 1641-2, the day after the lords had consented to pass the bill for depriving the bishops of their votes, he was elevated to the see of Chichester, being also presented to the rich rectory of Petworth in Sussex. He was residing at his episcopal palace when Chichester surrendered to the parliament in 1643. In his will he complains that his library was seized 'contrary to the condicōn and contracte of the Generall and Counsell of warre at the taking of that Cittie.' Walker (*Sufferings of the Clergy,* ii. 63) declares that he was 'most Barbarously Treated.' He was deprived of the rectory of Petworth, which was given by parliament to Francis Cheynell, and by a resolution of the House of Commons, 27 June 1643, his estates were ordered to be forthwith sequestrated, a petition for delay being rejected on 3 Oct. From 1643 to 1651 he lived in the house of his brother-in-law, Sir Richard Hobart of Langley, Buckinghamshire. In 1649 he published an elegy on Charles I, dated 'from my sad Retirement, March 11, 1648-9;' another elegy, 'A Deepe Groane . . . by D. H. K.,' has been doubtfully assigned to him. 'The Psalmes of David. . . . To be sung after the Old Tunes vsed in yᵉ Churches,' appeared in 1651; 2nd edit. 1671.

Shortly afterwards King retired to Ritchings, near Langley, the residence of Lady Salter (supposed to be a sister of Bishop Duppa), where other members of the King family and John Hales of Eton found refuge. In 1657 his scattered 'Poems,' 8vo, were collected. The unsold copies were reissued in 1664 with a new title-page and some additional elegies. In the edition of 1700 the additional elegies were cancelled, and the volume was entitled 'Ben Jonson's Poems, Paradoxes, and Sonnets.' Some of the poems had been published before 1657. The elegy on Gustavus Adolphus appeared in the 'Swedish Intelligencer,' pt. iii. 1633; another on Donne was prefixed to Donne's 'Poems,' 1633; another on Ben Jonson was contributed to 'Jonsonus Virbius,' 1638; and the epistle to George Sandys was printed in 1638. King did not prepare the volume for publication, and some of the poems appear not to belong to him. The verses on Lord Dorset's death are found in Bishop Corbet's poems. 'My Midnight Meditation' is ascribed on early manuscript authority to his brother Dr. John King, and two pieces are found among the poems attributed (often wrongly) to the Earl of Pembroke and Sir Benjamin Rudyard. A poem beginning 'Like to the falling of a star' is found among Francis Beaumont's poems; but probably it belongs neither to Beaumont nor King. The additional poems in the edition of 1664 include elegies on the Earl of Essex, Sir Charles Lucas, Sir George Lisle, and Lady Stanhope. King's best poem is his elegy on his wife.

In 1659 King was engaged in negotiations for supplying the vacant bishoprics, and in the next year returned to Chichester. Wood says that at the Restoration he 'became discontented, as I have heard, and a favourer thereupon of the presbyterians in his diocese.' On 29 May 1661, 'being the happy day of his majesties inauguration and birth,' he preached a sermon (published in 1661, 4to) at Whitehall, and on 24 April 1662 he delivered an impressive funeral sermon (published in 1662, 4to) on Bishop Duppa at Westminster Abbey. In 1662 he published 'Articles of Visitation and Enquiry,' 4to; in 1663 'A Sermon preached at Lewis in the Diocese of Chichester, Oct. 8, 1662;' and in 1664-5 'A Sermon preached the 30th of January at Whitehall, 1664.' His letter to Izaak Walton was printed before Walton's 'Life of Hooker,' 1665.

King died at Chichester 30 Sept. 1669, and was buried in the cathedral, where the widow of his son John erected a monument to his memory and that of her husband. His second son, Henry, died 21 Feb. 1668-9; his eldest son, John, died 10 March 1670-1. Izaak Walton (*Life of Donne*) describes King as 'a man generally known by the clergy of this nation, and as generally noted for his obliging nature,' and Wood (*Athenæ,* ed. Bliss, iii. 842) declares that he was 'the epitome of all honours, virtues, and generous nobleness, and a person never to be forgotten by his tenants and by the poor.' Vicars maliciously styles him 'a proud prelate' and 'a most pragmaticall malignant.'

King was among the contributors to 'Justa Oxoniensium,' 1612, on the death of Henry, prince of Wales; 'Epithalamia,' 1613, on the marriage of Princess Elizabeth; 'Justa Funebria Ptolemæi Oxoniensis, Thomæ Bodleii Equitis Aurati,' 1613-14; 'Jacobi Ara,' 1617; 'Annæ Funebria Sacra,' 1619; and 'Parentalia Jacobo,' 1625. In 1843 the late Archdeacon Hannah edited King's 'Poems and Psalms,' with an elaborate biographical notice. King's portrait hangs in Christ Church hall.

[Biographical notice by J. Hannah before King's Poems and Psalms, 1843; Welch's Alumni Westmonasterienses.]   A. H. B.

KING, HUMPHREY (*fl.* 1613), verse-writer, a seller of tobacco in London, was author of 'An Halfe-penny-worth of Wit, in a Pennyworth of Paper. Or, The Hermites Tale. The third impression,' London, 1613, 4to, pp. 48. No earlier edition is known, but it must have been printed some years previously. 'Robin the Devil his Two Penniworth of Wit in Half a Penniworth of Paper. By Robert Lee, a famous fencer of London, alias Robin the Devil' (London, for

N. Ling, 1607, 4to), is mentioned in West's 'Sale Catalogue,' 1773, and may have been an earlier edition, but it is not now known to be extant. As early as 1599 Nashe had dedicated his 'Lenten Stuffe' to 'his worthie good patron, Lustie Humfrey, according as the townsmen doo christen him, little Numps as the Nobilitie and Courtiers do name him, and Honest Humfrey, as all his friendes and acquaintance esteeme him, king of the Tobacconists *hic & ubique*, and a singular Mecænas to the Pipe and the Tabour:' and at the end of the dedicatory epistle refers to the forthcoming 'sacred Poeme of the Hermites Tale, that will restore the golden age amongst us.' Prefixed to King's poem is a jocular dedicatory epistle to the Countess of Sussex. He acknowledges that his work is 'a course homespun linsey woolsey webbe of wit;' but, seeing his 'inferiours in the gifts of learning, wisedome, and vnderstanding torment the Print daily,' he is 'the bolder to shoulder in amongst the.' The epistle is followed by an address to the reader, to which succeed three short copies of verses (the second being 'In discommendation of the Author'), and three unsigned sonnets. 'The Hermites Tale' takes the form of a dialogue between a hermit and a young man concerning the views and follies of the age. Complaint is made of the growth of luxury and decay of hospitality, and the puritans are vigorously assailed.

[Collier's Bibliographical Catalogue; Corser's Collectanea; Hazlitt's Handbook.] A. H. B.

KING, JAMES, LORD EYTHIN (1589?–1652?), born about 1589, was son of James King of Barracht, Aberdeenshire. He entered the service of the king of Sweden, and by 1632 had risen to be 'general-major.' In 1638, while commanding in Munster under the Swedish general Baner, King received orders to join Rupert and the Prince Palatine, who had raised a small army. At the battle of Lemgo, near Minden, in which the Elector was routed by Hatzfeldt, the Austrian general, King has been unfairly charged with misconduct and treachery (WARBURTON, *Prince Rupert*, i. 452). It appears that Rupert was attacked before his army was collected, and defeated before King could bring up the foot to support the cavalry, and that finally King rallied, and skilfully conducted the retreat of the troops. In January 1640 he was recalled to England (*Cal. State Papers*, Dom. 1639–40, p. 367), and was graciously received by the king, who gave him a diamond 'of good value' and a pension of 1,000l. a year (*ib.* 1640, pp. 208, 450). In the following July he was despatched to Hamburg and Gluck-

stadt, apparently to bring over horse and foot to be employed against the covenanters (*ib.* 1640, pp. 492, 502). He did not return, but retired to Stockholm (*ib.* 1640–1, p. 320). On being again pressed to enter Charles's service he came as far as Hamburg, whence he wrote an outspoken letter to Secretary Vane requesting a recognised position in the army and the regular payment of his pension (*ib.* pp. 579–80). He was given a command under Lord Newcastle (ELLIS, *Original Letters*, 1st ser. iii. 297). On 28 March 1643 he was created a peer of Scotland as Lord Eythin and Kerrey, the former title being probably derived from the river Ythan in Aberdeenshire. At the siege of Leeds in April of that year Eythin and all the old officers from Holland were of opinion that an assault was too dangerous, and in favour of raising the siege (*Letters of Henrietta Maria*, Caml. Soc., p. 189). According to Sir Philip Warwick (*Memoirs*, p. 264), he was the chief advocate of the policy of reducing Hull rather than marching south to join the king, and it was he who inspired Newcastle's defensive strategy during the campaign against the Scots, displaying a treacherous sympathy with his fellow-countrymen (*ib.* p. 277). So much did these accusations weigh with Eythin, that in April 1644 he seriously thought of retiring from the royal service, and returning to the continent. Both Charles and Henrietta pressed him to stay (*Letters of Henrietta Maria*, p. 238; ELLIS, iii. 298). On 26 July 1644 the Scottish parliament passed a decree of forfaulture against him, which was rescinded on 14 Jan. 1647, and on 19 Feb. following another act in his favour was passed (DOUGLAS, *Peerage of Scotland*, ed. Wood, i. 558). During the siege of York even Warwick (*Memoirs*, p. 278) admits that he 'showed eminency in soldiery' and 'no want of loyalty,' for now he 'fought not singly against his own nation.' At Marston Moor he opposed Rupert's desire to engage, and disapproved of the plan of battle. Eythin subsequently accompanied Newcastle to Hamburg. His conduct was severely condemned (CLARENDON, *History*, 1849, viii. 87), even, it seems, by Rupert, to whom Eythin wrote a letter in his defence (*Pythouse Papers*, p. 21). Eythin's last services in the royalist cause appear to have been performed in connection with the expedition of Montrose, under whom he was appointed lieutenant-general by warrant dated 19 March 1650. A letter of 13 March 1650 shows that he was also engaged in some negotiations for bringing Charles II to Sweden (*Cal. State Papers*, Dom. 1650, pp. 52, 611). Eythin died in Sweden some time between October 1651 and April 1652, and was buried in the Reddarholms

Church. He was married and had a daughter (ib. 1640, p. 443). Administration of his estate in Scotland was granted on 28 Oct. 1652 to Thomas Watson, a principal creditor (*Administration Act Book*, P. C. C. 1652, f. 186, where he is called Edward). A letter from Eythin to the Earl of Forth is in Patrick Ruthven's 'Correspondence' (Roxburghe Club, p. 81; cf. also p. xxxviii n.), and another from him to the Marquis of Hamilton, dated 12 Sept. 1638, in the Historical Manuscripts Commission's 11th Rep. (Appendix vi. p. 93).

[Duchess of Newcastle's Life of William, Duke of Newcastle (Firth), pp. 77, 370; notes kindly supplied by C. H. Firth, esq.; Memoirs of Sir J. Turner (Bannatyne Club), pp. 9, 11, 31; Letters of Henrietta Maria (Camd. Soc.), p. 149; Gardiner's Hist. of the Great Civil War (1642-9), i. 283, &c.]   G. G.

KING, JAMES (1750-1784), captain in the navy, second son of James King, curate of Clitheroe, Lancashire, and afterwards dean of Raphoe, was born at Clitheroe in 1750. Dr. Walker King, bishop of Rochester, was his younger brother. At the age of twelve he entered the navy under the patronage of his kinsman, Captain William Norton, brother of the first Lord Grantley, and at that time in command of the Africa guardship. He afterwards served under Captain Palliser on the Newfoundland station, where he must have had some acquaintance with Cook, who was then surveying that coast [see COOK, JAMES]; and he was in the Alarm with Captain Jervis, in the Mediterranean. He was promoted to be lieutenant in January 1771. In 1774 he spent some time in Paris, devoting himself principally to scientific study, and on his return settled at Oxford to be with his brother Walker, then a fellow of Corpus Christi College. Here he made the acquaintance of Dr. Thomas Hornsby [q.v.], who in 1776 recommended him as a competent astronomer to accompany Cook's third voyage. He was accordingly appointed to the Resolution as second lieutenant. At the time of Cook's death, 14 Feb. 1779, King was on shore, apparently taking sights. He had with him only a few men, but was reinforced by some of a boat's crew who had been rowing off the mouth of the bay before the disturbance with the natives began. This brought the number of the party up to twenty-four, and fortifying themselves in a neighbouring burial-place, they succeeded in repelling the attack of the natives, till they were relieved, two hours afterwards, by the ships' boats (*Gilbert's Journal*, quoted in BESANT, *Captain Cook*, pp. 162-3). On the death of Captain Charles Clerke [q.v.], 22 Aug.

1779, King succeeded to the command of the Discovery, and on arriving in England was advanced to post-rank, 3 Oct. 1780. He was then appointed to the Crocodile frigate, attached to the Channel fleet, and towards the end of 1781 was moved to the Resistance of 40 guns, in which he went out to the West Indies in charge of a convoy of five hundred merchant ships, which he succeeded in conducting safely to their destination; but the intense anxiety of the duty is said to have turned his hair grey. His constitution was never strong, and he came back to England in an advanced decline. It was under this disadvantage that he assisted in preparing Cook's journal of the third voyage for the press, and wrote the narrative of its conclusion, which formed the third volume. In 1783 the state of his health compelled him to go to Nice, and he died there in October 1784. He was buried at Nice, but there is a tablet to his memory in Clitheroe Church. King's 'Astronomical Observations' were published by order of the board of longitude in 1782 [see BAYLY, WILLIAM], and procured his election as F.R.S. The narrative of the voyage (3 vols. 4to, and atlas in fol.) was issued in 1784.

[Alice King's A Cluster of Lives, p. 137; Espinasse's Lancashire Worthies, 2nd ser. p. 195; Baines's History of Lancashire (edit. of 1836), iii. 218; Correspondence with Dr. John Douglas [q. v.] (afterwards bishop of Salisbury), 1780-4, in Egerton MS. 2180; and his own narrative already referred to.]   J. K. L.

KING, JOHN, D.D. (1559?-1621), bishop of London, born at Worminghall, Buckinghamshire, in or about 1559, was son of Philip King of that place, by Elizabeth, daughter of Edmund Conquest of Houghton Conquest, Bedfordshire. He was a great-nephew of Robert King [q.v.], the first bishop of Oxford. He received his education at Westminster School, and thence was elected to Christ Church, Oxford, in 1576 (WELCH, *Alumni Westmon.* ed. Phillimore, p. 53). He graduated B.A. in 1579-80, and commenced M.A. in 1582-3 (WOOD, *Fasti Oxon.* ed. Bliss, i. 212, 221). After taking holy orders he became domestic chaplain to John Piers, archbishop of York, by whom he was collated to the archdeaconry of Nottingham on 12 Aug. 1590. He proceeded B.D. on 2 July 1591. Strype gives extracts from a lecture delivered by King at York on the plague and the severe storms by which England was visited in 1593-4 (*Annals of the Reformation*, iv. 293, 8vo). On 17 Nov. 1594 King preached the sermon at the funeral of Archbishop Piers. Afterwards he was appointed chaplain to Sir Thomas Egerton, lord-keeper of the great seal. He was admitted to the rectory of St. Andrew, Holborn, on 10 May 1597, on the promotion of Richard Bancroft to the see of London, and to the prebend of Sneating in the church of St. Paul on 16 Aug. 1599, on the promotion of William Cotton to the see of Exeter (NEWCOURT, *Repertorium*, i. 211, 275). He also became one of Queen Elizabeth's chaplains. On 17 Dec. 1601 he was created D.D. at Oxford. He was appointed by the privy council to preach before James I on his entry into London, and the king retained him in his service as one of the royal chaplains, commending him as 'the king of preachers.' He became dean of Christ Church, Oxford, on 4 Aug. 1605, in accordance with the petition of thirty-two students there. Soon afterwards King was selected as one of the four preachers at the Hampton Court Conference. He was vice-chancellor of the university of Oxford from 1607 to 1610. On 16 Dec. 1610 he obtained the prebend of Milton Manor in the church of Lincoln (WILLIS, *Survey of Cathedrals*, ii. 223).

In 1611 the king bestowed upon him the bishopric of London, which had become vacant by the translation of Dr. George Abbot to the see of Canterbury. He was consecrated in Lambeth Chapel on 8 Sept., and had restitution of the temporalities on the 18th of the same month. In 1613 he was appointed a member of the commission engaged in hearing the Countess of Essex's suit for divorce (GARDINER, *Hist.* ii. 170). On 26 March 1620 he pleaded in a sermon preached at St. Paul's Cross in the king's presence for contributions to the repair of St. Paul's Cathedral. James selected the text, and popular curiosity was excited by rumours that King was instructed to declare James's resolve to intervene in the German wars in behalf of his son-in-law, the king of Bohemia; but although one of his hearers wrote that the bishop's heart was in Bohemia, he made no reference to European politics (*ib.* iii. 311–2). While bishop, King always preached on Sundays in some pulpit in or near London (FULLER, *Church Hist.* ed. Brewer, v. 500). He died on Good Friday, 30 March 1621, and was buried in the south aisle of St. Paul's Cathedral, under a plain stone on which was inscribed only the word 'Resurgam,' but on a mural tablet near it was a very long and eulogistic inscription to his memory (DUGDALE, *Hist. of St. Paul's*, ed. 1658, p. 73). Wood says 'he was a solid and profound divine, of great gravity and piety, and had so excellent a volubility of speech, that Sir Edward Coke would often say of him that he was the best speaker in the Star-chamber in his time' (*Athenæ Oxon.* ed. Bliss, ii. 295).

During his last illness and after his death a report was circulated that he had been reconciled on his deathbed to the church of Rome. Many catholics gave credence to the rumour, and in 'The Protestant's Plea for Priests and Papists,' a pamphlet issued in September 1621, King's conversion was announced as a matter of fact. Richard Broughton [q. v.] sent an account of the grounds of the report to Dr. Kellison, president of Douay College, but it does not clearly appear that he was himself convinced of the truth of the alleged conversion (DODD, *Church Hist.* i. 490; *Hist. MSS. Comm.* 5th Rep. p. 484). The bishop's son Henry indignantly denied the report in a sermon preached at St. Paul's Cross on 25 Nov. 1621, but the baseless statement was repeated in an anonymous book written by George Musket, afterwards president of Douay College, and entitled 'The Bishop of London his Legacy. Or Certaine Motives of D. King, late Bishop of London, for his change of Religion, and dying in the Catholike, and Roman Church. With a Conclusion to his Brethren, the LL. Bishops of England. Permissu Superiorum' [St. Omer], 1624, 4to, pp. 174 (GEE, *Foot out of the Snare*, ed. 1624, pp. 77–80, 99); BRYDGES, *British Bibliographer*, i. 505).

King married Joan, daughter of Henry Freeman of Staffordshire. His eldest son, Henry, is noticed separately. His second son, JOHN KING (1595–1639), educated with his brother at Westminster and Christ Church, Oxford (B.A. 1611, M.A. 1614, and B.D. and D.D. 1625), became prebendary of St. Paul's Cathedral (1616), public orator of Oxford (1622), canon of Christ Church (1624), archdeacon of Colchester and canon of Windsor (1625). He was also rector of Remenham, Berkshire. He died on 2 Jan. 1638–9, and was buried in Christ Church Cathedral. He published three Latin orations delivered as orator at Oxford (London, 1623, 4to, and Oxford, 1625), a separate sermon preached at Oxford in 1625, and poems in the university collections of 1613 and 1619.

The bishop contributed to many of the Oxford collections of poems, and published: 1. 'Lectures upon Jonas, delivered at Yorke in the yeare of our Lorde 1594,' Oxford, 1597, 4to, pp. 660. Dedicated to Sir Thomas Egerton, lord-keeper. Reprinted, Oxford, 1599 and 1600, 4to; London, 1611, 4to, 'newly corrected,' and again 1618. 2. 'A Sermon preached at the Funeralles of . . . John [Piers] late Arch-bishoppe of Yorke, Nov. 17, 1594,' Oxford, 1597, 4to (printed at the end of the 'Lectures upon Jonas'); separately Oxford, 1599, 4to. 3. 'The Fourth Sermon preached at Hampton Court on Tuesday the last of Sept. 1694,' Oxford, 1696, 4to. 4. ' Vitis Palatina. A Sermon appointed to be preached at Whitehall upon the Tuesday after the marriage of the Ladie Elizabeth her Grace,' London, 1614, 4to; reprinted in 'Conjugal Duty set forth in a collection of Wedding-Sermons,' 1732. A very singular composition, concluding with an ejaculation against the 'papists.' 5. ' A Sermon of Public Thanksgiving for the happie recoverie of his majestie from his late dangerous sicknesse,' London, 1619, 4to. 6. ' A Sermon at Paules Crosse on behalf of Paules Church,' London, 1620, 4to (cf. *Notes and Queries*, 1st ser. iii. 368-9). Some copies of his letters are in Brit. Mus. Addit. MSS. 29439, ff. 184*b*-192.

A portrait, by Cornelius Janssen, is preserved at Christ Church, Oxford. There are engravings by Simon Pass and Francis Delaram (GRANGER, *Biog. Hist. of England*, 5th edit. ii. 48).

[Belford's Blazon of Episcopacy; Collier's Church Hist. vii. 420, 421 ; Dodd's Church Hist. ii. 327, 351 ; Fuller's Church Hist. (Brewer), iii. 28, v. 266, 371, 420, 499 ; Fuller's Worthies (Nichols), i. 139 ; Godwin, De Præsulibus (Richardson), p. 194 ; Lansd. MS. 984, f. 3 ; Le Neve's Fasti (Hardy); Lowndes's Bibl. Man. (Bohn), pp. 63, 1273; Newcourt's Repertorium, i. 29 ; Cal. State Papers, Dom. (Addenda 1580-1625) pp. 621, 622, (1603-10) pp. 362, 445, 527, (1619-23) p. 675; Strype's Works (general index); Willis's Survey of Cathedrals, i. 107, ii. 440; Wood's Athenæ Oxon. (Bliss), ii. 294, 634, 861, iii. 839, Fasti, i. 248, 255; Wood's Annals (Gutch), ii. 295, 299, 300, 322, 788, 791 ; Wood's Colleges and Halls (Gutch), pp. 439, 458, 463, Appendix pp. 112, 118-19, 281, 289.]   T. C.

KING, SIR JOHN (d. 1637), Irish administrator, came of a family formerly seated at Feathercock Hall, near Northallerton, Yorkshire. By July 1585 he was acting as secretary to Sir Richard Bingham [q. v.], governor of Connaught (*Cal. State Papers*, Irish, 1574-85, p. 574). His services were rewarded by Queen Elizabeth with a lease of the abbey of Boyle, co. Roscommon. Under James I he enjoyed many profitable offices and privileges, and had lands granted to him in twenty-one different counties (*ib.* 1603-6, pp. 113, 269, &c.) On 12 July 1603 he was made clerk of the crown in chancery and clerk of the hanaper, both of which places he surrendered on 20 Jan. 1606, and with Francis Edgeworth had a new grant thereof on 29 Jan. (*ib.* 1603-6 p. 430, 1606-1608 pp. 81, 387). In 1603 he was receiver of the revenue (*ib.* 1606-8, p. 54), and in March 1605 deputy vice-treasurer (*ib.* 1603-1606, p. 420). In May 1607, being then constable of the abbey of Boyle, he commenced

to build, along with John Bingley, a massive castle on the river Boyle, and to cultivate much of the surrounding district (*ib.* 1606-1608, pp. 87, 150, &c.) On 11 May 1609 he was appointed mustermaster-general and clerk of the cheque for Ireland, with a reversionary grant of both offices to his eldest son : in June of the same year he was sworn of the privy council (*ib.* 1608-10, pp. 202, 218, 507), and on 7 July following he was knighted (METCALFE, *Book of Knights*, p. 161). In October 1611 he was a commissioner for compositions ; in 1613 was returned M.P. for co. Roscommon by the aid of Vice-president Oliver St. John's soldiery, and in 1614 was appointed to assist in the plantation of Wexford (*Cal. State Papers*, Irish, 1611-14, pp. 138, 362, 496). On 20 May 1615, when living at Baggotrath, near Dublin, he was appointed one of the council for the province of Munster ; and on 9 June following he was authorised, with Sir Thomas Rotherham, to act as governor of Connaught during the absence of the president and vice-president. On 24 Sept. 1616 he was joined in commission with Lord-deputy St. John and others to aid in the settlement of the British 'undertakers' in Ulster. On 23 Sept. 1617 he was nominated a commissioner of the court of wards in Ireland, and on 18 Jan. 1621 was made, with Francis Edgeworth, receiver of the fines of that court, and of all other fines upon letters and grants.

By privy seal (8 Aug. 1619) King was appointed a commissioner for the plantation of co. Longford and the territory of Elye O'Carroll in King's County, and on 15 July 1624 was constituted a commissioner, justice, and keeper of the peace in Leinster and Ulster during the absence of Lord-deputy Falkland. By commission dated 9 Dec. 1625 he was authorised, with four others, to examine abuses committed in the army in order to their redress, and to take a general muster of all the forces throughout the kingdom.

King died in the Close at Lichfield, Staffordshire, on 4 Jan. 1636-7, and was buried in the church of Boyle on 30 March following. He married Catherine (d. 1617), daughter of Robert Drury, nephew of Sir William Drury, lord deputy of Ireland. Of his six sons, Sir Robert King (1599?-1657) and Edward King (1612-1637), Milton's friend, are separately noticed. Of three daughters, Mary (d. 1663) married William Caulfeild, second baron Charlemont, and Margaret married Sir Gerard Lowther, chief justice of the common pleas in Ireland.

[Lodge's Peerage of Ireland (Archdall), iii. 223; Cal. State Papers, Irish, 1585-1625; Carew MSS. 1603-24.]   G. G.

KING, JOHN, first Lord Kingston (d. 1676), was eldest son of Sir Robert King (1599?–1657) [q.v.], by his first wife, Frances, daughter of Sir Henry Folliott, the first lord Folliott of Ballyshannon. His father, on going to England in 1642, entrusted him with the command of Boyle Castle, co. Roscommon. His abilities as a leader were displayed on many occasions, particularly at the relief of Elphin Castle and at the defeat of the Ulster army on 24 June 1650, when he took prisoner with his own hands the general of the catholic army, the popish bishop of Clogher. The parliament accorded him full powers, and on 26 July 1649 ordered him to be paid 100*l.* from delinquents' estates 'in consideration of long attendance' (*Cal. State Papers*, Dom. 1649–50, p. 582). He was then a colonel. On 7 June 1658 he was knighted by Henry Cromwell, lord deputy-general of Ireland (METCALFE, *Book of Knights*, p. 215). Having worked hard for the restoration of Charles II, he was created on 4 Sept. 1660 an Irish peer by the title of Baron Kingston, was sworn of the Irish privy council, and was appointed on 19 March 1660–1 a commissioner of the court of claims for the settlement of Ireland. On 8 May 1661 he took his seat in the Irish House of Lords, on 11 May he was made commissary-general of the horse, and on 31 May was added to the committee appointed to consider the erection of a college of physicians in Dublin. On 15 Nov. following he was appointed captain of a troop. With John, lord Berkeley, King was constituted on 2 April 1666 joint-president of Connaught, and on 5 May following sole governor of that province. On 20 April previously he was made colonel of a regiment of horse. On 1 Oct. 1670 he was appointed one of the commissioners to examine and state the arrears due to the king before the commencement of that year, of the farm of the revenue for seven years, and on 15 July 1674 had a grant by patent of a substantial yearly pension. It was also provided by the act of settlement that all his claims to land should be ratified and confirmed to him and his heirs. For his arrears of service before 5 June 1649 he received four several grants of land. By letters patent dated 25 Jan. 1664 he had confirmed to him the town and lands of Kilcolman, with other lands, amounting to some thousands of acres, in the counties of Limerick, Cork, and Kildare.

King died in 1676. He married Catherine (d. 1669), daughter of Sir William Fenton, knt., of Mitchelstown, co. Cork, and left two sons, Robert (d. 1693) [q.v.] and John, successively second and third lords Kingston.

[Lodge's Peerage of Ireland (Archdall), iii. 226.] G. G.

KING, Sir JOHN (1639–1677), lawyer, of a Huguenot family of Rouen, originally named Le Roy, was eldest son of John King, M.D., of Aldersgate Street, London, by his second wife, Elizabeth, youngest daughter of Barne Roberts of Willesden, Middlesex. He was born at St. Albans on 5 Feb. 1638–9, and was educated first at the free school there, and then, from the age of thirteen, at Eton, where he obtained a foundation scholarship and became head of the school. He proceeded to Queens' College, Cambridge, in November 1655, and graduated B.A. Though personally desirous of taking orders, by his father's desire in November 1660 he was admitted a member of the Inner Temple, and on 9 Feb. 1667 was called to the bar. He became a bencher of the inn 31 Jan. 1674, and treasurer in 1675. He began his practice by appearing before the commission for the rebuilding of London after the fire, but soon obtained business in Westminster Hall, and eventually a very large chancery practice. He was made a king's counsel and attorney-general to the Duke of York, and on 10 Dec. 1674 was knighted. In 1676 his fees amounted to 4,700*l.* His fine memory, his polished eloquence, his affable manners, and still more his incredible industry, had secured for him an enormous amount of work, and he was in the front rank of his profession in nine years from his call. Burnet says of him that the court party were weary of 'Sir William Jones' [q.v.], Attorney-general, and were raising Sir John King to vie with him, but he died in his rise, which indeed went on very quick' (*Hist. of his own Time*, fol. ed. i. 396). His health broke down under the strain of work, and in his later years he could not sleep more than three hours together. He died at his house in Salisbury Court on 29 June 1677. He was buried in the Temple Church on 4 July, where there is an inscription in the triforium and a stone in the churchyard to his memory.

King married, on 20 Feb. 1666–7, Joyce, daughter and heiress of William Bennett of High Rothing, Essex, by whom he had two sons and five daughters.

[From a family manuscript written by his father in 1677, and contributed to Gent. Mag. lii. 110, reprinted with additions in 1855; Roger North's Life of Lord Keeper Guildford; Chauncy's Hertfordshire, p. 467 a; Echard's History of England, ed. 1718, iii. 438.] J. A. H.

KING, JOHN (d. 1679), covenanting preacher, was for some time domestic chaplain to Henry Erskine, third lord Cardross, and in 1674 was apprehended and tried before the privy council of Scotland for holding conventicles. Lord Cardross was heavily fined at the same time for permitting King to conduct worship in his family. King was admitted to bail in five thousand merks to appear when called upon. In the following year he was again seized at Cardross House during the night; but in the morning the country people assembled and took him out of the hands of the soldiers. This incident was made the occasion of a letter from King Charles II to the Scottish council, dated 12 June 1675, complaining of their supineness (*Hist. MSS. Comm.* 11th Rep. App. pt. vi. p. 159). King was now by letters of intercommuning, 6 Aug. 1675, declared an outlaw. On 2 June 1679 he was apprehended in the town of Hamilton by Graham of Claverhouse. The battle of Drumclog took place next day, and Claverhouse's prisoners were rescued. King, however, was recaptured by stratagem on the estate of Blair, in the parish of Dalry, Ayrshire, shortly after the defeat of the covenanters at Bothwell, and was conveyed to Edinburgh. One of his escort of dragoons, being asked whither they were bound, is said to have answered, ' To carry King to hell.' The same day the dragoon was killed by the accidental discharge of his carbine. King was brought before the council on 9 July 1679, along with a fellow-minister, John Kid. After several appearances and a futile petition by counsel on their behalf, they were condemned and executed at the cross of Edinburgh on 14 Aug. following, their heads and limbs being severed from their bodies and placed on the Nether Bow port. Proclamation was made immediately before the execution of an indulgence to the 'ousted' ministers, and King and Kid were pressed by Robert Fleming the elder [q. v.], then a fellow-prisoner, to signify their approval of it, which they resolutely declined to do. King's last speech on the scaffold was printed. In it he makes mention of his wife and one child. The only sermon by him which is known to exist is included in the collection made by John Howie [q. v.] (Glasgow, 1779).

[Wodrow's History of the Sufferings of the Church of Scotland, Burn's ed. 1831, ii. 270-286, iii. 69-136; Crookshank's History of the Church of Scotland, ii. 32-65; Patrick Walker's Biographia Presbyteriana, i. 247-94.]   H. P.

KING, JOHN (1696-1728), classical writer, eldest son of John King (1652-1732) [q. v.], was born at Adstone, Northamptonshire, on 5 Aug. 1696. He was educated at Eton and King's College, Cambridge,

graduating B.A. 1718 and M.A. 1722, and being elected a fellow. Though he did not take a medical degree, he settled at Stamford as a physician, and soon acquired a great reputation. In 1727 he married Lucy, daughter of Thomas Morice, paymaster of the forces at Lisbon, and his intention then was to settle in London, under the direction of John Freind [q. v.], who married his wife's sister, but he was cut off by fever at Stamford, 12 Oct. 1728. He was buried at Pertenhall, Bedfordshire. His only son, John King, patron and rector of Pertenhall 1752-1800, and also fellow of King's College, Cambridge, died 6 Oct. 1812, aged 85.

King was author of: 1. 'Epistola ad Johannem Freind, in qua D. W. Trilleri epistolam Medico-criticam super primo et tertio Epidemicorum ad examen revocavit,' Cambridge, 1722; an attack on the remarks of Triller on the treatises of Hippocrates on epidemics. 2. 'Euripidis Hecuba, Orestes et Phœnissæ,' Cambridge, 1726; the original Greek, with a Latin translation; this had occupied him nearly five years, as he had collated ten manuscripts. Thomas Morell published for use at Eton in 1748 the same three plays, with the addition of 'Alcestis,' in which he gave nearly the whole of King's translation and notes. King was elected on 12 Aug. 1724 a member of the Gentlemen's Society at Spalding. In the ' Rel. Galeanæ ' (*Bibl. Topogr. Brit.* iii. 80) is the statement of Roger Gale, under date 1742, that he ' always took Dr. King's skill in medals to be more that of a trader than a scholar.'

[Nichols's Lit. Anecdotes, iii. 752, vi. 13, 93; Gent. Mag. October 1812, p. 405; Harwood's Alumni Eton. p. 294.]   W. P. C.

KING, JOHN (1652-1732), miscellaneous writer, born at St. Columb, Cornwall, 1 May 1652, matriculated at Exeter College, Oxford, as a poor scholar on 7 July 1674, being described as aged twenty, and as the son of John King of Manaccan in Cornwall. He graduated B.A. 1678 and M.A. 1680, and in 1688, when his friend Sir William Dawes [q. v.], afterwards archbishop of York, was its master, took the degree of D.D. at Catharine Hall, Cambridge. When first in clerical orders he was curate of Bray, Berkshire, where he married Anne, youngest daughter of William Durham, whose wife was Lætitia, granddaughter of Sir Francis Knollys, treasurer of the household of Queen Elizabeth. He had no children by his first wife. On 3 June 1690 King married, as his second wife, Elizabeth, daughter of Joseph Aris of Adstone, Northamptonshire, and widow of the Rev. John Eston, through whom he acquired the living of Pertenhall, Bedfordshire, to which he was at once instituted (7 June 1690). This benefice he vacated for institution to Chelsea on 22 Nov. 1694, the two preferments being then of equal value, but the income of his new living was greatly increased by the letting of the glebe for building. His other preferment was the prebendal stall of Weighton in York Cathedral, to which he was collated by Archbishop Dawes on 1 May 1718. King died at Chelsea 30 May 1732, and was buried in Pertenhall chancel on 13 June, a large mural monument being erected to his memory. His wife died at Chelsea on 22 June 1727, aged 61, and was also buried at Pertenhall. Their youngest daughter, Eulalia, married, on 20 Aug. 1732, John Martyn, professor of botany at Cambridge, and died on 13 Feb. 1748-9, aged 45 (LIPSCOMB, *Buckinghamshire*, i. 529). The eldest son, John (1686-1728), is separately noticed. Another son, Joseph, was buried at Ashby Canons (BAKER, *Northamptonshire*, ii. 16).

King wrote, in addition to two sermons: 1. 'Animadversions on a Pamphlet [by Increase Mather] intituled a Letter of Advice to the Nonconformists,' 1701, as ' by a Divine of the Church of England;' 2nd edit., with his name, 1702. 2. 'Case of John Atherton, Bishop of Waterford, fairly represented' (anon.), 1710. 3. 'Tolando-pseudologo-mastix, an Answer to Toland's "Hypatia"' (anon.), 1721. Among the Sloane MSS. at the British Museum is one by King (No. 4455), containing a supplement of remarks in 1717 on the life of Sir Thomas More, a letter on More's house at Chelsea, which is printed by Faulkner (pp. 269-99), epitaphs and verses. From a manuscript account of Chelsea by King in the possession of its rector long extracts are made by Lysons, Faulkner, and Beaver. King's diary and memoranda are in the Plymouth Proprietary Library. He was one of the earliest subscribers to the Society for Promoting Christian Knowledge.

[Nichols's Lit. Anecdotes, iii. 156, 638 ; Lysons's Environs, iii. 115; Halkett and Laing's Anon. Literature, i.95; Gorham's Martyn Family, pp. 48. &c.; Faulkner's Chelsea, pp. 53 7 ; Beaver's Chelsea, passim; McClure's Chapter in Church History, pp. 4-14.] W. P. C.

KING, JOHN (1788-1847), painter, was born at Dartmouth in 1788, and at the age of twenty entered the schools of the Royal Academy. He first exhibited at the British Institution in 1811 and at the Academy in 1817, and throughout his life was a frequent contributor to both of biblical, Shakespearean, and historical subjects, as well as of portraits. Meeting with little success in London he paid frequent and extended visits to Bristol, where his art was better appreciated ; for St. Thomas's Church in that city he painted in 1828 the 'Incredulity of St. Thomas,' and for St. Mark's Chapel the ' Dead Christ surrounded by His Disciples.' For the former, a very large but poor work, he received 200l.; the latter is smaller and of better quality. King also painted the portraits of many of the leading citizens of Bristol, and he is referred to in 'Felix Farley's Rhymes' as a member of the ' Bristol School.' His portrait of the Rev. Henry Francis Lyte [q. v.] the hymn-writer has been engraved by G. H. Phillips. King died of apoplexy at Dartmouth 12 July 1847.

[Redgrave's Dict. of Artists; Graves's Dict. of Artists, 1760-1880; Felix Farley's Bristol Journal, 17 July 1847; British Institution and Royal Academy Catalogues; George's Lyte's Cary Manor House, 1879, p. 11; information from the Rev. C. Taylor, vicar of St. Thomas's, Bristol.] F. M. O'D.

KING, JOHN DUNCAN (1789-1863), captain in the army and landscape-painter, born in 1789, entered the army in August 1806, and became lieutenant in February 1808. He served in the Walcheren expedition and in the Peninsular war, and was present at the battles of Busaco, Vittoria, and the Pyrenees, being wounded severely on 28 July 1813. He was present at the occupation of Paris by the allies in 1815. On 16 March 1830 he was promoted to be captain, and on 28 Dec. 1830 was placed on half-pay. King had a talent for painting, and in 1821 exhibited at the Royal Academy a view in Spain, from a drawing by Lieutenant-general Hawker. In 1836 he sent a view in Portugal, and subsequently was an occasional honorary exhibitor of views near Killarney, Boulogne, and other places. In 1843 he exhibited a picture called 'A Pilgrim.' He also exhibited thirty-nine landscapes at the British Institution; the last was sent in 1858. About 1852 King was made a military knight of Windsor, and resided in Windsor Castle until his death on 21 Aug. 1863.

[Gent. Mag. 3rd ser. 1863, pt. ii. p. 518; Redgrave's Dict. of Artists; Windsor and Eton Express, 19 Aug. 1863; Catalogues of the Royal Academy and British Institution ; Graves's Dict. of Artists.] L. C.

KING, JOHN GLEN, D.D. (1732-1787), divine, born in Norfolk in 1732, was educated at Caius College, Cambridge, where he graduated B.A. in 1752 and M.A. in 1763. After taking orders he was presented by the King in 1760 to the vicarage of Berwick Parva, Norfolk (BLOMEFIELD, *Hist. of Norfolk*, x. 297), and subsequently was appointed chaplain to the English factory at St. Petersburg. During his residence in Russia he was appointed medallist to the empress; and he devoted much time to the study of the history and liturgical rites of the Greek church. He became a fellow of the Society of Antiquaries of London on 10 Jan. 1771, and on 21 Feb. in the same year was elected a fellow of the Royal Society (THOMSON, *Hist. of the Royal Society*, Append. iv. p. liv). He was incorporated M.A. at Oxford, on 19 March 1771, as a member of Christ Church, and four days later took the degrees of B.D. and D.D. in that university. He was presented to the rectory of Wormley, Hertfordshire, by Sir Abraham Hume, bart., in July 1783; and in the summer of 1786 he purchased the chapelry of Spring Gardens, Somerset. He also purchased, though at what date is not stated, Dr. John Warner's chapel in Long Acre, London (NICHOLS, *Lit. Anecd.* ii. 446). He died at his house in Edward Street, London, after a few hours' illness, on 3 Nov. 1787, and was buried in the churchyard of Wormley.

He married, first, Ann Magdalene, daughter of Michael Combrune, by whom he had one daughter, Anna Henrietta; and secondly, in August 1776, at Greenwich, Jane, daughter of John Hyde, esq., of Blackheath (she died in August 1789).

He was the author of: 1. Verses in the Cambridge University collection on the death of Frederick, prince of Wales, 1752. 2. 'The Rites and Ceremonies of the Greek Church in Russia: containing an Account of its Doctrine, Worship, and Discipline,' London, 1772, 4to, dedicated to the king. A learned work, illustrated with copper-plate engravings. 3. 'A Letter to the Bishop of Durham, containing some Observations on the Climate of Russia, and the Northern Countries, with a View of the Flying Mountains at Zarsko Sello, near St. Petersburg,' 1778. Printed in the 'Westminster Magazine,' 1780, viii. 45. 4. 'Observations on the Barberini Vase,' 1786; in 'Archæologia,' viii. 307. 5. 'Catalogue of a small Library at St. Petersburg,' London, 1786, 8vo. 6. 'Nummi Familiarum et Imperatorum Romanorum' London? 1787?], 4to, consisting of 102 plates, without letterpress.

There is a neat print of him by Fourdrinier. Another portrait of him, painted by Falconet, was engraved by Gabriel Smith.

[Addit. MS. 5874, f. 45; Gent. Mag. vol. lvii. pt. ii. p. 1030, vol. lix. pt. ii. p. 916; Nichols's Lit. Anecd. iii. 623, 624, 760, ix. 6, 169; Cat. of Oxford Graduates, 1851, p. 385; Graduati Cantabr. 1823, p. 275; Lowndes's Bibl. Man. (Bohn), p. 1274.] T. C.

KING, MATTHEW PETER (1773–1823), musical composer, born in 1773, studied musical composition under Charles Frederick Horn. He lived mainly in London, where he died in January 1823.

King wrote the music to a number of dramatic pieces, most of which were produced at the Lyceum Theatre. These include: 'Matrimony,' comic opera, words by James Kenney [q. v.], 1804; 'The Invisible Girl' and 'The Weathercock,' 1806; 'False Alarms,' comic opera, music by King and Braham, words by J. Kenney, 1807; 'One o'Clock, or the Wood Demon,' comic opera, music by King and Kenney, words by M. G. Lewis, 1807; 'Ella Rosenberg,' melodrama, by J. Kenney, 1807; 'Up all Night, or The Smugglers' Cave,' comic opera, words by S. J. Arnold, 1809; 'Plots, or the North Tower,' melodramatic opera, words by S. J. Arnold, 1810; 'Oh! this Love,' comic opera, words by J. Kenney, 1810; 'The Americans,' music by King and Braham, 1811; 'Timour the Tartar,' romantic melodrama, by M. G. Lewis, 1811; 'Turn him out,' musical farce, words by J. Kenney, 1812; 'The Fisherman's Hut,' music by King and Davy, 1819.

King composed a number of glees, ballads, and pianoforte pieces, as well as an oratorio, 'The Intercession,' which was produced at Covent Garden in 1817. In this, Eve's lamentation, 'Must I leave thee, Paradise?' became very popular.

He was the author of 'Thorough Bass made easy to every Capacity,' London, 1796; 'A General Treatise on Music, particularly on Harmony or Thorough Bass,' a work of considerable repute, London, 1800, new edit. 1809; 'Introduction to the Theory and Practice of Singing at First Sight,' London, 1806; and he edited 'The Harmonist, a Collection of Glees and Madrigals from the Classic Poets,' London, 1814.

His son, C. M. King, published some songs in 1826.

[Grove's Dict. of Music, ii. 57; Brown's Dict. of Music, p. 359; Brit. Mus. Catalogues.] R. F. S.

KING, OLIVER (d. 1503), bishop of Bath and Wells, a native of London, became scholar of Eton in 1449 (HARWOOD, *Alumni Eton.* p. 107), and was elected fellow of King's College, Cambridge. He is said to have been secretary to Edward, prince of Wales, son of Henry VI, and in 1476 was appointed by Edward IV his chief secretary in French for life, being described as a 'master of the seven liberal arts' and a licentiate of laws. In 1480 he was made a canon of Windsor, resigning in that year a prebend at Hereford.

He was registrar of the order of the Garter, and in 1482 received the archdeaconry of Oxford. Richard III on his accession in 1483 deprived him of the office of secretary. Having been reinstated by Henry VII in 1485, he received a commission on 3 Dec. to meet the commissioners of Charles VIII of France, and treat for a prolongation of the truce. For his expenses on this embassy he received the following year fifty marks, and was further employed on a commission to ascertain the rights of the crown in Calais, Hammes, and Guisnes. He was appointed to the deanery of Hereford in 1487. A grant in 1488 to him, Lord Daubeny, and another of the next canonry which should fall vacant at Windsor is probably connected with a license granted to him in the same year to found the guild of the Holy Trinity at Windsor. On 12 July 1489 he was installed at Wells archdeacon of Taunton through his proctor (REYNOLDS, from *Liber Ruber*). Being appointed bishop of Exeter by a papal provision dated October 1492, he was consecrated to that see in St. Stephen's, Westminster, on 3 Feb. following. It is doubtful whether he ever entered his diocese (OLIVER). That he stood high in the king's favour is proved by the prominent part assigned to him in the ceremony of the creation of the king's son Henry as duke of York. In 1495 he was translated by a papal bull to the diocese of Bath and Wells. In September 1497 he wrote to acquaint the king of the landing of Perkin Warbeck in Cornwall, and on the 20th Henry wrote to him telling him of the progress of affairs. Three days later he was with the king at Woodstock. He accompanied the king on his march into Somerset, and entered Wells with him on the 30th, which seems to have been the bishop's first visit to his cathedral city. He is said to have visited Bath in 1499, and while there to have had a remarkable dream. The abbey church was in ruins. At night he had a vision of the Trinity and a ladder with angels ascending and descending, and at the foot an olive-tree supporting a crown. He heard a voice saying, 'Let an olive establish the crown, and a king restore the church' (HARINGTON). The words fitting his name, he applied them to himself, and, in conjunction with Prior Birde, began to rebuild the church, ordering that all the surplus revenues of the house, after the payment of certain fixed allowances to the prior, monks, and others, should be devoted to the work. His church, which he did not live to finish, is built on the nave only of the older church. He caused his dream to be represented on the west front,

with the lines, 'Trees going to chuse their king said, Be to us the olive king' (Judges ix. 8). The ladders and angels (now headless) of his dream are still to be seen on the west front. Sir John Harington represents him as apt to listen to wizards and soothsayers, and says that it was thought that he fell into a melancholy after the death of Prince Arthur in 1502, on account of a prophecy foretelling the evils which Henry, afterwards king, would bring on the church. He died on 29 Aug. 1503 (REYNOLDS, from *Liber Ruber*; WHARTON; GODWIN's date, 24 Jan., is wrong). He is said to have been buried, according to the directions in his will, on the north side of the choir of Bath Abbey, near the high altar, though it is also asserted that he was laid in the south aisle of St. George's Chapel at Windsor, within a chantry chapel which he founded and which still retains his name. In this chapel there is a tomb of grey marble which is assigned to him, and near it is an incomplete inscription concerning him. A statue of him, standing by the west door of Bath Abbey, was erected early in the seventeenth century.

[Le Neve's Fasti Eccl. i. 142, 167, 376, 477, 534, iii. 389 (Hardy); Rymer's Fœdera, xii. 26, 279, ed. 1711; Materials illustrative of Reign of Hen. VII, i. 193, 356, ii. 49, 104, 474 (Rolls Ser.); Letters, &c., Ric. III and Hen. VII, i. 392, ii. 407 (Rolls Ser.); Ellis's Orig. Letters, 1st ser. i. 31 sq.; Davies's York Records, p. 165; Harington's Nugæ Antiq. ii. 136, ed. 1804; Wharton's Anglia Sacra, i. 575; Oliver's Bishops of Exeter, p. 114; Cassan's Bishops of Bath and Wells, pp. 315–30; Godwin, De Præsulibus, p. 384; Reynolds's Wells Cathedral, pp. 179, 209; Warner's Bath, p. 131; Somerset Archæol. and Nat. Hist. Soc.'s Proc. xii. ii. 37, xxii. i. 29, xxv. ii. 64.]
W. H.

KING, PAUL (*d.* 1655), Irish Franciscan, was the son of Cornelius King, who was employed by Lord Upper Ossory as a clerk or secretary. His uncle, the Rev. Murtagh King, a convert to protestantism, and beneficed by William Bedell [q. v.], bishop of Kilmore, who employed him to translate the Old Testament into Irish. According to Richard Bellings [q. v.], King was christened David. His name in religion was Paulus a Spiritu Sancto. In early life he was imprisoned among the Moors, and owed his liberation to Luke Wadding [q. v.] In 1641 he taught moral theology at Brindisi, and in 1644 he was doing similar work at Kilkenny, where he was made guardian of the convent and, as it seems, of the whole province, by the nuncio Rinuccini, whose cause he espoused both against Ormonde and against tho supreme council of tho confederate catholics. In July 1648, when acting as the nuncio's confidential agent (CARDINAL MORAN, *Spicilegium Ossoriense*, i. 422), he was arrested by order of the council, and his guardianship of the convent conferred on Peter Walsh (*Aphorismical Discovery*, ed. Gilbert, i. 238). A few days later he wrote to Macmahon, bishop of Clogher, inviting Owen Roe O'Neill [q. v.] to seize Kilkenny and all the nuncio's enemies before Ormonde's arrival in Ireland. The letter was intercepted, and King fled to the continent. According to Bellings he had openly committed innumerable crimes, but the abortive plot to betray Kilkenny is alone mentioned. At Louvain he wrote a bitter diatribe against Rinuccini's opponents and the Anglo-Irish party generally; and this pamphlet, which professes to have been written from the Irish camp some months before, was carefully circulated by the wandering Franciscans in France, Spain, and Italy. Bellings dissects it sentence by sentence in the second part of the 'Vindiciae.' Innocent X is believed to have blamed the nuncio much, but the Franciscan order generally sustained him, and in 1649 King was made guardian of St. Isidore's at Rome (*Spicilegium Ossoriense*, i. 326). The famous John Colgan [q. v.] recommended him as a proper person to be commissary over the Franciscan colleges on the continent, and he was for some years secretary to the procurator-general of the order. Bellings regrets (*Vindiciae*, preface to part ii.) having had no opportunity of showing that punishment was deserved rather than promotion; but his antagonist John Ponce, himself a Franciscan, says King was worthy of even much greater honours, and defends him against a charge of publishing scurrilous verses. While at Rome King projected a book in ten volumes in honour of his order ('nostri seraphici ordinis'), but only lived to publish a kind of syllabus, which was licensed for the 'Index' as 'earnest of a great work.' King, who was a professor of theology, was learned in Greek and Hebrew. He records his preference for an obvious and easy style, and wrote with vigour, but incorrectly, though he was a pupil of the famous latinist, Bonaventure Baron [q. v.] He died, it is believed, at Rome, in 1665.

King's published writings, all in Latin, are: 1. Letter to the Bishop of Clogher, August 1648, printed in Bellings's 'Vindiciae,' i. chap. 14, and in Cox's 'Hibernia Anglicana.' 2. 'Epistola nobilis Hiberni ad amicum Belgam scripta ex castris catholicis ejusdem regni, die 4 Maii, anno 1649,' printed in 'Vindiciae,' pt. ii., and in Gilbert's 'Contemporary History,' ii. 211. 3. 'Idea Cosmographiae Seraphicae concepta et concinnata a Fr. Paulo King, Hiberno, ... Romae,' 1654. 4. An Elegy on Cardinal Ximenes.

[Vindiciae Catholicorum Hiberniae, authore Philopatro Irenaeo (Richard Bellings), Paris, 1650; John Ponce's Vindiciae Everso, Paris, 1653; Gilbert's Contemporary Hist. of Affairs in Ireland; information kindly supplied by the Rev. F. L. Carey, late guardian of St. Isidore's.]

R. B l.

KING, PETER, first LORD KING, BARON OF OCKHAM in Surrey (1669–1734), lord chancellor, son of Jerome King, grocer and drysalter, of Exeter, by Anne, daughter of Peter Locke, uncle of the philosopher John Locke, was born in Exeter in 1669. He was educated in Exeter at the nonconformist academy kept by Joseph Hallett (1656–1722) [q. v.] and bred to his father's business, but showed a studious disposition, and spent all his pocket-money in buying books. He was trained as a presbyterian, and interested himself in the early history of the Christian church. In 1691 he published anonymously 'An Enquiry into the Constitution, Discipline, Unity and Worship of the Primitive Church that flourished within the first three hundred years after Christ. Faithfully collected out of the extant Writings of those Ages,' London, 12mo. Locke was interested in the treatise, and persuaded King's father to send him to the university of Leyden, where he spent about three years. He was entered as a student at the Middle Temple on 23 Oct. 1694, and was called to the bar on 8 June 1698 by the recommendation of Chief-justice Treby [q. v.] He rapidly made his way both on circuit and at Westminster, and on 10 Jan. 1700-1 was returned to parliament in the whig interest for the close borough of Beeralston, Devonshire. The election gave the whigs an immense majority, and King, by Locke's advice, sacrificed the spring circuit to remain in town and watch the course of events. He made his maiden speech in the house in February 1702, and was, according to a congratulatory letter from Locke, well received. His first reported speech, however, was delivered in the debate on the Aylesbury election case in 1704, when he ably vindicated the rights of the electors. In 1705 he was appointed recorder of Glastonbury, and on 2? July 1708 recorder of London. He was knighted at Windsor on the ensuing 12 Sept., after conveying to the queen the congratulations of the city upon the battle of Oudenarde. At this time he was regarded as one of the mainstays of the whig party. In 1710 he was one of the managers of the impeachment of Sacheverell, and aggravated the doctor's

peevish censure of the Toleration Act into a
'malicious, scandalous, and seditious libel.'
On their return to power after the general
election, the tories retaliated by moving
(10 June 1712) that the preface to the recently published sermons of Fleetwood, bishop
of St. Asaph, deserved burning by the common
hangman, a motion which King stoutly, but
in vain, resisted. He defended gratuitously
William Whiston [q. v.], on his trial for
heresy in July 1713 (WHISTON, *Memoirs*,
1749, p. 227). On the arrival of George I
in the country, King, as recorder of London,
attended with the mayor and corporation to
receive him at St. Margaret's Hill, Southwark, on his progress from Greenwich to
St. James's (20 Sept. 1714). Soon afterwards, at the suggestion of Lord Cowper
[q. v.], he was designated to succeed Lord
Trevor [q. v.] in the common pleas, and
accordingly on 26 Oct. 1714 he took the
degree of serjeant-of-law, and on 22 Nov. the
oaths, as chief justice of the common pleas.
His salary was fixed at 2,000*l.*, double that
of his predecessor. On his consequent resignation of the recordership of London he
was presented by the mayor and corporation
with a piece of plate 'as a loving remembrance of his many good services done to
the city.' On 29 March 1715 he was sworn
of the privy council (BOYER, *Polit. State of
Great Britain*, ix. 238). During the tenure
of his new office King gained the reputation
of an eminently able, learned, and impartial
judge, but, as the business of his court was
entirely civil, had not much opportunity of
trying notorious cases. He tried the commoners implicated in the rebellion of 1715;
but these cases are not reported, though, from
some excerpts printed by Lord Campbell from
his manuscript report to the secretary of state,
he appears to have been lenient. In a case
tried by him in 1722 King has been censured
for putting too liberal a construction upon the
Coventry Act (22 & 23 Car. II. c. 1), which
made malicious maiming or wounding, with
intent to disfigure the person, felony, without
benefit of clergy. A man had been left for
dead by his intending murderers, but had recovered. King directed the jury that the
intent to murder included the intent to maim
or wound, and the prisoners were convicted
and executed.

In January 1717-18 King concurred with
the majority of his colleagues in advising
George I that the custody of the royal grand-
children was vested not in their father, but
in the crown, a fact which was probably
not forgotten when the Earl of Macclesfield
resigned the great seal in January 1724-5
(see PARKER, THOMAS, EARL OF MACCLES-

VOL. XXXI.

FIELD, 1666-1732]. King was at once commissioned to supply the late chancellor's
place as speaker of the House of Lords, in
which capacity he presided at his trial on the
articles of impeachment subsequently exhibited against Macclesfield, and read the sentence of the house on 25 May. On 28 May
he was raised to the peerage as Lord King,
baron of Ockham, Surrey, and took his seat in
the House of Lords on the 31st. On 1 June
the king delivered to him the great seal, and
he was forthwith sworn lord chancellor and
appointed one of the lords justices in whom
the regency was vested during the king's approaching visit to Hanover. A patent of the
office of lord chancellor was also made out
to him in the form 'quamdiu se bene gesserit,'
and besides the ordinary emoluments of his
office, which then consisted chiefly of fees, a
pension of 6,000*l.* a year was settled upon
him, with an additional 1,200*l.* a year in lieu
of the profits arising from the sale of offices,
then for the first time expressly declared illegal. He resigned the chief justiceship on
2 June. On the occasion of George I's last
visit to Hanover he was again nominated one
of the lords justices, 31 May 1727 (BOYER,
Polit. State of Great Britain, xxix. 500, 553,
xxxiii. 516). On 16 June following he surrendered the great seal to George II on his
accession, but immediately received it back,
and took the oaths as lord chancellor, being
informed by George (8 July) that he intended
to nominate to all benefices and prebends that
were in the gift of the chancellor. This pre-
tension King quietly, but firmly and successfully, resisted, hoping his majesty 'would not
put things out of their ancient course,' and
after some discussion the matter dropped.

Few chancellors ever took their seat on
the woolsack with greater reputation than
King, and quitted it with less. An admirable common lawyer, he was little versed in
either the theory or the practice of equity;
and though he diligently studied abridgments
and reports, and even took private lessons
from eminent counsel, he was never able to
acquire a competent knowledge of the law
he had to administer. He was morbidly diffi-
dent, and inclined to defer judgment as long
as possible, thus grievously aggravating the
dilatoriness of chancery procedure. Arrears
multiplied exorbitantly, and King was compelled to prolong his sittings far into the
night. Still the arrears were not overtaken,
and the decrees thus tardily pronounced were
only too frequently reversed by the House
of Lords. During the last few years of his
life he became so drowsy and inattentive that
the suitors were left almost entirely at the
mercy of the leading counsel, the decrees

L

being usually settled by Attorney-general Yorke and Solicitor-general Talbot.

Nevertheless King established some important legal principles, e.g. that a will of English land, though made abroad, must be made according to the formalities of English law; and that, where a husband had a legal title to his wife's personal estate, a court of equity would not help him to 'reduce it into possession' without compelling him to settle a part of it upon her, which did something to mitigate the harshness of the old law. He was the author of the act which substituted English for Latin as the language of writs and similar documents, and also of the statute 12 Geo. I, c. 32, which, by requiring masters in chancery to pay all sums deposited with them in their official capacity into the Bank of England as soon as received, rendered impossible a recurrence of the frauds perpetrated during Lord Macclesfield's tenure of office. He is charged by Whiston, whom he had offended by refusing to join his Society for Promoting Primitive Christianity, with being wholly guided by worldly considerations in dispensing church patronage, and with justifying subscription by unbelievers on the ground that 'we must not lose our usefulness for scruples' (WHISTON, Memoirs, pt. i. pp. 35, 162). As a minister he made no considerable figure. He was an F.R.S., a friend of Newton and one of his pall-bearers, a governor of the Charterhouse, a member of the Society for the Propagation of the Gospel in Foreign Parts and of a commission for the building of new churches.

A paralytic stroke compelled King to resign the great seal on 19 Nov. 1733. He was offered a pension of 4,000l., or a capital sum of 20,000l., and chose the latter. He died on 22 July 1734 at his seat at Ockham, and was buried in the parish church, where a splendid monument by Rysbrach perpetuates his memory. Lord Hervey has left a clever and ill-natured character, or perhaps caricature, of him in his 'Memoirs,' i. 280-1: an extravagant panegyric by the Duke of Wharton, written while he was still lord chief justice of the common pleas, will be found in the 'True Briton,' No. xxxix. (See also an absurd adulatory 'Letter to the Right Honourable the Lord Chief Justice King on his Lordship's being designed a Peer,' London, 1725, 4to.) King married, in September 1704, Anne, daughter of Richard Seys of Boverton, Glamorganshire, by whom he had four sons—John, Peter, William, and Thomas—and two daughters. Each of his sons in turn succeeded to the title. King's portrait by Daniel de Coning, painted in 1720, is in the National Portrait Gallery.

In 1702 King published a 'History of the Apostles' Creed: with Critical Observations on its several Articles.' It was received more favourably abroad than at home, and was highly praised in Bernard's 'Nouvelles de la République des Lettres' (November and December 1702). A Latin translation by Gottfried Olearius was published at Leipzig in 1706, and reprinted at Basel in 1750. Later English editions appeared in 1703, 1711, 1719, and 1737. This, the first attempt to trace the evolution of the creed, gave a great impulse to research, and determined the main lines upon which it was to be conducted. The creed, according to King, was originally a baptismal formula, which varied in different churches, and did not assume its present shape till four centuries after the close of the apostolic age. Later writers (see SCHAFF, Creeds of the Greek and Latin Churches, p. 52) have given 750 as the approximate date. John Simson, professor of divinity in Glasgow, accused of Arianism in 1727, tried to shelter himself behind some words in King's 'History.' King made no reply to this misrepresentation of his views, but was defended in a 'Vindication' by an anonymous author in 1731. Joseph Bingham in his 'Antiquities' frequently refers to King, and with invariable respect, though without accepting all his conclusions.

In 1712 and 1713 King published a second edition of his early 'Enquiry,' with a second part treating of ceremonies and worship. The book, though intended to promote the comprehension of the dissenters, is impartial and critical. A correspondence with Edmund Elys [q. v.] upon liturgical forms, occasioned by the first edition, is printed in Elys's 'Letters on several Subjects' (1694). In 1717 King was attacked by the anonymous author of 'The Invalidity of the Dissenting or Presbyterian Ordination,' and by William Sclater, a nonjuring clergyman, in his 'Original Draught of the Primitive Church.' Charles Daubeny [q. v.] in his 'Eight Discourses, &c.,' 1801, declares, but without justification, that King was himself converted by this work. John Wesley in 1746 read the 'Enquiry,' and, in spite of his high church prejudices, admitted it to be an 'impartial draught' (Journal). It was reprinted in 1839 and 1843, with an abridgment of Sclater by way of antidote, and was not really superseded until the publication in 1881 of the Bampton lectures of Edwin Hatch [q. v.] on 'The Organisation of the Early Christian Churches.'

King was erroneously identified by Mosheim with a 'Mr. K——,' who defended the legend of the thundering legion, in correspondence with Walter Moyle [q. v.] The real author was a London clergyman named Richard King.

During his tenure of the great seal King kept a diary chiefly of affairs of state, which was printed by his descendant, the seventh baron, as an appendix to his 'Life of Locke' [see KING, PETER, seventh LORD KING].

The reports of Peere Williams, W. Kelynge, and Mosely (the two latter works of slight authority) contain King's decisions while lord chancellor.

[Notes and Queries, 1st ser. xi. 327; Hist. Reg. Chron. Diary, 1734; Chaufepié's Nouveau Dict. Hist.; Biog. Brit.; Biog. Univ.; Lord King's Diary; Campbell's Lives of the Lord Chancellors; Foss's Lives of the Judges; Welsby's Lives of Eminent English Judges; Parl. Hist. vi. 294, 1155; Luttrell's Relation of State Affairs; Hearne's Collect. ed. Doble (Oxf. Hist. Soc.), ii. 32; Howell's State Trials, xv. 134 et seq., 418 et seq., 1222, 1323–1404, xxi. 767 et seq.; Lord Raymond's Rep. ed. Gale, 1318, 1319; Lords' Journ. xxii. 377; Collins's Peerage, ed. Brydges, vii. 223; Burke's Peerage. 'Lovelace;' Brayley and Britton's Surrey, iii. 112 et seq.] J. M. R.

KING, PETER, seventh LORD KING, BARON OF OCKHAM, Surrey (1776–1833), born 31 Aug. 1776, was eldest son of Peter, the sixth baron, by Charlotte, daughter of Edward Tredcroft of Horsham, and was great-grandson of Lord-chancellor King [see KING, PETER, first LORD KING]. He was educated at Eton and Trinity College, Cambridge, and succeeded to the title in 1793. After a short tour on the continent he returned to England on coming of age, and took his seat in the House of Lords. True to the whig traditions of his family, he acted with Lord Holland [see Fox, HENRY RICHARD VASSALL], whose motion for an inquiry into the causes of the failure of the expedition to the Low Countries he supported in his maiden speech, 12 Feb. 1800. His habits, however, were somewhat recluse, and except to oppose a Habeas Corpus Suspension Bill, or a bill to prolong the suspension of cash payments by the Banks of England and Ireland, begun in 1797, he at first rarely intervened in debate. Of the currency question he made a profound study, the fruit of which was seen in a pamphlet entitled 'Thoughts on the Restriction of Payments in Specie at the Banks of England and Ireland,' London, 1803, 8vo, 2nd edit. Much enlarged, it was reissued as 'Thoughts on the Effects of the Bank Restrictions,' 1804, 8vo, and was reprinted in 'A Selection' from King's speeches and writings, edited by Earl Fortescue, London, 1844, 8vo. In this classical tract King established that

the suspension had caused an excessive issue of notes, particularly by the Bank of Ireland, and a consequent depreciation of the paper and appreciation of bullion, and advocated a gradual return to the system of specie payment. It was reviewed by Horner in the 'Edinburgh Review' (ii. 402 et seq.), and attracted much attention, but produced no practical result; and, the depreciation increasing, King in 1811 gave his leasehold tenantry notice that he could no longer accept notes in payment of rent, except at a discount varying according to the date of the lease. Ministers, alarmed lest his example should be followed generally, hastily introduced a measure making notes of the Banks of England and Ireland payable on demand legal tender in payment of rent out of court, and prohibiting the acceptance or payment of more than 21s. for a guinea. King opposed the bill, and justified his own conduct in an able and spirited speech (afterwards published in pamphlet form); but it passed into law, and was followed in 1812 by a measure making the notes legal tender in all cases (stat. 51 Geo. III, c. 127, 52 Geo. III, c. 50). King was from the first, and as long as he lived, a determined opponent of the corn laws, which he denounced as a 'job of jobs.' He supported catholic emancipation and the commutation of tithes, and opposed grants in aid of the Society for the Propagation of the Gospel in Foreign Parts, pluralities and other abuses, and was suspected of a leaning to presbyterianism (see Hierarchia versus Anarchiam, &c., by Antischismaticus, London, 1831, 8vo, and A Letter to Lord King controverting the sentiments lately delivered in Parliament by his Lordship, Mr. O'Connell, and Mr. Sheil, as to the fourfold division of Tithes, by James Thomas Law, London, 1832, 8vo). A career of increasing distinction was, by his sudden death, cut short on 4 June 1833. King married, on 26 May 1804, Lady Hester Fortescue, daughter of Hugh, first earl Fortescue, by whom he had (with two daughters) two sons—William King, who was created Earl of Lovelace in 1838, and Peter John Locke King [q. v.]

Besides the tract on the currency, King published: 1. A pamphlet 'On the Conduct of the British Government towards the Catholics of Ireland,' 1807. 2. 'Speech in the House of Lords on the second reading of Earl Stanhope's Bill respecting Guineas and Bank Notes.' 3. 'The Life of John Locke, with extracts from his Correspondence, Journals, and Commonplace Books,' London, 1829, 4to; new edition, with considerable additions, 1830, 2 vols. 8vo; another in Bohn's Standard Library, London, 1858,

1 vol. 8vo. 4. 'A Short History of the Job of Jobs,' written in 1825, first published as an anti-cornlaw pamphlet, London, 1846, 8vo.

[The principal authority is A Selection from the Speeches and Writings of the late Lord King, with a short introductory Memoir by Earl Fortescue, London, 1844, 8vo. See also Gent. Mag. 1833, pt. ii. p. 80; Brougham's Historical Sketches of Statesmen who flourished in the time of Geo. III, 2nd ser. pp. 172 et seq.; Yonge's Life of Lord Liverpool, iii. 170; Lord Colchester's Diary, vol. iii.; Parl. Hist. and Hansard; Horner's Memoirs, ii. 92; Collins's Peerage (Brydges), vii. 226; Burke's Peerage, 'Lovelace;' Edinburgh Review, l. 1 et seq.] J. M. R.

KING, PETER JOHN LOCKE (1811–1885), politician, second son of Peter King, seventh baron King [q. v.], and brother of William King-Noel, first earl of Lovelace, was born at Ockham, Surrey, on 25 Jan. 1811. He was educated at Harrow and at Trinity College, Cambridge, where he graduated B.A. 1831, and M.A. 1833. In 1857 he unsuccessfully contested East Surrey, but was elected for that constituency on 11 Aug. 1847, and retained his seat until the conservative reaction at the general election in February 1874. He supported an alteration in the law of primogeniture for many sessions. On 15 March 1855 he delivered a speech in which he showed emphatically 'the crying injustice of the law.' On 11 Aug. 1854 he passed the Real Estate Charges Act, according to which mortgaged estates descend with and bear their own burdens. In the session of 1856 he was successful in obtaining the repeal of 120 sleeping statutes which were liable to be put in force from time to time. He also waged war against the statute law commission, and more than once denounced it as a job. King introduced a bill for abolishing the property qualification of members, which passed the House of Lords on 28 June 1858, and in eight successive sessions he brought forward the county franchise bill, on one occasion, 20 Feb. 1851, defeating and causing the resignation of the Russell ministry. He succeeded in carrying through the House of Commons a bill for extending the 10l. franchise to the county constituencies, so as to include every adult male who came within the conditions of the borough suffrage. He was also well known for his advocacy of the ballot and of the abolition of church rates, and for his strenuous opposition to the principle and practice alike of endowments for religious purposes. He died at Brooklands, Weybridge, on 12 Nov. 1885. He married, on 22 March 1836, Louisa Elizabeth, daughter of William Henry Hoare of Mitcham

Grove, Surrey. She died in 1884, leaving two sons and four daughters.

King was the author of: 1. 'Injustice of the Law of Succession to the Real Property of Intestates,' 1854; 3rd edit. 1855. 2. 'Speech on the Laws relating to the Property of Intestates,' 15 March 1855. 3. 'Speech on the Laws relating to the Property of Intestates in the House of Commons,' 17 Feb. 1859. 4. 'Speech on the Law relating to the Real Estates of Intestates,' 14 July 1869. Four letters which King wrote to the 'Times' in 1855 on 'Chancery Reform' are reprinted in 'A Bleak House Narrative of Real Life,' 1856, pp. 55–60.

[Hansard, 1849, ciii. 88 et seq.; Statesmen of England, 1862, No. 46, with portrait; Drawing-room Portrait Gallery, 2nd ser. 1859, with portrait; Foster's Peerage; Times, 14 Nov. 1885, p. 9.] G. C. B.

KING, PHILIP GIDLEY (1758–1808), first governor of Norfolk Island and governor of New South Wales, was born 23 April 1758 at Launceston in Cornwall, where his father, Philip King, was a draper; his mother was a daughter of John Gidley, attorney, of Exeter. He was educated at Yarmouth by a Mr. Bailey, but went to sea at the age of twelve as a midshipman in the Swallow frigate, Captain Shirley, and served five years in the East Indies, returning to England 'with much knowledge of his business and some acquaintance with the world' (PHILLIP, Voyage). In 1775 he went to Virginia with Captain Bellew in the Liverpool. His ship, after seeing some service, was wrecked in Delaware Bay, whereupon King entered on board the Princess Royal, October 1778. He was promoted to the Renown, with the rank of lieutenant, 26 Nov. following. In 1779 he again returned home, and for four years served in the Channel on board the Kite cutter and Ariadne frigate. He was associated as lieutenant with Captain Phillip of the Europe in 1783, and this officer's high appreciation of his qualities—his merit as a seaman and perseverance—led to his selection of King (25 Oct. 1786) for the post of second lieutenant on his own ship, the Sirius, when he commanded the famous 'First Fleet' which sailed for Australia on 13 May 1787, and arrived at Botany Bay in January 1788. Immediately after his landing Phillip appointed King commandant of Norfolk Island. King set sail thither on 14 Feb. 1788, taking with him only a petty officer, a surgeon's mate, two marines, two men who were supposed to understand the cultivation of flax, and nine male and six female convicts, for the purpose of settling the island as a branch colony. At that time Norfolk Island was covered with scrub, and to convert it into a source of supply for flax for the navy (an object dear to the home government, but never realised), and to form gardens and cultivated fields, was no easy task with the small force at King's command. In two years, however, by unflagging energy, he had some fifty acres of land under cultivation, and the population had risen to 418, besides the eighty men belonging to the Sirius. His duties were manifold; he was at once magistrate and chaplain, farmer and governor of convicts. Though he was obliged to have recourse to the lash, he was not unduly severe, and never abused his almost autocratic powers; indeed Sir Joseph Banks found fault with his too ready clemency (letter to King, 1804; BARTON, i. 239). In March 1790 he left Norfolk Island for Sydney Cove, whence he was sent in April with despatches from Phillip to the government. He sailed by way of Batavia, where he embarked on a small vessel of the Dutch East India Company. The captain and most of the crew fell ill with fever contracted at Batavia, and King had to navigate the ship with a crew of only four sound men. Seventeen of the crew died before they made Mauritius, and it was not till eight months after leaving Australia that he reached England (December 1790). Phillip had recommended him for promotion to the rank of master and commander in a letter to the secretary of state, 10 July 1788, as 'a very steady officer' who was doing good work in a difficult situation (ib. i. 329); and on his arrival in London with his despatches he was informed that the government had already appointed him lieutenant-governor of Norfolk Island with an allowance of 250l. a year (commission dated 28 Jan. 1790; letter from Lord Grenville, 1 Feb. 1790; BARTON, i. 194, 520). He obtained the rank of commander in March 1791. After giving the government every information in his possession on the condition, prospects, and present necessities of the new colonies at Sydney Cove and Norfolk Island, King sailed, 15 March 1791, with his wife, Anna Josepha Coombes of Bedford, whom he had recently married, on board the Gorgon, Captain Parker, and arrived at Port Jackson 21 Sept. (the voyage is described by Mrs. Parker, Voyage, &c., London, 1795); and on 26 Oct. he departed for Norfolk Island, where he remained at his post till he was appointed governor of New South Wales, 28 Sept. 1800. He retired on 12 Aug. 1806, returned to England, and died at Tooting, Surrey, 3 Sept. 1808. His son, Rear-admiral Philip Parker King, is noticed separately.

[Voyage of Governor Phillip to Botany Bay, 1789, with a portrait of King facing p. 96, drawn by J. Wright, 1789, and engraved by W. Skelton; John Hunter's Historical Journal of the Transactions at Port Jackson and Norfolk Island, 1793, containing King's Journal as commandant at Norfolk Island, 1788-90, and an account of his voyage home, at pp. 287-448; G. B. Barton's History of New South Wales from the Records, vol. i. 1889; Heaton's Australian Dict. of Dates, 1879. A manuscript journal by King (311 pp.), describing the voyage of the First Fleet, is in the possession of the Hon. P. G. King, M.L.C. of New South Wales.] S. L-P.

KING, PHILIP PARKER (1793-1856), rear-admiral, born at Norfolk Island 13 Dec. 1793, was son of Captain Philip Gidley King [q. v.] He entered the navy in November 1807, on board the Diana frigate; and after six years of active service in the Bay of Biscay, the North Sea, and the Mediterranean, was promoted by Sir Edward Pellew to be lieutenant of the Trident, 28 Feb. 1814. In the beginning of 1817 he was appointed to conduct a survey of the coast of Australia, and was sent out, a passenger in a transport, to take command of the Mermaid, a cutter of eighty-four tons, with a complement of eighteen officers and men. He arrived in Port Jackson in September 1817, and for the next five years was engaged, almost without intermission, on the work of the survey. During that time he examined and delineated the greater part of the west, north, and northeast coasts, and laid down a new route from Sydney to Torres Strait, inside the Barrier Reef. In December 1820 the Mermaid was found to be no longer seaworthy, and King was transferred to a newly purchased ship, which was renamed the Bathurst. This was about double the size of the Mermaid, and carrying twice the number of men, but the work on which she was employed was essentially the same. King was promoted to the rank of commander, 17 July 1821, but continued the survey till the April of 1822. In September the Bathurst sailed for England, where she arrived in April 1823, and during the next two years King was occupied with the narrative and the charts of his survey. The charts were published by the hydrographic office, and form the basis of those now in use; the 'Narrative of the Survey of the Intertropical and Western Coasts of Australia' (2 vols. 8vo) was published in 1827. Meantime, on 26 Feb. 1824, King was elected a fellow of the Royal Society; and in September 1825 was appointed to the Adventure, with instructions to undertake the survey of 'the southern coast of South America from the Rio Plata round to Chiloe, and of Tierra del Fuego.' In this service the Adventure was accompanied by the Beagle, commanded by Captain Stokes, and after the latter's death by Captain Robert Fitzroy [q.v.], and during the four years 1826–30 the work was carried on with unremitting diligence and an exactness which established the reputations of both King and Fitzroy in the very first rank of hydrographers. King was advanced to post-rank on 25 Feb. 1830, and in the following November the two ships returned to England. In April and May 1831 King read some account of the results of his voyage before the Royal Geographical Society, and in the following year he published a volume of 'Sailing Directions to the Coasts of Eastern and Western Patagonia, including the Straits of Magalhaen and the Sea-Coast of Tierra del Fuego.' In 1839 a more popular account of his and Fitzroy's voyage was published in the first volume of the 'Voyages of the Adventure and Beagle,' edited by Captain Fitzroy. King had no further service in the navy, but returning to New South Wales, settled in Sydney and entered busily into the affairs of the colony; he was for many years manager of the Australian Agricultural Society, and a member of the legislative council. In September 1855 he became a rear-admiral on the retired list. He died in February 1856, leaving a widow and a large family. He had married in 1817 Harriet, daughter of Christopher Lethbridge of Madford, Launceston, Cornwall.

[Marshall's Roy. Nav. Biog. x. (vol. iii. pt. ii.) 200; O'Byrne's Nav. Biog. Dict.; Gent. Mag. 1856, new ser. i. 426; Heaton's Australian Dict.; and King's works mentioned in the text.] J. K. L.

KING, Sir RICHARD, the elder (1730–1806), admiral, son of Curtis King, master in the navy, and afterwards master-attendant at Woolwich, and of his wife Mary, sister of Commodore Curtis Barnett [q.v.], was born at Gosport on 10 Aug. 1730. He entered the navy in 1738 on board the Berwick, of which his father was master, but was shortly afterwards moved into the Dragon, then commanded by his uncle, whom he accompanied to the Mediterranean and to the East Indies, where he was promoted to be lieutenant, 1 Feb. 1745–6. In 1754 he again went to the East Indies as lieutenant of the Tiger, from which he was moved into the flagship by the commander-in-chief, Rear-admiral Charles Watson [q.v.], formerly a lieutenant of the Berwick. On 23 July 1756 he was promoted to be commander of the Blaze fire-ship, and in the following January commanded the

boats and the landing party at the capture of Calcutta and Hoogly. He was then sent home with despatches, and was immediately ordered to the West Indies in the Bonetta sloop, from which he was posted, by Commodore Moore, to the Rye frigate, 29 Jan. 1759. In May he was moved to the Ludlow Castle and sent home with convoy. In January 1760 he was appointed to the Argo, in which he cruised with some success on the coast of France and in the North Sea. In 1762 he carried out General Draper to the East Indies; took part in the expedition to Manila [see DRAPER, SIR WILLIAM; CORNISH, SIR SAMUEL], and with Captain Hyde Parker (1713–1783) [q.v.] assisted in the capture of an extraordinarily rich galeon, his personal share in the prize-money amounting to upwards of 30,000l. In the following year he returned to England in command of the Grafton. In the Spanish armament of 1770 King commissioned the Northumberland; from her he was moved to the Ardent, and afterwards to the Asia, which he commanded for three years, as a guardship. In January 1778 he was appointed to the Monmouth, was soon afterwards transferred to the Pallas, and, in January 1779, to the Exeter of 64 guns, in which he went out to the East Indies with Sir Edward Hughes [q.v.] On arriving on the station he was ordered to wear a broad pennant as an established commodore and second in command. In the action off Sadras, 17 Feb. 1782, the Exeter was the rearmost ship of the English line, and was for some time in great danger of being overpowered, the French admiral having ably concentrated his attack on the English rear. She was almost entirely dismasted, had received several shot under water, had ten men killed and forty-seven wounded. The flag-captain, Reynolds, was killed, and his brains were dashed in King's face, temporarily blinding him, just as the master, seeing yet another enemy's ship bearing down on them, asked 'What was to be done?' Wiping his face with his handkerchief, King answered, 'There is nothing to be done but to fight her till she sinks.' A lucky shift of wind, however, enabled the van to tack to the assistance of the rear, when the French retired. In the other four actions between Hughes and Suffrein, the Exeter played a distinguished part, though not such an exceptional one as in the first, and on the passage home had to be condemned at the Cape of Good Hope as no longer seaworthy. On arriving in England King was knighted. He was promoted to be rear-admiral 24 Sept. 1787, was commander-in-chief in the Downs in 1790, and had a junior command in the fleet at Spithead in 1791. In 1792 he was created a baronet, and appointed governor and commander-in-chief at Newfoundland. He became a vice-admiral on 1 Feb. 1793, and returning to England was elected M.P. for Rochester. In December 1794 he was appointed commander-in-chief at Plymouth, and was advanced to the rank of admiral on 1 June 1795. He died 7 Nov. 1806. He married Susannah Margaretta, daughter of William Coker of Mappowder, Dorset, and left, besides three daughters, a son, Richard (1774–1834) [q. v.], who succeeded to the baronetcy. His portrait by Sir William Beechey is in the possession of the family.

[Charnock's Biog. Nav. vi. 369; Ralfe's Naval Biog. i. 225; Beatson's Nav. and Mil. Memoirs; Chevalier's Histoire de la Marine française (pt. i.); Commission and Warrant Books in the Public Record Office.]   J. K. L.

KING, RICHARD (1748–1810), divine, born on 30 Nov. 1748, was son of Henry King of St. Augustine, Bristol. He was admitted scholar of Winchester in 1762 (KIRBY, Winchester Scholars, p. 258), matriculated at Oxford from Queen's College on 4 April 1767, and was elected fellow of New College in 1768, graduating B.A. in 1772, and M.A. in 1776 (FOSTER, Alumni Oxon. 1715–1886, ii. 796). In 1782 he resigned his fellowship, receiving the college livings of Worthen, Shropshire, and Steeple Morden, Cambridgeshire. He died at the latter place on 30 Oct. 1810 (Gent. Mag. vol. lxxx. pt. ii. p. 589).

King wrote: 1. 'A Discourse on the Inspiration of the Scriptures,' 8vo, London, 1805. 2. 'Remarks on the Alliance between Church and State, and on the Test Laws,' 8vo, London, 1807. 3. 'Brother Abraham's Answer to Peter Plymley [i.e. to the "Letters on the subject of the Catholics to my brother Abraham, who lives in the Country," by Sydney Smith] . . . in two Letters; to which is prefixed a "Postliminious" Preface,' 8vo, London, 1808.

On 17 Aug. 1782 he married Frances Elizabeth, third daughter of Sir Francis Bernard, bart. [q. v.]

His wife, FRANCES ELIZABETH KING, was born on 25 July 1757. After the death of her husband she resided at Gateshead, Durham, so as to be near her two married daughters, and died there on 23 Dec. 1821 (Gent. Mag. vol. xcii. pt. i. p. 90). An intimate friend of Hannah More, she established under her guidance societies for visiting the sick poor and schools for their children. To the 'Reports' issued by the Society for Bettering the Condition of the Poor, under the editorship of her brother, Sir Thomas Bernard [q. v.], she contributed many papers. Her other writings are: 1. 'A Tour in France,' 12mo, London, 1803. 2. 'The Beneficial Effects of the Christian Temper on Domestic Happiness,' 2nd edit. 8vo, London, 1807; 6th edit. 1825. 3. 'Female Scripture Characters; exemplifying Female Virtues,' 16mo, London, 1813; 10th edit. 1826, to which her portrait, engraved by Scriven after Hastings, is prefixed. 4. 'The Rector's Memorandum Book, being Memoirs of a Family in the North' [anon.], 12mo, London, 1814 (and 1819). Her portrait was also engraved by Woolnoth.

[Memoir prefixed to Mrs. King's Female Scripture Characters, 3rd edit.; Evans's Cat. of Engraved Portraits, ii. 233.]   G. G.

KING, SIR RICHARD, the younger (1774–1834), vice-admiral, born in 1774, was only son of Admiral Sir Richard King [q. v.] He entered the navy in 1788 on board the Crown in the East Indies with Commodore (afterwards Sir William) Cornwallis [q. v.], by whom he was made lieutenant in 1791, commander in 1793, and captain in 1794. On his return to England he was appointed in November 1794 to the Aurora for cruising service in the Channel. During the continuance of the war he commanded different ships with credit in the Channel and the North Sea. In April 1804 he was appointed to the Achille of 74 guns, in which, on 21 Oct. 1805, he took part in the battle of Trafalgar. On the death of his father in November 1806, King succeeded to the baronetcy, but continued in the Achille, employed on the west coast of France or Spain till 1811, when he was appointed captain of the fleet to Sir Charles Cotton [q. v.] in the Mediterranean and afterwards in the Channel. He was promoted to be rear-admiral on 12 Aug. 1812, and for the rest of the war had his flag in the San Josef, in the Mediterranean, as second in command to Sir Edward Pellew [q. v.], afterwards Viscount Exmouth. He was nominated a K.C.B. 2 Jan. 1815, was commander-in-chief in the East Indies from 1816 to 1820, and became a vice-admiral on 19 July 1821. In July 1833 he was appointed commander-in-chief at the Nore, and died at Admiralty House, Sheerness, on 5 Aug. 1834. King was twice married, first, in 1805, to Sarah Anne, only daughter of Sir John Thomas Duckworth [q. v.]; secondly, in 1822, to Maria Susanna, daughter of Sir Charles Cotton, and left issue by both wives. His second son by the first marriage, Admiral SIR GEORGE ST. VINCENT DUCKWORTH KING, K.C.B. (d. 1891), succeeded to the baronetcy on the death of his elder brother in 1847, was captain of the Leander, and afterwards of the Rodney, in the Black Sea during the Russian war in 1854-5, and was second in command of the naval brigade at the siege of Sebastopol. He became a rear-admiral in 1863, was commander-in-chief in China from 1863 to 1867, was made vice-admiral in 1867, and admiral in 1875. He died on 18 Aug. 1891.

[Marshall's Royal Nav. Biog. vol. i. pt. ii. p. 545; Ralfe's Nav. Biog. iii. 126; O'Byrne's Nav. Biog. Dict. (s. n. 'King, George St. Vincent'); United Service Journal, 1834, iii. 232; see also Foster's Baronetage.]   J. K. L.

KING, RICHARD (1811?-1876), arctic traveller and ethnologist, was born about 1811, and educated at Guy's and St. Thomas's Hospitals. He became M.R.C.S. on 29 June, L.S.A. 16 Aug. 1832, and obtained in the following year the honorary degree of M.D. of New York. He was subsequently made a member of the court of examiners of the Apothecaries' Society in London. Shortly after qualifying as a medical man he obtained the post of surgeon and naturalist in the expedition led by Captain (afterwards Sir) George Back [q. v.] to the mouth of the Great Fish River between 1833 and 1835, in search of Captain Ross. He took a prominent part in the expedition, and he is frequently mentioned in Back's 'Narrative' (1836), to which he contributed botanical and meteorological appendices. He subsequently published an independent account of the expedition, entitled 'Narrative of a Journey to the Shore of the Arctic Ocean under command of Captain Back,' 2 vols. 8vo, 1836, in which he took a more sanguine view than his commander of the value of the Great Fish River as a basis for future arctic exploration. On 20 July 1842 King issued the prospectus which originated the Ethnological Society. He published an address to the society, of which he was the first secretary, in 1844, and when both it and its successor, the Anthropological Society, were in 1870 merged in the Anthropological Institute of Great Britain, King became a member of the council of the institute. He was also a member of the general council of the British Association. When in 1845 the admiralty proposed the Franklin expedition, King wrote very strongly to Lord Derby, then colonial secretary, recommending, in lieu of the polar sea journey, a polar land journey by the Great Fish River, and proffering his services. The admiralty lent a cold ear both to this project and to those which King would have substituted for the measures proposed for the relief of Franklin in 1849. King was, however, in 1850 appointed assistant-surgeon to the Resolute, in the expedition sent out to

search for Franklin under Captain Horatio Austin, and in 1857 he received the arctic medal for his services. In 1855 he drew up a summary of his correspondence with the admiralty on the subject, entitled 'The Franklin Expedition from first to last,' in which he animadverted very severely on the treatment he had undergone at the hands of the government. He received much sympathy in his grievances from the newspapers of the time, but his eccentricity and excitability were prejudicial to his advancement, and he died in obscurity at his residence in Blandford Street, Manchester Square, London, on 4 Feb. 1876.

King was a copious contributor to the Ethnological and Statistical Societies' Journals, to the 'Medical Times,' of which he was for some time editor, and to other papers. Besides the works mentioned above and two small medical books on the cause of death in still-born infants he published: 1. 'The Physical and Intellectual Character and Industrial Arts of the Esquimaux,' 1844. 2. 'The Natives of Vancouver's Island and British Columbia,' 1869. 3. 'The Manx of the Isle of Man,' 1870. 4. 'The Laplanders,' 1871. None of these works appears in the British Museum Library Catalogue.

[Medical Times, 12 Feb. 1876; Athenæum, 12 Feb. 1876; Medical Directory, 1875. and Obituary, 1876, where, however, the date of King's death is wrongly given as 18 Feb.; Markham's Arctic Navy List; information kindly supplied by J. B. Bailey, esq., Royal College of Surgeons; King's works in British Museum Library.]   T. S.

KING, RICHARD JOHN (1818-1879), antiquary, eldest son of Richard King, who married at Berry Pomeroy, Devonshire, in April 1816, Mary Grace Windeatt, was born on 18 Jan. 1818 at Montpelier, Pennycross, a chapelry attached to St. Andrew, Plymouth. His father died in April 1829; his mother survived until 13 Jan. 1884. He matriculated at Exeter College, Oxford, on 17 Nov. 1836, and graduated B.A. in 1841. On his father's death he inherited a considerable property, including the estate of Bigadon in Buckfastleigh, Devonshire, where he lived until 1854; but the lands were heavily mortgaged, and in that year they were sold under pecuniary pressure, when he was also forced to part with his father's collection of pictures and the magnificent library which he himself had amassed. King then withdrew to The Limes, Crediton, and supported himself by his writings. No one has in this generation equalled him in the knowledge of the literature and history of the west country, and he was gifted with the art of interesting others in the fruits of his researches. He was elected a member of the Devonshire Association in 1874, and filled the office of president in 1875, when his address dealt with the early history of Devonshire. He contributed several papers to its 'Transactions,' and at the time of his death was on no less than eight of its special committees. With several of its members he was engaged in translating and editing the 'Devonshire Domesday.' King died at The Limes, Crediton, on 10 Feb. 1879, and was buried in its churchyard, the east window of the lady-chapel being filled with stained glass in his memory. The east window and four smaller windows in Buckfastleigh Church were given by him when he was residing at Bigadon.

When an undergraduate King printed in 1840, for private distribution, thirty-three copies of two lectures read before the Essay Society of Exeter College. Their subjects were 'The Supernatural Beings of the Middle Ages' and 'The Origin of the Romance Literature of the XII and XIII Centuries,' and they were dedicated to the Rev. R. C. Powles, the schoolfellow and friend of Charles Kingsley. To the 'Oxford Essays' for 1856 (pp. 271–94) he contributed a paper on 'Carlovingian Romance,' which was afterwards included in his 'Sketches and Studies.' His first separate work consisted of 'Selections from Early Ballad Poetry,' 1842, to which were added many notes and preliminary observations. A novel by him, entitled 'Anschar: a Story of the North,' Plymouth, was published anonymously in 1850. It depicted the apostle of the north while engaged on his mission of converting the Norsemen to Christianity, but its success was not great. At one time he contemplated tracing 'The History of Devonshire from the British Period to our own Time,' but this enterprise proved too ambitious, and he contented himself with publishing the first two chapters, under the title of 'The Forest of Dartmoor and its Borders: an Historical Sketch.'

To Murray's series of handbooks to the English counties King was a large contributor. He prepared 'Handbooks to Kent and Sussex' (1858), 'Surrey and Hampshire' (1858), 'Eastern Counties' (1861), and 'Yorkshire' (1866–8). Those for 'Northamptonshire' (1872–7) and 'Warwickshire with Hertfordshire' (1872–5) were partly written by him, though the last volume has not yet been published, and the fifth and later editions of that for 'Devon and Cornwall' were supervised by him. He was the chief writer in the same publisher's series of 'Handbooks to the Cathedrals of England,'

which were issued during 1861–9, and in the subsequent volume on the 'Cathedrals of Wales' (1873). The 'Handbook to Hereford Cathedral' was struck off separately in 1864, and the account of the three choirs, Gloucester, Hereford, and Worcester, appeared in one volume in 1866. For many years he was a constant contributor to the 'Saturday Review,' the 'Quarterly Review,' and 'Fraser's Magazine.' A delightful selection from his articles was published in 1874 under the title of 'Sketches and Studies,' and in them his extensive learning was embodied in a permanent form. He frequently wrote in the 'Academy' and in 'Notes and Queries,' and to the ninth edition of the 'Encyclopædia Britannica' he supplied accounts of Cornwall and Devon. The first five parts of 'Our Own Country' were written by him for Cassell & Co., and he assisted in the compilation of 'Picturesque Europe.' His paper on 'Bristol Cathedral' appeared in the 'Transactions of the Bristol and Gloucestershire Archæological Society,' iii. 89–105, and a letter by him 'On the Family and Parentage of Judhael de Totnais' is in Cotton's 'Totnes,' App. pp. 77–88.

[Devon. Assoc. Trans. xi. 58–60; Academy, 1879, p. 165; Notes and Queries, 5th ser. xi. 180 (1879); information from Miss King, his sister, of Crediton, and from Mr. John Murray.]
W. P. C.

KING, ROBERT (d. 1557), bishop of Oxford, although stated to have belonged to the Devonshire family of that name, appears to have been second son of William King of Thame, Oxfordshire, yeoman, who was living in 1508 (F. G. LEE, Hist. of the Prebendal Church . . . of Thame, pp. 383, &c.; HANNAH, Poems and Psalms by Henry King, Bishop of Chichester, lxxxiii. lxxxvi.; Brit. Mus. Add. MS. 24488, ff. 1–3). His brother, William King of Thame and Worminghall, Buckinghamshire, gentleman, married Anne, daughter of Sir John Williams of Burghfield, Berkshire, and sister of Joan Williams, prioress of Studley, Oxfordshire, and of Sir John Williams of Thame; Robert King was thus connected with the same family as Thomas Cromwell [q. v.] He joined the Cistercians at Rewley Abbey, near Oxford, but, as was not unusual, passed some of his early years in the Oxford house of the Bernardines (cf. WOOD, City of Oxford, ed. Clark, Oxf. Hist. Soc., ii. 306–9). He proceeded B.D. in February 1506-7, was abbot of Bruern, Oxfordshire, in May 1515, and proceeded D.D. on 1 March 1518-19. John Longland [q. v.], bishop of Lincoln, was a patron of King, and helped him to obtain the office of abbot of Thame in 1530. King seems to have continued to hold Brewern, for at the dissolution he received a pension of 22*l.* a year in respect of it. King probably became suffragan to the Bishop of Lincoln on 7 Jan. 1527, taking the title Reonensis, from the name of a diocese in the province of Athens. He is thus described on 15 April 1535, when he received the prebend of Crackpole St. Mary in the cathedral of Lincoln. He exchanged this on 28 Nov. 1536, for Biggleswade, which he held till 1541.

On 22 Dec. 1537 King was elected abbot of Oseney, Oxfordshire, by the management of John London (q. v.) and John Tregonwell (q. v.), who acted on Cromwell's instructions. In 1539 he was a preacher at St. Mary's, Stamford, and is said to have preached there against those who used the English translation of the New Testament (STRYPE, *Cranmer*, i. 196). The abbey of Thame surrendered on 16 Nov., and that of Oseney on 17 Nov. 1539.

King was made bishop of Oseney and Thame probably in 1541 (*ib.*), but the letters patent were not issued till 1 Sept. 1542. He lived in Gloucester College until 9 June 1545, when he was made bishop of Oxford. He managed to retain his bishopric during the reigns of Edward VI and Mary. He sat at Cranmer's trial, and Foxe (*Acts and Monuments*, ed. Townsend, viii. 630), who is followed by Strype, includes 'King, Bishop of Thame,' among 'persecuting bishops that died before Queen Mary.' King died on 4 Dec. 1557, and was buried at Oxford, in Christ Church Cathedral, where a tomb was erected to his memory. This tomb, of which an engraving was published, was, with a stained window containing a portrait, moved later to another part of the cathedral by his great-grand-nephews, John and Henry King (q. v.), bishop of Chichester. Wood asserts that they found a coat of arms for the bishop which he never had or knew of himself. A painting of the window is at Tythorpe House, Oxfordshire.

[Authorities quoted: Strype's Annals, iv. 173; Memorials, i. ii. 407, ii. ii. 172; Cranmer, pp. 52, 481, 1049; Wood's Athenæ Oxon. (Bliss), ii. 774; Fasti Oxon. ed. Bliss, i. 18, 48; Wood's Hist. and Antiq. of the Univ. of Oxf. ed. Gutch, pp. 431, 629; Reg. of the Univ. of Oxf. ed. Boase (Oxf. Hist. Soc.), i. 47; Browne Willis's Hist. of Mitred Abbeys, ii. 172, 181, 187; Rymer's Fœdera, xiv. 755, xv. 12, 75, 671; Letters and Papers Henry VIII, ed. Gairdner, xii. i. 360, ii. 1246; Le Neve's Fasti, ii. 112, 138; Turner's Selections from the Records of the City of Oxf. pp. 152, 155; Oxf. City Docs. ed. Thorold Rogers (Oxf. Hist. Soc.), p. 133; Burnet's Hist. of the Reformation, i. i. 260, ii. 252; Godwin, De Præsulibus, p. 545.] W. A. J. A.

KING, Sir ROBERT (1599?–1657), Irish soldier and statesman, born in Ireland about 1599, was eldest son of Sir John King (*d.* 1637) [q. v.] He enjoyed the offices of mustermaster-general and clerk of the cheque in Ireland by virtue of his reversionary grant, dated 8 May 1618 (*Cal. State Papers*, Irish, 1615–25, p. 193), which was renewed to him on 11 Jan. 1637–8. On 19 Aug. 1621 he was knighted (METCALFE, *Book of Knights*, p. 179). He entered parliament as member for Boyle, co. Roscommon, in 1634, was re-elected in 1639, and in 1640 was returned for Roscommon county. In November 1641 he was appointed governor of Boyle Castle, and soon became conspicuous for his military skill and activity. During the Irish rebellion he distinguished himself at the battle of Balintobber, co. Roscommon, in 1642. But he lost heavily during the rebellion, and left Ireland in 1642 for London, where Cecil or Wimbledon House, in the Strand, had come to him through his second marriage. He now entered the service of the parliament, and was sent in October 1645 to Ulster, with two others, to manage the parliament's affairs. In 1647 he was one of the five commissioners appointed to receive the sword from the Marquis of Ormonde, the viceroy of Charles. He contrived to increase his estate by easy purchases and the allotment of lands in satisfaction of his arrears for service in Ireland. By act of parliament dated 8 March 1649–50 he was nominated a trustee for the new university of Dublin (*Cal. State Papers*, Irish, 1633–6, p. xcvii). On 15 Dec. following he was desired, along with the attorney-general, to have a complete inventory taken of all books and records concerning the herald's office.

On 24 Sept. 1651 King was empowered, with Colonel Hewson, to sign warrants for 2,000*l.* for payment of the Leinster forces, which order was renewed on 8 Oct. ensuing, and on 17 Nov. he was authorised to issue warrants for 1,000*l.* towards payment of the forces in Dublin. On 13 Dec. he was ordered to receive 100*l.* for his services as commissioner of the public revenue for one year, commencing on 1 May previously. On 23 May 1653 he was appointed an overseer of the poor within Dublin and parts adjacent, and was also made overseer for stating the accounts of the army. He was sworn a member of the council of state on 4 Nov. of that year (*ib.* Dom. 1653–4, p. 230), and sat in Cromwell's parliament of 1654 as member for Sligo, Roscommon, and Leitrim counties (*Official Return of Members of Parliament*, pt. ii.)

King died at Cecil House about June 1657.

He married, first, Frances (d. 1638), daughter of Sir Henry Folliott, the first lord Folliott of Ballyshannon, by whom he had John, first lord Kingston [q. v.], and three other sons and six daughters; and secondly, Sophia (d. 1691), daughter of Sir William Zouch of Woking, Surrey, and widow of Sir Edward Cecil, viscount Wimbledon, by whom he had two daughters.

[Lodge's Peerage of Ireland (Archdall), iii. 223–6; Cal. State Papers, Dom. 1644–57.]

G. G.

KING, ROBERT, LL.D. (1600–1676), master of Trinity Hall, Cambridge, born in 1600, was a native of Kent. He matriculated as a pensioner of Christ's College, Cambridge, 5 July 1617, graduated B.A. in 1620–1, and proceeded M.A. in 1624. In 1625 he was elected to a fellowship at Trinity Hall, which he held till 1636 (Harl. MS. 7073, ff. 142–3). On 16 June 1628 he was sworn and admitted a proctor in the Bishop of Ely's consistorial court by Dr. Thomas Eden (Addit. MS. 5808, f. 214). In 1636 he took the degree of LL.D. (Notitia Academiæ Cantabrigiensis, Lambeth MS. 770, p. 252), and on 10 Oct. 1641 was admitted an advocate of the court of arches at Doctors' Commons, London (MS. Admissions to College of Doctors of Law in Lambeth Library, ff. 50, 110). From 1641 to 1662 he was official to the Archdeacon of Suffolk, and from 1642–5 commissary of the Suffolk archdeaconry. He was commissary of Sudbury archdeaconry for 1645 only, and official to the archdeacon of Sudbury, 1645–1674.

On the death of Thomas Eden [q. v.] (18 July 1645), the parliament (20 Aug.) ordered the fellows of Trinity Hall to suspend the election of any master until the university regulations had been carried out; but the fellows on 26 Sept. petitioned for leave to elect in consequence of various inconveniences (Lords' Journals, vii. 600). Their prayer being granted, they elected John Selden (23 July), and upon his refusal to act King was chosen on 28 Oct., and his election approved by the lords on 6 Nov.; but the commons objecting, he was constrained to resign, and the fellows proceeded on 7 March 1646 to elect John Bond [q. v.], which election received the approval of both houses on 26 March (for particulars concerning these elections, see Baker MSS. xxv. 12, ff. 381–97 in Cambr. Univ. Libr.)

At the Restoration King was re-elected and admitted to the mastership, 20 Aug. 1660. He is addressed as chancellor of Ely by Bishop Wren in 1660 and 1661 (Harl. MS. 7043, ff. 21, 25). In 1661 he was

made vicar-general and principal official to Bishop Wren, who confirmed him in these offices by patent, dated 10 Dec. 1662 (Addit. MS. 5808, f. 214), and on 30 June 1662 the bishop placed him at the head of a commission to visit the diocese (Harl. MS. 7043, f. 30). On 2 Feb. 1661–2 he appeared before the house of convocation, and with other lawyers gave his written opinion that the bishops 'were in no danger of irregularity' by sitting with the lords in cases of high treason (Gibson, Codex, i. 145).

He retained his chancellorship of Ely under Bishop Laney, and was one of the commissioners for visiting the diocese in 1674 ('Registr. Laney,' quoted in Stevenson's Suppl. to Bentham's Ely, p. 11). A collection of forms of licenses, citations, sequestrations, &c., issued in his name, is preserved in the Cambridge University Library. King died on 6 Nov. 1676, aged 76, and was buried in the chapel of Trinity Hall. A black marble slab to his memory, with a Latin inscription and coat of arms, is placed near the altar. His arms also appear on a window in the master's lodge.

King married Frances, daughter of Jasper Wareyn of Great Thurlow, Suffolk. By her he had a son and daughter, who both predeceased him. Land which he had purchased at Great Thurlow he left by will to three grandsons, Robert, Henry, and Thomas King. His widow was buried at Great Thurlow on 18 April 1684.

[Cambridge Univ. Registers, communicated by the late Rev. H. R. Luard, D.D.; Stevenson's Suppl. to Bentham's Ely; Le Neve's Fasti, ed. Hardy, iii. 679; Blomefield's Norfolk, iii. 657–8, 661; Lords' Journals, vii. 524, 630, 678, viii. 237; Commons' Journals, iv. 228, 308, 489; Wilkins's Life of Selden prefixed to Works, pp. xxxvii, xxxviii; Carter's Cambridge, p. 106; Cooper's Annals of Cambr. iii. 376–7; Kennett's Register, pp. 222, 620, 882, 885; Gibson's Synodus Anglicana (Cardwell), p. 223; Le Neve's Monumenta Anglicana, iii. 172; Addit. MS. 5807, ff. 86, 93, 110; Blomefield's Collectanea Cantabrigiensia, pp. 106, 209, 211, 215; Prin. Prob. Reg. (Bence, 141); Addit. MS. 19138, f. 211 (Davy's Suffolk Collections); Cat. of MSS. in Cambr. Univ. Libr.; Todd's Cat. of MSS. at Lambeth Palace.]

B. P.

KING, ROBERT, second Lord Kingston (d. 1693), was eldest son of John, first lord Kingston [q. v.], by Catherine (d. 1669), daughter of Sir William Fenton, knt., of Mitchelstown, co. Cork. He was brought up by his uncle, Sir Robert King, who sent him to Brasenose College, Oxford, where he commenced M.A. on 25 June 1670. On 4 Jan. 1689 the protestant association for the county of Sligo chose King and Captain Chidley Coote their chief commanders. King arrived at Ballyshannon on 24 Jan. There he received a letter from the committee in Derry, with orders (as they said) from Colonel Lundy to keep the passes on the Erne Water. He obeyed these instructions with signal success, but on 15 April he received directions from Lundy to bring his men suddenly into the immediate neighbourhood of Derry. The scattered position of his troops rendered this impossible. He himself went at sunrise the next morning towards Derry to inquire into the situation of affairs, and learnt on coming within five miles of Raphoe that Lundy with his forces had fled to Derry, and that the Irish, who had reached Raphoe, would prevent him from approaching Derry. King thereupon hastened back to his troops, despatched orders for the horse to secure themselves in Enniskillen, and the foot at Donegal, Ballyshannon, and other places, and then with some of his officers went to Scotland in a French vessel, which they seized at Killybegs, co. Donegal, and hurried to give William an account of affairs (HARRIS, Life of William III, pp. 197-9). By Tyrconnel's proclamation of 7 March King was exempted from mercy or James's favour: he was attainted by the parliament on 7 May, and had his estate sequestered; but on 26 Aug. following he commanded a regiment of foot at the taking of Carrickfergus, and on the reduction of the kingdom took his seat in parliament on 5 Oct. 1692.

By deeds dated 19 and 20 Dec. 1693 King demised to Henry, lord Capel, Sir Robert King, and others the castle, manor, and lands of Newcastle, and part of the manor of Mitchelstown, in cos. Tipperary and Cork, for building, endowing, and establishing for ever a college in or near the borough of Boyle, co. Roscommon, to be called by the name of Kingston College, for one master and usher and a chaplain, with apartments for them and twenty poor widows, together with a free school and a chapel. He alienated his estate from his brother and successor, John, because he had become a Roman catholic and had married a servant girl: but John recovered it in 1708. King died without issue in December 1693.

[Lodge's Peerage of Ireland (Archdall), iii. 229 s.; A Vindication of Sir Robert King's Designs and Actions, 1699.] G. G.

KING, ROBERT (fl. 1684-1711), composer, was a member of the band of music to William and Mary under the mastership of Nicholas Staggins. He was the composer of several songs in 'Choice Ayres, Songs, and Dialogues,' 1684, and wrote the music for the songs in Crowne's most popular comedy, 'Sir Courtly Nice.' These were printed separately in the 'Theater of Musick' (vol. ii. ed. 1685). King was also a contributor to 'Comes Amoris,' 1687-93; 'The Banquet of Musick,' 1688-92; the 'Gentleman's Journal,' 1692-4; and 'Thesaurus Musicus,' 1695-6. In 1690 he set Shadwell's ode on St. Cecilia's day, 'O Sacred Harmony;' and in 1693 'an ode on the Rt. Hon. John Cecil, earl of Exeter, his birthday,' commencing 'Once more 'tis born the happy day,' the words of which were written by Peter Anthony Motteux [q. v.] In 1696 he took the degree of Mus.Bac. from St. Catharine College, Cambridge, and subsequently served in the band of music to Queen Anne. There are two songs by King, 'With thee for ever' and 'Only tell her,' among the manuscript collections of the Sacred Harmonic Society (Catalogue, p. 233), and a collection of twenty-four songs by him, entitled 'Songs for one, two, or three Voices, composed to a Thorough Basse for ye Organ or Harpsichord, engraved on copper,' was published by John Walsh (the elder) in 1711. King appears to have been living at this date, but the time of his death is not known.

[Grove's Dict. of Music, ii. 57; Fétis's Biog. Universelle des Musiciens, v. 33; Brown's Biog. Dict. of Musicians, p. 359; Graduati Cantabrigienses, p. 275.] T. S.

KING, ROBERT, second EARL OF KINGSTON (1754-1799), born in 1754, was eldest son of Edward, first earl of Kingston (1726-1797), by Jane, daughter of Thomas Caulfeild of Donamon, co. Roscommon (LODGE, Peerage of Ireland, ed. Archdall, iii. 237). As Viscount Kingsborough he was returned M.P. for co. Cork in 1783, 1790, and 1798, when he was called to the House of Lords (Official Return of Members of Parliament, pt. ii.) On 5 Dec. 1769 he married a cousin, Caroline, only daughter and heiress of Richard Fitzgerald of Mount Ophaly, co. Kildare, by the daughter and heiress of James, fourth and last baron Kingston. By their marriage the family estates were reunited. They had issue six sons and five daughters. Henry Gerard Fitzgerald, an illegitimate son of Lady Kingsborough's brother, was brought up with her own family. He became a colonel in the army, and was married, but in the summer of 1797 eloped with Mary Elizabeth, Lord and Lady Kingsborough's third daughter. Fitzgerald successfully deceived the girl's parents, but his guilt was discovered and the lady restored to her parents. Her brother, Colonel Robert Edward King (afterwards Viscount Lorton), fought a duel with Fitzgerald in Hyde Park on Sunday morning, 1 Oct. 1797. After exchanging no fewer than six shots they separated and agreed to meet at the same hour and place upon the following morning. Both, however, were put under arrest that day (*Gent. Mag.* vol. lxvii. pt. ii. pp. 1120–1). Fitzgerald in disguise soon pursued Miss King to the family residence at Mitchelstown, co. Cork, lodging in December 1797 at the inn there. The suspicions of Lord Kingsborough and his son, Colonel King, were aroused, and on the night of 11 Dec. they burst into his room at the Kilworth hotel. Colonel King grappled with him, and Lord Kingsborough, to protect his son, shot Fitzgerald dead (*Annual Reg.* 1797, xxxix. 55–7). True bills were found against father and son by the grand jury of co. Cork. But on 13 Nov. 1797 the first Earl of Kingston died, and Lord Kingsborough, on succeeding to the title, demanded to be tried by his peers. On 18 May 1798 the trial came on in the House of Lords, Curran appearing for the prisoner. No evidence was offered by the crown, and the accused was unanimously acquitted (*Lords' Journals*, Irish, viii. 83–92). Colonel King had been acquitted at the Cork assizes in the previous April.

Lord Kingston died at Mitchelstown House, which he had rebuilt in magnificent style, on 17 April 1799 (*Gent. Mag.* 1799, pt. i. pp. 350–1). His wife, from whom he had been separated for some years, survived until 13 Jan. 1823, and was buried in Putney cemetery (*ib.* 1823, pt. i. pp. 374–5, vol. xciv. pt. i. p. 648).

Miss King lived under a feigned name in the family of a clergyman in Wales. Her brilliant conversational powers made her a general favourite. She married, in April 1805, George Galbraith Meares of Clifton, and died at Shirehampton, Gloucestershire, in 1819 (*ib.* 1819, pt. i. p. 587).

[Burke's Peerage; Sharpe's Peerage; Madden's Revelations of Ireland, ch. iii.; Lecky's England in the Eighteenth Century, viii. 39–40; Barrington's Personal Sketches, i. 195, 201.] G. G.

KING, SAMUEL WILLIAM (1821–1868), traveller and man of science, eldest son of W. H. King, vicar of Nuneaton, Warwickshire, was born in 1821. He graduated B.A. 1845, and proceeded M.A. 1853 from St. Catharine's College, Cambridge. He became rector of Saxlingham Nethergate, Norfolk, in 1851. King was an enthusiastic entomologist and geologist, and helped Sir Charles Lyell, who was a personal friend, in his investigations both in England and abroad. In 1860 the two explored the de-

posits at Hoxne, Suffolk, together, and in 1865 King investigated the cave at Aurignac (cf. PROFESSOR BOYD DAWKINS in *Nature*, 13 July 1871). King travelled frequently on the continent, and was an enthusiastic mountain climber. His wife usually accompanied him, and the records of a long expedition made about 1855 are contained in King's only book, 'The Italian Valleys of the Pennine Alps,' London, 1858. It is illustrated from drawings made by the author. King was a fellow of the Royal Geographical Society (1858), the Geological Society (1860), and of the Society of Antiquaries. He died at Pontresina in 1868, and was buried there. His collection of fossil mammalia from the Norfolk forest beds he bequeathed to the Museum of Practical Geology, Jermyn Street, London.

[Information from Colonel W. Ross King; Crockford's Clerical Directory; Lyell's Antiquity of Man, 4th ed. pp. 132, 219, 261, 268.] W. A. J. A.

KING, THOMAS (d. 1769), portrait-painter, was a pupil of George Knapton [q. v.], and was an artist of ability, but eccentric and thriftless in his habits. Four of his portraits have been engraved in mezzotinto: Anthony Maddox the rope-dancer and Matthew Skeggs the actor, as Signor Bumbasto playing on a broomstick, both by R. Houston; John Keeling, J.P., by J. McArdell; and John Harrison the chronometer maker, by P. J. Tassaert. He died in John Street, Oxford Road, in 1769, and was buried in St. Marylebone churchyard.

[Edwards's Anecdotes of Painting; Chaloner Smith's British Mezzotinto Portraits.] F. M. O'D.

KING, THOMAS (1730–1805), actor and dramatist, born 20 Aug. 1730, in the parish of St. George's, Hanover Square, London, where his father was a tradesman, was educated at a grammar school in Yorkshire, whence he proceeded to Westminster School. According to the school-list preserved in the Harleian MSS. at the British Museum, Thomas King was in the second form at Westminster in 1730. Genest says (*Account of the Stage*, iv. 259): 'A gentleman told me that King's father kept a coffee-house, and that King, when a boy, had often brought him a dish of coffee.' Other accounts are that King was born in a northern town in which his father lived, and that he was descended from a respectable family in Hampshire. Articled to a London solicitor, he was taken to a dramatic school, and conceived such a fancy for the stage that in October, or, according to another account, May 1747, in company with Edward Shuter [q. v.], he ran away, and joined on sharing terms a travelling company at Tunbridge, where for the sum of fourpence he recited a prologue and an epilogue and acted the two characters of Hamlet and Sharp in the 'Lying Lover' of Garrick. After a short experience of acting in barns, in the course of which (June 1748) he played in a booth at Windsor, directed by Yates, he was seen by Garrick, who, on the recommendation of Yates, engaged him for Drury Lane. His first part was the Herald in 'King Lear,' presumably on 8 Oct. 1748. On 19 Oct., when Massinger's 'New Way to Pay Old Debts' was given for the first time at Drury Lane, he played Allworth, the occasion being disingenuously announced in the bills as his first appearance in any character. Salanio in the 'Merchant of Venice,' Cinthio in the 'Emperor of the Moon,' Truman in the 'Squire of Alsatia,' Tattoo in 'Lethe,' Clerimont in the 'Miser,' and Don Philip in 'She would and she would not,' followed during the season, in which also he was the original Murza in Dr. Johnson's 'Irene,' and played a part in the 'Hen-Peck'd Captain,' a farce said to be founded on the 'Campaigners' of D'Urfey. During the summer he played, with Mrs. Pritchard, Romeo, Benedick, Ranger, and George Barnwell, with much success, at Jacob's Well Theatre, Bristol. There he was seen by Whitehead, who formed a high estimate of him. On his return to Drury Lane he found himself announced for George Barnwell. During his second season he played, among other parts, the Younger Brother in 'Comus,' Rosse in 'Macbeth,' Claudio in 'Much Ado about Nothing,' and Ferdinand in the 'Tempest,' and was the original Duke of Athens in 'Edward the Black Prince,' by William Shirley, and Valeria in the 'Roman Father' of Whitehead. He also played in the 'Little French Lawyer' and the 'Spanish Curate,' converted after Garrick's fashion into farces. At the close of the season he went with a Miss Cole, a pleasing actress, to Dublin. His first appearance under Sheridan at the Smock Alley Theatre took place in September 1750 as Ranger in the 'Suspicious Husband.' Except for one season, beginning in September 1755, when he was the manager and principal actor at the Bath Theatre—a fact unrecorded by Genest—King remained at Smock Alley Theatre for eight years, and while there rose to the highest rank in comedy. Tom in the 'Conscious Lovers,' Jeremy in 'Love for Love,' Mercutio, Sir Andrew Aguecheek, Autolicus in 'Florizel and Perdita,' the Miser, Abel Drugger, Daretête, Marplot in the 'Busy Body,' Scrub, Lord Lace, Tattle,

Osric, Trinculo, Iago, Bayes, and Harlequin in the 'Emperor of the Moon,' were among his parts. On 23 Oct. 1758 he appeared at the Crow Street Theatre as Trappanti in 'She would and she would not.'

The difficulties and dissensions of the Dublin theatres at length drove him back to Drury Lane, where, as Tom in the 'Conscious Lovers,' he appeared on 2 Oct. 1759. He had greatly improved in style, and was assigned leading parts. With occasional visits to Dublin or to country towns, and with one season at Covent Garden and a summer visit to the Haymarket, he remained at Drury Lane, of which he became the mainstay, until 1802. On his reappearance at Drury Lane he was accompanied by Miss Baker, a hornpipe dancer, who then made her first appearance at Drury Lane. He married her in 1766, and she retired from the stage 9 May 1772. Genest gives a list of King's characters, which is confessedly incomplete. Nevertheless it extends to nearly one hundred and fifty parts, and embraces the whole range of comedy, from Falstaff, Sir Peter Teazle, Sir Anthony Absolute, and Puff, to Ben in 'Love for Love' and Scrub, from Benedick and Sir Harry Wildair to Parolles, Bobadil, and Cloten. At Drury Lane King was, on 31 Oct. 1759, the original Sir Harry's servant in 'High Life below Stairs,' and on 12 Dec. the original Squire Groom in Macklin's 'Love à la Mode.' He took part during the same season in the first production of Murphy's 'Way to Keep him,' and 'Every Woman in her Humour,' attributed to Mrs. Clive. Scribble in Colman's 'Polly Honeycombe,' Florimond in Hawkesworth's 'Edgar and Emmeline,' Sir Harry Beagle in Colman's 'Jealous Wife,' and Captain Le Brush in Reed's 'Register Office' were also among his original parts in the following season. But not until his performance of Lord Ogleby in the 'Clandestine Marriage' of Garrick and Colman, on 20 Feb. 1766, was the highest rank allotted to him. Garrick studied the part and resigned it to King, who accepted it with reluctance. Garrick was pleased with his conception, and his performance was declared to be in the same preeminent class with Garrick's Hamlet and Kemble's Coriolanus. In July 1766 King broke his leg, and was unable to act until the following November. His reputation attained its climax on 8 May 1777, when he was the original Sir Peter Teazle in the famous first representation of the 'School for Scandal.' Of that representation it was said a generation later that 'no new performer has ever appeared in any of the principal characters that was not inferior to the person who acted it originally' (GENEST, v. 555).

King also spoke Garrick's prologue. On 29 Oct. 1779, in the scarcely less famous original cast of the 'Critic,' King was Puff. Other original characters, to the number of about eighty, which he took at Drury Lane, and nearly all of which were of primary importance, include Mask in Colman's 'Musical Lady,' Prattle in his 'Deuce is in Him,' Spatter in his 'English Merchant,' Rufus Rubrick in his 'Spleen,' Sharply in Mrs. Sheridan's ill-starred piece, 'The Dupe,' Glib in Garrick's 'A Peep behind the Curtain'—which, on the strength of the line spoken by King,

I, Thomas King, of King Street, am the poet,

was for some time assigned to the actor—Cecil in Kelly's 'False Delicacy,' Dr. Cantwell in the 'Hypocrite,' Bickerstaffe's alteration of the 'Nonjuror,' Muskato in Kenrick's ''Tis well it's no worse,' Belcour in Cumberland's 'West Indian,' Mortimer in his 'Fashionable Lover,' General Savage in Kelly's 'School for Wives,' Nightshade in his 'Choleric Man,' Jack Hustings in his 'Natural Son,' Governor Tempest in his 'Wheel of Fortune,' Sir John Trotley in Garrick's 'Bon Ton,' Sir Miles Mowbray in his 'First Love,' Sir George Boncour in Fielding's 'Fathers,' Gradus in Mrs. Cowley's 'Who's the Dupe?' Sir Clement Flint in Burgoyne's 'Heiress,' Don Alexis in Mrs. Cowley's 'School for Greybeards,' Gabriel in Holcroft's 'Seduction,' Sir Paul Panick in Edward Morris's 'False Colours,' Sir Adam Contest in Mrs. Inchbald's 'Wedding Day,' the Fool in 'Vortigern,' Sir Solomon Cynic in Reynolds's 'Will,' Sir Marmaduke Maxim in Hoare's 'Indiscretion,' and Sir Valentine Vapour in 'Fashionable Friends.'

To these must be added the parts he played in his own pieces. 'Love at First Sight,' a not very brilliant ballad-farce, by him (8vo, 1763), was acted at Drury Lane on 17 Oct. 1763, King playing in it Smatter, a servant who personates his master. In a short preface King says it was conceived, written, and delivered to the managers within fifteen days, and neglects to add that it was forgotten within a similar space. 'Wit's Last Stake' (8vo, 1769), his second farce, was given at Drury Lane on 14 April 1768. It is an adaptation of 'Le Légataire Universel' of Regnard, and its great success was due to King's reading of the part of Martin, the Crispin of the original, a servant who personates a man supposed to be dying, and dictates a will by which he himself benefits. Under the title of 'A Will and no Will, or Wit's Last Stake,' it was revived on 24 April 1789 for King's benefit, on which occasion

King was Linger the invalid, and Bannister, jun., Martin.

Upon the death of William Powell [q. v.] King bought his share in the King Street Theatre, at which during the summer seasons of 1770 and 1771 he was actor and sole manager. He then sold his share to James William Dodd [q. v.], and purchased of the builder for 9,000l. three-fourths of Sadler's Wells, in which he was associated with Arnold. He made some changes in the performances, raised the prices of admission, and provided horse patrols, to guard through the dangerous district the fashionable visitors whom he attracted. His prices, three shillings boxes, eighteenpence pit, and a shilling gallery, entitled the visitor to receive a pint of wine at an added cost of sixpence. In 1778 King sold his share, and was succeeded by Wroughton. As successor to Garrick he was elected, on 14 Feb. 1779, master of the Drury Lane Theatrical Fund, and held the office until September 1782, when, on acceptance of the management of Drury Lane, he resigned it, the discharge of the functions of the two offices being held incompatible. His earnings as an actor were at that time 700l. a year. As manager and actor he found them reduced to 564l. 13s. 10d., being one-eighth share of the profits, his guaranteed remuneration. In June 1783, accordingly, he laid down his functions and issued an address, dated from Gerrard Street, in which he contradicted a rumour that he was about to retire from the stage, though he admitted it was 'barely possible' he might not act at Drury Lane during the coming season. He is said, accordingly, to have acted at Edinburgh and Glasgow as well as in Dublin. Mr. James C. Dibdin, the historian of the Edinburgh stage, does not mention his presence in this year, and speaks of his performance of Lord Ogleby on 28 March 1789 as his first appearance in Edinburgh. In October 1783 it was announced in the newspapers that King was not connected with the management of Drury Lane, but that his abilities and long service induced the management to offer him for his performance, advice, and attention a very liberal salary, stated to be 1,200l., but in fact only a thousand guineas. He delivered on his reappearance an address in verse, by Cumberland. In 1785 he seems to have resumed his management of Drury Lane, and is said to have been responsible for the successful pantomime of that year, 'Hurly Burly, or the Fairy of the Well,' for which he received 105l. In September 1788 he again resigned the management and his connection with the theatre, announcing as his reason, in an explanation which appeared on

13 Sept., that his authority had been nominal rather than real. Of Sheridan, who was authorised to negotiate with him, he spoke pleasantly, but said that when appointments were made he found Sheridan 'in a great hurry or surrounded by company,' until his patience being exhausted he wrote relinquishing his engagement in all its parts, and, for fear of being induced to reconsider his determination, left town. On 20 Nov. 1789 he made, as Touchstone, his first appearance at Covent Garden, and the same evening was the original Sir John Trotley in 'Bon Ton.' After playing several of his best-known characters, he appeared for his benefit on 2 Feb. 1790 as Sancho in 'Lovers' Quarrels,' an alteration, attributed to himself, of Vanbrugh's 'Mistake.' On 23 Oct. 1790, as Lord Ogleby, he reappeared at Drury Lane, and during the rebuilding of the theatre went with the company to the Haymarket Opera House. On 2 Aug. 1792 he played at the Haymarket Falstaff in the 'First Part of King Henry IV,' and on the 23rd was General Touchwood in 'Cross Partners,' a comedy announced as by a lady. In September 1792 he rejoined the Drury Lane company, then playing at the Haymarket, and in March 1794 appeared with them at their newly built home, where he remained till the close of his career. On 24 May 1802, for his last benefit, King played his great character of Sir Peter Teazle. At the close he spoke, amidst lively demonstrations of sympathy, an address written for him by R. Cumberland. When, much exhausted, he reached the greenroom, Mrs. Jordan presented him with a silver cup worth a hundred guineas, subscribed for by the company. Around the rim were engraved the lines from 'King Henry V' (act v. sc. 2), 'If he be not fellow with the best king, thou shalt find the best king of good fellows.'

About 1783 King had a villa at Hampton, and was at that date robbed by highwaymen on his journey home. He took to gambling in middle life, with disastrous results. One night, when he had recovered 2,000l. of his heavy losses, he made an oath, in the presence of Garrick and his wife, that he would never touch dice again. This he kept until the death of Garrick. In 1785 he entered his name at Miles's Club in St. James's Street. Shortly afterwards he yielded to the old temptation, lost all his savings, was compelled to forego a proposed purchase of a share in Drury Lane, to sell his villa at Hampton, and remove to a house in Store Street. There he died on 11 Dec. 1805. On the 20th he was buried in the vault of St. Paul's, Covent Garden. His pall-bearers included Pope, Moody, Wroughton, Palmer, Powell, H. Siddons, and other actors. A benefit for Mrs. King followed, and brought a respectable addition to a limited income. She died on 30 Nov. 1813.

Apart from his incapacity to resist the temptation to gambling, King was a worthy and an honourable man. Davies gives him exemplary eulogy: 'No man ever exerted his abilities to greater satisfaction of the public, or consulted the interests of his employers with more cordiality and assiduity. . . . Booth's character of the great actor, Smith, may be applied with justice to Mr. King: "By his impartial management of the stage and the affability of his temper he merited the respect and esteem of all within the theatre, the applause of those without, and the goodwill and love of all mankind"' (Dram. Misc. iii. 372). Dibdin likens King to Préville as regards his performance of valets, and adds: 'King is a performer who has thrown novelty into old characters, consequence into new, and nature into all' (Hist. of the Stage, v. 348). Of his acting, as of his life, he says that integrity is the guiding principle, and he credits King with the exercise of benevolence, good humour, and every other sacred virtue. Hazlitt describes his acting in later life as leaving 'a taste on the palate sharp and sweet like a quince; with an old, hard, rough, withered face, like a Johnapple, puckered up into a thousand wrinkles, with shrewd hints and tart replies;' he was 'the real amorous, wheedling, or hasty, choleric, peremptory old gentleman in Sir Peter Teazle and Sir Anthony Absolute; and the true, that is the pretended, clown in Touchstone, with wit sprouting from his head like a pair of ass's ears, and folly perched on his cap like the horned owl.' Churchill satirises King in his customary fashion for shamelessness acquired in Ireland.

His countenance is said to have been expressive of benignity and of archness, his action slow, his voice musical. In method of speech he was sententious, conveying always an idea of epigram. He was consequently most in request of any actor for the delivery of prologues, epilogues, and occasional addresses. King was also a fair singer. Besides the pieces mentioned, the 'Secret History of the Green-Room' credits him with the authorship of an interlude called 'A Dramatic Oglio' (sic), which was received with much favour. He also recited, at his benefit at Drury Lane on 29 April 1796, 'Kitty Connolly and Jack the Painter,' versified by himself. King kept a diary, now untraceable, in which were preserved some curious facts concerning Sheridan's management of Drury Lane. He announced, and then withdrew, a pamphlet called ' A Word or two at Parting, or a Letter to R. B. Sheridan, Esq.' &c., and was rather fond of addressing the public upon his grievances, real or imaginary. Some letters of his in the 'Garrick Correspondence' show that, though his relations with Garrick were friendly, there were occasional divergences of interests or opinion. Other letters appear in the 'Manager's Note-Book' contributed to the 'New Monthly Magazine.'

[Works cited; Genest's Account of the Stage; Biographia Dramatica; Thespian Dictionary; Theatrical Biography, 1772 ; Hazlitt's Dramatic Essays; Dutton Cook's Hours with the Players; Clark Russell's Representative Actors ; Dramatic Censor, 1770; Monthly Mirror, various years; Theatrical Inquisitor, various years; Bernard's Recollections; Life of F. Reynolds; O'Keeffe's Recollections; Jenkins's Bristol Stage; Dibdin's Edinburgh Stage; Georgian Era.]   J. K.

KING, WILLIAM (1624–1680), musician, born in 1624, son of George King, organist of Winchester Cathedral, was admitted a clerk of Magdalen College, Oxford, on 18 Oct. 1648, graduated B.A. 5 June 1649, and in 1652 was promoted to a chaplaincy at Magdalen. This he held until 25 Aug. 1654, when he became a probationer-fellow of All Souls' College. He was incorporated M.A. at Cambridge in 1655. On 10 Dec. 1664 he was appointed successor to Pickover as organist of New College, to preside over the new organ there at a salary of 50l. a year. He continued organist until his death on 7 Nov. 1680. He was buried in New College cloisters, where a Latin inscription marks his grave.

King composed a full service in B flat, and some anthems, preserved among the Elvey MSS. at the Bodleian. He also set to music Cowley's 'Mistress,' under the title, 'Poems of Mr. Cowley and others, composed into Songes and Ayres, with Thorough Basse for the Theorbo, Harpsecon, or Basse-Violl,' Oxford, 1668, fol.

[Bloxam's Magd. Reg. ii. 66, 158; Foster's Alumni Oxon. 1500–1714; Hawkins's Hist. of Music. v. 23; Grove's Dict. of Music, ii. 57; Brown's Dict. of Music, p. 360.]   T. S.

KING, WILLIAM, D.C.L. (1663–1712), miscellaneous writer, born in 1663, was the son of Ezekiel King, gentleman, of London, from whom he inherited a small estate in Middlesex. In his 'Adversaria' he mentions his great-grandfather, a merchant named La Motte, and his cousin Harcourt; and he had some connection with the Hyde family. In 1678 he was admitted a scholar of Westminster, and was elected student of Christ Church,

Oxford, where he matriculated on 16 Dec. 1681. On 8 Dec. 1685 he graduated B.A. as a grand compounder, proceeding M.A. on 6 July 1688, and B.C.L. and D.C.L. 7 July 1692. He early became fond of desultory reading. In 1688 he joined Edward Hannes [q. v.] in ' Reflections upon Mons. Varillas's History of Heresy,' chiefly in defence of Wycliffe. About 1690 he published an amusing ' Dialogue shewing the way to Modern Preferment.' In November 1692 he obtained a fiat from Archbishop Tillotson admitting him an advocate at Doctors' Commons. He continued to use his talents as a humorous writer upon the side of the tories and high church party. In 1693 he contributed a pamphlet to the famous Sherlock controversy (see MACAULAY, Hist. chap. xvii.) In 1694 he published 'Animadversions' on the account of Denmark, by Robert (afterwards Lord) Molesworth [q. v.], a sound whig, who had attacked the Danish system of government. The Danish envoy supplied materials to King, and he received the thanks of the university of Copenhagen. Prince George of Denmark also obtained his appointment as secretary to the Princess Anne.

Charles Boyle, in the book commonly called 'Boyle upon Bentley' [see under BENTLEY, RICHARD, 1662–1742], mentions an interview between Bentley and a bookseller at which King was present, and gives a letter from King describing Bentley's insolence. Bentley attacked King in his famous 'Dissertation' (1699); and in the same year appeared 'A Short Account of Dr. Bentley's Humanity and Justice,' with a second letter from King to Boyle. King probably gave other help to Boyle, and, according to Pope, as reported by Warburton, contributed the droll argument to prove that Bentley was not the author of the 'Dissertation' and the index (Letters from an Eminent Prelate, 1809, p. 11). King's 'Dialogues of the Dead,' 1699, one of his cleverest productions, attacks Bentley in a series of ten dialogues.

Another very characteristic work appeared, probably a few months earlier than the 'Dialogues of the Dead.' This was 'A Journey to London in the year 1698. After the ingenious method of that made by Dr. Martin Lister to Paris in the same year. Written originally in French, by Monsieur Sorbière, and newly translated into English,' 1699. This was a travesty of a very recent book upon Paris by Martin Lister [q. v.] Sorbière had published a much-abused book of travels in England (1664), and King adopts the name to insinuate a comparison between their styles. He thought this his best work, and described many of his later writings as ' by the author

VOL. XXXI.   M of "A Journey to London."' A poem, 'The Farmctory,' was published in 1699, and others were circulated in manuscript. In 1700 King published anonymously ' The Transactioner, with some of his Philosophical Fancies, in two Dialogues,' a satire upon Sir Hans Sloane, who edited the 'Transactions' of the Royal Society. In 1701 King defended his friend the Earl of Anglesea in an action for separation brought by the countess. He is said to have shown ability in spite of his usual indolence. Directly afterwards he was appointed judge of the admiralty court in Ireland, and, as appears by a letter in the British Museum (*Add. MS.* 28887, f. 369), was in Ireland by 13 Nov. 1701. He probably obtained his post through the influence of the Earl of Rochester, lord-lieutenant from 1700 to February 1703, or of Pembroke, then lord high admiral, to whose son he afterwards dedicated his ' Miscellanies.' On 10 Jan. 1703 King wrote to John Ellis, M.P., begging that an order might be sent to swear him, delay being caused by the obstinacy of a Scottish lord mayor, in whose hands was his commission. King also asked Ellis to support his request for the post (which he obtained) of vicar-general of Armagh (*ib.* 28890, f. 17). King was likewise sole commissioner of the prizes, but appears to have neglected all his duties. While idling at Mountown, near Dublin, the house of his friend Judge Upton, he wrote 'Mully of Mountown,' Mully being the red cow that furnished him with milk. It was surreptitiously published in 1704, together with another poem, 'Orpheus and Eurydice,' as the 'Fairy Feast.' King reprinted the poems, asserting that they had no hidden meaning, and added 'Some Remarks on the Tale of a Tub.'

In 1705, or a little later, King published a collection of 'Miscellanies.' On 19 June 1707 he was appointed keeper of the records in the Bermingham Tower at Dublin Castle, but resigned on 28 Nov. (LASCELLES, *Liber Munerum Publicorum Hiberniæ*, 1824, pt. ii. p. 78). Probably King returned to England at the close of 1707. It seems that he had by this time spent his private fortune, and had nothing to rely upon except his studentship at Christ Church. In February 1708 Lintot paid him 32*l.* 5*s.* for ' The Art of Cookery, in imitation of Horace's Art of Poetry; with some Letters to Dr. Lister and others, occasioned principally by the title of a book published by the Doctor, being the Works of Apicius Cœlius, concerning the Soups and Sauces of the Ancients.' It was published in the following month without date (*Daily Courant*, 13 March 1708). Two spurious editions of this amusing poem, perhaps his best work,

appeared, and it was coarsely attacked in ' A Letter to Dr. W. King, occasioned by his Art of Cookery.' In February 1709 Lintot paid King 32*l.* 5*s.* for ' The Art of Love,' in imitation of Ovid, but dealing with ' innocent and virtuous ' love, if not always within modern bounds of propriety.

In 1709 appeared also the amusing 'Useful Transactions in Philosophy and other sorts of Learning,' which were 'to be continued monthly, as they sell.' Three parts appeared, for each of which King received only 5*l.* These 'Transactions' are a parody of the ' Philosophical Transactions,' and the third part again satirises Sloane. The ' Memoirs of Martin Scriblerus ' probably owe some hints to this book.

King supported the high church party in the Sacheverell controversy by several pamphlets, including ' A Friendly Letter from honest Tom Boggy to the Rev. Mr. Goddard, Canon of Windsor;' 'A Second Letter to Mr. Goddard, occasioned by the late Panegyric given him by the Review,' 1710; 'A Vindication of the Rev. Dr. Sacheverell,' 1711 (in which King was assisted by Charles Lambe of Christ Church, and probably by Sacheverell himself); ' Mr. Bisset's Recantation, in a Letter to the Rev. Dr. Henry Sacheverell,' 1711 ; and 'An Answer to a second scandalous Book that Mr. Bissett is now writing, to be published as soon as possible.' King contributed to the early numbers of the ' Examiner,' started in August 1710, but it is not known that he had any connection with the paper after Swift undertook the management of it in November.

At the end of 1710 King published his ' Historical Account of the Heathen Gods and Heroes,' a compilation which was used in schools for many years, and for which the author was paid 50*l.* In 1711 he wrote a bitter attack upon the Duke of Marlborough, which was published late in the year, with the date 1712, entitled ' Rufinus, or an Historical Essay on the favourite Ministry under Theodosius and his son Arcadius,' with a poem, 'Rufinus, or the Favourite,' annexed. In December 1711 King, on Swift's recommendation, was appointed to succeed Steele in the post of gazetteer. King had been in great difficulties. Gay, writing earlier in the year, says, in 'The Present State of Wit,' that King deserved better than to ' languish out the small remainder of his life in the Fleet Prison.' Swift, in the ' Journal to Stella ' (19 Dec.), speaks of King as a ' poor starving wit;' but on 31 Dec. mentions the appointment to the 'Gazette,' which he values at 200*l.* a year. He afterwards (8 Jan. 1711–12) tells Archbishop King ' that it will be worth 250*l.*

per annum to him if he be diligent and sober.' King, however, was incapable of diligence. Upon the influx of an unusual amount of matter he had to sit up till three or four in the morning to correct the proofs. King therefore resigned the office on 1 July 1712. On the same day Lintot paid him 4l. 1s. 6d. for the 'Useful Miscellanies, Part the First,' containing the tragi-comedy of 'Joan of Hedington' and an 'Account of Horace's behaviour during his stay at Trinity College in Cambridge.' In August he published some verses, 'Britain's Palladium, or Lord Bolingbroke's Welcome from France.'

During the summer of 1712 King lived in a friend's house between Lambeth and Vauxhall. He visited his friends in London, especially his relation Lord Clarendon at Somerset House. In the autumn his health grew worse. Clarendon had him conveyed on 24 Dec. to a lodging opposite Somerset House. That night he made his will, by which he appointed his sister, Elizabeth King, sole executrix and residuary legatee; and on the following day he died. On 27 Dec. he was buried in the north cloister of Westminster Abbey. King seems to have been sincerely religious and moral in his life, though given to occasional conviviality. Pope told Lord Burlington in 1716, 'I remember Dr. King would write verses in a tavern three hours after he could not speak.' He sometimes said ill-natured things, but was generally amiable and easy-going. His 'Adversaria' proves the width of his general reading, and he was certainly well skilled in law. A eulogistic 'Pindarick Ode to the memory of Dr. William King' appeared after his death.

Many of King's writings were published anonymously, and some without date. Among the fragments left by him are an 'Essay on Civil Government' (reprinted by Dr. Johnson in 1776), and 'Crapulia,' translated from Joseph Hall's 'Mundus alter et idem.' King wrote also several papers for Harrison's continuation of the 'Tatler,' and a few songs and tales in verse, which are of little value. One of these, 'Apple Pye,' was printed in 'The Northern Atalantis,' 1713, and in the following year it was included in Hill's collection of 'Original Poems and Translations.' King in his early years translated some books from the French, and was one of the translators, from the French of De la Croix, of 'The Persian and the Turkish Tales compleat,' published in 1714, having begun the work, as the dedication states, at the request of Lady Theodosia Blye, baroness of Clifton. In 1732 King's 'Remains' were published, with an account of his life, and a

dedication to Lord Orrery; and in 1734 they were edited as 'Posthumous Works,' by Joseph Browne, M.D. A portrait, engraved by J. Vandergucht from a painting by Below, was prefixed to both collections. In 1776 the 'Original Works of William King, LL.D.,' in three volumes, were published, carefully edited by John Nichols. On the title-page is a portrait in a circle, engraved by Cook.

[Memoirs of Dr. King, prefixed to Nichols's edition of the Original Works; Biog. Brit.; Add. MSS. 28883 ff. 137, 180, 255, 28885 f. 169, 28887 f. 369, 28890 f. 17 (Brit. Mus.); Welch's Alumni Westmonasterienses, 1852, pp. 147, 183, 190–2; Swift's Works, ed. Scott, 1824, vols. i. ii. vi. x. xv.; T. Cibber's Lives of the Poets, iii. 228; Gent. Mag. 1776, 465; European Mag. vii. 400; Johnson's Lives of the Poets; Coote's Catalogue of Civilians, pp. 104–5; Monk's Life of Bentley, 1833; Oxford Graduates; Chester's Registers of Westminster, 1876, p. 275; Noble's Continuation of Granger, ii. 260; Pope's Works, ed. Elwin and Courthope, x. 207, 295; Ideal Commonwealths, 1885 (Morley's Universal Library), pp. 273–84; Nichols's Lit. Anecd. 1812, i. 25, 32–5, 327, iii. 227, iv. 715; D'Israeli's Quarrels of Authors (Miscellanies, 1840), pp. 206, 219–21. Dr. King is constantly confused especially in indexes, with Dr. William King [q. v.], archbishop of Dublin, or with Dr. William King [q. v.] of St. Mary Hall, Oxford, the author of 'The Toast.'] G. A. A.

KING, WILLIAM, D.D. (1650–1729), archbishop of Dublin, son of James King, a native of Barra in Aberdeenshire, the original seat of the family, was born on 1 May 1650 in the town of Antrim in Ireland, whither his father had migrated some time between 1639 and 1649, in order to escape the solemn league and covenant, and where he is said to have pursued the calling of a miller (Hist. MSS. Comm. 3rd Rep. p. 416; Noble, Continuation of Granger, ii. 103). At the age of twelve King was sent to a Latin school at Dungannon, co. Tyrone, and on 7 April 1666 (Mason, St. Patrick's, p. 207) he was admitted a sizar into Trinity College, Dublin. He studied hard, and having obtained a scholarship he graduated B.A. on 23 Feb. 1670, was ordained deacon by Dr. Robert Mossom, bishop of Derry, on 25 Oct. 1671 and proceeded M.A. in 1673. He failed to obtain a fellowship, but having attracted the attention of John Parker, archbishop of Tuam, he was by him ordained a priest on 12 April 1674, and was collated to the prebend of Kilmainmore on 14 July in the same year, and to the provostship of the cathedral church of Tuam on 26 Oct. 1676. On the translation of Parker to the see of Dublin in 1678 King was on 27 Oct. 1679 collated to the

M 2

chancellorship of St. Patrick's and the parish of St. Werburgh's annexed, where he laboured zealously to prevent the spread of Roman catholicism in the metropolis. Shortly after his appointment he was involved in a dispute with Dean Worth as to the right of the dean to visit independently of the chapter. Judgment was finally given against King in 1681, and as a punishment for his 'contentiousness' he was required to build a number of stalls in the chapter-house (ib. pp. 201-2). In 1687 King entered upon a prolonged controversy with Peter Manby (q. v.), sometime dean of Derry, who had been lately converted to the church of Rome. Manby's 'Considerations which obliged Peter Manby to embrace the Catholic Religion' drew from King an 'Answer to the Considerations,' in which Manby's motives were ascribed to a desire to curry favour with James II. Manby thereupon replied with 'A Reformed Catechism,' which King answered in 'A Vindication of the Answer to the Considerations,' 1688. Subsequently Manby, according to Harris (WARE, Bishops), 'dispersed a short paper, artfully written,' under the title 'A Letter to a Friend, shewing the vanity of this opinion, that every man's sense and reason is to guide him in matters of Faith,' which led to King's 'Vindication of the Christian Religion and Reformation against the Attempts of a late Letter.' Owing to some disparaging remarks about presbyterianism made by him during this controversy, King was vigorously attacked by Joseph Boyse (q. v.), a presbyterian minister in Dublin. On the death of Dean Worth in 1688, King was elected his successor, and was formally installed on 1 Feb. 1688-9, taking his degree of D.D. shortly afterwards. Hitherto he had been noted as a strenuous advocate of the doctrine of passive resistance (LESLIE, Answer, p. 113), but the government of Tyrconnel converted him into an ardent whig. He openly espoused the cause of the Prince of Orange, and falling under the suspicion of the Jacobite government he was arrested and confined to the castle. He was liberated after a short imprisonment by the good offices of Lord-chief-justice Sir Edward Herbert [q. v.], but continued to suffer insults and indignities in public till the beginning of 1690, when he was recommitted on a charge of having furnished treasonable information to the Duke of Schomberg (ib. p. 105). The battle of the Boyne, however, put an end to his sufferings. On 16 Nov. he preached before the lords justices Sidney and Coningsby in St. Patrick's Cathedral on the occasion of the thanksgiving for 'the preservation of his Majesty's person, his good success in our deliverance, and his

safe and happy return into England,' and on 9 Jan. 1690-1 he was promoted to the see of Derry. In 1691 he published his 'State of the Protestants of Ireland under the late King James's Government,' for which he had partly collected the materials during his imprisonment. Though more of a party pamphlet than an impartial history, it is a powerful vindication of the principles of the revolution, and was, as Bishop Burnet described it, 'not only the best book that hath been written for the service of the government, but without any figure it is worth all the rest put together, and will do more than all our scribblings for settling the minds of the nation.' Three editions were at once exhausted. An 'Answer' was published anonymously in 1692 from the pen of the nonjuror, Charles Leslie [q. v.] The charge of inconsistency in the matter of passive resistance was pressed home against King with considerable skill, and from certain memoranda still extant (Hist. MSS. Comm. 2nd Rep. p. 236) it would seem as if King at one time meditated a reply to Leslie's book. Immediately after his consecration (25 Jan. 1690-1) King proceeded to his diocese, where he busied himself in repairing the ravages created by the war, in restoring and rebuilding parish churches, towards which he himself contributed liberally, in enforcing the residence of his clergy, in augmenting the revenues of the see, and generally in endeavouring to restore the church under his care to a position of efficiency and respectability. In December 1693 he was appointed, along with Dopping, bishop of Meath, and Wiseman, bishop of Dromore, ecclesiastical commissioner for the visitation of the bishop and clergy of the diocese of Down and Connor, in consequence of which Bishop Hacket, satirically styled the bishop of Hammersmith, the archdeacon of Down, and several other clergymen were suspended (Lansdowne MS. 446, f. 36).

The prevalency of nonconformity in his diocese, and particularly in the city of Derry, where, as he expressed it, the presbyterians were 'mighty insolent,' caused King much annoyance. Mainly with the intention of repressing the growth of sectarianism he entered upon a lawsuit with the London Society in order to prevent the letting of waste lands to presbyterians. The case raised the whole question of the judicial independence of the Irish House of Lords, and led to much wider consequences than King had anticipated. Pending its settlement he published in 1694 a tract entitled 'A Discourse concerning the Inventions of Man in the Worship of God.' The pamphlet, according to Reid (Hist. of the Presbyterian Church, iii. 27), was a 'clever and plausible performance,' 'written in a spirit of affected friendship for presbyterians,' but 'full of unworthy insinuations and unfounded charges.' It was immediately reprinted in London. Joseph Boyse replied on behalf of presbyterianism in his 'Remarks' on the 'Discourse,' which King immediately answered in 'An Admonition to the Dissenting Inhabitants of the Diocese of Derry.' King denied that he wished to stir up old animosities, and declared himself solely anxious to remove the objections of those who refused to attend the established church. Boyse's 'Vindication' of his 'Remarks' and King's 'Second Admonition' closed the controversy so far as the chief combatants were concerned. But King's strictures on the ignorance of many presbyterians as to their own creed and the inadequacy of the means provided for their religious instruction stimulated the presbyterians to new and effective exertions.

Meanwhile King sought more profitably to meet the religious requirements of a colony of Scottish highlanders who had recently settled in the barony of Inishowen by providing them with clergymen able to speak their own language, and at a later period he promoted the teaching of Irish at Trinity College. In the parliament of 1695 he supported the penal legislation against the Roman catholics, opposed the Toleration Bill, and was one of the seven bishops and seven lay lords who in 1697 protested against the act to confirm the Articles of Limerick. He strongly resented the growing interference of the English parliament in Irish affairs, and chiefly for this reason opposed the bill for the preservation of the king's person in 1697. He denounced, too, the taxation by parliament of the clergy without their consent, and strenuously urged the necessity of summoning convocation. King's private letters of the time of Queen Mary's death, 1694, reveal his deep sense of the prevailing laxity in matters of religion. A severe attack of gout in the spring of 1696 nearly proved fatal, and led to a rumour that he was dead.

With the work of his diocese King managed to combine the preparation of his *magnum opus,* 'De Origine Mali,' which was published in 1702 simultaneously in Dublin and London, with a dedication to Sir Robert Southwell. The work attempts, on a Lockean basis, to reconcile the existence of evil, and particularly of moral evil, with the idea of an omnipotent and beneficent deity. It attracted immediate attention on the continent, where it was favourably noticed in 'Les Nouvelles de la République des Lettres' (May and June 1703), at that time under the editorship of Jacques Bernard. The review was criticised by Bayle adversely to King in his 'Réponse aux Questions d'un Provincial' (chaps. lxxiv–xcii.) Bernard replied in 'Nouvelles de la République,' January 1706, and Bayle, having read King's book, made several new observations upon it, which were published after his death in 'Réponse aux Questions d'un Provincial,' vol. v. Leibnitz also published a criticism 'Adnotationes in librum De Origine Mali haud ita pridem in Anglia evulgatum,' which was mainly directed to a confutation of King's doctrine of free will (*Opera,* ed. L. Dutens, i. 430–69; also *Lettre xvi. à M. Thos. Burnet, ib.* vi. 285). And J. C. Wolff, in his work 'Manichæismus ante Manichæos' (Hamburg, 1707), devotes considerable space to King's arguments. In England the book appears to have been neglected till it was translated by Edmund Law, afterwards bishop of Carlisle, in 1729, and the translation probably suggested to Pope some of the ideas contained in his 'Essay on Man.'

On 11 March 1702–3 King was by letters patent translated to the archbishopric of Dublin, in succession to Narcissus Marsh [q. v.] The appropriations and impropriations of ecclesiastical property in the diocese were very numerous, and King at once recognised how formidable an obstacle these would present to any attempt at reformation. In order the better to assert his authority in the matter, he therefore insisted on being consecrated by the dean and chapter of Christ Church, who alone appropriated twenty-seven parishes, many of them being not supplied at all, and most of them very indifferently. The dean and chapter refused to comply. King held a visitation, and in their absence pronounced sentence of contumacy against them. The case was transferred to England, and an inhibition was obtained against him in chancery. King thereupon appealed to the English House of Lords, and after much controversy the case was finally decided in 1724 in his favour. The dean and chapter then joined him in making provision for the cures dependent on them. Meanwhile King had been labouring successfully to promote the welfare of his diocese by building new and rebuilding old parish churches, by supplying them with capable clergymen, and by making better provision for their livelihood, partly by annexing the prebends of St. Patrick's as they fell vacant to the vicarages from which they had become separated, and partly by establishing a fund for the purchase of glebes and impropriate tithes. His endeavours to obtain for the church of Ireland the restoration of the first-fruits and twentieth parts brought him into close relationship with

Swift, whom he sent to London in 1707 to further the project. Four years later the matter was satisfactorily settled through Swift's exertions and his influence with Harley. The result raised Swift in King's estimation, but King only saw in him a clergyman of very unclerical habits, of considerable ability, but of ill-regulated ambition and of overweening egotism. His advice to him to turn his attention seriously to the study of theology, although well-intentioned, was unaccompanied by any substantial preferment, and consequently appeared to Swift impertinent, and even slightly malicious. Though there was no open breach, the friendly correspondence that had existed between them was interrupted between 1711 and 1716.

On 15 May 1709, after a severe attack of gout, King preached before the lord-lieutenant, the Earl of Wharton, at the opening of parliament, on ' Divine Predestination and Foreknowledge, consistent with the Freedom of Man's Will,' King attempting to reconcile the doctrine of predestination with that of free will. Our knowledge of God being of necessity limited, is, he argues, like the knowledge that a man born blind has of colour, only by way of analogy. This doctrine of analogical knowledge was attacked by Anthony Collins (q. v.) in his 'Vindication of the Divine Attributes,' 1710, and by Dr. John Edwards (1637–1716) (q. v.) in 'The Divine Perfections Vindicated,' 1710. On the death of Archbishop Marsh in 1713, King's whiggism led the English ministry to pass over his claims to the primacy in favour of Thomas Lindsay (q. v.), bishop of Raphoe. But at the time of Queen Anne's death he was joined with the Earl of Kildare and the Archbishop of Tuam in the commission for the government of Ireland, and it was, according to Harris, largely due to his prudence and influence ' that the city of Dublin was preserved steady . . . to the succession of the royal family of Hanover.' In 1717 he was reappointed one of the lords justices, and again in 1718; but having by his opposition to the Bill of Toleration incurred the displeasure of government, he was omitted from the commission in 1719. He manifested no resentment, and during the absence of the Duke of Grafton in 1721–3 was again included in the commission. On the death of Archbishop Lindsay, 13 July 1724, King was chosen administrator of the spiritualities of the see by the dean and chapter of Armagh, and the compliment was the more gratifying to him by reason of the appointment by the government for political considerations of Hugh Boulter [q. v.] to the primacy.

Though a whig, King was also an Irish patriot, that is to say, an advocate of the doctrines enunciated by William Molyneux (q. v.), and he was in effect the leader of the opposition to the party of the English interest in Ireland. His own suit with the London Society, in which the judgment of the Irish House of Lords had finally, in 1708, been reversed by that of England, had given point to Molyneux's argument. He had supported Swift's agitation against Wood's halfpence, and by his amendment to the address upon the lord-lieutenant's speech in September 1725, adding the words ' great wisdom' to his majesty's ' goodness and condescension' in putting an end to Wood's patent, he drew down upon himself the wrath of Archbishop Boulter. King was at the same time a high churchman; and having laboured all his life to advance the welfare of the church in Ireland by improving its revenues, and by raising up a body of efficient clergymen, he was indignant at the callous indifference with which the English ministry conferred the best preferments in the church on Englishmen, as rewards for their own or their friends' political subserviency. His protests proving unavailing, and old age and disease pressing heavily upon him, he gradually retired from active life. Since 1716 he had again been on terms of friendly if not very cordial intercourse with Swift, but an attempt on his part in 1727 to interfere in the affairs of the deanery, which Swift regarded as an encroachment on his personal liberty, led to a fresh explosion, and an open quarrel was only averted by King's timely withdrawal of his claim. In April 1728 he emerged from his retirement in order to support the Privileges of Parliament Bill. He died on 8 May 1729, and was buried on the 10th (his funeral sermon being preached by Richard D'aniel, dean of Armagh) in the north side of St. Mary's Church, Donnybrook, near Dublin, but, according to a wish expressed by him in his lifetime, no monument or memorial slab was erected. King was unmarried, and by his will he left all his property, amounting to nearly 17,000l., to public charities (Notes and Queries, 2nd ser. ix. 329, 5th ser. xi. 217). He founded in 1718 the Archbishop King's lectureship in divinity at Trinity College, Dublin.

At the time of his death there were at least three portraits of King in existence, in the possession respectively of Lord Carteret, Sir Hans Sloane, and Mr. Annesley. One of these was engraved by Faber. Mention also is made (Notes and Queries, 1st ser. vii. 430) of a small and rather curious engraving by Kane O'Hara, the celebrated burletta writer, published on 20 Sept. 1803 in London.

King was a voluminous letter-writer, and his letters throw a flood of light on the state of Ireland in his day. A number of these in the possession of Trinity College, Dublin, were printed by Mant in the second volume of his ' History of the Church of Ireland.' Others addressed to Sir Robert Southwell, forming two folio volumes, are in the Phillipps library of Cheltenham, Cat. No. 8556 (THORPE, Cat. 1834, pt. iv, p. 265). Another very valuable collection, including King's draft of a reply to Leslie's ' Answer,' and papers relating to his suit with the London Society, is that of Robert D. Lyons, esq., M.D., of Dublin. According to Mr. J. T. Gilbert (Hist. MSS. Comm. 2nd Rep. p. 235), who adds that there are other collections of King's extant in Ireland, these papers originally belonged to King's relative, the Rev. Robert Spence, rector of Donaghmore, co. Donegal. King's ' Diary,' written during the time of his imprisonment, with some other autograph manuscripts, are mentioned (ib. 3rd Rep. p. 416) as being in the possession of Colonel Ross-King of Kinellar, Aberdeenshire. A few letters and other papers will be found among the Egerton and Additional MSS. in the British Museum, but these have been utilised by Mant.

To the printed works mentioned above may be added: 1. ' A Sermon preached 7 Sept. 1704, being the Thanksgiving Day for the Victory . . . at Blenheim,' London, 1704, 4to. 2. ' Christian Humility: a Sermon preached before the Queen,' London, 1705, 4to. 3. ' The Advantages of Education, Religious and Political: a Sermon,' London, 1706, 4to. 4. ' The Mischief of Delaying Sentence against an Evil Work: a Sermon,' London, 1707, 4to. 5. ' The Right of Monarchy Asserted: a Sermon,' London, 1713, 8vo. 6. ' A Key to Divinity, or a Philosophical Essay on Free Will,' London, 1715, 12mo. 7. ' The Irish Historical Library: pointing at most of the Authors and Records in print or MS. which may be serviceable to the compiler of a General History in Ireland,' Dublin, 1724, 8vo.

[There is no regular biography of Archbishop King, nor any collected edition of his works. The life by Harris in his edition of Ware's Bishops, with the additional information furnished by Mant in his History of the Church of Ireland, is still the chief source of our information. The life in Willis's Irish Nation is chiefly abstracted from Mant. Some interesting and authentic matter will be found in Monck Mason's History of St. Patrick's. The correspondence between King and Swift, and to a less extent the earlier letters in the Journal to Stella, in Sir Walter Scott's edition of Swift's Works, throw much light on King's character and on the subject of the first-fruits. To these may be added, for incidental reference, J. W. Stubbs's Hist. of the University of Dublin; the Rev. John Richardson's Short Hist. of the Attempts to Convert the Popish Natives of Ireland, London, 1712; Cotton's Fasti Eccl. Hib.; Burdy's Life of Skelton; Bishop Nicholson's Letters on Various Subjects; Archbishop Boulter's Letters; Locke's Familiar Letters; George Faulkner's edition of Swift's Works, Dublin, 1763; Dublin Intelligencer, 10 May 1729; Notes and Queries; Hist. MSS. Comm. Reports, ii. 231–67, iii. 416; Leslie Stephen's English Thought in the Eighteenth Century; Craik's Life of Swift.] R. D.

KING, WILLIAM (1685–1763), principal of St. Mary Hall, Oxford, born at Stepney, Middlesex, on 16 March 1685, was the son of the Rev. Peregrine King and Margaret, daughter of Sir William Smyth, bart., of Radclive, Buckinghamshire (Anecdotes, p. 62; LYSONS, Environs, iii. 456). After attending Salisbury grammar school (Anecdotes, p. 136) he entered Balliol College, Oxford, on 9 July 1701, and graduated B.C.L. on 12 July 1709, D.C.L. on 8 July 1715. He was admitted a civilian on 20 Jan. 1716, but being possessed of a modest patrimony, he never sought practice (COOTE, English Civilians, pp. 111–12). He devoted his life to scholarship and literature, interested himself in politics, and was long at the head of the Jacobite party at Oxford. From want of ' human prudence ' he twice in his life lost the opportunity of acquiring a very large fortune ' in the most irreproachable manner,' and owing to the same defect his own fortune became much impaired (Anecdotes, pp. 2, 3). For a time he acted as secretary to the Duke of Ormonde and the Earl of Arran, when chancellors of the university, and he was elected principal of St. Mary Hall in 1719. He resigned his secretaryship in 1722, when he stood for the parliamentary representation of the university, but was easily defeated by George Clarke (1660–1736) [q. v.] (H. S. SMITH, Parliaments of England, ii. 7). A lawsuit about an estate in Galway to which he laid claim obliged him to go to Ireland in 1727. His learning, his turn for satire, and his hatred of the existing government recommended him to Swift. He thought himself injured in the course of his suit, and attacked his enemies in a mock-heroic poem, in two books, called ' The Toast,' supposed to have been originally composed in Latin by a Laplander, ' Frederick Scheffer,' and translated into English, with notes and observations, by ' Peregrine O'Donald, Esq.' The heroine, ' Mira,' is the Countess of Newburgh, who had secretly married as her third husband Sir Thomas Smyth, King's uncle. It was published in octavo at Dublin in 1732, a second volume being promised. Swift, after seeing the manuscript, declared that if he had read it when he was only twenty years of age he never would have written a satire. Hereupon 'The Toast' was completed in four books, inscribed to Swift, and printed in handsome quarto at London in 1736, with a frontispiece by H. Gravelot; it was reissued in 1747 (Notes and Queries, 1st ser. ii. 480, iii. 13, 4th ser. iv. 411, 5th ser. iii. passim). In his old age King regretted that he had not expunged many of the passages (Anecdotes, pp. 97-100), and at his death the remaining copies were burnt (NICHOLS, Lit. Anecd. viii. 241). The poem was reissued without the annotations in Almon's 'New Foundling Hospital of Wit.' A key to the characters is given in William Davis's 'Second Journey round the Library of a Bibliomaniac,' 1825, pp. 106-15, and an analysis of it in 'Bentley's Miscellany' for June 1857, pp. 616-25. About April 1737 King wrote a witty political paper called 'Common Sense,' in which he proposed a new scheme of government to the people of Corsica [i.e. Great Britain], advising them to make their king of the same stuff of which the Indians fashion their gods. He enclosed a copy in a letter to Swift, but both were intercepted at the post-office (SWIFT, Works, ed. Scott, 1824, xix. 81). It seems to be identical with 'Antonietti ducis Corsorum epistola ad Corsos de rege eligendo' included in King's collected writings. Through King, Swift endeavoured in the ensuing July to arrange for the publication in London of his 'History of the Four Last Years of the Queen.' King remonstrated, and ultimately Swift abandoned the intention for a time (POPE, Works, ed. Elwin and Courthope, vii. 363). In January 1738-9 Swift entrusted King with a copy of the verses on his own death, that they might be published in London. King, alarmed at the satire upon Walpole and Queen Caroline, omitted more than a hundred lines, 'in deference,' he said, 'to the judgment of Pope and other friends of Swift's,' but greatly to Swift's annoyance (ib. viii. 444; SWIFT, Works, xix. 176, 179). During the same year King met Nathaniel Hooke [q. v.] at Dr. Cheyne's house at Bath, and often acted as his amanuensis while he was translating Ramsay's 'Travels of Cyrus' (NICHOLS, Lit. Anecd. ii. 607). In this year also he issued his anonymous political satire entitled 'Miltoni Epistola ad Pollionem' (Lord Polwarth), 1738, fol., London, dedicated to Pope (Notes and Queries, 2nd ser. i. 255; Anecdotes, p. 151), of which a second edition appeared in

1740 (NICHOLS, Lit. Anecd. ii. 139). When honorary degrees were conferred upon the Duke of Hamilton, and Lords Lichfield and Orrery at Oxford in 1743, King delivered the Latin speeches, afterwards published as 'Tres Oratiunculæ habitæ in Domo Convocationis Oxon.,' 4to, London, Oxford (printed), 1743. The preface implies that he had been attacked by some anti-Jacobite canon. To keep up public interest in the affair, King himself wrote 'Epistola Objurgatoria ad Guilielmum King, LL.D.,' 4to, London, 1744, to which is attached a doggerel 'Epistola Canonici reverendi admodum ad Archidiaconum reverendum admodum.' Lastly appeared 'A Letter to a Friend occasioned by Epistola Objurgatoria, &c., by S. P. Y. B.,' 4to, London, 1744; the writer pretends to have been wrongly credited with the authorship of the 'Epistola.' The 'Letter' was doubtless by King, who thus in all probability created and wrote the whole controversy (Notes and Queries, 6th ser. xi. 33-4). Soon after the rebellion of 1745, King described the Duke of Cumberland as a man 'qui timet omnia præter Deum.' In 1748 he ridiculed Edward Bentham [q. v.], who had published a guide to intending students, in 'A Proposal for publishing a Poetical Translation, both in Latin and English, of the Reverend Mr. Tutor Bentham's Letter to a Young Gentleman of Oxford. By a Master of Arts,' 4to, London, 1748 (another edit. 8vo, 1749).

At the opening of Radcliffe's Library, on 13 April 1749, King delivered a Latin speech in the Sheldonian Theatre, in which he adroitly contrived to express his Jacobitism. He introduced six times in his peroration the word 'redeat,' pausing each time for a considerable space, amid loud applause from a distinguished audience (FITZMAURICE, Life of Lord Shelburne, i. 35). Thomas Warton, in his poem 'The Triumph of Isis,' eulogises King's powers of oratory. The oration (printed in 1749, and again in 1750) gave rise to violent attacks. King was charged with barbarous Latin, Jacobitism, and propagation of sedition in the university. John Burton (1696-1771) [q. v.], cousin and patron of Edward Bentham, published some virulent 'Remarks on Dr. K——'s Speech,' by 'Phileleutherus Londinensis,' 1750. King retorted savagely in 'Elogium Famæ inserviens Jaci Etonensis sive Gigantis; or, the Praises of Jack of Eton, commonly called Jack the Giant; collected into Latin and English Metre, after the Manner of Thomas Sternhold, John Hopkins, John Burton, and others. To which is added, a Dissertation on the Burtonian style. By a Master of Arts,' 8vo, Oxford, 1750. The satire also attacks William Bowyer the younger [q. v.], who had said something against King's latinity (NICHOLS, *Lit. Anecd.* ii. 223–5). King further translated all the abusive names which Burton had bestowed on him, and the complimentary phrases applied by Burton to himself, and printing the whole catalogue on a large sheet of coarse paper, gave it to a scavenger to be cried about the streets of Oxford, Windsor, and Eton (*Anecdotes*, pp. 153–7).

King was presented to the Pretender in September 1750. The Pretender was then paying a stealthy visit to England, and drank tea one evening at the doctor's lodgings at Oxford. They subsequently corresponded, but as the intimacy advanced King came to dislike the Pretender (*ib.* pp. 196–214).

King took part in the memorable contested election for Oxfordshire in 1754, and was in consequence vigorously libelled. He was accused of having defrauded subscribers for books never published to the extent of 1,500*l.*, was taunted with having offered himself to sale both in England and Ireland, and was accused of inspiring the Jacobite 'London Evening Post.' During the same year he published without his name a volume of fanciful essays called 'The Dreamer,' 8vo, London, 1754, which was assailed in the whig papers as tainted with Jacobitism. In February 1755 King had the pleasing duty of taking to Johnson his diploma of M.A., and found in him a warm admirer of both his scholarship and politics (BOSWELL, *Life of Johnson*, ed. G. B. Hill, i. 279). During the same year he replied to his assailants in a vigorously written pamphlet entitled 'Doctor King's Apology; or, Vindication of himself from the several matters charged on him by the Society of Informers,' 4to, Oxford, 1755 (2nd and 3rd editions the same year). He retaliated warmly on the authors of various libels which had appeared in the 'Evening Advertiser,' attacked a pestilent tract called 'A Defence of the Rector and Fellows of Exeter College,' and spoke severely of a canon of Windsor named Richard Blacow. Blacow thereupon printed a 'Letter to William King, LL.D.,' 8vo, 1755, in which he sought to make King responsible for a Jacobite demonstration by some undergraduates in February 1747.

On the Earl of Arran's death the Jacobite Earl of Westmoreland was elected chancellor. At his installation on 7 July 1759 King made a speech, at which Johnson 'clapped his hands till they were sore' (BOSWELL, i. 348). A collective edition of his writings was published as 'Opera Guilielmi King,' 4to, London, 1760 (cf. *Notes and Queries*, 5th ser. ix. 14). King publicly severed his connection with the Jacobite party in 1761, when he accompanied a deputation from the university to present the king with an address of congratulation on his marriage. He was personally introduced to the king by Lord Shelburne. His desertion did not escape censure (*Anecdotes*, pp. 189–196).

At the Encænia of 1763 King, amid great applause, delivered an oration with all his wonted animation and grace. Churchill, who was present, condescended to approve of his style, but afterwards sneered at his 'piebald Latin' in the 'Candidate' (NICHOLS, *Lit. Anecd.* viii. 236).

King died on 30 Dec. 1763, and was buried on 5 Jan. following at Ealing, Middlesex (LYSONS, ii. 236), where he had resided for many years on an estate called Newby, near the church. He was also lessee of the rectory of Ealing (FAULKNER, *Hist. of Brentford*, &c., 1845, pp. 177, 248). His heart, having been enclosed in a silver urn, was deposited by his own directions in the chapel of St. Mary Hall, where there is a monument to his memory, with a Latin epitaph written by himself (WOOD, *Colleges and Halls*, ed. Gutch, p. 675). His son, Charles King, born about 1711, was M.A. of St. Mary Hall, and in holy orders (FOSTER, *Alumni Oxon.* 1715–1886, ii. 794). His daughter Dorothy married William Melmoth the younger (1710–1799) [q. v.] (NICHOLS, *Lit. Anecd.* iii. 41).

Assisted by the contributions of old members of St. Mary Hall, King rebuilt the east side of the quadrangle, and added a new room to the principal's lodgings (WOOD, *Colleges*, &c., p. 674).

King wrote also an inscription for the collection of statues presented to the university in 1756 by the Countess Dowager of Pomfret (WOOD, *Antiquities of Oxford*, ed. Gutch, vol. ii. pt. ii. p. 811); an 'Elogium' in 1758 on Chevalier John Taylor the oculist, of which he printed a few copies to oblige his friends (*Anecdotes*, p. 136), and an epitaph on Beau Nash (*ib.* p. 248). His posthumous 'Political and Literary Anecdotes of his own Times,' 8vo, London, 1818 (2nd edit. 1819), mostly written in his seventy-sixth year to beguile the languor of a sick-room, and edited for the benefit of two of his lady relatives by Philip Bury Duncan [q. v.] (*Gent. Mag.* 3rd ser. xvi. 125), show him to have been a man of sense, acuteness, and cultivation. Throughout his life he was a water-drinker (*Anecdotes*, p. 11).

There is a striking likeness of King in the orator's rostrum in Worlidge's picture of the installation of Lord Westmoreland. His portrait by Williams hangs in the picture gallery at Oxford (NICHOLS, *Lit. Anecd.* viii. 241; WOOD, *Antiquities*, &c., vol. ii. pt. ii. p. 977). It was engraved by Faber; another portrait by Hudson was engraved by MacArdell; both are in mezzotint (EVANS, *Cat. of Engraved Portraits*, i. 197).

[Nichols's Lit. Anecd, ii. 607.] G. G.

KING, WILLIAM (1701–1769), independent minister, was born in Wiltshire on 9 June 1701, and educated at a local school, and afterwards at the university of Utrecht. He passed his trials there, returned to England in 1724, and was at once called by the independent church at Chesham, Buckinghamshire, where he was ordained on 25 April 1725. He removed to London in 1740, and on 14 Feb. in that year became pastor of the independent church in Hare Court, Aldersgate Street, as successor to Samuel Bruce. Shortly afterwards he received from a Scottish university a diploma creating him D.D. On 14 Jan. 1748 he was chosen Merchants' lecturer at Pinners' Hall, where he died on 3 March 1769. He was buried in Bunhill Fields. Besides 192 lectures at Pinners' Hall, of which at his death he was the eldest lecturer, he delivered evening lectures at Silver Street and Lime Street chapels. An oil-portrait of King, which has been engraved by Hopwood, is preserved in the vestry at Hare Court.

[Musgrave's Obituaries; Wilson's Dissenting Churches, iii. 299; Jones's Bunhill Memorials, p. 135; Evans's Cat. of Engraved Portraits, i. 196; Gent. Mag. 1769, p. 168; London Mag. 1769, p. 353; Funeral Sermon by Dr. James Watson, from Isaiah lx. 19.] T. S.

KING, WILLIAM (1786–1865), promoter of co-operation, born at Ipswich on 17 April 1786, was the son of the Rev. John King, many years master of the Ipswich grammar school. He was educated at Peterhouse, Cambridge, of which he became a fellow. He graduated B.A. in 1809 (as twelfth wrangler), M.A. in 1812, licensed by the university 11 June 1817, and commenced M.D. at Cambridge in 1819. He became a fellow of the Royal College of Physicians in 1820, and delivered the Harveian oration in 1843. He was for a time private tutor of Lord Overstone, who highly esteemed him. In 1823 he settled at Brighton, and became known as a writer on co-operation and social questions. King, who was remarkable for his conversational power, obtained the confidence of Lady Byron. He was her adviser in schemes for improving the condition of the poor upon her estates, and she actively promoted the co-operative system, of which he was a remarkable advocate.

From May 1828 to July 1830 he wrote a small monthly periodical, entitled 'The Co-operator,' the first which bore that name. No such publication before or since has excelled it in simplicity, persuasiveness, or in grasp of the ethical and economical principles to which the name of 'co-operation' was first given. Though each number consisted but of four pages, published at 1*d.*, and issued anonymously, it was the most influential publication of the kind at that time. Lady Byron left 300*l.* with a view to publishing a selection of King's writings. This has not yet been adequately done.

King died at Brighton on 20 Oct. 1865. He was consulting physician to the Sussex County Hospital (1842–1861), and first president of the Brighton 'Medical Chirurgical Society.' Besides the 'Co-operator,' he wrote: 'The Institutions of De Fellenberg,' 1842; 'Medical Essays,' 1850; 'Address to the Provincial Medical Surgical Society,' 1851; an 'Essay on Scrofula,' in the 'Medical Gazette;' and (posthumous) 'Thoughts on the Teaching of Christ,' 1872.

[Munk's Coll. of Phys. iii. 226; Gent. Mag. 1865, ii. 797; personal knowledge.] G. J. H.

KING, WILLIAM (1809–1886), geologist, was born at Hartlepool, Durham, in April 1809, and became in 1841 curator of the Museum of Natural History at Newcastle-on-Tyne; he was also lecturer on geology in the school of medicine there. In 1849, on the foundation of Queen's College, Galway, he was appointed professor of geology, and organised the formation of the geological museum. In 1870 the Queen's University of Ireland conferred on him its first honorary degree of D.Sc. In 1882 the professorship of natural history was added to King's other duties, but he resigned in 1883. The college nominated him emeritus professor of geology, mineralogy, and natural history, and presented him with a testimonial. King died at Glenoir, Taylor's Hill, Galway, on 24 June 1886, and was buried in the Galway new cemetery. He was married, and left issue. King's chief work was his 'Monograph of the Permian Fossils,' published by the Palæontographical Society, London, 1850. He also contributed a large number of papers on geological subjects to various scientific journals; a catalogue will be found in the printed 'Catalogue of the Library of Queen's College, Galway' (1877), pp. 403–8. With J. H. Rowney he published 'An Old Chapter of the Geological Record, with a new Interpretation,' London, 1881, 8vo.

[Nature, 1 July 1886; private information.] W. A. J. A.

KINGHORN, JOSEPH (1766–1832), particular baptist minister, was born at Gateshead-on-Tyne, Durham, on 17 Jan. 1766. His father, David Kinghorn (b. 3 Oct. 1737; d. 18 Feb. 1822), was a shoemaker and baptist preacher at Newcastle-on-Tyne, who was ordained on 1 May 1771 as minister of a baptist congregation at Burton-Bishop, East Riding of Yorkshire, where he remained till July 1789, when he retired to Norwich. Joseph was his eldest son by his second wife, Elizabeth (d. 25 Jan. 1810, aged 72), second daughter of Joseph Jopling of Satley, co. Durham. After four years' schooling, Kinghorn was taken on trial as apprentice to watch- and clock-making at Hull in 1779, but in March 1781 became a clerk in the white-lead works at Elswick, Northumberland. In April 1783 he was baptised by his father at Burton-Bishop, and looked forward to entering the ministry. He made the acquaintance of Robert Hall (1764–1831) [q. v.], and had thoughts of joining him at the university of Aberdeen. On 20 Aug. 1784 he entered the baptist academy at Bristol, under Caleb Evans, D.D. Among his fellow-students his most intimate friend was James Hinton, father of John Howard Hinton [q. v.] On leaving the academy he ministered for several months (from May 1788) at Fairford, Gloucestershire. He received an invitation from the baptist congregation at St. Mary's Chapel, Norwich, so called because it is situate in the parish of St. Mary-in-Coslany. On 27 March 1789 he settled in Norwich, and was ordained on 20 May 1790.

Kinghorn's ministry at Norwich, which lasted till his death, was one of much public usefulness. He was famed for the unction of his preaching, and his power of apt illustration was noted by Edward Irving. His old chapel was replaced in 1811 by a very handsome structure on the same site. On 2 Aug. 1804 he was invited to the headship of the Northern Baptist Academy, then on the point of being established in Bradford, but he preferred pastoral work. In a controversy with Robert Hall, which began in 1816, he took the side of close communion, making adult baptism a term of participation in the Lord's Supper. He made mission journeys to Scotland in 1818 and 1822, and in every enterprise connected with his own body he played a prominent part. The intellectual life of Norwich was in his time considerable. From 1790 he was a member of a 'speculative society,' of which William Taylor [q. v.], the German scholar, was the leading spirit, and in which the cultured Roman catholic was welcomed along with the representatives of all protestant churches. In later life Kinghorn gave much time to Hebrew and rabbinical studies. He died unmarried on 1 Sept. 1832, and was buried on 7 Sept. in the vestibule of St. Mary's Chapel; Joseph John Gurney [q. v.], the quaker philanthropist, spoke at his funeral; the sermon was preached by John Alexander, minister of Prince's Street congregational church.

A list of twenty of his publications is given by Wilkin, including: 1. 'A Defence of Infant Baptism its best confutation,' &c., Norwich, 1795, 12mo. 2. 'Public Worship,' &c., Norwich, 1800, 12mo. 3. 'Address . . . on Church Communion,' &c., Norwich, 1803, 1813, 1821. 4. 'Arguments . . . against the Roman Catholic Doctrines,' &c., Norwich, 1804. 5. 'Serious Considerations addressed to the House of Israel,' &c., 1811, 12mo. 6. 'The Miracles of Jesus not performed by the power of the Shemhamphorash,' &c., 1812. 7. 'Scriptural Arguments for the Divinity of Christ,' &c., Norwich, 1813, 12mo; 1814, 8vo. 8. 'Advice . . . to Young Ministers,' &c., Norwich, 1814, 12mo. 9. 'Baptism a Term of Communion,' Norwich, 1816, 8vo; two editions same year; 1876, 8vo; also 'A Defence' of this, Norwich, 1829, 8vo. 10. 'Practical Cautions to Students,' &c., Norwich, 1817, 8vo. 11. 'The Argument in support of Infant Baptism from . . . Circumcision,' &c. 1823, 12mo. 12. 'Arguments . . . against Mixed Communion,' &c., 1827, 12mo. 13. 'Sketch of the Life of the Rev. Isaac Slee,' &c., 1827, 12mo. 14. 'Remarks on . . . the Visible Church,' &c., Norwich, 1829, 12mo. He edited Robertson's 'Clavis Pentateuchi,' &c., Norwich, 1824, 8vo, and the 9th (1814) and 10th (1827) editions of Ash and Evans's 'Collection of Hymns' (1769). His sermon on the 'Separate State' is in vol. ii. of the 'British Preacher,' 1831. Wilkin enumerates twelve of his unpublished manuscripts, chiefly controversial. The catalogue of his library was published at Norwich, 1833, 8vo.

[Wilkin's Joseph Kinghorn, 1855; Browne's Hist. Congr. Norf. and Suff. 1877, p. 552; Todd's Brief Histor. Sketch of the Baptist Church in St. Mary's, Norwich [1886], pp. 14 sq.; Julian's Dictionary of Hymnology, 1892, p. 112.]   A. G.

KINGHORNE, third EARL OF. [See LYON, PATRICK, 1642–1695.]

KINGLAKE, ALEXANDER WILLIAM (1809–1891), historian of the Crimean war, born 5 Aug. 1809, was the eldest son of William Kinglake, banker and solicitor, of Taunton, Somerset, by Mary, daughter of Thomas Woodforde, esq., of Taunton. He had two brothers, Robert Arthur and John Hamilton. The Kinglake family is said to have been of Scottish origin, the original name being Kinloch, and to have come to England in the reign of James I, and settled in Somerset. It there acquired the estate of Saltmoor, which descended to the historian.

Kinglake says of his mother: 'The most humble and pious of women was yet so proud a mother that she could teach her first-born son no Watts's hymns, no collects for the day; she could teach him in earliest childhood no less than this—to find a home in his saddle and to love old Homer and all that Homer sang' (Eöthen, chap. iv.) The Homer, he adds, was Pope's. He retained his skill in horsemanship, and though he did not gain the usual scholastic honours, he certainly acquired a classical refinement of taste. He was educated at Eton under Keate, of whom he has left a most characteristic portrait (ib. ch. xviii.), and in 1828 he entered Trinity College, Cambridge. He was the college contemporary and friend of Thackeray and Lord Tennyson. He became B.A. in 1832, and M.A. in 1836. He entered Lincoln's Inn on 14 April 1832, and was called to the bar on 5 May 1837. He had about 1835 made the Eastern tour described afterwards in 'Eöthen, or Traces of Travel brought home from the East.' The Methley of that book was Lord Pollington. Mysseri, his dragoman, was an hotel-keeper at Constantinople during the Crimean war. The book, as the preface informs us, was the result of a third attempt after he had twice failed to satisfy himself, and did not appear until 1844. It showed Kinglake to be a master of a most refined style and subtle humour, although he thinks it necessary to apologise for the possible failure of his attempts to subdue the 'almost boisterous tone' of the original writing. He has endeavoured, he adds, and he thinks successfully, to exclude from it 'all valuable matter derived from the works of others.' In truth, though the book was rather absurdly compared with the ordinary records of travel, it is more akin to Sterne's 'Sentimental Journey,' and is a delightful record of personal impressions rather than outward facts.

Although a barrister, and obtaining some little employment as a conveyancer, Kinglake cared little for his profession. He had always been interested in military history, and in 1845 he went to Algiers and accompanied the flying column of St. Arnaud, whom he afterwards described from personal knowledge (Invasion of the Crimea, vol. ii. ch. i.) In 1854 he followed the English expedition to the Crimea, and was present at the battle of the Alma (20 Sept. 1854). A fall from his pony on the morning of the day introduced him to Lord Raglan, who happened to be near, and he dined with

Raglan in the evening. He stayed with the army until the opening of the siege. In 1856 Lady Raglan asked him to undertake the history of the campaign, and communicated to him all the papers in her possession. Kinglake undertook the task, and executed it with extraordinary care. He made the most elaborate inquiry into every incident of the war, carefully compared all the available evidence, and spared no labour in polishing the style of his narrative. The first two volumes of the 'Invasion of the Crimea' appeared in 1863, the third and fourth in 1868, the fifth in 1875, the sixth in 1880, and the seventh and eighth in 1887. The scale upon which he worked was probably excessive, and, as the interest in the war declined, readers had less patience with the full description of minute incidents. His strong prejudices, especially his moral indignation against Napoleon III and his loyalty to his friend Lord Raglan, gave a party tone to the narrative, for which allowance must be made. Military experts have found fault with some of the judgments of an amateur in war, though admitting his skill in dealing even with technical details. His friend Abraham Hayward defended him in 'Mr. Kinglake and the Quarterlys,' 1863. The literary ability in any case is remarkable; the spirit of the writing is never quenched by the masses of diplomatic and military information; the occasional portraits of remarkable men are admirably incisive; the style is invariably polished to the last degree, and the narrative as lucid as it is animated. Kinglake in 1857 was elected in the liberal interest for Bridgewater. He held his seat until 1868, in which year he was unseated upon petition and the borough disfranchised. Kinglake himself, however, was entirely incapable of the slightest complicity in the corruption which was disclosed, and was only too innocent to suspect its existence. A weak voice and feeble delivery prevented him commanding the attention of the house. He took a part, however, in defending all those whom he held to be victims of oppression. He moved the first amendment to the Conspiracy Bill in 1858, and in 1860 vigorously denounced the annexation of Savoy and Nice.

During many years Kinglake was fully occupied by his history. He lived in Hyde Park Place, and was a member of the Travellers' and the Athenæum Clubs. He constantly dined at the Athenæum, in company with his friends, Abraham Hayward [q. v.], Thomas Chenery [q. v.], and Sir Henry Bunbury. A singularly gentle and attractive manner covered without concealing the generosity of sentiment and chivalrous sense of honour which prompted his eloquent denunciations of wrong-doing. He suffered at the last from cancer of the tongue, and bore with admirable patience sufferings happily not very long protracted. He died on 2 Jan. 1891. He requested his executor, Dr. J. H. Kinglake, to 'prevent the publication of any writings of his that might be found,' and destroy all such papers as were not necessary to be preserved.

Kinglake is said to have contributed to the 'Owl,' with which his friend Laurence Oliphant was connected; and he wrote an article upon Mme. de Lafayette in 'Blackwood's Magazine' for September 1872. He wrote two articles in the 'Quarterly Review,' one upon the 'Rights of Women' (December 1844), the other 'The Mediterranean a French Lake' (March 1845). His only other works are mentioned above.

[Times, 3 Jan. 1891; Blackwood's Magazine for February 1891.] L. S.

KINGLAKE, ROBERT, M.D. (1765–1842), medical writer, born in 1765, graduated M.D. at Göttingen, and also studied at Edinburgh. After practising for some years as a surgeon at Chipping Norton, Oxfordshire, he removed to Chilton-upon-Polden, Somerset, and in 1802 to Taunton in the same county. At Taunton he frequently attended public meetings and made many eloquent speeches in support of the first Reform Bill. He died on 26 Sept. 1842 at West Monkton rectory, near Taunton, the residence of his son, the Rev. W. C. Kinglake (Gent. Mag. 1842, ii. 556). He was a member of the Royal Medical Society of Edinburgh, the Physical Society of Göttingen, and other learned bodies.

Kinglake attracted considerable attention by his writings on gout, in which he advocated the cooling treatment. His first papers on the subject appeared in 1801 and 1803 in the 'Medical and Physical Journal' (Nos. 33 and 48). His views were combated by Wadd, W. Perry, John Hunt, J. King, and others. He replied to his antagonists in: 1. 'A Dissertation on Gout' (with appendix), 8vo, London, 1804. 2. 'Reply to Mr. Edlin's two Cases of Gout,' 8vo, Taunton, 1804. 3. 'Additional Cases of Gout,' 8vo, Taunton, 1807. 4. 'Strictures on Mr. Parkinson's Observations on the Nature and Cure of Gout. ... To which are added, Two Letters to Dr. Haygarth, containing Remarks on the Opinions he has lately published on Acute Rheumatism,' 8vo, Taunton, 1807. He also published some curious 'Observations on the Medical Effects of Digitalis' in the 'Medical and Physical Journal' for 1800, iii. 120. In

Macnish's 'Anatomy of Drunkenness,' there is a short article by the author on Kinglake's experiment with ether.

[Watt's Bibl. Brit.]

KINGSBOROUGH, VISCOUNT. [See KING, EDWARD, 1795–1837.]

KINGSBURY, WILLIAM (1744–1818), dissenting minister, was born in Bishopsgate Street, London, on 12 July 1744. On the death of his father, Thomas Kingsbury, in 1753, he was placed at Merchant Taylors' School, but some two years later received a nomination from Sir John Barnard [q. v.] for Christ's Hospital. Leaving there in 1758 he entered the congregational academy at Mile End, where he studied under John Conder [q. v.] and Thomas Gibbons [q. v.] After much mental conflict he was converted towards the close of 1760, preached his first sermon at Bethnal Green in August 1763, and was ordained minister to the independent congregation at Southampton on 8 Aug. 1765. There he remained some forty-five years, attracting a large congregation by the evident earnestness of his preaching. In 1770, when John Howard the philanthropist was at Southampton, Kingsbury laid the foundations of a lifelong intimacy with him, and contributed some particulars to the life of Howard by James Baldwin Brown the elder [q. v.] Another close friend was John Newton [q. v.], the intimate of the poet Cowper. Kingsbury was a strong supporter of the movement which developed into the London Missionary Society, and in 1796 he drew up by request a circular letter of appeal to the independent churches throughout the country. Some disparaging remarks let fall in a sermon by Richard Mant, D.D., rector of All Souls', Southampton, in this same year, drew from Kingsbury his one controversial work, 'The Manner in which Protestant Dissenters perform Prayer in Public Worship vindicated,' London, 1796, 12mo; the tract rapidly passed through two editions. In 1809 Kingsbury, who had since 1772 conducted a small school in addition to his pastoral duties, found himself unequal to his work. He formally resigned his pastorate on 29 July in that year, when a stipend of 200l. per annum, of which he would only accept 120l., was offered him. He died at Caversham on 18 Feb. 1818, and a mural tablet was erected to his memory in the independent chapel at Southampton. Kingsbury married in November 1768 a Miss Andrews, daughter of Mordecai Andrews, an independent minister in London, by whom a son, Thomas, and a daughter, Sarah, who married one Jameson, survived him. A memoir, together with a devotional diary kept by Kingsbury during the latter years of his life, was published by John Bullar of Southampton in 1819.

Kingsbury published, besides the work mentioned above, a number of funeral sermons. A copy of one, which is not mentioned in the British Museum Catalogue, on the 'Life, Labors, and Departure of the Rev. Edward Ashburner,' delivered at Poole in Dorset, 6 July 1804, is in Dr. Williams's Library. Another sermon, published in 1789, on 'The Sickness and Recovery of King Hezekiah,' was 'occasioned by the happy recovery of his Majesty' (George III).

[Life by Bullar; Wilson's Dissenting Churches, i. 190, ii. 549, iii. 603; Biog. Dict. of Living Authors, p. 190; Brown's Life of Howard, p. 101; Darling's Cyclop. Bibl. 1732; Morison's Missionary Fathers.] T. S.

KINGSCOTE, HENRY ROBERT (1802–1882), philanthropist, was born on 25 May 1802. He was second son of Thomas Kingscote (d. 1811), who was brother of Robert Kingscote of Kingscote, Gloucestershire; his mother was Harriet, fourth daughter of Sir Henry Peyton of Dodington in the same county. He was educated at Harrow, and early became a cricketer and rider to hounds. He was six feet five inches in height. He played his first match at Lord's on 21 May 1823. In 1827 he was elected president of the Marylebone Cricket Club. A narrow escape from drowning turned his attention to religious matters; he became a friend of Bishop Blomfield, and with him was instrumental in founding the Church of England Scripture Readers' Association and the Metropolitan Visiting and Relief Association, of which he was a trustee all his life. In 1846 he published a pamphlet-letter to the Archbishop of Canterbury on the needs of the church, which ran through several editions, and in it he urged the extension of lay agency and the foundation of new bishoprics. In 1846 he helped to found the Southwark fund for schools and churches, and in 1847 he helped in alleviating the distress in Ireland. He sent out supplies to the troops during the Crimean war. In 1868 Kingscote was one of the founders of the British and Colonial Emigration Society; he was also the founder of the scheme for establishing workshops for the indigent blind, which was not very successful, and of the National Orphan Asylum at Ham Common. Kingscote died on 13 July 1882. He married, on 11 July 1833, Harriet Elizabeth Tower of Weald Hall, Essex, and by her had three sons and five daughters.

[Times, 14 July 1882; Lillywhite's Cricket Scores and Biographies, i. 468; Box's English Game of Cricket, p. 101; Nimrod's Hunting Tour, p. 198; Men of the Reign; Burke's Landed Gentry.] W. A. J. A.

KINGSDOWN, LORD. [See PEMBERTON-LEIGH, THOMAS, 1793–1867.]

KINGSFORD, MRS. ANNA (1846–1888), doctor of medicine and religious writer, daughter of John Bonus, was born at Maryland Point, Stratford, Essex, 16 Sept. 1846, and was baptised Annie. She married in 1867 Algernon Godfrey Kingsford, vicar of Atcham, Shropshire. From 1868 to 1872 she wrote stories in the 'Penny Post,' signed Ninon Kingsford and Mrs. Algernon Kingsford. In 1870 she was received into the Roman catholic church by Cardinal Manning, and she adopted the christian names Annie Mary Magdalen Maria Johanna. In 1872 she purchased and edited in her own name 'The Lady's Own Paper,' in which she strenuously supported the movement against vivisection, but she gave up the paper in 1873, and in 1874 went to Paris to commence medical studies. On 22 July 1880 she received the degree of M.D. from the faculty of Paris. She had then adopted vegetarian principles, and the title of her thesis was 'De l'alimentation végétale chez l'homme;' this, translated and enlarged, was published in London, 1881, as 'The Perfect Way in Diet.' Mrs. Kingsford soon engaged in the active practice of a London physician, but her attention was largely devoted to mystical subjects. She became president of the Theosophical Society in 1883, and founded in 1884 the Hermetic Society. In 1887 a cold caught while visiting M. Pasteur's laboratory on a snowy day developed into pulmonary consumption. She removed to the Riviera without benefit, and, returning to London, died at Wynnstay Gardens, Kensington, 22 Feb. 1888, being buried in Atcham church-yard. She left a daughter.

In person Mrs. Kingsford was singularly beautiful; as a doctor she was very successful with women; she also was one of the pioneers in the cause of the higher education of women. Much doubt exists as to the faith in which she died. Her aim as a religious teacher was to reconcile Christianity with her own mystical theories, and to bring prominently forward the connection of Christianity with eastern faiths, a connection which had in her opinion been long obscured. The Hermetic Society still exists in this country, and has a certain following in the United States.

Mrs. Kingsford's chief works were: 1. 'Beatrice, a Tale of the Early Christians,' London, 1863, 12mo, remarkable on account of the youthful age of the authoress. 2. 'River Reeds,' a volume of verse, anon., London,

1886. 3. 'The Perfect Way, or the Finding of Christ,' London, 1882, 4to: revised ed. 1887; 3rd ed. 1890: in this work Mr. Edward Maitland assisted. 4. 'The Virgin of the World,' translated, with a preface, from 'Hermes Mercurius Trismegistus,' 1885, 4to. 5. 'Astrology theologised,' 1886, 4to, a reprint, with a preface, of a work of Valentine Weigelius. 6. 'Health, Beauty, and the Toilet,' London, 1886, 8vo (2nd ed. same year), a reprint of letters which appeared, 1884-6, in the 'Lady's Pictorial.' These occasioned some adverse criticism, as sanctioning artificial aids to beauty. Posthumous, and edited by Mr. Edward Maitland, were: 7. 'Dreams and Dream Stories,' 1888, 8vo. 8. 'Clothed with the Sun,' New York, 1889, 4to, a curious collection of what are termed by the editor 'illuminations.'

[Times, 27 Feb. 1888; Lady's Pictorial, 3 March 1888 (portrait from a photograph and reminiscences by Mrs. Fenwick-Miller); Tablet, 1888 (letters from Mr. Edward Maitland as to whether Mrs. Kingsford died in the catholic faith); Hays's Women of the Day; private information.]   W. A. J. A.

KINGSLAND, Viscounts. [See Barnewall, Nicholas, 1592-1663, first Viscount; Barnewall, Nicholas, 1668-1725, third Viscount.]

KINGSLEY, CHARLES (1819-1875), author, son of the Rev. Charles Kingsley, first of Battramsley House in the New Forest, by his wife, daughter of Nathan Lucas of Barbadoes and Rushford Lodge, Norfolk, was born on 12 June 1819 at Holne Vicarage, Devonshire. His father, a descendant of an old family which had produced many soldiers, had been bred as a country gentleman; but, from the carelessness of his guardians during a long minority, had been forced to adopt a profession, and had taken orders after thirty. He became acquainted, while studying at Trinity Hall, Cambridge, with Herbert Marsh [q. v., then professor of divinity, and in 1819 bishop of Peterborough. He took a curacy in the fens, and afterwards at Holne, whence he moved to Burton-on-Trent and Clifton in Nottinghamshire. He held the valuable living of Barnack in Northamptonshire (between Peterborough and Stamford) from 1824 to 1830, until the son of Bishop Marsh could take orders. He caught ague in the fen country, and was advised to remove to Devonshire, where he was presented to Clovelly. He remained there till, in 1836, he became rector of St. Luke's, Chelsea. He died on 29 Feb. 1860 at the Chelsea rectory, in his seventy-eighth year.

Charles was a precocious child, writing sermons and poems at the age of four. He was delicate and sensitive, and retained through life the impressions made upon him by the scenery of the fens and of Clovelly. At Clovelly he learnt to boat, to ride, and to collect shells. In 1831 he was sent to a school at Clifton, and saw the Bristol riots of August 1831, which he says for some years made him a thorough aristocrat. In 1832 he was sent to the grammar school at Helston, Cornwall, then under Derwent Coleridge [q. v.], though it is said that E. C. Hawtrey [q. v.] wished him to go to Eton, from reports of his early promise. Kingsley was not a close student, though he showed great intellectual activity. He was not popular, rather despising his fellows, caring little for the regular games, although fond of feats of agility and of long excursions in search of plants and geological specimens. He wrote a good deal of poetry and poetical prose. In 1836 he went with his family to London, and became a student at King's College, London, walking in and out from Chelsea. He worked hard, but found London life dismal, and was not a little bored by the parish work in which his father and mother were absorbed. He describes the district visitors as ugly and splay-footed beings, 'three-fourths of whom can't sing, and the other quarter sing miles out of tune, with voices like love-sick parrots.' In October 1838 he entered Magdalene College, Cambridge, and at the end of his first year gained a scholarship. In the following vacation, while staying with his father in the country, he met, on 6 July 1839, his future wife, Fanny, daughter of Pascoe Grenfell. That, he said afterwards, was 'my real wedding-day.' They began an occasional correspondence, in which Kingsley confessed very fully to the religious doubts by which he, like others, was tormented at the time of the Oxford movement. He was occasionally so much depressed by these thoughts, and by the uncertainty of any fulfilment of his hopes, that he sometimes thought of leaving Cambridge to 'become a wild prairie hunter.' His attachment to Miss Grenfell operated as an invaluable restraint. He read Coleridge, Carlyle, and Maurice with great interest. Meanwhile, though his studies seem to have been rather desultory, he was popular at college, and threw himself into every kind of sport to distract his mind. He rowed, though he did not attain to the first boat, but specially delighted in fishing expeditions into the fens and elsewhere, rode out to Sedgwick's equestrian lectures on geology, and learnt boxing under a negro prize-fighter. He was a good pedestrian, and once walked to London in a day. His distractions, intellectual, emotional, and athletic, made him regard the regular course of study as a painful drudgery. He read classics with W. H. Bateson [q. v.], afterwards master of St. John's, during his first and third years, but could not be induced to work hard till his last six months. He then by great effort succeeded in obtaining the last place in the first class of the classical tripos of 1842. He was a 'senior optime' in the previous mathematical tripos. He had by this time decided to take orders, and in July 1842 was ordained by the Bishop of Winchester to the curacy of Eversley, Hampshire. Eversley is on the borders of Windsor Forest, a wild heather-covered country, with a then neglected population of 'broom squires' and deerstealers, and with a considerable infusion of gipsies. Kingsley disliked the Oxford school, which to him represented sacerdotalism, asceticism, and Manichæism, and was eagerly reading Maurice's 'Kingdom of Christ.' Carlyle and Arnold were also among his prophets. He soon became popular by hard work in his parish and genuine sympathy with the poor, but lived a secluded life, with little society beyond that of a few friends in the Military College at Sandhurst. A year's interruption in the correspondence with his future wife implies a cause for depression. In September 1843, however, he obtained through one of her relations, Lord Sidney Godolphin Osborne, a promise of a living from Lord Portman, and was advised to apply in the meantime for the curacy of Pimperne, near Blandford. The curacy was promised, and the correspondence was renewed. Early in 1844 he married. The living of Eversley fell vacant at the time, and the parishioners were anxious that he should succeed to it. In May 1844 he was accordingly presented to it by Sir John Cope, the patron, and settled there as rector soon afterwards.

Heavy dilapidations and arrears of poor-rate fell upon the new incumbent; the house was unwholesome, and much drainage was required. The church was empty; no grown-up labourers in the parish could read or write, and everything was in a state of neglect. Kingsley set to work vigorously, and in time successfully, to remedy this state of things. His only recreation was an occasional day's fishing, and sometimes a day with the hounds on an old horse 'picked up cheap for parson's work.' In 1844 he made acquaintance with Maurice, to whom he had written for advice upon some of his difficulties. Maurice soon became a revered friend, whom he delighted to call his 'master.' In 1845 he was appointed a canon of Middleham by

Dean Wood, father of an old college friend, a post which was merely honorary, though historically interesting.

In 1842, just after taking his degree, he had begun to write the life of St. Elizabeth of Hungary. He finally changed his original prose into a drama, which was accepted, after some refusals from publishers, by Messrs. Parker, and appeared at the beginning of 1848 with a preface by Maurice. The book excited interest both in Oxford and in Germany. It was much admired by Bunsen, and a review by Conington, though not very favourable, led to a friendship with the critic. While showing high poetical promise, and indeed containing some of his best work, it is also an exposition of his sentiments upon the social and religious movements of the day. Though expressing sympathy with mediæval life, it is a characteristic protest against the ascetic theories which, as he thought, tended to degrade the doctrine of the marriage bond. The events of 1848 led to a more direct utterance. His admiration for Maurice brought about a close association with the group who, with Maurice for leader, were attempting to give a Christian direction to the socialist movement then becoming conspicuous. Among others he came to know A. P. Stanley, Mr. Froude, Mr. Ludlow, and especially Mr. Thomas Hughes, afterwards his most intimate friend. He was appointed professor of English literature in Queen's College, Harley Street, just founded, with Maurice as president, and gave a course of weekly lectures, though ill-health forced him to give up the post a year later. His work at Eversley prevented him from taking so active a part as some of his friends, but he heartily sympathised with their aims, and was a trusted adviser in their schemes for promoting co-operation and 'Christian socialism.' His literary gifts were especially valuable, and his writings were marked by a fervid and genuine enthusiasm on behalf of the poor. He contributed papers to the 'Politics for the People,' of which the first number (of seventeen published) appeared on 6 May 1848. He took the signature 'Parson Lot,' on account of a discussion with his friends, in which, being in a minority of one, he had said that he felt like Lot, 'when he seemed as one that mocked to his sons-in-law.' Under the same name he published a pamphlet called 'Cheap Clothes and Nasty' in 1850, and a good many contributions to the 'Christian Socialist: a Journal of Association,' which appeared from 2 Nov. 1850 to 28 June 1851. The pamphlet was reprinted with 'Alton Locke' and a preface by Mr. Thomas Hughes in 1881. He produced his first two novels under the same influence. 'Yeast' was published in 'Fraser's Magazine' in the autumn of 1848. He had been greatly excited by the events of the previous months, and wrote it at night, after days spent in hard parish work. A complete breakdown of health followed. He went for rest to Bournemouth in October, and after a second collapse spent the winter in North Devon. A further holiday, also spent in Devonshire, became necessary in 1849. The expenses of sickness and the heavy rates at Eversley tried his finances. He resigned the office of clerk-in-orders at St. Luke's, Chelsea, which he had held since his marriage, but which he now felt to be a sinecure. To make up his income he resolved to take pupils, and by a great effort finished 'Alton Locke' in the winter of 1849-50. Messrs. Parker declined it, thinking that they had suffered in reputation by the publication of 'Yeast.' It was, however, accepted by Messrs. Chapman & Hall on the recommendation of Carlyle, and appears to have brought the author 150*l.* (*Kingsley*, i. 277). It was published in August 1850, and was described by Carlyle as a 'fervid creation still left half chaotic.'

Kingsley's writings exposed him at this time to many and often grossly unfair attacks. In 1851 he preached a sermon in a London church which, with the full knowledge of the incumbent, was to give the views of the Christian socialists, and was called 'The Message of the Church to the Labouring Man.' At the end of the sermon, however, the incumbent rose and protested against its teaching. The press took the matter up, and the Bishop of London (Blomfield) forbade Kingsley to preach in his diocese. A meeting of working-men was held on Kennington Common to support Kingsley. The sermon was printed, and the bishop, after seeing Kingsley, withdrew the prohibition.

The fear of anything called socialism was natural at the time; but Kingsley never adopted the socialist creed in a sense which could now shock the most conservative. In politics he was in later life rather a tory than a radical. He fervently believed in the House of Lords (see e.g. *Kingsley*, ii. 241-3), detested the Manchester school, and was opposed to most of the radical platform. 'Yeast' and 'Alton Locke' indeed show an even passionate sympathy for the sufferings of the agricultural labourer and of the London artisan. The ballad of the 'poacher's widow' in 'Yeast' is a denunciation of game-preservers vigorous enough to satisfy the most thoroughgoing chartist. But Kingsley's sentiment was thoroughly in harmony with the class of squires and country clergymen, who

required in his opinion to be roused to their duties, not deprived of their privileges. He therefore did not sympathise with the truly revolutionary movement, but looked for a remedy of admitted evils to the promotion of co-operation, and to sound sanitary legislation (in which he was always strongly interested). He strove above all to direct popular aspirations by Christian principles, which alone, as he held, could produce true liberty and equality. Thus, when the passions roused in 1848 had cooled down, he ceased to be an active agitator, and became tolerably reconciled to the existing order.

In 1851 he was attacked with gross unfairness or stupidity for the supposed immorality of 'Yeast,' and replied in a letter to the 'Guardian' by a *mentiris impudentissime*, which showed how deeply he had been stung. He sought relief from worry and work in the autumn of 1851 by his first tour abroad, bringing back from the Rhine impressions afterwards used in 'Two Years Ago.' One of his private pupils, Mr. John Martineau, has given a very vivid account of his home life at Eversley during this period (*Kingsley*, i. 297-308). He had brought things into better order, and after his holiday in 1851 was able for some time to work without a curate. Not being able to get another pupil, he was compelled to continue his work single-handed, and again became over-exhausted. His remarkable novel, 'Hypatia,' certainly one of the most successful attempts in a very difficult literary style, appeared in 1853, after passing through 'Fraser's Magazine.' It was well received in Germany as well as England, and highly praised by Bunsen (*Memoirs*, ii. 309). Maurice took a part in criticising it during its progress, and gave suggestions which Kingsley turned to account. Like his previous books, it is intended to convey a lesson for the day, dealing with an analogous period of intellectual fermentation. It shows his brilliant power of constructing a vivid, if not too accurate, picture of a past social state. The winter of 1853-4 was passed at Torquay for the sake of his wife, whose health had suffered from the damp of Eversley. Here his strong love of natural history led him to a study of seashore objects and to an article on the 'Wonders of the Shore' in the 'North British Review,' afterwards developed into 'Glaucus.' In February he gave some lectures at Edinburgh on the 'Schools of Alexandria,' and in the spring settled with his family at Bideford, his wife being still unable to return to Eversley. Here he wrote 'Westward Ho!' It was dedicated to Bishop Selwyn and Rajah Brooke. Brooke was a hero after his own heart, whom he knew personally and had heartily endeavoured to support (*Kingsley*, i. 222, 369-70, 444 5). It is in some ways his most characteristic book, and the descriptions of Devonshire scenery, his hearty sympathy with the Elizabethan heroes, and the unflagging spirit of the story, make the reader indifferent to its obviously one-sided view of history.

While staying at Bideford Kingsley displayed one of his many gifts by getting up and teaching a drawing class for young men. In the course of 1855 he again settled at Eversley, spending the winter at a house on Farley Hill, for the benefit of his wife's health. Besides frequent lectures, sermons, and articles, he was now writing 'Two Years Ago,' which appeared in 1857. Kingsley had been deeply interested in the Crimean war. Some thousands of copies of a tract by him, called 'Brave Words to Brave Soldiers,' had been distributed to the army. He always had keen military tastes; he studied military history with especial interest; many of the officers from Sandhurst and Aldershot became his warm friends; and he delighted in lecturing, preaching, or blessing new colours for the regiments in camp. Such tastes help to explain the view expressed in 'Two Years Ago,' which was then less startling than may now seem possible, that the war was to exercise a great regenerating influence. The novel is much weaker than its predecessors, and shows clearly that if his desire for social reform was not lessened, he had no longer so strong a sense that the times were out of joint. His health and prospects had improved, a result which he naturally attributed to a general improvement of the world.

The Crimean pamphlet had been published anonymously, on account of the prejudices against him in the religious world. The prejudices rapidly diminished from this time. In 1859 he became one of the queen's chaplains in ordinary. He was presented to the queen and to the prince consort, for whom he entertained a specially warm admiration. He still felt the strain of overwork, having no curate, and shrank from London bustle, confining himself chiefly to Eversley. In May 1860 he was appointed to the professorship of modern history at Cambridge, vacant by the death in the previous autumn of Sir James Stephen. He took a house at Cambridge, but after three years found that the expense of a double establishment was beyond his means, and from 1863 resided at Eversley, only going to Cambridge twice a year to deliver his lectures. During the first period his duties at Eversley were undertaken by the Rev. Septimus Hansard. The

salary of the professorship was 371*l.*, and the preparation of lectures interfered with other literary work. During the residence of the Prince of Wales at Cambridge a special class under Kingsley was formed for his benefit, and the prince won the affectionate regard of his teacher. The prince recommended him for an honorary degree at Oxford on the commemoration of 1863, but the threatened opposition of the high church party under Pusey induced Kingsley to retire, with the advice of his friends. Kingsley's tenure of the professorship can hardly be described as successful. The difficulties were great. The attempt to restore the professorial system had at that time only succeeded in filling the class-rooms with candidates for the ordinary degree. History formed no part of the course of serious students, and the lectures were in the main merely ornamental. Kingsley's geniality, however, won many friends both among the authorities and the undergraduates. Some young men expressed sincere gratitude for the intellectual and moral impulse which they received from him. Professor Max Müller says (*Kingsley*, ii. 263) 'history was but his text,' and his lectures gave the thoughts of 'a poet and a moralist, a politician and a theologian, and, above all, a friend and counsellor of young men.' They roused interest, but they did not lead to a serious study of history or an elevation of the position held by the study at the university. Kingsley's versatile mind, distracted by a great variety of interests, had caught brilliant glimpses, but had not been practised in systematic study. His lectures, when published, were severely criticised by writers of authority as savouring more of the historical novelist than of the trained inquirer. He was sensible of this weakness, and towards the end of his tenure of office became anxious to resign. His inability to reside prevented him from keeping up the intimacies with young men which, at the beginning of his course, he had rightly regarded as of great value.

In the beginning of 1864 Kingsley had an unfortunate controversy with John Henry Newman [q. v.] He had asserted in a review of Mr. Froude's 'History' in 'Macmillan's Magazine' for January 1860 that 'Truth, for its own sake, had never been a virtue with the Roman catholic clergy,' and attributed this opinion to Newman in particular. Upon Newman's protest, a correspondence followed, which was published by Newman (dated 31 Jan. 1864), with a brief, but cutting, comment. Kingsley replied in a pamphlet called 'What, then, does Dr. Newman mean?' which produced Newman's famous 'Apologia.' Kingsley was clearly both rush in his first statement and unsatisfactory in the apology which he published in 'Macmillan's Magazine' (this is given in the correspondence). That Newman triumphantly vindicated his personal character is also beyond doubt. The best that can be said for Kingsley is that he was aiming at a real blot on the philosophical system of his opponent; but, if so, it must be also allowed that he contrived to confuse the issue, and by obvious misunderstandings to give a complete victory to a powerful antagonist. With all his merits as an imaginative writer, Kingsley never showed any genuine dialectical ability.

Kingsley's health was now showing symptoms of decline. The 'Water Babies,' published in 1863, was, says Mrs. Kingsley, 'perhaps the last book, except his West Indian one, that he wrote with any real ease.' Rest and change of air had been strongly advised, and in the spring of 1864 he made a short tour in France with Mr. Froude. In 1865 he was forced by further illness to retire for three months to the coast of Norfolk. From 1868 the Rev. William Harrison was his curate, and lightened his work at Eversley. Mr. Harrison contributed some interesting reminiscences to the memoir (Kingsley, ii. 281–8). In 1869 Kingsley resigned his professorship at Cambridge, stating that his brains as well as his purse rendered the step necessary (ib. ii. 293). Relieved from the strain, he gave many lectures and addresses; he was president of the education section at the Social Science Congress held in October 1869 at Bristol, and delivered an inaugural address, which was printed by the Education League; about 100,000 copies were distributed. He had joined the league, which was generally opposed by the clergy, in despair of otherwise obtaining a national system of education, but withdrew to become a supporter of W. E. Forster's Education Bill. At the end of the year he sailed to the West Indies on the invitation of his friend Sir Arthur Gordon, then governor of Trinidad. His 'At Last,' a graphic description of his travels, appeared in 1870. In August 1869 Kingsley was appointed canon of Chester, and was installed in November. Next year he began his residence on 1 May, and found congenial society among the cathedral clergy. He started a botany class, which developed into the Chester Natural History Society. He gave some excellent lectures, published in 1872 as 'Town Geology,' and acted as guide to excursions into the country for botanical and geological purposes. A lecture delivered at Sion College upon the 'Theology of the Future' (published in 'Macmillan's Magazine') stated his views of the relations between scientific theories and theological doctrine, and for the later part of his life his interest in natural history determined a large part of his energy. He came to believe in Darwinism, holding that it was in full accordance with theology. Sanitary science also occupied much of his attention, and an address delivered by him in Birmingham in 1872, as president of the Midland Institute, led to the foundation of classes at the institute and at Saltley College (a place of training for schoolmasters) for the study of the laws of health.

In 1873 he was appointed canon of Westminster, and left Chester, to the general regret of his colleagues and the people. His son, Maurice, had gone to America in 1870, and was there employed as a railway engineer. Returning in 1873, he found his father much changed, and urged a sea-voyage and rest. At the beginning of 1874 Kingsley sailed for America, was received with the usual American hospitality in the chief cities, and gave some lectures. After a visit to Canada, he went to the west, saw Salt Lake city, San Francisco, the Yosemite valley, and had a severe attack of pleurisy, during which he stayed at Colorado Springs. It weakened him seriously, and after his return in August 1874 he had an attack at Westminster, by which he was further shaken. His wife had a dangerous illness soon afterwards. He was able to preach at Westminster in November, but was painfully changed in appearance. On 3 Dec. he went with his wife to Eversley, catching fresh cold just before. At Eversley he soon became dangerously ill. His wife was at the same time confined to her room with an illness supposed to be mortal, and he could only send messages for a time. He died peacefully on 23 Jan. 1875. He was buried at Eversley on 28 Jan., amid a great concourse of friends, including men of political and military distinction, villagers, and the huntsmen of the pack, with the horses and hounds outside the churchyard. Dean Stanley took part in the service, and preached a funeral sermon in Westminster Abbey (published) on 31 Jan. A cross was erected by his wife in Eversley churchyard. A Kingsley Memorial Fund provided a restoration of the church and a bust (by Mr. Woolner) in Westminster Abbey. A portrait is prefixed to the first volume of the 'Memoirs,' and an engraving from Mr. Woolner's bust to the second.

A civil list pension was granted to Mrs. Kingsley upon her husband's death, but she declined the queen's offer of rooms in Hampton Court Palace. She died at her residence

N 2

at Bishop's Tachbrook, near Leamington, on Saturday, 12 Dec. 1891, aged 77. Kingsley's four children, all born at Eversley, were: 1. Rose Georgina (b. 1845); 2. Maurice (b. 1847), now of New Rochelle in the state of New York; 3. Mary St. Leger (b. 1852), now wife of the Rev. W. Harrison, rector of Clovelly; and 4. Grenville Arthur (b. 1857), now resident in Queensland. Mrs. Harrison has written some well-known novels under the pseudonym 'Lucas Malet.'

Kingsley was above middle height, of spare but muscular and vigorous frame, with a strongly marked face, to which the deep lines between the brows gave an expression of sternness. He was troubled by a stammer. He prescribed and practised rules for its cure, but never overcame it in conversation, although in public speaking he could avoid it. The name of 'muscular Christianity,' first given in the 'Saturday Review,' and some of his verses suggested the tough athlete; but he had a highly nervous temperament, and his characteristic restlessness made it difficult for him to sit still through a meal (Martineau in *Kingsley*, i. 300). He had taken to smoking at college to soothe his nerves, and, finding the practice beneficial, acquired the love of tobacco which he expresses in 'Westward Ho!' His impetuous and excitable temper led him to overwork himself from the first, and his early writings gave promise of still higher achievements than he ever produced. The excessive fervour of his emotions caused early exhaustion, and was connected with his obvious weaknesses. He neither thought nor studied systematically, and his beliefs were more matters of instinct than of reason. He was distracted by the wide range and quickness of his sympathy. He had great powers of enjoyment. He had a passion for the beautiful in art and nature. No one surpassed him in first-hand descriptions of the scenery that he loved. He was enthusiastic in natural history, recognised every country sight and sound, and studied birds, beasts, fishes, and geology with the keenest interest. In theology he was a disciple of Maurice, attracted by the generous feeling and catholic spirit of his master. He called himself a 'Platonist' in philosophy, and had a taste for the mystics, liking to recognise a divine symbolism in nature. At the same time his scientific enthusiasm led him to admire Darwin, Professor Huxley, and Lyell without reserve. He corresponded with J. S. Mill, expressed the strongest admiration of his books, and shared in his desire for the emancipation of women. Certain tendencies of the advocates of women's rights caused him to draw back; but he was always anxious to see women admitted to medical studies. His domestic character was admirable, and he was a most energetic country parson. He loved and respected the poor, and did his utmost to raise their standard of life. 'He was,' said Matthew Arnold in a letter of condolence to his family, 'the most generous man I have ever known; the most forward to praise what he thought good, the most willing to admire, the most free from all thought of himself, in praising and in admiring, and the most incapable of being made ill-natured or even indifferent by having to support ill-natured attacks himself.' This quality made him attractive to all who met him personally, however averse to some of his views. It went along with a distaste for creeds embodying a narrow and distorted ideal of life—a distaste which biassed his judgment of ecclesiastical matters, and gives the impression that the ancient Greeks or Teutons had more of his real sympathies than the early Christians. He was a genuine poet, if not of the very highest kind. Some of his stirring lyrics are likely to last long, and his beautiful poem, 'Andromeda,' is perhaps the best example of the English hexameter.

Kingsley's works are: 1. 'The Saint's Tragedy,' 1848. 2. 'Twenty-five Village Sermons,' 1849. 3. 'Alton Locke,' 1850. 4. 'Yeast, a Problem,' 1851 (published in 'Fraser's Magazine' in 1848, and cut short to please the proprietors; for intended conclusion see *Kingsley*, i. 219). 5. 'Phaethon, or Loose Thoughts for Loose Thinkers,' 1852. 6. 'Sermons on National Subjects,' 1st ser. 1852, 2nd ser. 1854. 7. 'Hypatia,' 1853 (from 'Fraser's Magazine'). 8. 'Alexandria and her Schools' (lectures at Edinburgh), 1854. 9. 'Who causes Pestilence?' (four sermons), 1854. 10. 'Sermons for the Times,' 1855. 11. 'Westward Ho!' 1855. 12. 'Glaucus, or the Wonders of the Shore,' 1855. 13. 'The Heroes, or Greek Fairy Tales,' 1856. 14. 'Two Years Ago,' 1857. 15. 'Andromeda, and other Poems,' 1858; 'Poems' (1875) includes these and 'The Saint's Tragedy.' 16. 'The Good News of God,' a volume of sermons, 1859. 17. 'Miscellanies,' 1859. 18. 'Limits of Exact Science, as applied to History' (inaugural lecture at Cambridge), 1860. 19. 'Town and Country Sermons,' 1861. 20. 'Sermons on the Pentateuch,' 1863. 21. 'The Water Babies,' 1863. 22. 'David' (four sermons before the university), 1865. 23. 'Hereward the Wake,' 1866. 24. 'The Ancien Régime' (three lectures at the Royal Institution), 1867. 25. 'The Water of Life, and other Sermons,' 1867. 26. 'The Hermits' (Sunday Library, vol. ii.), 1868. 27. 'Discipline, and other Sermons,' 1868. 28. 'Madam How and Lady Why' (from 'Good Words for Children'), 1869. 29. 'At Last: a Christmas in the West Indies,' 1871. 30. 'Town Geology' (lectures at Chester), 1872. 31. 'Prose Idylls,' 1873. 32. 'Plays and Puritans,' 1873. 33. 'Health and Education,' 1874. 34. 'Westminster Sermons,' 1874. 35. 'Lectures delivered in America,' 1875. 36. 'All Saints' Day, and other Sermons' (edited by W. Harrison), 1878.

Kingsley also published some single sermons and pamphlets besides those mentioned in the text. Various selections have also been published. He wrote prefaces to Miss Wordsworth's translation of 'Tauler' and the 'Theologia Germanica,' and to Brooke's 'Fool of Quality.'

[Charles Kingsley: his Letters and Memories of his Life, by his Wife, 2 vols. 8vo, 1877; see also A. P. Stanley's Funeral Sermon; T. Hughes's Memoir prefixed to Alton Locke, 1881; Dr. Rigg's Memoir in Modern Anglican Theology, 3rd edit.; Life of F. D. Maurice, by his Son.]

L. S.

KINGSLEY, GEORGE HENRY (1827–1892), traveller and author, son of the Rev. Charles Kingsley of Battramsley House in the New Forest, was born at Barnack, Northamptonshire, 14 Feb. 1827. Charles Kingsley [q. v.] and Henry Kingsley [q. v.] were his brothers. He was educated at King's College School, London, at Edinburgh University, where he graduated M.D. in 1846, and at Paris, where he was slightly wounded during the barricades of 1848. Later in 1848 his activity in combating the outbreak of cholera in England was commemorated by his brother Charles in the portrait of Tom Thurnall in 'Two Years Ago.' He completed his medical education at Heidelberg, and returning to England about 1850, devoted himself from the commencement of his career to a special line of practice, the charge of individual patients. He adopted foreign travel as his method of treatment, and either in the capacity of medical adviser, or merely as travelling companion, he explored most of the countries of the world. Travelling in Polynesia between 1867 and 1870 with the young Earl of Pembroke, he recorded his experiences in the volume by which he is chiefly remembered, 'South Sea Bubbles by the Earl and the Doctor,' London, 1872, 8vo. Frank and unconventional in style, graphic and humorous in its descriptions, this book of travel and adventure won great and instant success, reaching a fifth edition by 1873.

Travelling subsequently with Lord Dunraven and other noblemen, Kingsley did much work as a field naturalist, and made numerous communications to the 'Field' under the signature of 'The Doctor.' A large amount of his manuscript on subjects connected with folklore and ethnology is now in the possession of his son. While acting as medical adviser to the Earl of Ellesmere's family, he had the partial care of the library at Bridgewater House, and in 1865 he edited, from a manuscript preserved there, Francis Thynne's 'Animadversions upon the Annotacions and Corrections of some Imperfections of Impressiones of Chaucer's Workes ... reprinted in 1598,' which was re-edited, with additions by Dr. Furnivall, for the Chaucer Society, in 1876.

Kingsley's genial manners, versatility, and store of picturesque information rendered him extremely popular in society. He was a keen and experienced sportsman, an excellent linguist, and a brilliant talker. Dying on Friday, 5 Feb. 1892, at his house, 7 Mortimer Road, Cambridge, he was buried on 15 Feb. in Highgate cemetery. He married in 1860 Mary Bailey, who died in April 1892, leaving a son, Charles, and a daughter.

Besides the works mentioned above Kingsley published: 1. 'Four Phases of 'Love. Translated from the German of Heyse,' 1857, 8vo. 2. 'A Gossip on a Sutherland Hillside,' 1861, 8vo: a descriptive sketch of a stalking expedition in Sutherland, included by Francis Galton in his 'Vacation Tourists and Notes of Travel.'

[Athenæum, 13 Feb. 1892; Cambridge Chron. 12 and 19 Feb.; Manchester Guardian, 8 Feb.; Brit. Mus. Cat.; private information.] T. S.

KINGSLEY, HENRY (1830–1876), novelist, third son of the Rev. Charles Kingsley, and younger brother of Charles Kingsley [q. v.] and George Henry Kingsley [q. v.], was born at Barnack, Northamptonshire, on 2 Jan. 1830. He was educated at King's College, London, and at Worcester College, Oxford, where he matriculated 6 March 1850. He left college in 1853 to go to the Australian goldfields with some fellow-students. After five years' desultory and unremunerative employment he returned to England, and soon afterwards made himself known by the spirited and successful novel, 'Geoffry Hamlyn,' in which his Australian experience was turned to account. It was followed in 1861 by 'Ravenshoe,' which also made its mark, and afterwards by many others. In 1864 he married his second cousin, Sarah Maria Kingsley, and settled at Wargrave, near Henley-on-Thames. He was afterwards for eighteen months editor of the 'Edinburgh Daily Review,' an organ of the free church. During his editorship the Franco-German war broke out, and Kingsley went out as correspondent for his paper. He was present at the battle of Sedan (1 Sept. 1870), and was the first Englishman to enter the town afterwards. After giving up the paper he settled for a time in London, and renewed his work as a novelist. He subsequently retired to the Attrees, Cuckfield, Sussex, where he died of a cancer in the tongue after some months' illness on 24 May 1876.

Kingsley's works are: 1. 'The Recollections of Geoffrey Hamlyn,' 3 vols. 1859. 2. 'Ravenshoe,' 3 vols. 1862. 3. 'Austin Elliott,' 2 vols. 1863 (French translation by Daurand Forgues, 1866). 4. 'The Hillyars and Burtons: a Story of two Families,' 3 vols. 1865. 5. 'Leighton Court : a Country House Story,' 2 vols. 1866. 6. 'Silcote of Silcotes,' 3 vols. 1867. 7. 'Mademoiselle Mathilde,' 3 vols. 1868. 8. 'Stretton,' 3 vols. 1869. 9. 'Old Margaret,' 2 vols. 1871. 10. 'The Lost Child' (illustrated by L. Frölich), 1871. 11. 'The Boy in Grey,' 1871. 12. 'Hetty, and other Stories,' 1871. 13. 'The Harveys,' 2 vols. 1872. 14. 'Hornby Mills, and other Stories,' 1872. 15. 'Valentin: a French Boy's Story of Sedan,' 1872. 16. 'Reginald Hetherege,' 3 vols. 1874. 17. 'Number Seventeen,' 2 vols. 1875. 18. 'The Grange Garden : a Romance,' 3 vols. 1876. 19. 'Fireside Studies,' 2 vols. 1876.

He also edited the Globe edition of 'Robinson Crusoe' in 1868, with a biographical introduction, and published in 1869 'Tales of Old Travels re-narrated.'

[Information from Mrs. Henry Kingsley.]

L. S.

KINGSLEY, WILLIAM (1698?–1769), lieutenant-general, son of William Kingsley and his wife Alice, daughter and heir of William Randolph of Maidstone, Kent, was born about 1698. He was a direct descendant from William Kingsley, archdeacon of Canterbury (d. 1647), from whom Charles Kingsley [q. v.] the novelist also traced his descent. The Kingsleys are stated to have been of Lancashire origin (BERRY), and a 'William Kingsley, gentleman, of Canterbury,' appears in a roll of Romancatholic estate-holders in Yorkshire (North Riding) during the period 1717–1780 (cf. Hist. MSS. Comm. 9th Rep. i. 346 a).

Kingsley seems to have become cornet in Honywood's dragoons (now 11th hussars) in May 1721. He was lieutenant and captain in the 3rd foot-guards (now Scots guards) in the company commanded by Lieutenant-colonel Wolfe, father of General James Wolfe. His commission bore date 29 June 1721 (Home Off. Mil. Entry Book, vol. xii. f. 238). He

was promoted captain-lieutenant in the same regiment in 1743; captain and lieutenant-colonel in 1745; brevet-colonel in 1750; and regimental major, with the rank of colonel of foot, on 29 Jan. 1751 (ib. vol. xxii. f. 173). He was aide-de-camp to his colonel, Lord Dunmore, at Dettingen, and was present with the 1st battalion of his regiment at the battle of Fontenoy, where a cannon-ball passed between his legs and killed four men behind him, on 11 May 1745. When the collected grenadier companies of the several regiments of guards marched from London for the north in the following December (the 'march to Finchley'), he was one of the officers sent ahead into Northamptonshire by the Duke of Cumberland to obtain information of the enemy's movements (HAMILTON, ii. 135). On 22 May 1756 Kingsley was made colonel of the 20th foot (now Lancashire fusiliers). James Wolfe, then lieutenant-colonel of the regiment at Devizes, wrote of him: 'Our new colonel is a sensible man, and very sociable and polite' (WRIGHT, p. 345). Kingsley was with his regiment in the Rochefort expedition of 1757, and afterwards went to Germany as major-general. He greatly distinguished himself at the battle of Minden on 1 Aug. 1759, at the head of a brigade composed of the 20th (Kingsley's), 25th (Home's), and 51st (Brudenell's) foot, which was very prominently engaged. 'Kingsley's grenadiers, as the 20th was popularly called, is said to have fought among some rose-gardens or hedges, a circumstance still commemorated by the regimental custom of wearing 'Minden roses' in the caps on each anniversary of the day. The regiment had six officers and eighty men killed and eleven officers and 224 men wounded, and was excused from all further duty on account of its losses. A general order of three days' later date announced that 'Kingsley's regiment of the British line will resume its share of the duty at its own request.' Kingsley was afterwards engaged at Ziezenberg and elsewhere. He became a lieutenant-general in December 1760, and was appointed to the command of a secret expedition, with William Draper [q. v.] as his quartermaster-general. The force was at first destined for eastward of the Cape, but was afterwards ordered to rendezvous at Quiberon for an attempt on Belle Isle on the coast of Brittany. The death of George II and other circumstances delayed the expedition, which was eventually countermanded (BEATSON, ii. 420, iii. 167 n.). Kingsley was not actively employed again. He was an outspoken, independent Englishman, extremely popular with his soldiers, and an active freemason. He was over seventy years of age and unmarried at the time of his death at Kingsley House, Stone Street, Maidstone, on 9 Oct. 1769 (*Scots Mag.* 1769). He was buried in the family vault at Kennington Ashford, Kent (see RUSSELL, *Hist. of Maidstone*, p. 340).

Kingsley's portrait was painted by Sir Joshua Reynolds in March 1760, and two engraved portraits are catalogued by Evans (*Cat. Engraved Portraits*, vol. ii.) Marginal notes by him appear in a history of the seven years' war in possession of the Hon. Mrs. Stopford Sackville (*Hist. MSS. Comm. 9th Rep.* iii. 81 *a*), and some of his letters are in British Museum Addit. MSS. 32732, 32890, 32918.

[Berry's Genealogies (Kent), p. 306; cf. Hist. MSS. Comm. 9th Rep. i. 346 *a*; also Hasted's Kent, fol. ed. iii. 268 *n*. Home Office Military Entry Books in Public Rec. Office, London, vols. xii–xxii., various; Georgian Era, vol. ii.; 'The Guards at Fontenoy,' in Colburn's United Service Mag. February 1868; Hamilton's Gren. Guards (London, 1872), vol. ii.; Wright's Life of Wolfe (London, 1864); Beatson's Nav. and Mil. Memoirs (London, 1794), vols. ii–iii.; Gent. Mag. 1759 pp. 385 et seq., 1760 pp. 44, 155, 485, 541; Cannon's Hist. Rec. 20th (East Devon) Regt.; Memoirs of Sir James Campbell (Callendar) (Edinburgh, 1832), vol. i.; Smith's Story of the 20th Regiment, 1688–1888 (London, 1888); Scots Mag. 1769, also afford incidental notices.]

H. M. C.

KINGSMILL, ANDREW (1538–1569), puritan divine, son of John Kingsmill of Sidmonton in Hampshire, was probably born at Sidmonton in 1538. He matriculated on 23 Aug. 1553 at Corpus Christi College, Oxford, and in 1558 was elected fellow of All Souls' College. He was admitted B.C.L. in the beginning of 1563, and acquired a high reputation as a student of civil law, but gradually turned towards divinity. He soon knew by heart considerable portions of the Old and New Testaments in Greek, and was a keen student of Hebrew. 'A young bachelor of All Souls' who frequently supplied the sermon at St. Mary's at the beginning of Elizabeth's reign is identified as Kingsmill by Wood. In order to qualify himself thoroughly for the ministry Kingsmill spent three years at Geneva, and removing thence to Lausanne, died there in September 1569. His papers came into the hands of his friend Francis Mills, sub-warden of All Souls, who describes him, in a short sketch of his life, as 'a phoenix among lawyers, and a rare example of godliness among gentlemen' (*View of Man's Estate*, Pref.)

Mills edited the following works by Kingsmill: 1. 'A Viewe of Mans Estate, wherein the greate Mercie of God in Mans free Justifi-

cation by Christ is verie comfortably declared. By Andrewe Kyngesmill. Divided into Chapiters in suche sorte as maie beste serve for the commoditie of the Reader. Whereunto is annexed a Godlie Advise given by the Author touchyng Mariage . . . London, by H. Bynneman,' 1574, 1576, 1580, 8vo. The 'Advise' is addressed to the author's sister, who had lost her first husband. 2. 'A most excellent and comfortable Treatise for all such as are any maner of way either troubled in Mynde or afflicted in Bodie. Made by Andrew Kingesmyl, Gentleman, sometime fellow of Alsoule Colledge in Oxford. Imprinted at London by Christopher Barkar,' 1577, 1578, 1585, 8vo. This also was written by Kingsmill for his sister. Printed along with this tract are two treatises usually ascribed to Kingsmill, but Mills, in his prefatory note, declares himself unable to conjecture the author of the second treatise, and says nothing about the third. They are entitled: 'A verie and learned Exhortation to suffer patiently all Afflictions for the Gospel of Christ Jesus,' 'A Conference conteyning a Conflict had with Satan,' &c. Wood ascribes to Kingsmill 'A Sermon on St. John iii. 16' (perhaps the 'View'); 'Resolutions concerning the Sacraments;' 'Resolutions of some Questions relating to Bishops, Priests, and Deacons,' and papers on 'other matters relating to the Reformation.' Strype mentions a long letter written by Kingsmill to Archbishop Parker 'against urging the habits.'

[Wood's Athenæ, ed. Bliss, i. 373; Fasti, i. 162; Boase's Reg. of Univ. of Oxford, i. 238, 250, n. ii. 10; Strype's Parker (Clar. Press, 1821), i. 313; Catalogues of Brit. Mus. and Bodleian Libraries; Lowndes's Bibliog. Manual.] R. B.

KINGSMILL, SIR ROBERT BRICE (1730–1805), admiral, son of Charles Brice, a captain in the army, was made a lieutenant on 29 April 1756, was appointed commander of the Swallow sloop in February 1761, and was confirmed in the rank on 3 July, consequent on his capture of a 10-gun privateer on the coast of France. In 1762 he commanded the Basilisk bomb at the reduction of Martinique and St. Lucia by Sir George Rodney, and on 26 May was posted to the Crescent. He returned to England in 1764. He had already married Elizabeth, only daughter of Hugh Corry of Newton, co. Down, and of his wife, Frances, only daughter of Sir William Kingsmill (*d.* 1698), knight, of Sidmonton, Hampshire. On the death of her last surviving maternal uncle, William Kingsmill, a bachelor, in 1766, Brice's wife succeeded to her grandfather's estates; on which Brice assumed by act of parliament the surname of

Kingsmill by royal license. He commanded the Vigilant of 64 guns in the action off Ushant on 27 July 1778 [see KEPPEL, AUGUSTUS, VISCOUNT], but after the courts-martial quitted the ship in disgust at the action of the admiralty. On the change of ministry in 1782 he was appointed to the Elizabeth, which after the peace was employed as a guardship. He was elected M.P. for Tregony, Cornwall, on 5 April 1784. In the Spanish armament of 1790 he commanded the Duke of 90 guns. On 1 Feb. 1793 he was promoted to be rear-admiral, and was shortly afterwards appointed commander-in-chief on the coast of Ireland, an arduous, though not brilliant post, which he held continuously till 1800, being advanced meanwhile to the rank of vice-admiral on 4 July 1794, and of admiral on 14 Feb. 1799. He was created a baronet on 24 Nov. 1800, and died without issue at Sidmouth on 23 Nov. 1805.

His brother Edward, principal surveyor of revenue at Belfast, also assumed the surname of Kingsmill in December 1787, and his son Robert succeeded his uncle as second baronet. On the second baronet's death in 1823 the title became extinct.

[Charnock's Biog. Nav. vi. 485; Ralfe's Nav. Biog. i. 354; Burke's Dormant and Extinct Baronetcies.] J. K. L.

KINGSMILL, THOMAS (*fl.* 1605), regius professor of Hebrew at Oxford, was seventh son of Sir John Kingsmill of Fribook, Hampshire. Entering Magdalen College, Oxford, as a demy, he graduated B.A. in 1559, M.A. in 1564, and supplicated for the B.D. degree in 1572 (*Oxf. Univ. Reg.*, Oxf. Hist. Soc., vol. i.) He was probationer fellow from 1559 to 1568, natural philosophy lecturer in 1563, Hebrew lecturer in 1565, and junior dean of arts in 1567. On 15 Dec. 1565 he was appointed public orator, and on 2 Nov. 1570 regius professor of Hebrew. He became mad for a time, and was obliged to resign his professorship in 1591.

He wrote: 1. 'A Complaint against Securitie in these perilous Times,' 8vo, London, 1602. 2. 'Classicum Pœnitentiale (Tractatus de Scandalo, &c.),' 2 pts. 4to, Oxford, 1605. 3. 'The Drunkards Warning: a Sermon,' 8vo, London, 1631.

[Wood's Athenæ Oxon. (Bliss), i. 758; Bloxam's Reg. of Magd. Coll., Oxford, iv. 153; Le Neve's Fasti, iii. 514, 534.] G. G.

KINGSNORTH, RICHARD (d. 1677), baptist minister, seems to have been a Kentish farmer, although it has been suggested that he was connected with the cloth-making trade. He was led to adopt baptist views through the arguments of the Rev. Francis Cornwell, vicar of Marden, Kent, who announced his own conversion to baptist views in a visitation sermon at Cranbrook in 1644. Christopher Blackwood [q. v.], vicar of Staplehurst, Kent, undertook to confute Cornwell, but, while considering his answer, also became a convert. After being baptised by William Jeffery of Sevenoaks, Blackwood and Kingsnorth founded a baptist congregation which met at Spilshill House, the residence of Kingsnorth, about half a mile from Staplehurst Church. Kingsnorth and most of the congregation were general baptists, and on this account he was chosen and ordained minister. Blackwood, who held the doctrine of particular election, assisted in the ministry until he joined the parliamentary army and went to Ireland.

The church increased under Kingsnorth, spread to adjacent parts, and held meetings at Headcorn, Smarden, and Frittenden. Kingsnorth died in 1677, at which time five of his sons were engaged in the ministry. He is said to have written two works vindicating the doctrine of universal redemption, entitled 'The Pearl of Truth, found out between two Rocks of Error,' printed in 1670 (HAZLEWOOD, *Smarden,* p. 198); and 'Gospel Certainty of Everlasting Felicity,' but they do not appear to be extant.

After his death a division arose in the church on the subject of the Trinity, and a separation was agreed upon. Two of Kingsnorth's sons, with several ministers and members of the congregation, withdrew and formed a separate church, meeting at Biddenden and Frittenden, while a brother and two other sons remained and upheld the leading tenets of the original foundation. A long list of elders and ministers is given in Hazlewood's 'Memorials of Smarden.'

[Taylor's General Baptists, i. 286-8; Ivimey's English Baptists, ii. 233-7; Bailey's Struggles for Conscience, or Religious Annals of Staplehurst, pp. 12-15; Hazlewood's Memorials of Smarden, pp. 198-9; Kent Examiner and Chronicle, 9 Dec. 1887; information from Mr. W. Tarbutt.] B. P.

KINGSTHORPE, RICHARD (*fl.* 1224), Franciscan. [See INGWORTH.]

KINGSTON, DUKES OF. [See PIERREPONT.]

KINGSTON, self-styled DUCHESS OF. [See CHUDLEIGH, ELIZABETH, 1720-1788.]

KINGSTON, EARLS OF, in the peerage of England. [See PIERREPONT.]

KINGSTON, EARL OF, in the peerage of Ireland. [See KING, ROBERT, second EARL, 1754-1799.]

KINGSTON, VISCOUNTS, in the peerage of Scotland. [See SETON.]

KINGSTON, LORDS. [See KING, JOHN, d. 1676, first LORD; KING, ROBERT, d. 1693, second LORD.]

KINGSTON, SIR ANTHONY (1519-1556), provost-marshal in Cornwall, born in 1519, was the son of Sir William Kingston [q. v.] of Gloucestershire, comptroller of the king's household. Anthony served at the head of a thousand Gloucestershire men under the Duke of Norfolk in the suppression of the Pilgrimage of Grace, 1536-7, and fought in the defeat (13 Oct. 1536) of the rebels at Louth. He was knighted by Henry VIII, 18 Oct. 1537, probably as a reward for his services. He held small offices about the court, such as that of serjeant of the king's hawks, at 2s. a day, and received grants of land belonging to the suppressed monasteries in Gloucestershire, including a regrant of the site of the Cistercian abbey of Flaxley.

After the death of Sir William Courtenay in 1535, Kingston married his widow, Mary, daughter of Sir John Gainsford, and left Gloucestershire to reside at Chudleigh, Devonshire, which, with Honiton, belonged to his wife's jointure. When the western rebellion broke out in 1549, under Edward VI—the rebels demanding the restoration of the old liturgy—Kingston was appointed provost-marshal of the king's army in Cornwall, and suppressed the outbreak at the expense of much bloodshed. His conduct has been compared with that of Judge Jeffreys. He is said to have entertained the mayor of Bodmin at a banquet and to have hanged him after dinner on the gallows which the mayor had himself been directed to make ready. The mayors of Clevedon and St. Ives shared a like fate. Carew defends Kingston on the score of the guilt of his victims, and says, 'He did nothing herein as a judge by discretion, but as an officer by direction' (CAREW, Survey of Cornwall, p. 294). No other writers, however, take this view. Kingston was a member of Edward VI's council for the marches of Wales. When Lady Jane Grey succeeded Edward, she sent orders to Kingston and Sir John St. Loe to levy forces and march towards Buckinghamshire (16 July 1553), but her reign was over before they had time to obey (Hist. MSS. Comm. 3rd Rep. p. 153). In 1552 Kingston was cited before Hooper, bishop of Gloucester, on a charge of adultery. Burnet quotes the case as an instance of Hooper's impartial administration of affairs in his diocese. At first Kingston refused to appear, and when at

length he came, he beat and abused the bishop, who sternly rebuked him, fined him 500l., and forced him to do penance (BURNET, Reformation, ed. 1829, iii. 402). He afterwards owned that Hooper had converted him from his evil life, and took a touching farewell of the bishop (8 Feb. 1555) before his martyrdom (FROUDE, Hist. vi. 320). Kingston sat in the House of Commons for Gloucestershire in the parliaments of 1545, 1552-3, and 1555. He was knight-marshal in the parliament of 1555 and 'a main stickler in it' for the protestant religion, as Burnet infers from his action against the catholic rebels in the west, under Edward (Reformation, ii. 650). It is said that he took the keys of the house away from the serjeant, with, it seems, the approval of the majority. But on 10 Dec., the day after parliament was dissolved, he was sent to the Tower on a charge of conspiring to put Elizabeth on the throne (Hist. MSS. Comm. 5th Rep. pp. xvi-155). He remained there till the 23rd, when he submitted, asked pardon, and was discharged (cf. MACHYN, Diary, Camd. Soc., p. 347). In the next year, 1556, however, Kingston was concerned in the plot to rob the exchequer in order to provide funds for the conspiracy devised by Sir Henry Dudley with the object of making Elizabeth queen and marrying her to Courtenay, earl of Devonshire (FROUDE, Hist. vi. 6-11). Six confederates were executed, but Kingston died 14 April 1556 at Cirencester, Froude says probably by his own hand from despair (Hist. vi. 442), while journeying from Devonshire to stand his trial in London. He left two illegitimate sons, Anthony and Edmund, on whom by a deed of feoffment he settled part of his estates in 5147 (cf. LODGE, Illustrations, i. 16).

[Polwhele's History of Cornwall, iv. 64, 65; Parochial History of Cornwall (Davies and Gilbert), i. 88, ii. 197; Bristol and Gloucestershire Archaeol. Soc. Trans. vi. 284 sq; Baker's Chronicle, p. 305; Cleaveland's History of the Courtenay Family, p. 29; Strype's Memorials, i, i. 15, ii. i. 9, ii. ii. 161; Fuller's Church History, iv. 49; Calendar of State Papers, Dom., Henry VIII, x. 333, 389, xi. 155, 290, 374; Rudder's Gloucestershire, pp. 146, 554; Tanner's Notitia Monastica, pp. xi, xxvii, xxviii; Metcalfe's Knights, p. 68; Nicolas's Privy Purse Expenses of Hen. VIII, pp. 226, 229.]   E. T. B.

KINGSTON, RICHARD (fl. 1700), political pamphleteer, was born about 1635. According to his own statements he was a M.A. of some university, and was ordained by the Bishop of Galloway, 17 July 1662, at Westminster, but Matthew Smith [q. v.] in 1700, when engaged with Kingston in a bitter political controversy, charged him, with some show of justification, with having forged his letters of orders (SMITH, *Reply to a Modest Answer*, p. 11). All the proof Kingston could bring of their validity was a certificate signed by one Thomas Beesly, asserting that he had been ordained at the same time, but Beesly had in 1700 been dead three years. Smith, among other charges, tells a scandalous story of Kingston's conduct in the west of England; but he does not seem to have had any benefice in the diocese of Exeter, as is thereby implied.

In 1665 Kingston became minister at St. James's, Clerkenwell, and worked hard during the plague, but he resigned this preferment before 17 Sept. 1667. In 1678 he received the living of Henbury in Gloucestershire, and on 6 Feb. 1681-2 was made chaplain in ordinary to Charles II. He asserts that a prebend and a rectory were added to Henbury. What the prebend was is uncertain, but he seems in 1688 to have been rector of Raydon in Suffolk. Kingston also states that he suffered for preaching against the Romanists. He remained at Henbury, where he had a small estate, till the revolution, when he sold his property and came up to London. He was soon lured by a pension to write for the government, but his pension fell into arrears and he suffered extreme poverty. A petition from him dated 1689 states that 600l. was due to him, that he had assisted as a witness at the conviction of three traitors, that he had brought 1,225l. into the treasury by the seizure of French silks, and that he had printed thirteen books on behalf of the government at his own expense.

In 1700 Kingston attacked Smith, who had just published his 'Memoirs of Secret Service,' and a violent controversy ensued. Kingston always attributed Smith's works to Tom Brown (1663-1704) [q. v.]. Kingston also intervened in the controversy which raged in 1707-9 about the so-called French Prophets. In 1707 his attack on Dr. John Freind's vindication of the Earl of Peterborough's conduct in Spain appeared, and he was promptly arrested by an order of the House of Lords. He was, however, released, 19 Jan. 1707-8, and the attorney-general was instructed to prosecute him. Kingston was married (perhaps he was the man who married Elizabeth Webb at St. James's, Clerkenwell, 28 Jan. 1667-8, see *Regist. of St. James's, Clerkenwell*, Harl. Soc. 138, cf. 189), and in 1689 had nine children. An engraved portrait of Kingston is said by Bromley to have formed the frontispiece to the 'Pillulæ Pestilentiales,' but it has disappeared from the copy in the British Museum.

Kingston wrote: 1. 'Pillulæ Pestilentiales,

a Sermon at St. Paul's,' London, 1665. 2. 'The Cause and Cure of Offences,' a sermon, London, 1682, 4to. 3. 'Vivat Rex,' a sermon preached before the Mayor of Bristol after the discovery of the Rye House plot, London, 1683, 4to. 4. 'God's Sovereignty and Man's Duty asserted,' London, 1688. 5. 'A True History of the several Designs and Conspiracies against his Majesties Sacred Person and Government from 1688 to 1697,' London, 1698. 6. 'Tyranny detected, and the late Revolution justified,' London, 1689. 7. 'A Modest Answer to Captain Smith's Immodest Memorial of Secret Service,' London, 1700. 8. 'Impudence, Lying, and Forgery detected and Chastiz'd,' London, 1700, an answer to Smith, and the chief source of information respecting Kingston's history. 9. 'A Discourse on Divine Providence,' London, 1702. 10. 'Impartial Remarks upon Dr. Freind's Account of the Earl of Peterborough's Conduct in Spain,' London, 1706. 11. 'Enthusiastick Impostors no Divinely Inspired Prophets,' part i. 1707, part ii. 1709. 12. 'Apophthegmata Curiosa, or Reflections, Sentences, and Maxims,' London, 1709. Kingston also mentions that he wrote a work called 'Cursory Remarks.'

[Pink's Clerkenwell, pp. 68, 283, 619-21 (citing Notes and Queries); Luttrell's Brief Hist. Rel. vi. 247-8; Bromley's Cat. of Engraved Portraits, p. 136; Matthew Smith's Works; Kingston's Works.] W. A. J. A.

KINGSTON, Sir WILLIAM (d. 1540), constable of the Tower, was of a Gloucestershire family, settled at Painswick. A brother George is mentioned in the inquisition taken after his death. William appears to have been a yeoman of the guard before June 1509 (*Letters and Papers Henry VIII*, i. 248). In 1512 he was an under-marshal in the army; went to the Spanish coast; was with Dr. William Knight [q. v.] in October of that year at San Sebastian, and discussed with him the course to be pursued with the disheartened English forces who had come to Spain under Thomas Grey, second marquis of Dorset [q. v.] (ib. p. 3451). He fought well at Flodden, was knighted in 1513, became sewer to the king, and later (1521) was carver (ib. iii. 1899). He seems to have been with Sir Richard Wingfield, the ambassador, at the French court early in 1520, for Wingfield wrote to Henry VIII (20 April) that the dauphin 'took a marvellous pleasure in young Kyngston, whom after he had seen once he called him beau fils, whom he would sometime have kneel down and sometime stand up' (ib. iii. 752). Kingston took part in the tilting at the Field of the Cloth of Gold, and

was at the meeting with Charles V in July. Henry seems to have liked him, and presented him with a horse of very great value. For the next year or two he was a diligent country magistrate and courtier, levying men for the king's service in the west, and living when in London with the Black Friars (ib. III. ii. App. 28, III. ii. 3274). In April 1523 Kingston joined Dacre on the disturbed northern frontier, and with Sir Ralf Ellerker had the most dangerous posts assigned him (ib. pp. 2955, 2960); he was present at the capture of Cessford, the stronghold of the Kers, on 18 May (ib. p. 3039). He returned rather suddenly to London, and was made knight of the king's body and captain of the guard. On 30 Aug. 1523 he landed at Calais in the army of the Duke of Suffolk (ib. p. 3288). Surrey wrote from the north lamenting his absence. On 28 May 1524 he became constable of the Tower at a salary of 100l. He appears among those who signed the petition to Clement VII for the hastening of the divorce, 13 July 1530.

In November 1530 Kingston went down to Sheffield Park, Nottinghamshire, to take charge of Wolsey. The cardinal is said to have been alarmed at his coming because it had been foretold that he should meet his death at Kingston. Kingston tried to reassure him, and was with him at the time of his death, riding to London to acquaint the king with the circumstances (CAVENDISH, Life of Wolsey, ed. 1827, pp. 371 sq.) On 11 Oct. 1532 he landed at Calais with Henry on the way to the second interview with Francis at Boulogne, and on 29 May 1533 he took an official part in the coronation of Anne Boleyn. He is said to have been of Catherine's party, though the emperor not unreasonably distrusted him (cf. FRIEDMANN, Anne Boleyn, ii. 61; Letters and Papers, viii. 327). On 21 Feb. 1535-1536 Kingston wrote to Lord Lisle, an old Gloucestershire neighbour, ' I have done with play, but with my lord of Carlisle, penny glerk, this is our pastime ' (ib. x. 336). He seems to have become prematurely old, but continued to be constable. He received Anne Boleyn 2 May 1536, when committed a prisoner to the Tower, and with his wife took charge of her and reported her conversations to Cromwell. To him Anne joked about the size of her neck and the skill of the executioner (ib. pp. 793, 797-8, 910). Kingston was made controller of the household 9 March 1539, and knight of the Garter 24 April following. He had many small grants, and on the dissolution of monasteries received the site of the Cistercian abbey of Flaxley, Gloucestershire. He died at Painswick, Gloucestershire, 14 Sept. 1540, and was buried there. He married, first, Elizabeth, of whom nothing seems known, and by her had Anthony, who is separately noticed, and Bridget, married to Sir George Baynham of Clearwell, Gloucestershire; secondly, Mary, daughter of Sir Richard Scrope of Upsall, Yorkshire, and widow of Sir Edward Jerningham of Somerleyton, Suffolk.

[Metcalfe's Knights; Nicolas's Testamenta Vetusta; Lodge's Illustr. of Brit Hist. i. 19; Chron. of Calais (Camd. Soc.), pp. 33, 41; Wriothesley's Chron. (Camd. Soc.), pp. 36, 37, 94 ; Fuller's Church Hist. v. 178 ; Trans. of the Bristol and Gloucestershire Arch. Soc. vi. 284 sq.; authorities quoted.]   W. A. J. A.

KINGSTON, WILLIAM HENRY GILES (1814-1880), novelist, born in Harley Street, London, 28 Feb. 1814, was eldest son of Lucy Henry Kingston, and grandson by the mother's side of Sir Giles Rooke [q. v.], justice of the common pleas. His father was in business in Oporto, and there for many years the son lived, making frequent voyages to England, and contracting a lifelong affection for the sea. He entered his father's business, but soon indulged his natural bent for writing. His newspaper articles on Portugal were translated into Portuguese, and assisted the conclusion of the commercial treaty with Portugal in 1842, when he received from Donna Maria da Gloria an order of Portuguese knighthood and a pension. His first book was ' The Circassian Chief,' a story published in 1844, and while still living in Oporto, he wrote ' The Prime Minister,' an historical novel, and ' Lusitanian Sketches,' descriptions of travels in Portugal Settling in England, he interested himself in the emigration movement, edited in 1844 ' The Colonist ' and ' The Colonial Magazine and East India Review,' was honorary secretary of a colonisation society, wrote in 1848 ' Some Suggestions for a System of General Emigration,' lectured on colonisation in 1849, published a manual for colonists, ' How to Emigrate,' in 1850, and visited the western highlands on behalf of the emigration commissioners. He was afterwards a zealous volunteer and worked actively for the improvement of the condition of seamen. But from 1850 his chief occupation was writing books for boys, or editing boys' annuals and weekly periodicals. The ' Union Jack,' a paper for boys, he started only a few months before his death. The best known of his stories, which numbered more than a hundred, are: ' Peter the Whaler,' 1851; ' Blue Jackets,' 1854; ' Digby Heathcote,' 1860; ' The Cruise of the Frolic,' 1860 ; ' The Fireships,' 1862; ' Foxholme Hall,' 1867; ' Ben Burton,' 1872 ; ' The Three Midshipmen,'

1873; 'The Three Lieutenants,' 1875; 'The Three Commanders,' 1876; and 'The Three Admirals,' 1878; 'Kidnapping in the Pacific,' 1879; and 'Hendriks the Hunter,' 1884. He travelled widely on the ordinary routes of travel, and described his experience for the young in 'Western Wanderings,' a Canadian tour, 1859; 'My Travels in Many Lands' (France, Italy, and Portugal), 1862; 'The Western World,' 1874; and 'A Yacht Voyage round England,' 1879. His popular records of adventure and of discovery included: 'Adventures in the Far West,' 1881; in Africa, 1883; in India, 1884; in Australia, 1885; a 'Life of Captain Cook,' 1871; 'Great African Travellers,' 1874; a 'Popular History of the Navy,' 1876; 'Notable Voyages from Columbus to Parry,' 1880, subsequently brought down to 1885; 'Livingstone's Travels,' 1886; 'Mungo Park's Travels,' 1886. He translated several of Jules Verne's stories from the French, and wrote many historical tales dealing with almost all periods and countries, from 'Eldol the Druid,' 1874, and 'Jovinian,' a tale of Early Papal Rome,' 1877, downwards, and undertook some popular historical compilations like 'Half-Hours with the Kings and Queens of England,' 1876. His writings occupy nine pages and a half of the British Museum Catalogue. They were very popular; his tales were quite innocuous, but most of them proved ephemeral. Feeling his health failing, he wrote a farewell letter in touching terms to the boys for whom he had written so much and so long on 2 Aug. 1880, and died three days later at Stormont Lodge, Willesden, near London.

[Boy's Own Paper, 11 Sept. 1880, which contains his portrait; preface to his novel James Braithwaite, 1882; Athenæum, 14 Aug. 1880; Times, 10 Aug. 1880.]   J. A. H.

KINLOCH, GEORGE RITCHIE (1796?–1877), editor of 'Ancient Scottish Ballads,' was born at Stonehaven, Kincardineshire, about 1796, and became a lawyer. He was clerk to three successive advocates-depute, and at Stirling, in 1817 or 1818, he acted for an absent crown-agent. For several years he was secretary to Scott's friend, George Cranstoun, Lord Corehouse, enjoying also the friendship of Lord Colonsay. Appointed in 1842 assistant-keeper of the register of deeds in Edinburgh Register House, he became head of his department in 1851, and retired in 1869. A noted philanthropist, Kinloch was for many years treasurer of the Patterson and Pope fund for relief of deserving poor. Dr. Jamieson, in the preface to the supplementary volume of his 'Scottish Dictionary,' 1825, acknowledged

indebtedness to him for valuable help. Kinloch died at Edinburgh, 19 April 1877.

In 1824 Kinloch projected, without publishing, a 'Collection of Scottish Proverbs.' In 1827 appeared his 'Ancient Scottish Ballads, recovered from Tradition, and never before published.' This collection fully deserves the commendation given to it by Scott in 'Border Minstrelsy,' i. 83. A miscellaneous 'Ballad Book' of little value, issued the same year, was reprinted in 1885. For the Maitland Club Kinloch edited, in 1830, Dr. Archibald Pitcairne's very droll and whimsical production. 'Babell; a Satirical Poem on the Proceedings of the General Assembly in 1692;' and the 'Chronicle of Fife, being the Diary of Mr. John Lamont of Newton, 1649–1671.' In 1848 he published 'Reliquiæ Antiquæ Scoticæ.'

[Scotsman newspaper of 21 April 1877; information from Mr. Thomas G. Stevenson, Edinburgh, and Mr. James O. M'Laren, Helensburgh.]   T. B.

KINLOCH, LORD (1801–1872), Scottish judge. [See PENNEY, WILLIAM.]

KINLOSS, LORD. [See BRUCE, EDWARD, 1549?–1611.]

KINMONT WILLIE (*fl.* 1596), border moss-trooper. [See ARMSTRONG, WILLIAM.]

KINNAIRD, ARTHUR FITZGERALD, tenth BARON KINNAIRD (1814–1887), philanthropist, third son of Charles Kinnaird, eighth baron Kinnaird (q. v.), was born at Rossie Priory, Perthshire, on 8 July 1814, and entered at Eton in 1829. Receiving an appointment in the foreign office, he was attached to the embassy at St. Petersburg from July 1835 to September 1837, and was for a time private secretary to the ambassador, the Earl of Durham. In 1837 he became a partner in the banking-house of Ransom & Co., Pall Mall East, London, in succession to his uncle, the Hon. Douglas James William Kinnaird [q. v.] He ultimately became head of the firm, which latterly was styled Ransom, Bouverie & Co. As a liberal he sat in the House of Commons for Perth from 29 July 1837 till August 1839. He was re-elected for that city on 15 May 1852, and continued to represent it until 7 Jan. 1878, when he succeeded his brother, George William Fox Kinnaird [q. v.], as Baron Kinnaird. While in the House of Commons he spoke frequently on Indian questions, of which he had a special knowledge, and he was a strong opponent of the bill for legalising marriage with a deceased wife's sister. He was keenly interested in all movements concerning the well-being of the working classes. There was no more familiar figure at the May meetings. In all efforts for raising women in the social scale he took a special interest, actively labouring in their behalf in connection with homes, refuges, and reformatories. Among the public institutions with which he was more especially connected were the Church Missionary Society, the Malta Protestant College, the Lock Hospital, Dr. Barnardo's Homes, the London City Mission, and the Aged Christians Society. He died at 2 Pall Mall East, London, on 26 April 1887, leaving issue one son, Arthur Fitzgerald, the present Baron Kinnaird, and five daughters.

Kinnaird was the author of: 1. 'Bengal: its Landed Tenure and Police System,' speech in the House of Commons, 11 June 1857. 2. 'Nine Months in the United States during the Crisis,' by G. Fisch, with an introduction by the Hon. A. Kinnaird, 1863. 3. His speech at the meeting of the Columbia mission, 27 Feb. 1862, was also printed.

His wife, MARY JANE, LADY KINNAIRD (1816–1888), philanthropist, daughter of William Henry Hoare of the Grove, Mitcham, Surrey, a London banker, was known for the interest she took in religious and educational works at home and missionary efforts abroad. She was born at Blatherwick Park, Northamptonshire, on 14 March 1816, and in 1821 went to reside with her maternal uncle, the Hon. and Rev. Baptist W. Noel, at Hornsey. In 1841 she instituted the St. John's Training School for Domestic Servants, with a branch at Brighton, an institution which was very successful. After her marriage, 28 June 1843, she held meetings in conjunction with her husband for philanthropic and religious purposes at 2 Pall Mall East. In 1848 she edited a volume of 'Servants' Prayers.' With Lady Canning she was associated in sending nursing and other aid to the wounded in the Crimean war. She was one of the founders of the British Ladies' Female Emigration Society, of the Foreign Evangelisation Society, of the Calvin Memorial Hall at Geneva, of the Union for Prayer, of the Zenana Bible and Medical Mission, and the Young Women's Christian Association. She died at Plaistow Lodge, near Bromley, Kent, on 1 Dec. 1888.

[Times, 27 April 1887, p. 9, 4 Dec. 1888, p. 10; Illustrated London News, 7 May 1887, p. 520; Foreign Office List, 1874, p. 125; Rock, 29 April 1887, p. 5; Record, 29 April 1887, p. 400; Fraser's Mary Jane Kinnaird, 1890, with portraits of Lord and Lady Kinnaird.] G. C. B.

KINNAIRD, CHARLES, eighth LORD KINNAIRD (1780–1826), the eldest surviving son of George, seventh baron Kinnaird, and of Elizabeth, only daughter of Griffin Ran-

som, banker, of Westminster, was born on 8 April 1780, and educated at the universities of Edinburgh, Cambridge, and Glasgow. His father's connection with the whigs enabled him to obtain a seat in the House of Commons as member for Leominster in 1802. From that time till the death of his father in 1805 he voted consistently with the whigs, and rendered valuable aid to the party in the repeated attacks made upon the Addington ministry. On his succession to the title his seat became vacant, but at the general election in 1806 he was chosen one of the Scottish representative peers, a position which had been held by his father. In 1807 he began the erection of Rossie Priory in the Carse of Gowrie, Perthshire, still the principal seat of the Kinnaird family in Scotland. Kinnaird resided much on the continent, and his refined taste led him to secure many works of art dispersed during the Napoleonic wars. The picture gallery at Rossie Priory contains both pictures by the old masters, and portraits of contemporaries, including Gainsborough's Sir William Johnstone Pulteney and Reynolds's splendid portrait of Sheridan. Kinnaird died 11 Dec. 1826. In May 1806 he married Lady Olivia Fitzgerald, youngest daughter of the second Duke of Leinster, and by her he had three sons and two daughters—George William Fox, ninth lord Kinnaird [q. v.]; Graham Hay St. Vincent de Ros, lieutenant royal navy, drowned off Bonn, 1838; and Arthur Fitzgerald, tenth lord Kinnaird [q.v.] There is a portrait of Lord Kinnaird by Northcote preserved at Rossie Priory, and a marble bust of him in the old kirk of Rossie, which is now reserved as the burying-place of the Kinnaird family.

[Douglas's Peerage of Scotland, ed. Wood, ii. 43; Millar's Historical Castles and Mansions of Scotland, i. 38 et seq.] A. H. M.

KINNAIRD, DOUGLAS JAMES WILLIAM (1788–1830), friend of Byron, fifth son of George, seventh baron Kinnaird, and younger brother of Charles, eighth lord Kinnaird [q. v.], was born on 26 Feb. 1788. He was educated first at Eton, and afterwards at Göttingen, where he acquired a thorough knowledge of German and French, and subsequently went to Trinity College, Cambridge, where he graduated M.A. in 1811. In 1813 he travelled with his friend John Cam Hobhouse [q. v.] on the continent, and was present at the battle of Culm. In the autumn of 1814 he travelled home from Paris with William Jerdan [q.v.] After his return to England he took an active share in the business of Ransom & Morland's bank, and upon the dissolution of the partnership with Sir F. B. Morland in 1819, assumed the chief management of the new firm. In 1815 he became, with Byron, Whitbread, Peter Moore, and others, a member of the sub-committee for directing the affairs of Drury Lane Theatre (MOORE, *Life of Lord Byron*, iii. 169-71, 185-7). In 1817 he visited Byron at Venice (SMILES, *Memoir of John Murray*, 1891, i. 386-7). At the general election in the summer of 1818 Kinnaird was nominated a candidate for the city of Westminster in the reform interest, but finding the contest hopeless withdrew after the third day's polling, and canvassed actively on behalf of Burdett (*Memoirs of Sir Samuel Romilly*, 1840, iii. 360-2). Kinnaird refused to be nominated again on the death of Sir Samuel Romilly, the senior member, in November 1818, and seconded his friend Hobhouse, who was defeated after a vigorous contest by George Lamb in March 1819. At a by-election in July 1819 Kinnaird was returned to the House of Commons for the borough of Bishops Castle, Shropshire, and in his maiden speech on 30 Nov. 1819 supported Lord Althorp's motion for a select committee on the state of the country (*Parl. Debates*, xli. 536-9). Kinnaird also took part in the debate on Hobhouse's anonymous pamphlet on 10 Dec. (*ib.* pp. 988-9, 1002), and contended that 'any conclusion might be drawn from it' rather than that it was meant as an excitement to rebellion. At the general election in March 1820 Kinnaird was included in the double return for Bishops Castle, but in the following June was declared 'not duly elected' by the select committee appointed to try the petition (*Journals of the House of Commons*, lxxv. 316). He made no further attempt to enter parliament, but frequently took part in the discussions at the India House. He died unmarried in Pall Mall East, London, after a long illness, on 12 March 1830, aged 42.

Kinnaird was a man of active mind, cultivated tastes, and a hasty temper. He was a member of the 'Rota,' a radical dinner club, to which Bickersteth, Burdett, and Hobhouse also belonged, and was famous for his 'mob dinners,' comprising some thirty or forty guests (BENTHAM, *Works*, 1843, x. 576). He was an intimate friend of Byron, who calls him 'my trusty and trustworthy trustee and banker, and crown and sheet anchor' (MOORE, *Byron*, vi. 103). He was frequently consulted by Byron upon his pecuniary negotiations with Murray (RUSSELL, *Moore*, iii. 295-6; see also SMILES, *Memoir of John Murray*, 1891, i. 367, 374, 402-3), and with Hobhouse insisted upon the destruction of the 'Memoirs' after Byron's death (RUSSELL, *Moore*, iv. 187-90, 332). It was at his request that Byron wrote the 'Hebrew Melodies' and the 'Monody on the Death of the Right Hon. R. B. Sheridan, spoken at Drury Lane Theatre' (*Poetical Works of Lord Byron*, 1855, ii. 13, 14, 57). Jerdan relates that Coleridge, when his tragedy 'Remorse' was under consideration by the Drury Lane authorities, was invited to read it to Kinnaird, who received him while dressing. After Coleridge had read two acts, Kinnaird remarked that he had 'listened to enough of your nonsense,' and invited his attention to 'a little two-act piece' of his own. His works are: 1. 'The Merchant of Bruges, or Beggar's Bush [a comedy by John Fletcher], with considerable alterations and additions, by Douglas Kinnaird, Esq. Now performing . . . at the Theatre Royal, Drury Lane,' London, 1815, 8vo. This comedy has been reprinted in several collections of plays. The first three songs in it were written by the Hon. George Lamb [q. v.], to whom it was dedicated, while Hobhouse was the author of the prologue and epilogue. 2. 'Remarks on the Volume of Hydrabad Papers printed for the use of the East India Proprietors [entitled "Papers relating to the pecuniary transactions of Messrs. W. Palmer & Co. with the Government of . . . the Nizam "],' London, 1825, 8vo.

[Moore's Life of Lord Byron, 1851; Lord John Russell's Memoirs of Thomas Moore, 1853; Annual Biography and Obituary, 1831, xv. 493-4; Gent. Mag. 1830, vol. c. pt. i. p. 465; Jerdan's Autobiography, vol. i. ch. v.; Annual Register, 1830, App. to Chron. p. 256; Burke's Peerage, 1890, p. 791; Grad. Cantabr. 1873, p. 236; Stapylton's Eton School Lists, 1864, p. 44; Price's Handbook of London Bankers, 1876, p. 116; Brit. Mus. Addit. MS. 27845; Official Return of Lists of Members of Parliament, pt. ii. pp. 276, 290; Brit. Mus. Cat.]
G. F. R. B.

KINNAIRD, GEORGE PATRICK, first LORD KINNAIRD (*d.* 1689), was eldest son of Patrick Kinnaird of Inchture, who was member for Perthshire in the conventions of 1625 and 1643. The family descended from Radulphus Rufus, who obtained a charter of the barony of Kinnaird in the Carse of Gowrie, Perthshire, from William the Lion, king of Scotland from 1165 to 1214. To this barony the neighbouring lands of Inchture were united in 1399 by the marriage of Reginald de Kinnaird with Margaret, the heiress of Sir John Kirkaldy of Inchture. During the civil war George Kinnaird espoused the royalist cause, and was an ardent supporter of the claims of Charles II. In 1659 he was on intimate terms with Monck. In the family charter-room at Rossie Priory are preserved two commissions—one dated 10 Oct. 1659 and signed by the noblemen, gentlemen, and heritors of Perthshire, appointing Kinnaird as their representative to treat with Monck at Edinburgh regarding the welfare of the country; the other, dated 3 Dec. 1659, directs Kinnaird to meet Monck for the same purpose at Berwick. Kinnaird actively engaged in bringing about the restoration of Charles II. There is a tradition still current in the Carse of Gowrie that shortly before Monck left Scotland to bring back the exiled monarch in 1660 he was greatly indebted to Kinnaird for provender for his army. Kinnaird was knighted by Charles II in 1661, and from an entry in Lamont's 'Diary' he appears to have been one of the first Scotsmen to receive the honour after the Restoration. He represented Perthshire in the Scottish parliament of 1662-3, and was sworn a privy councillor. On 28 Dec. 1682 he was raised to the peerage by patent, with the title of Baron Kinnaird of Inchture. He died on 29 Dec. 1689. By his marriage with Margaret, daughter of James Crichton of Ruthven, he had six sons, of whom the eldest, Patrick, second lord, and the youngest, George, alone left issue. The elder line became extinct in 1758, and the younger line is now represented by Arthur Fitzgerald, eleventh baron Kinnaird, son of Arthur, tenth baron Kinnaird [q. v.]

[Douglas's Peerage, ed. Wood; Hist. MSS. Comm. 5th Rep. p. 621; Millar's Historical Castles and Mansions of Scotland; Glamis Book of Record, p. 149.]   A. H. M.

KINNAIRD, GEORGE WILLIAM FOX, ninth BARON KINNAIRD (1807–1878), eldest son of Charles, eighth baron Kinnaird [q. v.], was born at Drimmie House, Perthshire—the family mansion before the erection of Rossie Priory—on 14 April 1807. He was educated at Eton, and entered the army as an officer of the guards, afterwards exchanging into the Connaught Rangers. He succeeded to the Scottish peerage on the death of his father, 11 Dec. 1826, and resigned his commission. His father and grandfather had both rendered great service to the whig party, and in recognition of their adherence Kinnaird was, in 1831, on the recommendation of Earl Grey, raised to the rank of a peer of the United Kingdom, with the title of Baron Rossie of Rossie, the name of a portion of the family estates at Inchture, Perthshire. In 1860 this title was exchanged for that of Baron Kinnaird of Rossie. During his youth Kinnaird spent much time in Italy. He inherited the antiquarian tastes

of his father, and conducted important excavations near Rome, bringing to this country many Roman antiquities, which are now preserved at Rossie Priory. On 15 Jan. 1840, while Melbourne was in office, Kinnaird was made a privy councillor, and was chosen a knight of the Thistle 6 July 1857. He was made lord-lieutenant of Perthshire 28 Feb. 1866, and retained that office till his death.

As a large landowner Kinnaird made himself practically acquainted with agriculture, and was one of the earliest reformers of the old style of husbandry prevailing in the Carse of Gowrie. Steam-ploughs and threshing-machines were first used in Scotland on his estate, and having an aptitude for mechanics, he himself devised various improvements in agricultural implements. He energetically sought to ameliorate the condition of the labouring classes, organising evening schools for the ploughmen, and establishing free reading-rooms and libraries about his estate. It was largely through his exertions that the railway system in the east of Scotland was developed, the line connecting Perth and Dundee, which ran through part of his property, being carried out principally under his supervision. He also helped to found and maintain industrial schools throughout the country, and his philanthropic aims extended to the reclamation of criminals, especially of juvenile delinquents. His principal legislative work was the drafting of the important measure for the closing of public-houses on Sunday, which is known as the 'Forbes Mackenzie Act' from the name of William Forbes Mackenzie [q. v.], M.P. for Peeblesshire, who introduced it in the House of Commons. It received the royal assent in 1853. Kinnaird similarly interested himself in the abatement of the smoke nuisance, the reform of the mint (on which subject he wrote several pamphlets), and the regulation of mines. He was chairman of the Mining Commission. As a whig politician he took a prominent part in the free trade agitation, was on terms of close intimacy with Ricardo, Cobden, and Bright, and presided at a great meeting of the Anti-Cornlaw League at Covent Garden Theatre. He gave further proof of his liberal views by aiding the Polish refugees, and by befriending Mazzini and Garibaldi. Science also interested him, and he spent much time, in company with Mr. Talbot, in developing photography, and in forming an extensive geological collection with the aid of Sir Charles Lyell. Kinnaird died at Rossie Priory on 8 Jan. 1878, when in his seventy-first year. He married in 1837 Lady Frances Ponsonby, daughter of Lord de Mauley, and had two sons and one daughter, all of whom predeceased him. The title and estates fell at his death to his eldest surviving brother, Arthur Fitzgerald Kinnaird [q. v.]

[Millar's Historical Castles and Mansions of Scotland; Dundee Advertiser, 9 Jan. 1878; private information.] A. H. M.

KINNEDER, LORD. [See ERSKINE, WILLIAM, Scottish judge, 1769-1822.]

KINNEIR, SIR JOHN MACDONALD (1782-1830), lieutenant-colonel H.E.I.C.S., traveller and diplomatist, born at Carnden, Linlithgow, on 3 Feb. 1782, was son of John Macdonald, comptroller of customs at Borrowstounness, and Mrs. Cecilia Maria Kinneir. In 1802 he was nominated to a cadetship by Sir William Bensley, under the name of Macdonald, which he retained in the Indian army lists up to his death. On 21 Sept. 1804 he was appointed ensign in the Madras infantry, but was not posted until the formation of the 24th (out of the 1st) Madras native infantry on 1 Jan. 1807, when he joined the new corps as lieutenant. He became captain in the same regiment on 14 April 1818, and afterwards attained the army rank of brevet lieutenant-colonel. For some time he was secretary to the officer commanding in Malabar and Canara. Afterwards he was attached to Sir John Malcolm's mission in Persia in 1808-9, during part of which time he was supernumerary agent at Bushire, and made numerous journeys in Persia, the list of which is given in his narrative of later travels (*Travels in Asia Minor in* 1813-14, App.) On the breaking up of the mission in 1810 Macdonald travelled from Bagdad, by way of Mosul and Diarbekr, to Constantinople, visited Magnesia and Smyrna, and returned to England through Spain and Portugal. Being unexpectedly ordered to rejoin his regiment, he started for Stockholm in January 1813 with Colonel Neil Campbell [see CAMPBELL, SIR NEIL, 1776-1827], one of the military commissioners then sent to the north of Europe, purposing to reach India through Russia and Persia; but, the retreat of the French from Moscow having left open a more southerly route, he accompanied Campbell from Stockholm to the czar's headquarters at Kilisch in Poland, and proceeded through Austria and Hungary to Constantinople. After visiting Asia Minor and Cyprus, he returned to Constantinople, and thence travelled through Armenia and Kurdistan to Bagdad and Bombay. A few years later he published a 'Narrative of Travels in Asia Minor, Armenia, and Kurdistan in 1813-14, with Remarks on the Marches of Alexander the Great and of the Ten Thousand Greeks' (London, 1818). From the title-page of the volume it appears that Macdonald had at this time taken his mother's surname of Kinneir, although there is no record in the India office of his change of name. He had previously published a 'Gazetteer of Persia,' with map (London, 1813). After 1813 he was for some years town-major of Fort St. George, Madras, and resident with the nawab of the Carnatic.

In 1823-4 it was proposed to withdraw the chargé d'affaires who had represented British interests at Teheran since 1815, and to replace him by an East India Company's envoy as formerly. The shah, Futteh Ali, consented reluctantly, and Kinneir was appointed envoy in 1824. He was conducted to Persia, and arrived at the shah's camp at Ahar in September 1826, where he found the Persians engaged in active hostilities with the Russians, and claiming the British subsidy to which by the treaty of Teheran Persia was entitled if attacked by a European power. Kinneir would not support the subsidy, holding that the aggression had been on the side of Persia. Various military operations followed, during which Kinneir was present with the Persian army, until, on 19 Oct. 1827, the frontier fortress of Erivan was stormed by Prince Paskievitch's troops; a Russian division was pushed on to Tabreez; the shah's chief minister, Ali Yar Khan, deserted him on the approach of the Russians, and fled to Ali Bengloo with Kinneir, who did his utmost to bring about a peace. The Russians, though declining to admit his official character, accepted his mediation in his private capacity. A treaty of peace was signed at Turkmanchi on 23 Feb. 1828 (see Treaties printed by order of the House of Commons, 11 March 1839), involving much loss of territory to Persia and the destruction of the paramount influence previously enjoyed by the British mission. No blame has been attributed to Kinneir, who won the respect of both Persians and Russians. He received the Persian order of the Sun and Lion, and on 17 Nov. 1829 was created a knight bachelor (see *London Gazette*, 29 Nov. 1829, in which his name is given as Macdonald).

Kinneir remained as envoy in Persia until his death at Tabreez on 11 June 1830, when a three months' mourning was observed by the shah and the inhabitants. Kinneir married Amelia Harriet, third daughter, by his first wife, of Lieutenant-general Sir Alexander Campbell, bart. [q. v.], who died commander-in-chief at Madras in December 1825. This lady, whose elder sister married Sir John Malcolm, long survived her husband, and died at Boulogne in 1860.

[Information supplied by the India Office; East India Registers and Army Lists; Kaye's Life and Corresp. of Sir John Malcolm (London, 1867). i. 395 et seq., ii. 1–54; Kinneir's Travels in Asia Minor, &c. (Lond. 1818); Mill's Hist. of India, ix. 216 et seq.; Lond. Gazettes, 1829; Gent. Mag. 1830, pt. ii. pp. 190, 649.]   H. M. C.

KINNOULL, EARLS OF. [See HAY, SIR GEORGE, 1572–1634, first EARL; HAY, GEORGE, d. 1758, seventh EARL; HAY, THOMAS, 1710–1787, eighth EARL.]

KINSEY, WILLIAM MORGAN (1788–1851), divine and traveller, born in 1788 at Abergavenny, Monmouthshire, was son of Robert Morgan Kinsey, solicitor and banker at Abergavenny, and Caroline Hannah, his wife, daughter of Sir James Harington, bart. He matriculated at Oxford on 28 Nov. 1805, became a scholar of Trinity College, graduated B.A. in 1809, and proceeded M.A. in 1813. In 1815 he was elected a fellow of his college, dean in 1822, vice-president in 1823, and bursar in 1824. In 1822 he proceeded to the degree of B.D. In 1827 Kinsey made a tour in Portugal with the intention of making the country better known to the English people. From his journals and a series of letters written to his friend Thomas Haynes Bayly [q. v., as well as from historical and other sources, Kinsey compiled a book, which appeared in 1828 under the title of 'Portugal Illustrated.' The work excited some little interest as a good account of the country, and was well illustrated with engravings by G. Cooke and Skelton, from drawings chiefly made by a companion during his tour. It was dedicated to Lord Auckland, to whom Kinsey was chaplain, and a second edition appeared in 1829. In 1830 Kinsey was travelling with Viscount Alford in Belgium, and, happening to be at Brussels at the outbreak of the revolution in August of that year, was an eye-witness of the conflict between the troops and the populace. About 1832 he was appointed minister of St. John's Church, Cheltenham, where he obtained some repute as a preacher, and published a few sermons. In 1843 he was appointed rector of Rotherfield Greys, Oxfordshire, where he resided until his death on 6 April 1851. He was the author of a few other pamphlets, and in January 1848 contributed a paper to the 'Gentleman's Magazine' entitled ' Random Recollections of a Visit to Walton Hall.'

[Gent. Mag. 1851, new ser. xxxvi. 95; Foster's Alumni Oxonienses; Kinsey's Portugal Illustrated.]   L. C.

KINSIUS (d. 1060), archbishop of York. [See KYNSIGE.]

VOL. XXXI.

KINTORE, EARL OF. [See KEITH, SIR JOHN, d. 1714, first EARL.]

KINWELMERSH, KYNWELMERSH, or **KINDLEMARSH, FRANCIS** (fl. 1570), poet, belonged to an Essex family, whose name is spelt in a variety of ways. Thomas Kinwolmersh of Much Dunmow, Essex, with William Kinwolmersh of Broxted, served in the war in France in 1513 as retainers of Henry Bourchier, earl of Essex, captain of the king's spears (Letters, &c., of Henry VIII, i. 596). The poet was probably son of Richard Kinwelmersh, who held in 1582 the manor of Newton Hall, now Great Dunmow (MORANT, Essex, ii. 424). He entered Gray's Inn in 1557. Two students of the same surname, Anthony and Robert, were admitted to the same inn in 1561 and 1563 respectively, and were probably Francis's brothers (FOSTER, Gray's Inn Reg. pp. 27, 29, 32). Francis became intimate with the poet, George Gascoigne [q. v.], who was his fellow-student at Gray's Inn, and in 1566 they produced conjointly a blank-verse rendering of Euripides's 'Phœnissæ,' which they entitled 'Jocasta.' It was performed in the hall of their inn in the course of 1566, and was first published in Gascoigne's 'Hundreth Sundrie Flowres' in 1572. Kinwelmersh was responsible for arts. i. and iv. Gascoigne wrote poems upon mottos suggested by Francis and his brother Anthony about 1566 (see GASCOIGNE, Works, ed. Hazlitt, i. 64–5). Francis was a contributor to the 'Paradyse of Daynty Devises,' 1576, and his initials, 'F. K.,' appear on the title-page in the list of 'sundry learned gentlemen' whose poems are included. In the title-pages of the editions of 1580 and 1600 the initials are expanded into 'F. Kindlemarsh.' Seven poems, chiefly on religious topics, bear the signature 'F. K.' in the first edition, and six in that of 1600. A poem ('For Whitsunday') in all the editions is signed 'M. Kindlemarsh,' and another piece is subscribed 'M. K.' In Bodenham's preface to ' Belvedere, or the Garden of the Muses,' 1600, ' Francis Kindlemarsh, Esq.,' figures, together with Norton, Gascoigne, Atchelow, and Whetstone, among deceased authors, to whose published and unpublished writings 'due right' is given by the compiler. According to a letter from Sir Francis Englefield [q. v.] to the Duchess of Feria [see DORMER, JANE, one 'Kindlemarsh,' who seems to have been friendly with the Dormer family, was at Louvain in August 1569 (Cal. State Papers, Dom. Add. 1566–79, p. 285). 'Francis Kynwelmarshe, Esq.,' was elected M.P. for Bossiney, Cornwall, on 27 April 1572, at the same time as Gascoigne was returned for Midhurst.

O

[Ritson's Biographia Poetica, p. 204; Brydges's Censura Literaria, i. 238, 264; Gascoigne's Works; Return of Members of Parl. i. 408; see art. GEORGE GASCOIGNE.]
S. L.

KIP, JOHANNES (1653 – 1722), draughtsman and engraver, born at Amsterdam in 1653, was married there in 1680 (contract on 5 April) to Elizabeth Breda of Amsterdam (Oud-Holland, iii. 77). He was employed in Amsterdam as an engraver, at first of book illustrations (cf. plate of 'The Siege of Groningen,' etched in 1672). In 1685 he etched a large view of Amsterdam, and in 1686 a long procession of William III and his wife, Mary of England, outside the Hague. Shortly afterwards Kip appears to have come to London, where he settled in Westminster. He was employed by the booksellers in engraving portraits, such as that of Marcellus Malphigi, M.D., prefixed to an edition of his works in 1697; frontispieces, such as that of an edition of 'Bibliotheca Patrum,' in 1693; book illustrations, such as plates of birds after Barlow, or separate prints, such as one of a new water-engine in the manner of J. Van der Heyden, a view of the Danish Church in London after C. G. Cibber, a view of the German Chapel, St. James's, a design for a fountain as a monument to the Duke of Marlborough, after Claude David, and a view of Bridge Town in Barbadoes in 1695. Kip's most important work, however, was the series of etchings done by him from the drawings of Leonard Knyff (q. v.), and published in London by David Mortier of Amsterdam. The first volume appears to have been published in 1708, with a title-page 'Britannia Illustrata, or Views of several of the Queen's Palaces, as also of the principal Seats of the Nobility and Gentry of Great Britain, curiously engraven on 80 copper-plates,' dated 1707, and a second title-page in French, commencing 'Nouveau Théâtre de la Grande Bretagne,' &c., dated 1708. This volume consists of a series of bird's-eye views drawn by L. Knyff and etched by Kip. Three other volumes followed in 1709 and subsequent years. The second volume consisted of similar bird's-eye views, drawn as well as etched by Kip; and subsequent volumes contained the works of other artists. A supplement contains the twenty-five views of Audley End engraved by Henry Winstanley in 1676. A later edition was published with a few additions by Joseph Smith in 1724–8. Though of little artistic merit this series of engravings is of the greatest archaeological interest. Copies of the work are frequently made up from the various editions. In 1710 Kip published a 'Prospect of the City of London, Westminster, and St. James's Park,' drawn by himself from Buckingham House, and engraved by himself on twelve sheets; a second edition of this was printed on eight sheets in 1726. From a view of St. Clement Danes Church we learn that Kip resided and sold prints in St. John's Street, near Storyes Back Gate in Westminster. He died in Westminster in April 1722, leaving a daughter, who was also an ingenious artist.

[Vertue's MSS. (Brit. Mus. Add. MS. 23069); Dodd's manuscript Hist. of English Engravers (ib. 33402); Immerzeel's Levens en Werken der Hollandsche Konstschilders, &c., and Kramm's supplement to the same; Lowndes's Bibl. Man.; Brunet's Manuel du Libraire.]
L. C.

KIPLING, THOMAS (d. 1822), dean of Peterborough, born at Bowes, Yorkshire, was son of William Kipling, cattle salesman. He received his early education at Scroton and Sedbergh schools, and was admitted a sizar of St. John's College, Cambridge, on 28 June 1764. He graduated B.A. in 1768, was elected a fellow of his college 29 Jan. 1770, and commenced M.A. in 1771. In 1773 he was elected one of the taxors of the university. He took the degree of B.D. in 1779. In 1782 he was elected Lady Margaret's preacher on the resignation of Dr. Richard Farmer (Addit. MS. 5874, f. 87). He was created D.D. in 1784, in which year he was presented by his college to the vicarage of Holme on Spalding Moor, Yorkshire. In 1787 he was appointed deputy regius professor of divinity, the professor, Dr. Richard Watson, being in ill-health. In 1792 he preached the Boyle lectures, but did not print the course (NICHOLS, Lit. Anecd. vi. 450).

In 1792 he was severely condemned by the liberal party in the university for promoting the prosecution of the Rev. William Frend (q. v.), fellow of Jesus College, who had attacked the established church. The errors in Kipling's edition of the 'Codex Bezæ' and the bad latinity of the preface were mercilessly censured, so that in the slang of the university a 'Kiplingism' came to be synonymous with a grammatical blunder (Gradus ad Cantabrigiam, 1824, p. 61). On 10 Feb. 1798 he was made dean of Peterborough. In the summer of 1802 he resigned the deputy professorship of divinity in consequence, it is said, of ill-health. When Dr. Lingard's 'Strictures' on Dr. Herbert Marsh's 'Comparative View of the Churches of England and Rome' appeared in 1815, Kipling took offence at the term 'modern church of England,' and imagining that it came within the category of 'seditious words, in derogation of the established religion,' wrote to

Lingard through the public papers informing him that unless within a reasonable time he should 'publish a vindication of his inflammatory language' he would be indicted and 'summoned to answer for his offensive demeanour in Westminster Hall.' By way of reply Lingard merely advertised his 'Strictures' in all the papers which had published the dean's letter; and Kipling, after another letter and a short rejoinder from Lingard, repeating the original offence, affected to discover that the latter was not, as he had supposed, 'a popish priest,' and entreated pardon for having entertained 'the erroneous notion.' Kipling died at his parsonage, after a lingering illness, on 28 Jan. 1822.

His principal work is: 'Codex Theodori Bezæ Cantabrigiensis, Evangelia et Apostolorum Acta complectens, quadratis literis, Græco-Latinus. Academia auspicante venerandæ has vetustatis reliquias, summa qua potuit fide, adumbravit, expressit, edidit, Codicis historiam præfixit, notasque adjecit T. Kipling,' Greek and Latin, 2 pts., Cambridge, 1793, fol., printed at the university press. The impression was limited to 250 copies. This edition of the 'Codex Bezæ' is a splendid specimen of typography, the types resembling the uncial characters of the original manuscript. It was criticised with severity in the 'Monthly Review,' new ser. xii. 241-6, and by Porson, who had a high opinion of Kipling's Greek scholarship, in two notices in the 'British Critic,' vol. iii. (1794); and the preface was coarsely attacked in a pamphlet entitled 'Remarks on Dr. Kipling's Preface to Beza. Part the first. By Thomas Edwards, LL.D.,' London, 1793, 8vo. No second part appeared. Horne remarks that Kipling's work, although imperfect, was unfairly underrated. The Rev. H. Scrivener, in the preface to his own edition of the 'Bezæ Codex Cantabrigiensis' (Cambridge, 1864), says: 'I have found the text of my predecessor less inaccurate than some have suspected: the typographical errors detected (eighty-three, of which sixteen are in his notes, &c.) I have recorded as a matter of duty, not of reproach :—perfect correctness is quite unattainable, yet Kipling has laboured faithfully, and not wholly in vain, to approach it as near as may be. His most serious fault is one of design and plan, in that he has placed in the body of the work those numerous changes which deform the pages of "Codex Bezæ."'

Kipling's other works are: 1. 'The Elementary parts of Dr. Smith's Complete System of Optics,' 1778, 4to. 2. 'The Articles of the Church of England proved not to be Calvinistic,' Cambridge, 1802, 8vo, which

was attacked by a writer under the signature of 'Academicus,' and drew forth a defence claiming to be by a friend of Kipling, but supposed to be by himself. 3. 'Certain Accusations brought lately by the Irish Papists against British and Irish Protestants, of every denomination, examined,' London, 1809, 8vo; reprinted in 'The Churchman armed against the Errors of the Time,' vol. ii. London, 1814, 8vo. This was elicited by a reprint of Ward's 'Errata of the Protestant Bible.'

[Cooper's Annals of Cambridge, iv. 378, 431, 557; Gunning's Reminiscences, i. 24, 281 seq., 312, 314, ii. 49-51; Gent. Mag. 1822, pt. i. p. 276; Literary Memoirs, i. 199, 312; Biog. Dict. of Living Authors, pp. 190, 440; Watt's Bibl. Brit.; Lowndes's Bibl. Man. (Bohn), pp. 764, 1278; Graduati Cantabr. 1846, pp. 185, 398; Public Characters, vi. 91; Tierney's Life of Dr. Lingard, p. 9; Annual Reg. 1822, Chron. p. 276; Nichols's Lit. Anecd. ix. 79; Annual Biog. vii. 449; Horne's Introduction to the Study of the Scriptures, 9th edit. v. 15; British Critic, xi. 619; Scrivener's Codex Cantabrigiensis Bezæ, Introd. pp. xii, xiii; Cooper's Memoir of W. Melmoth, pp. 285, 405; Christian Observer, vol. i. pref. pp. vii, 593; Le Neve's Fasti, ii. 541, iii. 645; Baker's Hist. of St. John's College, Cambridge, ed. Mayor. vol. ii.]   T. C.

KIPPIS, ANDREW, D.D. (1725-1795), nonconformist divine and biographer, was born at Nottingham on 28 March (O.S.) 1725. His father, Robert Kippis, a silk-hosier of Nottingham, maternally descended from Benjamin King of Oakham, Rutland, an ejected minister, was second of the three surviving sons of Andrew Kippis, who died in 1748, and is buried in Sleaford Church (Gent. Mag. lvi. pt. i. pp. 98, 198). His mother, Anne Ryther, was granddaughter of the Rev. John Ryther, who was ejected for nonconformity from the benefice of Ferriby, Yorkshire. Losing his father when he was five years old, he was placed under the care of his grandfather at Sleaford, Lincolnshire, where he was educated. By the advice of Mr. Merrivale, the local pastor, he resolved to enter the dissenting ministry. In 1741 he was admitted into the academy at Northampton, under the care of Dr. Philip Doddridge [q. v.], and after completing his course of five years in that seminary he accepted an invitation from Boston, Lincolnshire, where he settled in September 1746. Thence he removed to Dorking, Surrey, in 1750, as successor to the Rev. John Mason, author of a treatise on 'Self-Knowledge;' and in June 1753 he became pastor of the presbyterian congregation meeting in Princes Street, Westminster. On 21 Sept. 1753 he married Elizabeth, daughter of Isaac Bott, merchant, of Boston.

Kippis's pastorate at Westminster continued for forty-three years. He was soon elected a trustee of the presbyterian fund; he became a member of Dr. Williams's trust in 1762: and his association with many other charitable institutions in London and Westminster enabled him to effectively promote the nonconformist cause. In 1763 he was appointed to succeed Dr. David Jennings as classical and philological tutor in the Coward Academy at Hoxton; and in June 1767 he received the degree of D.D. from the university of Edinburgh, on the unsolicited recommendation of Professor Robertson. He was elected a fellow of the Society of Antiquaries on 19 March 1778, and a fellow of the Royal Society 17 June 1779 (THOMSON, *Hist. of the Royal Soc.* App. iv. 57). In both these learned societies he served on the council for about two years. He withdrew from the institution at Hoxton in 1784, and the two other tutors followed his example the next year, when the seminary was dissolved (BOGUE and BENNETT, *Hist. of Dissenters,* ii. 519). In 1786 he became one of the tutors in the new dissenting college established at Hackney, and although he retired from that office after a few years, he continued to support the college by a liberal subscription and by his interest with opulent friends. Among his pupils at Hackney were William Godwin and Samuel Rogers. Rogers subsequently apostrophised him, together with his colleagues Price and Priestley, in 'The Pleasures of Memory' (CLAYDEN, *Rogers and his Contemporaries,* i. 418). Kippis died at his residence in Crown Street, Westminster, on 8 Oct.1795. His funeral sermon was preached, and the oration at the grave in Bunhill Fields delivered, by the Rev. Dr. Abraham Rees.

Kippis was reverenced by dissenters, and his literary attainments secured for him the friendship and esteem of distinguished members of the established church. When about fourteen years old he renounced the principles of Calvinism, in which his relatives had brought him up (*Biog. Brit.* 2nd edit. iv. 3). Subsequently he inclined to Socinianism, though 'he highly disapproved the conduct of the modern Socinians, in assuming to themselves the exclusive appellation of unitarians' (WILSON, *Hist. of Dissenting Churches,* iv. 116). In his youth he was a most assiduous student. He informed Alexander Chalmers that he once read for three years at the rate of sixteen hours a day. One of the works which he read through was the 'General Dictionary,' in ten folio volumes, and he thus laid the foundation of his skill

in biographical composition (*Gent. Mag.* 1795, pt. ii. p. 803).

His editorial connection with the 'Biographia Britannica' constitutes his chief claim to remembrance. He was employed by the booksellers to prepare the second edition of that work, 'with corrections, enlargements, and the addition of new lives.' When he had been engaged for some time on this task he found it too vast for him to execute alone, and Dr. Towers was appointed as his associate. The letters K. and T. affixed to the new articles, or to the additions to the old articles, distinguish their respective shares. Only five volumes were published, all at London in folio—vol. i. in 1778, vol. ii. in 1780, vol. iii. in 1784, vol. iv. in 1789, and vol. v. in 1793, when the dictionary ends abruptly with the article 'Fastolf.' A first part of the sixth volume ('Featley' to 'Foster') was printed in 1795. To this half-volume, after the proprietors had for some time endeavoured to find a fitting successor to Kippis, Dr. George Gregory wrote a preface, intending to come forward as continuator of the work. Delays in its publication followed, and nearly the whole impression was consumed in the fire on Nichols's premises in February 1808, only three copies having been preserved (NICHOLS, *Lit. Anecd.* ix. 184 n.) The second edition of the 'Biographia Britannica' hardly deserves the high praise which has been sometimes bestowed upon it. The memoirs which were imperfect or incorrect in the original edition, instead of being rewritten, were textually reproduced, with notes by the editor pointing out omissions and inaccuracies. Thus it seemed as if a literary controversy were being carried on between the editor and the author. Again, many of the new memoirs were of inordinate length, and the prominence given to nonconformists laid the editor open to a charge of partiality. Moreover, he indulged too freely in the expression of opinions instead of confining himself mainly to the narration of facts; and many of the footnotes were far too long and irrelevant. Johnson told Boswell in 1777 that he had been asked to undertake the new edition of the 'Biographia Britannica,' but had declined it, 'which,' says Boswell, 'he afterwards said to me he regretted.' Although Boswell admitted that Kippis had discharged the task judiciously, and with more impartiality than might have been expected from a separatist, he complained that the work was 'too crowded with obscure dissenting teachers.' He subsequently, however, withdrew all censure (BOSWELL, *Johnson,* ed. G. B. Hill, iii. 174, iv. 376). According to Horace Walpole 'the "Biographia Britannica" ought to be called the Vindicatio Britannica, for that it was a general panegyric upon everybody' (cf. COWPER, *Works*, viii. 320). But in spite of these defects Kippis made a valuable addition to our national biographical literature.

Kippis began his literary career early in life by contributing to the magazines, especially the 'Gentleman's Magazine.' Afterwards he became a more constant writer in the 'Monthly Review.' He also largely contributed to 'The Library, or Moral and Critical Magazine,' which he edited for 1761-2. He laid the foundation of the 'New Annual Register,' and suggested the improved plan upon which that work was conducted. The 'History of Ancient Literature' and the 'Review of Modern Books' were at its first commencement written by him, and continued to 1784. He was also the author of the 'Review of the Transactions of the Present Reign' prefixed to the 'Register' for 1780, and of the 'History of Knowledge, Learning, and Taste in Great Britain' prefixed to the succeeding volumes to the year 1794.

His separate publications are: 1. 'A Vindication of the Protestant Dissenting Ministers with regard to their late application to Parliament in the matter of Subscription,' London, 1772 and 1773, 8vo. 2. Life of Sir John Pringle, bart., president of the Royal Society, prefixed to his 'Six Discourses, delivered on occasion of six annual assignments of Sir Godfrey Copley's medal,' 1783. 3. 'Considerations on the Provisional Treaty with America, and the Preliminary Articles of Peace with France and Spain,' 2nd edit. 1783. 4. 'Observations on the late Contests in the Royal Society' (concerning Dr. Hutton), London, 1784, 8vo, published with a view to allaying the animosities which existed in that body. 5. 'The Life of Captain James Cook,' London, 1788, 4to, translated into French by J. H. Castéra, 2 vols., Paris, 1789, 8vo. 6. Life of Dr. Nathaniel Lardner, prefixed to the complete edition of his 'Works,' 11 vols., 1788. 7. 'The Life of Anthony Ashley Cooper, first Earl of Shaftesbury,' privately printed (London, 1790?), 4to. The fourth Earl of Shaftesbury originally entrusted the work to Benjamin Martyn, who had free access to the family archives; but after the fourth earl's death in 1771, his son, the fifth earl, considering that Martyn's life was not sufficiently complete for publication, put it into the hands of Dr. Gregory Sharpe, master of the Temple, and afterwards engaged Kippis to revise it and prepare it for the press. An edition was eventually printed, but with the exception of two copies the whole impression was immediately destroyed. One of the extant copies is now in the British Museum. The work afterwards appeared under the title of 'The Life of the first Earl of Shaftesbury, from original documents in the possession of the family, by Mr. B. Martyn and Dr. Kippis, now first published. Edited by G. Wingrove Cooke, esq.,' 2 vols., London, 1836, 8vo. 8. Several single discourses, some of which are reprinted in his 'Sermons on Practical Subjects,' London, 1791 and 1878, 8vo. 9. 'An Address delivered at the Interment of Richard Price, D.D., F.R.S.,' 1791. 10. Life of Dr. Philip Doddridge, prefixed to the seventh edition of his 'Family Expositor,' 1792. 11. Life of Job Orton, prefixed to his 'Exposition of the New Testament,' 1822. This first appeared as a long note appended to the memoir of Philip Doddridge in the 'Biographia Britannica,' 2nd edit. v. 308 seq. Kippis also edited Doddridge's 'Lectures,' with a large number of additional references, and assisted in preparing 'A Collection of Hymns and Psalms for Public and Private Worship,' 1795, which was extensively used in dissenting chapels, and passed through several editions.

A portrait of Kippis was engraved (1792, folio) by F. Bartolozzi, from a painting by W. Artaud (BROMLEY, *Cat. of Engraved Portraits*, p. 364).

[Addit. MSS. 5874 ff. 71, 72, 28104 f. 51, 21553 f. 128; Evans's Cat. of Engraved Portraits, n. 6142; Sermon by John Evans, M.A., being a Tribute of Respect to the Memory of S. Stennett, A. Kippis, and R. Harris, 1795; Gent. Mag. 1795, pt. i. p. 10, pt. ii. pp. 803, 883, 913, 1796, pt. i. p. 5, 1804, pt. i. p. 35; Georgian Era, iii. 545; Brown's Nottinghamshire Worthies, pp. 299-302; Lowndes's Bibl. Man. (Bohn), pp. 205, 1278; Nichols's Illustr. of Lit.; Nichols's Lit. Anecd.; Notes and Queries, 3rd ser. x. 432, xi. 213; Phonetic Journal, xlv. 468; Funeral Sermon by Dr. Abraham Rees, 1795; Rees's Cyclopædia; Wilson's Dissenting Churches, iv. 103-17, 402; Jones's Bunhill Memorials, pp. 138, 140.]   T. C.

KIPPIST, RICHARD (1812-1882), botanist, was born at Stoke Newington, London, on 11 June 1812. His first experience was gained in the office of Joseph Woods the architect and a distinguished botanist. Kippist travelled with Woods and helped to compile the still useful 'Tourist's Flora.' After Woods retired to Lewes in 1830, Kippist entered the service of the Linnean Society, helping to distribute the vast herbarium amassed by Dr. Wallich, until, on the death of David Don the librarian in 1842, he was chosen to succeed him. After two or three years of broken health he retired in

1881 on a pension of his full salary, but died at Chelsea on 14 Jan. 1882. He had an excellent knowledge of plants, especially those of Australia, and twice has a genus been dedicated to him as *Kippistia*, but in both cases they have been merged in older genera.

[Proc. Linn. Soc. 1881–2, pp. 64–5.]

B. D. J.

KIRBY, ELIZABETH (1823–1873), writer for the young, youngest child of John Kirby, manufacturer, of Leicester, by his wife, Sarah Bentley, was born in Southgate Street, Leicester, on 15 Dec. 1823. She displayed at an early age a faculty for story-telling and a taste for literary composition both in verse and prose. In 1854 she published, under the title of 'The Discontented Children,' a story which she had frequently told to small audiences. She removed from Leicester to Norwich in 1855, and the new society and surroundings stimulated her literary zeal. After a few years her younger sister, Mary, married the Rev. Henry Gregg, rector of Brooksby, Leicestershire, and Miss Kirby settled in Melton Mowbray, to share for the rest of her life Mrs. Gregg's home. With her sister she wrote a long series of books for children. Twenty-four volumes under the joint authorship are in the British Museum Library. They are homely and unpretentious little works, written in a style specially calculated to interest children. Among the best are 'The Italian Goldsmiths, a Story of Cellini,' 1861, 16mo; 'Chapters on Trees,' 1873, 8vo; 'Stories about Birds of Land and Water,' 1873, 4to. Two little books on insects, 'Caterpillars, Butterflies, and Moths,' 1857, 18mo, and 'Sketches of Insect Life,' London, 1874, 8vo, embody much original observation. The sisters also published a number of serial tales, including 'The Desboroughs' and 'Deepdale Vicarage,' in various magazines. Miss Kirby's last work, a little story, entitled 'Hold fast by your Sundays,' was published in 1872. She died at Melton Mowbray in June 1873. 'Her literary talents,' says the 'Athenæum,' 'were at all times exercised for the good, intellectual and moral, of her readers.'

[Information kindly supplied by Mrs. Gregg and the latter's Leaflets from my Life (1887); Athenæum, 12 July 1873; Allibone, Supplement, ii. 956; Miss Kirby's Works.]

T. S.

KIRBY, JOHN (1690–1753), Suffolk topographer, born in 1690 at Halesworth, Suffolk, was originally a schoolmaster at Orford in that county, and afterwards occupied a mill at Wickham Market. In 1735 he published at Ipswich, in duodecimo, 'The Suffolk Traveller; or, a Journey through Suf-folk,' a road-book with antiquarian notices, from an actual survey which he made of the whole county in 1732, 1733, and 1734. Prefixed is a small map of the county. A new edition was published by subscription, with 'many alterations and large additions by several hands,' in 1764, 8vo, London, under the editorship of the Rev. Richard Canning, of which a reprint was issued from Woodbridge about 1800, containing some trifling additions, and a fourth edition, with additions, appeared as 'A Topographical . . . Description of the County of Suffolk,' 8vo, Woodbridge, 1829, with Ebden's map in place of Kirby's. A 'Supplement to the Suffolk Traveller' was published in 1844 by Augustine Page (cf. his Introduction, p. vi). In 1736 Kirby issued 'A Map of the County of Suffolk,' illustrated with coats of arms and views. An improved edition, engraved by John Ryland, was published on a larger scale in 1766 by his sons John Joshua and William Kirby (NICHOLS, *Lit. Anecd.* vi. 541–4). Kirby died on 13 Dec. 1753, at Ipswich, and was buried in the churchyard of St. Mary at Tower, Ipswich. His portrait, by Thomas Gainsborough, R.A., was in 1868 in the possession of the Rev. Kirby Trimmer. He married in 1714 Alice Brown; his eldest son, John Joshua Kirby, is separately noticed.

[Life of Mrs. Trimmer, i. 5; Cat. of the Third Exhibition of Portraits at South Kensington, 1868, No. 752.]

G. G.

KIRBY, JOHN JOSHUA (1716–1774), clerk of the works at Kew Palace, born in 1716 at Wickham Market, Suffolk, was the eldest son of John Kirby [q. v.] (PAGE, *Supplement to the Suffolk Traveller*, pp. 189–90). About 1738 he settled at Ipswich as a coach and house painter. An early friendship with Gainsborough induced him to attempt landscape-painting. He made a number of drawings of monasteries, castles, churches, and monuments in Suffolk for a projected county history, and of these he published twelve, with an 'Historical Account,' 8vo, Ipswich, 1748, the plates etched by himself, followed by a series engraved by J. Wood. He also studied linear perspective, upon which he lectured at the St. Martin's Lane Academy, London. In 1754 he printed at Ipswich, in quarto, 'Dr. Brook Taylor's Method of Perspective made easy, both in Theory and Practice,' 2 pts., founded upon Taylor's two treatises on linear perspective, published respectively in 1715 and 1719. The book is illustrated with a curious frontispiece by Hogarth, and fifty copperplates, mostly engraved by Kirby himself. It was reissued

in 1755, 1765, and in 1768, with additions.
Having secured warm friends in Hogarth and
Sir Joshua Reynolds, Kirby went to London.
Through the Earl of Bute he was appointed
teacher of perspective to the Prince of Wales,
afterwards George III, by whom he was appointed clerk of the works at Kew Palace.
Under the patronage of the king, who de-
frayed the expense of the plates, Kirby published in 1761 a splendid folio volume entitled
'The Perspective of Architecture, in two
parts, . . . deduced from the Principles of Dr.
Brook Taylor; and performed by two Rules
only of universal application.' He appears
to have designed in 1762 St. George's Chapel,
Old Brentford, Middlesex (Dict. of Architecture, Architect. Publ. Soc., vol. iv.) About
1767 he published 'Dr. Brook Taylor's Method
of Perspective compared with the Examples
lately published . . . as Sirigatti's by J.
Ware . . . being a Parallel between those
two Methods of Perspective. In which the
superior excellence of Taylor's is shewn,' 4to.
London. On 26 March 1767 he was elected
F.R.S. (THOMSON, Hist. of Royal Soc. App.
iv. p. lii), and F.S.A. on the following 4 June
(GOUGH, Chronological List of Soc. Antiq.
1798, p. 20). He was secretary, and in 1768
elected president, of the Incorporated Society
of Artists, in place of Francis Hayman (q.v.),
at the instance of a discontented clique; but
resigned the post the same year on the plea of
ill-health. From 1765 to 1770 he exhibited
with the society views in Richmond Park,
Kew, and the neighbourhood. His drawings
of Kew Palace were engraved by Woollett
in 1763 (REDGRAVE, Dict. of Artists, ed.
1878, p. 251). Kirby died on 20 June 1774,
aged 58, and was buried in Kew churchyard.
Such was Gainsborough's regard for Kirby,
that he made a special request in his will
that he might be buried by his side—a desire which was carried into effect (FAULK-
NER, Brentford, &c., 1845, pp. 128, 131, 156–
157). A portrait of Kirby by Hogarth was
in 1867 in the possession of Mr. George C.
Handford, and a portrait of Kirby and his
wife by Gainsborough was in 1868 in the
possession of the Rev. Kirby Trimmer. A
mezzotint portrait of Kirby, by J. Dixon,
from the painting by Gainsborough, and an
engraving by D. Pariset, from a picture by
P. Falconet, are also known (EVANS, Cat. of
Engraved Portraits, i. 197). Kirby married
Sarah Bull of Framlingham, Suffolk, who
died in 1775. His son William, who was in
1766 a member of the Incorporated Society
of Artists, died suddenly at Kew in 1771;
his daughter Sarah, afterwards married to
James Trimmer of Brentford, was a popular
writer of books for the young (see TRIM-

MER). Kirby was uncle of William Kirby
(1759–1850) [q. v.], the entomologist.

[Memoir, principally compiled by Mrs. Trim-
mer, in Nichols's Biog. Anecdotes of Hogarth,
No. 8; Life of Mrs. Trimmer; Catalogues of
the Second and Third Special Exhibitions of Nat.
Portraits at South Kensington; Gough's British
Topography, Suffolk; Edwards's Anecdotes of
Painters; Gent. Mag. new ser. xxxiv. 219.]
                                          G. G.

KIRBY, WILLIAM (1759–1850), entomologist, eldest son of William Kirby of
Witnesham Hall, Suffolk, and of Lucy Meadows, was born at Witnesham on 19 Sept.
1759. He derived a taste for natural history
from his mother, who died in 1776. He was
educated at Ipswich grammar school and
Caius College, Cambridge, where he graduated B.A. in 1781 and M.A. in 1815. In
1782 he took holy orders and obtained the
sole charge of Barham, Suffolk, held by the
Rev. N. Bacon with the vicarage of Codden-
ham in the same county. He remained at
Barham for the remainder of his life, the
vicar on his death in 1798 leaving him the
next presentation.

Kirby was already an excellent botanist,
when the accidental finding of a beautiful
insect determined him to study entomology.
His name appears in the first list of fellows of the Linnean Society, founded in
1788, and in 1793 he contributed to the society's 'Transactions,' the first of a long series
of papers. In 1802 he published his important monograph on English bees. He had
collected 153 wild specimens in his own
parish. In 1805 he made the acquaintance
of William Spence [q. v.] of Drypool, Hull,
whom he afterwards persuaded to be his coadjutor in the famous 'Introduction to Entomology,' first suggested in 1808. The form
chosen was that of letters on the most interesting subjects in entomology. Vol. i.
appeared in 1815, and a third edition was
issued with vol. ii. in 1817; vols. iii. and iv.,
containing the special systematic description
of insects, were written entirely by Kirby,
owing to his friend's ill-health. The sixth
edition was edited by Spence in 1843, when
Kirby's advanced age disabled him from
work. The seventh and subsequent editions, in one volume, consist of the first
two volumes of the sixth edition. During
the writing of the introduction Kirby had
(in 1811) contributed an important paper to
the Linnean Society, in which he founded the
new insect order of Strepsiptera, which has
held its ground. In 1818 he was elected
F.R.S. He took an active part in the Zoological Club of the Linnean Society, founded
in 1822, which afterwards developed into

the Zoological Society. In 1830 he began the Bridgewater treatise on 'The Habits and Instincts of Animals,' which was published in 1835. In his seventy-eighth year (1837) he completed the description of the insects brought home by Franklin's first two arctic expeditions. Kirby's descriptions formed the fourth part of 'Fauna Boreali-Americana.' In 1837 he was elected honorary president of the recently founded Entomological Society of London. He died of old age on 4 July 1850. His collection of insects was bequeathed to the Entomological Society. He married (1) in 1784 Sarah Ripper, who died in 1814, and (2) in 1816 Charlotte Rodwell, who died in 1844, but had no children.

Kirby was of middle height, broad-shouldered and strongly built, with broad forehead and small blue eyes, deeply set. His chief aim in life was to trace the benevolence and wisdom of the Creator in His works. Though no theological work of his, apart from sermons, was published, he wrote much on theology from the point of view of an orthodox anti-Calvinistic churchman. An excellent portrait of him by H. Howard, R.A., was painted about 1819, and an engraving of it was published by T. Lupton.

Besides many papers in the Linnean and other transactions, Kirby wrote: 1. 'Monographia Apium Angliæ,' 2 vols. 8vo, Ipswich, 1802. 2. 'Strepsiptera, a new order of Insects proposed,' 'Linnean Transactions,' xi. 86-122. 3. 'Introduction to Entomology,' jointly with James Spence, 4 vols. 8vo, London, 1815-26; vols. i. and ii. 6th edit., with much additional matter, London, 1843; 7th edit. of vols. i. and ii. 8vo, 1856, with Spence's account of the origin and progress of the work. 4. 'Seven Sermons on our Lord's Temptation,' London, 1829. 5. 'On the History, Habits, and Instincts of Animals, being the seventh Bridgewater Treatise,' London, 1835, 8vo, 2 vols. 17 plates; another edition in 12mo, in Bohn's Scientific Library, 1852. 2 vols., with notes by T. Rymer Jones. 6. 'Fauna Boreali-Americana,' pt. iv., the 'Insects,' 4to, Norwich, 1837.

[The Rev. J. Freeman's Life of Kirby, 1852.]

G. T. B.

KIRBYE, GEORGE (d. 1634), musician, was probably born either at Bury St. Edmunds or in its neighbourhood. The first mention of his name occurs in 1592. In that year Thomas East [q. v.] published his 'Whole Book of Psalms,' and Kirbye was employed among others to write new settings to the old psalm tunes for this work. In his preface East states that he had 'intreated the help' of such musicians as he knew to be

'expert in the Arte,' and as Kirbye contributed more to the book than any of the ten composers employed, except John Farmer, it may be assumed that he had made some reputation as a musician at the time. Some time before 1597 he entered the service of Sir Robert Jermyn of Rushbrooke, near Bury St. Edmunds, and it was while he was living at Rushbrooke that he composed and published what he calls the 'first fruites of my poore knowledge in Musicke,' namely 'The first set of English Madrigalls to 4. 5. & 6. voyces. Made & newly published by George Kirbye. London, Printed by Thomas Este, dwelling in aldersgate street, 1597.' The part-books contain twenty-four madrigals. Kirbye dedicated the work to 'Mistris Anne & Mistris Frauncis Iermin, daughters to the right worshipfull Syr Robert Iermin, Knight (his very good Maister).' In the same year (16 Feb. 1597-8) George Kyrby (sic) married Anne Saxye at Bradfield St. George, the neighbouring parish to Rushbrooke. His next publications were two madrigals composed for the 'Triumphs of Oriana,' 1601. In the copy of the 'Triumphs' belonging to the Music School, Oxford, Kirbye's contribution is a six-part madrigal, 'With Angells face and brightnesse,' not to be confounded with Norcome's five-part setting of the same words. In other copies this is replaced by a second six-part madrigal, 'Bright Phœbus greetes most cleerely.' The last named only is printed in Hawes's edition of the 'Triumphs of Oriana.'

After this date Kirbye published nothing, though the dedication of the first set of madrigals implies that he intended to publish other works.

In 1626 he was living in St. Mary's parish in Bury St. Edmunds; probably he had already bought the house in Whiting Street which he occupied till his death. On 11 June 1626 the burial of his wife Anne is recorded in the register of St. Mary's, Bury St. Edmunds, and in 1627-8 his name twice appears with another's at the foot of the same register, probably as one of the churchwardens. He died in 1634, and was buried at St. Mary's on 6 Oct. of that year. The will of Kirbye, 'musition,' dated 10 March 1633, was proved 7 Oct. 1634. He left 10l. each to his brother, Walter Kirbye, and his sister, Alice Moore, widow: and all the rest of his property, including his house in Whiting Street and his personal estate (except a few small sums), to his servant Agnes Seaman, kinswoman to his late wife. He appears to have left no children.

A new edition of Kirbye's 'First Set of Madrigals,' edited by the present writer, was published in 1891-2. In the library of the Royal College of Music are old manuscript copies of twenty-six madrigals by Kirbye, which include nine that are not found in his printed works. They are all imperfect except the seven four-part madrigals, of which only one is unpublished. In the Bodleian Library (MS. Mus. f. 16-19 and 20-4) are seven unpublished five-part madrigals and two four-part motets, all imperfect. In the library of Christ Church, Oxford, are copies of three madrigals from the 'First Set of Madrigals,' with different words.

[Registers of St. Mary's, Bury St. Edmunds, and of Bradfield St. George, near Bury St. Edmunds; Bury St. Edmunds Wills, Liber Colman 1631-5, fol. 368; Grove's Dict. of Music, ii. 59; Burney's Hist. of Music, iii. 123; Mus. Ant. Society's edition of Este's Whole Book of Psalms; works mentioned above; the present writer's edition of the First Set of Madrigals.]

G. E. P. A.

KIRK. [See also KIRKE.]

KIRK, JOHN (1724?-1778?), medallist, was probably born about 1724 (cf. HAWKINS, *Med. Illustr.* ii. 559-60). He became (about 1740?) the pupil of James Anthony Dassier [q. v.], and from about 1740 till 1776 produced a large number of medals signed KIRK or I. KIRK. He was a medallist of moderate ability. In 1745 Kirk was living in St. Paul's Churchyard, London (*ib.* ii. 603). In 1762 and 1763 he received premiums from the Society of Arts. He was a member of the Incorporated Society of Artists, and exhibited medals of the royal family, &c., in 1773-5-6. Redgrave states that Kirk died in London on 27 Nov. 1776; but several medals in the British Museum (cf. *Numismatic Chronicle*, 1890, p. 54, No. 7) signed by Kirk bear the date 1778, and are almost conclusive evidence that he was still alive in that year. Kirk's principal medals are: 1. Bust of George II (no reverse), signed 'I. Kirk F. ætate 16.' 1740(?) 2. Sir John Barnard, circ. 1744. 3. Recapture of Prague, 1744. 4. Loyal Association Medal, 1745. 5. Medals relating to the Rebellion of '45, 1745-6. 6. Tuesday Club of Annapolis, 1746. 7. Counters with heads of the Royal Family, 1746. 8. William, Prince of Orange, 1746. 9. Peace of Aix-la-Chapelle, 1749. 10. Free British Fishery Society, 1751. 11. Louisburg taken (from design by Cipriani), 1758. 12. Battle of Minden, 1759. 13. Lord-chancellor Camden, 1763. 14. Series of thirteen medalets given away to subscribers to the 'Sentimental Magazine,' 1773-5 (*Gent. Mag.* 1797, pp. 469, 471). 15. Duke of Athol, 1774.

16. Lord Bathurst (Six Clerks Office), 1776. 17. Death of Lord Chatham, 1778. 18. Lord Chesterfield, 1778. Certain medals of 1745 and 1746 were made and signed by John Kirk in conjunction with A. Kirk (HAWKINS, ii. 606, 608, 613; cf. 614). The editors of the 'Medallic Illustrations' conjecture (ii. 729) that this A. Kirk was a brother of John, and suppose that he died in 1761, apparently assuming that he was identical with the 'Mr. Kirk, senr.,' whose death in St. Paul's Churchyard is recorded in the 'Gentleman's Magazine' (1761, p. 539) as having taken place on 19 Nov. 1761.

[Hawkins's Medallic Illustrations, ed. Franks and Grueber, ii. 729; Redgrave's Dict. of Artists of Engl. School; Kirk's Medals in Brit. Mus.]

W. W.

KIRK, JOHN, D.D. (1760-1851), catholic divine and antiquary, son of William Kirk and his wife Mary Fielding, was born at Ruckley, near Acton Burnell, Shropshire, on 13 April 1760, and at ten years of age was sent to Sedgley Park school, Staffordshire. He was admitted into the English College at Rome on 5 June 1773, a few months before the suppression of the Society of Jesus by Clement XIV. He was thus the last scholar received at the college by the jesuits who had had the conduct of it, by favour of the holy see, for 193 years (FOLEY, *Records*, vi. 504). He was ordained priest on 18 Dec. 1784. Returning to England in August 1785, his first mission was at Aldenham Hall, Shropshire, in the family of Sir Richard Acton. In 1786 he became chaplain at Sedgley Park school, and as vice-president assisted the Rev. Thomas Southworth, whom he succeeded as president in 1793. He had previously removed to the small mission at Pipehill, near Lichfield, and he had had charge of the congregation at Tamworth. In July 1797 he left Sedgley to become chaplain and private secretary to Dr. Charles Berington [q. v.], vicar apostolic of the midland district, and after the bishop's sudden death (8 June 1798) he remained at the episcopal residence at Longbirch till the appointment of Dr. Gregory Stapleton to the vicariate in 1801. He then removed to Lichfield, where a chapel built by him was opened on 11 Nov. 1803; afterwards enlarged, it was converted in 1834 into the little Norman church of St. Cross. He also erected chapels at Hopwas, near Tamworth, and in Tamworth itself. By diploma dated 9 Nov. 1841, Pope Gregory XVI conferred upon him the degree of D.D. He died at Lichfield 21 Dec. 1851, aged 90.

Monsignor Weedall says of Kirk: ' He formed a perfect specimen of the olden times, a type of the fine old English priest; methodical, dignified, devout.' There is a portrait of him, engraved by Deere, in the 'Catholic Directory' for 1853.

During his residence in Rome, and for upwards of forty years of his long life, he was diligently preparing materials for a continuation of Dodd's 'Church History of England.' With infinite labour he transcribed or collected, and methodically arranged, letters, tracts, annals, records, diaries, and innumerable miscellaneous papers, forming upwards of fifty volumes in folio and quarto. An account of all these materials, specifically arranged under distinct heads, was published by him in a 'Letter to the Rev. Joseph Berington, respecting the Continuation of Dodd's Church History of England,' Lichfield, September 1826 (Catholic Miscellany, vi. 250, 328, 405). Finally he handed over the work to the Rev. Mark Aloysius Tierney [q. v.] of Arundel, who brought out a new edition of Dodd's 'History,' 5 vols. London, 1839–43, 8vo. This edition is incomplete, ending with the year 1625, and no portion of a projected continuation ever appeared. On Tierney's death in 1862 the manuscript materials were bequeathed to Dr. Thomas Grant, bishop of Southwark, and they are now in the possession of that prelate's successor, Dr. John Butt. Transcripts of some of Kirk's letters and manuscripts are preserved in the library of St. Francis Xavier's College at Liverpool (FOLEY, Records, vii. 20). Four small but closely written bundles of biographical collections by Kirk, mostly of a later date than Dodd, were in the possession of the late Cardinal Manning (GILLOW, Dict. of the English Catholics, i. Pref. p. xv).

About 1794 Kirk undertook the task of deciphering, copying, and preparing for publication the 'State Papers and Letters' of Sir Ralph Sadler, ambassador to Scotland in the time of Elizabeth. These were published in 3 vols. 1809, 4to, by Arthur Clifford, with a biographical sketch by Sir Walter Scott. The original papers were then in the possession of the Cliffords of Tixall, Staffordshire; they are now in the British Museum (Athenæum, 1 March 1890, p. 277).

Kirk wrote, in collaboration with the Rev. Joseph Berington, 'The Faith of Catholics confirmed by Scripture and attested by the Fathers of the first five centuries of the Church,' London, 1813 and 1830, 8vo: 3rd edit. revised and greatly enlarged by the Rev. James Waterworth, 3 vols. London, 1846, 8vo. There is a Latin translation in Joseph Braun's 'Bibliotheca Regularum Fidei,' Bonn, 1844, 8vo, vol. i. The work was attacked by the Rev. John Graham, M.A., in

a review printed at the end of his 'Annals of Ireland,' London, 1819, 8vo; and the Rev. Richard Thomas Pembroke Pope published 'Roman Misquotation; or, Certain Passages from the Fathers adduced in Kirk's work brought to the test of their originals,' London, 1840, 8vo. In consequence of some exceptions having been taken to the 'Propositions' which form the heading of 'The Faith of Catholics,' Kirk published 'Roman Catholic Principles in reference to God and the King. First published in the year 1680. To which is prefixed an inquiry respecting the Editions and the Author of that valuable tract,' London, 1815, 8vo. He proved by circumstantial evidence that the 'Principles' were drawn up by the Benedictine father James Corker [q. v.]

[Catholic Directory, 1853, p. 129; Catholic Magazine and Review, vol. v. p. ci; Gent. Mag. new ser. xxxvii. 304, ccxii. 509; Rambler, ix. 244–9, 425; Smith's Brewood, 2nd edit. 1874, p. 51; Monsignor Weedall in Tablet, 24 Jan. 1852, p. 51, and 31 Jan. p. 71.] T. C.

KIRK, ROBERT (1641?–1692), Gaelic scholar, was youngest son of James Kirk, minister at Aberfoyle, Perthshire, and was born presumably there about 1641. He studied at Edinburgh University (where he graduated M.A. in 1661), and afterwards at St. Andrews. In 1664 he became minister of Balquhidder, Perthshire, and in 1685 was appointed to his father's old charge at Aberfoyle, where he continued until his death on 14 May 1692. He was buried near the east end of the church, and his grave is marked by a stone with the inscription, 'Robertus Kirk, A.M., Linguæ Hibernæ Lumen.' He is said to have had a benefice in England (REID), but this is incorrect. He was twice married, and when his first wife died cut out with his own hands an epitaph for her (ib.), which is still to be seen at Balquhidder. His eldest son, Colin, became a writer to the signet, and another, Robert, was appointed minister of Dornoch, Sutherlandshire.

Kirk was an admirable Gaelic scholar, and most of his literary work lay in this direction. He was the author of the first complete translation of the Scottish metrical psalms into Gaelic, published at Edinburgh in 1684 under the title of 'Psalma Dhaibhidh an Meadrachd,' &c. ('Psalms of David in Metre,' &c.) This version bears a grant of 'privilidge' from the lords of the privy council, forbidding any one to print it for eleven years. During its preparation Kirk learned that the synod of Argyle intended to bring out a rival version, and some curious stories are told of the expedients to which he resorted in order to keep himself awake while working almost night and day in order to be first in the field (REID). Kirk's psalter is extremely rare, but copies are in the British Museum, Advocates' (Edinburgh), and Glasgow University Libraries. In 1689 Kirk was called to London to superintend the printing of the Gaelic Bible prepared under the direction of Bishop Bedell, and published in 1690. To this version he added a short Gaelic vocabulary (6 pp.), which was republished, with additions, 'by the learned Mr. Ed. Lhuyd,' in Nicolson's 'Historical Library' (8vo, London, 1702). He had a firm belief in fairy superstitions, and wrote a curious work bearing the title of 'The Secret Commonwealth; or an Essay on the Nature and Actions of the Subterranean (and for the most part) Invisible People heretofoir going under the name of Faunes and Fairies, or the lyke, among the Low Country Scots, as they are described by those who have the second sight,' 1691. One hundred copies of this work were reprinted by Ballantyne, Edinburgh, 1815 (4to, pp. 97).

[Reid's Bibliotheca Scoto-Celtica, Glasgow, 1832, p. 21; Nisbet's Heraldry, i. 420; Scott's Fasti Ecclesiæ Scoticanæ, ii. pt. ii. 718; Marshall's Historic Scenes in Perthshire, p. 393; New Statistical Account, vols. iii. and x.; Chambers's Domestic Annals; Scott's Demonology and Witchcraft.] J. C. H.

KIRK, THOMAS (1765?–1797), painter and engraver, born about 1765, was a pupil of Richard Cosway, R.A. [q. v.] He attained some excellence as a painter of historical subjects in the insipid prettiness of the time, and also as a miniature-painter in the style of Cosway. In 1785 he exhibited at the Royal Academy 'Venus presenting Love to Calypso,' and was an occasional exhibitor of Shakespearean, scriptural, and other subjects up to 1795, when he exhibited a number of drawings illustrating popular works of fiction. In 1796 he exhibited for the last time, sending 'Evening' and 'A Dream.' He made a number of graceful drawings, which were engraved as illustrations to Cooke's 'Poets.' Kirk also practised as an engraver in the stipple method, among his engravings being a portrait of the African prince Leboo, from a drawing by Miss Keate, 1789; 'Shepherds in Arcadia,' after G. B. Cipriani, 1789; and 'Titus Andronicus and Lavinia,' from his own painting, done for Boydell's 'Shakespeare,' 1793. He painted other pictures for Boydell, and also for Macklin's 'Bible.' Kirk died of consumption 18 Nov. 1797, and was buried in St. Pancras Church. He worked on an engraving up to the day before he died. There is a pretty admission ticket designed by him for a con-

cert of the Choral Fund at the Haymarket Theatre in 1796.

[Dayes's Sketches of Modern Artists; Redgrave's Dict. of Artists; Dodd's manuscript Hist. of English Engravers (Brit. Mus. Addit. MS. 33402); Royal Academy Catalogues.] L. C.

KIRK, THOMAS (1777–1845), sculptor, born in 1777 at Newry, co. Down, was son of William Kirk and Elizabeth Bible, his wife. His parents moved to Cork when he was a child, but Kirk settled in Dublin in early life and studied sculpture in the art school of the Dublin Society of Artists. He became noted for his fine work in relief on mantelpieces, monuments, &c.; two pieces of 'Spanish Banditti' and 'The Rokeby Cavern Scene' attracted especial attention. His busts also gained him rapid reputation, and they were considered remarkable for the delicate handling of the marble and for distinctness of detail. He exhibited with the Dublin Society, and on the foundation of the Royal Hibernian Academy in 1822 he was chosen one of the foundation members, contributing to their first exhibition several busts and the colossal statue of Thomas Spring-Rice, lord Monteagle, now at Limerick. Kirk was successful in the competition for the Nelson monument in Dublin, and executed the colossal statue of him on the memorial column in Sackville Street. He also executed the statue of George IV in the Linen Hall, that of the Duke of Wellington, and a model of that of George III for the bank in Dublin, which was carried out in marble by other hands. His most important work, however, was the statue of Sir Sidney Smith, commissioned by parliament and placed in Greenwich Hospital. Many busts from his hand are in the Dublin College of Surgeons, the Royal Dublin Society's rooms, the library of Trinity College, and elsewhere in Dublin. Among them are busts of Curran, Thomas Moore, J. Wilson Croker, Mme. Catalani, and other notabilities. Among his groups were 'The Young Champion' executed for Lord de Grey when lord-lieutenant, 'The Orphan Girl' in Christ Church Cathedral, 'The Young Dogstealer' for Viscount Powerscourt, &c. Kirk rarely exhibited in London, but he sent busts to the Royal Academy there in 1825, and occasionally afterwards. Kirk married a Miss Eliza Robinson, and died in 1845, leaving twelve children. One son, Mr. Joseph R. Kirk, inherited his father's skill as a sculptor, and is a member of the Royal Hibernian Academy; other of his sons are the Rev. William Boston Kirk, D.D., and the Very Rev. Francis J. Kirk of St. Mary of the Angels, Bayswater, London.

[Bolster's Quarterly Magazine, 1827, ii, 263; Sarsfield Taylor's Fine Arts in Great Britain and Ireland; Graves's Dict. of Artists, 1760-1880; information kindly supplied by Joseph R. Kirk, R.H.A.] L. C.

KIRKALL, ELISHA (1682 ?-1742), engraver, born at Sheffield in Yorkshire about 1682, was son of a locksmith, from whom he learnt to work and engrave on metal. Walpole, Redgrave, and others erroneously give him the christian name of Edward. About 1702 he came to London, where he was employed 'to grave arms, ornaments, etch and cut stamps in hard mettal for printing in books for several years' (see Vertue in Brit. Mus. Addit. MS. 23070). He also studied drawing in the new academy in Great Queen Street, Lincoln's Inn Fields. He married early in life, as appears from his trade card, preserved in the print room of the British Museum (reproduction in Linton's 'Masters of Wood-engraving'), which bears the names of Mr. Elisha and Mrs. Elizabeth Kirkall, and the date 31 Aug. 1707. This card was cut in relief on metal, and not on wood, as sometimes stated. Kirkall has been classed (see CHATTO and JACKSON's Treatise on Wood-engraving) as a wood-engraver, and credited with the revival of the art in the eighteenth century. He is also claimed as the first exponent in England of the white-line intaglio manner of wood-engraving, afterwards brought to such perfection by Thomas Bewick [q. v.] It is very doubtful, however, whether he engraved on wood at all. He engraved the copperplate frontispiece to W. Howell's 'Medulla Historiæ Anglicanæ' (1712), the plates for Maittaire's edition of the works of Terence (1713), for the translation of Ovid's 'Metamorphoses' (Tonson & Watts, 1717), and for Rowe's translation of Lucan's 'Pharsalia' (1718). Certain cuts in Maittaire's edition of 'Sallust' (1713) and Dryden's 'Plays' (Tonson & Watts, 1717), usually described as on wood and assigned to Kirkall, appear to be on metal. The attribution to him of the woodcuts in Croxall's edition of 'Æsop's Fables' (1722) rests on surmise only (see LINTON, loc. cit.) Some of the copperplates engraved by Kirkall show both artistic merit and technical skill. He is better known for his mezzotint engravings, frequently printed in green ink, and occasionally in a variety of colours. In this manner he published by subscription sixteen views of shipping by William Van de Velde the younger, the seven cartoons of Raphael, three hunting scenes by J. E. Ridinger, &c. In 1722 he introduced a new method of chiaroscuro engraving, produced by adding fresh tints to the coloured mezzotint engravings by the superimposition of wood blocks in the manner of the early Italian chiaroscuro engravers. In this method he produced a copy of Ugo da Carpi's chiaroscuro engraving of '.Æneas and Anchises,' after Raphael, and a number of reproductions of drawings by Italian masters. A collection of these is in the print room at the British Museum. He also engraved in a similar manner a portrait of Sir Christopher Wren, by John Closterman [q. v.], in an architectural frame designed by Henry Cook [q. v.], and a portrait of Dr. William Stukeley the antiquary, for whose antiquarian works he likewise engraved some ordinary copperplates. He continued to engrave plates for the booksellers, among others for Oldsworth and others' translation of Homer's 'Iliad' (B. Lintot, 1734), Pope's translation of the same work (B. Lintot, 1736), and the plates to an edition of Inigo Jones's 'Stonehenge' (1725). A portrait by Kirkall of Eliza Haywood [q. v.], prefixed to her 'Works' in 1724, earned for him a couplet in Pope's 'Dunciad.' Early in 1732 William Hogarth published his famous set of engravings, 'The Harlot's Progress.' As there was no legal protection at the time, they were quickly pirated, Kirkall being first in the field with a set of free copies in mezzotint, printed in green, and published at his house in Dockwell's Court, Whitefriars, in November 1732. Among other engravings by Kirkall may be noted a portrait of Senesino the singer, in mezzotint, after J. Goupy, thirty plates of flowers after Van Huysum, and some plates of shipping after T. Baston. He died in Whitefriars in December 1742, leaving a son, aged about twenty-two.

[Vertue's MSS. (Brit. Mus. Add. MSS. 23071. 23076, 23079); Dodd's manuscript History of English Engravers (ib. 33402); Walpole's Anecdotes of Painting, ed. Wornum; Austin Dobson's William Hogarth, 1891; The Portfolio, xv. 2; authorities mentioned in the text.] L. C.

KIRKBY, JOHN (d. 1290), treasurer and bishop of Ely, was in early life one of the clerks of the chancery of Henry III. He may have been of the same family as the John Kirkby who acted as justice in 1227 and 1236, and who was also, perhaps, parson of Kirkby Lonsdale, Westmoreland (Foss, Judges of England, ii. 377-8); but the name is a common one, and all such identification purely conjectural. In 1271 Kirkby received a grant from Henry III of rents worth 47s. 9d. a year in Medbourne, Leicestershire, along with the advowson of Medbourne Church (Cal. Rot. Pat. p. 44 b). On 7 Aug. 1272 the custody of the great seal was handed over to him on the death of the chancellor, Richard Middleton (Excerpta e Rot. Fin. ii. 575). On

16 Nov. Henry III died, whereupon Kirkby delivered up the seal to Archbishop Walter Giffard of York and the other councillors of the new king (*ib.* ii. 590). Under Edward I Kirkby remained attached to the chancery, and seems almost always to have been entrusted with the care of the great seal, when the chancellor, Bishop Burnell, was absent, either in his diocese or beyond sea. This was the case in February 1278, May 1279, February 1281, and March 1283 (Foss, iii. 111; Madox, *Hist. of Exchequer*, i. 71; *Cal. Rot. Pat.* pp. 48, 50). The name of vice-chancellor is given to him ('Ann. Dunst.' in *Ann. Mon.* iii. 305; *Deputy-Keeper's Seventh Report*, App. ii. 239), which suggests some sort of permanent official position. At least as early as 1276 he appears as a member of the royal council (*Parl. Writs*, i. 6).

In 1282 Edward I's finances were in a straitened condition through the expenses of the Welsh war. On 19 June he issued writs from Chester informing the sheriffs that he had appointed Kirkby as his commissioner for declaring verbally to all the shires (except Cornwall) certain arduous and important affairs (*ib.* i. 384). Walter of Agmondesham was associated with him, and all sheriffs and officials were instructed to assist him. Similar writs were sent to the boroughs, the religious houses, and the other local authorities. The object of Kirkby's mission was to persuade the various communities to make voluntary grants of money to the king. Kirkby spent the whole of the autumn in travelling about the country, and collected large sums of money. His mission is interesting as the last great attempt at carrying out the older conceptions of taxation, which rested on individual assent and grant (Stubbs, *Const. Hist.* ii. 124). Kirkby's activity drew upon him the anger of the monastic annalists (cf. *Parl. Writs*, i. 385, 387, 388; B. de Cotton, *Hist. Angl.* p. 162; the Continuator of Florence of Worcester, ii. 225, and the Dunstable and Worcester 'Annals' in *Annales Monastici*, iii. 302, iv. 487). But the sums collected were insufficient for the king's purpose. Edward therefore summoned two great parliamentary conventions of the clergy of the two provinces at York and Northampton, with meetings of lay representatives side by side with them. To the Northampton meeting Kirkby was sent as the royal representative on 5 Jan. 1283, along with Edmund, earl of Cornwall, and the abbot of Westminster, the treasurer (*Parl. Writs*, i. 11). Their exertions resulted in a grant by the commons of a thirtieth, from which, however, the sums previously collected by Kirkby were uniformly deducted (*ib.* i. 12).

Kirkby was rewarded for his services to the crown by so large a number of benefices that strict churchmen looked upon him as a scandalous pluralist. Though only in deacon's orders, and entirely occupied with affairs of state, he was rector of St. Berian's, Cornwall, dean of Wimborne, canon of Wells and York, and, after 1272, archdeacon of Coventry (Le Neve, *Fasti Eccl. Angl.* i. 568, ed. Hardy). In 1283 he was elected bishop of Rochester by the prior and convent of the cathedral. But Archbishop Peckham was resolutely opposed to rewarding mere officials with high ecclesiastical preferment, and exerted so much pressure that on 17 May Kirkby resigned his claims to the bishopric (Peckham, *Letters*, iii. 1032). Soon after the archbishop wrote to the monks of Rochester directing them to make a fresh election, on the ground that Kirkby's notorious pluralism made him an impossible candidate (*ib.* ii. 575-6). The statement in Prynne (*Records*, iii. 359) that Kirkby was elected bishop of Chester (Lichfield) seems a mere mistake in names.

On 6 Jan. 1284 Kirkby was appointed treasurer in succession to the abbot of Westminster, who had died suddenly (*Ann. Dunst.* p. 305). He held this post until his death. Early in 1285 Kirkby had a hot dispute with the Londoners. The mayor, to avoid appearing before the treasurer at an inquest held in the Tower, resigned his office. Thereupon Kirkby took possession of the city, and directed all the leading citizens to appear next day before the king at Westminster. Edward ordered a large number into custody, and Kirkby appointed two agents to take the sheriffs' part in collecting the customary ferm of the city ('Ann. Londin.' in *Chron. Edward I and II*, i. 94). In four days the prisoners were released, but the city was not under the rule of a warden, and did not recover its mayor until 1298 (*Monumenta Gildhallæ Lond.* i. 16-18, Rolls Ser.) Kirkby's high-handed action provoked much resentment.

From May 1286 to August 1289 Edward I was abroad. But on 8 July 1286 the king issued from Paris a license to the monks of Ely to elect a new bishop on the death of Hugh de Balsham [q. v.] On 26 July Kirkby was elected. Peckham offered no further opposition. On 7 Aug. Kirkby was presented before Edward at Melun, and on 17 Aug. Peckham confirmed the election at Saltwood in Kent. The temporalities were restored on 7 Sept., and on Saturday 21 Sept. Peckham himself ordained Kirkby priest at Faversham (Peckham, *Letters*, iii. 1041). Next day (22 Sept.) Peckham consecrated him bishop at Canterbury (Stubbs, *Registrum Sacrum*

Anglicanum, p. 47 ; Anglia Sacra, i. 638 ; Ann. Osney, p. 398 ; Ann. Dunstable, p. 326, say on 29 Sept.) Strict churchmen observed with disgust that the new bishop at once hurried back to the duties of the treasury (Ann. Dunst. p. 326). On 24 Dec. Kirkby was enthroned at Ely (Cont. Flor. Wig. ii. 237).

The continued absence of the king and his special need of large supplies (Madox, i. 357) imposed peculiar responsibilities upon the treasurer. In 1287 Kirkby was sent to South Wales, along with Earl Gilbert of Gloucester and the prior of St. John's, to put down the rebellion of Rhys ab Maredudd (Ann. Dunst. p. 338; cf. Ann. Osney, p. 310). Despite the remissness of Gloucester, Rhys was forced to flee to Ireland. In February 1289 the magnates were convoked at London, and Kirkby asked them to grant a general subsidy to defray the expenses incurred by the king in France. But the barons replied that they would pay nothing until the king came back. Thereupon Kirkby, as a last resource, began to tallage the cities, boroughs, and royal domains (Ann. Osney, p. 316). The crisis brought Edward home in August (ib. p. 323). He approved his treasurer's acts.

Early in the next year Kirkby was smitten by a sharp attack of fever (ib. p. 323), from which he recovered, but he died at Ely from a recurrence of the malady on Palm Sunday (26 March 1290) 'about the hour of compline' (Anglia Sacra, i. 638; Cotton, p. 174). He was buried in his cathedral, on the north side of the choir, before the altar of St. John the Baptist.

Kirkby was a liberal benefactor of his see. He gave an inn, called the Bell, opposite the convent of the Franciscans at London, to provide for celebrating his anniversary, and by will left his successors a house and nine cottages in Holborn. This house, called Ely Place, became the London residence of the bishops of Ely, and was given to Sir Christopher Hatton [q. v.] in 1577 (Bentham, Ely, 1771, pp. 151–2). A street formed out of the garden is still called Kirby Street. During his lifetime Kirkby had claimed a right to lodge at the Temple, but the master of the knights disputed his pretensions, and Kirkby seems to have made this bequest to avoid similar troubles in the future. In most respects Kirkby was a bad bishop, and a very unfavourable picture of him is drawn by the chroniclers, whose houses had suffered from his exactions. Cotton (p. 147) gives some Latin lines describing him as greedy, loquacious, self-assertive, and quarrelsome. But the Dunstable chronicler (p. 358) admits that he was just and truthful. His heir was

his brother, William Kirkby, who was thirty years old at his death (Calendarium Genealogicum, p. 146). He had also four sisters—Margaret, Alice, Matilda, and Mabel—all married, and at the time of his death aged thirty-eight, thirty-six, thirty-four, and thirty-two respectively. Probably he was himself not an old man. He had some landed property, and in 1279 had inherited the estate of Amicia de Gorham in Northamptonshire.

[Monachus Eliensis in Anglia Sacra, i. 637–8; Calendarium Genealogicum, Excerpta e Rotulis Finium, Calendarium Lit. Patentium, Fœdera, vol. i., all in Record Commission; Annals of Dunstable, Winchester, Osney, and Wykes, in Annales Monastici; Peckham's Letters, Chronicles of Edward I and II, B. de Cotton, all in Rolls Ser.; Continuation of Florence of Worcester, in Engl. Hist. Soc.; Le Neve's Fasti Ecclesiæ Anglicanæ, ed. Hardy; Bentham's History and Antiquities of Ely, 1771, pp. 151–2; Stubbs's Const. Hist. vol. ii.; Foss's Judges of England, iii. 110–12.]   T. F. T.

KIRKBY, JOHN de (d. 1352), bishop of Carlisle, was an Augustinian canon at Carlisle, and afterwards prior of the house. He was elected bishop of Carlisle on 8 May 1332, the royal assent was given on 18 May, the temporalities were restored on 9 July, and on 19 July he was consecrated by William de Melton, archbishop of York, at South Burton, near Beverley (Stubbs, Reg. Sacr. Angl. p. 53). He was present at the installation of Richard de Bury as bishop of Durham on 5 June 1334, and when Edward Baliol did homage for Scotland at Newcastle a fortnight later. In September 1337, in company with Thomas Wake and other barons, he plundered Teviotdale and Nithsdale during twelve days. When in October the Scots retaliated by invading England, and burnt the suburbs of Carlisle, the Lords Percy and Neville came to the rescue, and the Scots were defeated (17 Oct.) At the beginning of November the Scots besieged the English in Edinburgh; Kirkby and Ralph Dacre collected the men of Westmoreland and Cumberland, and marching into Scotland raised the siege. In 1341 the treasury was ordered to pay Kirkby 200l., part of arrears of 529l. 4s. due to him for carrying on the war with the Scots. Next year he accompanied Henry of Lancaster, earl of Derby, in an expedition to raise the siege of Lochmaben Castle. In 1343 he was a commissioner with Richard de Bury to treat for peace with Scotland (Fœdera, ii. pt. ii. p. 1230), and next year was directed to assist Edward Baliol (ib. iii. pt. i. p. 21). In 1345 the Scots, under Sir William Douglas, made a raid into Cumberland, and were defeated by Kirkby and Robert Oggill; the bishop, who distinguished himself by his valour, was unhorsed during the engagement and nearly captured. According to Geoffrey le Baker, Kirkby was also one of the English leaders at the battle of Neville's Cross on 17 Oct. 1346 (p. 87, ed. Thompson). In 1348 he was sent to escort Joan, daughter of Edward III, to her affianced husband, Alfonso of Castile. Kirkby died in 1352; permission to elect his successor was granted on 3 Dec. 1352. His episcopate was a troublous one, owing to the frequent Scottish raids. He also suffered from disorders within his own borders, and on at least three occasions, in 1333, 1337, and 1342, was attacked by brigands in the neighbourhood of his cathedral city (RAINE, *Letters from Northern Registers*, pp. 364–8, Rolls Ser.) As a consequence he was frequently compelled to hold his ordinations outside his diocese. Kirkby is said to have been engaged in many disputes with his chapter and archdeacons, and to have been excommunicated for the non-payment of tenths on certain lands to the pope.

[Walsingham's Historia Anglicana, i. 254, 266–7 (Rolls Ser.); Chron. Lanercost, pp. 276–277, 291–3 (Bannatyne Club); Nicolson and Burn's Hist. Westmorland and Cumberland, ii. 264–6; Jefferson's Carlisle, pp. 194–5; Le Neve's Fasti Eccl. Angl. iii. 235.] C. L. K.

KIRKBY, JOHN (1705–1754), divine, son of the Rev. Thomas Kirkby, is stated in the register of St. John's College, Cambridge, to have been born at 'Lowusborough,' i.e. Londesborough, Yorkshire, but he says himself that he was a native of Cumberland. He was educated at home by his father, and proceeded, 4 May 1723, aged 18, to St. John's College, Cambridge, where he graduated B.A. 1726 and M.A. 1745. According to his own account he began life as a poor curate in Cumberland. On 8 Dec. 1739 he was appointed vicar of Waldershare in Kent, and on 19 Nov. 1743 rector of Blackmanstone, Romney Marsh. 'A Demonstration from Christian Principles that the present regulation of ecclesiastical revenues in the Church of England is contrary to the design of Christianity,' which he published on behalf of the poorer clergy at Canterbury in 1743, is said to have excluded him from further preferment (cf. manuscript note in Brit. Mus. copy). To eke out his slender income he in 1744 became tutor to Edward Gibbon, then a boy of seven. He held, while at Putney with the Gibbons, some clerical appointment, but lost it by unluckily omitting the name of King George in the morning prayers, and so irritating his patron (GIBBON, 'Memoirs' in

Miscell. Works, i. 20). Gibbon liked and respected him, says that he had thought much on the subjects of languages and education, and seems to have regretted his hasty departure. Kirkby died 21 May 1754.

Kirkby's chief works are : 1. 'The Capacity and Extent of the Human Understanding, exemplified in the extraordinary case of Automathes, a young nobleman . . . accidentally left in his infancy upon a desert island,' London, 1745, 12mo; an attempt to illustrate the growth of men's ideas in a state of nature. A second edition appeared at Dublin in 1746. Gibbon describes it as a poor performance, and as a plagiarism of well-known romances. It seems largely borrowed from the 'History of Autonous' (1736). It is reprinted in Weber's 'Popular Romances' (Edinb. 1812, pp. 583–638). 2. 'The Impostor detected, or the Counterfeit Saint turn'd inside out,' London, 1750; a bitter attack on 'those diabolical seducers called Methodists.' 3. 'An Effectual and Easy Demonstration of the Truth of the coequal Trinity of the Godhead,' London, 1752. An introduction of thirteen pages gives an account of a ' new system of logic' projected by Kirkby. Kirkby also published in 1734, under the title 'The Usefulness of Mathematical Learning explained,' a translation from the Latin of the mathematical lectures of Dr. Isaac Barrow, and Gibbon credits him with a Latin and English grammar (1746), of which he speaks highly. De Morgan mentions as by Kirkby 'Arithmetical Institutions, containing a Compleat System of Arithmetic, Natural, Logarithmetical, and Algebraical,' 4to (*Arithmetical Books*, pp. 67, 71).

[Hasted's Hist. of Kent, iii. 432, &c.; Kirkby's books; Notes and Queries, 6th ser. xii. 68, 177; information kindly supplied by R. F. Scott, esq., of St. John's College, Cambridge.] R. E. A.

KIRKBY, RICHARD (d. 1703), captain in the navy, passed his examination for the rank of lieutenant under order of 28 March 1680. On 10 July 1689 he was appointed second lieutenant of the St. Michael, and was shortly afterwards promoted to be commander of the Success, employed in the convoy of the coasting trade. In 1694 he was appointed to the Southampton, with Admiral Russell in the Mediterranean, one of the ships present at the capture of the Content and Trident on 18–19 Jan. 1694–5, but excluded from sharing in the prize-money [see KILLIGREW, JAMES]. In 1696 the Southampton returned to England, and was sent out to the West Indies, where Kirkby is said to have 'behaved in a way very much to his credit' (CHARNOCK). The Southampton, however, does not appear to have been either a comfortable or a well-disciplined ship. Her chaplain was discharged, on her return from the Mediterranean, on account of some unpleasantness with the captain; the boatswain was broken and flogged, by sentence of court-martial, for disobedience and insolence; a seaman was sentenced to be flogged and 'towed ashore' for 'scandalous actions, to the great corruption of good manners;' and on her return from the West Indies in 1698 Kirkby himself was tried on charges of embezzling, plunder, and of cruelty and oppression. The alleged embezzlement admitted of a satisfactory explanation, and he was acquitted of cruelty, though it appeared that he had punished a seaman for straggling by ordering him to be 'tied up by the right arm and left leg for several hours,' the right foot being, however, allowed to rest on the deck. In February 1700-1 Kirkby was appointed to the Ruby, and again sent out to the West Indies. He arrived at Barbadoes in November, and in March went on to Jamaica. There he was moved into the Defiance. The death of Rear-admiral Martin had left him 'the oldest officer under the flag;' and though in May he was superseded from this position by the arrival of Rear-admiral Whetstone, he remained the senior captain on the station. He was thus second in command of the squadron which sailed in August under Vice-admiral Benbow [q. v.], and which met the French squadron off Santa Marta on the 19th. Benbow's signals to close the enemy and engage were not obeyed; a mutinous, disobedient, or cowardly spirit took possession of almost all the captains; and Kirkby, as the senior, appears to have been the prime mover in the crime. The result was that after a running skirmish of five days, those English ships that engaged were beaten off, and Benbow was himself mortally wounded. On the return of the squadron to Jamaica, Kirkby and his fellow-mutineers were tried by court-martial. One had died previously, two were suspended, one was cashiered, Kirkby and Wade were sent home in the Bristol [see ACTON, EDWARD], and were shot on board her on 16 April 1703, two days after her arrival in Plymouth Sound. Kirkby had written a long letter to the secretary of the admiralty, alleging that the admiral's injudicious and ignorant conduct was the cause of his defeat; that the court-martial was ordered in dread of an inquiry into his own fault, and that the same dread had made him desirous of hurrying on the execution, which the court-martial had not agreed to. His plea, however, is contradicted by the evidence of the court-martial, the witnesses, whether belonging to other ships or to the De-

fiance, agreeing with remarkable unanimity on the details of Kirkby's misconduct.

[Charnock's Biog. Nav. ii. 329; Barchett's Transactions at Sea; Lediard's Naval Hist.; minutes of courts-martial, letters and other documents in the Public Record Office.]

J. K. L.

KIRKCALDY or **KIRKALDY**, SIR JAMES (d. 1556), of Grange, lord high treasurer of Scotland, was descended from the elder branch of a family which at a very early period had been settled in Fifeshire, his father being William Kirkaldy of Grange. Introduced to the court of James V by his father-in-law, Sir John Melville of Raith, he soon became a special favourite of the king, who made him a lord of the bedchamber, and on 24 March 1537 appointed him lord high treasurer of Scotland. He was one of the chief opponents of the ambitious political projects of Cardinal Beaton and the ecclesiastics. It was chiefly owing to his persuasion that the king refused to sanction the punishment of a number of noblemen and barons whose names had been inscribed by Cardinal Beaton on a 'scroll' as guilty of heresy (KNOX, *Works*, i. 82-4; and more at length in SIR JAMES MELVILLE'S *Memoirs*, pp. 60-2). He also advised the king to check the power of the ecclesiastics and increase the revenues of the crown by retaking possession of the benefices as they fell vacant (*ib.* p. 63). The supporters of Beaton were afraid to oppose his statements in his presence; for, according to Sir James Melville, he was 'a stout, bold man,' ready to maintain his words at the point of the sword. But during his absence from court, at the marriage of his second son to the heiress of Kelly, they persuaded the king to grant a warrant for his imprisonment. Arriving, however, suddenly in Edinburgh, he obtained an interview with the king before the warrant could be executed, and got it countermanded (*ib.* p. 67). According to Melville it was during the absence of Kirkcaldy at this time that James V was induced to withdraw from his engagement to meet Henry VIII at York (*ib.*) After the rout of Solway (25 Nov. 1542) the king on his way to Falkland visited Kirkcaldy's house at Hallyards, but Kirkcaldy himself was absent (KNOX, i. 90). Chiefly by the persuasion of Kirkcaldy, the Earl of Arran, on the death of the king shortly afterwards, was induced to assume the regency, in order to counteract Cardinal Beaton's attempt to place himself and three other persons in the regency (*ib.* i. 93; SIR JAMES MELVILLE, *Memoirs*, p. 71). The cardinal nevertheless soon persuaded Arran to dismiss Kirkcaldy from the treasurership.

In the following year Crichton, laird of Brunston, informed Henry VIII that Kirkcaldy and the Master of Rothes were prepared to apprehend or slay the cardinal if assured of his support. Henry VIII approved of the scheme, but through precautions taken by the cardinal it was for the time frustrated (see especially 'Historical Remarks on the Assassination of Cardinal Beaton' in Appendix to TYTLER, *History of Scotland*). Kirkcaldy, however, never lost sight of his purpose; although he did not take an actual part in the assassination of the cardinal in 1546, he was one of its main instigators, and on the evening succeeding the assassination joined the murderers in the castle of St. Andrews. On 9 March he, along with others in the castle, signed a contract with the king of England, engaging to promote a marriage between Prince Edward and Mary Queen of Scots and to further the unity of the two realms. On the surrender of St. Andrews castle in the following July he was carried a prisoner to France, where he was confined in the castle of Cherbourg (KNOX, i. 225). According to Knox, strenuous efforts were made to induce Kirkcaldy and the other prisoners to attend the mass, but they remained obdurate (*ib.*) Through the intercession of the queen-dowager they were released in July 1550 (*ib.* p. 233). Kirkcaldy died some time in 1556. By his wife, Janet Melville, daughter of Sir James Melville of Raith, he had five sons: Sir William [q. v.], Sir James, hanged on the same scaffold with Sir William in 1573, Sir David, Thomas, and George. Of his four daughters: Marjory was married to Sir Henry Ramsay of Coluthie; Agnes, to Sir Robert Drummond of Carnock; Marion, to William Semple, second baron of Cathcart; and Elizabeth, to Sir John Mowbray of Barnbougle.

[Knox's Works; Sir James Melville's Memoirs; Crawford's Officers of State, pp. 374-5.]
T. F. H.

KIRKCALDY, Sir WILLIAM (*d.* 1573), of Grange, was the eldest son of Sir James Kirkcaldy [q. v.] Randolph, minister of Elizabeth, in a letter to him, 1 May 1570, refers to the time 'when we were both students in Paris,' but nothing further is known regarding Kirkcaldy's education. He was respected for his character and abilities both in England and in Scotland. In his father's absence he waited on James V at Hallyards, his father's house in Fifeshire, in November 1542, after the disaster at Solway Moss. Deputed by his father to superintend the arrangements for the murder of Cardinal Beaton at St. Andrews in May 1546,

he arrived at the city some time before the other conspirators. Getting entrance to the castle early in the morning of the 29th, while the drawbridge was let down to admit building material, he held the porter in parley till the approach of Norman Leslie [q. v.] with his company. The porter was then thrown into the fosse, and, while the other conspirators went to seek the cardinal, Kirkcaldy took charge of the privy postern to prevent his escape (*ib.* pp. 173-5; *Cal. State Papers*, Scott. Ser. i. 58). After the murder he proceeded to England to obtain assistance for the conspirators, who had taken refuge in the castle. He was brought back to the castle by English ships (KNOX, i. 182), and articles of agreement were entered into between the defenders and Henry VIII (*Cal. State Papers*, Scott. Ser. i. 61). On the surrender of the castle to the French in July of the following year, Kirkcaldy was carried a prisoner to France and confined in Mount St. Michael, Normandy; but by the aid of a page he and other Scottish prisoners there escaped, 5 Jan. 1549-50 (the eve of Epiphany), while the drunken garrison were asleep. Along with another Scotsman, Peter Carmichael, Kirkcaldy, in the guise of a mendicant, reached the French coast at Le Conquet, and ultimately, as 'poor mariners,' they embarked on a French ship, which conveyed them to the west coast of Scotland (KNOX, i. 231). Thence Kirkcaldy escaped south to England, where he obtained a pension from Edward VI, who employed him on secret diplomatic service. In February 1550-1 he was at Blois, acting as the secret agent of England, the name under which he is known in political correspondence being 'Coraxe' (*Cal. State Papers*, For. Ser. 1549-53, p. 77). Being deprived of his English pension on the accession of Mary, Kirkcaldy entered the service of France, and as captain of a hundred light horse (SIR JAMES MELVILLE, *Memoirs*, p. 256) distinguished himself in the campaigns against Charles V. According to Sir James Melville he acquired special repute both for his valour in battle and his skill in knightly contests, Henry II pointing him out on one occasion as 'one of the most valiant men of our time.' The French king conferred on him a pension, which, however, according to Melville, Kirkcaldy never drew (*Memoirs*, p. 257).

Although a special favourite of the French king, Kirkcaldy appears to have been secretly hostile to the influence exercised by France in Scotland, and was already taking means to thwart it. Writing to Queen Mary of England from Boissy, 30 Nov. 1556, Dr. Wotton states that Grange had offered 'to

F

serve her majesty for the like pension he had formerly in England whenever she pleases; and, whether in England, the Low Countries, or here, says he shall have good intelligence of the affairs of Scotland and France by his intimacy with those of both nations' (*Cal. State Papers*, For. Ser. 1553–8, p. 277). In another letter Wotton writes that Kirkcaldy is 'either a very great dissembler or else bears no goodwill at all to the French, and next to his own country has a good mind to England' (*ib.* p. 290). Mary refused his services, but the act of forfeiture against him and other murderers of Beaton was rescinded and he returned to Scotland about June 1557.

The severe treatment of his cousin, John Kirkcaldy, who had been taken prisoner by the English in a border skirmish, caused a breach in his friendly relations with England. To avenge his kinsman he challenged to a duel Lord Rivers, the English commander at Berwick, and it was subsequently accepted by Rivers's brother, Sir Ralph Rivers. The combat, according to Pitscottie, took place in sight of the English garrison of Berwick and the Scottish garrison of Eyemouth, Kirkcaldy running his adversary through the shoulder and unhorsing him. Subsequently Kirkcaldy had a principal share in the negotiations which resulted in the conclusion of the peace with England in May 1559. After its conclusion he, at the instigation of Knox (*Works*, ii. 22), entered into communication with Cecil to secure the support of England for the furtherance of the Reformation in Scotland. Even then he had taken no active steps against the queen-regent, but on 26 July Croft writes to Cecil that Kirkcaldy had now plainly declared himself a supporter of the protestants (*Cal. State Papers*, For. Ser. 1558–9, entry 1073). At the skirmish of Restalrig in the following November Kirkcaldy with a number of horsemen rendered important service in checking the French advance. The campaign was then transferred to Fife, where in the following spring the French burnt Kirkcaldy's mansion of Grange to the ground. Learning soon afterwards that Captain le Battu with a hundred Frenchmen had left Kinghorn to forage, he and the Master of Lindsay surrounded them in a village. After a desperate fight fifty of the Frenchmen with their commander were slain and the remainder taken prisoners (KNOX, ii. 11; BUCHANAN, *History*, bk. xvi.) The unremitting zeal of Kirkcaldy in annoying the enemy in Fife is highly lauded by Knox, who states that at Lundie he was shot under the left breast (vi. 106–8). On the arrival of the English fleet, Kirkcaldy by a rapid march succeeded in breaking down

the bridge across the Devon at Tullibody, with the view of hindering the French retreat westwards to Stirling, but the French cleverly repaired it by the use of material from the roof of the parish church. Regarding the part played by Kirkcaldy in the subsequent events of the war there is no information.

In the autumn of 1562 Queen Mary, after reaching Aberdeen, sent for Kirkcaldy to take the command of forces for the capture of Sir John Gordon, and protect her during her progress against the possible designs of Huntly (*Cal. State Papers*, For. Ser. 1562, entries 718 and 823). He doubtless rendered not unimportant aid in winning the battle of Corrichie. At the parliament held in May of the following year he was formally restored to his estates. He opposed the marriage of Mary to Darnley in 1565, and, disobeying the summons to appear at court after the marriage, was put to the horn. Thereupon he joined the Earl of Moray and others in their attempt to seize Edinburgh, but being received with a severe cannonade from the castle they retired, and, recognising that the sympathy of the nation was with the queen, they in October took refuge in England. Kirkcaldy was privy to the plot against Rizzio (Bedford to Cecil, 6 March 1566; *Cal. State Papers*, For. Ser. 1566–8, entry 102). On the night after the murder he arrived in Edinburgh along with Moray, and he took part in the subsequent deliberations in regard to the disposal of the queen. After the queen's escape to Dunbar he was, along with Moray, nominally restored to favour. He appears to have held aloof from the intrigues connected with the murder of Darnley. At this time he was a confidential correspondent of the English government, but his main purpose was probably to serve Moray and the protestant party. On 20 April 1567 he informed Bedford that 'if the Queen of England will pursue for the revenge of the late murder she shall win the hearts of all the honest men of Scotland again' (*ib.* 1119). He is the authority for the famous declaration of Mary that she would 'follow Bothwell to the world's end in a white petticoat' (*ib.*), and he also attributed the so-called 'ravishment' by Bothwell to the queen's own instigation (*ib.* 1131). With the bond in Bothwell's favour in Ainslie's tavern Kirkcaldy had no connection, and he explains that it had been signed by the majority 'in fear of their lives,' and 'against their honour and conscience' (*ib.* 1181). He affirmed that he was 'so suited to enterprise the revenge' that he 'must either take it on hand or else leave the country.' At first he determined on the latter course, and having disposed of 'all his corn and movables' (ib. 1234) had obtained a license to leave Scotland for seven years (ib. 1275), when his plans were altered by the resolution of the nobles in the beginning of June to seize Mary and Bothwell in Holyrood Palace. Kirkcaldy immediately joined the forces of the lords. At Carberry Hill he held command of the horse, and placed them in a position that would prevent a retreat towards Dunbar. Mary on learning this desired to have a conference with him. While they were in conversation a soldier sent by Bothwell took aim at him, but 'the Queen gave a cry and said that he should not do her that shame' (MELVILLE. *Memoirs*, p. 183). When Bothwell declared his willingness to maintain his innocency by single combat, Kirkcaldy with characteristic alacrity took up the challenge, but Bothwell, no doubt well aware of his prowess, declined to fight with one who was only a baron (ib.) Finally the queen surrendered to Kirkcaldy, and Bothwell was permitted to escape.

As Kirkcaldy had pledged his word for the queen's safety, he strongly opposed the harsh treatment accorded to her, and especially her removal to Lochleven, after her letter to Bothwell pledging herself to constancy was intercepted. Even then he was willing to excuse, and he hoped that further difficulties might be removed by Bothwell's capture. On 11 Aug. he received, along with Sir William Murray of Tullibardine, a commission to fit out ships for the pursuit of Bothwell (*Reg. P. C. Scotl.* i. 544-6). While Bothwell was on shore he came up with his ships in Bressay Sound; but, as Kirkcaldy himself confesses, he was 'no good seaman,' and subsequently Bothwell outsailed him and escaped to Norway (see HEPBURN, JAMES, fourth EARL OF BOTHWELL).

After his return to Scotland Kirkcaldy succeeded Sir James Balfour as governor of Edinburgh Castle. He attended the meeting of the 'lords of the secret council and others' on 4 Dec., when it was declared that Mary was a conspirator with Bothwell in the murder of the king. On Mary's escape from Lochleven he joined the forces of the regent against her, and at Langside the regent committed to him the 'special care as an experimented captain to oversee every danger' (SIR JAMES MELVILLE, *Memoirs*, p. 201). He rode from wing to wing, giving advice and direction at the most critical moments, and by his skilful generalship turned the tide of battle against the queen.

Kirkcaldy's subsequent transference to the queen's party is not difficult to explain.

When Mary, after the conferences in England, finally agreed to a divorce from Bothwell, he was of opinion that an arrangement with her was possible. He was doubtless also strongly influenced by the plausible schemes of Maitland of Lethington. Nevertheless he for some time disguised his sentiments. On 8 May 1568 he and the provost of Edinburgh had entered into a mutual band to retain the town and castle for the young king's party (printed in CALDERWOOD, ii. 412-413), and this severely hampered his subsequent action. His first decided step was the rescue in September 1569 of Maitland while under arrest in Edinburgh; but he pleaded as an excuse that the arrest was unjustifiable, and his professed purpose was to bring about a reconciliation with the regent. With that intent he in October had a friendly conference with Maitland at Kelso (Drury to Cecil, 22 Oct. 1569, *Cal. State Papers*, For. Ser. 1569-71, entry 479). From the castle Maitland wrote to Mary that Kirkcaldy would be 'conformable to a good accord' in her favour. The assassination of the regent on 20 Jan. 1569-70 somewhat altered the aspect of events. It rendered a peaceable arrangement impossible, and while it weakened the cause of Mary it deprived King James's party of an invaluable leader. So odious was the murder to 'all that faction' (including Maitland and Kirkcaldy) that they were 'presently all reconciled and vowed to revenge' (ib. 677). At the funeral of the regent Kirkcaldy bore his standard before the body (KNOX, vi. 571). But while shocked at the assassination Kirkcaldy was not minded to subject himself over far to any surviving member of the king's party (*Cal. State Papers*, For. Ser. 1569-71, entry 854), and when Lennox was chosen regent he refused either to come to the election or to permit a salute to be fired in his honour (ib. 1097). Still he continued for some time to profess neutrality, and it was not until a proclamation had been made forbidding any to serve him that he declared himself by announcing that for his own security and that of the castle he was 'forced to join with such of the nobility as would concur with him' (ib. 1668). His conduct in rescuing from the Tolbooth one of his followers who had been concerned in the slaughter of George Durie (for particulars see RICHARD BANNATYNE, *Memorials*, pp. 72 et seq.) had already caused Knox to denounce him as a 'murderer and throat-cutter.' Violent letters passed between them, and a reference by Knox in one of his sermons to Kirkcaldy's conduct provoked loud protestations on Kirkcaldy's part, who was present. The breach between them was never healed.

P 2

After his final declaration Kirkcaldy began to fortify the approaches to the castle from the city, mounting for this purpose cannon on the steeple of St. Giles and within the body of the church. He also appointed his son-in-law, Andrew Ker of Ferniehirst [q. v.] provost of the city, which, as well as the castle, was now held for the queen. So satisfied was Kirkcaldy with his preparations for resistance that he celebrated their completion in what Calderwood disparagingly terms a 'rowstie rhyme,' but which was really a very clever political squib (printed in full in SIR J. GRAHAM DALYELL's *Scottish Poems of the Sixteenth Century*; and in *Satirical Poems of the time of the Reformation*, Scottish Text Soc., i. 174-9). In September he despatched from the castle a force which made an unsuccessful attempt to capture the leaders of the king's party at Stirling. In the fray the regent Lennox was shot, but the murder was done solely at the instance of the Hamiltons, and was deeply regretted by Kirkcaldy, who declared that if he knew who had committed the foul deed or even directed it to be done he would avenge it with his own right hand (SIR JAMES MELVILLE, *Memoirs*, p. 242). Through the interposition both of the English and French representatives a truce was entered into on 1 Aug. 1572, which lasted to the following January. Knox on his deathbed sent word to Kirkcaldy that unless he 'was brought to repentance' he should be 'disgracefully dragged from his nest to punishment and hung on a gallows in the face of the sun' (*Works*, ii. 157). Morton, who succeeded Mar in the regency on the day of Knox's death, employed Sir James Melville to negotiate an agreement with Kirkcaldy. The negotiations promised to be successful, but on Kirkcaldy learning that Morton did not intend to include in them 'the rest of the queen's faction,' especially the Hamiltons, he, in the words of Melville, 'stood stiff upon his honesty and reputation,' and declined conditions which implied the ruin of his friends. While the negotiations were thus in suspense Morton received final pledges of assistance from England to enable him to capture the castle. Thereupon he came to terms with the Hamiltons, and refused to the defenders of the castle any conditions except the safety of their lives. The task of capturing it was entrusted to the English commander, Sir William Drury, who had brought with him English cannon and a force of fifteen hundred men, the besieging force being completed by about five hundred Scottish soldiers. From 17 May to the 20th they kept up a continuous cannonade day and night, and the spur was captured by assault. The position of the defenders, from lack of water and provisions, was now hopeless. Kirkcaldy, therefore, on the 28th sent privately to Hume and Crawford, who commanded the Scottish contingent, and delivered the castle into their hands, thus avoiding the surrender of it to the English. Next morning he gave up his sword to Sir William Drury, by whom he was treated with every courtesy. On 3 June he and Maitland wrote to Elizabeth that they had surrendered themselves to her, and hoped that she would not put them 'out of her hands to make any others, especially our mortal enemy, our masters;' but on the 18th they were delivered up to Morton. Every effort was made by Kirkcaldy's friends to save his life, and Morton candidly admitted the strength of the temptation which the offered bribes exerted on him. But he saw that the 'denunciations of the preachers' rendered the sacrifice of Kirkcaldy, which Knox had foretold, essential to his own continuance in power. Kirkcaldy was executed on the afternoon of 3 Aug. 1573, on the gibbet at the cross. After the accession of James VI his remains were removed to the ancestral burying-place at Kinghorn.

Sir James Melville describes Kirkcaldy as 'humble, gentle, and meek, like a lamb in the house and like a lion in the field, a lusty, stark, and well-proportioned personage, hardy, and of magnanimous courage' (*Memoirs*, p. 257). He also states that he refused 'even the office of regent' (*ib.* p. 258). Although his political career is chargeable almost throughout with inconsistency, he was not directly involved in the baser intrigues of his time, and was less influenced than most of his contemporaries by ulterior and selfish motives. His defence of the castle for the queen was not merely quixotic, but incompatible with the clear obligations into which he had entered. Nevertheless his chivalrous resolve and the constancy of his courage have secured him a place of honour in Scottish history.

[Knox's Works; Sir James Melville's Memoirs; Calderwood's Hist. of the Kirk of Scotland; Lindsay of Pitscottie's Chronicle; Buchanan's Hist. of Scotland; Spotiswood's Hist. of Scotland; James Melville's Diary; Richard Bannatyne's Memorials; Diurnal of Occurrents; Reg. Privy Council of Scotl. vols. i. and ii.; Cal. State Papers, Scott. Ser.; Cal. State Papers, For. Ser. 1549-73; Biographical Sketch of Sir William Kirkcaldy of Grange in Sir J. Graham Dalyell's Scottish Poems of the Sixteenth Century. 1801; Grant's Memoirs and Adventures of Sir William Kirkcaldy of Grange, 1849.]

T. F. H.

KIRKCUDBRIGHT, first LORD. [See MACLELLAN, ROBERT, d. 1641.]

KIRKE. [See also KIRK.]

KIRKE, EDWARD (1553–1613), friend of the poet Spenser, matriculated as a sizar of Pembroke Hall, Cambridge, in November 1571, but soon removing to Caius College, graduated there B.A. in 1574–5, and M.A. in 1578. Spenser had been admitted a sizar of Pembroke Hall in 1569, and Gabriel Harvey became fellow a year later. Kirke formed a warm friendship with these members of his college.

In the spring of 1579 was issued anonymously 'The Shepheardes Calender,' Spenser's earliest publication. On the title-page the work is inscribed to Sir Philip Sidney, but the volume opens with a long preface addressed, by a writer calling himself 'E. K.,' to 'his verie special and singular good friend,' Gabriel Harvey. 'E. K.' commends 'the new poet' to Harvey's patronage, anticipates that the poet's worthiness 'shall soon be sounded by the trump of Fame,' defends his employment of archaic words and turns of speech, and praises his wit, pithiness, 'pastoral rudnes,' 'morall wisenesse,' 'due observing of decorum,' 'strongly knit sentences,' and his modesty in concealing himself in the verses under the name of Colin. 'Hereunto,' 'E. K.' continues, 'haue I added a certaine glosse or scholia for the exposition of olde words and harder phrases: by means of some familiar acquaintance I was made priuie to his counsaile and secret meaning in them, as also in sundrie other workes of his.' In a postscript 'E. K.' entreats Harvey to publish his own English poems. He dates his preface 'from my lodgings at London thys 10 of April 1579.' In accordance with his promise he supplies an argument and a verbal commentary, with illustrations from classical and Italian poetry, to each of the twelve eclogues of the 'Calender.' In his notes in the ninth eclogue 'E. K.' announces that he owes one of his comments in part to the author.

The suggestion that 'E. K.' was Edward Kirke may be safely adopted, despite the attempts recently made to identify the commentator with Spenser himself. If Spenser were the author of 'E. K.'s' preface and notes, he would be exposed to a charge of repulsive immodesty in lavishing praise upon himself; but it is incredible that the poet, who disguised himself in his early works under the pseudonym of 'Immerito,' should be guilty of that offence. Nor does the tone of the preface, with its author's repeated expression of friendship for both Spenser and Harvey, make it capable of any but the obvious interpreta-

tion. Few of the arguments in favour of the theory of 'E. K.'s' identification with Spenser are worthy of attention. The chief lies in the fact that 'E. K.' introduces into his commentary on the eclogue for May an English rendering of two Latin hexameters, which appears almost word for word in a letter from Spenser to Harvey dated a year later (10 April 1580), and is there claimed by Spenser as his own 'extempore' effort. No literary interest attaches to the lines. It is quite possible that 'E. K.' had heard Spenser repeat them at some earlier time, and had appropriated them when he 'was made priuie' to the poet's 'counsaile.' Elsewhere (in the April eclogue) 'E. K.' quotes verses from Petrarch, which Harvey also quotes in a letter to Spenser; but that circumstance only illustrates the similarity of the literary sympathies of 'E. K.' and Harvey. 'E. K.'s' continued intimacy with his two college friends is further proved by Spenser's message to Harvey, writing from Leycester House, London, 16 Oct. 1579: 'Maister E. K. hartily desireth to be commended unto your worshippe, of whome what accompte he maketh, your selfe shall hereafter perceive by hys paynefull and dutiful verses of your selfe.' The verses referred to are not known to be extant. It is clear, moreover, that 'E. K.' edited another of Spenser's works in the same fashion as he treated the 'Calender.' 'I take beste,' the poet wrote to Harvey, 'my Dreames should come forth alone, being growen by meanes of the Glosse (running continually in maner of paraphrase) full as great as my Calender. Therein be some things excellently, and many things wittily discoursed of E. K.' These 'Dreames' have been identified with Spenser's 'Muiotaphin,' and his 'Visions of Du Bellay;' but it is more probable that they are to be numbered among his lost poems. Spenser also mentions in his correspondence with Harvey one 'Mistress Kerke,' to whose care his letters appear to have been addressed. But there is nothing to show her relationship to Kirke. It is conjectured that she was Kirke's mother, and that the poet lived while in London in 1579–80 in her house.

Kirke subsequently took holy orders, and on 26 May 1580 he was presented by the patron, Sir Thomas Kytson, to the rectory of Risby, Suffolk. The neighbouring rectory of Lackford was added to his preferment on 21 Aug. 1587. He died at Risby on 10 Nov. 1613, aged 60. His widow, Helen, was the executrix of his will, in which mention is made of a son-in-law, Richard Buckle, and of a godson, John Kirke, who may be identical with the dramatist noticed below. His property included a house at Bury St. Edmunds.

[Spenser's Works, ed. Grosart, vol. i. passim, iii. cviii-xiv (where Kirke's will is printed): Spenser's Shepheardes Calender, ed. by H. Oskar Sommer, Ph.D. (London, 1890), where are collected the arguments against the theory of 'E. K.'s' identification with Kirke, and the impossible solution is proposed that 'E. K.' was Spenser himself; Gabriel Harvey's Letters, 1580, reprinted in Harvey's and Spenser's Works in Dr. Grosart's editions; Cooper's Athenæ Cantabr. ii. 214.]   S. L.

KIRKE, JOHN (*fl.* 1638), dramatist, may be the John Kirke who is described in the will of Edward Kirke (q. v.), Spenser's friend, as the testator's godson. He was author of a popular tragi-comedy, entitled 'The Seven Champions of Christendome,' which was licensed for the press on 13 July 1638 (ARBER, *Stationers' Reg.* iv. 424). License was given at the same time for the publication of 'The Life and Death of Jack Straw and Watt Tyler by John Kirke' (*ib.*), but of this piece nothing is known. The play was published under the title 'The Seven Champions of Christendome. Acted at the Cockpit and at the Red Bull in St. John's Streete, with a generall liking, and never printed till the yeare 1638. Written by J. K.,' London, 1638, 8vo. The dedication is addressed to the author's 'much respected friend, Master John Waite.' It is written in both prose and verse, with a few songs interspersed, but it has few literary merits. It was reprinted in 'Old English Drama,' 1830. An unnamed play by Kirke was burned by Sir Henry Herbert, licenser of stage plays, in May 1642, for 'the offence that was in it,' but on 8 June following Herbert allowed Kirke's 'Irish Rebellion,' a play that is not now known to be extant. The dramatist was author of the dedication to Sir Kenelm Digby prefixed to Shirley's 'Martyred Soldier,' 1638.

[Hunter's Chorus Vatum (Addit. MS. 24492, f. 91); Fleay's Biog. Chron. of English Drama, ii. 236.]   S. L.

KIRKE, PERCY (1646?–1691), lieutenant-general, colonel of 'Kirke's Lambs,' is usually described as belonging to the ancient family of Kyrke or Kirke of Whitehaigh, Chapel-le-Frith, Derbyshire, now represented by Kirke of 'The Eaves' (see BURKE, *Landed Gentry,* 1886 edit. vol. i.; also the *Reliquary,* vi. 213 et seq.) The relationship is not established (CHESTER, *Westminster Register,* p. 295). His father, GEORGE KIRKE (*d.* 1675?), was gentleman of the robes to Charles I, and under Charles II groom of the bedchamber and keeper of Whitehall Palace. His first wife was Mistress Anne Killigrew, eldest daughter of Sir Robert Killigrew (q. v.), and sister of William [q. v.], Thomas [q. v.], and Henry

Killigrew D.D. [q. v.] (*ib.* p. 135 *n.* 6). A memorandum of the arms displayed by George Kirke on the occasion of her funeral in 1641, preserved at Heralds' College, shows that they are not the arms of Kirke of Chapel-le-Frith (*ib.* p. 295 *n.* 1). Chester supposes Lucy Hamilton Sands, an associate of Nell Gwyn, to have been one of Anne Killigrew's children (*ib.* p. 218 *n.* 6). George Kirke married, secondly, Mary, daughter of Aurelian Townshend, the successor to Ben Jonson as writer of masques for the court. She was 'an admired beauty of the tyme,' and given away by Charles I at Oxford on 26 Feb. 1646. This lady and her daughters—Mary, afterwards wife of Sir Thomas Vernor, and Diana, second wife of Aubrey de Vere, last earl of Oxford—were no better than other ladies at the court (cf. *Notes and Queries,* 1st ser. viii. 461–3). George Kirke probably died in 1675, when his wife was drawing a pension as a widow (CHESTER, p. 295 *n.* 1.)

Percy or Piercy Kirke, though generally described as a son of Anne Killigrew, was more probably one of the children by a second marriage. The earliest official notice of him is a petition (circa 1665?) praying that an annuity of 365*l.*, for which his father paid 2,000*l.* to Sir Charles Howard before the revolution, although he never benefited by it, might be renewed in his favour (*Cal. State Papers,* Dom. 1665–6, p. 153). On 10 July 1666 (*ib.*) the Duke of York obtained his appointment as ensign in Captain Bromley's company of the lord admiral's regiment (the yellow-coated 'maritime' regiment, with which the marine forces originated). Afterwards he appears to have been a subaltern in the Earl of Oxford's (his brother-in-law) regiment of horse, the Oxford Blues. Warrants to the commissary of musters direct that Kirke, at the time captain-lieutenant of the colonel's troop of the regiment, should be passed (as on duty) in 1673, when serving under the Duke of Monmouth in France, and again in 1680, when commanded to Tangier (*Hist. Rec. Royal Horse Guards or Blues,* note at p. 30). Cannon states (*Hist. Rec. 4th King's Own Foot,* p. 143) that Kirke was present, with the Duke of Monmouth's regiment in the pay of France, at the siege of Maestricht in 1673, and afterwards in two campaigns under Turenne on the Rhine, also under Marshal Luxembourg in 1676 and Marshal de Creci in 1677. On 13 July 1680 he was appointed lieutenant-colonel, and on 27 Nov. following colonel of the 2nd Tangier regiment, then raised, and afterwards the 4th King's Own, and now the King's Own Royal Lancaster regiment. Kirke raised the eight companies formed about London, and took the regiment out to Tangier, where it arrived in April 1681. He was sent on an embassy to the Emperor of Morocco at Mequinez and visited Fez. An account of his mission was published in 'Latest Accounts from Fez. By a Person of Quality,' London, 1683. Kirke succeeded Colonel Sackville as governor of Tangier in March 1682, and on 19 Sept. following was transferred to the colonelcy of the old Tangier or Governor's regiment, since the 2nd or Queen's, and now the Queen's Royal West Surrey regiment. The regiment had been raised for service at Tangier. The origin of its badge —a Paschal Lamb—is unknown. Cannon and other writers err in describing it as an emblem of the house of Braganza. Perhaps, as Macaulay suggests, it was thought a fitting device for a Christian regiment going to war against the infidels. An account of Kirke's two years' command, compiled from the 'Tangiers State Papers' in the Public Record Office, the Dartmouth MSS., and other sources, is given in Davis's exhaustive 'History of the Queen's Royal West Surrey Regiment,' London, 1888, i. 202–48, and conveys the impression that Kirke was an energetic and capable officer. Bishop Ken, then chaplain of the fleet under Lord Dartmouth, speaks of the dissolute tone of the garrison, and of a scandal caused by Kirke endeavouring to thrust one Roberts, the brother of his mistress, into the post of garrison-chaplain (PLUMPTRE, *Life of Ken*, London, 1888, vol. i.) Dr. Lawson, the garrison-physician, told Pepys that Kirke had done more to improve the town and defences than all the other governors put together (SMITH, *Life of Pepys*, i. 444). Lord Dartmouth [see LEGGE, GEORGE, 1648–1691], Kirke, and Pepys were joint-commissioners for arranging the abandonment of Tangier. On the evacuation of the place, early in 1684, Kirke, accompanied by his wife and two daughters, returned to England with his regiment (Kirke's Lambs), which was then stationed at Pendennis Castle and Plymouth. In an order dated 27 June 1684 the regiment is first styled the 'Queen Consort's.' Kirke's regiment, after the death of Charles II in February 1685, was called the 'Queen Dowager's,' the other Tangier regiment (afterwards the 4th King's Own) becoming for a time the 'Queen's.' Kirke's was ordered up to London from Pendennis in April 1685 (*Home Office Marching Books*, vol. i. order 1685, f. 10).

Made a brigadier-general on 4 July 1685, Kirke was present with part of both the late Tangerine regiments at the battle of Sedgmoor on 6 July 1685. He was appointed to command in the west of England by Lord Faversham, with whom he entered Bridgewater the day after the battle. A day or two later Kirke marched into Taunton with his 'Lambs,' escorting a convoy of prisoners and two cartloads of wounded. He at once hanged nineteen prisoners in the market-place (TOULMIN, *Hist. of Taunton*, ed. Glover), and appears to have claimed credit for not hanging more. The most exaggerated stories were circulated of his severities, and in London it was believed that he hanged over a hundred persons without any sort of trial within a week after the battle (LUTTRELL, vol. i.) He had his headquarters at the White Hart, at the corner of the High Street and the market-place, and, tradition asserts, used the signpost as a gallows. The little inn was afterwards kept for a time by the notorious murderers, the Mannings, and is now pulled down. The camping-ground of the 'Lambs' is yet called 'Tangier.' Kirke, a short-tempered, rough-spoken, dissolute soldier, was no doubt harsh and unscrupulous, but the accounts of his atrocities are fictitious or exaggerated (cf. MACAULAY, *Hist. of England*, i. 634–6; TOULMIN, *Hist. of Taunton*, ed. Glover, 1822, pp. 546–9). Despatches from Sunderland to Kirke, under dates 14–28 July 1685, express the king's disapproval of the severity shown, and of the living at free quarters enjoyed by the 'Lambs;' rebels (it was objected) were still at large, apparently a reference to delinquents from whom Kirke had taken bribes. He was recalled to London by an order dated 10 Aug. 1685 (*Home Office Marching Books*, i. 223). Another order, dated 31 Aug., directs his regiment to march from Taunton to London on relief by the Queen's (4th King's Own). Similar directions were sent to detached companies of Kirke's 'Lambs' still at Plymouth; other entries show that the orders were carried out, and disprove the unsupported statement that Kirke and his 'Lambs' formed the escort of Jeffreys during 'the bloody assizes.' Kirke's regiment was in the neighbourhood of London, and in the camps annually formed at Hounslow Heath, until 1688, when it formed part of a small force under his command at Warminster. Kirke, who had refused to abjure protestantism, saying he was pledged to the Emperor of Morocco to turn Mussulman if ever he changed his faith, was believed to be privy to the plot to seize James II at Warminster. Kirke was sent prisoner to London for refusing under some pretext to advance to Devizes. William III promoted him, his rank as major-general being dated (8 Nov. 1688) three days after the landing in Torbay. Oldmixon says he was among those who subsequently were in correspondence with the exiled king (BURNET, *Own Time*, addit. notes). In May 1689 Kirke was despatched with two regiments to relieve Derry. After much delay he forced the boom, in accordance with a peremptory order from Marshal Schomberg, preserved among the Nairne MSS. in the Bodleian Library. Kirke became governor of Londonderry, and served at the Boyne, the siege of Limerick, and elsewhere. He became a lieutenant-general 25 Dec. 1690, and in May 1691 returned from Ireland to London, whence he was sent to Flanders. He joined the army in camp at Gembloux, and made the campaign in Flanders of that summer. He died at Brussels (not Breda, as often stated) on 31 Oct. 1691. Bishop Wilson likens his end to that of Herod and other murderers, who died in the torments of loathsome disease (see *Notes and Queries*, 4th ser. i. 254). Some of Kirke's letters are preserved among the manuscripts of the Earl of Dartmouth (*Hist. MSS. Comm.* 11th Rep. App. v. 59–128).

Kirke married the Lady Mary Howard, daughter of George Howard, fourth earl of Suffolk, by his first wife, Catherine Allen, and granddaughter of Theophilus, second earl. There are references to her and her son Percy in the 'Calendar of Treasury Papers' from 1696 to 1701. She died in 1712.

His eldest surviving son, PERCY KIRKE (1684–1741), was also a lieutenant-general and colonel of the 'Lambs' from 1710 to 1741, during which time the regiment was successively known as the 'Queen Dowager's,' the 'Princess of Wales's,' and the 'Queen's Royal' (*Home Office Mil. Entry Book*, i. 480). At the age of three he appears as ensign in Trelawny's regiment (4th King's Own). He succeeded his father as keeper of the palace of Whitehall. At the age of twenty-four he was taken prisoner when lieutenant-colonel commanding the 'Lambs' at the battle of Almanza. He became colonel of the regiment on 19 Sept. 1710, and was with it in the Canada expedition. He died in London, a lieutenant-general, on 1 Jan. 1741, and was buried in Westminster Abbey, where in the north transept is a very elaborate monument to him, erected by his niece and heiress, Diann Dormer, daughter of John Dormer of Rousham, Oxfordshire, who married Diana Kirke. Diana Dormer (1710–1743) is buried in the same grave.

[Chester's Westminster Registers, footnotes under 'Kirke,' passim; Calendars of State Papers, Dom. 1658–9 p. 581, 1663–4 passim; Howard's Memorials of the Howard Family, p. 56; Calendars of Treasury Papers, 1696–1701, under 'Kirke,' Lady Mary;' Burnet's Own Time, with the additional notes to 1st edit. p. 82; Luttrell's Relation, vols. i-ii.; Strickland's Queens of England, vii. 317; Toulmin's Hist. of Taunton, ed. Glover, 1822; Davis's Queen's Royal West Surrey Regiment, 1888, vol. i.; Cannon's Hist. Records, Royal Horse Guards or Blues, 2nd or Queen's Foot, 4th or King's Own Foot (some of Cannon's statements respecting the elder Kirke in the second of these works are wrong); D'Auvergne's Campaigns in Flanders, 1736, vol. i. Kirke figures in Mr. Conan Doyle's romance, Micah Clarke.] H. M. C.

KIRKE, THOMAS (1650–1706), virtuoso, born on 22 Dec. 1650, was the son of Gilbert Kirke of Cookridge, near Leeds, Yorkshire, by Margaret, daughter of Francis Layton of Rawden in the same county. He was a distant relative and the intimate friend of Ralph Thoresby [q. v.], whom he often accompanied in his antiquarian rambles. In May 1677 he started on a three months' tour in Scotland, and kept a journal of his adventures, which Thoresby transcribed and placed in his museum (*Diary*, i. 320, 380, 403, 406). At Cookridge he devised a 'most surprising' labyrinth, which attracted visitors from all parts (THORESBY, *Ducatus Leodiensis*, ed. Whitaker, p. 158). He was elected F.R.S. on 30 Nov. 1693 (THOMSON, *Hist. Roy. Soc.*, Appendix, iv. p. xxix). He died on 24 April 1706. By his marriage, on 11 July 1678, to Rosamund, daughter and coheiress of Robert Abbot, he had a son, Thomas, who died in January 1709. He helped his father in the formation of a fine library and museum, which were sold by auction in 1710.

Kirke published anonymously a coarse satire entitled 'A Modern Account of Scotland . . . Written from thence by an English Gentleman,' 4to, 1679, reprinted in 'Harleian Miscellany,' ed. Park (vi. 135–42). The 'Journal' already mentioned was printed as an appendix to ' Letters addressed to R. Thoresby' (ii. 403). ' Journeyings through Northumberland and Durham in 1677' appeared in 1845 in vol. vii. of M. A. Richardson's 'Historical Tracts.' The original was preserved among the Thoresby MSS. To the 'Philosophical Transactions' he contributed two letters giving an 'Account of a Lamb suckled by a Wether Sheep for several months after the Death of the Ewe' (xviii. 263–4). Some of his correspondence is printed in Nichols's 'Illustrations of Literature' (i. 478, iv. 72–6). In the British Museum there is a letter from him to Sir Hans Sloane (Addit. MS. 4060, No. 924); also a humorous poetical 'Dialogue betwixt the Ghost of Thomas Kirke de Cookridge, Esq., and Milo Gale, rectro de Kighley,' 8 July 1706 (*ib.* 4457, No. 90). Thoresby (*Diary*, i. 465) wrote memoirs of Kirke intended for insertion in what he called the historical part of his 'Leeds Topography,' but it was never completed.

[Thoresby's Ducatus Leodiensis (Whitaker), p. 543 sq.; Gough's Brit. Topogr. ii. 569; Nichols's Illustr. of Lit. iv. 886; Taylor's Biog. Leodiensis, p. 161 a.]   G. G.

KIRKHAM, WALTER DE (*d.* 1260), bishop of Durham, was apparently of humble parentage, but became one of the royal clerks. His name first appears in 1225, when he is frequently mentioned in connection with the exchequer, was clerk of the wardrobe, and is spoken of as 'specialis et familiaris noster' (*Cal. Rot. Lit. Claus. in Turri Londinensi*, ii. 9 b, 49, 70 b). He received much ecclesiastical preferment, was chaplain of Eastrington, Yorkshire, in 1225, dean of Peneric in Ireland in 1226 (*ib.* p. 161 b), parson of Rudby, Yorkshire, in 1228, and dean of St. Martin's-le-Grand, London, on 10 Oct. 1229. He also held the prebend of Bole at York, and was appointed archdeacon of Salop some time after 1232. In 1241 he became dean of York, and on 21 April 1249, on the resignation of Nicholas de Farnham, he was elected bishop of Durham, in preference to the royal nominee, Aymer (*d.* 1260) [q. v.] The king would not give his consent till 27 Sept., and Kirkham was not consecrated at York till 5 Dec. His episcopate was uneventful. He appears in some commissions on affairs with Scotland, and in 1257 was at Stirling. He was present at the parliament of April 1253, and took part in the excommunication of the violators of the charters. In 1255 he was attacked by John de Baliol, some of whose servants he had excommunicated. The king, however, interfered in his favour. In the 'Osney Annals,' where he is called 'specialis regis,' he is said to have signed a blank charter at the king's request in 1255, and to have been sent by Henry with it to the Roman curia, where he pledged the English church for nine thousand marks (*Ann. Mon.* iv. 109, 110). In 1258 Kirkham quarrelled with Henry, and refused to come to court (MATT. PARIS, v. 675). He died, at a great age, at Howden, on 9 Aug. 1260, and was buried at Durham. He is described as of a generous and kindly disposition, and is said to have enjoyed a high reputation (*Chron. Lanercost*, p. 60; *Flores Hist.* ii. 454). He is, however, alleged to have connived at an attempt to deprive Bishop Farnham, his predecessor at Durham, of his share of the revenues of the see (MATT. PARIS, v. 83). He had inherited a long law-suit with the abbey of St. Albans, which he eventually composed (*ib.* vi. 326-32, 395;

Flores Hist. u.s.) He gave the churches of Hartburn and Eglingham for the support of hospitalities at St. Albans (MATT. PARIS, vi. 317-21). He compelled one of the barons of his palatinate, as a punishment for wrongdoing, to assign a sum of money for the support of students of Oxford. Some 'Constitutiones' which he issued in 1255 are printed in Wilkins's 'Concilia,' i. 704-8.

[Graystanes's Chronicle in Hist. Dun. Scriptt. Tres, pp. 42-4 (Surtees Soc.); Matt. Paris, Annales Monastici, Flores Historiarum (these three are in the Rolls Series); Chronicle of Lanercost (Bannatyne Club); Tanner's Bibl. Brit.-Hib. p. 458; Le Neve's Fasti, i. 573, iii. 121, 174, 287; Godwin, De Præsulibus, ed. Richardson, p. 742; Surtees's Hist. of Durham, i. p. xxix.]
                                                   C. L. K.

KIRKHOVEN or **KERCKHOVEN**, **CATHERINE**, LADY STANHOPE and COUNTESS OF CHESTERFIELD (*d.* 1667), governess to Mary, princess royal, daughter of Charles I, was the eldest daughter and coheiress of Thomas, second Lord Wotton of Marley, Kent, by Mary, daughter of Sir Arthur Throckmorton of Paulerspury, Northamptonshire. She married thrice, her first husband being Henry, lord Stanhope, son and heir to Philip Stanhope, first earl of Chesterfield. This marriage appears to have taken place about 1628. Lord Stanhope died in the lifetime of his father, on 29 Nov. 1634, leaving a son, Philip [q. v.], who succeeded to the earldom on the death of his grandfather, 12 Sept. 1656; and two daughters, Mary, who died unmarried in 1654, and Catherine, who married William, second lord Alington of Wimondley, Hertfordshire, and died without issue in 1662 (*Cal. State Papers*, Dom. 1629-31, p. 41). Still young and attractive, Lady Stanhope was courted by Lord Cottington and Vandyck, but refused them both. She was thought to be in love with Carey Raleigh, and was apparently offended with Vandyck for charging too much for her portrait (STRAFFORD, *Letters and Despatches*, ed. Knowles, ii. 48). She married in 1641 John Polyander à Kerckhoven, lord of Heenvliet in Sassenheim, chief forester of Holland and West Friesland, son of the celebrated divine of the same name, and one of the ambassadors from the States-general for the negotiation of the marriage between Prince William of Orange and the princess royal. After the betrothal of the prince and princess (12 May 1641), Lady Stanhope, as she still continued to be called, accompanied her husband to Holland, and acted as governess to the princess, while Kerckhoven filled the office of superintendent of the household. The Dutch poet, Kasper van Baerle, welcomed her to Holland in an epithalamium, which forms part of the third book of his 'Heroics' (*Cal. State Papers, Dom.* 1641-3, p. 296; VAN BAERLE, *Poemata,* ed. 1655, p. 526). As the princess grew to womanhood, Lady Stanhope became her chief lady of honour and her confidential friend and adviser, nor was her influence impaired by the accession of Prince William to the stadtholdership (14 March 1647 N.S.), while on his death (6 Nov. 1650) it became paramount, much to the discontent of Hyde and Nicholas, who believed, or affected to believe, that she had her own interest rather than that of the princess at heart [see HYDE, EDWARD, EARL OF CLARENDON, and NICHOLAS, SIR EDWARD, 1593-1669]. During the civil war Lady Stanhope gave Charles I substantial aid in arms, ammunition, and money, and after his death she was much esteemed and trusted by Charles II and Henrietta Maria, and was party or privy to most of the royalist plots that were hatched on the continent. Towards the end of 1651 she visited England, and was arrested on suspicion of complicity in a treasonable conspiracy, but was released on finding sureties to appear for examination before a committee of the council of state. She appeared, but nothing of importance was proved against her, and she received a passport for foreign parts on 30 June 1652.

She attended the princess on her visit with Charles II to Cologne in the autumn of 1654, and thence to Frankfort, when they went incognito to see the fair in the autumn of the following year; but at her own request she remained with her husband in Holland when the princess proceeded to Paris in the winter. This was intended to make it clear that the princess's visit had no political significance, Charles II being then more hopeful of help from Spain than from France. In the autumn of 1658 Lady Stanhope came to England with her husband on private affairs. Before the Restoration, however, they returned to Holland, where Heenvliet died on 10 March 1660 (N.S.) She appears to have been much attached to Heenvliet, to whose memory she raised a splendid monument in the Pieterskerk at Leyden. On 29 May 1660 she was created Countess of Chesterfield for life, her daughters by Lord Stanhope being granted precedence, as if he had succeeded to the earldom. Shortly afterwards she sailed for England, whither she was followed by the princess. During the short remainder of the princess's life she continued in her service, and tended her with much devotion during her last illness. Under her will she took a legacy of 500*l.*, payment of which she secured by retaining possession of some of the prin-

cess's effects. She also kept the princess's wardrobe as a perquisite. She now passed into the service of the Duchess of York, and married Daniel O'Neill [q. v.], whom she had met in Holland. On 1 June 1663 she was appointed lady of the bedchamber to the queen. On O'Neill's death (24 Oct. 1664) she surrendered his powder-monopoly for a pension of 3,000*l.*, but retained the postmaster-generalship. She died of dropsy on 9 April 1667, and was buried in the parish church of Boughton Malherbe, Kent, the manor of which she had inherited from her father.

By Heenvliet Lady Stanhope had one son, Charles Henry, and three daughters—Anne, who married Wigbolt van der Does, lord of Noordwyk and governor of Sluys; Magdalen, whose untimely death was the subject of one of Nyendal's Latin elegies (*Poemata,* ed. 1645, p. 455); and Emilia, who, with her brother, was naturalised by act of parliament on 13 Sept. 1660, and died unmarried in 1663. Another of Heenvliet's daughters, Walbrooke, wife of the Hon. Thomas Howard, brother of James, earl of Suffolk, master of the horse to the princess royal, and one of Thurloe's spies, cannot have been Heenvliet's legitimate issue, unless, which does not appear, Lady Stanhope was Heenvliet's second wife. She was appointed governess to the young prince in 1654, being then married.

The son, CHARLES HENRY KIRKHOVEN, BARON WOTTON and EARL OF BELLOMONT (d. 1683), was created Baron Wotton of Wotton in Kent, by letters patent dated at Perth 31 Aug. 1650. He was a great favourite with the princess royal, who made him the principal officer of her son's household, to the disgust of his Dutch attendants (*Harl. MS.* 4529, f. 528 b). He resided much in Holland, and was chief magistrate (*schout*) of Breda from 1659 to 1674. His house, Belsize, Hampstead, is praised by Evelyn and Pepys for its magnificent appointments and gardens. On 11 Feb. 1680 he was created Earl of Bellomont in the peerage of Ireland. He married Frances, daughter of William, lord Willoughby of Parham, Suffolk, and dying without issue was buried in Canterbury Cathedral on 11 Jan. 1683.

[Collins's Peerage, ed. Brydges, iii. 421-3, ix. 425; Visitation of the County of Nottingham (Harl. Soc.), p. 8; Lipscomb's Buckinghamshire, i. 14, 480; Hasted's Kent, i. 140, ii. 430; Baker's Northamptonshire, ii. 202; Letters of Philip, second Earl of Chesterfield; Biographisch Woordenboek (Polyander); Burke's Extinct Peerage ('Wotton' and 'Kirkhoven'); Lords' Journ. v. 681, xi. 145; Nicholas Papers (Camd. Soc.), i. 203-4, 218; Cal. State Papers, Dom. 1640-1 p. 501,

1651-2 pp. 95, 253, 547-8, 568, 1655 pp. 324-5, 1655-6 p. 31, 1663-4 p. 517, 1664-5 p. 77; Groen van Prinsterer's Archives de la Maison d'Orange-Nassau, 2ième série, tom. iv. and v.; Thurloe State Papers, i. 683, 700. 742, ii. 284, 513, 694, 701-2, vii. 131, 168, 228, 315, 334; Abelin's Theatr. Europ. ix. 222; Merc. Polit. 25 Oct. 1655; Parl. Intelligencer, 3-10 Sept. 1660; Merc. Pub. 13 and 20-7 Sept. 1660; Kingdom's Intelligencer, 1-8 June 1663; Lower's Relation, pp. 66, 71; Hist. MSS. Comm. 7th Rep. App. 129a; Pepys's Diary, 17 Aug. 1668; Evelyn's Diary, 2 June 1676; O'Hart's Irish Pedigrees, p. 385; Montgomery MSS. Belfast, 1830, p. 65; Van Goor's Beschryving der Stadt en Lande van Breda, 1744, p. 215; Granger's Biog. Hist. ed. 1779, iv. 169; Mrs. Everett Green's Lives of the Princesses of England.]   **J. M. R.**

KIRKLAND, THOMAS, M.D. (1721-1798), medical writer, a native of Scotland, was born in 1721. He practised at Ashby-de-la-Zouch, Leicestershire. In January 1760 he was called in to attend the steward of Lord Ferrers after he had been shot by his master. Despite Ferrers's threats of violence, Kirkland contrived the arrest of the murderer (*Gent. Mag.* xxx. 44, 230). By 1774 Kirkland had graduated M.D. at Edinburgh, and subsequently became a member of the Royal Medical Societies of Edinburgh and London. He died at Ashby-de-la-Zouch on 17 Jan. 1798.

Kirkland's writings are: 1. 'A Treatise on Gangrenes,' 8vo, Nottingham, 1754. 2. 'An Essay on the Methods of Suppressing Haemorrhages from Divided Arteries,' 8vo, London, 1763. 3. 'An Essay towards an Improvement in the Cure of those Diseases which are the cause of Fevers,' 8vo, London, 1767. 4. 'A Reply to Mr. Maxwell's Answer to his Essay on Fevers; wherein the Utility of the Practice of Suppressing them is further exemplified,' 8vo, London, 1769. 5. 'Observations on Mr. Pott's General Remarks on Fractures, etc.: with a Postscript concerning the Cure of Compound Dislocations,' 8vo, London, 1770 (Appendix, 1771). 6. 'A Treatise on Childbed Fevers . . . with two Dissertations, the one on the Brain and Nerves, the other on the Sympathy of the Nerves, etc.' (included in 'Essays on the Puerperal Fever,' published by the Sydenham Society in 1849), 8vo, London, 1774. 7. 'Animadversions on a late Treatise on the Kink-Cough [by Dr. William Butler]. To which is annexed an Essay on that Disorder,' 8vo, London, 1774, published anonymously. 8. 'Thoughts on Amputation; being a Supplement to the Letters on Compound Fractures, and a Comment on Dr. Bilguer's book on this operation; also, an Essay on the use of Opium in Mortifications,' 8vo, London, 1780. 9. 'An Essay on the Inseparability of the different Branches of Medicine,' 8vo (London, 1783). 10. 'An Inquiry into the Present State of Medical Surgery,' 2 vols. 8vo, London, 1783-6. (Appendix, edited by his son, James Kirkland, surgeon to the Tower, 1813). 11. 'A Commentary on Apoplectic and Paralytic Affections, and the Diseases connected with the Subject,' 8vo, London, 1792.

[Gent. Mag. 1798, pt. i. pp. 88-9, 254; Watt's Bibl. Brit.]   **G. G.**

KIRKMAN, FRANCIS (*fl.* 1674), bookseller and author, born in 1632, was apparently eldest son of Francis Kirkman (*d.* 1662), citizen and blacksmith, of London, by his wife Ellen (will of F. Kirkman registered in P. C. C. 67, Laud). By dint of private study he acquired some knowledge of French and Spanish, which he was afterwards able to turn to good account. From boyhood he was a collector of plays and romances. His father left him considerable property, which he appears to have squandered. In 1661 he established himself as a bookseller at the sign of 'John Fletcher's Head,' near St. Clement Danes Church, Strand, but removed before 1671 to Thames Street, in 1672 to St. Paul's Churchyard, and in 1673 to Fenchurch Street. With the bookselling business he combined that of a circulating library, his speciality being plays, poetry, and romances.

As early as 1657 Kirkman issued an edition of Marlowe's tragedy of 'Lusts Dominion' (12mo). In 1661 he printed a useful 'Catalogue of all the English Stage-Playes' then printed—690 in all. Ten years later he appended to John Dancer's translation of Corneille's 'Nicomède' (4to, 1671) a revised edition of this 'Catalogue,' brought down to date, and consisting of 806 plays. In an interesting 'Advertisement' he informs his readers that he had not only seen but had read all these plays, and possessed most of them, which he was ready either to sell or lend 'upon reasonable considerations.' He also states that he knew many curious particulars of the lives of the old dramatists from his having 'taken pleasure to converse with those who were acquainted with them.'

He also proposed to publish from time to time plays hitherto unprinted, the manuscripts of which he possessed; but he only issued Webster and Rowley's comedies of 'A Cure for a Cuckold' (1661) and 'The Thracian Wonder' (1661). During the same year he published in black letter Bishop Still's comedy of 'Gammer Gurton's Needle.' Under the title of 'The Wits, or Sport upon Sport,' he issued a collection of drolls and farces (2 pts. 12mo, London, 1673, pp.

72), which had been performed at fairs and taverns during the puritan ascendency by Robert Cox the comedian, and prefixed to it an introduction full of delightful gossip.

Kirkman is thought to be the author of 'The Presbyterian Lash; or, Noetroff's Maid Whipt, a tragy-comedy,' 4to, London, 1661, from the fact of the dedication to 'Master Zach. Noctroffe' bearing the initials 'K. F.' It is a personal and somewhat indecent satire on Zachary Crofton [q. v.], a presbyterian minister then living, who was accused of whipping his maid-servant (KENNETT, *Reg.* p. 797). In 1666 Kirkman reissued the 'English Rogue,' by Richard Head [q. v.], whom Wood wrongly describes as his partner. He himself wrote a second part, which appeared in 1671. During the same year third and fourth parts were issued, with intimation of a fifth part. Kirkman asserted that in the third and fourth parts Head and himself had collaborated, and the preface to the fourth part is signed by both. Head, however, disclaimed responsibility for any part except the first.

Kirkman wrote also: 1. 'The Famous and Delectable History of Don Bellianis of Greece, or the Honour of Chivalry,' 3 pts. 4to, London, 1673-71-72, which is founded on the Spanish romance by T. Fernandez. In the preface he gives an account of most of the romances which had then been published in English. 2. 'The Unlucky Citizen: Experimentally Described in the various Misfortunes of an Unlucky Londoner . . . intermixed with severall Choice Novels . . . illustrated with Pictures,' 8vo, London, 1673, to which is prefixed his portrait.

From the French he translated: 1. 'The famous and renowned History of Amadis de Gaule . . . being the sixt part never before published,' 4to, London, 1652. 2. 'The Loves and Adventures of Clerio & Lozia . . . a romance,' 8vo, London, 1652. 3. 'The History of Prince Erastus, son to the Emperour Dioclesian, and those famous Philosophers called the Seven Wise Masters of Rome . . . with . . . Pictures,' 8vo, London, 1674.

[Kirkman's Prefaces and Advertisements; Baker's Biog. Dram. (1812), i. 154, 418-19, iii. 178; Granger's Biog. Hist. of England (2nd ed.), iv. 58 n.; Evans's Cat. of Engraved Portraits, i. 198.]   G. G.

KIRKMAN, JACOB (*fl.* 1800), musical composer, was probably a nephew of Jacob Kirkman, who carried on the business of harpsichord-maker in Broad Street, Golden Square, London, about 1770. The younger Kirkman acquired some reputation as a pianist and composer of pianoforte works in London before the end of the eighteenth century. One Jacob Kirkman died in Upper Guilford Street, London, 29 April 1812, aged 67 (*Gent. Mag.* 1812, i. 596). Among his published works may be mentioned: 1. Duets for the pianoforte, Op. 5. 2. 'Trois Sonates à quatre mains, et une à deux Temps' (Amsterdam). 3. Three sonatas for harpsichord with violin, Op. 8. 4. A sonata for pianoforte. 5. Eight ballads dedicated to the Marchioness of Salisbury, Op. 10. 6. 'Six Lessons for Harpsichord or Pianoforte,' Op. 3 (London). 7. 'A Collection of Six Voluntaries for the Organ, Harpsichord, and Pianoforte,' Op. 9. Copies of the last two works are in Mr. Taphouse's library at Oxford. Kirkman and John Keeble [q. v.] together published 'Forty Interludes to be played between the verses of the Psalms.'

[Dict. of Mus. 1824.]   R. H. L.

KIRKPATRICK, JAMES (*d.* 1743), Irish presbyterian divine, son of Hugh Kirkpatrick, who was minister successively of Lurgan, co. Armagh, Ireland, Dairy and Old Cumnock in Scotland, and Ballymoney, co. Armagh (where he died in 1712), was probably born in Scotland while his father was minister there. In February 1691 he matriculated from the university of Glasgow, and in February 1694 his name appears in the university list of students in theology. On 7 Aug. (probably) 1699 he was ordained as minister of the congregation of Templepatrick, co. Antrim. The well-known 'Belfast Society,' which exercised an important influence on the ecclesiastical affairs of the north of Ireland, was founded in 1705, and Kirkpatrick was one of its earliest and most influential members. In 1706 he resigned his charge at Templepatrick on receiving an invitation from the presbyterian congregation in Belfast to take the place of their minister, John McBride [q. v.], who had been obliged to retire to Scotland owing to his non-abjuring opinions. Soon afterwards the congregation divided on account of its numbers, and he became minister of the second congregation, a new meeting-house having been built close to the first. In 1712 he was elected moderator of the synod of Ulster. In 1720 he came prominently into notice as one of the leaders of the non-subscribing party in the north of Ireland. In 1725 he was placed with the other non-subscribers in the presbytery of Antrim, which the synod in 1726 excluded from its judicatories. In his later days he took the degree of M.D., and combined the practice of a physician with the work of a clergyman. He is said to have died suddenly in Dublin, where he had gone on business with his wife. The date of his death is usually given as 1744, but a notice by James Blow, prefixed to Kirkpatrick's posthumous 'Defence of Christian Liberty,' shows that he died in 1743. A copy of his portrait is in the vestry of the first presbyterian church in Belfast.

Kirkpatrick is best known by his 'Historical Essay upon the Loyalty of Presbyterians in Great-Britain and Ireland from the Reformation to this present year 1713, &c.' (4to, pp. xv, 504, and index of ten pages, no place or printer's name, 1713), a work undertaken to meet the desire of the general synod to possess a history of their church, and specially called for by the persistent attacks of Tisdall, vicar of Belfast, on the presbyterian body. It preserves many valuable facts and documents, and gives a good idea of the state of public sentiment in Ireland in the days of Queen Anne. It was published anonymously. Kirkpatrick also wrote: 1. 'A Vindication of the Presbyterian Ministers in the North of Ireland, subscribers and non-subscribers, from many gross and groundless aspersions cast upon them in a late scandalous libel entitled "An Account of the Mind of the Synod,"' Belfast, 1721, 8vo (anon.; by 'A Lover of Truth and Peace'). 2. 'A Scripture Plea against a fatal rupture and breach of Christian Communion amongst the Presbyterians in the North of Ireland,' Belfast, 1724, 8vo. 3. 'An Essay upon the Important Question whether there is a Legislative Proper Authority in the Church,' Belfast, 1731, 8vo (anon.; by several hands, probably edited by Kirkpatrick). 4. 'An Account of the Success of Mrs. Stephens's Medicines for the Stone; in the case of James Kirkpatrick, Doctor of Divinity, M.D., &c.,' Belfast, 1739, 8vo. 5. 'A Defence of Christian Liberty, by a Member of the General Synod,' Belfast, 1743, 4to (unfinished).

[Witherow's Historical and Literary Memorials of Presbyterianism in Ireland; Reid's Hist. of the Presb. Church in Ireland; Scott's Fasti; Records of General Synod of Ulster, 1890, vol. i.; Catalogue of Early Belfast Printed Books; Disciple, 1882, pp. 171 sq.; information kindly supplied by the Rev. Alexander Gordon.]

T. H.

KIRKPATRICK, JOHN (1686?–1728), antiquary, born about 1686, was son of a native of Closeburn, Dumfriesshire, who had settled in the parish of St. Stephen, Norwich. He was apprenticed in the parish of St. Clement, and subsequently established himself in business as a linen merchant in St. Andrew, in partnership with John Custance. In 1726 Kirkpatrick was appointed treasurer of the Great Hospital in St. Helen's. He died without issue on 20 Aug. 1728, aged 42, and was buried in St. Helen's Church, Norwich

(mon. inscr. in BLOMEFIELD, Norfolk, 8vo ed. iv. 379). He married the youngest daughter of John Harvey, great-grandfather of Lieutenant-colonel Harvey of Thorpe Lodge, Norwich, where his portrait was preserved. It has been engraved by W. C. Edwards (EVANS, Cat. of Engraved Portraits, ii. 234). On 18 Feb. 1719 Kirkpatrick was elected F.S.A. (GOUGH, Chron. List of Soc. Antiq. 1798, p. 3).

Kirkpatrick accumulated copious materials for the history of Norwich. These he bequeathed, after the death of his brother Thomas, to the corporation of Norwich, together with his coins and many of his printed books. Of the manuscripts, which Kirkpatrick fondly hoped would be completed and published, eleven were safe in the custody of the corporation about 1815, but all are now dispersed, except some notes on the tenure of houses in Norwich. A thick quarto volume, devoted to the 'History of the Religious Orders and Communities, and of the Hospitals and Castle, of Norwich,' compiled by Kirkpatrick about 1725, was published at the expense of Hudson Gurney, under the editorship of Dawson Turner, in 1845. Turner, in an interesting preface, gives a list of the missing manuscripts. Extracts from Kirkpatrick's papers are cited in Robert Fitch's historical introduction to John Ninham's 'Views of the Gates of Norwich,' published by the Norfolk and Norwich Archæological Society in 1861.

Peter Le Neve was Kirkpatrick's intimate friend, and they mutually exchanged their collections for Norwich. Blomefield acknowledged the great assistance which he derived from their labours.

Kirkpatrick was a good draughtsman. In 1723 he published a large north-east prospect of Norwich, in two sheets, engraved by E. Kirkall, which he exhibited to the Society of Antiquaries, together with a plan and Saxon coins found at Norwich. In the previous year his friend Le Neve had shown the society a draft and description of Burgh Castle, Suffolk, by him. His north-east view of Norwich Cathedral was engraved by J. Harris in 1742, and his three views and a ground-plot of the gatehouse of St. Bennet in the Holm Abbey were published by the Society of Antiquaries in 'Vetusta Monumenta.' A list of his drawings is given in Gough's 'British Topography' (ii. 10, 14, 30, 34, 252).

[Dawson Turner's Preface referred to above; Nichols's Illustr. of Lit. iii. 418, 421, 433, 434; Norfolk Archæology, v. 233; Blomefield's Norfolk, 8vo ed. iv. 379–80; (John Chambers's) Norfolk, ii. 1181, 1208.]

G. G.

KIRKPATRICK, WILLIAM (1754–1812), orientalist, born in 1754, was eldest son of Colonel James Kirkpatrick, Madras army, and grandson of James Kirkpatrick, M.D., who died in 1770, and was the author of several poetical and medical works. Colonel James Kirkpatrick was the author of a pamphlet on the 'Organisation of a Body of Light Troops for Detached Service in the East Indies' (London, 1762: 2nd edit. 1781), and in a critical notice of that work is described as 'a cavalry leader of experience' (*Monthly Review*, 1762). He was in command of the troops at Fort Marlborough, Sumatra, in 1777, and returned home in 1779. He married Katherine, daughter of Alexander Monro, by whom he had three sons—William, George, in the Bombay civil service, and James Achilles. He died at his seat, Hollydale, Kent, in 1818, aged 89. William, his eldest son, a cadet of 1771, was appointed ensign in the Bengal infantry on 17 Jan. 1773, lieutenant 9 April 1777, captain 3 April 1781, major 1 March 1794, lieutenant-colonel 12th native infantry 1 Jan. 1798, lieutenant-colonel commandant 8th native infantry 30 June 1804, colonel 6th native infantry 25 April 1808, major-general 4 June 1811. He was Persian interpreter to Lieutenant-general Giles Stibbert, who was commander-in-chief in Bengal in 1777–9 and 1780–5, and prepared a Persian translation of the articles of war (printed 1782). Afterwards he was resident with Scindia at Gwalior (*Cornwallis Corresp.* i. 261), and served on Lord Cornwallis's staff as Persian interpreter in the Mysore war of 1790–1. In 1793, in consequence of disputes between the Nepaulese and the lama of Tibet, a Chinese army crossed Tibet, and took up a position near Katmandu, in view of the Ganges valley. The Nepaulese implored the aid of British arms. Cornwallis offered to mediate, and Kirkpatrick was deputed to meet the Nepaulese envoys at Patna, and afterwards proceeded to Nayakote, where the Nepaul rajahs held their court. The officers of the mission, Kirkpatrick and his suite, were the first Englishmen 'to pass the range of lofty mountains separating the secluded valley of Nepaul from the north-east part of Bengal' (*Account of Nepaul*, p. 1). Cornwallis testified that 'no one could have acquitted himself with more ability, prudence, and circumspection' (*Cornwallis Corresp.* ii. 570). In 1795 Kirkpatrick was appointed resident with the nizam of Hyderabad, but in 1797 was invalided to the Cape, being replaced by his brother, Lieutenant-colonel James Achilles Kirkpatrick. At Cape Town Kirkpatrick met the Marquis Wellesley, who took him back to India with him as confidential

military secretary. In a despatch dated 10 Jan. 1802 Wellesley declares himself indebted to Kirkpatrick 'for the seasonable information which enabled me to extinguish French influence in the Deccan, and to frustrate the vindictive projects of Tippoo Sultaun' (*Wellesley Desp.* vol. iii. pp. ix–xi). Kirkpatrick was appointed one of the commissioners for the partition of Mysore after the fall of Seringapatam, for which he received a sum of ten thousand pagodas, and in 1801 was made resident at Poona, but was compelled to finally quit India through ill-health the same year.

Kirkpatrick suggested and promoted the Bengal Military Fund. He translated various works from the Persian, and also published a translation of the 'Diary and Letters of Tippoo Sultaun' (London, 1804), and an 'Account of the Mission to Nepaul in 1793' (London, 1811). He helped to select the library deposited in the India House, Leadenhall Street, and now at the India Office. He was a man of mild and amiable manner, and in his skill in oriental tongues and knowledge of the manners, customs, and laws of India was declared by the Marquis Wellesley to be unequalled by any man he ever met in India. The future Duke of Wellington appears to have had a less favourable opinion of the Kirkpatrick brothers, particularly of Achilles (cf. *Wellington Suppl. Desp.* i. 95, 244. 250).

Kirkpatrick married at Calcutta, 26 Sept. 1788, Miss Maria Seaton Rawson (*Gent. Mag.* lvi. pt. i. p. 351), and left four daughters: Clementina, who married Admiral Sir John Louis, bart.; Barbara, who married Mr. Charles Buller, M.P.; Julia, who married Edward Strachey, father of the present Sir Edward Strachey, bart.; and Eliza, who died unmarried. Kirkpatrick died on 22 Aug. 1812, aged 58.

[Memoirs of the Family of Kirkpatrick of Closeburn, privately printed, London, 1885, pp. 60–3; information supplied by the India Office; East India Military Calendar, London, 1823, vol. ii.; Despatches of the Marquis Wellesley in India, London, 1837. A large number of Kirkpatrick's letters and memoranda are among the Mornington Papers in Brit. Mus. Addit. MSS.]

H. M. C.

KIRKPATRICK, WILLIAM BAILLIE (1802–1882), Irish presbyterian divine, was born near Ballynahinch, co. Down, in 1802. After spending some time at a classical school conducted by the Rev. Arthur Neilson of Rademon, he went to Glasgow College, where he proceeded to the degree of M.A. He studied theology at the old Belfast College, under the divinity professor of the synod of Ulster. In 1827 he was licensed by the presbytery of Armagh, and on 29 July 1829 ordained one of the ministers of Mary's Abbey Church, Dublin, by the presbytery of Dublin. He at once took high rank as a preacher and pastor. In 1850 he was moderator of the general assembly, and for many years convener of the home mission scheme and of the committee on the state of religion. He was appointed by government a commissioner of charitable donations and bequests, and a commissioner of endowed schools. During his ministry in Dublin a splendid new church was built in Rutland Square, at a cost of 13,000*l.*, for the Mary's Abbey congregation, by Mr. Alexander Findlater, J.P. He died 23 Sept. 1882, at Bray, co. Wicklow, and was buried in Mount Jerome cemetery, Dublin, leaving a widow, two sons, and six daughters. Besides many fugitive publications, he wrote 'Chapters in Irish History,' Dublin, n.d. [1875], which reached a second edition.

[Obituary notice in Belfast Witness; personal knowledge.] T. H.

KIRKSTALL, HUGH or (*fl.* 1200), historian, was received as a Cistercian monk at Kirkstall, Yorkshire, by Ralph Haget, who was abbot there from 1181 to 1190. He was certainly living at Kirkstall in 1207, when he determined to write the history of Fountains Abbey, and sought information from an aged monk named Serlo. Serlo had, by his own account, entered Fountains about 1138, and was afterwards sent in succession to Baronoldswic and Kirkstall, and was in the sixty-ninth year of his profession when he supplied Hugh with material for his history. For the literary form of the work Hugh would seem to be entirely responsible. The 'Narracio de Fundatione Monasterii de Fontibus' in its oldest extant form ends with Haget's translation to Fountains in 1190; the continuation down to 1219 may be by Hugh or by some other person. Leland saw and used a copy of the history, which contains matter not found in extant copies, and additions probably made after Hugh's death; his extracts are printed in the 'Collectanea,' vol. iv. Leland thus cites a reference to Stephen de Eston, abbot of Fountains from 1247 to 1252 (*Coll.* iv. 108). Tanner regarded this as proof that Hugh survived till that period, which, though possible, is not very likely. The only extant mediæval copy of the 'Narracio' is among the Gale MSS. at Trinity College, Cambridge. Bernard mentions a manuscript, 'De Fontanensis Monasterii Origine,' in the library of Sir Henry Langley, which cannot now be traced (*Cat. MSS. Angliæ*, ii. 216).

There are, however, three late copies which differ somewhat from the Gale MS., and are apparently due to a common abbreviation of the original. These are Lansdowne MS. 404 and Arundel MS. 51 in the British Museum, and Dodsworth MS. 26 in the Bodleian. From the second Dugdale printed the chronicle in his 'Monasticon Anglicanum' (v. 292–303). The fuller text has been printed in 'Memorials of Fountains Abbey' (i. 1–128), edited by Mr. J. R. Walbran for the Surtees Society in 1863. Hugh is also credited with a work, 'De Rebus a Cisterciensibus Monachis in Anglia Gestis,' which is probably identical with the 'History of Fountains.' Tanner suggests that he was the Hugh the monk whose verses, 'De Gestis et Laudibus Thurstini Eboracensis Archiepiscopi, cum aliis notabilibus quæ concernunt Ecclesiam Ebor.,' were formerly preserved in the library of the monastery of Sion. The fact that Thurstan was a patron of the Cistercians is favourable to this conjecture. Bale inadvertently calls Hugh 'Hugh of Kirkstede.'

[Leland, Commentarii de Scriptt. Brit. p. 245, and Collectanea, iv. 105–9 ; Bale, iii. 81 ; Pits, p. 297 ; Tanner's Bibl. Brit.-Hib. p. 419 ; Dugdale's Monasticon, v. 292–303, 530–2 ; Mr. Walbran's preface to Memorials of Fountains, vol. i. pp. vii-xxi.] C. L. K.

KIRKTON, JAMES (1620?–1699), Scottish divine and historian, was born about 1620. He graduated at the university of Edinburgh in 1647, and was ordained and admitted to the second charge of Lanark in 1655. He was afterwards translated to Mertoun in Berwickshire, and was deprived in 1662 on the restoration of episcopacy. Under the indulgence granted in 1672 he was appointed as minister of Carstairs, but he refused the appointment and went to England. In 1674 he was denounced as a rebel for holding conventicles, and in June 1676 he was seized in Edinburgh by a Captain Carstairs, but was rescued by his brother-in-law, Robert Baillie of Jerviswood [q. v.] He declined an invitation to become one of the ministers of the Scottish church in Rotterdam, but during the height of the persecution he and his family took refuge in Holland, and remained there till the proclamation of the Toleration Act of 1687. He then returned to Scotland, was appointed at a meeting of presbyterian ministers to officiate in Edinburgh, and preached to a large congregation in a meeting-house on the Castle Hill till the revolution, when he was reinstated in his former parish of Mertoun, and was one of the ministers appointed to 'purge' the university of Edinburgh of professors disaffected to the

new government. In 1091 he was admitted
minister of the Tolbooth parish, Edinburgh,
and remained there till his death, which took
place in 1609. Wodrow describes him as a
'minister of great zeal, knowledge, and learning, a most curious searcher into the natural,
civil, and ecclesiastical history of Scotland,'
and as a 'most successful and sententious
preacher of the gospel;' but, according to
episcopal pamphlets of the time, he was 'the
comedian of his party,' and his sermons were
'the chat of the tavern' and 'the divertis-
ment of the young people.' Kirkton married
Grissel, daughter of George Baillie of Jerviswood, and had three sons, and a daughter
who married Dr. A. Skene, besides other
children who died young.

Kirkton published two separate sermons in
1698 and 1699, and wrote a 'History of Mr.
John Welsh, Minister of the Gospel at Ayr,'
with whom he was connected by marriage.
He left in manuscript 'The Secret and True
History of the Church of Scotland from the
Restoration to the year 1678,' which was
edited, with biographical sketch and notes,
by Charles Kirkpatrick Sharpe, and published
in 1817, Edinburgh. The manuscript was of
great service to Wodrow in compiling his
'History of the Sufferings of the Church
of Scotland,' but he tones down Kirkton's
stories, some of which are coarse and scurrilous. The book contains a panegyric on
the church of Scotland during the commonwealth, which later historians have characterised as a 'romance and an enthusiastic fable.'

[Scott's Fasti; Wodrow's Hist. of the Suff. of
the Church of Scotland; Scots Presby. Eloq.;
Pitcairn's Assembly; M'Crie's Knox, biog.
sketch by Sharpe.]   G. W. S.

KIRKUP, SEYMOUR STOCKER
(1788–1880), artist, born in London in 1788,
was the eldest child of Joseph Kirkup,
jeweller and diamond merchant in London.
He was admitted a student of the Royal
Academy in 1809, and obtained a medal in
1811 for a drawing in the antique school
there. He became at this time acquainted
with William Blake (1757–1827) [q. v.] (see
WEMYSS REID, Life of Lord Houghton, ii.
222), and with B. R. Haydon [q. v.], with
whom he subsequently kept up an interesting correspondence (see HAYDON, Correspondence and Table-talk, edited by F. W. Haydon). About 1816 Kirkup began to suffer
from pulmonary weakness, and, after his
father's death, visited Italy. He eventually
settled in that country, living some time at
Rome, where, on 26 Feb. 1821, he was
present at the funeral of John Keats and
in 1822 at that of Shelley. He eventually settled at Florence, where he lived for

many years in a house on the Arno, adjoining the Ponte Vecchio. He was a good
artist, but practised painting in a 'dilettante'
fashion. He sent to the Royal Academy in
1833 a picture of 'Cassio,' and in 1836 a
lady's portrait. He also published a few
etchings. At Florence Kirkup became a
leader of a well-known literary circle. He
collected a valuable library, of which a catalogue was printed in 1871, and maintained
a large correspondence. Walter Savage
Landor, Robert and Elizabeth Browning,
Bezzi, E. J. Trelawny, Joseph Severn, and
others were his intimate friends, and his
name is of frequent occurrence in their biographies. He drew many portraits of his
friends; one of Trelawny is in the possession of Mr. J. Temple Leader at Florence,
and in the Scott collection of drawings in
the Scottish National Gallery at Edinburgh
there is a portrait drawn by Kirkup of John
Scott, editor of the 'Champion.' He was a
devoted and learned student of Dante, and
adopted the peculiar scheme of Dantesque
interpretation promulgated by his friend
Gabriele Rossetti. In 1840 Kirkup, Bezzi,
and Henry Wilde, an American, obtained
leave to search for the portrait of Dante,
painted, according to tradition, by Giotto, in
the chapel of the Palazzo del Podestà at
Florence. In this they were successful on
21 July 1840. Kirkup was able surreptitiously
to make a drawing and a tracing before an ill-
conceived restoration in 1841 destroyed the
truth and value of the painting. The drawing, which was issued in chromolithography
by the Arundel Society, was made from
Kirkup's sketch. The latter was also engraved by P. Lasinio. Kirkup gave his
tracing to Rossetti, who handed it on to his
son, Dante Gabriel Rossetti [q. v.] It was
sold after the latter's death. Kirkup made
some of the designs for Lord Vernon's splendid edition of Dante's works.

On the restoration of the Italian kingdom,
Kirkup was created for these services cavaliere
of the order of S. Maurizio e Lazzaro. Apparently through a misunderstanding he assumed that this gave him a right to the rank
of 'barone,' by which title he was known
for the rest of his life. Kirkup was below
middle stature, and in early life very good-
looking. Latterly he displayed much eccentricity in his dress and habits, and suffered
from increasing deafness. He was most of
his life a devoted believer in spiritualism, and
a disciple of Daniel Home [q. v.], under whose
influence he parted with his library and other
treasures. Kirkup had by a young Florentine
lady, Regina Ronti, who died 30 Oct. 1856,
aged 19, a daughter, Imogene, who married

Kirkwood   225   Kirkwood

Signor Teodoro Cioni of Leghorn, and died in 1878, leaving two children. On 16 Feb. 1875 he married, he being eighty-seven and his bride only twenty-two years of age, Paolina, daughter of Pasquale Carboni, English vice-consul at Rome. His widow afterwards married Signor Morandi of Bologna. Kirkup died at 4 Via Scali del Ponte Nuovo, Leghorn, where he had resided since 1872, on 3 Jan. 1880, and was buried on 5 Jan. in the new British cemetery there. A portrait of Kirkup, drawn by himself in 1844, is in the possession of Mr. Thomas Marchant at Lewisham.

[Athenæum, 29 May 1880; Spectator, 11 May 1850; Forster's Life of W. S. Landor; B. R. Haydon's Memoirs; Sharp's Memoirs of Joseph Severn; information kindly supplied by W. M. Rossetti, J. Temple Leader, the Rev. R. H. Irvine, Mr. T. Marchant, Duchessa di Sermoneta, Signora Morandi, Signor Cioni, Miss Browning, and others.]   L. C.

KIRKWOOD, JAMES (1650?–1708), advocate of parochial libraries, was born at Dunbar about 1650. He graduated M.A. from Edinburgh University in 1670, and after passing his trials before the presbytery of Haddington became domestic chaplain to John Campbell, earl of Caithness, afterwards first earl of Breadalbane [q. v.], by whom, on 12 May 1679, he was presented to the living of Minto. Deprived of this benefice after 1 Nov. 1681 for refusing to take the test, Kirkwood, following the example of a large number of 'outed ministers,' migrated to England, where, on 1 March 1685, through the friendship of Bishop Burnet, he was instituted to the small rectory of Astwick, Bedfordshire.

While residing in the highlands with Lord Breadalbane's family Kirkwood had been much impressed with the ignorance on the part of the Gaelic people of the scriptures, and, indeed, of all kinds of literature, and in 1680 he commenced a correspondence with the Hon. Robert Boyle [q. v.] on the subject. Boyle presented him with two hundred copies of his Bible in Irish for immediate circulation, and subscribed towards the printing of three thousand more copies, which Kirkwood succeeded in distributing over the north of Scotland, in spite of the opposition to his scheme in England, on the ground that it would obstruct the desired extirpation of the Gaelic tongue. In 1699 appeared anonymously a tract, now of great rarity, entitled 'An Overture for Founding and Maintaining Bibliothecks in every Paroch throughout the Kingdom.' This was printed at Edinburgh, the word 'overture' being the technical term for a proposal to the old Scottish parliament. Under the arbitrary and comprehensive scheme therein contained the parish minister's private books were to form the nucleus of each library, the parish schoolmaster was to act as librarian, and a uniform system of cataloguing was to be adopted throughout the country. Among other inducements which the scheme offered is mentioned the fact that 'it will in a short time carry away the whole trade of printing from all the rest of Europe.' The tract was reprinted by William Blades in 1889 from a copy preserved in the Public Library at Wigan. The only other copy known is in a private library at Glasgow. The 'Overture' is traced to Kirkwood by means of a second tract, of which only one copy is known; it is entitled 'A Copy of a Letter anent a Project for Erecting a Library in every Presbytery, or at least every County in the Highlands. From a Reverend Minister of the Scots Nation now in England' (no place nor date), to which is appended the following printed statement: 'The author of this Letter is a person who has a great zeal for propagating the knowledge of God in the Highlands of Scotland, and is the same who did promote contributions for the printing of Bibles in the Irish language, and sent so many of them down to Scotland.' The general assembly approved the project, but do not appear to have translated their approval into action. Charters, however, states that a library was established for the clergy in the highlands by Kirkwood in 1699 (Cat. of Scotish Writers, s. n. 'Girwod, James,' p. 61). In recognition of the activity displayed in these various projects Kirkwood was, on 4 March 1703, elected a corresponding member of the Society for Promoting Christian Knowledge (S. P. C. K. Minutes, pp. 217–43), and on 11 Nov. following were read at one of the society's meetings 'Letters and Papers from Mr. Kirkwood relating to the Erection of Lending Libraries in the Highlands.' The 'papers' are probably identical with the unique tract mentioned above, which contains elaborate suggestions and rules for the conduct of a lending library. A dry place was to be chosen; the books to be kept under lock and key. Some may be lent out, but no one to have more than two at a time, and the borrowers must be approved preachers, schoolmasters, and students. Each book to have its price against it in the catalogue, and every borrower to deposit a quarter more than the value, as a security for its safe return. Kirkwood had previously, on 7 Jan. 1702, been ejected from the living of Astwick for 'neglect in not abjuring according to the statute 13 and 14 William III.' No further mention of him has been traced, but

VOL. XXXI.

he appears to have died in 1708, when he bequeathed his books and papers with 'some other things' to the presbytery of Dunbar, his native place.

Besides the tracts mentioned, Kirkwood wrote ' A New Family Book, or the True Interest of Families. . . . Together with several Prayers for Families and Children and Graces before and after Meat.' The second edition of this work, with a preface by Dr. Anthony Horneck (q. v.) and a grotesque frontispiece engraved by M. Vandergucht, dated 1693, is preserved in the British Museum Library. Charters assigns the date 1692 to this work, but in a letter to Kirkwood, dated 18 Oct. 1690, Boyle acknowledges the receipt from the author of a 'pious and sensible book,' which, from other remarks that he lets fall, is evidently the 'New Family Book.' It must therefore have been published in or before 1690.

[Scott's Fasti, pt. ii. pp. 506, 756; Birch's Boyle, 1772, clxxxviii-cciv; Library Chronicle, 1888, p. 116; Notes and Queries, 3rd ser. v. 29; MacClure's A Chapter in English Church History, pp. 217, 243; Miller's Dunbar, pp. 207-9; notes kindly supplied by F. A. Blaydes, esq.]
T. S.

KIRKWOOD, JAMES (*fl.* 1698), Scottish teacher and grammarian, was born near Dunbar. In May 1674 he was acting as tutor or 'governour' to Lord Bruce at the college of Glasgow, where he lodged for some time in the same house with Dr. Burnet, and in the same year was offered by Sir Robert Milne of Barntoun, provost of Linlithgow, the mastership of the school in that burgh with a yearly salary of four hundred merks. At first he refused the offer, as he had 'a good hope of rising to a place of more credit and advantage,' but on 23 Jan. 1675 he accepted it. After serving for fifteen years, he quarrelled with the magistrates over a suggested reduction of his salary and a refusal on his part to attend the presbyterian 'meeting-house.' He was dismissed, and a long litigation ensued. Kirkwood got the better of his employers, who were mulcted in damages to the extent of four thousand merks for forcibly ejecting him and his wife—a Dutch lady, Goletine van Beest—from their house, and throwing his books and papers and Mrs. Kirkwood's fine Dutch furniture into 'the open and dirty street.' Kirkwood published an account of the litigation in 'A Short Information of the Plea betwixt the Town Council of Lithgow and Mr. James Kirkwood, Schoolmaster there, whereof a more full account may perhaps come out hereafter' [1690], 4to. Among other charges brought against Kirkwood was that he was 'a reviler of the gods of the people.' 'By gods,' says Kirkwood, 'they mean the twenty-seven members of the town council.' Many years afterwards he published ' The History of the Twenty Seven Gods of Linlithgow; Being an exact and true Account of a Famous Plea betwixt the Town-Council of the said Burgh, and Mr. Kirkwood, Schoolmaster there. Seria Mixta Jocis,' Edinburgh, 1711, 4to. It was dedicated to Sir David Dalrymple, whose elder brother, the 'Earl of Stair,' says the author, 'not only sent his son, the present earl, to my school at Lithgow, but tabled him in my house.' The work contains many curious particulars regarding the social and religious state of affairs during the contention for supremacy between the presbyterian and prelatic parties.

Kirkwood left Linlithgow and went, in March 1690, to Edinburgh, where he lived for a year without employment. He then started a school 'with above sevenscore of noblemen and gentlemen's sons.' He tells us that he afterwards refused the professorship of humanity in St. Andrews, a call to Duns, another call to be professor of Greek and Latin at Jamestown, Virginia, the mastership of the free school at Kimbolton, and of a free school in Ireland. He also states that he was invited to return to Linlithgow school.

Subsequently Kirkwood became, on the invitation of the Countess of Roxburgh, master of the school at Kelso. Here he was again involved in serious difficulties, which he narrated in 'Mr. Kirkwood's Plea before the Kirk, and Civil Judicatures of Scotland. Divided into Five Parts,' London, printed by D. E. for the author, 1698, 4to, dedicated to the Countess of Roxburgh. Kirkwood made a gross attack on the character of the minister, Dr. Jaques, who replied in a ' Vindication against Master Kirkwood's Defamation.' Kirkwood sent forth an 'Answer,' 4to, without an imprint.

Throughout his pamphlets Kirkwood claims high repute as a grammarian, and in Penney's 'History of Linlithgowshire' and Chalmers's 'Life of Ruddiman' he is spoken of as the first grammarian of the day. At the suggestion of Lord Stair, president of the court of session, he was consulted by the commissioners for colleges and schools as to the best Latin grammar to be used in Scotland. He pointed out the defects of Despauter, 'the Priscian of the Netherlands,' and was requested to edit Despauter's grammar, with the result that in 1695 he produced 'Grammatica Despauteriana, cum nova novi generis Glossa: cui subjunguntur singula primæ Partis Exempla Vernacule Reddita.' It was dedicated to the commissioners of schools and colleges, and secured the privy council's privilege for nineteen years. A second edition appeared in 1700.

a third in 1711, and a fourth in 1720, all published in Edinburgh. To the fourth edition is appended the note, 'Cui jam tandem Author postremam apposuit manum.' The book was superseded by Ruddiman's 'Rudiments' (1714). Kirkwood died before 1720, probably at Kelso.

In addition to the works named, Kirkwood was author of: 1. 'Grammatica facilis, seu nova et artificiosa methodus docendi Linguam Latinam : cui præfiguntur animadversiones in rudimenta nostra vulgaria, et Grammaticam Despauterianam ...,' Glasgow, 1674. 2. 'Prima pars Grammaticæ in metrum redacta,' Edinburgh, 1675. 3. 'Secunda pars Grammaticæ ...,' Edinburgh, 1676. 4. 'Tertia et quarta pars Grammaticæ,' Edinburgh, 1676. 5. 'All the Examples, both Words and Sentences, of the First part of grammar, translated into English by J. K.,' Edinburgh, 1676. 6. 'Grammatica delineata secundum sententiam plurium ...,' London, 1677. 7. 'Rhetoricæ Compendium ; cui subjicitur de Analysi Tractatiuncula,' Edinburgh, 1678.

[Chambers's Dict. of Eminent Scotsmen (Thomson); Miller's History of Dunbar, pp. 223–4 ; Wahlie's Hist. of Linlithgow ; Penney's Linlithgowshire, pp. 78, 215 ; Notes and Queries, 3rd ser. v. 29, 30 ; Anderson's Scottish Nation ; Catalogues of British Museum, Advocates' Library, Trinity College, Dublin, and Aberdeen University.]   G. S–n.

KIRTON, EDMUND (d. 1466), abbot of Westminster, belonged to the old family called Cobbledike, but took the name of Kirton, probably from the village where he was born. Villages of that name exist in both Lincolnshire and Suffolk, and the Cobbledikes are known to have spread themselves over the two counties. In 1403 Edmund was a monk of Westminster, and, while continuing a member of that monastery, graduated B.D. from Gloucester Hall (Worcester College), Oxford. According to his epitaph he was at Rome during the pontificate of Martin V, 1417–31, and preached before him. In 1423 he was prior of the Benedictine scholars at Gloucester Hall, and in the same year he was sent by the university to lay various letters, touching subsidies for the new divinity schools and other buildings at Oxford, before a general chapter of his order at Northampton. He was selected to preach before the council, and on his motion a vote of thanks was returned to John Whethamsted, abbot of St. Albans, as the chief benefactor and second founder of Gloucester Hall. In recognition of Kirton's services the chapter appointed him a visitor of the Benedictine monasteries, and requested the chancellor of the university to grant him a D.D. degree.

In 1437 he accompanied Paul Norreys, principal of University Hall, Oxford, to the council of Basle. Both seem to have been cited to appear there before Eugenius IV, on suspicion of heresy, but the influence of Humphrey, duke of Gloucester, and letters from their university enabled them to exculpate themselves. After having been a monk of Westminster thirty-seven years, Kirton was elected abbot between 27 May and 20 Aug. 1440. He resigned the post twenty-two years later (1462), probably on account of increasing age and infirmities, but received till his death (October 1466) an annual pension of two hundred marks. His oratory is spoken of as remarkable. His tomb in St. Andrew's Chapel, Westminster Abbey, formed part of a screen which Kirton himself had caused to be ornamented 'with carved birds, flowers, and cherubim, and with the arms, devices, and mottoes of the nobility,' but tomb and screen have long disappeared.

[Dart's History of Westminster Abbey, ed. 1723, vol. ii. p. xxxv; Widmore's History of the Church of St. Peter's, Westminster, p. 114; Dugdale's Monasticon, 1817, ii. 276; Wood's History of the University of Oxford (Gutch), i. 587 : Neale and Brayley's History of Westminster Abbey, i. 90.]   E. T. B.

KIRWAN, FRANCIS (1589 – 1661), bishop of Killala, the son of Matthew Kirwan and Juliana Lynch, was born at Galway in 1589, and educated there at a school kept by his maternal uncle, Arthur Lynch. He afterwards studied at Lisbon, and was ordained priest in Ireland in 1614. Next year he went to France, and taught philosophy at Dieppe. He returned to Ireland in 1620 with a commission as vicar-general from Florence Conry, archbishop of Tuam, and remained in charge of his diocese for nine years, during which he laboured incessantly, not only in the more settled districts, but in the wild Connaught mountains and in the oceanic islands. He was often accompanied by jesuits, and became much attached to the society. Conry died in 1629, but his successor, Malachy O'Queely, retained Kirwan as his vicar. In 1637 or 1638 he went again to France, spending some time at Rennes, Rouen, and Caen, and at Paris, where he became intimate with St. Vincent de Paul, but he did not escape abuse from some Irish students, whom he vainly endeavoured to organise for a mission to their own country. The *nolo episcopari* was genuine in his mouth, but even in his own despite he was consecrated bishop of Killala at St. Lazaire on 7 May 1645. Thirteen

Q 2

bishops, fifteen abbots, and thirty doctors of the Sorbonne were present. Kirwan's books and altar furniture were captured by pirates, but he himself reached Ireland safely and made his way to Kilkenny, where Rinuccini was then resident as nuncio, and took possession of his own see on 5 Oct. 1646. He joined Rinuccini in rejecting Ormonde's peace (June 1646), which left the future position of the Roman catholics mainly dependent on the king's will; but in the nuncio's later struggle with the supreme council—virtually one between the Celtic and the Anglo-Irish party—he sided with the latter and with Archbishop De Burgo of Tuam, who during the interdict forced a passage through the roof of the collegiate church at Galway, 'and himself, with the Bishop of Killala, celebrated mass there' (RINUCCINI, *Embassy in Ireland*, Engl. transl. p. 468). Kirwan was afterwards sorry for his resistance to papal or quasi-papal authority, and sued for absolution, which was readily given (CARDINAL MORAN, *Spicilegium Ossoriense*, ii. 175). He took an active part in the last struggles of the Irish in Connaught, and in the abortive negotiations with the Duke of Lorraine (PONCE, *Vindiciæ Eversæ*, Paris, 1653), and was on intimate terms with Clanricarde. He also worked in his own diocese from 1649 to 1652, in which year he became a fugitive, and underwent great hardships. Fearing to bring trouble on those who sheltered him, he surrendered in 1654, and after fourteen months' imprisonment was allowed to retire to France. He reached Nantes in August 1655, and spent the remainder of his life in Brittany, where charitable people, and even the provincial states, provided for the Irish exiles. He died at Rennes on 27 Aug. 1661, and was buried with great pomp in the jesuit church there, having been allowed to enrol himself in the society when at the point of death. His relics were long believed to have worked miracles.

Kirwan was a thorough ascetic, never sparing himself either in purse or person, and self-condemned to the scourge and the horsehair shirt, but cheerful and pleasant nevertheless. He loved to make peace among those committed to his charge, and some of his awards show considerable humour. A man who had put away his wife called upon the bishop to confirm the arrangement, but Kirwan found her innocent, and ordered him to take her back on pain of eternal damnation. 'I can,' said the man, 'bear the flames of hell better than my wife's company.' The bishop told him to begin by putting his hand into the candle; but a few seconds of this foretaste sufficed, and the couple were reconciled. Finding many gamblers among the priests, Kirwan ordered them to restore all they had won, at the same time forbidding other winners to make restitution to them. His opponents respected him, his people loved him, and he made friends wherever he went.

[A life of Kirwan by his nephew, John Lynch, archdeacon of Tuam, and author of Cambrensis Eversus, was published at St. Malo in 1669, under the title of Pii antistitis Icon, &c. This was reprinted at Dublin in 1848, with a translation and notes by the Rev. C. P. Meehan, who published a second edition (much improved) in 1884. See also a Contemporary Hist. of Affairs in Ireland, and a Hist. of the Confederation and War in Ireland, both edited by Mr. J. T. Gilbert, and the three books mentioned above.] R. B-L.

KIRWAN, OWEN (*d.* 1803), Irish rebel, was a tailor by trade, resident in Plunket Street, Dublin. He joined the conspiracy of Robert Emmet, and was employed in the manufacture of ammunition. Kirwan was specially attached to the Patrick Street depôt of arms, the sudden explosion at which place on 16 July 1803 precipitated the insurrection. On the evening of 23 July Kirwan's residence was used as a muster-place for a large party of rebels. A little before nine o'clock in the evening Kirwan, attired in a green uniform, took up a position outside his door to watch for the rocket which was to announce the rising. On its appearance he summoned the men waiting in his house, and led them with a pike on his shoulder down Plunket Street into Thomas Street. After his departure his house was used as a refreshment-place for another body of rebels. Kirwan was denounced by a neighbour, and arrested immediately after the rising. He was tried before Mr. Baron George on 1 Sept. He was eloquently defended by Curran, but the evidence against him was conclusive, and he was found guilty and executed on 3 Sept. 1803.

[Madden's United Irishmen, 3rd ser. vol. iii.; Hibernian Magazine for 1803; Trial of Owen Kirwan, in Howell's State Trials, vol. xxviii.] G. P. M-y.

KIRWAN, RICHARD (1733–1812), chemist and natural philosopher, was the second son of Martin Kirwan, esq., of Cregg, co. Galway, Ireland, by his wife Mary, daughter of Patrick French, esq., of Cloughballymore in the same county, where he was born in 1733 and brought up until his father's death in 1741. He was sent to Poictiers to complete his education, and read Latin eagerly. The death of his mother in 1751 caused him poignant grief. He entered the jesuit novitiate at St. Omer in 1754, but quitted it and returned to Ireland in 1755, when, his elder brother having been killed in a duel, he came into possession of the family estates. He was then (as described by Lady Morgan from her father's recollections) 'a tall, elegant, comely young man,' given to interlarding his discourse with foreign idioms. The morning after his marriage, in February 1757, with a daughter of Sir Thomas Blake of Menlo, co. Galway, he was thrown into prison for her debts. Yet they lived happily together for eight years, chiefly at Menlo, where Mrs. Kirwan died in 1765, leaving two daughters, of whom the elder married Lord Trimleston, the second Colonel Hill. In 1766 Kirwan, having conformed to the established church, was called to the Irish bar, but threw up practice after two years, and pursued scientific studies in London, exchanged for Greek at Cregg in 1773. He resided in London from 1777 to 1787, and became known to Priestley, Cavendish, Burke, and Horne Tooke. He corresponded with all the *savants* of Europe; his Wednesday evenings in Newman Street were the resort of strangers of distinction; the Empress Catherine of Russia sent him her portrait. His library, despatched from Galway to London on 5 Sept. 1780, was captured by an American privateer. Elected a fellow of the Royal Society on 24 Feb. 1780, he received the Copley medal in 1782 for a series of papers on chemical affinity (*Phil. Trans.* vols. lxxi–lxxiii.), promptly translated into German by Crell. His 'Elements of Mineralogy' (London, 1784; 3rd edition, 1810) was the first systematic treatise on the subject in English, and was translated into French, German, and Russian. 'An Estimate of the Temperatures of Different Latitudes' (London, 1787) was designed to pave the way for a theory of winds. As the representative work of the Stahlian school, Kirwan's celebrated 'Essay on Phlogiston' (London, 1787) was translated into French in 1788 by Madame Lavoisier, with adverse commentaries by Lavoisier, Monge, Berthollet, and De Morveau. Kirwan replied in a second English edition (1789), but in 1791 candidly acknowledged his conversion to the views of his opponents.

Delicate health compelling a more retired life, he settled in 1787 at No. 6 Cavendish Row, Dublin, joined the Royal Irish Academy, and became in 1799 its president. He presided as well over the Dublin Library and 'Kirwanian' Societies. A gold medal was voted to him by the Royal Dublin Society in acknowledgment of his services in procuring the Leskeyan cabinet of minerals for their museum, and his portrait by Hamilton hangs in their board-room. He was a member of

the Edinburgh Royal Society and of a number of foreign academies; and the university of Dublin conferred upon him in 1794 an honorary degree of LL.D. A baronetcy offered to him by Lord Castlereagh was declined; but he bore the honorary title of inspector-general of his majesty's mines in Ireland.

Kirwan's criticism in 1797 of the Huttonian theory of the earth (*Trans. R. Irish Acad.* vi. 233) involved him in a heated controversy. The publication of his 'Geological Essays' (London, 1799), delayed by the Irish rebellion, was anticipated by the appearance of a German version. 'An Essay on the Analysis of Mineral Waters' (1799) indicated valuable methods and contained much useful information. He wrote instructively besides on subjects connected with mining, bleaching, and the chemistry of soils, and was consulted as a weather-prophet by half the farmers in Ireland. His 'Logick' (2 vols. London, 1807) and 'Metaphysical Essays' (1811) had little success.

An accomplished linguist, a brilliant talker, and an adept in Italian music, he indulged as he grew old in some minor oddities, readily permitted to the 'Nestor of English chemistry.' Even in courts of justice or at viceregal levées he wore a slouched hat as a precaution against cold; received his friends, summer and winter, extended on a couch before a blazing fire; and, owing to a weakness of the throat, always ate alone, his diet consisting of ham and milk. Flies were his especial aversion; he kept a pet eagle, and was attended by six large dogs. He was a good landlord and philosophically indifferent to money. A unitarian form of belief was finally adopted by him, and he spent much time in scriptural study. He died, as the consequence of 'starving out' a cold, on 1 June 1812, in his seventy-ninth year, and was buried in St. George's Church, Lower Temple Street, Dublin. Between 1788 and 1808 he contributed thirty-eight memoirs to the 'Transactions' of the Royal Irish Academy; controverted in 1784 some of Cavendish's results (*Phil. Trans.* lxxiv. 154, 178); and presented to the Royal Society in 1785 'Remarks on Specific Gravities' (*ib.* lxxv. 267) and 'Experiments on Hepatic Air' (*ib.* lxxvi. 118), the latter included, in an Italian translation, among Amoretti's 'Opuscoli Scelti' (x. 40, Milan, 1787). Several of his essays on chemical subjects were reproduced in German in Crell's 'Annalen' (vols. i. and ii., 1800). The Royal Irish Academy possesses a good likeness of him, and his portrait was also painted by Comerford. There is a bust of him in the Dublin Library.

[Proc. R. Irish Acad. vol. iv. App. No. viii. p. lxxxi, 1850 (Michael Donovan), ib. p. 481 (Pickell); Philosophical Mag. 1802, xiv. 353 (portrait prefixed to volume); Gent. Mag. vol. lxxxii. pt. i. p. 669; Ann. Reg. 1812, p. 177; Thomson's Hist. R. Society, p. 483; Thomson's Hist. of Chemistry, 1831, ii. 137; Cuvier's Hist. des Sciences, v. 46; Poggendorff's Biog. Lit. Handwörterbuch; Watt's Bibl. Brit.]

A. M. C.

KIRWAN, STEPHEN (d. 1602?), bishop of Clonfert, a native of Galway, was educated partly at Oxford and partly at Paris. Conforming to the protestant religion he was, apparently while 'a student resident at Oxford,' appointed archdeacon of Annaghdown in 1558. On 13 April 1573 he was, on the recommendation of Sir William Fitzwilliam, advanced to the see of Kilmacdaugh, of which he was the first protestant bishop. His conduct giving satisfaction to the government, he was, on the recommendation of Lord Arthur Grey, translated to the bishopric of Clonfert on 24 May 1582, and on 15 July 1585 he was placed on a commission for compounding with the landowners in Connaught and Thomond for a certain rent in lieu of the uncertain cess accustomed to be paid by them to the crown. In 1587, 1588, 1597, and 1599 he was one of the commissioners of martial affairs in Connaught. On 20 Oct. 1602 Roland Lynch, bishop of Kilmacduagh, was appointed to the see of Clonfert *in commendam*, from which it seems likely that Kirwan died in that or the preceding year.

[Ware's Bishops, ed. Harris; Cotton's Fasti Eccl. Hib.; Cal. State Papers, Ireland; Cal. Fiants, Eliz.; Brady's Irish Reformation.]

R. D.

KIRWAN, WALTER BLAKE (1754–1805), dean of Killala, was born at Gortha, co. Galway, in 1754. His father being a Roman catholic, he was sent for education in early youth to the jesuit college at St. Omer. At the age of seventeen he went to St. Croix in the West Indies, along with a relative who had large property in that island. The climate did not suit him, the cruelty which he witnessed disgusted him, and after six years' residence he returned to Europe, and went to the university of Louvain, where he took orders, and was appointed professor of natural and moral philosophy. In 1778 he became chaplain to the Neapolitan ambassador at the British court, and the eloquence of the sermons which he preached in London in this capacity attracted marked attention. In 1787 he left the Roman catholic church, and on 24 June of that year preached his first sermon to a protestant congregation in St. Peter's Church, Dublin, where for some time he continued to officiate every Sunday, immediately taking rank as a pulpit orator of singular power. His services were eagerly sought for charity sermons, and the churches in which he preached had to be defended against the pressure of the crowds by guards and palisades. It was not uncommon for collections amounting to 1,000l. or 1,200l. to be taken up on such occasions, jewellery and gold watches being frequently laid upon the plates. In 1789 Kirwan was collated by the Archbishop of Dublin to the prebend of Howth, and was in the same year preferred to the living of St. Nicholas Without in the city of Dublin. In 1800 he was appointed dean of Killala. He died at his house, Mount Pleasant, near Dublin, on 27 Oct. 1805. His wife, Wilhelmina, youngest daughter of Goddard Richards of Grange, co. Wexford, whom he had married 22 Sept. 1798, survived him, with two sons—one of whom, Antony la Touche Kirwan, became afterwards dean of Limerick—and two daughters. His widow was granted by the crown a pension of 300l. per annum for life, with reversion to her daughters.

A volume of Kirwan's sermons was published posthumously, London, 1816.

[Memoir prefixed to Sermons.]

T. H.

KITCHIN, *alias* **DUNSTAN, ANTHONY,** (1477–1563), bishop of Llandaff, born in 1477, was a Benedictine monk of Westminster, who studied at Gloucester (now Worcester) College, a college built originally for Benedictine novices. He graduated at Oxford B.D. in 1525 and D.D. in 1538. In 1526 he was made prior of Gloucester College (see Foxe, *Acts and Mon.* v. 425). In 1530 he was appointed abbot of Eynsham, Oxford, and as abbot was a signatory to the king's supremacy (1534) and to the articles of 1536. On the dissolution of the lesser monasteries he, together with eight monks, surrendered his abbey, 4 Dec. 1539, receiving a pension of 133l. 6s. 8d., with the promise of a benefice and cure. He was also appointed king's chaplain, and in 1545 bishop of Llandaff. The oath he took on his consecration contains the fullest possible renunciation of the papal supremacy (STRYPE, *Cranmer*, p. 187). He clung to his bishopric through all changes, and wastefully reduced it from one of the wealthiest to one of the poorest sees. He did homage to Mary at her coronation, displayed zeal enough to burn a martyr (FOXE, vi. 646), and was one of the commissioners who sat on Hooper. At the accession of Elizabeth he again complied, being the only papist bishop who took the oath of supremacy, although he had dissented in the House of Lords from all the acts of restitution and reformation. He was included by Elizabeth in the two commissions which she drew for the consecration of Parker, but owing perhaps to pressure from Bonner he certainly did not act. No bishop consequently took part in the ceremony, a fact which gave rise to the great controversy as to the validity of English ordinations. It was in connection with this controversy that the Nag's Head story was invented. According to the later form of this fable, Kitchin was present at the dinner at the Nag's Head tavern on the day of the confirmation of Parker, 9 Dec. 1559, and was in vain importuned by Scory and the rest to consecrate him and other bishops-elect. Kitchin died 31 Oct. 1563, and was buried in the parish church of Matherne, Monmouthshire.

His name appears as Dunstan up to the time of his election as bishop; after that event as Kitchin.

[Strype's Cranmer, Annals, Memorials, and Parker; Foxe's Acts and Mon. loc. cit.; Oxford Registers; Dugdale's Mon. Anglic. vol. iii.; State Papers, Dom. 1559, p. 143, ibid. Hen. VIII, iv. 1762; Godwin, De Præsulibus Angliæ (makes Kitchin Cantabr. Acad. Alumnus); Wood's Ath. Oxon.; Le Neve; Burnet; Fuller; Lansdowne MS. 981, fol. 15; Cotton. MSS. Vit. cx. 92–100.]

W. A. S.

KITCHINER, WILLIAM, M.D. (1775?–1827), miscellaneous writer, was probably born at Beaufort Buildings, Strand, London, in 1775. His father, William Kitchiner, came to London from Hertfordshire, and began life as a porter at a coal wharf. By trading as a coal merchant he eventually realised a fortune of about 2,000l. a year. As a justice of the peace for Westminster he occasionally sat at Bow Street court-house. He died at Beaufort Buildings, Strand, London, on 19 July 1794, and was buried in a vault at St. Clement Danes Church. By a first wife he had a daughter, by a second an only son (Gent. Mag. July 1794, p. 678). The son was educated at Eton, and obtained the degree of M.D. from Glasgow. He therefore could not practise in London; but having inherited a handsome competence from his father he was independent of his profession, devoted himself to science, and showed hospitality to a circle of friends distinguished for genius and learning.

Though always an epicure, he was regular and even abstemious in his habits. Convinced that the health depends to a great extent on the proper preparation of the food, he experimented in cookery in his own house, being

aided in his work by Henry Osborne, who was cook to Sir Joseph Banks. He soon attained to a considerable culinary skill. His lunches, to which only a few were admitted, were far famed. His dinners were conducted with much ceremony, and no guest was admitted after the hour fixed. On Tuesday evenings he held conversazioni from seven to eleven. Among the most frequent guests at these gatherings were Charles Kemble and Kitchiner's most intimate friend, Dr. John Haslam [q. v.] His gastronomic experience he embodied in a work entitled 'Apicius Redivivus, or the Cook's Oracle,' which not only treated of delicacies, but also gave instructions in economical housekeeping. He likewise studied optics, and wrote 'An Essay on the size best adapted for Achromatic Glasses, with Hints to Opticians and Amateurs of Astronomical Studies on the construction and use of Telescopes' (Phil. Mag. 1815, xlvi. 122–9). He had a taste for music, played and sang with considerable feeling, and collected with care a library of manuscript and printed music. On 26 Feb. 1827 he dined with his friend John Braham at 69 Baker Street. On returning to his residence, 43 Warren Street, Fitzroy Square, he was attacked with spasms of the heart, and died early on the morning of 27 Feb. He was buried in the church of St. Clement Danes. On 2 Aug. 1799 he married Miss Oram; by her he had no children, and a separation took place. A natural son, who was educated at Cambridge, inherited the bulk of his property.

Kitchiner's writings are: 1. 'A Companion to the Telescope,' 1811. 2. 'Practical Observations on Telescopes, Opera-glasses, and Spectacles,' 1815; 3rd edit. 1818. 3. 'Apicius Redivivus, or the Cook's Oracle, being six hundred receipts, the result of actual experiments instituted in the kitchen of a physician, comprising a culinary code for the rational epicure,' 1817. The 3rd edition is entitled 'The Cook's Oracle;' 7th edit. 1827. 4. 'Peptic Precepts to prevent and relieve Indigestion,' 1821. 5. 'Observations on Vocal Music and Singing,' 1821. 6. 'The Pleasure of Making a Will,' 1822. 7. 'The Art of Invigorating and Prolonging Life by Food, Clothes, Air, Exercise, Wine, Sleep, &c., 1822, four editions. 8. 'Loyal, National, and Sea Songs of England. Selected from original manuscripts and early printed copies in the library of W. Kitchiner,' 1822. Reprinted in 'Songs of the late Charles Dibdin,' 1850, App. pp. 275–314. 9. 'A brief Memoir of Charles Dibdin, with some Documents supplied by Mrs. Lovat Ashe,' 1823. 10. 'The Economy of the Eyes, Precepts for the Improvement and Preservation of the Sight, and what Spectacles are best calculated for the Eyes, and an Account of the Pancratic Magnifier.' Part ii., 'Of Telescopes; being the result of thirty years' experience with fifty-one Telescopes in the possession of W. Kitchiner,' 1824–5. 11. 'The Housekeeper's Ledger; a Plan of keeping Accounts of the Expenses of Housekeeping. To which is added Tom Thrift's Essay on the Pleasure of Early Rising,' 1825. 12. 'The Traveller's Oracle, or Maxims for Locomotion,' 1827. 13. 'The Horse and Carriage Keeper's Oracle. By John Jervis. Revised by W. Kitchiner. Being Part 2 of the Traveller's Oracle,' 1827. 14. 'The Housekeeper's Oracle, containing a system of Carving, the Art of Managing Servants, and the Economist and Epicure's Calendar,' 1829. 15. 'The Shilling Kitchiner,' 1861.

[Gent. Mag. 1799, pt. ii. Suppl. p. 1190, May 1827, pt. i. pp. 470–2; John Bull Mag. August 1824, pp. 52–5; Jerdan's Men I have Known, pp. 282–7; Hood's Whims and Oddities, 1826, pp. 26–32.]   G. C. B.

KITCHINGMAN, JOHN (1740?–1781), painter, was a pupil at Shipley's drawing school and afterwards at the Royal Academy, and was awarded several premiums by the Society of Arts; he exhibited miniatures with the Free Society from 1766 to 1768, and from 1770 was a constant contributor to the Academy exhibitions, sending, besides portraits, figure-subjects and seapieces. His 'Beggar and Dog,' a subject from Mackenzie's 'Man of Feeling,' exhibited in 1775, was mezzotinted on a large scale by H. Kingsbury, and a set of four pictures representing the building, chase, unlading, and dissolution of a cutter, which appeared at the Academy in the last year of his life, was well engraved by B. T. Pouncy [q. v.]; his portraits of Mrs. Elizabeth Carter, Mr. Macklin as Shylock, and Mrs. Yates as Alicia in 'Jane Shore' have also been engraved. Kitchingman was fond of boating, and in 1777 won the Duke of Cumberland's cup in the annual sailing match on the Thames. He married when very young, but soon separated from his wife and fell into intemperate habits. He died in King Street, Covent Garden, 28 Dec. 1781. Edwards speaks of him as a miniaturist of good abilities.

[Edwards's Anecdotes of Painters; Redgrave's Dict. of Artists; Graves's Dict. of Artists, 1760–1880; Royal Academy Catalogues.]   F. M. O'D.

KITE, CHARLES (d. 1811), medical writer, was a member of the corporation of surgeons in London, and practised at Graves-

end, where he died in 1811. Besides contributing to the 'Memoirs' of the London Medical Society and other medical journals, he wrote: 1. 'An Essay on the Recovery of the Apparently Dead,' 8vo, London, 1788, to which the silver medal of the Humane Society was adjudged. 2. 'Essays and Observations, Physiological and Medical, on the Submersion of Animals, and on the Resin of the Acoroides Resinifera, or Yellow Resin of Botany Bay. . . . Select Histories of Diseases. . . . (Meteorological Tables,' &c.), 8vo, London, 1795.

[Watt's Bibl. Brit.; Reuss's Alphabetical Reg. of Authors.]   G. G.

KITE, JOHN (d. 1537), successively archbishop of Armagh and bishop of Carlisle, was a native of London, and, according to Wood, received his education in the university of Oxford, 'but in what house, or what degrees he took, it appears not' (Athenæ Oxon. ed. Bliss, ii. 747). It is much more probable, however, that he is the John Kite who was educated at Eton, and thence elected to King's College, Cambridge, in 1480 (COLE, Hist. of King's Coll. i. 93). After taking holy orders he became rector of Harlington, Middlesex, and on resigning that benefice in 1510 was admitted to the prebend of Stratton in the church of Salisbury, which he held till 1517. On 1 March 1510 he was presented to the church of Weye at Weyhill, in the diocese of Winchester (Letters, &c. of Henry VIII, i. 928). He was also a prebendary of Exeter and sub-dean of the king's chapel at Westminster (LELAND, Collectanea, i. 472).

By provision of Pope Leo X in the consistory of 24 Oct. 1513 he was appointed archbishop of Armagh. On 15 Nov. 1515 he took part in the ceremony of receiving the cardinal's hat sent to Wolsey (Letters, &c. Henry VIII, vol. ii. pt. i. p. 1153). In 1516 he came to England by the king's special command, attended the Princess Mary's christening, 21 Feb. 1516 (ib. p. 1573), and was granted 20 Sept. following a writ of protection for himself and his see during his absence (ib. p. 2375). In February 1518 he was sent with John Bourchier, lord Berners [q. v.], on a special embassy to Charles V to secure peace between Spain and England, and their interesting adventures in Spain are recorded in their letters to Wolsey, which are calendared in the 'Letters, &c. of Henry VIII' (cf. vol. ii. pt. ii. Nos. 4135–6–7, 4160–1, 4245, 4436). He left Saragossa in January 1519, and after visiting San Sebastian arrived in London on 10 March of that year (ib. vol. iii. pt. i. Nos. 10–11). In 1520 he was one of the deputy-commissioners of the jewel office, and he was one of the prelates who, in the same year, accompanied Henry VIII and Queen Catherine to the 'Field of the Cloth of Gold' (*Rutland Papers*, ed. Jerdan, p. 30). Attended by six horsemen, he was also present at the meeting between Henry and Charles V at Gravelines in July (*Letters, &c.*, vol. iii. pt. i. No. 900).

On 12 July 1521 he was translated by papal provision from Armagh to the bishopric of Carlisle. He was permitted to retain in the diocese of Armagh two canonries and one parochial church of the value of 60*l.*, and was allowed to assume the title of an archiepiscopal see. He accordingly took the title of archbishop of Thebes *in partibus* (BRADY, *Episcopal Succession*, i. 104, 216). Kite paid the pope for his translation 1,790 ducats, which the impoverished state of the papal exchequer rendered very welcome (*Letters, &c.*, vol. iii. pt. ii. Nos. 1430, 1477). The royal mandate for the restitution to Kite of the temporalities of the see of Carlisle is dated 11 Nov. 1521 (LE NEVE, *Fasti*, ed. Hardy, iii. 240). He also held the living of St. Stephen, Walbrook, London, which he resigned in 1534. For these preferments he was largely indebted to the influence of Wolsey, ' who conversed freely with him in his prosperity, and applied to him for necessaries as a faithful friend in his adversity' (CAVENDISH, *Life of Wolsey*, pp. 119, 146). In 1522 he was actively repressing disorders on the Scottish border, and proved very useful to the warden, Thomas Fiennes, eighth lord Dacre. His correspondence with Wolsey vividly illustrates the disturbed state of the border country. Writing on 25 June 1524, he pointed out that he had to make a circuit of sixty miles out of the direct route in order to avoid thieves and reach Carlisle in safety. In 1524, and again in 1526, he was one of the royal commissioners to treat for peace with the king of Scotland. In 1529 he signed an instrument approving the reasonableness of the king's scruples concerning his marriage with Catherine of Arragon, and advising recourse to the pope for a speedy decision of the cause (RYMER, *Fœdera*, xiv. 301, 405, 406). On 13 July 1530 he was one of the four bishops who, with Cardinal Wolsey, Archbishop Warham, and the whole peerage of England, signed the bold letter to Pope Clement VII demanding the king's divorce. He signed the renunciation of the pope's supremacy on 15 Feb. 1534, but was one of the prelates who, adhering to Lee, archbishop of York, in 1536, opposed the advanced proposals made by Cranmer and his party in convocation (FULLER, *Church Hist.* bk. v.

p. 212). During his occupancy of the see of Carlisle he made large additions to Rose Castle, the episcopal residence, one of the towers of which is still called by his name. After ruling pastorally, and 'kepyng nobyl Houshold wyth grete Hospitalitv,' but suffering in later years much ill-health, he died in London on 19 June 1537, and was buried in Stepney Church, where a marble slab, still extant, covers his remains, and bears a quaint English epitaph (cf. WEEVER, *Funerall Monuments*, pp. 539–40). By his will, dated the day before his death, he gave directions, which were disregarded, that his body should be buried near that of his father in St. Margaret's Church, Westminster.

[Letters and Papers of Henry VIII, passim; Nicolson and Burn's Westmorland and Cumberland, ii. 277; Cooper's Athenæ Cantabr. i. 62, 531; Cotton's Fasti Eccl. Hibernicæ; Fiddes's Life of Wolsey, p. 491; Froude's Divorce of Catherine of Aragon, p. 443; Fuller's Worthies; Giustinian's Four Years at the Court of Henry VIII, ii. 162, 184, 165, 253–5; Godwin's Cat. of Bishops, 1615, p. 682; Godwin, De Præsulibus (Richardson); Leland's Collectanea, 1770, ii. 347; Lysons's Environs, ii. 688; Maitland's London, ii. 786; Newcourt's Repertorium, i. 632; Percy's Household Book of the Earl of Northumberland, p. 430; Rymer's Fœdera, xiii. 759, xiv. 21, 29, 119, 301, 400, 406, 465; Ware's Bishops (Harris).]

T. C.

KITTO, JOHN (1804–1854), author of the 'Pictorial Bible,' son of John Kitto, a Cornish stonemason, and Elizabeth Picken, was born at Plymouth on 4 Dec. 1804. He was a sickly lad, caring for nothing but books. Between his eighth and eleventh years he was at four different Plymouth schools, and had no other schooling. In 1814 he was taken by his father to assist him at his trade. On 13 Feb. 1817, while carrying slates up a high ladder, he fell a distance of thirty-five feet, and was thenceforth stone-deaf. Being now unfit for work, he was left to spend his time as he pleased, and devoted himself to reading, selling scraps of old iron, and painting children's pictures and shop-labels to procure pence to buy books. On 15 Nov. 1819 he was sent to the workhouse, where he was set to learn shoemaking. In November 1821 he was apprenticed to a Plymouth shoemaker named Bowden, who treated him badly, and in May 1822 he was taken back into the workhouse. In July 1823 some gentlemen became interested in his case, made provision for his support, and obtained permission for him to read in the public library. In 1824 Mr. A. N. Groves, an Exeter dentist, took him as a pupil, giving him board, lodging, and a small salary. Shortly after he came under deep religious impressions, and in July 1825 went, at the suggestion of Mr. Groves, to the Missionary College at Islington, to be trained for employment by the Church Missionary Society as a printer at one of their foreign presses. In June 1827 he was sent by the society to Malta: but his predilections for literary work seem to have prevented his giving his whole attention to his duties, the committee became dissatisfied, and in January 1829 he returned to England. In June of that year he became a member of a private mission-party organised by Mr. Groves, and in company with him and others sailed for Persia; an interesting account of the journey appears in his 'Journals.' The party reached Bagdad in December, and Kitto, besides acting as tutor to Mr. Groves's children, opened an Armenian school. A terrible visitation of the plague destroyed fifty thousand of the inhabitants of Bagdad in little more than a month, and carried off five out of thirteen inmates of Mr. Groves's house. An inundation and a siege by Ali Pasha of Aleppo followed; the schools were broken up, and in September 1832 Kitto left Bagdad. On reaching England, after a journey of nine months, he obtained an introduction to some gentlemen connected with the Society for the Diffusion of Useful Knowledge, and was engaged to write for the 'Penny Magazine,' in which the 'Deaf Traveller' and other papers of his appeared. He also at this time contributed to the 'Companion to the Almanack,' the 'Companion to the Newspaper,' the 'Printing Machine,' and Knight's 'Cyclopædia.'

At the suggestion of Charles Knight [q. v.] he began in 1834 a series of narratives illustrative of the life of the blind and deaf and dumb, which were afterwards collected and published under the title 'The Lost Senses' (London, 1845); and in 1835 a 'Biblical Commentary,' which resulted in 'The Pictorial Bible.' This was originally published anonymously in monthly parts. It was completed in May 1838, and received by the public with great favour (3 vols. imperial 8vo, and 4 vols. 4to, London, 1835–8). The notes were afterwards published separately under the title 'The Illustrated Commentary' (5 vols. post 8vo, London, 1840). He next agreed with Knight to write a 'Pictorial History of Palestine and the Holy Land, including a complete History of the Jews,' which he completed after nearly three years of hard work (London, 1840). 'The Christian Traveller' was then projected, a work intended to give some account of the various missionary establishments for the propagation of Christianity in heathen lands; but the affairs of his publisher

became embarrassed, and only three parts of it appeared (London, 1841). Kitto now suffered much hardship. He had to sell his house at Islington, and remove to Woking. He transferred his services to Messrs. A. & C. Black, Edinburgh, for whom he wrote a school 'History of Palestine' (Edinburgh, 1841). He also now commenced the 'Cyclopædia of Biblical Literature,' on which he was at work till 1845 (2 vols. Edinburgh, 1845). In 1844, though a layman, he received the degree of D.D. from the university of Giessen, and in 1845 was made a fellow of the Society of Antiquaries. In 1848 he commenced the 'Journal of Sacred Literature' (London, 1848–1853), which he continued to edit until 1853, when he handed it over to the care of Dr. H. Burgess. Pecuniary difficulties continued to press upon him. The 'Journal of Sacred Literature' did not pay the cost of printing, and he was obliged to leave Woking for a cheaper house at Camden Town. In 1849 he commenced the preparation of the 'Daily Bible Illustrations' for Messrs. Oliphant of Edinburgh, to be published in quarterly parts. Vol. i. appeared in the December of that year, and the concluding volume in January 1854. A civil list pension of 100l. per annum was conferred on him in 1850 in recognition of his 'useful and meritorious literary works.' His health, never robust, began seriously to fail in 1851. In August 1854 he proceeded to Germany to try the effect of mineral waters, but on 25 Nov. 1854 died at Cannstadt, where he had settled. His remains were buried in the cemetery there, a tombstone being erected over them by Mr. Oliphant, his publisher.

Kitto married, on 21 Sept. 1833, Miss Fenwick. She and seven of his children survived him.

In addition to the works mentioned above, he was the author of the following: 1. 'Essays and Letters, with a Short Memoir of the Author,' Plymouth, 1825. 2. 'Uncle Oliver's Travels in Persia,' 2 vols. London, 1838. 3. 'Thoughts among Flowers,' London, 1843. 4. 'Gallery of Scripture Engravings, Historical and Landscape, with Descriptions, Historical, Geographical, and Critical,' London, 1841–3. 5. 'The Pictorial Sunday Book,' London, 1845. A portion of this was published separately, under the title 'The Pictorial History of our Saviour.' 6. 'Ancient and Modern Jerusalem.' 7. 'The Court and People of Persia.' 8. 'The Tartar Tribes,' London, 1846–9. 9. 'The Tabernacle and its Furniture,' London, 1849. 10. 'Scripture Lands,' London, 1850, 8vo. 11. 'The Land of Promise,' London, 1850, 8vo. 12. 'Eastern Habitations,' London, 1852, 8vo. 13. 'Sunday Reading for Christian Families,' London, 1853, 8vo.

[The Lost Senses; Memoirs by J. E. Ryland, M.A., Edinburgh, 1856.]   T. H.

KLITZ, PHILIP (1805–1854), musician and author, was born at Lymington, Hampshire, 7 Jan. 1805. His father, George Philip Klitz, drum-major of the royal Flintshire militia, and musical composer, was born at Biebrich, Germany, in 1777, and died at Lymington in 1839. In 1801 he married Elizabeth Lane of Boldre (1775–1838), and by her he had a large family, which included six sons, all well-known musicians: (1) Philip; (2) William, organist of St. Michael's Church, Basingstoke, died 31 May 1857; (3) Charles, organist of St. Thomas's Church, Lymington, died 16 Feb. 1864; (4) James Frederick, died at Northampton 2 Oct. 1870; (5) Robert John; (6) John Henry, died 6 Dec. 1880, who by will founded the Widow and Orphans British and Foreign Musical Society. Philip, the eldest, early became a composer of ball-room music. About 1829 he took up his residence at Southampton, where, besides classical music, he produced a variety of ballads, of which the words were frequently his own. He was a brilliant performer on the pianoforte and violin, and in 1831 conducted Paganini's concert in Southampton. His lectures on music, given in literary institutions and other places, were always well attended, and his advocacy of the Hullah system [see HULLAH, JOHN PYKE] met with much success. He was first organist of St. Lawrence and St. Joseph's Church, Southampton, and from 1845 to his death of All Saints' Church. In 1838 he printed 'Songs of the Mid-watch, the Poetry by Captain Willes Johnson, the Music composed for and dedicated to the British Navy.' These six songs were, by order of the admiralty, reprinted in a work entitled 'Songs of Charles Dibdin. Arranged by T. Dibdin,' 1850, pp. 315–20. Besides his musical works, he was the author in 1850 of a book entitled 'Sketches of Life, Character, and Scenery in the New Forest: a series of Tales, Rural, Domestic, Legendary, and Humorous.' To the masonic body he gave his support, and his composition, 'Faith, Hope, and Charity,' is still introduced at the entertainments of the Hampshire lodges. He was one of the first persons to write songs for the concerts of Ethiopian serenaders. 'Miss Ginger' and 'Dinah Dear,' both in 1847, became very popular ditties. He died at 24 Portland Place, Southampton, on 12 Jan. 1854. His wife was Charlotte Lyte, a half-sister of the well-known hymn-writer, the Rev. H. F. Lyte.

His son, George Klitz, was also a voluminous musical composer.

Klitz's best-known pieces, besides those already mentioned, were: 1. 'Song of the Spanish Cavalier,' 1835. 2. 'I never cast a Flower away,' 1853. 3. 'King Alfred in the Danish Camp.' 4. 'Napoleon's Grave.' But it is difficult to distinguish the pieces written by the father, the son, and the grandson.

[Gent. Mag. March 1854, p. 328; Hampshire Independent, 14 Jan. 1854, p. 5; information from Mr. Charles John Klitz.]   G. C. B.

KLOSE, FRANCIS JOSEPH (1784–1830), musical composer, born in London in 1784, was son of a professor of music, who gave him his first instruction. At a later period Klose studied pianoforte-playing and musical composition under Franz Tomisch, a pupil of Haydn. He was a member of the orchestra of the King's Theatre and of the Concerts of Antient Music, and an instrumental performer of great excellence. But he acquired so large a connection as a teacher of the piano that he gave up most of his public engagements and devoted himself almost entirely to teaching. As a composer he was much esteemed in his day for his pathetic and sentimental ballads; while his pianoforte music was considered excellent for teaching purposes. He died in Beaumont Street, Marylebone, on 8 March 1830, aged 46 (parish register).

Of his numerous published compositions the following proved most popular: 1. Piano, &c. Sonatinas for pianoforte and violin; Instruction book for pianoforte; Grand Sonata for pianoforte, violin, and flute; eight books of selected melodies; Grand Overture and ballets; 'Les Déguisemens Amoureux,' for the King's Theatre. 2. Songs.—'The Rose,' 'My Native Land,' 'Canst thou bid my heart.' Klose also published 'Practical Hints for acquiring Thoroughbass,' London, 8vo, 1822, which was very popular in its day.

[Dict. of Mus. 1824; Georgian Era, iv. 532; Gent. Mag. 1830, pt. i. [p. 472–3.] R. H. L.

KNAPP, JOHN LEONARD (1767–1845), botanist, born at Shenley, Buckinghamshire, 9 May 1767, was son of Primatt Knapp, rector of Shenley. Educated at Thame grammar school, Knapp entered the navy, but finding the sea unsuited to his health, resigned and subsequently served successively in the Herefordshire and Northamptonshire militia, becoming a captain in the latter. He lived for a time at Powick, near Worcester, and was then in the habit of making long summer botanical excursions. On one of these he visited Scotland in company with

George Don [q. v.], and collected several of the rarest species of British grasses. In 1804 he published 'Gramina Britannica, or Representations of the British Grasses on 119 coloured plates, with Descriptions,' 4to, the figures being executed by himself. This edition was, with the exception of a hundred copies, destroyed by a fire at Bensley's, the printers, and the book was not reissued until 1842. In 1818 Knapp published anonymously a poem entitled 'Arthur, or the Pastor of the Village,' and between 1820 and 1830 a series of articles, under the title of 'The Naturalist's Diary,' in 'Time's Telescope.' These formed the germ of his most successful work, the 'Journal of a Naturalist,' a botanical companion to White's 'Selborne,' which was published anonymously in 1829, and went through three editions during his lifetime. He lived till 1813 at Llanfoist, near Abergavenny, and subsequently at Alveston, near Bristol, where he died 29 April 1845. In 1804 he married Lydia Frances, daughter of Arthur Freeman of Antigua, by whom he had seven children; two sons and a daughter survived him.

Knapp became in 1798 a fellow of the Linnean Society, and was also a fellow of the Society of Antiquaries. The genus of grasses previously named *Mibora* by Adanson was called *Knappia* by Smith, and *Rhynchospermum* of Blume was similarly renamed by F. Bauer.

[Proc. Linnean Soc. i. 244; Athenæum, 1845, p. 463; Life-lore, 1889, i. 257.]   G. S. B.

KNAPP, WILLIAM (1698–1768), musical composer, was born at Wareham, Dorset (HUTCHINS), in 1698. He was for thirty-nine years parish clerk of Poole, and died there in September (he was buried on the 26th) 1768. He published 'A Sett of New Psalm Tunes and Anthems in Four Parts, with an introduction to Psalmody after a plain and familiar manner,' London, 1738, 7th edition, 1762, and 'New Church Melody,' London, 1753, with portrait prefixed. To the latter work is added an 'Imploration to the King of Kings, wrote by Charles I during his captivity in Carisbrook Castle, 1648.' Both works consist of original compositions, and each contains the long-metre psalm-tune called, after the composer's birthplace, 'Wareham,' which constitutes Knapp's chief claim to remembrance. In the first-named publication the tune appears under the title and in the form now known; in the other work it is called 'Blandford,' and is printed in common instead of triple time.

[Hutchins's Hist. of Dorset, 3rd ed. 1861–1873, i. 67; Noble's Continuation of Granger, iii. 306; Parr's Church of England Psalmody; information from the rector of Poole.] J. C. H.

KNAPTON, GEORGE (1698–1778), portrait-painter, born in London in 1698, was a son of James Knapton, a prosperous bookseller in Ludgate Street. He studied under Jonathan Richardson [q. v.], and at first practised chiefly in crayons. He spent some years in Italy, where he became known to English travellers as a sound judge of the works of the old masters, and an interesting account, which he sent to his brother Charles, on a visit to the newly-opened-up city of Herculaneum, was printed in the 'Philosophical Transactions' of 1740, No. 458. Knapton was an original member of the Society of Dilettanti and their first portrait-painter; at a meeting of the society, 4 Jan. 1740, it was ordered 'that every member of the society do make a present of his picture, in oil-colours, done by Mr. George Knapton, a member, to be hung up in the room where the society meets,' and at a meeting in February 1744 'that every member who has not had his picture painted by Mr. Knapton by the meeting in February next year shall pay one guinea per annum till his picture be delivered in to the secretary, unless Mr. Knapton declares it is owing to his want of time to finish the same.' Accordingly, before 1749 he painted the portraits of the first twenty-three members, most of them in fancy characters or costumes; these, which are some of his best works, include the Duke of Dorset as a Roman general, Viscount Galway as a cardinal, Sir Francis Dashwood as St. Francis adoring the Venus de' Medici, the Earl of Holdernesse as a waterman, Mr. Howe drawing a glass of wine from a terrestrial globe, the Earl of Bessborough as a Turk, and Sir Bourchier Wray holding a punch-bowl and ladle; they are all still in the possession of the society and were contributed to the National Portrait Exhibition of 1868. Knapton resigned the appointment in 1763, and was succeeded, after an interval of six years, by Sir Joshua Reynolds. In 1750 the Prince of Wales commissioned Knapton, in conjunction with Vertue, to prepare a critical catalogue of the pictures at Kensington, Hampton Court, and Windsor, and in 1765 he succeeded Stephen Slaughter [q. v.] as surveyor and keeper of the king's pictures; he also had charge of Lord Spencer's collection at Althorp, Northamptonshire. Knapton's largest work was the group of the widowed Princess of Wales and her family, painted in 1751, now at Hampton Court, but that of the Earl of Upper Ossory and his brother and sister, at Woburn, and the portrait of the Earl of Burlington, at

Hardwick Hall, are of better quality; the last has been engraved in Lodge's series. There are also portraits by Knapton of the Hon. John Spencer with his son, at Althorp, of Admiral Sir John Norris, at Greenwich, and of Francis, fifth duke of Leeds, in the possession of the present duke (a replica in the National Portrait Gallery); his portraits of Sir George Vandeput, bart., Archibald Bower, Nicholas Tindal, Hildebrand Jacob, Admiral Sir E. Hawke, and the singers, Carestini and Lisabetta du Parc, have been engraved. Knapton was a skilful painter, but not free from the stiffness and formality which characterised the art of his day. He assisted his brothers, John and Paul, who succeeded to and extended their father's business, in the production of several fine publications, including Birch's 'Lives' with heads by Houbraken, and Rapin and Tindal's 'History of England.' He died at Kensington December 1778, and was buried there on the 28th of that month.

KNAPTON, CHARLES (1700-1760), brother of George, engaged with Arthur Pond in the production of a volume of imitations of original drawings by the old masters, published in 1735. Of the seventy plates which constitute the work twenty-seven are by Knapton; these are chiefly after Guercino and are cleverly executed; they have been erroneously attributed to his brother. Charles Knapton died in 1760.

[Redgrave's Dict. of Artists; Walpole's Anecdotes (Dallaway and Wornum), p. 710; G. Scharf's Cat. of Pictures at Woburn Abbey, 1890; Vertue's manuscript collections in Brit. Mus.; Bromley's Cat. of Engraved British Portraits, 1793; An Account of the Portraits of the Dilettanti Society, 1885; Kensington parish register.]   F. M. O'D.

KNAPTON, PHILIP (1788-1833), musical composer, born at York in 1788, received his musical education mainly at Cambridge, at the hands of Dr. Hague. Returning to York, he followed music as a profession, and lived in that city until his death, on 20 June 1833. He was one of the assistant-conductors at the York festivals of 1823, 1825, and 1828.

He composed several overtures, pianoforte concertos, and other orchestral works, and arranged a number of fantasias on well-known airs for pianoforte and pianoforte and harp. His pianoforte arrangement of Lady Nairne's song 'Caller Herrin',' and his music for the song 'There be none of Beauty's Daughters,' enjoyed considerable popularity.

[Grove's Dict. of Music, ii. 65; Brit. Mus. Cat. of Music.]   R. F. S.

KNAPWELL, RICHARD (*fl.* 1286), Dominican. [See CLAPWELL.]

KNATCHBULL, SIR EDWARD (1781-1849), statesman, eldest son of Sir Edward Knatchbull of Mersham Hatch, Kent, eighth baronet of the name, by Mary, daughter and coheiress of William Western Hugessen of Provender in the same county, was born on 20 Dec. 1781, and succeeded to the baronetcy on 21 Sept. 1819. On 16 Nov. following he was returned to parliament for Kent in his father's room. He retained the seat until the dissolution of 1830, when he did not stand for re-election. During this period he distinguished himself by his stout opposition to corn-law reform and catholic emancipation. His speech on the second reading of the Catholic Relief Bill, in which he pointed his remarks on Peel's change of front with the apt quotation, 'Nusquam tuta fides,' made a deep impression, and marked him out as leader of the House of Commons in the event of the bill being defeated and the protestant party coming into power. In 1830 he moved an amendment to the address pledging ministers to take steps to alleviate the prevalent distress. It was lost by a majority of 158 to 105. A large number of country gentlemen voted for it, and the Duke of Wellington's government was, in fact, saved by the whigs. In the following November Knatchbull led his following of tory malcontents into the opposition division lobby on Sir Henry Parnell's motion for a reduction of the civil list. The government was placed in a minority, and resigned on 17 Nov. Knatchbull was offered a place in Lord Grey's government, but declined it because, though not altogether opposed to the extension of the franchise, he could not accept the ministerial scheme in its entirety; nor did he go to the polls at the general election. After the passing of the bill he was returned at the general election of 1832 for the eastern division of Kent, which he continued to represent until February 1845, when he accepted the Chiltern hundreds. On the accession of Peel to power in December 1834, he chose, though offered higher office, the subordinate place of paymaster of the forces, and was sworn of the privy council. Towards the close of this short-lived administration he is described by Greville as 'the only cabinet minister who has shown anything like a faculty to support Peel.' To Peel he adhered steadily in opposition, and returned to power with him in September 1841, taking the same office as before. His retirement in February 1845 was due solely to ill-health and domestic affliction, and has been erroneously attributed to the internal differences in Peel's cabinet, which did not occur until after his retirement. He died on 24 May 1849.

Knatchbull married twice: (1) on 25 Aug. 1806, Annabella Christiana, daughter of Sir John Honywood, bart.; (2) on 24 Oct. 1820, Fanny Catherine, eldest daughter of Edward Knight of Godmersham Park, Kent. He had several children by each wife. He was succeeded in the baronetcy by his eldest son, Norton Joseph, father of Sir Wyndham Knatchbull, the present baronet. Knatchbull's eldest son by his second wife, Edward Hugessen, is the present Lord Brabourne.

[Gent. Mag. 1849, pt. ii. p. 89; Roebuck's Hist. of the Whig Ministry of 1830, i. 136, 138, 158; Spencer Walpole's Hist. of England from the conclusion of the Great War in 1815, ii. 534; Greville Memoirs, Geo. IV–Will. IV, ii. 62, iii. 176–7, 226; Hansard's Parl. Deb. new ser. vi. 857, xv. 996, xvi. 131, 1041, 1270, xx. 1117; information from Lord Brabourne.]   J. M. R.

KNATCHBULL, Sir NORTON (1602–1685), scholar, son of Thomas Knatchbull (d. 1623) by his wife Eleanor, daughter of John Astley of Maidstone, born in 1602, matriculated at Cambridge as a fellow-commoner of St. John's College on 20 March 1618–19, and graduated B.A. in 1620. He was a nephew of Sir Norton Knatchbull, knight, of Mersham Hatch, Kent, who was sheriff of Kent in 1608, M.P. for Hythe in 1609, and founder of the free school at Ashford. The elder Sir Norton 'was,' says Philipot, in his 'Visitation of the County of Kent,' 'a person who, for his favour and love to learning and antiquities in times when they are both fallen under such cheapness and contempt, cannot be mentioned without an equivalent to so just a merit.' Sir Norton the younger succeeded to the family mansion and estate at Mersham Hatch upon his uncle's death in 1636. He at once confirmed the deed of endowment executed by his uncle in behalf of Ashford grammar school, continued to pay the master a yearly stipend of 30l., and subsequently added to the buildings. In 1639 Knatchbull was elected M.P. for Kent, and was knighted at Whitehall by Charles I. He was member for New Romney in the Long parliament, and was made a baronet on 4 Aug. 1641. On 12 Nov. 1642 he was summoned, with twenty-seven others, to appear before the House of Commons as a delinquent (Commons' Journals, ii. 845). But though a loyalist, Knatchbull seems to have remained in strict seclusion during the civil wars; and his name does not appear in the calendar of the committee for compounding. On 6 May 1661 he was again returned for New Romney (Members of Parl. i. 447, 495, 532).

In the year before the Restoration he published his 'Animadversiones in Libros Novi Testamenti. Paradoxæ Orthodoxæ, London. Guil. Godbid. in vico vulgo vocato Little-Brittain,' 1659. The work consists of a large number of critical emendations, based upon a fair knowledge of Hebrew, and showing considerable intrepidity for a critic of that period. A second edition with appendix was published in 1672, a third, 'auctæ et emendatæ,' Oxford, 1677; a fourth edition, in English, appeared in 1692, entitled 'Annotations upon some difficult Texts in all the Books of the New Testament,' Cambridge, 1693. The translation is, according to Darling (Cyclop. Bibl. 1738), the author's own. It is preceded by an 'Encomiastick upon the most Learned and Judicious Author,' by Thomas Walker, Sidney Sussex College. The original was reprinted at Amsterdam, and also at Frankfort, where it formed part of the supplement to N. Gurtler's edition of Walton's 'Polyglot,' 1695–1701. The work was held in great estimation for a century after its publication, and figures in a list of books annotated by the learned Ambrose Bonwicke (1652–1722) [q. v.] (NICHOLS, Lit. Anecd. v. 141). Kitto, however, says that Knatchbull's remarks 'are not entirely wanting in depth, and we cannot read them without wonder at the small amount of knowledge which procured for their author such a widespread reputation' (Cyclop. Bibl. ii. s.v.) In 1680 Peter du Moulin the younger [q. v.] dedicated to Knatchbull his 'Short View of the Chief Points in Controversy between the Reformed Churches and the Church of Rome,' being a translation from an unprinted manuscript by his father, Peter du Moulin the elder, which had been made over to him for purposes of publication by the baronet. James Duport [q. v.], the tutor of his son John, addressed three Latin odes in his 'Musæ Subsecivæ' to Knatchbull, and the latter, according to Ballard, himself acted as tutor to the learned Dorothy, lady Pakington.

Knatchbull died at his seat in Kent on 5 Feb. 1685 (N.S.), and was buried in the chancel of Mersham Church, where a Latin inscription describes him as 'Ciceronis et Chrysostomi facundia, Varronis et Hieronymi judicio ornatus.' He married, first, Dorothy, daughter of Thomas Westrow, sheriff of London, by whom he had eleven daughters and two sons. The elder son, Sir John, second baronet (1636–1696), was author of a manuscript diary for 1688–9, from which an interesting narrative of the arrest of James II at Faversham was printed in 'Notes and

Queries,' 3rd ser. vi. 1–3, 21–3. The younger son, Sir Thomas, was third baronet (d. 1711). By his second wife, Dorothy, daughter of Sir Robert Honywood [q. v.] of Charing, Kent, and relict of Sir Edward Stewart, kt., he had no issue. A contemporary half-length portrait of Knatchbull by Hoogstraten has been engraved (EVANS, ii. 234).

[Hasted's Kent, iii. 287, ii. 127, 444; Wotton's Baronetage, i. 462; Collins's English Baronetage, ii. 232; Addit. MS. 5520, ff. 257–8 (pedigree); M'Clintock and Strong's Cyclop. Eccles. Lit. v. 124; Duport's Musæ Subsecivæ, pp. 262, 295, 309, 311; Life of Dr. R. Warren, prefixed to his Sermons, 1739, pp. iiisq.; Knatchbull's Works in Brit. Mus. Library; information kindly supplied by R. F. Scott, esq.]   T. S.

KNELL, PAUL (1615?–1664), divine, graduated B.A. from Clare Hall, Cambridge, in 1635, and was incorporated D.D. at Oxford on 31 Jan. 1643. He was for some time 'chaplain to a regiment of cuirassiers in his majesty's army,' a fact which he is careful to mention on the title of each of his sermons. He appears subsequently to have lived at Woodford in Essex, where in 1650 he joined other clergymen and gentry in a petition, 'addressed to the charity of all good Christians,' in behalf of 'the King's servants to the number of forty, being in present distress by reason that their sole dependence was upon the late King's Majesty' (LYSONS, iv. 285). He became vicar of Newchurch, Romsey Marsh, in 1660, rector there in 1662, and vicar of St. Dunstan's, near Canterbury, in 1664. He died at St. Dunstan's, and was buried in the church 24 Aug. 1664 (HASTED, Kent, iii. 468, 594).

Knell published: 1. 'Israel and England Parallelled (sic) in a Sermon preached before the Honourable Society of Grayes Inn, 16 April 1648. Addressed to all those who are friends to Peace and King Charles.' 2. 'The Life Guard of a Loyal Christian. Preached at St. Peter's, Cornhill, 7 May 1648,' and preceded by a prayer for the king. 3. 'A Looking-glasse for Levellers, held out in a Sermon preached at St. Peter's, Paul's Wharf, 24 Sept. 1648.' A savage attack upon the army and the independents, anathematising in particular the conduct of Fairfax and his 'bloodhounds' at Colchester; this passed through several editions. These three sermons with two others were published collectively in 1660, and again in 1661, under the title 'Five Seasonable Sermons, preached before the King's Majesty beyond the Seas, and other eminent Auditories in England, formerly prohibited, but now published and dedicated to his Majesty.'

[Wood's Fasti, ed. Bliss, ii. 58; Foster's Alumni Oxon. 1500–1714; Brit. Mus. Cat.]   T. S.

KNELL, THOMAS (fl. 1570), divine and verse-writer, was made rector of Wareham, Dorset, in 1569; he was appointed rector of St. Nicholas Acons, London, on 6 March 1570, and resigned before 3 March 1573. On 21 May 1571 he was instituted to the vicarage of Hackney, Middlesex, and on 19 May 1573 to that of St. Bride's. The last preferment he resigned at once, probably because he had become chaplain to Walter Devereux, first earl of Essex [q. v.] With Essex he proceeded to Ireland, and was present at the earl's death on 22 Sept. 1576. A contemporary copy of an account which he drew up of Essex's last illness is preserved in the British Museum (Add. MS. 32092, f. 5). He favoured the current rumour that the earl was poisoned. Knell was author of: 1. 'Of the Hurt done in divers Parts of this Realm by a terrible Tempest, 20 Oct. 1570,' 1571 (?). 2. 'Epitaph on the Death of the Earl of Essex,' in English verse' (in Tanner's time among the Le Gros MSS.)

Knell has been confused with another author of the time, known as THOMAS KNELL, JUNIOR (fl. 1560–1581). The latter, who was probably Knell's son, and was also a clergyman, wrote: 1. 'An A B C to the Christian Congregation,' 1560(?), a broadside. 2. 'An Epitaph, or rather a short Discourse made upon the Life and Death of Dr. Boner,' London, 1569, 12mo, reprinted in vol. i. of the 'Harleian Miscellany.' 3. 'A pithy Note to Papists all and some that joy in Felton's Martyrdome,' London, 1570, 12mo. A copy of this rare work is in the Lambeth Library. It has been reprinted by Collier in vol. i. of 'Illustrations of Early English Popular Literature.' 4. 'An Answer at large to a most Hereticall and Papisticall Byll, in English Verse, which was cast abroade in the Streetes of Northampton, and brought before the Judges at the last Assizes there,' London, 1570. A copy of this work is in the library of St. John's College, Cambridge, and it has been reprinted in the 'Collection of Northamptonshire Reprints.' Another edition, also issued in 1570, was in the Heber Library, and is now in the possession of Mr. S. Christie Miller. The two editions differ in the 'Answer,' but the 'Bill' of course remains the same. The work is an answer to a Romish ballad ridiculing the marriage of the English clergy. 5. 'An Historical Discourse of the Life and Death of Dr. Story,' 1571, 12mo, in English verse. This has been attributed to the elder Knell. 6. 'A Treatise of the Use and Abuse of Prayer,' London, 1581 (TANNER). The younger Knell was also author of the 'Epistle to the Christian Reader' prefixed to Northbrook's 'Poore Man's Garden,' 1573. All the verses by Knell junior are characterised by a strong bias against the Roman catholics.

Thomas Knell, junior, has been erroneously identified by Collier with the KNELL (*fl.* 15—) mentioned (without a christian name) by Nashe in 'Pierce Penilesse' and by Heywood in his 'Apology for Actors' as a notable actor. Heywood speaks of him as dead before 1609. The actor seems to have been son of John Knell, a vintner, who was buried at St. James's, Garlick Hill, in 1574. He married at the same church one Alice Turner in 1568. John Heming or Hemminge q. v.] the actor married in March 1587–8 Rebecca, widow of William Knell. Collier conjectures that the latter was the actor to whose christian name we have no other clue. If Collier be right, Rebecca Knell was the actor's second wife. In 1601 a player named Nill lived in Southwark, and had a child, Alice, baptised on 13 Aug.

[Tanner's Bibl. Brit.; Newcourt's Repert. i. 317, 505, 620; Collier's Reg. of the Stationers' Company, ii. 3, &c.; Collier's Bibl. Cat. art. 'Knell;' Collier's Lives of the Actors (Shakesp. Soc.), p. 63; Heywood's Apol. for Actors, ed. Collier (Shakesp. Soc.), pp. 43, 64; Nashe's Works, ed. Grosart, ii. 93; Ritson's Bibl. Angl. Poet. p. 265; Devereux's Lives of the Earls of Essex. i. 110, 146.]   W. A. J. A.

KNELL, WILLIAM ADOLPHUS (*d.* 1875), marine-painter, first exhibited at the Royal Academy in 1825, sending a view at Eastbourne. He was a clever painter of shipping and the sea, and a frequent contributor to the Royal Academy and the British Institution, sending to the former in 1835 'Folkestone from the Dover Road,' in 1846 'Vessels off the Flemish Coast,' in 1852 'The Action in which Van Tromp was killed,' and in 1866 (the last year in which he exhibited) 'Outward-bound Vessel entering Funchal, Madeira.' Knell painted a picture of 'The Landing of Prince Albert,' which was purchased for the royal collection, and was engraved by Miller for the 'Art Journal' in 1857. He died on 10 July 1875, and was buried in the Abney Park cemetery, Stoke Newington.

[Redgrave's Dict. of Artists.]   L. C.

KNELLER, SIR GODFREY, whose original name was GOTTFRIED KNILLER (1646–1723), painter, born at Lübeck in North Germany on 8 Aug. 1646, was third son of Zacharias Kniller and Lucia Beuten his wife. His father, born at Eisleben in Thuringia on 16 Nov. 1611, was son of a landed proprietor at Halle in Saxony, who was surveyor-general and inspector of revenues for the mines belonging to the Count Mansfeldt; he left Eisleben, possibly through

the continued wars, and settled in Lübeck, where he practised as a portrait-painter, and from 1659 was master of the works to the church of St. Catherine. A portrait by him of Johannes Olearius was engraved. He married at Lübeck 31 Oct. 1639, and was the father of three sons, besides the eminent painter Johann, born 15 Dec. 1642. Johann Zacharias, born 6 Oct. 1644 (see below), and Andreas, born 23 Aug. 1649, afterwards organist to St. Peter's Church at Hamburg. The father died 4 April 1675, and was buried in St. Catherine's Church, where, in the following year, a portrait of him was painted and dedicated by his two painter-sons; a few portraits from his hand still exist at Lübeck.

Gottfried was destined for a military life, and was sent to Leyden to study mathematics and fortification. His inherited love of painting was, however, so strong that his father removed him to Amsterdam, where he became a pupil of Ferdinand Bol, with the additional privilege, as there seems no reason to doubt, of an occasional lesson in 1668 from the great Rembrandt himself. He then returned to Lübeck, where he soon found employment. Two portraits remain in the town library, one of an aged student, painted by Godfrey Kneller in 1668, and a companion portrait of a youthful scholar, by Godfrey's elder brother, John Zacharias, in the same year. Godfrey appears at first to have intended painting large scriptural or historical subjects in the style of Rembrandt's school, and one of 'Tobit and the Angel,' painted in 1672, remained in his own collection till his death. In 1672 the two brothers went to Italy to study historical painting. They first visited Rome, where Godfrey studied from the antique and the paintings of Raphael and the Carracci, and worked in the studios of Carlo Maratti and Bernini. The latter held him in high estimation. After spending some time in Naples they went to Venice, where Godfrey studied the works of Titian and Tintoretto, and laid the foundation of his future fame as a portrait-painter. There he was largely employed by the leading families, especially that of Bassadonna, for whom he painted a portrait of Cardinal Bassadonna, which was sent to Rome as a present to the pope. On his way home he visited Nuremberg, where he painted numerous portraits, and then found occupation at Hamburg. There he painted a large family portrait, which attracted much attention, for a wealthy merchant, Jacob del Böe, an amateur of art, who had inherited a valuable collection of Dutch paintings from his brother, Professor Sylvius of Leyden. The collection included fine works of Gerard Douw, Frans van Mieris, and others, and del

Bee gave the painter free access to them for study. After their father's death in 1675, Kneller, as he then wrote his name, purposed returning with his brother through France to Italy, and went to England on the way: he bore a letter of recommendation from del Bee to a wealthy Hamburg merchant in London, Jonathan Banks.

Banks gave Kneller a warm welcome, lodged him in his house, and commissioned him to paint portraits of himself and his family. These were seen by many people of consequence, including Mr. Vernon, secretary to the Duke of Monmouth, who had his own picture done, and secured for Kneller a suitable house in Durham Yard, where he resided for four years. When the duke saw Vernon's portrait he gave Kneller permission to execute one of himself, and he was so much pleased with the result (the picture is now in the collection of the Duke of Buccleuch) that he recommended Kneller to the king. Charles II was (1678) about to sit to Sir Peter Lely [q. v.], at the request of James, duke of York, when Monmouth obtained leave for Kneller to draw the king's portrait at the same sitting. The first sitting took place in the presence of the two royal dukes and other members of the court, and at the close Kneller had not only nearly completed the portrait, but had obtained so good a likeness as to excite the wonder of all present, including the king and Lely himself. Being still young and good-looking, with a graceful figure and confident manner, Kneller's success was from that date assured. Commissions poured in upon him, and he soon had to remove to a larger house in the Piazza at Covent Garden, where he continued to reside for twenty-one years. He painted Charles II more than once (one portrait, 1685, seated, being in the royal collection), and his queen, Catherine of Braganza. Not long before his death Charles sent Kneller to Paris to paint the French king, Louis XIV, and when, after the work was done, Louis offered him some mark of esteem, Kneller, at his own request, received permission to make a drawing of Louis for himself. He kept the drawing all his life. James II was as generous as his brother in the patronage which he bestowed on Kneller. Kneller painted so many portraits of the king, of his queen, Mary Beatrix, and of other members of the family, that he subsequently claimed to be a competent authority on the question of Prince James Edward's legitimacy, because of his exceptionally close acquaintance with the features and peculiarities of the royal family. It was while sitting to Kneller for a portrait, commissioned by Samuel Pepys, that

VOL. XXXI.

James heard the news of the landing of the Prince of Orange at Torbay. An engraving of this portrait by George Vertue adorns the folio edition of Rapin's 'History of England.' Kneller received further marks of favour from William III and Queen Anne. He was made principal painter to the king, and was knighted at Kensington on 3 March 1691, when the king presented him with a gold chain and medal worth three hundred guineas. On 7 June 1695 William granted him an annuity of 200l. (Addit. MS. 5763, f. 31). During the reign Kneller went to Brussels to paint the Duke of Bavaria (life-size, on horseback), and also painted the Czar, Peter the Great, of Russia during his visit to England. This portrait is now at Hampton Court.

Kneller's equestrian portrait of William III with allegorical figures, now at Hampton Court, is one of his best-known performances; it was painted in 1697 to celebrate the signing of the peace of Ryswyk. At Hampton Court there are also eight of the twelve portraits of 'Beauties,' painted by Kneller for Queen Mary in imitation of Lely's series of similar portraits at Windsor Castle: and the series of 'Admirals,' painted for the king, to which Kneller contributed some of his best work. Kneller retained all his dignities under Anne; the queen sat to him several times, as well as Prince George of Denmark and the youthful Duke of Gloucester. In 1703 Kneller painted the Archduke Charles, titular king of Spain, afterwards the Emperor Charles VI (now at Hampton Court), and was rewarded with the patent of a knight of the Roman empire by the Emperor Leopold I. Under Queen Anne he was paid 50l. for each portrait, 'besides fees' (Cal. Treas. Papers, 1710, cxxi. 23). George I treated Kneller with even greater favour than his predecessors. He was continued in his office of principal painter, and was created a baronet on 24 May 1715. Portraits of George I and his son, as Prince of Wales, are also at Hampton Court. In 1711, when the first academy of painting was founded in Great Queen Street, Lincoln's Inn Fields, Kneller was unanimously elected the first governor, and continued so for some years. Many artists subsequently bore testimony to the great advantages which they derived from his advice and supervision, and to the care and interest which he bestowed on the institution.

Kneller enjoyed continuous good health, and was thus able to accomplish an enormous amount of work up to the last year of his life. He amassed great wealth, and though he lost heavily in the speculations of the South Sea Bubble, he left a large fortune. About

1703 he purchased a house in Great Queen Street, Lincoln's Inn Fields, where he resided until his death, and he invested money in other property in London. He purchased an estate at Whitton, near Hounslow, where he built himself a magnificent house, decorated with mural paintings by Laguerre and with many of his own works. Here he resided some months of the year, and received visits from royalty and the nobility. The adulation paid him made him extremely vain, and there are many anecdotes of his eccentric displays of arrogance. He possessed, however, a shrewd wit and sound judgment, and as a justice of the peace for the county of Middlesex exercised a rough-and-ready sort of equity which commanded respect. Pope alludes to his methods of dispensing justice in the lines,

> I think Sir Godfrey should decide the suit,
> Who sent the thief that stole the cash away,
> And punished him that put it in his way

(*Pope*, ed. Elwin, iii. 380; WALPOLE, *Anecdotes of Painting*). He was churchwarden of Twickenham Church, and took an active part in its restoration in 1713. He was taken ill in London with a fever in May 1722, which an excellent constitution and the care of Dr. Richard Mead [q. v.] enabled him to partially conquer. But he never wholly recovered from its effect; and after being moved to Whitton in November was soon brought back to Great Queen Street, where he slowly sank, preserving his faculties to the last. He died during the night of 19 Oct. 1723 (*Hist. Register*, Chron. Diary, p. 50). On 7 Nov. he was carried in state to Whitton, and was buried in his garden. The register of the church at Twickenham records his burial. For some time before his death he was engaged in arranging his own monument, having models made by Francis Bird and Rysbrack. He intended it to be placed in Twickenham Church, but, being unable to obtain the particular spot in the church which he desired, he left money and directions in his will for Rysbrack's design to be carried out in Westminster Abbey. The monument was placed there in 1729, with an epitaph by Pope, imitated from the epitaph on Raffaelle.

Kneller married Susannah, daughter of the Rev. John Cawley, archdeacon of Lincoln and rector of Henley-on-Thames, and son of William Cawley [q. v.] the regicide. By her, who survived him, he left no children. She died in 1729, and was buried on 11 Dec. with her husband. Early in life, according to some accounts, before he left his native country, he had a mistress, a Mrs. Vos, who is stated elsewhere to have been the wife of

a quaker in Austinfriars, and to have served him as a model. By her Kneller had an illegitimate daughter, Agnes, whom he educated, and painted several times as St. Agnes, St. Catherine, &c. She married a Mr. Huckle, and had a son, Godfrey Kneller Huckle, to whom Kneller stood godfather. The son was Kneller's ultimate heir and assumed the name. By his marriage with Mary, daughter and heiress of Luke Weeks, Huckle became possessed of property at Donhead, Wiltshire. Kneller's will is dated 27 April 1723, with a codicil of 24 Oct. (printed at length in German in Heineken's 'Nachrichten von Künstlern und Kunstsachen,' Leipzig, 1768, p. 253). He left numerous legacies, including some to the six daughters of his brother Andreas at Hamburg. Upwards of five hundred portraits remained unfinished, to be completed by Edward Byng, who, with his brother, had been his regular assistant for many years. Mathias Oesterreich, afterwards director of the royal picture gallery at Dresden, is usually stated to have been Kneller's grandson; he was more probably his great-nephew. Kneller's house at Whitton still exists, though much altered; it is known as Kneller Hall, and is now used as the School of Military Music.

Ten reigning sovereigns in all sat to Kneller for their portraits. His sitters included almost all persons of rank, wealth, or eminence in his day, and examples of his brush may be found in nearly every historic mansion or palace in the kingdom. He kept a great number of assistants, to whom he delegated the less material portions of the painting, such as the draperies and accessories; latterly he seldom painted more than the face, and sometimes the hands, himself. His praises were sung by Dryden, Prior, Addison, Steele, and Tickell. Dryden addressed to him one of his best poems on receiving a copy of the 'Chandos' portrait of Shakespeare, done by Kneller as a present to the poet. The engravings from his works by his friend John Smith (whose portrait by Kneller is in the National Gallery), John Faber, and others form quite a school of mezzotint-engraving in themselves. Kneller is said to have tried his hand himself, and engraved his own portrait and a portrait of the Earl of Tweeddale, which, if really the work of Kneller and not of Smith, is an excellent performance. His paintings vary in excellence, the best being of the highest order, while others, even when authenticated, seem unworthy of a great reputation. He was always a student of the works of other great portrait-painters, and at one time quite changed his style of colouring, owing to his admiration for certain portraits by Rubens. The monotony of dress and attitude in Kneller's portraits is due much more to the compulsion of fashion and the imitative tendency in the English character than to the painter himself. His sitters themselves demanded that he should depict them in the one familiar attitude. Posterity has not endorsed the extravagantly high opinion in which Kneller's talents were held by his contemporaries.

Kneller can best be studied at Hampton Court. In his own opinion his finest portrait was the full-length portrait of Francis Couplet, a Chinese convert and jesuit missionary, now in the royal collection at Windsor Castle (engraved in mezzotint by John Faber, jun.) Among the most remarkable of his performances was the series of portraits of forty-eight members, including himself, of the Kit-Cat Club [see CAT, CHRISTOPHER], painted for Jacob Tonson [q. v.], the publisher, engraved in mezzotint by John Faber, jun., and published as a series in 1735, and now in the possession of Mr. Baker at Bayfordbury in Hertfordshire. Other of his best-known portraits are those of the Countess of Ranelagh at Cassiobury, the full-length of Queen Anne, and the Duchess of Marlborough at Grove Park, Lord-chancellor Cowper at Panshanger, the Grimston portraits at Gorhambury, and Sir Isaac Newton at Kade. He frequently painted his own portrait, and was specially invited by the Grand Duke of Tuscany to contribute his portrait to the gallery of artists' portraits, which still remain in the Uffizi at Florence. One of his own portraits of himself was engraved by T. Beckett in 1685, and another by John Smith in 1694. A portrait of him by David van der Plaes was engraved by P. Schenck. Kneller's drawings, of which there are some fair examples in the print-room at the British Museum, display more effectively his great artistic genius than many of the pictures finished by others and merely begun by him.

KNELLER or KNILLER, JOHN ZACHARIAS (1644–1702), painter, elder brother of Sir Godfrey Kneller, born at Lübeck on 6 Oct. 1644, accompanied his brother in all his travels on the continent in early life, and settled with him in England. Though he also practised as a portrait-painter, he never attained the same excellence. He is better known as a painter of architecture and ruins, and especially of still life, and in the last-named subject did some meritorious work. He died in London in 1702, and was buried in St. Paul's, Covent Garden. His brother painted a good portrait of him, which has been engraved.

[Vertue's Diaries (Brit. Mus. Addit. MSS. 23068–78); Walpole's Anecdotes of Painting, ed. Wornum; Notes and Queries, 4th ser. iv. 77, vi. 176, 262, 376, x. 328, 379; Sandrart's Teutsch Akademie, 1675; Houbraken's Groote Schonburgh, ed. von Wurzbach; W. Ackermann's Der Portraitmaler Sir Godfrey Kneller im Verhältniss zur Kunstbildung seiner Zeit, Lübeck, 1845; Heineken's Nachrichten von Künstlern und Kunstsachen; Chaloner Smith's British Mezzotinto Portraits; De Piles's Lives of the Painters; Le Neve's Pedigrees of Knights (Harl. Soc.); Burke's Extinct Baronetage; Hoare's Modern Wiltshire, iv. 31; R. S. Cobbett's Memorials of Twickenham; Miss Bradley's Popular Guide to Westminster Abbey.]   L. C.

KNEVET. [See also KNYVET and KNYVETT.]

KNEVET, RALPH (1600–1671), poet, was a native of Norfolk, and seems to have been closely associated as tutor or chaplain with the family of Sir William Paston of Oxnead. He is probably identical with the Ralph Knevet who was rector of Lyng, Norfolk, from 1652 till his death in 1671, at the age of seventy-one. He was buried in the chancel of his church (BLOMEFIELD, Norfolk, viii. 251–2).

Knevet published: 1. 'Stratisticon, or a Discourse of Militarie Discipline,' 1628, 4to, in verse. 2. 'Rhodon and Iris, a Pastoral, as it was presented at the Florists' Feast in Norwich, May 3, 1631,' London, 1631, 4to, dedicated to Nicholas Bacon, esq., of Gillingham, with an address to 'the Society of Florists,' and verses by Ri. Pert, Will. Deunye, and John Mingay. The scene is laid in Thessaly, and the metre is very irregular (Brit. Mus.) 3. 'Funerall Elegies, consecrated to the Immortal Memory of the Right Hon. Lady Katherine Paston, late Wife to the truly Noble and Heroicke William Paston of Oxned, esquire,' London, 1637, 4to, dedicated to Lady Katherine's sister, Lady Elizabeth Bertie, daughter of Robert, earl of Lindsey. The book is very rare. A copy is in the Grenville Library at the British Museum.

Among unpublished papers, now in the British Museum, of Sir William Paston and other members of the family, is a collection of sacred poems by Knevet, entitled 'A Gallery to the Temple. Lyricall Poemes upon sacred occasions, by Ra. Kneuett' (Addit. MS. 27447, ff. 11–67). The verse is imitated from George Herbert, and the collection is intended to form a supplement to Herbert's 'Temple.' Some of the poems are worth printing.

[Knevet's Works; W. C. Hazlitt's Bibliographical Handbook.]   S. L.

KNEWSTUBS or KNEWSTUB, JOHN (1544–1624), divine, born at Kirkby Stephen in Westmoreland in 1544, entered at St. John's College, Cambridge, whence he graduated B.A. 1564, and on 21 March 1567 was elected a fellow of the society. In 1568 he proceeded M.A., and in 1576 took his degree as B.D. He appears by this time to have become eminent as a controversialist, and was especially prominent as a writer against the teaching of Henry Nicholas, the founder of the sect known as the Family of Love. In 1576 he preached against their doctrines at Paul's Cross. The 'Evangelium Regni' of Nicholas, composed originally in German, had been translated into Latin, and in 1579 Knewstub translated a large portion of the Latin version into English, with comments in which he unsparingly denounced the tenets advanced. In the epistle dedicatory to 'his very good Lord and Maister, Ambrose, Earle of Warwick,' he says that 'the errours of the sect bee so many, so foule and so filthy, as woulde force the very penne in passing to stay and stop her nose.' The contents of the volume show that Knewstub was by this time well known at court, and on 13 Aug. 1579 he was presented by Sir William Spring to the rectory of Cockfield in Suffolk, in succession to Dr. Longworth, master of St. John's, and continued to hold the living for a period of forty-five years. Knewstub, however, was not less opposed to the teaching of Romanism, and under his influence Cockfield soon became a centre of puritan doctrine (cf. his *Answeare*).

About 1582, according to Fuller, an assembly of clergymen from Norfolk, Suffolk, and Cambridgeshire met in Cockfield Church 'to confer about the Common Prayer Book as to what might be tolerated and what totally rejected,' and also about 'apparel, holidays, fastings, injunctions, &c.' From Cockfield, according to Neal, they somewhat later repaired to Cambridge, and there again enunciated and disseminated their views. St. John's College was at that time noted for its leaning to puritanism, and Knewstub's teaching so far recommended him to the favour of his college that on the death in 1595 of the master, the celebrated theologian, William Whitaker, he was one of the most popular candidates for the office, but Richard Clayton [q. v.] was elected. His reputation continued to rise, and at the conference in Hampton Court in 1604 he appeared as one of the four ministers deputed to oppose conformity. On behalf of 'some honest ministers in Suffolk' he took especial exception to the use of the sign of the cross in baptism and also to the surplice, 'a kind of garment used

by the priests of Isis.' Barlow, the historian of the conference, describes him as speaking throughout the proceedings 'most affectionately,' but excuses himself from reporting all his interrogatories on the subject of baptism on the ground that 'he spoke so confusedly that his meaning is not to be collected therein' (*Sum of the Conference*, p. 65).

Knewstub died at Cockfield, where he was buried 31 May 1624. His epitaph, which has disappeared from his place of interment, has been preserved by Peck (*Desiderata Curiosa*, p. 216). He does not appear to have been married; but a Richard Knewstub, whose name occurs in the Cockfield parish registers, was probably a relative.

He founded in connection with his own college two exhibitions; one to be held by a scholar born and brought up at Kirkby Stephen, or, failing that place, at Appleby; and one from Cockfield, or, failing that place, from Sudbury.

He published: 1. 'A Sermon preached at Paules Crosse the Fryday before Easter, commonly called good Fryday, in the yeere of our Lorde, 1576. By John Knewstub.' b.l. 2. 'The Lectures of John Knewstub, upon the twentieth Chapter of Exodus, and certeine other places of Scripture. Seene and allowed according to the Queenes Majesties Injunctions. Imprinted by Lucas Harrison. Anno 1577;' 2nd edit. (see 'To the Reader'), b.l. 1578. The Lectures are dedicated to 'Anne, Countesse of Warwick,' as 'some remembrance of my thankfulnesse and dutie, towards any of that honourable house of Warwick, to the which I am (in the Lord) so many wayes indebted.' 3. 'A Confutation of monstrous and horrible Heresies, taught by H. N. and embraced of a number who call themselves the *Familie of Love*. By I. Knewstub. Imprinted in London at the three Cranes in the Vinetree, by Thomas Dawson, for Richard Sergier, 1579.' b.l. 4. 'An Answeare unto certayne assertions, tending to maintaine the Church of Rome to be the true and Catholique Church. By John Knewstub. Printed in London at the three Cranes in the Vintree, by Thomas Dawson for Richard Sergier, 1579.' b.l.

[Baker's Hist. of St. John's College. ed. Mayor; Barlow's Sum of the Conference (Phenix, vol. ii.); Neal's Hist. of the Puritans (ed. 1733), vol. ii.; Churchill Babington's Materials for a History of Cockfield.] J. B. M.

KNIGHT, CHARLES (1743–1827?), engraver, born in 1743, is sometimes stated to have been a pupil of F. Bartolozzi, R.A. [q. v.] He appears, however, to have practised stipple-engraving independently, and subsequently became quite as skilful as Bartolozzi himself. He was at first employed on somewhat indifferent prints for such works as Harding's 'Shakespeare Illustrated,' 'Memoirs of Grammont,' &c., but later obtained a good reputation, and was extensively employed on more important work. He engraved numerous subjects after H. W. Bunbury, Angelica Kauffmann, F. Wheatley, T. Stothard, J. H. Benwell, J. Hoppner, J. Northcote, J. R. Smith, and others, as well as many portraits after Sir Joshua Reynolds, Sir Thomas Lawrence, &c. Others are often credited with his work. His engraving of 'The Spirit of a Child borne to Heaven,' after W. Peters, is usually ascribed to W. Dickinson; and his fine full-length portrait of Elizabeth Farren, countess of Derby, has been ranked among the best productions of Bartolozzi. One C. Knight exhibited four miniatures at the Royal Academy between 1793 and 1816. Knight resided in 1781 in Berwick Street, Soho, in 1792 in Brompton, and later in Hammersmith, where he was still living in 1826, when he published, although aged 83, a portrait of the Rev. Thomas Stephen Attwood, minister of Hammersmith. He probably died soon after this. In 1803 Knight was one of the original governors of the abortive Society of Engravers. His daughter Martha also practised as an engraver.

[Dodd's manuscript History of English Engravers (Brit. Mus. Add. MS. 33402); Redgrave's Dict. of Artists, p. 253; Leblanc's Manuel de l'Amateur d'Estampes; Tuer's Bartolozzi and his Works.]   L. C.

KNIGHT, CHARLES (1791–1873), author and publisher, son of Charles Knight, bookseller of Windsor, was born in 1791. The elder Knight, a man of cultivation and public spirit, published the 'Microcosm,' written by George Canning, Robert Smith, John Frere, and other Eton boys in 1786 and 1787, and its successor, the 'Miniature,' edited by Stratford Canning sixteen years later. The father also spent much time on local affairs. He was on very friendly terms with George III, who used to come to turn over his books. One morning in 1791 he was horror-struck at finding the king in his shop poring over Paine's 'Rights of Man,' then just published. The king made no comment. In 1803 Knight was sent to a school kept by a Dr. Nicholas at Ealing. Before he could acquire more than a rudimentary knowledge of the classics, his father removed him from school, and took him as an apprentice in the summer of 1805. The elder Knight sold old as well as new books, and Knight acquired

a good bibliographical knowledge. An imperfect copy of the first folio Shakespeare, bought by the father in a library, was given by him to the son. Having access to a fount of similar type, and 'abundant flyleaves of 17th-century books which matched the paper,' Knight composed, with the aid of the facsimile, and printed himself every missing or defective page, and made his copy perfect. He sold it for a 'tempting price' to an Eton tutor; but his careful study of the text was of value to him in later days. About this time he began a lifelong habit of dabbling in verse. He wisely burnt his early attempts, but later he published a little of his work. In 1813 he wrote a play, 'Arminius,' which, though declined by the management of Drury Lane, was printed. On the marriage of Princess Charlotte he produced a 'mask,' entitled 'The Bridal of the Isles,' called by Leigh Hunt 'very crisp and luxuriant.' He was among the founders in 1810 of a short-lived 'Reading Society' at Windsor. The ambition to become a popular instructor already possessed him. His first idea was to achieve this end by journalism, and during the session of 1812 he began to learn the trade by reporting for the 'Globe' and 'British Press.' On 27 Feb. he was accidentally left alone to report a speech by Canning. In August 1812, as joint proprietor with his father, he started the 'Windsor and Eton Express.' His experience made him aware of the obstacles placed in the way of 'popular instruction' by the stamp, advertisement, and paper duties.

In 1818, his father being mayor of Windsor, Knight was appointed overseer of the parish. He threw himself into the work with his usual enthusiasm, startled his brother officials with a proposal that they should visit the 'out-poor' at home, and once successfully chased a supposed bigamist, who had left a wife 'on the parish' at Windsor, into Oxfordshire. He took the opportunity of visiting the house at Burford reported to have been Lord Falkland's, and pushed on to Wantage, that he might see the birthplace of King Alfred. In 1817 he edited and published an edition of Fairfax's 'Tasso' (Singer's edition appeared in the same year). He was still keen about popular instruction, and so early as 1814 had sketched out the plan of a weekly series, which should bring all kinds of knowledge, mixed with lighter matter, within the reach of the poorest. At last, on 1 Feb. 1820, in conjunction with Edward Hawke Locker [q. v.], Knight produced the first number of the 'Plain Englishman,' comprehending original compositions and selections from the best writers, under the heads of 'The Christian Monitor,' 'The British

Patriot,' 'The Fireside Companion.' J. B. Sumner (afterwards archbishop of Canterbury) wrote 'Conversations with an Unbeliever,' and apparently papers on political economy; J. M. Turner (bishop of Calcutta 1829-32) wrote on 'Naval Victories,' and Locker on 'The Bible and Liturgy.' The editor wrote a series of simple tales. In June 1820 Knight became editor and part proprietor of a London weekly paper, 'The Guardian,' in which he combined literature with politics, and (apparently) set the first example of summarising articles in the magazines. J. W. Croker, in spite of their political differences, helped him in both departments. 'Croker was,' says Knight, 'always ready to give me his opinion, as I believed honestly, and was always glad to gossip with me on subjects of literature.' The 'Plain Englishman' came to an end in December 1822; the 'Guardian' was sold at the same time; and in the course of 1823 Knight, partly at Croker's instigation, started as a publisher in London. In the course of the past two years, as an interlude to more serious business, he had been publishing the 'Etonian' (October 1820 to July 1821), and had by this means come into contact with W. M. Praed, J. Moultrie, W. S. Walker, and H. N. Coleridge, who now were Cambridge undergraduates. With the help of these, reinforced by Macaulay, Malden, and others, he started 'Knight's Quarterly Magazine,' edited by himself, and 'printed for Charles Knight & Co., 7 Pall Mall East' (1823-4). Matthew Davenport Hill, De Quincey, and others contributed (cf. *Notes and Queries*, 1st ser. ix. 103, 334); but the magazine was hardly successful, and practically dropped with the sixth number, though one other was published a year later. In 1824 Knight published Vieusseux's 'Italy and the Italians,' and in July 1825, for the Cambridge University Press, a translation by C. R. Sumner (afterwards bishop of Winchester) of Milton's 'Treatise on Christian Doctrine.' In November he was preparing a scheme for a 'national library,' a cheap series of books which should condense the information contained in voluminous and extensive works. But this was cut short by the financial panic. The prospectus ultimately appeared in the name of Messrs. Murray, and arrangements were even begun for the merging of Knight's business in that firm. These, however, fell through, and with them Knight's business. In the summer of 1827 he was compelled to place his affairs in the hands of trustees. After a short period of promiscuous literary work on James Silk Buckingham's paper, 'The Sphinx,' on the 'London Magazine,' of which he became part

proprietor in March 1828, and elsewhere, he undertook to superintend the publications of the Society for the Diffusion of Useful Knowledge, which (taking its title from that of an article in the 'Plain Englishman') had been organised a few months earlier by Brougham, M. D. Hill, and others. At first his duties were mainly those of 'reader' for the committee: subsequently he wrote and edited. He had not yet re-established himself as a publisher, and the first number (for 1828) of the 'British Almanack and Companion,' which he had long projected as an antidote to the trash which was still disseminated under the name of almanacks, and which the society now took up, bears the imprint of Baldwin & Cradock. But by 31 March 1829 he was again in Pall Mall East. On that day appeared 'The Menageries,' written by him as the first volume of the 'Library of Entertaining Knowledge.' From this time till its dissolution in 1846 Knight remained the society's publisher. In this capacity he produced the 'Quarterly Journal of Education,' 1831-6; the 'Penny Magazine,' 1832-1845—this by the end of its first year had a sale of two hundred thousand; the 'Penny Cyclopædia,' 1833-44; the 'Gallery of Portraits,' 1832; besides smaller works. Early in 1832 a new post, which it was proposed to create at the board of trade, for arranging official documents, was offered to him by Lord Auckland, then president. Knight wisely refused, for his nature, at once practical and impatient of restraint, would have chafed beyond endurance at the pedantries of a government department. However, in 1835, when the new poor law was coming into operation, Knight was appointed publisher by authority to the commission. About this time he removed his place of business to Ludgate Street. In 1831 and 1832 he wrote 'The Results of Machinery' (of which Spring Rice said 'that it had effected more good for the repression of outrage than a regiment of horse') and 'Capital and Labour.' These were afterwards reprinted in one volume under the title 'Knowledge is Power.' In 1836 he began to publish in parts the 'Pictorial Bible.' This was quickly followed by Lane's 'Arabian Nights;' then came the 'Pictorial History of England' by G. L. Craik and C. MacFarlane, with other contributors, published in monthly parts for seven years, from 1837, a book which is still unbeaten as a history of England for domestic use. 'London' (1841-4) was in great part written by Knight himself. From 1837 he had been occupied with what he himself probably regarded as his *magnum opus*. From the time of his boyish experience he had wished to edit Shakespeare. In 1838 appeared the first number of the 'Pictorial Shakespere.' Knight's edition has doubtless been superseded at many points. His faith in the first folio may possibly have been too unflinching; but H. N. Coleridge was not far wrong when he called it 'the first in the country conceived in a right spirit,' and no future editor can afford to neglect it. The 'Pictorial Shakespere' was completed in 1841. Before the last part appeared Knight had begun to publish 'a series of original treatises by various authors' under the name of 'Knight's Store of Knowledge for all Readers,' leading off himself with two numbers devoted to Shakespeare. The 'library edition' began to appear in January 1842, and during 1842 and 1843 Knight went to Stratford, Oxford, Edinburgh, Glasgow, in search of materials for the 'Biography,' upon which he was now at work. In the spring of 1844 appeared the twenty-seventh and last volume of the 'Penny Cyclopedia,' and the event was celebrated by a dinner, at which Knight was 'entertained' by his friends, Brougham being in the chair. The 'Weekly Volumes,' a series started largely owing to a suggestion of Harriet Martineau, were begun at this time. The first appeared on 29 June, the publisher opening with a biography of William Caxton. In this series (appearing every week for two years, and every month for two years more in the 'shilling volume') many well-known works made their first appearance: Miss Martineau's 'Tales,' G. H. Lewes's 'Biographical History of Philosophy,' Mrs. Jameson's 'Early Italian Painters,' Rennie's 'Insect Architecture,' 'The Camp of Refuge,' and many more. The 'Penny Magazine' was now drawing to an end, and with it Knight's connection with the Useful Knowledge Society. He made a short effort to continue the magazine in his own name; but this series only lived six months. Three months before this, in March 1846, the society itself had come to an end. Hitherto Knight had taken the risk of the various works brought out under its auspices, the society receiving a 'rent,' practically a royalty, in return for the prestige of its name. The 'Biographical Dictionary,' which it undertook at its own expense, failed after devoting seven excellent volumes to the letter A, when the loss was nearly 5,000l., and the society prudently wound up.

Knight gradually withdrew from miscellaneous publishing, though his pen was as active as ever. The 'Weekly Volumes' only paid their way, but he had for some time been carrying on with better success a series of 'picture-books, especially adapted for sale by

book-hawkers,' called 'The Pictorial World,' illustrative of natural history, English topography, &c. In 1847 he began his 'Half-hours with the Best Authors,' and 'The Land we Live in,' containing pictures and descriptions of everything noteworthy in England. To obtain materials he travelled all over the country. In 1848 he started a weekly periodical, 'The Voice of the People,' to which Miss Martineau contributed; but it failed after a career of three weeks on account, she says, of the dictatorial interference of whig officials (HARRIET MARTINEAU, Autobiography, ii. 298). In 1846 he had begun to publish in parts 'A History of the Thirty Years' Peace, 1815–1845.' After sixteen chapters had been written Miss Martineau took it up, completed it in 1849, and in the following year wrote an introduction, taking the history back to the opening of the century. This, published in 1851, would seem to be the last work of general literature bearing Knight's imprint. Since that time, with the exception of one or two reprints of his works, only official or semi-official publications have been issued by the house, which in his later years had migrated to Fleet Street. His own books were in future published chiefly by Bradbury & Evans; a few by Murray.

In 1851 Knight was invited by Dickens to take a part in Bulwer's comedy, 'Not so bad as we seem,' in connection with the 'Guild of Literature and Art.' He had already been connected with Dickens's amateur companies; but this seems to have been the first time that he was cast for a part. He played Jacob Tonson in the performance at Devonshire House.

In 1855 he was a juror at the Paris exhibition. In the same year, on the repeal of the stamp duty (to which his exertions had largely contributed), he started a 'Town and Country Newspaper.' The method (which failed at the time, though it has since been adopted) was to print general news in London, leaving a space blank for local news, to be supplied in the places to which the paper was sent. The 'English Cyclopedia' (1853–1861) was practically only the old 'Penny Cyclopedia' revised and brought up to date. Knight now set about the 'Popular History of England.' The plan of this was 'to trace through our annals the essential connection between our political history and our social,' to enable the people 'to learn their own history—how they have grown out of slavery, out of feudal wrong, out of regal despotism —into constitutional liberty, and the position of the greatest estate of the realm.' The history, in eight volumes, was completed by the end of 1862. In 1865 appeared an abridgment called the 'School History,' re-published in 1870 as the 'Crown History;' an excellent school book, the merits of which more recent works have obscured.

In 1864 and 1865 Knight wrote 'Passages of a Working Life,' being his own autobiography; and 'Shadows of the Old Booksellers.' Two series of 'Half-hours with the Best Letter-writers' appeared in 1867 and 1868, and in the former year he ventured with 'Begged at Court' into the field of fiction. His sight was, however, failing, and he had to be led by a friend at the dinner given to Dickens on 1 Oct. 1867. His remaining years were passed at Hampstead and at Addlestone in Surrey. He died at Addlestone 9 March 1873.

Knight was a man of middle stature, with finely cut features, and a countenance indicative of his character, in which a sanguine temperament somewhat preponderated over accurate judgment. His schemes, though often sound in themselves, were apt to be carried into effect somewhat prematurely, and without sufficient regard to probable obstacles. Consequently after all his great publishing operations he remained a poor man. He was thoroughly honourable in business and considerate to his fellow-workers. His temper was quick, and when moved he could speak and write strongly; but he bore no ill-will, and seems never to have made an enemy. The often-quoted jest with which Jerrold took leave of him one evening after a social meeting—'Good Knight'—gives the measure of the estimate formed of him by his friends. In politics he was a liberal, and was one of the earliest members of the Reform Club. When M. D. Hill was candidate for Hull in the first reformed parliament, Knight worked for him. 'Tell Mrs. Knight,' wrote Hill to his wife, 'that her husband is one of the best speakers I ever heard.'

He was also something of an inventor, and in 1838 took out a patent for 'improvements in the process and in the apparatus used in the production of coloured impressions on paper, vellum, parchment, and pasteboard by surface printing.' His proposal to collect the newspaper duty by means of a stamped wrapper is said to have given to Rowland Hill (q. v.) the first suggestion of the penny post.

In 1815 Knight married Miss Vinicombe. Of their children one son (Barry Charles Henry, 1828–1884) and four daughters, two of whom married respectively the Rev. C. F. Tarver and Robert Kerr, esq. (Mr. Commissioner Kerr), survived them. Another daughter, Mrs. G. Clowes, died before her parents; and a son and daughter died in infancy.

Knight's position as author, editor, and publisher makes it difficult to ascertain exactly how much is due to him in the first capacity. The following, however, seem undoubted, besides articles and pamphlets: 1. 'The Menageries,' 1828. 2. 'The Elephant,' 1830. 3. 'Results of Machinery,' 1831. 4. 'Capital and Labour,' 1831. 5. 'Trades Unions and Strikes,' 1834. 6. 'Shakspere's Biography,' 1843. 7. 'William Caxton,' 1844. 8. 'Old England' (first book and part of second), about 1844. 9. 'Studies of Shakespere,' 1849. 10. 'The Struggles of a Book against Excessive Taxation,' 1850. 11. 'Once upon a Time,' 1854. 12. 'The Old Printer and Modern Press,' 1854. 13. 'Knowledge is Power,' 1855. 14. 'Popular History of England,' 1856–1862. 15. 'Passages of a Working Life,' 1864–5. 16. 'Begged at Court,' 1867. 17. 'Shadows of the Old Booksellers,' 1867.

[Passages of a Working Life during Half a Century, by Charles Knight; Harriet Martineau's Autobiography, 1876; The Recorder of Birmingham, a Memoir of Matthew Davenport Hill, by his Daughters, 1878; obituary notices in the Times and Athenæum, &c.; private information.]
A. J. B.

KNIGHT, EDWARD (1774–1826), actor, commonly known as 'Little Knight,' and spoken of as a Yorkshireman, was born in 1774 in Birmingham. While practising as a sign-painter, or, as is sometimes said, an artist, he was stirred to emulation by the performance of a provincial company. He appeared accordingly at Newcastle, Staffordshire, as Hob in 'Hob in the Well,' and was so complete a victim to stage-fright that, despite the encouragement of a friendly audience, he ran off the stage and quitted the town. A year later at Raither in North Wales, with a salary of five shillings per week, he was fortunate enough to get in safety through the same part. Playing Frank Oatland in 'A Cure for the Heartache' he was seen and engaged by Nunns, the manager of the Stafford Theatre. In Stafford he stayed some years, increasing in reputation, and he married a Miss Clews, the daughter of a local wine merchant. Tate Wilkinson, to whom he introduced himself, engaged him for the York circuit about 1803. His reception was favourable. After a time he was gratified by the present from Wilkinson of a chest containing all the appliances of an actor's wardrobe, with the compliment: 'I have been long looking for some one who knew how to value them; you are the very man.' While at Leeds his wife died, and Knight, left with a young family, married in 1807 Susan Smith, who had succeeded her sister,

Sarah Bartley (q. v.), as leading lady, and, though an actress of no great power, was a remarkable favourite. Engaged by Wroughton, on the report of Bannister, for Drury Lane for three years, at a salary rising from 7l. to 9l., Knight arrived with wife and children in London, to find the theatre burnt down. At the Lyceum accordingly, whither the company betook itself, Knight made, 14 Oct. 1809, as Timothy Quaint in the 'Soldier's Daughter,' and Robin Roughhead in 'Fortune's Frolic,' his first appearance in London. The favourable impression he created in these characters, and as Label in the 'Prize,' was fortified by his creation of Jerry Blossom in Pocock's 'Hit or Miss,' 26 Feb. 1810, in which he and Mathews as Cypher retrieved the fortunes of the piece. Scrub in the 'Beaux' Stratagem,' Varland in the 'West Indian,' Zekiel Homespun in the 'Heir-at-Law,' Dominique in 'Deaf and Dumb,' Sam in 'Raising the Wind,' Gripe in the 'Confederacy,' and Risk in 'Love laughs at Locksmiths,' are among the parts he took at the Lyceum, where he was also the original Diego in the 'Kiss,' an alteration of Fletcher's 'Spanish Curate.' With the company he went to the new theatre in Drury Lane, to which he remained constant until his death. Simple in the 'Merry Wives of Windsor,' 23 Oct. 1812, is the first part in which he can be traced at this house. The Clown in 'Twelfth Night' and Little John in 'Robin Hood' were given during his first season. He played many parts, chiefly domestics, rustics, farm-labourers, and the like, and was the representative of scores of characters in feeble pieces by T. Dibdin, Pocock, Kenney, and other writers. Francis in 'King Henry IV,' Sim in 'Wild Oats,' Hawbuck in 'Town and Country,' Quiz in 'Love in a Camp,' Tom in 'Intrigue,' Gripe in the 'Two Misers,' Stephen Harrowby in the 'Poor Gentleman,' Solomon Lob in 'Love laughs at Locksmiths,' David in the 'Rivals,' Appletree in the 'Recruiting Officer,' Silky in the 'Road to Ruin,' Tester in the 'Suspicious Husband,' Peter in 'Romeo and Juliet,' Isaac in the 'Duenna,' Nym in 'King Henry V,' and Crabtree, represent the range of his abilities. Among his original parts, Tom in 'Intrigue' and Farmer Enfield in the 'Falls of Clyde' may be mentioned. During the season of 1825-6 he retired from the stage in consequence of illness. He died 2½ Feb. 1826 at his house in Great Queen Street, Lincoln's Inn Fields, and was buried on the 27th in a vault in St. Pancras New Church. His son by his first wife, John Prescott Knight, the portrait-painter, is separately noticed.

Knight was a shy, careful, benevolent, and retiring man, who shrank from social intimacies, and was wholly domestic in habits. His figure was small and pliable, his height being five feet two, his hair and eyes dark, his voice shrill, but not unmusical. He sang well and made up well, and in various lines of pert servants was unequalled. The 'Mirror of the Stage' calls him a very natural actor. Oxberry, a rival, says that Sim was his best part; that in characters such as Spado, Ralph, Trap, and Lingo he surpassed Harley, was inimitable in decrepit old men, was the best actor of the day in sharp footmen and cunning rustics, and, although capable of pathos, showed his art in squeezing tears to his eyes. His country boys (the same critic adds) are 'never unsophisticated; they are shrewd, designing, knowing.' Terry, in his 'British Theatrical Gallery,' says: 'There is always oddity, and sometimes pathos, in his acting,' but charges him with being 'a curious compound of quietude and restlessness.' Knight had a precise walk, a firm bearing, and a habit of laughing too much. He was author of a musical farce in two acts, entitled 'The Sailor and Soldier, or Fashionable Amusement,' which was produced for his benefit in Hull in 1805. It is without merit.

A famous engraved picture in the Mathews collection in the Garrick Club by Clint shows him as Ralph in 'Lock and Key,' with Munden as Old Brummagem, Mrs. Orger as Fanny, and Miss Cubitt as Laura. In the same collection are pictures of him by De Wilde as Robin Roughhead in 'Fortune's Frolic;' and by Foster as Jailor in 'Plots, or the North Tower,' and Jerry Blossom in 'Hit or Miss.' A coloured print after Clint of Knight as Hodge in 'Love in a Village' is in Terry's 'British Theatrical Gallery.'

[Books cited; Genest's Account of the Stage; Oxberry's Dramatic Biography, vol. ii.; Terry's British Theatrical Gallery; Biographia Dramatica; Theatrical Inquisitor and New Monthly Mag., various years; Georgian Era; Clark Russell's Representative Actors.] J. K.

KNIGHT, ELLIS CORNELIA (1757–1837), authoress, born in 1757, was the only child of the second marriage of Sir Joseph Knight, rear-admiral of the white. Though brought up in London, she was educated at a school kept by a Swiss pastor, and early obtained an acquaintance with continental languages and literature. She also became a good Latin scholar. Her mother, a woman of great accomplishments, was a friend of a sister of Sir Joshua Reynolds, and Miss Knight thus became acquainted with Johnson and his circle, of whom she has left several anecdotes. Admiral Knight died in 1775, and in the following year his widow and daughter, having failed to obtain a pension, went abroad from motives of economy. For many years they lived principally in Rome and Naples, mingling with the best society, and living on particularly intimate terms with Sir William and Lady Hamilton. In compliance with her mother's dying wishes, Miss Knight placed herself, after the latter's death in 1799, under Lady Hamilton's protection, and she returned to England with her protectress. Nelson accompanied them. Miss Knight was already intimate with the hero, and had obtained the title of his poet laureate by verses in celebration of his victories. She naturally found the position embarrassing. 'Most of my friends were very urgent with me to drop the acquaintance, but circumstanced as I had been I feared the charge of ingratitude.' Her autobiography passes very lightly over this period, but records her appointment as companion to Queen Charlotte in 1805. From this time there is an entire break until 1809, and little of importance is recorded until 1813, when the principal event in Miss Knight's life took place—her exchange of the companionship of Queen Charlotte for a similar position in the household of Princess Charlotte. By this step she gave mortal offence to the queen, who lost a useful attendant, and was probably aware that Miss Knight had a just grievance against the dull, uninteresting, and monotonous character of the life which she had perforce to lead at Windsor. Want of interest and monotony could not be imputed to her new employment, where she found herself entangled in intrigues, quarrels, misunderstandings, and recriminations among a number of persons inspired by self-interested views, and in general animated by most undisciplined tempers, especially when their rank placed them beyond the reach of contradiction [see CHARLOTTE AUGUSTA, PRINCESS OF WALES]. Miss Knight's autobiography is among the most valuable sources of information for the court history of those days. At length (July 1814) the princess's refusal to marry the Prince of Orange induced the regent to suddenly dismiss all her attendants, including Miss Knight. The princess consequently fled to her mother at Connaught Terrace, and general confusion ensued. Miss Knight afterwards wrote of her own part in these transactions: 'Either I ought to have remained with the queen, or I ought to have carried things with a higher hand to be really useful while I was with Princess Charlotte. I had the romantic

desire that Princess Charlotte should think for herself, and think wisely. Was that to be expected from a girl of seventeen, and from one who had never had proper care taken of her since early childhood?' In 1816 Miss Knight again went abroad, and, although frequently revisiting England, spent most of her life on the continent, mixing in the highest society, and collecting the anecdotes which appear in her journals. She died in Paris on 17 Dec. 1837.

The most important passages from her autobiography, with selections from her diaries, were edited in 1861 by Sir John William Kaye, or rather, as is virtually admitted in the preface, by Mr. James Hutton. They are justly appreciated by Kaye when he says: 'Miss Knight was no retailer of prurient scandal or frivolous gossip; she had too good a heart to delight in the one, and too good a head to indulge in the other. Some, therefore, may think that she neglected her opportunities.' In fact, her memoirs might easily have been more piquant without any breach of propriety. They are matter-of-fact records without any attempt at delineation of the persons concerned, but they bear the strongest impress of sincerity and truth. Miss Knight also wrote 'Dinarbas,' a kind of supplement to 'Rasselas' (1790); 'Flaminius, a View of the Military, Social, and Political Life of the Romans,' a didactic romance in the form of letters (1792), which was translated into German in 1794, and reached a second English edition in 1808; 'Sir Guy de Lusignan,' a romance (1833); translations of German hymns and prayers, privately printed at Frogmore in 1812, and published in 1832; besides her principal work, 'A Description of Latium, or La Campagna di Roma' (1805, 4to), with etchings by the author, a work of considerable value in its day, and interesting even now. T. L. Peacock says, writing to Lord Broughton, 22 Feb. 1842: 'I have read Miss Knight's autobiography. I have not for a long time read anything that pleased me so much; but I am not sure how much may belong to the book and how much to old associations. Her "Latium" has long been a favourite book with me.'

[Autobiography of Miss Cornelia Knight, 1861; Quarterly Review, vol. cxl.]   R. G.

KNIGHT, FRANCIS (d. 1589), socinian. [See KETT.]

KNIGHT, GOWIN (1713–1772), man of science and first principal librarian of the British Museum, baptised at Corringham, Lincolnshire, on 10 Sept. 1713, was son of Robert Knight, vicar of that place, and of

Elizabeth his wife. His father, a virtuoso who collected coins and medals, was appointed in 1724 to the vicarage of Harewood, near Leeds, where he remained until his death in 1747. According to the Wilson MSS. preserved in the Leeds Free Library, Knight was educated at the Leeds grammar school. He matriculated at Oxford from Magdalen Hall 5 April 1731, and held a demyship at Magdalen College from 1735 to 1746, proceeding B.A. 20 Oct. 1736, M.A. 22 June 1739, and M.B. 11 Feb. 1741–2. He afterwards settled in London and is said to have practised as a physician. In 1749 he was living in Lincoln's Inn Fields; he removed to a house in Crane Court, Fleet Street, about 1750 (cf. NICHOLS, *Literary Anecdotes*, v. 534).

Knight began the magnetical researches which gave him his reputation before 1744. His attention was directed to the subject by witnessing the effects of a flash of lightning upon a ship's compass, and the first results of his labours were presented to the Royal Society in 1744 (*Phil. Trans.* xliii. 161), when he exhibited some bar magnets of great power, and performed some experiments which proved that he was in possession of an entirely new method of magnetising bars. A paper read by him in 1745 (*ib.* xliii. 361) discusses the various positions of the poles of magnets. In recognition of the value of these researches the Royal Society in 1745 elected him a fellow, and in 1747 the Copley medal was awarded to him. He found a ready sale for his magnets, and in a further series of papers laid before the society in 1746–7 (*ib.* xliv. 656–72) dealt more particularly with the theoretical aspects of the question. He withheld a full disclosure of his methods of operating for fear of injuring the sale of his magnets, but he soon found in John Canton, who had also begun the manufacture of artificial magnets, a formidable rival [see CANTON, JOHN]. Knight's papers on magnetism were collected and published separately in 1758, with notes and additions by the author. It appears from T. H. Croker's 'Experimental Magnetism' (1761), p. 8, that Knight issued proposals in 1760 for publishing by subscription an extensive work on magnetism, in two volumes 4to, but the plan was never carried out. After his death his friend Dr. Fothergill read a paper before the Royal Society (*ib.* 1776, lxvi. 591), in which Knight's methods of magnetising were more fully disclosed. The paper also contains a description of his 'magnetic magazine' or battery, which was for many years in the possession of the Royal Society, but is now missing. In 1779 Benjamin Wilson (*ib.* lxix.

51) gave an account of Knight's method of making artificial loadstones, which consisted in cementing finely divided metallic iron into a solid mass by the admixture of linseed-oil varnish.

Knight's attention had meanwhile been turned to the mariner's compass, and in a paper read before the society in 1750 (*ib.* xlvi. 505) he stated that he had examined several compass-needles obtained from the best makers, and found them all defective, being either of feeble directive power or absolutely incorrect as regards direction. These defects were due to the shape of the needles, all of which were possessed of four poles. He recommended a plain rhomboidal bar, and he also suggested improved modes of suspension. Some further improvements already made in Knight's compass by Smeaton were communicated to the society at the same time.

Knight brought his improved compass under the notice of the admiralty, and there is an entry in the official minute book under date 4 April 1751 to the effect that the navy board and the Trinity House authorities had been consulted and various experiments made with the improved compass and bar magnets. Compasses were ordered to be supplied to the Glory, bound for Guinea, the Rainbow going to Newfoundland, the Swan sloop bound to Barbadoes, and to the Vulture and Fortune sloops in the Channel. On 11 Sept. in the same year there is a further order directing the captain of the Fortune to receive Dr. Knight on board at Harwich and to sail northwards according to his directions, for the purpose of experimenting with the new compass. He was accompanied on the voyage by Smeaton (see *Annual Register*, 1793, Chronicle, p. 250). The results of the trials appear to have been satisfactory (though the captain's reports cannot now be found), and by a minute dated 24 June 1752 the board recommended that Knight should be paid 300*l.* It appears from this minute that the compass had already been brought to the notice of the board of longitude, probably with a view to its use in determining the longitude by observation of the magnetic variation, but the minutes for this date are missing from the records of the board preserved at the Royal Observatory, Greenwich. There are other entries in the admiralty books relating to the matter, and it appears that Knight's instrument gradually came to be the standard compass for the royal navy. They were also used in the better class of merchant ships. The compasses were made, under Knight's direction, by George Adams the elder [q. v.] of Fleet Street, the mathematical instrument maker. Knight was in the habit of certifying each instrument by signing his name on the card. There is a compass preserved in the admiralty compass department at Deptford certified in this way. It is stated by Captain Flinders in a manuscript diary, now in the possession of his descendant, Mr. Flinders Petrie, that Knight occupied the position of inspector of compasses to the admiralty, and that J. H. de Magelhaens was his successor in the office. Captain Flinders had every opportunity of knowing the facts, but the statement is not borne out by the admiralty minute books. In 1766 Knight took out a patent (No. 850) for some further improvements in compasses, the main object of which was to check the vibration, the card and box being made to oscillate in equal times, so that the card always remained parallel to the glass. A reflecting azimuth compass is also described in the specification of this patent. The value of Knight's services to navigation does not seem to have received adequate recognition. A useful summary of Knight's work in this department of science is given in Snow Harris's 'Rudimentary Magnetism,' 1852, chap. ix.

Knight was an unsuccessful candidate for the post of secretary to the Royal Society in 1752, in opposition to Dr. Birch. But when the British Museum was first established at Montague House, Bloomsbury, in 1756, he was appointed principal librarian. The salary attached to the office was only 160l. per annum, but the librarian was allowed to act also as a 'receiver,' and received on that account an additional 40l. a year. He presented to the museum a set of his magnetical apparatus (which were shown in the early days of the institution, but cannot now be found), the Copley medal which he received from the Royal Society in recognition of his magnetical researches, and a collection of coins and medals bequeathed to him by his father. There are two papers in his hand among the Sloane MSS., one relating to alchemy and the other being notes of lectures on surgery, but without any indication of the time and place of delivery.

He seems to have led a secluded life, and during his later years was involved in financial difficulties. Dr. John Fothergill on one occasion advanced him a thousand guineas to save him from impending ruin due to some disastrous mining speculations (FOTHERGILL, Works, ed. Lettsom, vol. i. p. ciii), and Knight was never able to discharge this liability. By his will, dated 9 April 1772, he left everything to his 'good friend and principal creditor, John Fothergill of Harpur Street,' whom he appointed sole executor. It appears from the official records that Knight died at the museum on 8 June 1772 (not 9th, as in Gent. Mag. 1772, p. 295). His burial is recorded in the registers of St. George's, Bloomsbury, a few days afterwards, but it is probable that he was interred in the parochial cemetery near the Foundling Hospital. There is a portrait of him in the board room at the museum presented by his executor. It was probably painted by Benjamin Wilson, with whom he was on terms of intimacy, but it is not the original of the small etching in the Rembrandt manner bearing the inscription, 'Painted and etched by B. Wilson, 1751,' which is well known to collectors.

Although the bent of Knight's genius was decidedly experimental and practical, he published a speculative treatise in 1748 entitled 'An Attempt to demonstrate that all the Phenomena in Nature may be explained by two simple active principles, Attraction and Repulsion, wherein the attractions of Cohesion, Gravity, and Magnetism are more particularly explained.' The book consists of ninety-one propositions, and is of interest as showing marks of an epoch in which attempts were made to push the Newtonian doctrine into molecular speculations. It preceded Boscovich's better-known work on a similar subject by ten years. Knight also wrote a paper on the earthquake of 8 Feb. 1749-50 (Phil. Trans. xlvi. 603) and some remarks on W. Mountaine's letter on the effects of lightning (ib. li. 294). He was the inventor of 'dwarf venetian blinds,' which have since been largely used. He obtained a patent for the invention in 1760 (No. 750).

[Authorities cited; Foster's Alumni Oxonienses; Bloxam's Registers of Magdalen College, vi. 241; Nichols's Literary Illustrations, viii. 626; Nichols's Literary Anecdotes, v. 534; Athenæum, 6 Jan. 1849 pp. 5, 6, 15 Oct. 1849 p. 495; De Morgan in Notes and Queries, 2nd ser. x. 281.]

R. B. P.

KNIGHT, HENRIETTA, LADY LUXBOROUGH (d. 1756), friend of Shenstone, was the only daughter of Henry, viscount St. John, by his second wife, Angelica Magdalene, daughter of Georges Pillesary, treasurer-general of the marines, and superintendent of the ships and galleys of France under Louis XIV. Henry St. John, first viscount Bolingbroke [q. v.], was her half-brother. She married, on 20 June 1727, Robert Knight of Barrells, Warwickshire, eldest son of Robert Knight, cashier of the South Sea Company, created in 1746 Baron Luxborough of Shannon, and in 1763 Viscount Barrells and Earl of Catherlough in the peerage of Ireland. Horace Walpole describes her as 'high-coloured' and 'lusty,' with a 'great black bush of hair,' in which at first she wore the portrait of her husband, from whom she soon 'was parted ... upon a gallantry she had with Dalton, the reviver of Comus and a divine,' and 'retired to a hermitage on Parnassus.' The story may be a scandal, but Lady Luxborough was certainly separated from, or deserted by, her husband within a few years of their marriage; and was an intimate friend of Frances Seymour, countess of Hertford, afterwards duchess of Somerset [q. v.], in whose house Dalton resided as tutor to Lord Beauchamp [see DALTON, JOHN, 1709–1763]. The hermitage mentioned by Walpole was her husband's estate of Barrells, which she had laid out in the artificial style of landscape gardening. Here she was within easy reach of Shenstone, whom she frequently visited at the Leasowes, and with whom she kept up a regular correspondence. Shenstone celebrated their somewhat artificial Arcadia in his ode on 'Rural Elegance,' addressed to the Duchess of Somerset (1750). Lady Luxborough was also a friend of the poet William Somervile [q. v.] She died towards the end of March 1756, and was buried in the church of Wootton Wawen, the parish in which Barrells is situate, whence her remains were afterwards removed to a mausoleum near Barrells. Though she had been supposed to share her brother's religious opinions, she took the sacrament on her deathbed. By Lord Luxborough she had one son, Henry, who married, 21 June 1750, a daughter of Thomas Heath of Stanstead, Essex, and died without issue in the lifetime of his father; also two daughters, one of whom married a French count; the other, Henrietta, married Charles Wymondesold of Lockinge, Berkshire, but, eloping in 1753 with the Hon. Josiah Child, brother of John, second earl Tylney, was divorced, and married her paramour on 7 May 1754. Lady Luxborough's 'Letters to William Shenstone, Esq.,' published by Dodsley, London, 1775, are very insipid. Four little poems of slight merit, printed as 'by a lady of quality' in Dodsley's 'Collection of Poems by several hands' (1775), iv. 313, are attributed to her by Horace Walpole. See also Hull's 'Select Letters between the late Duchess of Somerset, Lady Luxborough ... and others,' London, 1778, 2 vols. 8vo.

[Collins's Peerage (Brydges), vi. 75; Add. MS. 23728; marginalia and other manuscript notes by E. Gulston in the British Museum copy of Lady Luxborough's 'Letters to Shenstone;' Mrs. Delany's Autobiography, ed. Lady Llanover; Gent. Mag. 1746 p. 384, 1754 p. 243, 1756 p. 206; Horace Walpole's Letters, ed. Cunningham; Horace Walpole's Cat. of Royal and Noble Authors, ed. Park, v. 260, where there is an engraving of Lady Luxborough's portrait by an unknown artist; Grenville Papers, ed. Smith, ii. 48; Cairird's Worthies of Warwickshire; Official Lists of Members of Parliament; Hist. MSS. Comm. 3rd Rep. App. p. 291; Nichols's Lit. Anecd. ii. 379, vi. 204; Burke's Extinct Peerage.]   J. M. R.

KNIGHT, HENRY GALLY (1786–1846), writer on architecture, born on 2 Dec. 1786, was the only son of Henry Gally Knight of Langold Hall, Yorkshire, barrister, by his wife Selina, daughter of William Fitzherbert of Tissington, Derbyshire. His grandfather, John Gally (who assumed the additional name of Knight), was M.P. for Aldborough and Boroughbridge, and a son of Henry Gally, D.D. [q. v.], the classical scholar. Knight was educated at Eton, and apparently at Trinity College, Cambridge, though his name does not appear in the list of graduates. In 1810 and 1811 he travelled in Spain, Sicily, Greece, Egypt, and Palestine, in company with the Hon. Frederick North and Mr. Fazakerly. His first publications were in verse, being 'Ilderim, a Syrian Tale,' 1816, 8vo; 'Phrosyne, a Grecian Tale;' 'Alashtar, an Arabian Tale,' London, 1817, 8vo; 'Eastern Sketches, in verse,' 3rd edit. London, 1830, 8vo. Byron (whose 'Giaour' was published in May 1813) bestowed praise on some of Knight's oriental verses (MOORE, Life of Byron, under 4 Dec. 1813, p. 218, in one-vol. ed. 1846; cf. ib. p. 245), though he does not seem to have relished 'Ilderim' (BYRON, Works, 'Versicles:' 'I tried at "Ilderim"—Ahem!') Knight turned from poetry to architecture. In May 1831 he landed at Dieppe, and during the year examined the buildings and libraries of Normandy. After his return to England he published 'An Architectural Tour in Normandy,' London, 1836, 12mo (French translation by M. A. Campion, Caen, 1838, 8vo). In August 1836 he started for Messina, and afterwards published 'The Normans in Sicily,' London, 1838, 12mo (French translation by M. A. Campion, Caen, 1839, 8vo; German translation, ed. C. R. Lepsius, Leipzig, 1841, 8vo), and 'Saracenic and Norman Remains to illustrate the "Normans in Sicily,"' London [1840], fol. He was assisted in his studies by professional architects: in Normandy by Richard Hussey, in Sicily by George Moore. In 1842–1844 he published 'The Ecclesiastical Architecture of Italy from ... Constantine to the 15th Century' (2 vols., London, fol.), with eighty-one litho-chromatic plates by Owen Jones. Knight was also the author of some minor works.

Knight, who had succeeded to the family estates on his father's death in 1808, was elected M.P. for Aldborough (between 1824 and 1628?); for Malton in 1830; for North Nottinghamshire in 1835 and in 1837. The last seat he held from 1837 till his death, which took place in Lower Grosvenor Street, London, on 9 Feb. 1846. He was buried in Firbeck Church, Yorkshire, on 17 Feb. Knight married in 1828 Henrietta, third daughter of Anthony Hardolph Eyre of Grove, Nottinghamshire, but had no issue. By his will he directed that his Langold estate should be sold for the benefit of some friends. His other estates at Firbeck, Kirton, and Warsop were left to his widow for her life; the Firbeck estate and mansion were to go after her death to the ecclesiastical commissioners for charitable uses. Some manuscripts relating to Knight's tour in 1810-11 remained in the hands of his family. In parliament Knight was a fluent but infrequent speaker. He was a kind landlord, and on 19 Oct. 1841 was presented by his tenants with his portrait, painted at a cost of 250 guineas. He held the office of deputy-lieutenant of Nottinghamshire, and was a member of the commission for the advancement of the fine arts. Tom Moore (*Diary*, v. 222) relates that Lord Wellesley, who once found Gally Knight overcome with sea-sickness, applied to his case the Horatian lines:

neque

Decedit *ærata triremi*, et

Post *equitem sedet atra cura*.

[Gent. Mag. 1846, new ser. xxv. 432-4; Athenæum, 14 Feb. 1846, p. 174; Brit. Mus. Cat.]

W. W.

KNIGHT, JAMES (*d.* 1719?), arctic voyager, for many years an agent of the Hudson's Bay Company, appears to have been governor of Fort Albany in 1693. In 1714 he was appointed governor of the Nelson River settlement, and in 1717 or 1718 established Prince of Wales's fort at the mouth of Churchill River. From the friendly Indians he heard of a mine, which may possibly have been copper, or more probably pyrites, such as had formerly beguiled Frobiser, but which his fancy at once set down as gold. He hastened to England and urged the company to fit out an expedition to search for it. The company reluctantly equipped two vessels, which sailed in June 1719, with instructions to search for the Straits of Anian and to discover gold and other valuable commodities to the northward. Except so far as related to the conduct of the ships, the command was vested in Knight. Nothing further was heard of them, and it was at first supposed that they had found the fabled straits and were returning to England from the Pacific. But in 1722 a search expedition was sent out

under the command of Captain John Scroggs. It met with no success, and the fate of Knight and his companions remained shrouded in mystery till in 1767 the ships' hulls, some of their guns and anchors, and other traces of the presence of Europeans were found at Marble Island by a whaling party. Further examination among the Eskimos elicited the facts that the ships had arrived late in the autumn, presumably of 1719, that in getting into the harbour one, or, more probably, both of them sustained serious damage, that the men built a house and sojourned there that winter and the next, suffering great hardships. At the beginning of the second winter the original fifty had dwindled to twenty, and at the end of that winter to five, all of whom died shortly after, in May or June 1721. As Knight is described as a very old man, verging on eighty, we may conjecture that he died among the first, that is in the end of 1719 or early months of 1720.

[Barrow's Chron. Hist. of Voyages into the Arctic Regions, p. 271; Joseph Robson's Account of Six Years' Residence in Hudson's Bay (1752), p. 36; Sam. Hearne's Journey from Prince of Wales's Fort in Hudson's Bay to the Northern Ocean (1795), p. xxviii; Report from the Committee appointed to Inquire into the State and Condition of the Countries adjoining to Hudson's Bay (1749), p. 49.]

J. K. L.

KNIGHT, JOHN (*d.* 1606), mariner, apparently of Scottish birth, was in 1605 associated with two other Scots, Cunningham and Lyon, in command of a Danish expedition to the coast of Greenland, which sailed from Copenhagen on 2 May. On the 30th, in lat. 59° 50', they sighted high land, which they called Cape Christian, but the ice prevented them from reaching it. On 12 June they sighted high land on the west coast of Greenland, and named Cape Anna after James I's queen, Cape Sophia after her mother, King Christian's Fjord, and Cunningham Fjord, in lat. 67° 10'. Some small islands off Cape Sophia were named Knight's Islands (Danish Gov. Chart, 1832). This marks the extent of their voyage, of which few particulars have been preserved. They returned to Copenhagen in August, and Knight, passing on to England, was in the next year employed by the East India merchants to discover the north-west passage. In the Hopewell of forty tons he sailed from Gravesend on 18 April 1606, and, leaving the Orkneys on 12 May, fell in with a large ice-field, and after a long passage made the coast of Labrador, in about lat. 57°, on 19 June. The ice was still very troublesome, and after pushing through it for a couple of days the Hopewell anchored. In a violent gale on the 23rd and 24th the cables parted and the ship drove ashore. She was got afloat again, but her rudder was torn off, and she was making a great deal of water. Gorrell, the mate, was sent on shore to look for a place where she could be beached for repairs, and as he was unsuccessful, on the next day, 26 June, Knight went himself with Gorrell and four men. Leaving two men in the boat, Knight and his three companions went inland over a hill, and were never seen again. It was concluded that they were killed by the natives—little people, tawny-coloured, flat-nosed, with thin or no beards. The survivors on board repaired the ship as they best could, not without opposition from the Eskimos, and so reached Newfoundland, whence they sailed on 22 Aug., and arrived at Dartmouth on 24 Sept.

[Markham's Voyages of Sir James Lancaster, &c. (Hakluyt Soc. vol. lvi.); Purchas his Pilgrimes, pt. iii. p. 827.]   J. K. L.

KNIGHT, Sir JOHN, 'the elder' (1612–1683), mayor of Bristol, third son of George Knight, provision merchant, by his wife Anne, daughter of William Dyos, was born in Bristol in 1612. He inherited his father's business in Temple Street, and became one of the most prosperous merchants in the city, and a prominent high church member of the common council. He was knighted by Charles II on 5 Sept. 1663, on the occasion of the king's visit to Bristol, and was elected mayor in the same year. His tenure of office was distinguished by his persecution of quakers, Knight paying large sums to have their houses watched, and concerting measures with Guy Carleton [q. v.], bishop of Bristol, for their punishment. Nine hundred and twenty persons are said to have suffered for their religion during his mayoralty, and many moderate churchmen were scandalised by the mayor's rushing out of church on Sundays in pursuit of recalcitrant nonconformists. Knight's intolerance, however, only increased with years, and in 1669 he denounced the other members of the common council, including his namesake, John Knight [see KNIGHT, JOHN, fl. 1670, under KNIGHT, Sir JOHN, 'the younger'], who was mayor of Bristol in the following year, as 'fanaticks.' He took a prominent part in the reception of Queen Catherine in 1677. In 1680, 'by reason of his infirmity,' he desired the city to nominate some other persons to take care of their affairs in the common council, but though he no longer had any official status he still occasionally acted as an informer. His antipathy to Roman catholics was quite as strong as that against

protestant nonconformists, and in 1681 he was fined for an assault, and for calling several members of the common council 'papists, popish dogs, jesuits, and popish devils.'

He had in the August of the previous year acted as emissary from William Bedloe [q. v. : to Chief-justice North previous to the latter's receiving Bedloe's dying deposition, and it is apropos of this that Roger North sums him up as 'the most perverse, clamorous old party man in the whole city or nation' (Examen, p. 253). Knight represented Bristol during the parliaments of 1661, 1678, and 1679, and was highly indignant at not being re-elected in 1681. He died in 1683, and was buried in the Temple Church, Bristol. By his wife Martha, daughter of Thomas Cole, esq., of Bristol, he left three sons and eight daughters.

[Le Neve's Knights, p. 175; Barrett's Bristol, p. 695; Seyer's Memoirs, ii. 543; Evans's Chronological Hist. p. 215; Garrard's Life and Times of Edward Colston, pp. 278, &c.]   T. S.

KNIGHT, Sir JOHN, 'the younger' (d. 1718), Jacobite, is supposed to have been a kinsman of his namesake, Sir John the elder [q. v.] He was a native of Bristol, and was sheriff of that city in 1681, when he rivalled his relative in his zeal against the dissenters. He was rewarded by being knighted during March 1682. A prosperous merchant, like his kinsman, Knight henceforth took an equally prominent part in the town's affairs, and the politics of the two men being very similar their identity has been inextricably confused. Macaulay seems to have confused them, and Garrard, in his 'Life of Edward Colston,' is undoubtedly wrong in attributing to Sir John the elder (who was dead at that time) the information given against a popish priest about which Sunderland speaks with irritation in a letter to the Duke of Beaufort dated May 1686. It appears from local records that on 25 April in this year Sir John 'the younger' seized eight or ten papists and their priest who were intending to celebrate mass in a house on St. Michael's Hill, and sent them to Newgate. Knight's anti-papist zeal was doubtless the real cause of his committal to the King's Bench prison in 1686, though the ostensible charge was that he had been in the habit of 'going with a blunderbuss in the streets to the terrifyeing of his majesty's subjects.' Elected a member of the convention in 1689 and mayor of Bristol in 1690, he signalised his tenure of the latter office by fostering a demonstration against the judges of assize and refusing to entertain them during their visit to the town (Hist. MSS. Comm. 5th

Rep. pt. ii. App. p. 382; LUTTRELL, *Diary*, September 1691). In the following year Knight was chosen to represent the city in parliament. The only occasion on which he took a prominent part in the house was in 1694, when, speaking with ability, though with great virulence, against the proposal for naturalising foreign protestants in England, he wound up a violent tirade with a proposal 'that the serjeant be commanded to open the doors, and let us first kick the Bill out of the house, and then all foreigners out of the kingdom.' The speech was shortly afterwards printed with a preface in which it was said that 'if other corporations and shires would take the like care as Bristol, they might be happy in their representatives; and then, and never till then, may we hope to see poor England become Old England again, rich and happy at home, glorious and renowned abroad.' The speech produced an extraordinary effect, and although, in deference to the indignation of the house, which ordered a copy of the printed speech to be burnt, Knight thought proper to disclaim any connection with the publication, his persecution, as it was considered, only served to render him more popular. 'The people,' says Macpherson, 'were inflamed to a degree of madness; as for Sir John Knight, he was discoursed of as a saviour, and in a manner adored, for having made so noble a stand in behalf of his country.' The government had to drop the bill. Hazlitt includes Knight's speech against the Dutch in his 'British Eloquence' (i. 226), and admits a preference for the speaker's 'downright passion, unconquerable prejudice, and unaffected enthusiasm over the studied eloquence of modern invective.'

At the very time that he delivered this speech, however, Knight was in correspondence with St. Germains, and engaged in a scheme for restoring James by the aid of French arms. On 18 March 1696, after the discovery of the assassination plot, he was arrested as a suspected Jacobite, but no definite charge being brought against him, he was bailed on 30 June, and set at liberty on 5 Sept. following. Having lost his seat at Bristol in the previous year, Knight henceforth lived in obscurity. Falling into poverty he gave much offence in Bristol by threatening to sue the corporation for his 'wages as a Parliament man,' but finally retired to Congresbury in Somerset, where he had a small estate. In October 1713 his daughter, Anne, set forth her 'deplorable estate' in a petition to the town council, and was granted 20*l.* In December 1717 Sir John himself made a similar appeal, asserting that he was reduced to great necessity and want by the unnatural treatment of his son, and praying for charitable assistance. Only 20*l.* was voted. The Merchants' Company had a few weeks previously granted Sir John an annuity of 20*l.*, but he did not live to enjoy it. He died at an advanced age in the following February 1718 (*Hist. Reg.* ii. 6). Macaulay calls Knight a 'coarse-minded and spiteful Jacobite,' and speaks of 'his impudent and savage nature.' There is, however, no specific evidence in support of these charges. His brother-Jacobite, Roger North, contrasts him with his kinsman, Sir John the elder, and describes him as 'a gentleman of as eminent integrity and loyalty as ever the city of Bristol was honoured with' (*Examen,* p. 253).

A third JOHN KNIGHT (*fl.* 1670), also of Bristol, was apparently no relation of his namesakes. He was at first in opposition to the dominant or royalist party in Bristol, and was in 1663 fined 400*l.* for refusing to become a member of the common council on election. He shortly afterwards became a convert to royalist views, and was elected mayor of Bristol in 1670, but his conversion did not prevent him from being denounced as a fanatic by Sir John Knight 'the elder' in the same year. He was summoned to London, and appeared before the privy council, but was cleared of all charges brought against him, returned home without delay, and 'was honourably brought into Bristoll with 235 horse.'

[Garrard's Edward Colston, passim; Parl. Hist. v. 850; Addit. MS. 5540, ff. 8, 27; Somers Tracts, iv. 272; Luttrell's Diary, passim; Macpherson's History, ii. 52; Macaulay's History; information kindly supplied by Mr. William George, Bristol; authorities cited for Sir John Knight the elder; J. Latimer's Annals of Bristol in the Eighteenth Century, in course of publication in the Bristol Mercury.] T. S.

KNIGHT, Sir JOHN (1748?–1831), admiral, son of Rear-admiral John Knight (*d.* 1788), was born at Dundee about 1748. He entered the navy in 1758, on board the Tartar frigate, commanded by his father, in the expedition against St. Malo and Cherbourg under Lord Howe. After the peace of 1763 he served in the Romney, carrying the flag of Lord Colville as commander-in-chief on the coast of North America. He was promoted to be lieutenant on 25 May 1770, and in 1775 went out to North America as second lieutenant of the Falcon sloop with Captain John Linzee, arriving there three days before the skirmish at Lexington. The Falcon was one of the vessels that covered the attack on Bunker's Hill. In the early part of the following year, in attempting to destroy a schooner which had been driven on shore in Cape Ann harbour, Knight was taken prisoner. He was exchanged in December 1776, and was appointed by Howe to command the Haerlem hired ship, in which he was actively employed against the enemy's coasting trade. He was afterwards ordered to join the flagship, and in her he returned to England, October 1778. In 1780 he was appointed to the Barfleur, going out to the West Indies with the flag of Sir Samuel (afterwards Lord) Hood [q. v.], and was first lieutenant of her in the action off Martinique on 29 April, and off Cape Henry on 5 Sept. 1781. On the 21st he was posted to the command of the Shrewsbury, from which in the following January he was moved back to the Barfleur as flag-captain, and commanded her in the engagements at St. Kitts, in the skirmish of 9 April, and in the battle of Dominica on 12 April 1782. In 1787–8 he was again captain of the Barfleur with Hood at Portsmouth, and in 1793, when Hood went out as commander-in-chief in the Mediterranean, Knight was flag-captain on board the Victory. In 1794 he returned to England with Hood; but on his going back to the Mediterranean, Rear-admiral Mann hoisted his flag on board the Victory, in the action of 13 July 1795. Knight shortly afterwards went home overland, and was appointed to the Montagu in the fleet under Admiral Duncan in the North Sea.

On the outbreak of the mutiny the Montagu was taken by her crew to the Nore, where her surgeon was tarred and feathered, rowed through the fleet, and afterwards put on shore with some other obnoxious officers. When the mutiny was quelled the Montagu rejoined Duncan, and took a distinguished part in the battle of Camperdown. In 1798 Knight commanded a detached squadron on the coast of Ireland, and in 1799–1800 took part in the blockade of Brest. On 1 Jan. 1801 he was promoted to be rear-admiral, and in the summer of 1805 succeeded Sir Richard Bickerton at Gibraltar. He became vice-admiral on 9 Nov. 1805, admiral on 4 Dec. 1813, and was made a K.C.B. on 2 Jan. 1815.

Knight died on 16 June 1831. He was twice married, and had a large family. Knight Island, to the south-east of New Zealand, in lat. 48° S., long. 166° 44′ E., was named after him by Captain W. R. Broughton [q. v.], who, as a midshipman of the Falcon, was a fellow-prisoner in America in 1776.

[Ralfe's Naval Biog. ii. 352; Marshall's Roy. Nav. Biog. i. 154; Naval Chron. (with a portrait), xi. 425.] J. K. L.

VOL. XXXI.

KNIGHT, JOHN BAVERSTOCK (1785–1859), painter, born at the parsonage, Langton, near Blandford, Dorset, on 3 May 1785, was second son of John Forster Knight, land-agent, and Sophia his wife. He was educated at home and in a commercial school at Child Okeford. He became assistant to his father as land surveyor and agent, but from a love of art, which his father encouraged, took to water-colour painting. His careful studies from nature brought him much local reputation, and he exhibited one or two architectural subjects at the Royal Academy. In 1816 he published some etchings of old buildings in Dorset, one of which, a view of Bradford Abbas Church, was published in the 'Gentleman's Magazine' for 1818. After the death of his father and his own marriage, the care of his mother and younger brother devolved on Knight, and this, coupled with increasing bad health, led him to abandon art as a profession. He died at West Lodge, Piddle Hinton, Dorset, on 14 May 1859. His works were favourably noticed by Henry Fuseli, Sir Thomas Lawrence, and other competent authorities. A neighbour and intimate friend of Knight's was Thomas Rackett [q. v.] the antiquary, rector of Spetisbury, Dorset.

[Gent. Mag. 3rd ser. 1859, vii. 310; Graves's Dict. of Artists, 1760–1880.] L. C.

KNIGHT, JOHN PRESCOTT (1803–1881), portrait-painter, son of Edward Knight [q. v.] the comedian, was born at Stafford in 1803. He began life in the office of a West India merchant in Mark Lane, London, who soon afterwards failed. He then took to drawing, according to his own statement, out of sheer idleness, and after a time his father, who had artistic tastes, consented to place him for six months with Henry Sass to correct his drawing, and for another six months with George Clint to improve his colouring. In 1823 he became a student of the Royal Academy, and in 1824 he contributed to its exhibition portraits of his father and of Alfred Bunn [q. v.], the manager of Drury Lane Theatre. The death of his father in 1826 left him early to depend on his own exertions, and for some time he continued to paint theatrical portraits, although sometimes producing pictures of a more fanciful character. His first appearance at the British Institution was in 1828, when he sent 'The Whist Party' and 'List, ye landsmen all, to me!' These were followed in 1829 by 'Auld Robin Gray;' in 1830 by 'Smugglers alarmed;' in 1831 by 'The Auld Friends' and 'The Pedlar;' in 1832 by 'A Bit of Courtship' and another 'Auld Robin Gray;' in 1833 by 'The Spanish Refugees' and 'John Anderson, my Jo,' and in 1834 by 'Sunset.' In 1835 he exhibited at the Royal Academy 'Tam o' Shanter,' in 1836 'The Wreckers,' in 1837 'The English Harvest,' in 1838 'The Saint's Day,' engraved by William Chevalier for the Art Union of London, and in 1839 'The Broken Heart.' Having been elected an associate of the Royal Academy in 1836, he was in 1839 appointed to the professorship of perspective, which he held until 1860, to the great advantage of the students. About 1840 he resumed portrait-painting and obtained much success, especially with his male sitters. The 'Heroes of Waterloo,' better known as the 'Waterloo Banquet,' in the possession of the Duke of Wellington, was exhibited in 1842, and engraved by Charles G. Lewis. In 1843 appeared 'John Knox endeavouring to restrain the violence of the people at Perth.' Knight became a royal academician in 1844, and in 1848 was elected secretary, after acting in that capacity for a year previously as deputy of Henry Howard (1769–1847) [q. v.]. This office he retained until 1873, and discharged its often irksome duties with much tact and ability. In 1848 also he exhibited the 'Peninsular Heroes,' which has been engraved by Frederick Bromley. Many of his works were presentation portraits, among them being those of James Walker, for the Institution of Civil Engineers; Arthur, duke of Wellington, for the City of London Club; Sir James Duke, bart., for the town-hall of Montrose; Sir Samuel Bignold, for St. Andrew's Hall, Norwich; Sir George Burrows, bart., for St. Bartholomew's Hospital; John Crossley, for the town-hall, Halifax; the Duke of Cambridge, for Christ's Hospital; and Sir Charles Lock Eastlake, P.R.A., presented by the painter to the Royal Academy. His sitters were very numerous, and some of his portraits have been engraved. He exhibited last in 1878, in which year he was nominated a knight of the Legion of Honour.

Knight died at 24 Maida Hill West, London, on 26 March 1881, and was buried in Kensal Green cemetery. He was an ardent follower of Edward Irving, and held high office in the catholic apostolic church. His wife, who died before him, exhibited at the British Institution and elsewhere between 1832 and 1837 a few pictures of domestic subjects.

[Art Journal, 1849 p. 200 (autobiographical sketch, with portrait), 1881 p. 159; Times, 30 March 1881; Illustrated London News, 9 April 1881, with portrait; Athenæum, 1881, i. 466; Bryan's Dict. of Painters and Engravers,

ed. Graves, 1886–9, i. 738; Sandby's History of the Royal Academy of Arts, 1862, ii. 174; Royal Academy Exhibition Catalogues, 1824–1878; Exhibition Catalogues of the British Institution (Living Artists) and Society of British Artists.]   R. E. G.

KNIGHT, JOSEPH PHILIP (1812–1887), composer of songs, was the youngest son of Francis Knight, D.D., vicar of Bradford-on-Avon, Wiltshire, where he was born 26 July 1812. He studied music under John Davis Corfe, organist of Bristol Cathedral, and began composing at the age of twenty, when he published a set of six songs under the name of 'Philip Mortimer' (1832). Among these were 'Old Times,' sung by Henry Phillips, and 'Go, forget me,' which became popular both here and in Germany. Under his own name, and in collaboration with Haynes Bayly, he subsequently produced very many songs, the most notable of which were 'The Veteran' and 'She wore a wreath of roses.' After these came, among other productions, a song, 'The Parting,' and a duet, 'Let's take this world as some wide scene,' words of both by Thomas Moore. In 1839 Knight visited America, and there composed his famous song 'Rocked in the cradle of the deep,' which will always be associated with Braham. On his return to England in 1841 he produced 'Beautiful Venice,' 'Say, what shall my song be to-night?' and 'The Dream,' words by the Hon. Mrs. Norton. Some years afterwards he took holy orders, and was appointed to the charge of St. Agnes in the Scilly Isles, where he remained for two years. He then married, and went to reside abroad, but finally returned to England and resumed composition. His death took place at Yarmouth, Norfolk, 1 June 1887. Knight's songs, duets, and trios number in all about two hundred. Many of these have enjoyed great popularity, but only 'She wore a wreath of roses' and 'Rocked in the cradle of the deep' seem likely to hold their ground. As a composer he had a remarkable command of pure English melody. He was an excellent organist, and was exceptionally skilful in extemporising.

[Grove's Dict. of Music; Brown's Dict. of Musicians.]   J. C. H.

KNIGHT, MARY ANNE (1776–1831), miniature-painter, born in 1776, was a pupil of Andrew Plimer [q. v.], and was a skilful painter of miniatures in his manner. She first exhibited at the Royal Academy in 1807, and continued to exhibit occasionally up to the date of her death. She resided for some years at 51 Berners Street, and latterly in

Grove End Road, St. John's Wood, London, where she died unmarried in 1831.

[Redgrave's Dict. of Artists : Graves's Dict. of Artists, 1760–1880 ; Bryan's Dict. of Painters and Engravers, ed. Graves.]   L. C.

KNIGHT, RICHARD PAYNE (1750–1824), numismatist, born in 1750, was the eldest son of the Rev. Thomas Knight (1697–1764) of Wormesley Grange, Herefordshire, rector of Bewdley and Ribbesford, Worcestershire, by his wife, Ursula Nash. Thomas Andrew Knight [q. v.], F.R.S., was his younger brother. Knight was called Payne after his grandmother, Elizabeth, daughter of Andrew Payne, and wife of Richard Knight (1659–1745), the founder of the Knight family, who acquired great wealth by the ironworks of Shropshire, and settled at Downton, Herefordshire. Richard Payne Knight being of weakly constitution as a boy was not sent to school till he was fourteen, and did not begin to learn Greek till he was seventeen. He was not at any university. About 1767 he went to Italy, and remained abroad several years.

Knight again visited Italy in 1777, and from April to June of that year was in Sicily in company with Philipp Hackert, the German painter, and Charles Gore. Knight kept a journal, which, under the title of 'Tagebuch einer Reise nach Sicilien,' was translated and published by Goethe in his biography of Hackert (GOETHE, *Werke*, xxxvii. 1850, pp. 146–218, cf. *Notes and Queries*, 4th ser. iii. 473). In 1785 he again travelled southwards, and in that year laid the foundation of his fine collection of bronzes by the purchase of an antique head ('Diomede') from Thomas Jenkins, the dealer at Rome (*Spec. Ant. Sculpt.* i. pl. 20, 21). When in Italy Knight spent much time at Naples, where his friend Sir William Hamilton (1730–1803) [q. v.] was the British envoy. About 1764 Knight had inherited the estates at Downton, Herefordshire. He ornamented the grounds, and there erected from his own designs (severely criticised by BURTON, 'Toddington,' 1840, 4to, p. 21) a stone mansion in castellated style. A view is given in Neale's 'Seats' (1826, 2nd ser. vol. iii., 'Downton Castle;' cf. *Dict. of Architecture*, Architect. Publ. Soc., s.v. 'Knight, R. P.') Knight invited Lord Nelson and Lady Hamilton to Downton Castle in 1802 (DUNCUMB and COOKE, *Hereford*, iii. 170). In London, he had a house in Soho Square (WALFORD, *Old and New London*, iv. 500), and used one of the large rooms as his museum. In 1780 he became M.P. for Leominster, and from 1784 to 1806 sat for Ludlow. In the House

of Commons he acted with Fox, but took no part in debate.

Knight's first published work was 'An Account of the Remains of the Worship of Priapus lately existing in Isernia; to which is added a Discourse on the Worship of Priapus, and its Connexion with the Mystic Theology of the Ancients,' 1786, 4to. The book was severely attacked by Mathias in the 'Pursuits of Literature' (Dial. i.), and Knight endeavoured to buy up the copies of his offending publication (cf. ALLIBONE, *Dict. of Engl. Lit.* art. 'Knight, R. P.') Professor Michaelis (*Anc. Marbles*, p. 122) says that the book is blameworthy, apart from the unpleasantness of its subject, for its adoption of the mythological fantasies of D'Hancarville, whose acquaintance Knight had made in 1784 at the house of Charles Townley. In 1791 Knight published 'An Analytical Essay on the Greek Alphabet,' London, 4to, with nine plates, reviewed by Porson in the 'Monthly Review' for 1794. Knight was the first to question in this work the genuineness of the Greek inscriptions stated to have been found by Fourmont in Laconia (BOECKH, *Corpus Inscr. Gr.* i. 61–104). He was the first to edit the 'Elean Inscription' (*ib.* No. 11). In 1808 he printed privately fifty copies (London, 8vo) of his 'Carmina Homerica, Ilias et Odyssea.' This consists of Prolegomena, the text being added in the later edition of 1820, 8vo. His object was to restore the text to its supposed original condition, and he introduced the digamma and various early forms. Knight printed privately 'An Inquiry into the Symbolical Language of Ancient Art and Mythology' (London, 8vo, reprinted in 'Classical Museum,' pp. xxiii–xxvii, and in 'Specimens of Ant. Sculpt.,' vol. ii.; new ed. by A. Wilder, New York, 1876). Knight also wrote for the 'Classical Museum,' the 'Philological Museum,' and in the 'Archæologia,' and contributed to the 'Edinburgh Review' (August 1810) an article on Barry, and a severe critique (July 1809) of Falconer's 'Strabo,' a publication of the Clarendon press. Copleston of Oriel defended the Oxford press and Oxford scholarship in a 'Reply' (Oxford, 1810), and a controversy ensued (see the joint article in *Edinb. Rev.* April 1810, pp. 158–87, by Sidney Smith, Playfair, and Knight, who wrote pp. 169–77). Knight was also the author of two didactic poems: 'The Landscape' (London, 1794, 8vo; 2nd edit. 1795), a protest against the gardening methods of Brown and Mason; and 'The Progress of Civil Society' (London, 1796, 8vo), written in a quasi-Lucretian vein, which was parodied in the 'Anti-Jacobin.' Knight's bad poetry and sceptical principles

s 2

were attacked by Walpole (*Letters*, ix. 462, '22 March 1796') and by Mathias (*Pursuits of Lit.*)

As a connoisseur and authority on ancient art Knight's reputation stood very high. A 'Quarterly Reviewer' described him (xiv. 533 f.) as 'the arbiter of fashionable virtu.' In 1808 he published two editions of 'An Analytical Inquiry into the Principles of Taste' (London, 8vo; 4th edit. 1808; noticed by Jeffrey, *Edinb. Rev.* May 1811, and censured by Professor Wilson, *Essays*, 1856, iv. 102). In 1781 he had joined the Dilettanti Society, and with his friend Charles Townley suggested to it the publication of 'Specimens of Antient Sculpture selected from several Collections in Great Britain,' vol. i. London, 1809, fol. Twenty-three specimens from Knight's own collection were included in the book, and Knight wrote the text, consisting of concise descriptions and a fairly creditable introduction on the history of ancient art. He was one of the contributors to the second volume of the 'Specimens,' edited by W. S. Morritt. Unlike the other dilettanti of the time, Knight cared little for ancient marbles, and his collection included only a few specimens. He chiefly appreciated bronzes, coins, and gems. He told Lord Elgin at a dinner-party that he had 'lost his labour' in bringing over the Parthenon marbles (HAYDON, *Life*, i. 272), some of which Knight supposed to be Roman, 'of the age of Adrian.' Knight gave evidence in 1816, before a select committee of the House of Commons, against the national acquisition of these monuments, which he said he 'had looked over.' The contrary evidence of Haydon was dispensed with, 'out of delicacy to Mr. Payne Knight.' Knight's evidence was severely commented on in the 'Quarterly Review' (xiv. 533 f.), and Knight himself issued a supplementary 'Explanation' of it. He valued the Elgin collection—including coins estimated by him at 1,000*l*.—at 25,000*l*. (ELLIS, *Elgin Marbles*, i. 8). In 1814 Knight had written to the 'Morning Chronicle' approving the national purchase of the Phigaleian marbles. As a collector of small antiques Knight had good taste and good luck. He used to speak of his 'jewels in bronze,' and his collection of bronzes far surpassed any other. Walpole sneered at the 'Knight of the Brazen Milk-pot.' Many of Knight's bronzes had belonged to the Duc de Chaulnes, who died at the beginning of the French revolution. Knight sent an agent as far as Russia to hunt up the bronzes from the Paramythia find, one specimen of which had reached England. His collection of Greek coins was no less

remarkable, and was especially rich in the money of Sicily and Magna Graecia, beautiful series which he had the good taste to appreciate (cf. Knight's article on Syracusan coins in the *Archæologia*, xix. 374 f.) He also collected some good gems, though he purchased as an antique, for 250*l*., from Bonelli, a cameo of Flora (now in the British Museum) which had been made by Pistrucci (*Quart. Rev.* xix. 539). Knight was vice-president of the Society of Antiquaries, and a member of the Eumelean Club, a literary society which met at Blenheim Tavern in Bond Street, London (NICHOLS, *Lit. Anecd.* ii. 638). The Latin inscription on the monument erected in 1813 to Sir Joshua Reynolds in St. Paul's Cathedral was written by Knight (LESLIE, *Reynolds*, ii. 637). Knight died at his house in Soho Square, London, on 23 April 1824, of 'an apoplectic affection' (*Gent. Mag.* 1824, pt. ii. p. 185). He was buried in Wormesley Church, Herefordshire, where there is a monument to him, with a Latin epitaph by Cornewall, bishop of Worcester. His Downton estate passed to his brother, Thomas Andrew Knight. He made to the British Museum, of which he had been Townley trustee since 1814, the munificent bequest of his bronzes, coins, gems, marbles, and drawings. The collection was valued at the time at sums varying from 30,000*l*. to 60,000*l*. The acquisition of the bronzes and coins immensely strengthened the national collection. The trustees of the British Museum printed and published in 1830 (London, 4to) Knight's own manuscript catalogue of the coins, with the title 'Nummi Veteres.' It consists of brief descriptions in Latin and of a few notes. Knight's manuscript catalogue of his gems, 'Sigilla antiqua,' is now in the department of Greek and Roman antiquities at the museum. The drawings—273 works by Claude —had been purchased by Knight for 16,000*l*. (FAGAN, *Handbook to Dept. of Prints*, p. 133; *Gent. Mag.* 1824, pt. ii. p. 104). The sole condition of the bequest was the appointment of a perpetual 'Knight family trustee.' This was arranged by a bill passed on 17 June 1824. A portrait of Knight was painted by Sir Thomas Lawrence in March 1792, and is now the property of the Dilettanti Society, to which it was presented by Knight in 1805 (*Account of the Portraits of the Dilettanti Soc.* 1885, p. 5, No. 27). He is described (*Gent. Mag.*) as reserved in his manners, though he was hospitable, and ready to give information on artistic subjects. When at Downton he passed a country gentleman's life, and was a good landlord. He was an insatiable reader, reading, it is said, for 'ten hours at a stretch.'

[Burke's Landed Gentry, s.v. 'Knight of Wormesley;' Penny Cyclopædia, 'Knight, R. P.;' Edwards's Lives of the Founders of the Brit. Mus. pp. 389, 401-12, 460; Michaelis's Ancient Marbles in Great Britain; Brit. Mus. Cat., and authorities cited in the article.]   W. W.

KNIGHT, SAMUEL, D.D. (1675-1746), biographer, born in 1675 in London (where his father was free of the Mercers' Company), received his education at St. Paul's School, where he was elected Paulin exhibitioner in 1696, and proceeded to Trinity College, Cambridge. He graduated B.A. in 1702 and M.A. in 1706. After taking holy orders he became chaplain to Edward, earl of Orford, who presented him to the vicarage of Chippenham, Cambridgeshire, and also to the rectory of Burrough Green in the same county (3 Nov. 1707). Afterwards he was collated by Bishop Moore to the seventh prebendal stall in the church of Ely, 8 June 1714, and was presented by him to the rectory of Bluntisham, Huntingdonshire, 22 June 1717. He became a fellow and one of the founders of the Society of Antiquaries in 1717, and he was also a member of the Gentlemen's Society at Spalding. In 1717 he was created D.D. at Cambridge. In 1727 he erected in Northwold Church, Norfolk, a monument to the memory of Dr. Robert Burhill [q. v.], a great antagonist of the Roman catholics (Addit. MS. 5847, pp. 147, 148). He was appointed chaplain to George II in February 1730-1. On 5 March 1734-5 he was collated by Bishop Sherlock to the archdeaconry of Berkshire; and in 1742 he was installed in the prebend of Leighton Ecclesia in the church of Lincoln. He died on 10 Dec. 1746, and was buried in the chancel of Bluntisham Church, where a monument of white marble was erected to his memory, with a Latin inscription composed by his friend Edmund Castle, dean of Hereford. According to William Cole (MS. xxx. f. 118) Knight was a very black and thin man, and had much the look of a Frenchman. The same authority says that he had been brought up a dissenter, which may account for his strong protestant bias.

He married in 1717 Hannah, daughter of Talbot Pepys, esq., of Impington, Cambridgeshire. She died on 14 April 1719, soon after the birth of their only child Samuel, who became a fellow of Trinity College, Cambridge, and who, with the ample fortune bequeathed to him by his father, purchased the manor of Milton, near Cambridge.

In addition to some single sermons he published: 1. 'The Life of Dr. John Colet, Dean of St. Paul's . . . and Founder of St. Paul's School: with an Appendix containing some account of the more eminent scholars of that

foundation, and several original papers relating to the said Life,' London, 1724, 8vo, dedicated to Spencer Compton, speaker of the House of Commons. Knight's draft of this work, which is largely founded on the collections of White Kennett [q. v.], is now in the Cambridge University Library. There is an index in the 'Life of Erasmus.' A second edition appeared in 1823. 2. 'The Life of Erasmus, more particularly that part of it which he spent in England; wherein an account is given of his learned friends, and the State of Religion and Learning at that time in both our Universities. With an Appendix containing several original papers,' Cambridge, 1726, 8vo, dedicated to Sir Spencer Compton. Both biographies are illustrated with portraits and other fine engravings by Vertue, and were published in German translations by Theodore Arnold at Leipzig in 1735 and 1736 respectively. Manuscript lives by Knight of Symon Patrick, bishop of Ely, and of John Strype, are in the University Library, Cambridge. His collections for the lives of Bishops Grossetete and Overall seem to be lost (PECK, Desiderata Curiosa, Pref. p. v).

[Addit. MSS. 5853 (index), 5874 f. 23, 32556 f. 116, 32699 f. 343, 32700 f. 72; Archæologia, vol. i. Introd. p. xxxvi; Bentham's Ely, i. 263; Blomefield's Norfolk, ii. 218; Charity Reports, xxxi. 131; Cooke's Preacher's Assistant, ii. 204; Dibdin's Library Companion, ii. 117; Faulkner's Fulham, p. 42; Gent. Mag. vol. lx. pt. i. pp. 85, 177; Reliquiæ Hearnianæ, ii. 647; Jortin's Life of Erasmus, pp. 530, 587, 617; Nichols's Lit. Anecd. vii. 218, x. 610, and Illustrations, ii. 414 (containing a contemptuous account of Knight by Warburton); Peck's Desiderata Curiosa, Pref. pp. xiv, xvii, 232; Secretan's Life of Nelson; Stacy's Norfolk, ii. 692; Sale Cat. of Dawson Turner's Library, p. 114; Ward's Hist. of Gresham College, p. i; Warton's Essay on the Genius and Writings of Pope, p. 184; Wilford's Memorials, p. 407.]   T. C.

KNIGHT, SAMUEL (1759-1827), vicar of Halifax, where he was born on 9 March 1759, was son of Titus Knight by a second marriage. His father, an independent minister at Halifax, came under Lady Huntingdon's influence in 1762, became minister of a methodist chapel in 1763, and for two months yearly assisted Whitefield at Tottenham Court Chapel and elsewhere. He died 2 March 1793 (see Life of Lady Huntingdon, ii. 285-7). The son, after attending Hipperholme grammar school, entered Magdalene College, Cambridge, as a sizar in 1779, graduated B.A. as seventh wrangler in 1783, and was elected fellow. In April 1783 he was appointed curate of Wintringham,

Lincolnshire, and took pupils. He proceeded M.A. in 1786. In 1794 he was presented to the vicarage of Humberstone, Lincolnshire, but continued to reside at Wintringham, where he received pupils into his house, and became also curate of Roxby, a neighbouring village. In 1798 he obtained the perpetual curacy of Holy Trinity, Halifax, being the first to fill that office, and removed thither with his pupils. In December 1817 he was instituted to the vicarage of Halifax. He died on 7 Jan. 1827. Knight was author of: 1. 'Forms of Prayer,' 12mo, York, 1791, which passed through sixteen editions during his lifetime. 2. 'On Confirmation,' 12mo, York, 1800 (four editions). His 'Sermons and Miscellaneous Works,' 2 vols. 8vo, Halifax, 1828, were edited by his son James (see below), with a memoir by another son, the Rev. William Knight. Prefixed is his portrait, engraved by W. T. Fry.

The son, JAMES KNIGHT (1793–1863), was scholar of Lincoln College, Oxford, from 1812 to 1815, graduated B.A. 1814, and proceeded M.A. 1817. He was appointed perpetual curate of St. Paul's Church, Sheffield, in 1824, and resigned the living in 1820. He died at Burton-on-Humber 30 Aug. 1863. He wrote: 1. 'Discourses on the principal Parables of Our Lord,' 1829. 2. 'Discourses on the principal Miracles of Our Lord,' 1831. 3. 'Discourses on the Lord's Prayer,' 1832. 4. 'A Concise Treatise on the Truth and Importance of the Christian Religion.'

[Memoir referred to; Gent. Mag. 1827 i. 282, 1863 ii. 515, 660; Darling's Cycl. Bibl. 1711; Foster's Alumni Oxon.] G. G.

KNIGHT, THOMAS (d. 1820), actor and dramatist, was born in Dorset of a family of more consideration than means. He was intended for the bar, and received from Charles Macklin (q. v.) the actor lessons in elocution. A favourite with Macklin, he accompanied him to the theatre, acquiring in his visits tastes which led him to adopt the stage as a profession. At an unrecorded date he appeared at the Richmond Theatre in Charles Surface, and failed conspicuously. He then joined Austin's company at Lancaster. Before leaving London he tried vainly to force upon Macklin a remuneration for his services as a teacher. Tate Wilkinson saw Knight, it is said, in Edinburgh, and engaged him for the York circuit. His first appearance was made in York in 1782 as Lothario to the Calista of Mrs. Jordan. Wilkinson, who was greatly disappointed with him, advised him to quit the stage, but Knight struggled on, playing Charles Oakley, Spatterdash in the 'Young Quaker,' Carbine in the 'Fair

American,' &c., and gradually grew in public favour. Wilkinson generously acknowledged the error of his former judgment, and during the five years in which Knight remained with the company he took the lead, and had only one quarrel with the management. Finding his name as Twineall in 'Such things are' put third on the list, the customary place for the character, he insisted on its place being first, and being refused did not appear. On 27 Oct. 1787 he played at the Bath Theatre as the Copper Captain. Spatterdash, Ramilie in the 'Miser,' Duke of Monmouth in 'Such things were,' and Marquis in the 'Midnight Hour' followed.

In 1787 Knight married at Bath Margaret Farren, sister of the Countess of Derby [see FARREN, ELIZABETH]. She had been seen at an early age in London, having played at the Haymarket, as Miss Peggy Farren, Titania in the 'Fairy Tale,' a two-act adaptation of the 'Midsummer Night's Dream,' 18 June 1777. She joined Wilkinson in 1782; left him to act in Scotland and Ireland; and rejoined him in 1786. In that year she played with Knight in York, where she was a favourite, and followed him by arrangement to Bath for their wedding. Soon afterwards she made her first appearance there as Miss Peggy in the 'Country Girl' to her husband's Sparkish. In the course of the same season Knight acted thirty characters, among which Touchstone, Trappanti, Claudio in 'Measure for Measure,' Trim in the 'Funeral,' Sir Charles Racket, and Pendragon may be mentioned. In Bath, as at Bristol, which was under the same management, he played during the nine years of his engagement an endless variety of comic parts—Charles Surface, Antonio in 'Follies of a Day,' Clown in 'All's well that ends well,' Mercutio, Duretête, Goldfinch, Dromio of Ephesus, Pistol, and Autolycus being among the most easily recognisable.

Knight's first appearance at Covent Garden took place on 25 Sept. 1795 as Jacob in the 'Chapter of Accidents' (when his wife played Bridget) and Skirmish in the 'Deserter.' Knight was seen in an endless number of parts at Covent Garden. The most important are Sim in 'Wild Oats,' Hodge, Bob Acres, Slender in 'Merry Wives of Windsor,' Roderigo, Gratiano, Dick Dowlas, Sir Benjamin Backbite, Tony Lumpkin, Sergeant Kite in the 'Recruiting Officer,' Sir Andrew Aguecheek, Touchstone, and Lucio in 'Measure for Measure.' His original parts included Young Testy in Holman's 'Abroad and at Home,' Count Cassel in Mrs. Inchbald's adaptation, 'Lovers' Vows,' Changeable in Thomas Dibdin's 'Jew and the Doctor,' Farmer Ashfield in Morton's 'Speed the 'Plough,' and Corporal Foss in the 'Poor Gentleman.' After acting with his wife for three years at Covent Garden, they went together to Edinburgh, where she played on 2 July 1799 Aura in the 'Farm House,' and he made what was called, probably in error, his first appearance in Edinburgh as Sir Harry Beagle in the 'Jealous Wife.' Mrs. Knight afterwards played at Newcastle and elsewhere, returned to Bath, where she was welcomed, and died there in 1804.

With Fawcett, Holman, Johnstone, Pope, H. Johnston, Munden, and Incledon, Knight signed the well-known statement of the 'Differences subsisting between the Proprietors and Performers of Covent Garden,' London, 1800, 8vo (3rd edit.) The lease of the Liverpool Theatre having come into the market, the house was taken by Knight in partnership with Lewis for fourteen years, at a rent elevated from 300l. to 1,500l., and was opened 6 June 1803 with 'Speed the Plough' and 'No Song, no Supper,' and an address by T. Dibdin, spoken by Knight. During this season Knight remained at Covent Garden, where his last performance took place for his benefit, 15 May 1804, as Farmer Ashfield in 'Speed the Plough,' and, for the first time, Lenitive in the 'Prize.' He also spoke an address. In 1802 he was living at 10 Tavistock Street, Covent Garden. While managing the Liverpool Theatre he lived first at Norton Hall, Lichfield, and subsequently at Woore, Shropshire. In 1817 a new lease was granted to Knight, Thomas Lewis, a son of his late partner, and Banks, with whom Knight became associated in the management of the Manchester Theatre. At the Manor House, Woore, 4 Feb. 1820, Knight died with 'appalling suddenness.'

Knight wrote many pieces himself. His 'Thelyphthora, or the Blessings of two Wives at once,' a farce, was acted at Hull in 1783, but neither printed nor apparently brought to London; 'Trudge and Wowski,' a prelude, supposedly from 'Inkle and Yarico,' was acted by Knight for his benefit in Bristol 1790, and 'Honest Thieves,' a two-act abridgment of the 'Committee' of Sir Robert Howard, was produced at Covent Garden with Knight as Abel, 9 May 1797. On 14 Nov. 1799 he appeared at Covent Garden as Robert Maythorn in his own 'Turnpike Gate.' This farce was printed in 8vo, 1799, was well received, went through five editions in two years, and kept possession of the stage. Munden made in it as Crack a noteworthy success. Knight's 'Turnpike Gate' and the 'Honest Thieves' are included in collections of acting plays by Oxberry, Cumberland, Mrs. Inchbald, &c. The anonymous author of the 'Managers' Note-book,' which appeared in the 'New Monthly Magazine,' attributes to Knight the 'Masked Friend,' an anonymous and unprinted reduction to three acts of Holcroft's 'Duplicity,' given at Covent Garden for the benefit of Mr. and Mrs. Knight, 6 May 1798, with the former as Squire Turnbull and the latter as Miss Turnbull, and 'Hints for Painters,' an unprinted farce, given on the same occasion; also 'What would the Man be at?' a one-act piece, unprinted, in which, for his benefit, he played Charles, George, and Will Belford, three brothers. Knight also wrote an 'Ode on the late Naval War and the Siege of Gibraltar,' Hull, 4to, 1784, and some comic songs or recitations.

Knight was an admirable actor, and a worthy man. Though living in good style, and consorting with men of science and letters, he realised an independence, which was augmented by a legacy from an uncle. His repertory was not unlike that of his namesake Edward Knight [q. v.] He had a light and elegant figure, a melodious voice, and much sense and tact. As Watty Cockney in the 'Romp,' chosen for his second part, he did not create much effect, and his wife's Priscilla Tomboy was a failure, the result being that both were relegated for a time into obscurity. His great parts were Jacob Gawkey, Plethora in 'Secrets worth knowing,' Count Cassel, and Farmer Ashfield, all very distinct impersonations. His Master Stephen in Ben Jonson's 'Every Man in his Humour,' which he revived for his benefit, also won much praise. During the latter part of his life he assumed the position of a country gentleman, and left a reputation for great liberality. A portrait of him, by Zoffany, as Roger in the 'Ghost,' is in the Garrick Club, where also are other portraits of him by De Wilde as Jacob, and by Wageman.

[The principal particulars are drawn from Tate Wilkinson's Wandering Patentee and from the Managers' Note-book. The European Magazine, the Monthly Mirror, and many other magazines have been consulted, as well as Genest's Account of the English Stage, the Biographia Dramatica, the Thespian Dictionary, Dibdin's Edinburgh Stage, &c.]   J. K.

KNIGHT, THOMAS ANDREW (1759–1838), vegetable physiologist and horticulturist, born at Wormesley Grange, near Ludlow, Herefordshire, on 12 Aug. 1759, was the younger son of Thomas Knight, rector of Ribbesford and Bewdley, Worcestershire, a member of an old Shropshire family, whose fortunes had been made by his father, Richard Knight, an ironmaster. Richard Payne Knight [q. v.] the numismatist was Thomas

Andrew Knight's elder brother. Knight was educated at Ludlow grammar school, at a school at Chiswick, and at Balliol College, Oxford, where he matriculated on 13 Feb. 1778. He was early distinguished as an eager sportsman, a good shot, and a keen observer. He settled at Elton, near Downton Castle, Herefordshire, his brother's residence, and began there his experiments in raising new varieties of fruits and vegetables. He was also a successful cattle-breeder, and was accordingly recommended by his brother to Sir Joseph Banks as a correspondent for the board of agriculture. In 1795 his work as a horticulturist first became generally known through some papers which he read before the Royal Society on grafting and the inheritance of disease among fruit trees. In 1803 Banks introduced him to Sir Humphry Davy, who soon became his greatest friend. Knight was an original member of the Horticultural Society (established in 1804), of which he was president from 1811 until his death, and he contributed to every part of its 'Transactions' issued during his lifetime from their first publication in 1807. He was in 1805 elected fellow of the Royal Society, and in 1806 received the Copley medal from the society. He became a fellow of the Linnean Society in 1807, and he was also a member of many American and other horticultural societies.

In 1809 his brother made over Downton Castle to him, and he thus had the management of an estate of ten thousand acres. In 1827 he entertained there, much to his satisfaction, the French physiologist, Dutrochet. In November of the same year he lost his only son, who was accidentally shot when in his thirty-second year. In 1836 he was awarded the first Knightian medal of the Horticultural Society, bearing his own portrait, by Wyon, and founded in his honour. Knight died in London on 11 May 1838, and was buried at Wormesley. He married in 1791 Frances, daughter of Humphrey Felton of Woodhall, near Shrewsbury. She survived him with three daughters, of whom Frances (b. 1793), a skilful botanical draughtswoman, who shared in his experiments, was married to Thomas Pendarves Stackhouse Acton (d. 1881); the second daughter married Sir William Rouse Boughton; and the third, Francis Walpole.

Knight raised new varieties of apples, cherries, strawberries, plums, nectarines, pears, potatoes, cabbages, and peas, many of which bear his name; and a genus of *Proteaceæ* was called *Knightia* by Robert Brown. Though he will always be associated with certain purely physiological experiments,

such as those on the influence of gravitation upon direction of growth, his main object was always utilitarian. His chief independent works were 'A Treatise on the Culture of the Apple and Pear, and on the Manufacture of Cider and Perry,' 8vo, 1797, 2nd edition 1801, 3rd 1808; and 'Pomona Herefordiensis,' 4to, 1811, with thirty coloured plates; but he was also the author of upwards of a hundred papers. Of these, one 'On the Aphis and Blights on Fruit Trees,' and another 'On the Fecundation of Vegetables,' are in Alexander Hunter's 'Georgical Essays,' vols. iv. and vi. 1803–4; while another, 'On Blight,' is in the 'Pamphleteer,' vol. iv. 1813. In 1841 was published 'A Selection from the Physiological and Horticultural Papers published in the Transactions of the Royal and Horticultural Societies by the late Thomas Andrew Knight, to which is prefixed a Sketch of his Life.' This volume was edited by George Bentham and John Lindley, the life being apparently by Mrs. Acton. It contains a lithographed portrait, and comprises eighty-two papers, sixty-three read before the Horticultural Society, together with fifteen on plants, and four, dealing with bees, and the influence of male and female parents on their offspring and hereditary instincts (dated 25 May 1837), which were presented to the Royal Society. The horticultural series treat, among other subjects, of sap, buds, germination, bark, roots, tendrils, early varieties, forcing-houses, layering, manure, ringing, mildew, and the supposed change of English climate. Only forty-six of his papers are enumerated in the Royal Society's 'Catalogue' (iii. 687–8), but it includes one 'On Variegation' from the Linnean 'Transactions' (vol. ix. 1808), one 'On the Direction of the Radicle and Germen,' from the Royal Institution 'Journal' (vol. ii. 1831), and fourteen others not included in the volume of 1841.

[Life prefixed to selection of papers, 1841; Athenæum, 1838, p. 358; Gent. Mag. 1838, ii. 99; Gardeners' Chronicle, 1841 p. 351, 1871 i. 169; Gardeners' Magazine, xiv. 303.] G. S. B.

KNIGHT, WILLIAM (1476–1547), bishop of Bath and Wells, born in London in 1476, entered Winchester School as a scholar in 1487, and proceeded in 1491 to New College, Oxford, where he became fellow in 1493. He afterwards proceeded D.C.L. 12 Oct. 1531 (*Reg. Univ. Oxf.*, Oxf. Hist. Soc., i. 166). In 1495 Knight went up to the court, where Henry VII is said to have made him one of his secretaries. He was frequently employed as an ambassador in the reign of Henry VIII. On 3 June 1512 he went with Sir Edward Howard to Spain, and, after many dangers from storms and sickness, reached Valladolid 18 Feb. 1512–13. He had received (30 Jan.) a commission dated 13 Dec. 1512, authorising him and John Stile to treat with Ferdinand of Aragon about the defence of the church. A long letter from Stile and Knight in cipher (of 3 March) is preserved in the British Museum (Cotton. MS. Vesp. C. i. 30). Knight remained at Valladolid till June 1513. On 3 April 1514 he was at Mechlin on the first of a long series of embassies to the Low Countries (cf. letter in *Cotton. MS. Galba*, B. iii. 13). Wingfield and Spinelly were with him (18 April), and on 12 June he was at the Hague with Sir Edward Poynings. In July he seems to have visited Switzerland (cf. misdated letter *ib.* Vesp. F. i. 51). Probably to better qualify him for diplomatic work, as well as in reward for past services, he received, on 14 July 1514, a grant of arms (party per fess or and gules, an eagle with two heads displayed sable; on its breast a demi-rose and a demi-sun conjoined into one, counterchanged of the field). In the grant he is described as prothonotary.

In May 1515 Knight is styled chaplain to the king, and in that month Henry lent him 100*l.*; in the same year he became dean of the collegiate church of Newark, Leicestershire. On 7 May he was appointed ambassador with Sir Edward Poynings to Prince Charles (afterwards Charles V), to renew the league of 9 Feb. 1505. They had a conference with Tunstal, 23 May, at Bruges, and an audience with Charles at Bergen-op-Zoom on 29 May. He remained in Flanders during the rest of 1515, and, like most of Henry's servants, found himself in pecuniary straits (cf. *Letters and Papers, Henry VIII*, II. i. 1235). In February 1515–16 the treaty had been concluded (cf. RYMER, *Fœdera*, xiii. 533, 539). He probably came to England in 1516, as he was in that year collated to the prebend of Farrendon-cum-Balderton in the cathedral of Lincoln (LE NEVE, *Fasti*, ii. 150). On 30 Dec. 1516 he was, in company with the Earl of Worcester, again appointed ambassador to the emperor (for his instructions see *Letters and Papers*, II. i. 2713), and he had an interview with Charles, 22 Jan. 1516–17. Throughout 1518 he was English representative to the Lady Margaret in the Low Countries, and sailed home from Calais 15 Feb. 1518–19. As one of Henry's chaplains and clerk of the closet he was at the Field of the Cloth of Gold in 1520 (*Rutland Papers*, Camden Soc., p. 33); and seems to have been made prebendary of Llanvair in Bangor Cathedral in the same year (LE NEVE, i. 120). On 10 June 1520 he was commissioned, with Sir Thomas More, John Hussee, and Hewester, to settle the disputes between the English merchants and the Teutonic Hanse, and went again to the Netherlands (cf. *Letters and Papers*, III. i. 868, 974). Sir Richard Wingfield, writing from Oudenard, 28 Oct. 1521, reported that Knight was to take his place as ambassador to the emperor (*ib.* III. ii. 1712), but it seems (*ib.* III. ii. 1777) that the emperor objected to his low birth, and expressed a preference for Wingfield's brother, Sir Robert (*ib.* III. ii. 2033, February 1521–2). Knight made a journey on diplomatic business into Switzerland in 1522; went on an embassy to the empire respecting the woolstaple, and was (11 Nov.) admitted archdeacon of Chester. In 1523 he concluded with the Duke of Bourbon a treaty against France (*ib.* III. ii. 3123, instructions. 3203, 3225, account of the journey), but was back at Brussels in August. On 11 Sept. 1523 he was appointed archdeacon of Huntingdon (LE NEVE, ii. 52). The next few years he chiefly passed in Flanders. About August 1526 he became secretary to the king.

In 1527, though he complained that he was old and losing his sight (*Letters and Papers*, IV. ii. 3300), Henry decided to send him to Rome to promote the divorce. Wolsey thought Jerome de Ghinucci, bishop of Worcester, would have been better suited for the work (*ib.* IV. ii. 3400). On 10 Sept. Knight saw Wolsey at Compiègne, and by his direction went on to Venice to watch for an opportunity to get access to the captive Pope Clement VII (*ib.* IV. ii. 3420; cf. 3422–4, 3497). The journey was dangerous from the disposition of the Spaniards, but he managed to get a safe-conduct by the aid of Gambara the prothonotary. He was, however, wellnigh murdered at Monterstundo (4 Dec. 1527), and when he entered Rome all that he could do was to send in his letters of credence with a minute of what the king wished (*ib.* IV. ii. 3638; cf. FROUDE, *Catherine of Aragon*, p. 51). On 19 Dec. 1527 Knight, while still in Italy, was made canon of Westminster. By the end of December, Jerningham wrote that the secret of Knight's negotiation had not been so well kept as it should have been, and that the emperor now knew Knight's business, and had written to the pope accordingly (*Letters and Papers*, IV. ii. 3687). Full instructions were thereupon sent to Knight, with a commission to Wolsey and another, which, if signed by the pope, would have empowered them to settle the divorce (*ib.* IV. ii. 3693; 3694, copy of bull). On 1 Jan. 1527–8, the pope being now at liberty, Knight visited him at Orvieto, and after Cardinal St. Quatuor (to whom two thousand crowns were given) had made some alterations in the commission, the pope signed it (*ib.* IV. ii. 3749). Leaving for England, Knight was ordered back to Orvieto when he had reached Asti, but he appears to have arrived in London in February 1528 (*ib.* IV. App. p. 143). He seems to have admitted the failure of this embassy (*ib.* IV. ii. 4185), and went (13 Dec. 1528), with some misgiving, on another mission with Benet to Montmorency, to confer about Italian affairs, and was instructed to proceed thence again to Rome (*ib.* IV. ii. 5023, 5028, 5148–50; 5179, their instructions). On 31 Jan. 1528–9, however, Gardiner joined Knight and Benet at Lyons and brought new instructions; Knight went back to Paris and acted through March and April with Sir John Taylor (master of the rolls) as ambassador; in June Suffolk and Fitzwilliam were with him. On 30 June 1529, Knight, with Tunstal, More, and Hacket, arranged the treaty of Cambray (*ib.* IV. iii. 5744). He was at the convocation of Canterbury of 1529, and was admitted archdeacon of Richmond on 7 Dec. (LE NEVE, iii. 141).

In February 1532 Hacket and Knight were appointed to treat with the emperor's commissioners about commercial intercourse, and the hope was expressed that they were well instructed, as they would have to meet 'the polytikist felows in all this londe.' The embassy did not bear much fruit (*Letters and Papers*, v. 804, 843, 946, 1056). Knight held at this time the rectory of Ronald Kirk, Yorkshire. In November 1533 he had difficulties as to jurisdiction with the Archbishop of York, who, he writes, 'deals very unkindly with me,' and 'cursed my official,' Dakyn, the vicar-general (*ib.* VI. 1440). The archbishop offered to submit the dispute to arbitration (*ib.* p. 1441). On 30 Jan. 1535 Knight was a commissioner for collecting the ecclesiastical tenths, and on 15 Oct. 1537 was present at the christening of Edward VI.

On 29 May 1541 he was consecrated bishop of Bath and Wells, in succession to John Clerk [q. v.] (LE NEVE, i. 144), and he resigned all his other preferments. At Wells Fuller relates that he built a market cross with the assistance of Dean Woolman. He died in 1547 at Wiveliscombe, Somerset, and was buried in Wells Cathedral next to Sugar's Chapel, where a pulpit which he had erected and which bears his arms served as a monument.

Knight was a faithful servant of Henry VIII, and a useful diplomatist of the old school, which regarded dissimulation as one of the requisites of success. He was a patron of Henry Cole [q. v.], whose education he seems to have paid for, and Cole calls him 'my master' (*Letters and Papers*, x. 321,

xi. 573). When in London Knight lived in a house in Cannon Row, Westminster, afterwards (1536) assigned, in accordance with an act of 27 Henry VIII, to the bishop of Norwich. By his will he left money to Winchester and New Colleges.

[Wood's Athenæ Oxon. ed. Bliss, ii. 752; Cassan's Bishops of Bath and Wells, i. 447, distinguishes Knight from William Knight of Merton College, Oxford, who lived about the same time; Fuller's Worthies, ed. 1662, p. 205; State Papers, Henry VIII; Dixon's Hist. of the Church of England, ii. 284, gives a character, Strype's Memorials, I. i. 86, 136, 188, II. i. 9, III. i. 452; Cranmer, pp. 77, 135; Thomas's Hist. Notes; Syllabus to Rymer's Fœdera; Nicolas's Privy Purse Expenses of Hen. VIII, p. 118; authorities quoted.] W. A. J. A.

KNIGHT, WILLIAM (*fl.* 1612), divine, a native of Arlington, Sussex, was matriculated as a pensioner of Christ's College, Cambridge, on 1 July 1579, went out B.A. in 1582–3, was subsequently elected a fellow of his college, and in 1586 commenced M.A. His friend Joseph Hall, afterwards bishop of Norwich, wrote, encouraging him to persist in the calling of the ministry, and commended his 'variety of tongues and style of arts.' Knight was instituted to the rectory of Barley, Hertfordshire, on 19 April 1598, but before the close of that year he exchanged the benefice, with Andrew Willet, for the rectory of Little Gransden, Cambridgeshire. On 12 July 1603 he was incorporated M.A. at Oxford. Willet terms him 'vir probus, prudens, doctus, mihique amicissimus.'

He was author of: 1. 'A Concordance Axiomatical, containing a Survey of Theological Propositions, with the Reasons and Uses in Holy Scripture,' London, 1610, fol. 2. Latin epistle prefixed to Joseph Hall's 'Mundus alter et idem,' Frankfort, n. d.

[Cooper's Athenæ Cantabr. iii. 16; Bishop Hall's Works (Pratt), vii. 251, x. 132; Heywood and Wright's Univ. Trans. i. 465, ii. 10; Horsfield's Sussex, i. 322; Newcourt's Repertorium, i. 800; Strype's Annals, iii. 400, App. p. 261 fol.; Willet's Epist. Ded. to Harmonie on 2 Samuel; Wood's Fasti Oxon. (Bliss), i. 229, 300.] T. C.

KNIGHT, WILLIAM (1786–1844), natural philosopher, son of William Knight, a bookseller, of Aberdeen, was born in that city on 17 Sept. 1786. In 1793 he entered the Aberdeen grammar school, where he was a contemporary of Lord Byron. Though not in the same class with him, he preserved a vivid recollection of the poet, whose disposition he described in later life as 'most damnable.' He entered the Marischal College and University in 1798, graduated M.A.

there in 1802, and delivered several courses of lectures to the students in natural history and chemistry between 1810 and 1816. In 1811 he was defeated in his candidature for the chair of natural philosophy, but was elected in 1816 to the professorship of natural philosophy in the Academical Institution, Belfast. In 1817 he received from Marischal College and University the degree of LL.D., and in the following year he published his chief work, entitled ' Facts and Observations towards forming a New Theory of the Earth,' Edinb. 1818, 8vo, being a series of desultory papers mainly on geological subjects. Knight returned to Aberdeen from Belfast in 1822, when he was appointed professor of natural philosophy at the Marischal College and University. His style of lecturing, says Professor Masson (*Macmillan's Magazine*, ix. 331), was characterised by much pungency, occasionally relieved by a ' sarcastic scurrility which no other lecturer ventured on, and which was far from pleasant.' Though his teaching was varied and interesting, its effect was greatly marred by the shallowness of his mathematical knowledge. Knight died at Aberdeen on 3 Dec. 1844, his class during the session 1844-5 being taken by Mr. Alexander Bain, afterwards professor of logic in the university of Aberdeen. He married, on 17 Sept. 1821, Jean, eldest daughter of George Glennie, professor of moral philosophy at Marischal College from 1798 to 1846. By her he had two sons and four daughters.

Besides the work mentioned above Knight published: 1. ' Outlines of Botany,' Aberdeen, 1813; 2nd edition, 1828. 2. ' First Day in Heaven, a Fragment,' London, 1820; a curious book, afterwards suppressed by the author. More important than any of his printed works are his eight volumes of manuscript collections relating to Marischal College, now in the library of the university of Aberdeen, which have formed the basis of the ' Fasti Academiæ Mariscallanæ,' edited by Mr. P. J. Anderson for the New Spalding Club. To these must be added some ' Autobiographical Collections,' now in the hands of relatives, which are full of racy criticisms of contemporaries.

[Information kindly supplied by Mr. P. J. Anderson, secretary, New Spalding Club, Aberdeen; Alma Mater (Aberdeen Univ. Mag.), January and February, 1889; James Riddell's Aberdeen and its Folk; Philos. Mag. xlviii. 384.]
T. S.

KNIGHT, WILLIAM HENRY (1823-1863), painter, was born on 26 Sept. 1823 at Newbury, Berkshire, where his father, John Knight, was a schoolmaster; he was articled to a solicitor in that town, but after having two pictures accepted by the Society of British Artists in 1844, abandoned the law, and in the following year came to London. He took lodgings in the Kennington Road, where he maintained himself by drawing crayon portraits while studying at the British Museum and in the schools of the Royal Academy. In 1846 he sent his first contribution to the Academy, ' Boys playing at Draughts,' which was purchased by Alderman Salomons, and from that year was a constant exhibitor; he also sent many pictures to the British Institution. Among his best works were ' A Christmas Party preparing for Blind Man's Buff,' 1850; ' Boys Snowballing,' 1853; ' The Broken Window,' 1855 (engraved in the ' Art Journal,' August 1865); ' The Village School,' 1857; ' Knuckle Down,' 1858; ' The Lost Change,' 1859; ' An Unexpected Tramp,' 1861; and ' The Counterfeit Coin,' 1862. These titles indicate the character of Knight's art, which was limited to scenes of everyday life, with children prominently introduced. His pictures are of cabinet size, very delicately finished. He died on 31 July 1863, leaving a widow and six children.

[Art Journal, 1863, p. 133; Redgrave's Dict. of Artists; Royal Academy Catalogues.]
F. M. O'D.

KNIGHT-BRUCE, SIR JAMES LEWIS (1791-1866), judge. [See BRUCE.]

KNIGHTBRIDGE, JOHN (d. 1677), divine, was the fourth son of John Knightbridge, attorney, of Chelmsford, Essex, by Mary, daughter of Charles Tucker of Lincoln's Inn (*Visitations of Essex*, Harl. Soc., vol. xiii. pt. i, p. 432). He graduated B.A. in 1642 as a member of Wadham College, Oxford, was translated to Peterhouse, Cambridge, on 3 May 1645, and five days later was admitted to a fellowship in place of Christopher Bankes of Yorkshire, who had been ejected (*Addit. MS.* 5874, f. 64). After resigning his fellowship in July 1659, he became rector of Spofforth, Yorkshire (ib. 5861, f. 267). In 1673 he proceeded D.D. (*Cantabr. Graduati*, 1787, p. 229). He died in the parish of St. Paul, Covent Garden, London, in December 1677 (*Probate Act Book*, P. C. C., 1677). By his will (P. C. C. 57, Reeve) he gave 40l. to the common fund of Wadham College, and the same sum to Peterhouse. He also gave to the master and fellows of Peterhouse as feoffees in trust his fee-farm rent of the manor of Heslington, near York, a house in the Minories, London, 7l. a year from his land in Chelmsford called Little Vinters, and another house and land, upon condition that they paid 50l. annually to a professor of moral theology or casuistical divinity. The first election to the chair, called the Knightbridge professorship, was made in 1683. He presented a library for the use of the clergy of Chelmsford and the neighbourhood, which is placed in a chapel on the north side of Chelmsford parish church.

[Addit. MS. 5861, ff. 298, 299, 300, 304, 305; Cambr. Univ. Calendar ; Trans. of Essex Arch. Soc. ii. 197.]   G. G.

KNIGHTLEY, Sir RICHARD (1533–1615), patron of puritans, born in 1533, was the eldest son of Sir Valentine Knightley (d. 1566) of Fawsley, Northamptonshire, by Anne (d. 1554), daughter of Edward Ferrers of Badesley Clinton, Warwickshire. The Knightleys were descended from an old Stafford-shire family, one branch of which settled in Northamptonshire, where they acquired numerous estates and vast wealth. Richard's father, Sir Valentine, was knighted at the coronation of Edward VI. His brother, Sir Edmund Knightley (d. 1542) (Richard's uncle), serjeant-at-law, was one of the chief commissioners for the suppression of religious houses. He was of a litigious temperament, and for obstructing the king's claim to some property in 1532 was committed to the Fleet. A curious letter to Cromwell begging for release is in the State Paper Office (September 1532). He made a very distinguished marriage with Ursula, widow of George, son of Andrew, lord Windsor, and sister and coheiress of John Vere, earl of Oxford. Between 1537 and 1542 he seems to have built the hall of Fawsley House. Dying on 12 Sept. 1542, he was buried at Fawsley (*Northamptonshire Notes and Queries*, i. 119–20).

Richard succeeded to landed property producing 13,000l. a year. He was knighted at Fotheringay in 1566 by the Earl of Leicester, with whom he seems to have been intimate. He was sheriff of Northamptonshire in 1568–9, 1581–2, and again in 1589, when he was present in his official capacity at the execution of Mary Queen of Scots. He was twice M.P. for the town of Northampton (in 1584 and 1585), and twice (in 1589 and 1598) for the county.

Knightley is said to have led a gay life in youth, but the family had always leaned to the reformed religion, and he ultimately became a rigid puritan.

In 1567, under Leicester's patronage, letters patent were granted making Knightley and others governors of the property of the ministers of the gospel in Warwickshire (*Cal. State Papers*, Dom. 1547–80, p. 304). When, in 1588, Penry and other advanced puritans began their determined onslaught on episcopacy by secretly issuing the tracts which they subscribed 'Martin Mar-Prelate,' they found a patron and abettor in Knightley. The travelling printing-press, whence came the famous tracts of Martin Mar-Prelate, was in the autumn of 1588 concealed in Knightley's house at Fawsley, and in a small upper room there, late in the year, the 'Epitome,' by Mar-Prelate, was printed. The press was removed after Christmas to Knightley's house at Norton, and was finally seized by the Earl of Derby in February 1588–9 at Manchester. Many arrests followed, and Knightley's complicity was discovered by the confessions of his servants. He was arraigned before the Star-chamber 'for maintaining seditious persons, books, and libels' on 31 Feb. 1588–9. Archbishop Whitgift, who had himself been a chief object of Mar-Prelate's attack, generously interceded for Knightley with the queen, and procured his release (see proofs against Sir R. Knightley, *Lansd. MSS.* cxxxviii. 327 ; Strype, *Whitgift*, ii. 511 ; Arber, *Introduction to the Martin Mar-Prelate Controversy*, pp. 114, 129–30). In February 1605 Knightley appears once more as a champion of the puritan party, when he, with two of his sons and other gentlemen of Northamptonshire, signed a petition against the suspension of the nonconformist ministers in his county. For this he was severely rebuked, was fined 10,000l. by the Star-chamber, and was deprived of his posts as lieutenant of Northamptonshire and commissioner of the peace (*Cal. State Papers*, James I, Dom. 1603–10, pp. 193, 435). An undated letter of thanks to Salisbury for the composition of this fine, and for some favour to his son, is also in the State Papers (ib. 1611–18, p. 130). Knightley and Sir Francis Hastings [q. v.] signed about 1608 a petition to parliament on behalf of the Roman catholics, hoping indirectly to benefit their own party by advocating religious toleration. Knightley died, aged 82, at Norton, 1 Sept. 1615, and was buried there with his second wife (d. 1602).

By his first wife, Mary, daughter of Sir Richard Fermor of Easton Neston, whom he married in 1556, he had three sons and three daughters; by his second wife, Elizabeth Seymour, youngest daughter of the protector Somerset, seven sons and two daughters. Knighthood was conferred on four of his sons: Valentine (d. 1618), Francis (d. 1620), who was cupbearer to James I, Seymour, and Ferdinand, who saw much foreign military service and was highly favoured by the electress. Through the extravagance of his elder sons, Sir Valentine and Edward (d. 1598), much of the Knightley property was sold and alienated during Sir Richard's lifetime ; in 1591 a final settlement was made, and the estates of Fawsley and Byfield were entailed upon his eight sons and his three brothers successively with their heirs male. The eldest son, Sir Valentine, who was sharply reprimanded for signing the Northamptonshire petition in 1605, inherited Fawsley, and on his death in 1618 it descended to his brother Edward's son Richard [q. v.]

There are two portraits of Sir Richard, at the ages respectively of thirty-three and eighty, at Fawsley Manor House.

[Fuller's Church History, ed. 1845, p. 131; Strype's Annals, Clar. Press, vol. iii. pt. ii. pp. 102, 602; Heylyn's History of the Presbyterians, p. 280; Baker's History of Northamptonshire, i. 380, 385; Betham's Baronetage, iv. 386; Excerpta Historica, p. 18; Northamptonshire Notes and Queries (1886), i. 120.]   E. T. B.

KNIGHTLEY, RICHARD (d. 1639), member of parliament, was son of Edward Knightley of Preston Capes, Northamptonshire, in right of his wife Mary, daughter of Peter Coles of that place. Sir Richard Knightley (1533-1615) [q. v.] was his grandfather, and on the death of his uncle, Sir Valentine, in 1618, he succeeded to the family property of Fawsley. He was returned to the House of Commons as member for Northamptonshire on 22 Nov. 1621, and he was re-elected for the same constituency on 23 Jan. 1623-4, and in 1625. From his first entrance into public life Knightley displayed the puritan leanings of his family, and in the first parliament of Charles I's reign he took his stand beside Sir John Eliot and the opponents of Buckingham and the court. A manuscript journal of this parliament, which is still extant among the Knightley family archives, was printed by the Camden Society in 1873. After the dissolution in August 1625 Knightley, like other deputy-lieutenants of Northamptonshire, was directed to search papists' houses in the county, and proceeding to Lord Vaux's house at Harrowden, was seriously assaulted by the owner. Knightley brought the matter before the privy council, and threatened his assailant with Star-chamber proceedings (Court and Times of Charles I, i. 56). Charles I seems to have already noticed Knightley's political hostility, and, in order apparently to exclude Knightley from his second parliament of 1626, he appointed him sheriff of Northamptonshire in that year. In January 1627 Knightley was reported to the council as one who refused to subscribe to the forced loan. When summoned to appear before the council he made a defiant speech, and accordingly was committed to the Fleet prison. He re-entered the House of Commons for his old constituency early in 1628, and acted through that and the following session in close alliance with Eliot and Hampden. He spoke in favour of the Remonstrance of 1628. When Eliot was arrested Knightley was his chief correspondent, and fourteen of Eliot's letters to him, written from the Tower, are extant (ELIOT, De Jure Majestatis and Letter-book, ed. Grosart, 1882, vol. ii.) The intimacy was of the closest and most congenial kind. Knightley was in similar relations with Pym, Hesilrigge, and Hampden. He appointed the puritan John Dod [q. v.] to the rectory of Fawsley in 1637, and was one of the Company of Adventurers for Providence Island (Cal. State Papers, Colonial, 1574-1660, p. 123). He died in November 1639, and was buried at Fawsley (11 Nov.) He married, in July 1614, Bridget, daughter of Sir Thomas Lucy of Charlecote, Warwickshire, but left no issue, and his property devolved on his cousin and the step-brother of his mother, Richard Knightley, with whom he is often confused. This Richard Knightley (1580-1650) was son of Thomas Knightley of Burgh Hall, Staffordshire (d. before 1621), and was a nephew of Sir Richard Knightley, the patron of Martin Mar-Prelate. His mother was Elizabeth, daughter of John Shuckburgh of Naseby, whose first husband was Peter Coles of Preston Capes. He was admitted to Gray's Inn 22 May 1601 (FOSTER, Reg. p. 101). He seems to have lived in retirement at Fawsley, and was buried there on 19 Sept. 1650. He married Anne, daughter of Sir Edward Littleton of Pillaton, Staffordshire, and left a son, Richard.

This son, SIR RICHARD KNIGHTLEY (1617-1661), was admitted to Gray's Inn 17 May 1633 (ib. p. 199), and about 1637 married Elizabeth, eldest daughter of John Hampden, who died in 1643, greatly to the distress of her father. As 'Richard Knightley, junior,' he sat in the Short parliament as member for Northampton. He fully shared the political sympathies of his family, and after the dissolution of the Short parliament in May 1640 he invited Hampden, Pym, and other of the opposition leaders to meet at Fawsley to concert a plan of action. He was re-elected member for Northampton to the Long parliament in October 1640, and acted consistently with the opposition. He and Sir Walter Earle were the tellers for their party on the vote on the Grand Remonstrance on 23 Nov. 1641. On 21 Jan. 1642-3 he subscribed a petition to the parliament from the freeholders of Northamptonshire expressing approval of the parliamentary policy. He signed the solemn league and covenant, and was a member of the parliamentary committee

for Northamptonshire in March 1643 (HUS-
BANDS, p. 942; cf. *Cal. State Papers*, 1645,
p. 411). Knightley strongly disapproved of
the plans for bringing the king to trial; was
consequently imprisoned by the army from
6 to 20 Dec. 1648, and was excluded from the
parliament (*A full Declaration of the true
state of the Secluded Members' Case*, 1660, 4to,
p. 55). He had a license to go abroad, 24 June
1651 (*Cal. State Papers*, 1651, p. 529), and
in December 1655 he was included in a list
drawn up by the quakers of those 'who do
not persecute but are loving to Friends' (*ib.*
1655 6, p. 64). He sat in Richard Cromwell's parliament in January 1658-9 as member for Northamptonshire, and was suggested
as speaker 9 March 1659, when he excused
himself from taking the office (cf. BURTON,
Diary, vol. iv.; *Clarendon State Papers*, iii.
433). As an opponent of the army he was
not summoned to the Rump—the restored
Long parliament in May 1659. But on 7 May
he and Prynne made an attempt to enter the
house (*A true and perfect Relation of what
was done between Mr. Prynne and the Secluded
Members and those now sitting*, 1659, pp. 4, 7).
On 17 Feb. 1659-60 he took part in the conference between the secluded and sitting
members, and as soon as the former members
took their places he was elected (23 Feb.)
member of the council of state which arranged
the recall of the king. At the coronation of
Charles II (April 1661) he was created a
knight of the Bath. He died in London on
22 June 1661, and was buried on 6 July at
Fawsley. He married in 1647 a second wife,
Ann, daughter of Sir William Courten, and
widow of Essex Devereux, son and heir of
Walter Devereux, fifth viscount Hereford.
His widow was buried at Fawsley on 5 Feb.
1702 3, aged 88. By her Knightley had two
sons, Richard (1647-1655) and Essex (1649-
1671). The latter's widow, Sarah, daughter of
Thomas Foley of Witley, married as second
husband John Hampden the younger [q. v.]

[Notes kindly supplied by C. H. Firth, esq.;
Le Neve's Pedigrees of Knights (Harl. Soc.),
pp. 17-18; Baker's Northamptonshire, i. 389 sq.;
Northamptonshire Notes and Queries, i. 120-1;
Beesley's Hist. of Banbury, 1841; Forster's Sir
John Eliot; Return of Members of Parliament.
A Richard Knightley, who, according to Wood,
joined the royalist standard in 1642, and on his
arrival with the Marquis of Hertford's army in
Oxford was created M.A. on 16 Jan. 1642-3
(Wood's Fasti, ed. Bliss, ii. 33), was probably son
of a distant connection of the family of Fawsley,
Edward Knightley, a royalist.] S. L.

KNIGHTON (or **CNITTHON**, as he himself spells the name), HENRY (*fl.* 1363),
historical compiler, was a canon of St. Mary's

Abbey, Leicester. He is the author of a
'Compilatio de eventibus Angliæ,' a work in
four books beginning with Edgar and ending
in 1366. His name, Henricus Cnitthon, is
supplied by the initial letters of the sixteen
chapters of each of the first three books. In
his prologue he states that he follows the
seventh book of Cestrensis (i.e. Higden),
and that he adds to his extracts from him
the accounts of other matters, 'quæ aspectui
meo sparsim se obtulerant.' But he carefully conceals that almost the whole of the
additional matter, with the exception of a
few references to Leicester and its abbey, is
transcribed from Walter of Hemingburgh.
When Hemingburgh speaks of his own monastery (Gisburn) as 'nostram,' this is altered to
its own name (e.g. 'quandam ecclesiam de
Gysburne,' TWYSDEN, col. 2522). At the end
of the third book he states that he is proceeding alone, and the fourth book, which is not
divided into chapters, and occupies from 1337
to 1366, may be original. It gives nearly
the same sequence of events as is found in
Robert of Avesbury. He speaks of being
present at the visit of Edward III to the
abbey of Leicester in 1363. As the history
breaks off abruptly in 1366, he probably did
not survive that year.

A fifth book is added in the manuscripts,
begun ten years later (1377), and carrying
on the history to 1395. This is clearly the
work of another writer, whose style as well
as 'his whole tone of speaking of church
matters' is very different from that of
Knighton. The documents preserved by the
continuator, the details respecting the rising
of 1381, and those of the history and opinions
of Wycliffe, are of great value. He 'is a partisan of the Duke of Lancaster,' and almost
'the only writer of that day on the less popular
side.' He was clearly, like Knighton, a canon
of St. Mary's, Leicester, but there is no clue
to his name. The book was in the library of
Leicester Abbey, as may be seen in Nichols's
'History of Leicester,' App. p. 102. It is
preserved in two manuscripts in the Cotton
collection in the British Museum, Claudius
E. 3 and Tiberius C. 7, from the latter of
which Twysden printed his edition in the
'Decem Scriptores.' A new edition is in
progress in the Rolls Series, under the editorship of the Rev. Dr. Lumby.

[Authorities given in text.] H. R. L.

KNIGHTON, SIR WILLIAM (1776-
1836), keeper of the privy purse to George IV,
son of William Knighton, was born at Beer
Ferris, Devonshire, in 1776. His family had
an estate at Grenofen, Whitchurch, Devonshire, but his father was disinherited, and,

dying very early, left his widow in poverty. Knighton, after a little schooling at Newton Bushell, Devonshire, was at an early age sent to study medicine under his uncle, Dr. Bredall, a surgeon of Tavistock. He afterwards studied for two years at Guy's Hospital, London. At the age of twenty-one he returned to Devonshire, and obtained through the influence of Dr. Geach, chief surgeon of the Royal Naval Hospital at Plymouth, an assistant-surgeon's post there, and a diploma from St. Andrews University. At the end of 1797 he settled in practice at Devonport. In 1800 he married Dorothea, youngest daughter of Captain Hawker, R.N., and in 1803 he removed to London. He began practice as an accoucheur, but shortly removed to Edinburgh. After three years' study there, he once more returned to London, received a degree from the Archbishop of Canterbury, and the degree of M.D. from the university of Aberdeen (21 April 1806), and began practice in Hanover Square. In July 1809 he attended the Marquis Wellesley as his physician on his embassy to Spain, and returned with him in October. By him he was in 1810 recommended to the Prince of Wales, with the result that he became one of the prince's physicians, and was shortly afterwards created a baronet (1812). The prince told Sir Walter Farquhar, in explanation of this appointment, that Knighton was the best-mannered doctor he had ever met. He had been an intimate friend of Sir John Macmahon, and when, on the latter's death in 1818, he came, as executor, into possession of some of his papers, which were compromising to the prince, he at once delivered them up, conduct which so charmed the regent that he appointed him to the auditorship of the duchy of Cornwall and of the duchy of Lancaster, and soon began more and more to consult him on matters of business.

Knighton's firmness of character appeared in his management of George IV's inextricably confused affairs. In spite of the king's extravagance, Knighton gradually reduced his finances to order, caused the debts to be steadily liquidated, and asserted over the king's weak mind an authority which few of the ministers enjoyed (cf. LORD ELLEN-BOROUGH, *Diary*, i. 384; *Greville Memoirs*, 1st ser. i. 100, 144; LORD COLCHESTER, *Diary*). The king wrote to him as 'dearest friend,' signed himself 'most affectionately yours,' and gave him written authority to notify the royal tradesmen that no goods were to be supplied or work done on account of the privy purse except upon Knighton's orders given in writing. Knighton had attended him on the continent in 1821, and received the degree of M.D. from the university

of Göttingen, and on the return of the court to England he was appointed private secretary to the king and keeper of the privy purse, in succession to Sir Benjamin Bloomfield. He thereupon gave up practice on 11 Sept. 1822. He was frequently employed on confidential missions for the king both at home and abroad, but their precise nature is unknown, as all his letters on the subject were destroyed by his widow. He was sent to Paris in 1823, and in 1824 made three journeys in rapid succession to Paris, Spain, and Sardinia. 'At a moment's notice,' he writes to his wife, 'the king has again ordered me abroad . . . my situation involves very heavy penalties on me.' These sudden and toilsome journeys, continued yearly and often several times a year till 1825 and 1826, probably contributed to bring on the severe illness which overtook him in 1827. He was highly esteemed by the royal family and by the ministry, having taken to heart the Duke of Wellington's advice to beware how he interfered in politics; but he became the object of considerable ill-will, owing to his undoubted influence with the king (see LORD COLCHESTER, *Diary*, iii. 527, 589; RAIKES, *Diary*, iii. 53, 54). A severe attack was made upon him by T. S. Duncombe in his maiden speech in the House of Commons on 18 Feb. 1828; but Peel met it by a point-blank denial (HANSARD, *Parl. Debates*, 2nd ser. xviii. 540). The attack appears to have been got up as a joke by Henry de Ros and Charles Greville (see *Greville Memoirs*, 1st ser. i. 128); but to Knighton, who was then abroad and unable to defend himself, it was very painful. He attended the king almost night and day during his last illness, was present even at political interviews in the royal closet, and appears not only to have been sincerely attached to the king, but also to have esteemed him. His vigilance prevented Lady Conyngham from profiting by the temporary disorder at Windsor during the king's illness to lay hands on any of the royal jewels, and after the king's death on 26 Jan. 1830 Knighton was busily occupied for several months in winding up his affairs. He subsequently gave up his house in London and retired into the country, which suited his failing health better than town. He died, however, in Stratford Place, Oxford Street, London, on 11 Oct. 1836 of an enlargement of the heart, and was buried at Kensal Green cemetery.

He had considerable taste, especially in painting, very great social tact, a sound business capacity, and honestly fulfilled the duties of a very delicate position. Though he long held a position where his court interest might have commanded almost any favour, he proved himself greedy neither of money nor honours, and kept aloof from all intrigue. He left a widow, one son, and one daughter.

[Memoirs published by his widow, 2 vols. 8vo, 1838, which, however, leave half the story of his latter years untold, and discover no secrets, political or other; Munk's Coll. of Phys. iii. 39; see also the Age, 16 Oct. 1836. This article has been revised by Sir W. Knighton's granddaughter, Mrs. Dawson.]　　　　　　　　J. A. H.

KNILL, RICHARD (1787–1857), dissenting minister, fourth child of Richard Knill, carpenter (d. 15 Dec. 1826), by Mary Tucker (d. 1826), was born at Braunton, Devonshire, on 14 April 1787. In 1804 he enlisted as a soldier, but was shortly afterwards bought out by his friends. He became a student of the Western Academy at Axminster in 1812, and under the influence of a sermon by Dr. Alexander Waugh, volunteered for missionary work. He was accepted by the London Missionary Society, and embarked for Madras 20 April 1816. Here he engaged in English services for the schools, soldiers, and residents, while studying the native languages. His health soon failed, and he was sent in September 1818 to Nágarkoil in Travancore, whence, after suffering from the cholera, he returned to England 30 Nov. 1819. A cold climate being recommended, he sailed on 18 Oct. 1820 for St. Petersburg, intending to proceed to Siberia as a missionary; but, on the persuasion of the British and Americans, consented to remain in that city. Here he laboured successfully, and obtained the support of the emperor and the royal family. A Protestant Bible Society was formed for supplying the bible in their own tongues to Germans, Finns, Poles, Livonians, and other persons not belonging to the Greek church. A school was opened for the children of foreigners, and a mission to the sailors at Cronstadt established. Returning to England in August 1823 to obtain funds for erecting a larger church in St. Petersburg, his labours were so successful in creating funds and friends for the London Missionary Society, that he was requested to remain at home, and for eight years he visited almost every place in the United Kingdom, advocating the claims of the foreign missions. Quite worn out by his incessant labours, he on 1 Jan. 1842 settled down as congregational minister at Wotton-under-Edge, Gloucestershire, where he remained until his removal to Chester in 1848. His last days were not the least useful, and his preaching in the Chester Theatre for twenty Sunday afternoons was most successful. Few men of his time had greater mastery over large assemblies of men. He died at 28 Queen Street, Chester, on 2 Jan. 1857. On 9 Jan. 1823 he married Sarah, daughter of James and Isabella Notman, a native of St. Petersburg, by whom he had five children.

Knill was the author of: 1. 'The Farmer and his Family,' 1814. 2. 'Memoir of the Life and Character of Walter Venning,' 1822. 3. 'The Influence of Pious Women in Promoting a Revival of Religion,' 1830. 4. 'Some Account of John Knill,' 1830. 5. 'The Happy Death-bed,' 1833. 6. 'A Traveller arrived at the End of the Journey,' 1836. 7. 'A Dialogue between a Romish Priest and R. Knill, Missionary,' 1841. 8. 'A Scotchman Abroad,' 1841.

[Birrell's Life of R. Knill, 1860, with portrait, new ed. 1878, with another portrait; Congregational Year-Book, 1857, pp. 212–14; Evangelical Mag. March 1857, pp. 137–45; Scottish Congregational Mag. April 1857, pp. 97–103, May, pp. 129–33; Waddington's Congregational History, 1880, v. 185–96; Nonconformist, 7 Jan. 1857, p. 16, 14 Jan. p. 24; Chester Chronicle, 3 Jan. 1857, p. 8, 10 Jan. p. 5.]　　　　G. C. B.

KNIPE, THOMAS (1638–1711), headmaster of Westminster School, son of the Rev. Thomas Knipe, was born in 1638, most probably in Westminster. He was educated at Westminster School, whence in 1657 he was elected to a studentship at Christ Church, Oxford, but did not matriculate till 31 July 1658. He graduated B.A. 22 Feb. 1660, and M.A. 1 Dec. 1663. In the interval he acted as usher at his old school, and in 1663 became second master there. Dr. Busby [q. v.], the head-master, is said to have appreciated Knipe's merits. Knipe succeeded to Busby's post by a patent dated the very day, 6 April 1695, of Busby's death, and, though scarcely so brilliant as his predecessor, was respected and beloved by his pupils. A letter addressed by Knipe to Henry, lord Herbert of Cherbury [see under HERBERT, HENRY, 1654–1709], whose son was at Westminster School, shows that he was a strict disciplinarian (cf. WARNER, Epistolary Curiosities, 1818, where Knipe's letter is printed). On 17 Oct. 1707 Knipe was installed a prebendary of Westminster, and died at Hampstead on 6 Aug. 1711 in his seventy-third year. He was buried on the 9th in the north cloister of Westminster Abbey, and a monument was put up to him by his widow in the south aisle. Knipe was married twice, first to a relative of Bishop Sprat, who died 26 Aug. 1685, and secondly to a widow, Alice Talbot, of St. Margaret's parish, who survived him until 8 March 1723; both his wives and several of his children also found sepulture in the abbey (see CHESTER, Registers of Westminster Abbey). A portrait of Knipe, painted by J. Dahl, has been engraved (see NOBLE, *Continuation of Granger*, ii. 119). Two of Knipe's descendants are also commemorated in the Abbey: Captain John Knipe, 90th regiment, who died at Gibraltar 25 Oct. 1798; and Captain Robert Knipe, 14th light dragoons, who was mortally wounded at the battle of Fuentes d'Onoro, 5 May 1811.

Knipe compiled and published two grammars for the use of Westminster scholars: 'Ἀπολλοδώρου τοῦ Ἀθηναίου Γραμματικοῦ Βιβλιοθήκη ἢ περὶ Θεῶν Βιβλίον,' &c., London, 1686; and 'Hebraicæ Grammaticæ Rudimenta,' 1704. He also certainly took some part in, and is even said to have been the author of, the 'Grammatica Busbeiana.' To Knipe were dedicated in laudatory terms the Greek dialogues (1706) of Maittaire, second master at Westminster, and the 'Historical Account of the Heathen Gods,' by Dr. William King, an old pupil of Westminster.

[Wood's Athenæ (Bliss), iv. 643; Wood's Fasti (Bliss), ii. 223, 266; Welch's Alumni Westmonast. 1852; Stanley's Memorials of Westminster Abbey; Le Neve's Fasti, iii. 364; Nichols's Illustr. iii. 270; Anecdotes, i. 26, 489, iv. 556.]
E. T. B.

KNIPP or **KNEP**, MRS. (*fl.* 1670), actress, probably made her *début* on the stage of the Theatre Royal as a member of Killigrew's company, as Epicene in Ben Jonson's 'Silent Woman' on 1 June 1664. Pepys made her acquaintance at his friend Mrs. Pierce's on 6 Dec. 1665, and thought her 'pretty enough, but the most excellent, mad-humoured thing, and sings the noblest that ever I heard in my life.' Her husband he describes as 'an ill, melancholy, jealous-looking fellow,' suspected of ill-treating her. On 2 Jan. 1665-6 he records the 'perfect pleasure' it gave him at Brouncker's 'to hear her sing, and especially her little Scotch song of Barbary Allen.' They soon became very intimate, corresponding with one another as 'Dapper Dicky' and 'Barbary Allen.' On 23 Feb. 1665-6 (his birthday) Pepys records that she came to see his wife, and he spent the whole night talking with her and teaching her his song 'Beauty, retire,' which she made 'go most rarely.' On 6 Aug. 1666 he took her to dine with him at a tavern in Old Fish Street. On 14 Nov. 1666 he visited her at her lodging, which he found 'very mean.' He took her husband into the city, left him there, and returned to dine with her *tête-à-tête*. Next year she chose him for her valentine, upon which he 'bought 32s. worth of things' for her. He also made her occasional presents of money. From this time, however, out of regard to his wife, who began to be seriously

VOL. XXXI.

jealous, Pepys allowed the intimacy to cool. He admired her in the part of the Widow in Beaumont and Fletcher's 'Scornful Lady 'on 28 Dec. 1666; in the Widow's part in the 'Custom of the Country,' 2 Jan. 1666-7; in 'Mrs. Weaver's great part' in Dryden's 'Indian Emperor,' 15 Jan.; and her singing in the 'Humorous Lieutenant,' 23 Jan.; and 'The Chances,' a comedy by the Duke of Buckingham, 5 Feb. She also took some part in the revival of Suckling's 'Goblins' on 23 Jan.; on 5 Oct. she appeared as Otrante in Rhodes's 'Flora's Vagaries;' on 19 Oct. as Savina in Lord Orrery's historical play of the 'Black Prince;' and with Nell Gwyn [q. v.] spoke the prologue to Sir R. Howard's 'Great Favourite, or the Duke of Lerma,' on 20 Feb. 1667-8, 'most excellently,' 'beyond any creature' Pepys had 'ever heard.' She appeared in Dryden's 'Mock Astrologer' and 'Tyrannick Love' in 1668 and 1668-9, and in 'The Heiress,' 2 Feb. 1668-9, entranced Pepys with her singing and a wink from the stage with which she honoured him. She appeared at Lincoln's Inn Fields, the Theatre Royal having been burned down, in 1671 2, as the nun Hippolita in Dryden's 'Assignation;' and in that or the following year as Lady Fidget in Wycherley's 'Country Wife.' In 1674 she played Eliza in Wycherley's 'Plain Dealer,' and spoke the epilogue to Duffet's 'Spanish Rogue.' She took the part of a priestess of Bellona in Lee's 'Sophonisba, or Hannibal's Overthrow,' in 1676; and that of a maid in 'Country Innocence, or the Chambermaid turned Quaker,' in 1677. Her last recorded appearance was as Mrs. Dorothy in D'Urfey's version of Fletcher's 'Trick for Trick.' Her subsequent history is wholly uncertain.

[Downes's Roscius Anglicanus, ed. Knight; Genest's Account of the English Stage, vol. i.; Pepys's Diary.]
J. M. R.

KNIVET. [See KNYVET.]

KNOLLES, RICHARD (1550?-1610), historian of the Turks, born about 1550, probably at Cold Ashby, Northamptonshire, seems to have been son of the Francis Knolles or Knowlis of Cold Ashby who married Frances Holmeby, his second wife, on 17 June 1560 (BRIDGES, *Northamptonshire*, i. 553, note 4). He graduated B.A. from Lincoln College, Oxford, on 26 Jan. 1564-5, and M.A. in July 1570. He was elected a fellow of his college, and was still in residence in 1571 (*Oxford Univ. Reg.*, Oxford Hist. Soc. ii. ii. 36). Sir Peter Manwood, son of Sir Roger Manwood [q. v.], hearing of Knolles's abilities, 'called him from the university,' and obtained for him the mastership

T

of the grammar school at Sandwich, Kent, a town to which Sir Peter and his father had proved liberal benefactors. According to Wood 'he did much good in his profession, and sent many young men to the universities,' although he lived 'in a world of trouble and cares.' He died at Sandwich in 1610, and was buried on 2 July in St. Mary's Church there, 'leaving behind him the character of an industrious, learned, and religious person.'

Sir Peter Manwood was fully justified in his estimate of Knolles's abilities. Owing to his persuasion and encouragement Knolles completed his 'Generall Historie of the Turkes from the first beginning of that Nation,' a specimen of carefully elaborated English prose, although its historical value is small. The book, which occupied Knolles about twelve years, was published in 1603 by Adam Islip in London, in a folio of nearly 1,200 pages, with a dedication to James I, and engraved portraits of the sultans by Lawrence Johnson [q. v.] A long list of Byzantine historians and other authorities is given, but Knolles seems to have largely followed Boissard's 'Vitæ et Icones Sultanorum Turcicorum' (Frankfort, 1596). Knolles's volume concludes with 'a brief discourse of the greatness of the Turkish Empire, and where the greatest strength thereof consisteth.' A second edition, with 'the lives of the Ottoman emperors and kings' continued to the date of publication, appeared in 1610, and third and fourth editions, with further continuations, were issued in 1621 and 1631 respectively. The fifth edition, 1638, included 'a new continuation' collected out of the despatches of Sir P. Wyche and others by Thomas Nabbes [q. v.] A later edition, revised by Paul Rycaut, is dated 1679, and the same editor, then Sir Paul Rycaut, brought out a final and extended edition, in three folio volumes, between 1687 and 1700, under the title of 'The General History of the Turks, with a Continuation by Sir Paul Rycaut.' An abridgment by John Savage appeared in 1701 in 2 vols. 8vo.

Dr. Johnson lavished somewhat excessive praise on Knolles's style. 'None of our writers,' he asserted in the 'Rambler,' No. 122, 'can in my opinion justly contest the superiority of Knolles, who in his "History of the Turks" has displayed all the excellencies that narration can admit. His style, though somewhat obscured by time, and sometimes vitiated by false wit, is pure, nervous, elevated, and clear. A wonderful multiplicity of events is so artfully arranged and so distinctly explained that each facilitates the knowledge of the next.' Only in the orations which Knolles places in the mouths of his leading personages does Johnson detect aught that is tedious or languid; and Knolles's limited reputation he attributes to his choice of a subject 'of which none desires to be informed.' Hallam commends Johnson's verdict : 'Knolles's descriptions are vivid and animated—circumstantial, but not to feebleness : his characters are drawn with a strong pencil.' Horace Walpole, on the other hand, found the style tiresome ; but Southey was an ardent admirer, and recommended Coleridge, when setting out for Malta, to 'look in old Knolles and read the siege of Malta before you go.' Byron acknowledged deep indebtedness to Knolles. Shortly before his death at Missolonghi, he wrote: 'Old Knolles was one of the first books that gave me pleasure when a child ; and I believe it had much influence on my future wishes to visit the Levant, and gave perhaps the oriental colouring which is observed in my poetry' (BYRON, Works, ix. 141; cf. Don Juan, bk. v. c. exlvii. 7).

Knolles also published a translation : 'The Six Bookes of a Common Weale written by J. Bodin, a famous Lawyer . . . out of the French and Latin copies, done into English.' London, 1606 (by Adam Islip), dedicated to Sir Peter Manwood (cf. BRYDGES, Censura Literaria, i. 319 sq.) Wood wrongly ascribes to Knolles 'Grammatica Latina, Græca et Hebr.' (1665), which is by Hanserd Knolly [q. v.] (Athenæum, 6 Aug. 1881, p. 176).

A manuscript English translation of Camden's 'Britannia' is among Ashmolean MSS. at the Bodleian Library, Oxford. A note describes this copy as once Camden's property, which was 'founde in his own library. lock't in a cupboard, as a treasure he much esteemed and since his death suffered to see light.' It has not been printed.

[Wood's Athenæ Oxon. ed. Bliss, ii. 79–82 ; Knolles's Works ; Brit. Mus. Cat.] S. L.

KNOLLES, THOMAS (d. 1537), president of Magdalen College, Oxford, was born in Westgate, York. He was a secular priest, educated at Magdalen College, Oxford, whence he graduated M.A., and became in 1495 fellow of the college, proceeding B.D. on 19 April 1515, and D.D. June 1518. He is said to have been rector of South Kirkby, Yorkshire. From 31 July 1502 till his death he was vicar of All Saints, Wakefield. Wood calls him 'a learned man,' and says he was much followed for his preaching in Yorkshire. From 1507 to 1529 he was subdean of York, and in 1529 became a prebendary of the cathedral. On the resignation of Laurence Stubbs in 1527 Knolles was elected president of Magdalen. He seems to have exerted some influence at the university, and was a friend of Cromwell, with whom he corresponded (see *Letters and Papers of Henry VIII*, vols. v. viii. ix. x.) On 3 Feb. 1535 he resigned his headship, in accordance with a promise made the year before to Cromwell, who desired the post for another friend (Marshall). The latter was, however, not elected. Knolles retired to Wakefield, where he died on 9 May 1537. By his will, which is still extant at York, he desired to be buried near his parents in the south aisle of All Saints' Church, Wakefield. The gravestone has disappeared, but Walker (see *Cathedral Church of Wakefield*, p. 191) copied the Latin inscription from Dodsworth's notes in the Bodleian Library.

[Le Neve's Fasti, iii. 131, 316, 561; Wood's Fasti, ed. Bliss, i. 35, 43, 48; Oxf. Univ. Reg. (Oxf. Hist. Soc.), i. 82; Sisson's Hist. of Wakefield Church, p. 15; Bloxam's Register of Magdalen College, ii. 321, iii. 82, iv. 7, 10, 46.]

E. T. B.

KNOLLYS, Sir FRANCIS (1514?–1596), statesman, was elder son of ROBERT KNOLLYS (d. 1521). The father is said by Dugdale to have been descended from Sir Robert Knollys or Knolles (d. 1407) [q. v.], the soldier, but the proofs are wanting. Sir Francis's pedigree cannot be authentically traced beyond Sir Thomas Knollys, lord mayor of London in 1399 and 1410, from whom Sir Francis's father was fifth in descent. Lord-mayor Knollys may, it is suggested, have been a nephew of the soldier. He was a member of the Grocers' Company; directed in 1400 the rebuilding of the Guildhall, and rebuilt St. Antholin's Church in Watling Street, where he was buried with his wife Joan. His will, dated 20 May 1435, was proved 11 July 1435 at Lambeth, where it is still preserved. Sir Thomas's son Thomas (d. 1440) possessed the manor of North Mimms, Hertfordshire. This passed to his heir, Robert, who died without male issue. It was the second son, Richard, who seems to have been grandfather of Sir Francis's father, Robert Knollys (*Herald and Genealogist*, vii. 553, viii. 289).

In 1488 the latter was one of Henry VII's henchmen, and late in that year was appointed to wait on 'the king's dearest son the prince' (Arthur). He received 5l. 'by way of reward' for each of the three years 1488 to 1490, and when Henry VII met Archduke Philip in 1500 he accompanied the English king as one of the ushers of the chamber (*Materials illustrative of Henry VII*, Rolls Ser. ii. 383, 394, 437, 562; *Letters of Richard III and Henry VII*, Rolls Ser. ed. Gairdner, ii. 89). He continued in the same office under Henry VIII, and received an annuity of 20l. on 15 Nov. 1509, and a grant of Upclatford, called Rookes Manor, in Hampshire—part of the confiscated property of Sir Richard Empson—on 10 Feb. 1510-11 (*Letters, &c., of Henry VIII*, i. 94, 218). The 'Robert Knolles,' a dyer of Wakefield, Yorkshire, who was given letters of protection on going to the war in France, in the retinue of Richard Tempest, in April 1513, can hardly be identical with the usher of the royal chamber (*ib.* i. 529, 546). On 9 July 1514 the usher and his wife were jointly granted the manor of Rotherfield Greys, near Henley-on-Thames, Oxfordshire, in survivorship, at an annual rental of a red rose at midsummer. The grant was confirmed on 5 Jan. 1517-18 by letters patent for their own lives and that of one successor. Other royal gifts followed (*ib.* i. 841, ii. pt. ii. 1217, iii. pt. i. 121, iv. pt. i. 231). Robert Knollys died in 1521, and was buried in the church of St. Helen's, Bishopsgate. His will, dated 13 Nov. 1520, was proved 19 June 1521. His widow, Letitia or Lettice, was daughter of Sir Thomas Penyston of Hawridge and Marshall, Buckinghamshire. After Robert Knollys's death she became the second wife of Sir Robert Lee of Burston, Buckinghamshire, son of Sir Henry Lee of Quarendon in the same county. Sir Robert Lee, by whom she had issue, died in 1537, when she became the second wife of Sir Thomas Tresham of Rushton, Northamptonshire, prior (under Queen Mary) of the Knights of St. John of Jerusalem. Her will, dated 28 June 1557, was proved 11 June 1558.

Robert Knollys's children included, besides Francis, a son Henry and two daughters, Mary and Jane. The latter married Sir Richard Wingfield of Kimbolton Castle. The son Henry (d. 1583) was in some favour with Edward VI and Queen Elizabeth. He went abroad with his brother Francis during Queen Mary's reign. In 1562 he was sent on a diplomatic mission to Germany, to observe the temper of German protestants (FROUDE, *Hist.* vi. 580), and in 1569 was temporarily employed in warding both Queen Mary of Scotland at Tutbury and the Duke of Norfolk in the Tower (*Hatfield MSS.* i. 443). He was M.P. for Reading in 1563, and for Christchurch in 1572. His will, dated 27 July 1582, was proved 2 Sept. 1583.

Francis, born about 1514, appears to have received some education at Oxford, but Wood's assertion that he was for a time a member of Magdalen College is unconfirmed. Henry VIII extended to him the favour that he had shown to his father, and secured to him in fee the paternal estate of Rotherfield Greys in 1538. Acts of parliament in 1540

T 2

1541 and in 1545–6 attested this grant, making his wife in the second act joint tenant with him. At the same time Francis became one of the gentlemen-pensioners at court, and in 1539 attended Anne of Cleves on her arrival in England. In 1542 he entered the House of Commons for the first time as member for Horsham. At the beginning of Edward VI's reign he accompanied the English army to Scotland, and was knighted by the commander-in-chief, the Duke of Somerset, at the camp at Roxburgh, 28 Sept. 1547 (NICHOLS, *Lit. Rem. of Edw. VI*, ii. 219). Knollys's strong protestant convictions recommended him to the young king and to his sister the Princess Elizabeth, and he spent much time at court, taking a prominent part not only in tournaments there (*ib.* ii. 389), but also in religious discussion. On 25 Nov. 1551 he was present at Sir William Cecil's house, at a conference between a few catholics and protestants respecting the corporeal presence in the Sacrament (STRYPE, *Cranmer*, 1848, ii. 356). About the same date he was granted the manors of Caversham in Oxfordshire and Cholsey in Berkshire. At the end of 1552 he visited Ireland on public business.

The accession of Mary darkened Knollys's prospects. His religious opinions placed him in opposition to the government, and he deemed it prudent to cross to Germany. On his departure the Princess Elizabeth wrote to his wife a sympathetic note, expressing a wish that they would soon be able to return in safety (GREEN, *Letters of Illustrious Ladies*, iii. 278–9). Knollys first took up his residence in Frankfort, where he was admitted a church-member, 21 Dec. 1557, but afterwards removed to Strasburg. According to Fuller, he 'bountifully communicated to the necessities' of his fellow-exiles in Germany (*Church Hist.* iv. 228), and at Strasburg he seems to have been on intimate terms with Jewel and Peter Martyr (cf. BURNET, *Reformation*, iii. 500). Before Mary's death he returned to England, and as a man 'of assured understanding and truth, and well affected to the protestant religion,' he was admitted to Elizabeth's privy council in December 1558 (HAYWARD, *Annals*, p. 12). He was soon afterwards made vice-chamberlain of the household and captain of the halberdiers, while his wife and her sister—first cousins of Elizabeth—became women of the queen's privy chamber (*Hatfield MSS.* i. 158). In 1560 Knollys's wife and son Robert were granted for their lives the manor of Taunton, part of the property of the see of Winchester. In 1559 Knollys was chosen M.P. for Arundel, and in 1562 for Oxford, of which town he was

also appointed chief steward. In 1572 he was elected member for Oxfordshire, and sat for that constituency until his death. Throughout his parliamentary career he was a frequent spokesman for the government on questions of general politics, but in ecclesiastical matters he preserved as a zealous puritan an independent attitude.

Knollys's friendship with the queen and Cecil led to his employment in many offices of anxious responsibility. In 1563 he was governor of Portsmouth, and was much harassed in August by the difficulties of supplying the needs in men and money of the Earl of Warwick, who was engaged on his disastrous expedition to Havre (see DUDLEY, AMBROSE; *Hatfield MSS.* i. 274–5). In April 1566 he was sent to Ireland to control the expenditure of Sir Henry Sidney, the lord deputy, who was trying to repress the rebellion of Shane O'Neil, and was much hampered by the interference of court factions at home; but Knollys found himself compelled, contrary to Elizabeth's wish, to approve Sidney's plans. It was, he explained, out of the question to conduct the campaign against the Irish rebels on strictly economical lines (cf. BAGWELL, *Ireland under the Tudors*, ii. 105–7). In August 1564 he accompanied the queen to Cambridge, and was created M.A. Two years later he went to Oxford, also with his sovereign, and received a like distinction there. In the same year (1566) he was appointed treasurer of the queen's chamber.

In May 1568 Mary Queen of Scots fled to England, and flung herself on Elizabeth's protection. She had found refuge in Carlisle Castle, and the delicate duty of taking charge of the fugitive was entrusted jointly to Knollys and to Henry Scrope, ninth baron Scrope. On 28 May Knollys arrived at the castle, and was admitted to Mary's presence. At his first interview he was conscious of Mary's powerful fascination. But to her requests for an interview with Elizabeth, and for help to regain her throne, he returned the evasive answers which Elizabeth's advisers had suggested to him, and he frankly drew her attention to the suspicions in which Darnley's murder involved her. A month passed, and no decision was reached in London respecting Mary's future. On 13 July Knollys contrived to remove her, despite 'her tragical demonstrations,' to Bolton Castle, the seat of Lord Scrope, where he tried to amuse her by teaching her to write and speak English (*Hatfield MSS.* i. 400). Knollys's position grew more and more distasteful, and writing on 16 July to Cecil, whom he kept well informed of Mary's conversation and conduct, he angrily demanded his recall (WRIGHT, *Queen Eliz.* i. 291). But while lamenting his occupation, Knollys conscientiously endeavoured to convert his prisoner to his puritanic views, and she read the English prayer-book under his guidance. In his discussions with her he commended so unreservedly the doctrines and forms of Geneva that Elizabeth, on learning his line of argument, sent him a sharp reprimand. Knollys, writing to Cecil in self-defence, described how contentedly Mary accepted his plain speaking on religious topics (8 Aug. 1568). Mary made in fact every effort to maintain good relations with him. Late in August she gave him a present for his wife, desired his wife's acquaintance, and wrote to him a very friendly note, her first attempt in English composition (ELLIS, *Orig. Letters*, 1st ser. ii. 252). In October, when schemes for marrying Mary to an English nobleman were under consideration, Knollys proposed that his wife's nephew, George Carey, might prove a suitable match. In November the inquiry into Mary's misdeeds which had begun at York, was reopened at Westminster, and Knollys pointed out that he needed a larger company of retainers in order to keep his prisoner safe from a possible attempt at rescue. In December he was directed by Elizabeth to induce Mary to assent to her abdication of the Scottish throne. In January 1569 he plainly told Elizabeth that, in declining to allow Mary either to be condemned or to be acquitted on the charges brought against her, she was inviting perils which were likely to overwhelm her, and entreated her to leave the decision of Mary's fate to her well-tried councillors. On 20 Jan. orders arrived at Bolton to transfer Mary to Tutbury, where the Earl of Shrewsbury was to take charge of her. Against the removal the Scottish queen protested (25 Jan.) in a pathetic note to Knollys, intended for Elizabeth's eye (LABANOFF, ii. 284-6), but next day she was forced to leave Bolton, and Knollys remained with her at Tutbury till 3 Feb. His wife's death then called him home. Mary blamed Elizabeth for the fatal termination of Lady Knollys's illness, attributing it to her husband's enforced absence in the north (WRIGHT, *Queen Eliz.* i. 308).

In April 1571 Knollys strongly supported the retrospective clauses of the bill for the better protection of Queen Elizabeth, by which any person who had previously put forward a claim to the throne was adjudged guilty of high treason. Next year he was appointed treasurer of the royal household (13 July), and he entertained Elizabeth at Reading Abbey, where he often resided by permission of the crown. The office of treasurer he retained till his death.

Although Knollys was invariably on good terms personally with his sovereign, he never concealed his distrust of her statesmanship. Her unwillingness to take 'safe counsel,' her apparent readiness to encourage parasites and flatterers, whom he called 'King Richard the Second's men,' was, he boldly pointed out, responsible for most of her dangers and difficulties. In July 1578 he repeated his warnings in a long letter, and begged her to adopt straightforward measures so as to avert such disasters as the conquest of the Low Countries by Spain, the revolt of Scotland to France and Mary Stuart, and the growth of papists in England (WRIGHT, *Queen Eliz.* ii. 74-6). He did not oppose the first proposals for the queen's marriage with Alençon which were made in 1579, but during the negotiations he showed reluctance to accept the scheme, and Elizabeth threatened that 'his zeal for religion would cost him dear.'

In December 1581 he attended the jesuit Campion's execution, and asked him on the scaffold whether he renounced the pope. He was a commissioner for the trials of Parry the jesuit in 1585, of Babington and his fellow-conspirators, whom he tried to argue into protestantism, in 1586, and of Queen Mary at Fotheringay in the same year. He urged Mary's immediate execution in 1587 both in parliament and in the council. In April 1589 he was a commissioner for the trial of Philip Howard, earl of Arundel. On 16 Dec. 1584 he introduced into the House of Commons the bill legalising a national association to protect the queen from assassination. In 1585 he offered to contribute 100*l.* for seven years towards the expenses of the war for the defence of the Low Countries, and renewed the offer, which was not accepted, in July 1586. In 1588-9 he was placed in command of the land forces of Hertfordshire and Cambridgeshire which had been called together to resist the Spanish Armada. Knollys was interested in the voyages of Frobisher and Drake, and took shares in the first and second Cathay expeditions.

Knollys never wavered in his consistent championship of the puritans. In May 1574 he joined Bishop Grindal, Sir Walter Mildmay, and Sir Thomas Smith in a letter to Parkhurst, bishop of Norwich, arguing in favour of the religious exercises known as 'prophesyings.' But he was zealous in opposition to heresy, and in September 1581 he begged Burghley and Leicester to repress such 'anabaptisticall sectaries' as members of the 'Family of Love,' 'who do serve the turn of the papists' (WRIGHT, ii. 152-4).

Writing to Whitgift, archbishop of Canterbury, 20 June 1584, he hotly condemned the archbishop's attempts to prosecute puritan preachers in the court of high commission as unjustly despotic, and treading 'the highway to the pope' (*Hatfield MSS.* iii. 35). He supported Cartwright with equal vehemence. On 24 May 1584 he sent to Burghley a bitter attack on ' the undermining ambition and covetousness of some of our bishops,' and on their persecutions of the puritans (*ib.* pp. 412-13). Repeating his views in July 1586, he urged the banishment of all recusants and the exclusion from public offices of all who married recusants. In 1588 he charged Whitgift with endangering the queen's safety by his popish tyranny, and embodied his accusation in a series of articles which Whitgift characterised as a foul and scandalous syllogism. In the parliament of 1588-9 he vainly endeavoured to pass a bill against non-residence of the clergy and pluralities (STRYPE, *Whitgift*, p. 193). In the course of the discussion he denounced the claims of the bishops ' to keep courts in their own name,' and denied them any 'worldly preeminence.' This speech, 'related by himself' to Burghley, was published in 1608, together with a letter to Knollys from his friend, the puritan Dr. Reynolds 'or Rainolds,' in which Bishop Bancroft's sermon at St. Paul's Cross (9 Feb. 1588-9) was keenly criticised. The volume was entitled ' Informations, or a Protestation and a Treatise from Scotland . . . all suggesting the Usurpation of Papal Bishops.' Knollys's contribution reappeared as ' Speeches used in the parliament by Sir Francis Knoles,' in William Stoughton's ' Assertion for True and Christian Church Policie' (London, 1642). Throughout 1589 and 1590 he was seeking, in correspondence with Burghley, to convince the latter of the impolicy of adopting Whitgift's theory of the divine right of bishops. On 9 Jan. 1591 he told his correspondent that he marvelled ' how her Majestie can be persuaded that she is in as much danger of such as are called Purytanes as she is of the Papysts' (WRIGHT, ii. 417). Finally, on 14 May 1591, he declared that he would prefer to retire from politics and political office rather than cease to express his hostility to the bishops' claims with full freedom.

Knollys's domestic affairs at times caused him anxiety. In spite of his friendly relations with the Earl of Leicester, he did not approve the royal favourite's intrigues with his daughter, Lettice, widow of Walter Devereux, first earl of Essex [q. v.], and he finally insisted on their marriage at Wanstead 21 Sept. 1578. The wayward temper of his grandson, Robert Devereux, second earl of Essex (son of his daughter Lettice by her first husband), was a source of trouble to him in his later years, and the queen seemed inclined to make him responsible for the youth's vagaries. Knollys was created K.G. in 1593, and died 19 July 1596. He was buried at Rotherfield Greys, and an elaborate monument, with effigies of seven sons, six daughters, and his son William's wife, is still standing in the church there. A poem on his death was penned by Thomas Churchyard, under the title 'A sad and solemne funerall,' London, 1596, 4to (see reprint in Park's 'Heliconia'). Two portraits of Knollys and one of his wife are said to have been in possession of a descendant at Fern Hill, near Windsor, in 1776.

Many of his letters are printed in Wright's ' Queen Elizabeth,' in the Calendars of the Hatfield MSS., and in Haynes's ' State Papers.' Wood states that a manuscript 'General Survey of the Isle of Wight, with all the Fortresses and Castles near adjoining,' belonged in his time to Arthur, earl of Anglesey. A manuscript ' Discourse of Exchange' by Knollys is at Penshurst (*Hist. MSS. Comm.* 3rd Rep. p. 230): his ' arguments against the cross in baptism and the surplice' are in Lansd. MS. 64, art. 14, and a ' project ' by him ' for security of the protestant religion by checking the ecclesiastical power' is in Lansd. MS. 97, art. 16.

Knollys married Catherine, daughter of William Carey, esquire of the body to Henry VIII, by Mary, daughter of Sir Thomas Boleyn, earl of Wiltshire, and sister of Queen Anne Boleyn. Lady Knollys was thus first cousin to Queen Elizabeth, and sister to Henry Carey, lord Hunsdon [q. v.] She died, aged 39, at Hampton Court, while in attendance on the queen, 15 Jan. 1568-9, and was buried in April in St. Edmund's Chapel in Westminster Abbey, at the royal expense (*Hatfield MSS.* i. 415). Elizabeth keenly felt her loss (*ib.* i. 400). A broadside epitaph by Thomas Newton, dated in 1569, belonged to Heber (cf. *Bibl. Heber.* ed. Collier, p. 55). She left seven sons and four daughters. Of the latter, Lettice (1540-1634) was wife successively of Walter Devereux, earl of Essex, Robert Dudley, earl of Leicester, and of Sir Christopher Blount [see under DUDLEY, ROBERT]: Cecilia, maid of honour to Queen Elizabeth, married Sir Thomas Leighton, captain of Guernsey (NICOLAS, *Hatton*, p. 281): Anne, married to Thomas, lord de la Warr; and Catherine, married (1) to Gerald Fitzgerald, lord Offaly, and (2) Sir Philip Boteler of Watton Woodhall.

All Knollys's sons were prominent courtiers in his lifetime. They were, according to Naunton, at continual feud with the Norris family, and, aided by Leicester's influence, kept their rivals in subjection until Leicester's death. Henry, the eldest son, described as of Kingsbury, Warwickshire, was educated at Magdalen College school, Oxford, and after accompanying his father to Germany, is said to have matriculated at the college, although his name does not appear in the university register, and to have obtained there the reputation of being a very cultivated and religious man. He was elected M.P. for Shoreham in 1562-3, and for Oxfordshire in 1572, and accompanied his brother-in-law, Walter Devereux, earl of Essex, to Ireland in 1574. He was an esquire of the body to Queen Elizabeth. His will, dated 21 Dec. 1582, was proved 14 May 1583. He married, before 11 April 1568, Margaret (1549?–1606), daughter of Sir Ambrose Cave, by whom he had two daughters, Elizabeth (dead before 1632), wife of Sir Henry Willoughby (d. 1649) of Risley, Derbyshire, and Lettice, wife of William, fourth lord Paget (d. 20 Aug. 1629), from whom descend the Marquises of Anglesey.

William, the second son, and eventual heir, is noticed separately.

Edward, the third son, was elected M.P. for Oxford 2 April 1571, and died about 1580.

Robert, the fourth son, was appointed keeper of Sion House in 1590, and usher of the Mint in the Tower, 5 Feb. 1578. He was M.P. for Reading from 1572 to 1589, and for Breconshire from 1589 to 1604, subsequently sitting for Abingdon, 1614, and again in 1623-4 and 1625, and for Berkshire in 1620. He was created K.B. 24 July 1603, and died in January 1625. He married Katherine, daughter of Sir Rowland Vaughan of Porthamel, Anglesey.

Richard, the fifth son, described as of Stanford-in-the-Vale, Berkshire, M.P. for Northampton in 1588 and for Wallingford in 1584, died at Rotherfield Greys 21 Aug. 1596, having married Joane, daughter of John Higham of Cliffords, Sussex, and sister of John Higham of Stanford. Her second husband was Francis Winchcombe of Bucklebury, Berkshire. She was buried at Rotherfield Greys 10 Oct. 1631. Sir Robert Knollys (d. 1659), her son by her first husband, was knighted 10 Jan. 1612-13, and acquired Rotherfield Greys from his uncle William 4 March 1630-1. The estate was finally alienated from the family in 1686.

Francis, sixth son, leased from the crown the manor of Battel, near Reading. He was well known at court as 'young Sir Francis,' and was M.P. for Oxford 1572-88, and for Berkshire in 1597 and 1625. His will was proved in 1648. He married Lettice, daughter of John Barrett of Hanham, Gloucestershire, by license dated 21 Dec. 1588. A son Sir Francis, who seems to have been M.P. for Reading in 1625-6-8 and 1640, died in 1643, and his daughter, Letitia or Lettice, was second wife of John Hampden [q. v.]

Thomas, apparently seventh son, distinguished himself in the warfare in the Low Countries, acting as governor of Ostend in 1586, and prominently aiding Peregrine Bertie [q. v.] in the siege of Bergen in 1588. He married Odelia, daughter of John de Morula, marquess of Bergen.

[Wood's Athenæ Oxon. i. 653-5; Cooper's Athenæ Cantabr. ii. 209, 548; Gent. Mag. 1846, pt. i. p. 250 (account of Lettice Knollys and her family); Froude's History; Lists of Members of Parliament; Cal. State Papers, Domestic, Colonial, and Scottish; Dr. F. G. Lee's History of the Prebendal Church of Thame, p. 593; Herald and Genealogist, vols. vii. viii.; Nicolas's Life of Sir Christopher Hatton; Devereux's Lives of Earls of Essex; Dugdale's Baronage; Strype's Whitgift, Eccl. Memorials, and Annals; Coates's Reading; Zurich Letters (Parker Soc.); Nichols's Lit. Remains of Edward VI (Roxb. Club); Naunton's Queen Elizabeth's Favourites; Pedigree of the family of Knollys and title to the manor of Rotherfield Greys, published by the House of Lords, 1810; Davenport's Lords-Lieutenants and Sheriffs of Oxfordshire, p. 60.]

S. L.

KNOLLYS, HANSERD (1599?–1691), particular baptist divine, was born at Cawkwell, Lincolnshire, about 1599. He was educated privately under a tutor, was for a short time at Great Grimsby grammar school, and afterwards graduated at Cambridge; his college is not mentioned. Leaving the university, he became master of the grammar school at Gainsborough, Lincolnshire. In 1629 he was ordained (29 June, deacon; 30 June, priest), and he was presented to the vicarage of Humberstone, Lincolnshire, by John Williams, then bishop of Lincoln. He preached also every Sunday in the neighbouring churches of Holton-le-Clay and Scartho, but in two or three years resigned his living owing to scruples about ceremonies and admission to the communion, continuing, however, to preach. By 1636 he had become a separatist, and renounced his orders. He removed to London with his wife and family, and shortly afterwards fled to New England to escape the high commission court. A warrant from that court reached him at Boston, but after a brief imprisonment he was allowed to remain unmolested. He preached at Dover, New Hampshire. Cotton

Mather enumerates him among 'godly ana-baptists;' the date of his adoption of this type of doctrine and practice is not clear.

On 24 Dec. 1641 he reached London on his return to this country at the instance of his aged father. He opened a boarding-school on Great Tower Hill. Soon afterwards he was elected to the mastership of the free school in the parish of St. Mary Axe. As a schoolmaster he was very successful, but after holding this office for about a year he gave it up to become an army chaplain. Dissatisfied with the spirit of the parlia-mentary commanders, he returned to London and to school-keeping. He learned Hebrew from Christian Ravy [Ravis] Berlinas, 'He-brew professor' in London. In 1644 we find him preaching in London and Suffolk churches and churchyards, and occasionally, in what afterwards became quaker fashion, endeavouring to supplement the regular ser-mon by a discourse of his own. This led, according to Edwards (*Gangræna*, 2nd ed. 1646, i. 129 sq.), to 'riots and tumults,' for which Knollys was twice brought before a committee of parliament, but on each occa-sion 'got off.' In fact he was absolved from blame and protected in his action. He gathered a church of his own in 1645, meet-ing first, for about a year, in Great St. Helen's, 'next door to the publique church,' then in Finsbury Fields, next in Coleman Street, subsequently in George Yard, Whitechapel, and ultimately at Broken Wharf, Thames Street. His most important convert was Henry Jessey [q. v.], whom he baptised in June 1645. A letter (11 Jan. 1646) from him to John Dutton of Norwich, in favour of toleration, printed by Edwards (*ib.* iii. 48), embittered the presbyterians against him. But his ministry was popular; though Ed-wards calls him 'a weak man, and a sorry disputant,' he attracted nearly a thousand hearers. He subscribed the second edition (1646) of the confession of faith issued by London baptists, but not the original edition (1644). On 17 Jan. 1649 parliament gave a commission to him and William Kiffin [q. v.] to preach in Suffolk, on petition from inhabi-tants of Ipswich. His name is attached to pleas for toleration addressed to parliament in 1651 and 1654, and to the lord protector on 3 April 1657.

Between 1645 and the Restoration Knollys met with no interference. He held some offices of profit under Cromwell's govern-ment, resigning on 29 March 1653 the post of examiner at the customs and excise, with a salary of 120*l.*, 'for more beneficial em-ployment.' He was clerk of the check till 23 May 1655. On the outbreak (7 Jan. 1661)

of Venner's insurrection he was committed to Newgate on groundless suspicion, and detained till the act of grace on the king's coronation (23 April) liberated him. It was not safe for him to resume his ministry in London; he made some stay in Wales, and twice sought a refuge in Lincolnshire. Sail-ing thence for Holland, he made his way to Germany, where he remained two or three years, returning at length to London by way of Rotterdam. In his absence, Colonel Legge, lieutenant of the ordnance, in the king's name took forcible possession of his property (a house and garden worth 700*l.*, and 200*l.* deposited with the Weavers' Com-pany).

In London he once more resumed his school and his pastorate, preaching also a morning lecture on Sundays at Pinners' Hall, Old Broad Street, then in the hands of indepen-dents. On 10 May 1670 he was arrested at his meeting in George Yard, under the second Conventicle Act, which had just come into force. He was committed to the Bishopsgate-compter, but was considerably treated and was allowed to preach to the prisoners; at the next Old Bailey sessions he obtained his discharge. He survived the Toleration Act, and, though in extreme old age, took a leading part in efforts made in 1689 for the consolida-tion of the baptist cause. He retained great vigour both of body and mind; when at-tacked by illness he discarded medicine, and resorted to anointing and prayer. He con-tinued preaching to the last, when he could scarcely stand or make his voice heard. Robert Steed was his assistant.

He died on 19 Sept. 1691, in his ninety-third year, and was buried in Bunhill Fields. The funeral sermon was preached by Thomas Harrison (1699–1702), particular baptist minister at Petty France, and afterwards at Loriners' Hall. His portrait, at the age of sixty-seven, was engraved; the print, as re-produced by Hopwood, is given in Wilson. An engraving by Van Hove, representing him in his ninety-third year, is prefixed to his 'Life.' He wore long hair, mostly covered by a loose skull-cap, and no beard. He mar-ried in 1630 or 1631; his wife died on 30 April 1671; he had at least three sons and a daughter; Isaac, his last surviving son, died on 15 Nov. 1671.

He published: 1. 'A Glimpse of Sion's Glory,' &c., 1641, 4to (this is probably his). 2. 'A Modest Answer to Dr. Bastwick's book called "Independency not God's Ordinance,"' &c., 1645, 4to. 3. 'Christ Exalted . . . ser-mon . . . at Debenham [Coless. iii. 11] . . . Also, another sermon [Ephes. i. 4],' &c., 1645, 4to; 2nd ed. 1646, 4to. 4. 'The Shining of a Flaming Fire in Zion,' &c., 1646, 4to (answer to 'The Smoke in the Temple' by John Saltmarsh [q. v.]). 5. 'The Rudiments of the Hebrew Grammar in English,' &c., 1648, 8vo. 6. 'Grammaticæ Latinæ, Græcæ et Hebraicæ Compendium,' &c., 1665, 8vo (Bodleian). 7. 'An Exposition of the Whole Book of the Revelation,' &c., 1688, 4to. 8. 'The Parable of the Kingdom of Heaven . . . first 13 verses of the 25th chapter of Matthew,' &c., 1674, 8vo. 9. 'An Essay of Sacred Rhetoric,' &c., 1675, 8vo. 10. An Exposition of the Eleventh Chapter of the Revelation,' &c., 1679, 4to. 11. 'The World that now is, and the World that is to come: or the First and Second Coming of Jesus Christ,' &c., 1681, 12mo. Also preface to 'The Exaltation of Christ,' 1646, 8vo, by Thomas Collier [q. v.], and to an edition of 'Instructions for Children' by Benjamin Keach (q. v.] Posthumous was: 12. 'The Life and Death of . . . Hanserd Knollys . . . Written with his own hand to the year 1672. . . . To which is added his Last Legacy to the Church,' &c., 1692, 12mo (edited and continued by Kiffin): reprinted 1812, 12mo. The Hanserd Knollys Society, for the reprinting of early baptist writings and the publication of original records, was instituted in London in 1845, and dissolved after issuing ten volumes.

[Life, 1692; Funeral Sermon by Harrison, 1694; Mather's Magnalia Christi Americana, 1702, iii. 7; Crosby's Hist. of English Baptists, 1738, i. 120 sq., 334 sq., ii. 91; Granger's Biographical Hist. of England, 1779, iii. 338; Wilson's Dissenting Churches of London, 1808, ii. 560 sq.; Brook's Lives of the Puritans, 1813, iii. 491 sq.; Confessions of Faith (Hanserd Knollys Society), 1854, pp. 23, 338; Records of the Churches at Fenstanton, &c. (Hanserd Knollys Society), 1854, pp. 303 sq.; Cal. State Papers, Dom. 1653 and 1655; Athenæum, 6 Aug. 1881.] A. G.

KNOLLYS or **KNOLLES**, SIR ROBERT (d. 1407), military commander, was a native of Cheshire. Walsingham calls him 'pauper mediocrisque valletus' (Hist. Angl. i. 280), and Malverne says that he was sprung 'quasi de infimo genere' (ap. HIGDEN, viii. 372); but, despite such expressions, Knolles was probably of honourable parentage. On 1 May 1354 the estate of Lea was entailed on Hugh, David, and Robert, sons of Richard (it should be David) de Calvylegh, while in the inquisition held on the death of Mabel de Calvylegh in 1361, 'Robert Knollus chivaler' is included in the entail with Hugh and David de Calveley (see CALVELEY, SIR HUGH], and may therefore possibly be their brother (ORMEROD, Cheshire, ii. 764, 768, ed. Helsby). Lysons, on the other hand, makes Knolles

the son of Richard Knolles by Eva de Calveley, and nephew, not brother, of Sir Hugh (LYSONS, Cheshire, p. 543). That there was some special connection between Calveley and Knolles seems to be proved by the appearance of Knolles's arms on Calveley's tomb, while Calveley's arms appear with those of Knolles at Sculthorpe, Norfolk; the arms of Sir Hugh Browe, whom we know to have been a cousin of Knolles, also appear on Calveley's tomb. No contemporary authority, however, mentions the two men as relatives. The date of Knolles's birth is uncertain; Fuller conjectures that it was at least as early as 1317, but it may well have been some years later. Jehan le Bel strangely asserts that Knolles was a German, and says that he had been a tailor (ii. 216).

Knolles's first military service was in Brittany, where he served with Calveley and Walter Hewett under Sir Thomas Dagworth at the siege of La Roche d'Orient, in July 1346 (OTTERBOURNE, p. 136, ed. Hearne). He was already a knight in 1351, when he took part in the famous 'Combat of the Thirty,' on which occasion he was one of the survivors who were made prisoners (see the poem 'Combat des Trente,' ap. FROISSART, xiv. 301-20, ed. Buchon). Knolles was soon released, and, remaining in Brittany, acquired great renown as a soldier. Jehan le Bel says that Knolles, Renault de Cervole, and Ruffin were the first leaders of the 'Companies,' i.e. of free lances and freebooters (ii. 210; cf. FROISSART, iv. 186). Knolles was with Walter de Bentley when he defeated Guy de Nesle at Mouron on 14 Aug. 1352 (GEOFFREY LE BAKER, p. 120, ed. Thompson). Previously to 10 July 1355 he was in charge of Fougeray and other castles in Brittany; he appears to have paid two thousand florins for their custody (Fœdera, iii. 307, 312, 622). When in 1356 Henry of Lancaster made a raid into Normandy in support of Philip of Navarre and Godfrey de Harcourt, Knolles came to his aid from Carentoir with three hundred men-at-arms and five hundred archers. The expedition started on 22 June and ravaged Normandy up to the walls of Rouen. Knolles displayed his valour in a successful skirmish at the end of the raid, in the middle of July (FROISSART, iv. 186-9, and lxx; AVESBURY, pp. 463-5, Rolls Ser.) He then went to besiege Domfront, and in September attempted to join the Prince of Wales in Poitou, but found the Loire so strongly guarded that he had to return (Chron. des Quatre Valois, pp. 45-6). In 1357 he served under Henry of Lancaster when he besieged Du Guesclin at Rennes, and at the end of June he and Sir James Pipe defeated the

French before Honfleur (BARNES, *Hist. of Edward III*, p. 531).

Next year Knolles was plundering in Normandy at the head of a numerous body known as the 'Great Company,' to whom his remarkable skill insured abundant booty; he is said to have received for his own share a hundred thousand crowns (WALSINGHAM, *Hist. Angl.* i. 286; FROISSART, v. 95). Eventually he established himself in the valley of the Loire, made himself master of forty castles, and ravaged all the country from Tonnerre to Vezelay and Nevers to Orleans. The suburbs of Orleans were sacked and burnt, while at Ancenis, on the Loire, the people were so frightened at the terror of his name that many threw themselves into the river. Knolles declared that he fought neither for the king of England nor for Charles of Navarre, but for himself alone, and displayed on his devices the legend—

Qui Robert Canolle prendera,
Cent mille moutons gagnera.

In October 1358 he captured the castle of Châteauneuf-sur-Loire, and on 10 March 1359 the town of Auxerre, which he sacked and held till 30 April, exacting an enormous ransom. Froissart wrongly states that he was with Philip of Navarre before St. Valery in April (*ib.* v. 144–7; cf. p. xlvii). On 2 May he captured Châtillon-sur-Loing, and a little later made a great raid through Berri into Auvergne, boasting that he would ride to Avignon and plunder the pope (Benedict XIII); Knighton states that he actually came within twelve leagues of the city, and caused great alarm (col. 2619). When the French of Auvergne and Rouergue came out to oppose him, Knolles eluded them by a stratagem, and retired into the Limousin. His ravages during these raids were so terrible that the charred gables which marked his route were called 'Knolles's mitres.' A contemporary epigram has been preserved:—

O Roberte Knollis, per te fit Francia mollis,
Ense tuo tollis præedas, dans vulnera collis.

On his return Knighton says that he sent to England to say that all the towns and castles which he had captured were at the king's disposal. Edward III, who was much pleased at his success, seems to have rewarded him by pardoning his informal proceedings, and it was probably to this that the commons referred in 1376, when they petitioned that Sir John Hawkwood [q. v.] might receive a pardon in like terms to the one granted to Knolles (KNIGHTON, col. 2620; BARNES, p. 563; *Rot. Parl.* ii. 372 *b*). According to Knighton, Knolles was captured about Mi-

chaelmas in an ambush, but was rescued by his comrade, Hannekin François. He served with Lancaster at the siege of Dinan, where he vainly endeavoured to arrange the quarrel between Du Guesclin and Thomas de Canterbury (CUVÉLIER, i. 82–94). Thence he was summoned to join Edward III in the campaign which immediately preceded the peace of Bretigny (*ib.* i. 97). There is, however, no record of Knolles's share in it, and he was in Brittany in April 1360, when his wife joined him with a reinforcement (*Fœdera*, iii. 480). M. Luce does not think Knolles took part in the expedition; it is certain that he defeated and took prisoner Bertrand du Guesclin at Pas d'Erran in Brittany, near the end of 1359 (*Hist. de B. du Guesclin*, pp. 311–12).

The struggle between the partisans of John de Montfort and Charles de Blois continued in spite of the peace, and Knolles remained in Brittany to support the former (cf. *Fœdera*, iii. 653, 662, 697). In 1363 he was at the siege of Bécherel (*Chron. du Guesclin*, p. 14, Panth. Littéraire), and next year was with Louis of Navarre in Auvergne, where they plundered the Bourbonnais and all the country between the Loire and Allier. In September 1364 he was with De Montfort at the siege of Auray in high command. When Du Guesclin and Charles de Blois advanced to the rescue, Knolles supported Oliver de Clisson in advising an attack, and in the battle of 29 Sept. was joined with Sir Walter Hewett and Sir Richard Burlegh in command of the first division. Charles de Blois was defeated and slain, Du Guesclin captured, and John de Montfort secured in possession of the duchy, a result largely due to the valour of Knolles, who took prisoner the Count of Auxerre (FROISSART, vi. 150–5; CUVÉLIER, i. 201–33). As a reward John de Montfort bestowed on Knolles, in 1365, the lands of Derval and Rougé, together with two thousand 'livres de rente' in the land of Conq (LUCE, vi. p. lxvi), whence Knolles is sometimes called Sire de Derval. Early in 1367 Knolles joined the Black Prince in his Spanish expedition with a chosen band of the 'Great Company' (WALSINGHAM, i. 303). He crossed the pass of Roncevaux with the third battle on 17 Feb., and joined Sir Thomas Felton [q. v.] in his reconnoitre and capture of Navaretta in Alava (LUCE, vii. p. vii). He was still with Felton in his successful skirmish against Henry of Trastamare, but was not present at his defeat a few days after. Froissart alludes to Knolles as one of those who were taken prisoners on that occasion (vii. 303), but Knolles was certainly present at the battle of Najara, 3 April, when he came to the support of Chandos on the left wing, and by his valour contributed largely to the victory (WALSINGHAM, i. 304; WRIGHT, *Pol. Songs*, i. 95, 108). On 2 May we hear of Knolles at Burgos (*Fœdera*, iii. 825). He returned with the prince to France, and soon after went back to Brittany.

When in 1369 the war broke out anew in Aquitaine, Knolles equipped a small force, and, embarking at Conq in April, landed at Rochelle and joined the Prince of Wales at Angoulême. The prince received him warmly, made him master of his household, and entrusted him with the command of a strong force. Knolles's first exploit was to induce Perducas d'Albret to rejoin the English; the free companies under other leaders then evacuated Cahors and fortified the priory of Duravel, where Knolles besieged them. Chandos came to join him, but the priory was so strongly fortified, and the weather so bad, that they had to raise the siege. Domme was next besieged for fifteen days without success, but after sending for reinforcements they captured Gramat, Fons, Rocamadour, and Villefranche. In July Chandos was recalled, and Knolles, refusing to remain without him, returned to Angoulême. He then went to Poitou and served with the Earls of Cambridge and Pembroke at the capture of Roche-sur-Yon. In January 1370 he was at Angoulême, and took part in the operations for the relief of Belleperche. In March he returned to Derval (FROISSART, vii. 139-50, 215, 370).

Knolles had scarcely been at Derval a month when he was summoned to England, and, landing at St. Michael's Mount, rode to Windsor (*ib.* vii. 220). The French were contemplating an invasion of Wales, and Edward III had therefore decided on two counter expeditions to France. One of these was to land at Calais, and Knolles had been chosen as its commander. After three months spent in preparation, the expedition, consisting of fifteen hundred men-at-arms and four thousand archers, sailed from Dover early in July (*Fœdera*, iii. 892, 894, 895-8; many references to the preparations will be found in BRANTINGHAM, *Issue Rolls*, see index, s. v. 'Knolles'). Leaving Calais about 22 July, Knolles marched to Teronenne, which was too strong for attack; Arras, where he sacked the suburbs; and so through Artois into Picardy and Vermandois. The English supported themselves by plunder, and the country people fled before them into the fortresses. Knolles, whose policy was to do as much damage as possible, did not attempt any sieges, and contented himself with the exaction of heavy ransoms. He vainly offered

battle before Noyon, and, after crossing the Oise and Aisne, made a demonstration before Rheims. Thence he directed his steps by the valley of the Marne and Seine towards Paris, in the hope that he might induce the French to fight. On 22 Sept. he encamped near Athis-Mons and Ablon, and on the 24th drew up in order of battle between Villejuif and Paris. But though the English army was so near that the smoke of the burning villages was visible from Paris, Charles V would not permit the French to offer battle. On the 25th the English marched off towards Normandy, and on the 29th sacked St. Gervais de Seez. Knolles was much hampered by dissensions in his army. The young nobles thought it a slight to be under the orders of one whom they regarded as an adventurer. Sir John de Menstreworth stirred up this feeling by calling Knolles 'the old brigand' (*vetus cispilio*), and eventually a considerable portion of the army broke away from its leader under Grandson and Menstreworth. Knolles thereupon decided to withdraw to Brittany; he marched by Chartres and Chateaudun, and spent November in subduing various small places in the valley of the Loire (LUCE, viii. p. iv, note 4; the account given by Froissart is inaccurate). Meantime Bertrand du Guesclin had been hastily summoned back from Aquitaine, and was marching in pursuit. Knolles, who was now in the marches of Brittany, determined to give battle. He summoned Sir Hugh de Calveley from St. Maur-sur-Loire, and ordered Grandson to rejoin him. Grandson was on his way when he was totally defeated by Du Guesclin at Pont Vallain on 4 Dec. (*ib.* viii. p. vi). Further action was now impossible, and the English dispersed to the neighbouring fortresses, Knolles going to his own castle of Derval (FROISSART, vii. 223-45, viii. 1-4; WALSINGHAM, i. 310; CUVÉLIER, ii. 123-4, 145-50, 185).

Although the expedition had ended disastrously, it had not been ineffectual; the invasion of Wales was averted, and the recall of Du Guesclin had relieved the English in Aquitaine. Menstreworth, however, on his return made the partial failure the ground of an accusation, and Knolles felt it necessary to send home two squires to represent his case. Sir Alan Buxhull [q. v.] also supported his late commander, and Knolles was fully acquitted on the ground that his ill-success was due to the pride and disobedience of his followers. Menstreworth fled over sea, and in 1377 was captured and executed as a traitor. Walsingham, however, adds that Edward III withdrew many presents which he had bestowed on Knolles (cf. BLOMEFIELD, vi. 282), and that Knolles could not return to England till he had purchased the royal favour by a large sum of money (WALSINGHAM, i. 310). This is confirmed by the articles of accusation against William, fourth lord Latimer [q. v.] in 1377, which charged him with having embezzled four-fifths of a fine of ten thousand marks sent to the king by Knolles (*Chron. Angliæ*, p. 78).

Knolles remained some years in Brittany to support John de Montfort. By 1373 Charles V had won over to the French side all the barons of the duchy except Knolles, and when John de Montfort went to England in that year he left Knolles as his lieutenant. Knolles went to Brest, leaving Derval in charge of his cousin, Sir Hugh Browe. In the summer Du Guesclin laid siege to Derval and Oliver de Clisson to Brest. Browe, soon reduced to extremities, gave hostages for the surrender of the castle if not relieved by a sufficient force within forty days; the time seems to have been afterwards prolonged. Knolles learnt of his straits through a spy, and by promising to surrender Brest if not relieved within one month by a force which could fight the French, induced De Clisson to raise the siege on 9 July. Knolles left Brest, and succeeded in entering Derval with a small following. When he arrived at Derval, Knolles disavowed the action of his lieutenant, Browe, and declared the agreement for the capitulation void. Thereupon Louis, duke of Anjou, who was now in command of the French, had Browe's hostages executed on 30 Sept. Knolles at once retaliated by beheading an equal number of prisoners, and throwing their bodies over the castle walls. These acts of cruelty seem to have been regarded as indefensible, but Knolles gained his object, for the French raised the siege of Derval (FROISSART, viii. 123–48, 158–60, and M. LUCE's notes on pp. lxxx and xciii; *Chron. du Duc Louis de Bourbon*, pp. 45, 47).

Knolles appears to have returned to England, and, probably towards the end of 1374, was sent with an expedition to Aquitaine; but after recapturing a number of places from the French, and among them Niort, he came home without securing any permanent advantage (*ib.* p. 74; *Eulog. Hist.* iii. 339). On 28 Nov. 1376 he was one of the conservators of the truce with France (*Fœdera*, iii. 1066). In 1377 he was one of the commanders of the fleet who were sent to attack the Spaniards at Sluys (WALSINGHAM, i. 344). Next year he was again captain of Brest, and while there defeated the Bretons (*ib.* i. 365; *Fœdera*, iii. pt. iii. p. 77). In April he left Brest for England, and at Whitsuntide was with the Earl of Arundel

when he attacked the French outside Harfleur (*Chron. des Quatre Valois*, p. 263). He then joined the Duke of Lancaster at the siege of St. Malo, and in company with Sir Hugh Browe plundered the neighbouring country. In 1379 Knolles was with John de Montfort in London, and in July returned with him to Vannes (FROISSART, vii. 275–6, ed. Buchon). Next year Knolles took part in the great expedition under Thomas, earl of Buckingham [see THOMAS OF WOODSTOCK, DUKE OF GLOUCESTER], which, landing at Calais early in July, marched through Artois, Vermandois, and Champagne, and eventually descended the valley of the Loire to Brittany. When near Vendôme Knolles's detachment had a skirmish, in which Knolles defeated the French leader, the Sire de Mauvoisin, and with his own hand took him prisoner. Buckingham established himself at Rennes, but John de Montfort was already wavering, and it was only after a mission in which Knolles took part that matters were for the time arranged. At the end of October the English laid siege to Nantes; Knolles was stationed with Thomas Percy at St. Nicholas's Gate, and his valour alone saved the English from defeat on 12 Nov. John de Montfort was negotiating with the French, and did not act heartily with his English allies, who were thus compelled to raise the siege on 2 Jan. 1381. Buckingham retired to Vannes, and Knolles went with Sir Hugh Calveley to Quimper Corentin, whence they probably returned with Buckingham to England in the following April (*ib.* vii. 316–428; WALSINGHAM, i. 444–5).

At the time of Wat Tyler's rebellion in July 1381 Knolles was residing in London, and guarded his treasure with 120 companions ready armed. After the murder of the archbishop in the Tower, the citizens put themselves under the leadership of Knolles. Knolles rode out with the king to Smithfield. When Richard asked him whether Tyler's followers should be massacred, he replied, 'No, my lord; many of these poor wretches are here against their will'; then, turning to the crowd, he bade them disperse on pain of death if found in the city after night. This is the account given in the 'Eulogium Historiarum' (iii. 353–4). Froissart transposes the parts taken by the king and Knolles, and says the latter was angry because Richard would not permit him to adopt violent measures (viii. 36, 55–7, ed. Buchon). The Londoners rewarded Knolles's services with the freedom of their city, and the king by the grant of the manor of St. Pancras to him and his wife (BLOMEFIELD, vi. 174).

The Monk of St.-Denys asserts that Knolles shared in the Flemish expedition of Henry Despenser [q. v.], bishop of Norwich, in 1383, and represents him as playing the part at Bergues which Froissart more correctly ascribes to Sir Hugh de Calveley (*Chron. Rel. de St.-Denys*, i. 258, 270, 272, Documents Inédits, &c.; FROISSART, viii. 442-4, ed. Buchon). Probably the remainder of his long life was spent in quiet retirement either in London or at his manorhouse at Sculthorpe, Norfolk. In 1384 there was a serious riot in London under one John Comerton; by Knolles's advice one of the ringleaders was beheaded, and the movement subsided. On 18 Aug. 1389 Knolles had license to go to Rome on a matter of conscience (*Fœdera*, iii. pt. iv. p. 46). The 'regal wealth' (WALSINGHAM, i. 286) which he had amassed in the wars enabled him to acquire large estates, chiefly in Norfolk, but also in Wiltshire, Kent, and London (*Cal. Inq. p. m.* ii. 305; HASTED, *Hist. of Kent*, ii. 674; *Rot. Parl.* iii. 258 b). He frequently assisted Richard II by loans on the security of jewels and plate (BLOMEFIELD, vi. 176). His munificence was notable. In 1380 he joined with Sir John Hawkwood and Calveley in the foundation of an English hospital at Rome (*Harl. MS.* 2111, f. 100 b). In 1388, together with John de Cobham, he re-built and endowed the bridge and chantry at Rochester; the bridge was destroyed in 1856 (*Eulog. Hist.* iii. 367; *Rot. Parl.* iii. 289 b; HASTED, *Hist. of Kent*, ii. 17-18). In London he was a liberal benefactor to the house of the Carmelites at Whitefriars, and in Norfolk he rebuilt the churches of Sculthorpe and Harpley; but his chief foundation was a college and hospital for a master, six priests, and thirteen poor men and women, at Pontefract, which was known as 'Knolles' Almeshouse.' The college was endowed with 180l. a year, from land chiefly in London and Norfolk; it was dissolved at the Reformation, but the almshouse, revived in 1563, still exists (BLOMEFIELD, vi. 21, 276; *Cal. Rot. Pat.* pp. 211, 220; *Rot. Parl.* v. 135, 366; LELAND, *Itinerary*, i. 43; DUGDALE, *Monasticon*, vi. 713-14).

Knolles died at Sculthorpe 15 Aug. 1407, and was buried at Whitefriars, London (WEEVER, *Funerall Monuments*, p. 436; *Coll. Top. et Gen.* viii. 321). His two wills in French and Latin, and dated 21 Oct. 1399 and 29 May 1404 respectively, are now extant at Lambeth. No mention is made of any children (*Herald and Genealogist*, viii. 289). As a soldier he must be placed among the most eminent of his age; Froissart speaks of him as 'the most able and skilful man of arms in all the companies,' and says that he was chosen for the

command in 1370 on account of his great skill and knowledge in handling and governing an army (iv. 186, vii. 223). His partial ill-success on that occasion was due to prejudices which he could scarcely have controlled, and he seems to have possessed some of the qualities of a true general as distinguished from a merely skilful soldier. In his own time and country he was scarcely less renowned than Hawkwood, whom he might have rivalled permanently but for his loyalty to his sovereign and his native land— a characteristic specially mentioned by Froissart (vii. 139). To Cuvélier he is 'Robert Canole qui moult greva Françoiz tous les jours de sa vie' . . . 'qui ne prise Françoiz deux deniers seulement' (i. 101, ii. 163). The Chandos herald calls him 'a man of few words' (ed. Coxe, l. 2725).

Knolles was married to his wife Constantia before 1360 (*Fœdera*, iii. 480). Leland says that she was a native of Pontefract and 'a woman of mene birth and sometime of a dissolute lyvyng before marriage' (*Itinerary*, i. 43). But her arms, 'argent a fess dancette between three pards' faces sable,' are those of the Yorkshire family of Beverley, to which she perhaps belonged (*Coll. Top. et Gen.* viii. 321). Dying a few days after her husband, she was buried by his side. Sir Robert left no legitimate male heirs, and it is very doubtful whether he was even, as some have supposed, the father of Emme or Margaret Knolles who married John Babington of Aldrington, Devon (*Herald and Genealogist*, v. 296; BLOMEFIELD, vi. 175). Sir Robert's name most usually appears in contemporary English writers as Knolles, but Knollis, Knowles, and Knollys also occur. French writers usually call him Canolles or Canole. The common statement that he was a knight of the Garter is not substantiated (ANSTIS, *Register of the Order of the Garter*, ii. 30-2).

[Froissart's Chroniques, ed. Luce (Soc. de l'Hist. de France), vols. iv-viii., and ed. Buchon (Collection des Chroniques), vols. vii. and viii.: M. Luce's valuable notes are sometimes referred to under his own name, his edition is the one used, except when otherwise stated; Chroniques de Jehan le Bel (Acad. Royale, Brussels); Chronique du Duc Louis de Bourbon, Chron. des quatre premiers Valois, Chronique Normande (all published by Soc. de l'Hist. de France); Cuvélier's Chron. de B. du Guesclin (Documents Inédits sur l'Hist. de France); the prose Chronique de B. du Guesclin in the Panthéon Littéraire; Walsingham's Historia Anglicana; Chronicon Angliæ, 1328-88; Eulogium Historiarum; Wright's Political Songs (the last four are contained in the Rolls Series); Knighton's Chronicle ap. Twysden's Scriptores Decem; Rymer's Fœdera, Record ed.; Blomefield's Hist. of Norfolk, ed. 1805-10, see index; Fuller's Worthies, i. 188-9, ed. 1811; Lobineau's Hist. de Bretagne; Morice's Hist. Eccl. et Civile de Bretagne; Barnes's Hist. of Edward III; Herald and Genealogist, v. 289–308, vii. 553-8.]   C. L. K.

KNOLLYS, WILLIAM, Earl of Banbury (1547–1632), second but eldest surviving son of Sir Francis Knollys [q. v.], was born in 1547, and was educated in early youth by Josceline or Julius Palmer, who fell a victim to the Marian persecution in 1556. William performed his first public service as captain in the army which was sent to repress the northern rebellion in 1569. He was elected M.P. for Tregony in 1572, and for Oxfordshire in 1584, 1593, 1597, and 1601. In November 1585 Queen Elizabeth sent him as 'one that appertaineth to us in blood'—his mother was the queen's first cousin—to James VI of Scotland to assure him that she had no intention of aiding the banished Scottish lords (Corresp. of Eliz. and James, Camd. Soc., p. 23). In the following January he accompanied Burghley's son Thomas in the expedition to the Low Countries under Leicester (Leycester Corresp., Camd. Soc., p. 58), and was knighted by Leicester on 7 Oct. 1586. He was colonel of the Oxford and Gloucester regiments of foot which were enrolled to resist the Spanish Armada in 1588, and was created M.A. of Oxford on 27 Sept. 1592.

Elizabeth extended to him the favour that she had shown his father, and on the latter's death in 1596 and the consequent changes in court offices, Knollys was made comptroller of the royal household and a privy councillor (30 Aug. 1596). He inherited his father's estates in Oxfordshire and Berkshire, and became joint lieutenant of those counties on 4 Nov. 1596, sole lieutenant in July 1601, and lord-lieutenant 22 March 1612-13. He was a commissioner to arrange a peace between the Dutch and the emperor in August 1598, and was granted the reversion to the office of constable of Wallingford Castle's Feb. 1601. At the final trial of the Earl of Essex (January 1601) he entered the witness-box to deny the statement of the defence that Sir Robert Cecil had in private conversation acknowledged the infanta's title to the crown of England (Cecil, Corresp., Camd. Soc., p. 70 n.), and in August 1601 he entertained his sovereign at his house at Caversham, and in May 1602 at his residence in St. James's Park. On 22 Dec. 1602 he succeeded Roger, lord North, as treasurer of the royal household, a position which his father had filled before him.

On James I's accession Knollys retained all his offices, and was further created, on 13 May 1603, Baron Knollys of Rotherfield Greys. He became cofferer of the household to Henry, prince of Wales, in 1606. In May 1613 he represented his cousin the Earl of Essex in the abortive conference held at Whitehall to arrange a separation between the earl and the earl's wife, Frances, who was a sister of Knollys's second wife. In 1614 he proved his loyalist zeal by putting down the names of persons as willing to subscribe to the benevolence of that year without consulting them. He acted as commissioner of the treasury from 24 Jan. to 11 July 1614, and was made master of the court of wards on 10 Oct. following. On 24 April 1615 he was elected a knight of the Garter, and was promoted in the peerage to the viscountcy of Wallingford on 7 Nov. 1616. In the following month he resigned the treasurership of the household. Wallingford's influence at court was at the time somewhat imperilled by his connection with the Howards, his wife's family. His sister-in-law Frances, then Countess of Somerset, was placed on her trial for the murder of Overbury in 1615, and all her kinsfolk were suspected of complicity. But the chief witness against the Howards, Mrs. Turner, had to admit, respecting Wallingford, 'if ever there was a religious man, it was he.' When Thomas Howard, earl of Suffolk [q. v.], his father-in-law, fell into disgrace in 1618, his wife openly attributed her family's misfortunes to Buckingham's malice; the words were reported to the king, who declared that he did not wish to be further served by the husband of such a woman. Wallingford was accordingly forced to resign the mastership of the wards (December 1618). He gradually recovered his position, and in April 1621 took a leading part in the House of Lords in the case of Bacon, insisting that the chancellor should furnish a full answer to the charges brought against him. In 1622 he and his wife's relatives patched up a reconciliation with Buckingham, and Wallingford sold to him his London residence, Wallingford House, for 3,000l.

The earldom of Banbury was conferred on Knollys by Charles I on 18 Aug. 1626, possibly, as Mr. Gardiner suggests, in order to complete the king's and Buckingham's reconciliation with the Howard family. The patent contained a clause that 'he shall have precedency as if he had been created the first earl after his Majesty's accesse to the crowne.' The lords resisted this grant of precedency as an infringement of their privileges, but when a committee met to consider the question, Charles sent a gracious message, desiring 'this may pass for once in this particular, considering how old a man this lord is, and childless.' Accordingly, on 9 April 1628, the lords resolved to allow the earl the 'place of precedency' 'for his life only.' On 15 April the earl took his seat 'next to the Earl of Berks,' the patent for whose earldom dated from 7 Feb. 1625-6. Banbury proved himself no compliant supporter of Charles I's despotic policy, and when in February 1628 he was invited to collect ship-money in Oxfordshire, bluntly declined. He died at the house of Dr. Grant, his physician, in Paternoster Row, London, on 25 May 1632, and was buried at Rotherfield Greys. His age is stated to have been eighty-five, although he 'rode a hawking and hunting' within half a year of his death. His will, which makes no mention of children, was dated 19 May 1630, and was proved by his widow, to whom he left all his possessions, on 2 July 1632. The funeral certificate at the College of Arms describes him as dying without issue. He sold Rotherfield Greys to his brother Richard's son, Sir Robert Knollys of Stanford-in-the-Vale, on 4 March 1630-1.

The earl was twice married. His first wife, by whom he had no children, was Dorothy, widow of Edmund Brydges, lord Chandos, and daughter of Edmund Braye, first lord Braye; she died 31 Oct. 1605. Less than two months later (23 Dec.) Knollys, who was then about fifty-eight, married a girl of nineteen, Elizabeth, daughter of Thomas Howard, earl of Suffolk; she was baptised at Saffron Walden, 11 Aug. 1586. A daughter of this marriage died young, before 1610; but the countess gave birth to a son, Edward, at her husband's house, on 10 April 1627, and on 3 Jan. 1630-1 another son, Nicholas, was born to her at Harrowden, Northamptonshire, the residence of Edward Vaux, fourth lord Vaux. The paternity of these two sons has given rise to much controversy.

Within five weeks of her husband's death (before 2 July 1632) Lady Banbury married Lord Vaux. She adopted Roman catholicism, the religion of her second husband, and was consequently an object of much suspicion to the Long parliament. On 19 Aug. 1643 the speaker issued a pass enabling her to go to France, and on 13 June 1644 the House of Commons resolved that should she return she should be seized and kept under restraint. She died in her seventy-second year, 17 April 1658, and was buried at Dorking, Surrey, near the residence of her second husband. The latter survived till 8 April 1661, and is said to have died without issue.

Although the legal doctrine, 'Pater est quem nuptiæ demonstrant,' assumes in all cases of children born in wedlock that the husband is the children's father, the House of Lords has repeatedly refused to admit the legitimacy of the Countess of Banbury's sons, or to allow the title to them or their descendants. Between 1641 and 1813 the question has been frequently discussed in the House of Lords and in the law courts, with the curious result that while the judges have distinctly acknowledged the children's legitimacy, the peers have persistently adhered to the contrary view, mainly on the grounds of the earl's age at the date of their birth, and his alleged ignorance of their existence at the time of his death. The peers' inference was that Lord Vaux was their father.

The long controversy opened with a legal decision in favour of the claim to legitimacy. Edward, the elder of the countess's two sons, was styled 'Earl of Banbury' in a chancery suit to which in February 1640-1 he was party as an infant, for the purpose of establishing his right to a plot of land at Henley, styled the Bowling Place, and to other property left by his father. Under orders of the court of wards an inquiry into the late earl's property was held at Abingdon 1 April 1641, and the court found that 'Edward, now Earl of Banbury, is, and at the time of the earl's decease was, his son and next heir.' Edward travelled in Italy in 1644, and in June 1645 was slain in a quarrel on the road between Calais and Gravelines. He was buried in the church of the Friars Minims at Calais.

His younger brother, Nicholas Knollys, called third Earl of Banbury (1631-1674), thereupon assumed the title. He had travelled to France with his mother in 1644, but both had returned before 19 Oct. 1646, when Lord Vaux settled all his lands at Harrowden on his wife (Knollys's mother), with remainder to Knollys himself, who was styled Earl of Banbury in the deed. At an early age Nicholas married his first wife, Isabella, daughter of Mountjoy Blount, earl of Newport, and soon fell into pecuniary difficulties. On 27 Feb. 1654-5, as Nicholas, earl of Banbury, he, with his wife, his mother, and Lord Vaux of Harrowden, petitioned Cromwell to remove the sequestration on Lord Vaux's estate, and to allow them to compound or sell some of the lands. The earl and countess, the petitioners stated, were both young, and owed 10,000l., on account of which debt the earl was confined at the time in the Upper Bench prison (Cal. State Papers, Dom. 1654-5, p. 55). Soon afterwards Knollys's first wife died, and he married at Stapleford, Leicestershire, on 4 Oct.

1655, Anne, daughter of William, lord Sherard of Leitrim. In June 1660 he attended the Convention parliament in the House of Lords, but it was not until 13 July 1660 that the first attempt was made to dispute his right to his seat there. It was then moved that 'there being a person that now sits in this house as a peer of the realm, viz. the Earl of Banbury, it is ordered that this business shall be heard at the bar by counsel' on the 23rd. Knollys attended the house daily in the week preceding that appointed for the hearing, and was present on the day itself. But no proceedings were taken, and on 24 July he was nominated, under the style of Earl of Banbury, to sit on the committee on the Excise Bill. On 21 Nov. it was ordered that the earl 'hath leave to be absent for some time.' On 29 Dec. the Convention parliament was dissolved.

No writ of summons was sent to Knollys for the new parliament, meeting 8 May 1661. He therefore petitioned the king for the issue of the writ and for all the old earl's rights of precedency. His petition when forwarded to the House of Lords was referred to a committee of privileges. This committee examined the servants who were at Harrowden at the time of his birth. The attorney-general argued on behalf of the king that the old earl had died childless, but the committee reported on 1 July 1661 that 'Nicholas, Earl of Banbury, is a legitimate person.' The House of Lords, after a long debate and an examination of witnesses before the whole house, declined to accept this report, and the committee was directed to reconsider it, and also to examine Knollys's title to the old earl's precedency. In the result another report was issued on 19 July declaring the claimant to be 'in the eye of the law' son of the late earl, but denying him his claim to precedency. The House of Lords adjourned before taking this second report into consideration, and after reassembling in November, although it was decided to discuss it on 9 Dec. following, a bill declaring Knollys illegitimate was, on that date, read for a first time. The report was never considered, nor did the bill go beyond the initial stage. When the house met on 26 Oct. 1669, nearly eight years later, the committee of privileges, at the suggestion of some friend of Knollys, was directed to examine the grounds on which the Earl of Banbury's name was omitted from the roll, but their report merely rehearsed the previous proceedings, without suggesting any conclusion. On 23 Feb. 1670 Knollys once more petitioned the lords to admit him to their house, but the petition was passed over without notice. On 14 March 1673-4 Knollys

died at Boughton, Northamptonshire. His widow survived till 10 March 1679-80.

CHARLES KNOLLYS, called fourth EARL OF BANBURY (1662-1740), son of the above by his second wife, was baptised at Boughton as 'Viscount Wallingford,' son of 'the Earl of Banbury,' 3 June 1662, and on 10 June 1685 petitioned the House of Lords for a writ of summons; the committee of privileges for a second time issued a report of the earlier history of the case, and the house resolved to hear counsel for and against the claim on 6 July, but owing to adjournments and prorogations the case was not heard. The controversy entered on a new phase in 1692. In that year Knollys fought a duel with his brother-in-law, Captain Philip Lawson, and killed him. He was arrested, and on 7 Dec. 1692 was indicted for murder under the style of 'Charles Knollys, esq.' He at once stated, in a petition to the House of Lords, that as Earl of Banbury he was entitled to a trial by his peers. On 9 Jan. 1692-3 the lords heard arguments for and against the plea. Finch and Sir Thomas Powis represented Knollys, while Sir John Somers, attorney-general, appeared for the crown and resisted his pretensions. A proposal to invite the opinion of the judges on points of law was rejected by the lords (17 Jan. 1692-3), and a resolution declaring the petitioner to have no right to the earldom was carried. Twenty peers protested against this decision. Meanwhile Knollys remained in Newgate, but he obtained a writ for the removal of his trial from the Middlesex sessions to the court of king's bench, and when arraigned there in Hilary term 1693 in the name of Charles Knollys, he pleaded a misnomer. The trial was delayed while this plea was under consideration in the law courts, and the prisoner was admitted to bail 3 May 1693. The attorney-general insisted that the resolution of the lords destroyed Knollys's case, but in Trinity term 1694 Lord-chief-justice Holt [q. v.], with the three other judges of the king's bench, unanimously quashed the indictment and set the defendant free on the ground that he was Earl of Banbury, and that his name was wrongly entered. In January 1698, on 19 May 1712, and on the accession of George II in 1727, Knollys again petitioned the crown to issue a writ of summons. On the first of these occasions the lords were once more invited to consider the question. Maintaining their hostile attitude a committee of privileges summoned Holt and the other judges to explain their recent judgment. Holt declined to offer any explanation, and the matter dropped. Owing to accidental circumstances the advisers of the crown arrived at no decision in 1712 and 1728. Knollys died in France in April 1740. One Elizabeth Price issued in 1696 a pamphlet entitled 'The True Countess of Banbury's Case relating to her Marriage rightly stated in a Letter to the Earl of Banbury,' Lond. 1696, sm. fol. The writer claimed, after living with Knollys at London, Paris, and Mantua, to have married him at Verona, 7 April 1692, but Knollys denied her statement, and was legally married at the time to Elizabeth, daughter of Edward Lister of Barwell, Leicestershire. The latter was his first wife. By his second wife, Mary (d. 1762), daughter of Thomas Woods of St. Andrew's, Holborn, he left a surviving son, Charles (1703-1771), of Christ Church, Oxford (B.A. 1725, M.A. 1728), who was titular Earl of Banbury, and was vicar of Barford, Oxfordshire, from 1750 till his death. The vicar's two sons, William (1726-1776) and Thomas Woods Knollys (1727-1793), both officers in the army, were also successively titular Earls of Banbury. The latter's son, WILLIAM KNOLLYS, called eighth EARL OF BANBURY (1763-1834), took legal steps to reassert his claim to the earldom. He was appointed ensign of the 3rd foot-guards in 1778, and lieutenant, with rank of captain, in 1788. He served throughout the campaign in Flanders in 1793, and became lieutenant-colonel in December of that year, and in 1796 brevet-colonel. He was with the grenadier battalion of guards throughout the expedition to Holland in 1797. In 1802 he was promoted major-general, and in 1808 lieutenant-general. In 1818 he became lieutenant-governor of St. John's, in 1819 general in the army, and was later governor of Limerick. In 1806 he petitioned the crown for his writ as a peer. On 17 Jan. 1808 the attorney-general, Sir Vicary Gibbs, reported that the resolution of the lords in 1692-3 was 'not a conclusive judgment' against the claim, and that no attempt had been made to reverse the decision of the court of king's bench, but that the legitimacy of the Nicholas Knollys, the first petitioner, was doubtful. After five years' discussion and a reconsideration of all the former proceedings by the committee of privileges of the House of Lords, the lords on 15 March 1813 resolved that the claimant was not entitled to the title of earl. An 'eloquent and forcible' protest, enunciating the illegality of this decision, was drawn up by Lord Erskine, and was signed by the Dukes of Kent, Gloucester, and Sussex, and six other peers. The general died at Paris of influenza, 20 March 1834 (see *Gent. Mag.* 1834, ii. 209), leaving

by his wife (a daughter of Ebenezer Blackwell of London) a son, Sir William Thomas Knollys [q. v.] Since the decision of 1813 the family have taken no steps to assert their right to the earldom of Banbury.

[For the life of William, earl of Banbury, see Dugdale's Baronage; Spedding's Bacon; Gardiner's Hist. of England; Nichols's Progresses; Doyle's Official Baronage. Much of the earl's official correspondence is in Brit. Mus. Addit. MSS. (cf. index for 1854-75). The fullest account of the peerage case is in Sir H. N. Nicolas's Treatise on the Law of Adulterine Bastardy (1836), which includes the reports of proceedings in the House of Lords from 1661 to 1813. A good summary of the litigation appears in G. E. [Cokayne]'s Complete Peerage, 1887, i. 229 sq. Burke's version of the story in Romance of the Peerage and in Extinct Peerage is unsatisfactory.]

S. L.

KNOLLYS, Sir WILLIAM THOMAS (1797-1883), general, born on 1 Aug. 1797, was eldest son of General William Knollys, called eighth Earl of Banbury, and until 1813 Sir William held the courtesy title of Viscount Wallingford [see under KNOLLYS, WILLIAM, EARL OF BANBURY, *ad fin.*] Educated at Harrow and Sandhurst, Knollys received his first commission in 1813, when little more than sixteen, in the 3rd (now the Scots) guards, and was almost immediately despatched with a draft to the Peninsula. Thence he crossed the Bidassoa into France with the victorious English army, and after the passage of the Adour was attached to the force which invested Bayonne. The first day he joined the headquarters of his battalion he was detailed for outpost duty, and on being shown the area which he was to guard by Lieutenant-colonel (afterwards Field-marshal) Sir Alexander Woodford, he found his own sentries stationed behind one hedgeside of a narrow lane, while the French sentries lined the other hedgeside. But Colonel Woodford explained that he need give himself no concern about this anomaly, for that the pickets of both nations had for some time held it a point of military honour and courtesy never to molest one another so long as the respective delimitations of ground were observed. Indeed Knollys was wont to dwell on the difficulty experienced in preventing this mutual forbearance merging into actual friendship, leading the opposing pickets to exchange presents of wine and tobacco, and thus allowing undesirable intelligence to leak out.

On the occasion of the French sortie from Bayonne, 14 April 1814, Knollys was again with the outposts. He had noticed an ominous stir in his front, and his suspicions had been strengthened by information brought in by a French deserter. He sent warnings to his superiors, but his information was unheeded; the surprise was complete, and the French penetrated so far within the English lines that after the fray Knollys found they had ransacked his tent. When most hotly engaged in the first onset, and as he was running along the ditch of the parallel, he stumbled in the dark almost into the arms of two French grenadiers, who made a clutch at their prize, but the lad escaped capture.

On the signing of peace he returned to England, but directly after the battle of Waterloo he was again sent with a draft to join his battalion in Paris, which formed part of the army of occupation. In 1821 he was appointed adjutant, and thence working his way through successive grades he became lieutenant-colonel of his battalion in 1844, and regimental colonel in 1850. He had had for his own adjutant the present general, Sir Frederick Stephenson, and under their joint efforts the regiment was held to be one of the best drilled, disciplined, and organised in the British army. Accordingly, Colonel Knollys was instructed to initiate Prince Albert, who was titular colonel of the Scots fusilier guards, into the art of soldiering. Beginning in 1850 and for successive seasons the prince was in the habit of attending battalion and brigade field days in Hyde Park at nine o'clock in the morning, diligently mastering, under Knollys's instruction, the intricacies which characterised the drill of forty years back, and afterwards studying the interior economy of the regiment. From this period Prince Albert became Knollys's steady supporter. In 1854 he was promoted major-general and appointed governor of Guernsey, whence in 1855 he was despatched on a mission to Paris to investigate the French system of 'intendance,' i.e. commissariat, transport, &c., which was supposed to have exemplified its superiority to our method in the Crimea.

At the same time the camp at Aldershot —the first conception of which was due to Prince Albert—was in process of formation, and Lord Hardinge, the commander-in-chief, entrusted Knollys, at the instance of Prince Albert, with the first conduct of the experiment in 1855. The army at the time utterly lacked administrative cohesion. It therefore fell to Knollys's lot not only to form his Aldershot staff and to organise the troops into brigades and divisions, but to initiate the diverse departments of commissariat, transport, stores, and even the medical and chaplain's departments. He found it necessary to instruct with his own hands some of the first arrivals in camp in pitching tents, and, while sharing with them a tent life, to teach them the elementary duties of soldiers in the field. On the death of General Bucknall Estcourt, chief of the staff in the Crimea, in June 1855, it was suddenly intimated to Knollys that he had been selected to succeed him; but before the date fixed for his embarkation the appointment was cancelled, on the ground of his seniority, which would have entailed the supersession of many other Crimean generals. Notwithstanding his disappointment, he resumed his labours at Aldershot with undiminished energy. Although Lord Hardinge was then commander-in-chief, the principal moving spirit in the English army, as regarded the practical training of the troops, was Prince Albert, and from him Knollys received the most encouraging support against the ill-will and obstruction of which Aldershot, at that time unpopular with the public, was the object. The queen and prince consort were frequent residents for days together at the Pavilion. Success exceeded expectation. General von Moltke was one of the foreign visitors to the camp, and on the rare occasions when he broke his habitual silence, he evinced his surprise and approval at the progress made by British troops. When Knollys's command came to an end in 1860, he had established Aldershot on a basis of efficient organisation, which in its main lines has continued up to the present day.

In 1861 he accepted, at the instance of the prince consort, the post of president of the council of military education. In 1862 he was selected by the queen as treasurer and comptroller of the household of the Prince of Wales, who had recently entered on his twenty-first year. For fifteen years, 1862–1877, he performed the responsible and laborious duties attached to this confidential position, frequently accompanying the prince, especially during the earlier period, in his travels abroad and in his visits to foreign courts. The honorary distinctions of LL.D. and D.C.L. had been conferred on him by the universities of Oxford and Cambridge in 1863 and 1864. In 1867 he was created a K.C.B., and in 1871 he was made a member of the privy council. In 1872 he had once more a short interlude of military duty, having been appointed, in conjunction with Sir Hope Grant, umpire in chief during the well-known Salisbury manœuvres. In 1877 he resigned his position in the household of the Prince of Wales, and accepted that of gentleman usher of the black rod. At the same time he was nominated to the honorary post of groom of the stole to the prince. In 1883 Knollys was gazetted to the colonelcy of the Scots guards, the regiment in which he had begun his soldier's life nearly seventy years previously. He only survived this honour three days. He died on 23 June 1883 at Black Rod's House, Westminster Palace, in his eighty-sixth year, and was carried to his grave in Highgate cemetery by sergeants of his old regiment. Knollys married in 1830 Elizabeth, daughter of Sir John St. Aubyn, and by her he left a numerous family of sons and daughters.

Knollys published 'Some Remarks on the Claim to the Earldom of Banbury,' London, 1835, 8vo, and 'A Journal of the Russian Campaign of 1812, translated from the French' of the Duc de Fezensac, London, 1852, 8vo.

[Private information, personal knowledge, and family records.]   H. K.

KNOTT, EDWARD (1582–1656), jesuit, whose real name was MATTHEW WILSON, was born at Catchburn, a township in the parish of Morpeth, Northumberland, in 1582. After studying humanities in the college of the English jesuits at St. Omer, he was on 10 Oct. 1602 admitted an alumnus of the English College at Rome, under the assumed name of Edward Knott, which he retained through life. He was ordained priest on 27 March 1606. He entered the Society of Jesus on 2 Oct. the same year, and upon the expiration of his novitiate in 1608 he was appointed penitentiary in Rome. For some time he was prefect of studies in the English College. He was raised to the rank of a professed father of the Society of Jesus on 30 Sept. 1618.

During 1625 he was a missioner in the Suffolk district. He was apprehended in 1629, and was committed to the Clink prison in Southwark, but at the instance of the queen he was released and banished in February 1632–3. In 1633 he served in the London district, acting as vice-provincial to Father Richard Blount, the provincial. In 1636 he was, in the same district, vice-provincial to Father Henry More, whom he succeeded as provincial of the English province in 1643. In that capacity he assisted at the eighth general congregation of the Society of Jesus, held in November 1645, when Vincent Carafa was elected seventh general of the order in the place of Father Mutius Vitelleschi. Soon afterwards he returned to the English mission, and thenceforward resided for the most part in London. He was reappointed provincial on 23 March 1652–3, in succession to Father Francis Foster. He died in London on 4 Jan. (O.S.) 1655–6, and was buried the next day in St. Pancras Church. His religious fervour and intellectual vigour

were both remarkable (cf. FOLEY, Records, v. 632; OLIVER, Jesuit Collections, p. 128).

His works are: 1. 'A Modest Briefe Discussion of some points taught by M. Doctour [Matthew] Kellison [q. v.], in his Treatise of the Ecclesiasticall Hierarchy,' Rouen, 1630, 8vo. It appeared in Latin, Antwerp, 1631, 12mo. This work, which relates to the disputes between the secular and regular clergy, was published under the pseudonym of Nicholas Smith, and was composed by Knott in the Clink prison. Another reply to Kellison was published by Father John Floyd [q. v.], and both these works were censured by the archbishop of Paris 30 Jan. 1631, and by the Sorbonne 15 Feb. 1631. Father Charles Plowden believed the two books to be ' very deserving of censure, in the sense in which the Parisian doctors supposed them to have been delivered' (Remarks on Panzani, p. 247). Knott was attacked by an anonymous writer in a work entitled 'A Reply to M. Nicholas Smith, his Discussion of some pointes of M. Doctour Kellison his Treatise of the Hierarchie. By a Divine,' Douay, 1630, 8vo. A. B. justified Knott in 'A Defence of N. Smith against a Reply to his Discussion,' &c., 1630, 8vo. On 9 May 1631 Pope Urban VIII issued the brief 'Britannia,' in which he lamented the divisions sown among the English catholics, and commanded them to cease. But the controversy continued until the issue of Urban VIII's brief dated 19 March 1633. 2. 'Charity Mistaken, with the want whereof Catholickes are unjustly charged, for affirming as they do with grief, that Protestancy unrepented destroyes Salvation' [London], 1630, 16mo. This was answered by Dr. Christopher Potter, provost of Queen's College, Oxford, and afterwards dean of Worcester, in his 'Want of Charity justly charged,' Oxford, 1633, 8vo; 2nd edit. 1634. 3. 'Mercy and Truth, or Charity maintayned by Catholykes,' a reply to Potter [St. Omer], 1634, 4to. William Chillingworth subsequently replied to the first part of this work in 'The Religion of Protestants,' 1638. 4. 'A Direction to be observed by N. N. [William Chillingworth] if hee meane to proceede in answering the booke entitled "Mercy and Truth,"' London, 1636, 8vo. Knott, who had heard of Chillingworth's intention to reply to 'Mercy and Truth,' here sought to put his adversary out of court by accusing him of Socinianism. 5. 'Christianity Maintained; or, A Discouery of sundry Doctrines tending to the Ouerthrowe of Christian Religion: Contayned in the Answere to a Booke entituled, "Mercy and Truth"' [St. Omer], 1638, 4to (anon.) The dedication to Charles I is signed I. H. 6. 'Infidelity Unmasked, or the Confutation of

v 2

Chillingworth's "Religion of Protestants,"' Ghent, 1652, 4to. In Daille's 'Apologie for the Reformed Churches,' Cambridge, 1653, is 'The Judgement of an University-man [Thomas Smith] concerning Mr. Knot's last book against Mr. Chillingworth,' described by Knott himself as a 'witty, erudite, and solid work.' 7. 'Protestancy Condemned by the express verdict and sentence of Protestants' (anon.), Douay, 1654, 4to. 8. 'Monita utilissima pro patribus Missionis Anglicanae.' Never printed.

[Biog. Brit. Suppl.; Birch's Life of Chillingworth; De Backer's Bibl. de la Compagnie de Jésus; Des Maizeaux's Life of Chillingworth; Dodd's Church Hist. iii. 106; Foley's Records, v. 629, vi. 225, vii. 850; Halkett and Laing's Dict. of Anonymous Lit. iii. 2040; Lowndes's Bibl. Man. (Bohn), p. 1286; Orthodox Journal, v. 117; Panzani's Memoirs, p. 124; Southwell's Bibl. Scriptorum Soc. Jesu, p. 185; Wood's Athenæ Oxon. (Bliss), iii. 91, 92, 181, 995.]
T. C.

KNOWLER, WILLIAM (1699–1773), divine, third son of Gilbert Knowler, gent., of Stroud House, at Herne in Kent, was baptised on 9 May 1699 (NICHOLS, Literary Anecdotes, ii. 129). He was educated at St. John's College, Cambridge, graduated B.A. in 1720, M.A. in 1724, and LL.D. in 1728. On leaving Cambridge, Knowler became chaplain to Thomas Watson Wentworth, then Lord Malton, who was in 1746 created Marquis of Rockingham. Lord Malton had inherited the papers of his great-grandfather, Thomas Wentworth, earl of Strafford [q. v.], and charged his chaplain with the task of publishing a selection from them. This appeared in 1739 under the title of 'The Earl of Strafford's Letters and Despatches,' London, 2 vols. folio. They were selected, says Knowler, in the dedication he addressed to his patron, by Lord Malton himself, and published according to his instructions, in order to vindicate Strafford's memory from 'the aspersions of acting upon arbitrary principles, and being a friend to the Roman catholics.' It is possible that the editor derived some assistance from an 'Essay on Epistolary Writings with respect to the Grand Collection of Thomas, Earl of Strafford,' which William Oldys had written in 1729, and dedicated to Lord Malton (THOMS, Memoir of William Oldys, 1862, p. viii; BOLTON CORNEY, Curiosities of Literature Illustrated, p. 113). Knowler was presented by his patron, first to the living of Irthlingborough, or Artleburrow, between Wellingborough and Higham Ferrers, and afterwards to the living of Boddington, both in Northamptonshire (NICHOLS, Lit. Anecdotes, ii. 129). In 1765 he prepared for the press a translation of Chrysostom's 'Commentary on St. Paul's Epistle to the Galatians,' which was never printed (ib. ii. 130). He died in December 1773.

A pedigree kindly communicated by the Rev. T. W. Openshaw of Bristol describes Knowler as marrying Mary Dalton in 1749. Nichols, quoting the 'Gentleman's Magazine' (lxxv. 90), describes Mrs. Knowler as the daughter of Mr. Presgrove, surgeon in Westminster, and states that she died in 1805 (ib. viii. 401). This may have been a second wife. A letter from Knowler to the Rev. John Lewis is printed by Nichols in 'Illustrations of Literature,' iv. 427; others relating to the publication of the 'Strafford Papers' will be published in the next volume of the 'Camden Miscellany,' from manuscripts of Knowler's in the possession of the author of this article.

[Authorities cited.] C. H. F.

KNOWLES. [See also KNOLLYS.]

KNOWLES, SIR CHARLES (d. 1777), admiral, reputed son of Charles Knollys, titular fourth earl of Banbury [see under KNOLLYS, WILLIAM, EARL OF BANBURY], is said to have been born about 1697, but the course of his service in the navy points rather to a date not earlier than 1704. He entered the navy in March 1718 on board the Buckingham with Captain Charles Strickland, whom in April he followed to the Lennox, with the rating of captain's servant, and so continued till December 1720. During the greater part of this time the Lennox was in the Mediterranean under the orders of Sir George Byng, afterwards Viscount Torrington [q. v.], and it appears from Knowles's own papers that in the battle off Cape Passaro he was serving actually on board the Barfleur, Byng's flagship, but of this there is no note in the Lennox's pay-book, on which he was borne for the whole time. He was afterwards, from June 1721 to June 1726, in the Lyme frigate with Lord Vere Beauclerk, and during the first eighteen months of this period with the rating of captain's servant. For the rest of the time he was rated 'able seaman.' During the five years of the Lyme's commission she was stationed in the Mediterranean, and it has been supposed that Knowles spent much of this time in being educated on shore. It is certain that in his riper years he not only spoke French as a Frenchman, but that his attainments in mathematics and mechanics were very far in advance of what was then usual in the navy. After paying off from the Lyme, Knowles served in the Winchester guardship at Portsmouth; in the Torbay, carrying the flag of

Sir Charles Wager; in the Kinsale, again with Lord Vere Beauclerk; in the Feversham and in the Lion, till on 30 May 1730 he was promoted to be lieutenant of the Trial. In the following March he was moved to the Lion, flagship of Rear-admiral Charles Stewart [q. v.] in the West Indies.

In 1732 he was promoted to be commander of the Southampton, a 40-gun ship, but apparently for rank only, as he did not take post till 4 Feb. 1736-7, when he was appointed to the Diamond. In her he went out to the West Indies in 1739, and joined Vice-admiral Edward Vernon (1684-1757) [q. v.] at Porto Bello. The place had already been taken, but he was ordered to take charge of the destruction of the forts, which proved to be a work of some difficulty. Still in command of the Diamond, Knowles was sent in the following March to examine the approach to Chagres, and had the immediate command of the bombs and fireships in the attack on the town, 22 March; on its surrender he was appointed governor of the castle pending the destruction of the defences. The work was completed by the 28th, when the squadron withdrew. Towards the end of the year he returned to England and was appointed to the Weymouth of 60 guns, one of the fleet which went out to the West Indies with Sir Chaloner Ogle [q. v.] In the Weymouth, Knowles took part in the expedition against Cartagena in March-April 1741, and acted throughout as the surveyor and engineer of the fleet, examining the approaches to the several points of attack, cutting the boom across the Boca Chica, taking possession of the Castillo Grande, and destroying the captured works before the fleet left.

The pamphlet 'An Account of the Expedition to Carthagena, with Explanatory Notes and Observations' (8vo, 1743), which, written in a very bitter tone against the army, was much spoken of at the time and ran through several editions, was generally attributed to Knowles. The preface to the 'Original Papers relating to the Expedition to Carthagena' (8vo, 1744), published with Vernon's sanction, describes the author of the pamphlet as 'an officer of approved abilities and resolution, who did not depend on hearsay and uncertain reports, but was himself an eye-witness of most of the transactions that he has given an account of.'

After the failure at Cartagena, Knowles was moved into the Lichfield, and in the course of 1742 into the Suffolk of 70 guns. In her he commanded a squadron, sent by Sir Chaloner Ogle in the beginning of 1743 to act against the Spanish settlements on the Caraccas coast. No pains were taken to keep the expedition a secret; the Spaniards had two months' warning for their preparations; and the Dutch, though allies of the English, supplied them with powder. The result was that when the squadron attacked La Guayra on 18 Feb. 1742-3 it was beaten off with very heavy loss, and when, having refitted at Curaçoa, it attacked Porto Cabello on 15 April and again on the 24th, it had no better success. On 28 April a council of war decided that 'the squadron was no longer in a condition to attempt any enterprise against the enemy,' and Knowles, sending the ships and troops to their respective stations, returned to Jamaica.

He was then appointed an 'established' commodore, or as it is now called a first-class commodore, with his broad pennant in the Superbe and afterwards in the Severn, and continued during 1743-4-5 as second in command on the Jamaica and West Indian station under Ogle. Towards the end of 1745 he returned to England, and after a short time in the Downs, as second in command under Vice-admiral William Martin [q. v.], he was, early in 1746, sent out as governor of Louisbourg, which had been captured from the French a few months before [see WARREN, SIR PETER]. There he remained for upwards of two years, repairing and renewing the defences of the fortress. In the large promotion of 15 July 1747 he was made rear-admiral of the white, and at the same time was appointed commander-in-chief at Jamaica.

In February 1747-8, with his flag on board the Cornwall, he took the squadron along the south coast of Cuba, and after capturing Port Louis on 8 March arrived off Santiago on 5 April. An attack was immediately attempted, but Captain Dent in the Plymouth, who led in, found the passage blocked by a boom, which he judged too strong to be forced. He turned back, and the ships following did the same. A second attempt was considered unadvisable. Knowles was much annoyed by the failure. Dent, who as senior officer had been for a short time commander-in-chief before Knowles's arrival, was not, perhaps, inclined to undertake any extraordinary service, the credit of which, if successful, would be placed to the account of the newly arrived admiral. Knowles doubtless believed this to be the case, and sent Dent home to be tried on a charge of not having done his utmost. Nearly a year later the court-martial took place and relieved Dent of all blame.

Meanwhile Knowles, having refitted the ships at Jamaica, took them for a cruise off Havana in hopes of intercepting the Spanish plate fleet. On 30 Sept. he was joined by Captain Charles Holmes [q. v.] in the Lennox, with the news that he had been chased the day before by a squadron of seven Spanish ships. These came in sight the next morning (1 Oct.) in the southern quarter. When first seen, the Spaniards were straggling in two divisions. By closing with them at once, and before they could get into compact order, Knowles thought that he would risk losing the weather-gage, without which —according to the Fighting Instructions— no attack would be possible. He accordingly spent some time in working to windward, and when at last he steered for the enemy, the unequal sailing of his ships disordered his line, and rendered the attack ineffective. The leading ships, too, misunderstood or disobeyed the signal to engage more closely, and took little part in the action. The brunt of it fell on the Strafford, commanded by Captain David Brodie [q. v.], and on Knowles's flagship, the Cornwall, which, owing to the disordered state of the line, was singly opposed to three of the enemy's ships, and sustained severe damage. She did, however, beat the Africa, the enemy's flagship, out of the line; the Conquistador struck to the Strafford, and the Canterbury, which had been delayed by the bad sailing of the Warwick, coming up, the Spaniards took to flight. It was then just dark. Knowles made the signal for a general chase; but the Cornwall had lost her main topmast and was disabled, and as the Conquistador just then rehoisted her flag and endeavoured to escape, Knowles contented himself with compelling her to strike again and with taking possession of her. In the pursuit the Africa was driven on shore by the Strafford and the Canterbury, and was afterwards burnt. The other Spanish ships escaped.

In writing of the engagement to Anson, Knowles spoke of the 'bashfulness—to give it no harsher term,' of some of the captains; and he publicly animadverted on the conduct of Captain Powlett of the Tilbury, the leading ship. Powlett applied for a court-martial, which was granted; but he was afterwards allowed to withdraw his application. When, however, it was openly said on board the Cornwall, the Strafford, and the Canterbury that the captains of the other four ships had been 'shy,' they retaliated by officially accusing the admiral of having given 'great advantage to the enemy by engaging in a straggling line and late in the day, when he might have attacked much earlier;' of having 'kept his majesty's flag out of action;' and of having 'transmitted a false and injurious account 'to the admiralty. A court-martial on Knowles

was accordingly ordered, and sat at Deptford in December 1749. Captain Innes of the Warwick acted as prosecutor, in the name of the four captains. The trial, based exclusively on points of seamanship and tactics, was necessarily extremely technical. The court decided that Knowles was in fault in taking his fleet into action in such a straggling line, and also in not going on board another ship and leading the chase in person. He was sentenced to be reprimanded. The four captains who had acted as prosecutors were then put on their trial. Holmes of the Lennox was honourably acquitted; but Powlett and Toll, who had commanded the two leading ships, were reprimanded, and Innes was suspended for three months. Many duels followed. After the trials Knowles, who received four challenges, interchanged shots with Holmes on 24 Feb. A meeting took place between Innes and Clarke, the captain of the Canterbury, the principal witness against him, on 12 March 1749-50, and Innes was mortally wounded. Several more duels were pending, when the king not only forbade them, but ordered the challengers into custody (Gent. Mag. xx. 22, 137).

In 1752 Knowles was appointed governor of Jamaica, and held the office for nearly four years. He offended the residents by insisting on the supreme jurisdiction of the English parliament, and by moving the seat of government to Kingston, thus causing a depreciation of property in Spanish Town. A petition for his removal, signed by nineteen members of the assembly, was presented to the king, and charges of 'illegal, cruel, and arbitrary acts' were laid before the House of Commons. After examination by a committee of the whole house, the action of the assembly of Jamaica was condemned as 'derogatory to the rights of the crown and people of Great Britain,' and Knowles's conduct, by implication, fully justified. But Knowles had already returned to England and resigned the governorship, January 1756.

On 4 Feb. 1755 he had been promoted to be vice-admiral, and in 1757, with his flag in the Neptune, was second in command under Sir Edward (afterwards Lord) Hawke [q. v.] in the abortive expedition against Rochefort. On the return of the fleet public indignation ran very high, and though for the most part levelled against the government and Sir John Mordaunt (1697–1780) [q. v.], Knowles was also bitterly reproached. He published a pamphlet entitled 'The Conduct of Admiral Knowles on the late Expedition set in a true light;' but this met with scant favour, and a notice of it in the 'Critical Review' (May 1758, v. 432) so far exceeded what was then considered decent, that the editor, Tobias Smollett [q. v.], was tried for libel, sentenced to a fine of 100*l.*, and to three months' imprisonment in the King's Bench. Nevertheless, Knowles's share in the miscarriage, and still more his championship of Mordaunt, offended the government. He was superseded from his command in the grand fleet, and though he had his flag flying for some time longer in the Royal Anne, guardship at Portsmouth, he had no further active service in the English navy.

On 3 Dec. 1760 he was promoted to the rank of admiral; on 31 Oct. 1765 he was created a baronet; and on 5 Nov. 1765 was nominated rear-admiral of Great Britain. This office he resigned in October 1770 on accepting a command in the Russian navy. Russia was at that time at war with Turkey [see ELPHINSTON, JOHN], but Knowles's service seems to have been entirely administrative, and to have kept him at St. Petersburg or the neighbourhood. On the conclusion of peace in 1774 he returned to England, and in 1775 published a translation of 'Abstract on the Mechanism of the Motions of Floating Bodies,' by M. de la Croix; in the prefatory notice he said that he had verified the author's principles by a number of experiments, and had also found them 'answer perfectly well when put into practice in several line-of-battle ships and frigates that I built whilst I was in Russia.' He died in Bulstrode Street, London, on 9 Dec. 1777, and was buried at Guildford in Surrey.

Few naval officers of high rank have been the subject of more contention or of more contradictory estimates than Knowles. He was beyond question a man that made many and bitter enemies, and when in command was neither loved nor feared, though he may have been hated. On the one hand, he has been described as vain, foolish, grasping—even dishonest—tyrannical, 'a man of spiritless and inactive mind, cautious of incurring censure, but incapable of acquiring fame.' On the other, Charnock, who in this may be supposed to represent the traditions he had received from Captain Locker, 'believes him to have been a man of spirit, ability, and integrity; but to have thought too highly of his own merit in regard to the two first, and to have wanted those conciliating and complacent manners which are absolutely necessary to render even the last agreeable and acceptable.'

Knowles was twice married: first, in 1740, to Mary, eldest daughter of John Alleyne, and sister of John Gay Alleyne, created a baronet in 1769; she died in March 1741-2, leaving one son, Edward, who was lost in command

of the Peregrine sloop in 1762. Secondly, at Aix-la-Chapelle in July 1750, to Maria Magdalena Theresa, daughter of Comte de Bouget, by whom he had, besides a daughter, a son, Charles Henry, who is separately noticed. A portrait by T. Hudson has been engraved.

[Charnock's Biog. Nav. iv. 345; Naval Chronicle, i. 89, ii. 256, xvi. 415; commission and warrant books, official letters, minutes of courts-martial and other documents in the Public Record Office; information from Rear-admiral Sir Charles G. F. Knowles. The minutes of the court-martial on Knowles, December 1749, were printed; so also was the defence of Captain Dent at his trial in March 1749. Knowles's correspondence with Anson is in Add. MS. 15956, ff. 119-74. Besides the pamphlets noted in the text, there are many others relating to different passages in Knowles's career. Among these may be noted: Journal of the Expedition to La Guira and Porto Cavalles in the West Indies, under the command of Commodore Knowles . . . 1744, 8vo; Relacion de la gloriosa y singular victoria que han conseguido las armas de S. M. Catolica contra una escuadra Britanica que invadió el dia 2 de Marzo de 1743 la plaza de la Guaira, comandada . . . por Don Carlos Wnoles (reprinted Caracas, 1858, 8vo. A manuscript note in the copy in the British Museum says that the original, which bears neither place nor date, but probably Cadiz, is extremely rare); Authentick Papers concerning a late Remarkable Transaction, 1746, a curious correspondence between Knowles and the Bank of England respecting a large quantity of silver he brought home in the Diamond; The Jamaica Association Develop'd, 1755. There are also some pamphlets about the case of Captain John Crookshanks [q. v.], and many relating to the Rochefort expedition. See also Beatson's Naval and Military Memoirs, vols. i. and ii.]

J. K. L.

KNOWLES, SIR CHARLES HENRY (1754-1831), admiral, only surviving son of Admiral Sir Charles Knowles [q. v.], was born in Jamaica 24 Aug. 1754. He entered the navy in 1768 on board the Venus with Captain the Hon. Samuel Barrington [q. v.], and was afterwards in the Seaford with Captain Macbride. Three years later he was again with Macbride in the Southampton on the home station, and from 1773 to 1776 in the flagship in the West Indies with Sir George Rodney and Rear-admiral Gayton. Gayton promoted him, 28 May 1776, to be lieutenant of the Boreas. In August the Boreas was sent to New York, and in the following January Knowles went home in the Asia in order to be with his father, whose health was failing. In June he again went out to North America, and was appointed by Lord Howe to the Chatham, but on the news of his father's death, 9 Dec. 1777, and his own succession to the baronetcy, he returned to England to arrange his private affairs. Afterwards he went out to join Barrington in the West Indies, was appointed to the Ceres, and in her was present in the action in the Cul-de-Sac of St. Lucia, 15 Dec. 1778. A few days later the Ceres was captured by the French squadron, and Knowles being shortly afterwards exchanged was appointed by Barrington to his own flagship, the Prince of Wales, in which he took part in the action off Grenada on 6 July 1779, when he was slightly wounded. He returned to England with Barrington, and in the following December went as a volunteer in the Sandwich with Sir George Rodney, who promoted him at Gibraltar to the command of the Minorca sloop, 26 Jan. 1780, and a week later, 2 Feb. 1780, to be captain of the Porcupine.

For the next two years Knowles continued in the Mediterranean, sometimes at Gibraltar, more commonly at Minorca, convoying or sending vessels loaded with provisions, or engaging French or Spanish privateers or cruisers. He returned to England in the spring of 1782, and, being ordered to resume the command of the Porcupine at Gibraltar, took a passage on board the Britannia with Admiral Barrington in the grand fleet under Howe. He was then appointed to command the San Miguel, a Spanish line-of-battle ship, which was blown ashore and captured, and on the departure of Captain Curtis [see CURTIS, SIR ROGER] remained at Gibraltar as senior officer until the peace. In 1793–4 Knowles commanded the Dædalus frigate on the coast of North America, and after his return to England commanded the Edgar of 74 guns in the North Sea. Towards the end of 1795 he was appointed to the Goliath of 74 guns; in her he joined the Mediterranean fleet in the summer of 1796, and took part in the battle of Cape St. Vincent on 14 Feb. 1797, for which, with the other captains, he received the thanks of parliament and the gold medal. On the return of the fleet to Lisbon he was appointed to the Britannia of 100 guns, but his ill-health compelled him to resign the command and return to England. He had no further service, though promoted in due course to be rear-admiral 14 Feb. 1799, vice-admiral 23 April 1804, and admiral 31 July 1810. On the accession of George IV he was nominated an extra G.C.B. He died 28 Nov. 1831, and was succeeded in the baronetcy by his son Sir Francis Charles (1802–1892), whose son Charles George Frederick is the present baronet.

Knowles was the author of numerous pamphlets on technical subjects (see also *British Museum Catalogue*).

[Ralfe's Nav. Biog. ii. 227; Marshall's Royal Nav. Biog. i. 113; Burke's Peerage and Baronetage.]   J. K. L.

KNOWLES, GILBERT (*fl.* 1723), botanist and poet, born in 1674, is known only for his ' Materia Medica Botanica ' (London, 1723, 4to). This work is dedicated to Dr. Richard Mead [q. v.], and consists of 7355 Latin hexameters. Four hundred plants of the materia medica are described and their uses in medicine explained. Various episodes, some of which may yet be read with pleasure, are interwoven with the subject for the sake of ornament. Knowles alludes to his verses as being written ' rudi Minerva,' and evidently was a close student both of Virgil's style and matter.

A portrait engraved in mezzotint by John Faber from a painting by T. Murray, subscribed ' Mr. Gilbert Knowles, ætatis 49, anno 1723,' is prefixed to the volume.

[Knowles's book in Brit. Mus.; Nichols's Lit. Illustrations, viii. 442–3; Pulteney's Sketches of the Progress of Botany, i. 283.]   M. G. W.

KNOWLES, HERBERT (1798–1817), poet, was born at Gomersal, near Leeds, in 1798. His parentage is said to have been very humble, but it is also stated that he was the brother of J. C. Knowles, subsequently Q.C. He lost both parents at an early age, and was about to enter a merchant's office at Liverpool when his talents attracted the notice of three benevolent clergymen, who raised 20l. a year towards his education on condition of his friends contributing 30l. more. He was sent to Richmond grammar school, Yorkshire, ' totally ignorant,' he tells Southey, of classical and mathematical literature. It had been hoped that he might obtain a sizarship at St. John's College, Cambridge, but the inability of his relations to fulfil their engagements seemed likely to put an end to the project, when Knowles conceived the idea of applying to Southey, sending him at the same time the poem of ' The Three Tabernacles,' which he had composed on 7 Oct. 1816. Southey, with his usual generosity, entered warmly into the matter, promised 10l. a year from his own means, and procured 20l. more by application to Earl Spencer and Rogers. Knowles was actually elected a sizar on 31 Jan. 1817, but he was already in a hopeless decline, and died on 17 Feb. following, at Gomersal. A letter from him to Southey, dated 28 Dec. 1816, conveys the most favourable impression of his modesty, candour, and good sense. He deprecates all extravagant expectations of his academical success, but undertakes to 'strive that my passage through the university, if not splendid, shall be respectable.' Verses from his pen were printed in the 'Literary Gazette' for 1819 and 1824, and the 'Literary Souvenir' for 1825 (reprinted in the 'Saturday Magazine,' vol. xvi.); and a correspondent of 'Notes and Queries' states himself to be in possession of several unpublished pieces. His reputation, however, entirely rests on the poem sent to Southey, entitled by himself 'The Three Tabernacles,' but better known as 'Stanzas in Richmond Churchyard,' which had a large circulation on a separate sheet, and first appeared in book form in Carlisle's 'Endowed Grammar Schools.' It would be difficult to overpraise this noble masterpiece of solemn and tender pathos, exquisite in diction and melody, and only marred by the anticlimax of the last stanza, fine in itself, but out of keeping with the general sentiment of the poem. If this had been omitted and the two preceding stanzas transposed, the impression would have been one of absolute perfection. Even as they stand the stanzas are unparalleled as the work of a schoolboy for faultless finish and freedom from all the characteristic failings of inexperience. This extraordinary maturity discriminates Knowles from other examples of precocious genius, such as Keats, Blake, and Chatterton, and insures him a unique place among youthful poets. His intellect must have been as active as his emotional nature; and even had the poetical impulse deserted him, he could not have failed to achieve distinction in some manner.

[Southey's Life and Correspondence, iv. 221-227; Quarterly Review, vol. xxi.; Notes and Queries, 2nd ser. vol. viii.; Carlisle's Endowed Grammar Schools.]   R. G.

KNOWLES, JAMES (1759-1840), lexicographer, born in 1759, was son of John Knowles of Dublin, by Frances, daughter of the Rev. Dr. Sheridan of Quilca, the friend of Swift. His mother's brother, Thomas Sheridan, author of a 'Pronouncing Dictionary,' and father of Richard Brinsley Sheridan, directed his education and intended him for the church; but an early marriage led Knowles to establish a school in Cork in 1780, which prospered until 1793. In that year Knowles, who was a liberal as well as a protestant, first signed a petition for catholic emancipation, and a little later went bail for the editor of a liberal paper, who had been prosecuted at the instance of the government. His pupils, who were the sons of protestant gentry, deserted him, and he went to London, where, according to his son's account, he was helped by his first cousin,

Richard Brinsley Sheridan. He continued his career as a schoolmaster, and in 1813, mainly by his son's influence, he was appointed head-master of the English department in the Belfast Academical Institution. In 1816 he was dismissed by the directors, on the ground of inability to maintain discipline. Knowles declined to be dismissed, and prepared to resist ejectment; but eventually he gave way, and in 1817 published 'An Appeal to the Dignified Visitors, and the Noblemen and Gentlemen, Proprietors,' invoking the principles of the British constitution to prove that he had suffered injustice. Before leaving Belfast he received a testimonial from some of the leading citizens. He returned to London, where he appears to have carried on his profession as 'teacher of reading, elocution, grammar, and composition' for several years. In 1829 he seems to have joined his son in Glasgow, where he brought out a little book on 'Orthoëpy and Elocution.' About this time, though he was now seventy and suffering from a painful disease, he began the compilation of a dictionary. This was published in London in 1835, under the name of 'A Pronouncing and Explanatory Dictionary of the English Language.' A dispute with the printer led to a protracted lawsuit, of which most of the expenses were borne by his son, James Sheridan Knowles [q. v.] Knowles died at his son's house, Alfred Place, Bedford Square, London, on 6 Feb. 1840, and was buried at Highgate.

Knowles married, first, Jane, daughter of Andrew Peace, medical practitioner, of Cork, widow of a Mr. Daunt, and after her death, in 1800, a Miss Maxwell. James Sheridan was the offspring of the first marriage.

[R. B. Knowles's Life of James Sheridan Knowles; Gent. Mag. 1840.]   T. B. S.

KNOWLES, JAMES SHERIDAN (1784-1862), dramatist, born at Cork on 12 May 1784, was son of James Knowles [q. v.] the lexicographer, by his first wife. Richard Brinsley Sheridan, from whom he derived his second name, was his father's first cousin. At the age of six he was placed in his father's school at Cork, but in 1793 moved with the family to London. There he made early efforts in verse, and at the age of twelve attempted a play, in which he acted with his juvenile companions, as well as the libretto of an opera on the story of the Chevalier de Grillon. A few months later he wrote 'The Welch Harper,' a ballad, which was set to music and became popular. He was befriended by the elder Hazlitt, an acquaintance of the family, who helped him with advice and introduced him to Coleridge and Lamb.

His mother, from whom he received much encouragement, died in 1809; and on his father's second marriage to a Miss Maxwell soon afterwards, Knowles, unable to agree with his stepmother, left the parental roof in a fit of anger, and lived for some time from hand to mouth, helped by his friends. During this period he served as an ensign in the Wiltshire, and afterwards (1805) in the Tower Hamlets militia; studied medicine under Dr. Willan, obtained the degree of M.D. from the university of Aberdeen, and became resident vaccinator to the Jennerian Society. Meanwhile he was writing small tragedies and 'dabbling in private theatricals.' Eventually he abandoned medicine and took to the provincial stage. He made his first appearance probably at Bath. Subsequently he played Hamlet with little success at the Crow Street Theatre, Dublin. In a company at Wexford he met, and on 25 Oct. 1809 married, Miss Maria Charteris of Edinburgh. They acted together in Cherry's company at Waterford, and there Knowles made the acquaintance of Edmund Kean, for whom he wrote 'Leo, or the Gipsy,' 1810, which was performed with favour at the Waterford Theatre. About the same time he published a small volume of poems. After a visit to Swansea, where his eldest son was born, Knowles appeared on the boards at Belfast. There he wrote, on the basis of an earlier work of the same name, a play entitled 'Brian Boroihme, or the Maid of Erin,' 1811, which proved very popular.

But these efforts produced a very small income, and Knowles was driven to seek a living by teaching. He opened a school of his own at Belfast, and composed for his pupils a series of extracts for declamation under the title of 'The Elocutionist,' which ran through many editions. In 1813 he was invited to offer himself for the post of first head-master in English subjects in the Belfast Academical Institution; but this appointment he declined in favour of his father, contenting himself with the position of assistant. Three years later the dismissal of his father made it necessary for the son to leave Belfast, and Knowles removed to Glasgow, where he carried on a school for about twelve years.

On 13 Feb. 1815 his tragedy of 'Caius Gracchus' had been brought out with great success at the Belfast Theatre. When Kean visited Glasgow he suggested to Knowles a play on the subject of Virginius. Though at this period he was teaching thirteen hours a day, Knowles wrote the drama in three

months; but by the time it was ready Kean had accepted another play on the same theme, which was not performed at Drury Lane until 29 May 1820 (GENEST, Hist. Stage, ix. 36). Knowles meanwhile produced his drama at Glasgow, where Tait, a friend of Macready, saw it, and brought it under that actor's notice. It was afterwards performed at Covent Garden on 17 May 1820, with Macready in the title-rôle, Charles Kemble as Icilius, Miss Foote as Virginia, and Mrs. Faucit as Servia; and although Genest denounces it as dull, it ran successfully for fourteen nights (ib. pp. 56–7). Among the congratulations which Knowles received was one in verse from Charles Lamb. Knowles then remodelled his 'Caius Gracchus,' and Macready brought it out at Covent Garden on 18 Nov. 1823. At Macready's suggestion he afterwards wrote a play on 'William Tell,' in which the actor appeared with equal success two years later. Knowles's reputation was thus established, and Hazlitt in his 'Spirit of the Age,' 1825, spoke of him as the first tragic writer of his time. But Knowles made little money by his dramatic successes. In 1823 and 1824 he added to his income by conducting the literary department of the 'Free Press,' a Glasgow organ of liberal and social reform. His school did not prosper, and he took to lecturing upon oratory and the drama, a field in which he won the praises of Professor Wilson in the 'Noctes Ambrosianæ.'

Knowles's first comedy, 'The Beggar's Daughter of Bethnal Green,' was produced at Drury Lane on 28 May 1828. It was based on the well-known ballad, which had already inspired a play by Henry Chettle and John Day (written about 1600, and printed London, 1659). Though expectation ran high, Knowles's play was damned at the first performance; the verdict was perhaps unduly emphasised by the presence of many ill-wishers from the rival house of Covent Garden, then temporarily closed. Knowles at once set to work to redeem the failure. In 1830 he and his family left Glasgow and settled near Newhaven, by Edinburgh, and there, while working at a new comedy, he put the last touches to his 'Alfred the Great, or the Patriot King.' This came out at Drury Lane on 28 April 1831, and met with some success, partly, perhaps, from the political circumstances of the time.

Knowles's second comedy, 'The Hunchback,' was meanwhile accepted by the authorities at Drury Lane, with some qualification as to the underplot, which, in Macready's judgment, was defective. The play was remodelled, and again offered to Drury Lane at the beginning of 1832, but there was delay in producing it. Knowles demanded his manuscript back, and took it to Charles Kemble at Covent Garden. It was produced there on 5 April 1832; Julia was played by Miss Kemble, and Master Walter by the author himself, who thus returned to his early calling. The comedy was a great success, and enjoyed an almost uninterrupted run till the end of the season, but Knowles's acting did not meet with much approval. On taking 'The Hunchback' to Glasgow and Edinburgh, he was received with enthusiasm by his former friends and pupils. When his next important play, 'The Wife,' was brought out at Covent Garden on 24 April 1833, Charles Lamb wrote both prologue and epilogue; and an article in the 'Edinburgh Review' at this date described Knowles as the most successful dramatist of the day.

On 10 Oct. 1837 appeared 'The Love Chase,' which, with the exception of 'The Hunchback,' has retained more public favour than any of Knowles's plays. With Strickland as Fondlove, and Elton, Webster, Mrs. Glover, and Mrs. Nisbett as Waller, Wildrake, Widow Green, and Constance respectively, the play was a brilliant success, and ran until the end of December.

Knowles, notwithstanding adverse criticism, continued to act up till 1843, and by his own account thus made a fair income. He acted in 'Macbeth' and in some of his own plays at the Coburg Theatre, and also in the provinces and in Ireland. After playing with Macready in 'Virginius' before an enthusiastic London audience, he paid, in 1834, a very successful visit of nine months to the United States. Between his return from America and 1843 he brought out eight more plays of his own (see list below), besides adapting Beaumont and Fletcher's 'Maid's Tragedy' under the name of 'The Bridal,' and later on the same authors' 'Noble Gentleman;' the latter, however, was not acted. In 1841 he composed the libretto of a ballad-opera, 'Alexina,' which after his death was re-arranged and brought out as a play under the name, 'True unto Death.' He also wrote tales in the magazines and continued his public lectures. Two novels by him—'George Lovell' and 'Fortescue'—appeared in 1846–7, but neither of them is remarkable. Although he was now in receipt of a comfortable income, his resources were hampered by his ready charity and his chivalrous efforts to discharge his father's debts. In 1848 Knowles was granted a civil-list pension of 200l. He was an original member of the committee formed for the purchase of Shakespeare's birthplace at Strat-

ford-on-Avon, and it was reported in 1848, when the purchase was completed, that the custodianship was offered to him. He never filled the office, but at his death the trustees of the birthplace recorded their belief that he had been in receipt of the dividends of 1,500l., invested in the names of Forster and Dickens, 'for the ostensible purpose of founding a custodianship of the birthplace,' and inquiries were made into the investment and appropriation of the dividends (extract from Trustees' Minute-book, 31 Dec. 1862).

Knowles had always had strongly religious and philanthropic interests, and had in early days been greatly impressed by the preaching of Rowland Hill at the Surrey Chapel. About 1844 he embraced an extreme form of evangelicalism and joined the baptists, professing that he had hitherto lived 'without God and without hope in the world.' He delivered sermons from chapel pulpits and at Exeter Hall. He denounced Roman catholicism, attacked Cardinal Wiseman on the subject of transubstantiation, and wrote two books of controversial divinity; but he avoided preaching against the stage. He was a great believer in the water-cure. In his last years he visited various parts of the kingdom, and in 1862, soon after entering his seventy-ninth year, was entertained at a banquet in his native city of Cork. On 30 Nov. of the same year he died at Torquay. He was buried in the Necropolis at Glasgow. His first wife died in 1841, and in the following year he married a Miss Elphinstone, a former pupil, who had played Meeta in his 'Maid of Mariendorpt.' His son by his first wife, Richard Brinsley Knowles, is noticed separately.

There is a portrait of Knowles in the 'Life' by his son, Richard Brinsley Knowles, and an outline sketch of him in Maclise's 'Portrait Gallery.'

Judged by literary tests alone, Knowles's plays cannot lay claim to much distinction. His plots are conventional, his style is simple, and, in spite of his Irish birth, his humour is not conspicuous. Occasionally he strikes a poetical vein, and his fund of natural feeling led him to evolve many effective situations. But he is a playwright rather than a dramatist. As an actor, his style, from a want of relief and transition, was apt to become tedious, but his unmistakable earnestness strongly recommended him to audiences with whom, as a dramatist, he was in his lifetime highly popular (see WESTLAND MARSTON, *Our Recent Actors*, ii. 122).

His published works may be conveniently divided into three classes. The dates given are those of first publication.

I. Dramatic works: 'Caius Gracchus,' a tragedy in five acts, 1815; 'Virginius,' a tragedy in five acts, 1820; 'William Tell,' a play in five acts, 1825 (manuscript copy, Brit. Mus. Addit. MS. 27710, f. 29); 'Alfred the Great, or the Patriot King,' an historical play in five acts, 1831; 'The Hunchback,' a play in five acts, 1832; 'The Wife, a Tale of Mantua,' a play, 1833; 'The Beggar of Bethnal Green,' a comedy in three acts, 1834 (an abridgment of 'The Beggar's Daughter of Bethnal Green,' 1828); 'The Daughter,' a play, 1837; 'The Love Chase,' a comedy in five acts, 1837; 'Woman's Wit,' 1838; 'The Maid of Marien-dorpt,' a play, 1838; 'Love,' a play, 1839; 'John of Procida, or the Bridals of Messina,' a tragedy, 1840; 'Old Maids,' a comedy, 1841; 'The Rose of Arragon,' 1842; 'The Secretary,' a play in five acts, 1843. All of the above are in verse, with the exception of parts of 'Caius Gracchus,' 'The Hunchback,' and 'The Beggar's Daughter.'

II. Miscellaneous poetical works and adaptations: 'The Welch Harper,' a ballad, 1796; 'Fugitive Pieces,' 1810; 'Leo, or the Gipsy,' 1810 (a fragment preserved in Proctor's 'Life of Edmund Kean'); 'Brian Boroihme, or the Maid of Erin' (adapted from D. O'Meara), 1811; 'A Masque on the Death of Sir Walter Scott,' 1832; 'The Bridal,' 1837 (adapted from Beaumont and Fletcher's 'Maid's Tragedy'); 'Alexina,' a drama in two acts, published posthumously as 'True unto Death,' 1863; various political poems and songs set to music.

III. Miscellaneous prose writings: Tales and novelettes printed in various forms between 1832 and 1843; lectures on dramatic literature, 1820-50; 'Lectures on Oratory, Gesture, and Poetry, to which is added a Correspondence with four Clergymen in defence of the Stage' (these tales and lectures, together with various dramatic works coming under class II, were revised, edited, and privately issued in five volumes by Francis Hervey in 1873-4; only twenty-five copies of each volume were printed. A complete set is in the British Museum); 'The Elocutionist,' a collection of pieces in prose and verse, peculiarly adapted to display the art of reading, 3rd edit. Belfast, 1823, 28th edit. London, 1883; various articles in the 'Free Press' of Glasgow, 1823-4; 'George Lovell,' a novel, 1846; 'Fortescue,' a novel, 1847; 'The Rock of Rome, or the Arch Heresy,' 1849; 'The Idol Demolished by its own Priest,' an answer to lectures on transubstantiation delivered by Cardinal Wiseman, 1851; 'The Gospel attributed to Matthew is the Record of the whole original Apostlehood,' 1855.

[Life of J. S. Knowles by his son, Richard Brinsley Knowles, revised and edited by Francis Hervey, London, 1872; only twenty-five copies printed, one in British Museum. This gives full information, and refers to contemporary authorities. For special criticisms see Hazlitt's Spirit of the Age, London, 1825; Edinburgh Review, October 1833; Horne's New Spirit of the Age, London, 1845; Dublin University Magazine, October 1852; Athenæum, February 1847; Blackwood's Edinburgh Magazine, October 1863; see also Macready's Reminiscences; Doran's Their Majesties' Servants, ii. 556-7; Maclise's Portrait Gallery.] T. B. S.

KNOWLES, JOHN (*fl.* 1646–1668), antitrinitarian, probably a native of Gloucester, first appears as a lay preacher among the independents there. In 1648 he described himself as 'a preacher of the gospel, formerly in and near Gloucester.' He was well acquainted with the Greek text of the New Testament and with Latin commentators, and his antitrinitarian sentiments were the result of his own scriptural studies. He admits having 'had upon occasion some communion' with 'one who appeared infected therein;' a clear reference to John Biddle [q. v.], who left Gloucester in 1646. But he did not adopt Biddle's specific opinions, his doctrine being of the Arian, not the Socinian type. He expressly states in 1668 that he had not read any of the writings of F. P. Socinus. By the parliamentary committee at Gloucester he was examined (1646?) on suspicion of unsoundness in the article of the Trinity, and gave in a written statement in which he owns to having 'had some questionings,' but gives his reasons for being now satisfied of 'the Godhead of the Holy Ghost.' He seems to have left Gloucester for London, where he lodged with Edward Atkinson, an antitrinitarian, in Aldersgate Street. Joining the parliamentary army, he belonged in 1648, according to his own account, 'to the lifeguard of his excellency Sir Thomas Fairfax.' He still continued to preach, publishing a defence of 'a private man's preaching.' Early in 1650 he became 'public preacher to the garrison' at Chester, in succession to Samuel Eaton [q. v.] The biographer of John Murcot [q. v.], writing in 1657, speaks of Knowles as having been 'a formidable and blazing comet at Chester,' where 'in public sermons, private conferences, and by a manuscript' he 'denied Jesus Christ to be the Most High God.' A short paper of arguments for the deity of Christ, sent by Eaton to Chester from Dukinfield, was published by Knowles in 1650, with his own reply. The pamphlet purports to have been 'printed by T. S. for Gyles Calvert,' the well-known publisher of eccentric theology; and in July 1650 John Whittell, girdler, of Milk Street, London, was brought before the council of state on the charge of having caused it to be printed. Replies were published by Eaton (1650 and 1651), and by Thomas Porter of Whitchurch, Shropshire (1651). The imprimatur of Porter's pamphlet, entitled 'A Serious Exercitation,' is dated 26 Dec. 1650, and by that time Knowles was 'late preacher at Chester.' He appears to have returned to Gloucester, for on 19 Nov. 1650 the mayor of that city was directed by the council of state to examine witnesses on oath respecting Knowles's preaching against the divinity of Christ. He removed to Pershore, Worcestershire, where he lived some fifteen years as 'a professed minister.'

At Pershore he was apprehended on 9 April 1665 by Thomas, seventh baron Windsor, and imprisoned first at Worcester, and then in the Gatehouse, Westminster, on 23 May. Papers found in his house were made the basis of charges of heresy; he had been invited on 5 June 1662 by H. Hed of Huntingdon to meet Christopher Crell, the exiled Polish antitrinitarian, at Oxford; on 19 Nov. 1664 he had been invited to London by Thomas Firmin [q. v.] Letters from his friends were construed as implying that he was ready to countenance sedition. A collection on behalf of the Polish exiles was thought to be really for English rebels. On 23 June and again on 7 July he petitioned (writing also to Monck, duke of Albemarle) for liberty to go out on bail, as the plague was then raging in London. His petition was repeated on 2 Feb. 1666, and he gained his liberty soon afterwards. On his release he mixed in controversial talk with London clergy, who respected his learning and sincerity. With his publication in reply to 'Justification onely upon a Satisfaction,' &c., 1668, 12mo, by Robert Ferguson (d. 1714) [q. v.], he drops out of notice. A pamphleteer of 1698 states that he bequeathed some valuable books to a library at Gloucester.

He published: 1. 'A Modest Plea for Private Men's Preaching,' &c., 1648, 4to (published 30 March; in answer to 'Private Men no Pulpit Men,' &c., 1646, 4to, by Giles Workman). 2. 'A Friendly Debate . . . by Writing betwixt Mr. Samuel Eaton and Mr. John Knowles,' &c., 1650, 4to. 3. 'An Answer to Mr. Ferguson's Book,' &c. [1668?], 8vo. In this last he mentions other projected publications, but he is not known to have issued anything further.

[Grounds and Occasions of the Controversy concerning the Unity of God, 1698, p. 16; Wallace's Antitrinitarian Biog. 1850, i. 154, iii. 210 sq.; Urwick's Nonconformity in Cheshire, 1864, pp. 16 sq., 465 sq.; Cal. of State Papers, Dom. 1862, 1665.]   A. G.

KNOWLES, JOHN (1600?–1685), nonconformist divine, was born in Lincolnshire about 1600. He was educated at Magdalene College, Cambridge, his chamber-fellow being Richard Vines [q. v.] In 1625 he was elected fellow of Catharine Hall, and acquired great repute as a tutor. On the advice of the master, Richard Sibbes, he joined in electing to a fellowship Laud's nominee, John Ellis (1606?–1681) [q. v.], an act of compliance which he afterwards regretted. In 1635 the corporation of Colchester elected him to a lectureship in that town. Here he exercised considerable public influence. He was intimate with the noted puritan, John Rogers, vicar of Dedham, Essex; preached his funeral sermon in 1636, and obtained the appointment of Matthew Newcomen [q. v.] as his successor. A vacancy in the mastership of Colchester grammar school was filled in 1637 by the appointment of William Dugard [q. v.], on Knowles's recommendation, in opposition to a candidate favoured by Laud. 'The getting in of a schoolmaster,' says Calamy, 'proved the outing of a lecturer.' Knowles had laid himself open to interference by opposing the ceremonies. Laud reprimanded him and threatened further proceedings. Ultimately his license was revoked; Knowles resigned his lectureship before the end of 1637, and left Colchester. In 1639 he embarked for New England.

For about ten years he was 'teacher,' i.e. lecturer, as colleague with George Philips, at Watertown, Massachusetts, 'in a cold wilderness.' After this he went (7 Oct. 1642) on a mission to Virginia. The governor prohibited him from public preaching, as he would not use a surplice or the prayer-book. The governor's chaplain, Thomas Harrison, D.D. (1619–1682) [q. v.], seems to have acted a double part, openly favouring, but privately opposing, the puritan preachers. Knowles preached in private houses with much acceptance until he and others were expelled. He returned to Watertown, and was still in New England on 31 Dec. 1650, on which day he signed a letter addressed to Oliver Cromwell. Soon afterwards he returned to England, and was appointed lecturer in the cathedral at Bristol. On 18 Oct. 1653 an augmentation was ordered to be paid to 'John Knowles of Bristol cathedral.' He was several times interrupted by quakers. On 17 Dec. 1654 Elizabeth Marshall, a quakeress, was sent to prison for delivering 'a message' to Knowles at the close of the service. On 20 June 1657 his sermon in All Hallows Church was disturbed by Nathaniel Milner, and on 6 Oct. 1659 Thomas Jones was committed for assailing Knowles's door with a chopping-knife.

The Restoration deprived him of his post at Bristol, and he repaired to London. In 1661 he was lecturer at All Hallows the Great on Mondays, Wednesdays, and Fridays. The Uniformity Act, 1662, made his preaching illegal, but he continued to exercise his ministry as opportunity served. In August 1664 he was reported as having 1,000l. in his hands for the benefit of 'godly men.' During the great plague of 1665 he was assiduous in giving his services to the sufferers. On the indulgence of 1672 he became colleague to Thomas Kentish in the charge of a presbyterian congregation meeting in the parish of St. Catherine-in-the-Tower, afterwards in Eastcheap (ultimately at the King's Weighhouse). He had many narrow escapes from arrest after the cancelling of the Act of Indulgence in 1673. He died on 10 April 1685.

[Cotton Mather's Magnalia Christi Americana, 1702, iii. 3, 216 sq.; Calamy's Account, 1713, pp. 605 sq.; Wilson's Dissenting Churches of London, 1808, i. 154 sq.; Davids's Evang. Nonconformity in Essex, 1863, pp. 547 sq.; Pike's Ancient Meeting-Houses, 1870, pp. 336 sq.; Calendar of State Papers (Domestic), 1653, 1664.]   A. G.

KNOWLES, JOHN (1781–1841), biographer of Henry Fuseli [q. v.], born in 1781, early in life became a clerk in the surveyor's department of the navy office. He attained the chief clerkship there about 1806, and held this post until 1832. He published two or three works on naval matters, including 'The Elements and Practice of Naval Architecture,' 1822. For his scientific researches he was elected a fellow of the Royal Society. Knowles is best known, however, from his long, intimate friendship with Henry Fuseli the painter, and the circle to which that artist belonged. He was the executor of Fuseli's will, and a devoted admirer of his art. In 1830 he published an edition of Fuseli's 'Lectures on Painting,' and in 1831, in 3 vols. 8vo, the life of Fuseli, written as a labour of love, to which was added an edition of the painter's writings on art. As a biography the work has some merit. Knowles died, unmarried, at Ashburton, Devonshire, on 21 July 1841, aged 60. He was one of the original members of the Athenæum Club, and his portrait, drawn by C. Landseer, is No. 25 of the series of lithographs, published as 'Athenæum Portraits,' by Thomas McLean. He was corresponding member of the Philosophical Society of Rotterdam.

[Gent. Mag. new ser. 1841, xvi. 331; Knowles's Life and Writings of H. Fuseli; Smith's Nollekens, ii. 425–7; private information.]   L. C.

KNOWLES, Mrs. MARY (1733–1807), quakeress, eldest daughter of Moses and Mary Morris of Rugeley, Staffordshire, was born on 6 May 1733. She was witty and beautiful. One of her accomplishments was working in worsted what Dr. Johnson called 'sutile pictures' (CROKER). Specimens having been shown to the queen, she was sent for and commissioned to execute portraits of George III and the young princes, which were much approved. She married Dr. Thomas Knowles, graduate of Leyden 1772, L.R.C.P. 1784, and author of 'Tentamen Medicum,' Leyden, 1722. They travelled abroad, and were received at the Hague and at Versailles. Dr. Knowles died in Lombard Street 16 Nov. 1784, leaving considerable wealth. Mrs. Knowles was intimate with Dr. Johnson. She was a brilliant conversationalist, and said of Johnson's reading that 'he tore the heart out of a book.' She wrote, about 1770, a 'Compendium of a Controversy on Water-Baptism' between Rand, a clergyman of Coventry, and herself; 'A Poetic Correspondence' between her and a Captain Morris was printed in the 'British Friend,' April 1848, p. 110. Other verses by her appeared as small tracts without date. Boswell records her talents, but declines to accept as authentic her account of a 'Dialogue between Dr. Johnson and Mrs. Knowles' respecting the conversion to quakerism of Miss Jane Harry, which Mrs. Knowles forwarded to him while engaged on the biography of Johnson. Its authenticity was corroborated by Miss Seward, who was present at the interview. Mrs. Knowles published it in the 'Gentleman's Magazine,' June 1791, p. 500, and it has been many times reprinted separately. Mrs. Knowles had one son, George. She died in London 3 Feb. 1807.

[Smith's Catalogue; Boswell's Life of Johnson, ed. Croker, 1831, iii. 440–2, iv. 142–5; Monthly Repository of Theol. March 1807, ii. 160; Lady's Monthly Museum, November 1803, with engraved portrait; Letters of Anna Seward, 6 vols., Edinb. 1811, passim.]   C. F. S.

KNOWLES, RICHARD BRINSLEY (1820–1882), journalist, son of James Sheridan Knowles [q. v.], dramatist, was born at Glasgow on 17 Jan. 1820, and about 1838 held an appointment in the registrar-general's office, Somerset House, London. He was admitted a student of the Middle Temple on 14 Nov. 1839, and called to the bar 26 May 1843. His tastes, however, inclined towards literature, and on 19 Nov. 1845 he produced at the Haymarket Theatre a comedy, 'The Maiden Aunt,' which, aided by the acting of William Farren and Mrs. Glover, had a run of thirty nights. In 1849 he joined the church of Rome, and became editor of the 'Catholic Standard,' a publication which was subsequently purchased by Henry Wilberforce, and re-named the 'Weekly Register.' From 1853 to 1855 he edited the 'Illustrated London Magazine,' a series of five volumes. He was one of the chief writers on the 'Standard' from 1857 to 1860, but some display of religious intolerance on the part of the proprietors led to an abrupt termination of his engagement. Professor John Sherren Brewer [q. v.], who was then conducting the paper, indignant at the treatment of his colleague, at once relinquished his editorship. Knowles was afterwards editor of the 'London Review,' but in later years his chief engagement was on the 'Morning Post,' until ill-health obliged him to resign his connection with that paper. He edited the 'Chronicles of John of Oxenedes,' a manuscript copy of which was found in the Duke of Newcastle's collection; and his edition was published in 1859 in the 'Rolls Series.' In 1871 he was engaged under the royal commission on historical manuscripts, and described many valuable collections of family muniments, chiefly belonging to Roman catholic families. Among these were the collections of the Marquis of Bute, the Earl of Denbigh, the Earl of Ashburnham, and Colonel Townley. He was the author in 1872 of 'The Life of James Sheridan Knowles,' an edition of twenty-five copies for private circulation. He died suddenly at 29 North Bank, Regent's Park, London, 28 Jan. 1882, having married on 25 Oct. 1845 Eliza Mary, youngest child of Peter and Elizabeth Crowley of Dublin, and sister of Nicholas Joseph Crowley(1819-1857) [q. v.], painter.

[Athenæum, 4 Feb. 1882, p. 156; Times, 30 Jan. 1882, p. 7; Law Times, 25 Feb. 1882, p. 301; Hist. MSS. Comm. 3rd Rep. 1872, p. 209, and succeeding reports: information from his son, Richard Brinsley Sheridan Knowles, esq.] G. C. B.

KNOWLES, THOMAS, D.D. (1723-1802), divine, born at Ely in 1723, was son of one of the vergers and master of the works of Ely Cathedral. He received his education in Ely grammar school and Pembroke Hall, Cambridge, where he graduated B.A. in 1743 and M.A. in 1747. He was elected a fellow of his college on 2 March 1748-9. On 10 Jan. 1748 he was instituted to the rectories of Ickworth and Chedburgh, Suffolk. He was also chaplain to Lady Hervey, baroness dowager of Ickworth. In 1752 he had a dispensation to hold with Ickworth the living of Feversham, Cambridgeshire. He was made

D.D. by Archbishop Secker in 1753. From about 1771 till his death he was lecturer of St. Mary's, Bury, and on 10 Oct. 1779 he was collated to a prebend at Ely (LE NEVE, Fasti, ed. Hardy, i. 362). In 1791 he became rector of Winston, Suffolk. He died on 6 Oct. 1802, and was buried in his church of Chedburgh. One of his daughters married Benjamin Underwood, rector of Great Barnet, and the other, Eliza, married Sir Edmund Lacon, afterwards baronet.

His principal publications are: 1. 'The Existence and Attributes of God not demonstrable *a priori*, in Answer to the Argument of . . . Dr. Clarke and his Followers, and more particularly to a late Pamphlet, entitled "The Argument *a priori*, &c., stated and considered,"' Cambridge, 1746, 8vo. This elicited 'Some Thoughts concerning the Argument *a priori*,' anon., London, 1748, 8vo. 2. 'The Scripture Doctrine of the Existence and Attributes of God, as manifested by the Works of Creation and Providence. In twelve Sermons.' With a preface, in answer to the pamphlet, entitled 'Some Thoughts,' &c., Cambridge, 1750, 8vo. 3. 'An Answer to an Essay on Spirit,' London, 1753, 8vo. 4. 'Observations on the Divine Mission and Administration of Moses,' London, 1762, 8vo. 5. 'A preparatory Discourse on Confirmation,' 6th edit. Ipswich, 1770, 8vo; 10th edit. Ipswich, 1784, 8vo. 6. 'Letters between Lord Hervey and Dr. Middleton concerning the Roman Senate. Published from the original manuscripts,' London, 1778, 4to. 7. 'The Passion; or a Description of Christ's Sufferings,' London, 1780, 12mo; 2nd edit. London, 1796, 12mo; a new edit., with additions by the Rev. Henry Hasted, M.A., London, 1830, 8vo. 8. 'Primitive Christianity,' London, 1789, 8vo. Capel Lofft wrote 'Observations' on the first part of this work, 1789, and James Edward Hamilton published 'Strictures' upon it, 1790. 9. 'Advice to a young Clergyman upon his entering into Priest's Orders. In six Pastoral Letters,' 2nd edit. London, 1797, 8vo.

[Addit. MSS. 5874 f.21 b, 19167 f. 13; Hawes and Loder's Framlingham, p. 285; Cat. of the Library of John Holmes, ii. 97; Gent. Mag. 1802 pt. ii. p. 980; Tyms's Hist. of St. Mary's Church, Bury, pp. 131, 132; Nichols's Lit. Illustr. vi. 468.] T. C.

KNOWLTON, THOMAS (1692-1782), gardener and botanist, born in 1692, superintended from an early age the botanic garden of Dr. Sherard at Eltham in Kent. In 1728 he entered the service of Richard Boyle, third earl of Burlington [q. v.], at Lanesborough, Yorkshire, and there he appears to have remained for the rest of his life. He became known as a botanist of merit, corresponded with Mark Catesby, E. M. Da Costa [q. v.], and other members of the Royal Society, and won the esteem of Sir Hans Sloane. To him is due the first discovery in England of the 'moor-ball,' a species of fresh-water algæ of the conferva family, called by Linnæus *Ægagropila*, from its resemblance to the hairy balls found in the stomachs of goats (DILLWYN, *British Confervæ*, 1809, pl. 87). In order to find even a moderate number of these balls, he had to spend many hours wading in the lake at Wallingfen, in water from two to over three feet deep. Knowlton was also something of an antiquary. He discovered the exact site of the ancient city of Delgoricia, near Pocklington in Yorkshire, and communicated some observations on this and other subjects to the 'Philosophical Transactions' (xliv. 100, 102, 124). Two large deer's horns which he discovered, one resembling the horn of an Irish elk, are figured in the same volume (plate 422). Knowlton died in 1782 at the age of ninety. A botanical genus of the order *Ranunculaceæ*, comprising five or six species of plants indigenous to the Cape of Good Hope, has been named after him. A John Knowlton, gardener to Earl Fitzwilliam, whose will was proved in February 1782 (P. C. C. Gostling, fol. 95), was probably a brother of the botanist, and Charles Knowlton, who graduated M.A. from St. John's College, Cambridge, in 1751, and was presented, on 7 April 1753, by the Earl of Burlington to the small living of Keighley in Yorkshire, was almost certainly his son (WHITAKER, *Deanery of Craven*, ed. Morant, p. 202).

[Pulteney's Progress of Botany, ii. 240; Biog. Universelle, xxii. 498; Nicholson's Dict. of Gardening, ii. 220; Nichols's Illustrations, iv. 469, 748, 785, where several letters to and from Knowlton are printed.] T. S.

KNOX, ALEXANDER (1757–1831), theological writer, born at Londonderry, 17 March 1757, was descended from the Scottish family to which John Knox the reformer belonged. The father was a well-to-do member of the corporation of Derry. In 1765 John Wesley, while in Ireland, became acquainted with Mr. and Mrs. Knox, who both joined his society. Alexander formed an intimacy with Wesley, which was kept up until Wesley's death in 1791. Knox always expressed the deepest obligation to Wesley's influence, but denied that he owed to him his early religious impressions, which he attributed entirely to his mother (Letter to Mr. Butterworth in 1807). When he was twelve years old he lost his

father. At an early age he became for a time a member of Wesley's society, but 'a growing disposition to think for himself' caused his 'relish for their religious practises to abate before he was twenty.' His weak health prevented him from passing through any regular course of education at all, though his writings prove that he managed to pick up a considerable knowledge of the classics and of general literature. He attributes his low spirits to his having been brought up to no regular employment; but he was also subject to epileptic fits. Twenty letters to him from Wesley, published in the 'Remains,' gave him much pious and rational advice. For a while he threw himself into politics. He was a good public speaker, as well as writer, in support of parliamentary reform in Ireland. His alarm at the proceedings of the United Irishmen convinced him that 'any degree of popular reform would infallibly lead to complete democracy,' and he finally became 'an unqualified supporter of the existing constitution.' In 1797 he renewed an intimacy with John Jebb [q. v.], which had commenced when Jebb was a boy at Derry school. He was private secretary to Lord Castlereagh during the rebellion of 1798 and afterwards. After the union Lord Castlereagh urged him to accept an offer of representing his native city, Derry, in the united parliament, and also to write a history of the union. Knox, however, retired from public life and devoted himself to theology, in which his chief interest had always lain. He lived a recluse life in lodgings in Dawson Street, Dublin. He spent 1801 and 1802 in England, where he made the acquaintance of Hannah More, William Wilberforce, and others of similar tendencies. This society, perhaps, deepened his religious impressions, for after his return to Ireland he commenced in 1803 a stricter course of life; but he always differed widely on many important points from the evangelical party. He now made the acquaintance of the La Touche family, and spent much of his time at their country residence, Bellevue, near Delgany, amid the Wicklow mountains. Bellevue became practically his home, though he still retained his lodgings in Dawson Street, Dublin, whither he retired on the death of Peter La Touche in 1827, and where he died, unmarried, 17 June 1831. He kept up a close intimacy with many attached friends, the chief among whom were John Jebb, bishop of Limerick; Charles Brodrick, archbishop of Cashel; Hannah More, whom he enthusiastically admired; William Wilberforce, whom he charmed with his conversational powers; and the whole family of the La Touches; Joseph Butterworth, to whom several of his most interesting letters are addressed. George Schoales, J. S. Harford, and Adam Clarke were among his frequent correspondents in his later years.

Knox was universally admitted to be an admirable conversationalist; and people used to visit him in Dawson Street, much in the same way as people used to visit S. T. Coleridge at Highgate. Unfortunately no records of his talk have been preserved. Coleridge and Knox resemble each other as having done much to stimulate thought by unsystematic methods, and to influence the succeeding generation. But, as Cardinal Newman points out, Knox differed from Coleridge in that 'he realises his own position, and is an instance in rudiment of those restorations which he foresaw in development' (*British Critic* for April 1839).

Knox published a volume of 'Essays on the Political Circumstances of Ireland during the Administration of Lord Camden; with an Appendix containing Thoughts on the Will of the People' (1799). This is merely a collection of 'papers intended in almost every instance for insertion in newspapers, or for circulation in the form of handbills.' They were written at intervals between 1795 and 1797, in a bright, lively, popular style. In 1802 he published a pamphlet in defence of Wesley against a Calvinistic clergyman, James Walker, fellow of Trinity College, Dublin, who had published an 'Expostulatory Address to the Members of the Methodist Society in Ireland.' Knox's 'Remarks' on this address called forth a 'Defence' from Walker. A little later he wrote two articles for the 'Eclectic Review.' In 1820 he issued a short tract 'On the Doctrine respecting Baptism held by the Church of England,' in which he shows the doctrine of baptismal regeneration in the case of infants to be that of the church of England. In 1822 he contributed some short but interesting 'Remarks,' which were inserted at the end of the second edition of Southey's 'Life of Wesley.' In 1824 he published 'An Enquiry on Grounds of Scripture and Reason into the Use and Import of the Eucharistic Symbols.' He also published prefaces to Jebb's two editions of Burnet's 'Lives.'

'The Remains of Alexander Knox,' edited by Mr. Hornby of Winwick, appeared in 4 vols. 8vo in 1834-7, and in 1834 appeared 'Thirty Years' Correspondence between Bishop Jebb and Alexander Knox,' edited by the Rev. C. L. Forster, Bishop Jebb's biographer. These letters show his close agreement in many points with the leaders of the Oxford movement, then beginning. In an article in the 'Contemporary Review,' August 1887, Professor Stokes traced the movement of thought from Wesley to Knox, from Knox to Jebb, and from Jebb to Hugh James Rose, Newman, and Pusey. The theory was impugned by Dr. Church, dean of St. Paul's, and defended by Professor Stokes in the 'Guardian' (7, 14, 21, and 28 Sept. 1887); but both agree that Knox anticipated much of what was afterwards insisted upon by the leaders of the revival. Keble, while admiring Knox, thought him an eclectic, looking down upon all schools with an air of superiority (COLERIDGE, *Memoir*, p. 241).

Knox contends that 'the church of England is neither Calvinian nor Augustinian, but eminently and strictly catholic, and *catholic* only;' that 'our vitality as a church is in our identity of organisation with the church catholic;' that the church of England is not protestant, but a reformed branch of the church catholic; that the English church is the only representative of the spirit of the *Greek* fathers, and that we ought to aim at union with the Greek church. He dislikes Calvinism in every form; and he argues that our justification is an *imparted*, not an *imputed*, righteousness. This last view was specially obnoxious to the evangelicals, and was opposed, among others, by G. S. Faber [q. v.] in 'The Primitive Doctrine of Justification investigated' (1837). Knox laments the general deadness of the services as conducted in his day; he rebels against the identification of churchmanship with toryism, and takes the primitive church in ancient times, and the seventeenth century in modern, as his models. Like Wesley, he admired mystical writers like À Kempis, De Sales, and De Renty. He had no tendency to Rome, although he was a steady advocate of catholic emancipation and a supporter of Maynooth.

He exercised a great influence through his friend Bishop Jebb. The appendix to Jebb's sermons in 1815 (not quite accurately described as the first publication that recalled men's attention to Anglo-catholic principles) was avowedly the joint production of Knox and Jebb, and it is plain that Knox was really the inspirer of the thought expounded by Jebb.

[Remains of Alexander Knox, Esq., 4 vols.; Thirty Years' Correspondence between John Jebb and Alexander Knox, 2 vols.; Alexander Knox, by the late Mrs. Alexander Leeper, an article in the Churchman, July 1889; Alexander Knox and the Oxford Movement, an article by Professor G. T. Stokes in the Contemporary Review, August 1887; Guardian, 7, 14, 21, and 28 Sept. 1887; Wesley's Journals; Forster's Life of Bishop Jebb; letters from Knox in the Castlereagh Correspondence, vols. i. and iv.]
J. H. O.

KNOX, ALEXANDER ANDREW (1818–1891), journalist and police magistrate, son of George Knox, landed proprietor in Jamaica, was born in London 5 Feb. 1818. He was educated at Blundell's school, Tiverton, whence he proceeded with a scholarship to Trinity College, Cambridge. In June 1842 he was ordered to the south for his health, and he travelled with Mrs. Shelley (the widow of the poet) and her son Percy, his college friend. The party was joined by another of Knox's Cambridge friends, Robert Leslie Ellis [q.v.], and during this interesting experience of Italian travel Knox met Trelawny, the friend of Byron and of Shelley. Owing to ill-health Knox was unable to compete for honours, but graduated B.A. in 1844 and M.A. in 1847. He was called to the bar as member of Lincoln's Inn in 1844. In 1846 he became a writer of leading articles on the staff of the 'Times,' and continued to write for that paper till 1860, when he accepted Sir George Cornewall Lewis's offer of the office of police magistrate at Worship Street. In 1862 he was transferred to the Marlborough Street court, and remained there till 1878, when a paralytic seizure compelled him to retire. On three occasions he received the special thanks of the home office for his magisterial services.

Knox was a man of wide culture, a good linguist, and a brilliant talker. He was a frequent guest of Dr. Paris, at whose house in London he met Faraday, Sir B. Brodie, Babbage, and other men of science. Among his intimate friends were Rajah Brooke, Admiral Sherard Osborn, Kinglake, Sir Spencer St. John, Kingsley, Thomas Mozley, Wingrove Cooke, and Miss Marianne North. He died in London 5 Oct. 1891. In 1857 he married Susan, daughter of James Armstrong, esq., of the Bengal civil service.

Knox published 'The New Playground, or Wanderings in Algeria,' in 1881. Besides his work on the 'Times,' he contributed articles to the 'Edinburgh Review,' 'Blackwood,' and many other periodicals.

[Article by the present writer, 'Alexander Knox and his Friends,' in Temple Bar, April 1892.] C. A. H. C.

KNOX, ANDREW (1559–1633), bishop of Raphoe, the second son of John Knox of Ranfurly in Renfrewshire, was born in 1559. He was educated at the university of Glasgow, where he graduated M.A. in 1579. In 1581 he was ordained minister of Lochwinnoch in Renfrewshire, and in 1585 was translated to the abbey church of Paisley. On 6 March 1589–90 he was appointed on a commission of select clergymen to promote subscription to the confession of faith and covenant over the whole kingdom. In December 1592 he was instrumental in arresting George Kerr on the Isle of Cumray as he was on the point of sailing for Spain, and was thereby the means of bringing to light and frustrating on the eve of its execution the dangerous conspiracy of the Earls of Huntly, Errol, and Angus. In 1597 he was appointed a commissioner, with others whom he thought 'meitest to employ,' to seek and apprehend 'all excommunicat papistis, jesuitis, seminarie preistis and suspect trafficquaris with the King of Spayne,' and having in the execution of his office accidentally caused the death by drowning of Hew Barclay of Ladyland, who had intended to capture and fortify Ailsa Craig against the coming of the Spaniards, he was by parliament exonerated from all consequences arising therefrom, and commended for his 'loyall and gud seruice to his Majestie and his cuntry' (*Acta Parl. Scot.* iv. 148). About this time Knox, who appears to have been of a contentious disposition, was involved in several discreditable disputes with his fellow-citizens (*Genealogical Memoirs of the Family of Knox*, p. 11; *Registers of the Privy Council.* v. 171, vii. 52). During the course of one of them Knox so far forgot himself as to strike his adversary, George Stewart, burgess of Paisley, in public court. The outrage was reported to the presbytery. He was suspended 4 Oct. 1604, and was ordered to do public penance in his church on Sunday the 19th following. 'This being done, the bailies and sum of the honest men of the paroch sall receive him be the hand' (*Genealogical Memoirs*, p. 12). On 2 April 1606 (the episcopacy having been restored in Scotland) Knox was created bishop of the Isles, and having obtained leave from the presbytery he immediately proceeded to his diocese. On 31 July he was commissioned along with others 'to meit with David, Lord Scone, comptroller, and hear the offers made by the inhabitants of the Isles and the Highlands anent their obedience and suritie for his Majesties rents.' In January 1606–7 he was appointed constant moderator of the presbytery of the Isles, and on 4 June he took the oath of allegiance. His absence from his charge at Paisley causing some inconvenience, the presbytery suggested the appointment of a colleague, but his parishioners would only accept the proposal if 'he would altogether denuide himself of the bishopric and tak to the ministerie.' Knox preferred to resign, and on 12 Nov. 1607 he was relieved of his charge.

In accordance with King James's intention to reform the Western Isles and highlands, Knox was on 8 March 1608 joined in a commission with Andrew, lord Stewart of Ochiltree, to take the matter in hand. In May he visited the king at Greenwich, and brought back instructions for a military expedition against the Isles, of which Lord Ochiltree was to be commander, assisted by a council, of which Knox was to be the head with a salary and bodyguard of his own. The expedition sailed early in August, and the castles of Dunivaig and Lochgorme in Isla having been surrendered by Angus Macdonald, Ochiltree opened a court at the castle of Aros in Mull on 15 Aug. The chieftains showing some reluctance to come to terms, Ochiltree, acting on the advice of Knox, induced them to visit him on board his vessel on pretence of a dinner and a sermon from the bishop. Having thus succeeded in kidnapping them, Ochiltree sailed to Glasgow. On his return Knox accompanied Ochiltree to London, and was commended by the king for his zeal in the service.

The chief obstacle to a settlement of the isles was thus removed, and Knox was in February 1609 appointed one of a commission to negotiate with the chieftains for the purpose of devising a scheme for the civilisation of the Western Islands. In May he was the bearer of a confidential message from his colleagues to the king. He returned in June with instructions for a fresh expedition, of which he himself was to be the head, and he conducted the business with great credit to himself. Before the end of July he met the principal chieftains at Iona, and with their consent enacted the statutes of Icolmkill. He returned to Edinburgh in September, but immediately proceeded to London. He seems to have been detained at court till the following July, when he returned to Edinburgh, and made formal redelivery of 'the Band and Statutes of Icolmkill' before the council. On 15 Feb. 1610 he was appointed a member of the court of ecclesiastical high commission for the province of Glasgow, and on 8 May steward of the whole Western Isles, with instructions to make the castle of Dunivaig his headquarters. In the same year he was preferred to the bishopric of Raphoe (patent 26 June 1611) 'to the effect that by his panes and travellis the ignorant multitude within that Diocie may be reclamed from their superstitious and Papishe opinionis' (LAING, Original Letters, i. 427). He continued to hold both bishoprics till 22 Sept. 1619, when he resigned that of the Isles in favour of his eldest son, Thomas.

Having established a garrison in the castle of Dunivaig, he immediately proceeded to Ireland, and in April 1611 transmitted to Lord Salisbury a report of the state of religion in his diocese. In consequence of his report the king instructed Sir Arthur Chichester to require the Archbishop of Armagh to convene a meeting of the bishops of his province in order to consider the reformation of ecclesiastical abuses in the north of Ireland (the report of their proceedings will be found in RUSSELL and PRENDERGAST, Calendar of Irish State Papers, iv. 142). On 13 Oct. 1611 Chichester wrote of Knox: 'He is a good bishop for that part of the kingdom, and zealously affected to correct and reform the errors and abuses of the priests and people, and has done more good in church government in the short time of his being among them than his predecessor in all his time' (ib. iv. 149). It was probably in consequence of Chichester's report that on 13 Feb. 1612 the king authorised his admission to the privy council. As a reward for his good success in reforming the Western Isles, James addressed a letter to the council of Scotland on the 24th of the same month, requiring them (1) to make payment to him of all arrears of a pension formerly granted to him out of the duties of the Isles, in compensation for his expense in maintaining a garrison at Dunivaig; (2) to grant him a charter in feu farm for life of the Isle of Barra; (3) to restore as far as possible all the lands belonging to his bishopric that had by chance been alienated; (4) to reannex to his bishopric the abbey of Icolmkill and the priory of Ardchattan, formerly held in commendam with it. In 1614 the castle of Dunivaig was surprised by the Macdonalds, and Knox, attempting to retake it with insufficient force, was defeated and compelled to treat. He consented to solicit a lease of the crown lands of Isla for Angus Oig Macdonald, together with the proprietary rights in the castle of Dunivaig, and a free pardon for all crimes up to date, and to leave his son Thomas and his nephew John Knox of Ranfurly as hostages for his good faith. The council, however, refused these terms, and prepared to reduce the Macdonalds by force. Knox, who was alarmed for the safety of his hostages, openly counselled the employment of deceit in dealing with the Macdonalds, to be followed by their total extirpation, and the plantation of their lands by honest men from the north of Ireland and the west of Scotland. His scheme was in part realised. The Earl of Argyll desired to drive the Macdonalds into desperate courses on behalf of his kinsman, John Campbell of Calder, who had undertaken their reduction on condition of succeeding to their inheritance. One John Graham, who acted, it was supposed, at Argyll's

x 2

instigation, contrived that Thomas and John Knox should be set at liberty, and on 6 Jan. 1616 Campbell of Calder, with the assistance of Sir Oliver Lambart [q. v.], captured Dunivaig. Some time during his life-time Knox had carried off the two principal bells from the abbey of Icolmkill to Raphoe. These his successor, Bishop John Lesley, was by royal edict compelled to restore on 14 March 1635 (*Collectanea de rebus Albanicis*, p. 187).

Knox resigned the bishopric of the Isles in 1619, but continued bishop of Raphoe till his death on 27 March 1633. He married his cousin-german Elizabeth, daughter of William Knox of Silvieland (though, by another account, the daughter of John Knox, merchant, in Ayr). By her he had three sons, Thomas, James, and George, and two daughters, Margaret, who married John Cunningham of Cambuskeith, son of James, seventh earl of Glencairn, and another, who married John Hamilton of Woodhall. The three sons took orders in the church. Thomas, the eldest, was educated at Glasgow University, where he graduated M.A. in 1608. He became incumbent of Sorabie in Tiree, and on 4 Aug. 1617 he was constituted dean of the Isles. In February 1619 he succeeded his father as bishop of the Isles, and in 1622 was appointed non-resident rector of the parish of Clandevadock in the diocese of Raphoe. He was B.D., and died in 1628 without issue, and is reported to have been a man of learning and piety.

Knox's house, 25 High Street, Paisley, is said (*Genealogical Memoirs of the Family of Knox*, 1879) to be still standing, and in an oak panel over the chimney of the principal room are engraved his initials and those of his wife.

[C. Rogers's Genealogical Memoirs of the Family of Knox (Grampian Club). 1879; Collectanea de rebus Albanicis (Iona Club), 1839; Laing's Original Letters (Bannatyne Club), 1851; Book of the Thanes of Cawdor (Spalding Club), 1859; Register of the Privy Council of Scotland, vols. v.–ix.; Donald Gregory's Hist. of the Western Highlands; Collections upon the Lives of the Reformers (Maitland Club), 1834; Calderwood's Hist. of the Kirk; Spotiswood's Hist. of the Church; George Crawfurd's Hist. of Renfrewshire; Bishop Keith's Cat. of Scottish Bishops; Cotton's Fasti Eccl. Hib.; Reid's Hist. of the Presbyterian Church in Ireland; Russell and Prendergast's Cal. of State Papers, Ireland.]

R. D.

KNOX, JOHN (1505–1572), Scottish reformer and historian, was born in 1505 at Giffordgate, Haddington, in a house opposite the east end of the abbey, on the other side of the Tyne from the burgh. It was standing in 1785, but has since been pulled down. The conjecture that his birthplace was in the neighbouring parish of Morham, founded on his statement that his 'father, gudeschir, and grandschir' fought under the Earls of Bothwell, who had lands in that parish, but not in Haddington, is ingenious, but not proved so as to displace the argument of Laing in favour of Giffordgate. The reformer's father, William Knox, is supposed to have been a cadet of the family of Knox of Ranfurly in Renfrewshire. But the name is too common to support this descent, which is opposed by the fact that the reformer calls himself 'of base condition,' and is described as 'of lineage small' by John Davidson in the panegyrical poem published the year after his death, while his personal character indicates a burghal rather than a gentle ancestry. His mother was a Sinclair, and a note to one of his manuscript letters, signed John Sinclair, mentions 'this was his mother's surname, whilk he wearit in time of trubell.' A brother, William, mentioned in two of his letters and in his will, was a trader with England, and settled in Preston.

Knox was educated at the school of Haddington. In 1522 his name appears in the register of the university of Glasgow among the students incorporated on St. Crispin's day, 25 Oct. He was attracted to Glasgow by the fame of John Major [q. v.], himself born at Gleghornie, not far from Haddington, and probably educated at the burgh school. On 9 June 1523 Major was transferred to the university of St. Andrews; so Knox, unless he followed Major to that university, of which there is no proof, can have been his pupil only one session, yet this may have sufficed to disgust Knox, like Buchanan and other of Major's hearers, with the scholastic logic, of which he retained little except the argumentative spirit.

The name of Knox does not appear in the list of graduates of either university. The tradition that he was led by the study of Augustine and the fathers to abandon scholastic theology is so far confirmed by the citation in his writings of Augustine as 'that learned Augustine,' Chrysostom as 'the ancient godlie writer,' and Athanasius as 'that notable servant of Jesus Christ.' With Latin, still the language of education, he was of course familiar, though he rarely used it. He is the first, almost the only, great prose writer in the vernacular, though his Scotch has been criticised for its intermixture with English and French words and idioms. Of Hebrew he confessed his ignorance, but also 'his fervent thirst to have sum entrance thairin' (letter to Bishop of Durham), which he to some extent gratified when he went to the continent. He also studied law, and the next clearly ascertained fact in his life is that he acted as a notary in Haddington and the neighbourhood. In his writings he more than once cites the Pandects. He appears as pro-curator for James Ker in Samuelston, a vil-lage about three miles from Haddington, at the market-cross of that burgh, on 13 Dec. 1540; as umpire, along with James Ker, in a dispute on 21 Nov. 1542 as witness to a deed concerning Rannelton, Berwickshire, in a Haddington protocol book, 28 March 1543; and as the notary who wrote a notarial instru-ment on 27 March 1543, still extant among the Earl of Haddington's papers at Tynninghame. In the earliest of these documents he is de-signed 'Schir John Knox,' and in the notarial instrument he designs himself 'Johannis Knox sacri altaris minister sancte Andree diocesis authoritate apostolica notarius.' These designations prove that he had been admitted to minor orders (KNOX, *Works*, i. 555). He used as his motto as notary 'Non falsum testimonium perhibeo,' and as witness ' Per Christum fidelis cui gloria Amen.' He may have served at the chapel of St. Nicholas at Samuelston, but he held no cure, and in the preface to his sermon published in 1566 he dates his study of the scriptures as com-mencing within twenty years. A Romanist contemporary, Archibald Hamilton, alleged within five years of his death that, 'although very illiterate, he contrived to be made a presbyter, and employed himself in teaching in private houses to young people the rudi-ments of the vulgar tongue' (*De Confessione Calvinianæ Sectæ apud Scotos*, fol. 64, Paris, 1577–8). Between 1523 and 1544 the record of his life is blank. From 1544 we follow his life in the pages of his 'History,' which is largely an autobiography. It is truthful and substantially accurate, except as to dates, but vehement and prejudiced, and requiring to be checked by contemporary writings.

Rejecting the career of a priest, which his adoption of the principles of the reformers made impossible, and abandoning that of a notary, which can scarcely have been more congenial, he adopted, perhaps earlier, but certainly in 1544, the vocation of a tutor. His pupils were Francis and John, sons of Hugh Douglas of Longniddry, near Trauent in East Lothian, and Alexander Cockburn, eldest son of the Laird of Ormiston, boys about twelve years of age. Their studies were grammar, the Latin classics (*Humanæ Literæ*), the catechism, and the gospel of St. John. It was while thus engaged that George Wishart [q. v.], a champion of Lu-theran doctrines, came to Lothian to es-

cape the persecution of Cardinal Beaton. He had friends among the gentry of that shire, and the fathers of Knox's pupils, Dou-glas and Cockburn and Crichton of Brunston, gave him an asylum in their houses. Knox was constantly with him in Lothian, and accompanied him before 1546 to Hadding-ton, where Wishart preached on two days in succession, 15 and 16 Jan. of that year. After the second sermon, whose invective shows the model on which Knox formed his own style, Wishart bade Knox go back to Long-niddry. The same evening, 16 Jan., Wishart was seized at Ormiston by Bothwell, and was burnt at St. Andrews for heresy on 1 March. On 29 May Cardinal Beaton was murdered in revenge for Wishart's death [see LESLIE, NORMAN]. The participators in the deed shut themselves up in the castle of St. An-drews, and, having opened communication by sea with England, held it in spite of a siege. Knox had intended about this time to visit the German universities to avoid persecution. He approved, though he had no hand in, the cardinal's murder, which he calls 'the godly act of James Melvine,' in a marginal note to his 'History,' and at Easter, 10 April 1547, he was persuaded by the fathers of his pupils to go with them to the castle of St. Andrews. In the chapel of the castle he continued to teach them the gospel of St. John, beginning where he left off at Long-niddry, and after the siege was raised he cate-chised them publicly in the parish kirk. The leaders of the party in the castle, and espe-cially John Rough [q. v.], a preacher, Henry Balnaves, a lawyer, and Sir David Lyndsay [q. v.], the poet, seeing his ability, urged him to assume the office of preacher. He refused, as he had not received a call. This was speedily supplied. Rough, after a sermon on the election of ministers, charged Knox, ' in the name of God and Christ, and of those that presently call you by my mouth, not to refuse this holy vocation.' The congregation publicly expressed their approval. The call was irregular, but it asserted for the first time in Scotland the claim of the congregation to choose their spiritual guide. Knox accepted it, and on the next Sunday, appointed for his sermon, preached from a text in the seventh chapter of Daniel upon the corruption of the papacy, as seen in the lives of the popes and the bishops. He ended with a challenge to his old master, John Major, or any of his hearers, to dispute his conclusions. The chal-lenge was accepted, and a conference held in ' the yards of St. Leonard's.' Certain theses drawn from Knox's sermon were proposed for debate, such as that ' the pope is ane anti-christ,' that ' the sacraments of the New

Testament ought to be ministered as they were instituted by Christ, and nothing added to or taken from them,' that ' the mass is abominable idolatry,' and that ' there is no purgatory, and there are no bishops unless they preach themselves.' Winram, the sub-prior, first disputed with Knox, but left the conclusion of the argument to Arbuckle, a grey friar, whom Knox, according to his own narrative—the only account preserved—easily overcame by a combination of texts, logic, and ridicule. Knox refers, for his share in the debate, to 'a treatise he wrote in the galleys,' containing the pith of his doctrine and the confession of his faith. This has not been preserved, unless the reference be to the letter he wrote to his brethren in Scotland in 1548, when he sent them Balnaves's 'Confession and Treatise on Justification.' The friars attempted to stifle a voice they could not answer by occupying the pulpit at St. Andrews Sunday about, but Knox evaded this device by preaching on the weekdays and protesting that if the friars preached in his absence the people ought to suspend their judgment till they heard him again. The effect of his preaching was that many in the town as well as the castle accepted the reformed doctrine, and communicated at the Lord's Table after the reformed rite. On 31 June 1547 the French galleys, under Strozzi, prior of Capua, appeared in the Forth and besieged the castle on 18 July. The regent soon after joined in the siege on the land side. On 31 July the castle capitulated. By the terms of the capitulation the prisoners, of whom Knox was one, were to be sent to France in the galleys, and either liberated there or sent to any other country they chose except Scotland. They were taken to Fécamp, a port of Normandy, and thence up the Seine to Rouen, but, in breach of the terms of their surrender, were dispersed in several prisons. Knox remained with the galleys, which sailed to Nantes and lay in the Loire all the winter. In the summer of 1548 the galleys returned to the Scotch coast. The prisoners' treatment, though strict, was not very rigid.

Balnaves composed his 'Treatise on Justification by Faith' in the castle of Rouen, and managed to send it to Knox in the galley Notre Dame. Knox digested it into chapters and forwarded it, with an epistle, to the congregation of the castle of St. Andrews in 1548. It reached the hands of his friends at Ormiston, but was first published in 1584 by the French printer Vautrollier, who explains, in a dedication to Lady Sandilands, the mother of Knox's pupil Cockburn, that it had been unsuccessfully sought for by Knox after his return to Scotland, and accidentally

recovered by Richard Bannatyne [q. v.], Knox's amanuensis, in the hands of some children at play. As the earliest of his known writings, it is remarkable for the clearness with which it propounds the Lutheran doctrine that ' faith is only justifiable before God, without all aid and merit of our works.' In February 1549 his own release was effected, probably by the intercession of Edward VI, and he came to England.

On 7 April 1549 Knox received 5l., ' by way of reward, from the king's privy council,' and was sent by the council to preach at Berwick, where he remained two years, attracting a large congregation. While there he prepared and probably issued a tract, of which the first edition extant was published in 1554: ' A Declaration what true Prayer is, how we should pray, and for what we should pray.' On 4 April 1550 he was summoned, at the instance of Tunstall, the Romanist bishop of Durham, to answer for having upheld in his preaching ' that the mass was idolatry.' His defence, afterwards printed along with a letter to Mary of Guise, the queen regent, in 1556, was a syllogistic argument: ' All service invented by the brain of man in the religion of God, without his own express command, is idolatry. The mass is invented by the brain of man without the command of God; therefore it is idolatry.' He explained that the mass was abomination, and concluded by distinguishing the Lord's Supper of the protestants at the communion-table from the sacrifice of the mass, which the priest offered at the altar. Neither Tunstall nor any one else answered him. Probably most of the council were lukewarm or favourable. Nothing came of this, his first prosecution.

A tract of two or three pages, containing ' in a Sum, according to the Holy Scriptures, what opinions we Christians haif of the Lordis Supper, callit The Sacrament of the Bodie and Blude of our Saviour Jesus Christ,' printed without date, was probably issued in the same year for general circulation. About the end of 1550 he removed to Newcastle, where he served as preacher in the church of St. Nicholas, and in autumn 1551 he was appointed one of six royal chaplains, with a salary of 40l., of which the first payment was made by the privy council on 27 Oct. 1552. While at Newcastle he denounced from the pulpit the execution of Somerset. As king's chaplain he took part in the revision of the second prayer-book of Edward VI, issued 1 Nov. 1552, and is credited with the ' black rubric,' which explained that the act of kneeling meant no adoration of the bread and wine, ' for that idolatry is to be abhorred by all faithful Christians.' A letter from John Utenhove to Bullinger, dated London, 12 Oct. 1552, doubtless refers to Knox as 'a pious preacher, chaplain to the Duke of Northumberland,' who, in a sermon before the king, 'inveighed with great freedom against kneeling at the Lord's Supper.' He went to London in connection with the preparation of the church articles, which were submitted on 20 Oct., before their issue, to the royal chaplains, but soon returned to Newcastle. On 27 Oct. Northumberland wrote to Cecil, recommending the king to appoint Knox to the Rochester bishopric. On 23 Nov. the duke again reminded the king's secretaries that 'some order be taken for Knox, otherwise you shall not avoid the Scots from out of Newcastle;' but on 7 Dec., after he had seen Knox at Chelsea by Cecil's request, and found him not so pliable as he thought the offer of a bishopric should have made him, Northumberland altered his tone. He had found Knox 'neither grateful nor pleasable,' and wishes to have 'no more to do with him than to wish him well.' On Christmas day 1552 Knox was again at Newcastle, where he preached and declared that 'whosoever in his heart was enemy to Christ's gospel then preached in England was enemy also to God, a secret traitor to the crown and commonwealth of England.' A letter Northumberland received from Knox in January 1553, when the latter had been threatened with an accusation by Lord Wharton and Brandling, mayor of Newcastle, encouraged that nobleman again to befriend him, but in a way which shows he no longer regarded him as a man of much consequence. He calls him repeatedly 'poor Knox,' says 'his letter shows what perplexity the poor soul remaineth in,' and, dropping all mention of the bishopric, asks only that something 'might be done for his comfort.' In March new charges, to which Knox refers in his letters to Mrs. Bowes, were made to Lord Westmoreland, but these, too, broke down, for on the 23rd he says : 'This assault of Satan has been to his confusion and to the glory of God.'

Knox himself states that he declined the bishopric because he was unwilling to accept even the modified formularies of the English church as leaning to Roman doctrine, though he was favourable to an office similar to the bishop's. A warrant of 2 Feb. 1553 to the archbishop to appoint him to the living of All Hallows, in Bread Street, London, was perhaps a compliance with Northumberland's last request, but in April he declined this preferment, and was summoned before the privy council. After a long debate between him and the council, in which he set forth his objections to the English ministry, he was dismissed with the gentle admonition 'that they were sorry he was of a contrary mind to the common order,' to which he replied 'that he was more sorry that a common order should be contrary to Christ's institution.' In the same month he preached his second and last sermon before Edward VI on the text 'He that eateth bread with me hath lifted up his heel against me,' in which he affirmed that the most godly princes had most ungodly officers. Citing the example of the good king Hezekiah, he applied it to the English court. No wonder the bold preacher had enemies at court. But the English reformers could not afford to dispense with his services; and on 2 June 1553 he was sent as a preacher to Buckinghamshire, an office which gave him more liberty, and which his conscience distinguished from a settled charge. On the 6th of the following month Edward VI died, and as Mary Tudor for a time tolerated the protestants, he continued his preaching tour in Buckingham and Kent till October. England was fast becoming unsafe for a man of Knox's opinions, and a tract entitled 'A Confession and Declaration of Prayer upon the Death of that most virtuous and famous King, Edward VI,' issued in July 1554, though it contained a prayer 'to illuminate the heart of our Sovereign Lady Queen Marie with pregnant gifts of Thy Holy Ghoste,' had to conceal its place of printing under the ironical imprint, ' At Rome, before the Castel of St. Angel, at the signe of Sanct Peter.'

Knox returned to Newcastle in December, but before the publication of his tract he had fled to Dieppe, where he remained from 20 Jan. 1554 to the end of February. While resident at Berwick in 1549 he had made the acquaintance of the family of Bowes of Streatham Castle in Durham, and gained the friendship of Elizabeth, wife of Richard Bowes, captain of Norham [see BOWES, ELIZABETH]. This lady accepted him as her spiritual adviser, and promised him the hand of her fifth daughter, Marjory. Their marriage, or betrothal, opposed by her father, was probably not celebrated till July 1553, after which he refers to Marjory as his wife. To her mother he had long used the signature 'your Son.' Mrs. Bowes was about his own age. The correspondence that passed between her and her son-in-law was always affectionate : she was confiding and importunate, he consolatory and invigorating, though as time went on he found his position as her spiritual guide somewhat tiring—'faschious' is his expressive Scotch word. Mrs. Bowes was afflicted with the religious melancholy which the Calvinistic doctrine of assurance sometimes produced. Knox himself in one letter to her admits that he was also on one occasion oppressed by a doubt whether he was one of the elect. This was for him the rarest experience. A complete conviction that his sins were forgiven, and that he and those who believed with him were the chosen people, accompanied him through life. As Mrs. Bowes subsequently left her husband and joined Knox and her daughter at Geneva, the connection gave rise to unwarranted scandal (cf. KNOX, *Answer to a Letter of a Jesuit named Tyrie*, 1572, advertisement). Just as he was leaving Dieppe in the end of February 1554, he sent home two tracts: 'An Exposition of the Sixth Psalm,' in a letter addressed to Mrs. Bowes signed, 'at the very point of my journey, your Son, with sorrowful heart, J. K.,' part of which had been written in London. A longer letter was entitled 'A Godly Letter sent to the Faithful in London, Newcastle, and Berwick;' of this there are two editions, one with the colophon 'from Wittemberg, by Nicholas Dorcaster, anno 1554, the 8th of May,' and the other with the fictitious imprint, 'In Rome, before the Castel of St. Angel, at the signe of Sanct Peter, in the month of July in the year of our Lord 1554,' and the device of Hugh Singleton. A manuscript copy has the postscript, 'The peace of God rest with you all, from ane sore-troubled heart upon my departure from Diep 1553, whither God knoweth.' It is a vehement denunciation of the mass. In the spring (1554) he journeyed through France and Switzerland, and at Geneva met Calvin for the first time. Calvin gave him an introduction to Bullinger, the reformer of Zurich. Knox sent, on 10 and 20 May, epistles to his afflicted brethren in England after returning to Dieppe to learn the position of affairs in England and Scotland. 'Since the 28th of January,' he wrote in the earlier letter, 'I have travelled through all the congregations of Helvetia, and reasonit with all the pastours and many other learned men upon sic matters as now I cannot submit to writing.' The matters were indeed dangerous, and involved the questions ' whether a female can rule a kingdom by divine right, and transfer the right to her husband;' 'whether obedience is to be rendered to a magistrate who enforces idolatry;' and 'to which party must godly persons attach themselves in the case of a religious nobility resisting an idolatrous sovereign.' Bullinger reported to Calvin the cautiously vague replies that he made to Knox. In the same year Knox published 'A Faithful Admonition to the Professors of God's Faith in England, 1554,' which was printed on 20 July at 'Kalykow,' perhaps a pseudonym for Geneva

or Dieppe. He there directs the whole force of his attack against the Spanish marriage of Mary Tudor.

In the summer of 1554 Knox returned to Geneva, and remained there till November, when he accepted the call which the English congregation at Frankfort-on-Maine had sent him on 24 Sept. to be one of their pastors. He accepted it unwillingly, he says in his 'History,' 'at the commandment of that notable servant of God, John Calvin.' The difficulties which he had foreseen soon arose. The English congregation at Frankfort had been formed in the end of July 1554 by a few refugees from the Marian persecution. The magistrates, with the friendly co-operation of a French protestant congregation already established, allowed the English the use of the French church. The English subscribed the French confession of faith, and were allowed the English order of service, with some modifications, the omission of the responses, the litany, and parts of the sacramental liturgy which were deemed superstitious. Soon after Knox's arrival, the English exiles in Strasburg offered to join their fellow-countrymen in Frankfort, but first inquired what parts of the English service book were sanctioned at Frankfort. Knox and other members of his congregation answered (3 Dec.) that whatever in that book could be shown to stand with God's word was admissible. It was agreed to submit the English service-book, of which Knox and Whittingham and others made a summary in Latin, to Calvin. Calvin, while counselling moderation, recommended a new order for a new church. Knox, Whittingham, and three others were directed by the congregation to draw up 'some order meant for their state and time,' and accordingly compiled the liturgy, afterwards published in 1556, and known as 'The Order of Geneva.' But the work proved unsatisfactory to many, and Knox, Whittingham, and two others were invited to make a second attempt. Some modification was agreed upon; Knox counselled concessions, and it was determined that the new 'order' should be observed till the end of April 1555. If any further dispute arose, it was to be referred to Calvin, Martyr, and Bullinger, and two other divines. A reconciliation followed, and 'the holy communion was upon this happy agreement ministered.' But the cessation of hostilities was temporary. On 13 March Dr. Richard Cox [q. v.] came with others from England. The small band of protestant exiles were thereupon divided into Coxians and Knoxians. At church the newcomers insisted on making responses after the minister, although Knox and the seniors of the church had previously admonished them to desist.

Knox one Sunday charged the Coxians from the pulpit with breaking the agreement. The matter was fully debated on the Tuesday following. Knox urged, in a spirit of bravado, that the Coxians should be admitted to vote as members of the congregation. He bade them condemn him if they dared. He was taken at his word, and the majority declared against him. He was now prohibited from preaching, and another conference of three days failed to reconcile the conflicting parties. On the third day Knox passionately denounced the proposal to use in the morning service prescribed words of prayer and praise not to be found in scripture. He was thereupon accused before the magistrates by a friend of Cox of treason in describing the emperor, in his 'Admonition to the People of England,' 'as no less enemy to Christ than Nero,' and in attacking Mary. The magistrates finally, through Williams and Whittingham, two of his friends, sent him an order to leave Frankfort. The night before he left he preached at his lodgings to some fifty persons on the Resurrection and the joys prepared for the elect. Escorted by his friends for a few miles, he proceeded at once to Geneva, where he was well received by Calvin, who condemned the proceedings of the majority. Ridley wrote to Grindal shortly before his own martyrdom, lamenting 'that our brother Knox could not bear with our Book of Common Prayer,' and while admitting that 'a man (as he is) of wit and learning may find plausible grounds of dissent, doubted that he could soundly disprove it by God's word.' But to Knox any colour of Roman ritual necessarily meant Roman doctrine, and was therefore anti-Christian.

On his return to Geneva, he and his friend Christopher Goodman [q. v.] were chosen ministers of the English congregation, but his heart still turned homewards. The register of the church of Nostre Dame la Neuve, to the south-east of the cathedral, where the congregation was allowed to worship, records in 1555 that Goodman and Anthony Gilby [q. v.] were appointed to fill Knox's place as minister in his absence. In August 1555 he went to Dieppe, crossed to the east coast of Scotland, and in November joined Mrs. Bowes and her daughter at Berwick. The comparative toleration which the regent was at that time allowing to the protestants enabled him to spend about nine months in his native country. The progress of the Reformation since he left Scotland had been rapid. He found houses open to him in every town, and, when the churches were closed, the seats of the country gentlemen became preaching centres. The converts to the new doctrines belonged to every class. Knox went through the country preaching, discussing, and writing. At Edinburgh he lodged with a burgess, James Sym, to whose house Erskine of Dun, in Angus, and many countrymen and their wives came to hear him. Among other topics he discussed at a supper given by the Laird of Dun the question, then much agitated, whether it was lawful to go to mass. Lethington was of the company, and 'nothing was omitted,' says Knox, 'that might make for the temporiser;' but every point was so fully answered that Lethington at last confessed, 'I see that our shifts will save nothing before God, seeing they stand us in so small stead before man.' From Edinburgh he went to Dun, where he stayed a month, preaching daily to the principal men of the county. From Dun he returned to Calder in West Lothian, the residence of Sir James Sandilands, one of whose sons was preceptor of Torphichen and head of the Knights Hospitallers in Scotland. He met there, besides many gentlemen, three young nobles, who became leaders in the Reformation: Lord Erskine, afterwards sixth earl of Mar, Lord Lorne, afterwards fifth earl of Argyll, and Lord James Stewart, prior of St. Andrews, afterwards the regent Murray. During the winter of 1555-6 he taught in Edinburgh, and after Christmas went to Kyle in Ayrshire, where the doctrine of the lollards still lingered, and preached in the houses of county gentlemen, chiefly small barons, who supported Knox in large numbers, while the burgesses were even more enthusiastic. For a time a common cause united burgh and country. Before Easter, 5 April 1556, Knox was summoned by the Earl of Glencairn to Finlayston, near Port Glasgow, and preached and administered the sacrament. He then returned to Calder, where disciples from Edinburgh and the country came to hear him, and to sit for the first time at the Lord's Table —a scene painted by Wilkie. A union, perhaps a formal bond of smaller numbers but of similar character to later covenants, 'to maintain the true preaching of the gospel to the uttermost of their power,' was hallowed by participation in the most sacred office of religion. Alarmed at the success of his preaching, the bishops summoned Knox to appear at the Blackfriars kirk in Edinburgh on 15 May 1556. He came, attended by John Erskine [q. v.] of Dun and a number of other gentlemen, like a feudal lord with his retainers, and the bishops suddenly dropped proceedings. Knox, instead of appearing as a criminal, preached in the Bishop of Dunkeld's lodging to a larger audience than before. He continued to preach forenoon and afternoon for ten days, and after William Keith, earl Marshal, and Henry Drummond had heard him, they desired him to write to the regent to try to move her to hear the word of God. He sent his famous letter, printed in 1556 (enlarged edition, Geneva, 1558), entitled 'The Letter to the Queen Dowager,' which Glencairn presented, but Mary of Guise passed it on to Beaton, bishop of Glasgow, saying, 'Please you, my lord, to read a pasquil.' This term, derived from the scurrilous lampoons Italian satirists circulated under the eyes of the pope and cardinals, irritated Knox. Before issuing the letter from the press he added words declaring, in the prophetic strain he affected, 'God will shortly send his messengers, with whom she would not be able to jest.'

About this time a call reached him from the English church at Geneva, which he accepted. His farewell services in Scotland were held for several days at Castle Campbell, near Dollar, with the old Earl of Argyll and others of his clan and neighbourhood. In July he crossed to Dieppe, whither he had sent his wife and mother-in-law, and they went straight to Geneva. The bishops, after he was gone, again summoned him to Edinburgh, and in his absence condemned him, and burnt his effigy at the cross. But before the end of harvest 1556 he had reached Geneva. On 16 Dec. in the three following years, 1556, 1557, and 1558, Knox and Goodman were chosen ministers by the congregation. Closer contact brought him into terms of warm friendship with Calvin, who directed not only the spiritual, but the temporal affairs of the Swiss republic. As Knox learnt from Wishart how to preach, he now learnt from Calvin how to govern.

In May 1557 James Sym and James Barrow, Edinburgh burgesses, came to Geneva with a letter from Glencairn and other nobles, which entreated him to return to Scotland, now that the persecution was diminishing. Knox, after consulting Calvin and others, replied that he would come as soon as he might 'put in order the dear flock committed to his charge.' Whittingham was chosen to fill his place, and on 23 Oct. he arrived at Dieppe. He found there letters of a contrary purport, dissuading him from coming to Scotland, and at once sent on 27 Oct. a sharp letter rebuking his Scottish friends for their vacillation. When this letter was received, along with another afterwards published to the whole nobility, and special missives to the lairds of Dun and Pittarrow, a consultation was held;

and the nobles, including old Argyll and his son Lorne, Glencairn, Morton, and Erskine of Dun, and other gentry, signed a bond at Edinburgh on 3 Dec. 1557 by which they promised, 'before the Majesty of God and his congregation, with all diligence to . . . establish the most blessed word of God and his congregation.' They also sent urgent letters to Calvin and Knox urging his return, which were delivered in November. Knox, on 1 and 17 Dec., sent letters to the brethren in Scotland and to the nobility, with exhortations to maintain their principles, not to suddenly disobey authority in things lawful, but 'to defend their brethren from persecution and tyranny, be it against princes or emperors.' He finally resolved not to run the risk of returning; otherwise he might possibly have shared the fate of Walter Milne [q. v.], who was burnt for heresy by Archbishop Hamilton.

While still at Dieppe he wrote on 7 Dec. a preface to an 'Apology for the Protestant in Prison in Paris,' which he translated, with additions of his own, for the benefit of his Scottish brethren. He at the same time officiated in the protestant congregation not only at Dieppe but also at Rochelle, where he declared that within two or three years he hoped to preach in St. Giles in Edinburgh.

Early in 1558 he returned to Geneva. In that busy year he published six tracts, which covered the whole ground of the conflict raging in Scotland. The titles of four were respectively 'The First Blast of the Trumpet against the Monstrous Regiment of Women,' 'A Letter to the Queen Dowager Regent of Scotland, augmented and explained by the Author,' 'The Appellation from the Sentence pronounced by the Bishops and Clergy, addressed to the Nobility and Estates of Scotland,' and 'A Letter addressed to the Commonalty of Scotland.' The 'Appellation' was appended to Gilby's 'Admonition' (Geneva, 1558), and, like the 'Letter,' restated his doctrinal views, and was addressed to the commons in the tone of a democratic leader. It included a summary of the 'Second Blast . . . against Women,' the only form in which the 'First Blast' was continued. In a fifth publication of the same year he bade the inhabitants of Newcastle and Berwick stand by his doctrine; and in a sixth he briefly exhorted England to embrace the gospel speedily. The last two were written at fever-heat, and in his most fiery style. To the exhortation which he addressed to England he appended a list of the names of nearly three hundred Marian martyrs, 'in thee and by thee, O England, most cruelly murdered by Fire and Imprisonment for the testimony of Christ Jesus and his eternal

Verity, whose Blood from under the Altar crieth aloud to be avenged.'

The attitude of Knox, avowed in the 'First Blast,' towards the political government of women was dictated by the hostility to the Reformation already displayed by Mary Tudor, Catherine de' Medici, and Mary of Guise. Knox laboured to prove that 'to promote a woman to bear rule, superiority, dominion, or empire above any realm is repugnant to nature, contrary to God, and, finally, it is the subversion of good order, of all equity and justice.' His work was published without his name, but the authorship was well known, and it was intimated that he would himself announce it when he blew his third 'Blast,' which never appeared. The 'Blast' did not produce the effect intended. Foxe the martyrologist expostulated with Knox, who replied on 18 May 1558, admitting his vehemence, but adding, 'To me it is enough to say that black is not white, and man's tyranny and foolishness is not God's perfect ordinance.' Calvin, more inclined to compromise, assured Cecil two years later that 'for a whole year he was ignorant of its publication,' that he had never read it, and that he dissuaded Knox from publishing it. On 17 Nov. 1558, within the year of its publication, Mary Tudor died and Elizabeth reigned. It was then seen how imprudent had been the argument of Knox. The new queen, the most powerful ally of the reformers among crowned heads, treated the work as a personal insult, and would not allow Knox to pass through England. Her attitude through life towards the Scottish reformation was affected by the untimely publication. It required all the tact of Cecil to prevent an open breach. It was in vain that Knox attempted to explain. 'My First Blast,' he writes, 'hath blown from me all my friends in England.' John Aylmer [q. v.], afterwards the bishop of London, one of the English exiles, wrote an answer to it, in which he speaks favourably of Knox's 'honesty and godliness,' and even says that he will not disdain to hear better reasons. Knox has been sometimes represented as having withdrawn his opinion out of deference to Elizabeth, but he himself wrote later to the queen: 'I cannot deny the writing of a Book against the usurped Authority and unjust Regiment of Women; neither yet am I minded to retract or call back any principal point or proposition of the same till truth and verity do further appear.' Still he felt he had gone too far, and in the summary of the 'Second Blast' his propositions are altered from special application to women to a general argument that a king can only lawfully reign over a people professing Christ by election, not by birth nor propinquity—a doctrine as little palatable, though not so irritating, to Elizabeth.

Knox left Geneva on 7 Jan. 1559, after receiving the freedom of the city. Reaching Dieppe in March, he sailed for Leith on 22 April, and arrived at Edinburgh on 2 May. Next day he wrote to Mrs. Lock, one of his English friends: 'I am come, I praise my God even in the heart of the battle. . . . Assist me, sister, with your prayers, that now I shrink not when the battle approacheth.' Remaining only two nights, he went straight to Dundee, where the reformers of Angus and Mearns were assembled. With them he advanced to Perth. John Erskine of Dun brought in May the news that Mary of Guise was, contrary to her promise, proceeding with the trial of the ministers who championed the Reformation. Knox was included in the number, and was one of those who were outlawed for not appearing. On the day of Erskine's arrival in Perth, Knox preached against the mass as idolatry. A priest began to celebrate by opening the tabernacle on the high altar. A riot followed, stones were thrown, and the altar was soon demolished. The people, proceeding to seek 'some spoil' (in Knox's phrase), sacked the monasteries of the Grey and Black Friars and the Charterhouse. In two days only the walls remained of the religious foundations in the city. Knox calls these the acts of 'the rascal multitude,' but his voice gave the signal. He stayed in Perth to instruct the people who were 'young and rude in Christ,' while the men of Angus returned home; but hearing that Mary of Guise was determined to avenge the monasteries, they came back, fortified the town, and on 22 May addressed a letter to her, declaring that they had taken up arms solely because pursued for conscience sake, and threatening to appeal to the king of France, Mary their queen, and her husband. Knox probably was the author of this letter, and of another addressed to the nobility, claiming their aid. In reply to messengers sent by Mary of Guise to ask the meaning of the movement in Perth, it was stated by the leaders of the reforming party that if the regent 'would suffer the religion then begun to proceed, they, the town, and all they had were at her command.' But Knox went to the messengers' lodgings on 25 May, and boldly directed them to tell Mary in his name that she was fighting not against man, but God. This speech was reported, according to Knox, 'so far as they could.' Her reply was to send the Lyon herald, ordering Knox and his friends to leave Perth under pain of treason. Meanwhile the Earl of Glencairn reached Perth, with the news that the congregations of Kyle and Cunningham were advancing to the reformers' relief. But after negotiations, Mary's envoys (Argyll and Lord James Stewart) on 28 May 1559 persuaded the reformers to evacuate Perth on condition of an amnesty, and that no French garrison should be left in the town. Argyll and Lord James promised that if the condition was not kept they would join the congregations. Next day Knox preached, thanking God there had been no bloodshed, but exhorting all to be ready, for the promise would not be kept. On the 30th, Argyll and Lord James before leaving entered into a bond with Glencairn to support the congregations if anything was attempted against them, and shortly after they left Perth they rejoined the reformers at St. Andrews, and issued a summons to the men of Angus to meet them on 4 June for reformation in Fife. Dun, Wishart of Pittarrow, and the provost of Dundee kept the appointment, and brought Knox with them. On Friday, 2 June, he preached at Crail, on Saturday at Anstruther, and announced his intention of preaching on Sunday at St. Andrews. Archbishop Hamilton sent a message that if Knox preached in his town he would be saluted with culverins. The queen with her French troops lay at Falkland. The reformers hesitated how to act, but on Sunday Knox mounted the pulpit, and the archbishop fled to Falkland. Taking as his text the ejection of the buyers and sellers from the Temple, he applied it to the corruption of the papacy, and as a result the town, headed by the magistrates, proved their zeal by removing all 'the monuments of idolatry with expedition.' Knox continued his preaching for three days, and the doctors were as dumb, he says, as the idols burnt in their presence.

The French troops of the queen regent, under the Duke of Chatelherault and D'Oisell, were meantime advancing towards St. Andrews. The lords, the gentlemen of Fife and Angus, and the burghers of Dundee and St. Andrews collected at Cupar Muir to resist their approach. A force came to the reformers' aid from the other side of the Forth. It 'rained men' is Knox's forcible expression. But neither side wished to risk an engagement, and a truce or assurance to last for eight days was made. Both sides at once complained of infringements of the agreement. Perth was retaken by the reformers before Sunday, 25 June, and the abbey of Scone demolished. Knox represents himself as sent to try to save it, but before he came

the 'idols and dormitory were pulled down,' and all he could do was to preserve the bishops' girnal. Stirling was next taken. On 28 June 1559 'The Congregation,' as the main body of reformers was called, came to Edinburgh, accompanied by Knox and Goodman. Knox preached the same day at St. Giles, and on the morrow in the church of the abbey. On 7 July the inhabitants met in the Tolbooth, and chose him for their minister. He seems shortly afterwards to have revisited St. Andrews, but was again in Edinburgh by the 20th. The queen regent, at Dunbar, declined to make terms, and marched on Edinburgh. Leith opened its gates to her, and Lord Erskine, who commanded the castle of Edinburgh, was friendly, or at least neutral. Placed between two fires, the congregation was forced to a truce on 24 July, in accordance with which Knox and the congregation left Edinburgh on the 26th, and marched by Linlithgow to Stirling, where they subscribed a bond, binding themselves not to negotiate with the regent except by common consent. The regent temporised with the lords of the congregation, and issued proclamations to the people in expectation of the arrival of French troops from Francis and Mary, now, by the death of Henry II, king and queen of France.

Immediately after Cupar Muir, Knox had pointed out to Kirkcaldy of Grange the necessity of seeking English aid. Kirkcaldy had consequently entered into communication through Sir Henry Percy with Cecil, who received the overtures in a cautious but friendly manner. Knox, who had already written to Cecil from Dieppe, without receiving a reply, again addressed Cecil on 20 July, enclosing his letter to Queen Elizabeth. He addressed the latter as 'The virtuous and Godlie Queen Elizabeth,' and made a double-edged apology for the 'Blast,' which he said neither touched her person nor was prejudicial to liberty, if the time when it was written was considered. To Cecil he said that the time was come for the union of the protestant party in England and Scotland, and that he had a communication he wished to make if some one were appointed—the sooner the better—to meet him. Percy in reply, by Cecil's orders, invited him to Alnwick, and Cecil requested a personal interview at Stamford. This arrangement was never carried out. Cecil, writing to Knox from Oxford on 28 July, the day he expected to have met him at Stamford, declared he was ready to meet him if duly accredited, but forbore till then to 'descend to the bottom of things.'

About the beginning of August, Knox and

another minister, Robert Hamilton, went by sea from Pittenweem to Holy Island, and in Percy's absence Knox visited Sir James Croft at Berwick. He had received on 1 Aug. 1559 instructions from the congregation at Stirling urging the necessity of a league with England to suppress the Roman antichrist, and to maintain the liberties of England and Scotland against foreign violation. Knox now suggested to Croft that money should be granted to support a garrison in Stirling and forces sent by sea to Dundee and Perth, and to seize the fort at Broughty Ferry; he added that pensions would be acceptable to some of the nobility. On 6 Aug. Knox wrote to Croft of his safe return to Stirling; and urged the English council to be ' more forward in the common action.' The lords of congregation wrote to the same purport, and a convention meeting at Glasgow on 10 Aug. appealed to Cecil for a plainer answer. Writing from St. Andrews on the 15th, Knox frankly informed Cecil ' that unless without delay money be furnished to pay their soldiers, . . . they will be compelled every man to seek the next way for his own safety,' and added in a postscript : ' Haste answer of the former articles, for we have great need of comfort at the present.' At last, on 24 Aug., Sir Ralph Sadler, who was on his way to Scotland, was directed to secretly furnish a little money to Knox's friends. The convention again met on 10 Sept. at Stirling, where Arran joined the congregation, and through him Chatelherault, who as Duke of Hamilton claimed to be next heir to the crown. On 21 Sept. Knox wrote to Croft from St. Andrews, again pressing that money should be given to the particular men of whom he had furnished a list. The regent had vainly attempted to detach individuals from the reforming party. Knox and others refused to receive her letters because of the pledge they had given not to treat with her separately. In his second letter to her he asserted that he had never shown any hate against her, but only gave her good counsel, yet threatened God's plague upon her and her posterity if she persisted in her malice against Christ Jesus, his religion, and ministers. This letter Lockhart, the regent's messenger, declined to deliver to his mistress.

Encouraged by the adhesion of so many of the chief nobles and the hope of English support, and alarmed by the fortification of Leith and the arrival of more French troops, the convention in Edinburgh, on 21 Oct. 1559, proceeded to the bold step of deposing the regent. The sentence, owing to Knox's counsel, was worded as one of suspension.

The reformers now laid siege to Leith, but there was dissension among their leaders, and a sally made on Edinburgh by the besieged French garrison forced the reformers to withdraw to Stirling on 5 Nov. 1559. Next day Knox preached on the 80th Psalm, and ascribed their discomfiture to their own sins and dissensions, applying his discourse to the Duke of Hamilton and his friends who were present, and whom he specially distrusted. He ended with a strong assurance that God would give his children the victory in the end. The council met on the afternoon of this sermon, and Lethington, formerly the regent's secretary, who had joined the congregation before it left Edinburgh, was sent to London to implore the help of Elizabeth.

Knox was still writing urgent letters to Croft, Cecil, and others, pressing not merely for money, but for troops and experienced commanders. In one letter he adroitly alluded to Mary's claim to the English crown, an argument for supporting the congregation which touched Elizabeth, he knew, more nearly than the principles of the Scottish Reformation. At length these tactics succeeded. Elizabeth sent a fleet to the Forth under Admiral Winter before the end of January, and a treaty between her and the lords of the congregation was concluded at Berwick on 27 Feb. 1559-60.

Knox had remained in St. Andrews since November 1559, and the French troops in their raids on Fife had come within eight miles of the town and placed him in imminent danger. The arrival of the English ships filled him with exultation. The French troops withdrew from the neighbourhood. Towards the end of March the English land forces joined the reformers, and Leith was again besieged. Knox returned to Edinburgh in April 1560, and was active both in preaching and in counsel. On 1 April Mary of Guise took refuge in the castle of Edinburgh. On 7 May an assault on Leith failed, and Mary, watching from the castle wall the corpses of her enemies lying in the sun along the wall, exclaimed, ' Yonder is the fairest tapestry I ever saw.' Knox denounced her cruel speech in the pulpit, and affirmed ' that God would revenge the cruelty done to his image,' a prophecy which he believed was fulfilled by her death from dropsy on 16 June 1560. Two days before preliminaries had been adjusted at Berwick for a treaty between France and England, which was concluded at Edinburgh on 6 July, and which provided for the withdrawal of English and French troops.

The Scottish parliament met on 1 Aug. The commissioners of the burghs, with some of the nobility and barons, had previously been appointed to see to the ' equal distribution of ministers,' a phrase and idea of Knox's. Knox himself was appointed to Edinburgh, and in all the proceedings which quickly followed for the ecclesiastical settlement he took the foremost part. During the sittings of parliament in August 1560 he preached from Haggai, with special application to the times, and to the duty of providing for the temporal wants of the church. A commission was at once given to Knox and others to draw up in several heads the sum of the reformed doctrine. In four days the confession of faith, which Knox had already at his fingers' ends, was completed. It was adopted on 17 Aug. without alteration of a sentence.

Three short acts abolished the authority of the bishop of Rome, idolatry, and the mass. Death was enacted as the penalty for a third offence in celebrating the mass. Letters were directed to Francis and Mary requiring them to ratify these acts according to the terms agreed to in the treaty of peace, but there can have been little expectation that such ratification would be obtained. Knox boldly declares in his 'History' that the want of ratification mattered nothing. 'The sword and sceptre is rather a glorious vain ceremony than a substantial point of necessity required to a lawful parliament.' The thin veil of a monarchy, whose representative was absent, was easily rent, and the democratic Reformation stood revealed.

Parliament rose on 25 Aug., and after its dissolution a consultation was held, which led to a commission to Knox and other ministers to draw up in a volume 'the policy and discipline of the kirk as well as they had done the doctrine.' The result was the compilation of the 'First Book of Discipline,' as it was called to distinguish it from the second, of which Andrew Melville was chief author. The first embodied the opinions which Knox had thought out for himself or embraced at Geneva. A more rigid discipline, rather than the absence of set forms of worship, was his standard of a true church. Although little of the correspondence between Calvin and Knox is preserved, Knox evidently kept the Swiss leader informed of the fortunes of the Reformation in Scotland, and received from him counsels of moderation, which Knox did not always approve. At a critical moment in the conflict with the regent Knox consulted Calvin whether the children of idolaters and excommunicated persons should be baptised until their parents testified their repentance. Calvin answered in the affirmative, but Knox inclined to the negative. In regard to ceremonies, Calvin wrote subsequently: 'I think that your strictness, although it may displease many, will be regulated by discretion.

. . . Certain things not positively opposed must be tolerated.' Knox's 'Book of Discipline' showed little toleration: it treated (1) of office-bearers, organising the kirk on the Calvinistic model of presbyterian synods and general assemblies; (2) of worship; (3) of discipline, or the penal law of the kirk, and (4) of the patrimony of the kirk. Although many of the laity disliked the third point, which placed, despite the institution of lay elders, too much power in the hands of the ministers, it was chiefly on the last that Knox and the ministers differed from the nobles and gentry. The proposal made in the book was that the whole revenues of the old church should be devoted to the maintenance of education in the parish and burgh schools, the expenses of the ministers, and the relief of the aged and infirm poor, for able-bodied poor were to be compelled to work. The nobles had already whetted their appetites with the benefices transferred to lay impropriators, and the lairds had ceased to pay tithes. After perusing the book many days, the opposition was found so formidable that its adoption was delayed. Lethington called it a 'devout imagination.' Lord Erskine, the future regent Mar, led the opposition. No wonder, remarked Knox, 'if the poor, the schools, and the ministers had their own, his kitchen would lack two parts and more of that he unjustly possesses.' On 20 Dec. 1560 the first general assembly, of which Knox was of course a member, met, and after passing acts, chiefly relating to procedure, adjourned till 15 Jan. 1561. A certain number of the nobility, and among them the leaders of the reformed party, however, signed their approval of the 'Book of Discipline' on 27 Jan. 1561, but the dissent of others and their own lukewarmness caused it to remain a dead letter.

Knox soon afterwards compiled the form and order of the election of superintendents and the order of election of elders and deacons, published 9 March 1561. The Book of Common Order, which took the place of the English Book of Common Prayer until the time of Charles I and Laud, with the Psalms in metre and a translation of Calvin's catechism, were issued on 26 Dec. 1564, and were chiefly prepared by him.

Meanwhile, the only one of his works on which a claim can be made for him to be called a theologian, his 'Treatise on Predestination,' written in 1559, was first published at Geneva in 1560. Its title ran, 'An Answer to a great number of Blasphemous Cavillations written by an Anabaptist and Adversarie to God's Eternal Predestination, and confuted by John Knox, minister of God's Word in Scotland.' With an intense belief in the omnipotence of God and the corruption of man, he accepts the necessitarian hypothesis, and substituting the will of God for law, applied the doctrine of necessity to the spiritual as modern science does to the physical world.

About this time Knox lost his wife, the faithful companion of his exile. Calvin, consoling him, calls her ' Your friend and wife, whose like is not found everywhere,' and refers to her in a letter to Goodman as ' the most delightful of wives.' Knox felt her death, but his few extant letters to her, and a letter to Foxe the martyrologist, in which he says, 'I used the help of my left hand, that is of my wife, in scribbling these few lines to you,' do not present him in the character of a fond husband. His opinion of the inferiority of the sex was too firmly rooted to admit exception, even in his own household.

Queen Mary's husband, Francis II, died 5 Dec. 1560, and in the convention of estates, 15 Jan. 1561, the confession was read, and a debate on the mass was held by Knox on the one side, and Lesley, bishop of Ross, on the other. The noblemen present readily accepted Knox's views. By the convention's order, Lord James Stewart was sent to Queen Mary in France, and found her at St. Dizier on 15 April. Before his departure Knox had warned him that if he consented to her having mass publicly or privately within Scotland he betrayed the cause of God. While opposed to public Lord James was willing to concede private celebration, asking who could stop her. Against this Knox protested, and in a letter to Calvin, on 24 Oct. 1561, Knox sends the greeting of James Stewart, the queen's brother, ' who, alone of those who frequent the court, opposes himself to impiety : yet he is fascinated amongst the rest.' There can be no doubt that Lord James gave his sister assurance that her own religious observances would not be interfered with.

While Lord James was absent a riot occurred in Edinburgh between the common people, who wished to play Robin Hood, and the magistrates, who put it down and sentenced the ringleaders. Knox was asked to intercede for the latter, but declined, for, as he pointed out, he feared the mob as little as the sovereign or the nobles.

On 19 Aug. 1561 Mary Stuart returned to Scotland, and the conflict that Knox had foreseen between her Roman catholic convictions and the protestant convictions of so many of her subjects at once commenced. On Sunday, 24 Aug., mass was celebrated in the chapel of Holyrood, Lord James keeping the door to prevent a riot. Next Sunday Knox preached, declaring ' one mass was more fearful to him than 10,000 armed

enemies.' Four years later Knox reproached himself for want of fervency, that ' I did not what in me lay to have suppressed that idol in the beginning.' He was summoned to the queen's presence, and the first of the interviews which he has so vividly described—we have only his own account of them—took place at Holyrood. Mary accused him of raising her subjects against her mother and herself, and of writing against ' the Regiment of Women.' He answered he had only rebuked idolatry and taught people to worship God according to his word, and that the book had been written against the wicked Jezebel of England. While he maintained his opinion, he promised not to hurt her authority if she did not defile her hands with the blood of the saints. A conversation followed, in which he asserted the right of subjects to rise against a sovereign who opposed God's word. The queen declared the Roman kirk was hers, and that Knox wished her subjects to obey him instead of their sovereign. On leaving he prayed God she might yet be another Deborah, but when asked his thought of her by his friends, he answered, ' If there be not in her a proud mind, a crafty wit, and indurate heart against God and his word, my judgment faileth me,' and he wrote to Cecil, ' In communication with her I espied such craft as I have not found in such age.'

In the autumn of 1561, after Mary's return from a tour through the country, mass was again celebrated at Holyrood on All Hallows' day (1 Nov.) A conference was at once held in James Macgill's house between the leaders of the congregation to consider the situation. Lord James, Morton, the Earl Marshal, Lethington, Bellenden the justice clerk, and Macgill himself were there, with Knox and other ministers. Macgill expressed the opinion that ' her subjects might not lawfully take her mass from her.' But the ministers were of a contrary mind, and proposed that letters should be sent to Geneva for the opinion of that church. Knox offered to write, but Lethington shrewdly remarked that there lay much in the information sent, and proposed to act himself as secretary. The lords prevailed, and no letter was written. In December the general assembly met, but Lethington objected to its sitting without the queen's sanction, to which Knox replied : ' Take from us the freedom of assemblies and you take from us the evangel.' The knotty point of the ' Book of Discipline' was again brought forward. To objections raised by Lethington, Knox rejoined ' that the book had been read publicly and all knew its contents.' He failed again to carry its adoption, but resolutions were passed that idolatry should be suppressed, the churches planted with true ministers, and 'some certain provision made for them according to equity and conscience.' The discussion ended with the concession that the churchmen (i.e. the lay or ecclesiastical impropriators) should have two-thirds of these benefices, and the remaining third should be in the hands of a committee for such uses as should be afterwards settled. The third was afterwards reduced to a fourth, with the proviso that if a fourth was not found enough for the support of the ministers and the queen, a third or more might be taken. A return which was ordered of all ecclesiastical revenues was apparently never made. Knox inveighed against this compromise. 'I see twa partis,' he said, 'freely given to the devil, and the third may be divided betwixt God and the devil. It will not be long before the devil shall have three parts of the third, and judge you then what God's portion shall be.'

The ministers' stipends were at last fixed at a hundred merks for the ordinary, and three hundred for the chief charges. The superintendents got double. Knox himself had two hundred and a free house. On 8 Feb. 1562 Lord James, who had been created Earl of Murray, was married at St. Giles to the daughter of the Earl Marshal. Knox officiated, and in the nuptial address warned Murray that if he became less favourable to the reformers it would be said his wife had changed his nature. He was much offended at the vanity of the dresses and banquets, and the divergence between his views and those of the future regent now began to show itself. Early in 1562 Knox made vain endeavours to reconcile James Hepburn, fourth earl of Bothwell [q. v.], and James Hamilton, third earl of Arran [q. v.]

On a Sunday towards the end of the same year (1562) Knox preached another violent sermon against the queen and her court, in which he denounced dancing and other vanities. He was sent for by Mary. Murray, Morton, Lethington, and some of the guard were present. According to Knox's account, he said that he did not utterly condemn dancing provided those who practised it did not neglect their principal vocation, and did not dance for the pleasure they took in the displeasure of God's people. Mary dismissed him, saying stronger words had been reported, and Knox grumbled at being called away from his book. He left her with 'a reasonably merry countenance.' Some of the bystanders wondering that he was not afraid, he remarked, 'Why should the pleasing face of a gentlewoman frighten one who had looked on the faces of many angry men without fear?' The assembly presented a supplication to the queen, in which the hand of Knox is visible, demanding reformation of the mass, punishment of vice, provision for the poor, the restoration of the glebes to the ministers, obedience to the superintendents, and, lastly, support of the ministers out of the thirds. Knox was appointed to visit Kyle and Galloway, and met the barons and gentlemen of these districts at Ayr on 4 Sept., when they subscribed a declaration promising to assist the whole body of protestants. He then passed by Nithsdale to Galloway, where he induced the Master of Maxwell to write to Bothwell to be on his good behaviour, and wrote to Chatelherault warning him against his bastard brother, the new archbishop of St. Andrews. While in Ayrshire Knox was challenged to a disputation by Quintin Kennedy [q. v.], abbot of Crosraguel, on the doctrine of the mass. It was held at Maybole in Ayrshire in September, and the substance of it was printed by Lekprevik at Edinburgh next year. Both sides claimed the victory, but it was a drawn battle. With another Roman apologist, Ninian Winzet [q. v.], schoolmaster of Linlithgow, who sent Knox a paper with questions in February 1562, the reformer had an epistolary but incomplete correspondence. In the beginning of 1563 he acted as one of the commissioners appointed by the assembly of 1562 for the trial of Paul Methven, minister of Jedburgh, for immorality, and takes credit for the condemnation of Methven as a contrast to the license the Roman church conceded to its ecclesiastics.

In the middle of April the queen sent for him to Lochleven, and in an audience of two hours before supper urged him to stay the persecution of the Romanists for saying mass, especially in the western shires. Knox, in return, exhorted her to administer the laws, and reminded her that the sword of justice belonged to God and not to any temporal sovereign. Next morning, before daybreak, she again summoned him to meet her when hawking near Kinross. Without going back on their former conference she started fresh topics—the offer of a ring to her by Ruthven, the appointment of Gordon, bishop of Athens, afterwards of Galloway, as a superintendent, and the quarrel between the Earl of Argyll and his wife, her bastard sister, in which she asked Knox to mediate. She concluded by promising to put the law in force as he had requested. Knox reports this conversation, to 'let the world see,' he says, 'how deeply Mary Queen of Scotland could dissemble.' While at Glasgow on 2 May, on his way to Dumfries, where he was sent to assist in the election of a superintendent, Knox wrote a severe letter to Argyll, whom he had already once before reconciled with his wife, although he was unable to heal the breach permanently. During the parliament which met in the Tolbooth on 20 May 1563, the barons, especially Murray, showed signs of yielding to Mary, against the wish of Knox and the ministers. Knox accordingly quarrelled with Murray, reminding him of his rise, and, in his habitual vein of prophecy, warning him that if he bore with impunity pestilent papists he would lose God's favour. In the result they ceased to speak to each other for eighteen months. Parliament confirmed Murray in his earldom, and passed an act of amnesty; but while pretending to take up the subject of discipline and the assignment of manses and glebes, the acts passed were so modified as to be of no value. Before the session closed Knox preached a political sermon, recalling to the nobility how he had been with them in the hour of danger, and exhorted them to let the queen understand that they 'would agree with her in God,' but were not bound 'to agree with her in the Devil.' He concluded by saying that he heard of many suitors for the queen's hand, but if they consented that an infidel, and 'all Papists are infidels,' should be head of their sovereign, they would so far as in their power banish Christ from the realm, and bring God's vengeance upon the country, themselves, and their sovereign. Incensed by such language the queen again summoned Knox to her presence. When he came she burst out in invectives, mingled with tears, and vowed revenge. 'The chamber-boy could scarcely get napkins,' says Knox, with grim mirth, 'to dry her eyes.' 'What have you to do,' she broke in, 'with my marriage?' What are you in this commonwealth?' To which he made the memorable answer, 'A subject born within the same, and though neither earl, lord, nor baron, God has made me a profitable member,' after which he repeated his denunciation of a papist marriage. Mary once more resorted to the feminine argument of tears, but Knox told her 'he never delighted in the weeping of any of God's creatures, and could scarcely abide the tears of his own boys when he flogged them. But as he had only spoken truth he must sustain, though unwillingly, the royal tears rather than hurt his conscience or injure the commonwealth by silence.' Mary, still more offended, ordered him out of her cabinet, and to remain in the antechamber. He obeyed, but occupied his time in warning her maids of honour that all their 'gay gear' would avail them nothing at the coming of the 'knave Death.' After the queen had ordered him to go to his own

house she wished to have him prosecuted, but was advised to let him alone, and the 'storm quieted in appearance but never in the heart.'

In the summer of 1563 she travelled through the west, and everywhere had the mass celebrated. On hearing this Knox began to use a daily prayer at table, 'Deliver us, O Lord, from Idolatry.' Soon after he wrote to the brethren in all quarters to come to Edinburgh for the defence of a zealous protestant, John Cranstoun, who was being prosecuted for violently denouncing the altar at Holyrood. His letter was divulged by a minister at Ayr to Henry Sinclair, president of the College of Justice, and communicated to the queen. The council decided it imported treason, and Knox was summoned to answer for it in the middle of December 1563. When he came his fearless and constant courage divided the hostile camp. The Master of Maxwell reproved Knox for convoking the lieges, and their friendship ceased, but Spens of Condie, the queen's advocate, stood by him, saying, 'You will be accused, but God will assist you.'

Murray and Lethington made vain efforts to induce Knox to confess his offence, and in a few days he was summoned before the council. He came with so great a following that the stairs and passage leading to the chamber were full. When the queen had taken her seat, and saw Knox bareheaded at the other end of the table, she burst out laughing, and said: 'Yon man garred me greet and grat never tears himself. I will see gif I can gar him greet.' When Lethington asked if he had written the offending letter, he acknowledged the writing, and at the court's request read it aloud. After it was read the queen, looking round, said: 'Heard ye ever a more treasonable letter?' Knox denied that he had committed any offence, and the nobles voted in his favour. When on 25 Dec. the assembly met, Knox remained silent until pressed to speak, when he asked the assembly whether he had done more in his letter than obey their commands. After he had been removed from the bar the vote was taken, and the whole kirk found that a charge had been given him to summon the brethren as often as danger appeared, and the act of writing was not his only but that of all.

In the beginning of 1564 the dancing and banqueting of the court went on, notwithstanding the threatenings of Knox and the preachers, who pointed to the great rain and frost in January and the meteors in February as warnings from heaven. Knox now surprised both friends and foes by marrying for a second time Margaret Stewart, daughter of Lord Ochiltree, 'a very near kinswoman of the duke's, a lord's daughter, a young lass not above sixteen years of age' (Randolph to Cecil, January 1564). The queen 'stormed wonderfully,' for the bride was 'of the blood and name.' 'If Mary keeps promise,' Randolph proceeded, 'he shall not long abide in Scotland. If I be not much deceived, there will be much ado before he leaves it.' Knox himself does not mention the marriage, nor are any letters between him and his second wife preserved, but the union proved happy. He cannot be charged with marrying for money or rank. His father-in-law was one of his debtors in his will. The daughter of a smaller baron who embraced the reformed doctrine was not, in the opinion of its followers, disparaged by a union with a leader like Knox.

The assembly met on 25 June 1564, and Knox opened it with exhortation and prayer. It was attended only by the ministers and commissioners of provinces. The court party and the officers of state were absent. A conference between committees of the two parties was arranged, Knox being one of the representatives of the popular party, but nothing was to be decided on without the consent of the whole assembly. The principal subject of discussion was Knox's refusal of all compromise respecting the mass and his willingness to pray for the queen only on condition of her abandoning it. Lethington maintained passive obedience, Knox open resistance to the civil authority, however high, if opposed to God's ordinances. Knox resisted Lethington's proposal that a vote should be taken on the question 'Whether it was proper to take the queen's mass from her' unless the matter was submitted to the whole assembly. A few votes on subsidiary points were, however, taken, and Macgill, the clerk register, finding the votes going against the court, revived a suggestion that Knox should write to Calvin. The assembly broke up without coming to any conclusion.

Although Knox, like the rest of the protestant party, was opposed to the marriage with Darnley, and seems to have favoured the Earl of Leicester as a suitor for Mary's hand, he did not openly oppose the Darnley marriage. It was uncertain whether the young king might not turn protestant. On 19 Aug. 1565 Darnley went in state to St. Giles to hear Knox preach. The text was from Isaiah xxvi, beginning with the 13th verse, 'O Lord our God, other lords beside thee have ruled us, but we will remember thee only and thy name;' and quoted the passage, 'I will give children to be their princes, and babes shall rule over them. Children are their oppressors and women rule

over them.' He also referred to the punishment of Ahab because he did not correct the idolatry of Jezebel. Darnley left the church in displeasure. In the afternoon Knox was brought before the privy council and prohibited from preaching so long as the king and queen were in Edinburgh. The town council passed a resolution that they would 'in no manner of way consent or grant that his mouth should be closed.' Knox published this sermon, the only one of his we have in full. From the preface we learn that his practice was to preach without writing, and that he considered his vocation was to teach 'by tongue and lively voice in these most corrupt days rather than to compose books for the ages to come.' The printed sermon concludes: 'The terrible roaring of guns and the noise of armour doe so pierce my heart that my soul thirsteth to depart. The last of August 1565, at four at afternoon, written indignantly, but truly as memory would serve of these things, that in public preaching I spake upon Sunday, the 19 of August.' Mary and Darnley left Edinburgh on 25 Aug. The castle was still held for the queen, though the insurgent lords, led by Murray, occupied the town before the 31st. It does not clearly appear where Knox was during the troubled months of the Roundabout Raid. But if the statement in his 'History' is accurate, that the superintendents of Lothian met on 1 Oct. at Edinburgh, 'all the ministers under his charge,' he was probably present and joined in the supplication then sent to the king and queen for payment of ministers' stipends, to which a seemingly favourable but dilatory answer was returned, that 'they would cause order to be taken to their contentment.'

On 25 Dec. 1565 the assembly met in Edinburgh, and Knox received a commission along with John Craig (1512?–1600) [q. v.] to 'set down the Form of a Public Fast and cause Robert Lekprevik to print it.' The tract was published early in 1566, under the title of 'The Ordour and Doctrine of the General Faste appointed be the Generall Assemblie of the Kirkes of Scotland.' 'The Form of Excommunication,' published in 1569, completed his labours on the standards of discipline, doctrine, and ritual of the reformed church of Scotland. As in the case of Knox's liturgical books, he emphasised the distinction between a public or general fast and the private fasting on set days of the Roman church. This fast was limited to a week, from the last Sunday of February 1566, of which only from Saturday at eight to Sunday at five was to be a time of abstinence, the rest being devoted to preaching and prayer. One of the main ends of the fast he declared to be a protest against the mass. It was subsequently postponed for a week, but commenced on Sunday, 3 March 1566. On Saturday, the 9th, Rizzio was murdered. On the following day Murray and his party returned to Edinburgh, and a proclamation was issued in the king's name that all papists should quit the town. Where Knox was at this time, and whether he was privy to the murder of Rizzio, is not clearly ascertained. The language of the 'History,' 'The next day, which was the second Sunday of our Fast in Edinburgh,' suggests that he was still in Edinburgh, but there is no sufficient proof that this passage was written by Knox. In a list of the conspirators sent in a letter, on 21 March, by Randolph to Cecil, the names of Knox and Craig occur, but as they are described as being 'at the death of Rizzio,' which they were not, 'as well as privy thereunto,' and their names are omitted in a second list, sent in a letter of 27 March by Randolph and Bedford to the English privy council, it is fair to infer that the foreknowledge of the murder is not brought home to Knox. His approval of it is scarcely open to doubt, and he appears to have remained in Edinburgh till Sunday, 17 March, when the queen returned along with her vacillating husband and a force, which compelled Murray and the rest of his party once more to take to flight. The same date is given by the 'Diurnal of Occurrents,' a contemporary diary, for Knox's departure from Edinburgh. The fifth book of the 'History of the Reformation' substantially agrees with the 'Diurnal,' for it states: 'Now a little before the Queen's entrance into the town [i.e. the 18th] . . . Knox passed west to Kyle.'

In the assembly in December Knox obtained leave to visit England on condition that he returned before June 1567. Before leaving Scotland he wrote, along with the other ministers, to Beza, now head of the Genevese congregation, offering to send a copy of the Scottish confession, and pointing out that they did not dare to acknowledge the festivals of the life of Christ, because they were not prescribed by scripture. He also sent a letter in the name of the superintendents and ministers in Scotland to the bishops and pastors of God's church in England in favour of the clergy who refused to wear vestments. He probably had a share in the supplication of the general assembly of 25 Dec. 1566 to the nobility, exhorting the council to recall the commission granted by the queen to the Archbishop of St. Andrews. He received a safe-conduct from Elizabeth, and a letter was entrusted him to the English bishops,

asking for toleration in favour of the clergy who objected to vestments. What parts of England he visited does not clearly appear, but it seems to have been chiefly the north, and probably the county of Durham, where his sons were residing with their mother's relations.

He was absent when Darnley met Rizzio's fate, but returned home after the flight of Bothwell from Carberry Hill and the imprisonment of Mary in Lochleven. Throgmorton, the English envoy, mentions that Knox came to Edinburgh on 17 July 1567, and that he had several meetings with him, when he found him 'very austere.' In his sermon on the 19th, which Throgmorton heard, he inveighed vehemently against the queen, and the envoy tried to persuade the privy council to advise him and other ministers not to meddle with affairs of state. The attempt was vain, for Knox continued his custom of preaching daily against the queen and Bothwell, in favour of the English alliance, and against the French alliance.

The assembly appointed him, John Douglas, John Row, and John Craig commissioners to request the lords who had hitherto remained neutral or belonged to the party of the Hamiltons to come to Edinburgh and join with the lords in the settlement of God's true worship, the maintenance of the ministers, and the support of the poor. But the commissioners did not succeed in their mission, and the articles which ratified the reformation of 1560 were the joint work of the assembly and the nobles of Murray's party alone. After Mary's forced abdication and the call of Murray to the regency, Knox went to Stirling for the coronation of James, and preached the sermon on 29 July 1567 from the text 'I was crowned young,' in the Book of Kings, relating to the coronation of Joash. He refused to take part in the ceremony of unction. On 22 Aug. Murray was solemnly invested with the regency, and a parliament was summoned for the middle of September. From this time Murray and Knox were again closely associated. Before parliament met the regent appointed a committee of nobles and burgesses to prepare the business. Knox and four other ministers were added to it in ecclesiastical matters. The parliament at last made an arrangement as to the thirds of benefices favourable to the ministers, but the provision for education, on which Knox set great store, was still delayed.

While the presbyterian reformation was confirmed no notice was taken of the 'Book of Discipline.' In the assembly which met on 25 Dec. Knox was appointed to join the superintendent of Lothian in his visitation from Stirling to Berwick, and thereafter to visit Kyle, Carrick, and Cunningham. His name stands first, with that of Craig, on the list of the standing committee which was to concur with the committee of the privy council on all matters touching the church. He was probably not made a superintendent only because he disliked an office which might lead, as in fact it did, to the restoration of a modified prelacy. In February 1568 Knox wrote a letter to John Wood of Tullidavy, the secretary of Murray, in which, in answer to a request that he should publish his history, he states that he proposed leaving it to his friends after his death to decide whether it should be suppressed or come to light, and sturdily maintains that his 'Blast against the Regiment of Women' had never been answered, implying, no doubt, that its argument had been confirmed by the conduct of Mary Stewart. He concludes with a declaration that he would gladly end his days with the dispersed little flock of Geneva, as it had pleased God to prosper the work in Scotland, for which he had left it. But the situation at home was still full of anxiety during the four remaining years of his life, which he passed in increasing bodily suffering. While Murray and the Scottish commissioners were at York and Westminster seeking to press home the charge against Mary Stewart, Knox recalled in a letter to Wood (September 1568) a passage of a sermon in which he had expressed his fear that some of those professing the Evangel would follow the example of Judas when the expectation of gain failed, and he now applied his prophecy to the conduct of Hamilton, who was daily expected with French troops 'to restore Satan to his kingdom.' He impressed upon his correspondent the necessity of the English alliance. The rumour of Mary's marriage to Norfolk roused all Knox's old fury. 'It shows,' he told his friend, 'that England is more foolish than foolish Scotland.' Well might Lethington, who favoured the marriage project, write to Mary, 'I have of late dealt with divers ministers here who will not be repugnant to a good accord, however I think Knox inflexible.'

On 2 Jan. 1570 Knox wrote briefly to Cecil, 'If ye strike not at the root, the branches that appear to be broken will bind again.' It is difficult not to detect a counsel to put Mary to death, which comes painfully from one who signs himself 'yours to command in God, John Knox, with his one foot in the grave.'

On 23 Jan. Murray was shot at Linlithgow, and on 14 Feb. was buried in the south aisle of St. Giles. Knox preached the funeral sermon from the text 'Blessed are the dead who die in the Lord.' Despite the general affection inspired in the Scottish people by the regent, there were not wanting contrary voices which accused him of aiming at the crown by the death of his sister, and, if necessary, even of his nephew. A satirical pamphlet, chiefly aimed at Murray, by a brother of Lethington, described a pretended conference between Murray, Knox, and others, in which Knox was made to persuade Murray to seize the throne. Knox never gave any such advice, either from the pulpit or in private.

Neither Lennox, who succeeded to and held the regency till his assassination in September 1571, nor his successor, Mar, who was regent till his death in October 1572, was a friend of Knox, and his influence in politics decreased, though he continued to direct ecclesiastical affairs. In October 1570 his bodily infirmity culminated in a stroke of apoplexy, which, though of the milder kind called by physicians resolution, threatened, to the joy of his adversaries, to silence his tongue. But his indomitable spirit knew no decay, and within a short time he so far recovered as to resume preaching on Sundays. The course of events in Scotland more than his own illness preyed upon his mind. The party of the nobles headed by the Duke of Hamilton, and supported by Lethington and Knox's former friend and supporter, Kirkcaldy of Grange, now openly raised Queen Mary's standard. Edinburgh Castle, garrisoned by its governor, Kirkcaldy, for the queen, made war upon the town. One of Grange's soldiers having killed at Leith Henry Seton, a soldier in the opposite camp, Knox on the Sunday following, 24 Dec. 1570, in his sermon at St. Giles, boldly inveighed against this outrage. The same afternoon Kirkcaldy sent a ticket or short writing to Craig, which he required him to read from the pulpit, in which he declared that he was not a murderer, as Knox intimated, and called upon God to prove his vengeance on the man who was most desirous of innocent blood. He also sent a charge of slander against Knox to the kirk session. Craig refused to read the ticket, and the session to take any action. Recrimination followed recrimination. In the spring the assembly met in Edinburgh, and Kirkcaldy renewed his accusation against Knox, when Bannatyne, his secretary, appeared and protested. Knox himself wrote a long answer to the accusation. More acrimonious correspondence followed, until, Kirkcaldy having received the Hamiltons into the castle, Knox was reluctantly persuaded that it was prudent for him to quit Edinburgh and go to St. Andrews. He left on 5 May 1571, and remained at St. Andrews till 17 Aug. 1572. While there he resided in lodgings near the abbey, and, infirm though he was, his sickbed became the seat of presbyterian ecclesiastical government. He wrote to the brethren in Edinburgh, exhorting them to stand by the good cause and avoid jealousies. 'Be faithful and loving to one another,' he writes with unwonted calmness, 'let bitterness and suspicions be far out of your hearts, and let every one watch for the preservation of another without grudging or murmuring.'

The general assembly met in Stirling in August, and he addressed it in similar terms. To Douglas of Drumlanrig he wrote denouncing the traffic held with 'that Babylon the Castle of Edinburgh.' To Wishart of Pittarrow he condemned in even stronger language 'the murtherers assembled' in the Castell of Edinburgh,' and denounced the self-seeking of the nobles. He added, 'out of my bed and from my book I come not but once in the week.'

Of one of his weekly sermons, which, in spite of infirmities, he still delivered with his old vigour, James Melville [q.v.], then a young student of St. Andrews, has given the often quoted account : ' I saw him every day of his doctrine [preaching] go hulie and fairly [slowly and carefully], with a furring of martricks about his neck, a staff in the ane hand, and guid godlie Ricard Bannatyne holding up the other oxtar [armpit], from the abbey to the paroch kirk, and by the said Richard and another servant lifted up to the pulpit, whar he behovit to lean at his first entry ; bot or he had been done with his sermon, he was so active and vigorous that he was lyk to ding that pulpit in blads and flee out of it. . . . The threatenings of his sermons were very sore, and so particular that such as liked them not took occasion to reproach him as a rash ranter without warrant. . . . And Mr. Robert Hamilton asking his warrant of that particular threatening against the Castell of Edinburgh—that it should run like a sand-glass ; it should spew out the captain with shame ; he should not come out at the gate, but down over walls and sich lyk—Mr. Knox answered, God is my warrant, and ye sall see it.' But Knox had gentler moments, and would ' come and repose himself in our college ground [i.e. St. Leonard's], and call us scholars unto him, and bless us and exhort us to know God and his work in our creation, and stand by the guid cause.' He even took part in amusements, and was present at the marriage of Mr. Colvin, when a play was acted representing the taking of the castle and the captain according to 'Mr. Knox's doctrine.'

In St. Andrews, though the college of St. Leonard's was on his side, and he was supported by many, he had fierce opponents—including Robert Hamilton, the minister of the town, John Rutherford, the provost of St. Salvator, and Homer Blair, a young student of that college, who attacked him in a public oration. One Archibald Hamilton retaliated on him for stating that all ' Hamiltons were murderers' by saying that 'John Knox was a greater murderer than any, for his hand would be found to the bond for Darnley's death.' Knox indignantly denied the calumny, and his faithful servant Bannatyne tried, but in vain, to extract an apology. Another slander was that he would take no part in the inauguration of Robert Douglas, the first tulchan bishop, although desired to do so by Morton, because he sought a bishopric himself ; to which he was able to retort with effect that if he had wished this he could have had a greater bishopric from a greater man, referring to Cecil's offer of the see of Rochester.

When the general assembly met at Perth in August 1572, he sent it a farewell letter, in which he exhorted them ' above all things to preserve the kirk from the bondage of the universities. Persuade them to rule themselves peaceably and order their schools in Christ, but subject never the pulpit to their judgment, neither yet except them from your jurisdiction.' The accompanying articles have been erroneously interpreted as a proof that Knox accepted the modified episcopacy sanctioned by the convention of ministers at Leith through the influence of Morton. Their aim really was, assuming a modified episcopacy to be re-established, to curb its power and apply its revenues to the general benefit of the church. The assembly informed Knox that his articles seemed reasonable and would be adopted as far as possible. The same assembly granted the request of commissioners from Edinburgh to choose a new minister in the place of Craig, who had fallen out with his congregation, on account of suspected leanings to the party in the castle. The commissioners had already selected Knox, and after the assembly closed they went to St. Andrews to announce their choice. He was to have as colleague James Lawson, sub-principal of the college of Aberdeen. Knox consented to return, on condition that he should not be expected in any way to bridle his tongue or cease to speak against the treasonable doings of the castle of Edinburgh. On 17 Aug. 1572 he left St. Andrews and

reached Leith on the 22nd, when, after a rest of a day or two, he came to Edinburgh. On the first Sunday after, and every Sunday till confined to his deathbed, he was carried to the pulpit, not, it would seem from a letter of Killigrew, the English envoy, at St. Giles's, but at some smaller place, where he preached with his old vehemence. Through Killigrew he sent a message of the respect that he felt for Cecil. In September 1572 the news of the massacre of St. Bartholomew reached Edinburgh, and added another to the causes of grief and disappointment of his last years. On the 21st he preached in the Tolbooth, which had been specially prepared for him, and on 9 Nov. he was able to preside at the admission of his colleague, Lawson, when he preached on the duties of a pastor and his flock. On leaving the pulpit he returned home, leaning on his staff and attended by the congregation. He never left his house again, being seized next day with a violent cough, and gradually losing strength till the night of 24 Nov., when he breathed his last. The house in which he lived and died has been identified on the evidence of tradition with the picturesque residence in Netherbow Port, whose projecting angle still forms one of the prominent features of the High Street of old Edinburgh. A recent controversy on the point led to no absolutely certain result. Two accounts—one by Bannatyne, his secretary, and the other probably by his colleague, Lawson—describe the closing fortnight of his life. The second account was published by Thomas Smeaton in his 'Answer to the Violent Dialogue of Archibald Hamilton on the Calvinistic Sect in Scotland.' Both accounts treat of those who visited him, his conversation with them, the passages of Scripture he desired to be read, his prayers for the church, his bitter message to Kirkcaldy, his excuse for his vehemence, and his last prayer, 'Lord Jesus, receive my spirit.' 'Surely,' concludes Smeaton, 'whatever opprobrious persons may say, in him God hath set us an example both of living and dying well.'

On 26 Nov. Knox was buried in the kirkyard of St. Giles, now the paved courtyard of the Parliament House, where the initials 'J. K.' mark the spot. His coffin he had himself ordered. In this, as in the discharge of his servants' wages and in making his last will, his long illness had not deprived him of the power of punctually performing the last earthly duties. His funeral was attended by Morton, who had been appointed regent. His will, dated 13 May 1572, was confirmed on 13 Jan. 1573 in the commissary court of Edinburgh, where it is still preserved. The sums owing to the testator amounted to

880l. 19s. 6d. Scots. He owed nothing. His wife and three daughters were executors.

By his first wife Knox had two sons: Nathaniel, born at Geneva, May 1557, and Eleazar, baptised at Geneva 29 Nov. 1558. They were brought up by their mother's family, and sent to St. John's College, Cambridge, of which they became fellows (COOPER, Athenæ Cantabrigienses, i. 430,568; ROGERS, Genealog. Mem. of Knox, pp. 138–9). Nathaniel died in 1580. Eleazar was vicar of Clacton, Essex, from 1587 till his death in 1591. Neither son left issue. Knox's second wife, who survived him, was granted by the general assembly, at Morton's suggestion, the sum of five hundred merks. In 1574 she married Andrew Ker of Faldonside, Roxburghshire, who died 19 Dec. 1599. She herself died about 1612. By Knox she had three daughters: Martha (1565?–1592), wife of Alexander, son of Robert Fairlie, laird of Braid, and left issue; Margaret (b. 1567?), married Zachary Pont, archdeacon of Caithness, in 160s, by whom she had two sons; and Elizabeth (1570?–1625), married John Welsh, minister of Ayr [q. v.] Descendants of this daughter are still traceable. The line of descent from Knox's other daughters is believed to be extinct.

Morton's words at his tomb, 'Here lies one who never feared the face of man, were not biassed by intimate friendship. They are confirmed by his life, and reveal the source of his power. Bannatyne calls him 'the light of Scotland, the comfort of the kirk, the mirror and example to all true ministers in purity of life, soundness in doctrine, and boldness in reproving of wickedness.' He died, worn out by a life of continuous conflict, and although he won only a part of that for which he fought, the cause into which he flung all his strength ultimately triumphed, and that largely through his influence. Rarely has any country produced a stronger will. In British annals Oliver Cromwell is his nearest parallel; but, while both are examples of the power of self-confident faith, Knox mastered his countrymen by the influence of speech, without the stain of self-aggrandisement. His egotism was not vanity. It was the spirit required for the reformation he desired, the essence of the character of a people which prizes independence and self-reliance above humility and reverence. The breach of continuity with the Roman church that Knox effected was a sign of the continuity of Scottish history. Robert Bruce also had defied the pope. Knox was a Scottish patriot, with two important modifications. His patriotism was limited to the body of believers, and extended beyond the bounds of his own country to all of like belief. He had a strong attachment to that part of the English nation which afterwards became puritan and republican, and to the reformed churches of the continent. He carried the Scottish people with him, and for a time, during the crisis of the Reformation, he was political leader of the Scottish nobles and the guide in Scottish affairs of the English statesmen. But the real aim of both these allies differed from his. Through their selfishness, as he thought, he died with the reformation of religion he wished only partially accomplished, and the reformation of education, which was an integral part of his endeavours, scarcely begun. The spectacle of a single democratic leader holding the chief influence, not as Calvin in a republican city, but in an aristocratic country still governed by a monarch, commanded the attention of the cotemporary world. He left a still deeper mark on his own countrymen, whose ecclesiastical polity has continued largely to reflect his spirit.

It is easy to detect his faults. They lay on the surface, yet sprang from the depths of his character. Bellesheim, the modern Romanist historian, dwells on the cruelty shown by his approval of Beaton's murder, and the enactment of a death-penalty for the third celebration of the mass, his inordinate love of power, his vehement language in prayers as well as in sermons, and his meagre store of theology. It is erroneous to charge him with inconsistency as to his views on episcopacy, or with profiting by Lord Ochiltree's wealth. He was narrow, fierce, with regard to some subjects coarse, and with regard to some persons unforgiving. At his best he resembled a prophet of the Old Testament, not an evangelist of the New. At his worst he was a political partisan and ecclesiastical bigot, who could see no merit in an opponent, and could overlook any faults in a follower. Yet he was unselfish in a time of self-seeking, straightforward in an age of deceit. A strain of humour saved him from pedantry, and his severity was occasionally exchanged for a tenderness, more valued because so rare. A shrewd discerner of the character of others, and a close observer of civil as well as religious politics, his foresight was mistaken for a prophetic gift. As an author his reputation rests on 'The History of the Reformation,' unequal and incomplete, but unsurpassed for its vigorous representation of the principal acts and actors of the historic drama in which he himself plays the leading part.

A portrait of Knox, painted by Vaensoun, was sent by James VI in 1580, along with one of himself, to Beza, and was engraved in Beza's 'Icones,' Geneva, 1580. The best

reproduction is that by Jodocus Hondius (q. v.), in Verheiden's 'Præstantium aliquot Theologorum,' Hague, 1602. It was again engraved by Boissard in the 'Bibliotheca Chalcographica,' 4th edition, Frankfort, 1650. This portrait, undoubtedly genuine, presents a long straight nose, large eyes, sunk cheeks, firm brow, strong under-lip, and 'a river of a beard.' In 1836 another quite different head was given in Knight's 'Gallery of Portraits,' from a picture in the possession of Lord Somerville. This represents a face with an oblique nose, which gives an unpleasant expression to somewhat commonplace eyes, and a weak chin, covered by a short pointed beard. The white tippet covering the shoulders, which takes the place of the high ruff or collar in Beza's portrait, should have put any one on his guard against accepting it as a divine of the sixteenth century. The costume belongs to the seventeenth. Unfortunately, Carlyle in his old age insisted that it was the only likeness of Knox, and was backed up in his opinion by Boehm the sculptor, and by injudicious friends with no qualifications to offer an opinion on such a point. Mr. James Drummond, R.S.A., conclusively refuted Carlyle in a paper read to the Royal Scottish Antiquarian Society in 1878 entitled 'The Portraits of John Knox and Buchanan.'

After Knox's death the general assembly granted Bannatyne 40l. (March 1572-3) to enable him to put in order Knox's manuscript 'History of the Reformation of Religion within the Realme of Scotland,' which he had completed as far as 1564, but nothing was heard again of the work till 1584, when Vautrollier printed in London the first three books. Most of the copies were seized and destroyed by order of the Archbishop of Canterbury (February 1586-7). In 1664 an edition of the whole five books by David Buchanan was published (London, fol.); but Buchanan's interpolations destroy much of the value of his labours (cf. NICOLSON, Scottish Hist. Library, 1776, p. 109). An improved edition, called the fourth, edited by Ruddiman, is dated 1732. The best edition is in the first two volumes of David Laing's Knox's 'Works' (vols. i-ii. 1846-8). His other works have been already described.

[Knox's Correspondence supplements the History as the chief source of his biography. The other sources are the Narrative of Richard Bannatyne and the Memoirs of James Melville, published for the Bannatyne Club; Thomas Smeaton's Account of his last Illness and Death, published by Charteris in 1579, reprinted in Laing's edition of Knox's Works, vi. 647; the English State Papers or Letters of Randolph

Throckmorton Crofts and Cecil's Correspondence or Memoranda are collected in the Calendars of Documents relating to Scottish Affairs in the English Records; the Correspondence and Writings of Maitland of Lethington, and his brother's satire, the substance of which is given in a picturesque style in Skelton's Maitland of Lethington, Edinburgh, 1889; the Zürich Letters of the English Reformers, published by the Parker Society; the Livre des Anglois, or register of the English Church at Geneva, printed in facsimile with notes by Professor Mitchell of St. Andrews; the Roman catholic writers, Winzet, Tyrie, Kennedy, abbot of Crossraguel, with whom he had controversies, and the tract of Archibald Hamilton, De Confusione Calvinianæ Sectæ apud Scotos; but the last is too controversial to be of much historical value. Of modern authors, the Life of Knox, by Thomas M'Crie, 1st ed. 1813, 7th ed. 1872, is, in spite of its partisanship and prejudices, an excellent biography, which leaves few facts unascertained, and allows any reader to correct its bias—it requires, however, to be read along with the standard edition of the Works of John Knox, Edinburgh, 1864, 6 vols., collected and edited by David Laing, whose notes are of great value. A German life, John Knox, von Friedrich Brandes, Elberfeld, 1862, has nothing original. The lives and correspondence of Calvin and Beza contain less than might be expected. Both the civil and ecclesiastical histories of Tytler and Burton, Cunningham, Grub, and Bellesheim, require to be consulted. Froude in his History of England has given a characterisation of Knox, which in the main agrees with that of Carlyle. As regards Knox's own writings, a full bibliography of the different editions is given by M'Crie, and they are all published with exact bibliographical details by Laing. See also Lorimer's John Knox and the Church of England and Rogers's Genealogical Memoirs of Knox, 1879; Essay on John Knox and his Relation to Women by R. L. Stevenson; and Buckle's Civilisation, iii. 75 sq.] Æ. M.

KNOX, JOHN (1555?–1623), Scottish presbyterian divine, born about 1555, appears to have been third son of William Knox, a merchant of Preston, the reformer's brother (ROGERS, Geneal. Memoirs of Knox, p. 70). But there is some ground for the belief that his father was the Preston merchant's eldest son, William Knox, minister of Cockpen from 1567 till his death in April 1592 (HEW SCOTT, Fasti Eccl. Scot. pt. i. pp. 271-2, pt. ii. p.519). John graduated M.A. at the university of St. Andrews in 1575, and in the following year became minister at Lauder. He was a member of the general assemblies in October 1581 and October 1582, and in 1584 was transferred to the ministry of Melrose. Knox was a resolute champion of the ecclesiastical principles of his great kinsman and namesake, and gained great influence in the twelve general assemblies of which he was a member. In 1585 he declined to subscribe the articles of religion promulgated by Secretary Maitland. He was elected moderator of the synod in October 1586, and on 6 March 1589 he was one of the commissioners appointed by the privy council to secure the preservation of religion in the sheriffdom of Edinburgh. In 1596 he was one of the commissioners for the south who were directed to meet daily the Edinburgh presbytery in order to consult means of resistance to the actions of the excommunicated popish earls and their adherents. His uncontrolled zeal is said to have led to his discharge from the assembly on 7 March 1597. He was, however, a member of the assembly in 1601, when he refused to vote for the royal recommendation concerning the translation of ministers. He was accordingly regarded as hostile to the government. When nominated moderator of the assembly of 1606 he declined to accept the office, and was accordingly put to the horn. In 1608, however, he had regained favour with the government, and was appointed to visit the kirks of Annandale, Ewesdale, and Eskdale with the Archbishop of Glasgow. On 4 May 1609 he also attended the conference at Falkland. He led the resistance to the re-establishment of episcopacy, admonishing the Archbishop of St. Andrews in the assembly of 1617; and in a sermon delivered by him at the synod of Perth (November 1618), which had been called to acknowledge obedience to the Articles of Perth, he exhorted his hearers to uphold the liberty and government of the church as it was before the introduction of bishops. He died in 1623, aged about 68. Livingston mentions him and others as 'eminent for grace, gifts, faithfulness, and success.'

JOHN KNOX (fl. 1621–1654), who was laureated at St. Andrews about 1613, and was minister of Bowden, on the presentation of James VI, from 22 Nov. 1621 till 26 July 1654, is said to have been son of the above. He gave 10l. towards building the library of the college at Glasgow on 1 Aug. 1632, was member of the assembly in 1638, and of the commissions of 1646 and 1648 (HEW SCOTT, Fasti Eccl. Scot. pt. ii. pp. 544-5).

[Hew Scott's Fasti Eccl. Scot. pt. ii. p. 559; Wodrow's Miscellanea; Calderwood's Historie of the Kirk; James Melville's Autob. (Wodrow Soc.); Livingston's Characters.]

KNOX, JOHN (d. 1688), presbyterian divine, was younger son of John Knox, minister of Bowden in Teviotdale, Roxburghshire, and grandson of John Knox (1555?–1623) [q. v.], minister of Melrose, who is said to have been nephew of John Knox the reformer. He graduated M.A. at Edinburgh University on 15 July 1641. When still a probationer he joined the royalist army as chaplain to Sir John Brown's regiment of horse, and was present at the royalist defeat at Inverkeithing on 19 July 1651. He shortly afterwards became chaplain to Archibald Douglas, earl of Ormonde (1609–1655) [q. v.], or, as he is more often called, Earl of Angus. He was one of the inmates of Tantallon Castle when it was besieged by Colonel Lambert, and during the progress of the siege was selected to escort the Countess of Ormonde and her sister-in-law, Lady Alexander Douglas, to North Berwick, whence it was arranged that they should cross to Fife to place themselves under the protection of the royalist army. At North Berwick, while waiting for the tide, the party was surprised by a body of the enemy, upon which the lieutenant and troops, to whose protection they had been entrusted, made a hurried escape in fishing boats, leaving Knox and the ladies to the care of a sergeant and a few sentinels. Knox offered to surrender on being allowed to convey the ladies to a boat, and as the rank of his charges was unsuspected his terms were accepted, and the countess, together with her infant son and sister-in-law, was safely put on board. By a bold and dashing stroke Knox subsequently managed to escape from his captors, and, riding off on their officer's horse, rejoined the garrison in Tantallon. There he remained until the castle was surrendered, when he was carried a prisoner to Edinburgh. He appears to have regained his liberty in 1653, in which year he received a letter under the king's own hand, dated St. Germains, 31 Aug. 1653, and asking for a 'seasonable obligation' in the shape of a loan. (The letter is given in full in Wodrow, iv. 39.) In this same year he was ordained minister of North Leith, but at the Restoration his services were forgotten, and in consequence of his firm adherence to the presbyterian church he was in 1662 deprived of his charge by the privy council. Indulged by the council in September 1672, he ministered at West Calder until 16 Sept. 1684, when he appeared before the council on a charge of breaking his confinement, not keeping Restoration day (29 May), and baptising children of other parishes. Convicted of these offences, he was imprisoned until the close of Charles II's reign. (Wodrow's statement, iv. 41, that he was confined on the Bass Rock, is disputed by M'Crie in his 'History of Bass Rock,' p. 386.) Liberated on 5 March 1685, 'under bond to re-enter, when called upon, under pain of five thousand merks,' he returned to his charge at Leith, where he continued unmolested until his death in March 1688.

Knox married, on 23 June 1659, Jean Dalgleish of Cramond. She died on 26 Oct. 1673, leaving a son and a daughter, Jean, who married, on 20 Feb. 1691, the Rev. John Tullidelph, minister of Dunbarney, Perthshire, son of Principal Tullidelph of St. Leonard's College, St. Andrews.

[Hew Scott's Fasti, pt. i. pp. 94–5, pt. ii. p. 544; Rogers's Memoirs of John Knox, pp. 72–3; Wodrow's Hist. ed. Burns, iv. 38, 39, 214; Crichton's Life of Col. Blackader, p. 382.]   T. S.

KNOX, JOHN (1720–1790), Scottish philanthropist, a native of Scotland, born in 1720, followed for many years the trade of bookseller in the Strand, London, retired with a large fortune, and from 1764 until his death devoted himself to the improvement of the fisheries and manufactures of Scotland. Between 1764 and 1775 he made sixteen tours through Scotland. The Highland Society of London gave him every assistance and encouragement, and he was a leading member of the British society formed in Scotland for extending the fisheries and improving the sea-coast. This society was incorporated by act of parliament in 1786.

Knox's earliest work, 'A View of the British Empire, more especially Scotland, with some Proposals for the Improvement of that Country, the Extension of its Fisheries, and the Relief of the People,' was published anonymously in 1784, while Knox was living at Richmond, Surrey, and was dedicated to 'the members of the British Society.' A 'third edition, greatly enlarged,' in two volumes, was issued in 1785. Among other suggestions, Knox recommended the formation of three canals in Scotland—between the Forth and Clyde, between Lochfyne and the Atlantic, and between Fort William and Inverness. All have since been constructed (see BUCKLE, Hist. of Civilisation, iii. 183). After the publication of Knox's next work, 'Observations on the Northern Fisheries, with a Discourse on the Expediency of Establishing Fishing Stations or Small Towns in the Highlands of Scotland and the Hebride Islands' (1786), the British Fishery Society, which had collected 7,000l. for the purpose of establishing fishing villages, commissioned Knox to make 'a more extensive journey in the highlands and isles than had ever been performed by an individual.' On his return the society voted him a gold medal, and at its request he published his journal in 1787, under the title, 'A Tour through the Highlands of Scotland and the Hebride Isles in MDCCLXXXVI.' (cf. Gent. Mag. 1787, pt. ii.

pp. 704–7). The work was translated by T. Mandat into French (2 vols. Paris, 1790). Knox proposed, on the four hundred miles of coast from the Mull of Cantire to the Dornoch Frith, and the six hundred miles of the Hebrides, 'to erect 40 stations, or fishing towns, at 25 miles from each other, more or less, as circumstances suit, to consist of about 16 houses of two stories and two rooms, with an inn and school-house, and an acre, or half an acre, to each. Each town to cost 2,000*l*., and the whole number 80,000*l*. Each town to have 50 Scots acres.' To meet the emergencies of war, Knox recommended that Great Britain should always hold two hundred thousand seamen in readiness.

Before his death Knox projected an elaborate work on the 'Picturesque Scenery of Scotland,' which was to be 'one of the most splendid publications ever attempted in this or any other country.' His 'Address to the Public' explaining his plan appeared in the 'Gentleman's Magazine,' 1789 (pt. i. pp. 326–328). Joseph Farington [q. v.] and Charles Catton the younger [q. v.] were among those who were engaged to prepare drawings and plates. But the project was abandoned owing to the death of Knox at Dalkeith, near Edinburgh, on 1 Aug. 1790.

[Imp. Dict. xii. 108; Scots Mag. August 1790; Gent. Mag. 1786 pt. ii. p. 794, 1787 pt. ii. pp. 704 et seq., 1790 pt. ii. p. 857; Nouvelle Biographie Générale.]   G. S.-H.

KNOX, ROBERT (1640?–1720), writer on Ceylon, born in 1640 or 1641, was the son of Robert Knox, a Scot, and commander in the East India Company's service. His parents were strict puritans. His boyhood was passed at Wimbledon, Surrey, where his mother was buried in 1655 or 1656. In January 1657 he sailed with his father to Fort George. On the homeward voyage in November 1659 a storm obliged them to put into Cottiar Bay, Ceylon, where Knox, his father, and fourteen others were made prisoners and carried into the interior of the island. His father died in captivity on 9 Feb. 1660. Knox remained a prisoner at large for nineteen years and a half, during which time he supported himself by knitting caps, lending out corn and rice, and hawking goods about the country. He made several unsuccessful attempts to escape. The rajah pressed him to enter his service, but Knox chose to risk losing his head rather than do so. The East India Company did what they could to obtain his release. At length, on 22 Sept. 1679, Knox, along with a faithful comrade named Stephen Rutland, contrived to elude the vigilance of

the sentinels, and after a dangerous journey reached Aripo, a Dutch settlement on the north-west coast, on 18 Oct. Here he was hospitably received, sent to Batavia, and thence to England, which he reached in September 1680. The East India Company acted generously towards him, and took him into their service. In October of the same year he sailed as fourth mate of the New London, then bound for Bantam, and on his arrival he had the option of serving in India by sea or land at a salary of 40*l*. a year. In May 1681 he was entrusted with the command of a merchantman bound to the South Seas. He was appointed in 1684 to take the Tonquin to Madagascar, there to ship a cargo of negroes for St. Helena; and in 1685 he appears as commander of the same vessel in the fleet sent to India for the intended capture of Chittagong. In January 1694 he arrived at Cork from India, probably one of his last voyages (HEDGES, *Diary*, Hakluyt Soc., vol. ii.). He died, a well-to-do bachelor, in July 1720, in the parish of St. Peter-le-Poor, London (*Probate Act Book*, P. C. C., 157, Shaller, 1720). His executor was his sister's son, Edward Lascelles. His numerous letters to his cousin, John Strype [q. v.], now preserved in the University Library, Cambridge (*Cat. of MSS.* v. 151), show him to have been a man of morose temper, rough manners, and a woman-hater (cf. *Addit. MS.* 5874, f. 5).

Knox wrote 'An Historical Relation of the Island of Ceylon in the East Indies; together with an Account of the detaining in Captivity the Author and divers other Englishmen now living there, and of the Author's Miraculous Escape. Illustrated with figures and a map of the island,' fol., London, 1681. A preface was furnished by Robert Hooke, M.D. [q. v.], who probably assisted in the compilation. The book, which is both delightful and trustworthy, is the first account of Ceylon in the English language. It was reprinted in J. Harris's 'Navigantium Bibliotheca' (vol. ii.), with additions from the history of J. Ribeyro, fol., London, 1705, and as an appendix to the 'History of Ceylon,' by Philalethes, A.M. Oxon. (Robert Fellowes [q. v.]), 4to, London, 1817. It was translated into Dutch by S. de Vries, 4to, Utrecht, 1692, and into French, 2 vols. 12mo, Amsterdam, 1693; while a German version appeared in vol. viii. of J. J. Schwabe's 'Allgemeine Historie der Reisen,' 4to, 1747, &c. Knox bequeathed to his nephew, Knox Ward, 'my Booke of Ceylone, with manuscripts of my owne Life.'

Knox's portrait was engraved by R. White in 1695.

[Tennent's Ceylon; Knox's Ceylon; Noble's Cont. of Granger's Biog. Hist. of England, i. 268–269. Copies of some of Knox's Letters to Strype are in Brit. Mus. Addit. MS. 5853.]   G. G.

KNOX, ROBERT (1791–1862), anatomist and ethnologist, descended from a family of Kirkcudbright farmers, was the eighth child and fifth son of Robert Knox (d. 1812), mathematical master at Heriot's Hospital, Edinburgh, and Mary Sherer or Schrerer, daughter of a farmer of German extraction. Knox was born on 4 Sept. 1791 at Edinburgh, and early lost the sight of his left eye through a virulent attack of small-pox. At the Edinburgh High School he rapidly rose to the head of every class, and was dux and gold medallist of the school in 1810. In November of that year he began medical study at Edinburgh University, and was twice president of the Royal Medical Society before his graduation. Failing once in his examination in anatomy, he entered as a pupil of John Barclay (1758–1826) [q. v.], and gained a masterly knowledge of the subject. He graduated M.D. in 1814. His thesis, 'On the Effects of Stimulants and Narcotics on the Healthy Body,' was followed in January 1815 by an important paper on 'The Diurnal Variations of the Pulse and other Functions,' especially as affected by muscular exertion (Edinb. Med. and Surg. Journ. xi. 52–65, 104–167). In 1815 he obtained a commission as assistant-surgeon in the army, and was sent to Brussels, where he gained much surgical experience after Waterloo. In April 1817 he was sent to the Cape with the 72nd Highlanders, and made ethnological, zoological, geographical, meteorological, and medical researches, becoming at the same time a practised shot and keen collector. He returned to England on half-pay on Christmas-day, 1820, and remained in Edinburgh, contributing papers to the Wernerian Society. In the autumn of 1821 he obtained permission to study for a year on the continent, and spent the time in Paris under Cuvier, Geoffroy St.-Hilaire, De Blainville, and Larrey. At the end of 1822 he returned to Edinburgh. He remained on army half-pay till 1832, when he received 100l. as a commutation payment. During the next few years he contributed to the Wernerian and Royal Societies of Edinburgh zoological and anatomical papers, some of which contained important discoveries on the structure and physiology of the eye. He succeeded in persuading the Edinburgh College of Surgeons to form an adequate museum of comparative anatomy and pathology, and was appointed its conservator in 1825, becoming also a fellow of the college. He advised the purchase and arranged for the transfer of the collection of Sir Charles Bell from London, and worked actively in the museum until 1831. In 1824 he privately married a person beneath him in station, and thus greatly injured his prospects. His wife died in 1841, having borne him six children, of whom only one son, Edward, survived him.

His old teacher, Barclay, being desirous to retire, Knox signed articles of partnership with him on 2 March 1825, undertaking the whole of the work. Barclay's death in 1826 left his anatomical school entirely under Knox's control. He at once took first rank as an anatomical lecturer, and his classes increased until his students numbered 504 in 1828–9, when he lectured for three hours daily.

Naturally Knox, who was an enthusiast for practical dissection, was the best customer of the 'resurrectionists,' from whom alone 'subjects' for dissection could be procured. He gave higher prices than others, and consequently offered a tempting market in 1828 for the victims of Burke and Hare [see BURKE, WILLIAM, 1792–1829]. The populace involved Knox in the obloquy of the murderers, and mobbed and burnt him in effigy. For months he was in danger of violence, but attempted no public defence of himself. He was caricatured in lithographic prints, termed 'Wretch's Illustrations of Shakespeare,' in one of which the devil was represented with a big pair of shears in his hand about to crop 'a nox-i-ous plant;' in another he was depicted as Richard III looking for Tyrrel, whom he finds in Burke. Burke in his confession exonerated Knox from all blame, but John Wilson, in 'Blackwood' ('Noctes,' March 1829), attacked him savagely. On 17 March 1829 Knox addressed a letter to the 'Caledonian Mercury,' with the report of an influential committee, including John Robinson, secretary to the Royal Society of Edinburgh, Russell, professor of surgery, W. P. Alison, professor of medicine, and Sir W. Hamilton, bart., to whom he had given every facility for ascertaining the facts. This committee reported that they had 'seen no evidence that Dr. Knox or his assistants knew that murder was committed in procuring any of the subjects brought to his rooms,' and 'firmly believed' in his complete innocence. There were circumstances calculated to excite suspicion of murder, but no proof that they did excite such suspicion. They thought that Knox had acted incautiously in the reception of subjects, and especially in allowing his assistants to receive them without making particular inquiry whence they came. Many did not consider Knox cleared by this verdict, and his chief assistants, T. W. Jones, William (afterwards Sir William) Fergusson, and Alexander Miller, shared in his unpopularity. Sir R. Christison thought Knox had rather wilfully shut his eyes to suspicious circumstances. The difficulty of procuring subjects was at last remedied by the Anatomy Act of 1832.

Knox's pupils were enthusiastic in his favour, and on 11 April 1829 presented him with a gold vase, acquitting him of every imputation and expressing sympathy with his mental sufferings. He continued his anatomical work, published various books and papers, and especially devoted himself to anatomising and describing a fine whalebone whale in 1831–4.

When the College of Surgeons vacated their old hall in Surgeons' Square in 1832, he moved thither from Barclay's old premises, and built a large class-room, in which he repeated his morning's lecture each evening. On Saturdays he lectured with eminent success on 'Comparative and General Anatomy and Ethnology,' often rousing enthusiastic cheers. In January 1833 Dr. John Reid [q. v.] joined Knox and Fergusson. Soon afterwards Knox's popularity in Edinburgh declined, partly in consequence of his heterodoxy and of his sarcastic and passionate habits of speech, and in 1836 Reid left him, to lecture on physiology at the Argyle Square school, and Fergusson almost gave up his work as assistant. Knox had now to rely principally on his younger brother, Frederick John, but anatomical material was scarce, and the students at Edinburgh decreased. Knox's 'Edinburgh Dissector,' brought out anonymously in 1837, to rival the 'Dublin Dissector' of Harrison, fell flat. In the same year he unsuccessfully contested the professorship of pathology, vacated by Dr. John Thomson. In April 1839 he failed to induce John Goodsir to join him, but Henry Lonsdale, his biographer, became his demonstrator and partner in May 1840. Alexander Lizars about this time gained the professorship of anatomy at Aberdeen, and Knox took his place at the Argyle Square medical school as anatomical lecturer. In the 'Medical Gazette' of 30 Oct. 1840 Knox announced as his own a discovery respecting the placenta which had been previously shown him by Dr. John Reid. Reid strongly censured Knox, and public opinion went against him, although he claimed to have given his new views to his class in 1839. Unfortunately it became evident that Knox's truthfulness or memory could not be strictly trusted. In 1841 he was a scarcely serious candidate for the professorship of the institutes of medicine (physiology) at Edinburgh, vacated by W. P. Alison. In his letter of application he sarcastically criticised not only the university course, but the other candidates, Allen Thomson, who was elected, John Reid, and W. B. Carpenter, and spoke of the chairs of the university as having 'fallen much below the income of a steady-going retail grocery or bakery.' After having formally resigned his right to give separate lectures in Edinburgh (with the idea, it is believed, of emigrating to the United States), he announced a course of anatomy there in November 1842, but got no class. In the following session he attempted a course of physiology with a similar result. For lack of better occupation he joined the small Portland Street school of medicine in Glasgow in November 1844, but returned his fees to his pupils before the end of the month. From 1842 to 1846 he was very unsettled, now living with an old pupil, now seeking employment in London. In 1846 he lectured on 'The Races of Men' at Newcastle-on-Tyne, Manchester, and other towns, and gained considerable popular reputation. He believed that the races of men, like the species of animals, were distinct, and that the secondary laws of evolution, as well as the origin of life, were beyond human inquiry. In 1846 he vainly sought a government appointment. In 1852 he tried to obtain office in the British Museum. Meanwhile he was delivering popular lectures, and was incessantly writing papers in the scientific journals and popular periodicals. Some of these were successful, and the proceeds, together with those from his text-books, enabled him to keep his family in Edinburgh. In May 1854 the death of his son Robert greatly distressed him. He shortly afterwards made application to be sent as surgeon to the Crimea, and when his application failed he retaliated by attacks on the administration in the 'Morning Advertiser' and other newspapers, based on letters from correspondents in the field. In October 1856 he was appointed pathological anatomist to the Cancer Hospital at Brompton. In his latter years he took to medical practice, especially obstetrics, in the Hackney district, continuing to lecture at public institutions in London and large towns. In 1860 he was made an honorary fellow of the Ethnological Society of London, and in 1862 honorary curator of its museum. Early in 1861 he was elected foreign member of the Anthropological Society of Paris. He formed many abortive projects, and in the autumn of 1862 talked of writing his own life. On 9 Dec. he had an apoplectic seizure after returning from his duties at the Cancer Hospital, and died on 20 Dec. 1862, at 9 Lambe Terrace, Hackney, aged 71. He was buried at Woking on 29 Dec.

Knox was slightly above middle height, with strong muscular body and firm, upright gait. His features were coarse and marred by small-pox. His left eye was atrophied, but the right was very vivid and expressive. In speech he was agreeable and persuasive, and in lecturing he rose to high eloquence. He dressed for lectures in the highest style of fashion. He may be ranked among the greatest anatomical teachers, though, owing to his disappointments and his untamed eccentricities, he failed to produce works of permanent value. His religious opinions were deistic.

Knox wrote, besides many memoirs in scientific transactions and contributions to medical, scientific, and other journals: 1. 'The Edinburgh Dissector,' Edinb. 1837, 12mo. 2. 'The Races of Men,' a fragment, 1850; 2nd edition, with supplementary chapters, 1862, London, 8vo. 3. 'A Manual of Artistic Anatomy,' London, 1852, 8vo. 4. 'Great Artists and Great Anatomists' (Leonardo, Michael Angelo, Raphael, Cuvier, Geoffroy St.-Hilaire). London, 1852, 12mo. 5. 'A Manual of Human Anatomy,' London, 1853, 8vo. 6. 'Fish and Fishing in the Lone Glens of Scotland,' London, 1854, 8vo. 7. 'Man, his Structure and Physiology popularly explained,' London, 1857, 8vo. 8. 'The Greatest of our Social Evils, Prostitution. By a Physician,' 1857. He also translated or edited Scarpa's 'Engravings of the Cardiac Nerves,' with descriptive letterpress, 1829, 4to; Cloquet's 'System of Human Anatomy,' with notes, 1829, 8vo, 2nd edition, 1831; Béclard's 'Elements of General Anatomy,' 1830, 8vo; Quételet's 'Treatise on Man and the Development of his Faculties,' 1842, 8vo; J. Fau's 'Anatomy of the External Form of Man,' 1849, 8vo and 4to; Milne-Edwards's 'Manual of Zoology,' 1856, 8vo. His name also appeared in 1834 on the title-page of a new edition of 'Anatomy of the Bones of the Human Body,' after Sue and Albinus, with explanations by Dr. Barclay.

[Lonsdale's excellent Life of Knox, 1870, with two portraits; Life of Sir R. Christison, vol. i. passim; H. Cockburn's Memorials of his Time, pp. 457–8; Journal of Anthropology, 1870–1, pp. 332–8, by C. C. Blake; Lancet, 1863, i. 1, 19; Medical Times, 27 Dec. 1862 (by Dr. Druitt); Wretch's Illustrations of Shakespeare, Edinburgh, 1829; Noxiana (six caricatures), Edinburgh, 1829.]   G. T. B.

KNOX, ROBERT (1815–1883), Irish presbyterian divine, third son of Hugh Knox, who was for forty years a ruling elder of the parish of Urney, co. Tyrone, was born at Clady in that parish in 1815. In 1834 he entered Glasgow University, where in 1837 he took M.A. He subsequently studied at the old Belfast College, where during his student days he was an active promoter of the union between the synod of Ulster and the secession synod, which resulted in the formation of the general assembly of the presbyterian church in Ireland in 1840. He was licensed to preach in 1840, and sent as a missionary to the south of Ireland, being ordained by the presbytery of Strabane in April of that year. Several congregations owed their origin to his labours. On 10 June 1842 he was installed as assistant and successor to the Rev. John Whiteside, pastor of the second congregation of Coleraine. Next year he became minister of the Linenhall Street Church, Belfast.

Knox was soon one of the most energetic of the Belfast clergy, being particularly active in promoting the erection of new churches and school-houses, and in furthering the work of the town mission, of which he became honorary secretary. He established and edited a monthly periodical entitled the 'Irish Presbyterian,' and published many sermons. A prolonged newspaper controversy with the Rev. Theophilus Campbell of Trinity Church, Belfast, afterwards dean of Dromore, on the question of baptismal regeneration, brought him into much prominence. The letters were subsequently collected and published. In 1863 he received the degree of D.D. from the university of Schenectady, U.S. He was one of the founders of the Sabbath School Society for Ireland in connection with the presbyterian church, and one of the earliest and most enthusiastic promoters of the presbyterian alliance, in which all the presbyterian churches of the world are represented. While actively engaged in preparations for the meeting of this body in Belfast, arranged for 1884, he died on 16 Aug. 1883, leaving a widow, daughter of William Gilbert, esq., of Belfast, who subsequently married the Rev. George Matthews, D.D., of Quebec. Dr. Knox was buried in the Belfast borough cemetery.

[Personal knowledge; obituary notice in Belfast Witness.]   T. H.

KNOX, THOMAS FRANCIS, D.D. (1822–1882), superior of the London Oratory, born on 24 Dec. 1822, was the eldest son of John Henry Knox, M.P., third son of Thomas Knox, first earl of Ranfurly. His father died on 27 Aug. 1872. His mother was Lady Mabella Josephine, eighth daughter of Francis Jack Needham (q. v.), first earl of Kilmorey. He was educated at Trinity College, Cambridge, where he graduated B.A. in 1845, coming out in the first class of the classical tripos and as second chancellor's medallist.

On 16 Nov. in the same year he and Frederick William Faber [q. v.] were received into the Roman catholic church at Northampton. At the beginning of 1848 he was admitted a member of the congregation of the Oratory by Father Newman at Maryvale, and in the following year he went with Father Faber to found the London Oratory, in which he remained till his death. He was created D.D. by Pope Pius IX in 1875, at which time he held the office of superior of the London Oratory. His learning and prudence were highly valued by Cardinal Manning. He held for several years the office of 'Defensor Matrimoniorum' in the archdiocese of Westminster, and he took a leading part in promoting the canonisation of the English martyrs. He died at the Oratory, South Kensington, on 20 March 1882, and was buried in the private cemetery of the Oratorian fathers at Sydenham.

His works are: 1. 'Life of Blessed Henry Suso, by himself. Translated from the German,' London, 1865, 8vo. 2. 'When does the Church speak infallibly? or the Nature and Scope of the Church's Teaching Office,' London, 1867, 8vo; 2nd edit., enlarged, London, 1870, 8vo; also translated into German and Italian. 3. 'The last Survivor of the ancient English Hierarchy, Thomas Goldwell, Bishop of St. Asaph' (London, 1876, 8vo). Reprinted from the 'Month and Catholic Review,' January and February 1876, and republished by the Rev. T. E. Bridgett, in his 'True Story of the Catholic Hierarchy deposed by Queen Elizabeth,' London [1889], 8vo. Knox prefixed 'Historical Introductions' to the 'Diaries' of the English College, Douay (1878), and Cardinal Allen's 'Letters' (1882), which form respectively vols. i. and ii. of 'Records of the English Catholics under the Penal Laws.' He also edited the Rev. Thomas Whytehead's 'College Life. Letters to an Undergraduate,' Cambridge, 1845, 8vo.

[Bowden's Life of Faber, pp. 238, 363, 424; Browne's Annals of the Tractarian Movement, 3rd edit. p. 101; Graduati Cantabr.; Tablet, 25 March 1882, p. 471, 1 April, p. 511; Times, 25 March 1882, p. 12, col. 1; Weekly Reg. 25 March 1882, pp. 365, 369, 1 April, p. 386.]
T. C.

KNOX, SIR THOMAS GEORGE (1824–1887), consul-general in Siam, born in 1824, was eldest surviving son of James Spencer Knox, D.D. (1789–1862), rector of Maghera, co. Derry, and his wife Clara, daughter of the Right Hon. John Beresford, and was grandson of William Knox [q. v.], bishop of Derry. On 17 April 1840 he was appointed ensign 65th foot, and on 7 Oct. 1842 was promoted to a lieutenancy in the 98th. After serving with the 98th in China and India, he sold out in December 1848. He subsequently served with the Siamese army from 1851 to 1857. He was appointed interpreter at the consulate of Bangkok on 7 July 1857, was acting consul there from December 1859 to May 1860, was appointed consul on 30 Nov. 1864, and promoted to be consul-general in Siam on 18 July 1868, and agent and consul-general in Siam on 8 Feb. 1875. He retired on a pension on 26 Nov. 1879, and was made K.C.M.G. in April 1880. He died at Eaux Chaudes, Pyrenees, on 29 July 1887. Knox married in 1854 a Siamese lady, Prang, daughter of Phya (Count) Somkok and Mäe Yen of Somkok and Bangkok.

[Foster's Peerage under 'Ranfurly;' Do I's Knightage, 1887; Hart's Army List, 1848; Foreign Office List, 1887.]
H. M. C.

KNOX, VICESIMUS (1752–1821), miscellaneous writer, only son of the Rev. Vicesimus Knox, B.C.L., by his wife Ann, daughter of Devereux Wall, was born at Newington Green, Middlesex, on 8 Dec. 1752. His father was a master at Merchant Taylors' from 1753 to 1772, when he was appointed head-master of Tunbridge School. In the probation lists of Merchant Taylors' his name is given as 'Nock,' and he signed himself 'Knock' until 1772, when he adopted the spelling of 'Knox' (ROBINSON, Merchant Taylors' School Register, ii. 90 n.) Young Knox was sent to Merchant Taylors' in 1764, whence he was elected to St. John's College, Oxford, where he matriculated on 13 July 1771, and graduated B.A. 1775, M.A. 1779. He was one of the speakers at the encænia in July 1773, when Lord North was installed chancellor of the university (Gent. Mag. xliii. 351). Knox became a fellow of his college, and resided some four years after taking his bachelor's degree, devoting his attention chiefly to the study of English literature and composition. Before leaving Oxford Knox sent the manuscript of his 'Essays Moral and Literary' anonymously to Charles Dilly [q. v.] the publisher, giving him the option of publishing or destroying them. Dilly obtained a highly favourable opinion of them from Johnson, and published them in one volume in 1778. In 1778 Knox succeeded his father (who had resigned) as head-master of Tunbridge School. Resigning this post in 1812, he retired to London, where he purchased a house on the Adelphi Terrace, Strand. Knox was ordained priest by Bishop Louth about 1777 (Notes and Queries, 5th ser. x. 503), and was rector of Runwell and Ramsden-Crays, Essex, receiving a dispensation to hold these livings, both of which were in his own patronage, in 1807 (Gent.

Mag. vol. lxxvii. pt. ii. p. 1056). He was also minister of the parochial chapelry of Shipborne, Kent, to which he was presented by Lord Vane. The degree of D.D. was conferred on him by the university of Philadelphia. He died at Tunbridge on 6 Sept. 1821, aged 68, and was buried in the chancel of Tunbridge Church, where a monument was erected to his memory. An engraving by William Ward, after a portrait of Knox by A. J. Oliver, is prefixed to the first volume of his collected 'Works,' which were published in 1824 in seven volumes (London, 8vo). Knox married a daughter of Thomas Miller of Tunbridge, by whom he had three sons and an only daughter, Sarah, who became the wife of Robert Clement Sconce of Plymouth, and died on 17 June 1818. Mrs. Knox died on 29 May 1809. Vicesimus, the elder of their two surviving sons, was called to the bar at the Inner Temple in 1804, became the recorder of Saffron Walden and a bencher of his inn, and died on 25 Jan. 1855. Thomas, the younger son, succeeded his father as head-master of Tunbridge School, and held that post until his death, which occurred on 23 July 1843.

Knox was a good scholar, an impressive preacher, and a popular and voluminous writer. He was a staunch whig, and, though a strenuous supporter of the establishment, was strongly in favour of Roman catholic emancipation. A sermon which he preached on the unlawfulness of offensive war at the parish church at Brighton on 18 Aug. 1793 attracted notice, and some indignant militia officers drove him and his family out of the Brighton Theatre. He subsequently published extracts from this sermon in a 'Narrative of Transactions' (1793; 3rd edit., corrected, 1794), and the whole of it is printed at length in his 'Works' (vi. 351-70).

Boswell says that Knox 'appears to have the *imitari ereo* of Johnson's style perpetually in his mind; and to his assiduous, though not servile, study of it we may partly ascribe the extensive popularity of his writings' (*Life of Johnson*, iv. 390-1). Though as an original writer Knox has been forgotten, he is still remembered as the compiler of the once familiar 'Elegant Extracts.' Besides two single sermons and anonymously issued editions of 'Juvenal and Persius' (1784) and of 'Catullus' (1784; reprinted 1824), he published: 1. 'Essays Moral and Literary,' anon. Lond. 1778, 8vo; 2nd edition, corrected and enlarged, Lond. 1779, 8vo; 'Volume the Second' [containing thirty-nine additional essays] was published in 1779, Lond. 8vo, after the second edition of the original volume had appeared with Knox's name on the title-page; 12th edition, New York, 1793, 12mo, 2 vols.; another edition, Basil, 1800, 8vo; 17th edition, Lond. 1815, 12mo, 3 vols.; in Ferguson's 'British Essayists,' 2nd edition, vols. xxxv-vii. Lond. 1823, 12mo; new edition, Lond. 1823, 12mo, 3 vols., a duplicate of the preceding, without the collective title-pages; another edition in Lynam's 'British Essayists,' vol. xxii. and xxiii., Lond. 1827, 12mo. Other editions are given in Lowndes's 'Bibliographer's Manual' (Bohn). 2. 'Liberal Education, or a Practical Treatise on the Methods of acquiring Useful and Polite Learning,' Lond. 1781, 8vo; 10th edition, Lond. 1789, 8vo, 2 vols., with a letter to Lord North. 3. 'Elegant Extracts, or Useful and Entertaining Passages in Prose, selected for the improvement of Scholars at Classical and other Schools in the Art of Speaking, in Reading, Thinking, Composing, and in the Conduct of Life,' anon. Lond. 1783, 4to; 10th edition, anon. Lond. 1816, 8vo, 2 vols. 'The Prose Epitome, or Elegant Extracts abridged,' anon. Lond. 1791, 12mo. 4. 'Winter Evenings, or Lucubrations on Life and Letters,' anon. Lond. 1788, 12mo, 3 vols.; 2nd edition, Lond. 1790, 8vo, 2 vols.; 3rd edition, Lond. 1795, 12mo, 3 vols.; new edition, Basil [printed], Paris, 1800, 8vo, 2 vols.; new edition, Lond. 1823, 12mo, 3 vols.; another edition is contained in Lynam's 'British Essayists,' vols. xxix. and xxx., Lond. 1827, 12mo. 5. 'Elegant Extracts, or Useful and Entertaining Pieces of Poetry, selected for the improvement of Youth,' anon. Lond. 1789, 8vo; other editions, anon. Lond. 1801, 1805, and 1816; 'The Poetical Epitome, or Elegant Extracts abridged,' &c., anon. Lond. 1807, 12mo. 6. 'Elegant Epistles, or a copious Collection of Familiar and Amusing Letters, selected for the improvement of young Persons, and for general Entertainment,' Lond. 1790, 8vo; another edition, Dublin, 1791, 8vo. The 'Elegant Extracts,' both in prose and verse, and the 'Elegant Epistles' were frequently reprinted together; an edition was published by Sharpe in 1810, 18mo (18 vols.); 'a new edition ... prepared by J. G. Percival,' 1842, Boston, Mass., 8vo (6 vols.); sometimes the 'Family Lectures' were added. 7. 'Family Lectures, or Domestic Divinity; being a copious Collection of Sermons, selected from ... Divines of the present century, for the Use of Schools,' &c. [anonymously edited by Knox], Lond. 1791-5, 8vo, 2 vols.; the second, or 'new volume,' has a somewhat altered title; reprinted in 1815, and subsequently published in 1 vol. 8vo to match the 'Elegant Extracts.' 8. 'Sermons, chiefly intended to promote Faith, Hope, and Charity,' Lond. 1792, 8vo; 2nd edition, corrected, Lond. 1793, 8vo.

9. 'Personal Nobility, or Letters to a young Nobleman on the Conduct of his Studies and the Dignity of the Peerage,' anon. Lond. 1793, 16mo; this was dedicated to Charles James Fox. 10. 'Antipolemus, or the Plea of Reason, Religion, and Humanity against War; a Fragment, translated from Erasmus and addressed to Aggressors,' anon. Lond. 1794, 8vo. 11. 'The Spirit of Despotism . . . London, printed in the year 1795; Philadelphia, reprinted . . . Nov. 28, MDCCXCV,' 12mo; four editions, 'dedicated to Lord Castlereagh,' and 'edited by the author of the "Political House that Jack Built"' [W. Hone], were published in 1821, Lond. 8vo; another edition by the same editor appeared in 1822, Lond. 8vo, with Knox's name on the title-page; the 10th edition appeared in the fifth volume of Knox's collected 'Works;' 11th edition, with 'A Preliminary Dissertation on Government, Law, and Reform, and the Life and Character of Dr. Knox, the Author, &c.,' Lond. 1837, 8vo, with portrait; Hone states that the book was 'first privately printed at London in 1795, during the war against France, in a duodecimo volume of 360 pages;' it is said to have been shortly afterwards suppressed by Knox, and that only three copies were left in existence, one of which went to America, and another subsequently fell into Hone's hands; no trace, however, of the three copies is now discoverable, and in all probability the American edition was really the first one (*Notes and Queries*, 5th ser. xi. 43, 174, 6th ser. vii. 407). 12. 'Christian Philosophy, or an Attempt to Display the Evidence and Excellence of Revealed Religion,' Lond. 1795, 12mo, 2 vols.; 3rd edition, with an appendix on Mr. Paine's 'Pamphlet on Prayer, on Psalmody, and a short List of Books for the use of the . . . unlearned reader,' &c., Lond. 1798, 12mo; 'First American edition, with a translation of all the . . . quotations annexed,' Philadelphia, 1804, 12mo; another edition, with an introductory essay by the Rev. Henry Stebbing, appeared in vol. xix. of Cattermole and Stebbing's 'Sacred Classics,' Lond. 1835, 8vo; other editions, Lond. 1854, 8vo, &c. 13. 'Considerations on the Nature and Efficacy of the Lord's Supper,' &c., Lond. 1799, 8vo; 2nd edition, abridged, Lond. 1800, 12mo. 14. 'Remarks on the tendency of certain Clauses in a Bill now pending in Parliament to degrade Grammar Schools. With cursory Strictures on the national importance of preserving inviolate the Classical discipline prescribed by their Founders,' Lond. 1821, 8vo; the 'second edition . . . corrected,' in the 'Pamphleteer,' Lond. 1822, 8vo, vol. xix.

[Biographical preface to the first volume of Knox's Works, 1824; Memoir prefixed to J. G. Percival's edition of Elegant Extracts, 1842; Life and Character prefixed to the eleventh edition of the Spirit of Despotism, 1837; Rivington's History of Tunbridge School, 1869, pp. 124–38; Annual Biography and Obituary for 1822, vi. 350–63; Monthly Magazine, 1821, pt. ii. vol. lii. pp. 275–6; European Magazine, 1822, lxxxi. 195–9 (with portrait); Public Characters of 1803–4, 1804, pp. 519–30; Gent. Mag. 1821, vol. xci. pt. ii. pp. 276–81; Annual Register, 1821, App. to Chron. p. 242; Boswell's Life of Johnson, ed. G. B. Hill, i. 222, iii. 13–14, iv. 330, 390–1; Georgian Era, 1834, iii. 562–70; Foster's Alumni Oxon. 1888, pt. ii, p. 806; Robinson's Register of Merchant Taylors' School, 1882–3, ii. 90, 126; Clode's Memorials of the Guild of Merchant Taylors, 1875, pp. 681, 682; Notes and Queries, 5th ser. x. 448, 593–4, xi. 306, 414; Dictionary of Living Authors, 1816; Halkett and Laing's Dict. of Anon. and Pseudon. Lit. 1882–8; Watt's Bibl. Brit. 1824; Lowndes's Bibl. Man. (Bohn); Allibone; Brit. Mus. Cat.; information from Mr. Alan H. Sterring.]

G. F. R. B.

KNOX, WILLIAM (1732–1810), official and controversialist, was born in Ireland in 1732. He received the rudiments of his political education from Sir Richard Cox [q. v.]. Lord Halifax appointed him 'one of his majesty's council and provost-marshal of Georgia,' when Henry Ellis [q. v.] was made governor of the colony. Ellis and Knox arrived at Savannah on 16 Feb. 1757, and Knox did not return to England until 1761. Lord Grosvenor was then his friend and patron; they were at Paris together in 1763, and it was probably through Grosvenor's influence that Knox obtained his introduction to George Grenville. He became agent in Great Britain for Georgia and East Florida, and in the interests of the colonies sent a memorial to Lord Bute, recommending the creation of a colonial aristocracy and the inclusion in parliament of representatives of the colonies; but his services as agent were dispensed with by resolution of the Georgia assembly on 15 Nov. 1765, for two pamphlets written in defence of the Stamp Act, which he considered to be the least objectionable mode of taxation. In the same year (1765) he gave evidence before a committee of the House of Commons on the state of the American colonies, and from the institution of the secretaryship of state for America in 1770 to its suppression by Lord Shelburne in 1782, he acted as the under-secretary. His views formed a basis for the conciliatory propositions of Lord North in 1776; he suggested the creation of a separate loyalist colony in Maine in 1780, which was approved by the king and ministers, but abandoned through legal difficulties, and to his zeal were ascribed many of the measures taken against the American colonies. On the suppression of his post he sought for compensation, but it was refused on the ground that his services were sufficiently rewarded in the two pensions of 600l. a year each bestowed by the state on him and his wife for the loss, as loyalists, of their property in America. In 1772 the 'reversion of the place of secretary of New York' (*Calendar of Home Office Papers*, 1770-2, p. 581) was granted to him, but it never brought him any emolument. Knox continued to be consulted even after his dismissal from office. He drafted in July 1783 an order in council excluding American shipping from the West Indies, and on his suggestion the province of New Brunswick was created in 1784, and lands were granted to the expelled loyalists of New York and New England. After the death of Sir James Wright in 1786 the loyalists of Georgia made him their attorney to press their claims to compensation, but his active life then ceased. He died at Ealing, near London, on 25 Aug. 1810.

Knox published numerous pamphlets. The chief were: 1. 'A Letter to a Member of Parliament, wherein the Power of the British Legislature and the case of the Colonists are briefly and impartially considered' [anon.], 1764. 2. 'The Claim of the Colonies to an Exemption from Internal Taxes imposed by authority of Parliament examined' [anon.], 1765. These were the two pamphlets that lost him his post of agent. 3. 'Three Tracts respecting the Conversion and Instruction of the Free Indians and Negroe Slaves in the Colonies' [anon.], n. p. or d. [1768]; new edit., with his name, 1789. They were written at the desire of Archbishop Secker. 4. 'The Present State of the Nation, particularly with respect to its Trade, Finances, &c.' [anon.], 1768; 4th edit. 1769. It was written by Knox, with the assistance of George Grenville, and many portions which were translated into French and Spanish were openly attributed to Grenville. Many of its prognostications were very gloomy, and it contained numerous reflections on Rockingham's friends. These provoked Burke into replying with 'Observations on the Present State of the Nation,' in which he ridiculed his opponent as writing 'a funeral sermon' (*Works*, 1852 ed., iii. 7–108). Burke's tract went through several editions, and evoked from Knox 'An Appendix to the Present State of the Nation, containing a Reply to the Observations on that Pamphlet' [anon.], 1769. Walpole says that from the 'same

mint' of Grenville and his friends had previously come 'Considerations on Trade and Finance' (*Memoirs of George III*, 1845 ed., iii. 333–5). 5. 'Controversy between Great Britain and her Colonies reviewed' [anon.], 1769, republished 1793. In this Knox was also assisted by Grenville. 6. 'A Defence of the Quebec Act,' 1774, two editions. 7. 'Considerations on the State of Ireland' [anon.], 1778, reprinted in 'Extra-Official State Papers,' App. i. 22–61. 8. 'Helps to a Right Understanding the Merits of the Commercial Treaty with France,' 1788. Knox's desire to augment Irish trade is shown in this tract, and in his letters described in the Hist. MSS. Comm. 8th Rep. App. i. p. 200, and App. iii. p. 39. 9. 'Extra-Official State Papers addressed to Lord Rawdon and others. By a late Under-Secretary of State,' 1789, 2 vols. 8vo. 10. 'Considerations of the Present State of the Nation, addressed to Lord Rawdon and others. By a late Under-Secretary of State,' 1789. 11. 'Observations upon the Liturgy, with a Proposal for its Reform. By a Layman of the Church of England, late an Under-Secretary of State,' 1789. 12. 'Letter from W. K., Esq., to W. Wilberforce,' 1790, respecting the latter's exertions for the slaves. 13. 'Letter to the People of Ireland upon the intended Application of the Roman Catholics to Parliament for the Exercise of the Elective Franchise,' 1792. 14. 'Friendly Address to the Clubs in St. Ann, Westminster, associated to obtain a Reform in Parliament,' 1793. 15. 'Considerations on Theocracy, by a Layman of the Church of England,' 1796, in favour of 'universal goodwill towards our fellow-creatures.' Watt attributes to Knox 'The Revealed Will of God the sufficient Rule of Men,' 1803, 2 vols. Several letters to and from George Grenville are in the 'Grenville Papers,' vols. iii. and iv., and Knox's opinions are often mentioned in Thomas Hutchinson's 'Diary.'

[Almon's Biog. Anecdotes, ii. 112–15; Drake's Dict. of American Biog.; Corresp. of George III and Lord North, ii. 402–3; Gent. Mag. 1810, pt. ii. p. 197; Halkett and Laing's Anon. Lit. pp. 409, 505, 866, 1791, 2004.]   W. P. C.

KNOX, WILLIAM (1789–1825), Scottish poet, was born at Firth, parish of Lilliesleaf, Roxburghshire, 17 Aug. 1789. After receiving elementary education at Lilliesleaf and Musselburgh, he farmed without success near Langholm, Dumfriesshire, from 1812 to 1817. He 'became too soon his own master,' says Scott, 'and plunged into dissipation and ruin' (*Journal*, i. 39). His farming career over, he returned to his native place. In 1820 the family settled in Edinburgh, and Knox became a journalist. Sir Walter Scott, Professor Wilson, and others befriended him, and Scott frequently gave him substantial pecuniary relief. His convivial habits undermined his health, and he died at Edinburgh of paralysis, 12 Nov. 1825.

Besides a prose 'Visit to Dublin' and a Christmas tale, 'Mariamne, or the Widower's Daughter,' Knox published 'The Lonely Hearth, and other Poems,' 1818; 'The Songs of Israel,' 1824; and 'The Harp of Zion,' 1825. His lyrics are graceful and thoughtful. Scott thought Knox in 'The Lonely Hearth' superior to Michael Bruce, and 'Mortality,' in 'Songs of Israel,' was a favourite with President Lincoln. A complete edition of Knox's poems appeared in 1847.

[Sir Walter Scott's Journal as in text; Lockhart's Life of Scott, vi. 152, ed. 1837; Rogers's Scottish Minstrel, vol. iii.]   T. B.

KNOX, WILLIAM (1762-1831), bishop of Derry, fourth son of Thomas, first Viscount Northland, a title now merged in the earldom of Ranfurly, was born 14 June 1762. At the age of about sixteen he entered Trinity College, Dublin, where in 1781 he graduated B.A. In 1785 he became rector of Pomeroy in the diocese of Armagh, after which he obtained the rectory of Callan in the diocese of Ossory, and became chaplain to the Irish House of Commons. On 21 Sept. 1794 he was consecrated bishop of Killaloe in St. Peter's Church, Dublin, by the Archbishop of Dublin, assisted by the Bishops of Limerick and Kilmore. In 1803 he was translated to the see of Derry, where he was enthroned on 9 Sept. of that year. During his tenure of this diocese he became widely known for his philanthropy and benevolence, and was held in high esteem by people of all denominations. He died in London on 10 July 1831. He published several sermons. Knox married in 1785 Anne, daughter of James Spencer, esq., by whom he had twelve children, eight daughters and four sons. His eldest son, James Spencer Knox, D.D., was father of Sir Thomas George Knox [q. v.]. George, the third son (1793-1884), was lieutenant-colonel in the Coldstream guards.

[Cotton's Fasti; Burke's and Foster's Peerage.]   T. H.

KNYFF, LEONARD (1650-1721), painter, born at Haarlem, on 10 Aug. 1650, was third son of Wouter Knyff, painter, by his second wife, Lydia Leenderts of Delft, widow of Jacob Bas of Haarlem. Knyff was known as a painter of birds and animals. He came to England about 1680, and settled in Westminster. He devoted himself in England to topographical drawing and painting, and made many drawings in Westminster and its vicinity. He is known principally by the series of bird's-eye views of palaces and gentlemen's seats in Great Britain, drawn by him and engraved by his fellow-countryman and neighbour in Westminster, Johannes Kip [q. v.], for vol. i. of 'Britannia Illustrata,' or 'Nouveau Théâtre de la Grande Bretagne,' published by Mortier in 1708. Knyff does not appear to have contributed to the later volumes. These drawings, though stiff and uninteresting as artistic productions, are of great archaeological value. A good specimen, 'The North Prospect of Windsor Castle,' is in the possession of Mr. John H. Arkwright (Eton Loan Exhibition, 1891). Knyff died in Westminster in 1721. His collection of pictures was sold by auction in May 1723.

[Vertue's MSS. (Brit. Mus. Add. MSS. 23069, 23073); Vander Willigen's Artistes de Haarlem; Walpole's Anecdotes of Painting, ed. Wornum.]   L. C.

KNYVET or KNEVET, SIR EDMUND (d. 1546), sergeant-porter to Henry VIII. was the second son of Edmund Knyvet of Buckenham Castle, Norfolk, by his wife Eleanor, sister of Sir James Tyrrell, knt. Sir Thomas Knyvet [q. v.] was his elder brother. One Edmund Knevet was grand-nephew of the mother of Dean Colet; he is believed to be the 'Edmund' who received religious instruction from the dean and was a legatee under Colet's will in 1519 (see COLET, JOHN). The sergeant-porter married Joan, daughter and heiress of John Bourchier, lord Berners [q. v.], and thus came into possession of Ashwellthorpe, Norfolk. In 1524 Knyvet is mentioned as sergeant of the king's gates, and in 1539 was made in addition keeper of the king's woods in Rockingham Forest. He was also receiver of the revenues of the royal domains in Denbigh, North Wales. Numerous grants of land were made him by Henry VIII. Early in 1541 Knyvet struck Thomas Clere, a Norfolk gentleman, and retainer and friend of the Earl of Surrey, so as to draw blood within the tennis-court of the king's house. A recent statute had adjudged the penalty of losing the right hand to any one guilty of such an offence. At first both Knyvet and Clere were arraigned on 28 Feb. 1541, and bound in a recognisance of five hundred marks each to attend the privy council daily till dismissed. On 27 April they were formally accused and were committed to the porter's ward to await trial. On 10 June Knyvet was arraigned before the king's justices at Greenwich, and found guilty by a quest of gentlemen and a quest of yeomen of maliciously striking Clere. He was condemned to lose his right hand, and there is a detailed account in Stow's 'Annals,' p. 581, of all the different household officials required to assist in what was evidently a new form of punishment. The assistants include the master cook for the king with the knife, the sergeant of the larder to set the knife right in the joint, the sergeant of the poultry with a cock, its head to be smitten off on the same block and by the same knife to be used for the criminal's hand, finally the sergeant of the cellar with ale and beer. All being ready, Knyvet was brought out, and after humbly confessing his guilt begged that the left instead of the right hand might be taken. 'For,' quoth he, 'if my right hand be spared I may hereafter do such good service to his grace as shall please him to appoint.' The justices, pleased by this submission, interceded with Henry VIII, who, 'moved by the gentle heart of the said Edmund and the good report of lords and ladies,' granted him a free pardon. Knyvet died on 1 May 1546, and was buried in Ashwellthorpe Church, in a chapel adjoining the chancel; the inscription on his tomb is given in Weever's 'Funeral Monuments,' p. 815. His widow survived him till 17 Feb. 1561, and was also buried at Ashwellthorpe. Their son John, born, it is said, in 1524, died before his mother, and by his wife Agnes, daughter of Sir John Harcourt of Stanton Harcourt, Oxfordshire, was father of Sir Thomas Knyvet (d. 9 Feb. 1616-1617), who unsuccessfully claimed the title of Lord Berners. The signature 'E. K.' attached to poems in a manuscript collection preserved in the British Museum (Addit. MS. 17492) is explained as that of Knyvet; the principal contributors to the collection are Wyatt and Sir Thomas Howard.

[Holinshed, iii. 953; Dugdale's Baronage, ii. 424; Nichols's Proceedings of the Privy Council; Cobbett's State Trials, i. 443; Blomefield's Norfolk, i. 379; Cal. of State Papers; Le Neve's Pedigrees of Knights, p. 21; Notes and Queries, 6th ser. v. x. 269, 379, 477; Lupton's Life of Colet.]
E. T. B.

KNYVET or **KNIVETT**, SIR JOHN (d. 1381), chancellor of England, was eldest son of Richard Knyvet of Southwick, Northamptonshire, and custos of the forest of Clyve in that county, by Joanna, daughter and heiress of Sir John Wurth. Knyvet was practising in the courts as early as 1347; in 1357 he was called to the degree of serjeant-at-law, and on 30 Sept. 1361 was appointed a justice of the court of common pleas. On 29 Oct. 1365 he was raised to the office of chief justice of the king's bench (Fœdera, iii. 777, Record ed.) In the parliament of 1362 he served as a trier of petitions for Aquitaine

and other lands over sea, and afterwards in each parliament down to 1380, except while he was chancellor, as a trier of petitions for England, Scotland, Wales, and Ireland (Rot. Parl. vols. ii. and iii.) On 30 June 1372, after the death of Sir Robert Thorpe, who had been appointed chancellor in consequence of a petition by the commons that the great seal should be entrusted to laymen, Knyvet was appointed his successor. Knyvet held the office for four years and a half, acting with great wisdom and discretion; three speeches which he made at the opening of parliament in 1372, 1373, and 1376 respectively, are given in the 'Rolls of Parliament' (ii. 309 a, 316 a, 321 a). In January 1377 Edward III, under the influence of John of Gaunt, reverted to the custom of appointing ecclesiastical chancellors, and Adam de Houghton [q. v.] was appointed to succeed Knyvet on 11 Jan. Knyvet did not again hold judicial office, though he was appointed with the two chief justices to decide a question between the Earl of Pembroke and William la Zouch of Haryngworth (Rot. Parl. iii. 79). Knyvet died in 1381. Sir Edward Coke speaks of him as 'a man famous in his profession,' and praises his administration of the law (Fourth Inst. 78, 79). Further testimony to his worth is given by his appointment as executor of Edward III, and of other eminent persons. He married Eleanor, daughter of Ralph, lord Basset of Weldon, and by her left two sons, John and Ralph (cf. BRIDGES, History of Northamptonshire, ii. 354-5). He owned large estates in various counties, but especially in Northamptonshire (Cal. Inq. p. m. ii. 333, iii. 30).

[Authorities quoted: Foss's Lives of the Judges, iii. 451-3; Campbell's Lives of the Chancellors, i. 264-8.]
C. L. K.

KNYVET, SIR THOMAS (d. 1512), officer in the navy, eldest son of Edmund Knyvet of Buckenham in Norfolk, by Eleanor, sister of Sir James Tyrrell of Gipping, Suffolk, was brother of Sir Edmund Knyvet [q. v.] Thomas was knighted by Henry VIII in 1509, became master of the horse 20 Feb. 1509-10, and held among other offices that of keeper of the New Park belonging to the lordship of Berkeley (27 Aug. 1510). He married the widow of John Grey, second viscount Lisle, whose christian name appears in the 'State Papers' as Marcella, and in the genealogies as Muriel. She was daughter of Thomas Howard, second duke of Norfolk, and thus sister of Sir Edward Howard, lord high admiral [q. v.] In 1512 Knyvet was captain of the Regent, the largest ship in the navy royal, one of the fleet with his brother-in-law off Brest. In

z 2

the engagement of 10 Aug. the Regent was grappled by the Marie la Cordelière, the largest ship in the French fleet, commanded by the Sieur de Portzmoguer, whose house had been burnt a few months before. Owing to an outbreak of fire on board the Cordelière, both ships burnt and blew up, with the loss of almost all their men, estimated at about seven hundred on board the Regent and one thousand on board the Cordelière. It was said that Howard, who was warmly attached to his brother-in-law, swore that he would not see the king's face till he was revenged on the French for his death; and it was probably the desire to wreak this revenge that prompted the enterprise in which, in the following April, he lost his life. Knyvet left four sons and a daughter. Sir Edmund, his heir, succeeded him at Buckenham. Sir Henry, his third son, obtained the estate of Charlton, Wiltshire. The name has been spelt in many different ways. No signature of Sir Thomas's can be found, but the spelling here adopted is that now followed by his representative, Sir Rowland Knyvet Wilson.

[Letters and Papers of Henry VIII. i. 1491, 3398; Jal, in Annales Maritimes et Coloniales (1844), lxxxvi. 993; Egerton MS. 1075, f. 26 b; Addit. MS. 5530, ff. 168-70; Metcalfe's Book of Knights; Chronicle of Calais (Camden Soc.), p. 9; Blomefield's Norfolk, i. 379.]   J. K. L.

KNYVET, THOMAS, LORD KNYVET OF ESCRICK (d. 1622), was second son of Sir Henry Knyvet of Charlton, Wiltshire, by Anne, daughter of Sir Christopher Pickering of Killington, Westmoreland. Edmund Knyvet [q. v.], sergeant-porter to Henry VIII, was his grand-uncle. He was educated at Jesus College, Cambridge, became a gentleman of the privy chamber to Queen Elizabeth, and was created M.A. on her visit to Oxford on 29 Sept. 1592. He sat for Thetford in the parliament of 1601. On 5 Aug. 1603 James I gave him the manor of Stanwell, Middlesex, to which a neighbouring property was added by royal grant in 1613, and he gained much favour with the king. He was knighted at the Tower on 14 March 1603-4. In his capacity of justice of the peace for Westminster, and as a gentleman of the privy chamber, Knyvet made the search of the cellars of the houses of parliament on the evening of 4 Nov. 1605, and discovered the powder; to him Fawkes made a confession of the plot. Knyvet was shortly afterwards appointed a privy councillor, member of the council of Queen Anne, and warden of the mint. James confided his daughter Mary to him to be educated, and she died at Stanwell on 16 Sept. 1607. On 4 July 1607 Knyvet was summoned to parliament as Baron Knyvet of Escrick, Yorkshire, and had gifts of 500l. from the king in 1612 and 1613. He regularly frequented the court, and seems to have had a town house in King Street, Westminster. He took part in the trial of the pyx, at which James was present in 1611, and was at the funerals of the Prince of Wales in 1612 and of the queen in 1619. Knyvet died on 27 July 1622, and was buried with his wife at Stanwell, where there is a large monument, with effigies in the chancel of the church. He had married, at St. Pancras Church, Soper Lane, London, on 21 July 1597, Elizabeth, daughter of Sir Roland Hayward, and widow of Richard Warren of Essex. She died on 5 Sept. 1622; her two daughters predeceased her. By his will he left 20l. a year for a school for boys at Stanwell; he settled Stanwell on a nephew, John Cary, and on a niece, Catherine, who married as her second husband Thomas Howard, first earl of Suffolk, and whose seventh son was Edward, created lord Howard of Escrick [q. v.] Lord Knyvet must not be confounded with his cousin, Sir Thomas Knyvet of Buckenham, the head of the family, who was knighted on 11 May 1603.

[Lysons's Parishes in Middlesex not described in the Environs of London, 'Stanwell;' Gardiner's Hist. of England, i. 250; Cooper's Memorials of Cambridge, i. 374; Burke's Extinct Peerage; Davy's Suffolk Collections, lxii., Brit. Mus. Add. MS. 19138 (pedigree); Lodge's Illustr. of Brit. Hist. iii. 203; Wood's Fasti Oxon. ed. Bliss, i. 260; Jardine's Gunpowder Plot, p. 101; Gent. Mag. 1794, pt. i. 313 (tomb); Cal. of State Papers, Dom. 1603-23 (very few notices); Nichols's Progresses of King James, passim.] W. A. J. A.

KNYVETT, CHARLES (1752-1822), musician, descended from the family of Knyvet or Knyvett of Fundenhall, Norfolk, was born in 1752. He possessed a fine alto voice, and was one of the chief singers at the Handel commemoration of 1784. On 6 Nov. 1786 he was appointed gentleman of the Chapel Royal. In 1789, in partnership with Samuel Harrison, he directed a series of oratorio performances at Covent Garden. In 1791, again in partnership with Harrison, and with the additional assistance of his brother William, he established at Willis's Rooms the Vocal Concerts, which were successfully carried on for three years. On 25 July 1796 he was appointed organist of the Chapel Royal, vice Thomas Sanders Dupuis, deceased. In 1801, with the co-operation of his brother William, his son Charles, and Messrs. Greatorex and Bartleman, he revived the Vocal Concerts at the Hanover Square Rooms, but in the following year he withdrew from the management. In 1808 he resigned his post of gentleman of the Chapel Royal, and was succeeded by his son Charles. Knyvett was a member of the Royal Society of Musicians from 4 Jan. 1778. He was for many years secretary to the Noblemen's and Gentlemen's Catch Club, whose meetings were held at the Thatched House Tavern, St. James's Street, and he was a frequent visitor at the meetings of the Madrigal Society. For one season he replaced Joah Bates [q. v.] as conductor at the Concerts of Antient Music. He died in Blandford Street, Pall Mall, on 19 Jan. 1822, and was succeeded as organist of the Chapel Royal by Sir G. T. Smart. He had purchased an estate at Sonning in Berkshire.

Parke (Musical Memoirs, ii. 77, 236) states that he considered Knyvett ' one of the best singers of glees,' and ' perhaps the best catch singer in England.' Knyvett married in his twenty-first year, and had three sons, Charles (see below), William [q. v.], and one who entered the army.

His eldest son, CHARLES KNYVETT (1773–1852), born in 1773, was a chorister of Westminster Abbey under Sir William Parsons. He was educated at Westminster School, where he formed a close friendship with Lord Dudley and Ward which lasted until his death. He studied the organ and pianoforte under S. Webbe, and in 1802 was appointed organist of St. George's, Hanover Square. In 1801 he assisted his father in the revival of the Vocal Concerts. He died, after many years of retirement, on 2 Nov. 1852.

He published in 1815 ' Six Airs harmonised for three and four voices;' and also edited, in 1800, a 'Collection of favourite Glees, Catches, and Rounds presented by the Candidates for the Premiums given by the Prince of Wales in the year 1800.'

[Grove's Dict. of Music, ii. 67, iv. 319; Burke's Extinct Baronetage; Benrose's Choir Chant Book, App. p. xxiii; Gent. Mag. 1822 pt. i. 561; Georgian Era, iv. 536; Records of Royal Soc. of Musicians; Records of Madrigal Soc.; Chapel Royal Cheque Book; Cat. of Music in British Museum.] R. F. S.

KNYVETT, WILLIAM (1779–1856), musical composer, third son of Charles Knyvett (1752–1822) [q. v.], musician, was born on 21 April 1779, most probably in London, and educated by his father, by Samuel Webbe, the glee composer, and by Signor Cimador. In 1788 he sang in the treble chorus at the Concerts of Antient Music, and in 1795 appeared there as the principal alto. In 1797 he was appointed one of the gentlemen of the Chapel Royal, and soon after a lay vicar of Westminster Abbey. He succeeded Dr.

Samuel Arnold in 1802 as one of the composers of the Chapel Royal. In singing he took the alto or contra-tenor parts, invariably employing his falsetto, though nature had supplied him with a deep bass. He attached himself to the Harrison and Bartleman school, and became the third of a fashionable vocal triumvirate. For upwards of forty years he sang at the best London concerts and at the provincial festivals. Callcott's glee, ' With sighs, sweet Rose,' was composed expressly for him. In 1832, on the death of Thomas Greatorex, he became conductor of the Concerts of Antient Music, an office which he resigned in 1840. He was the conductor of the Birmingham festivals from 1834 to 1843, and of the York festival of 1835. With the exception of Sir George Smart, he was the last of the musical leaders who inherited the Handel traditions as to the method of conducting an oratorio. He produced vocal works that were very popular, many of which will be remembered for their sweet melody and good harmony. Among them were ' There is a flower,' ' My love is like the red, red rose,' 1803; ' The Bells of St. Michael's Tower,' 1810; ' The Bonnie Rows,' 1810; ' The Midges' Dance,' and ' As it fell upon a day,' 1812. He also wrote ' When the fair rose,' a glee for which he gained a prize at the Harmonic Society in 1800, presented to him by his steady patron, the Prince of Wales. Upwards of thirty-five of his compositions were printed. His unpublished works include the grand anthem, ' The King shall rejoice,' produced officially for the coronation of George IV, and ' This is the day the Lord has made,' written for the coronation of Queen Victoria.

Knyvett impoverished himself by unsuccessful speculations. He died at Clarges House, Ryde, Isle of Wight, 17 Nov. 1856. His second wife, whom he married in 1826, was Miss Deborah Travis of Shaw, near Oldham. She was celebrated in her day for her knowledge of Handel's music and her superior mode of delivering it. She sang at the Concerts of Antient Music in 1813 and at the principal London concerts from 1815 to 1843. She died on 10 Feb. 1876.

[Gent. Mag. 1857, pt. i. 621–2; Grove's Dictionary of Music, 1880, ii. 67; Champlin's Cyclopedia of Music, 1889, ii. 380.] O. C. B.

KŒHLER, GEORGE FREDERIC (d. 1800), brigadier-general, captain royal artillery, a German (cf. Gent. Mag. vol. lxxi. pt. i. p. 377), was appointed to a direct commission as second lieutenant in the royal artillery at Gibraltar during the siege on 20 Jan. 1780. The official records do not show clearly whether he had previously served there or arrived as a volunteer with Rodney's relief.

His subsequent British commissions were: first lieutenant royal artillery, 1 Dec. 1782; brevet-major, October 1793; captain-lieutenant royal artillery, 5 Dec. 1793; brevet-lieutenant-colonel, April 1794; captain royal artillery, 9 Dec. 1796; brevet-colonel, 1 Jan. 1800.

Kœhler distinguished himself during the defence of Gibraltar in 1782 by the invention of a gun-carriage allowing the axis of the gun to be depressed to an angle of seventy degrees, the model of which is now in the royal military repository, Woolwich. The accuracy of the fire was so great that at the first trial, on 15 Feb. 1782, twenty-eight shot out of thirty fired took effect in one traverse of the Spanish San Carlos battery, at a distance of fourteen hundred yards (DRINKWATER, p. 101). George Augustus Eliott, lord Heathfield (q. v.), the governor, who is said to have disliked Kœhler at first (BROWNE, p. 60), took him on his staff. In a letter to Sir Robert Murray Keith (q. v.), soon after the siege, Heathfield speaks of Kœhler, then at Pisa on his way to Vienna, as 'my most confidential aide-de-camp' (SMYTH, Memoirs and Corresp. of Keith, ii. 163).

Kœhler is stated to have been at one time in Turkey, probably during the war with Austria and Russia in 1788, and to have acquired the language. He afterwards accompanied Lord Heathfield to the continent, and was with him on his way to Aix-la-Chapelle when the Flemings began their attempt to throw off the Austrian yoke. They applied for the services of a skilled artillerist, and Heathfield, through Count Dillon, recommended Kœhler, who received the rank of colonel of artillery, and afterwards of major-general in the service of the Belgian united states. He commanded the patriot troops in repeated engagements with the Austrians in 1790, in one of which, at Ardennes, 13 July 1790, he speaks of the fighting as having lasted from 3 A.M. to 7 P.M. Kœhler's reports to the 'Sovereign Congress of the Belgian United States' were published at Brussels in 1790. Divided counsels frustrated the Belgian attempt, and Kœhler rejoined his company of artillery at Gibraltar, and served with it at Toulon in 1793. When the place was evacuated in December 1793, Kœhler was left with two hundred men in Fort Malgore to cover the embarkation and spike the guns, a service he successfully accomplished (DUNCAN, ii. 67-8).

With Gilbert Elliot, afterwards first Earl of Minto (q. v.), and Lieutenant-colonel (afterwards Sir John) Moore, Kœhler was sent in 1794 to Corsica to confer with General Paoli. Lord Minto has left an amusing ac-

count of the mission (Life and Letters, 1751-1806, ii. 211 et seq.) Kœhler was quartermaster-general of the British troops at the subsequent reduction of the French garrisons in Corsica (DUNCAN, ii. 68), and was afterwards assistant quartermaster-general of the north-eastern district of England, with headquarters at Newcastle-on-Tyne. When the French gained a footing in Egypt in 1798, a military mission of artillery and engineer officers, with detachments of royal artillery and royal military artificers, was sent to organise the Turkish army. Kœhler was placed at its head, with the local rank of brigadier-general. The mission arrived at Constantinople in June 1799, and in January 1800 Kœhler with some of his staff, disguised as Turks, proceeded overland to Syria, returning in April. On 15 Jan. 1800 the whole party proceeded to the seat of war in Syria, arriving at Jaffa on 2 July. At the grand vizier's request plans were prepared for the defence of Jaffa. Attended by a large body of Turkish troops, the mission made a sort of royal progress towards Jerusalem. Kœhler and his men were jealously watched, but prayers were read every day in the camp without molestation. A malignant fever, produced by the filthy surroundings, carried off Kœhler's wife on 14 Dec. 1800, and Kœhler was soon afterwards attacked, and died near Jaffa 29 Dec. 1800. The remainder of the party subsequently marched with the Turkish army to join the British troops in Egypt in 1801. A narrative of the mission was subsequently published by the medical officer in charge, Dr. W. Wittman.

Kœhler died intestate. The balance of Kœhler's estate (7,842l. 8s. 4d.) was in 1814 paid over to the crown. In 1820 one Christian Bauer of Cronberg, Hesse-Nassau, labourer, and Elizabeth his wife filed a bill in the (now abolished) exchequer court at Westminster claiming Kœhler's estate as surviving next of kin. It was stated that he was the only son of George Kœbler, native of Bingen, who had enlisted in the British artillery and been killed in the service of the East India Company. After long legal inquiries it was finally decided in 1859 by Vice-chancellor Kindersley that the sum was due to his legal representatives, certain persons of the names of Kœhler and Schmidt, and after an appeal to the House of Lords in 1861 the decision was confirmed, and the original sum, together with 14,429l. 12s. 6d. interest, was restored to these claimants.

[Kane's List of Officers, Royal Artillery (Woolwich, revised ed. 1869); Browne's England's Artillerymen (London, 1865); Drinkwater's Siege of Gibraltar (London, 1844 ed.); printed bulletins of the revolt in the Netherlands, indexed in Brit. Mus. Cat. under Kœhler's name, with the accounts in Ann. Reg. 1791, and Flemish MS., forming Brit. Mus. Addit. MS. 23058; Duncan's Hist. Royal Artillery (London, 1872), vol. ii.; Life and Letters of Gilbert Elliot, first Earl of Minto, 1751–1806 (London, 1874, 3 vols.), vol. ii.; Letter from Kœhler to the Marquis Wellesley in Wellesley Desp. vol. i.; W. Wittman's Travels in Turkey, &c. (London, 1802). See also Preston's Unclaimed Money (London, 1880); the Records of the Court of Exchequer and Court of Chancery in the Public Record Office, London, 1820–60: Bauer v. the Solicitor-general and the Attorney-general v. Köhler and others.]   H. M. C.

KOLLMAN, AUGUST FRIEDRICH CHRISTOPH (1756–1829), organist and composer, was born at Engelbostel, near Hanover, in 1756. His christian name is erroneously given by Fétis as 'August Friedrich Karl,' a mistake which is followed by Grove and Brown, and which is possibly due to a confusion with his brother, Georg Christoph Kollman, who was an organist of some repute in Hamburg. The correct form of the name is given in full upon the title-page of the original editions of three of Kollman's theoretical works. His father was schoolmaster and organist at Engelbostel. He received his first musical training at the hands of the pastor of the village, and at the age of fourteen was sent to school at Hanover for two years. He studied music and the organ under J. C. Büttner, and in 1779 was admitted to the normal school of the electorate of Hanover. Two years later he obtained the post of organist to a private chapel at Lune, near Lüneberg. On 9 April 1784 he was appointed chapel-keeper and schoolmaster at the German Chapel, St. James's Palace. From this time Kollman lived in London, and became an Englishman by adoption.

In 1792 George III presented an organ to the German Chapel, and Kollman played it until his death. He was a man of considerable vigour, and is said on the occasion of a fire in St. James's Palace in 1809 to have saved the German Chapel from destruction by standing in the doorway and preventing the firemen from entering it. During his later years he taught music in many noble families in London. He died on Easter day 1829. His son, George August, succeeded him as organist to the German Chapel, and he in his turn was succeeded by his sister, Johanna Sophia.

Kollman was the author of the following theoretical works: 1. 'An Introduction to the Art of Preludising and Extemporising,' London, 1791. 2. 'An Essay on Musical Harmony,' London, 1796. 3. 'An Essay on Practical Musical Composition,' London, 1799. 4. 'A Practical Guide to Thorough Bass,' London, 1801. 5. 'A Vindication of a Passage in the " Practical Guide " against an Advertisement of Mr. M. P. King,' London, 1802. 6. 'A New Theory of Musical Harmony,' London, 1806. 7. 'A Second Practical Guide to Thorough Bass,' London, 1807.

He instituted the 'Quarterly Musical Register,' London, 1812, of which only two numbers appeared. Some 'Remarks' of Kollman's upon Logier's system of teaching, which were originally contributed to the 'Allgemeine Musikalische Zeitung' of Leipzig, were collected and published in pamphlet form, together with remarks on the same subject by C. F. Müller, at Munich in 1822.

His published compositions include: 'The Shipwreck, or the Loss of the East Indiaman "Halsewell," an orchestral symphony' (programme music), London, 1787; 'The First Beginning on the Pianoforte, according to an Improved Method of Teaching Beginners,' Op. 5, London, 1796; 'An Analysed Symphony for the Pianoforte, Violin, and Bass,' Op. 3, London, 1799; 'Concerto for Pianoforte and Orchestra,' Op. 8, London, 1804; 'The Melody of the One Hundredth Psalm, with examples and directions for a hundred different harmonies in four parts,' Op. 9, London, 1809; 'Rondo on the Chord of the Diminished Seventh,' London, 1810; 'Twelve Analysed Fugues for Two Performers,' Op. 10, London, 1810, 2nd edit. 1823; 'An Introduction to Extemporary Modulation,' Op. 11, London, 1820; and several songs, sonatas, and other pianoforte pieces.

Kollman also edited an edition of Bach's 'Wohltemperirtes Clavier.'

[Grove's Dict. of Music, ii. 68, iv. 692; Fétis's Biog. Univ. des Musiciens, v. 81; Brown's Biog. Dict. of Music, p. 364; Kollman's works in Brit. Mus. Library.]   R. F. S.

KONIG or KÖNIG, CHARLES DIETRICH EBERHARD (1774–1851), mineralogist, was born in Brunswick in 1774, educated at Göttingen, and came to this country to arrange the collections of Queen Charlotte at the end of 1800. On the completion of this work he became assistant to Dryander, librarian to Sir Joseph Banks. In 1807 he succeeded Dr. Shaw as assistant-keeper of the department of natural history in the British Museum, and on the death of his superior in 1813 he took his place. Afterwards he turned his attention to minerals and fossils, and arranged the recently acquired collections of Mr. Greville. At the time of his sudden death, 6 Sept. 1851, in London, he had charge of the mineralogical department of the British Museum.

Besides various papers in journals, he was associated with Dr. Sims in the issue of 'Annals of Botany,' 1805 7.

[Athenæum, 1851, p. 954.] B. D. J.

KOTZWARA or KOCSWARA, FRANZ (1750?-1793), musician, of Bohemian origin, was born in Prague about 1750. He seems to have led a vagabond life in Germany and Holland previous to 1784, when he was attracted to England by the Handel commemoration in Westminster Abbey, in which he took part as a member of the band. He was subsequently in Ireland, but returned to London in 1791, when he was engaged by Giovanni Gallini [q. v.] as a double-bass player at the new Italian opera-house. He was about the same time engaged by various music-sellers to compose trios and quartets. His sonata, the 'Battle of Prague,' for pianoforte, violin, and violoncello (which is still performed), at once achieved popularity and success. He wrote also three sonatas for piano and violin, three for the piano alone, besides some serenades, and three solos for the viola. In the spring of 1792 he was travelling on the continent, and François Joseph Fétis, then a boy of eight years old, describes a visit which Kotzwara paid to his father at Mons. After Kotzwara had heard Fétis play a sonata of Mozart, he invited him to play at sight on the harpsichord his 'Battle of Prague.' Fétis's father accompanied him on the violin, and Kotzwara himself on the 'cello.

Kotzwara was very versatile, and played a great number of instruments with fluency if not distinction. He was, however, as dissipated as he was clever, and on 2 Feb. 1793 he was discovered hanging in a house of ill-fame in Vine Street, Covent Garden. He had been making experiments in hanging in the company of some half-drunken women, and his death was the result of an accident; the parties implicated were arrested, but were ultimately acquitted.

[Fétis, v. 380; Imperial Dict. of Biog. pt. xii. p.115; Reissmann's Musikalisches Conversations-Lexikon; Champlin's Cyclop. of Music, ii 388; Dictionary of Music (1827), ii. 24; Grove, ii. 69; Brown's Dict. of Musicians, p. 364. The five last-mentioned authorities all give the date of Kotzwara's death wrongly as 1791.] T. S.

KRABTREE. [See CRABTREE.]

KRATZER, NICHOLAS (1487-1550?), mathematician, was born at Munich, Bavaria, in 1487, and studied in the universities of Cologne and Wittemberg, graduating B.A. at the latter place. Coming to England he made the acquaintance of Richard Foxe, bishop of Winchester, who on 4 July 1517 appointed him to a fellowship in his newly founded college of Corpus Christi, Oxford, and on 20 Feb. 1522-3 he was incorporated B.A. He proceeded M.A. 18 March, when he was described in the 'University Register' as 'notissimus & probatissimus et in mathematicis et in philosophicis.' Kratzer lectured on astronomy in Oxford, and soon afterwards was appointed mathematical reader there by Cardinal Wolsey He was skilled in the construction of sun-dials, and erected two in Oxford, one in the garden of Corpus Christi, and another in the south churchyard of St. Mary's Church (removed in 1744). After the assembly of bishops and divines which met at Wolsey's house in 1521 had condemned Luther's doctrines, 'a testimony was sent to Oxford, and fastned on the Dial in St. Marys churchyard by Nich. Kratzer, the maker and contriver thereof.' Leland refers to this dial in his 'De Encomiis.'

In 1520 Kratzer was at Antwerp on a visit to Erasmus, where he met Albert Dürer, then on his famous journey to the Netherlands. On 12 Oct. 1520 Tunstal wrote to Henry VIII saying that he had met Kratzer at Antwerp, 'an Almayn deviser of the King's Horologes,' and he asked that he should be allowed to remain until the pending election of the emperor was over. 'Being,' Tunstal added, 'born in High Almayn, and having acquaintance of many of the Princes, he might be able to find out the mind of the Electors touching the affairs of the Empire' (Letters and Papers Henry VIII, iii. i. 1018). In the same year among Henry's payments appears the quarterly salary of 100l. to 'Nicholas Craser an Estronomyer' (ib. p. 408). Dürer drew Kratzer's portrait, but it is not known to be extant. On 24 Oct. 1524 Kratzer wrote to Dürer from London a letter asking him to draw him a model of an instrument for measuring distances, which is in the collection of Herr Lempertz at Cologne; the reply from Dürer to Kratzer is in the Guildhall Library in London. When Hans Holbein [q. v.] came to London, Kratzer was one of his earliest friends. Holbein painted a magnificent portrait of Kratzer at a table on which are many mathematical instruments: this picture is now at the Louvre, and was painted in 1528, when Kratzer was forty-one years of age. A good copy was lent by Viscount Galway to the Tudor Exhibition, 1890 (No. 129). In 1529 Kratzer was sent with Hugh Bozvell and Hans Bour to search the king's woods and mines in Cornwall and to try to melt the ore (*ib.* v. 314). Among Cromwell's 'Remembrances' for 1533 is an item 'To send to Nich. Cracher for the conveyance of Christopher Mount's letters.' Nicolas Bourbon, the French poet, in a letter to Thomas Soliman, the king's secretary, prefixed to Bourbon's 'Παιδαγωγεος,' Lyons, 1536, sends greetings among other friends, including Holbein, ' D. Nic. Cratzero regio astronomo, viro honestis salibus, facetiisque ac leporibus concreto.' Payments to Nicolas, the king's astronomer, frequently occur in the accounts of the royal household.

In the preface to Guido Bonatus's treatise on astronomy (Basel, 1550) Kratzer is praised as a mathematician, ' qui ita bonus & probus est ut majore quam mathematicorum fortuna sit dignus.' He died soon after 1550. Many of his books came into the hands of Dr. John Dee [q. v.] and Richard Forster.

Kratzer left two books in manuscript, copies of which are found in Corpus Christi (clii.) and the Bodleian (MS. 504) Libraries at Oxford. First, 'Canones Horopti,' dedicated to Henry VIII, with a concluding note to intimate that the subjects of his Oxford lectures were ' Astronomiam super sphæram materialem Johannis de Sacro Bosco, compositionem astrolabis, & geographiam Ptolemæi.' His second work, 'De Compositione Horologiorum,' contains ' (1) Compositio & utilitates quadrantis; (2) De arte metrica sive mensurandi; (3) Compositio cylindri & aliorum instrumentorum mathematicorum; (4) Scripta plurima mathematica per N. Kratz.' In the Cottonian MSS. is a letter from N. Kracerus to T. Cromwell, dated London, 24 Aug. 1538, and conveying information received from Germany about the Turks.

[Notes kindly supplied by Lionel Cust, esq., F.S.A.; Wood's Athenæ Oxon. i. 59, 62, 190, ii. 457; Tanner's Bibl. Brit. p. 460; Hessel's Eccles. Lond. Batav. Archiv. i. 3, 888–9; Wood's Hist. and Antiq. of Univ. of Oxford (Gutch), vol. ii. pt. ii. p. 830, pt. i. p. 19; Notes and Queries, 2nd ser. iii. 144; Leland, De Encomiis, ed. 1589, p. 19; Thausing's Albert Dürer's Life and Works (Engl. trans. 1882); Woltmann's Hollbein und Seine Zeit, 1874–6; Cusel van Mander's Livre des Peintres, ed. Hymans, 1884; Privy Purse Expenses of Henry VIII; Clark's Oxford Colleges, 1891.]   R. E. A.

KRAUSE, WILLIAM HENRY (1796–1852), Irish divine, was born on 6 July 1796 in the island of St. Croix, West Indies. At an early age he was brought to England, and placed for education in a school at Fulham, from which he was afterwards sent to another at Richmond. In 1814, having made up his mind to enter the army, he obtained a commission in the 51st light infantry, then in the south of France. Next year he was present at the battle of Waterloo. On the termination of the war he was placed on half-pay, and soon afterwards returned to St. Croix, where his father still resided. In 1822, being on a visit at the house of a brother officer in Ireland, he came under deep religious impressions and resolved to take holy orders. It was a long time, however, before he succeeded in receiving ordination. In 1826 he was appointed by the Earl of Farnham ' moral agent ' on his Irish estates, his duty being to look after the schools and endeavour to promote the religious and moral welfare of the tenantry. While discharging these functions with great zeal, he also entered himself at Trinity College, Dublin, and on 27 Feb. 1838 received the degree of M.A. On 26 March 1838 he was ordained for the curacy of Cavan by the Bishop of Kilmore, and for two years ministered most earnestly there. In 1840 he was appointed incumbent of the Bethesda Chapel, Dublin, and soon became one of the most noted of the evangelical clergy of that city. He died on 27 Feb. 1852. Three volumes of his ' Sermons' were published after his death (Dublin, 1859).

[Memoir by the Rev. C. S. Stanford, D.D., Dublin, 1854.]   T. H.

KUERDEN, RICHARD, M.D. (1623–1690?), antiquary. [See JACKSON.]

KUPER, SIR AUGUSTUS LEOPOLD (1809–1885), admiral, son of William Kuper, D.D., chaplain to Queen Adelaide, was born on 16 Aug. 1809. He entered the navy in April 1823, and after serving on the South American and Mediterranean stations was promoted to be lieutenant on 28 Feb. 1830. During the next seven years he served almost continuously on the home station and the coast of Spain or Portugal, and in July 1837 was appointed first lieutenant of the Alligator, with his father-in-law, Captain Sir James John Gordon Bremer [q. v.] He assisted Bremer in forming the settlement of Port Essington in North Australia, and on 27 July 1839 was promoted by him to the command of the Pelorus. In a violent hurricane at Port Essington the Pelorus was driven on shore, high and dry, and was got off with great difficulty and labour after eighty-six days. On 5 March 1840 Bremer, being then senior officer in India, appointed Kuper acting captain of the Alligator, and in June 1841 moved him to the Calliope, in which he was confirmed by the admiralty with seniority 5 June 1841. In the Alligator, and afterwards in the Calliope, he was actively employed during the first Chinese war, and was honourably mentioned for his conduct at the capture of Chusan in July 1840, at the reduction of the Bogue forts in February 1841, and in the operations leading up to the capitulation of Canton. In acknowledgment of his services during this period he was nominated a C.B. on 21 Jan. 1842. From 1850 to 1853 he commanded the Thetis frigate in the Pacific, and the London in the Mediterranean for a few months in 1855.

On 29 July 1861 he was promoted to be rear-admiral, and in the autumn of 1862 succeeded Sir James Hope [q. v.] as commander-in-chief in China, where affairs were still in a very unsettled state, owing to the rebellion of the Taepings. It was Kuper's first business to lead an expedition against them, to defeat them, and capture their stronghold Kahding on 23 Oct. 1862. He was quickly called away to arrange matters in Japan, where the great nobles were in a state of fierce excitement and indignation, consequent on the treaties with occidental nations and the threatened introduction of foreigners and foreign customs. On 14 Sept. 1862 a small party of English riding in the country was savagely attacked by the retainers of the Daimio of Satsuma, and one was killed. Reparation and compensation had been demanded both from the imperial government and from the Prince of Satsuma, and as they were not given, Kuper was requested to bring the squadron into the bay of Yokohama. He arrived there in March 1863, and under this threat, following the suspension of diplomatic relations, the Japanese government agreed to pay the 100,000l. demanded. But Satsuma proved less compliant, and on 14 Aug. the admiral brought the squadron before Kagosima. On the 15th three steamers belonging to the refractory prince were seized. Thereupon his batteries opened fire and were speedily silenced. The prince's palace was shelled, and by an accident the greater part of the town was burnt. On the 16th the prince submitted to the English demands.

The following year the Daimio of Nagato, whose batteries commanded the Straits of Simonoseki, the ordinary and most convenient channel into the inland sea, asserted his right to close the navigation to all foreigners. The French and Dutch squadrons, as well as one ship of the United States navy, made common cause with the English, and acted for the occasion under the orders of the English admiral. The ships opened fire at 4 P.M. on 5 Sept., and by the next day all the batteries had been silenced and stormed, despite the gallant fighting of the Japanese. On the 7th negotiations began, and it was soon agreed

that 'all ships of all countries passing through the Straits of Simonoseki shall be treated in a friendly manner.' The battle led not only to the opening of the inland sea, but to the downfall of the old 'country' party in Japan, and to a social and political revolution in the organisation of the empire.

In the course of 1865 Kuper returned to England. He had no further service. He had been nominated a K.C.B. on 25 Feb. 1864, in acknowledgment of his services at Kagosima; and on 2 June 1869 he was advanced to the grand cross of the order. On 6 April 1866 he became a vice-admiral, and admiral on 20 Oct. 1872. He died on 29 Oct. 1885. He married, in June 1857, Emma Margaret, eldest daughter of Sir Gordon Bremer, but had no issue.

[O'Byrne's Naval Biog. Dict.; Rennie's British Arms in China and Japan; Annual Register, 1863; Parl. Debates, 9 Feb. 1864; Correspondence respecting Affairs in Japan (Parl. Paper), 1864; Times, 16, 17, and 19 Nov. 1864.]

J. K. L.

KURZ, SULPIZ (1833?–1878), botanist, was a native of Munich, and a pupil of Martius the Brazilian traveller, and professor of botany. Having quarrelled with his family, he sailed to Java and entered the Dutch service, in which he stayed for several years. In 1864 he was induced by Dr. T. Anderson, who was visiting the Dutch possessions, to return with him to Calcutta as curator of the herbarium, which post he held till his death, to the great advantage of Indian botany. Kurz had an intimate acquaintance with Indian and Malayan plants, and was frequently despatched on botanical missions. He explored Burma and Pegu, and spent three months in the Andaman Islands, of which he gave an exhaustive report in 1870. His most extensive work is his 'Forest Flora of Burma,' Calcutta, 1877, 2 vols. 8vo, and many articles in the 'Journal of the Asiatic Society of Bengal' and the 'Journal of Botany.' He died at Pulo-Penang on 15 Jan. 1878, his death being probably hastened by neglect of the precautions needful when exploring tropical countries.

[Journ. Bot. 1878, p. 127; Jackson's Guide Lit. Bot. p. 397.]

B. D. J.

KYAN, ESMOND (d. 1798), Irish rebel, was a landowner, residing at Monamolin, near Oulart, co. Wexford, Ireland. On the outbreak of the rebellion in Wexford, early in 1798 Kyan joined the insurgents. He commanded the rebel artillery at the battle of Arklow, where he lost an arm. Owing to this wound he was compelled to remain for some time in Wexford itself. According to the unanimous authority of contemporary writers, Kyan distinguished himself by his efforts to prevent the massacre of loyalist prisoners by the rebels on Wexford bridge. After the fall of Wexford he joined a band of insurgents who tried to penetrate the county Carlow, and took a part in the last scenes of the war in the Wicklow mountains. On the suppression of the rebellion Kyan returned home in disguise to see his relatives, but was discovered and arrested. He was executed in July 1798, after a short trial before a court-martial.

[Webb's Compendium of Irish Biography; George Taylor's History of the Wexford Rebellion of 1798; Memoirs of Miles Byrne. See also Lecky's England during the Eighteenth Century, vol. viii.]   G. P. M-Y.

KYAN, JOHN HOWARD (1774–1850), inventor of the 'kyanizing' process for preserving wood, son of John Howard Kyan of Mount Howard and Ballymurtagh, co. Wicklow, was born in Dublin, Nov. 27, 1774. His father was the owner of valuable copper mines in Wicklow (now worked by the Wicklow Copper Mines Company), and for some time at the end of the last century worked them himself. The son was educated to take part in the management of the mines, but soon after he entered the concern its fortunes declined, and in 1804 his father died almost penniless. For a time Kyan was employed at some vinegar works at Newcastle-on-Tyne, but subsequently removed to London, to Greaves's vinegar brewery in Old Street Road. The decay of the timber supports in his father's copper mines had already directed his attention to the question of preserving wood, and as early as 1812 he began experiments with a view to discovering a method of preventing the decay. Eventually he found that bichloride of mercury, or corrosive sublimate, as it is commonly called, gave the best results, and, without revealing the nature of the process, he submitted a block of oak impregnated with that substance to the admiralty in 1828. It was placed in the 'fungus pit' at Woolwich, where it remained for three years exposed to all the conditions favourable to decay. When taken out in 1831, it was found to be perfectly sound, and after further trials it still remained unaffected. Kyan patented his discovery in 1832 (Nos. 6253 and 6309), extending the application of the invention to the preservation of paper, canvas, cloth, cordage, &c. A further patent was granted in 1836 (No. 7001). The preservative action of a solution of bichloride of mercury was previously well known, and Kyan's process merely consisted in the submersion of timber or other materials in a tank containing a solution of corrosive sublimate in water. It was maintained by the inventor that permanent chemical combination took place between the mercurial salt and the woody fibre, but this was contested. The process attracted great attention. Faraday chose it as the subject of his inaugural lecture at the Royal Institution on 22 Feb. 1833, on his appointment as Fullerian professor of chemistry. Dr. Birkbeck gave a lecture upon it at the Society of Arts on 9 Dec. 1834, and in 1835 the admiralty published the report of a committee appointed by the board to inquire into the value of the new method. In 1836 Kyan sold his rights to the Anti-Dry Rot Company, an act of parliament being passed which authorised the raising of a capital of 250,000*l*. Tanks were constructed at Grosvenor Basin, Pimlico, at the Grand Surrey Canal Dock, Rotherhithe, and at the City Road Basin. Great things were predicted of 'kyanising,' as the process then began to be called. A witty writer in 'Bentley's Miscellany' for January 1837 told how the muses had adopted Kyan's improvement to preserve their favourite trees. At a dinner given to celebrate the success which attended the experiment, a song, which became popular, was first sung. The opening verse runs:

Have you heard, have you heard
Anti-dry Rot's the word?
Wood will never wear out, thanks to Kyan, to
    Kyan!
He dips in a tank any rafter or plank,
And makes it immortal as Dinn, as Dian!

Among the early applications of the process was the kyanising of the palings round the Inner Circle, Regent's Park, which was carried out in 1835 as an advertisement, small brass plates being attached to the palings at intervals stating that the wood had been submitted to the new process. The plates soon disappeared, but the original palings still remain in good condition. The timber used in building the Oxford and Cambridge Club, British Museum, Royal College of Surgeons, Westminster Bridewell, the new roof of the Temple Church, and the Ramsgate harbour works was also prepared by Kyan's process. When wooden railway sleepers became general (in place of the stone blocks used on the early lines), a very profitable business for Kyan's company was anticipated, and for a time these hopes were realised. But it became evident that iron fastenings could not be used in wood treated with corrosive sublimate, on account of the corrosive action, and it was said that the wood became brittle. The salt was somewhat expensive, and Sir William Burnett's method of preserving timber by chloride of zinc, and afterwards the application of creosote for that purpose, proved severe competitors. Doubts began to be expressed as to the real efficiency of kyanising (see *Proceedings of the Institution of Civil Engineers*, 11 Jan. 1853, pp. 246-243), and the process gradually ceased to be employed.

Besides the invention with which his name is associated, Kyan took out patents in 1833 (No. 6554) for propelling ships by a jet of water ejected at the stern, and in 1837 (No. 7489) for a method of obtaining ammoniacal salts from gas liquor. He was also the author of 'The Elements of Light and their Identity with those of Matter radiant or fixed,' 1838. He died on 5 Jan. 1850 at New York, where he was engaged on a plan for filtering the water supplied to that city by the Croton aqueduct.

[Faraday's *Prevention of Dry Rot in Timber*, a Lecture at the Royal Institution on 22 Feb. 1833; Birkbeck's *Preservation of Timber by Kyan's Patent*, a Lecture at the Society of Arts on 9 Dec. 1834; Report of Admiralty Committee on Kyan's Process (Parl. Paper, No. 367 of 1835); An Act to enable John Howard Kyan to assign certain Letters Patent, 6 Will. IV, cap. 26, 1836; Burke's *Landed Gentry*, 4th edit. 1868; art. 'Kyan's Process' in Architectural Publication Society's *Dict. of Architecture*.] R. B. P.

KYD, ROBERT (*d.* 1793), founder of the Botanical Gardens, Calcutta, obtained a cadetship in 1764, was appointed ensign in the Bengal infantry 27 Oct. 1764, lieutenant 16 Oct. 1765, captain 3 April 1768, major 4 Sept. 1780, lieutenant-colonel 7 Dec. 1782. On the latter date he was appointed secretary to the military department of inspection in Bengal, which post he seems to have held until his death. He was a man of cultivated tastes, fond of botany and horticulture. About 1786 he laid out the Botanical Garden, near Calcutta, which was taken over by the company, and of which Dr. Roxburgh was appointed superintendent on Kyd's death. Sir Joseph Hooker, describing a visit to these gardens in 1848, has said that ' they have contributed more useful and ornamental tropical plants to the public and private gardens of the world than any other establishment before or since ' (*Himalayan Journals*, i. 3-4). Kyd died at Calcutta 26 May 1793.

Derozario (*Complete Monumental Register*) states that Kyd was buried in the old burial-ground of Fort William, under a flat marble slab level with the ground, on the right of the entrance. A memorial urn, executed by the sculptor, Thomas Banks, was put up in the centre of the gardens, where it still stands. Some of Kyd's letters to Warren Hastings are in the British Museum (Addit.

MSS. 29162 f. 311, 29171 f. 327, 29172 ff. 40, 424), and other letters are among Lord Braybrooke's manuscripts (*Hist. MSS. Comm. 8th Rep. i.* 250 sq.)

Writers on India sometimes confuse Robert Kyd with Lieutenant-general Alexander Kyd, Bengal engineers, who built the government dockyard at Kidderpur, near Calcutta, which village is named after him. Alexander Kyd was the author of some tidal observations on the Hooghly, and died in London 25 Nov. 1826.

[Information supplied by the India Office. As the Cadet Papers there commence in 1789, it has not been possible to get details of Kyd's parentage, &c. Hunter's *Gazetteer of Bengal*, vol. viii. (Kidderpur); Murray's *Handbook of Bengal*; Derozario's *Complete Monumental Register*, Calcutta, 1815.] H. M. C.

KYD, STEWART (*d.* 1811), politician and legal writer, a native of Arbroath, Forfarshire, went at the age of fourteen from Arbroath grammar school to King's College, Aberdeen. Abandoning a design of entering the church, he settled in London, and was called to the bar from the Middle Temple. He became a firm friend of Thomas Hardy [q. v.] and John Horne Tooke, whose political opinions he admired. In November 1792 he joined the Society for Constitutional Information. On 29 May 1794 he was arrested and examined by the privy council, but was soon discharged. On 4 June he was again summoned before the council, and three days later was committed to the Tower on a charge of high treason, with Hardy, Tooke, and ten others. On 25 Oct. all the prisoners were brought up for trial before a special commission at the Old Bailey, but after the acquittal of Hardy, Tooke, and Thelwall, the attorney-general declined offering any evidence against Kyd, and he was discharged. In June 1797 he ably defended Thomas Williams, a bookseller, who was indicted for blasphemy in publishing Paine's ' Age of Reason.' His speech was printed during the same year. Kyd died in the Temple on 26 Jan. 1811 (*Scots Mag.* lxxiii. 159). His portrait has been engraved.

Besides a continuation of Comyn's 'Digest' (8vo, London, 1792), Kyd published: 1. 'A Treatise on the Law of Bills of Exchange and Promissory Notes,' 8vo, London, 1790; 3rd edit. 1795; 2nd American edit., Albany, New York, 1800. 2. 'A Treatise on the Law of Awards,' 8vo, London, 1791; 2nd edit. 1799. 3. 'A Treatise on the Law of Corporations,' 2 vols. 8vo, London, 1793-4. 4. 'The Substance of the Income Act,' 8vo, London, 1799, two editions. 5. 'Arrangement under distinct Titles of all the Provisions of the several Acts of Parliament relating to the Assessed Taxes,' 8vo, London, 1799 (Postscript, 1801).

[Gent. Mag. 1811. pt. i. p. 190 ; Cobbett and Howell's State Trials, vols. xxiv. xxv. xxvi. ; Bridgman's Legal Bibliogr. ; Evans's Cat. of Engraved Portraits, vol. ii. ; Reuss's Reg. of Authors, 1790–1803, pt. i. p. 589 ; Rivers's Memoirs of Living Authors, i. 352–3 ; Notes and Queries, 6th ser. ii. 12.]   G. G.

KYD or KID, THOMAS (1557?–1595?), dramatist, appears to be identical with Thomas Kydd, the son of Francis Kydd, a London scrivener, who entered Merchant Taylors' School on 26 Oct. 1565 (ROBINSON, *Merchant Taylors' School Reg.* i. 9). John Kyd, apparently the dramatist's brother, was admitted a freeman of the Stationers' Company on 18 Feb. 1583–4 (ARBER, *Transcripts*, ii. 691). John published some pamphlets of news and popular narratives of exciting crimes, but very few of his publications are extant. He died late in 1592. Mention is made of his widow in the Stationers' Registers on 5 March 1592–3 (*ib.* i. 595, ii. 621).

The dramatist was well educated. He could write a rough sort of Latin verse, which he was fond of introducing into his plays, and he knew Italian and French sufficiently well to translate from both. He also gained a slight acquaintance with Spanish. He was probably brought up to his father's profession of scrivener or notary. But he soon abandoned that employment for literature, and thenceforward suffered much privation. Kyd's career doubtless suggested to Nashe (in his preface to GREENE's *Menaphon*, 1589) his description of those who, leaving 'the trade of noverint whereto they were born,' busy themselves with endeavours of art, pose as English Senecas, attempt Italian translations or twopenny pamphlets, and 'botch up a blank-verse with *ifs* and *ands*.' Of all these offences Kyd was guilty, although his blank-verse is undeserving of such summary condemnation, and marks an advance on earlier efforts. When Nashe proceeds to point out that Seneca's famished English followers imitate 'the Kidde in Aesop,' he is apparently punning on the dramatist's name.

Kyd's earliest published book was a rendering from the Italian of 'The Householders Philosophie, first written in Italian by that excellent orator and poet, Torquato Tasso, and now translated by T. K.,' London, 1588. (An imperfect copy is in the British Museum.) It is signed at the end after Kyd's manner, with his initials beneath a Latin pentameter, and is dedicated to 'Maister Thomas Reade.' In 1592 Kyd wrote for his brother, the publisher, a pamphlet describing a recent murder. The title ran, 'The Truethe of the most wicked and secret Murthering of John Brewen, Goldsmith, of London, committed by his owne wife.' This was licensed for the press on 22 Aug. 1592. A unique copy is at Lambeth, and it was reprinted in J. P. Collier's 'Illustrations of Early English Popular Literature' in 1863. Murderous topics were always congenial to the dramatist, and it is quite possible that he was also the author of the 'True Reporte of the Poisoninge of Thomas Elliot, Tailor, of London,' which his brother published at the same date.

But it was as a writer of tragedies which clothed blood-curdling incident in 'the swelling bombast of bragging blank-verse' (to use Nashe's phrase) that Kyd made his reputation. Two plays from his pen, with Hieronimo or Jeronimo, marshal of Spain, for their hero, achieved exceptional popularity. They are the best extant specimens of that 'tragedy of blood' in which Elizabethan playgoers chiefly delighted before Shakespeare revolutionised public taste. The one dealing with the earlier events in the career of Jeronimo or Hieronimo was not published till 1605, when it appeared anonymously in the only edition known with the title 'The First Part of Jeronimo. With the Warres of Portugall and the Life and Death of Don Andrea' (London, for Thomas Pauyer). The other piece, dealing with the murder of the hero's son Horatio, and the hero's consequent madness and death, was licensed for the press to Abel Jeffes in October 1592, under the title of 'The Spanish Tragedy of one Horatio and Bellimperia' (Horatio's lady-love), but the earliest extant copy is a second and revised edition of 1594 (British Museum), which bears the title, 'The Spanish Tragedie, containing the lamentable end of Don Horatio and Bellimperia, with the pitiful death of old Hieronimo. Newly corrected and amended of such grosse faults as passed in the first impression' (London, by Edward Allde). A later edition, printed by William White, is dated 1599. All impressions appeared anonymously, but the authorship is established by Thomas Heywood's incidental mention of 'M. Kid' as the writer of 'The Spanish Tragedy' in his 'Apology for Actors,' 1612 (*Shaksp. Soc.* 45), and there is adequate internal evidence for assigning 'The First Part of Jeronymo' to the same pen.

The date of the production of these pieces is only ascertained from two contemptuous references made by Ben Jonson to their stubborn hold on popular favour. In 1600, in the induction to 'Cynthia's Revels,' Jonson assigns above a dozen years to the age of 'the old Hieronimo as it was first acted ;' and writing in 1614, in the induction to his 'Bartholomew Fair,' he declares that those who still commend 'Jeronymo, or Andronicus,' represent the popular opinion of 'five-and-twenty or thirty years' back. The pieces, it may therefore be stated with certainty, first saw the light between 1584 and 1586. There is nothing to show which of the two plays should claim precedence in point of time. In Henslowe's 'Diary' (p. 21), mention is first made under date 23 Feb. 1591-2 of the performance of the 'Spanes Comodye —Donne Oracoe,' doubtless an ignorant description of 'The Spanish Tragedy.' This play was far more popular than its companion, and it is quite possible that after its success was assured 'The First Part of Jeronimo' was prepared, in order to satisfy public curiosity respecting the hero's earlier life. Throughout 1592 Henslowe confusedly records performances of 'Don Oracoe,' 'The Comodey of Jeronymo,' and 'Jeronymo,' the first two titles being applied indifferently to 'The Spanish Tragedy,' and the third title to 'The First Part.' Contrary to expectation, 'The First Part' seems to have been usually played on the night succeeding that on which 'The Spanish Tragedy' was represented. Dekker, in his 'Satiromastix,' insinuated that Ben Jonson was the creator of the hero's rôle, but according to the list of Burbage's chief characters supplied in the 'Elegy' on his death, the part was first played by that actor, and was one of his most popular assumptions.

The title-page of a new edition of 'The Spanish Tragedy' in 1602 described it as enlarged, 'with new additions of the Painter's part and others, as it hath of late been divers acted.' The new scenes exhibit with masterly power the development of Hieronimo's madness, and their authorship is a matter of high literary interest. Despite the abuse lavished on 'the old Hieronimo' by Ben Jonson, and despite the superior intensity of the added scenes to anything in Jonson's extant work, there is some reason for making him responsible for them. Charles Lamb, who quoted the added scenes—'the salt of the old play' —in his 'Specimens of English Dramatic Poets,' detected in them the agency of some more potent spirit than Jonson, and suggested Webster. Coleridge wrote that 'the parts pointed out in Hieronimo as Ben Jonson's bear no traces of his style, but they are very like Shakespeare's' (*Table Talk*, p. 191). On the other hand Henslowe supplies strong external testimony in Jonson's favour. On 25 Sept. 1601 he lent Jonson 2*l*. 'upon his writings of his adicions in Geronymo,' and on 24 June 1602 he advanced 10*l*. to the same writer 'in earneste of a boocke called Richard Crockbacke, and for new adicyons for Jeronymo' (HENSLOWE, *Diary*, pp. 202, 223). Later editions of the revised play were issued in 1610, 1611, 1623, and 1633.

Many external proofs of the popularity of 'Jeronimo' are accessible. Between 1599 and 1628 at least seven editions appeared of a ballad founded on the play and entitled 'The Spanish Tragedy, containing the lamentable murders of Horatio and Bellimperia: with the pitiful death of old Hieronimo. To the tune of Queen Dido. In two parts . . . printed at London for H. Gosson.' A curious woodcut adorns the publication (*Roxburghe Ballads*, ii. 454 sq.) Before 1600 a portion of the play was adapted to the German stage by Jacob Ayrer, in his 'Tragedia von dem Griegischen Keyser zu Constantinopel vnd seiner Tochter Pelimberia, mit dem geheugten Horatio' (*Opus Theatricum*, i. 177; TIECK, *Altdeutsches Theater*, i. 200; COHN, *Shakespeare in Germany*, p. lxv). In 1608 A. van den Berghen published at Amsterdam a Dutch version, 'Don Jeronimo Maerschalck van Spanien, Treurspiel,' which was republished in 1683. At home Richard Brathwaite stated, in his 'English Gentlewoman' in 1631, that a lady 'of good rank' declined the consolations of religion on her deathbed, and died exclaiming 'Hieronimo, Hieronimo, O let me see Hieronimo acted!' Prynne, when penning his 'Histriomastix' in 1637, found in this story a convenient text for moralising. Two of Hieronimo's expressions—'What outcry calls me from my naked bed!' his exclamation on being roused to learn the news of his son's death, and the warning which he whispers to himself when he thinks he has offended the king, 'Beware, Hieronimo, go by, go by'—were long used as expletives in Elizabethan slang. Kit Sly quotes the latter in the vernacular form, 'Go by, Jeronimy,' in Shakespeare's 'Taming of the Shrew' (cf. HOLYDAY, *Shoemaker's Holiday*, 1600); while as late as 1640 Thomas Rawlins, in his 'Rebellion,' introduces derisively, 'Who calls Jeronimo from his naked bed?' amid many parodies of Kyd's grandiloquence. Ben Jonson was never weary of ridiculing both the bombastic style of Kyd's masterpiece and the vulgar taste which applauded it. In his 'Every Man in his Humour' and his 'Poetaster' a number of 'its fine speeches' are quoted with bitter sarcasm.

The sole play to which Kyd set his name was a translation of a French tragedy by Robert Garnier. On 26 Jan. 1593-4 'a booke called Cornelia, Thomas Kydde being the author,' was licensed for publication. It appeared in 1594 anonymously, but a dedication to the Countess of Sussex is signed

'T. K.,' and the title-page of a new edition of 1595 runs: 'Pompey the Great his faire Cornelias Tragedie: effected by her father and husbandes downecast, death, and fortune . . . translated into English by Thomas Kid,' London (Nich. Ling), 1593, 4to. In his dedication the author writes that he endured 'bitter times and privy broken passions' in writing the piece, and promises to deal hereafter with Garnier's 'Portia' ('Porcie'), a promise never fulfilled. 'Cornelia' follows the Senecan model, and is very tedious. The speeches in blank-verse are inordinately long, and the rhymed choruses show little poetic feeling. Unlike 'The Spanish Tragedy,' the piece seems to have met with a better reception from cultured critics than from the general public. In 1594 the author of an 'Epicedium' on Lady Helen Branch, who is doubtfully identified with Sir William Herbert, d. 1593 (q. v.), bestowed equal commendation on Shakespeare, the poet of 'Lucretia,' and on him who 'pen'd the praise of sad Cornelia.' A year later William Clerke, in his 'Polimanteia,' wrote that 'Cornelia's Tragedy, however not respected, was excellently well done.'

On strong internal evidence Kyd has been credited with two more anonymous tragedies of the 'Jeronimo' type, closely resembling each other in plot. One, first printed by Edward Allde for Edward White in 1589, was entitled 'The Rare Triumphs of Love and Fortune,' and may be identical with 'A History of Love and Fortune' which was acted at court before 23 Dec. 1582. Collier reprinted it for the Roxburghe Club in 1851. The other piece was 'The Tragedye of Solyman and Perseda. Wherein is laid open Loves Constancy, Fortunes Inconstancy, and Deaths Triumphs.' The play was licensed for the press to Edward White on 20 Nov. 1592, but an edition dated 1599, printed, like 'Love and Fortune,' by Allde for White, is the earliest extant, and in some copies is described as 'newly corrected and amended.' The plot is drawn from H. W.'s 'A Courtlie Controversie of Cupids Cautels,' 1578, which Collier assigns to Wotton, and the dramatist's description of the beauty of the heroine Persida is partly borrowed from a sonnet in Watson's 'Ekatompathia,' 1582. Kyd makes the whole story the subject of the play with which Hieronimo entertains the Spanish court in 'The Spanish Tragedy.' Greene refers familiarly to the leading theme, 'the betrothed faith of Ernsto to his Persida,' in both his 'Mamillia,' 1583, and his 'Gwydonius,' 1587, and the tragedy was probably written in the former year. Its popularity is attested by Shakespeare's direct allusion in 'King John' (i. 1, 244) to its comic exposure of the cowardice of Basilisco, a vainglorious knight (ed. Dodsley, v. 272).

Other plays have been attributed to Kyd on less convincing grounds. Malone believed that he had a hand in the 'Taming of a Shrew,' 1594, whence Shakespeare adapted his well-known comedy, and in 'Titus Andronicus,' which recalls 'The Spanish Tragedy' in some of its revolting incidents, and is alluded to by Jonson in close conjunction with 'Jeronimo.' But in neither case is the internal evidence strong enough to admit of a positive conclusion. Mr. Fleay's theory that he wrote 'Arden of Feversham' is unsatisfactory. But the argument in favour of Kyd's authorship of a pre-Shakespearean play (now lost) on the subject of Hamlet deserves attention. Nashe in 1589, when describing the typical literary hack, who at almost every point suggests Kyd, notices that in addition to his other accomplishments 'he will afford you whole Hamlets, I should say, handfuls of tragical speeches.' Other references in popular tracts and plays of like date prove that in an early tragedy concerning Hamlet there was a ghost who cried repeatedly 'Hamlet revenge!' and that this expression took rank, beside the quotations from 'Jeronimo,' in Elizabethan slang (cf. HALLIWELL-PHILLIPPS, Memoranda on Hamlet, pp. 7-21). The resemblance between the stories of 'Hamlet' and 'Jeronimo' suggests that the former would have supplied Kyd with a congenial plot. In 'Jeronimo' a father seeks to avenge his son's murder, in 'Hamlet' the theme is the same, with the position of father and son reversed. In 'Jeronimo' the avenger resolves to reach his end by arranging for the performance of a play with those whom he suspects of the crime, and there is good ground for crediting the lost tragedy of 'Hamlet' with a similar play-scene. Shakespeare's debt to the lost tragedy is a matter of conjecture, but the stilted speeches of the play-scene in his 'Hamlet' read like intentional parodies of Kyd's bombastic efforts in 'The Spanish Tragedy,' and it is quite possible that they were directly suggested by an almost identical episode in a lost 'Hamlet' by the same author.

Kyd's reputation as one of the best-known tragic poets of his time, and his close personal relations with the leading dramatist, Marlowe, strengthen the assumption that he was directly concerned in the composition of many popular anonymous plays. Immediately after Marlowe's death in 1593 he was charged with holding scandalous opinions regarding morality and religion. According to memoranda made from contemporary documents concerning that charge, and now preserved among Thomas Baker's manuscripts (MS. Harl. 7042, f. 401), 'one Mr. Thomas Kydde had been accused to have consorted with and to have maintained Marlowe's opinions, who seems to have been innocent, and wrote a letter to the lord keeper Puckering to purge himself from these aspersions.' Sir Walter Ralegh was similarly involved in these proceedings, but no further clue to them seems accessible.

Kyd is said to have died in poverty in 1595. His name was remembered long afterwards. In Clerke's 'Polimanteia' (1595) he is numbered among the chief tragic poets; in Meres's 'Palladis Tamia' (1598) mention is made of him among the best writers 'for tragedy.' Ben Jonson, in his elegy on Shakespeare (1623), points out Shakespeare's superiority to 'Sporting Kyd and Marlowe's mighty line;' the punning epithet 'sporting' is derisively inappropriate. Heywood writes of 'Famous Kid' in his 'Hierarchie of Blessed Angels' (1635), and Dekker speaks of 'Industrious Kyd' in his 'Conjuring Knight.' Quotations from Kyd's works figure in Allot's 'England's Parnassus' and in Bodenham's 'Belvedere' (1600).

The four plays, 'The First Part of Jeronimo,' 'The Spanish Tragedie,' 'Cornelia,' and 'Solyman and Perseda,' are reprinted in Dodsley's 'Old Plays,' ed. Hazlitt, vols. iv. and v.

[Some useful notes on Kyd's biography, with a discussion of the authorship and date of Solyman and Perseda, appear in Englische Studien, xv. pt. ii. (by G. Sarrazin), xvi. pt. iii. pp. 238 sq. (by E. Koeppel). For Kyd's relations with both the old play of Hamlet and Shakespeare's tragedy see Anglia (neue Folge, i. 117 sq., by G. Sarrazin). See also Fleay's Biographical Chronicle of the English Drama, ii. 26 sq.; Dodsley's Old Plays, ed. Hazlitt, vols. iv. v.; Nares's Glossary. ed. Halliwell; Greene's Menaphon, with Nashe's preface, ed. Grosart; Notes and Queries, iv. i. 462; Halliwell's Dict. of Plays; Collier's reprints of Kyd's tract on Brewen and of Love and Fortune (Roxb. Club), 1851; Henslowe's Diary, ed. Collier; Hunter's manuscript Chorus Vatum.]   S. L.

KYDERMYNSTER.   [See KEDERMYSTER.]

KYFFIN, MAURICE (d. 1599), poet and translator, was the second son of Richard Kyffin of Glasgoed, in the parish of Llansilin, Denbighshire (WILLIAMS, Eminent Welshmen, 1852, p. 270). In 1587 he published 'The Blessednes of Brytaine, or a Celebration of the Queenes Holyday. . . . Composed, and set foorth, in due Reuerence, and joyfull Memoriall, of her Maiesties present entrance into the Thirtieth yeere of her most triumphant raigne,' &c., 4to, London, of which a reprint was issued by the Cymmrodorion So-

ciety in 1885, from a copy then supposed to be unique in the Lambeth Palace Library. There is, however, a second but much mutilated copy in Archbishop Harsnett's Library at Colchester; Cat. of Harsnett Library, 1888, pp. xxxi-ii, 95). An inaccurate reprint had previously appeared in Huth's 'Fugitive Tracts in Verse,' 1st series, 1875. This fine piece of versification is a eulogy on the government of Queen Elizabeth, and an exhortation to loyalty, provoked, as it would seem, by Babington's conspiracy, in which two Welshmen were implicated. A second edition was issued in 1588 'newly set foorth with a New Addition containing the late Accidents and Occurrents of this yeere 88,' of which the only two copies known are those in the British Museum and Huth Library (Cat. of Huth Library, iii. 10-11). Kyffin, in dedicating his poem to the Earl of Essex, gratefully refers to the kindnesses received by his deceased father at the hands of the earl's grandfather and father. In the same year appeared his prose translation of the 'Andria' of Terence, 4to, London, 1588. He had nearly finished, but abandoned, a translation in verse. The tone of his dedicatory epistles to William, Henry, and Thomas Sackville, sons of Lord Buckhurst, makes it clear that he had been their tutor. In May 1592 Kyffin held the office of vice-treasurer of Normandy (Cal. State Papers, Dom. 1591–4, p. 219). In 1594 or 1595 he issued his Welsh translation of Bishop Jewel's 'Apologia pro Ecclesia Anglicana,' a work remarkable for its pure idiomatic diction. It was republished in 1671 by Charles Edwards of Rhydycroesau, and again in 1808 by T. Charles of Bala. In his preface Kyffin announced his intention of making a translation of the Psalms into Welsh verse, which, however, never appeared. He seems to have died unmarried in 1599, as on 20 April of that year administration of his estate (with will annexed) was granted by commission to his brother Edward Kyffin, 'preacher,' his cousin William Meredith first renouncing executorship of the will (registered in P.C.C. 31, Kidd). Kyffin was a devout believer in astrology, and bequeathed 10l. to John and Jane Dee of Mortlake; he also left 5l. to Hugh Broughton 'towards the printinge and publishinge of some of his observacōns on the Bible.' There are commendatory verses by him before Sir Lewis Lewkenor's translations of Olivier de la Marche's 'The Resolved Gentleman,'1594, and of Contarini's 'Commonwealth and Government of Venice,' 1599. An anonymous tract entitled 'A Defence of the Honorable Sentence and Execution of the Queene of Scots,' 4to, London,

1587, has been wrongly assigned to Kyffin (J. P. COLLIER, *Bibliographical and Critical Account*, ii. 207–8). Gabriel Harvey mentions Kyffin with respect in his 'Pierces Supererogation,' 1593 (p. 194 of Collier's reprint).

[Hunter's *Chorus Vatum* (Addit. MS. 24488, f. 382); Rowlands's *Cambrian Bibliography*; Cat. Advocates' Library, iv. 391; Baker's Biog. Dram. 1812, i. 442, ii. 38; Notes and Queries, 2nd ser. xii. 5, 142.]   G. G.

KYLE, JAMES FRANCIS, D.D. (1788–1869), Scottish catholic prelate, born at Edinburgh on 22 Sept. 1788, was received into the seminary of Aquhorties, on the banks of the Don, in Aberdeenshire, on 23 Oct. 1799; was appointed professor in that seminary in 1808, and was ordained priest in 1812. He remained at Aquhorties till January 1826, when he was sent to St. Andrew's, Glasgow. On 13 Feb. 1827 papal briefs were issued appointing him bishop of Germanicia, *in partibus*, and vicar-apostolic of the newly formed northern district of Scotland. He was consecrated at Aberdeen 28 Sept. 1828 by Dr. Penswick, vicar-apostolic of the northern district of England, assisted by Bishops Paterson and Scott. He died at Preshome, in the Enzie of Banff, on 23 Feb. 1869.

Kyle collected many early documents, some formerly in the Scots College, Paris, relating to the history of catholicism in Scotland. He computed that his letters and papers connected with the ecclesiastical history of Scotland from about 1597 to a comparatively modern period amounted to thirty thousand. Kyle also supplied Prince Labanoff with valuable materials for his 'Collection of the Letters of Queen Mary of Scotland.' Kyle's collections are now in the library at Buckie, on the coast of Moray Firth, together with volumes of materials, collected either by Kyle himself or under his directions, for a history of the catholic religion in Scotland since the Reformation.

[Brady's *Episcopal Succession*, iii. 474; Catholic Directory, 1891, p. 62; Hist. MSS. Comm. 1st Rep. 120; London and Dublin Orthodox Journal, 1837, iv. 121; Register and Magazine of Biography, i. 290; Stothert's Catholic Mission in Scotland, pp. 509, 643.]   T. C.

KYLMINGTON or KYLMETON, RICHARD (d. 1361), dean of St. Paul's and theologian, was educated at Oxford, where he graduated as doctor of divinity before 1339. He was afterwards a clerk of Richard de Bury (WHARTON, *De Episc. Lond.* p. 221), and seems to have been a friend of Richard Fitzralph [q. v.] In July 1339 he was employed in the embassy sent to negotiate with Philip of France (*Fœdera*, iii. 1084,

Record ed.) On 18 March 1348 he was appointed archdeacon of London, which position he held for two years. In 1353 he was made dean of St. Paul's (LE NEVE, *Fasti Eccl. Angl.* ii. 311, 321). He died in 1361, and was buried in St. Paul's Cathedral. Kylmington is memorable for his share in the controversy on evangelical poverty between Richard Fitzralph, archbishop of Armagh, and Roger of Conway [q. v.] the Franciscan. According to Wood, Kylmington was the first to oppose Conway (*Hist. and Antiq. Univ. Oxford*, i. 475, ed. Gutch). Kylmington's contributions to the controversy were: 1. 'Pro Armachano contra fratres,' inc. 'Quod dominus archiepiscopus Armachanus.' 2. 'Contra Rogerum Conway,' inc. 'Licet ex responsione Armacbani mei.' 3. 'Contra mendicitatem otiosam.' None of these seem to be extant. His other writings were: 4. 'Sermo de Adventu Domini' (*Bodleian MS.* Auct. F. inf. 1.21: this manuscript also contains some seventy other anonymous sermons. 5. 'Opuscula Logica,' in manuscript at St. Peter's College, Cambridge, No. 37 (BERNARD, *Cat. MSS. Angliæ*, ii. 140). 6. 'Quæstiones Theologicæ.' 7. 'De generatione ac corruptione.' Leland calls him 'most Aristotelian;' in Bodleian MS. Auct. F. inf. 1.2, he is spoken of as 'fratribus mendicantibus infensissimus.' His name appears in a variety of different forms, Kilmyngton, Chillington, Kylcyngton, Chelmeston.

[Leland's Comment. de Script. Brit. p. 455; Bale, v. 95; Pits, p. 499; Tanner's Bibl. Brit.-Hib. p. 990; Wharton, De Episcopis et Decanis Londinensibus, p. 221.]   C. L. K.

KYMER, GILBERT (d. 1463), dean of Salisbury and chancellor of the university of Oxford, was educated at Durham College, on the site of which the present Trinity College stands. He graduated as master of arts and philosophy, bachelor of laws, and doctor of medicine previously to 1420 (TANNER). In 1412–13 he served the office of proctor, and from 1412 to 1414 was principal of Hart Hall. On 16 Dec. 1420, being still a layman, he was presented to the living of Latterworth, Leicestershire, by William, lord Ferrers of Groby; this preferment he resigned in 1422. In 1427 he became dean of Wimborne Minster; on 28 June of that year was appointed treasurer of Salisbury, and on 28 Feb. 1427–8 was ordained sub-deacon by William, bishop of London, and priest on 29 May following. In 1431 he was chosen chancellor of the university, and held office two years. On 12 Feb. 1434 he was presented to St. Martin's Vintry, London (NEWCOURT, *Repertorium*, i. 422), and previously to 1447 became prebendary of Wells and Gillingham and rector of Fordingbridge, Hampshire (*Munimenta Acad.* ii. 575). In 1446 he once more became chancellor of Oxford, and on this occasion retained his office for seven years, resigning on 11 May 1453. In 1447 he was one of those who became sureties for the carrying out of Cardinal Beaufort's bequest for the building of the new schools at Oxford (*ib.* ii. 568). In 1451 he is described as of Coventry Hall in St. Martin's parish (WOOD, *Hist. and Antiq.* App. p. 53). On 16 June 1449 he was elected dean of Salisbury, and died in that city on 16 May 1463. He was buried in the cathedral, having made a bequest for the endowment of a chantry. There is an effigy of him, with a Latin inscription, in a window of the south transept.

Kymer was a physician of reputation, and in that capacity attached to the household of Humphrey, duke of Gloucester, whom he probably induced to give his library to Oxford. In June 1455 he was called in to attend Henry VI at Windsor (*Fœdera*, ix. 366, orig. edit.) Kymer was author of a treatise which he addressed to Duke Humphrey, 'Dietarium de Sanitatis Custodia.' Two chapters of the work, together with the titles of the remainder, were published by Hearne in the appendix to his 'Liber Niger Scaccarii,' pp. 550–9. It exists in manuscript in Sloane MS. 4, ff. 63–98, in the British Museum. The treatise was written in 1424 in Hainault, whither Kymer had no doubt accompanied Duke Humphrey (*Lib. Nig. Scacc.* Pref. pp. xxxiv and 559).

[Tanner's Bibl. Brit.-Hib. p. 461; Le Neve's Fasti Eccl. Angl. ii. 616, 646, iii. 467, 489, 582; Munimenta Academica (Rolls Ser.); Aubrey and Jackson's Wiltshire, p. 386; Maxwell Lyte's Hist. Univ. Oxf. pp. 319, 337.] C. L. K.

KYNASTON, EDWARD (1640?–1706), actor, son of Edward Kynaston or Kinaston, was born in London about 1640, and was apparently related to the Kynastons of Oteley in Shropshire. According to Downes and Gildon, he was Betterton's under-apprentice at the sign of the Bible, a bookseller's shop in Charing Cross. The shop was kept by one Rhodes, who had been a wardrobe-keeper to the king's company of comedians before the civil wars, and who in the year before the Restoration set up a company in the Cockpit in Drury Lane, where Kynaston first appeared in women's parts in 1659 [see BETTERTON, THOMAS]. Kynaston probably left Rhodes's company when it migrated from the Cockpit to Salisbury Court. It is not known precisely when this occurred, but it is certain that Kynaston was acting with the more distinguished company known as 'Old Actors' at the Cockpit on 18 Aug. 1660,

when Pepys saw him play a female part in the 'Loyal Subject,' and says 'he made the loveliest lady that ever I saw in my life,' adding, 'after the play Kinaston and another by Captain Ferrars' means came and drank with us.' Some of the female parts played by Kynaston at this time were Arthiope in the 'Unfortunate Lovers,' the Princess in the 'Mad Lover,' Aglaura in Suckling's play of that name, and Ismenia in the 'Maid of the Mill.' Shortly after this he was engaged with other of the 'Old Actors' in Thomas Killigrew's famous company of 'his majesty's servants,' who from 8 Nov. 1660 played in the theatre at Vere Street. Here on 7 Jan. 1661 Kynaston appeared as Epicœne in the 'Silent Woman,' and somewhat later as Evadne in the 'Maid's Tragedy.' Pepys saw him double a male and female part in the same month, and declares that he made successively the handsomest man and the prettiest woman in the house. It is often asserted that Kynaston was the queen on the occasion when, in reply to the king's inquiry why the actors were not ready, the master of the company 'fairly told his majesty that the queen was not shaved' (see BELJAME, *Le Public et les Hommes de Lettres en Angleterre*, p. 33). This is, it would appear, only an inference, from the fact that Cibber relates the anecdote when speaking of Kynaston, but it is certain that Kynaston was, with James Nokes or Noke [q. v.], the last male actor of female parts, as he was not improbably the best. His forte consisted in moving compassion and pity, 'in which,' says Downes, 'it has since been disputable among the judicious whether any woman that succeeded him so sensibly touched the audience as he.' At the same time 'he was,' says Cibber, 'so beautiful a youth that the Ladies of Quality prided themselves in taking him with them in their Coaches to Hyde Park in the theatrical Habit after the Play' (*Apology*, ed. Lowe, i. 119–21).

Kynaston's first important male part was Peregrine in the 'Fox,' which he played with the king's company at their new theatre in Covent Garden on 14 Jan. 1665. Other important parts played by him at the Theatre Royal between this date and 1682 were: Harcourt in the 'Country Wife,' 1673; Freeman in the 'Plain Dealer,' 1674; Morat in 'Aurengzebe,' 1675; Scipio in 'Sophonisba,' 1676; Cassander in the 'Rival Queens,' 1677; and Cassio in 'Othello,' 1682. Although his personal beauty and imperious mien made him a general favourite, his conceit could hardly fail to make him some enemies. He was particularly vain of his personal resemblance to one of the chief wits and beaux of the time, Sir Charles Sedley, whose dress and demeanour he imitated as closely as possible. Sedley, to show his resentment of what he considered a gross insult, hired a bravo to chastise the actor in St. James's Park in the spring of 1668, under the pretext that he mistook him for the baronet. Some time later Sedley, for the further instruction of Kynaston, introduced the incident into his play, 'The Mulberry Garden,' acted on 18 May 1668. The actor, however, was so far from taking the hint that he proceeded to impersonate Sedley on the stage, with the result that on the night of 31 Jan. 1668–9 ' he was exceedingly beaten with sticks by two or three men who saluted him, so that he is mightily bruised and forced to keep his bed' (PEPYS, v. 103). 'They say,' continues Pepys, ' that the king is very angry with Sir Charles Sedley for his being beaten, but he do deny it.' In spite of this severe treatment Kynaston was able to appear on 9 Feb., when Pepys saw him in the 'Island Princess.'

On 14 Oct. 1681 a memorandum was signed by Hart and Kynaston of the king's company, with Davenant, Betterton, and Smith of the Duke's Theatre, by which the two former, for a consideration of 5s. each for every day on which there should be a play at Dorset Garden, undertook to do everything in their power to break up the king's company. The object of the intrigue was to counteract the declining support from which both the patent theatres were at the time suffering. In the result a union between the two houses was formed on 16 Nov. 1682, when at the Theatre Royal Kynaston played the King of France to Betterton's Duke in Dryden's 'Duke of Guise.' Between this date and 1685, when he followed Betterton to Lincoln's Inn Fields, his most important parts were Sir Philip Luckless in the 'Northern Lass,' and Mark Anthony in 'Julius Cæsar,' with Betterton, Mountfort, Jevon, Underhill, and Leigh in the cast, 1684; Lord Bellgard in Crowne's 'Sir Courtly Nice,' 1685; Belmour in 'Lucky Chance,' and King of Tidore in Tate's 'Island Princess,' 1690; Sir Thomas Delamore in 'Edward III,' and Duke of Guise in D'Urfey's 'Bussy d'Ambois,' 1691. In 1693 he was prevented by illness from playing Lord Touchwood in Congreve's 'Double Dealer' before Queen Mary, and was replaced by Colley Cibber (q.v. (STRICKLAND, Queens, vii. 405).

At fifty Kynaston's powers were in no way impaired, and he was, says Genest, ' remarkable for a piercing eye and a quick impetuous vivacity in his voice, which painted the Tyrant truly terrible, particularly in Morat and Muley Moloch in "Don Sebastian," while in "Henry IV," when he whispered to Hot-spur, "Send us your prisoners, or you'll hear of it," he conveyed a more terrible menace than the loudest intemperance of voice could swell to.' After 1695 he took less important parts, but 'even at past sixty,' says Cibber, 'his teeth were all sound, white, and even as one could wish to see in a reigning toast of twenty.' His chief fault as an actor seems to have been his strident voice, concerning which an anecdote more pertinent than pleasing is given by Davies, and repeated by Genest (ii. 174). That characteristic, as well as his stately step, has been attributed to his early experience in female parts. Cibber praises him highly, and when he took Syphax in 'Cato,' played it ' as he thought Kynaston would have done.'

Kynaston appears to have retired in 1699, and to have died in January 1705–6. He was buried on 18 Jan. in St. Paul's, Covent Garden (Parish Reg. 1703–39, p. 190). Another Edward Kynaston, of St. Giles's-in-the-Fields, was buried in the same church 30 July 1712 (ib.) The actor had made a considerable sum of money, with the help of which he set up his son of the same name as a mercer. The latter had a large shop in Bedford Street, Strand, where Kynaston spent the last years of his life. Davies, in his 'Miscellanies,' states that he met Kynaston's grandson, who was a clergyman, but he was not disposed to be communicative about his ancestry, though he mentioned his kinship with the Kynastons of Oteley.

[Colley Cibber's Apology, ed. Lowe, passim; Downes's Roscius Anglicanus; Genest, i. 492, ii. 174; Malone's Historical Account, p. 130; Pepys's Diary, i. 128, 173 ; Gildon's Betterton, pp. 5, 9 ; Curll's English Stage, pp. 91, 116 ; Lowe's Betterton ; Doran's English Stage, i. 71–4 ; Davies's Dramatic Miscellanies, iii. 337 ; Dibdin's Hist. of the Stage, iv. 232 ; Russell's Representative Actors, pp. 9–11 ; Wheatley and Cunningham's London, i. 148–9.]   T. S.

KYNASTON or **KINASTON**, SIR FRANCIS (1587–1642), poet and scholar, born in 1587 at Oteley, Shropshire, was eldest son of Sir Edward Kinaston, by Isabel, daughter of Sir Nicholas Bagenall. His father, whose family originally came to Oteley from Stoke, near Ellesmere, was sheriff of Shropshire in 1599. On 11 Dec. 1601 Francis matriculated at Oriel College, Oxford, and graduated B.A. from St. Mary Hall on 14 June 1604. According to Wood he was more addicted ' to the superficial parts of learning, poetry and oratory (wherein he excelled), than to logic and philosophy ' (WOOD, Athenæ Oxon. ed. Bliss, iii. 38). Kinaston removed to Trinity College, Cambridge, where he graduated M.A. in 1609, but was incorporated

A A 2

M.A. at Oxford on 11 Nov. 1611. He was called to the bar at Lincoln's Inn in 1611. On leaving the university in 1613, he married Margaret, daughter of Sir Humphry Lee, bart., by whom he had one son. He was knighted by James I at Theobalds on 21 Dec. 1618 (LE NEVE, *Knights*, p. 112), was M.P. for Shropshire in 1621-2, was taxor of Cambridge University in 1623, and was proctor there in 1634. He became esquire of the body to Charles I on his accession.

At court Kinaston was the centre of a brilliant literary coterie. In 1635 he founded an academy of learning, called the Musæum Minervæ, for which he obtained a license under the great seal, a grant of arms, and a common seal (RYMER, *Fœdera*, xix. 638, &c.) Charles also contributed 100l. from the treasury (11 Dec. 1635; *Cal. State Papers,* Dom. Charles I, 1635-6, pp. 213, 551; *Notes and Queries*, 3rd ser. vi. 265). Kinaston gave his own house in Bedford Street, Covent Garden, for the college, which he furnished with 'books, manuscripts, musical and mathematical instruments, paintings, statues, &c.,' at his own expense. He was himself the regent, and his friends Edward May, Michael Mason, Thomas Hunt, Nicolas Phiske, John Spiedal, and Walter Salter were professors. According to the 'Constitutions of the Musæum Minervæ,' published by Kinaston in 1636, only the nobility and gentry were to be admitted to the college, the object of which was 'to give language and instruction, with other ornaments of travel, unto our gentlemen . . . before their undertaking long journeys into foreign parts.' The approval of the king and some lords of the privy council was claimed in the preface, and the universities and inns of court were assured that no rivalry was intended. A long list of the studies follows; the full course was to occupy seven years, the students who completed it to be called septennals, with privileges over those (called the triennals) who only finished the half-course. No gentleman was 'to exercise himself at once about more than two particular sciences, arts, or qualities, whereof one shall be intellectual, the other corporall.' The regent taught the following subjects: heraldry, a practical knowledge of deeds and the principles and processes of common law, antiquities, coins, husbandry. Music, dancing and behaviour, riding, sculpture, and writing formed important parts of the curriculum. On 27 Feb. 1635-6 Prince Charles, the Duke of York, and others visited the museum, and a masque by Kinaston, entitled 'Corona Minervæ,' was performed in their presence. In July of the same year Sir George Peckham [q. v.], the friend of Lilly

the astrologer, bequeathed 10l. to the institution. Very shortly after this, Kynaston was for a long time much occupied with a certain 'hanging furnace,' recommended by him to the lords of the admiralty for ships of war. Between 1637 and 1639 there are several letters and petitions in the 'State Papers' concerning a quarrel between Kinaston and his father with regard to the settlement of the latter's estates. The king and Laud both interfered on the son's behalf, but no result seems to have been arrived at (*Cal. State Papers*, Dom. Charles I, 1635-9). Kinaston died in 1642, and was buried at Oteley. The museum appears to have perished with the death of its founder. Its site is still marked by Kynaston's Alley, Bedfordbury.

Kinaston published, besides the 'Constitutions,' a translation of Chaucer's 'Troilus and Cressida,' with a commentary, prefaced by fifteen short poems by Oxford writers, including Strode and Dudley Digges (Oxford, 1635, 4to, Bodl.) Waldron proposed to reprint the 'Troilus and Cressida' in 1795 in monthly parts, but no more than the first part appeared. Kinaston also contributed to the 'Musæ Aulicæ' by Arthur Johnston [q. v.], a rendering in English verse of Johnston's Latin poems, London, 1635, and was author of an heroic romance in verse, 'Leoline and Sydania,' containing some of the legendary history of Wales and Anglesey, published with some sonnets addressed by Kinaston to his mistress under the name of Cynthia (London, 1642, 4to). In the preface he boasts of having many pieces of 'real and solid learning' ready for the press, and apologises for sending forth this trifle. The sonnets, which do not technically deserve that title, are often of genuine merit. They were probably published earlier in a separate volume. Ellis (*Specimens of Early English Poets*, iii. 265) quotes from an edition dated 1641.

[Dwnn's Heraldic Visitations of Wales and part of the Marches, ed. Meyrick. 1846, i. 320; Hunter's Chorus Vatum, Addit. MS. 24488, fol. 280; Nichols's Progresses of James I, iii. 498, 762; Faulkner's Chelsea; Brydges's Censura Literaria, ii. 333; Oxf. Univ. Reg. (Oxf. Hist. Soc.), ii. i. 359, ii. 254, iii. 247; Collectanea (Oxf. Hist. Soc.), ed. Fletcher, 1885, i. 280; Corpus Christi College, Oxford, MS. 307, No. 83, f. 75; Foster's Alumni Oxon. 1500-1714; Cal. State Papers, 1635-9.]   E. T. B.

KYNASTON, HERBERT (1809-1878), high-master of St. Paul's School, second son of Roger Kynaston, by Georgiana, third daughter of Sir Charles Oakeley, governor of Madras, was born at Warwick in 1809 and educated at Westminster from 1823. He was elected to Christ Church, Oxford, in 1827, and matriculated on 30 May. He obtained the college prize for Latin verse (subject, 'Scythæ Nomades') in 1829, took a first-class in classics in 1831, and was appointed tutor and Greek reader in 1836. He graduated B.A. in 1831, M.A. in 1833, and B.D. and D.D. in 1849. At the university he was select preacher in 1841, and was subsequently a lecturer at his college in philology, a subject to which he was much devoted, and to which he continually directed the attention of his pupils. In 1834 he was ordained, and served as curate of Culham, Oxfordshire. Four years later, at the early age of twenty-eight, he was elected to the high-mastership of St. Paul's School, London, on the retirement of Dr. John Sleath. During the thirty-eight years of his successful rule he numbered among his scholars many who grew up to be distinguished men. MM. Demogeot and Montucci, the French commissioners who visited the school in 1865, especially mention the paternal manner in which the high-master dealt with the boys. Lord Truro, an old Pauline, presented him in 1850 to the city living of St. Nicholas, Cole Abbey, with St. Nicholas Olave, which he held until the parishes were amalgamated with St. Mary Somerset in 1866. He resigned the mastership of St. Paul's in 1876, and the only preferment which he held at the time of his death was the prebendal stall of Holborn in St. Paul's Cathedral, to which he was presented by Bishop Blomfield in July 1853. He died at 31 Alfred Place West, South Kensington, on 26 Oct. 1878, and was buried at Friern Barnet on 2 Nov. He married Elizabeth Selina, daughter of Hugh Kennedy of Cultra, co. Down.

Kynaston's taste and scholarship led to his selection as a candidate for the chair of poetry at Oxford in 1867, but he was defeated by his college contemporary, Sir Francis Hastings Doyle. Few scholars of his age surpassed him as a composer of Latin verse. He was the author of numerous poetical compositions in praise of Dean Colet, the founder of St. Paul's School, which were produced each year at the apposition. Among these the 'Number of the Fish,' 1855, and the 'Lays of the Seven Half-centuries,' written for the seventh jubilee (1859), are the best known. To the outer world he was most familiar as a writer and translator of hymns. In the library at St. Paul's School are an engraved portrait of Kynaston and a marble bust by G. Halse.

Kynaston's chief works were: 1. 'Psittacus suum Naipæ,' 1840. 2. 'Miscellaneous Poetry,' 1841 (contains reminiscences of his life as a curate). 3. 'Prolusiones Literariæ in D.

Pauli Schola recitatæ comitiis maximis,' 1841. 4. 'Terentii Adelphorum Prologus et Epilogus,' 1842. 5. 'Strena Poetica,' 1849. 6. Commemoration Address in praise of Dean Colet, 1852. 7. ''Ο Άριθμός τῶν ἰχθύων. By the Scholæ Paulinæ Piscator primarius,' 1856. 8. 'Ipsum Audite. Hymnus super fundatione D. Pauli Scholæ,' 1857. 9. 'The Glory of Paradise. By Peter Damiani,' edited, with a translation, 1857. 10. 'Puerorum centum quinquaginta trium canticum centenarium. Rhythmus in D. Pauli Scholæ auditorio modis admixtis recitatus,' 1858. 11. 'Rete Coletinum,' 1861. 12. 'Saturnalium Intermissio. Carmen Latinum in divi Pauli Schola recitatum,' 1862. 13. 'Occasional Hymns. Original and Translated,' 1862; 2nd ser. 1864. 14. 'The Number of the Fish. A Poem on St. Paul's School,' 1864. 15. 'Doce, Disce aut Discede. Carmen elegiacum anniversarium,' 1864. 16. 'Cantica Coletina, quotidiana anniversaria centenaria,' 1867. Besides a number of minor pieces in pamphlet form, among which 'Coleti Torquis,' 1867, 'Comitiorum Coletinorum Intermissio,' 1871, 'Missiones Coletinæ,' 1873, 'Coleti Sepulcrum,' 1873, may be mentioned, Kynaston also wrote a long series of Latin hymns in the 'Guardian,' the last of which, entitled 'Ιχθύων κατάλογος,' was recited at the 'Winter Speeches' of 1876, when Kynaston retired from office.

[Forshall's Westminster School, 1884, p. 326; Gardiner's St. Paul's School, 1884, p. 298; Athenæum, 2 Nov. 1878, p. 563; Academy, 2 Nov. 1878. p. 428; Guardian, 2 Nov. 1878; Times, 29 Oct. 1878. pp. 1, 4; article in Leisure Hour, March 1879, pp. 180-2, by the Rev. J. H. Lupton.]   G. C. B.

KYNASTON, JOHN (1728–1783), author, born on 5 Dec. 1728, was son of Humphrey Kynaston, mercer. On 20 Feb. 1744-5 he was admitted to Manchester grammar school; proceeded with an exhibition to Brasenose College, Oxford, where he matriculated on 20 March 1745-6; was elected a scholar on 1 Aug. following, and graduated B.A. in 1749, M.A. in 1752 (FOSTER, Alumni Oxon. 1715–1886, ii. 807). He was elected fellow on 14 June 1751, and died at Wigan in June 1783.

Kynaston published in 1761 a Bridgman oration spoken in Brasenose College chapel, 'De Impietate C. Cornelio Tacito falso objectata.' In 1764 he issued 'A Collection of Papers relative to the Prosecution now carrying on in the Chancellor's Court in Oxford against Mr. Kynaston, by Matthew Maddock, Clerk, . . . for the charge of Adultery alleged against the said M. Maddock.'

He was a frequent contributor to the 'Gentleman's Magazine.' Nichols, in his 'Literary Anecdotes' (ii. 42 n.), acknowledges valuable help from Kynaston. The Latin inscription on the monument of Dr. Peter Francis le Courayer [q. v.] in Westminster Abbey was written by him. He also took an active part in behalf of Mary Blandy [q. v.]

[Smith's Reg. Manchester Grammar School (Chetham Soc.), i. 27, 224; Chalmers's Biog. Dict. xix. 435–7; Gent. Mag. liii. ii. 627–8, 803.]   G. G.

KYNDER, PHILIP (*fl.* 1665), miscellaneous writer, born on 12 April 1597, was second son of William Kynder of Snenton, Nottinghamshire, by Katherine, daughter of William Dunn of Nottingham (*Reliquary*, xv. 167). He was educated at Pembroke Hall, Cambridge, graduated B.A. in 1615–1616, and received a license to practise physic (*Notes and Queries*, 2nd ser. viii. 386). In 1620 he was practising at Leicester. He was at York when Charles I was preparing for his expedition against the Scots in 1640, and compiled a description of York Minster and of the coats of arms therein, but his notes were stolen, or perished at the plunder at Nottingham in 1643. In October 1643 he was employed at Oxford to draw the patent for creating Henry Hastings (*d.* 1667) [q. v.] (second son of Henry, earl of Huntingdon) Baron Loughborough, and was appointed an agent for all other affairs at court, but he complains of being ill requited for his services. For some years he received an annuity from Robert, earl of Kingston, which probably ceased at the latter's death in 1643. In 1654 he was in great distress, and had to remind various influential acquaintances of their promises to help him. These appeals he afterwards collected together in manuscript, under the title of 'The Aqua-vitæ Bottle, or Letters Expostularie.' He sought relief from his troubles in angling, and in the society of his friends Charles Cotton and Selden. Another of his favourite diversions was composing ornate Latin epitaphs on his deceased friends and relations. He raised an imposing cenotaph to his father's memory at Snenton (*Reliquary*, vol. xvi.) In August 1665 he was living at Nottingham. His wife was Elizabeth, daughter of John Barkley of Warwickshire.

Kynder's only known publication is entitled 'The Surfeit. To A. B. C.' [anon.], 8vo, London, 1656, reprinted by Philip Bliss in the appendix to his 'Reliquiæ Hearnianæ.' The authorship of this curious volume was long attributed to Philip King, archdeacon of Lewes (*Gent. Mag.* 3rd ser. xix. 220–1). He has verses before William Sampson's

'Virtus post funera vivit,' 1636; and in Latin before Sir John Beaumont's 'Poems,' 1629; and was a contributor to the collection of elegies on the death of Henry, lord Hastings of Ashby-de-la-Zouch, entitled 'Lachrymæ Musarum,' 1649 and 1650. He was also author of the Latin monumental inscription to Lord Hastings which is printed on a folded leaf bound up with the elegies. He wrote complimentary verses on Charles Cotton's 'Poems.'

Kynder's 'Booke,' a collection of miscellaneous tracts, observations, letters, and poems by him, is preserved in the Bodleian Library (MS. Ashmol. 788). It contains eighty-six different pieces relating to theology, medicine, poetry and the drama, astrology, genealogy, mathematics, topography, stenography, and the universal character. He incidentally mentions that at the age of eighteen he wrote a Latin comedy or pastoral founded on Sir Philip Sidney's 'Arcadia,' entitled 'Silvia.' The most valuable piece in the collection, his quaint 'Historie of Darbyshire,' was transcribed in 1882 by the Rev. W. G. Dimock Fletcher, and printed in the 'Reliquary' (vol. xxii.)

[Addit. MS. 24488, ff. 334–5; Black's Cat. Ashmol. MSS., cols. 404, 408, 410; Lysons's Magna Britannia, 'Derbyshire,' p. iv and elsewhere.]   G. G.

KYNEWULF, CYNEWULF, or CYNWULF (*fl.* 750), Anglo-Saxon poet, flourished in the eighth century. All the poems, with certainty and uncertainty, ascribed to him are contained in two manuscripts: the 'Exeter Codex,' a volume of Anglo-Saxon poetry given by Leofric, bishop of Exeter, in 1046, to his cathedral library, where it still remains; and the 'Vercelli Codex,' a book of Anglo-Saxon poetry preserved in the cathedral library at Vercelli, where it was found and made known by Dr. Friedrich Blume in 1832 and 1834. Both these manuscripts are written in West-Saxon (the literary dialect) by hands of the tenth century. In 1840 J. M. Kemble in England (*Archæologia*, xxviii. 360–2) and Jacob Grimm in Germany(*Andreas und Elene*, ed. Grimm, Cassel) independently found that the runic letters interwoven with the text of 'Crist' and 'Juliana,' two of the Exeter pieces, and 'Elene,' one of the Vercelli, formed in each case the name of the author 'Cynewulf.' Professor A. Napier recently found 'Cynwulf' in 'Fata Apostolorum,' another Vercelli poem. With these four poems Cynewulf is now credited with certainty.

The 'Crist,' which fills sixteen leaves of the Exeter book, was first printed by Thorpe as fifteen separate poems. But Dietrich recognised that the pieces form a cycle on the three-fold coming of Christ; they are now accordingly treated as one poem. The runes occur near the end of the first half. The 'Passion of St. Juliana' appears in the middle of the Exeter book. In the Vercelli book the poem of 'Elene,' the subject of which is the old legend of Constantine's banner and the invention or finding of the cross by his mother, Helena, is preceded (though not immediately) by a shorter poem of much beauty, describing the poet's vision, or 'Dream of the Cross.' From comparison of passages in the two, and other internal evidence, ten Brink and Sweet conclude (as it seems justly, although Wülker disagrees with them) that Cynewulf was the author of both. The 'Dream' is, in fact, an introduction to 'Elene.' These poems,—all religious narratives,—combine with their devout Christian fervour much patriotic feeling. Their poetic value varies, but the 'Dream' displays very realistic imagination.

Many more poems in the two manuscript books have been attributed to Cynewulf on more or less substantial grounds. If we admit his responsibility for all the lyrics and descriptive pieces that have been placed to his credit, he would be the most versatile and prolific, as well as one of the loftiest, of Old-English poets. Dr. Sweet (*A.-S. Reader*, 4th ed. 1884, p. 169) ascribes to him the majority of the poems preserved in the Exeter book, including a collection of poetical 'Riddles,' ninety-three in number according to Thorpe, eighty-nine according to Grein, but written in the manuscript in three groups. Leo believed that the first of the 'Riddles' in the Exeter book was a charade (not a riddle in the ordinary sense as many of them have proved to be), which in his hands yielded the three-syllable name Cyn-e-wulf, Cen-e-wulf, or Coen-e-wulf. Rieger agreed with him; but Leo's solution of this riddle has been keenly contested by Trautmann and H. Bradley on the ground that Cynewulf and Coenewulf are etymologically and phonetically distinct, and Mr. Henry Morley disputes Leo's interpretation by arguments other than etymological. Ten Brink, following Dietrich, Leo, and Rieger, is equally comprehensive; besides the 'Riddles' his list embraces the 'Dream,' 'Christ,' 'Descent into Hell,' 'Phoenix' (Exeter MS.), 'Life of St. Guthlac' (Exeter MS.), 'Juliana,' 'Andreas' (Vercelli MS.), and 'Elene;' but he rejects the 'Wanderer,' 'Sea-farer,' 'Rhyming Poem,' and several short poems. Grein credits Cynewulf with even more.

Of the new inquirers led by Wülker, Ramhorst contends that Cynewulf wrote 'Andreas,' while Gäbler supports Dietrich's ascription of the 'Phoenix' to him. Charitius and Lefèvre discuss 'Guthlac,' a portion of which, at least, they allow to Cynewulf. Wülker in 1877 (*Anglia*, i. 483) came to the conclusion that all previous theories required more investigation; but he admitted Cynewulf's responsibility for the 'Riddles,' which Trautmann only in part accepted.

It seems that Cynewulf was a professional minstrel, a Northumbrian, and that he probably wrote in that dialect. Towards the close of 'Elene' he tells us that in his joyful youth hunting, the bow, and the horse were his pleasures; that he was known in festive halls, and rewarded for his song with golden gifts; and that as he became an old man he studied many books, and the mystery of the cross, over which he had often pondered, became clear to him. Kemble and Thorpe thought the poet might be identical with Kenulphus, made abbot of Peterborough in 992 and bishop of Winchester in 1006; Dietrich tried to identify him with Cynwulf (so spelt in the 'Saxon Chronicle' and in Cotton MS. Vesp. b. vi.), who was bishop of Lindisfarne A.D. 737-780; while Grimm supposed him to be a scholar or a contemporary of Aldhelm.

H. Leo, in 1857, first tried to prove, from the runic letters forming the poet's name (in the three first poems above named), that Cynewulf was a Northumbrian. He contended that the form should be Cynevōlf, although Dietrich pointed out that *wulf*, not *wolf*, is the Northumbrian form. On the assumption that Cynewulf is the author of the 'Riddles,' his northern origin is corroborated by the existence in a manuscript at Leyden of a riddle in Northumbrian dialect which is evidently one of the Exeter riddles (both in SWEET, *Oldest English Texts*, Early English Text Soc., 1885, p. 150). At Ruthwell, Dumfries, moreover, stands a large cross of the eighth century covered with runes; Kemble and others succeeded in deciphering these, which are found to correspond to a fragment of the 'Dream' in Northumbrian dialect. Dr. Sweet declares that 'this inscription cannot well be later than the middle of the eighth century,' and 'holds fast to the opinion' that it is a part of the 'Dream,' the work of Cynewulf; and 'that the complete original text of the Ruthwell cross poem is that from which the Vercelli recension was copied' (*ib.* p. 125).

The Exeter and Vercelli MSS. must, according to these conclusions, be renderings of the poet's eighth-century Northumbrian work into West-Saxon of the tenth century. This theory is further borne out by the occasional presence of traces of the northern dialect, such as a copyist or translator imperfectly understanding his text would leave, as is found in the somewhat analogous case of

Cædmon. The positive assertion of ten Brink, Sweet, and Grein that 'Cynewulf was a Northumbrian' is denied by Wülker and Morley, but it has the greatest concurrence of probability on its behalf.

The text of Cynewulf's poems may be found in print in 'Codex Exoniensis,' with translation by B. Thorpe, London, 1842, of which a new edition, with a translation by Mr. I. Gollancz, is shortly to appear (Early English Text Soc.); in 'The Poetry of the Codex Vercellensis,' with translation by J. M. Kemble, Ælfric Society, 1844 and 1856; in Grein's 'Bibl. der A.-S. Poesie,' 1857, i. 149-232, 238-48, 362-5, ii. 7-146, 369-407; and in Wülker's edition of Grein, Kassel, Bd. i. 1883, Bd. ii. 1888 (not yet completed). The 'Elene' has been edited by J. Zupitza, 3rd ed. Berlin, 1888; and by Charles W. Kent, Boston, U.S.A., 1889.

Translations of Cynewulf into German appear in 'Dichtungen der A.-S. stabreimend übersetzt, von C. W. M. Grein,' Göttingen, 2nd ed. 1859. The following English translations have been issued: 'Elene,' by R. F. Weymouth, 1888, and by J. M. Garnett, Boston, U.S.A., 1889; 'Dream' and 'Seafarer,' by H. Sweet in Warton's 'History of English Poetry,' ed. Hazlitt, 1871, ii. 17-19; 'Dream of the Cross,' in H. Morley's 'English Writers,' 1888, ii. 237; 'Wanderer,' by Miss Hickey, in 'Academy,' 14 May 1881.

[The difficult questions involved in Cynewulf's works and life are generally discussed by ten Brink in History of English Literature, vol. i., Kennedy's translation, revised by author, 1883, pp. 385-9, and in Zeitschrift (Anzeiger) für deutsches Alterthum, xxiii. 60; by Fra. Dietrich in Ueber Crist, in the same Zeitschrift, 1853, ix. 193-214, and in his Disputatio de Cruce Ruthwellensi, Marburg, 1865; by Rieger in Ueber Cynewulf, in Zacher's Zeitschrift für deutsche Philologie, i. 215, 313; by Dr. Sweet in Sketch of Hist. of A.-S. Poetry in Warton's Hist. English Poetry, ed. Hazlitt, 1871, ii. 16-19; by R. P. Wülker in Anglia, i. 483-507, and ib. v. 451 (account of Vercelli MS.); by Henry Morley in English Writers, 1888, ii. 192-248. The Riddles are considered by H. Leo in Que de se ipso Cynewulfus . . . tradiderit, Halle, 1857; by Dietrich in Ebert's Jahrbuch, i. 241, in Zeitschrift für deutsches Alterthum, xi. 448, xii. 232, and in Commentatio de Kynewulfi poetæ ætate, Marburg, 1860; by Trautmann in Anglia, 1883, vi. 158 of Anzeiger; by A. Prehn, in Komposition und Quellen der Rätsel des Exeterbuches, Paderborn, 1883; and by H. Bradley in Academy, xxxiii. 198. Guthlac is treated by Charitius, Anglia, ii. 265; and by Lefevre, ib. vi. 181. The Phœnix by Gäbler, ib. iii. 488. Andreas by Fritzsche, ib. ii. 441 (F. Ramhorst opposes this in Der heiligen Andreas und der Dichter Cynewulf, Leipzig, 1886). Quellen der Elene, by O. Glöde,

Anglia, ix. 271, and Juliana, ib. xi. 146; Holtbuur, ib. viii. 1, and Rösger, viii. 338, treat of the use of the genitive in certain of the poems. E. Sievers, ib. xiii. 1, 1890, discusses the name and runes announced by Napier in Zuft. für deu. Alterthum, xxxiii. 70. For fuller bibliography see R. P. Wülker's 'Cynewulf und sein Kreis' (an important article in Grundriss zur Geschichte der A.-S. Litteratur, pp. 147-217, Leipzig, 1885), and Wülker's edition of Grein's Bibliothek der Angel-sächsischen Poesie, Bd. ii. Hälfte i. 210, as well as Zupitza's and Kent's editions of Elene.]
L. T. S.

KYNGESBURY or **KYNBURY, THOMAS,** (fl. 1390), Franciscan and D.D. of Oxford, was twenty-sixth provincial minister of the English Minorites from 1380 to 1390, or longer. At the beginning of the great schism he induced the English Franciscans to take an oath of adherence to Urban VI. He was in favour at court; Richard II urged Boniface IX to provide him to the next vacant bishopric (c. 1390). Perhaps Thomas died soon afterwards. He was buried at Nottingham. Though no writings of his remain, he clearly encouraged the study of science in his order.

[Mon. Franciscana, i.; English Hist. Rev. vi. 747; Bodl. MSS. 692, fol. 33; Digby, 90, fol. 6 b; Cotton Faust. A. ii. f. 1, Vesp. E. vii. f. 4.]
A. G. L.

KYNNESMAN, ARTHUR (1682-1770), schoolmaster, son of Harold Kynnesman, was born in London on Christmas day 1682. He was educated at Christ's Hospital, and admitted to Trinity College, Cambridge, 30 June 1702, whence he graduated B.A. 1705, and M.A. 1709. For some time he was an usher at Westminster School, but in 1715 resigned this appointment on becoming master of the grammar school at Bury St. Edmunds. Here he worked for thirty years, and secured for the school a high reputation. Richard Cumberland (1732-1811) [q. v.] was a pupil, and has left some account of Kynnesman. On one occasion, speaking to Bentley (Cumberland's grandfather), he said that he would make Cumberland as good a scholar as his grandfather, to which Bentley replied, 'Pshaw! Arthur, how can that be, when I have forgot more than thou ever knewst?' Kynnesman became rector of Barnham, in 1751 he was reader of St. James's, Bury, for a few months, and in 1766 he obtained the living of Eriswell; all three places are in Suffolk. He resigned the mastership of the grammar school in 1765, and died 10 July 1770 at Bury. He married a Miss Maddocks of Troston, Suffolk; she died in 1766, and both were buried at Barnham.

A portrait of Kynnesman and his wife was

at Troston Hall in the possession of Capell Lofft the elder 'q. v.'. A portrait of Kynnesman by Webster is at the Bury grammar school. It was engraved in mezzotint, at the cost of fourteen old pupils, by James Watson. Kynnesman wrote 'A Short Introduction to Grammar,' Ipswich, 1708; 2nd edition 1775.

[Davy's Suffolk Collections, &c. (Brit. Mus. Add. MS. 19166); Cumberland's Memoirs, ed. Flanders, pp. 25, 26, 31, 33, 38, 43; Nichols's Lit. Anecd. viii. 433, ix. 534; Nichols's Lit. Illustr. iii. 290, 291, 848, iv. 319, 376.]

W. A. J. A.

KYNSIGE, KINSIUS, KINSI, or **CYNESIGE** (*d.* 1060), archbishop of York, who, it is said, was brought into the world by a Cæsarean operation (*Chronicle of Archbishops*), was a monk of Peterborough, and became one of the chaplains or clerks of Edward the Confessor. He was consecrated archbishop of York in 1051, and in 1055 went to Rome to fetch his pall, which he received from Pope Victor. He gave gifts to Peterborough, which Queen Eadgyth [see EDITH] afterwards took away, one of them being a copy of the gospels splendidly enriched with gold and jewels. At Beverley he built a tower to the minster, hung two bells in it, and enriched the church with books and ornaments. He also gave bells to Southwell and Stow. While his household lived at great expense he is said to have practised abstinence, and when travelling from place to place to preach, as his custom was during Lent, to have gone on foot. In 1059 he and Egelwine, bishop of Durham, and Earl Tostig joined in conducting Malcolm, king of Scots, to King Edward. On 5 May 1060 he dedicated Earl Harold's (1022?–1066) [q. v.] new church at Waltham, Stigand, archbishop of Canterbury, being held to be a schismatic. On 22 Dec. following he died at York, and was buried, in accordance with his wish, at Peterborough, on the north side of the choir near the high altar, where his tomb and his bones were discovered in the seventeenth century.

[Raine's Fasti Ebor. p. 137; A.-S. Chron. ann. 1053, 1055, 1060 (Rolls Ser.); Symeon of Durham, Hist. Regum, an. 1059, ap. Symeonis Opp. i. 174 (Rolls Ser.); Chron. of Archbishops of York, ap. Historians of York, ii. 343; Hugo Candidus, p. 45 (Sparke); De Inventione Crucis, c. 10 (Stubbs).]

W. H.

KYNTON, JOHN (*d.* 1536), divinity professor at Oxford, was a Franciscan friar, though his connection with the Oxford convent seems to have been slight. He received the chancellor's license to incept as D.D. in 1500. He appears as vice-chancellor and *senior theologus* in 1503, 1504, 1506, 1507, 1510, 1512, and 1513. He preached the university sermon on Easter Sunday 1515. He was among the four doctors of divinity appointed by the university in 1521 to consult with Wolsey about the Lutheran doctrines, and he assisted in a further examination of the reformer's works undertaken by the theologians of Oxford at the king's command; he is said to have written on this occasion a treatise 'Contra Doctrinam Mart. Lutheri.' He was divinity reader to Magdalen College, and third Margaret professor of theology; he resigned the latter post in 1530; the date of his election is unknown. In 1530 he was one of the leading members of the committee of Oxford theologians to whom the question of the validity of the king's marriage was referred. Kynton died on 20 Jan. 1535–6, and was buried in the chapel of Durham College, now Trinity College, Oxford.

[Oxf. Univ. Archives, Acta Cur. Cancell. G, H, EEE.; Pocock's Records of the Reformation, vol. i.; Wood's Athenæ, i. 94; Fasti, i. 6, &c.; Lyte's Oxford.]

A. G. L.

KYNWELMARSH, FRANCIS (*fl.* 1570), poet. [See KINWELMERSH.]

KYNYNGHAM or **CUNNINGHAM, JOHN** (*d.* 1399), Carmelite, was a native of Suffolk, and since he appears to have been older than Wycliffe, must have been born about 1320. Kynyngham entered the Carmelite order at Ipswich, and thence went to study at Oxford, where he graduated as doctor of divinity previously to 1363, the probable date of his first controversy with Wycliffe (*Fasciculi Zizaniorum*, p. 454). He was present at the council of London on 19 May 1382, when Wycliffe was condemned, and preached the sermon at its conclusion (KNIGHTON, col. 2650). He was present at the condemnation of Henry Crump [q. v.] at the council of Stamford on 28 May 1392. Previously to the latter date he had been appointed confessor to John of Gaunt. He was chosen twenty-first provincial of his order in a council held at Yarmouth in 1393, and held the office till his death. In 1398 he was appointed to take part in the deliberations at Oxford relative to the termination of the great schism (WOOD, Hist. and Antiq. Univ. Oxford, i. 534, ed. Gutch). He died in the house of his order at York 12 May 1399. Kynyngham is described as gentle of disposition and speech, though a strenuous opponent of Wycliffe and of his doctrines during many years (Fasc. Ziz. p. 3). The Bollandists speak of him as 'blessed' (Acta Sanctorum, July, ii. 249 F).

Kynyngham's controversies with Wycliffe

are said to have embraced such subjects as logic, the humanity of Christ, civil dominion, and the endowment of the church. Those works of his which have survived are: 1. 'Ingressus contra Wicclyff.' 2. 'Acta contra ideas magistri Johannis Wyclif,' an answer to a tract by Wycliffe. 3. 'Secunda determinatio contra Wycliff. De ampliatione temporis,' a rejoinder to Wycliffe's reply. 4. 'Tertia determinatio contra Wycliff. De esse intelligibili creaturæ.' These four tracts, which may be referred to 1303, are contained in 'Fasciculi Zizaniorum' (MS. E. Mus. 86 in the Bodleian), which was edited for the Rolls Series in 1858 by the Rev. W. W. Shirley (pp. 4–103). Another manuscript of these tracts is in Corpus Christi College, Cambridge, 103. Bale speaks of a fifth tract of Kynyngham's, 'Determinatio quarta ad auctoritates J. Wyclif,' inc. 'Jam restat dicere ad auctoritates,' &c., but this is only a portion of No. 4 (cf. *Fasciculi Zizaniorum*, p. 80). Other treatises ascribed to Kynyngham are: 1. 'Sermones de tempore.' 2. 'Sermones de Sanctis.' 3. 'Contra propositiones Wiclivi,' inc. 'Ut ait Cassiodorus.' 4. 'Super Sententias, lib. v.' 5. 'De Angelis,' or 'De Natura Angelica.' 6. 'De Nativitate Christi.' 7. 'De ejus Passione.' 8. 'De Spiritu Sancto.' 9. 'Commentarii Metaphysices.' 10. 'Ad quasdam loca allegata.' 11. 'Quæstiones Varii.' 12. 'In Scripturas Commentarii.' Bale gives the first words of some of these, but none of them seem to be extant.

Kynyngham's name is sometimes spelt Kenyngham and Kiningham, while Wycliffe calls him Kylyngham. The form Cunningham is probably due to Dempster, who claimed him for Scotland, and attached him to the family of the Earls of Glencairn. Dempster also states that he studied at Paris, and was offered but refused the bishopric of Paderborn (*Hist. Eccl.* x. 763).

[*Fasciculi Zizaniorum*, ed. Shirley (Rolls Ser.), see index; Leland's Comment. de Scriptt. Brit. p. 386; Bale's Heliades, Harleian MS. 3838, ff. 30, 31, 73; Bale, De Scriptt. Brit. vi. 4; Pits, pp. 564–5; Tanner's Bibl. Brit.–Hib. p. 213, s.v. 'Cunningham;' C. de Villiers's Bibl. Carmelitana, ii. 24–3.]   C. L. K.

KYRLE, JOHN (1637–1724), the Man of Ross, born at the White House, in the parish of Dymock, Gloucestershire, on 22 May 1637, was eldest son of Walter Kyrle of Ross, Herefordshire, where the family had been settled for centuries, by Alice, daughter of John Mallet of Berkeley, Gloucestershire. From his father, who was a barrister, a justice of the peace for his county, and M.P. for Leominster in the Long parliament, Kyrle inherited in 1650 estates at Ross and elsewhere worth about 600*l.* a year. He was educated at the Ross grammar school and at Balliol College, Oxford, where he matriculated on 20 July 1654, but took no degree. A silver tankard holding five pints, embossed with his arms and inscribed with the words 'Poculum charitatis ex dono Johannis Kyrle de Ross in agro Herefordiensi et hujus Collegii commensalis,' but without date, is still preserved at the college. Kyrle was admitted a student of the Middle Temple in 1657.

After leaving the university Kyrle retired to Ross, where he lived a life of extreme simplicity, devoting his surplus income to works of charity and the improvement of the town and countryside. He owes his fame largely to the eulogy of him which Pope introduced into his third 'Moral Epistle' (1732) on information supplied by Jacob Tonson. An enthusiastic amateur architect, builder, and landscape gardener, nothing pleased Kyrle better than to advance a neighbour the funds necessary for enlarging or rebuilding his house, stipulating only that he should himself plan and superintend the execution of the work. His own estate he greatly improved by extensive plantations of timber. His favourite tree was the elm, of which he planted two avenues on either side, east and west, of Ross Church. He also acquired from Lord Weymouth in 1693 a lease for five hundred years of a small eminence near the church called the Prospect, which he dedicated to the public and laid out in walks shaded by ornamental trees interspersed with shrubberies. In the centre he erected a fountain, which, having become ruinous, was removed in 1794. The right of the public in this plantation, having been disputed in 1848, was, after prolonged litigation, secured in 1857 by a conveyance of the land to the town commissioners in perpetuity. Pope's lines plainly attribute to Kyrle the construction both of Ross Church and the raised stone causeway which connected the town with Wilton. Both, however, were in existence for centuries before Kyrle's time. It is said in a letter of 1746 (SPENCE, *Anecdotes*, 1820, pp. 423–5) that he gave a gallery and pulpit to the church, the spire of which was reconstructed in 1721; and the same letter implies that a fine avenue of elms along the causeway was planted by him. Pope's further statement that he fed the poor in the market-place possibly means, as suggested in Chambers's 'Book of Days,' ii. 557, that he acted as almoner to the lord of the manor in the distribution of a weekly dole. 'He feeds yon almshouse' may refer to Rudhall's Hospital, which was in close proximity to Kyrle's house. The character of general mediator attributed to him by Pope is supported by Hearne (*Diary*, April 1733), who says that 'when any litigious suits fell out' Kyrle 'would always stop them and prevent people going to law.' That, however, he did not succeed in exterminating the local attorneys is proved by the fact that towards the close of his life he was himself involved in litigation. Pope does not confirm the tradition that Kyrle used to release poor debtors from prison and re-establish them in life. He took a lively interest in a dame's school in the town, paying it a visit of inspection every week, and making minute inquiries into the behaviour of the children, and reproving delinquents with 'Od's bud, Od's bud, but I will mend you.' Though his rank in the county was but that of a squire who worked like a yeoman on his land, and lived on intimate terms with his labourers, he was chosen sheriff in 1683. He had little literary culture. Strictly temperate, he was fond of entertaining his friends with solid joints, washed down with cider, perry, or ale. The fragments of the repast were always given to the poor. He usually smoked two pipes of tobacco a day. He remained a bachelor all his life, his house being kept by one of his female relations, Miss Judith Bubb, and he died of old age on 7 Nov. 1724. The body, after lying in state for nine days, was buried in the chancel of Ross Church, without any monument or inscription. A blue slate stone, with the inscription, 'John Kyrle, Esq., 7 Nov. 1724, æt. 88,' was placed to mark the spot in 1749. The existing monument was erected in 1776 by Colonel James Money, executor of Kyrle's cousin Constantia, Lady Dupplin, pursuant to a direction in her will. It is a pyramidal marble tablet on the north wall of the chancel, with a bust of Kyrle in relief, and three allegorical figures, with coat of arms and motto. It is inscribed as 'In memory of Mr. John Kyrle, commonly called the Man of Ross.' A more recent monument is the Kyrle Society, started by the efforts of Misses Miranda and Octavia Hill, and inaugurated by Prince Leopold in 1877. The society endeavours, by giving popular concerts, promoting the conversion of waste plots of ground into gardens, and encouraging the growth of flowers and decoration of cottages, to brighten the lives of the working classes in the large towns (see *Good Words*, xxii. 609). Kyrle left the estates to his kinsman, Vandervort Kyrle, for life, with remainder to his sons in tail male.

Kyrle's house continued for some years to be occupied by the family, but was afterwards converted into the King's Arms Inn, and finally into shops. It faced the south-east corner of the market, on which Kyrle had inscribed a monogram intended to signify 'Love King Charles from the heart.' Kyrle refused to sit for his portrait; but it was painted from a sketch taken without his knowledge in church. This, or a copy, long hung in the King's Arms, whence it was removed in 1795 to the Swan Inn, Tewkesbury, and thence to the Talbot Inn, Shrewsbury, and was ultimately purchased by Sir Mark Sykes of Strettington Hall, near Malton, Yorkshire. A print of it is in the 'European Magazine' for 1786, ii. 161. There was also a copy in the King's Head Inn at Ross. Heath (*Excursion down the Wye*, 1826) states that Lord Muncaster was supposed to be in possession of the original. In person Kyrle was tall, broad-shouldered, and well built, red-faced and hearty, with a large nose and a loud voice. He wore a short bushy wig and brown suit.

[Robinson's Mansions and Manors of Herefordshire, p. 280; Reg. Matric. Oxford; Foster's Alumni Oxon.1500-1714; Pope's Works, ed. Elwin and Courthope, iii. 150, 529; Heath's Excursion down the Wye, 8th edit., 1826; Cooke's Collections ... of the County of Hereford, pp. 108 et seq.; Strong's Ross and Archenfield, p. 12; Gent. Mag. 1786, pt. ii. p. 1026; Notes and Queries, 1st ser. vi. 542, 2nd ser. xi. 466, xii. 72, 4th ser. vi. 154; Burke's Landed Gentry, 'Money Kyrle.']

J. M. R.

KYRTON, EDMUND (*d.* 1466), abbot of Westminster. [See KIRTON.]

KYTE, FRANCIS (*fl.* 1710-1745), mezzotint-engraver and portrait-painter, was author of a few fair mezzotint-engravings, mostly published by Edward Cooper, for whom he probably worked. They include two portraits of Thomas Parker, earl of Macclesfield, after Kneller (one dated 1714), Henrietta, countess of Godolphin, after Kneller, Harriet, duchess of Newcastle, after Kneller, two of John Gay after W. Aikman, Archbishop Sharpe, and a set, engraved with John Faber, junior, of 'The Worthies of Great Britain.' In 1725 Kyte was convicted of forging a bank-note, and sentenced to the pillory. Later in life he seems to have devoted himself to portrait-painting. Among his sitters were Edward Cave, printer (1740), engraved by T. Worlidge; William Caslon, type-founder (1740), engraved by J. Faber, jun.; the Rev. George Whitefield, whole length (1743), engraved by J. Faber, jun.; and George Francis Handel (1742), engraved by Lewis (now in the possession of Mr. W. H. Cummings) (see KEITH MILNES, *Memoir relating to a Portrait of Handel*, 1829).

[Chaloner Smith's British Mezzotinto Portraits; Dodd's manuscript Hist. of English Engravers (Brit. Mus. Add. MS. 33402).] L. C.

KYTE, JOHN (d. 1537), archbishop of Armagh and bishop of Carlisle. See KITE.

KYTELER, DAME ALICE (*fl.* 1324), reputed witch. See KETTLE.

KYTSON, SIR THOMAS (1485–1540), sheriff of London, son of Robert Kytson of Warton in Lancashire, was born in 1485. He came to London in his youth, and was apprenticed to Richard Glasyer, mercer, and on the expiration of his indentures was admitted a freeman of the Mercers' Company in 1507. He twice served the office of warden of the company, in 1525 and 1534, and held the office of master in 1535. In 1521 Kytson purchased of the Duke of Buckingham the manor of Hengrave, Suffolk, and the manor of Colston Basset in Nottinghamshire for 2,340*l.*, the estates being valued at 115*l.* yearly. On the attainder and execution of the Duke of Buckingham in the following year, Kytson was for a time deprived of the estates, but they were ultimately restored to him, and were confirmed to him by an act of parliament of 1524, which describes him as a 'citizen and mercer of London, otherwise called Kytson the merchant.'

At Hengrave he obtained a license from Henry VIII to build an embattled manorhouse on a magnificent scale. The building was begun in 1525, and finished in 1538. An elaborate inventory of the furniture and goods at Hengrave, taken in 1603 (GAGE, *History of Hengrave*, pp. 21–37), illustrates its great extent and elegance, and the vast wealth of its owner. In the valuation of the lands and goods of the inhabitants of London, taken in 1522, Kytson was assessed in goods at a thousand marks (altered to four thousand marks), and in lands at six hundred marks (*State Papers*, Hen. VIII, iii. pt. ii. p. 1052). In the following year he appears indebted to the crown for 600*l.*, and at the time his financial dealings with the crown were on a large scale (*ib.* p. 1530, vol. iv. pt. iii. p. 2771, vol. ix. p. 567, iii.) His mercantile transactions were very extensive. He was a member of the Merchant Adventurers' Company, and traded at the cloth fairs or staples held by that company at Antwerp, Middelburg, and other places in Flanders. Like many other wealthy London merchants, he appears to have had a house and staff of 'servants' at Antwerp (*ib.* vii. 106).

Kytson served the office of sheriff of London in 1533, and on 30 May in that year was knighted, an honour which was not conferred upon his co-sheriff, William Forman (*ib.* vi. 279). In May 1534 he was associated with

Roland Lee, bishop of Coventry and Lichfield, in receiving oaths of fealty from priests and monks (*ib.* vii. 283). Kytson was assessed for the subsidy of 1535 at four thousand marks (*ib.* viii. 184).

Subsequently he purchased several other manors in Suffolk of the crown of the yearly value of 202*l.* 4*s.* 7*d.*, for which he paid 3,710*l.* 1*s.* 8*d.* From an inventory of his effects taken after his death, it appears that his warehouses in London were stored with cloth of gold, satins, tapestry, velvets, furs, fustians, bags of pepper, cloves, madder, &c., to the value of 1,181*l.* 15*s.* 1*d.*, and the ready money and debts (good, doubtful, and desperate) amounted to a very considerable sum. He had a dwelling-house in Milk Street (with a chapel attached), the 'implements' in which were valued at 154*l.* 8*s.* 3½*d.*; a garden in Coleman Street, and a house and chapel at Stoke Newington. Besides Hengrave, he had houses at Westley and Risby in Suffolk, and at Torbrian in Devonshire.

Kytson died 11 Sept. 1540, and was buried with much state in Hengrave Church (cf. GAGE, pp. 112–15). In the north-east angle of the chapel is a well-executed tomb to the memory of Margaret, countess of Bath (his widow), and her three husbands. A recumbent figure of Kytson in armour is placed on the step in front of the tomb, the frieze of which contains an inscription to his memory. On 22 Sept. 1540 allegations were taken to prove his nuncupative will, by which he left his manors of Hengrave and Feltons and all his other property to his wife, Dame Margaret. The will is dated 11 Sept. (P. C. C. Spert, 30).

Kytson was twice married. By his first wife, whose name is not known, he had Elizabeth, wife of Edmund Crofts of Westowe in Suffolk. By his second wife, Margaret, only child of John Donnington of Stoke Newington in Middlesex and Elizabeth Pye, he had a posthumous son, afterwards Sir Thomas Kytson, and four daughters: (1) Katherine, married to Sir John Spencer of Wormleighton, Warwickshire; (2) Dorothy, married to Sir Thomas Packington of Westwood, Worcestershire; (3) Frances, wife of John, lord Fitzwarren, eldest son of John Bourchier, earl of Bath; and (4) Anne, wife of Sir William Spring of Pakenham, Suffolk.

Dame Margaret (d. 1561) was married secondly to Sir Richard Long, and afterwards to the Earl of Bath.

A portrait of Kytson by Holbein is at Hengrave, and was engraved by Sievier for Gage's 'History of Hengrave' (p. 106).

[Records of the Corporation of London and of the Mercers' Company.] C. W-R.

L

LABELYE, CHARLES (1705–1781?), architect of the first Westminster Bridge, son of François Dangeau Labelye, was born at Vevey, Switzerland, in 1705. He was baptised at Vevey on 12 Aug. 1705 as 'Danjau, Charles Paul, fils de M. François Danjau La Bélye et de Mme. Elisabeth Grammont sa femme.' In the entry of the baptism of a subsequent child in 1709 the father is described as 'Monsieur François Dangeau, Sieur de la Bélye, refugié en cette ville par sa Religion.' One of the godmothers of another child, baptised in 1714, was the Madame de Warens celebrated by J. J. Rousseau (J. CHAVANNES, *Les Réfugiés Français dans le Pays de Vaud*, Lausanne, 1874, p. 262). The father is said to have been related to the well-known Marquis de Dangeau, a prominent figure in the court of Louis XIV, and the author of a volume of 'Memoirs.' Some confusion appears to have arisen in consequence of the various modes in which Labelye's name is written, but with one exception he always called himself Charles Labelye. He probably came to England about 1725, as he states in the preface to his account of Westminster Bridge that he 'never heard a word of English spoken till I was near twenty years of age.' He appears to have become acquainted with John Theophilus Desaguliers [q. v.], to whom he addressed a letter dated 15 April 1735, dealing with a certain view of the laws of motion then prevalent, and displaying much mathematical knowledge. It is signed 'Charles de Labelye,' is printed in Desaguliers's 'Course of Experimental Philosophy' (1745, ii. 77), and is the earliest authentic evidence of his presence in this country. He is said to have been employed in Hawksmoor's office as a draughtsman, but the only evidence for this seems to be that Hawksmoor, in his 'Propositions for Erecting a New Stone Bridge at Westminster,' 1736, gives at p. 18 the results of some calculations made by Labelye to determine the probable effect of the bridge upon the current of the river.

The original act of parliament for building Westminster Bridge was passed in 1736 (9 Geo. II, cap. 29), but it was not until May 1738 that Labelye was appointed 'engineer,' a word which had not been previously employed in the sense of 'architect.' His salary was 100*l.* per annum, and 10*s.* per day subsistence money. The appointment of a youthful foreigner gave offence to the English

architects, and especially to Batty Langley, who, in a drawing in one of his books, shows 'the Swiss impostor' hanging in mid-air from one of the arches of the bridge.

The original idea was to build a bridge with a wooden superstructure, and Labelye's commission only extended to the construction of the stone piers. The foundations were laid in what are known as caissons, being huge wooden tanks, open at the top, eighty feet by thirty feet, constructed on shore, floated into position, and then sunk until the bottom rested on the bed of the river, a cavity having been previously excavated for their reception. The pier was then built in the caisson, and when it had reached above the level of high water the sides were removed. Labelye was not the inventor of this mode of building, as it was mentioned by Batty Langley in his 'Design for the Bridge at New Palace Yard' (1736), but it had never been carried out on any large scale. The first pile was driven on 13 Sept. 1738, and the first caisson launched on 15 Jan. of the following year. On the 29th of the same month the first stone was laid by the Earl of Pembroke. About a year afterwards the commissioners changed their plans, deciding upon a bridge entirely of stone. Labelye submitted a design, which was accepted, and the bridge was practically finished at the end of 1746; but soon after a serious failure of one of the piers became apparent. The public grew alarmed, and a ballad was written, 'The Downfall of Westminster Bridge, or my Lord in the Suds,' in which 'My Lord' (the Earl of Pembroke), the commissioners, and the architect were severely handled. The cause of the disaster was attributed to the unsoundness of the foundations. 'The Crace Collection of London Views' in the British Museum contains two contemporary drawings of the broken arch' (portfolio v. Nos. 93, 94). The bridge was consequently not open for public traffic until 18 Nov. 1750. It was the largest work of the kind executed up to that time, and was an object of admiration for many years. The views of it which were published are very numerous, and had Labelye carried out his original intention of laying the caissons on a foundation of piles instead of on the unprotected bed of the river, the bridge would probably have stood longer. In this, as in other respects, he seems to have been swayed by considerations of expense.

Labelye published in 1729 'A short Account of the Method made use of in Laying the Foundations of Westminster Bridge,' and in 1743 'The Present State of Westminster Bridge in a Letter to a Friend' (anon.) But it was Labelye's intention to publish a full description of the bridge, and in 1744 he issued a detailed prospectus of the proposed work. It appeared in 1751 under the title 'A Description of Westminster Bridge,' which is practically a second edition of the 'Short Account,' bringing the history of the bridge down to the date of its completion, and containing the prospectus of 1744 by way of appendix. Both works are said to contain engravings, which, however, were never published. The original drawings are to be found in the library of the Institution of Civil Engineers, bound up in a copy of Labelye's 'Short Account', together with a number of other drawings relating to the bridge. This volume was presented to the institution by Mr. Page, the architect of the present bridge. The drawings are signed 'T. Gayfere,' a clerk or draughtsman employed by the contractors, who subsequently became 'college mason' at Westminster Abbey. Labelye states in the 'Description' that as his health was failing he had arranged that all his papers were to pass into the hands of a competent person who would carry on the work in case of his death before its completion.

Labelye also published 'The Result of a View of the Great Level of the Fens' (1745), an abstract of his 'Report relating to the Improvement of the River Wear and Port of Sunderland' (1748), and a plan of a new harbour at Sandwich, engraved by Harris, but none of the suggested works were executed. He supplied Desaguliers with a description and drawings of Newsham's fire-engine, printed in the 'Course of Experimental Philosophy,' ii. 535. In 1746 he became a naturalised British subject by act of parliament (19 Geo. II, cap. 26), in which he is described as 'Charles Labelye, son of Francis Labelye, by Elizabeth his wife,' and his birthplace, Vevey, is wrongly placed 'in the canton of Bern in Switzerland.'

Upon the completion of the bridge in 1751 Labelye suddenly vanished. It is asserted by certain French writers that he retired to Paris, disgusted with the treatment which he had received in England. Not a trace of this dissatisfaction is to be found in his published works, and the greatest harmony seems to have prevailed between the commissioners and their engineer. On 26 Feb. 1751 the commissioners presented him with an honorarium of 2,000l. 'for his great fidelity and extraordinary labour and attendances, skill and diligence.' According to Le Sage (Recueil de divers mémoires extrait de la Bibliothèque des Ponts et Chaussées, 2me partie, p. 275, Paris, 1810), Labelye made the acquaintance in Paris of Perronet (the head of the department of Ponts et Chaussées), to whom he bequeathed his papers and a model of Westminster Bridge. The collection at the Ecole des Ponts et Chaussées contains a model of the bridge and some drawings, but nothing which can with certainty be attributed to Labelye. He appears, however, to have been in communication with the French engineers of that time, since Belidor (Architecture Hydraulique, ii. 198, Paris, 1753) gives a description and drawing of the mole of laying the foundations of the bridge, which are not to be found elsewhere. Le Sage also has a drawing of the machine invented by Labelye for cutting off piles under water, the particulars of which can hardly have been obtained from any one but the inventor.

The date of his death is uncertain, though all the accounts agree that it took place in Paris. The 'Gentleman's Magazine' states that it occurred 18 March 1762. According to Le Sage (op. cit.) he died about 1770, and this is to some extent borne out by a letter in the 'Journal Helvétique,' September 1770, p. 51, from Ritter, an architect of Berne, who writes as a friend of Labelye to correct an error in Grosley's book 'Londres.' Ritter writes throughout as if Labelye was no longer living. But the real date of his death is probably 17 Dec. 1781, which is that given in 'Le Conservateur Suisse,' 1817, viii. 226, and also by Albert de Montet in his 'Dictionnaire Biographique des Genevois et des Vaudois,' Lausanne, 1877.

[The chief authorities are cited above. A very full description of Westminster Bridge was presented to the Institution of Civil Engineers in 1838 by Mr. Francis Whishaw, who was rewarded with the Telford medal. A short abstract only appeared in the Proceedings, 1838, i. 44, but the manuscript is still preserved. This paper is particularly valuable, as the author had access to all the minute books and documents of the bridge commissioners, which are not now to be found, and have probably been destroyed. The British Museum possesses the journal and letter-book of Andrews Jelfe and Samuel Tuffnell, the contractors for the bridge (Add. MS. No. 27587), which contain many curious particulars. The name of Thomas Gayfere, already referred to, frequently occurs in this book.] R. B. P.

LABLACHE, FREDERICK (1815-1887), vocalist, eldest son of Luigi Lablache [q. v.], vocalist, was born on 29 Aug.

1815, and educated by his father. About 1837 he appeared at the King's Theatre, London, in Italian opera, and afterwards frequently sang at Manchester with Mario, Grisi, and Favanti. In 1844 he took a part in 'Cosi fan tutte' at Her Majesty's Theatre, and in 1846 in 'Il Matrimonio Segreto.' He played the part of Count Rodolphe to Jenny Lind's Amina on her first visit to Manchester, 28 Aug. 1847, and he also appeared with her in other characters under the management of Michael Balfe in 1849. About 1865 he withdrew from the stage, and devoted himself to teaching. He died at 51 Albany Street, Regent's Park, London, 30 Jan. 1887. His son, Luigi Lablache, is a well-known actor.

His wife, FANNY WYNDHAM LABLACHE (d. 1877), vocalist, whose maiden name was Wilton, was born in Scotland, studied at the Royal Academy of Music, London, 1836-7, and then made her début at the Lyceum Theatre, afterwards appearing at Her Majesty's Theatre. She was a serviceable vocalist and a teacher of much skill. After her marriage she retired from the stage, and died in Paris 23 Sept. 1877.

[Times, 4 Feb. 1887, p. 11; Theatre, March 1887, p. 173; Brown's Biog. Dict. of Musicians, 1886, p. 369.] G. C. B.

LABLACHE, LUIGI (1794-1858), vocalist, son of Nicholas Lablache, merchant, of Marseilles, by an Irish lady, was born at Naples 6 Dec. 1794. He was educated from 1806 at the Conservatorio della Pietà de' Turchini, where Gentili taught him the elements of music, and Valesi instructed him in singing, while at the same time he studied the violin and violoncello. His voice was a beautiful contralto, and just before it broke he sang the solos in the requiem of Mozart on the death of Haydn in 1809. Before long he became possessed of a magnificent bass, which gradually increased in volume until at the age of twenty it attained a compass of two octaves from E flat below to E flat above the bass stave. In 1812, when only eighteen, he was engaged at the San Carlo Theatre, Naples, and appeared in 'La Molinara' of Fioravanti. Two years later he married Teresa Pinotti, the daughter of an actor. In 1817, at La Scala in Milan, he took the part of Dandini in 'Cenerentola.' The opera of 'Elisa e Claudio' was now (1821) written for him by Mercadante; his position was made, and his reputation spread throughout Europe. From Milan he went to Turin, returned to Milan in 1822, then appeared at Venice, and in 1824 at Vienna. Going back to Naples after an absence of twelve years, he created a great sensation as Assur in 'Semiramide.' On 30 March 1830, under Ebers's management, he was first heard in London as Geronimo in 'Il Matrimonio Segreto,' and thenceforth appeared there annually, also singing in many provincial festivals. His success in England was assured from the first. His voice was at all times extraordinarily powerful, but he could produce comic, humorous, tender, or sorrowful effects with equal ease and mastery. As an actor he excelled equally in comic and tragic parts. His chief rôles were Leporello (his greatest part), Geronimo the Podestà in 'La Gazza Ladra,' Dandini in 'La Prova d'un' Opera Seria,' Henry VIII in 'Anna Bolena,' the Doge in 'Marino Faliero,' and Oroveso in 'Norma.' Towards the close of his career he played two new characters of quite different types with great success, Shakespeare's Caliban and Gritzenko, the Kalmuck, in Scribe's 'L'Etoile du Nord.' At the funeral of Beethoven in 1827 he was one of the thirty-two torchbearers who surrounded the coffin. He taught singing to Queen Victoria. He died at Naples 23 Jan. 1858, and was buried at Maison-Lafitte, Paris.

[Grove's Dict. of Music, 1880, ii. 79-81; Dramatic and Musical Rev. 1844, iii. 267-8, 377-9; You have Heard of Them, by Q., 1854, pp. 82-90; Lumley's Reminiscences of the Opera, 1864, pp. 135-8, 369; L. Engel's From Mozart to Mario, 1886, i. 23, ii. 81, 373; Illustrated London News, 1842 i. 124 (with portrait), 1843 ii. 275 (with portrait); Morley's Journal of a London Playgoer, 1866, pp. 91 et seq.] G. C. B.

LABOUCHERE, HENRY, BARON TAUNTON (1798-1869), elder son of Peter Cæsar Labouchere of Hylands, Essex, and Over Stowey, Somerset, by his wife, Dorothy Elizabeth, third daughter of Sir Francis Baring, bart., was born on 15 Aug. 1798. The family of Labouchere left France at the time of the edict of Nantes, and established themselves in Holland. Peter Cæsar Labouchere, a partner in the great mercantile firm of Hope, was the first of his family who settled in England. His son Henry was educated at Winchester, and on 24 Oct. 1816 matriculated at Christ Church, Oxford, where he took a first class in classics Easter term 1820, and graduated B.A. 1821, and M.A. 1828. He was admitted a member of Lincoln's Inn on 30 April 1817, but was never called to the bar. In 1824 he travelled with Lords Derby, Ossington, and Wharncliffe through Canada and the United States. At a by-election in April 1826 Labouchere was returned to the House of Commons for Michael Borough in the whig interest, and at the general election in the following June was re-elected. His first reported speech in the house was made during the debate on the civil government of the Canadas in May 1828 (*Parl. Debates*, new ser. xix. 316–18), when he drew attention to the abuses of the system of government, and declared that if 'we could not keep the Canadas with the good will of the inhabitants, we could not keep them at all.' At the general election in August 1830 he was returned at the head of the poll for the borough of Taunton, and continued to represent that constituency until his retirement from the House of Commons. In June 1832 he was appointed a lord of the admiralty in Lord Grey's administration, a post which he resigned on Sir Robert Peel's accession to office. Upon the formation of Lord Melbourne's second ministry in 1835, Labouchere became master of the mint, and on offering himself for re-election was opposed by Benjamin Disraeli, whom he defeated by 452 to 282 votes. On 6 May he was admitted to the privy council, and was further appointed vice-president of the board of trade. Labouchere filled the post of under-secretary of war and the colonies from February to August 1839, when resigning the vice-presidentship, in which he was succeeded by R. Lalor Shiel, but retaining the mastership of the mint, he was appointed president of the board of trade (29 Aug.) in succession to Poulett Thomson, and was admitted to the cabinet. On the resignation of Lord Melbourne in September 1841, Labouchere retired from office with the rest of his colleagues, and upon the formation of Lord John Russell's first administration in July 1846 became chief secretary to the lord-lieutenant of Ireland (John William Ponsonby, Earl of Bessborough, q. v.) The authorisation of reproductive employment by the famous 'Labouchere letter' of 5 Oct. 1846 (O'Rourke, *History of the Great Irish Famine of* 1847, &c., 1875, pp. 519–51) failed as a remedy for the widespread distress (Sir Charles Trevelyan, *Irish Crisis*, 1880, p. 49). Some two months after Lord Bessborough's death Labouchere was succeeded as chief secretary by Sir W. M. Somerville, and was reappointed president of the board of trade (22 July 1847) in the place of Lord Clarendon, the new lord-lieutenant. While holding this office Labouchere successfully carried through the House of Commons the bill by which the navigation laws were repealed (12 & 13 Vict. c. 29), in spite of the strong opposition of the shipping interest, and was also instrumental in passing the Mercantile Marine Acts (13 & 14 Vict. c. 93, and 14 & 15 Vict. c. 96) and the Seaman's Fund Act (14 & 15 Vict. c. 102). He retired with the rest of his colleagues on Lord John Russell's overthrow in February

1852, and took no part in Lord Aberdeen's administration. Though not an original member of Lord Palmerston's first ministry, Labouchere was appointed secretary of state for the colonies (21 Nov. 1855), in the place of Sir William Molesworth, after the refusal of the post by Lord Derby and Sidney Herbert ((Greville, *Memoirs*, 1887, 3rd ser. i. 292, 295), and continued to hold this office until Lord Palmerston's resignation in February 1858. Upon Lord Palmerston's return to power Labouchere was created Baron Taunton of Taunton in the county of Somerset, by letters patent dated 18 Aug. 1859. He took his seat in the House of Lords for the first time on 24 Jan. 1860 (*Journals of House of Lords*, xcii. 5): but though he took part in the debates from time to time, he held no further ministerial offices. He spoke for the last time in the House of Lords on 9 July 1869 (*Parl. Debates*, 3rd ser. cxcvii. 1493). He died at No. 27 Belgrave Square, London, on 13 July 1869, aged 70, and was buried at Over Stowey Church on the 20th following.

Taunton was a highly respected public man, and a hard-working administrator. Lord Campbell describes him 'as a very pretty speaker,' and 'such a perfect gentleman that in the House of Commons he is heard with peculiar favour' (*Life*, 1881, ii. 210). He served as one of the commissioners for the Exhibition of 1851, and presided over the commission appointed on 22 June 1853 'to inquire into the existing state of the corporation of the city of London' (*Parl. Papers*, 1854, vol. xxvi.), as well as over the schools inquiry commission appointed on 28 Dec. 1864. (For First Report see *Parl. Papers*, 1867–8, vol. xxviii. pt. 1).

He married, first, on 10 April 1840, his cousin, Frances, the youngest daughter of Sir Thomas Baring, bart., by whom he had three daughters, viz., 1. Mary Dorothy, who married, on 19 Sept. 1872, Edward James Stanley of Cross Hall, Lancashire; 2. Minna Frances, who married, on 2 May 1844, Captain Arthur Edward Augustus Ellis of the grenadier guards; and 3. Emily Harriet, who married, on 18 Oct. 1881, the Hon. Henry Cornwallis Eliot, now fifth Earl of St. Germans. His first wife died on 25 May 1850, and on 13 July 1852 he married, secondly, Lady Mary Matilda Georgiana Howard, the youngest daughter of George, sixth earl of Carlisle, by whom he had no children. In default of male issue the barony of Taunton became extinct upon his death. There is a fine whole-length engraving of Labouchere, when young, with his brother John (the father of Mr. Henry Labouchere, now M.P. for Northampton), by Watt, after Sir Thomas Lawrence. Another engraving 'from a picture in his own possession,' taken later in life, was published by Thomas Collius. Two of his speeches which he delivered in the House of Commons were published separately, viz. his speech on the sugar duties on 10 May 1841, and his speech on moving the resolution for the abolition of the navigation laws on 15 May 1848.

[Spencer Walpole's Hist. of England, vols. iii. and iv.; Sir D. Le Marchant's Memoir of John, third Earl of Spencer, 1876, pp. 52, 229, 232, 343; Lord Beaconsfield's Correspondence with his Sister, 1886, pp. 34–6; Times, 14 and 22 July 1869; Illustrated London News, 24 July 1869; Dod's Peerage, &c., 1869, pp. 589–90; Burke's Extinct Peerage, 1883, p. 309; Foster's Alumni Oxon. 1888, pt. iii. p. 808; Honours Register of the Univ. of Oxford, 1883. p. 206; Lincoln's Inn Registers; London Gazettes; Haydn's Book of Dignities, 1851; Official Return of Lists of Members of Parliament, pt. ii. pp. 285, 301, 320, 332. 344, 356, 369, 386. 404, 429, 436, 452; Notes and Queries, 4th ser. v. 175, 211, 457, 7th ser. x. 168, 215, 393; Brit. Mus. Cat.]
G. F. R. B.

LACEY, WILLIAM (1584–1673), jesuit, whose real name was WOLFE, born at Scarborough in 1584, was son of a tanner and leather dealer. He was sent to Oxford by an uncle, became a student in Magdalen College in 1600, and graduated B.A. on 2 July 1606 (Oxford Univ. Reg., Oxf. Hist. Soc., vol. ii. pt. iii. p. 264). Having become a convert to the Roman catholic religion, he was well received by the jesuits at St. Omer; was admitted an alumnus of the English College at Rome in 1608; and, after receiving minor orders, left for Lorraine, 2 Sept. 1611, in order to enter the Society of Jesus in the novitiate at Nancy. After his tertianship at Ghent, and a course of teaching at St. Omer, he was sent to England, and in 1625 was a missioner in the Lancashire district. In 1633 he was in the Oxfordshire district, or St. Mary's 'residence,' and two years later in St. George's 'residence,' which comprised Worcestershire and Warwickshire. He was professed of the four vows 21 Nov. 1637. In 1649 he was again at St. Mary's, where he remained, as missioner at Oxford, until his death. He died at Oxford on 17 July 1673. He was buried in the parish church of Somerton, Oxfordshire. Wood says 'he was esteemed by all, especially by those of his own opinion' (Athenæ Oxon. ed. Bliss, iii. 995).

He was the author of: 1. 'The Judgment of an University-Man concerning M. William Chillingworth his late Pamphlet, in Answere to Charity Maintayned,' 4to (anon.), 1639. Probably printed at St. Omer. A reply to Chillingworth's ' Religion of Protes-

tants' [see KNOTT, EDWARD]. 2. 'Heavtomachia. M. Chillingworth against himselfe,' 4to, pp. 46. Printed as an appendix to the preceding work. Wood and Oliver erroneously ascribe to him another attack on Chillingworth, 'The Totall Svmme,' 1639, 4to, which was the work of the jesuit Father John Floyd [q. v.]

[Birch's Life of Chillingworth; Dodd's Church Hist. iii. 320; Foley's Records, iv. 598, vi. 251, vii. 856; Oliver's Jesuit Collections, p. 128; Southwell's Bibl. Scriptorum Soc. Jesu, p. 315.]
T. C.

LACHTAIN (d. 622), Irish saint, whose name also appears in Irish literature as Laichtin (Martyrology of Donegal, p. 80), Lachtnain (Annala Rioghachta Eireann, i. 244), Lachtoc, and Molschtoc (Felire Oengusa, ed. Stokes, pp. 57, 64), belonged to the tribe called Muscraighe, who claimed descent from Conaire MacModhlamha, a king of Ireland in the second century. His father's name was Torben, and he was born in Munster. He became a disciple of Comgall [q. v.] of Beannchair and founded two churches, one in Ossory at Achadh-úir, now Freshford, county Kilkenny, the other at Bealach Feabhradh, of which the site is now uncertain. A later church, with an Irish inscription of the eleventh century over the door, represents his earlier edifice at Freshford, and near it is a holy well, called after him Tobar Lachtain. He died in 622. In the museum of the Royal Irish Academy, Dublin, is a silver reliquary, made in the twelfth century, to contain an arm of this saint. His feast is celebrated 19 March.

[Colgan's Acta Sanctorum Hibernia; Martyrology of Donegal, Irish Archæological and Celtic Society, 1864; O'Donovan's note in Annals R. E., i. 244–5; Leabhar Breac, facs. fol. 83; Dunraven's Notes on Irish Architecture, 1877, ii. 91; Mo Tures ar Lachtain, 1877.]
N. M.

LACKINGTON, GEORGE (1768–1844), bookseller, born in 1768, was a 'third cousin' of James Lackington [q. v.], and entered the latter's bookselling business in Chiswell Street, London, at the age of thirteen (J. LACKINGTON, Confessions, 1804, p. viii). His father was a prosperous coal merchant, and provided his son with the necessary capital to purchase a share in Lackington, Allen, & Co.'s great shop, known as the 'Temple of the Muses,' in Finsbury Square. He became head of the firm in 1798. The first volume of their 'Catalogue, Michaelmas 1799 to Michaelmas 1800,' described upwards of two hundred thousand volumes; the second volume, which described upwards of eight hundred thousand volumes, was issued in 1803. Selling cheaply in large quantities for cash only continued to be the main feature of the business, to which were afterwards added many publishing speculations. Besides Lackington the other members of the firm were Allen, who possessed a great knowledge of books acquired from early training with James Lackington, and Hughes. The latter was also lessee of Sadler's Wells. Subsequent partners were A. Kirkman, Mayor, a son of Dr. Mayor of Woodstock, and Jones. In 1822 the business was conducted under the style of Lackington, Hughes, Harding, Mavor, & Lepard. On the retirement of Lackington, Joseph Harding became the chief partner, and the business was removed to Pall Mall East by Harding and Lepard. Many well-known booksellers received their training in this famous house. 'The last of the Lackingtonians,' Kames James Ford, died 11 Dec. 1886, at the age of ninety-four (*Bookseller*, 16 Dec. 1886).

The Egyptian Hall in Piccadilly was bought by Lackington, and let for miscellaneous exhibitions (WHEATLEY and CUNNINGHAM, *London Past and Present*, ii. 7). He was usually known as the 'nephew' of the elder Lackington, and Nichols speaks of him as 'well educated and gentlemanly' (*Lit. Anecd.* iii. 646). In his later years he was an official assignee of bankrupts in London. He married a daughter of Captain Bullock, R.N., and left two daughters. He died at St. John's Wood 31 March 1844, aged 76.

[Nichols's Illustrations, viii. 516; Timperley's Encyclopædia, 1842, p. 862; Sir E. Brydges's Autobiography, 1834, 2 vols.; also Reasons for Amendment of Act 54 Geo. III. c. 156; Gent. Mag. 1817 pt. ii. pp. 153-5, 1818 pt. i. p. 350, May 1844 p. 549.] H. R. T.

LACKINGTON, JAMES (1746–1815), bookseller, born 31 Aug. 1746 at Wellington, Somerset, was the eldest son of George Lackington, a journeyman shoemaker. His grandfather was a gentleman farmer at Langford, near Wellington. Young Lackington's father was a drunkard, but his mother was a woman of remarkable energy. The son showed his business capacity when ten years old as an itinerant meat pieman (*Memoirs*, 1792, pp. 57–65). In 1760 he was bound apprentice to George Bowden, a shoemaker at Taunton, and two years later became a professed methodist. He worked as a journeyman at Bristol and other places. While living at Bristol he bought books and read much. Although he could not write he composed ballads, which were sung about the streets. In 1770 he married his first wife, Nancy Smith. He went to London in August 1773, with the traditional half-crown, but without his wife. The following year he opened a bookstall and shoemaker's shop in Featherstone Street, St. Luke's, commencing with a sackful of old theological books, which he bought for a guinea, and a few scraps of leather. He was able to borrow five pounds from a fund started by 'Mr. Wesley's people' to assist deserving members of their body. The exercise of great industry and frugality, in which virtue his wife excelled, enabled him in six months to increase his stock in value from five to twenty-five pounds. He gave up his shoemaking and removed to 46 Chiswell Street, where his wife died a few months after. On 30 Jan. 1776 he married Dorcas Turton, who was a lover of books, and who became very helpful in the business. The reading of Amory's 'John Buncle' upset Lackington's methodism, and gave him a sceptical turn. The business prospered, and John Denis, an oilman and collector of books on alchemy and mystical divinity, brought in some capital. In 1779 the firm of Lackington & Co. produced their first catalogue of twelve thousand volumes, all described by Lackington. The partnership with Denis only lasted two years, but Lackington was afterwards joined by Allen, who had worked his way upwards from boyhood in the business, and the firm became famous as Lackington, Allen, & Co.

In 1780 Lackington determined to sell for cash only at the lowest possible price, and four years later published catalogues of twelve and thirty thousand volumes respectively. He broke through the trade custom of destroying all but a few copies of remainders, and sold the whole stock at little profit. From buying books in small quantities he rose to purchasing entire libraries, and was able to set up a carriage and a country house at Merton. His shop occupied a large block at one of the corners of Finsbury Square, with a frontage of 140 feet. It was known as 'The Temple of the Muses,' and was one of the sights of London. Charles Knight remembered a visit there in 1801. A dome, in which stood a flag, was a conspicuous object at the top of the building. In the middle of the shop was an immense circular counter. A broad staircase led to the 'lounging rooms,' and the first of a series of circular galleries around which books were displayed, growing cheaper and shabbier in condition as one ascended (*Shadows of the Old Booksellers*, 1865, pp. 282–3). Some years later the shop was destroyed by a fire. There is an engraving of 1789 (F. CRACE, *Catalogue*, 1878, p. 492), and many later prints.

In 1787, and again in 1790, Lackington travelled through England to Edinburgh.

In 1791, when he calculated he was selling about one hundred thousand volumes each year at a profit of 4,000*l.* (*Memoirs*, p. 399), he published the first edition of his well-known 'Memoirs,' which give an interesting picture of bookselling life. The 'original humourous stories and droll anecdotes' with which the book is disfigured are said to have been furnished by the pen of a friend (P. PINDAR, *Ode to the Hero of Finsbury Square*, p. 30). In 1794 appeared 'The second volume of Lackington's Catalogue, from September 1793 to March 1794, consisting of above one hundred thousand volumes.' His second wife, Dorcas, died 27 Feb. 1795, aged 45 (*Gent. Mag.* 1795, pt. i. p. 173), and on 11 June, with his usual promptness, he married a relative of hers (*ib.* p. 526). He is said to have advertised for a wife with 20,000*l.* (P. PINDAR, *Ode*, p. 30). Lackington made over the whole of his part in the business to his cousin, George Lackington [q. v.], in 1798, retaining 'no share or interest in it' (*Confessions*, Pref. p. vii). He thereupon took up his residence at Thornbury in Gloucestershire. In 1804 were published his 'Confessions' to make amends for having 'publicly ridiculed a very large and respectable body of Christians.' The book is much less interesting than his previous volume: some prurient and entirely irrelevant remarks about girls' boarding-schools are appended. He subsequently purchased two small estates in Alveston, and in 1805 erected a small chapel for the Wesleyan methodists. He became a local preacher. In the following year he removed to Taunton, and built and endowed another chapel. A dispute arose between him and the conference in 1810. Two years afterwards he went to Budleigh Salterton in Devonshire, where he also erected and endowed a chapel. He died at Budleigh on 22 Nov. 1815, in his seventieth year (*Memoirs*, 1827, pp. 345-7; *Gent. Mag.* 1815, pt. ii. p. 640).

Lackington was a vain but warm-hearted, shrewd man of business, whose first object in life was to make money. As soon as he had acquired a fortune he seems to have lost any love of books which he may have had. A portrait by Scott, after Keenan, is prefixed to the 'Memoirs' (1792). There is a different portrait by Goldar and memoir in the 'New Wonderful Magazine' (iii. 119-32). In Peter Pindar's 'Ode' (1795) a caricature represents the bookseller stepping into his carriage, which bears the motto, 'Small profits do great things.'

His works are: 1. 'Memoirs of the first Forty-five Years of the Life of James Lackington, the present Bookseller in Chiswell Street, Moorfields, London, written by himself in a Series of Letters to a Friend,' London [1791], 8vo. 'A new edition, corrected and much enlarged,' London, 1792, 8vo, portrait: further enlarged, eight editions to 1794. 'Thirteenth edition, with index,' London [1810?], sm. 8vo. A German version, 'Anekdoten,' from the fifth edition, was printed at Hamburg in 1795, sm. 8vo. 2. 'The Confessions of J. Lackington, late Bookseller at the Temple of the Muses, to which are added two Letters on the bad Consequences of having Daughters educated at Boarding Schools,' London, 1804, sm. 8vo; Nos. 1 and 2 (the last in abstract) form vol. xviii. of the 'Autobiography' series, 1827, sm. 8vo. 'Lackington's Confessions rendered into Narrative by Allan Macleod [pseudonym],' London, 1804, sm. 8vo, is an attack upon Lackington in the form of a running commentary on his 'Confessions.'

[J. Lackington's Memoirs, 1792, and Confessions, 1804; C. Knight's Shadows of the Old Booksellers, 1865; two articles by A. L. Humphreys in Bookworm, May and June 1888; Humphreys's History of Wellington, 1889, 8vo; C. H. Timperley's Encyclopædia, 1842, p. 862; New Wonderful Mag. iii. 119-32; Nichols's Lit. Anecd. iii. 646, Illustrations, viii. 516; Gent. Mag. 1815 pt. ii. p. 640, 1812 pt. i. p. 673; Notes and Queries, 2nd ser. iii. 50; Biog. Dict. of Living Authors, 1816, p. 193.] H. R. T.

LA CLOCHE, JAMES (*fl.* 1668), natural son of Charles II, was born in Jersey in 1647, when his father was just seventeen. According to Charles, the boy's mother was 'a young lady of one of the noblest families in his dominions.' Her name is unknown. He was brought up as a protestant in France and Holland. In 1665 he was removed secretly to London; but his equivocal position caused him much disquietude there, and he returned of his own accord to the continent in 1667. He carried with him a formal acknowledgment of his parentage, signed and sealed by the king on 27 Sept. 1665, and a deed of settlement, dated 7 Feb. 1667, assigning to him a pension of 500*l.* In the first document Charles writes of him as 'our natural son James Stuart,' and states that he has borne various feigned names, and was now to take that of 'De La Cloche du Bourg de Jersey.' A few months afterwards he was received into the Roman catholic church at Hamburg, under the auspices, it would seem, of Queen Christina of Sweden, and in the latter part of the same year he entered the novitiate of the Jesuit Society at Rome under the name of James La Cloche, apparently with the knowledge and approval of Charles. In August 1668 the king, in search of some secret means of entering into communication with Rome,

B B 2

wrote to the general of the jesuits, F. Oliva, requesting that La Cloche should be sent to him in London. At the same time he sent a letter to La Cloche to the same effect (GIUSEPPE BOERO, *Istoria della Conversione alla Chiesa Cattolica di Carlo II*, 1863). La Cloche set out in October, travelling under the name of Henri de Rohan. Arrived in London, he obtained, in pursuit of the king's instructions, audience of the queen and the queen-mother, and was by them secretly brought to his father. No details of La Cloche's mission are accessible. The last of the king's letters to Oliva is dated 18 Nov., and suggests that some important determination had been arrived at. La Cloche finally returned to Rome as his father's 'secret ambassador to the father-general,' charged with commissions only to be explained orally, and with a stipulation that so soon as he had fulfilled them he was to return to England.

Further notice of La Cloche is wanting. Probably owing to the repeated change of name, his later career cannot be traced in the registers of the society, but he doubtless continued a member until his death. Boero is of opinion that after his return to England he remained there under an assumed name, that he continued secretly to visit his father at intervals, and that he was, in fact, the 'foreign ecclesiastic' who was sent for by the Duke of York, but who 'could not be found,' in the last illness of the king.

[Gent. Mag. 1866, i. 26–8, 226–7, 531 ; Boero's Istoria della Conversione . . . di Carlo II, 1863.]
G. G.

LACROIX, ALPHONSE FRANÇOIS (1799–1859), missionary, born in the canton of Neuchâtel on 10 May 1799, was educated there under the care of his uncle until he was seventeen years of age. In 1816 he went to Amsterdam as a tutor, and while there was stirred by the news of the overthrow of idolatry in Tahiti to offer himself for missionary labour. He was first appointed an agent of the Netherlands Missionary Society at Chinsurah, near Calcutta, but on the cession of the settlement to the East India Company he transferred his services to the London Missionary Society, and became a British subject. He married at Chinsurah, and continued there until 1827, when he removed to Calcutta, the principal sphere of his labours. While at Calcutta he inaugurated a remarkable religious movement in the small but numerous villages to the south and east of the metropolis as well as in the district of the Sunderbunds. He also preached with success in Saugor Island,

made various itinerant visits to the rivers Isamutty and Mattabhanga, and devoted his leisure to revising the Bengali scriptures and to training native preachers. During the thirty-eight years that he was thus honourably employed he paid only one visit to Europe, in 1842–3, when he spent his holiday in Switzerland, France, and England, and aroused an especial interest in his mission work throughout Switzerland, and particularly at Geneva. He pursued his pastorate of the native churches at Calcutta until his death there on 8 July 1859. He was tall and handsome, and of dignified presence, and was an animated, natural, and expressive preacher. He spoke English well, but felt more free in expressing himself on the continent in French, or at Calcutta in Bengali, of which language he was a perfect master.

[Brief Memorials of the Rev. Alphonse François Lacroix, by the Rev. Dr. Mullens, London Missionary Society; Chronicle of London Missionary Society, art. iv., by the Rev. E. Storrow, L.M.S., February 1882]
S. P. O.

LACY, FRANCIS ANTONY (1731–1792), Spanish general and diplomatist, born in 1731, was the son of an Irish officer who went to Spain with the Duke of Berwick, probably the Lacy who was a general at the Spanish siege of Oran in 1730. Francis Antony commenced his military career as ensign in the Irish infantry regiment of Ultonia in the Spanish service, during the disastrous campaign in Italy in 1747. He commanded the same regiment in the war with Portugal in 1762. As lieutenant-general he commanded the Spanish artillery at the famous siege of Gibraltar (DRINKWATER, p. 167). After the peace of 1783 Lacy was sent as Spanish minister-plenipotentiary to the courts of Stockholm and St. Petersburg, where he was very popular. On his return he was made commandant-general of the coast of Grenada, member of the supreme council of war, and commandant-general and sole inspector-general of the artillery and of all ordnance-manufacturing establishments in Spain and the Indies. The Spanish artillery school of Segovia was indebted to him for improved discipline and the establishment of classes for chemistry, mineralogy, and pyrotechnics. In March 1789 he was made governor and captain-general of Catalonia, where he was conspicuous by his active efforts to prevent the spread of French revolutionary doctrines. He married a daughter of the Marquis d'Abbeville, by whom he had a son and daughter. He died at Barcelona 31 Dec. 1792.

Lacy had the grand cordon of Charles III, was a commander of St. Januarius, and titular of the rich commandery of Casas Buenas, Merida. According to some he owed his success to his ready wit and imposing stature rather than to any military talent ; but his conciliatory disposition and his unswerving loyalty to the country of his adoption are generally admitted. Lacy is stated to have been uncle of Don Luiz Lacy (1775–1817), Spanish general and governor of Catalonia, whose name often appears in histories of Wellington's Peninsular campaigns, and who was executed at the castle of Belver, Majorca, on 5 July 1817, after his abortive attempt, in conjunction with General Milans, to re-establish the cortes and proclaim a constitution on 5 April in that year. Three years later the Spanish cortes, to honour his memory, named his son first grenadier of the Spanish army (*Biog. Univ.* Nouvelle edit. xxii. 421).

[Printed Sketch-Pedigree of General Maurice De Lacy [q. v.] of Grodno, of which there are copies in the British Museum ; Biog. Univers. vol. xxii., 'Lacy, François Antoine,' and 'Lacy, Luiz;' Grant's Cavaliers of Fortune, pp. 164–77 ; Drinkwater's Siege of Gibraltar, London, 1844 ed.]

H. M. C.

LACY, HARRIETTE DEBORAH (1807–1874), actress, daughter of a London tradesman named Taylor, was born in London in 1807. Her parents acquiescing in her desire to go on the stage she received lessons in elocution from Mrs. Bartley, wife of the Covent Garden manager, and made her *début* as Julia in the 'Rivals' under the management of Bellamy at the Bath Theatre on 5 Nov. 1827, when she was described on the bill as 'Miss Taylor from Richmond.' She obtained almost instant popularity, and in the course of the two following seasons Bellamy assigned her such parts as Portia, Helen McGregor, Lady Macbeth, and Catherine in the 'Taming of the Shrew.' She first appeared in London at Covent Garden, where, on 30 Oct. 1830, she played Nina in Dimond's 'Carnival of Naples,' and 'burst upon us,' says the 'Theatrical Journal' of that date, 'with a natural freshness and power that must at once secure her fame, and prove of signal advantage to the house.' Subsequent parts were Rosalind, in which Bannister compared her to Mrs. Jordan, and Helen to Sheridan Knowles's Hunchback in his play of that name, in which her performance excited the author's warmest admiration. She played Aspatia, to Macready's Melantius and Miss Huddart's Evadne, in the 'Bridal' under Benjamin Webster's management at the Haymarket in 1837, and in the following year she joined the company with which Macready com- menced his management of Covent Garden. There in August 1838 she played Lady Teazle to the Charles Surface of Walter Lacy, whom she shortly afterwards married. For some twelve years further she 'played leading comedy, tragedy, and Vestris business,' mainly at Covent Garden. Among her best performances were Nell Gwynne in Jerrold's play of that name (with the once well-known song, 'Buy my Oranges'), the original heroine in the same writer's 'Housekeeper,' and Ophelia, a part in which, according to Madame Vestris, she surpassed any actress of her time. She retired from the stage in 1848, making her farewell appearance at the Olympic. She died on 28 July 1874 at Montpellier Square, Brighton.

[Era, 2 Aug. 1874 ; Clark Russell's Representative Actors, Appendix, p. 441 ; Pascoe's Dramatic List, p. 242 ; Archer's Macready, pp. 107, 110.]

T. S.

LACY, HENRY DE, third EARL OF LINCOLN of the Lacy family (1249 ?–1311), was son of Edmund de Lacy, earl of Lincoln, by Alice, elder daughter of Manfred III, marquis of Saluzzo, and grandson of John de Lacy, first earl [q. v.] Henry was probably born in the latter part of 1249, since in April 1296 he was in his forty-seventh year (*Monast. Anglic.* v. 643). He succeeded his father on 21 July 1257. In 1269 he was involved in a quarrel with John de Warrenne, earl of Surrey, as to certain pasture land, and a threatened appeal to arms was only prevented by the king's intervention. The regular trial which followed was decided in De Lacy's favour (*Flores Historiarum*, iii. 17). On 5 April 1272 he was made custos of Knaresborough Castle, and on 13 Oct. of the same year was knighted by the king on the occasion of the wedding of Edmund, earl of Cornwall (*Ann. Mon.* ii. 111). About the same time he received full investiture of his earldom. In 1276 he served in the Welsh war, and was in command of a division which marched against Castle Baldwin, and next year besieged and took the castle of Dolvorwyn (*Brut y Tywysogion*, pp. 365–6, Rolls Ser.) In March 1278 he was one of the escort appointed to attend Alexander III of Scotland on his visit to England (*Cal. Docts. Scotland*, ii. 107). In 1279 he was joint-lieutenant of England during the king's absence from 27 April to 19 June (*Fœdera*, i. 568). Three years later he was again employed in Wales. Lincoln accompanied the king on his three years' visit to Gascony, from 1286 to 1289. In October 1289 he was appointed with Robert Burnell [q. v.] to hear the complaints against Ralph Hengham [q.v.]

and other judges. He was one of the commissioners appointed to treat with the guardians of Scotland in 1290, and in this capacity was present at the parliament of Brigham (STEVENSON, *Docts. illustr. of Hist. of Scotland*, i. 159, 163, 171). He was also present at Norham in 1291, and at Berwick in 1292 during the deliberations relative to the Scottish succession, and in the latter year was one of those appointed to decide on the claims of William de Ros and John de Vaux. In 1292 Lincoln was one of the sureties for Gilbert de Clare, eighth earl of Gloucester [q. v.] (*Rot. Parl.* i. 75–7).

In 1293 Lincoln served on an embassy to France to treat for peace. In the following year he was on his way to Gascony, but while still at Portsmouth was recalled by the outbreak of war in Wales. While proceeding to relieve his castle of Denbigh he was defeated by his own Welshmen on 11 Nov.; Lincoln himself escaped with difficulty. He remained in Wales till the spring of 1295. On 14 Jan. 1296 he sailed from Plymouth with Edmund, earl of Lancaster, on his way to Gascony. After pillaging St. Matthieu, near Cape Finisterre, they landed at Blaye in mid-Lent and marched against Bordeaux, which they besieged without success. On the death of Edmund on 5 June, Lincoln was chosen to succeed him by the voice of the whole army. He defeated Robert of Artois before Bourg-sur-Mer, and besieged Aux for seven weeks in July and August with great vigour, but was at length forced to retire to Bayonne. In February 1297 the citizens of Bellegarde, who were besieged by the French, appealed for assistance. Lincoln marched out to their aid, but was defeated and forced to retreat once more to Bayonne. However, in the summer he made a successful raid towards Toulouse, which lasted till Michaelmas. He then went back to Bayonne till after Christmas, and about Easter 1298 returned to England. On 15 May he was appointed to arrange the marriage between Edward, prince of Wales, and Isabella of France (*Fœdera*, i. 905). He was one of the nobles who swore on the king's behalf that he would reconfirm the charters on his return from the Scottish war. He accompanied Edward to Scotland, and was present at the battle of Falkirk on 22 July. In July 1299 he was summoned to attend the council at York to deliberate on the affairs of Scotland. In 1300 he was again in Scotland, and present at the siege of Caerlaverock in July, when he commanded the first division. On 26 Sept. 1300 he was sent with Hugh Despenser on a mission to the pope to complain of the injury done by the Scots (RISHANGER,

pp. 195–6, 451), and was also entrusted with a mission to the king of France on 14 Oct. In March 1301 he was directed to attend the Prince of Wales in person on his invasion of Scotland at midsummer, and during September and October was engaged in Galloway (*Cal. Docts. Scotl.* ii. 1191, 1224, 1235, 1240). During the next two years he was constantly employed in negotiations with the French king. Finally, after proclaiming peace at Paris on 20 May 1303 (*Fœdera*, i. 952–5), he went to Gascony to take possession of it in Edward's name; he remained there for the following year (*Chron. Edw. I and II*, i. 127–9; HEMINGBURGH, ii. 230). On 16 Sept. 1305 he was one of the commissioners appointed in the parliament at Westminster to arrange the affairs of Scotland, and in the same parliament was a receiver and trier of petitions from Gascony (*Rolls of Parliament*, i. 267, 159). On 15 Oct. he was sent on a mission to Lyons with presents for Pope Clement V (*Fœdera*, i. 974). He returned to London on 16 Feb. 1306, and was publicly received by the mayor (*Chron. Edw. I and II*, i. 143–4). Later in the year he went to Scotland with the Prince of Wales, who was ordered to act by his advice (*Chron. Lanercost*, p. 204). In January 1307 he was one of the commissioners appointed to hold a parliament at Carlisle (*Rolls of Parl.* i. 188–9). In the summer he accompanied Edward on his march to Scotland, and was present at the king's death on 7 July.

Lincoln attended Edward II into Scotland, and in the following year, 1308, was present at the coronation on 25 Feb., when he carried the sword. The monk of Malmesbury says that Lincoln gave his assent to the creation of Piers Gaveston [q. v.] as Earl of Cornwall, in August 1307, and advised Edward II that the separation of this earldom from the crown was within his power (*Chron. Edw. I and II*, ii. 155). The same authority says that, after the king, Lincoln was Gaveston's chief supporter, but that through the latter's ingratitude he came to be the chief of his enemies (*ib.* ii. 158). Lincoln's enmity to the favourite was already active in February 1308 (*Chron. Lanercost*, p. 211). He was, however, once more won over to Gaveston's side in July 1308, only to be speedily alienated by the nickname of 'burst-belly' (*boele crevée*), which Gaveston applied to him. As a consequence Lincoln joined with his son-in-law, Thomas of Lancaster, and other earls, in refusing to attend the council at York in October 1309 (HEMINGBURGH, ii. 275). He had joined in the letter of the barons to the pope at Stamford on 6 Aug. previously. On 16 March 1310 he was one of the petitioners for the ordinances, and was himself one of the ordainers who were in consequence appointed. An anonymous letter of this time, while stating that Lincoln had remonstrated with Edward II, alleges that there was in reality a secret understanding between the king and earl (*Cal. Docts. Scott.* iii. 177). Edward appointed Lincoln to be guardian of the kingdom when he went to Scotland in September 1310. Lincoln spent the Christmas at Kingston in Dorset (*ib.* iii. 197), and soon afterwards returned to London, where he died at his house in Holborn on 5 Feb. 1311. He was buried in the lady-chapel of St. Paul's Cathedral on 28 Feb.

Lincoln was 'the closest counsellor of Edward I' (STUBBS, *Const. Hist.* ii. 319, ed. 1877). His action during the reign of Edward II was perhaps due to the conflict between loyalty to his old master's son and his old master's policy. A later story represents him on his deathbed as counselling his son-in-law to opposition to the royal authority (WALSINGHAM, i. 130; TROKELOWE, pp. 72–3). Hemingburgh describes him as 'courteous, handsome, and active' (ii. 74), and elsewhere he is called 'active in war and ripe in counsel' (TROKELOWE, p. 72).

Lincoln was earl of Salisbury in right of his first wife. He held the barony of Renfrew in Scotland before 1280, and he also obtained a grant of the lands of James, steward of Scotland, which he afterwards surrendered in return for four thousand marks (*Cal. Docts. Scott.* ii. 1121, 1857, iii. 58, 98). He founded in April 1283 the abbey of Whalley, Lancashire, whither his great-grandfather's foundation of Stanlaw, Cheshire, was then transferred (*Mon. Angl.* v. 639). He also contemplated in 1306 the foundation of a college for thirteen scholars at Oxford (*Fœdera*, i. 990; *Calend. Genealogicum*, ii. 724). He also contributed largely to the 'new work' at St. Paul's Cathedral (DUGDALE, *St. Paul's*, ed. 1818, p. 11). His house in London was on the site of the present Lincoln's Inn, which owes its name to this circumstance (FOSS, *Judges of England*, iv. 256–7). He was the builder of Denbigh Castle, over the gate of which was his statue (LELAND, *Itin.* v. 61).

Lincoln married in 1257 Margaret Longespée, grand-daughter and heiress of William Longespée, second earl of Salisbury. By her he had two sons, Edmund, who was drowned in a well at the Red Tower in Denbigh Castle (*ib.*), and John, killed by a fall at Pontefract; also two daughters, Margaret, who died young, and Alice, born in 1283. Margaret, countess of Lincoln, died in 1309, and her husband then married Joan, sister of William, sixth baron Martin of Kemys. Alice de Lacy married Thomas, earl of Lancaster, on 28 Oct. 1294, but left him in 1318 and took refuge with John, earl of Warrenne (*Chron. Edw. I and II*, ii. 54). On the occasion of this marriage Lincoln surrendered his lands to the king and obtained a fresh grant of the whole, with remainder to his daughter and son-in-law. After Thomas's death, Alice de Lacy married Eubulo L'Estrange before October 1328. He died in September 1335, and his widow then married, in February 1336, Hugh le Freyne, who died the same year. Alice, who always styled herself Countess of Lincoln and Salisbury, died 2 Oct. 1348. Her husbands were styled Earls of Lincoln and Salisbury in her right. She left no children, and her titles consequently became extinct. Henry de Lacy endowed a kinsman, possibly a bastard son, with lands at Grantchester (LELAND, *Itin.* iv. 1). The 'Compoti of the Lancashire and Cheshire Manors of Henry de Lacy ... in 24 and 33 Edward I' were published by the Chetham Society in 1884.

[Chronicles Edward I and II; Flores Historiarum; Langtoft's Chronicle; Annales Monastici; Walsingham's Historia Anglicana; Rishanger's Chronicle, and the Annales Regni Scotiæ, printed in the same volume; Trokelowe and Blaneford's Chronicles (all these are in the Rolls Series); Hemingburgh's Chronicle (Engl. Hist. Soc.); Chronicle of Lanercost (Bannatyne Club); Calendar of Documents relating to Scotland, vols. ii. and iii.; Rymer's Fœdera, Record ed.; Nicolas's Song of Caerlaverock, pp. 5, 93–5; Dugdale's Baronage, vol. i.; Doyle's Official Baronage, ii. 374–6; Burke's Dormant and Extinct Peerage, p. 311; preface to the Compoti.]
C. L. K

LACY, HUGH DE, fifth BARON LACY by tenure, and first LORD OF MEATH (*d.* 1186), one of the conquerors of Ireland, was no doubt the son, and not, as has sometimes been stated, a younger brother, of Gilbert de Lacy (cf. DUGDALE, *Mon. Angl.* vi. 135).

GILBERT DE LACY (*fl.* 1150), fourth baron Lacy, was son of Emma, daughter of Walter de Lacy, first baron [q. v.] His father's name is not known. After the death of his uncle, Hugh de Lacy, the family estates were taken into the royal hands, but Gilbert assumed the name of Lacy. In the reign of Stephen he at first supported the Empress Matilda, in whose behalf he attempted to capture Bath in 1138 (*Gesta Stephani*, iii. 38, Rolls Series). But by 1146 he had gone over to the king, perhaps because the empress kept Joce de Dinan in possession of Ludlow Castle. So far as there is any truth in the early part of the 'Romance

of Fulk Fitzwarine,' Gilbert, and not his grandson Walter, must be the hero. That Joce and Gilbert were opponents is an historical fact. Gilbert appears to have obtained the favour of Henry II, and recovered his uncle's lands; in 1158 he was excused the 'donum' to the king. A little later he joined the knights of the Temple, and went to the Holy Land. There he became preceptor of his order in the county of Tripoli, in which capacity he took part in Geoffrey de Lusignan's successful expedition against Noureddin in 1163 (WILLIAM OF TYRE, xix. 8). He gave the templars twelve hides of land, and one virgate in Guttinges, and also five burgages in Winchcombe. He is described as a prudent man and skilful soldier.

Hugh de Lacy is said to have had a dispute with Joce de Dinan as to certain lands in Herefordshire in 1154 (WRIGHT, Hist. of Ludlow, p. 54). He was in possession of his father's lands before 1163, and in 1165–6 held fifty-eight and three-quarters knights' fees, and had nine tenants without knight service (EYTON, Shropshire, v. 263). In October 1171 he went over to Ireland with Henry II, and early in 1172 was sent to receive the submission of Roderic, king of Connaught. Before Henry's departure about the end of March Lacy was granted Meath by the service of fifty knights and with almost royal authority; he was also put in charge of Dublin Castle. Later in the year Lacy arranged a meeting with Tiernan O'Rourke to take place at Tlachtgha, now called the Hill of Ward, near Athboy in Meath. The meeting ended in a quarrel, which both parties attributed to the treachery of the other; Tiernan was slain, and Hugh only escaped with difficulty. Lacy seems to have left Dublin in charge of Earl Richard de Clare by the king's orders, and to have commenced securing Meath by the erection of castles. Among these was the castle of Trim, which was put in charge of Hugh Tyrel. After this Lacy went back to England (REGAN, ll. 3152–3238). On 29 Dec. 1172 he was at Canterbury, where, according to a story preserved by Giraldus, he reproved Archbishop Richard for his boastful language (Opera, vii. 69). Next year he was fighting for Henry in France, and held Verneuil against Louis VII for a month; but at the end of that time the town was forced to capitulate. Hugh de Lacy is mentioned as one of those who were sent by the king with his treasure to Jerusalem in May 1177 (Gesta Henrici, ii. 159). Another version names Henry de Lacy, and in any case it cannot be our Hugh, who was at the same time sent over to Ireland as procurator-general, Richard de Clare having

died shortly before. The grant of Meath was now confirmed, with the addition of Offelans, Offaly, Kildare, and Wicklow (ib. ii. 161, 163–4; GIRALDUS, v. 347).

As governor of Ireland Lacy secured Leinster and Meath by building numerous castles, while he maintained peace and good order by making it his first care to preserve the native Irish in possession of their lands. By his liberal and just conduct he won the hearts of the Irish; but his friendly relations with the native chiefs soon led to an accusation that he intended to seize the sovereignty of the island for himself (ib. v. 352–353, 356). The author of the 'Gesta Henrici,' however, says that Lacy lost his favour with Henry in consequence of complaints of his injustice by the Irish (ii. 221). In 1181, he was recalled from his government for having married the daughter of Roderic, king of Connaught, without leave (ib. ii. 270). But in the following winter Hugh was sent back, though with a coadjutor in the person of one of the royal clerks, Robert of Shrewsbury. When, early in 1185, Henry sent his son John over to Ireland, the young earl complained to his father that Hugh would not permit the Irish to pay tribute. This led to fresh disgrace, but Hugh remained in Ireland, and occupied himself as before with castle-building. He had erected a castle at Durrow, in what is now King's County, and on 25 July 1186 had gone out to view it, when 'one of the men of Teffia, a youth named Gilla-gan-inathar O'Meyey, approached him, and with an axe severed his head from his body' (Four Masters, iii. 73). The murderer was a foster-son of Sinnach O'Caharny, or 'the Fox,' chief of Teffia, by whose instigation he is said to have done the deed. A later story described him as one of the labourers on the castle, but there does not appear to be any authority for this older than Holinshed (ib. iii. 73–5 n.) William of Newburgh says that Henry was very glad at Hugh's death, and repeats the story that he had aspired to obtain the crown of Ireland for himself (Chron. Stephen, Henry II, &c. i. 239–40, Rolls Ser.) Certainly Lacy had made himself formidable to the royal authority, and Earl John was promptly sent over to Ireland to take possession of his lands (Gesta Henrici, ii. 350).

Lacy was buried at Durrow, but in 1195 his body was removed to the abbey of Bective in Meath, and his head to St. Thomas's Church at Dublin. Afterwards a controversy arose between the canons of St. Thomas and the monks of Bective, which ended in 1205 in the removal of the body to Dublin, where it was interred, together with the head, in the tomb of De Lacy's first wife (*Reg. St. Thomas, Dublin*, pp. 348-50).

Giraldus describes Lacy as a swarthy man, with small black sunken eyes, a flat nose, and an ugly scar on his cheek; muscular in body, but small and ill-made. He was a man of resolute character; for temperance a very Frenchman, careful in private affairs, and vigilant in public business. Despite his experience in military matters he sustained many reverses in his campaigns. He was lax in his morality, and avaricious, but eager beyond measure for honour and renown (*Opera*, v. 354). Hugh was a benefactor of Lanthony Abbey, and also of many churches in Ireland, including the abbey of Trim.

Hugh's first wife was Rose or Roysya de Monemue (Monmouth); by her he had two sons, Walter (*d.* 1241) and Hugh, both of whom are noticed separately, and also a daughter, Elayne, who married Richard de Beaufo. By the daughter of Roderic O'Connor, whose name is also given as Rose, he had a son, William (called Gorm or 'Blue'), who acted in close connection with his half-brothers. William de Lacy took a prominent part in the resistance to William Marshal in 1224, and was killed fighting against Cathal O'Reilly in 1233 (*Four Masters*, iii. 269; HENNESSEY, *Book of Fenagh*, pp. 72-7). He married a daughter of Llewelyn, prince of North Wales. Pierce Oge Lacy, the famous rebel of Elizabeth's time, was eighteenth in descent from him, and from him also descend the Lynches of Galway (*Four Masters*, iii. 75 n.; *Reg. St. Thos. Dublin*, pp. 7, 419-20; SHIRLEY, *Royal and Historical Letters*, i. 223-4, 499, 500-2, Rolls Ser.) Hugh had another son, Gilbert, who was alive in 1222 (*Cal. Rot. Claus.* i. 527 b), and two daughters, one married to Geoffrey de Marisco [q. v.] (MATT. PARIS, iii. 277), and the other to William FitzAlan (EYTON, v. 240), but by which wife is not clear. The daughter of the king of Connaught was alive in 1224; she had at least two other sons, Thomas and Henry, whose surname is given as Blund. Since William de Lacy is also sometimes called Le Blund, they may have been brothers of the whole blood (SHIRLEY, u.s. i. 502).

[Annals of the Four Masters, ed. O'Donovan; Annals of Loch Cé; Hoveden's Chron.; Gesta Henrici II ascribed to Benedict Abbas; Chron. St. Peter's, Gloucester; Chartularies of St. Mary, Dublin; Reg. St. Thomas, Dublin; Giraldus Cambrensis, Expugnatio Hiberniæ, in Opera, vol. v. (all these are in the Rolls Ser.); Anglo-Norman Poem on the Conquest of Ireland, ascribed to Regan, ed. Michel; Gilbert's Viceroys of Ireland; Stokes's Ireland and the Anglo-Norman Church; Eyton's Shropshire, v. 248-56; Dugdale's Baronage, i. 96.] C. L. K.

LACY, HUGH DE, EARL OF ULSTER (*d.* 1242?), second son of Hugh de Lacy (*d.* 1186) [q. v.], by his first wife, Rose or Roysya de Monemue (Monmouth). While his elder brother Walter (*d.* 1241) [q. v.] eventually succeeded his father in Meath, Hugh went into Ulster. Mr. Gilbert (*Viceroys of Ireland*, pp. 55, 59, 65) is mistaken in speaking of him as having been viceroy of Ireland in 1189-90, and again in 1203 and 1205; for the records show that John de Courci [q. v.] and Meiler FitzHenry [q. v.] held office uninterruptedly. Nor is it clear that Hugh is the 'son of Hugo de Lacy' who in 1195 joined John de Courci in his warfare with the English of Leinster and Munster, and afterwards in assisting Cathal Crobhderg, king of Connaught, against Cathal Macdermot (*Loch Cé*, i. 191; *Four Masters*, iii. 101-103; see under LACY, WALTER DE, *d.* 1241). But a little later, when Walter de Lacy was absent in France, Hugh acted for him in Meath, and in 1199 accompanied John de Courci to assist Cathal Crobhderg at Kilmacduagh. There Cathal Carragh attacked and defeated them with great slaughter, pursuing them to Randown on Lough Rec, near Athlone. But soon afterwards Hugh took Cathal Carragh by treachery, and confined him in his castle of Nobber, co. Meath, till he purchased his release (*Four Masters*, iii. 121 and notes; *Loch Cé*, i. 219-23, sub anno 1201). After this Hugh de Lacy became the chief opponent of John de Courci. When, in 1201, De Courci was fleeing from Walter de Lacy, Hugh treacherously made him prisoner, and would have handed him over to the king had not De Courci's followers rescued their lord by force (HOVEDEN, iv. 176). In 1203 Hugh again attacked De Courci and drove him out of Down. Next year the war was renewed and De Courci taken prisoner. Hugh's services were rewarded on 31 Aug. 1204 by the promise of eight cantreds of De Courci's land in Ulster, and the confirmation of six cantreds in Connaught, granted to him by the king while Earl of Moretain (*Cal. Rot. Pat.* i. 45; *Charter Rolls*, p. 148). In March 1205 Hugh went over to England, and on 2 May obtained a grant of all the lands which John de Courci held in Ulster on the day when Hugh defeated him and took him prisoner in the field; on 29 May the grant was confirmed, and Hugh made Earl of Ulster (*ib.* p. 151; *Cal. Rot. Pat.* i. 54). This is the earliest creation of an Anglo-Norman dignity in Ireland of which there is any extant record.

On 30 June 1205 Hugh de Lacy was sent back to Ireland, Meiler FitzHenry the justiciar being ordered to act by his advice (*Cal.*

Rot. Claus. i. 40). According to a legend preserved in the 'Book of Howth' (p. 112), Hugh now banished the traitors who had betrayed John de Courci, and on their return through stress of weather had them all hanged. In 1206 he led an army into Tyrone, where he burnt many churches, but could exact no pledge from Hugh O'Neill. His power, however, was already making him obnoxious to the English king, and on 30 Aug. 1206 he was ordered to render obedience to Meiler Fitzhenry the justiciar (*Cal. Rot. Pat.* i. 67). But next year found him at open war with Meiler, whose people were in consequence nearly ruined. In May 1207 King John wrote to the De Lacys and other barons of Leinster in consequence of their opposition to the justiciar, and bade them to desist from their attempt to create a new assize (*ib.* i. 72). The war, however, still went on, and in 1208 Hugh and Walter de Lacy captured the castle of Ardnurcher after a siege of five weeks, and also took the territory of Fircal (in King's County), compelling Meiler to leave the country (*Four Masters,* iii. 157; *Loch Cé,* i. 233, 239, gives date of siege as 1207). During 1208 Hugh was also engaged in warfare in Ulster, where he burnt several churches. Partly owing to the turbulence of the De Lacys during these years, and partly owing to the protection they afforded to William de Braose [q. v.], King John landed at Waterford in the latter part of June 1210. After expelling Walter de Lacy from Meath he marched into Ulster. Hugh retreated to Carrickfergus, and thence, before the king could arrive, fled in a small boat to Scotland (*Annales Cambriæ,* pp. 66–7 and note, Rolls Ser.) According to some accounts, the expulsion of the De Lacys from Ireland was due to their having treacherously slain Sir John de Courci of Rathenny (GRACE, *Annals,* p. 25; *Ann. Hib.* in *Chart. St. Mary, Dublin,* ii. 311).

After a short stay in Scotland at St. Andrews, Hugh crossed over to France, where, according to a later legend, he and his brother Walter worked at the monastery of St. Taurin, Normandy, in the most menial offices. At length the abbot recognised them, and interceded with the king for their pardon (*ib.*) In point of fact, Hugh was not pardoned till long after his brother, and it seems probable that he was the Hugh de Lacy who took part in the crusade against the Albigensians; for the 'Dunstable Annals' allude expressly to him in this connection (*Annales Monastici,* iii. 75). However, William of Tudela's statement, that he was with Simon de Montfort in 1209, is clearly inaccurate; but there is no other obstacle

to the identification. In 1211 he advised Simon to take the offensive against the Count of Toulouse, and in 1214 he appears as lord of Castelnaudry and Laurac. In 1216 he was with Simon at Beaucaire, and accompanied him to the siege of Toulouse, where he served during the next two years, and was present at the crusading leader's death on 25 June 1218. In 1219 he took part in the fight at Baziège (*Chanson de la Croisade contre les Albigeois,* Soc. de l'Hist. de France, see index; *Recueil des Historiens de la France,* xix. 181; GARLAND, *De Triumphis Ecclesiæ,* p. 86, Roxburghe Club). On 17 Sept. 1221 Hugh de Lacy had a safe-conduct to come to England (SWEETMAN, i. 1012), and accordingly returned soon after; the 'Dunstable Annals' add that he had been expelled by the Albigensians. On his arrival in England Hugh petitioned for the restoration of his lands. This was refused, but a pension of three hundred marks was granted for his support. In April 1215 Hugh had been informed that his brother had paid a fine on his behalf, but that his lands would be retained by the king on account of his neglect to seek pardon, 'although we have been near to you' (no doubt an allusion to John's French campaign in 1214). In July 1215 Matthew de Tuit, one of Hugh's knights, had leave to come to England to treat for his lord. The negotiation, however, seems to have failed; for in August Walter de Lacy received charge of some of his brother's lands (*Cal. Rot. Pat.* i. 134, 150). In November 1216 Hugh was again offered restitution if he would return to his fealty (*Fœdera,* i. 145, Record edit.)

After the refusal of his petition for restitution Hugh went over to Ireland without the king's consent, and in the summer of 1222 Cathal Crobhderg wrote to the king in complaint of Hugh's conduct (SHIRLEY, i. 183). Hugh de Lacy had allied himself with Hugh O'Neill, destroyed the castle of Coleraine, and ravaged Meath and Leinster. Nevertheless, a scheme was proposed for the conditional return of Hugh's lands; but the intended sureties would not accept the responsibility, and it consequently fell through (*Cal. Rot. Claus.* i. 501, 527 b, 549 b). In 1223 Hugh went over to Wales, and joined Llewellyn ap Iorwerth [q. v.] in his warfare with William Marshal (MATT. PARIS, iii. 82). Llewellyn was defeated, and Hugh then formed a fresh scheme for the invasion of Ireland, whither he returned by stealth early next year. He arranged for assistance to come from Norway in the summer (SHIRLEY, i. 219), and rejoining Hugh O'Neill took up arms against the English and their Irish ally.

Hugh or Aedh, son of Cathal Crobhderg. The Anglo-Irish under the justiciar, Henry of London, archbishop of Dublin, were forced to come to terms, and in consequence William Marshal the younger was sent over to Ireland in June 1224. Marshal took Trim, which was held by William de Lacy [see under LACY, HUGH DE, d. 1186], and sent William Grace to relieve Carrickfergus, which was besieged by Hugh de Lacy. Hugh's fleet attempted without success to oppose Grace, and the siege was then raised. Marshal meantime had captured William de Lacy and his crannog of O'Reilly (ib. i. 500–2). Eventually Hugh made an agreement with Marshal under which he surrendered and was sent over to England (SWEETMAN, i. 1219). Hugh de Lacy there received absolution from the sentence of excommunication which had been passed on him by the pope's command, but could not obtain the royal pardon (Ann. Mon. iii. 91; Cal. Rot. Claus. i. 549 b). On 12 May 1226 Walter de Lacy received charge of all Hugh's lands in Ulster, to hold them for three years (SWEETMAN, i. 1371–4). However, on 20 April 1227 Hugh was at length restored to possession of his castles and lands (Cal. Rot. Claus. ii. 182 b).

After this Hugh de Lacy appears as a supporter of the royal authority in Ireland. In 1228 he was summoned for the French war with four knights, being more than were demanded of any Anglo-Irish noble except his brother Walter (SHIRLEY, i. 358). On the coming of Richard Marshal, earl of Pembroke [q. v.], into Ireland, Hugh de Lacy supported Maurice Fitzgerald, the royal justiciar, against the earl, and was present at the conference between the earl-marshal and his opponents at the Curragh, and the earl's defeat on 1 April 1234. Afterwards Hugh was summoned to England to advise the king, and he was subsequently thanked by Henry for his services (ib. i. 437, 478; SWEETMAN, i. 2113). In 1235 he took part in the great raid of Richard de Burgh (d. 1243) [q. v.] into Connaught. In the same year Alan of Galloway, who had married Hugh's daughter in 1228 (Chron. Lanercost, p. 40), died, leaving three daughters by a former wife and a bastard son, Thomas, who endeavoured to seize his father's lands. In April 1236 Hugh gathered a great army from Ireland and the Isle of Man, and joined Thomas in his rebellion. But Alexander II of Scotland soon compelled them to come to terms (MATT. PARIS, iii. 344–6; FORDUN, Scotichronicon, iii. 753). On 25 April 1237 Hugh was summoned to England to advise the king (SWEETMAN, i. 2384). In 1238 some of Hugh's followers killed an Irish chieftain, whereupon Donnell MacLoughlin, chief of Cenel Owen, took up arms and drove Hugh out of Ulster. Hugh returned with FitzMaurice the justiciar at harvest time, and after expelling MacLoughlin gave Tyrone to Brian O'Neill. In 1239 MacLoughlin recovered his lordship, but was speedily expelled once more. It was probably a later phase of this struggle which caused the great dissensions against Hugh in Ulster in 1240 (Four Masters, iii. 301 n.)

Hugh died at Carrickfergus at the end of 1242 or beginning of 1243 (MATT. PARIS, iv. 232; SWEETMAN, i. 2616, says he was certainly dead before 25 April 1243). He was buried in the church of the Dominican friars at Carrickfergus (Book of Howth, p. 124). Matthew Paris calls him 'a most renowned warrior, and the glorious conqueror of a great part of Ireland' (iv. 232). As Hugh was certainly the most turbulent, so also he was perhaps the most powerful of all the Anglo-Irish nobles of his age. The careers of himself, his father and brother, illustrate well the course of the English conquest of Ireland, and the peculiar difficulties which the royal authority had to encounter through the excessive power granted to or acquired by the chiefs of the English settlement. The grant of Ulster to Hugh included all authority except that of episcopal investiture, and Hugh held it exempt and separate from every county, having his own court and chancery (SWEETMAN, i. 200, 283; Carew MSS. v. 450). The earldom of Ulster of this creation came to an end at Hugh's death, for he left no male heir; and the allegation that a daughter of his married Walter de Burgh, and conveyed to her husband her father's rights in the earldom, is incorrect [see under BURGH, WALTER DE].

Hugh married Emmeline (sometimes called Leveline), daughter of Walter de Redelesford. She was alive as late as November 1267, but died before 1278 (SWEETMAN, ii. 834; Calendarium Genealogicum, i. 256). Besides the daughter who married Alan of Galloway, Hugh had another daughter, who married Miles MacCostelloe (Four Masters, iii. 349). One of his daughters was called Roysya (Carew MSS. v. 412). He had two sons, Walter and Roger, who were alive in 1226 (SWEETMAN, i. 1372). A son of his was killed during the war with MacLoughlin in 1238 (Four Masters, iii. 239 n.) There is no evidence as to whether these children were illegitimate or not; the 'Dunstable Annals' allege that in 1225 Hugh had abandoned his wife, and was living with an adulteress (Ann. Mon. iii. 91).

Hugh is said to have given the monks of St. Taurin a cell at Ruskey, near Carlingford.

He founded the house of the Dominicans at Carrickfergus, and was a benefactor of the canons of St. Thomas, Dublin, and also of St. Andrew's Church in Scotland (*Chart. St. Mary's, Dublin*, ii. 311; *Reg. St. Thos. Dublin*, pp. 7, 9, 13, 49–50; SWEETMAN, i. 2408).

[Annals of Loch Cé; Roger of Hoveden's Chronicle; Matthew Paris's Chronica Majora; Annales Monastici; Shirley's Royal and Historical Letters of the Reign of Henry III; Annales Cambriæ; Register of St. Thomas, Dublin; Chartulary of St. Mary's, Dublin (all these are in the Rolls Series); Annals of the Four Masters, ed. O'Donovan; Calendars of Patent Rolls, Close Rolls, and Charter Rolls, published by the Record Commission; Sweetman's Calendar of Documents relating to Ireland; Carew MSS., vol. v., containing the Book of Howth. Among modern writers reference may be made to Gilbert's Viceroys of Ireland, and Stokes's Ireland and the Anglo-Norman Church.]   C. L. K.

LACY, JOHN DE, first EARL OF LINCOLN of the Lacy family (*d.* 1240), was son of Roger de Lacy, second earl [q. v.], by Maud de Clere. He was probably a minor at the time of his father's death in January 1212, as he did not receive full livery till September 1213, when, although a part of the fine was remitted, his castles of Pontefract and Donington were still retained in the king's hands. Donington was restored in July 1214, Lacy giving hostages for his good conduct (*Cal. Rot. Claus.* i. 151, 167, 169). In 1215 he was one of the confederate barons, and was among the twenty-five appointed to see to the observance of the Great Charter. Afterwards he appears for a time to have gone over to the king, for on 1 Jan. 1216 he received the royal pardon, and his lands were restored, and in August he received letters of protection (HARDY, *Cal. Rot. Pat.* pp. 162, 176, 179, 180). Nevertheless he had been excommunicated by Innocent III with the other barons, and his fortress of Donington was destroyed by order of the king (MATT. PARIS, ii. 639, 643). In September 1216 his land at Navesby, Nottinghamshire, was entrusted to Ernald de Ambleville, but he was finally pardoned and his lands restored in August 1217 (*Cal. Rot. Claus.* i. 289, 318, 330). In 1218 he went on the crusade with Earl Randulf of Chester [see BLUNDEVILL, RANDULF DE], and was present at the siege of Damietta (MATT. PARIS, iii. 41); he had taken the cross as early as March 1215 (GERVASE OF CANTERBURY, ii. 109). After his return to England, about August 1220, he joined with Earl Randulf in his opposition to the king's government, but submitted at the same time as his leader, and surrendered his castles. In September 1227 he was sent on an embassy to Antwerp (*Fœdera*, i. 187), and on 6 Sept. 1230 was a commissioner to treat for a truce with France. After the death of Earl Randulf, Lacy was made Earl of Lincoln on 22 Nov. 1232, in right of his wife, Margaret, daughter of Robert de Quincy, and Hawise, countess of Lincoln, a sister of Earl Randulf. In 1233 he at first supported Richard Marshal, earl of Pembroke [q. v.], in his opposition to Peter des Roches, but was eventually won over by a bribe of a thousand marks from the bishop. His followers in Ireland refused to submit to Gilbert Marshal (*Ann. Mon.* i. 91). In 1236 Lincoln appears as one of the witnesses to the confirmation of the charters, and at the queen's coronation attended as constable of Chester. On 20 Nov. 1237 he was one of those who were sent by the king to the legate Otto and the council at St. Paul's to forbid them from taking any action. Lincoln had by this time attached himself completely to the court party, and he is mentioned in this year along with Simon de Montfort as one of the king's unpopular counsellors (MATT. PARIS, iii. 412). He used his position to secure the marriage of his daughter Maud to Richard de Clare, earl of Gloucester, and his influence over the king was so great that Earl Richard of Cornwall made it a subject of reproach against his brother. Lincoln, however, made his peace with Earl Richard by means of prayers and presents. He died on 22 July 1240, and was buried at Stanlaw Abbey, Cheshire, of which he, like his father, had been a great benefactor; Dugdale gives two epitaphs (*Mon. Angl.* v. 648). Lincoln had acted as a justice itinerant in Lincolnshire and Lancashire in 1226, and in the former county in 1233, and was sheriff of Cheshire in 1237 and 1240. He was twice married: first, to Alice, daughter of Gilbert de l'Aigle; and, secondly, before 21 June 1221, to Margaret de Quincy (*Cal. Rot. Claus.* i. 462), who after his death married Walter Marshal, earl of Pembroke, in 1241. By his second wife he left a son Edmund (*b.* 1227) and two daughters. It is sometimes said that Edmund was never Earl of Lincoln, but he is so styled on 5 Sept. 1255. Edmund married, in May 1247, Alicia, elder daughter of Manfred III, marquis of Saluzzo, and died on 21 July 1257, leaving an only son Henry, third earl of Lincoln [q. v.]

[Matthew Paris; Annales Monastici (both in Rolls Ser.); Monasticon Anglicanum, v. 534, 647–648; Dugdale's Baronage, i. 101–2; Doyle's Official Baronage, ii. 373; Foss's Judges of England, ii. 379–80.]   C. L. K.

LACY, JOHN (*d.* 1681), dramatist and comedian, of humble extraction, was born near Doncaster, and came in 1631 to London, where he was apprenticed to John Ogilby [q. v.], translator and dancing-master. Lacy was himself for some time a dancing-master, being, according to the 'Lives and Characters of the English Dramatic Poets,' probably by Charles Gildon [q.v.], 'of a rare shape of body and good complexion.' Ben Jonson obtained from Lacy Yorkshire words and proverbs for his 'Tale of a Tub,' 1633. During the civil war he was a lieutenant and quartermaster under Colonel Charles Gerard, afterwards earl of Macclesfield [q. v.] An original member of the king's company (Killigrew's), he speedily rose to be one of its chief supports, and retained his connection with it until his death. The first part associated with his name is Scruple, a nonconformist, in John Wilson's comedy the 'Cheats,' written in 1662, and played about the same time, presumably at Vere Street Theatre. A too vivacious mimicry by Lacy of some well-known nonconformist is supposed to have been the reason why the play was temporarily suppressed. Pepys, who bears constant testimony to the merits of Lacy, saw him, 12 June 1663, as Teague, an original part, in the 'Committee' of Sir Robert Howard. He calls it 'a merry but indifferent play,' adding 'only Lacy's part, an Irish footman, is beyond imagination.' Evelyn bestows similar commendation on Lacy's performance, 27 Nov. 1662. In 1664 Lacy appears to have played Captain Otter in the 'Silent Woman' and Annuias in the 'Alchemist,' and in 1665 Sir Politick Wouldbe in the 'Fox,' all by Ben Jonson.

Before the last date Lacy wrote his best play, 'The Old Troop, or Monsieur Raggou,' in which he utilised his experiences during the civil war, giving an animated if exaggerated and farcical description of the repute in which cavalier troopers were held by the country-folk, together with some particulars of the kind of plundering to which the soldiers were addicted. Scott makes use of this piece in 'Woodstock,' the twentieth chapter of which contains many references to the habit of eating children, with which, according to Lacy, Samuel Butler, and other writers, 'Lunsford's horse' were credited ('Woodstock', ii. 38, ed. 1868). In a note to the same volume Scott quotes from the piece what he calls a scene of 'coarse but humorous comedy,' which Swift 'had not, perhaps, forgotten when he recommended the eating of the children of the poor as a mode of relieving the distress of their parents' (ib. ii. 402). In the epilogue to the 'Vestal Virgin' of Sir Robert Howard, acted at the Theatre Royal, 4 Jan. 1865-6, Lacy, who delivered the epilogue, spoke of himself as a poet and threatened to 'turn Raggou into a tragedy.' This, with references in the piece to the

Dutch war, fixes the date of production as earlier than 1665. Lacy is believed to have been the original Raggou, a French servant. Under the date 31 July 1668 Pepys writes: 'To the King's house to see the first day of Lacy's "Monsieur Ragou," now new acted. The king and court all there, and mighty merry; a farce.' Of neither of these representations is any cast preserved. The play was first published in 1672; a second edition was printed in 1698. Bowen at the Haymarket, 31 July 1707, is the first recorded Raggou and Verbruggen the first Lieutenant. It was further revived at Drury Lane in 1714 and 1717. Langbaine conjectures, not too happily, that it was founded on some French original.

On 27 Dec. 1666, on the resumption of performances after the cessation of the plague, Lacy was Sir Roger in the 'Scornful Lady' of Beaumont and Fletcher. 'Sawny the Scot,' an execrable adaptation of the 'Taming of the Shrew,' of the authorship of which Lacy is accused, was seen by Pepys 9 April 1667. Pepys says it 'hath some very good pieces in it, but generally is but a mean play, and the best part, Sawny, done by Lacy [Lacy], and hath not half its life, by reason of the words, I suppose, not being understood, at least by me.' Sawny is a Scotch servant of Petruchio, whose language might well be incomprehensible both sides of the Tweed. He is an inexpressibly coarse, tedious buffoon. The piece was first printed in 4to, 1698, and was reissued in 1708. No cast earlier than that of the revival of 1698 at Drury Lane is extant, when Bullock, Powell, Joe Haines, Mrs. Verbruggen, and Mrs. Cibber enacted the chief parts. It was given at Lincoln's Inn Fields so late as 18 May 1725. To its popularity the profanities to which the 'Taming of the Shrew' was frequently submitted on the stage may be largely ascribed. In the same season (1667), according to Pepys, Lacy played a Country Gentleman in 'Change of Crowns,' an unprinted piece by Edward Howard, and Jonny (sic) Thump in 'Love in a Maze,' otherwise 'The Changes.' Concerning the earlier presentation, Pepys, 15 April 1667, says: 'Lacy did act the Country Gentleman come up to Court, who do abuse the Court with all imaginable wit and plainness about selling of places and doing everything for money.' So angry was Charles II 'at the liberty taken by Lacy's part to abuse him to his face' that he commanded the company should act no more, and committed Lacy to the Porter's Lodge. Mohun obtained forgiveness for the company and for Lacy, but the play remained under censure. After Lacy's release he met Howard, and cursed him because 'his nonsensical play' had been the cause of his imprisonment, telling him, moreover, that 'he was more of a fool than a poet.' A scuffle followed, and Howard complained to the king, who again silenced the company on 20 April 1667. To 1669 Genest assigns 'The Dumb Lady, or the Farrier made a Physician.' This is a miserable and highly indecent piece, far coarser than the originals compounded by Lacy from 'Le Médecin malgré lui' and 'L'Amour Médecin' of Molière. It was not printed until 1672, and no cast is given, but Lacy, no doubt, played Drench (Sganarelle).

Lacy was on 7 Dec. 1671 the original Bayes of the 'Rehearsal,' the prologue to which says that if the burlesque exercises the desired effect Lacy will boast that he had reformed the stage. At Lincoln's Inn, whither, after the destruction of the Theatre Royal, Killigrew's company migrated, Lacy was the original Alderman Gripe in Wycherley's 'Love in a Wood, or St. James's Park,' and in 1675, at the new theatre in Drury Lane, was the original Intrigo in Sir Francis Fane's 'Love in the Dark, or the Man of Business.' His editors doubtfully assert that he also played the French Dancing-Mistress in a play so named. Genest says that he probably acted Bobadil, and was the original Frenchlove in the 'English Mounseer,' by the Hon. James Howard, 1666; Pinguister in 'All Mistaken, or the Mad Couple,' by the same author, 1667; Tartuffe in 'Tartuffe, or the French Puritan,' adapted from Molière by Matthew Medbourne [q. v.], 1670; French Valet in 'Mock Duellist, or the French Valet,' by P. B., 1675, and the English Lawyer in the play of that name adapted by Ravenscroft from the Latin play of 'Ignoramus.' He also played Falstaff, in which, according to Davies, he succeeded Cartwright, and in 'Variety,' by the Duke of Newcastle. Lacy died on 17 Sept. 1681, in Drury Lane, two doors off Lord Anglesey's house, and near Cradle Alley, and was buried the Monday following 'in the farther churchyard' of St. Martin's-in-the-Fields. On 19 Oct. 1681, 20l. was ordered to be paid by Edward Griffin, esq., treasurer of the chamber, to John Lacy, assignee of Charles Killigrew, master of the revels, for two plays acted before his majesty in February and March 1678-9 (see AKERMAN, Secret Service Money, Camd. Soc., p. 34). Lacy gave lessons to Nell Gwynn, and is said to have been one of her lovers.

After Lacy's death appeared, in 1684, at Dorset Garden Theatre, a comedy, entitled 'Sir Hercules Buffoon, or the Poetical Squire,' which was published in the same year. A prologue by D'Urfey describing Lacy as the author and an epilogue by Joe Haines [q. v.] were spoken by the latter. Genest speaks of the play disparagingly.

Lacy was praised in his own day. His dancing seems to have been his chief attraction until age disabled him. Downes commends his acting of Scruple in the 'Cheats,' Jonny Thump, Teague, and Bayes. Pepys seldom mentions him without praise, and describes, under date 19 Jan. 1668-9, the dances which he introduced between the acts of 'Horace,' 'a silly tragedy.' Langbaine says that Lacy 'performed all parts that he undertook to a miracle, insomuch that I am apt to believe that as this age never had, so the next never will have his equal, at least not his superior.' Lacy, says Langbaine, was so approved by Charles II that the king caused his picture to be drawn in three several figures in the same table, viz. that of Teague in the 'Committee,' Mr. Scruple in the 'Cheats,' and M. Galliard in the 'Variety;' the picture is still at Windsor Castle. A copy was sold in 1819. A second, or the same, painted by M. Wright (1675), is in the Garrick Club.

[A not too trustworthy Life of Lacy is prefixed to the edition of his plays by Maidment and Logan. See also Aubrey's Letters by Eminent Persons, 1813. Pepys's Diary, Langbaine's Lives (which is far too favourable to Lacy). Downes's Roscius Anglicanus, Genest's Account of the Stage, and the Biographia Dramatica are the principal sources of information. Wheatley and Cunningham's London Past and Present; the History of the Stage assigned to Betterton; Davies's Dramatic Miscellanies, vol. i.; Wilkes's (Derrick's) General View of the Stage, &c., have also been consulted.]   J. K.

LACY, JOHN (fl. 1737), pseudo-prophet, was born at Saffron Walden, Essex, in 1664. He received some classical education, and as a younger son was sent to London to earn his own living in 1680. In 1706 he was a married man with a family, in good repute for his parts and piety, and one of the wealthiest members of Dr. Calamy's congregation at Westminster. The loss of a lawsuit in that year preyed upon his mind, and at the same time he fell under the influence of the so-called 'French prophets,' then lately arrived in England. In 1707 he published a translation of the 'Théâtre Sacré des Cévennes,' by Francis Maximilian, under the title 'A Cry from the Desert, or Testimonials of the Miraculous Things lately come to pass in the Cevennes verified upon Oath and by other proofs,' London, 8vo. A second edition, with an able preface in favour of the miraculous character of the phenomena, appeared the same year. This he followed up with 'Prophetical Warnings of Elias Marion, heretofore one of the Commanders of the Protestants that had taken Arms in the Cevennes: a Discourse uttered by him in London under the Operation of the Spirit, and faithfully taken in Writing whilst they were spoken,' London, 1707, 8vo, and a collection of his own prophetical utterances, in three parts, entitled 'The Prophetical Warnings of John Lacy, Esq., pronounced under the Operation of the Spirit and faithfully taken in writing whilst they were spoken,' London, 1707, 8vo. These curious outpourings are all in the first person, as if spoken by the spirit, and consist mainly of vague vaticinations of coming woes. Some of them are in bad French, others in worse Latin. In the preface Lacy states that while in his ecstasies his mind, tongue, and fingers were directed by an invisible 'foreign agent,' by whom also his body was agitated and contorted, and sometimes carried round or across the room, and that the seizures began suddenly on 12 June 1707. Calamy and others who witnessed the ecstasies testify to his physical agitation, or 'quaking,' and describe his utterance as preceded by much hiccoughing, gasping, sighing, and groaning, and, though perfectly articulate, broken and unnatural. Lacy also claimed the power of working miracles, and in particular to have restored her sight to a prophetess called Betty Gray, cured her of paralysis, and removed a tumour in her throat by the 'operation of the Spirit.' Blindness, paralysis, and tumour were alike imaginary. He also predicted the resurrection from the dead upon 25 May 1708 of Thomas Emes [q. v.], buried in Bunhill Fields on Christmas day 1707 (see *Harl. Misc.* vii. 191-6). Such crowds collected to witness the fulfilment of the prophecy that the trainbands were called out. The ministers and elders of the French church in the Savoy had early tried in vain to check the excitement by censuring the prophets as impostors. The latter were then indicted (4 July 1707) before Lord-chief-justice Holt for publishing false and scandalous pamphlets and holding tumultuous assemblies, were convicted, fined, and put in the pillory. A prosecution was also instituted by the attorney-general against Lacy and his chief coadjutor, Sir Richard Bulkeley (1644-1710) [q.v.], but was eventually abandoned. There were soon more than four hundred persons prophesying in different parts of the country. The clergy denounced them, and Calamy censured Lacy at Westminster in some sermons published as 'A Caveat against New Prophets,' London, 1708, 8vo. Lacy replied by going into one of his ecstasies in his own house in Calamy's presence, and rebuking him in the name of the Spirit. His formal answer appeared as 'A Relation of the Dealings of God to his unworthy servant, John Lacy, since the time of his believing and professing himself Inspired,' London, 1708, 8vo. Lacy was also attacked by Dr. Josiah Woodward [q. v.] in 'Remarks on the Modern Prophets,' London, 1708, 8vo, and replied in a 'Letter to the Rev. Dr. Josiah Woodward concerning his Remarks on the Modern Prophets,' London, 1708, 8vo, to which Woodward published an 'Answer.' Failing to convert his wife, Lacy deserted her in 1711, and went to live in Lancashire with Betty Gray. This he called leaving Hagar for Sara. About 1713 Whiston had been to his house and tried vainly to reason him out of his delusion. The Jacobite rising in 1715 elicited from him an appropriate 'Vision of J. L., Esq., a Prophet,' London, 1715, 8vo. His last publication was 'The Scene of Delusions, by the Rev. Mr. Owen of Warrington, at his own earnest request considered and confuted by one of the Modern Prophets; and as it proves partly by himself,' London, 1723, 8vo. He was committed to Bridewell in 1737 for opening an 'oratory' at Villiers Street, York Buildings, London. The date of his death is uncertain.

[Besides the writings mentioned in the text the principal authorities are Calamy's Historical Account of my own Life, ed. Rutt, ii. 72 et seq.; Whiston's Memoirs, 1749, p. 138; Luttrell's Relation of State Affairs, vi. 244, 307; Kingston's Enthusiastick Impostors no Divinely inspired Prophets; An Account of the Tryal, &c., of Elias Marion, London, 1707, 1st pt.; Predictions concerning the Raising the Dead Body of Mr. Thomas Emes, &c., London, 1708 (?), 4to; The Honest Quaker, or the Forgeries . . . of the pretended French Prophets . . . expos'd in a letter . . . giving an Account of a Sham Miracle performed by John L—y, Esq., on the body of Elizabeth Gray on the 17th of August last, London, 1707, 8vo; Humphrey's Account of the French Prophets, &c., and Farther Account in two letters to Sir Richard Bulkeley, London, 1708, 8vo; A Letter from John Lacy to Thomas Duton, being Reasons why the former left his wife, and took E. Gray, a Prophetess, to his bed (dated 6 March 1711); A Brand plucked from the Burning, exemplified in the Unparallel'd Case of Samuel Keimer, &c., London, 1718, 8vo; Lettres d'un Particulier à Monsieur Misson L'honnête Homme, London, 1707-8, 8vo; Boyer's Polit. State, iv. 37, 210, cf. art. See ANNX.]

J. M. R.

LACY, JOHN WILLIAM or **WILLIAM** (1780?-1865?), singer, born about 1780, was about 1795 a pupil, at Bath, of Venanzio Rauzzini (1747-1810). Some three years later he appeared at various concerts in London, but being dissatisfied with his own powers, he went to Italy for further study; there he 'entirely mastered both the language and style of singing of the natives.' Returning to England soon after 1800, he sang repeatedly at the Lenten Oratorio and other important concerts, but owing to weak health he never succeeded in taking the prominent position among contemporary vocalists for which his natural ability and great talent qualified him. In 1812 Lacy married Jane (1776-1858), the widow of Francesco Bianchi (1752-1810), an Italian opera composer, and teacher of Sir Henry Bishop. She was the daughter of an apothecary named John Jackson in Sloane Street, Chelsea, and married Bianchi in 1800. Like Lacy, she was a singer of repute, making her first appearance in London on 25 April 1798, and singing as Miss Jackson at the Concerts of Antient Music in 1800. While Mrs. Bianchi she often sang at Windsor in the presence of George III and Queen Charlotte, and was considered one of the finest singers of Handel's music. She was a good linguist, pianoforte-player, and painter. With Lacy she took part in the concerts of Billington, Naldi, and Braham at Willis's Rooms on 1 March 1809 (PARKE, *Musical Memoirs*, ii. 35), and at the Vocal Concerts, Hanover Square Rooms, 2 March 1810 (*ib.* p. 49). In 1818 the Lacys accepted an engagement at Calcutta, where they remained seven years, giving frequent performances at the court of the king of Oude. After returning to England about 1826 they retired into private life. For some years they resided at Florence and other continental cities, but eventually settled in England. Lacy died while on a visit to Devonshire about 1845. His wife died at Ealing 19 March 1858.

Lacy possessed a bass voice of great excellence. So highly was he esteemed by the Italians that he was offered lucrative engagements at the Operas of Milan and Florence, and later at the King's Theatre in London (*Quart. Mus. Mag. and Rev.* i. 338 n.) He was 'considered by competent judges to be without question the most legitimate English bass singer, the most accomplished in various styles, and altogether the most perfect and finished that has appeared in this country. He was endowed by nature with organs of great strength and delicacy; his voice was rich and full-toned, particularly in the lower notes; his intonation perfect, and his finish and variety in graces remarkable' (*Dict. of Music*, 1824, ii. 33).

[Authorities given above; Grove's Dict. of Music; Brown's Dict. of Music; Quarterly Musical Magazine and Review, i. 333 sq. (1818); private information.] R. H. L.

LACY or DE LACY, MAURICE (1740-1820), of Grodno, Russian general, belonged to a branch of the family of Peter, count Lacy [q. v.] He was born apparently at Limerick during the 'great frost' of 1739-40 (see LENIHAN, p. 332), and is described (*Printed Sketch-Pedigree*) as son of Patrick de Lacy (*d.* 1790) by Lady Mary Herbert of Templeagleton and grandson of 'old Patrick Lacy' of Rathcahill, who died in 1741. Maurice, who was said to have been brought up in an Irish convent, obtained a commission in the Russian army, in which he fought against the Turks, and attained general's rank, with which he revisited Ireland in 1792-3. He went back to Russia, and held command under Marshal Suwarrow in the campaigns against the French in Switzerland and Italy. Sir Henry Edward Bunbury [q. v.], who was quartermaster-general of the small British force sent to Naples under Sir James Henry Craig [q. v.] in 1805, speaking of an auxiliary force of fourteen thousand Russians and two thousand wild Montenegrins sent thither from the Greek islands, under the Russian general, D'Anrep, observes that D'Anrep was subordinate to old General Lacy, who was residing at Naples under the pretence of ill-health, but prepared by his sovereign's order to take the chief command when the time should come to put the troops in movement. He had been a brave and meritorious officer, 'but showed no traces of ever having been a man of talent or information.' Bunbury, who is wrong on some points, adds: 'He spoke English with the strongest brogue I ever heard, and with peculiarities that I have never met with, except in the Teagues of our old comedies.' He used to bring his nightcap in his pocket when he attended a council of war, and put it on and go to sleep while others discussed the business. 'But the old gentleman was simple and kind-hearted, and, in his own words, "always for fighting"' (BUNBURY, pp. 191-2). Lacy played no prominent part in later campaigns. He was governor of Grodno, where he possessed estates. Lacy and his sister, Mrs. Johanna O'Brien, who died before him, outlived all their numerous brothers and sisters. His nephew, Maurice Pierse, entered the Russian service and died before Adrianople during the war of 1827-9 (see *United Service Magazine*, November 1844). Lacy, who is described (*Printed Sketch-Pedigree*) as 'the last lineal descendant of the great Hugh de Lacy,' died unmarried at Grodno, Russia, in January 1820.

[Printed Sketch-Pedigree of General Maurice de Lacy of Grodno, two copies of which are in the British Museum Library, signed by Mrs.

De Lacy Nash, the surviving representative of Lacy's sister, Mrs. Johanna O'Brien; see also Lenihan's Hist. of Limerick, Dublin, 1866; D'Alton's Illustrations of King James's Army Lists, Dublin, 2nd edit. 1861; Bunbury's Narrative of Passages in the late War with France, London, 1854.] H. M. C.

LACY, MICHAEL ROPHINO (1795–1867), violinist and composer, was born at Bilbao in Spain on 19 July 1795 (not in 1765 as stated in Fétis's 'Biographie Universelle'). His father, an Englishman, was engaged in mercantile pursuits in Bilbao; his mother was Spanish. He commenced to learn the violin at the age of five, and at six he made his public début at a concert given in Bilbao by Andreossi, an Italian violinist. He played a concerto of Jarnowick (or Giornovichi), and aroused the utmost enthusiasm, although he was so small that he had to stand up on a table before the audience could see him. Until 1802 he was patronised by the court of Madrid as an infant prodigy. In 1802 he commenced his education at the college of Bordeaux, and after spending eighteen months there proceeded to a lycée at Paris where his scholastic successes were amazing. While in Paris he was a pupil of Kreutzer, under whom he made rapid progress, and in 1805 he played a violin solo as 'le petit Espagnol' at the Tuileries. Meanwhile his father was ruined by some American speculations, and Lacy was brought to England in 1805 to study under Viotti. On the journey he played in various Dutch towns, and became a great favourite at the Hague. He arrived in England at the age of ten years and three months. At this time, we are told, he was able to speak fluently English, French, Italian, and Spanish, and had a fair knowledge of Latin. His performances roused much enthusiasm in England, where he was at first known merely as 'the young Spaniard;' his real name was not publicly revealed until May 1807, when there was published an engraved portrait of him by Cardon, from a drawing by Smart, on which was the legend 'Master M. M. J. R. Lacy, the celebrated young Spaniard, born in Bilbao 19 July 1795.' Among his patrons were the Prince of Wales, the Duke of Sussex, the Duchess of York, and Count Stahremberg, the Austrian ambassador. His first concert in London was given at the Hanover Square Rooms, and soon after he played at Catalani's first concert in Dublin, where the lord-lieutenant, the Duke of Richmond, and the duchess warmly patronised him. For performances at Corri's concerts in Edinburgh he received the large fee of twenty guineas per night. Subsequently his father caused him to abandon the musical for the

dramatic profession, and for about ten years (1808–18) he filled 'genteel comedy parts' in Edinburgh, Dublin, and Glasgow, only playing the violin in public at his benefits. In 1818, at the invitation of the directors, he succeeded Yaneviez as first violin and director of the Liverpool concerts, which were recruited from the best talent in London. At the end of 1820 Lacy returned to London, and until 1823 directed the ballets and composed most of the ballet-music for the Italian opera. In 1823, in consequence of disagreements with the musical director, he returned to the management of The Liverpool concerts, but resumed his position at the Italian opera in 1824. From this time until his retirement and death, which took place at Pentonville on 20 Sept. 1867, he devoted himself principally to composition and to the adaptation of foreign libretti, for which his linguistic talents eminently fitted him. It is to Lacy that we owe the first English adaptations of 'Semiramide,' 1829, 'Armida,' 'Cenerentola,' 'Cinderella,' and 'William Tell,' 1830, 'Fra Diavolo,' 1831, and others of minor importance. He is known as the composer of an oratorio entitled 'The Israelites in Egypt,' 1833, and of a re-adaptation of Weber's 'Freischütz,' 1839, as well as of several minor pieces of some merit, notably a set of rondos for the pianoforte and a quintett for two violins, tenor, flute, and violoncello, with pianoforte accompaniment. He also collaborated in Schœlcher's 'Life of Handel.'

[Fétis's Biographie Universelle des Musiciens; Grove's Dictionary of Music; A Dictionary of Musicians (anon.), 1822; private sources.]
E. H.-A.

LACY, PETER, COUNT LACY (1678–1751), Russian field-marshal, a kinsman of Colonel Pierce Lacy of Bruff, co. Limerick, who claimed descent from Hugh de Lacy (d. 1186) [q. v.], is said to have been second son of Peter Lacy and his wife, Maria Courtenay, and grandson of John Lacy of Ballingarry, co. Limerick. He was born at Killedy or Killeedy, in that county, on 29 Sept. (O.S.) 1678. At the age of thirteen he served King James II at the defence of Limerick, as an ensign in the Prince of Wales's regiment of Irish foot, of which his uncle, Quartermaster-general and brigadier James Lacy, was colonel. He left Ireland with Sarsfield's troops after the capitulation, landed at Brest in January 1692, and proceeded to Nantes to join the regiment of Athlone of the Irish brigade, in the service of France, in which he was appointed ensign (see O'CALLAGHAN, pp. 135–9, for the history of the corps). His father, who was afterwards a captain in King James's Irish guards, and two other sons, are said to have left Ireland about the same time, and all to have fallen in the service of France. Young Peter Lacy marched with his regiment to Piedmont, joined the army under the Marquis de Catinat, and fought at Marsaglia or Val de Marseilles on 4 Oct. 1693, where his uncle, James Lacy, was mortally wounded (cf. *ib.* pp. 176–8), and in the subsequent campaigns in Italy in 1693–6. In 1697 he accompanied his regiment to the Rhine; but the peace of Ryswick led to the disbanding of Athlone and other Irish regiments. Disappointed of employment in Hungary against the Turks, Lacy entered as a lieutenant in the Polish service under Marshal the Duc de Croy, by whom he was presented to the czar, Peter the Great (D'ALTON). The czar selected Lacy as one of a hundred foreign officers to be employed in training the Russian troops, and appointed him captain in the infantry regiment of Colonel Bruce. He served against the Swedes in Livonia and Ingria (a Russo-Finnish province, now part of the government of St. Petersburg), and after the fall of Jamburg was appointed to command a company called the Grand Musketeers, composed of one hundred Russian nobles armed and horsed at their own expense. When attending the czar in Poland in 1705, he was made major of the regiment of Schomeritoff, with which he served against the Swedes under Lewenhaupt, and in 1706 lieutenant-colonel of the regiment of Polotsk, where he was appointed to train and instruct three regiments. In 1707 he greatly distinguished himself at the siege of Bucko in Poland. In 1708 he was made colonel of the regiment of Siberia, and repeatedly distinguished himself in the operations against Charles XII and his ally, Mazeppa, on the Dnieper, particularly at the seizure of Rumna in December of that year. The following year the czar gave him a regiment of grenadiers. At the battle of Pultowa Lacy commanded a brigade of the right wing, although he did not attain the rank of brigadier until four years later. According to Russian authorities, the success of the day was largely due to an order issued by the czar, at Lacy's suggestion, directing the troops to reserve their fire for close quarters. From 1709 to 1721 Lacy was frequently engaged against the Danes, Swedes, and Turks. He became a brigadier-general in August 1712, major-general the month after, and lieutenant-general in July 1720. He signalised himself in the war of 1720–1 by his many successful descents on the Swedish coast, in one of which he anchored with 130 galleys, and encamped his advance-guard on shore within twelve miles of Stockholm (cf. SCHUY-

LER, ii. 517). In 1723 Lacy was summoned to St. Petersburg to take his seat at the council of war, and at the coronation of the Czarina Anne the year after, he rode behind the imperial carriage, throwing gold and silver coins among the populace. In 1725 he was made a knight of the Alexander Nevsky order, and was appointed commander-in-chief in St. Petersburg, Ingria, and Novogorod, to which the governments of Esthonia and Courland were added the year after. In 1727, when Maurice de Saxe (afterwards the famous marshal) was, in opposition to the court of St. Petersburg, made Duke of Courland, Lacy was sent to expel him from the duchy, and was afterwards appointed governor of Livonia and Esthonia. In 1733 he was engaged with Marshal Münnich in establishing Augustus of Saxony on the throne of Poland, in opposition to the deposed Stanislas. On the fall of Danzig, after a siege of 135 days in open trenches, during which the Russians lost eight thousand men, including two hundred officers, Lacy received from Augustus the order of the White Eagle, and his portrait set in brilliants. Lacy remained in Poland until the victory of Busawitza, where, with fifteen hundred dragoons, eighty hussars, and five hundred Cossacks, he put to rout twenty thousand Stanislasites, and the surrender of the rest of the Poles under Czerski, in April 1735, decided the contest in favour of Augustus. After a brilliant reception at Warsaw, Lacy was detached with a contingent of fifteen thousand (subsequently reduced to ten thousand) Russian troops, to join the imperialist forces collected near Mannheim, under Prince Eugene, in consequence of the declaration of war between Austria and France. Peace between Austria and France being agreed upon, Lacy repaired early in 1736 to Vienna, and on his way thence to St. Petersburg met a courier bearing his patent as a Russian field-marshal.

War having been declared against Turkey, Lacy was sent to reduce Azov. During the months of May and June 1736 Lacy carried on the approaches against Azov by sap, the Turkish garrison making repeated sallies, during one of which Lacy was wounded. At the beginning of July, the town being a heap of ruins from the Russian shells, and provisions running short, the Turkish bashaw capitulated, marching out with 3,463 men, and leaving behind some three hundred pieces of ordnance and 291 Christian captives, who were set at liberty. Lacy then marched to assist Münnich on his return from a disastrous expedition in the Crimea, and afterwards, with his own troops and the remnant of Münnich's force, went into winter quarters in the Ukraine. In 1737 Lacy was appointed to command a fresh expedition into the Crimea. With forty thousand men he unexpectedly crossed an arm of the sea at Arabat, stormed and blew up the Tartar lines at Perecop, and by the end of September returned to the Ukraine, having, 'without knowing why he was sent into the Crimea, conducted the campaign with great glory to himself and very little sickness to the army.' When Münnich was acting against the Turks the year after, Lacy was again sent to the Crimea with a force, inclusive of Cossacks, not exceeding thirty-six thousand men. With this he captured Kaffa, the stronghold of the Crimea; but finding the interior of the country too impoverished to support his troops, and a naval armament on the Sea of Azov, which was to co-operate with him, having been destroyed by a great storm, he returned to Perecop, razed the lines there, and went into winter quarters early. In 1739 his troops were kept in reserve in the Ukraine, in consequence of war with Sweden. Complaints against Münnich's severities and mismanagement were now so loud that the czarina asked Lacy to undertake the investigation of his colleague's conduct. Lacy declined the invidious task; but Münnich appears to have accused him of detraction, and a violent scene ensued, in which the marshals drew on each other, but were separated by Lewenhaupt, who threatened them both with arrest by order of the empress. In 1741 Lacy was appointed to command against the Swedes in Finland, with James Francis Edward Keith [q. v.] as his second in command. The event of the year was the capture in September of the important Swedish post of Wilmanstrand. Administrative difficulties stopped the enterprise, and Lacy returned to St. Petersburg, where he entertained at his palace the Swedish commander, Von Wrangel, who had been wounded and taken prisoner.

Lacy is said to have taken no part in the intrigues which raised Elizabeth to the throne in December 1741, but was confirmed in his rank and offices. His promptitude in suppressing a dangerous mutiny in the Russian guards on Easter Sunday 1742, when the foreign officers were savagely ill-treated by the mutineers, was said 'to have saved St. Petersburg, and perhaps the empire.' Towards the end of May 1742 Lacy reviewed at Viborg an army of thirty-five thousand to thirty-six thousand men, to be employed against the Swedes in Finland. In June the troops entered Finland, traversing a country having 'the worst roads in the universe,' where in many places two hundred men posted behind an abattis might stop an army. On 10 July,

the name-day of the Grand-duke Peter (afterwards Peter III), a solemn Te Deum was sung in the Russian camp, to celebrate the capture of Fredericsham, the only fortified place in Finland, without the loss of a man. Orders were then sent to conclude the campaign; but Lacy, after calling a council of war, pushed on to Helsingfors, where a Swedish army of seventeen thousand men capitulated. The operations of the following year were carried on by galleys, supported by a squadron of larger vessels under Admiral Golowin. On 14 May 1743 the army embarked. High mass according to the Greek ritual was celebrated with much pomp on board Lacy's galley, which was attended by the czarina in person, who presented Lacy with a ring of great value and a golden cross. After delays occasioned by the ice and head-winds, Lacy, who appears to have been desirous to win a victory by sea, sent orders to Admiral Golowin to attack the Swedish fleet at Hango. Lacy manœuvred his galleys very skilfully, and got the weather-gage of the enemy, but a fog favoured the escape of the Swedes. On 23 July Keith, who was in command of a separate squadron, joined Lacy, and preparations were made for a descent in the neighbourhood of Stockholm, when the treaty of Abo put an end to the war. In September the czarina sent her own yacht to bring Lacy to St. Petersburg, and great rejoicings were held. Lacy, after more than fifty years' campaigning, now retired to his estates in Livonia, of which province he was governor, and there resided until his death on 11 May 1751 (30 April Russian style), at the age of seventy-three. He left a fortune equivalent to 60,000l., and large estates, acquired, his will states, 'through long and hard service, and with much danger and uneasiness.' Lacy was in person tall and well made. He was cool in judgment, ready in resource, prompt and decided in action. Frederick the Great called him the 'Prince Eugene of Muscovy.' He was much esteemed in the army for his soldierly example and his unremitting care of his troops. To him belongs in a very large degree the credit of having converted the Russians from the worst into some of the best troops in Europe. A division of the Russian army was in 1891 named after him.

Lacy married the Countess Martha Feuchen de Loeser, by whom he had five daughters, married respectively to Major-general Boye, the privy councillor Lieven, Generals Stuart, Browne, and Von Witter, and two sons, the elder of whom was at one time an officer of cuirassiers in the Polish-Saxon service, royal chamberlain, and a count of the holy Roman empire. The younger was the famous Austrian field-marshal, Maurice Francis Lacy (Lasey), who was born in St. Petersburg in 1725, and at the age of twelve was placed by his father in the Austrian army, in the regiment of his kinsman, Ulysses Maximilian, count Brown [q. v.], with whom he made the campaign in Italy in 1747. He was favourably noticed by Daun, and served with great distinction in the seven years' war. In a family manuscript dated Vienna, 30 Nov. 1800, the emperor wrote to him, 'You created my army.' Frederick the Great also said of him: 'I admire the disposition of Lacy (Lasey), but tremble at the onset of Loudon.' Maurice Francis Lacy died at Vienna on 24 Nov. 1801 (see *N. Deutsche Biog.* vol. xxii.) A Count Lacy, who was a Russian major-general under Field-marshal Peter Lacy in the Finland war of 1741-3, and the Austrian general, Count Maurice Tanner Lacy, who died in 1819, are believed to have belonged to the same family as Peter, count Lacy. The Russian general, Maurice Lacy or De Lacy [q. v.] of Grodno, also belonged to the family.

[O'Callaghan's Hist. of the Irish Brigades in the Service of France, Glasgow, 1870, pp. 481-99, embody researches in the Lacy Family Papers (including some diaries of Field-marshal Peter Lacy and a copy of his will); then in possession of Richard MacNamara, esq., solicitor, 31 North Great George Street, Dublin. Confusion of christian names renders it utterly impossible to identify with certainty the immediate ancestors of Peter Lacy (cf. the notices of Colonel John Lacy and Colonel Pierce Lacy in D'Alton's Illustrations of King James's Army Lists, Dublin, 2nd edit. 1861, ii. 388-94; in Hist. MSS. Comm. 10th Rep. iii. 270-1, and in Ferrar and Lenihan's histories of Limerick). A useful summary of the campaigns in which Peter Lacy figured is furnished in Cust's Annals of the Wars of the Eighteenth Century, London, 1866. Some account of the Russian army in Lacy's time will be found in Schuyler's Peter the Great, London, 1886, vol. i. Notices of Peter, count Lacy, occur in Hist. MSS. Comm. 9th Rep. pt. ii. 10th Rep. pt. i. pp. 166, 188, 193, 268.] H. M. C.

LACY, ROGER DE (d. 1212), justiciar, and constable of Chester, was son of John de Lacy, by Alice de Vere, sister of William de Mandeville, earl of Essex [q. v.] JOHN DE LACY (d. 1190) was son of Richard Fitz-Eustace, constable of Chester, by Alberda, daughter of Robert de Lisours and Alberda, aunt of Robert de Lacy (d. 1193), the last male representative of Ilbert de Lacy, who came over at the Conquest (*Herald and Genealogist*, vii. 182). John de Lacy assumed his cousin's name as heir to his estates. He was in charge of Dublin in 1181, and, going on the crusade, died at Tyre on 11 Oct. 1190 (GIRALD. CAMBR. v. 355; HOVEDEN, ii. 253,

iii. 88). John de Lacy founded Stanlaw Abbey, Cheshire, about 1172; it was afterwards transferred to Whalley in 1296, by his descendant Henry de Lacy, third earl of Lincoln [q.v.] The charter, dated 1178, is printed by Dugdale. John de Lacy also founded the hospital of Castle Donington (*Mon. Angl.* vi. 639, 641, 765).

On his father's death Roger de Lacy became constable of Chester. In 1192, having been entrusted by the chancellor with the custody of the castles of Tickhill and Nottingham, he hanged two knights who had conspired to surrender these castles to John. John in revenge plundered Lacy's lands. In April 1199 Lacy swore fealty to John on his accession, and from this time remained in high favour with the new king. In November 1200 he was sent to escort William the Lion to Lincoln, and was present when the Scottish king did homage there to John on 22 Nov. In 1201 he was sent with William Marshal, earl of Pembroke, in command of one hundred knights to defend the king's possessions in Normandy. In 1203 Philip Augustus besieged him in the famous Château Gaillard, which he defended with incomparable fidelity for nearly a year, and only surrendered through stress of famine on 5 March 1204. Matthew Paris relates that the French king, in recognition of his gallant defence, put him in free custody. Lacy was ransomed by John's assistance for a thousand marks (*Rot. Claus.* i. 4). He was further rewarded by being made sheriff of York and Cheshire, which offices he held till 1210. In 1209 he was a justiciar. He is said to have rescued Earl Randulf of Chester (see BLUNDEVILL, RANDULF DE) when besieged by the Welsh at Rhuddlan, Flintshire. His fierce raids against the Welsh are said to have earned him the name of 'Roger of Hell.' Lacy was on familiar terms with John, and a record is preserved of the king's losses to him 'in ludo ad tabulas.' He died in January 1212, and was buried at Stanlaw. He was a benefactor of that abbey, and also of Fountains. Dugdale prints an epitaph on him from Cotton. MS. Cleop. C. iii. (*Mon. Angl.* v. 648). Dugdale's statement that he was present at the sieges of Acre and Damietta is due to a confusion with his father and son. Roger de Lacy married Maud de Clere, sister of the treasurer of York Cathedral, and left by her two sons, John, earl of Lincoln [q. v.], and Roger.

[Roger de Hoveden; Matt. Paris; Annales Monastici (all these are in the Rolls Ser.); Dugdale's Monasticon, v. 533-4, 647-8; Dugdale's Baronage, i. 100-1; Foss's Judges of England, ii. 87-8.] C. L. K

LACY, THOMAS HAILES (1809–1873), actor and theatrical publisher, was born in 1809, and from an early age was connected with the theatrical profession. His first recorded appearance in London was on Easter Monday 1828 at the Olympic Theatre, as Lenoir in the 'Foundling of the Forest.' After being manager for Montague Penley at the Windsor Theatre, he succeeded to the lesseeship, and in 1841 became manager of the Theatre Royal, Sheffield. Here in January 1842 he married Frances Dalton Cooper [see below] of Covent Garden Theatre, and in May played Jacques in 'As you like it' to his wife's Rosalind, Gustavus Vaughan Brooke [q. v.] being the Orlando. Next year Lacy included the Nottingham and Doncaster theatres in his circuit. In May 1844 he joined S. Phelps and Mrs. Warner at Sadler's Wells, acting on the opening night Banquo to Phelps's Macbeth. At the end of the year he went with his wife on a provincial tour. He then withdrew from the stage and entered into business as a theatrical bookseller, first in 1849 at 17 Wellington Street, Strand, London, and from 1857 at 89 Strand. He soon commenced publishing acting editions of dramas. 'Lacy's Acting Edition of Plays,' published between 1848 and 1873, ran to ninety-nine volumes, and contained 1,485 pieces. He was also the proprietor of 'John Cumberland's British Theatre' (399 dramas contained in forty-eight volumes), and of 'Cumberland's Minor Theatre' (152 plays in sixteen volumes). He retired in the spring of 1873, when his business was transferred to Samuel French of New York. He died at Benhill Street, Sutton, Surrey, 1 Aug. 1873, aged 64, and was buried at Sutton Church on 6 Aug. He left 8,000l. to the General Theatrical Fund. His library was sold 24–9 Nov. 1873 for 2,650l., and his theatrical portraits on 8 Dec. for 1,970l.

Lacy was the author of: 1. 'The Pickwickians,' a drama in three acts, 1837. 2 (with Thomas Higgie). 'The Tower of London,' a drama, 1840. 3 (with Dennis Lawler). 'The School for Daughters,' a comedy in three acts, 1843. 4 (with Thomas Higgie). 'Martin Chuzzlewit,' a drama in three acts, 1844. 5 (with John Courtney). 'Clarissa Harlowe,' a tragic drama in three acts, 1846. 6. 'A Silent Woman,' a farce, 1851. 7 (with Thomas Higgie). 'Belphegor, or the Mountebank,' a drama from the French of E. Philippe and M. Tournier, 1851. 8. 'Jeannette's Wedding Day,' a farce from 'Les Noces de Jeannette,' 1855. He edited 'The Comic Reciter,' 1864, and 'The Dramatic Reciter,' 1866, and many collections of costume plates (1865, 1868, and 1872).

His wife, FRANCES DALTON LACY (1819–1872), a capable and intelligent actress, was born in London in 1819, and at the age of fourteen played at the Reading Theatre as Sophia in the 'Road to Ruin.' Her first appearance in London was at the Haymarket on 16 April 1838 as Lydia in the 'Love Chase.' She became a member of Madame Vestris's company at Covent Garden 7 Sept. 1840, and after remaining there for three years went to Sadler's Wells, where she held a prominent position for several seasons. Mrs. Lacy died at 89 Strand, London, 23 April 1872 (*Era*, 28 April 1872, p. 11).

[*Era*, 10 Aug. 1873, p. 11, 30 Nov. p. 7; Illustrated London News, 20 Sept. 1873, p. 279.]

G. C. B.

LACY, WALTER DE, first BARON LACY by tenure (d. 1085), was sprung from a family settled at Lassy in the arrondissement of Vire in Normandy, and was a relative, perhaps a brother, of Ilbert de Lacy, ancestor of Roger de Lacy. [q. v.] He is mentioned by Wace as fighting for the conqueror at Hastings (*Roman de Rou*, p. 220, ed. Taylor), and afterwards obtained a grant of lands in the Welsh marches. The principal estates of the Lacy family were at Ewyas Lacy, Stanton Lacy, and Weobley, and also included Ludlow Castle. Walter certainly held some land at Ewyas (*Domesday Book*, i. 184–5), and also at Stanton, but other lands were due to grants to his sons, and it is impossible to say what proportion was Walter's. In 1071 Walter de Lacy was fighting against the Welsh (ORDERICUS VITALIS, ii. 218, Société de l'Hist. de France), and took part against the rebel earls three years later (FLOR. WIG. ii. 11). He was a benefactor of St. Peter's, Gloucester, and founder of St. Peter's, Hereford. He died 27 March 1085, having fallen from a ladder while superintending the building of the latter church. He was buried in the chapter-house at Gloucester. By his wife, Ermeline, he left three sons, Roger, Hugh, and Walter, and two daughters, Ermeline and Emma. Roger de Lacy appears in 'Domesday' as holding lands in Berkshire, Gloucestershire, Worcestershire, Herefordshire, and Shropshire (i. 62 b, 167 b, 176 b, 184–5, 260 b). He took part in the rebellions against William Rufus in 1088 and 1094, and for this was banished and his lands given to his brother Hugh. Hugh was founder of Lanthony Abbey, and died in Wales before 1121, without offspring; he was buried at Weobley (LELAND, *Itin.* viii. 89 a). Walter de Lacy (1073–1139) entered St. Peter's, Gloucester, in 1080, became abbot in 1130, and died in 1139 (*Chron. St. Peter, Gloucester*, i. 16–17,

92). Henry I seems to have taken the Lacy estates into his own hands, but Gilbert, son of Hugh's sister, Emma, assumed the name of Lacy and claimed to represent the family [see under LACY, HUGH DE, d. 1186].

[Florence of Worcester (Engl. Hist. Soc.); Chron. St. Peter, Gloucester (Rolls Ser.); Dugdale's Baronage, i. 97; Burke's Extinct Peerage, p. 310; Eyton's Shropshire, v. 5-7, 238-41.]

C. L. K.

LACY, WALTER DE, sixth BARON LACY by tenure and second LORD OF MEATH (d. 1241), was elder son of Hugh de Lacy (d. 1186) [q. v.], by Rovsya de Monemue (Monmouth), and was elder brother of Hugh de Lacy, earl of Ulster (d. 1242?) [q. v.] On his father's death he became entitled to the ancestral estates in Normandy and England, and to his father's conquest of Meath in Ireland, but the last was taken into the king's hands, and he did not obtain seisin of the English or Norman lands till 1189 (EYTON, v. 256-7); it is, of course, possible that he may have been a minor at his father's death. He does not seem to have had possession of Meath till 1194, at which time he seized Peter Pippard, one of the Irish justiciars (HENRY OF MARLEBUROH ap. BUTLER, Hist. of Trim, p. 6). It seems probable that he is the 'son of Hugh de Lacy' who supported John de Courci in 1195 in his warfare with the English of Leinster and Munster (Four Masters, iii. 101-3), for we know that his lands were escheated about this time, and that in 1198 he paid a fine of 2,100 marks (EYTON, v. 257-8; STAPLETON, Rot. Normanniæ, ii. lxxi); moreover, in 1197 Ludlow Castle was in the royal hands (HOVEDEN, iv. 35), and on 4 Sept. 1199 reference is again made to Walter de Lacy having been concerned with John de Courci in ravaging the king's lands in Ireland (SWEETMAN, i. 90). But before this he had made his peace with the king, and in October 1199 was with John in Normandy. In the autumn of 1200 he came over to England, and remained there till early in 1201 (Charter Rolls, pp. 24, 67, 69, 79 b, 84 b). He then crossed over to Ireland, and shortly afterwards attempted to kill John de Courci at a conference there (HOVEDEN, iv. 176). In 1203 he accompanied Meiler Fitz-Henry [q.v.] on his invasion of Munster to expel William de Burgh [see under FITZALDHELM, WILLIAM], and in March next year was appointed at the head of a commission to hear the complaints against Meiler (Cal. Rot. Pat. i. 39 b). During these years Walter had also assisted his brother Hugh against John de Courci, and on 31 Aug. 1204 was rewarded by the promise of eight cantreds of De Courci's land in Ulster. When in 1205 De Courci attempted

to re-enter Ireland, it was Walter de Lacy who drove him away (MUNCH, Chron. Manniæ, p. 15). Walter also supported his brother in his warfare with Meiler Fitz-Henry in 1207-8. On 14 April 1207 he was summoned to England on pain of forfeiture, and before 16 July left Ireland. He spent the winter in England, and after making his peace with the king, obtained, on 23 April 1208, a confirmation of Meath at fifty knights' service, and of Fingall at seven. He returned to Ireland in June (Cal. Rot. Pat. i. 70 b, 80 b, 84 b; Cal. Rot. Claus. i. 81, 106 b; Charter Rolls, 167 b, 170 b, 173 b, 178).

No doubt it was Walter's influence which secured for William de Braose [q. v.] the support of the De Lacys, who were consequently expelled from Ireland. Walter made his submission to John on 28 June 1210, almost immediately after the king's landing in Ireland; he pleaded that both he and his tenants had suffered much from his brother Hugh (SWEETMAN, i. 402). Both his English and Irish estates were taken into the king's hands, and he probably retired to France; for though the story of his sojourn at St. Taurin is somewhat legendary, he had special leave to come to England on 1 July 1213 (Cal. Rot. Claus. i. 134 b). On 29 July 1213 all his English lands except Ludlow Castle were restored to him (ib. i. 147). Walter de Lacy took part in John's expedition to the south of France in 1214, landing at La Rochelle with Henry Fitz-Count in March; in April he was sent on a mission to Narbonne to purchase horses (Cal. Rot. Pat. i. 112, 113 b). After his return Ludlow was restored to him on 23 Oct. 1214, and next year he recovered his Irish lands, except the castles of Drogheda and Airemaill, on paying a fine of four thousand marks (ib. i. 131, 132 b, 151, 181; Cal. Rot. Claus. i. 175, 224). During the next two years he was actively employed in John's service in England, and apparently stood high in the royal favour (see numerous references in the Close and Patent Rolls). On 18 Aug. 1216 he was put in charge of the castle and county of Hereford, and retained his office as sheriff of that county till November 1223 (Cal. Rot. Pat. i. 193 b; SHIRLEY, i. 508). After John's death Walter de Lacy became one of the chief supporters of the young king (Fœdera, i. 145, Record ed.). In 1219 he was appointed on the forest inquisition for Gloucestershire (Cal. Rot. Claus. i. 435). In 1219 or 1220 he was sent into Ireland on the royal service, being given full seisin of his lands except the castle of Drogheda (ib. i. 408 b, 415 b, 427; Lock Co, i. 261; Four Masters, iii. 189). In 1220 he led an army to Athliag, now Ballyleague, being part of Lanesborough in Connaught, and began to erect a castle, which the Irish, however, soon destroyed (*ib.* iii. 201). During this year he also captured the crannog of O'Reilly. Walter was at this time in charge of the lands of his brother Hugh, which had been entrusted to him in 1215 (*Cal. Rot. Pat.* i. 150; *Cal. Rot. Claus.* i. 501). In 1223 he was in England on the royal service, but next spring was sent over to Ireland on account of the war which his brother had raised (*ib.* i. 575b, 590b). In consideration of the excesses committed by his men of Meath in support of Hugh de Lacy, Walter had to make an agreement with the king, under which he put his castles of Trim and Ludlow into the royal hands for a period of two years from Easter 1224, and agreed to go over to Ireland and exert all his influence in opposition to his brother (SHIRLEY, i. 507). Walter was in Ireland by 30 March (*Cal. Rot. Claus.* i. 590b). How far he kept his promise to act against his brother is not clear; one statement in the ' Annals of Loch Cé' (i. 271) implies that he actually supported him. At any rate it was not thought prudent that he should remain in Ireland after the suppression of the rebellion, and his Irish estates were for a time taken into the royal hands. On 15 May 1225 he paid a fine of three thousand marks for seisin of these lands, but Trim, Drogheda, and other castles were not yet restored. Walter, moreover, was kept in England, and did not recover full seisin till 4 July 1226 (*Cal. Rot. Claus.* ii. 39b, 64, 104, 126). Previously he had been put in charge of his brother's lands in Ulster for three years, but he only held them till the following April (*ib.* ii. 182b; SWEETMAN, i. 1371–4). By August Walter was once more in Ireland, when Geoffrey de Marisco reported that no danger was to be apprehended from him on account of the agreement which his son Gilbert had made with William Marshal. De Marisco at the same time reported that the king of Connaught had been summoned to Dublin under conduct of Walter de Lacy (SHIRLEY, i. 292). Walter was summoned for the French war in 1228 with four knights (*ib.* i. 358). In June 1230 he was one of those appointed to hold the assize of arms in Herefordshire (*ib.* i. 374). On 26 Aug. he had leave to go to Ireland (SWEETMAN, i. 1850), and there assisted Geoffrey de Marisco in his invasion of Connaught, commanding one of the three divisions of the army (MATT. PARIS, iii. 197). On 15 Dec. 1233 he was again sent to Ireland on the royal service (SWEETMAN, i. 2079), and next year appears, like his brother

Hugh, in opposition to Richard Marshal. In 1235 he took part in the raid into Roscommon (*Loch Cé*, i. 321). In his later years Walter became blind and infirm (SWEETMAN, i. 2429, December 1237). He died early in 1241, apparently before 24 Feb. (*Excerpta e Rot. Finium*, i. 337; MATT. PARIS, iv. 174, ' circa Paschalem'). The ' Annals of Clonmacnoise' describe him as the ' bountifullest foreigner in steeds, attire, and gold that ever came to Erin' (*Four Masters*, iii. 302 n.; GILBERT, p. 101). Matthew Paris calls him ' the most eminent of all the nobles of Ireland' (iv. 43).

Walter de Lacy figures in the earlier part of the ' Romance of Fulk Fitzwarine' as the opponent of Joce de Dinan and the captor of Ludlow Castle. So far as Walter is concerned this is pure legend, and Joce's true adversaries were Walter's father and grandfather, Hugh and Gilbert de Lacy. The substitution of Walter's name in the romance may, however, serve to show the fame which he acquired as a great marcher lord. It is interesting to find Walter de Lacy twice mentioned in connection with Fulk Fitzwarine; on the first occasion in 1207, with reference to the quarrel between the king and William de Braose, when they were opponents (*Cal. Rot. Claus.* i. 92), and secondly, nearly twenty years later, when Walter de Lacy asked Hubert de Burgh to forward a marriage between his niece, the daughter of Madoc ab Griffith of South Wales, and Fulk's son (SHIRLEY, i. 306).

Walter de Lacy married, before November 1200, Margaret, daughter of William de Braose [q. v.], who was still living in 1255. By her he had two daughters, Egidia, who married Richard de Burgh (*d.* 1243) [q. v.], and Katherine, who was alive in 1267; also a son, Gilbert, who married Isabella, daughter of Ralph Bigod, and died in 1234, leaving a son, Walter, and two daughters, Matilda and Margaret. Walter de Lacy the younger was alive in 1238 (SWEETMAN, i. 2451); he married a daughter of Theobald Butler (*Reg. St. Thomas, Dublin*, p. 420), but died without issue in his grandfather's lifetime; possibly it is his death which the ' Annals of Clonmacnoise' record in 1240 (*Four Masters*, iii. 301 note x). Margaret and Matilda thus became their grandfather's heirs. Margaret married John de Verdon, son of Theobald Butler. Matilda married (1) in 1240 Peter de Geneva, a foreigner of low extraction, and (2), in 1249, Geoffrey de Genville, or Joinville, a brother of the famous Sieur de Joinville (MATT. PARIS, v. 91). Geoffrey de Genville held Ludlow and part of Meath, and was for a time justiciar of Ireland under

Edward I. His wife died 11 April 1303, and he himself on 19 Oct. 1314; their son Peter, who died in 1292, left a daughter, Johanna, who brought her inheritance to Roger Mortimer, earl of March (d. 1330) [q. v.] (see further, DUGDALE, *Mon. Angl.* vi. 135–6; EYTON, *Shropshire,* v. 240).

Walter de Lacy is said to have brought monks from St. Taurin and settled them at Fore in Westmeath (*Chartulary of St. Mary's, Dublin,* ii. 11). He was also a benefactor of St. Thomas, Dublin (*Reg. St. Thomas,* p. 11), and founder of Beaubec Abbey in Meath (ARCHDALL, *Monast. Hibern.* pp. 516, 711). In England he founded Cresswell Priory, Herefordshire, and was a benefactor of the two Lanthony priories in Monmouthshire and Gloucestershire. His wife founded the nunnery at Acornbury, Herefordshire, before 1218 (*Cal. Rot. Claus.* i. 368 b; SWEETMAN, i. 1909; DUGDALE, *Monast. Anglic.* vi. 138, 489, 569, 1034, 1129).

[For authorities, see under LACY, HUGH DE (d. 1242?), where also fuller information will be found on some points. See also the Romance of Fulk Fitzwarine, ed. T. Wright for the Warton Club; Eyton's Antiquities of Shropshire, v. 256–72; Butler's History of the Castle of Trim.]   C. L. K.

LACY, WILLIAM (1610?–1671), royalist divine, son of Thomas Lacy of Beverley and his wife, 'Elizabeth, daughter of Richard Franceys of Beckenham in co. Nott' (DUGDALE, *Visitation of the County of Yorke,* 1665–6), was a descendant of the noble family of Lacy. He was educated at St. John's College, Cambridge, where he was probably admitted before 1629, as his name does not appear in the admission registers of the college, which commence with that year. He proceeded B.A. in 1632, M.A. in 1636, was admitted fellow of his college on 5 April 1636, and was tutor during 1640–2. He obtained the degree of B.D. in 1642, and was made preacher at St. John's at Michaelmas 1643. He was associated with John Barwick [q. v.] and others in writing 'Certain Disquisitions' against the covenant, which was seized by the parliamentary party, but reissued at Oxford.

Lacy was ejected from his fellowship in 1644, after which he joined the royal army, and became chaplain to Prince Rupert. He was taken prisoner at the storming of Bridgewater by Sir Thomas Fairfax on 23 July 1645 (FAIRFAX, *Letter to Lenthall,* p. 6), was for some time in prison, where, being in great want, he was relieved by John Barwick, and in 1649 compounded for his estate by paying 26l., one-sixth of its value (*Royalist Composition Papers* in Record Office). Towards the end of 1651 he was in great want of money (*Cal. of Committee for the Advance of Money,* 1642–56, pt. iii. p. 1382).

At the Restoration he was restored to his fellowship by a letter from the Earl of Manchester, dated 27 Aug. 1660 (*Cal. State Papers,* Dom. 1661–2, p. 24). He was admitted to a senior fellowship on 4 Nov. 1661, and recommended by the king for the degree of D.D. on 3 Oct. 1662 (*ib.* p. 505). On 23 Oct. 1662 he was presented by Sir George Savile to the rectory of Thornhill, Yorkshire. Lacy died there on 12 May 1671, and was buried in the church, where there is a tablet to his memory. He married 'Ann, daughter of William Sherman of Newarke, near Leycester, gent.' (DUGDALE, *Visitation*), and had a son, who died in infancy in 1663.

While at Thornhill he rebuilt the rectory-house, which had been destroyed during the civil wars. In his will, dated 7 Sept. 1670, he left 350l. to found two scholarships of 8l. each at St. John's College, Cambridge, for the benefit of students of the grammar school at Beverley (POULSON, *Beverlac,* p. 459). He contributed 5l. towards the building of the third court at St. John's College in 1669.

[Baker's Hist. of St. John's Coll. Cambr. pp. 238, 295, 327, 335; Kennett's Register, pp. 239, 524; Peter Barwick's Life of John Barwick, pp. 33–40, 107, 349–50; Walker's Sufferings of the Clergy, pp. 149, 277; Mayor's Admission Registers of St. John's Coll. Cambr. pp. 54, 63; Cole's Cambr. B.As. in Addit. MS. 5885, f. 103; Harleian MS. 7028, ff. 476, 488; Notitia Academiæ Cantabrigiensis, Lambeth MS. 770, f. 265; Whitaker's Loidis and Elmete, pp. 324, 326; monument in Thornhill Church; parish registers kindly communicated by the Rev. F. R. Grenside.]   B. P.

LADBROOKE, ROBERT (1768–1842), landscape-painter, born in a humble position at Norwich in 1768, was apprenticed when very young to an artist and printer named White, and for some years worked as a journeyman printer. While so engaged he made the acquaintance of John Crome [q. v.], then a lad of about his own age, who was working for a house- and sign-painter, and having congenial tastes they became fast friends, living together, and devoting all their spare time to sketching and copying. They married, early, two sisters of the name of Berney, and for two years worked in partnership, Ladbrooke painting portraits and Crome landscapes, which they sold for very small sums. Subsequently Ladbrooke also turned to landscape-painting, in which he was highly successful. Crome and Ladbrooke took a leading part in the establishment of the celebrated Norwich Society of Artists in

1803, and to its first exhibition in 1805 the latter contributed fourteen works. In 1808, when Crome became president, Ladbrooke was elected vice-president. In 1816 he, with Stannard, Thirtle, and a few other members, having ineffectually urged a modification of some of the rules, seceded from the society, and started a rival exhibition, but this proved a failure, and was abandoned after three years. Between 1804 and 1815 Ladbrooke was an occasional exhibitor at the Royal Academy, and up to 1822 at the British Institution. He engaged successfully in teaching, and was able to retire with a competence many years before his death. He died at his house on Scoles' Green, Norwich, on 11 Oct. 1842.

Ladbrooke was a clever painter, chiefly of views of Norfolk scenery; but his reputation has never been more than local. He published aquatints of two of his pictures, 'A View of the Fellmongers on the River near Bishop's Bridge' and 'A View of Norwich Castle.' His 'Views of the Churches of Norfolk,' a series of over 650 lithographic plates, were published in five volumes in 1843. Two of Ladbrooke's sons were well-known artists.

LADBROOKE, HENRY (1800–1870), the second son, was born at Norwich on 20 April 1800. He wished to enter the church, but at his father's desire adopted landscape-painting as a profession. He acquired some reputation, especially for his moonlight scenes, and exhibited occasionally at the British Institution and the Suffolk Street Gallery. He died on 18 Nov. 1870.

LADBROOKE, JOHN BERNEY (1803–1879), Robert Ladbrooke's third son, was born in 1803. He became a pupil of John Crome (his uncle by marriage), whose manner he followed, and excelled in the representation of woodland scenery. He exhibited at the Royal Academy in 1821 and 1822, and frequently at the British Institution and the Suffolk Street Gallery up to 1873. He died at Mousehold, Norwich, on 11 July 1879.

[Norwich Mercury, 15 Oct. 1842; Wodderspoon's John Crome and his Works, 1876; Redgrave's Dict. of Artists; Royal Academy and British Institution Catalogues; Graves's Dict. of Artists, 1760–1880; Times, 29 July 1879.]
F. M. O'D.

LADYMAN, SAMUEL, D.D. (1625–1684), divine, son of John Ladyman of Dinton, Buckinghamshire, was born in 1625. He entered Corpus Christi College, Oxford, as a servitor 3 March 1642-3, graduated B.A. on 13 July 1647, was made fellow by the parliamentary visitors in 1648, and graduated M.A. on 21 June 1649. He became a frequent preacher and, according to Wood, was 'a noted person among the presbyterians.' This seems an error; he became an independent, and in this capacity was placed as minister at Clonmel, co. Tipperary, with a salary of 170l. under the civil establishment of 1655. In May 1658 he was one of some thirty ministers summoned to Dublin by Henry Cromwell, for consultation on church finance and other matters; he signed the submissive address presented to Cromwell by nineteen of them. At the Restoration he conformed, and received the vicarage of Clonmel. He was prebendary of Cashel in 1677; subsequently he became archdeacon of Limerick and D.D. He died in February 1683–4, and was buried in the chancel of St. Mary's, Clonmel, where there is a tablet to his memory. By his will (dated 1683) he left 5l. per annum for educating ten poor children, and 5l. to be given annually in alms. He married Grace (d. March 1663 or 1664), daughter of Dr. William Hutchinson of Oxford, and had several children, of whom Samuel, Francis, and Grace died in infancy; John died on 9 Dec. 1675, aged 20; and Jane died on 27 Sept. 1681, aged 21. John Ladyman of Knockgraffon, buried at Cashel on 2 Oct. 1731, was probably his grandson.

He published 'The Dangerous Rule,' &c., 1658, 12mo (sermon before the judges at Clonmel).

[Wood's Fasti (Bliss), ii. 121; Reid's Hist. Presb. Church in Ireland (Killen), 1867, ii. 558 sq.; information from the Dean of Cashel and from the rector of Clonmel, with copy of monumental inscription.]
A. G.

LAEGHAIRE or LOEGHAIRE (d. 458), king of Ireland, succeeded Dathi, his first cousin, as king in 428, and was the eldest of the fourteen sons of Niall Noighiallach, king of Ireland, slain in 405. None of the chronicles mention the year of his birth, but as he was the eldest of his family, and as his son was in an independent chieftainry about 430, it may probably be fixed near 380. At Easter 432 St. Patrick came towards Tara. Easter Eve came very near the time of lighting the spring fire, which the king himself, in accordance with ancient custom, used to light upon the hill of Tlaghta in Meath. All fires were extinguished and relighted in succession to this. Patrick lit a great fire of his own in the plain, easily seen from Tara, and thus at once excited the attention and the anger of Laeghaire. When Patrick on the next day came slowly up the hill of Tara, singing his famous song, 'Faed Fiadha,' Laeghaire expressed a wish that he and his clerics should be killed at once; but neither the king nor his followers ventured to attempt what seemed likely to be followed by uncertain supernatural consequences, and he became awed by the powers which Patrick asserted that he possessed. 'It is better for me,' said Laeghaire, 'to believe than to die' (Book of Armagh, f. 5, b. 1), and was forthwith baptised. Two tales called 'Comthoth Laeghaire' and 'Siabur Charput Conculaind,' of which there is a manuscript written before 1106 (Leabhar na h-Uidri, f. 117 and f. 113), describe his unwilling conversion, relapse, and death. He is made to demand that Patrick should give experimental proof of his assertions about his power and a future state by raising Cuchullain from hell, where he stated that the heroes of ancient Ireland were. After some conversation with the famous champion of Ulster, as to the reality of whose spectre the king at first expresses some doubt, he yields, and is baptised. The account of his unwilling resignation of paganism is everywhere to be found in Irish literature, and is confirmed by the fact that the historians record no Christian acts of his. He founded no church, relieved no poor, hated his enemies to the last, made vows by the elements and not upon the gospels, and received a pagan funeral. The fixing of the primacy of Ireland at Armagh, and not in Meath, is confirmatory evidence of his hostility to Christianity. The story that he caused the revision of the native law by three kings, three bishops, and three sages (Brit. Mus. Harleian MS. 432), forming the body of law known as the Senchus Mor, contains several obvious anachronisms, and does not appear in any early authority. In 453 he made war upon the Leinster men and defeated them, and in the following year celebrated at Tara the Feis Temrach, a sort of general assembly with games. In 457 he was defeated and taken prisoner by the Leinster men in the battle of Athdara, a ford of the river Barrow. He swore by sun and moon and all the elements never to come against them again, and was set free. In the next year, disregarding his oath, he tried to levy upon them an obsolete tax, claimed by the kings of Tara as an eric for a very ancient injury by the king of Leinster to the daughter of an ardrigh, called from its celebrity by Irish poets and historians, 'An Borama,' or 'The Tribute.' He claimed fifteen thousand cows, pigs, and sheep, thirty white cattle with red ears and trappings for driving, a huge cauldron capable of boiling twelve pigs, a quantity of cloth and of silver, and a number of smaller cauldrons (Book of Leinster, f. 295). The war began by his seizing cattle at Sidh Neachtain, near the source of the Boyne. He was attacked by superior force, and had to retreat, and fought a battle on the banks of Caissi, a small stream in the territory of Ui Faelan. Here he was defeated and slain by the Leinster men. A very ancient verse about his death, beginning 'Atbath Loeghaire MacNeill, for toebh Caissi,' is often quoted by Irish writers. He desired to be buried in the outer rampart of his dun at Tara, standing upright in the ground, fully armed, and with his face southwards towards his foes, the Leinster men. The site of his dun is discussed by Petrie (History and Antiquities of Tara Hill), and some part of what is probably this earthwork remains on the slope of the hill towards Trim, but has been much injured in recent years. The O'Coindealbhains of the country round Trim claimed descent from him.

LAEGHAIRE LORC, a much earlier and probably mythical king of Ireland, is the subject of many Irish tales. The chroniclers assign B.C. 593–5 as the date of his reign, and say that he was son of Ugaine Mor, and that he was slain at Wexford. There is a story of his murder in Keating (Foras Feasa ar Eirinn), and a poem on the loss of his crown in the 'Dindsenchas' (Book of Leinster), printed with translation by the present writer, London, 1883.

[The earliest account of Laeghaire occurs in Muirchu Maccu-Machtheni's composition in the Book of Armagh. The date of the manuscript is 807, and of the composition about 690. Various parts of his history are to be found in Leabhar na h-Uidri (1106), Book of Leinster (1200), and the Annals of Tigernach (1088). Book of Lecan (1400). Flann Mainistrech [see FLANN] and all the later annals agree with these authorities. Points in relation to him are discussed in O'Donovan's Topographical Poems of John O'Dubhagain and Gilla na naomh O'Huidhrin, Dublin, 1862; Petrie's History and Antiquities of Tara Hill; O'Beirne Crowe's 'Siabur-Charput' in Journal of Royal Hist. and Archæological Assoc. of Ireland, 1871, vol. i. pt. ii.; W. Stokes's Tripartite Life of St. Patrick, 1887, and 'The Boroma' in Revue Celtique, January 1892; O'Clery's Annals Rioghachta Eireann, under the years 438–58.] N. M.

LAFFAN, SIR JOSEPH DE COURCY (1786–1848), physician, third son of Walter Laffan of Cashel, by Eleonora, daughter of Richard de Courcy, a distant relative of the family of Kinsale, was born at Cashel on 8 May 1786. His eldest brother was Robert Laffan (d. 1833), Roman catholic archbishop of Cashel, and Laffan himself was originally destined for the Roman catholic priesthood, and placed at the college of Maynooth. Leaving Maynooth, however, he proceeded to Edinburgh University, turned his attention to medicine, graduated M.D. on 24 June 1808, and was admitted L.R.C.P. 22 Dec. 1808, from which date until 1812 he practised in Orchard Street, Portman Square. In October 1809 he proffered his services to the government in behalf of the fever-stricken troops lately returned from the Walcheren expedition. These were accepted, and the aptitude which Laffan showed for military practice led to his appointment in 1812 as physician to the forces. He served in Spain and Portugal during the latter part of the Peninsular war, and was eventually made physician in ordinary to the Duke of Kent. At the termination of the war he stayed at Paris, and practised there with brilliant success until desire for more rest led him to Rochester, where he remained until he was disabled by disease. After his retirement he settled at Otham in Kent. His successful treatment of an illness of the Duke of York, brother to George IV, led to his being created a baronet by patent dated 15 March 1828, and in 1836 he was also created a knight of the Hanoverian Guelphic order. He died at Vichy, in France, on 7 July 1848, in his sixty-third year. His body was brought to Rochester and interred in a vault in St. Margaret's Church. Laffan married in 1815 Jemima, daughter of Paul Pilcher of Rochester, and widow of a Colonel Symes, formerly English envoy at Ava in Burmah. He had no issue, and the title has become extinct. He devoted the greater part of his fortune to found a cancer ward for women in the Middlesex Hospital, and a full-length portrait of him is preserved in the hospital board-room.

[Gent. Mag. 1848, pt. ii. p. 318; Munk's Coll. of Phys. iii. 70-1; Pantheon of the Age, ii. 521; information kindly supplied by Lady Laffan and by the Rev. L. Lagier of Lausanne, who married a Miss Symes, Laffan's step-daughter.] T. S.

LAFFAN, Sir ROBERT MICHAEL (1821-1882), governor of Bermuda, third son of John Laffan, esq., of Skehana, cos. Clare and Limerick, was born on 24 Sept. 1821. Educated at the college of Pont Levoy, near Blois, France, he went to the Royal Military Academy, Woolwich, in September 1835, and on 5 May 1837 was gazetted a second lieutenant in the royal engineers. After serving for two years at Chatham and Woolwich, and becoming first lieutenant on 1 April 1839, he was sent to South Africa, where he was employed in frontier service. He was one of the officers summoned by the governor, Sir George Napier, to a council of war in order to concert measures for the relief of Colonel Smith and the garrison of Natal, then closely beleaguered by a strong body of emigrant Boers under their chief, Pretorius. It devolved upon Laffan to organise the engineering arrangements of the expedition, which,

under Sir Josiah Cloete, succeeded in effecting the relief of the British garrison.

From the Cape, Laffan was sent to Mauritius, where he was promoted captain on 1 May 1846. On his return home in 1847 he was appointed commanding royal engineer at Belfast, and at the close of the year was nominated an inspector of railways under the board of trade, an office he held until the autumn of 1852, when he was sent to Paris and Antwerp to report on the defences for the information of Sir John Burgoyne, the inspector-general of fortifications.

Laffan represented the borough of St. Ives, Cornwall, in the House of Commons from 1852 to 1857 in the conservative interest. In 1854 he was appointed commanding royal engineer in the London district, and in 1855 he was sent by the Duke of Newcastle, then secretary of state for war, with Sir William Knollys and Sir George Maclean, to report upon the organisation of the French ministère de la guerre. On his return to England in May 1855 he was appointed deputy inspector-general of fortifications at the war office. From 1858 to 1860 he was absent on sick leave in the south of France and Switzerland. Laffan was promoted brevet-major on 26 Oct. 1858, and became a regimental lieutenant-colonel on 28 Nov. 1859. On his return from sick leave he was stationed at Portsmouth for a short time, and towards the end of 1860 he was sent to Malta as commanding royal engineer. He remained there for five years, during which the armament of the fortress was completely revised. He was promoted brevet-colonel on 28 Nov. 1864.

In 1865 Laffan was sent to Ceylon as a member of a commission to investigate and report on the military expenditure of the colony and the strength of the force to be maintained there in time of peace. He was at the same time deputed to report specially to the secretary of state for war on the defences. On his way home, under instructions from the war office, he visited the Suez Canal in company with M. de Lesseps, and he made a report to the secretary of state for war. He revisited Egypt at the invitation of M. de Lesseps, to witness the opening of the canal in November 1869.

In 1866 Laffan was appointed commanding royal engineer at Aldershot, where he acquired no small reputation in peace manœuvres. He transformed the appearance of the camp by planting trees and laying down grass, and the old Queen's Birthday Parade has lately been renamed Laffan's Plain in his memory. Laffan was promoted regimental colonel on 9 Feb. 1870. In

January 1872 he was sent to Gibraltar as commanding royal engineer, and remained there for five years.

On 27 April 1877 Laffan was appointed governor and commander-in-chief of the Bermudas, with the rank of brigadier-general, and on 30 May the same year was made a K.C.M.G. In the 'Gazette' of 2 Oct. 1877 he was promoted major-general, and under the provisions of the royal warrant then just issued his rank was antedated to 8 Feb. 1870. He was promoted lieutenant-general on 1 July 1881. Laffan's ability, prudence, and tact made him a popular and successful governor of the Bermudas at a critical time in the political history of the colony. He died there, at Mount Langton, 22 March 1882. His body lay in state for two days, and was buried with military honours in Pembroke churchyard, Bermuda.

Laffan married in 1852 Emma, daughter of W. Norsworthy, and left a daughter and four sons.

[Corps Records; Royal Engineers' Journal, vol. xii.; Bermuda Royal Gazette, 28 March 1882.] R. H. V.

LAFOREY, Sir JOHN (1729?-1790), admiral, was the second son of Lieutenant-colonel John Laforey (d. 1753), one of the French Huguenot family La Forêt which settled in England in the time of William III. On 12 April 1748 he was promoted to be lieutenant; and to be commander of the Ontario by Commodore Keppel on 24 May 1755, while serving on the coast of North America. Continuing on that station, he was moved in 1756 into the Hunter, which he commanded off Louisbourg, under Admiral Holburne, in 1757, and at the capture of Louisbourg by Admiral Boscawen in 1758. On 25 July he commanded a division of the boats which burnt the Prudent and took the Bienfaisant in the harbour of Louisbourg, and was posted to the Echo frigate by Boscawen on the following day, 26 July 1758. In the following year the Echo was attached to the fleet under Sir Charles Saunders, during the operations in the St. Lawrence, culminating in the capture of Quebec, and was afterwards sent to the West Indies in the squadron under Sir James Douglas and at the reduction of Martinique by Sir George Rodney in February 1762. Laforey was then moved into the Levant frigate, in which he returned to England towards the end of 1763. He had married, at Antigua, Eleanor, daughter of Colonel Francis Farley of the artillery, and his eldest daughter was born in London in March 1764. As his only son was born in Virginia in December 1767, it appears probable that he was at that time in America on his private affairs; he had no naval appointment till 1770, when he commanded the Pallas frigate for a few months. In September 1776 he commissioned the Ocean of 90 guns, and in her took part in the action off Ushant on 27 July 1778; and at the subsequent court-martial gave evidence strongly in favour of Admiral Keppel. In November 1779 he was appointed commissioner of the navy at Barbadoes and the Leeward islands, with instructions to reside at Antigua and to act as commander-in-chief in the absence of a flag officer or senior captain.

In February 1783 he was moved to Plymouth, and was still there on 24 Sept. 1787, when a promotion of flag officers was made, extending below him. He, however, was passed over on the grounds that he had accepted a civil appointment. He disputed the justice of this decision, and eventually, on 10 Nov. 1789, was promoted to be rear-admiral of the red, with seniority of 24 Sept. 1787, in the place on the list which he would have held if promoted in due course. He was at the same time (3 Nov.) created a baronet; and a few days later went out as commander-in-chief at the Leeward islands. He was still there when war with France broke out in February 1793, and on the news reaching him led an expedition to Tobago, which surrendered on 15 April. He was shortly afterwards relieved by Rear-admiral Gardner and returned to England in July. He had been promoted to be vice-admiral on 1 Feb. 1793. He was reappointed commander-in-chief at the Leeward islands, and sailed on 9 May 1795 in the Amiable frigate, commanded by his son. He became admiral on 1 June 1795. During the year of his command a serious revolt of the negroes in St. Vincent, Grenada, and Dominica was suppressed, and Demerara, Essequibo, and Berbice were captured. He soon after resigned the command to Sir Hugh Christian, and sailed for England in the Majestic. He died of yellow fever on the passage, 14 June 1796, two days before the ship made the land. He was buried at Portsea on 21 June.

Laforey's son, Sir FRANCIS LAFOREY (1767-1835), who succeeded to the baronetcy, commanded the Spartiate in the battle of Trafalgar; was commander-in-chief at the Leeward islands 1811-14; was made K.C.B. in 1815; and died, admiral of the blue, 17 June 1835, when the baronetcy became extinct.

[Naval Chronicle, xxv. 177; Charnock's Biog. Nav. vi. 319; Ralfe's Naval Biog. i. 231; commission and warrant-books in the Public Record Office.] J. K. L.

LAGUERRE, LOUIS (1663-1721), painter, born at Paris in 1663, was son of a Spaniard, a native of Catalonia, who entered the service of Louis XIV, and was appointed 'maitre de la ménagerie' to the king. The father was much favoured by the king, who stood sponsor to his son. Louis was educated at the Jesuits' College, Paris, but having shown an early inclination for drawing, was sent by his parents to study in the school of the French Academy. Subsequently he worked for a time under Charles le Brun. At the Academy he obtained in 1682 the third prize for a painting of 'Cain building the Town of Enoch,' and in 1683 the third prize for a sculpture of 'Tubal Cain.' In the latter year he came to England with an architectural painter, called Ricard; they were employed as assistants by Verrio, who was then engaged on his paintings at St. Bartholomew's Hospital. Laguerre showed so much skill that he quickly found employment among the nobility in painting halls, staircases, or ceilings. He did much work at Burleigh House, Stamford; at Petworth House, Sussex, where he painted an allegorical history of Elizabeth, countess of Somerset; at Blenheim Palace, where he painted on the ceiling the Duke of Marlborough in triumph; at Berkeley or Devonshire House in Piccadilly (destroyed by fire); at the Earl of Radnor's, in St. James's Square; at Buckingham House (now rebuilt as Buckingham Palace); at Chatsworth, and elsewhere. At Marlborough House, in Pall Mall, he painted a series of Marlborough's victories, which have been engraved. He received a commission to paint the cupola of St. Paul's Cathedral, and had actually begun the designs, when the commission was withdrawn, and eventually the work was entrusted to Sir James Thornhill [q. v.] Laguerre was much esteemed by William III, who gave him apartments at Hampton Court. Here he painted in chiaroscuro 'The Labours of Hercules' in the fountain court, and was employed to 'restore' the sadly damaged tempera-paintings by Andrea Mantegna of 'The Triumph of Cæsar.' He was one of the directors of the Academy of Painting in Great Queen Street, Lincoln's Inn Fields, and might have become governor on the resignation of Sir Godfrey Kneller had he pushed his candidature more resolutely. Laguerre also painted small pictures, portraits (one of William, earl Cadogan, was engraved in mezzotint by J. Simon), and designs for engraving or tapestry. His figure-drawing was rated very highly, and was much imitated. Laguerre is also credited with an etching of 'The Judgment of Midas,' and for a club of virtuosi Laguerre painted, at the tavern in Drury Lane where they met, a Bacchanalian procession.

His early education was of great use to him in his allegorical and mythological compositions. Pope's depreciatory line,

Where sprawl the Saints of Verrio and Laguerre,

has caused posterity to treat their works with unmerited contempt. He was of an indolent and careless disposition, or he might have amassed a large fortune.

Laguerre's first wife was daughter of Jean Tijou, a worker in iron, who executed some of the ironwork at Hampton Court. For him he designed a frontispiece to a book of designs for ironwork, engraved by Paul Van Somer, and published by Tijou in 1693. After his first wife's death he married again. Late in life he became dropsical, and fell into general ill-health from neglect of medical advice. On Thursday, 20 April 1721, he went with his wife and a party of friends to Lincoln's Inn playhouse to see the 'Island Princess,' in which his son John was going to sing. Before the performance commenced he was stricken with apoplexy, and died in the theatre. He was buried in St. Martin's-in-the-Fields.

LAGUERRE, JOHN (d. 1748), painter and actor, son of the above, was born in London. He was educated by his father as a painter, and showed some skill, but was of too indolent and careless a nature to succeed in that art. Instead he went on the stage, having considerable vocal powers, and achieved some success. He also painted scenery for the theatre. He is best known by a series of drawings, representing the history of 'Hob in the Well,' which were engraved by Claude Dubosc, and were very popular. A plate called 'The Theatrical Revolt' was etched by him, representing a humorous occurrence in his stage life. He painted a portrait of Mary Tofts [q. v.] the impostor, which was engraved in mezzotint by John Faber the younger. He died in poor circumstances in March 1748.

[Walpole's Anecdotes of Painting, ed. Wornum; Vertue's MSS. (Brit. Mus. Add. MSS. 23068-75); Dodd's manuscript Hist. of English Engravers (Brit. Mus. Add. MS. 33402); Dussieux's Les Artistes Français à l'Etranger; Abcedario de P. J. Mariette; Chaloner Smith's British Mezzotinto Portraits.] L. C.

LAIDLAW, WILLIAM (1780-1845), friend of Sir Walter Scott, was born 19 Nov. 1780, at Blackhouse, Selkirkshire, where his father was a sheep-farmer. After receiving an elementary education at Peebles he assisted his father for a time. James Hogg [q. v.], the Ettrick Shepherd, whose mother was his distant cousin, was employed at Blackhouse for ten years, and formed a lasting friendship with Laidlaw. According to Hogg's 'Autobiography' Laidlaw was one of his first appreciative critics. In 1801 Hogg and Laidlaw helped Scott with materials for the 'Border Minstrelsy.' After two unsuccessful attempts at farming, in Peeblesshire and Midlothian respectively, Laidlaw in 1817 became steward to Sir Walter Scott at Abbotsford. Master and man suited each other exactly, Laidlaw proving himself not only an exemplary servant but a worthy counsellor and a devoted friend. He was valued in the field, on the stream, and in the study. In 1819, when Scott was recovering from an illness, Laidlaw and Ballantyne wrote to his dictation most of the 'Bride of Lammermoor,' and subsequently 'The Legend of Montrose,' and nearly all 'Ivanhoe.' 'St. Ronan's Well' may have been due to Laidlaw's suggestion that Scott should devote a novel to 'Melrose in July 1823' (LOCKHART, *Life*, v. 285, ed. 1837). When ruin fell upon Scott, he wrote to Laidlaw that it was 'not the least painful consideration' amid his troubles that he could no longer be useful to him (*Journal*, i. 97). After an interval, however, Laidlaw became his amanuensis, retaining the post till Scott's death in 1832. Subsequently he was factor to Sir Charles Lockhart Ross, Balnagowan, Ross-shire. Retiring in feeble health, he died in the house of his brother at Contin, near Dingwall, Ross-shire, 18 May 1845.

Laidlaw wrote several lyrics, but he is remembered only for his tender song, 'Lucy's Flittin',' published in Hogg's 'Forest Minstrel,' 1810. After 1817 he compiled, under Scott's management and direction, 'part of the 'Edinburgh Annual Register,' and contributed articles to the 'Edinburgh Monthly Magazine' (afterwards 'Blackwood's'). He is also said to have written on the geology of Selkirkshire.

[Lockhart's Life of Scott, passim, and Scott's Journal; Rogers's Scottish Minstrel, vol. ii.; Borland's Yarrow, its Poets and Poetry; Gent. Mag. 1845, pt. ii. p. 213.] T. B.

LAING, ALEXANDER (1778–1838), antiquary, the illegitimate son of an Aberdeen advocate named Michie, was born at Coull, Aberdeenshire, in 1778. He was tolerably well educated and possessed good natural abilities, but his erratic temperament precluded his advancement. For some years previous to his death he was employed as a book canvasser and flying stationer, in allusion to which he was commonly known

in the country as 'Stashie Laing.' The first of Laing's antiquarian writings, 'The Caledonian Itinerary, or a Tour on the Banks of the Dee, with Historical Notes from the best Authorities,' appeared at Aberdeen in 1819. During the three subsequent years Laing edited an annual, the first two issues of which were entitled 'The Eccentric Magazine,' and the third 'The Lounger's Commonplace Book,' being a collection of anecdotes, apophthegms, and literary and historical curiosities. In 1822 he published 'Scarce Ancient Ballads never before published, with Notes,' Aberdeen, 12mo, and in the following year a similar collection under the title 'The Thistle of Scotland' (*Advocates' Library Cat.*) In 1828 appeared his chief work, 'The Donean Tourist, interspersed with Anecdotes and Ancient National Ballads,' Aberdeen, 1828, 8vo, a volume on the history and traditions of the river Don, which, though somewhat loosely compiled, constitutes a rich mine of Scottish historical lore, and 'exhibits,' says Jervise, 'an incredible amount of patience' and labour (*Epitaphs and Inscriptions*, i. 284). This is the only work by Laing in the British Museum Library. His last work was 'An Cluaran Albannach, a Repository of Ballads, many never before published, to which are appended copious Notes, Historical, Biographical, Illustrative, and Critical,' Aberdeen, 1834, 12mo. Laing died in 1838 at Boltingstone, a roadside inn between Tarland and Strathdon, and was buried in the churchyard of Coldstone, Aberdeenshire.

All his works are now scarce and coveted by Scottish bibliophiles. 'Not a ruin or a battlefield by Dee or Don, which history or tradition gave name to, but Laing visited and viewed with a devotion almost sacred in its intensity. Ballads, family histories and genealogies, in all the unmethodical delightfulness of a tinker's wallet, lay jumbled up in his capacious brain, to be reproduced in various books with a confusing prolixity' (WALKER, *Bards of Bonaccord*, p. 650).

[Notes kindly supplied by John Bullock, esq., editor, Scottish Notes and Queries; Irving's Dict. of Eminent Scotsmen, p. 260; Men of the Reign, p. 507; Brit. Mus. Cat.] T. S.

LAING, ALEXANDER (1787–1857), the Brechin poet, was born at Brechin, Forfarshire, 14 May 1787. His father was an agricultural labourer. Laing spent only two winters at school, and when eight years old became a herd, but devoted much of his leisure to reading and writing. At the age of sixteen he was apprenticed to a flaxdresser, and followed this occupation for fourteen years, when an accident permanently disabled him. He afterwards earned a modest competency as a pedlar, and died at Brechin, 14 Oct. 1857.

Laing contributed to local newspapers and to the following poetical miscellanies: 'Harp of Renfrewshire,' 1819; R. A. Smith's 'Scottish Minstrel,' 1820; Struthers's 'Harp of Caledonia,' 1821; Whitelaw's 'Book of Scottish Song,' 1844; and 'Whistle Binkie,' 1832–47. He also furnished anecdotes to the Scottish story-book 'The Laird of Logan,' 1835. In 1846 he published a collection of his poetry under the title 'Wayside Flowers,' of which a second edition appeared in 1850. He writes vigorous and melodious lowland Scotch, and is both pathetic and humorous. Laing edited popular editions of Burns and Tannahill, supplied various notes to Allan Cunningham's 'Scottish Songs,' 1825, and biographical notices to the 'Angus Album,' 1838.

[Preface to Jervise's Epitaphs and Inscriptions; Rogers's Scottish Minstrel, vol. iv.; Grant Wilson's Poets and Poetry of Scotland, vol. ii.]   T. B.

LAING, ALEXANDER GORDON (1793–1826), African traveller, born 27 Dec. 1793, was eldest son of William Laing, A.M., of Edinburgh, by his wife, the daughter of William Gordon of Glasgow Academy, writer of an English translation of Livy and of various educational books. William Laing, a very popular private teacher in his day, opened the first classical academy in Edinburgh. There Alexander was taught until the age of thirteen, when he entered Edinburgh University. At fifteen he was an assistant-master in Bruce's classical academy at Newcastle-on-Tyne, but afterwards went back to Edinburgh to help his father. In 1810 he was made an ensign in the Prince of Wales's regiment of loyal Edinburgh volunteers, and in 1811 he went out to Barbadoes. His mother's brother, Colonel (afterwards General) Gabriel Gordon (cf. Gent. Mag. 1855), who was deputy quartermaster-general there, employed him as an extra clerk in his office, and in that capacity he came under the notice of General Sir George Beckwith [q. v.] On 11 March 1813 he was appointed ensign in the York light infantry, a corps, composed chiefly of foreigners, formed for West India service. He became lieutenant 28 Dec. 1815, and served with the corps in Antigua. When it was disbanded at the peace he effected, after a brief interval on half-pay, an exchange into the 2nd West India regiment in Jamaica, and was employed there as deputy assistant quartermaster-general. To cure a violent attack of liver complaint he subsequently

sailed to Honduras, where the governor, Colonel (afterwards Sir) George Arthur [q.v.], employed Laing as fort-major; but ill-health soon drove him home, and a reduction in the strength of his regiment placed him on half-pay from 25 Dec. 1818. In 1820 he was brought back into the 2nd West India regiment as lieutenant and adjutant, and on 3 April 1822 was promoted to a company in the royal African corps, to which (and not to the 2nd West India, as stated by CHAMBERS) he belonged at the time of his death.

Early in 1822 Sir Charles MacCarthy, the governor of Sierra Leone, where Laing was serving with his corps, despatched him into the Kambian and Mandingo countries to ascertain the disposition of the natives regarding trade, and their sentiments respecting the abolition of the slave-trade. After staying at Kambia long enough to fulfil his instructions, he crossed the Scarcies to Melacourie, on the Melageah, and afterwards tried to reconcile Amara, the Mandingo king, described as 'a crafty Mohammedan,' with the rival chief Sannassee of Melacourie. To attain this object permanently, Laing, after his return to Sierra Leone, undertook a second journey, and for six days was without shelter by day or night. On 16 April 1822 he began a journey through the Timmannee and Koornoko countries to Falaba, the capital of Soolima, where he had learned that abundance of gold and ivory was to be found. He was well received, and remained some months. He ascertained the source of the Rokell, and was within three days of the supposed source of the Niger, which he was not allowed to visit. In October 1823 he was ordered to join his corps on the Gold Coast, in consequence of the menacing attitude of the Ashantees. He organised and commanded a large native force on the frontier during the greater part of 1823, in the course of which he frequently engaged and defeated the Ashantees. His success secured the allegiance of all the Fantee tribes, and he compelled the king of Ajucaman to put his troops under British control. When the Ashantees carried off a British sergeant, Laing offered to proceed on a mission to Coomassie to rescue him; but Sir Charles MacCarthy considered the enterprise too perilous (cf. Ann. Reg. 1824, pp. 124–36). After the fall of MacCarthy in action with the Ashantees, 21 Jan. 1824, Colonel Chisholm, on whom the chief command devolved, sent Laing home to report the position of affairs to Henry, third lord Bathurst [q. v.], then colonial secretary. While at home he began to prepare for the press his journals, subsequently published under the title, 'Travels in Timmannee, Kooranko, and Soolima, Countries of Western Africa,' London, 1825.

Late in 1824 Laing received instructions from Lord Bathurst to undertake an expedition, by way of Tripoli and Timbuctoo, to ascertain the source and course of the Niger. Full of enthusiasm, he left England 5 Feb. 1825. He proceeded to Tripoli by way of Malta, where he was treated with marked attention by the governor, the Marquis of Hastings. At Tripoli he contracted a close friendship with the British consul, Mr. Warrington, whose daughter, Emma Maria Warrington, he married 14 July 1825. Two days later he set out for Timbuctoo, in company with Babani, a sheikh of good repute, who undertook his safe conduct thither in ten weeks' time. The ordinary route was deemed unsafe, and, after a tedious and roundabout journey of a thousand miles through part of Fezzan, the travellers reached Ghadamis on 13 Sept. Laing was well received. Although many of his instruments had been damaged, and the stock of his only rifle had been broken by a charging elephant, he hopefully left Ghadamis 27 Oct., and on 3 Dec. 1825 reached Ensala, a town on the eastern frontier of the province of Tuat, belonging to the Tuaric, where he repaid a kindly reception by rendering medical aid to the sick. On 10 Jan. 1826 he quitted Ensala, and a fortnight later entered the flat, sandy, cheerless desert of Tenezaroff. Of his subsequent movements there is no detailed information. According to letters received by his father-in-law, and dated 10 May and 1 July 1826, after suffering from fever, he and his party were attacked and plundered by the Tuaric, and he was severely wounded. The sheikh Babani, who was dead at the time, was not in Laing's opinion wholly blameless. Laing was then the sole survivor of his party. According to another letter, his last, dated Timbuctoo (Timbuctû) 21 Sept. 1826, Laing reached that city on 18 Aug. 1826 (which entitled him to the 3,000l. offered by a society in London to the first European arriving there). The city answered all his expectations, except as regarded size. His position was very unsafe, owing to the hostility of Bello, chief of the Foulahs of Massina, who had dispossessed the Tuaric. He proposed leaving the city in three days' time. From information afterwards collected from various sources, it appeared that Laing left Timbuctoo at the time intended, and was surprised and murdered by Arabs in his bivouac on the night of 26 Sept. 1826. Facts, which were established at Tripoli in 1829 to the entire satisfaction of the British, Dutch, Danish, Swedish, and Sardinian consuls there, showed that the sheikh Babani, who was sent

with Laing from Tripoli, was under the secret direction of Hassunah d'Ghies, son of the prime minister of the bashaw of Tripoli; that it was by d'Ghies's direction that the actual murderer, the ferocious Bourabouschi, was appointed to be Laing's guide on the return journey from Timbuctoo; that Laing's papers, forming a packet fourteen inches long and seven inches thick, were placed in d'Ghies's hands shortly after the murder, and that the packet was known to be secreted in Tripoli in August 1828. It was also alleged that the documents were given by d'Ghies to the French consul, Baron de Rosseau, who was in correspondence with the conspirators during the greater part of Laing's journey. Mohammed, brother of Hassunah d'Ghies, gave most of this information. A summary of the evidence is given in the 'Quarterly Review,' March 1830 (No. lxxxiv.) No further explanation has appeared. The Geographical Society of Paris presented to Mrs. Laing a gold medal in recognition of her late husband's services to science.

[The most authentic memoir of Laing is that in Chambers's Eminent Scotsmen, vol. ii., with a portrait from a painting in the possession of the family. A few corrections have been made here from war office sources. See also Thomas Nelson's Memoirs of Oudney, Clapperton, and Laing, 1830; Quarterly Review, 1830, No. lxxxiv.; Dict. Universelle, under 'De Caillé' and 'Laing, Alexander Gordon;' and Johnston's Dict. of Geogr., under 'Niger' and 'Timbuctoo.' The only notices of Laing in the Journals of the Roy. Geogr. Soc. London, are in vol. ii. p. i. viii. 298, xxii. 191.]   H. M. C.

LAING, DAVID (1774–1856), architect, son of a merchant in the city of London, was born in 1774, and articled to Sir John Soane [q. v.] about 1790. In 1811 he was appointed surveyor of buildings at the custom house, and was directed to prepare designs for a new custom house on a site to the westward of Sir Christopher Wren's structure. In five years (1813–17) the building was completed and occupied, but in 1825 the beech piling and planking used as the substratum of the foundation decayed, and the front fell down. Much litigation followed, and ultimately, under Sir Sydney Smirke's advice, a new foundation was put in, and the whole building rearranged and altered.

Tite, one of Laing's pupils, laid the foundation of his reputation as joint architect with Laing of the church of St. Dunstan-in-the-East in 1817–19. Laing, who was a fellow of the Society of Antiquaries, died at 5 Elm Place, West Brompton, London, on 27 March 1856, aged 82. He was the author of 'Hints for Dwellings, consisting of Original Designs for Cottages, Farmhouses, Villas, &c.,' 1800, new edit. 1841, and of 'Plans, Elevations, and Sections of Buildings, Public and Private, executed in various parts of England, &c., including the new Custom House, London,' &c., 1818.

[Builder, 5 April 1856, p. 189; Gent. Mag. 1856, i. 650.]   G. C. B.

LAING, DAVID (1793–1878), Scottish antiquary, born in Edinburgh 20 April 1793, was second son of William Laing, bookseller [q. v.] in that city. David was educated at the Canongate grammar school, and afterwards attended the Greek classes of Professor Dalzell at the Edinburgh University. In his fourteenth year he became apprentice to his father, and by his youthful enthusiasm as a bookseller he soon attracted the notice of literary men. His father at this time was the only bookseller in Edinburgh who dealt in foreign literature, and David occasionally travelled abroad in search of rare or curious books. On one such journey through Holland he made at Rotterdam the acquaintance of John Gibson Lockhart [q. v.], who, in 'Peter's Letters to his Kinsfolk' (1819), describes him as ' by far the most genuine specimen of a true old-fashioned bibliopole that I ever saw exhibited in the person of a young man,' and makes mention of his ' truly wonderful degree of skill and knowledge in all departments of bibliography.' The first fruits of his industry appeared in a reprint of the 'Auctarium Bibliothecæ Edinburgenæ sive Catalogus Librorum quos Gulielmus Drummondus ab Hawthornden D.D.Q. Anno 1627,' which was issued in 1815. Laing was a candidate for the keepership of the Advocates' Library, which fell vacant in 1818, but Dr. David Irving [q. v.] was elected. In 1821 Laing became partner in his father's business, and he now devoted himself to the study and editing of old Scottish ballads and metrical romances. In 1821 he reprinted Sir Thomas Craig's 'Epithalamium on the Marriage of Darnley and Mary Stuart' and the poems of Alexander Scot. He also edited, conjointly with David Irving, the poems of Alexander Montgomery. In the same year he began the publication in parts of 'The Select Remains of the Ancient Popular Poetry of Scotland,' and in the following year he issued a reprint of 'The Pleasing History of Roswall and Lillian.' In 1823 (27 Feb.) Sir Walter Scott founded the Bannatyne Club, which was to consist of thirty-one members, for the printing of inedited materials or rare tracts relating to the history and literature of Scotland. Sir Walter was the first president, and his friend Laing was

secretary and chief organiser until the dissolution of the club thirty-eight years later. Twenty-seven of the publications of the club were edited entirely, or conjointly with others, by Laing. He at first continued to confine himself mainly to ancient Scottish poetry, editing the 'Buke of the Howlat' and the poems of George Bannatyne for the club, and on his own account the first volume of his 'Fugitive Scottish Poetry, principally of the Seventeenth Century' (1823–5), 'Early Metrical Tales' in 1826, and in 1827 'The Knightly Tale of Golagrus and Gawane,' from the unique copy preserved in the Advocates' Library of this the first book known to have been printed in Scotland. But he soon enlarged the field of his research. In 1826 he was elected a fellow of the Society of Antiquaries of Scotland, and for the following fifty years there was scarcely a volume of the society's transactions to which he did not contribute a paper.

In 1830 he edited for the Bannatyne Club 'The Affairs of the Kirk of Scotland,' 1637–1638, by John, earl of Rothes. In 1834 he brought out the first collected edition of the poems of William Dunbar, to which he added a supplement in 1846. In 1836 he edited, from a manuscript in the Advocates' Library, Nicoll's 'Diary of Public Transactions, 1650–1657,' and in the following year the 'Seven Sages' of John Rolland of Dalkeith.

On 21 June 1837 Laing was elected librarian to the Society of Writers to H.M. Signet, in succession to Professor Macvey Napier [q. v.]. Laing thereupon gave up his business as a bookseller, and disposed of his stock by public sale. The Signet Library, when he became its librarian, contained about forty thousand volumes. He left it at his death, forty-one years later, with seventy thousand.

In 1840 he edited, with Adam Urquhart, Sir John Lauder's 'Memorable Occurrents,' 1680–6; and in conjunction with John Hill Burton, for the Abbotsford Club, which had been started in 1834, the 'Jacobite Correspondence of the Athole Family, 1745–6.' In the following year he published the valuable 'Letters and Journals of Robert Baillie,' 1637–62, in which, according to Carlyle, he exhibited his usual industry, sagacity, and correctness (London and Westminster Review, 1841).

For the Wodrow Society he edited in 1841 Row's 'History of the Kirk of Scotland from 1558 to 1639,' and for the same society he issued in 1846 the first volume of his most important work, 'The Collected Works of John Knox,' which was completed by the publication of the sixth volume in 1864.

His 'Notes of Ben Jonson's Conversations with Drummond of Hawthornden' (Shakespeare Society) appeared in 1842, and his edition of Sir Gilbert Hay's 'Buke of the Order of Knighthood' in 1847. Another inedited work of Sir John Lauder, his 'Historical Notices of Scottish Affairs from 1661 to 1688,' was published by him in 1848. In 1849 he issued to the members of the Abbotsford Club two volumes of ancient poetry from the Auchinleck Manuscript: 'Sirre Degarre, a Metrical Romance of the end of the Thirteenth Century,' and 'A Penni worth of Witte; Floriee and Blauncheflour,' &c. These were followed by two volumes of 'Original Letters relating to the Ecclesiastical Affairs of Scotland, 1603–25' (Bannatyne Club, 1851), and Lodge's 'Defence of Poetry, Music, and Stage Plays,' &c. (Shakespeare Society, 1853).

In 1854 Laing was elected honorary professor of antiquities to the Royal Scottish Academy. In 1855 he issued a volume of etchings (1773–9) by John Clerk of Eldin [q. v.], to which he prefixed an account of the artist, for the Bannatyne Club, and wrote the preface to Mr. Blew's edition of the 'Aberdeen Breviary.' In 1858 he edited the 'Letters of John Colville, 1582–1603,' and, conjointly with Mr. Macknight, 'Memoirs of the Insurrection,' 1715, by John, master of Sinclair. In the same year appeared his 'Catalogue of the Graduates of the University of Edinburgh from 1580 to 1858.' In 1859 he edited the 'Registrum Cartarum Ecclesix S. Egidii de Edinburgh, 1344–1567,' and in 1861 the 'Registrum Domus de Soltre necnon Ecclesiæ Collegiatæ S. Trinitatis prope Edinburgh,' &c., both for the Bannatyne Club.

In 1863 Laing edited for the Spalding Club 'Extracts from the Diary of Alexander Brodie of Brodie, 1652–80, and of his son James Brodie, 1680–5.' In the following year he received the honorary degree of LL.D. from the university of Edinburgh. In 1865 he contributed to the Abbotsford Club a volume of poems by Stephen Hawes, and in 1867 to the Bannatyne Club a volume of papers relating to the colonisation of New Scotland, 1621–38. In 1865 appeared also his edition of the poetical works of Robert Henryson. His edition of 'The Gude and Godlie Ballates' appeared in 1868, followed in 1871 by his popular edition of the works of David Lyndsay. In 1871–2 he published 'Wyntoun's Chronicle' for the series of 'Historians of Scotland,' and in 1873 he issued for the Hunterian Club the 'Poetical Works of Alexander Craig of Rose Craig, 1604–31.' In 1875 he published, in two volumes, the 'Correspondence of Sir Robert Kerr, first Earl

of Ancram, and his son, third Earl of Lothian, 1616–67.' In 1878 he edited, in one volume, for the Hunterian Club, Garden's 'Theatre of Scottish Worthies,' and the 'Lyf, Doings, and Deathe of William Elphinstoun, Bishop of Aberdeen.' In the year of his death he issued as a present to his friends a facsimile reproduction of the copperplates which illustrated the French translation of Boccaccio's 'Fall of Princes,' printed at Bruges in 1476, and prefixed to the volume an account of the origin of engraving.

Laing died unmarried, in his eighty-sixth year, at Portobello 18 Oct. 1878. His unrivalled knowledge of books, and all that concerned books, in every department of literature and art, with his well-known readiness to assist all inquirers, brought round him a large circle of friends. 'Sitting in that fine Signet Library, of which he holds the keys,' said Professor Cosmo Innes, ' he is consulted by everybody in every emergency. No wise man will undertake a literary work on Scotland without taking counsel with Mr. Laing.'

His large private library of printed books was, by his direction, sold by auction. The sale, conducted by Messrs. Sotheby, Wilkinson, & Hodge, occupied thirty-one days (1879–80), and realised 16,137l. 9s. He bequeathed a collection of drawings to the Royal Scottish Academy, and a valuable collection of manuscripts to the university of Edinburgh.

His portrait, painted by Robert Herdman, R.S.A., for the Society of Antiquaries, on the fiftieth anniversary of Laing's admission as a fellow, is preserved in the hall of the society. Another portrait was painted by Sir William Fettes Douglas, R.S.A., and was presented by the artist to the Royal Scottish Academy in 1863.

[Notices of David Laing, LL.D., with List of his Publications and Lectures on Scottish Art, &c., by T. G. Stevenson, Edinburgh (privately printed), 1878; Biographical Memoir (with portrait) prefixed to new edition of the Select Remains of Ancient Popular and Romance Poetry of Scotland, drawn up by John Small, M.A., Edinburgh, 1885.]   T. G. L.

LAING, JAMES (1502–1594), professor of theology in the university of Paris, was born in 1502 at Auchterless in Aberdeenshire. Having shown much aptitude at school in Scotland, he continued his studies at the university of Paris, where he applied himself to theology and entered holy orders. He is inscribed on the records of that university as a Scotsman, of the diocese of St. Andrews, and of the German nation. On 20 Oct. 1556 he was elected procurator of his nation, whereby he had the right to represent it in the rector's court, the governing body of the university. This honour was conferred on him on many later occasions—on 27 Aug. 1558, on 10 Feb. and 27 Oct. 1560, on 21 Oct. 1568, and on 14 Jan. 1571. About this latter date he obtained the degree of doctor of theology. He preached during several years in Paris. Jean de Rouen, privy councillor, royal almoner, rector and censor of the university, in his treatise on the Sorbonne, mentions Laing in very laudatory terms. He was a violent enemy of the Reformation, and very abusive in his personal attacks on the reformers. In 1581 he wrote 'De Vita et Moribus atque Rebus Gestis Hæreticorum nostri temporis.' The notices of Calvin are translated from the French of the earlier treatise of Bolsec. Laing's first sentence regarding Knox concludes, 'ab initio suæ pueritiæ omni genere turpissime facinoris infectus fuit.' In 1585 he wrote a second treatise of a similar character, 'De Vita et Moribus Theodori Bezæ, omnium hæreticorum nostri temporis facile principis, et aliorum hæreticorum brevis recitatio. Cui adjectus est libellus de morte Patris Edmundi Campionis et aliorum quorundam Catholicorum qui in Anglia pro fide Catholica interfecti fuerunt, primo die Decembris, anno Domini 1581. Authore Jacobo Laingvo, Doctore Sorbonico,' Paris, 1585. The book is dedicated conjointly to Queen Mary Stuart and to James VI. He is said to have written other unpublished works of a less polemical nature, including a commentary on Aristotle's philosophy, which Dempster relates he saw in manuscript with the author. His name is appended to a document drawn up in the form of an oath of fealty signed and addressed by the principal members of the Paris faculties to Henry IV on his accession, 22 April 1594. He died during this year, and was buried, according to his wish, in the chapel of the Sorbonne.

[Du Boulay's Histoire de l'Université, tome vi.; Dempster's Hist. Eccl. Gent. Scot.; Conwus's De Stat. Religione apud Scotos, ii. 167; Beza's Life of Calvin; Hist. de la Vie, Actes, Doctrine, et Mort de Jean Calvin, par Bolsec, Paris, 1582.]
J. G. F.

LAING, JOHN (d. 1483), bishop of Glasgow and chancellor of Scotland, was a native of Edinburgh, and belonged to the family of the Laings of Reidhouse, Midlothian, whose last male representative was John Laing, Lord Reidhouse, lord of session under James VI. As he inherited a house in the High Street of Edinburgh, and his kinsmen held property within that city, his father was probably a wealthy burgess. The earliest notice of him in public documents is in a charter of 1463, in which he is described as secretary to Mary of Gueldres, queen-dowager of James II. At this time he probably held the office of rector of Tannadyce in Forfarshire. According to Crawfurd (Officers of State, p. 39), he was 'preferred to the treasurer's place in 1465.' The evidence on which this statement is founded is a charter dated 13 Oct. 1465, but Dr. Thomas Dickson has shown that the true date of this charter is 1472, and there is proof extant to show that the office of lord high treasurer was held by Sir David Guthrie [q. v.] of Kincaldrum in 1465 (Accounts of the Lord High Treasurer, Preface, p. xxx). On 12 Feb. 1470 Laing's name first appears as 'Rector of Tannadyce, Treasurer.' In several charters dated September 1470 he is described as 'Vicar of Linlithgow, King's Treasurer,' and he was at that time engaged in administering the affairs of the late queen. The rectories of Southwick and of Newlands were conferred upon him in 1472, at which date he was treasurer and clerk of the king's rolls and register. The oldest extant rolls of the treasury were written by Laing while he was in that post. He appears to have resigned his office of treasurer on 1 Dec. 1474, having then been promoted to the see of Glasgow. Crawfurd's theory that Laing was reappointed to the office of treasurer is not supported by documentary evidence, but he still took an active part in state affairs, and it is said that the reconciliation between James III and the Duke of Albany was effected principally through Laing's intercession. In 1476 he founded the Franciscan monastery or 'Greyfriars' of Glasgow, in conjunction with Thomas Forsyth, rector of Glasgow. So highly was he esteemed by the king that when the office of lord high chancellor became vacant at the close of 1482, through the resignation of Lord Evandale, Laing was chosen as his successor. He held office till his death on 11 Jan. 1483.

[Registrum Magni Sigilli; Origines Parochiales Scotiæ; J. F. S. Gordon's Scotichronicon, ii. 511.]
A. H. M.

LAING, JOHN (1809–1880), bibliographer, was born in 1809 at Edinburgh, but spent his early youth at Dalmeny, where his father was for many years factor to the Earl of Rosebery; his mother was Mary Fyfe, daughter of a Banffshire gentleman. After the usual course of study at Edinburgh University in arts and theology, he was in 1842 appointed minister of the parish of Livingston, Linlithgowshire. At the disruption in the following year he withdrew from the establishment, joined the newly formed free church, and for a time continued his ministry

D D 2

in the same parish. In 1840 he became chaplain to the presbyterian soldiers at Gibraltar and afterwards at Malta. Failing health, together with an invincible repugnance to appear in public, caused him to resign his charge. In 1850 he was appointed librarian in New College, Edinburgh, where his love of books found free scope, and his researches into bibliography began. After the death of Samuel Halkett [q. v.] in 1871, the materials collected by the latter for a dictionary of anonymous literature were entrusted to him, and Laing more than doubled the store. But he died 3 April 1880, before the work went to press. The whole, with the exception of the indices, was arranged and edited by his elder surviving daughter, and appeared with the title 'A Dictionary of Anonymous and Pseudonymous Literature of Great Britain,' 4 vols. 8vo, between 1882 and 1888. Laing published the 'Catalogue of the Printed Books and Manuscripts in the Library of New College, Edinburgh,' 4to, 1868.

On 29 Aug. 1843 he married at Livingston Catherine Fyfe, daughter of a West India proprietor, and had three daughters, the eldest of whom predeceased him.

[Library Chronicle, 1888; private information.]   J. K-r.

LAING, MALCOLM (1762–1818), Scottish historian, son of Robert Laing, of an old Orkney family, and elder brother of Samuel Laing [q. v.], was born at the paternal estate of Strynzia in 1762. He received his education at the grammar school of Kirkwall and the university of Edinburgh, and was called to the Scottish bar on 9 July 1785. Of the art of oratory he knew nothing, and his speeches in the court were 'uttered with an almost preternatural rapidity and in harsh and disagreeable tones' (Edinburgh Annual Reg. vol. ii. pt. i. p. 249). Lord Cockburn nevertheless states that 'his speech in 1794 for Gerald, charged with sedition, was the best that was made for any of the political prisoners of that period.' His practice, however, was never great, and he devoted much of his time to historical studies. On the death of Dr. Robert Henry [q. v.] he, at the request of that historian's executors, undertook to complete vol. vi. of Henry's 'History of Great Britain,' which with a short life of Henry appeared in 1793. In 1802 Laing published a 'History of Scotland from the Union of the Crowns, on the Accession of King James VI to the Throne of England, to the Union of the Kingdoms. With two Dissertations, Historical and Critical, on the Gowrie Conspiracy, and on the supposed authenticity of Ossian's Poems.' Though somewhat awkward and ungainly in style,

the thoroughness of its research still renders it of considerable value. The dissertation on Ossian's poems is a somewhat merciless exposure of the Ossian delusion, and caused much perturbation and no little indignation in the highlands. In 1804 Laing published a second and corrected edition of his 'History of Scotland' in four volumes, the first two being occupied with a 'Dissertation on the participation of Mary Queen of Scots in the Murder of Darnley,' and appendices of original papers connected therewith. He attempts to establish the authenticity of the Casket Letters, and his dissertation is an able statement of the case against the queen. In the same year he edited 'The Life and Historie of James VI,' and in 1805 published in two volumes the 'Poems of Ossian, containing the Poetical Works of James Macpherson in Prose and Verse, with Notes and Illustrations.'

Laing was a liberal in politics, a friend of Charles James Fox, and from 1807 to 1812 he represented Orkney and Shetland in parliament. In 1808 he finally removed from Edinburgh to his estate in Orkney. Latterly nervous weakness necessitated the discontinuance of all work, and he never left the bounds of his estate. Sir Walter Scott describes a visit paid to him there in August 1814. 'Our old acquaintance,' he writes, 'though an invalid, received us kindly; he looks very poorly, and cannot walk without assistance, but seems to retain all the quick, earnest, and vivacious intelligence of his character and manner' (LOCKHART, Life of Scott, ed. 1842, p. 271). He died on 6 Nov. 1818.

Laing married Miss Carnegie of a Forfarshire family, but left no issue. There is a tablet to his memory on the wall of the north nave of Kirkwall Cathedral. 'Depth, truth, and independence as an historian were,' says Lord Cockburn, 'the least of his merits, for he was a firm, warm-hearted, honest man, whose instructive and agreeable companionship was only made the more interesting by a hard, peremptory, Celtic manner and accent' (Memorials, p. 349).

[Edinb. Ann. Reg. vol. ii. pt. i. (1818) pp. 249–251; Lord Cockburn's Memorials, 1851; Archibald Constable and his Literary Correspondence, 1873, ii. 194–210; Lockhart's Life of Scott; Chambers's Eminent Scotsmen.]   T. F. H.

LAING, SAMUEL (1780–1868), author and traveller, younger brother of Malcolm Laing [q. v.], born at Kirkwall, Orkney, on 4 Oct. 1780, was educated at Kirkwall grammar school and the university of Edinburgh. Leaving the university without a degree about 1800, he spent eighteen months at Kiel in

Schleswig-Holstein, studying German. In 1805 he entered the army as an ensign in the staff corps stationed at Hythe, with which he saw service under Sir Arthur Wellesley and Sir John Moore in the Peninsular war. Returning to England after the battle of Corunna (16 Jan. 1809), he retired from the army, and through his brother's influence obtained employment as a manager of mines at Wanlockhead, in the south of Scotland. In 1818 he returned to Orkney to organise for a London firm the herring fishery on the coasts of the island, an enterprise in which he was completely successful. His brother dying the same year, he succeeded to his heavily encumbered estates, resided at Kirkwall, of which he was for some years provost, and engaged in the kelp trade. At the general election of 1832-3 he unsuccessfully contested Orkney and Shetland as a radical against the whig candidate, George Traill, and publicly accused Jeffrey, then lord advocate, of interfering with the freedom of election in Traill's interest (*Address to the Electors of Scotland by Samuel Laing of Papdale*, Edinburgh, 1833, 8vo). Reduced to comparative poverty by the failure of kelp, which ruined so many of the west highland and island proprietors, he left Orkney in 1834, and travelled in Norway and Sweden, studying the economic and social condition of the inhabitants. The results of his observations he gave to the world in two works which were much read, not only by the general public, but by economists and political thinkers. These were—(1) 'Journal of a Residence in Norway during the years 1834, 1835, and 1836, made with a view to inquire into the Moral and Political Economy of that Country and the Condition of its Inhabitants,' London, 1836, 8vo; and (2) 'A Tour in Sweden in 1838; comprising Observations on the Moral, Political, and Economical State of the Swedish Nation,' London, 1839, 8vo. The former work was little less than an unqualified panegyric upon Norway, whose free, industrious, and enterprising peasant proprietors Laing, a strong and somewhat *doctrinaire* radical of the old school, painted as patterns of native virtue; in the latter he denounced the union of Sweden and Norway as a flagitious act, inveighed against the privileged nobility and priesthood of Sweden as destitute alike of public spirit and private virtue, and denounced the entire nation as the most immoral in Europe. This elicited from Count Björnstjerna, Swedish ambassador at the British court, a pamphlet 'On the Moral State and Political Union of Sweden and Norway, in Answer to Mr. Laing's Statement,' London, 1840, 8vo, to which Laing published a trenchant rejoinder in the 'Monthly Chronicle,' reprinted in the preface to his next work, 'Notes of a Traveller on the Social and Political State of France, Russia, Switzerland, Italy, and other parts of Europe during the Present Century,' London, 1842, 8vo; 2nd edition the same year. About half of this book is devoted to Prussia, whose system of 'functionarism' Laing severely criticised, prophesying the success of the French in the next war. A German translation of this part, by Adolph Heller, appeared in 'Preussen der Beamtenstaat in seiner politischen Entwickelung und seinen social-ökonomischen Zuständen. Dargestellt durch Benjamin Constant und Samuel Laing,' Mannheim, 1844, 8vo. The whole was reprinted between 1851 and 1854, with the 'Residence in Norway,' in the 'Traveller's Library,' vol. iii. London, 8vo.

Laing's most considerable work was a translation of the Icelandic chronicle known as the 'Heimskringla,' published as 'The Heimskringla, or Chronicle of the Kings of Norway, translated from the Icelandic of Snorro Sturleson, with a preliminary Dissertation,' London, 1844, 3 vols. 8vo. The 'Dissertation' undoubtedly exhibits less judgment than enthusiasm, and the translation is more vigorous than accurate, but is interesting as a first attempt to familiarise Englishmen with the life, beliefs, and achievements of their Viking ancestors, and was the principal source of Carlyle's 'Early Kings of Norway.' A revised edition by Rasmus B. Anderson, LL.D., United States minister to Denmark, appeared in London, 1889, 4 vols. crown 8vo. The ferment caused at home by the Maynooth grant, and abroad by the pilgrimage to Trèves in 1844, elicited from Laing, who was opposed to the grant, 'Notes on the Rise, Progress, and Prospects of the Schism from the Church of Rome called the German Catholic Church, instituted by Johannes Ronge and I. Czerzki in 1844, on occasion of the Pilgrimage to the Holy Coat at Trèves,' London, 1845, 8vo (reviewed by W. R. Greg [q. v.] in a pamphlet entitled 'The German Schism and the Irish Priests'). Resuming his travels on the continent, Laing published a second and third series of 'Notes of a Traveller,' entitled 'Observations on the Social and Political State of the European People in 1848 and 1849,' London, 1850, 8vo, and 'Observations on the Social and Political State of Denmark and the Duchies of Sleswick and Holstein in 1851,' London, 1852, 8vo. In the former of these works he showed an appreciation of the better sides of some English institutions, and of the disadvantages of peasant proprietorship, and was reproached with inconsistency by J. S. Mill, who had founded part of his argument in favour of that mode of land tenure upon Laing's 'Residence in Norway' (see J. S. MILL, *Political Economy*, 6th ed. book 11. chap. vi. § 3, and chap. vii. § 5 note). The same tendency towards conservatism is equally marked in the work on 'Denmark and the Duchies.' For the rest of his life Laing resided principally in Edinburgh, where he died at the house of his daughter, Mrs. Elizabeth Baxter, on 23 April 1868. He was buried in the Dean cemetery.

Laing married, in March 1809, Agnes, daughter of Captain Francis Kelly of Kelly, Devonshire. By her, who died in November 1812, he had issue the daughter above mentioned and a son, Samuel, formerly M.P. for Orkney, both of whom still live.

[Information kindly supplied by S. Laing, esq.; introduction to Anderson's edition of the Heimskringla; Army List, 1806; Observations on the Social and Political State of Denmark and the Duchies of Sleswick and Holstein in 1851, p. 33; Blackwood's Edinburgh Mag. x. 728; Foster's Members of Parliament (Scotland), 1357–1882, p. 207 note; Edinburgh Review, lxxxii. 267 et seq., lxxxiii. 100 et seq.]

J. M. R.

LAING, WILLIAM (1764–1832), bookseller, born in Edinburgh on 20 July 1764, was educated at the grammar school in the Canongate. Leaving school in 1779 he was apprenticed to a printer, but left that employment in consequence of defective eyesight, and set up in 1785 as a bookseller in the Canongate. He subsequently removed lower down the street to Chessel's Buildings, where he remained until 1803, when he removed to South Bridge. From 1786 he began to issue annual catalogues, and his reputation as a collector of and authority on best editions and valuable books generally, both English and foreign, steadily increased. That as a collector he was not only indefatigable, but also intrepid, is shown by his visit to revolutionary Paris in 1793. Learning in 1790 that Christian VII of Denmark had been advised to dispose of the numerous duplicates in the Royal Library at Copenhagen, and being instigated by Niebuhr the historian, then a student at Edinburgh University, Laing promptly journeyed to Denmark and negotiated the purchase of the duplicates from the king's librarian, Dr. Moldenhawer. He made a rapid tour in search of book rarities in France and Holland during the breathing space afforded by the peace of Amiens. When the war recommenced he devoted his attention to the production in Edinburgh of a worthy edition of the Greek classics. He commenced this attempt in 1804 by the publication of 'Thucydides, Græce et Latine; accedunt indices; ex editione Wassii et Dukeri,' in 6 vols. sm. 8vo. This was followed by editions of Herodotus and Xenophon, to which Laing contemplated adding the works of Plato and Demosthenes, but was prevented by the difficulty of procuring competent editors. Towards the close of his life Laing, who had acquired considerable wealth, and whose shop had become a 'veritable Herculaneum of the treasures of past ages,' became one of the original directors of the Commercial Bank of Scotland. He died at his house, Ramsay Lodge, Lauriston, Edinburgh, on 10 April 1832, leaving a widow and nine children. His second son, David Laing the antiquary (1793–1878), is separately noticed.

[Chambers's Biog. Dict. of Eminent Scotsmen, ii. 459; Gent. Mag. 1832, ii. 278–9; Irving's Eminent Scotsmen, p. 261; Timperley's Cyclopædia, p. 920.]

T. S.

LAIRD, JOHN (1805–1874), shipbuilder, eldest son of William Laird, shipbuilder, of Birkenhead, and brother of Macgregor Laird [q. v.], was born at Greenock in 1805. At an early age he was associated with his father in the firm of William Laird & Son, of which he was for some years the managing partner. He was one of the earliest to turn his attention to the use of iron for the construction of ships, and in 1829 built a lighter of sixty tons for use on the Irish lakes and canals, the first, or one of the first, iron vessels ever constructed. In 1833 the style of the firm was changed to John Laird; he built the Lady Lansdowne, an iron paddle-wheel steamer, for the City of Dublin Steam Packet Co.; she was sent from Liverpool in pieces, and was put together on Loch Derg. In 1834 he built the John Randolph, paddle steamer, for Savannah, U.S.; this also was sent out in pieces, and was the first iron vessel ever seen in American waters. Among other vessels built by him were the steamers in which Francis Rawdon Chesney [q. v.] explored the Euphrates in 1836; a steamer built to the order of Mehemet Ali in 1837 for the navigation of the Nile; transports for use on the Indus and Sutlej; the Nemesis, for the East India Company, the first iron vessel carrying guns [see HALL, SIR WILLIAM HUTCHEON]; and the famous Birkenhead. In 1861 Laird retired from the business, which has since been carried on by his sons, under the style of Laird Brothers, and in the same year was elected the first M.P. for Birkenhead, then newly formed into a parliamentary borough, which he continued to represent, in the conservative interest, till his death, 29 Oct. 1874. He was a D.L. and J.P. for the county of Chester, a government nominee member of the Mersey docks and harbour board, and for many years chairman of the Birkenhead improvement commission. He married in 1829 Elizabeth, daughter of Nicholas Hurry of Liverpool, by whom he had issue.

[Times, 30 Oct. 1874; information from Mr. John Laird, of Laird Brothers.]   J. K. L.

LAIRD, MACGREGOR (1808-1861), African explorer, younger son of William Laird, founder of the famous Birkenhead firm of shipbuilders, and brother of John Laird [q. v.], was born at Greenock in 1808, and after finishing his education at Edinburgh, entered into partnership with his father, a position he soon afterwards relinquished to take part in the formation of the company started at Liverpool for the commercial development of the recent discoveries of the brothers Lander on the river Niger [see LANDER, RICHARD LEMON]. In 1832 the company despatched an expedition in charge of Richard Lemon Lander in two small vessels, one of which, the Alburka, a little paddle-wheel steamer of 55 tons burden, built by Laird, was the first iron vessel that made an ocean voyage. The expedition, which Laird accompanied, left Milford Haven on 24 July 1832, but did not reach Cape Coast Castle until the beginning of October. Melancholy loss of life attended it, only nine Europeans surviving out of forty-eight who started with it. The steamers entered the Nun mouth, and ascended the Niger as far as the confluence with the Tchadda, whence Laird, although suffering much from the effects of the climate, and being carried on a litter the greater part of the way, penetrated as far as Fundah (see Athenæum, 15 Feb. 1834 ; Journ. Roy. Geogr. Soc. 1834). Laird returned to Liverpool in 1834, with his health much impaired by the hardships he had endured, and he never fully recovered from the effects. He published a spirited narrative of the expedition ; was elected a F.R.G.S. London ; and gave important evidence before the parliamentary commission on the navigation of the Indus in the year of his return. In 1837 Laird was one of the promoters of the British and North American Steam Navigation Company, formed to run steamers from England to New York. The company built and owned the Great Western, and her ill-fated consort, the President. The Great Western was despatched to New York in April 1838, and, like the Sirius, despatched by the same company some days previously, performed the voyage out and back under steam. The few steamers that had before crossed the Atlantic had depended chiefly on their sails, and the success of the new company's two steamers practically refuted the predictions of the impossibility of relying wholly on steam-propulsion at sea—predictions of which Dr. Dionysius Lardner [q. v.], then the great authority on steam, was the chief exponent. 'As well talk of steaming to the moon,' Lardner had loudly declared. In 1844 Laird removed to Birkenhead, and took an active part in the development of that place, his name appearing with that of his father among the founders of St. James's Church. Some years later he came to London, and in 1850 he patented improvements in the construction of metallic ships, materials for coating ships' bottoms, and steering gear (patent 12934, 19 Jan. 1850).

The last twelve years of Laird's life were devoted exclusively to the development of the resources of Africa, and more especially towards establishing trade with the interior. He had persistently advocated that policy as the best means of counteracting and extinguishing slavery. He established himself as a merchant at 3 Mincing Lane, London, and having obtained a contract from government, started the African Steamship Company, to keep up monthly communication with all parts of the west coast as far as Fernando Po. Not content with developing the coast trade, he formed the idea of cutting off the trade in slaves by introducing habits of peaceful industry into the interior, and rendering the Niger the highway of legitimate commerce with Central Africa. With these views, he fitted out in 1854 a trading and exploring expedition at his own cost and risk, but with government support. The explorers ascended the river Tchadda in the steamer Pleiad 150 miles beyond the furthest point previously reached. Not a single death occurred during the expedition, a result due to the general excellence of the equipment and arrangements, and the liberal use of quinine. Encouraged by this result, Laird prevailed on the government to enter into contracts for annual voyages up the river, for which purpose he built the steamers Dayspring, Sunshine, and Rainbow, and made repeated ascents with them. The Dayspring, having reached Rabba on the Niger in safety, was lost on a rapid a few miles above that plain. Trading depôts were established at the confluence of the Niger and Tchadda, and at various places lower down. Laird pursued these undertakings with little or no prospect of personal advantage. He was married and left issue, and died on 9 Jan. 1861, aged 53.

Laird was author of 'A Journal of the Niger Expedition . . . by Macgregor Laird and D. N. R. Oldfield,' London, 1834, 2 vols.; also of a pamphlet on the sugar duties. He was a constant writer in newspapers on subjects in which he was interested, but usually wrote under a pseudonym, and burned all his papers, so that very few literary remains are in possession of his family. One of his lectures, signed 'Cerebus,' in the 'Spectator,' 9 Sept. 1851, pointed out the advantages of gun-vessels of the class of the Nemesis, Phlegethon, Pluto, &c., which had been built some time before by Messrs. Laird for the secret committee of the East India Company, and had done excellent service in Indian and Chinese waters.

[Presidential address of Sir Roderick Murchison in Journal Roy. Geogr. Soc., London, 1861, vol. xxxi. p. cxxvii; Address of Lord Ravensworth, President of the Institution of Naval Architects, in Marine Engineer, 1 May 1887; Lists of Patents; Brit. Mus. Cat. Printed Books, under 'Laird, Macgregor;' private information. A lecture on the river Niger, with a short account of Laird's explorations and expeditions, by Archibald Hamilton, appears to have been printed, but is not in the British Museum or Guildhall Library.]
H. M. C.

LAKE, ARTHUR (1569 1626), bishop of Bath and Wells, the son of Almeric Lake, esq., and brother of Sir Thomas Lake [q. v.], was born in the parish of St. Michael's, Southampton, in September 1569. He commenced his education in the free school of his native town, whence he passed to Winchester College, of which he was admitted a scholar 28 Dec. 1581. He became a fellow of New College, Oxford, in 1589, and graduated as B.A. 4 June 1591. His subsequent degrees were M.A. 3 May 1595, B.D. and D.D. 16 May 1605. On 16 Jan. 1600-1 he was admitted a fellow of Winchester, and in 1603 became master of the hospital of St. Cross, where he increased the allowance of the poor brethren. In July 1607 he was appointed archdeacon of Surrey. The following year he was made dean of Worcester. While dean he aided his chapter in buying in a long lease of some of the cathedral lands which had been illegally made, and gave an organ to the cathedral. In 1613, though not a candidate for the office, he was unanimously elected warden of New College, where he established at his own cost lectureships in Hebrew and mathematics. He served the office of vice-chancellor in 1616, during which year he was appointed to succeed Bishop Montague, whom he had previously succeeded in the deanery of Worcester, as bishop of Bath and Wells. He

was consecrated at Lambeth 8 Dec. 1616. 'His promotion,' Fuller says, 'was due, not so much to the power of his brother, the Secretary of State, as to his own desert as one whose piety might be justly regarded exemplary to all of his order' (Church History, vi. 38); 'making,' in Walton's words, 'the great trust committed to him the chief care and great business of his life' (Life of Sanderson). Lake as bishop was magnificently liberal. He was diligent in preaching both in his own cathedral and in the adjacent parishes. Before conferring holy orders he examined the candidates personally, and after ordination his care of his clergy and of their families was tender and paternal. Though his triennial visitations were carried out strictly, and convicted offenders never escaped canonical punishment, yet he was always welcome. At the confirmations, which, according to the custom of the age, took place contemporaneously with his visitations, the rite was never administered 'in a tumultuary manner, and, as we say, "hand over head,"' but only to those 'of whose fitness he was certified.' He was firm in maintaining ecclesiastical discipline, sitting in person with his chancellor in his consistorial court, and refusing to allow penance to be commuted for a pecuniary fine. He commonly saw the penances duly performed, and usually preached 'a sermon of mortification and repentance,' after which he would invite the offenders to dine with him in his palace, and dismiss them with his blessing and exhortation to amendment. His character is thus summed up by his biographer: 'To his city he was an oracle, to scholars a living library, to the whole church a priest whose lips did preserve knowledge.' At the coronation of Charles I he was selected, with Bishop Neile, to walk by the side of the king beneath the canopy of state. He held the college living of Stanton St. John, Oxfordshire, in commendam with his bishopric till his death. He died 4 May 1626, at the age of fifty-nine, having made his confession to Bishop Andrewes a few hours before he breathed his last. He was buried in the south choir aisle of his own cathedral, a small brass plate marking his grave. There are portraits in the bishop's palace at Wells and at New College, Oxford. An engraving by J. Payne was copied by Hollar in 1640.

He appears to have published nothing himself, but after his death a folio volume, entitled 'Sermons with some Religious and Divine Meditations,' with a life by the Rev. John Harris, D.D., was issued, London, 1629. The sermons include several preached at public penances. In 1640 were published his 'Ten Sermons preached at Paul's Cross, &c.,' and in 1641 his 'Theses de Sabbato.'

[Harris's Life prefixed to his Sermons; Fuller's Church Hist. vi. 27, 38, Worthies, i. 406; Wood's Athenæ, i. 750, ii. 398, 969, Fasti, i. 192, 254, 270, 280, 306, 307, 365, ii. 67; Walton's Life of Sanderson; Lansd. MS. 984, f. 145; Cassan's Bishops of Bath and Wells, ii. 27 sq.] E. V.

LAKE, SIR EDWARD (1600?–1674), royalist, born about 1600, was the eldest son of Richard Lake of Irby, Lincolnshire, by Anne, youngest daughter and coheiress of Edward Wardell of Keelby in the same county. He graduated B.A. at Cambridge as a member of St. Catharine Hall, was incorporated in the same degree at Oxford on 15 Dec. 1627, and was admitted B.C.L. on 24 Jan. 1628 as a member of St. Alban Hall (WOOD, Fasti Oxon. ed. Bliss, i. 435). He ultimately took his doctor's degree, practised as a civilian, and became advocate-general for Ireland. On the outbreak of the civil war he both fought and wrote on the king's side. At the battle of Edgehill he received sixteen wounds, and having lost the use of his left hand by a shot, he placed his horse's bridle between his teeth and fought with his sword in his right hand. He was taken prisoner and detained seven weeks at Great Crosby, Lancashire, but managed to escape, and by Christmas 1642 was safe at Bangor, Carnarvonshire. On 20 Oct. 1643 he arrived at Oxford, and on the 23rd, the anniversary of Edgehill, was kindly received by the king. He was promised a baronetcy and an augmentation to his arms, besides some compensation for the loss of his estate in England and Ireland. Two months afterwards the king sent him to Worcester. At the Restoration Lake petitioned for preferment and a grant of forfeited lands (Cal. State Papers, Dom. 1660-1, pp. 41, 53), but had to content himself with the chancellorship of the diocese of Lincoln. He did not assume the title of baronet until after 1662. In 1666 a republican barrister named Edward King of Ashby, Lincolnshire, charged him before the committee of parliament for grievances with extortion and illegal conduct. King printed his petition and circulated it throughout the county. Lake published an elaborate 'Answer,' fol., London (1666), which apparently satisfied the committee. He died on 18 July 1674, and was buried in Lincoln Cathedral, where his monument describes him as of Bishop's Norton, Lincolnshire (COLLINS, English Baronetage, iv. 134-5). By his wife Anne, eldest daughter and coheiress of Simon Bibye of Buckden, Huntingdonshire,

he had a son, Edward, who died an infant before 1666. He was succeeded in the title by his grand-nephew, Bibye Lake. To the church of Normanton, Yorkshire, the ancient seat of his family, he gave a handsome clock and a sum of money 'for the maintaining and keeping of it for ever.'

Lake wrote: 1. An account of his interviews with Charles I, which was edited from the original manuscript in 1858 by T. P. Taswell-Langmead for vol. iv. of the Camden Society's 'Miscellany.' 2. 'Memoranda: touching the Oath Exofficio, pretended Self-Accusation, and Canonical Purgation. Together with some notes about the making of some new, and alteration and explanation of some old, laws. All most humbly submitted to the consideration of this Parliament,' 4to, London, 1662.

An engraving of the fine oil portrait of Lake preserved in the family, with his autograph and seal, may be seen in Thane's 'British Autography' (vol. iii.)

[Wood's Athenæ Oxon. (Bliss), iii. 633 ; Taswell-Langmead's Introduction to Lake's Account (Camd. Soc.); Burke's Peerage, 1890, p. 801.] G. G.

LAKE, EDWARD (1641–1704), archdeacon of Exeter, born in Exeter on 10 Nov. 1641, was the son of a clergyman. In 1658 he entered Wadham College, Oxford, a commoner, was elected a scholar in 1659, but removed to Cambridge before graduating. In early life he seems to have been connected with the Earl of Bath's family. About 1670 he became chaplain and tutor to the princesses Mary and Anne, daughters of James, duke of York. He was made prebendary of Exeter on 13 Dec. 1673 (LE NEVE, Fasti, ed. Hardy, i. 425), and archdeacon of Exeter on 24 Oct. 1676 (ib. i. 396). In 1676 he was created D.D. at Cambridge by royal mandate (Cantabr. Graduati, 1787, p. 230). On 5 Jan. 1681 he was elected a brother of St. Katharine's Hospital, of which he was also a commissary. He resigned his patent for the last-named office on 10 Nov. 1698 (Ducarel's 'Hosp. of St. Katharine,' in NICHOLS, Bibl. Top. Brit. vol. ii. Appendix, pp. 90, 93). On 30 Nov. 1682 he was instituted to the rectory of St. Mary-at-Hill, to which was annexed in 1700 that of St. Andrew Hubbard, London (NEWCOURT, Repertorium, i. 451). His preaching was greatly admired. He died on 1 Feb. 1703-4, and was buried in St. Katharine, Tower Hill (Bibl. Top. Brit. Appendix, p. 8). The inscription on his monument shows that his friends shared his own opinion that he had been inadequately rewarded. By his wife Margaret (1638-1712) he had a daughter, Frances, married in 1695 to William Taswell, D.D., Mary, and Anne (will reg. in P. C. C. 44, Ash).

Lake wrote primarily for the use of his royal pupils a very popular manual entitled 'Officium Eucharisticum. A preparatory service to a devout and worthy reception of the Lord's Supper,' 12mo, London, 1673, which reached a thirtieth edition in 1753. In 1843 it was republished at Oxford with a preface by A. J. Christie. In the later editions the text underwent some material alterations; but these in all probability were made after the author's death. The 'Meditation for every Day in the Week' appended to the third (1677) and subsequent editions seems to have been written by another divine. The 'Prayers before, at, and after the Holy Communion' were reprinted in T. Dorrington's 'Reform'd Devotions,' 12mo, 1700, 1701, 1727.

Lake's 'Diary in 1677–8' was edited in 1846 by a descendant, G. P. Elliott, from the manuscript in his possession for vol. i. of the Camden Society's 'Miscellany.' Sixteen of his 'Sermons preached upon Several Occasions' (including a 'Concio ad Clerum Londinensem,' 1685) were published by his son-in-law, W. Taswell, 8vo, London, 1705. Prefixed is Lake's portrait engraved by M. Vandergucht, a copy of which, by G. Vandergucht, adorns some of the editions of the 'Officium Eucharisticum.'

[Wood's Athenæ Oxon. (Bliss). iv, 735–6; Elliott's Introduction to Lake's Diary (Camd. Soc.); Taswell-Langmead's Introduction to Sir E. Lake's Account (Camd. Soc.), p. x; Granger's Biog. Hist. of England, 2nd ed., iii. 266.]

G. G.

LAKE, EDWARD JOHN (1823–1877), major-general in the royal engineers, born at Madras on 19 June 1823, was son of Edward Lake (d. 1829), major in the Madras engineers, who served with distinction in the Mahratta war of 1817, and was author of 'Sieges of the Madras Army.' Sent to England with a sister at an early age, Edward was left an orphan when six years old by the foundering at sea of the ship Guildford, in which his parents with their four younger children were on passage home. He was brought up by his grandfather, Admiral Sir Willoughby Lake, who placed him at a private school at Wimbledon. He afterwards entered the military college of the East India Company at Addiscombe, and passed through the course in three terms instead of the usual four. He obtained a commission as second lieutenant in the Bengal engineers on 11 June 1840. After a year at the royal engineers' establishment at Chatham, he went to India, and was posted to the Bengal sappers and miners at Delhi.

Shortly after his arrival at Delhi, Lake as sent with a company of sappers to suppress an outbreak at Kythul, near Kurnaul. He there made the acquaintance of Henry and John Lawrence, and was employed for a time in road-making under the former. He was promoted lieutenant on 19 Feb. 1844. During the autumn of 1845 he served as a settlement officer in the Umballa district under Major Broadfoot. On the outbreak of the Sikh war in the same year he was ordered to the Sutlej, and joined Lord Hardinge in time to be present at the battle of Moodkee on 20 Dec., when he had a horse shot under him and was himself severely wounded in the hand. After the battle he was sent to the frontier station of Loodiana, where he strengthened the defences and forwarded troops and supplies to the army in the field. When Sir Harry Smith's camp equipage fell into the hands of the enemy just before the battle of Aliwal, Lake was able to replace it, and received the commendation of the governor-general for his zeal and promptness. He was present at the battle of Aliwal, and received a medal and clasp for his services in the campaign.

On the restoration of peace in March 1846, the trans-Sutlej territory of the Jalundhur Doab was made over to the British as a material guarantee. John Lawrence was appointed commissioner for the newly acquired territory, and Lake was nominated one of his assistants and placed in charge of the Kangra district, with headquarters at Noorpoor, whence he was soon moved to Jalundhur.

In May 1848, when Sir Henry Lawrence, the commissioner of the Punjab, had left India on furlough to England, open hostility was manifested by Mulraj, governor of Mooltan, and his turbulent Sikhs; Patrick Alexander Vans Agnew [q. v.] and Lieutenant Anderson were foully murdered, and the Punjab was in a blaze. Herbert Edwardes, who was in political charge of the Dera Ismail Khan district and nearest to Mooltan, hastily collected a body of Pathans and managed to hold his own against Mulraj. Lake was specially selected as political officer to the nawab of Bahawalpoor, a friendly Mahometan chief, whose territories adjoined the Punjab, and in virtual command of the nawab's troops he co-operated with his old friend Edwardes. He took part on 1 July in the second battle of Suddoosam, close to Mooltan, and for seven months was engaged in the operations for the reduction of Mooltan before it fell. During these stirring times

Lake, then only a lieutenant like Edwardes, was in fact commander-in-chief of the Davodpootra army, and although directed to co-operate with Edwardes, and in no way under his orders, he nevertheless magnanimously subordinated himself, and was content to do his utmost to further his friend's plans (ED-WARDES, *A Year in the Punjab*). On the fall of Mooltan, Lake was again in the field, and took part in the final victory of Gujerat on 21 Feb. 1849. He accompanied General Gilbert to the Indus in his pursuit of the Afghans, and was present at Rawul Pindee when the Sikh army laid down its arms. The war over, Lake received a medal and two clasps. Going to Batala, he next had charge, under John (afterwards Lord) Lawrence, for two years of the northern portion of the country between the rivers Beas and Ravee. In 1852 he went home on furlough, travelling through Russia, Prussia, Norway, and Sweden. He returned to India in 1854, having been promoted captain on 21 Aug., and a brevet-major on 22 Aug. for his services in the Punjab campaign. He took up his old charge in the trans-Sutlej province at Kangra as deputy-commissioner. In 1855 he was appointed commissioner of the Julundhur Doab. When the mutiny broke out in 1857, Lake occupied and secured the fort of Kangra against the rebels, and held it until the mutiny was suppressed. His calmness and resource were a tower of strength to the government throughout the crisis.

In 1860 his health failed, and he was obliged to go to England. He was promoted lieutenant-colonel on 18 Feb. 1861, and in July married the youngest daughter of T. Bewes, esq., of Beaumont, Plymouth. He returned to his post at Jalundhur in the same year. In 1865 he was appointed financial commissioner of the Punjab, and the following year was made a companion of the Star of India. In 1867 ill-health again compelled him to go to England, and subsequently to decline Lord Lawrence's offer of the much-coveted appointment of resident of Hyderabad. He had been promoted colonel on 31 Dec. 1868, and on 1 Jan. 1870 he retired on a pension with the honorary rank of major-general. After he left India the 'Lake Scholarship' was founded by public subscription in January 1870 in his honour at the Lahore High School.

About 1855 Lake had come under deep spiritual impressions, and was thenceforth earnestly religious. At home he became honorary secretary of the East London Mission Relief Fund in 1868, and worked hard between 1869 and 1876 as honorary lay secretary of the Church Missionary Society.

From April 1871 to June 1874 he was sole editor of the 'Church Missionary Record,' and contributed articles to the 'Church Missionary Intelligencer,' the 'Sunday at Home,' &c. In the summer of 1876 lung disease made it necessary for him to remove from London to Bournemouth, and in the following spring he went to Clifton, where he died on 7 June 1877. He was buried on 13 June 1877 in Long Ashton churchyard, near Clifton. In 1873 he edited the fifth edition of the 'Church Missionary Atlas,' and was engaged on another edition at the time of his death.

Lake was a man of slight and delicate frame, but of a very cheery and lovable disposition. He had great aptitude for business, and remarkable tact in the management of natives, by whom he was known as Lake Sahib, and was much beloved. Lord Lawrence, Sir Robert Montgomery, and other great Indian administrators had a very high opinion of him. Sir R. Montgomery wrote: 'The names of Herbert Edwardes, Donald McLeod, and Edward Lake will ever be remembered as examples of the highest type of public servants and devoted friends.'

[In Memoriam Edward Lake, two Memoirs by the Rev. John Barton and General Maclagan, R.E., 2nd ed. Lond. 1878; Edwardes's A Year in the Punjab Frontier in 1848-9, 8vo, Lond. 1851; Royal Engineers Journal, vol. vii.]

R. H. V.

LAKE, GERARD, first VISCOUNT LAKE of Delhi and Leswurree (1744-1808), general, elder son of Launcelot Charles Lake and his wife, Elizabeth, was born on 27 July 1744. He was a descendant of Sir Thomas Lake (q. v.), secretary of state, and was grandson of Warwick Lake, who married the heiress of Sir Thomas Gerard, bart., of Flamberds, Harrow-on-the-Hill (see BURKE, *Extinct Baronetage*). His mother was daughter of Joseph Gumley of Isleworth, Middlesex. One of her sisters married William Pulteney, first earl of Bath, and another was mother of George Colman the elder [q. v.], the dramatist. Lake was appointed ensign in the 1st footguards (now grenadier guards) 9 May 1758. His subsequent steps, all in the same regiment, were lieutenant and captain 3 Jan. 1762, captain-lieutenant 11 Jan. 1770, captain and lieutenant-colonel 19 Feb. 1776, regimental (3rd) major 20 Oct. 1784, regimental lieutenant-colonel 1 Aug. 1792. He became major-general in 1790, lieutenant-general 1797, and general 1802.

Lake served with the 2nd battalion of his regiment in the campaigns in Germany in 1760-2, and some years later was aide-de-camp to General Sir Richard Pierson, K.B., an old 1st guardsman, in Ireland. As lieutenant-colonel he went out with drafts to America in the spring of 1781, made the campaign in North Carolina under Lord Cornwallis [see CORNWALLIS, CHARLES, first MARQUIS], and commanded the grenadiers of the guards and of the old 80th royal Edinburgh regiment in a sortie, under Colonel Robert Abercromby, from the British lines at York Town, which inflicted heavy loss on the French and American besiegers, on 11 Oct. that year. After the surrender of Cornwallis's force (17 Oct.), Lake remained prisoner on parole until the end of the war (HAMILTON, ii. 252–8). On the first formation of a separate household for the Prince of Wales, afterwards George IV [q. v.], Lake was appointed his gentleman-attendant, and afterwards first equerry and chief commissioner of the stables. Wraxall speaks of him as a 'pleasing exception' to the prince's list of undesirable companions (*Memoirs*, v. 383). Lake was a member of the suite up to his death, but had apparently little to do with the prince. His younger brother, Warwick Lake, a commissioner of stamps and gentleman of the bedchamber, who died in 1821 (*Gent. Mag.* xci. pt. i. p. 1881, was the prince's adviser in racing, and was much mixed up with his unfortunate transactions with the Jockey Club (for details see RICE, *Hist. British Turf*, i. 64–85).

Lake represented Aylesbury in the House of Commons from 1790 to 1802. War was declared by the French on 1 Feb. 1793, and on 26 Feb. Lake embarked in command of a brigade composed of the first battalions of the three regiments of foot-guards, which reached Helvoetsluys on 1 March, and after some desultory operations joined the allied armies at Tournay on 23 April. These battalions, the first British troops actually engaged in the war, were present in the affairs at St.-Amand and Famars, and at the siege of Valenciennes. During the siege, on 18 Aug. 1793, the Prince of Orange was driven out of some forts which he had captured near Lille by a French force, with the loss of six pieces of cannon. The English guards were sent to the rescue. Unable to rally the Dutch, Lake promptly decided to attack the works singlehanded. He carried them at the point of the bayonet, driving out the French, who confessed to twelve battalions present, and taking twelve guns, including the six left behind by the Dutch. The French were raw troops, whom the guardsmen hustled and cuffed 'like a London mob' (HAMILTON, ii. 280), but Lake's brigade lost 38 killed and 143 wounded out of 1,122 of all ranks. The action, which is inscribed on the colours of the three regiments of guards, was spoken of at the time as the

most brilliant affair of the year. When the Duke of York retired from Valenciennes towards Dunkirk, Lake's brigade did good service in covering the rear. In September he had a dangerous illness, and was sent home the month after, 'to the regret of the whole army, in which he was universally respected and beloved' (*ib.* ii. 289). He rejoined the Duke of York's army at Cateau in the following spring, but went home again at the end of April 1794, and was not employed on the continent afterwards. He had by this time sold his regimental lieutenant-colonelcy in the 1st guards, and had been appointed colonel 53rd foot, from which he was subsequently transferred to the colonelcy of the 73rd foot. He was also promoted from the lieutenant-governorship of Berwick-on-Tweed to the governorship of Limerick in the same year.

In December 1796 Lake was appointed to the command in Ulster, which he held under Henry Luttrell, lord Carhampton, and Sir Ralph Abercromby [q. v.] as commander-in-chief until April 1798. He became a lieutenant-general in January 1797. He was chiefly engaged during this time in disarming the population and counteracting the plans of the United Irishmen. A number of his autograph letters, addressed to Thomas Pelham, afterwards second earl of Chichester, then Irish secretary, are in Brit. Mus. Addit. MSS. 33102, 33105. His Ulster proclamation of 13 Jan. 1797, requiring all persons other than peace-officers and soldiers to deliver up their arms, was denounced in debates in the Irish and English Houses of Commons, the former led by Henry Grattan [q. v.] and the latter by Charles James Fox [q. v.] When Abercromby, after vainly remonstrating against the license of the troops, resigned in disgust, Lake, as next senior, succeeded as commander-in-chief from 25 April 1798, and he has been accused of making no effort to check military license. On 24 May the rebellion broke out. His most important service was the rout of the rebel forces entrenched on Vinegar Hill, overlooking the town of Enniscorthy, co. Wexford, on 21 June 1798. 'The carnage was dreadful,' wrote Lake to Lord Castlereagh; 'the rascals made a tolerable good fight of it' (*Castlereagh Despatches*, i. 224). He marched into Wexford the day after, putting to death all rebels found with arms. He expressed his deep regret at the necessity of making examples (*ib.* i. 225). Lecky says that his indiscriminating severity wrought much harm (*History*, viii. 163). Meanwhile Cornwallis had arrived in Dublin on 20 June 1798 as lord-lieutenant and commander-in-chief, and Lake reverted to the position of next in seniority, with the command in Leitrim. On the news of the landing of the French in Killala Bay in August, Cornwallis despatched Lake to Galway, to assume the command beyond the Shannon, while he moved forward from Dublin in support. At midnight on 29 Aug. 1798 Lake arrived at Castlebar, where General Hutchinson [see HELY-HUTCHINSON, JOHN, second EARL OF DONOUGHMORE] had already taken up a position. On the morrow followed the disgraceful affair remembered as 'Castlebar Races.' Cornwallis appears to have laid the blame on Hutchinson for his risky disposition of his untrustworthy troops (*Cornwallis Correspondence*, ii. 411). Lake reformed his troops at Tuam, and after four days' hard marching, in conjunction with Colonel Vereker and Cornwallis, came up with the French under Humbert, who had advanced into the country, receiving little support. Humbert's force laid down their arms to Lake at Ballinamuck, near Cloone, on 8 Sept. 1798. Lake was brought into the Irish parliament by the government as member for Armagh to vote for the union. He retained his military command until late in 1799, when he resigned it and the mastership of Kilmainham, and returned to London, in view of obtaining an Indian command, most probably through the interest of Lord Castlereagh. His relations with Cornwallis appear to have been cordial. Cornwallis, however, speaks of William Neville Gardiner [q. v.] as 'much better than Lake as a soldier and a man of business' (*ib.* iii. 77–81).

Lake was appointed commander-in-chief and second member of council in India on 13 Oct. 1800. He took over the command in succession to Sir Alured Clark [q. v.] at Calcutta on 31 July 1801, and after a tour of inspection resided near Cawnpore, and applied himself vigorously to the development of the company's military resources. Lake paid great attention to the formation and training of the Bengal native light cavalry, which did good service in his subsequent campaigns. He introduced the plan of attaching two light pieces of the newly organised horse artillery to each cavalry regiment, under the name of 'gallopers,' an arrangement which proved of great utility. He established a system of 'flankers' in each regiment of native infantry—picked shots, who, at a given signal, fell out from their respective companies and formed a company of skirmishers. No light troops had previously existed in the Bengal army, both flank companies of each native battalion then and for some years afterwards consisting of grenadiers (WILLIAMS, pp. 274–276). Lord Wellesley's first letter to Lake,

dated in February 1802, insists on the paramount necessity of military retrenchment (*Wellesley Despatches in India*, ii. 619, 624). Next year, however, saw the development of the marquis's plans for breaking up the great Mahratta confederacy and rendering British influence paramount in Southern India, and on 28 June 1803 Lake was ordered to have a force ready to act to the southward should Dowlut Rao Scindia, maharajah of Gwalior, who had in his service numerous battalions officered by M. Perron and other Frenchmen, attempt to oppose the measures for the restoration of the peishwa at Poonah (*ib.* iii. 164–7). On 27 July (after the tidings of the fresh rupture with France) Wellesley directed Lake to commence operations at once against the powers of Gwalior and Berar (*ib.* iii. 180). In a later despatch Wellesley testified that the subsequent successes were due to Lake's 'matchless energy, ability, and valour' (*ib.* iii. 382). Lake, indeed, had a wonderful power of infusing spirit into his subordinates, and appears from the first to have thoroughly grasped two great principles of success in Indian warfare—boldness and swiftness in striking, and tenacity in following up every advantage gained. On 7 Aug. 1803 he marched from Cawnpore with 10,500 men; on 14 Aug. he entered Mahratta territory; on 29 Aug. he drove off a large body of Mahratta horse drawn up near Alyghur, himself charging at the head of the 27th (afterwards 24th) dragoons, with some new regiments of Bengal cavalry in support. Coel was occupied, and on 4 Sept. Alyghur, the chief depot of Perron's battalions, was stormed in the most gallant style by the 76th foot. On 11 Sept. Lake reached Delhi, and the same day his toil-worn troops, in a pitched battle, defeated the bulk of Perron's battalions, whose losses were estimated at three thousand men and sixty-eight guns. On 14 Sept. Lake was received in Delhi by Shah Allum, once the opponent of Clive; but now deprived of his sight, he had long been a puppet in the hands of the Mahrattas. Shah Allum, 'seated in rags under a tattered canopy, the sole remnant of his former state, and surrounded by every external token of misery,' conferred on Lake the titles of saviour of the state, the invincible in war, &c. Lake's laconic report contrasts well with the bombast of the government despatches (*ib.* iii. 318; cf. MILL, *Hist. of India*, vi. note to p. 510). Lake's successes brought the entire country between the Ganges and Jumna (the Doab), which Scindia had so laboriously annexed, under British control. On 23 Sept. the combined forces of Scindia and the rajahs of Berar were defeated at Assaye, 220 miles from

Bombay, by Arthur Wellesley. On 17 Oct. Lake took Agra after eight days' siege. On 1 Nov. at Leswarree, a village eighty miles south of Delhi, Lake routed and destroyed a body of Scindia's troops detached from the Deccan, with which was the remnant of Perron's battalions escaped from Delhi (ib. vi. 512-17). The conflict was, perhaps, more remarkable for daring than generalship, but its results were decisive. It demoralised Scindia's forces before the final rout of the maharajah's forces by Wellesley at Argaum on the 29th of the same month, which ended the war (MALLESON, *Decisive Battles of India*, p. 293). During the battle Lake had two horses killed under him, and his son, Lieutenant-colonel George A. F. Lake, was wounded by a cannon-shot at his side as Lake was mounting to head the decisive charge of the 76th. A painting of the incident by Sir William Beechey, R.A., was among the king of Oude's treasures destroyed in the Alumbagh in 1857. Thus, in a little over two months (29 Aug.–1 Nov. 1803), with a force at no time exceeding eight thousand combatants, Lake destroyed thirty-one of Scindia's European-trained battalions, captured the strong fortress of Alyghur, entered the imperial city of Delhi as a conqueror, took Agra, captured 426 pieces of cannon, and defeated the enemy in four pitched battles, the last being one of the most decisive ever fought in India (ib. p. 294). Lake received the thanks of parliament, and on 1 Sept. 1804 was raised to the peerage as Baron Lake of Delhi and Leswarree and of Aston Clinton, Buckinghamshire, the latter being his seat, near Tring. Lake chose for his supporters a grenadier of the 76th foot and a Bengal sepoy. The inhabitants of Calcutta presented him with a sword of great value, and his officers gave him a magnificent service of plate. Peace with Scindia was finally signed at Berhampore in February 1804.

The French power in India having thus been hopelessly destroyed, and the influence of Gwalior and Berar checked, Wellesley next sought to curb the powers of another suspected Mahratta chieftain, Jeswunt Rao Holkar, maharajah of Indore. Holkar subsequently attacked Delhi, which was gallantly defended by David Oehterlony and James Baron. Lake, who had followed Holkar from Muttra to Delhi, started thence in pursuit on 31 Oct. 1804, with the 8th light dragoons (now hussars), the 24th (late 27th), and 25th (late 29th) light dragoons, with their galloper-guns, some regiments of Bengal light cavalry, and a considerable body of irregular cavalry. Between 31 Oct. and 17 Nov. he covered 350 miles. Before day-

break on 17 Nov., his troops having marched, it is said, seventy miles during the preceding twenty-four hours, Lake surprised Holkar's camp near Furruckabad, and routed and dispersed his army with terrible slaughter. Hearing that the rajah of Bhurtpore, who had been our ally, was aiding Holkar, Lake marched against him. On Christmas day 1804 the fortress of Deig was captured by Majorgeneral John Henry Fraser, 88th foot, and on 2 Jan. 1805 Lake broke ground against the famous fortress of Bhurtpore. He was unprovided with a battering train, or other means of prosecuting a siege. Four desperate but unsuccessful attempts were made to carry the place by storm, with an aggregate loss of 388 killed and 1,924 wounded, and the enterprise was then abandoned (cf. MILL, vol. vi. note pp. 605-10). But the rajah, wearied of the war and of Lake's stubborn pertinacity, soon after offered terms of peace, which were accepted. From Bhurtpore Lake moved in the direction of Gwalior, halting at Dholpore. Holkar had then retired from the neighbourhood of Bhurtpore. Wellesley's last despatch to Lake, dated 17 May 1805, expresses the hope that further military operations will be unnecessary, but insists on the need of preparation (*Wellesley Despatches in India*, iv. 535-41).

On 29 July 1805 Cornwallis, Wellesley's successor, arrived at Calcutta, invested with joint powers as governor-general and commander-in-chief. Lake, as second in seniority, then took the Bengal presidency command. Cornwallis came pledged to a more pacific policy, and with an expressed determination 'to bring this wretched and unprofitable war to an end.' His views were diametrically opposed to those held by Lake, and in a friendly letter to Lake he announced his supersession in the military command-in-chief (see *Cornwallis Correspondence*, iii. 543 et seq., 555-6). Lake appears to have addressed a strong remonstrance to Cornwallis, which was never answered, as Cornwallis died at Ghazepore, when on his way up country, on 5 Oct. 1805. Lake, learning that Holkar had gone off towards the Punjab to seek aid from the Sikhs, started with a force in pursuit as far as the Sutlej (Hyphasis). Disappointed of the expected aid from the Sikh chieftains, Holkar offered terms of peace, which were accepted by Lake at Umritsar in December 1805. Lake appears to have proposed to make the Sutlej the boundary of British India. No notice was taken of the suggestion at the time, although it was acted upon by Lord Minto some years later. Cornwallis's successor as governor-general (acting), Sir George Hilaro Barlow [q. v.], was not only as pacific in his policy as Cornwallis, but by his orders for the restoration of territory annexed by Lake sacrificed the hard-bought military advantages acquired. Lake commenced his return march to British territory on 9 Jan. 1806. On 19 Feb. 1806 he was formally reappointed commander-in-chief by the court of directors. He spent some time at Delhi, arranging affairs there, and, leaving Ochterlony in command, proceeded to Cawnpore, and thence at the end of the year to Calcutta. There he embarked for England on 9 Feb. 1807, receiving such a farewell from Europeans and natives alike as never had been accorded to any public servant before. After his return to England he was advanced to a viscounty under his former titles (31 Oct. 1807). A violent cold, caught while attending the court-martial at Chelsea on Lieutenant-general Bulstrode Whitelocke, ended fatally. He died at his town residence in Lower Brook Street on 20 Feb. 1808, aged 64, and was buried at Aston Clinton.

Few men possessed a larger circle of personal friends than Lake, and no commander-in-chief was more generally popular with all ranks. His influence over his soldiers was unbounded; and his calmness in danger, and his self-reliance and power of inspiring confidence in others, have never been surpassed. 'He had but one way of dealing with the native armies of India, that of moving straight forward, of attacking them wherever he could find them. He never was so great as on the battle-field. He could think more clearly amidst the rain of bullets than in the calm of his own tent. In this respect he resembled Clive. It was this quality which enabled him to dare almost the impossible. That which in others would have been rash was in Lake prudent daring' (MALLESON, *Decisive Battles of India*, p. 294). At the time of his death Lake was a full general, colonel of the 80th Staffordshire volunteer regiment of foot, governor of Dumbarton Castle, equerry to the prince of Wales, and receiver-general and a member of council for the duchy of Cornwall. He died a poor man. A pension of 2,000l. a year was settled on the two next successors to the title; but the vote for a public monument was not pressed by Lord Castlereagh (*Parl. Debates*, x. 871). A portrait of Lake is in the Oriental Club.

Lake married, in 1770, Elizabeth, only daughter of Edward Barker of St. Julians, Hertfordshire, sometime consul at Tripoli. She died 22 July 1788, and was buried at Aston Clinton. Besides five daughters, there were three sons by the marriage: 1. Francis Gerard, page of honour and afterwards equerry to the Prince of Wales, and sometime an officer in the 54th, 1st guards, and 60th royal Americans. He succeeded his father in the title, and rose to the rank of lieutenant-general. He died without male heirs in 1836. 2. George Augustus Frederick, page to the Prince of Wales, and afterwards in the 94th Scotch brigade and 29th regiments. He was a very popular and distinguished officer of his father's staff in India, and was killed as lieutenant-colonel commanding 29th foot, when driving the enemy from the heights of Roleia (Roliça), in Portugal, on 17 Aug. 1808. There is a monument to him in Westminster Abbey, erected by the officers and men of the 29th regiment. 3. Warwick, who rose to the rank of post-captain in the royal navy, but was dismissed the service by sentence of court-martial in 1810 for an act of gross cruelty when in command of H.M.S. Recruit, three years before, in abandoning on a desert island in the West Indies a seaman, one Richard Jeffery by name (see JAMES, *Naval Hist.* iv. 273–5; also *Parl. Debates* under date). He succeeded his brother as third viscount. At his death, which took place in London on 24 June 1848, the title, in default of male heirs, became extinct.

[Lipscomb's Buckinghamshire, ii. 75 (pedigree); Collins's Peerage, 1812 edit. vi. 432–53; Burke's Extinct Peerage, 1882 edit., under title; Hamilton's Hist. Grenadier Guards, 1872, vol. ii.; Dunfermline's Life of Sir Ralph Abercromby, 1858, chap. iv.; Lecky's Hist. of England, 1890, vol. viii.; Cornwallis Correspondence, vols. i–iii.; Castlereagh Despatches and Correspondence, vol. i.; Wellesley Despatches in India, 1836–7, vols. ii–iv.; Mill's Hist. of India, ed. Wilson, vol. vi.; Thorn's Narrative of Campaigns under Lord Lake, 1818; Memoirs of John Shipp, new edit., 1890, pp. 81–130; Williams's Hist. Bengal Native Infantry, 1817; Georgian Era, vol. ii.; M[alleson] Essays on Indian Historical Subjects, from Calcutta Review, 1862; Malleson's Decisive Battles of India, 1883, 'Leswarree;' European Mag. April 1808; Brit. Mus. Addit. MSS.; Wellesley Papers and Pelham Papers.]

H. M. C.

LAKE, SIR HENRY ATWELL (1808–1881), colonel of the royal engineers, third son of Sir James Samuel William Lake, fourth baronet, by his marriage with Maria, daughter of Samuel Turner, was born at Kenilworth, Warwickshire, in 1808. He was educated at Harrow and at the military college of the East India Company at Addiscombe. On 15 Dec. 1826 he obtained a commission as second lieutenant in the Madras engineers, and went to India. Until 1854 he was employed in the public works department of India, and principally upon irrigation works. He became lieutenant 4 March 1831, brevet-captain 22 July 1840, regimental captain in 1852, and brevet-major 20 June 1854.

While in England on leave of absence in 1854 he volunteered his services for the Russian war, and was sent to Kars, in Asia Minor, as chief engineer, and second in command to Colonel (afterwards Sir) William Fenwick Williams. He became lieutenant-colonel on 9 Feb. 1855. He strengthened the fortifications of Kars, and took a very prominent part in the defence, including the repulse of the Russian forces under General Mouravieff on 29 Sept. 1855. On the capitulation of Kars he was sent, with the other British officers, as a prisoner of war to Russia, where he remained until the proclamation of peace in 1856.

For his services at Kars he received the thanks of parliament, was transferred to the royal army as an unattached lieutenant-colonel, and was made a companion of the Bath, aide-de-camp to the queen, and colonel in the army from 24 June 1856. He received a medal with clasp for Kars, the second class of the Medjidie, was appointed an 'officer' of the Legion of Honour, and was given the rank of major-general in the Turkish army. On his arrival in England he was presented with a sword of honour and a silver salver by the inhabitants of Ramsgate, where his mother then resided, and where his family was well known.

Lake was placed on half-pay on 12 Sept. 1856, but next year accompanied the Earl of Eglinton, lord-lieutenant of Ireland, to Dublin as principal aide-de-camp, and in the following year retired from the army on his appointment as a commissioner of the Dublin metropolitan police. Subsequently he became chief commissioner of police in Dublin. In 1875 he was made a K.C.B. of the civil division for his civil services, and in 1877 he retired upon a pension. He died at Brighton on 17 Aug. 1881.

He was twice married: first, in 1841, to Anne, daughter of the Rev. Peregrine Curtois of the Longhills, Lincolnshire—she died in 1847; secondly, in 1848, to Ann Augusta, daughter of Sir William Curtis, second baronet—she died in 1877. Of his family of two daughters and five sons, Atwell Peregrine Macleod is a captain R.N., Edward a lieutenant-colonel R.A., Noel Montagu a major R.E., and Hubert Atwell a lieutenant R.A.

Lake was the author of: 1. 'Kars and our Captivity in Russia, with Letters from General Sir W. Fenwick Williams, Bart., Major Teesdale, and the late Captain Thomson,' London, 8vo, 1856; 2nd edition, published same year. 2. 'Narrative of the Defence of Kars, Historical and Military, from Authentic Documents, illustrated by Lieutenant-Colonel C. Teesdale and W. Simpson,' London, 8vo, 1857.

[Corps Records; Royal Engineers Journal, vol. xi.; Sandwith's Siege of Kars, 1857; Monteith's Kars and Erzeroum, 1857; Athenæum, 1856 p. 951, 1857 p. 626.]　　R. H. V.

LAKE, JOHN (1624–1689), bishop of Chichester, son of Thomas Lake, 'grocer,' of Halifax in Yorkshire, was born there in the autumn of 1624. He was educated in the Halifax grammar school, and at the age of thirteen was admitted to St. John's College, Cambridge (4 Dec. 1637). Soon after he had graduated B.A., 'his college being made a prison for the royal party, he was kept a prisoner there,' for, being a staunch royalist, he refused to take the 'covenant.' He managed to make his escape and fled to Oxford, where he joined the king's army and continued to serve in it as a volunteer for four years. He was at Basing House when it was taken, and at Wallingford, which was one of the last garrisons that held out for Charles I. In 1647 he received holy orders from one of the deprived bishops, probably Skinner, bishop of Oxford. He seems to have purposed settling in his native place, Halifax, where he preached his first sermon, but he was not permitted to remain there, because he refused to take the 'Engagement.' He consequently removed to Oldham, whence Robert Constantine had been ejected, holding the living at first as a supplier, and then by order of the committee for plundered ministers. In spite of charges of malignancy brought by the Constantine party in 1652, he managed to remain at Oldham till the close of 1654, when Constantine was restored (SHAW, Manchester Presbyterian Classis, Chetham Soc., iii. 375 sq.) Immediately after the Restoration he was presented to the vicarage of Leeds, but the puritans, who desired to have a Mr. Bowles as vicar, raised such opposition that at his induction soldiers had to be called in to keep the peace. In 1661 the degree of D.D. was conferred upon him by the university of Cambridge by royal mandate. He was appointed to preach the first 'synod sermon' at York after the Restoration. Dr. Hitch, afterwards dean of York, showed a copy of the sermon, without Lake's knowledge, to the Bishop of London, Dr. Sheldon, who sent for the preacher, and on 22 May 1663 collated him to the important living of St. Botolph's, Bishopsgate. In this post he remained for some years and was made prebendary of Holborn (4 June 1667). While in London he formed an intimate friendship with Sancroft, who was then dean of St.

Paul's. In 1669 he was appointed to the living of Prestwich in Lancashire, and in 1671 to the prebend of Fridaythorpe in York Cathedral. In 1680 he was installed archdeacon of Cleveland, but none of these preferments were of his own seeking. He attacked a bad custom of lounging about the nave of York Minster during divine service in the choir by going into the nave and pulling off the hats of all whom he found wearing them. He determined to put a stop to a revel held by the apprentices in the church on Shrove Tuesday, and defied the rabble, saying that he had faced death in the field too often to dread martyrdom. Although advised to retire to his country living, he stayed at his post until he succeeded in putting a stop to the desecration of the minster. In 1682 he was nominated by the Earl of Derby to the bishopric of Sodor and Man, and 'sacrificed a rich prebend for a poor bishopric.' In 1684, through the influence of Bishop Turner with the Duke of York, he was translated to the bishopric of Bristol, and soon after was entrusted by his old friend, now Archbishop Sancroft, with a commission to visit the diocese of Lichfield and Coventry. During the Monmouth rebellion he gave great satisfaction to the king by leaving his parliamentary duties in London to keep order in Bristol. James was so much pleased with his conduct as to promise him advancement. Lake had been opposed by the dean of Bristol in projects for improving the cathedral, and especially in an attempt to establish the weekly communion. He complained piteously to his friend Sancroft, and this may have been one of the reasons why Sancroft strongly urged James II to remove his friend from Bristol. In 1685 the king gladly appointed Lake to the see of Chichester. While at Chichester he established the weekly communion and restored the old custom of preaching in the nave of the cathedral. After his first visitation in 1682 he wrote to Sancroft a lamentable account of the state of the diocese and exerted himself to rectify it. In September 1688 he made 'a visitation extraordinary throughout his diocese,' and was received by the gentlemen of the district with such respect as 'was wont to be paid to the primitive bishops.' Lake, however, declined to sanction King James's illegal acts; he petitioned to be excused from reading the king's declaration of liberty of conscience, and was one of the seven committed to the Tower in 1688. He was also one of the bishops who refused to take the oaths of allegiance to William and Mary. 'He considered that the day of death and the day of judgment were as certain as the first of August [the day of suspension] and the

first of February [the day of deprivation], and acted accordingly.' Lake did not live to suffer actual deprivation. On 27 Aug. 1689, feeling his end was drawing near, he dictated a declaration to Jenkin, his chaplain. In this he solemnly and impressively asserted his fidelity to the church of England and his adherence to its distinctive doctrine of non-resistance. Holding this belief, he would rather have died than taken the oaths. The bishop signed this in the presence of the five gentlemen who communicated with him, and died three days later (30 Aug.) He was buried 3 Sept. in the church of St. Botolph, Bishopsgate. The paper was published as 'The Dying Profession of Bishop Lake on the Doctrine of Passive Obedience as the Distinguishing Character of the Church of England.' It produced many answers and defences, one of the latter being published anonymously by Robert Jenkin [q. v.], who gives the earliest account of the bishop's life.

Lake's whole life shows that he said truly, 'He thanked God he never much knew what fear was, when he was once satisfied of the goodness of his cause.' In 1670 he printed a sermon which was preached at Whitehall before the king on 29 May 1670, and in 1671 one entitled 'Ἐπιφανὴς πιστός, or the true Christian Character and Crown described,' a funeral sermon on William Cade. He also wrote a life of his tutor at St. John's, Cambridge, John Cleveland the poet [q. v.], which was prefixed to 'Clievelandi Vindiciæ,' 1677, an edition of the poet's works prepared by Lake in conjunction with his friend Samuel Drake, d. 1673 [q. v.]

[A Defence of the Profession which John, Bishop of Chichester, made upon his Death-bed, &c., together with an Account of some Passages of his Life, 1690 ; Agnes Strickland's Lives of the Seven Bishops committed to the Tower; Hearne's Collections, ed. Doble (Oxf. Hist. Soc.), iii. 12, 51, 68; Admissions to St. John's College, Cambridge, ed. Mayor, p. 38 ; T. Lathbury's History of the Nonjurors ; information kindly supplied by Mr. W. A. Shaw.] J. H. O.

LAKE, SIR THOMAS (1567?–1630), secretary of state, son of Almeric Lake of Southampton, and brother of Arthur Lake [q. v.], was born in St. Michael's parish, Southampton, about 1567. He was educated in the grammar school of his native town, while Hadrian a Saravia [q. v.] was head-master there, and is said to have subsequently proceeded to Cambridge. One 'Mr. Lake' of Clare Hall, who took the part of Trico in the performance of 'Ignoramus' at Cambridge in 1614, has been identified very doubtfully with Sir Thomas (RUGGLES, Ignoramus, ed. Hawkins, pp. xxiv, xxv). The actor is more likely to have been Sir Thomas's son. The father took no degree at Cambridge. On leaving the university he became amanuensis to Sir Francis Walsingham, and his dexterity and despatch gained for him in that capacity the nickname of 'Swiftsure,' after a well-known ship. He displayed some interest in antiquities, and joined the Elizabethan Society of Antiquaries, founded by Archbishop Parker. A paper on sterling money, read to the members by Lake, appears in Hearne's 'Curious Discourses,' i. 10. Queen Elizabeth took notice of his abilities, and about 1600 made him clerk of the signet. On 27 Sept. 1592 he was created M.A. at Oxford during the queen's visit. In her last days he is said to have read Latin and French to her. Three days after her death (27 March 1603) he and George Carew were sent by the council to James in Scotland, to acquaint him with the position of affairs in England. He impressed the new king favourably, and after James's arrival in London he was appointed the king's secretary of the Latin tongue, and was knighted (20 May 1603). On 1 June following he was made keeper of the records at Whitehall, and on 9 March 1603–4 was elected M.P. for Launceston. He was returned to parliament for the county of Middlesex in 1614.

Lake justified the royal favour by steadily championing the interests of the king's Scottish friends at court, and thus incurred the enmity of many English courtiers. He 'had no pretensions to be anything more than a diligent and ready official' (GARDINER), but despite his modest qualifications he was a recognised candidate for the post of secretary of state on Salisbury's death in 1612, and offered a bribe to secure the appointment. The king finally determined, for the time at least, to fill the office himself. Lake, however, performed the official duties of secretary at the wedding of Princess Elizabeth to the elector in December 1612, and he incurred much ridicule by his reading aloud with a very bad accent and translating into very poor English the French contract of marriage. In 1613, when the question of choosing a secretary of state was again discussed, the Howard influence at court was openly cast in Lake's favour. In 1614 he was made a privy councillor, and at the meeting of the council in September 1615, when the king's financial position called for serious consideration, Lake pressed on James the necessity of staying his hands from gifts, and recommended some modifications in the levy of the disputed impositions. About the same time Lake became a pensioner of Spain, and entered into intimate relations with

Gondomar, the Spanish ambassador. But James had no obvious ground for depriving him of his confidence, and on 3 Jan. 1615–16 conferred on him the coveted post of secretary of state. It was reported that James soon afterwards said of him that he was a minister of state fit to serve the greatest prince in Europe. In 1617 Lake and his son Thomas accompanied the king to Scotland. Early in 1619 Lake imperilled his position by communicating to his patron Howard, earl of Suffolk, some severe remarks which James I made to him about the venal character of Suffolk's wife. Buckingham had been introduced to James I's notice in 1614, in part through Lake's agency, and Lake, perceiving the insecurity of his relations with the king, flung himself on the favourite's mercy. He offered Buckingham a bribe of 15,000l. if he could help him to regain the full favour of the king. Buckingham at first was obdurate, but Lake gained the ear of Lady Compton, and Buckingham was induced by her to act in accordance with Lake's wishes.

Meanwhile a quarrel in Lake's family was hastening his ruin. His eldest daughter had married in 1616 William Cecil, lord Roos, a grandson of Thomas Cecil, first earl of Exeter (q. v.) The union proved unhappy, and husband and wife soon separated. But Roos had previously mortgaged to Lake his estates at Walthamstow, and after the separation Lake intimidated him into an agreement that the mortgaged estates should become the property of his wife. Roos's grandfather, the Earl of Exeter, declined to assent to the alienation of the lands. The dispute accordingly grew hotter, and Lady Roos's brother Arthur brutally assaulted Roos, and she and her mother threatened to charge him with an incestuous connection with the Countess of Exeter, his grandfather's young wife. The persecution drove Roos to take refuge in Rome, and he died at Naples in 1618. Lady Roos thereupon turned her artillery against the young Countess of Exeter. Forged letters were forthcoming to show that the countess, besides committing offences against morality, had attempted to poison Lake and his daughter. Late in 1618 Lady Exeter charged Lake, his wife, son, and daughter with defamation of character in the Star-chamber, and a host of witnesses were examined for five days together early in February 1618–19. The evidence showed that Lake had imprisoned one Gwilliams for refusing to swear falsely against the countess, and although less blameworthy than his fellow-prisoners he had undoubtedly sanctioned the circulation of his daughter's libels, and that in spite of a warning from the king that would be safer for him to withdraw them. On 13 Feb. 1618–19 James pronounced sentence against the defendants. All were ordered to be imprisoned during the king's pleasure, and Lake and his wife were also to pay a fine of 5,000*l.* each, with 1,000*l.* damages to Lady Exeter; Lady Roos was fined ten thousand marks, and Arthur Lake 300*l.*

Chamberlain reported on 14 Feb. 1618–19 that Lord Digby and Bacon extenuated Lake's guilt, and that the success of his cause had been prayed for by the catholics generally, and especially by those at Louvain. Lady Roos confessed her guilt on 19 June 1619, and was released. Lake himself admitted the justice of his sentence on 28 Jan. 1619–20, and was thereupon liberated. His wife did not gain her freedom till 2 May 1621. The fines were afterwards commuted to one payment of 10,200*l.*, in addition to the damages awarded to Lady Exeter.

The proceedings necessarily led to Lake's dismissal from the office of secretary. He spent the remainder of his life in retirement, chiefly at his estate of Canons, in the parish of Little Stanmore or Whitchurch, Middlesex, which he had purchased in 1604. He seems to have renewed his friendly relations with Buckingham, who visited him apparently in London in July 1621. He was elected M.P. for Wells in 1625, and for Wootton Bassett, Wiltshire, in 1626. He died at Canons on 17 Sept. 1630, and was buried at Whitchurch on 19 Oct. following. The erroneous statement that he was a benefactor to St. John's College, Oxford (HEARNE, *Discourses,* ii. 436), seems to have arisen from his purchase of a picture hanging in the president's lodgings there in 1616.

Lake married Mary, daughter and coheiress of Sir William Ryder, alderman of London. She was buried at Whitchurch on 25 Feb. 1642–3. By her he was father of three sons and four daughters. The eldest son, Thomas, and the second son, Arthur, were both knighted in 1617. The former was elected M.P. for Wells in 1625, and died in 1653. The latter was M.P. for Bridgwater in the parliaments of 1625 and 1626, and died in 1633. The third son, Lancelot (*d.* 1646), left a son, Lancelot, who was M.P. for Middlesex in the convention of 1660 and in the parliament of 1661, and was knighted at Whitehall on 6 June 1660, and died in 1680. Sir Lancelot had two sons, Thomas, and Warwick, the ancestor of Gerard, lord Lake [q. v.] The elder son, Thomas, who was knighted on 4 Dec. 1670, married Rebecca, daughter of Sir John Langham of Cotesbrooke, and had a daughter Mary, first wife of James Brydges, first duke of Chandos

[q. v.], to whom the estate of Canons ultimately passed.

[Le Neve's Pedigrees of Knights (Harl. Soc.), pp. 243–4; Lloyd's State Worthies, 1766, ii. 63, 75; Wood's Fasti Oxon. ed. Bliss, i. 360–1; Return of Members of Parliament; Goodman's Court of James I; Court and Times of James I; Weldon's Court of James I; Brydges's Peers of England; Saunderson's James I; Fuller's Worthies; Spedding's Bacon; Gardiner's History, vols ii. and iii.; Lysons's Environs, iii. 405, 412; Cal. State Papers, Dom.; Nichols's Progresses of James I; Burke's Extinct Peerage, s.v. 'Lake;' notes kindly supplied by J. Willis Clark, esq., registrary of the university of Cambridge, by L. Ewbank, esq., of Clare College, and by the Rev. W. H. Hutton, of St. John's College, Oxford.]
S. L.

LAKINGHETH, JOHN DE (*d.* 1381), chronicler, was a native of Norfolk, and a monk of Bury St. Edmunds in the time of Edward III and Richard II, and was 'custos baroniæ,' an office which, no doubt, brought him into close connection with the tenants of the monastery. He thus became very unpopular, and in the peasant rising of 1381 the insurgents clamoured that he should be surrendered to them. In order to save the monastery this was done, and he was beheaded. Lakingheth compiled 'Kalendare Maneriorum Terrarum . . . ad Monasterium S. Edmundi Buriensis spectantium,' which is preserved in Harl. MS. 743, no doubt his own autograph. The contents of this calendar are described in the 'Monasticon Anglicanum,' iii. 121–2, and some documents from it are printed on pp. 135–6, 138–9. The second article in the volume is a 'Short History of the Abbots down to the Death of John de Brynkele in 1379;' to this has been added a list of the abbots down to the dissolution. This history is printed in the 'Monasticon,' iii. 155–6.

One Sir John de Lakingheth was captain of Conq in Brittany in May 1375, when the town was captured by Oliver de Clisson (FROISSART, viii. 140, ed. Luce); afterwards in 1376 he was one of the captains of Brest (*Fœdera,* iii. 1062). A third John de Lakingheth was rector of Bircham Tofts, Norfolk, in 1375 (BLOMEFIELD, *Norfolk,* x. 287).

[Tanner's Bibl. Brit.-Hib. p. 462; Walsingham's Historia Anglicana, ii. 5 (Rolls Ser.); other authorities as quoted.]
C. L. K.

LALOR, JAMES FINTON (*d.* 1849), politician, was eldest son of Patrick Lalor, a gentleman farmer, of Tinakill, Queen's County, Ireland, who took a prominent part in the anti-tithe movement there and was M.P. for his county, 1832–5. Peter Lalor [q. v.] was his brother. Deaf, near-sighted, ungainly, and deformed, James led a secluded life, brooding over his own schemes for securing the freedom of his country, until 1847, when he sent to Charles Gavan Duffy, editor of the 'Nation,' a letter published on 11 Jan., in which he advocated physical force, land confiscation, and a struggle for national independence. He thus secured a place among the contributors to that paper, and wrote a series of letters, which were 'marvels of passionate, persuasive rhetoric.' He devised a scheme for a strike against rent, which, in spite of the strong disapproval of Duffy, he induced Mitchell to adopt; and he also endeavoured to form a land league of his own. On 18 Sept. 1847 he summoned a meeting of tenant farmers at Holycross, Tipperary, to found a land league on the footing of a 'live and thrive' rent, but his want of practical ability and his fierce self-opinionativeness caused the failure of the meeting. His resolutions were carried, but the association was abortive. He continued to play a prominent part in revolutionary circles until the outbreak of 1848. On 26 May of that year John Mitchell was transported and the 'United Irishman' suppressed. Thereupon John Martin arranged for the publication of the 'Irish Felon,' successor to the 'United Irishman.' The first number was dated 24 June 1848, and to its pages Lalor was the chief contributor. After Martin's arrest in July, Lalor practically edited it. It came to an end on 22 July with its fifth number. On 29 July a proclamation appeared calling on all persons to arrest P. J. Smyth, Lalor, and others. Lalor had been arrested the day before at Ballyhane. He was imprisoned under the Habeas Corpus Suspension Act, but after he had spent some months in gaol his health became impaired, and he was released. He immediately planned schemes for a new conspiracy and a new insurrection, but died 27 Dec. 1849. 'Endowed with a will and a persuasiveness of prodigious force,' says Duffy, 'of all the men who have preached revolutionary politics in Ireland, this isolated thinker, who had hitherto had no experience either as a writer or as an actor in public affairs, was the most original and intense;' but his intellectual pride in his own work was so great and his temper so irritable, that he was an impracticable colleague.

[Charles Gavan Duffy's Young Ireland and his Four Years of Irish History, 1845–9; William Dillon's Life of Davis; John Savage's '98' and '48,' New York, 1884; Nation, 1847; Times, 31 Dec. 1849.]   J. A. H.

LALOR, JOHN (1814–1856), journalist and author, son of John Lalor, a Roman catholic merchant, was born at Dublin in 1814, and educated at a Roman catholic school at Carlow and at Clongowes College. On 6 June 1831 he entered Trinity College, Dublin, where he graduated B.A. in 1837. After collecting important evidence as an assistant poor-law commissioner, he left Ireland in 1836, and became connected with the daily press in London, first as a parliamentary reporter, and afterwards for five or six years as one of the principal editors of the 'Morning Chronicle,' having social and domestic questions wholly under his direction. In 1838 he was admitted a solicitor in Dublin. In 1839 he obtained the prize of one hundred guineas awarded by the Central Society of Education for an essay on 'The Expediency and Means of Elevating the Profession of the Educator in Society.' He was brought up as a Roman catholic, but about 1844 he joined the unitarian church, and undertook the editorship of the unitarian weekly paper, 'The Inquirer.' He himself contributed vigorous articles on the Factory Bill, Ireland, and on education. His last work for the press was 'Money and Morals: a Book for the Times,' 1852, a portion of which was reprinted in 1844 under the title of 'England among the Nations.' He died, after much ill-health, at Holly Hill, Hampstead, London, on 27 Jan. 1856, aged 42.

[Inquirer, 9 Feb. 1856, pp. 83–4; Gent. Mag. March 1856, pp. 319–20; information kindly supplied by the Rev. Dr. Stubbs, of Trin. Coll. Dublin.]   G. C. B.

LALOR, PETER (1823–1889), colonial legislator, younger brother of James Finton Lalor [q. v.], was born at Tinakill, Queen's County, Ireland, in 1823, and educated at Trinity College, Dublin. He subsequently became a civil engineer, and shortly after the discovery of gold in Australia he sailed for Melbourne in 1852. Proceeding to Ballarat in 1853, he, with his companions, took up rich claims on the Eureka lead and gravel pits, from which they were hoping to obtain a fortune, when in Nov. 1854 the outbreak of the miners took place. Lalor played a leading part among the insurgents. It had been customary for the diggers to pay a monthly license to the government; but at a meeting on 29 Nov. 1854 it had been decided not to pay any further licenses, and the existing official documents were burnt. Parties of the 12th and 40th regiments, accompanied by police, attacked the miners on 3 Dec. at the Eureka stockade, when twenty-two of the rioters were killed, twelve wounded, and

125 taken prisoners. Lalor, who commanded the rebels, received a ball near the shoulder, and ultimately lost an arm. He, however, escaped, and a reward of 200l. offered for his capture did not result in his arrest. Subsequently representation was given to the gold-fields, and in November 1855 Lalor was without opposition elected as member for Ballarat. Shortly after taking his seat the government appointed him inspector of railways. At the next election, in 1856, he was returned for South Grant, and was appointed chairman of committees by the legislative assembly, an office in which he gained much distinction. He sat for South Grant till 1871, when he was defeated at the poll, but in 1875 he was again returned for the same constituency. In August of that year he became commissioner for customs in Graham Berry's first administration. In the following October he resigned with his chief. After the general election, in May 1877, Berry again took office, and Lalor resumed his former post. In 1868, after retiring from the chairmanship of the committees, he devoted much attention to his interest in the New North Clunes and the Australian mines. He was chairman of the Clunes water commission, with a large salary, and was a director of the New North Clunes mining company. Through his efforts in 1870 and 1871, the bill was carried for the Clunes waterworks, which were completed at a cost of 70,000l. On the formation of the third Berry ministry, in 1877, Lalor was appointed commissioner for trade and customs, and in 1878 became postmaster-general as well. He was appointed speaker of the house in 1880, and held this post until 1888, when he retired in consequence of ill-health. He was thereupon awarded a vote of thanks, with a grant of 4,000l. He died at Melbourne on 10 Feb. 1889.

[Men of the Time, Victoria, 1878, pp. 100–1; Heaton's Australian Dictionary of Dates, 1879, vol. x. pt. ii. p. 246; Times, 14 Feb. 1889, p. 5, 30 March p. 13.]   G. C. B.

LAMB. [See also LAMBE.]

LAMB, ANDREW (1565?–1634), bishop of Galloway, was probably son or relative of Andrew Lamb of Leith, a lay member of the general assembly of 1560. He became minister of Burntisland, Fifeshire, in 1593, was translated to Arbroath in 1596, and to South Leith in 1600. The same year he was appointed one of the members of the standing commission of the church, and in 1601 was made a royal chaplain, and in that capacity accompanied the Earl of Mar when he went as ambassador to the English court. He received a pension from the abbey of Arbroath for 'service done to the king, and for his earnest care in discharging his ministerial functions, and in the common affairs of the kirk tending to the establishment of discipline,' and in 1607 was made titular bishop of Brechin. He was a member of the assembly of 1610 which allowed spiritual jurisdiction to the bishops, and was one of the three Scottish prelates who were consecrated at London in October of that year. In 1615 he presented a beautiful brass chandelier to the cathedral of Brechin, still to be seen there. He was translated to the see of Galloway in 1619, and died in 1634. In his later years he became blind, and resided chiefly in Leith, where he had property. He was a favourite of King James, and a willing supporter of his measures for the introduction of episcopacy and the English ceremonies, but he was of a conciliatory temper, and the anti-prelatic party had nothing worse to say of him than that he 'loved not to be poor.' It is said by the biographers of Samuel Rutherford that, at his admission to the parish of Anwoth, Kirkcudbrightshire, Lamb connived at his ordination by presbyters only. There is no evidence for this, but he was tolerant to Rutherford and others who did not conform to the articles enjoined by the Perth assembly. He left a son James and two daughters, one of whom married Lenox of Cally and the other Murray of Broughton, both in the stewartry of Kirkcudbright. Several of his letters have been published in 'Original Letters relating to the Ecclesiastical Affairs of Scotland.'

[Scott's Fasti; Keith's Scottish Bishops; Row's, Calderwood's, and Lawson's Histories; Black's Brechin; Murray's Life of Rutherford.]   G. W. S.

LAMB, BENJAMIN (fl. 1715), was organist of Eton College and verger of St. George's Chapel, Windsor, about 1715. He wrote much church music and some songs. Among the former may be mentioned his anthems, 'Unto Thee have I cried,' 'O worship the Lord,' 'If the Lord Himself,' 'I will give thanks,' and an evening service in E minor, all of which are in the Tudway Collection (Brit. Mus. Harl. MSS. 7341–2).

[Grove's Dict. of Music; Dict. of Music, 1824; Harl. MSS.]   R. H. L.

LAMB, LADY CAROLINE (1785–1828), novelist, only daughter of Frederick Ponsonby, third earl of Bessborough, by his wife, Lady Henrietta Frances Spencer, the younger daughter of John, first earl of Spencer, was born on 13 Nov. 1785. At the age of three she was taken to Italy, where she remained six years, chiefly under the charge of a servant. She was then sent to Devonshire

House to be educated with her cousins, and was subsequently entrusted to her grandmother, Lady Spencer, who, alarmed at her eccentricities, consulted a doctor as to her state of mind. She was married on 3 June 1805 to the Hon. William Lamb, afterwards Lord Melbourne [q. v.] She was soon passionately infatuated with Byron, of whom she wrote in her diary, after his introduction to her, that he was 'mad, bad, and dangerous to know' [see under BYRON]. After Byron's rupture with her in 1813, Lady Caroline's temper became so ungovernable that her husband reluctantly determined upon a separation. While the legal instruments were being prepared she wrote and sent her first novel, 'Glenarvon,' to the press. On the day fixed, however, for the execution of the deed of separation, a sudden reconciliation took place, and Lady Caroline was found seated beside her husband, 'feeding him with tiny scraps of transparent bread and butter,' while the solicitor was waiting below to attest the signatures (TORRENS, *Memoirs of Viscount Melbourne*, i. 112). 'Glenarvon' was published anonymously in 1816 (London, 12mo, 3 vols.) It was written, she says, 'unknown to all (save a governess, Miss Welsh), in the middle of the night' (cf. *Lady Morgan's Memoirs*, ii. 202). This rhapodical tale owed its brief success to the caricature portrait of Byron which it contained. Moore, in a fit of indignation, wrote a review of it for the 'Edinburgh,' but on second thoughts did not send it (TORRENS, *Memoirs of Viscount Melbourne*, i. 112). Byron, in a letter to Moore, says: 'If the authoress had written the truth ... the romance would not only have been more romantic, but more entertaining. As for the likeness, the picture can't be good; I did not sit long enough' (MOORE, *Life of Lord Byron*, p. 330). An Italian translation of the novel appears to have been printed in Venice in 1817 (*ib.* p. 363). It was reprinted in one volume in 1865, under the title of 'The Fatal Passion' (London, 8vo). On hearing that Byron, when questioned by Madame de Staël, had laughed at her book as 'that insincere production,' Lady Caroline burnt at Brocket 'very solemnly, on a sort of funeral pile, transcripts of all the letters which she had received from Byron, and a copy of a miniature (his portrait) which he had presented to her; several girls from the neighbourhood, whom she had dressed in white garments, dancing round the pile, and singing a song which she had written for the occasion,' Burn, fire, burn, &c."' (ROGERS, *Table Talk*, 1856, p. 236). Caring little for politics, but always craving for notoriety, she energetically canvassed the Westminster electors in 1819 on

behalf of her brother-in-law, George Lamb, and succeeded in gaining over a number of doubtful voters. In the same year she published 'A New Canto' (anon. London, 8vo). Her second novel, 'Graham Hamilton,' which was sent to Colburn's in 1820, 'with an earnest injunction neither to name the author nor to publish it at that time,' was published in 1822 (anon. London, 12mo, 2 vols.) The design of this novel is said to have been suggested to her by Ugo Foscolo, whose advice was, 'Write a book which will offend nobody; women cannot afford to shock.' It was succeeded in 1823 by 'Ada Reis; a Tale' (anon. London, 12mo, 3 vols.), another edition of which was published in the following year (Paris, 12mo, 2 vols.) In July 1824 she accidentally met Byron's funeral procession on its way to Newstead. Though she partially recovered from this sudden shock, her mind became more affected, and in the following year she was separated from her husband. During the remainder of her life she lived for the most part at Brocket with her father-in-law and her only surviving child, George Augustus Frederick Lamb, a hopeless invalid, who died unmarried on 27 Nov. 1836, aged 29. She died at Melbourne House, Whitehall, in the presence of her husband, who had hastened over from Ireland, on 26 Jan. 1828, aged 42, and was buried at Hatfield.

Lady Caroline was a clever, generous, and impulsive woman, inordinately vain, and excitable to the verge of insanity. In person she was small and slight, with pale, golden-coloured hair, 'large hazel eyes, capable of much varied expression, exceedingly good teeth, and a musical intonation of voice' (*The Life of Edward Bulwer, Lord Lytton*, i. 328). Her powers of conversation were remarkable, full of wild originality, and combining great and sudden contrasts, while her manners 'had a fascination which it is difficult for any who never encountered their effect to conceive' (*Literary Gazette*, 1828, p. 108). Lord Lytton has left on record a curious account of his brief and sentimental attachment to her (*Life*, i. 334-6). She is supposed to have been the original of Mrs. Felix Lorraine in 'Vivian Grey,' of Lady Monteagle in 'Venetia' (HITCHMAN, *Public Life of the Earl of Beaconsfield*, 1879, i. 30, 127), of Lady Melton in 'De Lindsay,' Lady Clara in 'Lionel Hastings,' and of Lady Bellenden in 'Greville' (*Life of Edward Bulwer, Lord Lytton*, i. 357-358). She wrote poetry for the annuals, and several of her pieces were set to music by Isaac Nathan and others. Some of her verses have been collected in Isaac Nathan's 'Fugitive Pieces and Reminiscences of Lord Byron ... also some original Poetry, Letters, and

Recollections of Lady Caroline Lamb' (1829). Eleven letters written by her to her friend Lady Morgan are preserved in 'Lady Morgan's Memoirs' (i. 412-3, ii. 174-9, 203-4, 206-13, 210), and seven written to William Godwin in Mr. C. K. Paul's 'William Godwin, his Friends and Contemporaries,' 1876 (ii. 266-8, 285-6, 302-4). There is a whole-length engraving of Lady Caroline Lamb with her boy by Cheeseman, and a charming print by W. Finden, from 'an original drawing in the possession of Mr. Murray,' will be found in Finden's 'Illustrations of the Life and Works of Lord Byron,' 1833, vol. ii.

[Torrens's Memoirs of Viscount Melbourne, 1878, vol. i.; Lady Morgan's Memoirs, ed. by W. H. Dixon, 1863; Smiles's Memoir and Corr. of John Murray, 1891; Life of Edward Bulwer, Lord Lytton, by his Son, 1883, i. 327-30, 333-58; Moore's Life of Byron, 1847; article by Mr. S. R. Townshend Mayer in Temple Bar, liii. 174-92; G. and P. Wharton's Queens of Society, 1867, pp. 435-50; Literary Gazette, 1828, pp. 107-8; Monthly Magazine, 1828, new ser. v. 436-7; Ann. Biog. and Obituary for 1829, xiii. 51-7; Ann. Reg. 1784 and 1785 pp. 249, 1828 App. to Chron. pp. 216-17; Gent. Mag. 1828, pt. i. p. 269; Burke's Extinct Peerage, 1883, p. 313; Notes and Queries, 7th ser. x. 88, 125, 167, 193, 107, 235, 256, 315, 356; Halkett and Laing's Dict. of Anon. and Pseudon. Literature, 1882-8; Brit. Mus. Cat.]   G. F. R. B.

LAMB, CHARLES (1775-1834), essayist and humourist, was born on 10 Feb. 1775 in Crown Office Row in the Temple, London. His father, John Lamb, who is described under the name of Lovel in Charles Lamb's essay 'The Old Benchers of the Inner Temple,' was the son of poor parents in Lincolnshire, and had come up as a boy to London and entered domestic service. He ultimately became clerk and servant to Samuel Salt, a bencher of the Inner Temple, and continued to fill that position until Salt's death in 1792. He married Elizabeth Field, whose mother was for more than fifty years housekeeper at Blakesware in Hertfordshire, a few miles from Ware, a dower-house of the Plumers, a well-known county family. This Mary Field, Charles Lamb's grandmother, played an important part in the early development of his affections, and is a familiar presence in some of the most characteristic and pathetic of his writings.

To John and Elizabeth Lamb, in Crown Office Row, were born a family of seven children, of whom only three survived their infancy. The eldest of these three was John Lamb, born in 1763; the second Mary Ann, better known as Mary, born in 1764; and the third Charles, baptised 10 March 1775 'by

the Rev. Mr. Jeffs.' The baptisms of the entire family duly appear in the registers of the Temple Church, and were first printed by Mr. Charles Kent in his 'Centenary Edition of Lamb's Works' in 1875.

The block of buildings in which Samuel Salt occupied one or more sets of chambers, and in which the Lamb family were born and reared, is at the eastern end of Crown Office Row, and though considerably modified since in its interior arrangements, still bears upon its outer wall the date 1737.

Charles Lamb received his earliest education at a humble day-school kept by a Mr. William Bird in a court leading out of Fetter Lane (see Lamb's paper, 'Captain Starkey,' in HONE's *Every-day Book*, 21 July 1825). It was a school for both boys and girls, and Mary Lamb also attended it. At the age of seven Charles obtained a nomination to Christ's Hospital (the 'Blue Coat School'), through the influence of his father's employer, and within its venerable walls he passed the next seven years of his life, his holidays being spent with his parents in the Temple or with his grandmother, Mrs. Field, in Hertfordshire.

What Charles Lamb learned at Christ's Hospital, what friendships he formed, and what merits and demerits he detected in the arrangements, manners, and customs of the school, are all familiar to us from the two remarkable essays he has left us, 'On Christ's Hospital, and the Character of the Christ's Hospital Boys,' published in the 'Gentleman's Magazine' in 1813, and the later essay 'Christ's Hospital Five-and-thirty Years Ago,' one of the Elia series, in the 'London Magazine' of November 1820. On the whole he seems to have been happy in the school, and to have acquired considerable skill in its special studies, notably in Latin, which he was fond of reading, and in a rough-and-ready way writing, to the end of his life. At the time of quitting the school he had not attained the highest position, that of 'Grecian,' but the nearest in rank to it, that of deputy Grecian. Perhaps the school authorities were not careful to promote him to the superior rank, seeing that he was not to proceed to the university. As a Grecian Lamb would have been entitled to an exhibition, but it was understood that the privilege was intended for those who were to enter holy orders, and a fatal impediment of speech—an insurmountable and painful stutter—made that profession impossible for him even if his gifts and inclinations had pointed that way. He left Christ's Hospital in November 1789, carrying with him, among other precious possessions, the friendship of

Samuel Taylor Coleridge, a friendship destined to endure, and to be the main living influence upon his mind and character till the latest year of his life. Coleridge was two years Lamb's senior, and remained at the school till 1772, when he went to Cambridge.

At the date of Lamb's leaving school his elder brother John was a clerk in the South Sea House, and a humbler post in the same office was soon found for Charles through the good offices of Samuel Salt, who was a deputy-governor of the company. But early in 1792 he was appointed to a clerkship in the accountant's office of the India House, and remained a member of the staff for the next thirty years. The court minutes of the old India House record that on 5 April 1792 'William Savory, Charles Lamb, and Hutcher Trower' were appointed clerks in the accountant's office on the usual terms. Another entry of three weeks later tells that the sureties required by the office were in Lamb's case Peter Peirson, esq., of the Inner Temple, and John Lamb 'of the Inner Temple, gentleman.' The name of Peter Peirson recalls one of the most touching passages in the essay on the 'Old Benchers.'

Samuel Salt died in this same year, leaving various legacies and other benefactions to his faithful clerk and housekeeper. The Lamb family had accordingly to leave the Temple, and there is no record of their place of residence until 1796, when we hear of them as lodging in Little Queen Street, Holborn. The family were poor, Charles's salary, and what his sister could earn by needlework, in addition to the interest on Salt's legacies, forming their sole means of subsistence, for John Lamb the younger, a fairly prosperous gentleman, was living an independent life elsewhere. John Lamb the elder was old and sinking into dotage. The mother was an invalid, with apparently a strain of insanity. Mary Lamb was overworked, and the continued strain and anxiety began to tell upon her mind. On 22 Sept. 1796 a terrible blow fell upon the family. Mary Lamb, irritated with a little apprentice-girl who was working in the family sitting-room, snatched a knife from the table, pursued the child round the room, and finally stabbed her mother, who had interposed in the girl's behalf. The wound was instantly fatal, Charles being at hand only in time to wrest the knife from his sister and prevent further mischief. An inquest was held and a verdict found of temporary insanity. Mary Lamb would have been in the ordinary course transferred to a public lunatic asylum, but interest was made with the authorities, and she was given into the custody of her brother, then only just of age, who undertook to be her guardian, an office which he discharged under the gravest difficulties and discouragements for the remainder of his life. Mrs. Lamb was buried in the graveyard of St. Andrew's, Holborn, on 26 Sept. 1796, and Charles Lamb, with his imbecile father and an old Aunt Hetty, who formed one of the household, left Little Queen Street. (The house no longer stands, having been removed with others to make room for a church, which now stands on its site.) The family removed to 45 Chapel Street, Pentonville, with the exception of Mary, who was placed under suitable care at Hackney, where Charles could frequently visit her. In February 1797 old Aunt Hetty died, and Charles was left as the solitary guardian of his father until the latter's death in 1799.

The letters of Charles Lamb, through which his life may be henceforth studied, open with a correspondence with Coleridge, beginning in May 1796. The earliest of these letters records how Charles Lamb himself had been for six weeks in the winter of 1795-6 in an asylum for some form of mental derangement, which, however, seems never to have recurred. It is likely that this tendency was inherited from the mother, and that moreover the immediate cause, in this case, may have been a love disappointment. This at least is certain, that already Charles Lamb had lost his heart to a girl living not far from Blakesware, his grandmother's home in Hertfordshire. The earliest intimation of the fact is afforded by the existence of two sonnets which Lamb submits to Coleridge in 1796 as having been written by him in the summer of 1795 (see Lamb's Letters, i. 4). Both poems refer to Hertfordshire, and the second distinctly reveals an attachment to a 'gentle maid' named Anna, who had lived in a 'cottage,' and with whom 'in happier days' he had held free converse, days which, however, 'ne'er must come again.' At that early date, therefore, it is clear that the course of love had not run smooth, and it is reasonable to connect Lamb's mental breakdown in the following winter with this cause. A year later, in writing to Coleridge after his mother's death, he speaks of his attachment as a folly that has left him for ever. All that is certain of this episode in Lamb's life is that the girl's name was Ann Simmons, that she lived with her mother in a cottage called Blenheims, within a mile of Blakesware House, and that she ultimately married a Mr. Bartram, a silversmith, of Princes Street, Leicester Square (she is mentioned under that name in the essay 'Dream Children'). Thus far all is certain. The whole pedigree of the Simmons family is in the present writer's possession, but an old inhabitant of Widford (the village adjoining Blakesware), and intimate friend of the Lambs, from whom he obtained it, had never heard of the circumstances attending Lamb's unsuccessful wooing.

In the spring of 1796 Coleridge made his earliest appearance as a poet in a small volume published by Cottle of Bristol, 'Poems on Various Subjects, by S. T. Coleridge, late of Jesus College, Cambridge,' and among these were four sonnets by Lamb. 'The effusions signed C. L. were written by Mr. Charles Lamb of the India House. Independently of the signature, their superior merit would have sufficiently distinguished them.' Two of these sonnets refer also to Anna with the fair hair and the blue eyes. This was Lamb's first appearance in print. The sonnets are chiefly remarkable as reflecting the diction and the graceful melancholy of William Lisle Bowles [q. v.], whose sonnets had in a singular degree influenced and inspired both Lamb and Coleridge while they were still at Christ's Hospital. A year later, in 1797, Coleridge produced a second edition of his poems, 'To which are now added Poems by Charles Lamb and Charles Lloyd' (1775–1839) [q. v.] Among these were included the 'Anna' sonnets, and the lines entitled 'The Grandame,' written on his grandmother, Mrs. Field, who had died at Blakesware in 1792. (These latter had already appeared in print, in a handsome quarto, with certain others of Charles Lloyd's.)

In the summer of 1797 Lamb devoted his short holiday (only one week) to a visit to Coleridge at Nether Stowey, where he made the acquaintance of Thomas Poole [q. v.], and met Wordsworth and others (see Mrs. Sandford, Thomas Poole and his Friends; and Lamb's Letters, i. 79). The following year, 1798, saw the publication of a thin volume, 'Blank Verse, by Charles Lamb and Charles Lloyd,' containing the touching verses on the 'Old Familiar Faces.' Later appeared Lamb's prose romance, 'A Tale of Rosamund Gray and Old Blind Margaret,' a story of sentiment written under the influence of Mackenzie, and having the scene laid in Lamb's favourite village of Widford in Hertfordshire. During this year Cottle of Bristol had a portrait taken of Lamb by Hancock, an engraving of which appeared many years later in Cottle's 'Recollections of Coleridge.' This is the earliest portrait of Lamb we possess. In November 1798 Coleridge, with Wordsworth and his sister, left England

for Germany, and for the next eighteen months Lamb was thrown for literary sympathy upon other friends, notably on Southey, with whom he began a frequent correspondence. In these letters Lamb's individuality of style and humour became first markedly apparent.

In the spring of 1799 Lamb's father died, and Mary Lamb returned to live with her brother, from whom she was never again parted, except during occasional returns of her malady. But rumours of this malady followed them wherever they went. They had notice to quit their rooms in Pentonville in the spring of 1799, and they were accepted as tenants for a while by Lamb's old schoolfellow, John Mathew Gutch [q. v.], then a law-stationer in Southampton Buildings, Holborn. Here they remained for nine months, but the old difficulties arose, and the brother and sister were again homeless. Lamb then turned to the familiar precincts of the Temple, and took rooms at the top of King's Bench Walk (Mitre Court Buildings), where he remained with his sister for nearly nine years. They then removed to Inner Temple Lane for a period of another nine years.

Lamb's letters to Thomas Manning [q. v.], the mathematician and orientalist, and to Coleridge on his return from Germany, begin at the date of his settling in the Temple, and continue the story of his life. Manning's acquaintance he had made at Cambridge while visiting Charles Lloyd. Lamb now began to add to his scanty income by writing for the newspapers (see his Elia essay, Newspapers Thirty-five Years Ago). He contributed for some three years facetious paragraphs and epigrams to the 'Morning Post,' 'Morning Chronicle,' and the 'Albion.' In 1802 he published his 'John Woodvil,' a blank-verse play of the Restoration period, but showing markedly the influence of Massinger and Beaumont and Fletcher, full of felicitous lines, but crude and undramatic. It was reviewed in the 'Edinburgh Review,' April 1803, not unfairly, but ignorantly. The Elizabethan dramatists were still sealed books save to the antiquary and the specialist. Meantime Charles and Mary Lamb were struggling with poverty, and with worse enemies. Lamb's journalistic and literary associates made demands on his hospitality, and good company brought its temptations. In 1804 Mary Lamb writes that they are 'very poor,' and that Charles is trying in various ways to earn money. He was still dreaming of possible dramatic successes, but these were not to be. In 1803 he sends Manning his well-known verses on Hester

Savory, a young quakeress with whom he had fallen in love, though without her knowledge, when he lived (1797–1800) at Pentonville, and who had recently died a few months after her marriage. In September 1805 he is still thinking of dramatic work, and has a farce in prospect. The project took shape in the two-act farce, 'Mr. H.,' accepted by the proprietors of Drury Lane, and produced on 10 Dec. The secret of Mr. H.'s real name (Hogsflesh) seemed trivial and vulgar to the audience, and in spite of Elliston's best efforts, the farce was hopelessly damned. Lamb was himself present, and next day recorded the failure by letter to several of his friends. He now turned to a wider field of work in connection with the drama. He made Hazlitt's acquaintance in 1805, and Hazlitt introduced him to William Godwin, who had turned children's publisher. For Godwin Lamb and his sister agreed to write the 'Tales from Shakespeare,' published in January 1807, a second edition following in the next year. Lamb did the tragedies and Mary the comedies. This was Lamb's first success, and first brought him into serious notice. It was followed by a child's version of the adventures of Ulysses, made from Chapman's translation of the 'Odyssey,' for Lamb's knowledge of Greek was moderate. This appeared in 1808. A much more important work was at hand. The publishing house of Longmans commissioned him to edit selections from the Elizabethan dramatists. This also appeared in 1808, under the title of 'Specimens of English Dramatic Poets contemporary with Shakespeare.' Lamb was at once recognised as a critic of the highest order, and of a kind as yet unknown to English literature, and from this time forward his position as a prose writer of marked originality was secure among the more thoughtful of his contemporaries, though it was not till some ten years later that he reached the general public. Between 1808 and 1818 his chief critical productions were the two noble essays on Hogarth and on the tragedies of Shakespeare, published in Leigh Hunt's 'Reflector' in 1811, while the 'Recollections of Christ's Hospital,' in the 'Gentleman's Magazine' of 1813, and the 'Confessions of a Drunkard,' contributed to his friend Basil Montagu's 'Some Enquiries into the Effects of Fermented Liquors' in 1814, were the first specimens of the miscellaneous essay in the vein he was to work later, with such success, in the 'Essays of Elia.' Meantime he was strengthening his position and widening his interests by new and stimulating friendships, Talfourd, Proctor, Crabb Robinson, Haydon,

and others appearing among his correspondents, while the old relations with the Wordsworths and Coleridge remained among the best influences of his life.

In the autumn of 1817 Lamb and his sister left the Temple for lodgings in Great Russell Street, Covent Garden. Soon after a young bookseller, Charles Ollier, induced him to publish a collection of his miscellaneous writings in verse and prose, including some, like 'John Woodvil' and 'Rosamund Gray,' long out of print. These appeared in two volumes, dedicated to Coleridge, in 1818, and at once obtained for Lamb a wider recognition. A more important result was to follow. The 'London Magazine' made its first appearance in January 1820. Hazlitt, who was on the staff, introduced Lamb to the editor, John Scott, and he was invited to contribute occasional essays. The first of these, 'Recollections of the South Sea House,' appeared in August 1820. In writing the essay, Lamb remembered an obscure clerk in that office during his own short connection with it as a boy, of the name of Elia, and as a joke appended that name to the essay. In subsequent essays he continued the same signature, which became inseparably connected with the series (see letter of Lamb to his publisher, John Taylor, in July 1821). 'Call him Ellia,' writes Lamb, and it seems probable that the name was really thus spelled. Between August 1820 and December 1822 Lamb contributed five-and-twenty essays, thus signed, at the rate of about one a month. These were reprinted in a single volume in 1823: 'Elia—Essays that have appeared under that signature in the "London Magazine."'

Meantime, Lamb's elder brother John had died (November 1821), and to the increasing loneliness of his existence we owe the beautiful essay, 'Dream Children.' In 1822 Charles and his sister for the first time went abroad, paying a short visit to their friend James Kenney (q. v.) the dramatist, who lived at Versailles, and whose son, born in 1823, was christened Charles Lamb Kenney (q. v.) During this absence from England Mary Lamb had one of her now more frequent attacks of mental derangement. The next year brought a new anxiety into Lamb's life, in the form of a criticism from the pen of an old friend on the 'Elia' volume of 1823. Southey, in reviewing a work by Grégoire upon deism in France, drew a moral from the hopeless tone of one of Lamb's essays—that on 'Witches and other Night Fears'—adding that the essays as a whole lacked a 'sound religious feeling.' The charge pained Lamb keenly, both as coming from an old friend and as touching a vein of real sorrow and anxiety in his mental history. He replied to the charge in the well-known 'Letter of Elia to Robert Southey, Esq.,' in the 'London Magazine' for October 1823. Southey, in reply, wrote a loving and generous letter of explanation to Lamb, and the breach between the old friends was at once healed. The same year that brought Lamb this distress was to bring compensation in a new interest added to his life. He and his sister were in the habit of spending their autumn holiday at Cambridge, where they had a friend, Mrs. Paris, sister of Lamb's old friend, William Ayrton. Here the Lambs met a little orphan girl, Emma Isola, daughter of Charles Isola, one of the esquire bedells of the university. They invited her to spend subsequent holidays with them, and finally adopted her. During the remaining ten years of Lamb's life the companionship of the young girl supplied the truest solace and relief amid the deepening anxieties of the home life. Lamb and his sister devoted themselves to her education, and though in after years she left them at times to become herself a teacher of others, their house was her home until her marriage with Edward Moxon, the publisher, in 1833. Mrs. Moxon died in March 1891.

In August 1823 the Lambs left their rooms in Russell Street, Covent Garden, 'over the Brazier's,' and took a cottage in Colebrooke Row, Islington, the New River flowing at the foot of their garden. Lamb describes the house in a letter of 2 Sept. to Bernard Barton (q.v.), the quaker poet of Woodbridge, who was one of Lamb's later friends, acquired through the 'London Magazine.' To him many of Lamb's happiest letters are addressed. Meantime Lamb was writing more 'Elia' essays, though with weakening health and increasing restlessness. Already he was considering the chances of retirement from the India House, and a severe illness in the winter of 1824-5 brought the matter to an issue. His doctors urgently supported his application to the directors, and the happy result was made known to him in March 1825, when it was announced that a retiring pension would be awarded him, consisting of three-fourths of his salary, with a slight deduction to insure an allowance for his sister in the event of her surviving. 'After thirty-three years' slavery,' he wrote to Wordsworth, 'here am I a freed man, with 441l. a year for the remainder of my life.' The first use that Lamb made of his freedom was to pay visits of varying length in the country, always in the direction of his favourite Hertfordshire. The brother and sister took lodgings occasionally at the Chace,

Enfield, and after two years became sole tenants of the little house. Meantime the trials of having nothing to do became very real to them both. Lamb was an excellent walker, and in the summer months he found great pleasure in exploring the scenery of Hertfordshire, with the comforting remembrance that he was still in easy touch with London and friends. But old friends were dying, and Lamb's loyal nature found little compensation in the cultivation of new ones. That devoted friend of his childhood, Mr. Randal Norris, sub-treasurer of the Inner Temple, died in January 1827, and is the subject of a pathetic letter to Crabb Robinson—'To the last he called me Charley. I have none to call me Charley now.' Randal Norris left two daughters, who set up a school at Widford, to which village their mother had belonged. The younger, Mrs. Arthur Tween, who was well known to the present writer, died at an advanced age at Widford in July 1891. During the few remaining years of Lamb's life it was a favourite excursion for him and Miss Isola to walk over to Widford and beg a half-holiday for the girls and tell them stories.

In 1828 Lamb obtained some literary work of a kind thoroughly congenial. He wished to assist Hone, then producing his 'Table Book,' and undertook to make extracts (after the model of his 'Dramatic Specimens' of 1808) from the Garrick plays in the British Museum. He had written also for the 'New Monthly Magazine,' in 1826, his essays called 'Popular Fallacies.' He wrote also occasional verse, and at times in his happiest and most characteristic vein, such as the lines 'On an Infant dying as soon as born,' written on the death of Thomas Hood's first child, in 1828. Acrostics also, and other such trifles, and album verses, became increasingly in request among his young lady friends. And in 1830, to help his friend Moxon, then newly starting as publisher, he made a collection of these, under the title of 'Album Verses, with a few others.' In the summer of 1829 the brother and sister had again to change their residence. Mary's health was steadily weakening, her attacks and periods of absence from home became longer, and the cares of housekeeping proved intolerable. They moved, accordingly, to the adjoining house in Enfield Chace, and boarded with a retired tradesman and his wife, a Mr. and Mrs. Westwood. The immediate effects were satisfactory, and for a while Mary Lamb seemed to improve in health and spirits. But Charles meantime became less at ease in country life. The next year brought him new distractions. Emma Isola, for whom the Lambs had found a situation as governess in Suffolk, had a serious illness, during which Lamb visited her, and finally brought her home, convalescent, to Enfield. In 1833 the Lambs moved once more, and for the last time. Mary's improvement in health had been merely temporary, and it became necessary for her to be under more skilful and constant nursing. During previous illnesses she had been placed under the care of a Mr. and Mrs. Walden, at Bay Cottage, Edmonton (the parish adjoining Enfield), and now the brother and sister moved together, to spend, as it proved, the last two years of their united lives under the Waldens' roof.

In the same year Emma Isola became engaged to Edward Moxon, and the marriage took place in July 1833, leaving Charles Lamb yet more lonely, and without social resource. The 'Last Essays of Elia,' mainly from the 'London Magazine,' were published this year by Moxon, and but for an occasional copy of verses for a friend's album, Lamb's literary career was closed. In July 1834 Coleridge died, and with this event Lamb's last surviving friend passed from him. He himself, more and more lonely and forlorn, bore his heavy burden five months longer. One day in December, while walking on the London Road, he stumbled and fell, slightly wounding his face. A few days later erysipelas supervened, and he had no strength left to battle with the disease. He passed away without pain, on 27 Dec. 1834, and was buried in Edmonton churchyard. His sister survived him nearly thirteen years, dying at Alpha Road, St. John's Wood, on 20 May 1847; she was buried beside her brother. Charles left her his savings, amounting to about 2,000l., and she was also entitled to the pension reserved to her by the terms of Lamb's retirement from the India House.

No figure in literature is better known to us than Lamb. His writings, prose and verse, are full of personal revelations. We possess a body of his correspondence, also of the most confidential kind, and his friends have left descriptions of him from almost every point of view. He numbered among his earliest friends Coleridge, Southey, Wordsworth, and among his later Procter, Talfourd, Hood, Leigh Hunt, Hazlitt, Crabb Robinson, while many of his most characteristic letters were written to men who have attained general fame mainly through Lamb's friendship. Notable among these are Thomas Manning and Bernard Barton. No man was ever more loved by a wide and varied class of friends. His life-long devotion to his sister, for whose sake he abjured all thoughts of

marriage; the unique attachment between the pair; Lamb's unfailing loyalty to his friends, who often levied heavy taxes on his purse and leisure; his very eccentricities and petulances, including his one serious frailty—a too careless indulgence in strong drinks—excited a profound pity in those who knew the unceasing domestic difficulties which he surmounted so bravely for eight-and-thirty years. It is likely that the necessity of protecting and succouring his sister acted as a strong power over his will, and helped to preserve his sanity during the hardship of the years that followed. But one result of the taint of insanity inherited from his mother was that a very small amount of alcohol was enough at any time to throw his mind off its balance. He was afflicted, moreover, all his life with a bad stutter, and the eagerness to forget the impediment, which put him at a disadvantage in all conversations, probably further encouraged the habit. The infirmity, which has been in turn denied and exaggerated by friends and enemies, never interfered with the regular performance of his official duties, or with the assiduous and wise control of his money matters and his domestic responsibilities.

The extant portraits of Lamb are the following: 1. By Hancock of Bristol, 1798; engraved in Joseph Cottle's 'Reminiscences of Coleridge,' 1837. 2. By William Hazlitt, 1805, in a fancy dress; engraved in Barry Cornwall's 'Memoir,' 1866. 3. By G. F. Joseph, A.R.A., 1819; water-colour drawing made to illustrate a copy of 'English Bards and Scotch Reviewers;' engraved in the present writer's edition of 'Lamb's Letters.' 4. Etching on copper by Brook Pulham, a friend of Lamb's in the India House, 1825. 5. By Henry Meyer, 1826; engraved in Mr. Charles Kent's 'Centenary Edition of Lamb's Works.' 6. By T. Wageman, 1824 or 1825; engraved in Talfourd's 'Letters of Charles Lamb,' 1837. 7. Charles Lamb and his sister together, by F. S. Cary, 1834; engraved in Moxon's 1868 edition of Lamb's 'Works,' vol. i. 8. By Maclise, sketch in 'Fraser's Magazine,' 1835.

Lamb's writings published in book form are: 1. 'Poems on Various Subjects, by S. T. Coleridge, late of Jesus College, Cambridge,' 1796, contains four sonnets by Lamb signed 'C. L.,' referred to by Coleridge in his preface as by 'Mr. Charles Lamb of the India House.' 2. 'Poems by S. T. Coleridge, 2nd edit., to which are now added Poems by Charles Lamb and Charles Lloyd,' 1797. 3. 'Blank Verse by Charles Lloyd and Charles Lamb,' 1798. 4. 'A Tale of Rosamund Gray and Old Blind Margaret, by Charles Lamb,' 1798. 5. 'John Woodvil, a Tragedy, by Charles Lamb,' &c.,

1802. 6. 'Mrs. Leicester's School,' &c., 1807, by Charles and Mary Lamb, Charles contributing three of the stories, 'The Witch Aunt,' 'First Going to Church,' and the 'Sea Voyage.' 7. 'Tales from Shakespeare, &c., by Charles Lamb,' 1807. The bulk of the tales were written by Mary Lamb, Charles contributing the tragedies. 8. 'The Adventures of Ulysses, by Charles Lamb,' 1808. 9. 'Specimens of English Dramatic Poets, with Notes by Charles Lamb,' 1808. 10. 'Poetry for Children, entirely original, by the author of "Mrs. Leicester's School,"' anonymous, by Charles and Mary Lamb. The respective shares of the two writers were not indicated. A few of Lamb's verses were reprinted by him in his 'Collected Works' in 1818. 11. 'Prince Dorus,' a poetical version of an ancient tale, 1811. 12. 'The Works of Charles Lamb,' in 2 vols. London, 1818. 13. 'Elia—Essays which have appeared under that signature in the "London Magazine,"' 1823. 14. 'Album Verses, with a few others,' by Charles Lamb, 1830. 15. 'Satan in Search of a Wife,' 1831. 16. 'The Last Essays of Elia,' 1833. In this list are not included Lamb's occasional contributions to periodical literature, such as albums and keepsakes, prologues and epilogues to plays, and the like, almost all of which are to be found collected in posthumous editions of his works. As to Lamb's authorship of a child's book, done for Godwin, on the fairy tale of 'Beauty and the Beast,' there is no direct evidence, while all the indirect evidence points to an opposite conclusion.

[Excepting short memoirs, which appeared after Lamb's death, by Forster, Moxon, B. Field, and others, the first biography was Talfourd's Letters of Charles Lamb, with a Sketch of his Life, 1837. After Mary Lamb's death, in 1847, Talfourd produced a supplementary volume, the Final Memorials of Charles Lamb, 1848. An independent memoir, based upon personal recollections, by Barry Cornwall—Charles Lamb, a Memoir—appeared in 1866. In 1868, and again in 1875, Talfourd's two books were reissued, digested into a continuous narrative, with many additions, prefixed to new editions of the Works, the second of these edited by Mr. Percy Fitzgerald. In 1886 Mr. W. C. Hazlitt edited afresh Talfourd's two works, again digested into one, with additions, both to the letters and Talfourd's own text. Meantime, in 1875, Mr. Charles Kent prefixed a short memoir of Lamb to Routledge's one-volume Centenary Edition of the Works, adding several new facts of interest, including a letter from Fanny Kelly regarding the essay 'Barbara S.' In 1882 the present writer furnished the memoir of Lamb in the Men of Letters Series, since revised and enlarged, 1888. An annotated edition of Lamb's complete Works and Correspondence, by the same writer, was pub-lished in six volumes (1883-8). Other works referring in various ways to Lamb are Cottle's Early Recollections of Coleridge, 1837; Patmore's My Friends and Acquaintances, 1854; Hood's Literary Reminiscences (Hood's Own, 1st ser.); Crabb Robinson's Diary; Leigh Hunt's Autobiography; Memoirs of W. Hazlitt; Mr. and Mrs. Cowden Clarke's Recollections of Writers; Mary Lamb, by Mrs. Gilchrist, in the Eminent Women Series. The best attempt at a complete bibliography of Lamb's writings is that by Mr. E. D. North, appended to Martin's In the Footprints of Charles Lamb, New York, 1890.]

A. A.

LAMB, EDWARD BUCKTON (1806-1869), architect, born in 1806, had considerable reputation as an architect in the modern Gothic style, and obtained a large practice. From 1824 he frequently exhibited at the Royal Academy. In 1849 he exhibited a design for the Smithfield Martyrs' Memorial Church in St. John Street Road, Clerkenwell. Some of his designs were published in lithography. Lamb published in 1830 'Etchings of Gothic Ornament,' in four parts, and in 1846 'Studies of Ancient Domestic Architecture, principally selected from Original Drawings in the Collection of Sir W. Burrell.' He died at his residence in Hinde Street, Manchester Square, on 30 Aug. 1869.

[Obituary notices; Royal Academy Catalogues.]

L. C.

LAMB, FREDERICK JAMES, third VISCOUNT MELBOURNE and BARON BEAUVALE (1782-1853), the third son of Peniston, first viscount Melbourne, was born on 17 April 1782, and was educated at Eton. In 1800, together with his brother William [q. v.], he became a resident pupil of Professor Millar of Glasgow University (Lord Melbourne's Papers, p. 5). Lamb took his M.A. degree from Trinity College, Cambridge, in 1803. He entered the diplomatic service; in 1811 was appointed secretary of legation, and in 1812 minister plenipotentiary ad interim at the court of the Two Sicilies. In 1813 he was secretary of legation at Vienna, and in August was appointed minister plenipotentiary ad interim pending the arrival of Lord Stewart, afterwards Marquis of Londonderry. From 1815 to 1820 Lamb was minister plenipotentiary at the court of Bavaria. In 1822 he was sworn of the privy council, and in 1827 nominated a civil grand cross of the Bath in consideration of his diplomatic services. On 18 Feb. 1825 he was appointed minister plenipotentiary to Spain, to which court he was attached until 1827. He was then (28 Dec.) sent to Lisbon as ambassador. There he saw from the first an evident intention on the part of Dom Miguel, the queen's uncle, to usurp the throne. Accordingly he detained, on his own responsibility, the British force which had been sent to Portugal. The Wellington ministry endorsed the act of their representative, but decided nevertheless on recalling the troops (Lamb's despatches are in vol. xvi. of the *State Papers*; see also ASHLEY, *Palmerston*, i. 130-1). He was in England in August 1828, when he made no secret of his opinion that our government had acted 'very ill and foolishly in first encouraging and then abandoning the wretched constitutionalists to their fate' (GREVILLE, i. 141). On the formation of Grey's ministry, Lamb acquired much influence over his brother, Lord Melbourne, the home secretary, although Melbourne was rather jealous and perplexed by Frederick's severe strictures on the whigs. On 13 May 1831 he was appointed ambassador at the court of Vienna, where he remained until November 1841, his adroitness and social qualities enabling him to work well with Metternich, whose foreign policy was entirely congenial to him. He was very handsome, and made many friends. In 1836 he was directed by the government to sound the Duke of Wellington upon the Eastern question, and drew up an able paper, which elicited from the duke a reply dated 6 March 1836 (*Lord Melbourne's Papers*, p. 342). In 1839 he was created a peer of the United Kingdom by the title of Baron Beauvale. During the following year he was strongly opposed to Palmerston's Syrian policy, and told the ministry that he considered it impossible to execute the convention for the maintenance of the integrity of the Porte. Nevertheless, he carried out Palmerston's instructions with great ability (see especially *Parliamentary Papers*, 1841, vol. xxix.) When the crisis had abated, Beauvale—if Greville was correctly informed—suppressed a despatch of Palmerston's in which the vacillation of the Austrian cabinet was reviewed in a very offensive style (GREVILLE, pt. ii. vol. ii. p. 389). It was possibly at this time that Melbourne sent him a hint through Lady Westmorland that he could not remain at Vienna if he opposed Palmerston so often.

On his retirement in 1841 Beauvale received a pension of 1,700*l*. He had the good fortune 'at sixty years old, and with a broken and enfeebled constitution,' to marry, on 25 Feb. 1841, 'a charming girl of twenty,' the Countess Alexandrina Julia, daughter of the Count of Maltzahn, the Prussian minister at Vienna (she was born in 1818). Greville describes her unceasing devotion to him, and her grief for his death. Beauvale's last years were spent in the retirement of a valetudinarian; he had a great liking for political gossip, and carried on a correspondence with Madame de Lieven. He succeeded to Lord Melbourne's title in 1848, and died on 29 Jan. 1853.

Beauvale's estates devolved on Lady Palmerston, and through her to the present Earl Cowper, his titles becoming extinct. Lady Beauvale married secondly, on 10 June 1856, John George, second baron Forester.

[Greville Journals, especially the elaborate character of Beauvale in pt. iii. vol. i. pp. 35-7. For his appointments see Haydn's Book of Dignities. The facts of his career are correctly given in the Annual Reg. and Gent. Mag. for 1853.] L. C. S.

LAMB, GEORGE (1784-1834), politician and writer, fourth and youngest son of Peniston, first viscount Melbourne, was born 11 July 1784. At the age of two he was painted by Maria Cosway as 'the infant Bacchus.' Lamb was educated at Eton, and at Trinity College, Cambridge (M.A. 1805). In the same year Lord Minto met him at dinner at Lord Bessborough's, and recorded that he was 'merely a good-natured lad,' something like the Prince of Wales (MINTO, *Life and Letters*, iii. 361). He was called to the bar at Lincoln's Inn, and went the northern circuit for a short time, but soon abandoned law for literature. He was one of the earlier contributors to the 'Edinburgh Review,' and in consequence was satirised by Byron in his 'English Bards and Scotch Reviewers' (1809) in the passage—

> to be misled
> By Jeffrey's heart, or Lamb's Boeotian head.

The expression was afterwards allowed by Byron to have been unjust (MOORE, *Byron*, p. 81). Lamb was a good amateur actor (Miss BERRY, *Journal*, ii. 235), and on 10 April 1807 his two-act comic opera, 'Whistle for it,' was produced at Covent Garden, and performed some three times. It was printed in the same year, and is above mediocrity. Together with Byron and Douglas Kinnaird he was member of the committee of management of Drury Lane in 1815, and wrote the prologues to the revivals of old English plays, but almost gave up prologuising when Byron compared him to Upton, who wrote the songs for Astley's (MOORE, *Byron*, p. 288). His adaptation of 'Timon of Athens' was produced on 28 Oct. 1816, and published in the same year with a preface, in which it is described as 'an attempt to restore Shakespeare to the stage, with no other omissions than such as the refinement of manners has rendered necessary' (GENEST, *Hist. of the Stage*, viii. 584-6). In 1821 he tried to get

Moore to write a play on 'Lalla Rookh' (MOORE, *Diary*, iii. 294). In the same year Lamb published his most important literary work, 'The Poems of Caius Valerius Catullus translated, with a Preface and Notes' (2 vols.) Though it was savagely attacked in 'Blackwood's Magazine' for 21 Aug. (ix. 507–16), evidently by Christopher North), the translation has the merit of smooth versification and some pretensions to scholarship. It has been republished in Bohn's 'Classical Library' (1854). Lamb is said to have written some minor poems, but they were never collected.

On the death of Sir S. Romilly in 1819, Lamb was persuaded to stand for Westminster in the whig interest against the radicals Hobhouse and Major Cartwright. He was elected, after a very disorderly contest, lasting fifteen days, having polled 4,465 votes, against Hobhouse's 3,861 and Cartwright's 38 (*An Authentic Narrative of the Events of the Westminster Election*, published by order of Hobhouse's committee; ASHLEY, *Palmerston*, i. 87). At the general election of 1820 he was defeated, the numbers being: Burdett 5,327, Hobhouse 4,882, Lamb 4,436. In June 1826 he was returned for Dungarvan, co. Waterford, a borough of the Duke of Devonshire's. In 1830, on the formation of Grey's ministry, he became under-secretary of state to his brother, Lord Melbourne [see LAMB, WILLIAM], in the home department. He contrived to keep on good terms with O'Connell, who in 1831 offered to bring him in free of expense for co. Waterford (*O'Connell's Life and Times*, ed. Fitzpatrick, i. 259). He consented, however, to represent Dungarvan. In December 1830 he was sent by Lord Melbourne to request Francis Place [q. v.] to make a manifesto to the working classes against acts of violence. Place, a sound radical, declined to take the advice of a lukewarm reformer (*Place MSS.* i. 85). He died on 22 Jan. 1834. Lamb married, 17 May 1821, Caroline Rosalie Adelaide St. Jules, and left no issue. His married life was one of great happiness, and he was universally popular as an amiable and kind-hearted man.

[*Gent. Mag.* 1834, p. 438, where, however, Charles Lamb's farce, 'Mr. H.,' is wrongly attributed to George Lamb; Torrens's *Memoirs of Lord Melbourne*, vol. i. passim.] L. C. S.

LAMB, JAMES (1599–1664), orientalist, baptised on 2 Feb. 1598–9 in All Saints Ash, Oxford, was son of Richard Lamb, by his second wife. After attending Magdalen College school he matriculated as a commoner of Brasenose College on 2 July 1613 (*Oxf. Univ. Reg.*, Oxf. Hist. Soc., vol. ii. pt. ii. p. 331), and graduated B.A. in 1615–

1616, and M.A. as a member of St. Mary Hall in 1619–20 (*ib.* vol. ii. pt. iii. p. 341). He became chaplain to Thomas Wriothesley, earl of Southampton. On 23 July 1660 he was installed prebendary of Westminster (LE NEVE, *Fasti*, ed. Hardy, iii. 360), was created D.D. at Oxford on 9 Aug. following, and on 4 Jan. 1662–3 was presented to the rectory of St. Andrew, Holborn. He died on 18 Oct. 1664, and was buried on the 20th in Westminster Abbey, leaving a widow, Elizabeth, of the Bromfield family of Kent (CHESTER, *Registers of Westminster Abbey*, p. 161). He bequeathed many of his books to the Abbey library. In the Bodleian Library are the following manuscripts by Lamb: 1. 'Grammatica Arabica,' 3 vols. 4to. 2. 'Danielis Prophetiæ liber, Syriacè,' 4to. 3. 'Collectanea ad Lexicon Arabicum spectantia,' 4 vols. oblong 8vo. 4. 'Flexio Verborum Arabicorum,' 8vo.

[Wood's Athenæ Oxon. (Bliss), iii. 668.] G. G.

LAMB, SIR JAMES BLAND (1752–1824), politician and miscellaneous writer. [See BURGES.]

LAMB, JOHN, D.D. (1789–1850), master of Corpus Christi College, Cambridge, and dean of Bristol, born at Ixworth, Suffolk, on 28 Feb. 1789, was son of John Lamb, perpetual curate of Ixworth, vicar of Haxey, Lincolnshire, and rector of Stretton, Rutland, by his wife Maria, daughter of William Hovell of Backwell Ash, Suffolk. He studied at Corpus Christi College, Cambridge, where he graduated B.A. in 1811 as fifteenth and last wrangler, and proceeded M.A. in 1814, B.D. in 1822, and D.D. in 1827. In 1822 he was chosen master of his college, in succession to Philip Douglas, D.D. In 1824 he was presented by the college to the perpetual curacy of St. Benedict in Cambridge; on 20 Oct. 1837 he was nominated by the crown to the deanery of Bristol; and in 1845 he was instituted, on the presentation of the dean and chapter of Bristol, to the vicarage of Olveston, Gloucestershire, which he held till his death with his mastership and deanery. In politics he maintained whig principles. He died on 19 April 1850, at the lodge of Corpus Christi College, Cambridge, and was buried in a vault under the college chapel.

He married, on 19 March 1822, Anne, daughter of James Hutchinson, rector of Cranford, Northamptonshire, and had issue ten sons and four daughters. One of the sons, John Lamb, was a fellow and bursar of Gonville and Caius College; and another, James Henry Lamb, was a fellow of Christ's College, and is now (1892) rector of Burnham-Westgate, Norfolk. One of the daughters, Emily, is the wife of Norman Macleod Ferrers, D.D., the present master of Gonville and Caius College.

His works are: 1. 'An Historical Account of the XXXIX Articles,' Cambridge, 1829, 4to; second edit. 1835, 4to. 2. 'Masters's History of the College of Corpus Christi in the University of Cambridge; with additional matter and a continuation to the present time,' Cambridge, 1831, 4to. 3. 'Hebrew Characters derived from Hieroglyphics. The original pictures applied to the interpretation of various words and passages in the Sacred Writings, and especially of the History of the Creation and Fall of Man,' London, 1835, 8vo; second edit. Cambridge, 1835, 8vo. 4. 'The Table of Abydos correctly interpreted: corroborative of the Chronology derived from the Sacred Writings,' London, 1836, 8vo. 5. 'A Collection of Letters, Statutes, and other Documents from the MS. Library of Corpus Christi College, illustrative of the History of the University of Cambridge during the time of the Reformation, from A.D. MD. to MDLXXII.,' London, 1838, 8vo. 6. 'The Phænomena and Diosemeia of Aratus, translated into English Verse, with Notes,' London, 1848, 8vo.

[Private information; Gent. Mag. new ser. ix. 333, xxxiii. 667; Graduati Cantabr. (Romilly); Le Neve's Fasti (Hardy), i. 225, 445, iii. 682.]
T. C.

LAMB, MARY ANN (1764–1847), sister of Charles Lamb. [See under LAMB, CHARLES.]

LAMB, SIR MATTHEW (1705–1768), politician, second son of Matthew Lamb or Lambe, an attorney of Southwell, and the legal adviser of the Cokes of Melbourne Hall, Derbyshire, was born in 1705, was educated to the law, and was called to the bar at Lincoln's Inn. Robert, bishop of Peterborough [q. v.], was his elder brother. In 1734 the death of his uncle Peniston Lamb, who had been a successful 'pleader under the bar,' placed him in the possession of a considerable fortune. He rapidly extended his business, became the confidential adviser of Lord Salisbury and Lord Egmont, and according to Hayward (Celebrated Statesmen, i. 332), feathered his nest at their expense. He was probably the Councillor Lamb of Lincoln's Inn who in 1738 was appointed solicitor to the revenue of the post office (Gent. Mag. 1738). Two years later he married Miss Charlotte Coke, who, on the unexpected death of her brother, George Lewis Coke, in 1751, inherited Melbourne Hall. He acquired Brocket Hall, Hertfordshire, by purchase from the repre-

sentatives of Sir Thomas Winnington in 1746. Lamb was already in parliament, having been returned for Stockbridge in 1741, and was elected for Peterborough in 1747, which borough he represented until his death. On 17 Jan. 1755 he was created a baronet, and in the following year removed from Red Lion Square to Sackville Street, Piccadilly. He died on 5 Nov. 1768, leaving property estimated at nearly half a million, besides half a million in ready money. Lamb had three children: Peniston, who succeeded to the baronetcy, and was created first lord (1770) and viscount (1781) Melbourne in the Irish peerage; Charlotte, who married Henry, second earl of Fauconberg, in 1766, and died in 1790; and Anne, who died unmarried in 1768.

[Torrens's Memoirs of Lord Melbourne, vol. i. chap. i.; Lord Melbourne's Papers, ed. Sanders, chap. i.]
L. C. S.

LAMB, WILLIAM, second VISCOUNT MELBOURNE (1779–1848), second son of Peniston, first viscount Melbourne (1748–1819), by Elizabeth (1749–1818), only daughter of Sir Ralph Milbanke, bart., of Halnaby, Yorkshire, was born 15 March 1779. His father, son of Sir Matthew Lamb [q. v.], inherited a large property, which he promptly squandered. He was member for Ludgershall in the House of Commons from 1768 to 1784, when he was a silent follower of Lord North. He afterwards sat for Malmesbury and Newport, Isle of Wight (1784–93); was created an Irish baron in 1770 by the title of Lord Melbourne of Kilmore, and an Irish viscount in 1781. He was appointed gentleman of the bedchamber to the Prince of Wales in 1784, and created an English peer in 1815. Lady Melbourne (who was married 13 April 1769) was a remarkable woman. Though Horace Walpole thought her affected (Letters, ed. Cunningham, vii. 63), and she was the object of some scandal (WRAXALL, Memoirs, ed. Wheatley, v. 370; HAYWARD, Celebrated Statesmen, p. 336; and GREVILLE, pt. ii. vol. iii. p. 241), Byron on her death, 6 April 1818, called her 'the best, and kindest, and ablest female I have ever known, old or young' (MOORE, Byron, p. 379; see also p. 200). The rise of the family was due to her brilliant qualities. She was thrice painted by Reynolds; in 1770, mezzotint by Finlayson, and twice in 1771, together with her eldest child Peniston (born 3 May 1773). The first picture was engraved by Watson; the second, 'Maternal Affection,' by Dickinson.

William Lamb was his mother's favourite child, and she set herself to form his character. His childhood was passed at Brocket

Hall, Hertfordshire, and at Melbourne House, Piccadilly (now the Albany), which was purchased from Lord Holland in 1770, and became an important whig centre. In 1790 he was painted by Reynolds, together with his brothers Peniston and Frederick [q. v.], in the picture 'The Affectionate Brothers' (see HAYDON, *Autobiography*, ii. 343, and C. R. LESLIE, *Autobiographical Recollections*, pp. 103, 170). The picture was engraved by Bartolozzi and S. M. Reynolds. He went to Eton in 1790, where he reached the sixth form, and in July 1796 was entered a fellow-commoner of Trinity College, Cambridge, going into residence in the following October. He was also entered at Lincoln's Inn on 21 July 1797. In Michaelmas term 1798 he won the Trinity declamation prize by an oration on 'The Progressive Improvements of Mankind,' which was praised by Fox in the House of Commons (*Speeches of C. J. Fox*, vi. 472). He proceeded to his degree on 1 July 1799, having spent most of his time at Cambridge in private study. He wrote an 'Epistle to the Editor of the Anti-Jacobin,' published in the 'Morning Chronicle' of 17 Jan. 1798, the reply answered by Canning, and an epilogue to 'Sheridan's 'Pizarro,' performed at Drury Lane on 24 May 1799. In the winter of 1799 he went with his brother Frederick to Glasgow as a resident pupil of Professor Millar. His letters to his mother (*Lord Melbourne's Papers*, pp. 5-30) show that he worked hard and took a keen interest in literature. At the same time he was rather precocious and an extreme whig in his opposition to the French war. He wrote many essays at this time, contributed to the 'Bugle,' a weekly paper, written by the guests at Inverary Castle, under the editorship of 'Monk' Lewis (*Memoirs of M. G. Lewis*, i. 199), and wrote an epilogue on 'The Advantages of ance' for Miss Berry's 'Fashionable Friends,' acted May 1802 (see *Miss Berry's Journal*, 1905). Lamb was called to the bar in Michaelmas term 1804, and went the northern circuit. At the Lancashire sessions he was much pleased at receiving a complimentary brief through Scarlett (Lord Abinger). On death of his elder brother Peniston, on Jan. 1805, he gave up the bar for politics. 3 June he married Lady Caroline Ponsonby, only daughter of the third Earl of Bessborough, by whom he had been previously rejected [see LAMB, LADY CAROLINE]. On 31 Jan. 1806 Lamb was returned for Leominster in the whig interest. Soon afterwards he inscribed some passable lines in the pedestal of the bust of Charles James Fox. On 19 Dec. 1806 he made his maiden speech as mover of the address. In the fol-

lowing March he began to keep a diary, which he continued during the two following years. It records the downfall of the 'Talents' administration, in defence of whose conduct Lamb on 9 April seconded a resolution moved by Mr. Brand. At the general election he was returned for Portarlington (23 May 1807). He had now lost his boyish zeal for Napoleon, and took a deep interest in the success of the Peninsular war. Though he rarely spoke, he was selected on 31 Dec. 1810 to move an amendment to the Regency Bill. His speech was commended by Canning, whom, in spite of early prejudices, he had already begun to follow. In consequence of this, when Lamb lost his seat in 1812 for his support of catholic emancipation, Brougham wrote to Grey that his defeat at the polls was not to be regretted (*Brougham's Life and Times*, ii. 25, 64).

Lamb was out of parliament for four years. In 1813 his wife's temper led him to attempt a separation, which was not, however, carried out till 1825. From certain entries in his commonplace-book, quoted in 'Lord Melbourne's Papers' (pp. 71, 72), it may be gathered that the husband and wife were from the first an ill-assorted couple. Lamb was certainly a kind, if too indulgent, husband. He sought distraction from domestic troubles in sport, society, and literature. He was an excellent shot, and something of a field naturalist. But literature was his chief solace, and his commonplace-book contains a record of his studies, which embraced the greater part of the classics and many English historians. No record of his theological reading has been preserved. His reflections on society, suggested by his studies, are couched in a very cynical vein. In spite of his learning, however, he shrank from authorship, though he was an occasional contributor to Jerdan's 'Literary Gazette' (JERDAN, *Autobiography*, ii. 284-6, where a poem of Lamb's is identified), and wrote a sketch of the early part of Sheridan's political life, which in 1819 he handed over to Moore (MOORE, *Diary*, ii. 300, 308). Lamb subsequently regretted the step (MRS. NORTON, in *Macmillan's Magazine*, vol. iii.)

Lamb was returned to the House of Commons on 16 April 1816 as member for Northampton, and on 29 Nov. 1819 was elected one of the members for Hertfordshire, but retired from a contest for Hertford borough in 1825, because the electors preferred the uncompromising radicalism of Thomas Duncombe [q. v.] He had made little mark as yet, though Castlereagh and the regent and others foresaw his future eminence. He was a lukewarm whig, and though in 1819 he supported Lord Althorp's motion for an inquiry into the state of the country, he voted against his party for the Suspension of the Habeas Corpus Acts in 1816, and supported the Six Acts in 1819–1820. His commonplace-book shows that he was in favour of catholic emancipation and against reform. When Canning became prime minister in 1827, a vacancy was found for Lamb at Newport, Isle of Wight (24 April), and he was appointed Irish secretary, taking his seat for Bletchingley on 7 May. His tenure of office was unimportant, though he was a popular secretary, and though a memorandum, dated 19 Sept. 1827, exhibits a considerable knowledge of affairs (TORRENS, i. 241 6). O'Connell hoped that he would 'un-orange Ireland,' and was anxious to secure his return for Dublin (O'Connell's Correspondence, ed. Fitzpatrick, i. 148–9). After the departure of Wellesley, the lord-lieutenant, early in December, he carried on the government of the country, and had to face the renewal of the agitation for emancipation. Lamb left Ireland in January 1828, and consented to retain office under the new prime minister, the Duke of Wellington. His letters to the home secretary, Sir R. Peel, favoured the administration of Ireland through the ordinary law (PEEL, Memoirs, pt. i. pp. 24–46). In April, however, after more than one ministerial crisis, he and the other Canningites resigned in consequence of the division on the East Retford Bill. Lamb had voted with the government, but followed his friends into opposition 'because he thought it was more necessary to stand by them when they were in the wrong than when they were in the right' (GREVILLE, pt. ii. vol. iii, p. 376). George IV communicated through Bulwer (Lord Dalling) his especial wish that Lamb should remain, but he declined (BULWER, Palmerston, i. 272). Upon his father's death Melbourne took his seat in the House of Lords on 1 Feb. 1829, and on the 24th spoke on the bill for the suppression of the Catholic Association. In the Michaelmas term he appeared before the court of king's bench as co-respondent in an action for divorce brought by Lord Brandon, but the case was non-suited, and in the ecclesiastical court it was withdrawn. On 1 Feb. 1830 he spoke on the Portuguese question, but his speech was a failure, owing to his limited knowledge of the subject (GREVILLE, i. 277). In July 1830 overtures to rejoin the government were made to Melbourne and the other Canningites, but they had thrown in their lot with the whigs.

In the Grey ministry Melbourne was appointed home secretary (19 Nov. 1830). Greville's first opinion was 'Melbourne too idle,' but he soon became quite enthusiastic in his favour, and a similar view is to be found in Sydney Smith's second letter to Archdeacon Singleton (SYDNEY SMITH, Works, p. 625). In dealing with a country on the verge of revolution, he relied upon the ordinary law as administered by the magistrates, especially in the north. In the south, where rick-burning was prevalent, he declined to employ spies, but the machinery-breakers of Hampshire were suppressed by military force, and a special commission brought one thousand individuals to justice at Winchester. The Bristol rioters were treated in the same fashion. He had great difficulty in persuading William IV that special legislation was unadvisable in the case of political unions, such as that of Birmingham. But he dissuaded Burdett from taking part in the National Political Union at Westminster, and induced the other leaders to abandon a monster meeting which had been fixed for 7 Nov. The union was pronounced an illegal body on 22 Nov., but continued its proceedings. Melbourne only supported the Reform Bill because he felt it to be inevitable. Though opposed to a creation of peers, he took little interest in the attempt of the waverers to arrange a compromise (GREVILLE, ii. 254). When the bill passed he thought that its result would be 'a prevalence of the blackguard interest in parliament' (Papers, p. 146). On the appointment of the factory commission of 1833, Melbourne, after they had been at work for two months, insisted on their reporting in a week. Meanwhile disturbances continued in the agricultural districts, and in 1834 the conviction and transportation of the six Dorsetshire labourers for administering illegal oaths aroused great indignation. The trades unions of London got up a monster demonstration (21 April) which presented itself at Whitehall as a deputation demanding the recall of the labourers. Melbourne calmly refused to receive it, and the unionists were persuaded to march on to Newington. As home secretary Melbourne was the cabinet minister responsible for the administration of Ireland. Though he was at first willing that O'Connell should be master of the rolls, he soon saw that no terms were to be made with him, and approved of the suppression of his meetings and of his arrest. He also instructed Anglesey, the lord-lieutenant, to enforce with vigour the law for the collection of tithe, and was a strong advocate of the Coercion Bill of 1833. On the resignation of Anglesey he declined the lord-lieutenancy. He appears to have been averse to the subsequent modifications of the Tithe Bill, and wished the Coercion Bill to be reintroduced in its integrity. Hence he was very angry when Wellesley, the lord-lieutenant, acting on the private advice of Brougham, recommended the abandonment of the clauses for the suppression of meetings (19 June 1834), especially as the letter was addressed to the prime minister, not to himself. The ministry resigned over the misunderstanding thus produced, and Melbourne never forgave Wellesley or Brougham.

On the resignation of Grey, Melbourne was summoned by the king, and obeyed, having ascertained that Lansdowne would not be premier. He declined to form a coalition with Wellington, Peel, and Stanley, and reconstructed the old ministry, placing Duncannon, with a seat in the lords, at the home office, and making Hobhouse first commissioner of woods and forests (Letter to the king of 15 July 1834 in *Melbourne Papers*). A coercion bill was passed minus the meetings clauses, the lords threw out the Tithe Bill, and parliament was prorogued on 15 Aug. It was evident that the government was fast breaking up. O'Connell, whom Melbourne thought irreconcilable, published a violent attack on the whigs; Lansdowne threatened resignation because of blunders connected with the Irish poor-law commission; and Brougham raised a storm of criticism by his tour in Scotland and public altercation with Durham. Lord John Russell also quarrelled with Durham, and, without consulting Melbourne, obtained from the king permission to vindicate himself in parliament. Hence the king was evidently prejudiced against the ministry, and when Althorp's removal to the upper house necessitated a reconstruction of the cabinet, he readily availed himself of Melbourne's hint that he was ready to resign. An audience at Brighton on 14 Nov., which the king expressed alarm at the inquiry into the Irish church, and thought that Russell would make 'a wretched figure' leader of the commons (STOCKMAR, i. 329), as followed by a letter dismissing the ministry. Melbourne bore the summons to Wellington, and wrote that night to Grey: 'I am not surprised at his (the king's) decision, nor do I know that I can entirely condemn it.' Incensed by Brougham's communication to the 'Times,' the king insisted on the resignation of the ministry before their successors were appointed. His conduct in that instance was high-handed, but throughout the crisis he acted less unadvisedly than is stated in most histories.

Melbourne refused an earldom and the Garter, and retired to Melbourne House. At Derby he made two speeches in explanation of his position, the second of which was considered by Greville to be a retractation of the first, compelled by the menaces and reproaches of Duncannon (GREVILLE, iii. 170). But the speech does not bear out this conclusion. Before Christmas he was in the neighbourhood of London, and in correspondence with Grey and Holland. Holland was eager for an immediate attack on the Peel government. Melbourne hesitated, being afraid of radical violence, and unable to see his way to a coalition with Stanley. He was determined, however, that Brougham, Durham, and O'Connell should be excluded from a future liberal government, and explained his reasons to the first in remarkably plain terms. He was also strongly opposed to the negotiations with O'Connell, of which Duncannon was the agent, and which had issue in the so-called Lichfield House compact. But he acquiesced in the opposition to the re-election of Manners Sutton as the speaker, though he found the rival claims of Spring Rice and Abercromby difficult to adjust, and appears to have raised no objections to the Appropriation resolution, on which Peel was forced to resign (8 April 1835).

Melbourne was again summoned, together with Lansdowne, after Grey had declined to form a ministry, and once more refused to form a coalition government. The great seal was placed in commission in order to soothe Brougham's feelings, but Melbourne was unsuccessful in persuading Grey to accept, and Palmerston to relinquish, the foreign office. At the same time he had some difficulty in disposing of the king's objections, which embraced any attempt to meddle with the Irish church, or to alter the royal household. On 18 April, however, the arrangements were complete, and Melbourne's second government began, supported only by a small majority in the commons, and opposed by the pronounced hostility of the king and a strong majority in the House of Lords. Lord Mulgrave's viceregal entry into Dublin, at which banners bearing inscriptions in favour of repeal were freely displayed, gave great offence. The lords rejected the appropriation clauses of the Irish Tithe Bill, and the measure was lost after Melbourne had made an important speech in its favour (*Hansard*, 20 Aug. 1835). The legislative measure of the session was that for the reform of the municipal corporations, which became law in spite of the profuse amendments of Lyndhurst, and though the king wished to proceed by granting new charters rather than by act of parliament. The king's anger also found vent on the occasion of Durham's mission to St. Petersburg, and Sir Charles Grey's appointment as member of the Canadian commission. On the first occasion Melbourne manfully took the blame

F F 2

upon himself, and on the second a ministerial remonstrance against his reflections on Glenelg, the colonial secretary, was read to the king by the premier. The king also objected strongly, in a letter to Melbourne of 19 Oct., to the reception of O'Connell at the table of the lord-lieutenant, more especially after his crusade against the House of Lords in the north of England and Scotland. Melbourne exonerated Mulgrave at his own expense. He was more successful in gaining the king's consent to the promotion of Pepys to the chancellorship, and compensation of Campbell by the elevation of his wife to the peerage (January 1836). In spite of the success of the Irish administration, the Irish Tithe Bill and the Irish Municipal Corporation Bill were again rejected by the Lords, and the debates on the Orange lodges damaged the government. On the other hand, the English Tithe Bill was passed and the marriage law reformed. As a whole, the session was a failure, and the appointment of Renn Dickson Hampden [q. v.] to the regius professorship of divinity at Oxford was most unpopular. On 22 June, too, Melbourne appeared as co-respondent in the divorce case Norton v. Norton and Melbourne in the court of common pleas. The verdict was for the defendants, and the king expressed his satisfaction (TORRENS, ii. 188–92; LORD CAMPBELL, Life, ii. 82–5; HAYWARD, Celebrated Statesmen, i. 379–80, where Melbourne is said to have twice reiterated his denial of the alleged adultery; see also NORTON, CAROLINE ELIZABETH SARAH). At the close of the session Lyndhurst delivered a terrific attack on the ministry, and at a cabinet meeting of 9 Aug. Melbourne owned that it was doubtful if they could go on. There was a fresh quarrel with the king on the subject of Canada, as William IV was very unwilling to admit the electoral principle into the constitution of the lower province. William also raised serious objections to the enlistment of the British legion in the service of Spain. In Ireland the creation of the National Association by O'Connell aroused the protestants to a great indignation meeting at Dublin, and Melbourne with difficulty dissuaded Mulgrave from dismissing Lords Downshire and Donoughmore from their lieutenancies. In spite of the strong objections of the king, the Church Rates Bill was introduced on 3 March; but it received feeble support, and ministers had nothing but defeat before them, when on 20 June William IV died. Melbourne, who had managed him throughout with the utmost tact, declared him to have been 'a being of the most uncompromising and firmest honour that ever it

pleased Divine Providence to set upon the throne.'

At the general election the whigs were confirmed in power, and Melbourne assumed the position of adviser to the youthful sovereign, than which, as Greville remarked, 'none was ever more engrossing, or involved greater responsibility.' He spent the greater part of his time at Windsor, where he discharged the duties of the queen's secretary, and contrived to make his unconventional manners conform to a somewhat rigid etiquette (see especially, GREVILLE, pt. ii, vol. i. pp. 145–9; and STOCKMAR, Memoirs, i. 377–391). 'I wish,' said the Duke of Wellington, 'that he was always there.' Meanwhile, rebellion was imminent in Canada, and Lord Howick (the present Lord Grey) strongly remonstrated with Melbourne for his apparent apathy (27 Dec. 1837). After the rebellion had been crushed, Lord Durham was sent out on a special mission, and Melbourne was compelled to remonstrate with him for giving appointments to men of damaged character like Turton and Gibbon Wakefield, as well as for the ordinance by which he banished some of the rebels and sentenced others to death. Hence he could only make a weak defence when Durham's conduct was attacked by Brougham in the House of Lords. The excuse he gave for his silence on one occasion to Russell was: 'The fellow was in such a state of excitement that if I had said a word he would have gone stark, staring mad.' Towards Durham after his resignation he was disposed to be more conciliatory (November 1838) than most of his colleagues. At the same time he was not afraid of him or his friends. 'He should be alarmed,' he wrote, 'at the prospect of a stand-up fight with Cribb or Gully, but not of a set-to with Luttrell or old Rogers.' Though at first averse to giving constitutional government to the French in Lower Canada, he finally consented to the union of the provinces, which was carried out by Poulett Thomson (Lord Sydenham).

Meanwhile, Melbourne's government had gained some credit by passing the Irish Poorlaw Bill, in spite of O'Connell's denunciation of the measure (July 1838), which was neutralised by the abandonment of the Irish Corporation Bill, and of the appropriation clauses of the Irish Tithe Bill, which had hitherto been the cardinal principle of the administration. At the beginning of the session Melbourne had intentionally set Brougham at defiance, and, in the opinion of Greville, came out of the ordeal with tolerable success. In spite of the open mutiny of the radicals, the political state of affairs ended as it had begun. But the establishment of O'Connell's 'Precursor Association,' followed by the murder of Lord Norbury, produced the resignation of Mulgrave, and the reconstruction of the ministry did not add to its strength. In January 1839 Roden carried a motion for an inquiry into the Irish administration, in spite of Melbourne's declaration that he should consider the motion a pure censure on the government; but the vote was reversed in the House of Commons. On 7 May the ministry resigned, having obtained a bare majority of five in the commons on the Jamaica Bill. Peel, however, failed to form a government, in consequence of the bedchamber question, and Melbourne, 'unwilling to abandon his sovereign in a situation of difficulty and distress,' resumed office. In so acting he was constitutionally wrong, but was averse from placing an inexperienced sovereign in a difficult position until the feeling of the country had been decisively declared. He also thought of 'the poor fellows who would have to give up their broughams.' He had little sympathy with the education scheme, which was carried in a modified form before the close of the session, and threw cold water on the proposal to establish a liberal morning paper. During the remainder of its career his ministry was divided and discredited, and the premier himself was involved in the Lady Flora Hastings affair [see HASTINGS, LADY FLORA]. Before the meeting of parliament, 16 Jan. 1840, the government had committed itself to wars with Persia, Afghanistan, and China, while the discontent of the working classes had found vent in the chartist riots at Newport and Birmingham. They escaped Buller's vote of want of confidence by 308 to 287, but the management of the questions connected with Prince Albert's allowance and precedence did not gain them much respect (STOCKMAR, ii. 24–46; Early Years of the Prince Consort, pp. 251, 263). The Irish Municipal Bill was passed after Melbourne had induced Russell to forego his opposition to Lyndhurst's amendments.

During the summer the cabinet was divided in mind on the Syrian question, in which Palmerston's diplomacy seemed about to commit us to a war with France. Greville has much contempt for Melbourne's conduct during the crisis. But his letters show that, though he was intensely anxious to prevent resignations, particularly that of Russell, he consistently supported Palmerston, and argued that by yielding to the threats of France we should lose influence, and encourage the French in a menacing policy, likely to end in war. He is even said by Hayward to have

terminated the crisis by addressing a strong remonstrance to Louis Philippe through the king of the Belgians (Celebrated Statesmen, i. 41). There can be no doubt that some such communication was written (RAIKES, Journal, ii. 202).

Melbourne was always opposed to any tampering with the corn laws. It was with much reluctance that he consented to a low fixed duty being made an 'open question' in 1838, as he 'could not but doubt whether a large labouring population, dependent in any considerable degree upon foreign corn, was in a safe position.' In 1841 he agreed to its being brought forward as a government proposal. After the cabinet dinner, at which the resolution was taken, he is said to have called from the stairs to his departing colleagues : 'Stop a bit ! Is it to lower the price of bread, or isn't it ? It doesn't much matter which, but we must all say the same thing.' The government were defeated by ten votes on the sugar duties, and on 27 May by one on a direct vote of want of confidence proposed by Peel. Much against Melbourne's better judgment, recourse was had to a dissolution, with the result that the government candidates were generally unsuccessful. The retirement of Plunket from the Irish chancellorship in favour of Campbell (Life of Lord Plunket, ii. 333), which was effected by pressure put upon Plunket by Melbourne, added to the unpopularity of the ministry. They were defeated in both houses on the address, and Melbourne announced their resignation on 30 Aug. The queen parted with him with the utmost regret, and after his resignation he did his best to establish cordial relations between her majesty and Peel (GREVILLE, pt. ii. vol. ii. 39–43).

Melbourne continued to lead the opposition until after an attack of paralysis on 23 Oct. 1812, when he left the leadership to Lansdowne, and seldom afterwards ventured to speak. He was very indignant with Peel's conversion to free trade, and broke out at Windsor with 'Ma'am, it's a damned dishonest act' (GREVILLE, pt. ii. vol. ii. p. 351). But he attended a meeting of the peers at Lansdowne House on 28 May 1846, and advised them not to oppose the abolition of the corn laws (MR. GLADSTONE, in Nineteenth Century, January 1890). He continued to cling to the idea that he would be minister again, and was mortified when no place was offered him in the Russell ministry of 1846, though he acknowledged that he was too ill to accept office (Papers, p. 528). The statements that Melbourne, in his old age, was neglected by his friends have no foundation. He gave his last vote upon the Jewish disabilities question on 25 May 1848, and died on 24 Nov. of the same year, leaving no heir.

Melbourne's manners were unconventional, and his talk interlarded with oaths. His conversation was a piquant mixture of learning, shrewdness, and paradox (for specimens see especially GREVILLE, pt. i. vol. iii. pp. 129–33, HAYDON, *Life*, ii. 370–405 passim; LESLIE, *Autobiography*, i. 169 et seq.) Thus he said that Croker would dispute with the Recording Angel about the number of his sins, and of the results of the Catholic Emancipation Bill—' the worst of it is, the fools were in the right.' At the same time his was a peculiarly pensive and solitary mind. As a statesman he has been thought wanting in purpose and firmness. But Lady Palmerston declared that earnestness was the essential element of his character, and he was certainly firm enough with Brougham and William IV. The truth seems to be that he was a genuine liberal on many points, notably that of religious equality, and a conscientious supporter of the programme bequeathed to him by Grey. Further than that he was not inclined to go, and opposed an invariable ' Why not leave it alone ?' to the proposals of the radical section of his party. As the instructor of a young sovereign he won universal approbation.

[Torrens's Memoirs of Lord Melbourne, 2 vols.; Lord Melbourne's Papers, edited by Lloyd C. Sanders, with preface by Earl Cowper; Hayward's Essay on Lord Melbourne (a reprint, with additions, from the Quarterly Review for January 1878), in his Celebrated Statesmen and Writers; Greville Memoirs, especially pt. ii. vol. iii. pp. 241 et seq.; Sir H. Taylor's Autobiography; Miss E. J. Whately's Life and Correspondence of Archbishop Whately; Lord Houghton, in the Fortnightly Review, vol. xxix.; Earl Cowper in the Nineteenth Century, vol. xv.; Spencer Walpole's Life of Lord John Russell and Hist. of England, vol. iii.; Sir D. Le Marchant's Memoir of Lord Althorp; Sir T. Martin's Life of the Prince Consort, vol. i.; Dunckley's Lord Melbourne (Queen's Prime Ministers Ser.)]

L. C. S.

LAMBARDE, WILLIAM (1536–1601), historian of Kent, born in the parish of St. Nicholas Acon, London, on 18 Oct. 1536, was the eldest son of John Lambarde, draper, alderman, and sheriff of London, by his first wife, Julian, daughter and ultimately heiress of William Horne of London. On the death of his father in August 1554, he inherited the manor of Westcombe in Greenwich, Kent. He was admitted of Lincoln's Inn on 12 April 1556, and studied Anglo-Saxon and history with Laurence Nowell (q. v. (WOOD, *Athenæ*

Oxon. ed. Bliss, i. 426). His first work, undertaken at the request of Nowell, was a collection and translation, or rather paraphrase, of the Anglo-Saxon laws published under the title of ' Ἀρχαιονομία, sive de priscis Anglorum legibus libri, sermone Anglico vetustate antiquissimo, aliquot abhinc seculis conscripti, atq; nunc demum . . . e tenebris in lucem vocati, G. Lambardo interprete,' 4to, London, 1568; republished with Bede's ' Historia Ecclesiastica' in 1644, fol., by Abraham Wheelock. Some notes and corrections for ' Ἀρχαιονομία' by Francis Junius (q. v.] are in the Bodleian Library (ib. iii. 1142). In 1570, when residing at Westcombe, Lambarde completed the first draft of his ' Perambulation of Kent: containing the Description, Hystorie, and Customes of that Shyre,' and sent it to his friend Thomas Wotton. It was read in manuscript and commended by Archbishop Parker and Lord treasurer Burghley. Wotton printed it with the author's additions in 1576, 4to, London. This, the earliest county history known, is justly considered a model of arrangement and style. The first edition contains ' The Names of suche of the Nobilitie and Gentrie as the Heralds recorded in their Visitation 1574,' which is omitted in subsequent issues. A second edition appeared in 1596, a third edition is undated, and others were issued in 1640 and 1656. A reprint of the second edition, with a life of Lambarde, was published at Chatham in 1826, 8vo. From Lambarde's own letter to Wotton, accompanying the second edition, it appears that he had already collected materials for a general account of England, of which the ' Perambulation' was an instalment. He abandoned his design upon learning that Camden was engaged on a similar undertaking (cf. his letter to Camden, dated 29 July 1585, in *Camdeni Epistolæ*, p. 28). His materials, however, were published from the original manuscript in 1730, 4to, London, as ' Dictionarium Angliæ Topographicum et Historicum,' &c., with his portrait engraved by Vertue. Camden, in acknowledging his obligations to ' Perambulation,' eulogises Lambarde as ' eminent for learning and piety' (*Britannia*, ' Kent,' Introduction); the ' piety' apparently refers to his having founded almshouses at East Greenwich called the College of the Poor of Queen Elizabeth. The queen granted letters patent for the foundation of this charity in 1574, and it was opened on 1 Oct. 1576.

On 9 Feb. 1578–9 Lambarde was chosen a bencher of Lincoln's Inn, and on 6 Aug. of the same year was appointed a justice of the peace for Kent. He fulfilled his duties honourably, and expounded them in ' Eirenarcha: or of the Office of the Justices of Peace, into two bookes: gathered 1579, and now revised and firste published,' &c., 8vo, London, 1581. Written in a clear and unaffected style, this manual remained for a long time the standard authority (FULBECK, *Preparative*, p. 64). Blackstone (1 *Blk. Comm.* c. 9) recommends its study. It was reprinted seven times between 1582 and 1610. To the last three editions was added 'The Duties of Constables, Borsholders, Tithing-men, and such other Lowe Ministers of the Peace. Whereunto be also adjoyned the severall Offices of Churchwardens, of Surveyors for amending the Highwayes,' &c., another useful handbook by Lambarde, first published in 1583, 8vo, London, and reissued with additions six times between 1584 and 1610. An able and interesting letter from Lambarde to Burghley, dated 18 July 1585, 'contayning reasons why her Majestie should with speed embrace the action of the defence of the Lowe ñ 'ountries,' is printed in Nichols's' Bibliotheca Topographica Britannica' (vol. i. App. viii. pp. 527–9). In 1591 he completed another work, entitled 'Archeion; or, a Commentary upon the High Courts of Justice in England,' which was published in 1635 (8vo, London), by his grandson, Thomas Lambarde, from the author's manuscript. Another edition, of inferior authenticity, appeared in the same year.

On 22 June 1592 Lambarde was appointed a master in chancery by Lord-keeper Sir John Puckering, and made keeper of the records at the Rolls Chapel by Lord-keeper Sir Thomas Egerton on 26 May 1597. In 1597 he was nominated by William Brooke, lord Cobham, as one of his executors and trustees for establishing his college for the poor at Cobham, Kent (*Archæologia Cantiana*, xi. 206, 210, 214–15), and he drew up the rules for the government of the charity. He was personally noticed by the queen in 1601, and appointed on 21 Jan. keeper of the records in the Tower. On 4 Aug. of the same year he presented Elizabeth with an account of the Tower records, which he called his 'Pandecta Rotulorum,' and he has left behind a delightfully quaint note of their conversation in the queen's privy chamber at East Greenwich (NICHOLS, *Bibliotheca*, vol. i. App. vii. pp. 525–6).

Lambarde died at Westcombe on 19 Aug. 1601 and was buried in Greenwich Church. On the rebuilding of the church his monument was removed by his son Sir Multon Lambarde to Sevenoaks, then as now the family seat. His will is printed in 'Archæologia Cantiana' (v. 253–6). He married, first, on 11 Sept. 1570, Jane (1553–1573), daughter of George Multon of St. Cleres,

Ightham, Kent; secondly, on 28 Oct. 1583, Sylvestra (1554–1587), widow of William Dallison and daughter and heiress of Robert Deane of Halling, Kent; and, thirdly, on 13 April 1592, Margaret, daughter of John Payne of Frittenden, Kent, widow first of John Meryam of Boughton-Monchelsea in the same county, and secondly of Richard Reder. He had issue by his second wife alone three sons and a daughter (*Archæologia Cantiana*, v. 247–53).

Many of Lambarde's manuscripts are at Sevenoaks, including several 'Charges to Juries' from 1581 to 1600, and a 'Treatise of the service called the Office of Compositions for Alienations,' 1590 (list in NICHOLS, *Bibliotheca*, vol. i. App. i. pp. 510–12). In the Cottonian manuscripts are his 'Collectanea ex diversis antiquis historicis Anglicanis' (Vesp. A. v. i.), his 'Cycle of Years, from 1571 to 1600' (Julius, c. ix. 105), and his 'Letter to Camden,' 1585 (Julius, c. v. 9).

[Nichols's Bibl. Top. Brit. i. 493–532, from the family papers; Hasted's Kent (Drake), i. 51–2; Marvin's Legal Bibliography; Smith's Bibliotheca Cantiana; Archæologia Cantiana, viii. 300, 301, 309; Lowndes's Bibl. Manual (Bohn), iii. 1301.]   G. G.

LAMBART. [See also LAMBERT.]

LAMBART, CHARLES, first EARL OF CAVAN (1600–1660), the eldest son of Oliver Lambart, first baron Lambart in the Irish peerage [q. v.], and Hester, daughter of Sir William Fleetwood of Carrington Manor, Bedfordshire, was born in 1600. He is said to have been educated at Cambridge. On the death of his father on 23 May 1618 he became second Baron Lambart, and was given in wardship to his mother on 26 April 1619. On 8 Aug. 1622 he had a grant of 1,296 acres of land in Westmeath and King's County as part of a scheme for the plantation of Leinster. Lambart represented Bossiney, Cornwall, in the English parliaments of 1625 and 1627, and on 4 Nov. 1634 made his first appearance in the Irish House of Lords, where he frequently spoke. On 6 March 1627 he was appointed seneschal for the government of the county of Cavan and the town of Kells. Henceforth he lived in Ireland, and on 17 May 1628 he succeeded to the command of Lord Moore's company of foot. On the outbreak of the rebellion in 1641 Lambart's estates suffered very severely; in November of that year he raised a regiment of a thousand foot. On 12 Nov. 1641 he was one of those appointed to confer with the rebels in Ulster. Lambart now became a notable commander; he was with Ormonde in February 1643 at the rout of Kilsaghlan, and when in 1642 Sir Charles Coote the elder [q. v.] left Dublin, Lambart became military governor, and was continued in this position by order of council of 12 May 1642, on the receipt of the news of Coote's death. He was also made a privy councillor. But he had difficulties with a discontented military party under Sir John Temple, and with the civil authorities, who disliked his contempt for the common law and somewhat hasty procedure. In May 1643 he marched with a thousand horse into Wicklow on a foraging expedition. He helped to arrange the cessation from hostilities of 1643, its renewal in 1644, and the examination of the Earl of Glamorgan in December 1645. On 1 April 1647 he was made Earl of Cavan and Viscount Kilcoursie.

After the reduction of Ireland by the parliament Cavan was in poor circumstances, but he had a lease granted to him of Clontarf and Arlaine, and a pension of 30s. a week for himself and 1l. for his wife. He died on 25 June 1660, and was buried in St. Patrick's Cathedral, Dublin. He married Jane (d. 1655), daughter of Richard, lord Robartes, and by her had a numerous family, of whom Richard, the second earl, was a lunatic, and Oliver, the third son, surviving the second son, succeeded to the family estates under the will of his father.

[Lodge's Peerage, ed. Archdall, i. 353; G. E. C[okayne]'s Complete Peerage, art. 'Cavan;' Gilbert's Hist. of the Irish Confederation, passim; Carte's Ormonde, i. 263, &c.]   W. A. J. A.

LAMBART, Sir OLIVER, LORD LAMBART (d. 1618), Irish administrator, son and heir of Walter Lambart, esq., of Preston in the West Riding of Yorkshire, and his first wife, Rose, daughter of Sir Oliver Wallop, was by profession a soldier. He went to Ireland about 1580, acting in the first instance as a volunteer. He served under Sir John Norris in the expedition conducted by the deputy Sir John Perrot against the Scots in Clandeboye in the summer of 1584, and falling into the hands of the enemy 'he was so sorely wounded that besides the loss of some limbs'—dextro succiso poplite—' he hardly was saved with life' (State Papers, Ireland, Eliz. cxv. 16). Proceeding to Dublin for the sake of surgical assistance, he had the further misfortune to be ' betrayed ' by O'Cahan into the hands of Shane's sons Hugh and Art O'Neill; but they were anxious to come to terms with the government, and Lambart was made the bearer of their message to the lord deputy (ib. cxi. 25). On his recovery he proceeded to England with letters of recommendation from Sir John Perrot, Sir John Norris, and his uncle Sir Henry

Wallop to Lord Burghley and Walsingham. In August 1585 he accompanied Sir John Norris into the Netherlands. He was present at the capture of Doesburg in September 1586, and was subsequently, it would appear (Cott. Galba D. viii. ff. 71, 84, 110), made governor of that town. In June 1591 he greatly distinguished himself at the attack on Deventer, but being seriously wounded at the siege of Steenwyck in June 1592, he was prevented from taking part in the campaign in France and obliged to proceed to Ostend (State Papers, Dom. 2 July 1592). In 1596 he took part in the expedition against Cadiz, and for his valour on that occasion he was knighted (CAMDEN, Annales). He returned to the Netherlands in 1597, but in 1599 his company of 150 foot, forming part of Sir Charles Percy's regiment, was drafted into Ireland to support the Earl of Essex in the war against the Earl of Tyrone. On Essex's departure from Ireland in September, Lambart was made master of the camp, and subsequently sergeant-major of the army. In 1600 1601 he was actively engaged against the rebels in Leix and Offaly, and on the recommendation of Lord Mountjoy he was on 19 July 1601 appointed governor of Connaught, when he immediately began to build the fort of Galway, which was finished in the following year. He was present at the siege of Kinsale, and after the capitulation of the Spaniards he was occupied in suppressing the last traces of rebellion in Connaught (Cal. Carew MSS. iv. passim). On 9 Sept 1603 he was created a privy councillor, and received a grant of 100l. a year in crown lands. On the flight of the Earls of Tyrone and Tyrconnel becoming known, he was appointed to convey official information of it to the king, and having 'diligently attended to the business he came for,' returned to Ireland with such 'marks of the king's favour, which increase his state and fortune' (RUSSELL and PRENDERGAST, ii. 322). At the same time it is to be noted that in the document which Tyrconnel drew up of his grievances Lambart is charged with having 'purposely drawn the plot of the Earl's ruin' (ib. ii. 374).

Immediately on the outbreak of O'Dogherty's rebellion in April 1608, Lambart and Sir Richard Wingfield were despatched to the north 'with all available forces both of horse and foot' (ib. ii. 501). On 20 May they arrived at Derry, where they left a ward in the church, and proceeded to Birt Castle, three miles distant from Culmore, in viewing which Lambart received a slight bullet wound in the right shoulder (ib. ii. 541). In the meanwhile he had succeeded, by methods which, if legal, were not always strictly honourable (*ib.* iii. 397), in accumulating considerable real property in the county of Roscommon and elsewhere. In 1610 his name appears in the list of 'servitors thought meet to be undertakers' in the plantation of Ulster (*ib.* iii. 428), and he was of considerable assistance to Chichester in arranging the details of that plantation. He had made choice of him, Chichester wrote to Salisbury in November, to lay the scheme before the English council, because, 'albeit he is not the best orator,' 'he is well acquainted with the country and the condition of the people, having long travelled and bled in the business here when it was at the worst, and has seen many alterations since he came first into the land' (*ib.* iii. 527). He returned to Ireland in April 1611, and the plantation being put into execution, he received on 26 June as his allotment two thousand acres in Claumahon, co. Cavan. From Pynnar's 'Survey,' 1618–19 (HARRIS, *Hibernica*), it appears that he had not only complied with the conditions of the plantation so far as to build a stone house and lawn upon it, but had also purchased another portion of one thousand acres in the same precinct. All these and other lands acquired by him were confirmed to his family by patent on 16 Feb. 1621. He sat for the county of Cavan in the parliament of 1613, though his return was petitioned against by the Roman catholic freeholders on the ground that the election had been conducted illegally, and that Lambart himself did not reside in the county (*ib.* iv. 361, 363–4).

In November 1614 Lambart was appointed to command an expedition to assist in recovering the castle of Dunivaig in Islay from the Macdonalds, who had taken it, partly by stratagem, partly by force, from the constable Andrew Knox [q. v.], bishop of Raphoe. The expedition sailed in December, but it was not till the end of January 1615 that the weather permitted an attack to be made. On 2 Feb. the castle surrendered (cf. *Cal. Carew MSS.* vi. 287, and RUSSELL and PRENDERGAST, *Cal. Irish Papers*, v. 6–10). On 21 April the king directed Chichester to return his royal thanks to Lambart for his successful management of the business, and on 17 Feb. 1618 he was created Lord Lambart, Baron of Cavan in the Irish peerage. He died 23 May in the same year in London, and was buried 10 June in Westminster Abbey. He married Hester, daughter of Sir William Fleetwood of Carrington Manor, Bedfordshire, and by her (who died 12 March 1639, and was buried in St. Patrick's, Dublin) had two sons and three daughters, viz. Charles

[q. v.], who succeeded him; Cary, who was knighted and lived at Clonebirne in co. Roscommon, and died in 1627 unmarried; Jane who married Sir Edward Leech of Sauley in Derbyshire; Rose, who married, first, Nicholas, son and heir to Sir Nicholas Smith of Larkbear in Devonshire, and secondly Sir Daniel Blagrave of Southcot in Berkshire; and Lettice, who died young.

Sir Oliver Lambart, though he wrote his name Lambert, must be distinguished from Captain O[swald] Lambert, who was wounded at the siege of Guisnes in 1558 (CHURCHYARDE, *Choise*).

[Lodge's Peerage, ed. Archdall; Berry's Hampshire, p. 77; Cal. State Papers, Domestic and Ireland; Cal. Carew MSS.; Hist. MSS. Comm. 3rd Rep. pp. 264, 284, 4th Rep. p. 606, 8th Rep. p. 381; Rawlinson's Life of Sir John Perrot; Motley's United Netherlands; W. Harris's Hibernica; Hill's Plantation of Ulster; Reg. Privy Council, Scotland, vol. x.; Gregory's Western Highlands; Trevelyan Papers (Camd. Soc.), vol. iii.; Camden's Annales; Chester's Reg. of Westminster Abbey.] R. D.

LAMBART, RICHARD FORD WILLIAM, seventh EARL OF CAVAN (1763–1836), general, born 10 Sept. 1763, was only son of Richard, sixth earl, by his second wife, Elizabeth, eldest daughter of George Davies, a commissioner of the navy. He succeeded his father in the title 2 Nov. 1778. He was appointed ensign Coldstream guards 2 April 1779, lieutenant 1781, captain-lieutenant 1790, captain and lieutenant-colonel 23 Aug. 1793, second major 9 May, and first major 19 Nov. 1800, having in the meantime attained major-general's rank in 1798. His name is not in the roll of the officers of his regiment who served in America (MACKINNON, vol. ii.) He was wounded at Valenciennes 3 Jan. 1793, commanded a brigade in Ireland (Londonderry) in 1798–9, and in the Ferrol expedition and before Cadiz in 1800. He commanded a line brigade in Egypt in 1801, and when General Ludlow [see LUDLOW, GEORGE JAMES, third EARL LUDLOW] was removed to a brigade of the line on 9 Aug., Cavan succeeded to the command of the brigade of guards. As part of Eyre Coote's division the brigade was sent to attack Alexandria from the westward. The city surrendered 2 Sept. 1801. When Lord Hutchinson [see HELY-HUTCHINSON, JOHN, second EARL OF DONOUGHMORE] left in October, Cavan succeeded to the command of the whole army remaining in Egypt, including the troops under David (afterwards Sir David) Baird [q. v.] Cavan held a brigade command in the eastern counties in England during the invasion alarms of 1803–4, and in

1805 was lieutenant-general commanding in the Isle of Wight. Cavan was a knight of the Crescent, and was one of the six officers, besides Lord Nelson, who received the diamond aigrette. He became a full general in 1814, and was in succession colonel-commandant of a second battalion 68th foot, and colonel of the 2nd West Indian and 45th regiments. He was governor of Calshot Castle, Hampshire. Cavan died in London 21 Nov. 1836. He married, first, in 1782, Honora Margaretta, youngest daughter and coheiress of Sir Henry Gould the younger [q. v.] (she died in 1813); and, secondly, in 1814, Lydia, second daughter of William Arnold of Slatswood, Isle of Wight. He left issue by both marriages.

[Foster's Peerage under 'Cavan;' Mackinnon's Coldstream Guards, London, 1832, vol. ii.; Gent. Mag. 1838, new ser. ix. 92.]   H. M. C.

INDEX

TO

THE THIRTY-FIRST VOLUME.

END OF THE THIRTY-FIRST VOLUME.

www.ingramcontent.com/pod-product-compliance
Lightning Source LLC
Chambersburg PA
CBHW031052110726
47900CB00003B/896